THE BIG BOOK OF THE CONTINENTAL OP

DASHIELL HAMMETT

Samuel Dashiell Hammett was born in Saint Mary's County, Maryland, and grew up in Baltimore. Hammett left school at the age of fourteen and held a variety of jobs thereafter—messenger boy, newsboy, clerk, and stevedore, finally becoming an operative for Pinkerton's National Detective Agency. He served as a sergeant in the U.S. Army in World War I and World War II. In the late 1920s, Hammett became the unquestioned master of detective-story fiction in America. In *The Maltese Falcon* (1930), he first introduced his famous private eye, Sam Spade. *The Glass Key* (1931) introduced political fixer Ned Beaumont. *The Thin Man* (1934) offered another immortal sleuth, Nick Charles. *Red Harvest* (1929) and *The Dain Curse* (1929), included here, feature the Continental Op.

The

BIG BOOK

OF THE

CONTINENTAL

OP

The

BIG BOOK

OF THE

CONTINENTAL

OP

DASHIELL HAMMETT

Edited by

RICHARD LAYMAN AND JULIE M. RIVETT

VINTAGE CRIME/BLACK LIZARD
Vintage Books
A Division of Penguin Random House LLC
New York

A VINTAGE CRIME/BLACK LIZARD ORIGINAL, NOVEMBER 2017

Compilation copyright © 2017 by The Dashiell Hammett Literary Property Trust

All rights reserved. Published in the United States by Vintage Books, a division of Penguin Random House LLC, New York, and distributed in Canada by Random House of Canada, a division of Penguin Random House Canada Limited, Toronto.

Vintage is a registered trademark and Vintage Crime/Black Lizard and colophon are trademarks of Penguin Random House LLC.

Several stories first appeared in *The Continental Op: The Complete Case Files*, edited by Richard Layman and Julie M. Rivett, published as an eBook by Mysterious Press, New York, in 2016. Pages 737–38 constitute an extension of this copyright page.

The Cataloging-in-Publication Data is on file at the Library of Congress.

Vintage Crime/Black Lizard Trade Paperback ISBN: 978-0-525-43295-1

Book design by Christopher M. Zucker

www.blacklizardcrime.com

Printed in the United States of America
10 9 8 7 6 5 4 3 2 1

Contents

SECTION ONE: THE SUTTON YEARS

SECTION TWO: THE CODY YEARS

CONTENTS

SECTION THREE: THE SHAW YEARS

BONUS: THE UNFINISHED OP

SECTION FOUR: THE CONTINENTAL OP NOVELS

Foreword

"THROUGH MUD AND BLOOD AND DEATH AND DECEIT"

THIS LONG-AWAITED VOLUME you hold in your hands is the first and only collection to assemble every one of Dashiell Hammett's pioneering Continental Op adventures—twenty-eight stand-alone stories, two novels, and Hammett's only known unfinished Continental Op tale. It is truly definitive. And it has been many decades in the making. At the time of this writing, the first Op story is ninety-four years old and the last is seventy-nine, not including "Three Dimes," an undated draft fragment conserved in Hammett's archives, first published in 2016. The gritty sleuth Hammett described as a "little man going forward day after day through mud and blood and death and deceit" has weathered gunshots, grifters, criminal conspiracies, class struggles, temptations, neglect, and more. This volume is testament to his tenacity. He is a survivor, a working-class hero, and a landmark literary creation.

The Continental Op stories are rooted in Hammett's experiences as an operative for Pinkerton's National Detective Agency. Although Hammett worked for Pinkerton's for a scant five years—before and after his service in the U.S. Army during World War I—the job inspired both his writing career and his worldview. Some influences are plain. The Continental Detective Agency, for example, is modeled on Pinkerton's, their Baltimore office located in the Continental Trust Company Building, where Hammett had been hired. Hammett said his cases largely involved forgeries, bank swindles, and safe burglaries, a solid factual basis for the Op's fictional adventures, albeit considerably enlivened. "As much happens to one of my detectives in a page and a half as happened to me in six months when I was a real-life detective," Hammett wrote. While his salary was a mere $21 a week (roughly $500 in 2017 dollars), the training was invaluable, even in what Hammett called the "easiest thing a sleuth has to do": shadowing. Despite being more than six feet tall, Hammett was reportedly an excellent shadow man, knowing to hang back, keep his cool, and catalog all available clues. Faces were only one aspect of the descriptive package. Close observation of "tricks of carriage, ways of wearing clothes, general outline, individual mannerisms—all as seen from the rear—are much more important to the shadow than faces," Hammett wrote in a letter to *Black Mask* magazine in 1924. It's easy to imagine the Op's vivid narratives as extended versions of what his reports to the Continental would have been: physical detail in wry tone, succinct, but with enough specifics to allow colleagues to identify shared quarry and continue the chase. Hammett's case reports for Pinkerton's are lost to history (or fire), but it's safe to say that his experience as a shadow man was stellar preparation for his new class of scrupulously observed crime fiction.

Hammett identified the assistant manager of Pinkerton's Baltimore office, James Wright, as his mentor and a model for the Op. The claim bears truth in its implication, if not in actual fact. "James Wright" was a pseudonym that had been shared among Pinkerton agents for decades. Hammett's sly suggestion—that the Op is an anonymous amalgamation—holds with his later remarks on the origins of the character. "The 'op' I use," explained Hammett, "is the typical sort of private detective that exists in our country today. I've worked with half a dozen men who might be he with few changes. Though he may be 'different' in fiction, he is almost pure 'type' in life." Part of that "type" is defined by a code of honor intrinsic to the detectives' profession, which Hammett absorbed and integrated into his own life and worldview. According to the code, detectives maintain anonymity and resist publicity, sequestering themselves within a veil of secrecy. Their lives are safer that way. Detectives strive for objectivity, refusing emotional entanglements with cops, clients, crooks, anyone. Dispassionate logic is key to personal well-being, procedure, and justice. And detectives steer by their own moral constellations, balancing their obligation to the jobs they are assigned against personal standards of right and wrong. Legal and social norms—and even their bosses' expectations—tend to weigh lightly in thorny situations. Detectives are pragmatic by nature and necessity.

In a story called "Magic," unpublished during Hammett's lifetime, Hammett wrote "to the extent that one becomes a magician one ceases to be a man . . . this same thing might hold true for sailors and jewelers and bankers." The changeover certainly holds true for Hammett's detectives. The Op's personality—like his name—is subsumed to the parameters of his job. The result is jaded and cynical, but not inhumane, and not entirely invulnerable. He is willing to destroy evidence to protect a friend; to convict a real crook on a false charge; to fudge his reports to deflect culpability, sometimes his own. The Op introduced moral ambiguities that complicated conventional good versus bad binaries of detective fiction and, importantly, laid ground for Sam Spade. In what was perhaps a passing of the torch, *The Maltese Falcon* was published in hardcover in February 1930, the same month as the Op's penultimate appearance in *Black Mask* magazine in "The Farewell Murder." Ellery Queen had suggested casting the Op in the role of Sam Spade's older brother. "He's just as hard, just as hardbitten, just as hardboiled," wrote Queen. "A less spectacular workman at times (but only at times), he is equally brutal and efficient as a manhunter." The body of work collected in this volume made Sam Spade possible and has helped to pave the way for modern literary crime fiction, creating a bridge between the raw brawls-and-bullets thrillers common to post–World War I pulp magazines and the realistic, morally complex crime literature so enormously popular among twenty-first-century readers. The Op has been and remains one of American literature's most influential fictional creations.

The Continental Op stories were published individually during the early years of Hammett's writing career, between 1923 and 1930. All but two were featured in *Black Mask*, the leading light of pulp magazines—a favorite among working-class readers, crime-fiction aficionados, and anyone who longed for a coin's worth of well-crafted thrills. In June 1929, near the end of the run, Hammett sent a note to Harry Block, his editor at Alfred A. Knopf. He had just sent Block a draft of his third novel, *The Maltese Falcon*, which he described as "by far the best thing" he'd done so far. He goes on to say:

Also I've about two hundred and fifty thousand words of short stories in which the Continental Op appears. I know you're not likely to be wildly enthusiastic about the short-story idea; but don't you think that something quite profitable for both of us could be done with them by making a quite bulky collection of them—selling them by the pound, as it were? I don't know anything about the manufacturing costs—how far bulkiness could be carried at a fairly low cost without eating up the profits. I'd want to rewrite the stories we included, of course, and there are possibly fifty or sixty thousand of the quarter-million that I'd throw out as not worth bothering about. In the remainder there are some good stories, and altogether I think they'd give a more complete and true picture of a detective at work than has been given anywhere else.

Almost immediately Hammett had second thoughts about republishing the Op tales. "I'd rather forget them," he told Block. The hard-boiled pioneer was ready, in contemporary lexis, to retool his brand—to abandon the constraints and expectations of the crime-fiction genre and shift his focus from the Continental Detective Agency's anonymous foot soldier to more sophisticated conflicts starring independent detectives, non-detectives, and ex-detectives. It wasn't long before the Continental Op's work-a-day exploits were overshadowed by the deeper, darker, and splashier successes of Sam Spade (*The Maltese Falcon*, 1930), Ned Beaumont (*The Glass Key*, 1931), and Nick Charles (*The Thin Man*, 1934). Hammett's hardworking, hard-boiled protagonist was relegated to the sidelines.

During the thirteen-year hiatus that followed Hammett's change of direction, the Continental Op was available to readers primarily in Hammett's first two novels, *Red Harvest* and *The Dain Curse*. Both novels had been reworked from sets of linked stories originally published in *Black Mask*—*Red Harvest* in fall/winter 1927-28 and *The Dain Curse* in fall/winter

1928–29—and both were published by Knopf in 1929. *Red Harvest* was ahead of its time—a vivid and exquisitely informed exploration of corruption, pragmatism, and ambiguity, set in Montana mining country. Although *Red Harvest* was made into a film, released by Paramount as *Roadhouse Nights* in 1930, Hammett's fans could easily have overlooked the Op's dubious debut as Willie Bindbugel in Ben Hecht's wildly divergent adaptation of the novel. Willie played an investigative reporter, rather than a hard-boiled detective, in a story that was more action-comedy than crime. Today, the film is most notable as a vehicle for Jimmy Durante in his first big-screen appearance.

The Dain Curse, Hammett's second novel, featured the Op negotiating family drama, religious fervor, insanity, and drug-induced confusion in a tangled contest between the supernatural and sober reality. Hammett titled the expository final chapter "The Circus" and later described the book as a "silly story." It is generally considered the least of his five novels. Still, *The Dain Curse* was a solid performance that garnered largely favorable reviews, earned a spot on the *New York Times* recommended holiday books list, and won the Op (and Hammett) his first printing in England.

The Continental Op's fortunes rebounded in 1943, when Lawrence Spivak (with Frederic Dannay and his cousin Manfred B. Lee, jointly known as Ellery Queen) made arrangements to publish a string of digest-size paperback collections featuring Hammett's short fiction. Hammett, serving in Alaska with the U.S. Army Signal Corps, agreed unenthusiastically to a deal with Spivak's Mercury Publications. "I signed the contract," he told Lillian Hellman, "but don't take that as a hint that I want it especially." Hellman was by then an established playwright, a dozen years into what would be an intimate but tempestuous, three-decade-long relationship with Hammett. All but one of the twenty-eight Continental Op stand-alone tales were reprinted (in sometimes liberally reedited form) between 1943 and 1951, under Bestseller Mystery, Jonathan Press Mystery, Mercury Mystery, and Ellery Queen Selects imprints, many subsequently reprinted in Dell paperback editions. Once again, the Op was widely available in the working-class world he represented.

Between 1951 and 1961—the last decade of Hammett's life—virtually no one published the Op, Sam Spade, Ned Beaumont, Nick Charles, or any of Hammett's fiction. It was the era of the Red Scare, with its blacklists and committee hearings, and the beginnings of the Cold War, rife with anti-Soviet fearmongering and jingoistic conservatism. Hammett had made no secret of his left-wing affiliations, and with the taint of the Red brush, he became unmarketable. His income was devastated, his publishers wary, the radio shows based on his work canceled.

"Financially," Hammett told his wife, Jose, in March 1951, "this year's going to be a holy terror and so—from the looks of things right now—are the next few years to come." Hammett's estimation was dead-on. He spent five of the last six months of 1951 imprisoned on a contempt of court charge after claiming his Fifth Amendment rights in U.S. District Court. He would neither name the contributors to the Civil Rights Congress of New York bail fund he chaired nor provide information on the whereabouts of four Communist Party leaders who had skipped out on bail the CRC fund had provided. Hammett served his time without regret, but when he was released on December 9, both his health and his finances had crumbled beyond repair. His final efforts at political engagement, teaching, and innovative fiction withered away over the course of the next two years. He lived in increasing seclusion and frugality in upstate New York, dependent on the kindness of friends and his monthly veteran's pension of $131.10.

Hammett died on January 10, 1961. His only significant asset—$7,914.23 held in escrow by his publisher, Alfred A. Knopf—was dwarfed by federal and New York State tax liens totaling nearly $175,000. While a portion of the shortfall might be attributed to slipshod tax reporting on Hammett's part—he had failed to file returns for two years he was serving in the army during World War II—the bulk was a bitter by-product of the U.S. government's retaliatory anticommunist campaigns. Lillian Hellman attached another $40,000 in claims for repayment of personal loans, in addition to his final medical, funeral, and administrative expenses. She was executrix for the Dashiell Hammett estate, and with the approval of the IRS she put the rights to Hammett's entire body of work up for auction, with the understanding that the sale price (a minimum of $5,000) would settle his outstanding debt.

Lillian Hellman wrote to Hammett's daughters Mary and Jo to ask if they would be willing to go in with her to make an offer. There is no record of Mary's reply. But Jo wrote back in June 1963: "We will be able to send the thousand but it will be a month or six weeks before the cash is available. Is this satisfactory? Please let us know what has developed with the proposed tax settlement." Hellman ignored Jo's letter, disregarded her request for updates, and chose instead to pool resources with her friend Arthur Cowan. At the sale in November, she and Cowan won all rights to Hammett's works with the minimum bid of $5,000. One year later Cowan was killed in a car accident, leaving his share of the Hammett library under Hellman's control. "I am now the sole owner of the estate," she told Jo.

Having captured Hammett's literary rights at a bargain-basement rate, Hellman set herself to an ambitious campaign to restore his stifled reputation. She arranged for Random House to publish *The Novels of Dashiell Hammett* in 1965, bringing Hammett's five major works back into the marketplace. The timing was right. Americans' McCarthy-era prejudices had faded, international esteem for Hammett was growing, and critics, for the most part, were disposed to warmly welcome Hammett's reissues. "What can one say about the novels of Dashiell Hammett," wrote Philip Durham in *The New York Times*, "except that they are as superbly written as one remembers them from thirty years ago?" Dell paperback editions of *The Maltese Falcon*, *The Glass Key*, and *The Thin Man* followed in 1966.

The Continental Op stories also made their comeback in 1966, five years after Hammett's death, in what mystery reviewer Anthony Boucher celebrated as a "Hammett summer." *The Big Knockover* collection was edited and introduced by Lillian Hellman. All but one of the nine Op tales she selected had been published originally between 1925 and 1929—which is to say, Hellman focused primarily on the second half of Hammett's Op oeuvre, appended by Hammett's semiautobiographical fragment "Tulip." "They read well, most of them," wrote Robert Kirsch in the *Los Angeles Times*, "in that taut and stripped prose, that crackling dialogue, which was the Hammett hallmark." Hellman's introduction offered tribute and reminiscence, her glowing portrait of Hammett and her relationship with him pointedly sentimental rather than squarely factual. Reviewers described her comments as evocative, intimate, moving, and, in one case, as interesting as the stories themselves. In the five decades since, biographers and historians have learned to be skeptical of Hellman's recollections, but in that moment, with her introduction, Hellman set the stage for a chivalric rendering of Hammett that she would cultivate for the rest of her life.

The Continental Op followed in 1974, edited and introduced by Steven Marcus. He was a friend of Hellman and a respected literary and cultural scholar, but even so, Hellman maintained tight control over the editorial process. Early on, Marcus suggested twenty-four pieces of Hammett fiction, broken into three sections: Op stories; non-Op stories; and the first, unfinished draft of *The Thin Man*. Hellman objected, again and again; the book got shorter and shorter. "I do agree with you that Dash grew as a writer . . . but I don't think we can base an anthology on the growth since most readers would properly be more interested in the results of the growth," she argued. In the end the collection included just seven Op selections, hopscotching between 1924 and 1930. Critics, nonetheless, cheered new access to more Op adventures. Richard Fuller in *The Philadelphia Inquirer* raved, saying "Hammett's Continental Op saga is a rough, rugged, but sturdy log cabin in the town of American literature." Reactions to Marcus's introduction (also published in *Partisan Review* in 1974) were mixed, but his philosophical and academic interpretations of Hammett's writing helped to forever tilt perceptions of the Op's narratives toward the serious, literate, more durable side of library aisles.

Through all of this, barring his appearance in *Roadhouse Nights*, the Op was noticeably absent from Hollywood. Hellman did what she could to capitalize on the character's film and television potential, but it was tough going. Film rights to *Red Harvest* had been sold to Knopf along with print rights in 1929, as was then the standard. Knopf assigned rights to Paramount Famous Lasky Corporation (a precursor to Paramount Pictures), who later assigned rights to PEA Films—whose claims continue to constrain *Red Harvest*'s film and television prospects. The handful of deals Hellman made for film or television projects based on shorter Op stories failed to reach production. *The Dain Curse*, perhaps improbably, broke the Op's dry streak in 1978 with a three-part miniseries on CBS, starring James Coburn as detective Hamilton Nash. The Op had a name and, at last, a legitimate film credit. In the decades before and after, filmic roles for Hammett's seminal gumshoe have been more inspirational (and uncredited) than sanctioned or celebrated.

When Lillian Hellman died in 1984, control of the Hammett literary estate passed into a literary trust administered by three of her friends. While the trustees' oversight was uneven, under their tenure two important story collections came to fruition. The first was *Nightmare Town*, comprising twenty pieces of short fiction, spanning eleven years. *Nightmare Town* was published in 1999, with an introduction by William F. Nolan, who rightly described the anthology as "the largest collection of [Hammett's] shorter works and by far the most comprehensive." Seven stories featuring the Continental Op were included.

Just two years later, the prestigious Library of America published *Dashiell Hammett: Crime Stories and Other Writings*, succeeding *Nightmare Town* as the most comprehensive compilation of Hammett's short fiction. Steven Marcus, then free from Hellman's oversight, selected twenty-seven pieces, including all but eight of the twenty-eight Op stories. Contractual limitations dealing with reprints in competing publications made full inclusion problematic. Nevertheless, the volume is handsome and enlightening. Margaret Atwood, a long-standing Hammett fan, said it took readers "back to the beginning of the line" and showed why Hammett's popularity had risen so rapidly. The mere presence of *Crime Stories and Other Writings* among Library of America's illustrious editions is proof of esteem for Hammett's work that survived his pulp-fiction origins nearly eight decades earlier.

Lillian Hellman's appointees to the Dashiell Hammett literary trust ceded control to the Hammett family in 2003. What followed was a new season of engagement and publication, particularly abroad. Hammett never ventured overseas, but his Op is a veteran traveler, with recent editions in Brazil, Italy, Romania, Poland, Germany, England, and, most notably, France, where a Hammett renaissance has resulted in a flock of new translations and compilations, as well as, in 2011, an omnibus volume that collected virtually all of Hammett's available fiction.

With the twenty-first century, of course, came new technological opportunities. The Op made the leap into modern media in *The Continental Op: The Complete Case Files* e-book, released by Mysterious Press in 2016. It was the first electronic publication of Dashiell Hammett's collected Continental Op stories to be licensed by either Hammett or his estate—and the first English-language volume of any kind to include all twenty-eight of the Op's stand-alone stories. Versions of some of the prefatory materials included here also appear in that volume.

The Big Book of the Continental Op comes more than nine decades after Dashiell Hammett's nameless operative for the Continental Detective Agency narrated his first investigation in *Black Mask* magazine in 1923. This volume includes not only Hammett's twenty-eight Op stories but also, for the first time since their initial publication in *Black Mask* magazine between November 1927 and February 1929, the original serialized texts of *Red Harvest* and *The Dain Curse*. Differences between the *Black Mask* and Knopf editions are substantial, often instructive, and for decades largely undiscoverable for general readers. This volume fills that gap, with Hammett's original Op, from beginning to end, from his earliest publications.

The stand-alone stories are presented chronologically, with section introductions providing context and insights into Hammett's evolution under his three *Black Mask* editors—George W. Sutton, Philip C. Cody, and Joseph Thompson Shaw. *Red Harvest* and *The Dain Curse* are introduced separately. Headnotes original to each publication are reprinted, along with Hammett's remarks in letters to the editors. "Three Dimes"—an incomplete Continental Op adventure preserved in Hammett's archive at the Harry Ransom Center, University of Texas at Austin—is included as a bonus, along with Hammett's brief plot and character notes. The editors' only modifications are silent corrections to spelling, typographical errors, and irregularities discovered in the elusive, fragile pages of Hammett's original magazine offerings, along with footnotes identifying topical references and the rich slang of Hammett's 1920s. We are pleased to provide to modern readers this unparalleled opportunity to feast on the Continental Op's comprehensive canon—what Hammett called a "complete and true picture of a detective at work"—and to honor and illuminate his creator, who changed the face of not only American crime fiction but the literary tradition worldwide.

JMR

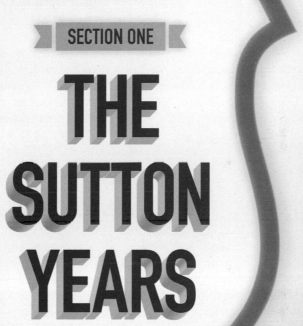

SECTION ONE

THE SUTTON YEARS

Introduction

THE SUTTON YEARS: 1923–1924

DASHIELL HAMMETT MAY HAVE been born with the urge to write, we can't know, but it was happenstance that set the course for his literary fame. His first choice of career was private investigation. When he turned twenty-one, he joined Pinkerton's National Detective Agency as an operative, a job he enjoyed for three years, from 1915 to 1918, before joining the army. He served in a medical unit at Fort Bragg, Maryland, an intake center for soldiers infected with Spanish influenza returning from the war in Europe. Hammett contracted the flu himself, and that activated a latent strain of tuberculosis probably spread from his mother. He left the army after just less than a year with a sergeant's rating, an honorable discharge, and a disability rating that fluctuated over the next ten years between 20 and 100 percent, usually hovering midway in between.

After a period of convalescence, Hammett returned to detective work sporadically, until he was hospitalized with tuberculosis for some six months from November 1920 to the following May. Upon his release from the hospital, he moved to San Francisco and married his nurse, Josephine Dolan, in July 1921. Their daughter

Mary was born in October. Hammett tried to support his new family as a detective, but he was unable. He retired permanently from the agency in either December 1921 or February 1922, depending on which evidence you choose to accept, due to disability. He was twenty-six, often a virtual invalid, and he needed money.

In February 1922 he commenced a year and a half of study at Munson's School for Private Secretaries, with a "newspaper reporting objective," as he wrote in his disability log for the Veterans Bureau. Though he apparently dropped out early, the training shows. His early fiction has a journalistic quality about it—in the best sense. It is clearly written, detail oriented, and plainly narrated, without the strained and sensationalistic flourishes that mark the fiction of other early pulp writers. In October 1922 he began submitting humorous and ironic sketches to *The Smart Set*, the high-brow magazine edited and partially owned by H. L. Mencken and George Jean Nathan. At their suggestion, after publishing three of his sketches, he lowered his sights to pulp magazines, which offered him steady, if not hefty, paychecks but required that he alter his subject matter. He made his living during most of the twenties on the back of what soon became his series character, the Continental Op, a professional agency detective.

Hammett's Continental Op is inseparable from the pulp magazine *Black Mask*, which was barely three years old and under new ownership when the Continental Op was introduced. Twenty-six of the twenty-eight published Op stories first appeared there between October 1923 and November 1930, as well as two four-part serial novels featuring the Op. Founded in 1920 by Mencken and Nathan to publish what Mencken called in *My Life as Author and Editor* "hacks of experience," writing for "murder fans." *Black Mask* had no literary pretensions in the beginning. Its sole purpose was to make money. Mencken claimed in a 1933 letter to his friend Philip Goodman that he and Nathan could "get out a 128-page magazine at a cash outlay of no more than $500," and did so. With "no desire to go on with the *Black Mask*," Mencken and Nathan sold it in summer 1921 to Eugene Crowe and Eltinge Warner (just before Crowe's death), having earned about $25,000 each for their efforts. From the beginning, the magazine was aimed at a blue-collar audience who wanted entertaining stories. Though it is known now as the publication that pioneered hard-boiled detective fiction, in the October 10, 1923, issue, the editor bragged that *Black Mask* published "rugged adventure and real man and woman romance; rare Western yarns, swift-acting logical detective stories, weird, creepy mystery tales, and the only thrilling, convincing ghost stories to be found anywhere." In that mix, Hammett found no models, and his sure-footed stories stood out—initially because of their confident, plausible prose and notable absence of gratuitous violence.

Hammett used pseudonyms for his earliest *Black Mask* stories, usually Peter Collinson (from theater slang for a phantom person). One might guess, and it is only a guess, that he was embarrassed to appear in the cheap pulps—certainly he spoke disparagingly of them later in his life. But he dropped his guard when he was asked for a comment about "The Vicious Circle," a story about a politician reacting to blackmail published in the June 15, 1923, *Black Mask* as by Collinson. Hammett replied that the story, which does not feature the Op, was based on cases he experienced as a private detective. He signed the response "S. D. Hammett" and soon afterward abandoned the Collinson pseudonym altogether. Editor George W. Sutton missed the reference. Even though Hammett took particular care in those early stories to describe accurately how a private detective went about his job and in "Zigzags of Treachery" (March 1, 1924) provided specific how-to advice, it wasn't until later that Sutton's successor recognized the real-life experience that shaped the Op's workmanlike approaches to his cases.

Writers rarely develop in a vacuum. In Hammett's case, the course of his literary development seems clearly enough to have been molded by his editors. He came to write detective fiction because Mencken saw no future for him among the smart set, and at *Black Mask* he clearly was guided in the beginning by his editors' ideas about what would sell in their market, ideas that changed with the man in charge. Sutton, the *Black Mask* editor who agreed after three months on the job to publish "Arson Plus," had no literary qualifications. He described himself this way in a farewell message to readers in the March 15, 1924, issue, the last for which he had responsibility:

The Editor is primarily a writer of automobile and motorboat articles, and all during the wonderful period that he has been at the helm of BLACK MASK, he has continued his automobile departments in various publications; using the afternoons and most of every night, every Sunday and holiday, to read the thousands of stories which come in to BLACK MASK—editing them, consulting with authors and artists, writing to readers, and attending to the thousands of details that make up the work necessary to getting out a "peppy" fiction magazine.

Sutton's "various publications" included *Vanity Fair, Collier's, Town & Country, Popular Mechanics*, and newspaper syndication.

In 1923 Sutton wrote a memo to prospective writers called "The Present needs of Black Mask," in which he lamented that "BLACK MASK finds it very difficult to get exactly the kind of stories it wants. We can print stories of horror, supernatural but explainable phenomena and gruesome tales which no other magazine in the country would print, but they must be about human beings, convincing, entertaining, and interest impelling." Sutton warned in his memo: "We do not care for purely scientific detective stories which lack action; and we are prejudiced by experience against the psychological story which is not very rugged and intense."

Though *Black Mask* is regarded, appropriately, as the birthplace of hard-boiled fiction, the hard-boiled story was still in gestation under Sutton. While crime was a staple of his *Black Mask*, it was but one ingredient of the editorial mix, and only the earliest stories of Carroll John Daly, featuring cartoonishly violent protagonists acting out what seem to be the author's homicidal, tough-guy fantasies, could properly be called hard-boiled. Hammett set out to fulfill *Black Mask*'s needs with stories about a short, portly, tough, nameless detective for the Continental Detective Agency, based obviously on Pinkerton's, who described his cases in procedural detail.

Hammett was known to Sutton and his associate editor Harry North only through correspondence and his fiction. Hammett lived in San Francisco; the editorial offices were in New York. Sutton made an effort to stay in touch with his writers and his readers, though. He solicited letters from his writers about the genesis of their stories, and he encouraged readers to write in with their reactions, which he published, criticisms and all. Hammett responded to Sutton's requests regularly, and his letters are included here after the stories on which they comment.

By the time his fourth Op story was published, Hammett was advertised by Sutton as having "suddenly become one of the most popular of *Black Mask* writers, because his stories are always entertaining, full of action and very unusual situations." They were also notably restrained by *Black Mask* standards. In those first four stories the Op does not carry a gun. In the first two there are no deaths; in the third there is one offstage murder and one murder before the story begins; and in the fourth there is one offstage murder and one shooting. In the next five stories, Hammett's last under Sutton's editorship, there are a total of five murders during the action. Though the Op had an occasional fistfight, under Sutton he never killed a person; the crooks are the murderous ones. But Sutton went back to motorsports at the end of March 1924—his *Camping by the Highway: Autocamper's Handbook and Directory of Camp Sites* was published by Field and Stream Publishing Company in 1925—and though Hammett was among the core writers on whose talents Sutton's successors planned to build, the new editor had different ideas about what makes an entertaining story.

RL

BLACK MASK, OCTOBER 1, 1923

Arson Plus

BY PETER COLLINSON

(Author of "The Vicious Circle," etc.)*

This is a detective story you'll have a hard time solving before the end. Form your ideas of the outcome as you go along and then see how near you guessed it.

JIM TARR PICKED UP the cigar I rolled across his desk, looked at the band, bit off an end, and reached for a match.

"Fifteen cents straight," he said. "You must want me to break a *couple* of laws for you this time."

I had been doing business with this fat sheriff of Sacramento County for four or five years— ever since I came to the Continental Detective Agency's San Francisco office—and I had never known him to miss an opening for a sour crack; but it didn't mean anything.

"Wrong both times," I told him. "I get two of them for a quarter; and I'm here to do you a favor instead of asking for one. The company

that insured Thornburgh's house thinks somebody touched it off."

"That's right enough, according to the fire department. They tell me the lower part of the house was soaked with gasoline, but God knows how they could tell—there wasn't a stick left standing. I've got McClump working on it, but he hasn't found anything to get excited about yet."

"What's the layout? All I know is that there was a fire."

Tarr leaned back in his chair, turned his red face to the ceiling, and bellowed:

"Hey, Mac!"

The pearl push-buttons on his desk are ornaments as far as he is concerned. Deputy sheriffs McHale, McClump and Macklin came to the door together—MacNab apparently wasn't within hearing.

---

* "The Vicious Circle" is a story without a detective published in the June 15, 1923, issue of *Black Mask*.

6

"What's the idea?" the sheriff demanded of McClump. "Are you carrying a bodyguard around with you?"

The two other deputies, thus informed as to who "Mac" referred to this time, went back to their cribbage game.

"We got a city slicker here to catch our firebug for us," Tarr told his deputy. "But we got to tell him what it's all about first."

McClump and I had worked together on an express robbery, several months before. He's a rangy, towheaded youngster of twenty-five or six, with all the nerve in the world—and most of the laziness.

"Ain't the Lord good to us?"

He had himself draped across a chair by now—always his first objective when he comes into a room.

"Well, here's how she stands: This fellow Thornburgh's house was a couple miles out of town, on the old county road—an old frame house. About midnight, night before last, Jeff Pringle—the nearest neighbor, a half-mile or so to the east—saw a glare in the sky from over that way, and phoned in the alarm; but by the time the fire wagons got there, there wasn't enough of the house left to bother about. Pringle was the first of the neighbors to get to the house, and the roof had already fell in then.

"Nobody saw anything suspicious—no strangers hanging around or nothing. Thornburgh's help just managed to save themselves, and that was all. They don't know much about what happened—too scared, I reckon. But they did see Thornburgh at his window just before the fire got him. A fellow here in town—name of Handerson—saw that part of it too. He was driving home from Wayton, and got to the house just before the roof caved in.

"The fire department people say they found signs of gasoline. The Coonses, Thornburgh's help, say they didn't have no gas on the place. So there you are."

"Thornburgh have any relatives?"

"Yeah. A niece in San Francisco—a Mrs. Evelyn Trowbridge. She was up yesterday, but there wasn't nothing she could do, and she couldn't tell us nothing much, so she went back home."

"Where are the servants now?"

"Here in town. Staying at a hotel on I Street. I told 'em to stick around for a few days."

"Thornburgh own the house?"

"Uh-huh. Bought it from Newning & Weed a couple months ago."

"You got anything to do this morning?"

"Nothing but this."

"Good! Let's get out and dig around."

We found the Coonses in their room at the hotel on I Street. Mr. Coons was a small-boned, plump man with the smooth, meaningless face, and the suavity of the typical male house-servant.

His wife was a tall, stringy woman, perhaps five years older than her husband—say, forty—with a mouth and chin that seemed shaped for gossiping. But he did all the talking, while she nodded her agreement to every second or third word.

"We went to work for Mr. Thornburgh on the fifteenth of June, I think," he said, in reply to my first question. "We came to Sacramento, around the first of the month, and put in applications at the Allis Employment Bureau. A couple of weeks later they sent us out to see Mr. Thornburgh, and he took us on."

"Where were you before you came here?"

"In Seattle, sir, with a Mrs. Comerford; but the climate there didn't agree with my wife—she has bronchial trouble—so we decided to come to California. We most likely would have stayed in Seattle, though, if Mrs. Comerford hadn't given up her house."

"What do you know about Thornburgh?"

"Very little, sir. He wasn't a talkative gentleman. He hadn't any business that I know of. I think he was a retired seafaring man. He never said he was, but he had that manner and look. He never went out or had anybody in to see him, except his niece once, and he didn't write or get any mail. He had a room next to his bedroom fixed up as a sort of workshop. He spent most of

7

his time in there. I always thought he was working on some kind of invention, but he kept the door locked, and wouldn't let us go near it."

"Haven't you any idea at all what it was?"

"No, sir. We never heard any hammering or noises from it, and never smelt anything either. And none of his clothes were ever the least bit soiled, even when they were ready to go out to the laundry. They would have been if he had been working on anything like machinery."

"Was he an old man?"

"He couldn't have been over fifty, sir. He was very erect, and his hair and beard were thick, with no gray hairs."

"Ever have any trouble with him?"

"Oh, no, sir! He was, if I may say it, a very peculiar gentleman in a way; and he didn't care about anything except having his meals fixed right, having his clothes taken care of—he was very particular about them—and not being disturbed. Except early in the morning and at night, we'd hardly see him all day."

"Now about the fire. Tell us the whole thing—everything you remember."

"Well, sir, I and my wife had gone to bed about ten o'clock, our regular time, and had gone to sleep. Our room was on the second floor, in the rear. Some time later—I never did exactly know what time it was—I woke up, coughing. The room was all full of smoke, and my wife was sort of strangling. I jumped up, and dragged her down the back stairs and out the back door, not thinking of anything but getting her out of there.

"When I had her safe in the yard, I thought of Mr. Thornburgh, and tried to get back in the house; but the whole first floor was just flames. I ran around front then, to see if he had got out, but didn't see anything of him. The whole yard was as light as day by then. Then I heard him scream—a horrible scream, sir—I can hear it yet! And I looked up at his window—that was the front second-story room—and saw him there, trying to get out the window. But all the woodwork was burning, and he screamed again and fell back, and right after that the roof over his room fell in.

"There wasn't a ladder or anything that I could have put up to the window for him—there wasn't anything I could have done.

"In the meantime, a gentleman had left his automobile in the road, and come up to where I was standing; but there wasn't anything we could do—the house was burning everywhere and falling in here and there. So we went back to where I had left my wife, and carried her farther away from the fire, and brought her to—she had fainted. And that's all I know about it, sir."

"Hear any noises earlier that night? Or see anybody hanging around?"

"No, sir."

"Have any gasoline around the place?"

"No, sir. Mr. Thornburgh didn't have a car."

"No gasoline for cleaning?"

"No, sir, none at all, unless Mr. Thornburgh had it in his workshop. When his clothes needed cleaning, I took them to town, and all his laundry was taken by the grocer's man, when he brought our provisions."

"Don't know anything that might have some bearing on the fire?"

"No, sir. I was surprised when I heard that somebody had set the house afire. I could hardly believe it. I don't know why anybody should want to do that."

"What do you think of them?" I asked McClump, as we left the hotel.

"They might pad the bills, or even go South with some of the silver, but they don't figure as killers in my mind."

That was my opinion, too; but they were the only persons known to have been there when the fire started except the man who had died. We went around to the Allis Employment Bureau and talked to the manager.

He told us that the Coonses had come into his office on June second, looking for work; and had given Mrs. Edward Comerford, 45 Woodmansee Terrace, Seattle, Washington, as reference. In reply to a letter—he always checked up the references of servants—Mrs. Comerford had written that the Coonses had been in her employ for a number of years, and had been "extremely satisfactory in every respect." On June thirteenth, Thornburgh had telephoned the bureau, asking that a man and his wife be sent out to keep house for him; and Allis had sent two couples that he had listed. Neither had been employed by Thornburgh, though Allis considered them more desirable than the Coonses, who were finally hired by Thornburgh.

All that would certainly seem to indicate that the Coonses hadn't deliberately maneuvered themselves into the place, unless they were the luckiest people in the world—and a detective can't afford to believe in luck or coincidence, unless he has unquestionable proof of it.

At the office of the real estate agents, through whom Thornburgh had bought the house—Newning & Weed—we were told that Thornburgh had come in on the eleventh of June, and had said that he had been told that the house was for sale, had looked it over, and wanted to know the price. The deal had been closed the next morning, and he had paid for the house with a check for $4,500 on the Scamen's Bank of San Francisco. The house was already furnished.

After luncheon, McClump and I called on Howard Handerson—the man who had seen the fire while driving home from Wayton. He had an office in the Empire Building, with his name and the title "Northern California Agent, Instant-Sheen Cleanser Company," on the door. He was a big, careless-looking man of forty-five or so, with the professionally jovial smile that belongs to the salesman.

He had been in Wayton on business the day of the fire, he said, and had stayed there until rather late, going to dinner and afterward playing pool with a grocer named Hammersmith—one of his customers. He had left Wayton in his machine, at about ten-thirty, and set out for Sacramento. At Tavender he had stopped at the garage for oil and gas and to have one of his tires blown up.

Just as he was about to leave the garage, the garage-man had called his attention to a red glare in the sky, and had told him that it was probably from a fire somewhere along the old county road that paralleled the State Road into Sacramento; so Handerson had taken the county road, and had arrived at the burning house just in time to see Thornburgh try to fight his way through the flames that enveloped him.

It was too late to make any attempt to put out the fire, and the man upstairs was beyond saving by then—undoubtedly dead even before the roof collapsed; so Handerson had helped Coons revive his wife, and stayed there watching the fire until it had burned itself out. He had seen no one on that county road while driving to the fire.

"What do you know about Handerson?" I asked McClump, when we were on the street.

"Came here, from somewhere in the East, I think, early in the summer to open that Cleanser agency. Lives at the Garden Hotel. Where do we go next?"

"We get a machine, and take a look at what's left of the Thornburgh house."

An enterprising incendiary couldn't have found a lovelier spot in which to turn himself loose, if he looked the whole county over. Tree-topped hills hid it from the rest of the world, on three sides; while away from the fourth, an uninhabited plain rolled down to the river. The county road that passed the front gate was shunned by automobiles, so McClump said, in favor of the State Highway to the north.

Where the house had been, was now a mound of blackened ruins. We poked around in the ashes for a few minutes—not that we expected to find anything, but because it's the nature of man to poke around in ruins.

A garage in the rear, whose interior gave no evidence of recent occupation, had a badly scorched roof and front, but was otherwise undamaged. A shed behind it, sheltering an ax, a shovel, and various odds and ends of gardening tools, had escaped the fire altogether. The lawn in front of the house, and the garden behind the shed—about an acre in all—had been pretty thoroughly cut and trampled by wagon wheels, and the feet of the firemen and the spectators.

Having ruined our shoe-shines, McClump and I got back in our machine and swung off in a circle around the place, calling at all the houses within a mile radius, and getting little besides jolts for our trouble.

The nearest house was that of Pringle, the man who had turned in the alarm; but he not only knew nothing about the dead man, but said he had never seen him. In fact, only one of the neighbors had ever seen him: a Mrs. Jabine, who lived about a mile to the south.

She had taken care of the key to the house while it was vacant; and a day or two before he bought it, Thornburgh had come to her house, inquiring about the vacant one. She had gone over there with him and showed him through it, and he had told her that he intended buying it, if the price, of which neither of them knew anything, wasn't too high.

He had been alone, except for the chauffeur of the hired car in which he had come from Sacramento, and, save that he had no family, he had told her nothing about himself.

Hearing that he had moved in, she went over to call on him several days later—"just a neighborly visit"—but had been told by Mrs. Coons that he was not at home. Most of the neighbors had talked to the Coonses, and had got the impression that Thornburgh did not care for visitors, so they had let him alone. The Coonses were described as "pleasant enough to talk to when you meet them," but reflecting their employer's desire not to make friends.

McClump summarized what the afternoon had taught us as we pointed our machine toward Tavender: "Any of these folks could have touched off the place, but we got nothing to show that any of 'em even knew Thornburgh, let alone had a bone to pick with him."

Tavender turned out to be a crossroads settlement of a general store and post office, a garage, a church, and six dwellings, about two miles from Thornburgh's place. McClump knew the storekeeper and postmaster, a scrawny little man named Philo, who stuttered moistly.

"I n-n-never s-saw Th-thornburgh," he said, "and I n-n-never had any m-mail for him. C-coons"—it sounded like one of these things butterflies come out of—"used to c-come in once a week t-to order groceries—they d-didn't have a phone. He used to walk in, and I'd s-send the stuff over in my c-c-car. Th-then I'd s-see him once in a while, waiting f-for the stage to S-s-sacramento."

"Who drove the stuff out to Thornburgh's?"

"M-m-my b-boy. Want to t-talk to him?"

The boy was a juvenile edition of the old man, but without the stutter. He had never seen Thornburgh on any of his visits, but his business had taken him only as far as the kitchen. He hadn't noticed anything peculiar about the place.

"Who's the night man at the garage?" I asked him, after we had listened to the little he had to tell.

"Billy Luce. I think you can catch him there now. I saw him go in a few minutes ago."

We crossed the road and found Luce.

"Night before last—the night of the fire down the road—was there a man here talking to you when you first saw it?"

He turned his eyes upward in that vacant stare which people use to aid their memory.

"Yes, I remember now! He was going to town, and I told him that if he took the county road instead of the State Road he'd see the fire on his way in."

"What kind of looking man was he?"

"Middle-aged—a big man, but sort of slouchy. I think he had on a brown suit, baggy and wrinkled."

"Medium complexion?"

"Yes."

"Smile when he talked?"

"Yes, a pleasant sort of fellow."

"Curly brown hair?"

"Have a heart!" Luce laughed. "I didn't put him under a magnifying glass."

From Tavender, we drove over to Wayton. Luce's description had fit Handerson all right; but while we were at it, we thought we might as well check up to make sure that he had been coming from Wayton.

We spent exactly twenty-five minutes in Wayton; ten of them finding Hammersmith, the grocer with whom Handerson had said he dined and played pool; five minutes finding the proprietor of the pool-room; and ten verifying Handerson's story.

"What do you think of it now, Mac?" I asked, as we rolled back toward Sacramento.

Mac's too lazy to express an opinion, or even form one, unless he's driven to it; but that doesn't mean they aren't worth listening to, if you can get them.

"There ain't a hell of a lot to think," he said cheerfully. "Handerson is out of it, if he ever was in it. There's nothing to show that anybody but the Coonses and Thornburgh were there when the fire started—but there may have been a regiment there. Them Coonses ain't too honest looking, maybe, but they ain't killers, or I miss my guess. But the fact remains that they're the only bet we got so far. Maybe we ought to try to get a line on them."

"All right," I agreed. "I'll get a wire off to our Seattle office asking them to interview Mrs. Comerford, and see what she can tell about them as soon as we get back in town. Then I'm going to catch a train for San Francisco, and see Thornburgh's niece in the morning."

Next morning, at the address McClump had given me—a rather elaborate apartment building on California Street—I had to wait three-quarters of an hour for Mrs. Evelyn Trowbridge to dress. If I had been younger, or a social caller, I suppose I'd have felt amply rewarded when she finally came in—a tall, slender woman of less than thirty; in some sort of clinging black affair; with a lot of black hair over a very white face, strikingly set off by a small red mouth and big hazel eyes that looked black until you got close to them.

But I was a busy, middle-aged detective, who was fuming over having his time wasted; and I was a lot more interested in finding the bird who struck the match than I was in feminine beauty. However, I smothered my grouch, apologized

for disturbing her at such an early hour, and got down to business.

"I want you to tell me all you know about your uncle—his family, friends, enemies, business connections, everything."

I had scribbled on the back of the card I had sent into her what my business was.

"He hadn't any family," she said; "unless I might be it. He was my mother's brother, and I am the only one of that family now living."

"Where was he born?"

"Here in San Francisco. I don't know the date, but he was about fifty years old, I think—three years older than my mother."

"What was his business?"

"He went to sea when he was a boy, and, so far as I know, always followed it until a few months ago."

"Captain?"

"I don't know. Sometimes I wouldn't see or hear from him for several years, and he never talked about what he was doing; though he would mention some of the places he had visited Rio de Janeiro, Madagascar, Tobago, Christiania. Then, about three months ago—some time in May—he came here and told me that he was through with wandering; that he was going to take a house in some quiet place where he could work undisturbed on an invention in which he was interested.

"He lived at the Francisco Hotel while he was in San Francisco. After a couple of weeks, he suddenly disappeared. And then, about a month ago, I received a telegram from him, asking me to come to see him at his house near Sacramento. I went up the very next day, and I thought that he was acting very queerly—he seemed very excited over something. He gave me a will that he had just drawn up and some life insurance policies in which I was beneficiary.

"Immediately after that he insisted that I return home, and hinted rather plainly that he did not wish me to either visit him again or write until I heard from him. I thought all that rather peculiar, as he had always seemed fond of me. I never saw him again."

"What was this invention he was working on?"

"I really don't know. I asked him once, but he became so excited—even suspicious—that I changed the subject, and never mentioned it again."

"Are you sure that he really did follow the sea all those years?"

"No, I am not. I just took it for granted; but he may have been doing something altogether different."

"Was he ever married?"

"Not that I know of."

"Know any of his friends or enemies?"

"No, none."

"Remember anybody's name that he ever mentioned?"

"No."

"I don't want you to think this next question insulting, though I admit it is. But it has to be asked. Where were you the night of the fire?"

"At home; I had some friends here to dinner, and they stayed until about midnight. Mr. and Mrs. Walker Kellogg, Mrs. John Dupree, and a Mr. Killmer, who is a lawyer. I can give you their addresses, or you can get them from the phone book, if you want to question them."

From Mrs. Trowbridge's apartment I went to the Francisco Hotel. Thornburgh had been registered there from May tenth to June thirteenth, and hadn't attracted much attention. He had been a tall, broad-shouldered, erect man of about fifty, with rather long brown hair brushed straight back; a short, pointed brown beard, and healthy, ruddy complexion—grave, quiet, punctilious in dress and manner; his hours had been regular and he had had no visitors that any of the hotel employees remembered.

At the Seamen's Bank—upon which Thornburgh's check, in payment of the house, had been drawn—I was told that he had opened an account there on May fifteenth, having been introduced by W. W. Jeffers & Sons, local stock brokers. A balance of a little more than four hundred dollars remained to his credit. The cancelled checks on hand were all to the order

of various life insurance companies; and for amounts that, if they represented premiums, testified to rather large policies. I jotted down the names of the life insurance companies, and then went to the offices of W. W. Jeffers & Sons.

Thornburgh had come in, I was told, on the tenth of May with $4,000 worth of Liberty bonds that he wanted sold. During one of his conversations with Jeffers, he had asked the broker to recommend a bank, and Jeffers had given him a letter of introduction to the Seamen's Bank.

That was all Jeffers knew about him. He gave me the numbers of the bonds, but tracing Liberty bonds isn't the easiest thing in the world.

The reply to my Seattle telegram was waiting for me at the agency when I arrived.

MRS. EDWARD COMERFORD RENTED APARTMENT AT ADDRESS YOU GIVE ON MAY TWENTY-FIVE GAVE IT UP JUNE SIX TRUNKS TO SAN FRANCISCO SAME DAY CHECK NUMBERS GN FOUR FIVE TWO FIVE EIGHT SEVEN AND EIGHT AND NINE

Tracing baggage is no trick at all, if you have the dates and check numbers to start with—as many a bird who is wearing somewhat similar numbers on his chest and back, because he overlooked that detail when making his getaway, can tell you—and twenty-five minutes in a baggage-room at the Ferry and half an hour in the office of a transfer company gave me my answer.

The trunks had been delivered to Mrs. Evelyn Trowbridge's apartment!

I got Jim Tarr on the phone and told him about it.

"Good shooting!" he said, forgetting for once to indulge his wit. "We'll grab the Coonses here and Mrs. Trowbridge there, and that's the end of another mystery."

"Wait a minute!" I cautioned him. "It's not all straightened out yet! There's still a few kinks in the plot."

"It's straight enough for me. I'm satisfied."

"You're the boss, but I think you're being a

little hasty. I'm going up and talk with the niece again. Give me a little time before you phone the police here to make the pinch. I'll hold her until they get there."

Evelyn Trowbridge let me in this time, instead of the maid who had opened the door for me in the morning, and she led me to the same room in which we had had our first talk. I let her pick out a seat, and then I selected one that was closer to either door than hers was.

On the way up I had planned a lot of innocent-sounding questions that would get her all snarled up; but after taking a good look at this woman sitting in front of me, leaning comfortably back in her chair, coolly waiting for me to speak my piece, I discarded the trick stuff and came out cold-turkey.

"Ever use the name Mrs. Edward Comerford?"

"Oh, yes." As casual as a nod on the street.

"When?"

"Often. You see, I happen to have been married not so long ago to Mr. Edward Comerford. So it's not really strange that I should have used the name."

"Use it in Seattle recently?"

"I would suggest," she said sweetly, "that if you are leading up to the references I gave Coons and his wife, you might save time by coming right to it?"

"That's fair enough," I said. "Let's do that."

There wasn't a half-tone, a shading, in voice, manner, or expression to indicate that she was talking about anything half so serious or important to her as a possibility of being charged with murder. She might have been talking about the weather, or a book that hadn't interested her particularly.

"During the time that Mr. Comerford and I were married, we lived in Seattle, where he still lives. After the divorce, I left Seattle and resumed my maiden name. And the Coonses _were_ in our employ, as you might learn if you care to look it up. You'll find my husband—or former husband—at the Chelsea apartments, I think.

"Last summer, or late spring, I decided to return to Seattle. The truth of it is—I suppose all my personal affairs will be aired anyhow— that I thought perhaps Edward and I might patch up our differences; so I went back and took an apartment on Woodmansee Terrace. As I was known in Seattle as Mrs. Edward Comerford, and as I thought my using his name might influence him a little, perhaps, I used it while I was there.

"Also I telephoned the Coonses to make tentative arrangements in case Edward and I should open our house again; but Coons told me that they were going to California, and so I gladly gave them an excellent recommendation when, some days later, I received a letter of inquiry from an employment bureau in Sacramento. After I had been in Seattle for about two weeks, I changed my mind about the reconciliation— Edward's interest, I learned, was all centered elsewhere; so I returned to San Francisco."

"Very nice! But—"

"If you will permit me to finish," she interrupted. "When I went to see my uncle in response to his telegram, I was surprised to find the Coonses in his house. Knowing my uncle's peculiarities, and finding them now increased, and remembering his extreme secretiveness about his mysterious invention, I cautioned the Coonses not to tell him that they had been in my employ.

"He certainly would have discharged them, and just as certainly would have quarreled with me—he would have thought that I was having him spied upon. Then, when Coons telephoned me after the fire, I knew that to admit that the Coonses had been formerly in my employ, would, in view of the fact that I was my uncle's heir, cast suspicion on all three of us. So we foolishly agreed to say nothing about it and carry on the deception."

That didn't sound all wrong, but it didn't sound all right. I wished Tarr had taken it easier and let us get a better line on these people, before having them thrown in the coop.

"The coincidence of the Coonses stumbling

into my uncle's house is, I fancy, too much for your detecting instincts," she went on, as I didn't say anything. "Am I to consider myself under arrest?"

I'm beginning to like this girl; she's a nice, cool piece of work.

"Not yet," I told her. "But I'm afraid it's going to happen pretty soon."

She smiled a little mocking smile at that, and another when the doorbell rang.

It was O'Hara from police headquarters. We turned the apartment upside down and inside out, but didn't find anything of importance except the will she had told me about, dated July eighth, and her uncle's life insurance policies. They were all dated between May fifteenth and June tenth, and added up to a little more than $200,000.

I spent an hour grilling the maid after O'Hara had taken Evelyn Trowbridge away, but she didn't know any more than I did. However, between her, the janitor, the manager of the apartments, and the names Mrs. Trowbridge had given me, I learned that she had really been entertaining friends on the night of the fire— until after eleven o'clock, anyway—and that was late enough.

Half an hour later I was riding the Short Line back to Sacramento. I was getting to be one of the line's best customers, and my anatomy was on bouncing terms with every bump in the road; and the bumps, as "Rubberhead" Davis used to say about the flies and mosquitoes in Alberta in summer, "is freely plentiful."

Between bumps I tried to fit the pieces of this Thornburgh puzzle together. The niece and the Coonses fit in somewhere, but not just where we had them. We had been working on the job sort of lop-sided, but it was the best we could do with it. In the beginning we had turned to the Coonses and Evelyn Trowbridge because there was no other direction to go; and now we had something on them—but a good lawyer could make hash of our case against them.

The Coonses were in the county jail when I got to Sacramento. After some questioning they had admitted their connection with the niece, and had come through with stories that matched hers in every detail.

Tarr, McClump, and I sat around the sheriff's desk and argued.

"Those yarns are pipe-dreams," the sheriff said. "We got all three of 'em cold, and there's nothing else to it. They're as good as convicted of murder!"

McClump grinned derisively at his superior, and then turned to me.

"Go on! You tell him about the holes in his little case. He ain't your boss, and can't take it out on you later for being smarter than he is!"

Tarr glared from one of us to the other.

"Spill it, you wise guys!" he ordered.

"Our dope is," I told him, figuring that McClump's view of it was the same as mine, "that there's nothing to show that even Thornburgh knew he was going to buy that house before the tenth of June, and that the Coonses were in town looking for work on the second. And besides, it was only by luck that they got the jobs. The employment office sent two couples out there ahead of them."

"We'll take a chance on letting the jury figure that out."

"Yes? You'll also take a chance on them figuring out that Thornburgh, who seems to have been a nut all right, might have touched off the place himself! We've got something on these people, Jim, but not enough to go into court with them! How are you going to prove that when the Coonses were planted in Thornburgh's house—if you can even prove they were—they and the Trowbridge woman knew he was going to load up with insurance policies?"

The sheriff spat disgustedly.

"You guys are the limit! You run around in circles, digging up the dope on these people until you get enough to hang 'em, and then you run around hunting for outs! What the hell's the matter with you now?"

I answered him from half-way to the door— the pieces were beginning to fit together under my skull.

"Going to run some more circles! Come on, Mac!"

McClump and I held a conference on the fly, and then I got a machine from the nearest garage and headed for Tavender. We made time going out, and got there before the general store had closed for the night. The stuttering Philo separated himself from the two men with whom he had been talking Hiram Johnson,[*] and followed me to the rear of the store.

"Do you keep an itemized list of the laundry you handle?"

"N-n-no; just the amounts."

"Let's look at Thornburgh's."

He produced a begrimed and rumpled account book and we picked out the weekly items I wanted: $2.60, $3.10, $2.25, and so on.

"Got the last batch of laundry here?"

"Y-yes," he said. "It j-just c-c-came out from the city t-today."

I tore open the bundle—some sheets, pillowcases, table-cloths, towels, napkins; some feminine clothing; some shirts, collars, underwear, sox that were unmistakably Coons's. I thanked Philo while running back to my machine.

Back in Sacramento again, McClump was waiting for me at the garage where I had hired the car.

"Registered at the hotel on June fifteenth, rented the office on the sixteenth. I think he's in the hotel now," he greeted me.

We hurried around the block to the Garden Hotel.

"Mr. Handerson went out a minute or two ago," the night clerk told us. "He seemed to be in a hurry."

"Know where he keeps his car?"

"In the hotel garage around the corner."

We were within two pavements of the garage, when Handerson's automobile shot out and turned up the street.

"Oh, Mr. Handerson!" I cried, trying to keep my voice level and smooth.

He stepped on the gas and streaked away from us.

"Want him?" McClump asked; and, at my nod, stopped a passing roadster by the simple expedient of stepping in front of it.

We climbed aboard, McClump flashed his star at the bewildered driver, and pointed out Handerson's dwindling tail-light. After he had persuaded himself that he wasn't being boarded by a couple of bandits, the commandeered driver did his best, and we picked up Handerson's tail-light after two or three turnings, and closed in on him—though his machine was going at a good clip.

By the time we reached the outskirts of the city, we had crawled up to within safe shooting distance, and I sent a bullet over the fleeing man's head. Thus encouraged, he managed to get a little more speed out of his car; but we were definitely overhauling him now.

Just at the wrong minute Handerson decided to look over his shoulder at us—an unevenness in the road twisted his wheels—his machine swayed—skidded—went over on its side. Almost immediately, from the heart of the tangle, came a flash and a bullet moaned past my ear. Another. And then, while I was still hunting for something to shoot at in the pile of junk we were drawing down upon, McClump's ancient and battered revolver roared in my other ear.

Handerson was dead when we got to him—McClump's bullet had taken him over one eye.

McClump spoke to me over the body.

"I ain't an inquisitive sort of fellow, but I hope you don't mind telling me why I shot this lad."

"Because he was Thornburgh."

He didn't say anything for about five minutes. Then: "I reckon that's right. How'd you guess it?"

We were sitting beside the wreckage now, waiting for the police that we had sent our commandeered chauffeur to phone for.

"He had to be," I said, "when you think it all over. Funny we didn't hit on it before! All that stuff we were told about Thornburgh had a fishy

---

[*] progressive U.S. senator from California, 1917–1945

sound. Whiskers and an unknown profession, immaculate and working on a mysterious invention, very secretive and born in San Francisco—where the fire wiped out all the old records—just the sort of fake that could be cooked up easily.

"Then nobody but the Coonses, Evelyn Trowbridge and Handerson ever saw him except between the tenth of May and the middle of June, when he bought the house. The Coonses and the Trowbridge woman were tied up together in this affair somehow, we knew—so that left only Handerson to consider. You had told me he came to Sacramento sometime early this summer—and the dates you got tonight show that he didn't come until after Thornburgh had bought his house. All right! Now compare Handerson with the descriptions we got of Thornburgh.

"Both are about the same size and age, and with the same color hair. The differences are all things that can be manufactured—clothes, a little sunburn, and a month's growth of beard, along with a little acting, would do the trick. Tonight I went out to Tavender and took a look at the last batch of laundry, and there wasn't any that didn't fit the Coonses—and none of the bills all the way back were large enough for Thornburgh to have been as careful about his clothes as we were told he was."

"It must be great to be a detective!" McClump grinned as the police ambulance came up and began disgorging policemen. "I reckon somebody must have tipped Handerson off that I was asking about him this evening." And then, regretfully: "So we ain't going to hang them folks for murder after all."

"No, but we oughtn't have any trouble convicting them of arson plus conspiracy to defraud, and anything else that the Prosecuting Attorney can think up."

BLACK MASK, OCTOBER 1, 1923

FROM THE AUTHOR OF "ARSON PLUS"

I'm glad you liked "Arson Plus"—it cost me gallons of sweat and acres of chewed finger nails! It went along nicely until I tried to bring it to an end—then it was hell-bent on running two or three thousand words further; but I finally fought it into reasonable length.

This detective of mine: I didn't deliberately keep him nameless, but he got through "Slippery Fingers" and "Arson Plus" without needing one, so I suppose I may as well let him run along that way. I'm not sure that he's entitled to a name, anyhow. He's more or less of a type: the private detective who oftenest is successful: neither the derby-hatted and broad-toed blockhead of one school of fiction, nor the all-knowing, infallible genius of another. I've worked with several of him.

Apropos of Charles Somerville's excellent article on capital punishment in the June 15th issue: under a law passed about two years ago, Nevada uses lethal gas for executions. The condemned man is placed in the lethal chamber during the week set by the court for his death. The gas is turned on while the condemned is asleep, the warden selecting the night of the week.

DASHIELL HAMMETT
San Francisco, Cal.

BLACK MASK, OCTOBER 1, 1923

Crooked Souls

BY DASHIELL HAMMETT

We've all seen the modern girl. She's a rare bird and here she is in all her glory—if that's what it is. A good detective yarn, this, with lots of action and some real people. Go to it.

HARVEY GATEWOOD HAD issued orders that I was to be admitted as soon as I arrived, so it only took me a little less than fifteen minutes to thread my way past the door-keepers, office boys, and secretaries who filled up most of the space between the Gatewood Lumber Corporation's front door and the president's private office. His office was large, all mahogany and bronze and green plush, with a mahogany desk as big as a bed in the center of the floor.

Gatewood, leaning across the desk, began to bark at me as soon as the obsequious clerk who had bowed me in bowed himself out.

"My daughter was kidnapped last night! I want the . . . that did it if it takes every cent I got!"

"Tell me about it," I suggested, drawing up the chair that he hadn't thought to offer me.

But he wanted results, it seemed, and not questions, and so I wasted nearly an hour getting information that he could have given me in fifteen minutes.

He's a big bruiser of a man, something over two hundred pounds of hard red flesh, and a czar from the top of his bullet head to the toes of his shoes that would have been at least number twelves if they hadn't been made to measure.

He had made his several millions by sand-bagging everybody that stood in his way, and the rage that he's burning up with now doesn't make him any easier to deal with.

His wicked jaw is sticking out like a knob of granite and his eyes are filmed with blood—he's in a lovely frame of mind. For a while it looks as if the Continental Detective Agency is going to lose a client; because I've made up my mind that he's going to tell me all I want to know, or I'm going to chuck up the job. But finally I got the story out of him.

His daughter Audrey had left their house on Clay street at about seven o'clock the preceding evening, telling her maid that she was going for a walk. She had not returned that night—though Gatewood had not known that until after he had read the letter that came this morning.

The letter had been from someone who said that she had been kidnapped. It demanded fifty thousand dollars for her release; and instructed Gatewood to get the money ready in hundred-dollar bills, so that there might be no delay when he is told in what manner it is to be paid over to his daughter's captors. As proof that the demand was not a hoax, a lock of the girl's hair, a ring she always wore, and a brief note from her, asking her father to comply with the demands, had been enclosed.

Gatewood had received the letter at his office, and had telephoned to his house immediately. He had been told that the girl's bed had not been slept in the previous night, and that none of the servants had seen her since she started out for her walk. He had then notified the police, turning the letter over to them; and, a few minutes later, he had decided to employ private detectives also.

"Now," he burst out, after I had wormed these things out of him, and he had told me that he knew nothing of his daughter's associates or habits, "go ahead and do something! I'm not paying you to sit around and talk about it!"

"What are you going to do?" I asked.

"Me? I'm going to put those . . . behind the bars if it takes every cent I've got in the world!"

"Sure! But first you can get that fifty thousand ready, so you can give it to them when they ask for it."

He clicked his jaw shut and thrust his face into mine.

"I've never been clubbed into doing anything in my life! And I'm too old to start now!" he said. "I'm going to call these people's bluff!"

"That's going to make it lovely for your daughter. But, aside from what it'll do to her, it's the wrong play. Fifty thousand isn't a whole lot to you, and paying it over will give us two chances that we haven't got now. One when the payment is made—a chance to either nab whoever comes for it or get a line on them. And the other when your daughter is returned. No matter how careful they are it's a cinch that she'll be able to tell us something that will help us grab them."

He shook his head angrily, and I was tired of arguing with him. So I left him, hoping that he'd see the wisdom of the course I had advised before too late.

At the Gatewood residence I found butlers, second men, chauffeurs, cooks, maids, upstairs girls, downstairs girls, and a raft of miscellaneous flunkies—he had enough servants to run a hotel.

What they told me amounted to this: The girl had not received a phone call, note by messenger, or telegram—the time-honored devices for luring a victim out to a murder or abduction—before she left the house. She had told her maid that she would be back within an hour or two; but the maid had not been alarmed when her mistress failed to return all night.

Audrey was the only child, and since her mother's death she had come and gone to suit herself. She and her father didn't hit it off very well together—their natures were too much alike, I gathered—and he never knew where she was; and there was nothing unusual about her remaining away all night, as she seldom bothered to leave word when she was going to stay overnight with friends.

She was nineteen years old, but looked several years older; about five feet five inches tall, and slender. She had blue eyes, brown hair,—very thick and long,—was pale and very nervous. Her photographs, of which I took a handful, showed that her eyes were large, her nose small and regular, and her chin obstinately pointed.

She was not beautiful, but in the one photograph where a smile had wiped off the sullenness of her mouth, she was at least pretty.

When she left the house she had worn a light tweed skirt and jacket with a London tailor's labels in them, a buff silk shirtwaist with stripes a shade darker, brown wool stockings, low-heeled brown oxfords, and an untrimmed gray felt hat.

I went up to her rooms—she had three on the third floor—and looked through all her stuff. I found nearly a bushel of photographs of men, boys, and girls; and a great stack of letters of varying degrees of intimacy, signed with a wide assortment of names and nicknames. I made notes of all the addresses I found.

Nothing there seemed to have any bearing on her abduction, but there was a chance that one of the names and addresses might be of some-one who had served as a decoy. Also, some of her friends might be able to tell us something of value.

I dropped in at the agency and distributed the names and addresses among the three operatives who were idle, sending them out to see what they could dig up.

Then I reached the police detectives who were working on the case—O'Gar and Thode—by telephone, and went down to the Hall of Justice to meet them. Lusk, a post office inspector, was also there. We turned the job around and around, looking at it from every angle, but not getting very far. We were all agreed, however, that we couldn't take a chance on any publicity, or work in the open, until the girl was safe.

They had had a worse time with Gatewood than I—he had wanted to put the whole thing in the newspapers, with the offer of a reward, photographs and all. Of course, Gatewood was right in claiming that this was the most effective way of catching the kidnappers—but it would have been tough on his daughter if her captors happened to be persons of sufficiently hardened character. And kidnappers as a rule aren't lambs.

I looked at the letter they had sent. It was printed with pencil on ruled paper of the kind that is sold in pads by every stationery dealer in the world. The envelope was just as common, also addressed in pencil, and post-marked "San Francisco, September 20, 9 P.M." That was the night she had been seized.

The letter reads:

"SIR:

WE HAVE YOUR CHARMING DAUGHTER AND PLACE A VALUE OF $50,000 UPON HER. YOU WILL GET THE MONEY READY IN $100 BILLS AT ONCE SO THERE WILL BE NO DELAY WHEN WE TELL YOU HOW IT IS TO BE PAID OVER TO US.

WE BEG TO ASSURE YOU THAT THINGS WILL GO BADLY WITH YOUR DAUGHTER SHOULD YOU NOT DO AS YOU ARE TOLD, OR SHOULD YOU BRING THE POLICE INTO THIS MATTER, OR SHOULD YOU DO ANYTHING FOOLISH.

$50,000 IS ONLY A SMALL FRAC-TION OF WHAT YOU STOLE WHILE WE WERE LIVING IN MUD AND BLOOD IN FRANCE FOR YOU, AND WE MEAN TO GET THAT MUCH OR. . . . . . . !

THREE."

A peculiar note in several ways. They are usually written with a great pretense of partial illiterateness. Almost always there's an attempt to lead suspicion astray. Perhaps the ex-service stuff was there for that purpose . . . or perhaps not.

Then there was a postscript:

"WE KNOW A CHINAMAN WHO WILL BUY HER EVEN AFTER WE ARE THROUGH WITH HER—IN CASE YOU WON'T LISTEN TO REASON."

The letter from the girl was written jerkily on the same kind of paper, apparently with the same pencil.

"Daddy—
Please do as they ask! I am so afraid—
Audrey"

A door at the other end of the room opened, and a head came through.

"O'Gar! Thode! Gatewood just called up. Get up to his office right away!"

The four of us tumbled out of the Hall of Justice and into a machine.

Gatewood was pacing his office like a maniac when we pushed aside enough hirelings to get to him. His face was hot with blood and his eyes had an insane glare in them.

"She just phoned me!" he cried thickly, when he saw us.

It took a minute or two to get him calm enough to tell us about it.

"She called me on the phone. Said, 'Oh, daddy! Do something! I can't stand this—they're killing me!' I asked her if she knew where she was, and she said, 'No, but I can see Twin Peaks from here. There's three men and a woman, and—' And then I heard a man curse, and a sound as if he had struck her, and the phone went dead. I tried to get central to give me the number, but she couldn't! It's a damned outrage the way the telephone system is run. We pay enough for service, God knows, and we . . ."

O'Gar scratched his head and turned away from Gatewood.

"In sight of Twin Peaks! There are hundreds of houses that are!"

Gatewood meanwhile had finished denouncing the telephone company and was pounding on his desk with a paperweight to attract our attention.

"Have you people done anything at all?" he demanded.

I answered him with another question: "Have you got the money ready?"

"No," he said, "I won't be held up by anybody!"

But he said it mechanically, without his usual conviction—the talk with his daughter had shaken him out of some of his stubbornness. He

was thinking of her safety a little now instead of altogether of his own fighting spirit.

We went at him hammer and tongs for a few minutes, and after a while he sent a clerk out for the money.

We split up the field then. Thode was to take some men from headquarters and see what he could find in the Twin Peaks end of town; but we weren't very optimistic over the prospects there—the territory was too large.

Lusk and O'Gar were to carefully mark the bills that the clerk brought from the bank, and then stick as close to Gatewood as they could without attracting attention. I was to go out to Gatewood's house and stay there.

The abductors had plainly instructed Gatewood to get the money ready immediately so that they could arrange to get it on short notice—not giving him time to communicate with anyone or make any plans.

Gatewood was to get hold of the newspapers, give them the whole story, with the $10,000 reward he was offering for the abductors' capture, to be published as soon as the girl was safe—so that we would get the help of publicity at the earliest moment possible without jeopardizing the girl.

The police in all the neighboring towns had already been notified—that had been done before the girl's phone message had assured us that she was held in San Francisco.

Nothing happened at the Gatewood residence all that evening. Harvey Gatewood came home early; and after dinner he paced his library floor and drank whiskey until bedtime, demanding every few minutes that we, the detectives in the case, do something besides sit around like a lot of damned mummies. O'Gar, Lusk and Thode were out in the street, keeping an eye on the house and neighborhood.

At midnight Harvey Gatewood went to bed. I declined a bed in favor of the library couch, which I dragged over beside the telephone, an extension of which was in Gatewood's bedroom.

At two-thirty the bell rang. I listened in while Gatewood talked from his bed.

A man's voice, crisp and curt: "Gatewood?"

"Yes."

"Got the dough?"

"Yes."

Gatewood's voice was thick and blurred—I could imagine the boiling that was going on inside him.

"Good!" came the brisk voice. "Put a piece of paper around it, and leave the house with it, right away! Walk down Clay street, keeping on the same side as your house. Don't walk too fast and keep walking. If everything's all right, and there's no elbows tagging along, somebody'll come up to you between your house and the waterfront. They'll have a handkerchief up to their face for a second, and then they'll let it fall to the ground.

"When you see that, you'll lay the money on the pavement, turn around and walk back to your house. If the money isn't marked, and you don't try any fancy tricks, you'll get your daughter back in an hour or two. If you try to pull anything—remember what we wrote you about the Chink! Got it straight?"

Gatewood sputtered something that was meant for an affirmative, and the telephone clicked silent.

I didn't waste any of my precious time tracing the call—it would be from a public telephone, I knew—but yelled up the stairs to Gatewood:

"You do as you were told, and don't try any foolishness!"

Then I ran out into the early morning air to find the police detectives and the post office inspector.

They had been joined by two plainclothes men, and had two automobiles waiting. I told them what the situation was, and we laid hurried plans.

O'Gar was to drive in one of the machines down Sacramento street, and Thode, in the other, down Washington street. These streets parallel Clay, one on each side. They were to drive slowly, keeping pace with Gatewood, and stopping at each cross street to see that he passed.

When he failed to cross within a reasonable time they were to turn up to Clay street—and their actions from then on would have to be guided by chance and their own wits.

Lusk was to wander along a block or two ahead of Gatewood, on the opposite side of the street, pretending to be mildly intoxicated, and keeping his eyes and ears open.

I was to shadow Gatewood down the street, with one of the plainclothes men behind me. The other plainclothes man was to turn in a call at headquarters for every available man to be sent to Clay street. They would arrive too late, of course, and as likely as not it would take them some time to find us; but we had no way of knowing what was going to turn up before the night was over.

Our plan was sketchy enough, but it was the best we could do—we were afraid to grab whoever got the money from Gatewood. The girl's talk with her father that afternoon had sounded too much as if her captors were desperate for us to take any chances on going after them rough-shod until she was out of their hands.

We had hardly finished our plans when Gatewood, wearing a heavy overcoat, left his house and turned down the street.

Farther down, Lusk, weaving along, talking to himself, was almost invisible in the shadows. There was no one else in sight. That meant that I had to give Gatewood at least two blocks' lead, so that the man who came for the money wouldn't tumble to me. One of the plainclothes men was half a block behind me, on the other side of the street.

Two blocks down we walked, and then a little chunky man in a derby hat came into sight. He passed Gatewood, passed me, went on.

Three blocks more.

A touring-car, large, black, powerfully engined, and with lowered curtains, came from the rear, passed us, went on. Possibly a scout! I scrawled its license number down on my pad without taking my hand out of my overcoat pocket.

Another three blocks.

A policeman passed, strolling along in ignorance of the game being played under his nose; and then a taxicab with a single male passenger. I wrote down its license number.

Four blocks with no one in sight ahead of me but Gatewood—I couldn't see Lusk any more.

Just ahead of Gatewood a man stepped out of a black doorway—turned around—called up to a window for someone to come down and open the door for him.

We went on.

Coming from nowhere, a woman stood on the sidewalk fifty feet ahead of Gatewood, a handkerchief to her face. It fluttered to the pavement.

Gatewood stopped, standing stiff-legged. I could see his right hand come up, lifting the side of the overcoat in which it was pocketed—and I knew the hand was gripped around a pistol.

For perhaps half a minute he stood like a statue. Then his left hand came out of his pocket, and the bundle of money fell to the sidewalk in front of him, where it made a bright blur in the darkness. Gatewood turned abruptly, and began to retrace his steps homeward.

The woman had recovered her handkerchief. Now she ran to the bundle, picked it up, and scuttled to the black mouth of an alley, a few feet distant—a rather tall woman, bent, and in dark clothes from head to feet.

In the black mouth of the alley she vanished.

I had been compelled to slow up while Gatewood and the woman stood facing each other, and I was more than a block away now. As soon as the woman disappeared I took a chance, and started pounding my rubber soles against the pavement.

The alley was empty when I reached it.

It ran all the way through to the next street, but I knew that the woman couldn't have reached the other end before I got to this one. I carry a lot of weight these days, but I can still step a block or two in good time. Along both sides of the alley were the rears of apartment buildings, each with its back door looking blankly, secretively at me.

The plainclothes man who had been trailing behind me came up, then O'Gar and Thode in their machines, and soon, Lusk. O'Gar and Thode rode off immediately to wind through the neighboring streets, hunting for the woman. Lusk and the plainclothes man each planted himself on a corner from which two of the streets enclosing the block could be watched.

I went through the alley, hunting vainly for an unlocked door, an open window, a fire-escape that would show recent use—any of the signs that a hurried departure from the alley might leave.

Nothing!

O'Gar came back shortly with some reinforcements from headquarters that he had picked up, and Gatewood.

Gatewood was burning.

"Bungled the damn thing again! I won't pay your agency a nickel, and I'll see that some of these so-called detectives get put back in a uniform and set to walking beats!"

"What'd the woman look like?" I asked him.

"I don't know! I thought you were hanging around to take care of her! She was old and bent, kind of, I guess, but I couldn't see her face for her veil. I don't know! What the hell were you men doing? It's a damned outrage the way . . ."

I finally got him quieted down and took him home, leaving the city men to keep the neighborhood under surveillance. There was fourteen or fifteen of them on the job now, and every shadow held at least one.

The girl would naturally head for home as soon as she was released and I wanted to be there to pump her. There was an excellent chance of catching her abductors before they got very far if she could tell us anything at all about them.

Home, Gatewood went up against the whiskey bottle again, while I kept one ear cocked at the telephone and the other at the front door. O'Gar or Thode phoned every half hour or so to ask if we'd heard from the girl. They had still found nothing.

At nine o'clock they, with Lusk, arrived at the house. The woman in black had turned out to be a man, and had gotten away.

In the rear of one of the apartment buildings

that touched the alley—just a foot or so within the back-door—they found a woman's skirt, long coat, hat and veil—all black. Investigating the occupants of the house, they had learned that an apartment had been rented to a young man named Leighton three days before.

Leighton was not at home when they went up to his apartment. His rooms held a lot of cold cigarette butts, and an empty bottle, and nothing else that had not been there when he rented it.

The inference was clear: he had rented the apartment so that he might have access to the building. Wearing woman's clothes over his own, he had gone out of the back door—leaving it unlatched behind him—to meet Gatewood.

Then he had run back into the building, discarded his disguise, and hurried through the building, out the front door, and away before we had our feeble net around the block; perhaps dodging into dark doorways here and there to avoid O'Gar and Thode in their automobiles.

Leighton, it seemed, was a man of about thirty, slender, about five feet eight or nine inches tall, with dark hair and eyes; rather good-looking, and well-dressed, on the two occasions when people living in the building had seen him, in a brown suit and a light brown felt hat.

There was no possibility, according to the opinions of both of the detectives and the post office inspector, that the girl might have been held, even temporarily, in Leighton's apartment.

Ten o'clock came, and no word from the girl.

Gatewood had lost his domineering bull-headedness by now and was breaking up. The suspense was getting him, and the liquor he had put away wasn't helping him. I didn't like him either personally or by reputation, but at that I felt sorry for him this morning.

I talked to the agency over the phone and got the reports of the operatives who had been looking up Audrey's friends. The last person to see her had been an Agnes Dangerfield, who had seen her walking down Market street near Sixth, alone, on the night of her abduction—some time between 8:15 and 8:45. Audrey had been too far away for the Dangerfield girl to speak to her.

For the rest, the boys had learned nothing except that Audrey was a wild, spoiled youngster who hadn't shown any great care in selecting her friends—just the sort of girl who could easily fall into the hands of a mob of highbinders!*

Noon struck. No sign of the girl. We told the newspapers to turn loose the story, with the added developments of the past few hours.

Gatewood was broken; he sat with his head in his hands, looking at nothing. Just before I left to follow a hunch I had, he looked up at me, and I'd never have recognized him if I hadn't seen the change take place.

"What do you think is keeping her away?" he asked.

I didn't have the heart to tell him what I was beginning to suspect, now that the money had been paid and she had failed to show up. So I stalled with some vague assurances, and left.

I caught a street-car and dropped off down in the shopping district. I visited the five largest department stores, going to all the women's wear departments from shoes to hats, and trying to learn if a man—perhaps one answering Leighton's description—had been buying clothes that would fit Audrey Gatewood within the past couple days.

Failing to get any results, I turned the rest of the local stores over to one of the boys from the agency, and went across the bay to canvass the Oakland stores.

At the first one I got action. A man who might easily have been Leighton had been in the day before, buying clothes that could easily fit Audrey. He had bought lots of them, everything from lingerie to a cloak, and—my luck was hitting on all its cylinders—had had his purchases delivered to T. Offord, at an address on Fourteenth street.

At the Fourteenth street address, an apartment house, I found Mr. and Mrs. Theodore Offord's names under the vestibule telephone for apartment 202.

I had just found them when the front door

_____

* Chinese thugs

opened and a stout, middle-aged woman in a gingham house-dress came out. She looked at me a bit curiously, so I asked:

"Do you know where I can find the manager?"

"I'm the manager," she said.

I handed her a card and stepped indoors with her.

"I'm from the bonding department of the North American Casualty Company"—a repetition of the lie that was printed on the card I had given her—"and a bond for Mr. Offord has been applied for. Is he all right so far as you know?" With the slightly apologetic air of one going through with a necessary but not too important formality.

She frowned.

"A bond? That's funny! He is going away tomorrow."

"Well, I can't say what the bond is for," I said lightly. "We investigators just get the names and addresses. It may be for his present employer, or perhaps the man he is going to work for wherever he's going has applied for it. Or some firms have us look up prospective employees before they hire them, just to be safe."

"Mr. Offord, so far as I know, is a very nice young man," she said, "but he has been here only a week."

"Not staying long, then?"

"No. They came here from Denver, intending to stay, but the low altitude doesn't agree with Mrs. Offord, so they are going back."

"Are you sure they came from Denver?"

"Well," she said, "they told me they did."

"How many of them are there?"

"Only the two of them; they're young people."

"Well, how do they impress you?" I asked, trying to get the impression that I thought her a woman of shrewd judgment over.

"They seem to be a very nice young couple. You'd hardly know they were in their apartment most of the time, they are so quiet. I am sorry they can't stay."

"Do they go out much?"

"I really don't know. They have their keys, and unless I should happen to pass them going in or out I'd never see them."

"Then, as a matter of fact, you couldn't say whether they stayed away all night some nights or not. Could you?"

She eyed me doubtfully—I was stepping way over my pretext now, but I didn't think it mattered—and shook her head.

"No, I couldn't say."

"They have many visitors?"

"I don't know. Mr. Offord is not—"

She broke off as a man came in quietly from the street, brushed past me, and started to mount the steps to the second floor.

"Oh, dear!" she whispered. "I hope he didn't hear me talking about him. That's Mr. Offord."

A slender man in brown, with a light brown hat—Leighton perhaps.

I hadn't seen anything of him except his back, nor he anything except mine. I watched him as he climbed the stairs. If he had heard the manager mention his name he would use the turn at the head of the stairs to sneak a look at me.

He did. I kept my face stolid, but I knew him. He was "Penny" Quayle, a con man who had been active in the East four or five years before. His face was as expressionless as mine. But he knew me.

A door on the second floor shut. I left the manager and started for the stairs.

"I think I'll go up and talk to him," I told her.

Coming silently to the door of apartment 202, I listened. Not a sound. This was no time for hesitation. I pressed the bell-button.

As close together as the tapping of three keys under the fingers of an expert typist, but a thousand times more vicious, came three pistol shots. And waist-high in the door of apartment 202 were three bullet holes.

The three bullets would have been in my fat carcass if I hadn't learned years ago to stand to one side of strange doors when making uninvited calls.

Inside the apartment sounded a man's voice, sharp, commanding.

"Cut it, kid! For God's sake, not that!"

A woman's voice, shrill, bitter, spiteful screaming blasphemies.

Two more bullets came through the door.

"Stop! No! No!" The man's voice had a note of fear in it now.

The woman's voice, cursing hotly. A scuffle. A shot that didn't hit the door.

I hurled my foot against the door, near the knob, and the lock broke away.

On the floor of the room, a man—Quayle—and a woman were tussling. He was bending over her, holding her wrists, trying to keep her down. A smoking automatic pistol was in one of her hands. I got to it in a jump and tore it loose.

"That's enough!" I called to them when I was planted. "Get up and receive company."

Quayle released his antagonist's wrists, whereupon she struck at his eyes with curved, sharp-nailed fingers, tearing his cheek open. He scrambled away from her on hands and knees, and both of them got to their feet.

He sat down on a chair immediately, panting and wiping his bleeding cheek with a handkerchief.

She stood, hands on hips, in the center of the room, glaring at me.

"I suppose," she spat, "you think you've raised hell!"

I laughed—I could afford to.

"If your father is in his right mind," I told her, "he'll do it with a razor strop when he gets you home again. A fine joke you picked out to play on him!"

"If you'd been tied to him as long as I have, and had been bullied and held down as much, I guess you'd do most anything to get enough money so that you could go away and live your own life."

I didn't say anything to that. Remembering some of the business methods Harvey Gatewood had used—particularly some of his war contracts that the Department of Justice was still investigating—I suppose the worst that could be said about Audrey was that she was her father's own daughter.

"How'd you rap to it?" Quayle asked me, politely.

"Several ways," I said. "First, I'm a little doubtful about grown persons being kidnapped in cities. Maybe it really happens sometimes, but at least nine-tenths of the cases you hear about are fakes. Second, one of Audrey's friends saw her on Market street between 8:15 and 8:45 the night she disappeared; and your letter to Gatewood was post-marked 9 P.M. Pretty fast work. You should have waited a while before mailing it, even if it had to miss the first morning delivery. I suppose she dropped it in the post office on her way over here?"

Quayle nodded.

"Then third," I went on, "there was that phone call of hers. She knew it took anywhere from ten to fifteen minutes to get her father on the wire at the office. If time had been as valuable as it would have been if she had gotten to a phone while imprisoned, she'd have told her story to the first person she got hold of—the phone girl, most likely. So that made it look as if, besides wanting to throw out that Twin Peaks line, she wanted to stir the old man out of his bullheadedness.

"When she failed to show up after the money was paid I figured it was a sure bet that she had kidnapped herself. I knew that if she came back home after faking this thing we'd find it out before we'd talked to her very long—and I figured she knew that too, and would stay away.

"The rest was easy, as I got some good breaks. We knew a man was working with her after we found the woman's clothes you left behind, and I took a chance on there being no one else in it. Then I figured she'd need clothes—she couldn't have taken any from home without tipping her mitt—and there was an even chance that she hadn't laid in a stock beforehand. She's got too many girl friends of the sort that do a lot of shopping to make it safe for her to risk showing herself in stores. Maybe, then, the man would buy what she needed for her. And it turned out that he did, and that he was too lazy to carry away his purchases, or perhaps there was too many of them, and so he had them sent out. That's the story."

Quayle nodded again.

"I was damned careless," he said, and then, jerking a contemptuous thumb toward the girl, "but what can you expect? She's had a skin full of hop ever since we started. Took all my time and attention keeping her from running wild and gumming the works. Just now was a sample—I told her you were coming up and she goes crazy and tries to add your corpse to the wreck!"

The Gatewood reunion took place in the office of the captain of inspectors, on the second floor of the Oakland City Hall, and it was a merry little party. For an hour it was a toss-up whether Harvey Gatewood would die of apoplexy, strangle his daughter, or send her off to the state reformatory until she was of age. But Audrey licked him. Besides being a chip off the old block, she was young enough to be careless of consequences, while her father, for all his bullheadedness, had had some caution hammered into him.

The card she beat him with was a threat of spilling everything she knew about him to the newspapers, and at least one of the San Francisco papers had been trying to get his scalp for years. I don't know what she had on him, and I don't think he was any too sure himself; but, with his war contracts even then being investigated by the Department of Justice, he couldn't afford to take a chance. There was no doubt at all that she would have done as she threatened.

And so, together, they left for home, sweating hate for each other at every pore.

We took Quayle upstairs and put him in a cell, but he was too experienced to let that worry him. He knew that if the girl was to be spared, he himself couldn't very easily be convicted of anything.

BLACK MASK, OCTOBER 15, 1923

Slippery Fingers

BY PETER COLLINSON

(Author of "The Vicious Circle")

You'll have the time of your life trying to solve this crime before you get to the end of the story. You'll think some of the characters don't act logically, but when you figure it out afterward you'll decide they were all pretty wise.

"YOU ARE ALREADY FAMILIAR, of course, with the particulars of my father's—ah—death?"

"The papers are full of it, and have been for three days," I said, "and I've read them; but I'll have to have the whole story first-hand."

"There isn't very much to tell."

This Frederick Grover was a short, slender man of something under thirty years, and dressed like a picture out of *Vanity Fair*.* His almost girlish features and voice did nothing to make him more impressive, but I began to forget these things after a few minutes. He wasn't a sap. I knew that downtown, where he was rapidly building up a large and lively business in stocks and bonds without calling for too much help

---
* stylish American magazine, founded in 1913, featuring fashion and popular culture

from his father's millions, he was considered a shrewd article; and I wasn't surprised later when Benny Forman, who ought to know, told me that Frederick Grover was the best poker player west of Chicago. He was a cool, well-balanced, quick-thinking little man.

"Father has lived here alone with the servants since mother's death, two years ago," he went on. "I am married, you know, and live in town. Last Saturday evening he dismissed Barton—Barton was his butler-valet, and had been with father for quite a few years—at a little after nine, saying that he did not want to be disturbed during the evening.

"Father was here in the library at the time, looking through some papers. The servants' rooms are in the rear, and none of the servants seem to have heard anything during the night.

27

"At seven-thirty the following morning—Sunday—Barton found father lying on the floor, just to the right of where you are sitting, dead, stabbed in the throat with the brass paper-knife that was always kept on the table here. The front door was ajar.

"The police found bloody finger-prints on the knife, the table, and the front door; but so far they have not found the man who left the prints, which is why I am employing your agency. The physician who came with the police placed the time of father's death at between eleven o'clock and midnight.

"Later, on Monday, we learned that father had drawn $10,000 in hundred-dollar bills from the bank Saturday morning. No trace of the money has been found. My finger-prints, as well as the servants', were compared with the ones found by the police, but there was no similarity. I think that is all."

"Do you know of any enemies your father had?"

He shook his head.

"I know of none, though he may have had them. You see, I really didn't know my father very well. He was a very reticent man and, until his retirement, about five years ago, he spent most of his time in South America, where most of his mining interests were. He may have had dozens of enemies, though Barton—who probably knew more about him than anyone—seems to know of no one who hated father enough to kill him."

"How about relatives?"

"I was his heir and only child, if that is what you are getting at. So far as I know he had no other living relatives."

"I'll talk to the servants," I said.

The maid and the cook could tell me nothing, and I learned very little more from Barton. He had been with Henry Grover since 1912, had been with him in Yunnan, Peru, Mexico, and Central America, but apparently he knew little or nothing of his master's business or acquaintances.

He said that Grover had not seemed excited or worried on the night of the murder, and that nearly every night Grover dismissed him at about the same time, with orders that he be not disturbed; so no importance was to be attached to that part of it. He knew of no one with whom Grover had communicated during the day, and he had not seen the money Grover had drawn from the bank.

I made a quick inspection of the house and grounds, not expecting to find anything; and I didn't. Half the jobs that come to a private detective are like this one: three or four days—and often as many weeks—have passed since the crime was committed. The police work on the job until they are stumped; then the injured party calls in a private sleuth, dumps him down on a trail that is old and cold and badly trampled, and expects—Oh, well! I picked out this way of making a living, so . . .

I looked through Grover's papers—he had a safe and a desk full of them—but didn't find anything to get excited about. They were mostly columns of figures.

"I'm going to send an accountant out here to go over your father's books," I told Frederick Grover. "Give him everything he asks for, and fix it up with the bank so they'll help him."

I caught a street-car and went back to town, called at Ned Root's office, and headed him out toward Grover's. Ned is a human adding machine with educated eyes, ears, and nose. He can spot a kink in a set of books farther than I can see the covers.

"Keep digging until you find something, Ned, and you can charge Grover whatever you like. Give me something to work on—quick!"

The murder had all the earmarks of one that had grown out of blackmail, though there was—there always is—a chance that it might have been something else. But it didn't look like the work of an enemy or a burglar: either of them would have packed his weapon with him, would not have trusted to finding it on the grounds. Of course, if Frederick Grover, or one of the servants, had killed Henry Grover . . . but the finger-prints said "No."

Just to play safe, I put in a few hours getting a line on Frederick. He had been at a ball on the night of the murder; he had never, so far as I could learn, quarreled with his father; his father was liberal with him, giving him everything he wanted; and Frederick was taking in more money in his brokerage office than he was spending. No motive for a murder appeared on the surface there.

At the city detective bureau I hunted up the police sleuths who had been assigned to the murder; Marty O'Hara and George Dean. It didn't take them long to tell me what they knew about it. Whoever had made the bloody finger-prints was not known to the police here: they had not found the prints in their files. The classifications had been broadcast to every large city in the country, but with no results so far.

A house four blocks from Grover's had been robbed on the night of the murder, and there was a slim chance that the same man *might* have been responsible for both jobs. But the burglary had occurred after one o'clock in the morning, which made the connection look not so good. A burglar who had killed a man, and perhaps picked up $10,000 in the bargain, wouldn't be likely to turn his hand to another job right away.

I looked at the paper-knife with which Grover had been killed, and at the photographs of the bloody prints, but they couldn't help me much just now. There seemed to be nothing to do but get out and dig around until I turned up something somewhere.

Then the door opened, and Joseph Clane was ushered into the room where O'Hara, Dean and I were talking.

Clane was a hard-bitten citizen, for all his prosperous look; fifty or fifty-five, I'd say, with eyes, mouth and jaw that held plenty of humor but none of what is sometimes called the milk of human kindness.

He was a big man, beefy, and all dressed up in a tight-fitting checkered suit, fawn-colored hat, patent-leather shoes with buff uppers, and the rest of the things that go with that sort of combination. He had a harsh voice that was as empty of expression as his hard red face, and he held his body stiffly, as if he was afraid the buttons on his too-tight clothes were about to pop off. Even his arms hung woodenly at his sides, with thick fingers that were lifelessly motionless.

He came right to the point. He had been a friend of the murdered man's, and thought that perhaps what he could tell us would be of value.

He had met Henry Grover—he called him "Henny"—in 1894, in Ontario, where Grover was working a claim: the gold mine that had started the murdered man along the road to wealth. Clane had been employed by Grover as foreman, and the two men had become close friends. A man named Denis Waldeman had a claim adjoining Grover's and a dispute had arisen over their boundaries. The dispute ran on for some time—the men coming to blows once or twice—but finally Grover seems to have triumphed, for Waldeman suddenly left the country.

Clane's idea was that if we could find Waldeman we might find Grover's murderer, for considerable money had been involved in the dispute, and Waldeman was "a mean cuss, for a fact," and not likely to have forgotten his defeat.

Clane and Grover had kept in touch with each other, corresponding or meeting at irregular intervals, but the murdered man had never said or written anything that would throw a light on his death. Clane, too, had given up mining, and now had a small string of race-horses which occupied all his time.

He was in the city for a rest between racing-meets, had arrived two days before the murder, but had been too busy with his own affairs—he had discharged his trainer and was trying to find another—to call upon his friend. Clane was staying at the Marquis hotel, and would be in the city for a week or ten days longer.

"How come you've waited three days before coming to tell us all this?" Dean asked him.

"I wasn't noways sure I had ought to do it. I wasn't never sure in my mind but what maybe Henny done for that fellow Waldeman—he disappeared sudden-like. And I didn't want to do nothing to dirty Henny's name. But finally I decided to do the right thing. And then there's another thing: you found some finger-prints in Henny's house, didn't you? The newspapers said so."

"We did."

"Well, I want you to take mine and match them up. I was out with a girl the night of the murder"—he leered suddenly, boastingly—"all night! And she's a good girl, got a husband and a lot of folks; and it wouldn't be right to drag her into this to prove that I wasn't in Henny's house when he was killed, in case you'd maybe think I killed him. So I thought I better come down here, tell you all about it, and get you to take my finger-prints, and have it all over with."

We went up to the identification bureau and had Clane's prints taken. They were not at all like the murderer's.

After we pumped Clane dry I went out and sent a telegram to our Toronto office, asking them to get a line on the Waldeman angle. Then I hunted up a couple of boys who eat, sleep, and breathe horse racing. They told me that Clane was well known in racing circles as the owner of a small string of near-horses* that ran as irregularly as the stewards would permit.

At the Marquis hotel I got hold of the house detective, who is a helpful chap so long as his hand is kept greased.† He verified my information about Clane's status in the sporting world, and told me that Clane had stayed at the hotel for several days at a time, off and on, within the past couple years.

He tried to trace Clane's telephone calls for me but—as usual when you want them—the records were jumbled. I arranged to have the girls on the switchboard listen in on any talking he did during the next few days.

Ned Root was waiting for me when I got down to the office the next morning. He had worked on Grover's accounts all night, and had found enough to give me a start. Within the past year— that was as far back as Ned had gone—Grover

had drawn out of his bank-accounts nearly fifty thousand dollars that couldn't be accounted for; nearly fifty thousand exclusive of the ten thousand he had drawn the day of the murder. Ned gave me the amounts and the dates:

May 6, 1922, $15,000
June 10, 5,000
August 1, 5,000
October 10, 10,000
January 3, 1923, 12,500

Forty-seven thousand, five hundred dollars! Somebody was getting fat off him!

The local managers of the telegraph companies raised the usual howl about respecting their patrons' privacy, but I got an order from the Prosecuting Attorney and put a clerk at work on the files of each office.

Then I went back to the Marquis hotel and looked at the old registers. Clane had been there from May 4th to 7th, and from October 8th to 15th last year. That checked off two of the dates upon which Grover had made his withdrawals.

I had to wait until nearly six o'clock for my information from the telegraph companies, but it was worth waiting for. On the third of last January Henry Grover had telegraphed $12,500 to Joseph Clane in San Diego. The clerks hadn't found anything on the other dates I had given them, but I wasn't at all dissatisfied. I had Joseph Clane fixed as the man who had been getting fat off Grover.

I sent Dick Foley—he is the agency's shadow-ace—and Bob Teal—a youngster who will be a world-beater some day—over to Clane's hotel.

"Plant yourselves in the lobby," I told them. "I'll be over in a few minutes to talk to Clane, and I'll try to bring him down in the lobby where you can get a good look at him. Then I want him shadowed until he shows up at police headquarters tomorrow. I want to know where he goes and who he talks to. And if he spends much time talking to any one person, or their conversation seems very important, I want one of you boys to trail the other man, to see who he is and what he does. If

---

* derogatory term for a team of horses, such as plow horses
† paid off

Clane tries to blow town, grab him and have him thrown in the can, but I don't think he will."

I gave Dick and Bob time enough to get themselves placed, and then went to the hotel. Clane was out, so I waited. He came in a little after eleven and I went up to his room with him. I didn't hem-and-haw, but came out cold-turkey:

"All the signs point to Grover's having been blackmailed. Do you know anything about it?"

"No," he said.

"Grover drew a lot of money out of his banks at different times. You got some of it, I know, and I suppose you got most of it. What about it?"

He didn't pretend to be insulted, or even surprised by my talk. He smiled a little grimly, maybe, but as if he thought it the most natural thing in the world—and it was, at that—for me to suspect him.

"I told you that me and Henny were pretty chummy, didn't I? Well, you ought to know that all us fellows that fool with the bang-tails* have our streaks of bad luck. Whenever I'd get up against it I'd hit Henny up for a stake; like at Tijuana last winter where I got into a flock of bad breaks. Henny lent me twelve or fifteen thousand and I got back on my feet again. I've done that often. He ought to have some of my letters and wires in his stuff. If you look through his things you'll find them."

I didn't pretend that I believed him.

"Suppose you drop into police headquarters at nine in the morning and we'll go over everything with the city dicks," I told him.

And then, to make my play stronger:

"I wouldn't make it much later than nine—they might be out looking for you."

"Uh-huh," was all the answer I got.

I went back to the agency and planted myself within reach of a telephone, waiting for word from Dick and Bob. I thought I was sitting pretty. Clane had been blackmailing Grover—I didn't have a single doubt of that—and I didn't think he had been very far away when Grover

_____
* horses

was killed. That woman alibi of his sounded all wrong!

But the bloody finger-prints were not Clane's—unless the police identification bureau had pulled an awful boner—and the man who had left the prints was the bird I was setting my cap for. Clane had let three days pass between the murder and his appearance at headquarters. The natural explanation for that would be that his partner, the actual murderer, had needed nearly that much time to put himself in the clear.

My present game was simple: I had stirred Clane up with the knowledge that he was still suspected, hoping that he would have to repeat whatever precautions were necessary to protect his accomplice in the first place.

He had taken three days then. I was giving him about nine hours now: time enough to do something, but not too much time, hoping that he would have to hurry things along and that in his haste he would give Dick and Bob a chance to turn up his partner: the owner of the fingers that had smeared blood on the knife, the table, and the door.

At a quarter to one in the morning Dick telephoned that Clane had left the hotel a few minutes behind me, had gone to an apartment house on Polk Street, and was still there.

I went up to Polk Street and joined Dick and Bob. They told me that Clane had gone in apartment number 27, and that the directory in the vestibule showed this apartment was occupied by George Farr. I stuck around with the boys until about two o'clock, when I went home for some sleep.

At seven I was with them again, and was told that our man had not appeared yet. It was a little after eight when he came out and turned down Geary Street, with the boys trailing him, while I went into the apartment house for a talk with the manager. She told me that Farr had been living there for four or five months, lived alone, and was a photographer by trade, with a studio on Market Street.

I went up and rang his bell. He was a husky of thirty or thirty-two with bleary eyes that looked as if they hadn't had much sleep that night. I didn't waste any time with him.

"I'm from the Continental Detective Agency and I am interested in Joseph Clane. What do you know about him?"

He was wide awake now.

"Nothing."

"Nothing at all?"

"No," sullenly.

"Do you know him?"

"No."

What can you do with a bird like that?

"Farr," I said, "I want you to go down to headquarters with me."

He moved like a streak and his sullen manner had me a little off my guard; but I turned my head in time to take the punch above my ear instead of on the chin. At that, it carried me off my feet and I wouldn't have bet a nickel that my skull wasn't dented; but luck was with me and I fell across the doorway, holding the door open, and managed to scramble up, stumble through some rooms, and catch one of his feet as it was going through the bathroom window to join its mate on the fire-escape. I got a split lip and a kicked shoulder in the scuffle, but he behaved after a while.

I didn't stop to look at his stuff—that could be done more regularly later—but put him in a taxicab and took him to the Hall of Justice. I was afraid that if I waited too long Clane would take a run-out on me.

Clane's mouth fell open when he saw Farr, but neither of them said anything.

I was feeling pretty chirp* in spite of my bruises.

"Let's get this bird's finger-prints and get it over with," I said to O'Hara.

Dean was not in.

"And keep an eye on Clane. I think maybe he'll have another story to tell us in a few minutes."

We got in the elevator and took our men up to the identification bureau, where we put Farr's

_____

* lively

fingers on the pad. Phels—he is the department's expert—took one look at the results and turned to me.

"Well, what of it?"

"What of what?" I asked.

"This isn't the man who killed Henry Grover!"

Clane laughed, Farr laughed, O'Hara laughed, and Phels laughed. I didn't! I stood there and pretended to be thinking, trying to get myself in hand.

"Are you sure you haven't made a mistake?" I blurted, my face a nice, rosy red.

You can tell how badly upset I was by that: it's plain suicide to say a thing like that to a finger-print expert!

Phels didn't answer; just looked me up and down.

Clane laughed again, like a crow cawing, and turned his ugly face to me.

"Do you want to take my prints again, Mr. Slick Private Detective?"

"Yeah," I said, "just that!"

I had to say something.

Clane held his hands out to Phels, who ignored them, speaking to me with heavy sarcasm.

"Better take them yourself this time, so you'll be sure it's been done right."

I was mad clean through—of course it was my own fault—but I was pig-headed enough to go through with anything, particularly anything that would hurt somebody's feelings; so I said:

"That's not a bad idea!"

I walked over and took hold of one of Clane's hands. I'd never taken a finger-print before, but I had seen it done often enough to throw a bluff. I started to ink Clane's fingers and found that I was holding them wrong—my own fingers were in the way.

Then I came back to earth. The balls of Clane's fingers were too smooth—or rather, too slick—without the slight clinging feeling that belongs to flesh. I turned his hand over so fast that I nearly upset him and looked at the fingers. I don't know what I had expected to find but I didn't find anything—not anything that I could name.

"Phels," I called, "look here!"

He forgot his injured feelings and bent to look at Clane's hand.

"I'll be—" he began, and then the two of us were busy for a few minutes taking Clane down and sitting on him, while O'Hara quieted Farr, who had also gone suddenly into action.

When things were peaceful again Phels examined Clane's hands carefully, scratching the fingers with a finger-nail.

He jumped up, leaving me to hold Clane, and paying no attention to my, "What is it?" got a cloth and some liquid, and washed the fingers thoroughly. We took his prints again. They matched the bloody ones taken from Grover's house!

Then we all sat down and had a nice talk.

"I told you about the trouble Henny had with that fellow Waldeman," Clane began, after he and Farr had decided to come clean: there was nothing else they could do. "And how he won out in the argument because Waldeman disappeared. Well, Henny done for* him—shot him one night and buried him—and I saw it. Grover was one bad actor in them days, a tough *hombre* to tangle with, so I didn't try to make nothing out of what I knew.

"But after he got older and richer he got soft—a lot of men go like that—and must have begun worrying over it; because when I ran into him in New York accidentally about four years ago it didn't take me long to learn that he was pretty well tamed, and he told me that he hadn't been able to forget the look on Waldeman's face when he drilled him.

"So I took a chance and braced Henny for a couple thousand. I got them easy, and after that, whenever I was flat I either went to him or sent him word, and he always came across. But I was careful not to crowd him too far. I knew what a terror he was in the old days, and I didn't want to push him into busting loose again.

_____
* killed

"But that's what I did in the end. I 'phoned him Friday that I needed money and he said he'd call me up and let me know where to meet him the next night. He called up around half past nine Saturday night and told me to come out to the house. So I went out there and he was waiting for me on the porch and took me upstairs and gave me the ten thousand. I told him this was the last time I'd ever bother him—I always told him that—it had a good effect on him.

"Naturally I wanted to get away as soon as I had the money but he must have felt sort of talkative for a change, because he kept me there for half an hour or so, gassing about men we used to know up in the province.

"After a while I began to get nervous. He was getting a look in his eyes like he used to have when he was young. And then all of a sudden he flared up and tied into me. He had me by the throat and was bending me back across the table when my hand touched that brass knife. It was either me or him—so I let him have it where it would do the most good.

"I beat it then and went back to the hotel. The newspapers were full of it next day, and had a whole lot of stuff about bloody finger-prints. That gave me a jolt! I didn't know nothing about finger-prints, and here I'd left them all over the dump.

"And then I got to worrying over the whole thing, and it seemed like Henny must have my name written down somewheres among his papers, and maybe had saved some of my letters or telegrams—though *they* were wrote in careful enough language. Anyway I figured the police would want to be asking me some questions sooner or later; and there I'd be with fingers that fit the bloody prints, and nothing for what Farr calls a alibi.

"That's when I thought of Farr. I had his address and I knew he had been a finger-print sharp in the East, so I decided to take a chance on him. I went to him and told him the whole story and between us we figured out what to do.

"He said he'd dope my fingers, and I was to come here and tell the story we'd fixed up, and have my finger-prints taken, and then I'd be safe no matter what leaked out about me and Henny. So he smeared up the fingers and told me to be careful not to shake hands with anybody or touch anything, and I came down here and everything went like three of a kind.

"Then that little fat guy"—meaning me—"came around to the hotel last night and as good as told me that he thought I had done for Henny and that I better come down here this morning. I beat it for Farr's right away to see whether I ought to run for it or sit tight, and Farr said, 'Sit tight!' So I stayed there all night and he fixed up my hands this morning. That's my yarn!"

Phels turned to Farr.

"I've seen faked prints before, but never any this good. How'd you do it?"

These scientific birds are funny. Here was Farr looking a nice, long stretch in the face as "accessory after the fact," and yet he brightened up under the admiration in Phels's tone and answered with a voice that was chock-full of pride.

"It's simple! I got hold of a man whose prints I knew weren't in any police gallery—I didn't want any slip up there—and took his prints and put them on a copper plate, using the ordinary photo-engraving process, but etching it pretty deep. Then I coated Clane's fingers with gelatin—just enough to cover all his markings—and pressed them against the plates. That way I got everything, even to the pores, and . . ."

When I left the bureau ten minutes later Farr and Phels were still sitting knee to knee, jabbering away at each other as only a couple of birds who are cuckoo on the same subject can.

BLACK MASK, OCTOBER 15, 1923

FROM THE AUTHOR OF "SLIPPERY FINGERS"

Since writing "Slippery Fingers" I have read an article in the San Francisco *Chronicle* wherein August Vollmer, chief of police of Berkeley, California, and president of the International Association of Chiefs of Police, is quoted as saying that although it is possible successfully to transfer actual finger-prints from one place to another it is not possible to forge them—"Close inspection of any forged finger-print will soon cause detection."

It may be that what Farr does in my story would be considered by Mr. Vollmer a transference rather than a forgery. But whichever it is, I think there is no longer reasonable room for doubt that finger-prints can be successfully forged. I have seen forged prints that to me seemed perfect, but not being even an amateur in that line, my opinion isn't worth much. I think, however, that quite a number of those qualified to speak on the subject will agree with me that it can be, and has been, done.

In the second Arbuckle trial, if my memory is correct, the defense introduced an expert from Los Angeles who testified that he had deceived an assembly of his colleagues with forged prints.

The method used in my story was not selected because it was the best, but because it was the simplest with which I was acquainted and the most easily described. Successful experiments were made with it by the experts at the Leavenworth federal prison.

Sincerely,
S. D. HAMMETT.

BLACK MASK, JUNE 1925

FINGER-PRINTS

(A LETTER FROM DASHIELL HAMMETT)

Since this finger-print argument is to be a free-for-all, I should like to have my little say in reply to Mr. Reeves' article in the April issue. This is really my second say; I used the juggling of prints as the basis for a story entitled "Slippery Fingers," published in BLACK MASK for October 15, 1923. Before I start, however, let me make it clear I am not an expert, not even one of Mr. Reeves' "half-baked (half-boiled?) potatoes." What I am turning loose here is simply an opinion or two accumulated in a few years of dabbling in criminal affairs as private detective, writer, and idle spectator.

Mr. Reeves says: "The infallibility of finger-prints as an *absolute means* of identification is based on the three following iron-clad facts: First, they never change. Second, they cannot be counterfeited. Third, no two are alike." Let us look at these facts.

They never change. This is still only probably true. Not enough proof has been piled up to convince a properly skeptical, that is to say a scientific, mind. It is certain that with the years the pattern areas become distorted, or may become distorted. How far this distortion may go without altering the patterns themselves is an open question. Then, too, the ridges disintegrate, as in the case of the prints of Sir William Herschel, whose prints (the first in 1856 and the second in 1914 or 1916) establish, I think, the longest record of persistence. Those prints are both recognizable as the prints of the same man. But what has been done to determine the effects an altogether new manner of living may have on a man's prints and because a hundred men may have this year the same patterns of ridges and pores they had twenty or fifty years ago, is that sufficient evidence to lay down laws purporting to include all the hundreds of millions of varying men in the world?

Experiments have been made to determine whether a person can change the patterns of his fingers. It has been definitely established that if the finger-ends are rubbed smooth, or cut, the old patterns grow out again, in every respect as they were originally. But these experiments have been, so far as I have knowledge of them, rather crude affairs, dealing with the surface of the fingers only. If, as is certain, these patterns to some government, perhaps of the nerves and glands, what might not be done in the way of alteration by tampering with these sources? Isn't it likely that a skillful surgeon might—and may someday actually—learn to alter the design of these ridges and pores by killing certain nerves, or otherwise manipulating them and the glands?

They cannot be counterfeited. Counterfeited is, like forgery, a tricky word in this connection. What Mr. Reeves must mean, to support his contention, is that a finger-print put on any surface by any other means that the pressure of the finger to which it belongs will not deceive a man who has at his disposal the training and instruments of the modern finger-print expert. Certainly Mr. Reeves is right when he says he can tell the difference between a print made by a finger and one made by a rubber stamp. Abut that degree of expertness is not quite all that is required. Personally, I am of the opinion that an engraver who gave the matter sufficient study could, with Mr. Reeves' microscope and a few simple tools, sit down to a fresh print and duplicate it, oil, pores, ridges and all. His counterfeit might not be philosophically accurate, but it would be exact enough to fool the very finite mind of the keenest expert who ever lived. I have never heard of anything so simple as a finger-print that could not be counterfeited.

But I am not an expert, so we will throw my opinion on that point out. There is a simpler and easier way of juggling prints than forging them—the transferring of the actual print from one place to another. I shall quote August Vollmer, one-time president of the International Association of Chiefs of Police, because he is known as a staunch believer in finger-print identification.

Discussing some experiments of E. O. Brown, a former secret service agent, later connected with the San Francisco post office, Chief Vollmer told W. T. Amis, of the San Francisco *Chronicle*: "Brown's method of transferring finger-prints will work only with a fresh print, and consists merely of the moving of the mark from one location to another. When a person's finger is placed on a smooth surface, such as glass or highly polished metals, there is an oily substance deposited, which is usually invisible to the eye, but can be developed by the use of chemicals. It is this fresh mark that is necessary for the transferring of the finger-print from one location to another. Brown has shown us that he is able to take this oily deposit and place it where he pleases.

"The greatest trouble to result in this discovery no doubt will be that a criminal, who knows the method employed, and wishes to cover up his crime, will be able to leave the print of another person around the place . . . and throw suspicion on the innocent man. . . . These finger-prints that the criminal might wish to use could very easily be obtained in an innocent manner and by means of the method be placed on a window of the place he has robbed . . . or on a safe or elsewhere as he chooses.

"Fortunately, however, the method is not known to more than half a dozen men at present, and all efforts will be made to keep it a secret of trusted police officials."

No two are alike. I have not gone into this angle very deeply. My understanding of the matter has always been that the most that finger-prints claimed was a ridiculously small likelihood of two men's prints being alike. I remember Wesley Turner, of the Spokane police identification bureau giving me the figures once: one chance in some enormous number of millions of two prints being alike. But I do not believe that there is, or that there ever can be, demonstrable grounds for saying, *no two are alike.* How could it possibly be proved? Think of all the people who now live, of all who lived before them in this old world, and of all who will some day live. No, honestly, don't you think Nature is going to run out of variations some day? And, erratic as Nature is, can we trust her to duplicate—when duplication becomes necessary—only the fingers of the long-dead? But, seriously, there is no proof that each man's pattern is peculiar to him, and there can be no proof until everybody, everywhere, has been examined. The chance of two men with identical proofs coming together is slight—ridiculously slight, perhaps—but if you have fooled around with crap games as much as I have, you know what chance can do to the laws of probabilities when it sets its mind to it.

Our three facts seem to be: (1) There is no proof that finger-prints change, and thus far experiments have not found a method for changing them; (2) there seems to be some confusion as to whether finger-prints can be actually forged, but they can be moved from place to place readily enough; and (3) there is nothing to show that two men with similar prints are likely to be in the same neighborhood at that same time.

Unfortunately, the most valuable data on this subject—and there seems to be a vast amount of it—is kept under cover, as is suggested in the last paragraph of my quotation from chief Vollmer. We would get a lot more truth out of our experts and police officials if it were not for their fear that confessions of fallibility will discredit the system, thus leaving the experts jobless and the police minus an effective weapon. These fears are, I think, groundless. The truth will put finger-print classification where it belongs: it is a valuable adjunct to the detective's and the prosecuting attorney's repertory, but it is not infallible when it stands alone, and it may then be dangerous.

The same thing holds true of all the devices of "scientific" detecting. Many of them are excellent when kept to their places, but when pushed forward as infallible methods, they become forms of quackery, and nothing else. The trouble is that criminals are so damned unscientific, and always will be so long as the most marked trait criminal is the childish desire for a short-cut to wealth. The chemist and the photographer and the rest make excellent assistants to our old friend, the flat-footed, low-browed gumshoe, but he's the boy who keeps the jails full of crooks in the long run. But, as I have said, these other things help him now and then. Take, for example, that species of nonsense which, in one shape or another, is commonly called the "lie detector." Usually it is attached somehow to the suspect, and purports to register his nervous glandular or heart reactions, on the naïve theory that a congenital liar or a half-animal thug will get all worked up over having to tell a fib. Nevertheless, these machines are, in their small way not without value: sometimes a crook is picked up who really believes in them, thinks he can't beat them, and so tells the truth when the dingus is tied on him.

There is no doubt that finger-prints are a valuable part of the anti-criminal arsenal, but they are only a part of it. As evidence goes, I favor what is usually called "circumstantial evidence," as against the testimony of witnesses, but I haven't a very high opinion of a jury that will condemn a man on the unsupported evidence of finger-prints, if there is a reasonable— and I don't mean overwhelming—amount of contrary evidence. Neither have I much faith in experts who claim infallibility in any field except, perhaps, abstract mathematics.

Sincerely,
DASHIELL HAMMETT.
San Francisco, March 28, 1925

BLACK MASK, NOVEMBER 1, 1923

It

BY DASHIELL HAMMETT

Calling a detective to solve a crime that turns out to be something quite different from the first diagnosis makes a very unusual story of this. You'll be surprised!

"NOW LISTEN, MR. ZUMWALT, you're holding out on me; and it won't do! If I'm going to work on this for you I've got to have the whole story."

He looked thoughtfully at me for a moment through screwed-up blue eyes. Then he got up and went to the door of the outer office, opening it. Past him I could see the bookkeeper and the stenographer sitting at their desks. Zumwalt closed the door and returned to his desk, leaning across it to speak in a husky undertone.

"You are right, I suppose. But what I am going to tell you must be held in the strictest confidence."

I nodded, and he went on:

"About two months ago one of our clients, Stanley Gorham, turned $100,000 worth of Liberty bonds over to us. He had to go to the Orient on business, and he had an idea that the bonds might go to par during his absence; so he left them with us to be sold if they did. Yesterday I had occasion to go to the safe deposit box where the bonds had been put—in the Golden Gate Trust Company's vault—and they were gone!"

"Anybody except you and your partner have access to the box?"

"No."

"When did you see the bonds last?"

"They were in the box the Saturday before Dan left. And one of the men on duty in the vault told me that Dan was there the following Monday."

"All right! Now let me see if I've got it all straight. Your partner, Daniel Rathbone, was supposed to leave for New York on the twenty-seventh of last month, Monday, to meet an R. W. DePuy. But Rathbone came into the office that day with his baggage and said that important personal affairs made it necessary for him to postpone his departure, that he had to be in San Francisco the following morning. But he didn't tell you what that personal business was.

"You and he had some words over the delay, as you thought it important that he keep the New York engagement on time. You weren't on the best of terms at the time, having quarreled a couple of days before that over a shady deal Rathbone had put over. And so you—"

"Don't misunderstand me," Zumwalt interrupted. "Dan had done nothing dishonest. It was simply that he had engineered several transactions that—well, I thought he had sacrificed ethics to profits."

"I see. Anyhow, starting with your argument over his not leaving for New York that day, you and he wound up by dragging in all of your differences, and practically decided to dissolve partnership as soon as it could be done. The argument was concluded in your house out on Fourteenth Avenue; and, as it was rather late by then and he had checked out of his hotel before he had changed his mind about going to New York, he stayed there with you that night."

"That's right," Zumwalt explained. "I have been living at a hotel since Mrs. Zumwalt has been away, but Dan and I went out to the house because it gave us the utmost privacy for our talk; and when we finished it was so late that we remained there."

"Then the next morning you and Rathbone came down to the office and—"

"No," he corrected me. "That is, we didn't come down here together. I came here while Dan went to transact whatever it was that had held him in town. He came into the office a little after noon, and said he was going East on the evening train. He sent Quimby, the bookkeeper, down to get his reservations and to check his baggage, which he had left in the office here overnight. Then Dan and I went to lunch together, came back to the office for a few minutes—he had some mail to sign—and then he left."

"I see. After that, you didn't hear from or of him until about ten days later, when DePuy wired to find out why Rathbone hadn't been to see him?"

"That's right! As soon as I got DePuy's wire I sent one to Dan's brother in Chicago, thinking perhaps Dan had stopped over with him, but Tom wired back that he hadn't seen his brother. Since then I've had two more wires from DePuy. I was sore with Dan for keeping DePuy waiting, but still I didn't worry a lot.

"Dan isn't a very reliable person, and if he suddenly took a notion to stop off somewhere between here and New York for a few days he'd do it. But yesterday, when I found that the bonds were gone from the safe deposit box and learned that Dan had been to the box the day before he left, I decided that I'd have to do something. But I don't want the police brought into it if it can be avoided.

"I feel sure that if I can find Dan and talk to him we can straighten the mess out somehow without scandal. We had our differences, but Dan's too decent a man, and I like him too well, for all his occasional wildness, to want to see him in jail. So I want him found with as much speed and as little noise as possible."

"Has he got a car?"

"Not now. He had one but he sold it five or six months ago."

"Where'd he bank? I mean his personal account?"

"At the Golden Gate Trust Company."

"Got any photos of him?"

"Yes."

He brought out two from a desk drawer—one full-face, and the other a three-quarter view. They showed a man in the middle of his life, with shrewd eyes set close together in a hatchet face, under dark, thin hair. But the face was rather pleasant for all its craftiness.

"How about his relatives, friends, and so on—particularly his feminine friends?"

"His only relative is the brother in Chicago.

As to his friends: he probably has as many as any man in San Francisco. He was a wonderful mixer.

"Recently he has been on very good terms with a Mrs. Earnshaw, the wife of a real estate agent. She lives on Pacific Street, I think. I don't know just how intimate they were, but he used to call her up on the phone frequently, and she called him here nearly every day. Then there is a girl named Eva Duthie, a cabaret entertainer, who lives in the 1100 block of Bush Street. There were probably others, too, but I know of only those two."

"Have you looked through his stuff, here?"

"Yes, but perhaps you'd like to look for yourself."

He led me into Rathbone's private office: a small box of a room, just large enough for a desk, a filing cabinet, and two chairs, with doors leading into the corridor, the outer office, and Zumwalt's.

"While I'm looking around you might get me a list of the serial numbers of the missing bonds," I said. "They probably won't help us right away, but we can get the Treasury Department to let us know when the coupons come in, and from where."

I didn't expect to find anything in Rathbone's office and I didn't.

Before I left I questioned the stenographer and the bookkeeper. They already knew that Rathbone was missing, but they didn't know that the bonds were gone too.

The girl, Mildred Narbett was her name, said that Rathbone had dictated a couple of letters to her on the twenty-eighth—the day he left for New York—both of which had to do with the partner's business—and told her to send Quimby to check his baggage and make his reservations. When she returned from lunch she had typed the two letters and taken them in for him to sign, catching him just as he was about to leave.

John Quimby, the bookkeeper, described the baggage he had checked: two large pigskin bags and a cordovan Gladstone bag. Having a book-keeper's mind, he had remembered the number of the berth he had secured for Rathbone on the evening train—lower 4, car 8. Quimby had returned with the checks and tickets while the partners were out at luncheon, and had put them on Rathbone's desk.

At Rathbone's hotel I was told that he had left on the morning of the twenty-seventh, giving up his room, but leaving his two trunks there, as he intended living there after his return from New York, in three or four weeks. The hotel people could tell me little worth listening to, except that he had left in a taxicab.

At the taxi stand outside I found the chauffeur who had carried Rathbone.

"Rathbone? Sure, I know him!" he told me around a limp cigarette. "Yeah, I guess it was about that date that I took him down to the Golden Gate Trust Company. He had a coupla big yellow bags and a little brown one. He busted into the bank, carrying the little one, and right out again, looking like somebody had kicked him on his corns. Had me take him to the Phelps Building"—the offices of Rathbone & Zumwalt were in that building—"and didn't give me a jit* over my fare!"

At the Golden Gate Trust Company I had to plead and talk a lot, but they finally gave me what I wanted—Rathbone had drawn out his account, a little less than $5,000, on the twenty-fifth of the month, the Saturday before he left town.

From the trust company I went down to the Ferry Building baggage-rooms and cigared† myself into a look at the records for the twenty-eighth. Only one lot of three bags had been checked to New York that day.

I telegraphed the numbers and Rathbone's description to the agency's New York office, instructing them to find the bags and, through them, find him.

Up in the Pullman Company's offices I was told that car "8" was a through car, and that they could let me know within a couple hours

---

* nickel

† bribed with a cigar

whether Rathbone had occupied his berth all the way to New York.

On my way up to the 1100 block of Bush Street I left one of Rathbone's photographs with a photographer, with a rush order for a dozen copies.

I found Eva Duthie's apartment after about five minutes of searching vestibule directories, and got her out of bed. She was an undersized blonde girl of somewhere between nineteen and twenty-nine, depending upon whether you judged by her eyes or by the rest of her face.

"I haven't seen or heard from Mr. Rathbone for nearly a month," she said. "I called him up at his hotel the other night—had a party I wanted to ring him in on—but they told me that he was out of town and wouldn't be back for a week or two."

Then, in answer to another question:

"Yes, we were pretty good friends, but not especially thick. You know what I mean: we had a lot of fun together but neither of us meant anything to the other outside of that. Dan is a good sport—and so am I."

Mrs. Earnshaw wasn't so frank. But she had a husband, and that makes a difference. She was a tall, slender woman, as dark as a gypsy, with a haughty air and a nervous trick of chewing her lower lip.

We sat in a stiffly furnished room and she stalled me for about fifteen minutes, until I came out flat-footed with her.

"It's like this, Mrs. Earnshaw," I told her. "Mr. Rathbone has disappeared, and we are going to find him. You're not helping me and you're not helping yourself. I came here to get what you know about him.

"I could have gone around asking a lot of questions among your friends; and if you don't tell me what I want to know that's what I'll have to do. And, while I'll be as careful as possible, still there's bound to be some curiosity aroused, some wild guesses, and some talk. I'm giving you a chance to avoid all that. It's up to you."

"You are assuming," she said coldly, "that I have something to hide."

"I'm not assuming anything. I'm hunting for information about Daniel Rathbone."

She bit her lip on that for a while, and then the story came out bit by bit, with a lot in it that wasn't any too true, but straight enough in the long run. Stripped of the stuff that wouldn't hold water, it went like this:

She and Rathbone had planned to run away together. She had left San Francisco on the twenty-sixth, going directly to New Orleans. He was to leave the next day, apparently for New York, but he was to change trains somewhere in the Middle West and meet her in New Orleans. From there they were to go by boat to Central America.

She pretended ignorance of his designs upon the bonds. Maybe she hadn't known. Anyhow, she had carried out her part of the plan, but Rathbone had failed to show up in New Orleans. She hadn't shown much care in covering her trail and private detectives employed by her husband had soon found her. Her husband had arrived in New Orleans and, apparently not knowing that there was another man in the deal, had persuaded her to return home.

She wasn't a woman to take kindly to the jilting Rathbone had handed her, so she hadn't tried to get in touch with him, or to learn what had kept him from joining her.

Her story rang true enough, but just to play safe, I put out a few feelers in the neighborhood, and what I learned seemed to verify what she had told me. I gathered that a few of the neighbors had made guesses that weren't a million miles away from the facts.

I got the Pullman Company on the telephone and was told that lower 4, car 8, leaving for New York on the twenty-eighth, hadn't been occupied at all.

Zumwalt was dressing for dinner when I went up to his room at the hotel where he was staying.

I told him all that I had learned that day, and what I thought of it.

"Everything makes sense up until Rathbone left the Golden Gate Trust Company vault on the twenty-seventh, and after that nothing does! He had planned to grab the bonds and elope with this Mrs. Earnshaw, and he had already drawn out of the bank all his own money. That's all orderly. But why should he have gone back to the office? Why should he have stayed in town that night? What was the important business that held him? Why should he have ditched Mrs. Earnshaw? Why didn't he use his reservations at least part of the way across the country, as he had planned? False trail, maybe, but a rotten one! There's nothing to do, Mr. Zumwalt, but to call in the police and the newspapers, and see what publicity and a nation-wide search will do for us."

"But that means jail for Dan, with no chance to quietly straighten the matter up!" he protested.

"It does! But it can't be helped. And remember, you've got to protect yourself. You're his partner, and, while not criminally responsible, you are financially responsible for his actions. You've got to put yourself in the clear!"

He nodded reluctant agreement and I grabbed the telephone.

For two hours I was busy giving all the dope we had to the police, and as much as we wanted published to the newspapers, who luckily had photographs of Rathbone, taken a year before when he had been named as co-respondent in a divorce suit.

I sent off three telegrams. One to New York, asking that Rathbone's baggage be opened as soon as the necessary authority could be secured. (If he hadn't gone to New York the baggage should be waiting at the station.) One to Chicago, asking that Rathbone's brother be interviewed and then shadowed for a few days. And one to New Orleans, to have the city searched for him. Then I headed for home and bed.

News was scarce, and the papers the next day had Rathbone spread out all over the front pages, with photographs and descriptions and wild guesses and wilder clews that had materialized somehow within the short space between the time the newspapers got the story and the time they went to press.

I spent the morning preparing circulars

and plans for having the country covered; and arranging to have steamship records searched.

Just before noon a telegram came from New York, itemizing the things found in Rathbone's baggage. The contents of the two large bags didn't mean anything. They might have been packed for use or for a stall. But the things in the Gladstone bag, which had been found unlocked, were puzzling.

Here's the list:

Two suits silk pajamas, 4 silk shirts, 8 linen collars, 4 suits underwear, 6 neckties, 6 pairs sox, 18 handkerchiefs, 1 pair military brushes, 1 comb, 1 safety razor, 1 tube shaving cream, 1 shaving brush, 1 tooth brush, 1 tube tooth paste, 1 can talcum powder, 1 bottle hair tonic, 1 cigar case holding 12 cigars, 1 .32 Colt's revolver, 1 map of Honduras, 1 Spanish English dictionary, 2 books postage stamps, 1 pint Scotch whiskey, and 1 manicure set.

Zumwalt, his bookkeeper, and his stenographer were watching two men from headquarters search Rathbone's office when I arrived there. After I showed them the telegram the detectives went back to their examination.

"What's the significance of that list?" Zumwalt asked.

"It shows that there's no sense to this thing the way it now stands," I said. "That Gladstone bag was packed to be carried. Checking it was all wrong—it wasn't even locked. And nobody ever checks Gladstone bags filled with toilet articles—so checking it for a stall would have been the bunk! Maybe he checked it as an afterthought—to get rid of it when he found he wasn't going to need it. But what could have made it unnecessary to him? Don't forget that it's apparently the same bag that he carried into the Golden Gate Trust Company vault when he went for the bonds. Damned if I can dope it!"

"Here's something else for you to dope," one of the city detectives said, getting up from his examination of the desk and holding out a sheet of paper. "I found it behind one of the drawers, where it had slipped down."

It was a letter, written with blue ink in a firm, angular and unmistakably feminine hand on heavy white note paper.

Dear Dannyboy:

If it isn't too late I've changed my mind about going. If you can wait another day, until Tuesday, I'll go. Call me up as soon as you get this, and if you still want me I'll pick you up in the roadster at the Shattuck Avenue station Tuesday afternoon.

More than ever yours,
"Boots."

It was dated the twenty-sixth—the Sunday before Rathbone had disappeared.

"That's the thing that made him lay over another day, and made him change his plans," one of the police detectives said. "I guess we better run over to Berkeley and see what we can find at the Shattuck Avenue station."

"Mr. Zumwalt," I said, when he and I were alone in his office, "how about this stenog of yours?"

He bounced up from his chair and his face turned red.

"What about her?"

"Is she—How friendly was she with Rathbone?"

"Miss Narbett," he said heavily, deliberately, as if to be sure that I caught every syllable, "is to be married to me as soon as my wife gets her divorce. That is why I canceled the order to sell my house. Now would you mind telling me just why you asked?"

"Just a random guess!" I lied, trying to soothe him. "I don't want to overlook any bets. But now that's out of the way."

"It is," he was still talking deliberately, "and it seems to me that most of your guesses have been random ones. If you will have your office send me a bill for your services to date, I think I can dispense with your help."

"Just as you say. But you'll have to pay for a full day today; so, if you don't mind, I'll keep on working at it until night."

"Very well! But I am busy, and you needn't bother about coming in with any reports."

"All right," I said, and bowed myself out of the office, but not out of the job.

That letter from "Boots" had *not* been in the desk when I searched it. I had taken every drawer out and even tilted the desk to look under it. The letter was a plant!

And then again: maybe Zumwalt had given me the air because he was dissatisfied with the work I had done and peeved at my question about the girl—and maybe not.

Suppose (I thought, walking up Market Street, bumping shoulders and stepping on people's feet) the two partners were in this thing together. One of them would have to be the goat, and that part had fallen to Rathbone. Zumwalt's manner and actions since his partner's disappearance fit that theory well enough.

Employing a private detective before calling in the police was a good play. In the first place it gave him the appearance of innocence. Then the private sleuth would tell him everything he learned, every step he took, giving Zumwalt an opportunity to correct any mistakes or oversights in the partners' plans before the police came into it; and if the private detective got on dangerous ground he could be called off.

And suppose Rathbone was found in some city where he was unknown—and that would be where he'd go. Zumwalt would volunteer to go forward to identify him. He would look at him and say, "No, that's not him," Rathbone would be turned loose, and that would be the end of that trail.

This theory left the sudden change in Rathbone's plans unaccounted for; but it made his return to the office on the afternoon of the twenty-seventh more plausible. He had come back to confer with his partner over that unknown necessity for the change, and they had decided to leave Mrs. Earnshaw out of it. Then they had gone out to Zumwalt's house. For what? And why had Zumwalt decided not to sell the house? And why had he taken the trouble to give me an explanation? Could they have cached the bonds there?

A look at the house wouldn't be a bad idea!

I telephoned Bennett, at the Oakland Police Department.

"Do me a favor, Frank? Call Zumwalt on the phone. Tell him you've picked up a man who answers Rathbone's description to a T; and ask him to come over and take a look at him. When he gets there stall him as long as you can—pretending that the man is being fingerprinted and measured, or something like that—and then tell him that you've found that the man isn't Rathbone, and that you are sorry to have brought him over there, and so on. If you only hold him for half or three-quarters of an hour it'll be enough—it'll take him more than half an hour traveling each way. Thanks!"

I stopped in at the office, stuck a flashlight in my pocket, and headed for Fourteenth Avenue.

Zumwalt's house was a two-story, semi-detached one; and the lock on the front door held me up about four minutes. A burglar would have gone through it without checking his stride. This breaking into the house wasn't exactly according to the rules, but on the other hand, I was legally Zumwalt's agent until I discontinued work that night—so this crashing in couldn't be considered illegal.

I started at the top floor and worked down. Bureaus, dressers, tables, desks, chairs, walls, woodwork, pictures, carpets, plumbing—I looked at everything that was thick enough to hold paper. I didn't take things apart, but it's surprising how speedily and how thoroughly you can go through a house when you're in training.

I found nothing in the house itself, so I went down into the cellar.

It was a large cellar and divided in two. The front part was paved with cement, and held a full coal-bin, some furniture, some canned goods, and a lot of odds and ends of housekeeping accessories. The rear division, behind a plaster partition where the steps ran down from the kitchen, was without windows, and illuminated only by one swinging electric light, which I turned on.

A pile of lumber filled half the space; on the other side barrels and boxes were piled up to the ceiling; two sacks of cement lay beside them, and in another corner was a tangle of broken furniture. The floor was of hard dirt.

I turned to the lumber pile first. I wasn't in love with the job ahead of me—moving the pile away and then back again. But I needn't have worried.

A board rattled behind me, and I wheeled to see Zumwalt rising from behind a barrel and scowling at me over a black automatic pistol.

"Put your hands up," he said.

I put them up. I didn't have a pistol with me, not being in the habit of carrying one except when I thought I was going to need it; but it would have been all the same if I had had a pocket full of them. I don't mind taking chances, but there's no chance when you're looking into the muzzle of a gun that a determined man is holding on you.

So I put my hands up. And one of them brushed against the swinging light globe. I drove my knuckles into it. As the cellar went black I threw myself backward and to one side. Zumwalt's gun streaked fire.

Nothing happened for a while. I found that I had fallen across the doorway that gave to the stairs and the front cellar. I figured that I couldn't move without making a noise that would draw lead, so I lay still.

Then began a game that made up in tenseness what it lacked in action.

The part of the cellar where we were was about twenty by twenty feet and blacker than a new shoe. There were two doors. One, on the opposite side, opened into the yard and was, I supposed, locked. I was lying on my back across the other, waiting for a pair of legs to grab. Zumwalt, with a gun out of which only one bullet had been spent, was somewhere in the blackness, and aware, from his silence, that I was still alive.

I figured I had the edge on him. I was closest

to the only practicable exit; he didn't know that I was unarmed; he didn't know whether I had help close by or not; time was valuable to him, but not necessarily so to me. So I waited.

Time passed. How much I don't know. Maybe half an hour.

The floor was damp and hard and thoroughly uncomfortable. The electric light had cut my hand when I broke it, and I couldn't determine how badly I was bleeding. I thought of Tad's[*] "blind man in a dark room hunting for a black hat that wasn't there," and knew how he felt.

A box or barrel fell over with a crash—knocked over by Zumwalt, no doubt, moving out from the hiding-place wherein he had awaited my arrival.

Silence for a while. And then I could hear him moving cautiously off to one side.

Without warning two streaks from his pistol sent bullets into the partition somewhere above my feet. I wasn't the only one who was feeling the strain.

Silence again, and I found that I was wet and dripping with perspiration.

Then I could hear his breathing, but couldn't determine whether he was nearer or was breathing more heavily.

A soft, sliding, dragging across the dirt floor! I pictured him crawling awkwardly on his knees and one hand, the other hand holding the pistol out ahead of him—the pistol that would spit fire as soon as its muzzle touched something soft. And I became uneasily aware of my bulk. I am thick through the waist; and there in the dark it seemed to me that my paunch must extend almost to the ceiling—a target that no bullet could miss.

I stretched my hands out toward him and held them there. If they touched him first I'd have a chance.

He was panting harshly now; and I was breathing through a mouth that was stretched as wide as it would go, so that there would be no rasping of the large quantities of air I was taking in and letting out.

Abruptly he came.

Hair brushed the fingers of my left hand. I closed them about it, pulling the head I couldn't see viciously toward me, driving my right fist beneath it. You may know that I put everything I had in that smack when I tell you that not until later, when I found that one of my cheeks was scorched, did I know that his gun had gone off.

He wiggled, and I hit him again.

Then I was sitting astride him, my flashlight hunting for his pistol. I found it, and yanked him to his feet.

As soon as his head cleared I herded him into the front cellar and got a globe to replace the one I had smashed.

"Now dig it up," I ordered.

That was a safe way of putting it. I wasn't sure what I wanted or where it would be, except that his selecting this part of the cellar to wait for me in made it look as if this was the right place.

"You'll do your own digging!" he growled.

"Maybe," I said, "but I'm going to do it now, and I haven't time to tie you up. So if I've got to do the digging, I'm going to crown you first, so you'll sleep peacefully until it's all over."

All smeared with blood and dirt and sweat, I must have looked capable of anything, for when I took a step toward him he gave in.

From behind the lumber pile he brought a spade, moved some of the barrels to one side, and started turning up the dirt.

When a hand—a man's hand—dead-yellow where the damp dirt didn't stick to it—came into sight I stopped him.

I had found "it," and I had no stomach for looking at "it" after three weeks of lying in the wet ground.

NOTE: In court, Lester Zumwalt's plea was that he had killed his partner in self-defense. Zumwalt testified that he had taken the Gorham bonds in a futile attempt to recover losses in the stock market; and that when Rathbone—who had intended taking them and going to Central

---

[*] Thomas Aloysius Dorgan, syndicated cartoonist whose work normally appeared on the sports page. Hammett is describing one of his famous cartoons.

America with Mrs. Earnshaw—had visited the safe deposit box and found them gone, he had returned to the office and charged Zumwalt with the theft.

Zumwalt at that time had not suspected his partner's own dishonest plans, and had promised to restore the bonds. They had gone to Zumwalt's house to discuss the matter; and, Rathbone, dissatisfied with his partner's plan of restitution, had attacked Zumwalt, and had been killed in the ensuing struggle.

Then Zumwalt had told Mildred Narbett, his stenographer, the whole story and had persuaded her to help him. Between them they had made it appear that Rathbone had been in the office for a while the next day—the twenty-eighth—and had left for New York.

However, the jury seemed to think that Zumwalt had lured his partner out to the Fourteenth Avenue house for the purpose of killing him; so Zumwalt was found guilty of murder in the first degree.

The first jury before which Mildred Narbett was tried disagreed. The second jury acquitted her, holding that there was nothing to show that she had taken part in either the theft of the bonds or the murder, or that she had any knowledge of either crime until afterward; and that her later complicity was, in view of her love for Zumwalt, not altogether blameworthy.

BLACK MASK, DECEMBER 1, 1923

Bodies Piled Up

BY DASHIELL HAMMETT

Author of "It," "The Second-Story Angel," "Crooked Souls," etc.

One of our best detectives is this nameless sleuth of Mr. Hammett's. He's deductive, practical, and maybe a little unromantic. Probably that's why he runs into such wild adventures and takes such horrible chances. In this story he walks into a whirlwind of death. Go to it.

THE MONTGOMERY HOTEL'S regular detective had taken his last week's rake-off from the hotel bootlegger in merchandise instead of cash, had drunk it down, had fallen asleep in the lobby, and had been fired. I happened to be the only idle operative in the Continental Detective Agency's San Francisco branch at the time, and thus it came about that I had three days of hotel-coppering while a man was being found to take the job permanently.

The Montgomery is a quiet hotel of the better sort, and so I had a very restful time of it—until the third and last day.

Then things changed.

I came down into the lobby that afternoon to find Stacey, the assistant manager on duty at the time, hunting for me.

"One of the maids just phoned that there's something wrong up in 906," he said.

We went up to that room together. The door was open. In the center of the floor stood a maid, staring goggle-eyed at the closed door of the clothespress. From under it, extending perhaps a foot across the floor toward us, was a snake-shaped ribbon of blood.

I stepped past the maid and tried the door. It was unlocked. I opened it. Slowly, rigidly, a man pitched out into my arms—pitched out backward—and there was a six-inch slit down the back of his coat, and the coat was wet and sticky.

That wasn't altogether a surprise: the blood on the floor had prepared me for something of the sort. But when another followed him—facing me, this one, with a dark, distorted face—I dropped the one I had caught and jumped back.

And as I jumped a third man came tumbling out after the others.

From behind me came a scream and a thud as the maid fainted. I wasn't feeling any too steady myself. I'm no sensitive plant, and I've looked at a lot of unlovely sights in my time, but for weeks afterward I could see those three dead men coming out of that clothespress to pile up at my feet: coming out slowly—almost deliberately—in a ghastly game of "follow your leader."

Seeing them, you couldn't doubt that they were really dead. Every detail of their falling, every detail of the heap in which they now lay, had a horrible certainty of lifelessness in it.

I turned to Stacey, who, deathly white himself, was keeping on his feet only by clinging to the foot of the brass bed.

"Get the woman out! Get doctors—police!"

I pulled the three dead bodies apart, laying them out in a grim row, faces up. Then I made a hasty examination of the room.

A soft hat, which fitted one of the dead men, lay in the center of the unruffled bed. The room key was in the door, on the inside. There was no blood in the room except what had leaked out of the clothespress, and the room showed no signs of having been the scene of a struggle.

The door to the bathroom was open. In the bottom of the bath tub was a shattered gin bottle, which, from the strength of the odor and the dampness of the tub, had been nearly full when broken. In one corner of the bathroom I found a small whisky glass, and another under the tub. Both were dry, clean, and odorless.

The inside of the clothespress door was stained with blood from the height of my shoulder to the floor, and two hats lay in the puddle of blood on the closet floor. Each of the hats fitted one of the dead men.

That was all. Three dead men, a broken gin bottle, blood.

Stacey returned presently with a doctor, and while the doctor was examining the dead men, the police detectives arrived.

The doctor's work was soon done.

"This man," he said, pointing to one of them, "was struck on the back of the head with a small blunt instrument, and then strangled. This one," pointing to another, "was simply strangled. And the third was stabbed in the back with a blade perhaps five inches long. They have been dead for about two hours—since noon or a little after."

The assistant manager identified two of the bodies. The man who had been stabbed—the first to fall out of the clothespress—had arrived at the hotel three days before, registering as Tudor Ingraham of Washington, D. C., and had occupied room 915, three doors away.

The last man to fall out—the one who had been simply choked—was the occupant of this room. His name was Vincent Develyn. He was an insurance broker and had made the hotel his home since his wife's death, some four years before.

The third man had been seen in Develyn's company frequently, and one of the clerks remembered that they had come into the hotel together at about five minutes after twelve this day. Cards and letters in his pockets told us that he was Homer Ansley, a member of the law firm of Lankershim and Ansley, whose offices were in the Miles Building—next door to Develyn's office, in fact.

Develyn's pockets held between $150 and $200; Ansley's wallet contained more than $100; Ingraham's pockets yielded nearly $300, and in a money belt around his waist we found $2200 and two medium-sized unset diamonds. All three had watches—Develyn's was a valuable one—in their pockets, and Ingraham wore two rings, both of which were expensive ones. Ingraham's room key was in his pocket.

Beyond this money—whose presence would seem to indicate that robbery hadn't been the motive behind the three killings—we found nothing on any of their persons to throw the slightest light on the crime. Nor did the most thorough examination of both Ingraham's and Develyn's rooms teach us anything.

In Ingraham's room we found a dozen or more packs of carefully marked cards, some crooked dice, and an immense amount of data on racehorses. Also we found that he had a wife who lived on East Delavan Avenue in Buffalo, and a brother on Crutcher Street in Dallas; as well as a list of names and addresses that we carried off to investigate later. But nothing in either room pointed, even indirectly, at murder.

Phels, the police department Bertillon man, found a number of fingerprints in Develyn's room, but we couldn't tell whether they would be of any value or not until he had worked them up. Though Develyn and Ansley had apparently been strangled by hands, Phels was unable to get prints from either their necks or their collars.

The maid who had discovered the blood said that she had straightened up Develyn's room between ten and eleven that morning, but had not put fresh towels in the bathroom. It was for this purpose that she had gone to the room in the afternoon. She had found the door unlocked, with the key on the inside, and, as soon as she entered, had seen the blood and telephoned Stacey. She had seen no one in the corridor nearby as she entered the room.

She had straightened up Ingraham's room, she said, at a few minutes after one. She had gone there earlier—between 10:20 and 10:45—for that purpose, but Ingraham had not then left it.

The elevator man who had carried Ansley and Develyn up from the lobby at a few minutes after twelve remembered that they had been laughingly discussing their golf scores of the previous day during the ride. No one had seen anything suspicious in the hotel around the time at which the doctor had placed the murders. But that was to be expected.

The murderer could have left the room, closing the door behind him, and walked away secure in the knowledge that at noon a man in the corridors of the Montgomery would attract little attention. If he was staying at the hotel he would simply have gone to his room; if not, he would have either walked all the way down to the

street, or down a floor or two and then caught an elevator.

None of the hotel employees had ever seen Ingraham and Develyn together. There was nothing to show that they had even the slightest acquaintance. Ingraham habitually stayed in his room until noon, and did not return to it until very late at night. Nothing was known of his affairs.

At the Miles Building we—that is, Marty O'Hara and George Dean of the police department homicide detail, and I—questioned Ansley's partner and Develyn's employees. Both Develyn and Ansley, it seemed, were ordinary men who led ordinary lives: lives that held neither dark spots nor queer kinks. Ansley was married and had two children; he lived on Lake Street. Both men had a sprinkling of relatives and friends scattered here and there through the country; and, so far as we could learn, their affairs were in perfect order.

They had left their offices this day to go to luncheon together, intending to visit Develyn's room first for a drink apiece from a bottle of gin someone coming from Australia had smuggled in to him.

"Well," O'Hara said, when we were on the street again, "this much is clear. If they went up to Develyn's room for a drink, it's a cinch that they were killed almost as soon as they got in the room. Those whisky glasses you found were dry and clean. Whoever turned the trick must have been waiting for them. I wonder about this fellow Ingraham."

"I'm wondering, too," I said. "Figuring it out from the positions I found them in when I opened the closet door, Ingraham sizes up as the key to the whole thing. Develyn was back against the wall, with Ansley in front of him, both facing the door. Ingraham was facing them, with his back to the door. The clothespress was just large enough for them to be packed in it—too small for any of them to slip down while the door was closed.

"Then there was no blood in the room except what had come from the clothespress. Ingraham, with that gaping slit in his back, couldn't have been stabbed until he was inside the closet, or he'd have bled elsewhere. He was standing close to the other men when he was knifed, and whoever knifed him closed the door quickly afterward.

"Now, why should he have been standing in such a position? Do you dope it out that he and another killed the two friends, and that while he was stowing their bodies in the closet his accomplice finished him off?"

"Maybe," Dean said.

And that "maybe" was still as far as we had gone three days later.

We had sent and received bales of telegrams, having relatives and acquaintances of the dead men interviewed; and we had found nothing that seemed to have any bearing upon their deaths. Nor had we found the slightest connecting link between Ingraham and the other two. We had traced those other two back step by step almost to their cradles. We had accounted for every minute of their time since Ingraham had arrived in San Francisco—thoroughly enough to convince us that neither of them had met Ingraham.

Ingraham, we had learned, was a book-maker and all around crooked gambler. His wife and he had separated, but were on good terms. Some fifteen years before, he had been convicted of "assault with intent to kill" in Newark, N. J., and had served two years in the state prison. But the man he had assaulted—one John Pellow—had died of pneumonia in Omaha in 1914.

Ingraham had come to San Francisco for the purpose of opening a gambling club, and all our investigations had tended to show that his activities while in the city had been toward that end alone.

The fingerprints Phels had secured had all turned out to belong to Stacey, the maid, the police detectives, or myself. In short, we had found nothing!

So much for our attempts to learn the motive behind the three murders.

We now dropped that angle and settled down to the detail-studying, patience-taxing grind of picking up the murderer's trail. From any crime to its author there is a trail. It may be—as in this case—obscure; but, since matter cannot move without disturbing other matter along its path, there always is—there must be—a trail of some sort. And finding and following such trails is what a detective is paid to do.

In the case of a murder it is possible sometimes to take a short-cut to the end of the trail, by first finding the motive. A knowledge of the motive often reduces the field of possibilities; sometimes points directly to the guilty one. It is on this account that murderers are, as a rule, more easily apprehended than any other class of criminals.

But a knowledge of the motive isn't indispensable—quite a few murder mysteries are solved without its help. And in a fair proportion—say, ten to twenty per cent—of cases where men are convicted justly of murder, the motive isn't clearly shown even at the last, and sometimes is hardly guessed at.

So far, all we knew about the motive in the particular case we were dealing with was that it hadn't been robbery; unless something we didn't know about had been stolen—something of sufficient value to make the murderer scorn the money in his victims' pockets.

We hadn't altogether neglected the search for the murderer's trail, of course, but—being human—we had devoted most of our attention to trying to find a short-cut. Now we set out to find our man, or men, regardless of what had urged him or them to commit the crimes.

Of the people who had been registered at the hotel on the day of the killing there were nine men of whose innocence we hadn't found a reasonable amount of proof. Four of these were still at the hotel, and only one of that four interested us very strongly. That one—a big rawboned man of forty-five or fifty, who had registered as J. J. Cooper of Anaconda, Montana—wasn't, we had definitely established, really a mining man, as he pretended to be. And our telegraphic communications with Anaconda failed to show that he was known there. Therefore we were having him shadowed—with few results.

Five men of the nine had departed since the murders; three of them leaving forwarding addresses with the mail clerk. Gilbert Jacquemart had occupied room 946 and had ordered his mail forwarded to him at a Los Angeles hotel. W. F. Salway, who had occupied room 1022, had given instructions that his mail be readdressed to a number on Clark Street in Chicago. Ross Orrett, room 609, had asked to have his mail sent to him care of General Delivery at the local post office.

Jacquemart had arrived at the hotel two days before, and had left on the afternoon of the murders. Salway had arrived the day before the murders and had left the day after them. Orrett had arrived on the day of the murders and had left the following day.

Sending telegrams to have the first two found and investigated, I went after Orrett myself. A musical comedy named "What For?" was being widely advertised just then with gaily printed plum-colored hand-bills. I got one of them and, at a stationery store, an envelope to match, and mailed it to Orrett at the Montgomery Hotel. There are concerns that make a practice of securing the names of arrivals at the principal hotels and mailing them advertisements. I trusted that Orrett, knowing this, wouldn't be suspicious when my gaudy envelope, forwarded from the hotel, reached him through the General Delivery window.

Dick Foley—the agency's shadow specialist—planted himself in the post office, to loiter around with an eye on the "O" window until he saw my plum-colored envelope passed out, and then to shadow the receiver.

I spent the next day trying to solve the mysterious J. J. Cooper's game, but he was still a puzzle when I knocked off that night.

At a little before five the following morning Dick Foley dropped into my room on his way home to wake me up and tell me what he had done for himself.

"This Orrett baby is our meat!" he said. "Picked him up when he got his mail yesterday afternoon. Got another letter besides yours. Got an apartment on Van Ness Avenue. Took it the day after the killing, under the name of B. T. Quinn. Packing a gun under his left arm—there's that sort of a bulge there. Just went home to bed. Been visiting all the dives in North Beach. Who do you think he's hunting for?"

"Who?"

"Guy Cudner."

That was news! This Guy Cudner, alias "The Darkman," was the most dangerous bird on the Coast, if not in the country. He had only been nailed once, but if he had been convicted of all the crimes that everybody knew he had committed he'd have needed half a dozen lives to crowd his sentences into, besides another half-dozen to carry to the gallows. However, he had decidedly the right sort of backing—enough to buy him everything he needed in the way of witnesses, alibis, even juries, and—so the talk went—an occasional judge.

I don't know what went wrong with his support that one time he was convicted up North and sent over for a one-to-fourteen-year hitch; but it adjusted itself promptly, for the ink was hardly dry on the press notices of his conviction before he was loose again on parole.

"Is Cudner in town?"

"Don't know," Dick said, "but this Orrett, or Quinn, or whatever his name is, is surely hunting for him. In Rick's place, at 'Wop' Healey's and at Pigatti's. 'Porky' Grout tipped me off. Says Orrett doesn't know Cudner by sight, but is trying to find him. Porky didn't know what he wants with him."

This Porky Grout was a dirty little rat who would sell out his family—if he ever had one—for the price of a flop. But with these lads who play both sides of the game it's always a question of which side they're playing when you think they're playing yours.

"Think Porky was coming clean?" I asked.

"Chances are—but you can't gamble on him."

"Is Orrett acquainted here?"

"Doesn't seem to be. Knows where he wants to go but has to ask how to get there. Hasn't spoken to anybody that seemed to know him."

"What's he like?"

"Not the kind of egg* you'd want to tangle with offhand, if you ask me. He and Cudner would make a good pair. They don't look alike. This egg is tall and slim, but he's built right—those fast, smooth muscles. Face is sharp without being thin, if you get me. I mean all the lines in it are straight. No curves. Chin, nose, mouth, eyes—all straight, sharp lines and angles. Looks like the kind of egg we know Cudner is. Make a good pair. Dresses well and doesn't look like a rowdy—but harder than hell! A big game hunter! Our meat, I bet you!"

"It doesn't look bad," I agreed. "He came to the hotel the morning of the day the men were killed, and checked out the next morning. He packs a rod, and changed his name after he left. And now he's paired off with The Darkman. It doesn't look bad at all!"

"I'm telling you," Dick said, "this fellow looks like three killings wouldn't disturb his rest any. I wonder where Cudner fits in."

"I can't guess. But, if he and Orrett haven't connected yet, then Cudner wasn't in on the murders; but he may give us the answer."

Then I jumped out of bed.

"I'm going to gamble on Porky's dope being on the level! How would you describe Cudner?"

"You know him better than I do."

"Yes, but how would you describe him to me if I didn't know him?"

"A little fat guy with a red forked scar on his left cheek. What's the idea?"

"It's a good one," I admitted. "That scar makes all the difference in the world. If he didn't have it and you were to describe him you'd go into all the details of his appearance. But he has it, so you simply say, 'A little fat guy with a red forked scar on his left cheek.' It's a ten to one that that's just how he has been described to Orrett. I don't look like Cudner, but I'm his size

* person

and build, and with a scar on my face Orrett will fall for me."

"What then?"

"There's no telling; but I ought to be able to learn a lot if I can get Orrett talking to me as Cudner. It's worth a try anyway."

"You can't get away with it—not in San Francisco. Cudner is too well known."

"What difference does that make, Dick? Orrett is the only one I want to fool. If he takes me for Cudner, well and good. If he doesn't, still well and good. I won't force myself on him."

"How are you going to fake the scar?"

"Easy! We have pictures of Cudner, showing the scar, in the criminal gallery. I'll get some collodion—it's sold in drug stores under several trade names for putting on cuts and scratches—color it, and imitate Cudner's scar on my cheek. It dries with a shiny surface and, put on thick, will stand out just enough to look like an old scar."

It was a little after eleven the following night when Dick telephoned me that Orrett was in Pigatti's place, on Pacific Street, and apparently settled there for some little while. My scar already painted on, I jumped into a taxi and within a few minutes was talking to Dick, around the corner from Pigatti's.

"He's sitting at the last table back on the left side. And he was alone when I came out. You can't miss him. He's the only egg in the joint with a clean collar."

"You better stick outside—half a block or so away—with the taxi," I told Dick. "Maybe brother Orrett and I will leave together and I'd just as leave have you standing by in case things break wrong."

Pigatti's place is a long, narrow, low-ceilinged cellar, always dim with smoke. Down the middle runs a narrow strip of bare floor for dancing. The rest of the floor is covered with closely packed tables, whose cloths are always soiled; and the management hasn't yet verified the rumor that the country has gone dry.

Most of the tables were occupied when I came in, and half a dozen couples were dancing. Few of the faces to be seen were strangers to the morning "line up" at police headquarters.

Peering through the smoke, I saw Orrett at once, seated alone in a far corner, looking at the dancers with the set blank face of one who masks an all-seeing watchfulness. I walked down the other side of the room and crossed the strip of dance-floor directly under a light, so that the scar might be clearly visible to him. Then I selected a vacant table not far from his, and sat down facing him.

Ten minutes passed while he pretended an interest in the dancers and I affected a thoughtful stare at the dirty cloth on my table; but neither of us missed so much as a flicker of the other's lids.

His eyes—gray eyes that were pale without being shallow, with black needle-point pupils—met mine after a while in a cold, steady, inscrutable stare; and, very slowly, he got to his feet. One hand—his right—in a side pocket of his dark coat, he walked straight across to my table and sat down opposite me.

"Cudner?"

"Looking for me, I hear," I replied, trying to match the icy smoothness of his voice, as I was matching the steadiness of his gaze.

He had sat down with his left side turned slightly toward me, which put his right arm in not too cramped a position for straight shooting from the pocket that still held his hand.

"You were looking for me, too."

I didn't know what the correct answer to that would be, so I just grinned. But the grin didn't come from my heart. I had, I realized, made a mistake—one that might cost me something before we were done. This bird wasn't hunting for Cudner as a friend, as I had carelessly assumed, but was on the war path.

I saw those three dead men falling out of the closet in room 906!

My gun was inside the waist-band of my trousers, where I could get it quickly, but his was in his hand. So I was careful to keep my own hands motionless on the edge of the table, while I widened my grin.

His eyes were changing now, and the more I looked at them the less I liked them. The gray in them had darkened and grown duller, and the pupils were larger, and white crescents were showing beneath the gray. Twice before I had looked into eyes such as these—and I hadn't forgotten what they meant—the eyes of the congenital killer!

"Suppose you speak your piece," I suggested after a while.

But he wasn't to be beguiled into conversation. He shook his head a mere fraction of an inch and the corners of his compressed mouth dropped down a trifle. The white crescents of eyeballs were growing broader, pushing the gray circles up under the upper lids.

It was coming! And there was no use waiting for it!

I drove a foot at his shins under the table, and at the same time pushed the table into his lap and threw myself across it. The bullet from his gun went off to one side. Another bullet—not from his gun—thudded into the table that was upended between us.

I had him by the shoulders when the second shot from behind took him in the left arm, just below my hand. I let go then and fell away, rolling over against the wall and twisting around to face the direction from which the bullets were coming.

I twisted around just in time to see—jerking out of sight behind a corner of the passage that gave to a small dining room—Guy Cudner's scarred face. And as it disappeared a bullet from Orrett's gun splattered the plaster from the wall where it had been.

I grinned at the thought of what must be going on in Orrett's head as he lay sprawled out on the floor confronted by two Cudners. But he took a shot at me just then and I stopped grinning. Luckily, he had to twist around to fire at me, putting his weight on his wounded arm, and the pain made him wince, spoiling his aim.

Before he had adjusted himself more comfortably I had scrambled on hands and knees to Pigatti's kitchen door—only a few feet away—and had myself safely tucked out of range around an angle in the wall; all but my eyes and the top of my head, which I risked so that I might see what went on.

Orrett was now ten or twelve feet from me, lying flat on the floor, facing Cudner, with a gun in his hand and another on the floor beside him.

Across the room, perhaps thirty feet away, Cudner was showing himself around his protecting corner at brief intervals to exchange shots with the man on the floor, occasionally sending one my way. We had the place to ourselves. There were four exits, and the rest of Pigatti's customers had used them all.

I had my gun out, but I was playing a waiting game. Cudner, I figured, had been tipped off to Orrett's search for him and had arrived on the scene with no mistaken idea of the other's attitude. Just what there was between them and what bearing it had on the Montgomery murders was a mystery to me, but I didn't try to solve it now. I kept away from the bullets that were flying around as best I could and waited.

They were firing in unison. Cudner would show around his corner, both men's weapons would spit, and he would duck out of sight again. Orrett was bleeding about the head now and one of his legs sprawled crookedly behind him. I couldn't determine whether Cudner had been hit or not.

Each had fired eight, or perhaps nine, shots when Cudner suddenly jumped out into full view, pumping the gun in his left hand as fast as its mechanism would go, the gun in his right hand hanging at his side. Orrett had changed guns, and was on his knees now, his fresh weapon keeping pace with his enemy's.

That couldn't last!

Cudner dropped his left-hand gun, and, as he raised the other, he sagged forward and went down on one knee. Orrett stopped firing abruptly and fell over on his back—spread out full-length. Cudner fired once more—wildly, into the ceiling—and pitched down on his face.

I sprang to Orrett's side and kicked both of his guns away. He was lying still but his eyes were open.

"Are you Cudner, or was he?"

"He."

"Good!" he said, and closed his eyes.

I crossed to where Cudner lay and turned him over on his back. His chest was literally shot to pieces.

His thick lips worked, and I put my ear down to them.

"I get him?"

"Yes," I lied, "he's already cold."

His dying face twisted into a triumphant grin.

"Sorry . . . three in hotel . . ." he gasped hoarsely. "Mistake . . . wrong room . . . got one . . . had to . . . other two . . . protect myself . . . I . . ."

He shuddered and died.

A week later the hospital people let me talk to Orrett. I told him what Cudner had said before he died.

"That's the way I doped it out," Orrett said from out of the depths of the bandages in which he was swathed. "That's why I moved and changed my name the next day."

"I suppose you've got it nearly figured out by now," he said after a while.

"No," I confessed, "I haven't. I've an idea what it was all about but I could stand having a few details cleared up."

"I'm sorry I can't clear them up for you, but I've got to cover myself up. I'll tell you a story, though, and it may help you. Once upon a time there was a high-class crook—what the newspapers call a Master Mind. Came a day when he found he had accumulated enough money to give up the game and settle down as an honest man.

"But he had two lieutenants—one in New York and one in San Francisco—and they were the only men in the world who knew he was a crook. And, besides that, he was afraid of both of them. So he thought he'd rest easier if they were out of the way. And it happened that neither of these lieutenants had ever seen the other.

"So this Master Mind convinced each of them that the other was double-crossing him and would have to be bumped off for the safety of all concerned. And both of them fell for it. The New Yorker went to San Francisco to get the other, and the San Franciscan was told that the New Yorker would arrive on such-and-such a day and would stay at such-and-such a hotel.

"The Master Mind figured that there was an even chance of both men passing out when they met—and he was nearly right at that. But he was sure that one would die, and then, even if the other missed hanging, there would only be one man left for him to dispose of later."

There weren't as many details in the story as I would have liked to have, but it explained a lot.

"How do you figure out Cudner's getting into the wrong room?" I asked.

"That was funny! Maybe it happened like this: My room was 609 and the killing was done in 906. Suppose Cudner went to the hotel on the day he knew I was due and took a quick slant at the register. He wouldn't want to be seen looking at it if he could avoid it, so he didn't turn it around, but flashed a look at it as it lay—facing the desk.

"When you read numbers of three figures upside-down you have to transpose them in your head to get them straight. Like 123. You'd get that 3-2-1, and then turn them around in your head. That's what Cudner did with mine. He was keyed up, of course, thinking of the job ahead of him, and he overlooked the fact that 609 upside-down still reads 609 just the same. So he turned it around and made it 906—Develyn's room."

"That's how I doped it," I said, "and I reckon it's about right. And then he looked at the key-rack and saw that 906 wasn't there. So he thought he might just as well get his job done right then, when he could roam the hotel corridors without attracting attention. Of course, he may have gone up to the room before Ansley and Develyn came in and waited for them, but I doubt it.

"I think it more likely that he simply happened to arrive at the hotel a few minutes after they had come in. Ansley was probably alone in the room when Cudner opened the unlocked door and came in—Develyn being in the bathroom getting the glasses.

"Ansley was about your size and age, and close enough in appearance to fit a rough description of you. Cudner went for him, and then Develyn, hearing the scuffle, dropped the bottle and glasses and rushed out, and got his.

"Cudner, being the sort he was, would figure that two murders were no worse than one, and he wouldn't want to leave any witnesses around.

"And that is probably how Ingraham got into it. He was passing on his way from his room to the elevator and perhaps heard the racket and investigated. And Cudner put a gun in his face and made him stow the two bodies in the clothespress. And then he stuck his knife in Ingraham's back and slammed the door on him. That's about the—"

An indignant nurse descended on me from behind and ordered me out of the room, accusing me of getting her patient excited.

Orrett stopped me as I turned to go.

"Keep your eye on the New York dispatches," he said, "and maybe you'll get the rest of the story. It's not over yet. Nobody has anything on me out here. That shooting in Pigatti's was self-defense so far as I'm concerned. And as soon as I'm on my feet again and can get back East there's going to be a Master Mind holding a lot of lead. That's a promise!"

I believed him.

BLACK MASK, JANUARY 1, 1924

The Tenth Clew

BY DASHIELL HAMMETT

(A Complete Mystery-Detective Novelette)
(Author of "It," "Bodies Piled Up," etc.)

There were enough clews in this crime to give Mr. Hammett's nameless detective a year or so of work. But solving a mystery in that length of time didn't appeal to him. He wanted faster action—and he got it in good measure. So will you if you begin this entertaining novelette.

CHAPTER I

"DO YOU KNOW . . . EMIL BONFILS?"

"MR. LEOPOLD GANTVOORT is not at home," the servant who opened the door said, "but his son, Mr. Charles, is—if you wish to see him."

"No. I had an appointment with Mr. Leopold Gantvoort for nine or a little after. It's just nine now. No doubt he'll be back soon. I'll wait."

"Very well, sir."

He stepped aside for me to enter the house, took my overcoat and hat, guided me to a room on the second floor—Gantvoort's library—and left me. I picked up a magazine from the stack on the table, pulled an ash tray over beside me, and made myself comfortable.

An hour passed. I stopped reading and began to grow impatient. Another hour passed—and I was fidgeting.

A clock somewhere below had begun to strike eleven when a young man of twenty-five or -six, tall and slender, with remarkably white skin and very dark hair and eyes, came into the room.

"My father hasn't returned yet," he said. "It's too bad that you should have been kept waiting all this time. Isn't there anything I could do for you? I am Charles Gantvoort."

"No, thank you." I got up from my chair, accepting the courteous dismissal. "I'll get in touch with him tomorrow."

"I'm sorry," he murmured, and we moved toward the door together.

As we reached the hall an extension telephone in one corner of the room we were leaving buzzed softly, and I halted in the doorway while Charles Gantvoort went over to answer it.

His back was toward me as he spoke into the instrument.

"Yes. Yes. Yes!"—sharply—"*What?* Yes"—very weakly—"Yes."

He turned slowly around and faced me with a face that was gray and tortured, with wide shocked eyes and gaping mouth—the telephone still in his hand.

"Father," he gasped, "is dead—killed!"

"Where? How?"

"I don't know. That was the police. They want me to come down at once."

He straightened his shoulders with an effort, pulling himself together, put down the telephone, and his face fell into less strained lines.

"You will pardon my—"

"Mr. Gantvoort," I interrupted his apology, "I am connected with the Continental Detective Agency. Your father called up this afternoon and asked that a detective be sent to see him tonight. He said his life had been threatened. He hadn't definitely engaged us, however, so unless you—"

"Certainly! You are employed! If the police haven't already caught the murderer I want you to do everything possible to catch him."

"All right! Let's get down to headquarters."

Neither of us spoke during the ride to the Hall of Justice. Gantvoort bent over the wheel of his car, sending it through the streets at a terrific speed. There were several questions that needed answers, but all his attention was required for his driving if he was to maintain the pace at which he was driving without piling us into something. So I didn't disturb him, but hung on and kept quiet.

Half a dozen police detectives were waiting for us when we reached the detective bureau. O'Gar—a bullet-headed detective-sergeant who dresses like the village constable in a movie, wide-brimmed black hat and all, but who isn't to be put out of the reckoning on that account—was in charge of the investigation. He and I had worked on two or three jobs together before, and hit it off excellently.

He led us into one of the small offices below the assembly room. Spread out on the flat top of a desk there were a dozen or more objects.

"I want you to look these things over carefully," the detective-sergeant told Gantvoort, "and pick out the ones that belonged to your father."

"But where is he?"

"Do this first," O'Gar insisted, "and then you can see him."

I looked at the things on the table while Charles Gantvoort made his selections. An empty jewel case; a memoranda book; three letters in slit envelopes that were addressed to the dead man; some other papers; a bunch of keys; a fountain pen; two white linen handkerchiefs; two pistol cartridges; a gold watch, with a gold knife and a gold pencil attached to it by a gold-and-platinum chain; two black leather wallets, one of them very new and the other worn; some money, both paper and silver; and a small portable typewriter, bent and twisted, and matted with hair and blood. Some of the other things were smeared with blood and some were clean.

Gantvoort picked out the watch and its attachments, the keys, the fountain pen, the memoranda book, the handkerchiefs, the letters and other papers, and the older wallet.

"These were father's," he told us. "I've never seen any of the others before. I don't know, of course, how much money he had with him tonight, so I can't say how much of this is his."

"You're sure none of the rest of this stuff was his?" O'Gar asked.

"I don't think so, but I'm not sure. Whipple could tell you." He turned to me. "He's the man who let you in tonight. He looked after father, and he'd know positively whether any of these other things belonged to him or not."

One of the police detectives went to the telephone to tell Whipple to come down immediately.

I resumed the questioning.

"Is anything that your father usually carried with him missing? Anything of value?"

"Not that I know of. All of the things that

hc might have been expected to have with him seem to be here."

"At what time tonight did he leave the house?"

"Before seven-thirty. Possibly as early as seven."

"Know where he was going?"

"He didn't tell me, but I supposed he was going to call on Miss Dexter."

The faces of the police detectives brightened, and their eyes grew sharp. I suppose mine did, too. There are many, many murders with never a woman in them anywhere; but seldom a very conspicuous killing.

"Who's this Miss Dexter?" O'Gar took up the inquiry.

"She's well—" Charles Gantvoort hesitated. "Well, father was on very friendly terms with her and her brother. He usually called on them—on her several evenings a week. In fact, I suspected that he intended marrying her."

"Who and what is she?"

"Father became acquainted with them six or seven months ago. I've met them several times, but don't know them very well. Miss Dexter—Creda is her given name—is about twenty-three years old, I should judge, and her brother Madden is four or five years older. He is in New York now, or on his way there, to transact some business for father."

"Did your father tell you he was going to marry her?" O'Gar hammered away at the woman angle.

"No; but it was pretty obvious that he was very much—ah—infatuated. We had some words over it a few days ago—last week. Not a quarrel, you understand, but words. From the way he talked I feared that he meant to marry her."

"What do you mean 'feared'?" O'Gar snapped at that word.

Charles Gantvoort's pale face flushed a little, and he cleared his throat embarrassedly.

"I don't want to put the Dexters in a bad light to you. I don't think—I'm sure they had nothing to do with father's—with this. But I didn't care

especially for them—didn't like them. I thought they were—well—fortune hunters, perhaps. Father wasn't fabulously wealthy, but he had considerable means. And, while he wasn't feeble, still he was past fifty-seven, old enough for me to feel that Creda Dexter was more interested in his money than in him."

"How about your father's will?"

"The last one of which I have any knowledge—drawn up two or three years ago—left everything to my wife and me jointly. Father's attorney, Mr. Murray Abernathy, could tell you if there was a later will, but I hardly think there was."

"Your father had retired from business, hadn't he?"

"Yes; he turned his import and export business over to me about a year ago. He had quite a few investments scattered around, but he wasn't actively engaged in the management of any concern."

O'Gar tilted his village constable hat back and scratched his bullet head reflectively for a moment. Then he looked at me.

"Anything else you want to ask?"

"Yes. Mr. Gantvoort, do you know, or did you ever hear your father or anyone else speak of an Emil Bonfils?"

"No."

"Did your father ever tell you that he had received a threatening letter? Or that he had been shot at on the street?"

"No."

"Was your father in Paris in 1902?"

"Very likely. He used to go abroad every year up until the time of his retirement from business."

CHAPTER II

"THAT'S SOMETHING!"

O'Gar and I took Gantvoort around to the morgue to see his father, then. The dead man wasn't pleasant to look at, even to O'Gar and me, who hadn't known him except by sight. I remembered him as a small wiry man, always smartly tailored, and with a brisk springiness that was far younger than his years.

He lay now with the top of his head beaten into a red and pulpy mess.

We left Gantvoort at the morgue and set out afoot for the Hall of Justice.

"What's this deep stuff you're pulling about Emil Bonfils and Paris in 1902?" the detective-sergeant asked as soon as we were out in the street.

"This: the dead man phoned the agency this afternoon and said he had received a threatening letter from an Emil Bonfils with whom he had had trouble in Paris in 1902. He also said that Bonfils had shot at him the previous evening, in the street. He wanted somebody to come around and see him about it tonight. And he said that under no circumstances were the police to be let in on it—that he'd rather have Bonfils get him than have the trouble made public. That's all he would say over the phone; and that's how I happened to be on hand when Charles Gantvoort was notified of his father's death."

O'Gar stopped in the middle of the sidewalk and whistled softly.

"That's something!" he exclaimed. "Wait till we get back to headquarters—I'll show you something."

Whipple was waiting in the assembly room when we arrived at headquarters. His face at first glance was as smooth and mask-like as when he had admitted me to the house on Russian Hill earlier in the evening. But beneath his perfect servant's manner he was twitching and trembling.

We took him into the little office where we had questioned Charles Gantvoort.

Whipple verified all that the dead man's son had told us. He was positive that neither the typewriter, the jewel case, the two cartridges, or the newer wallet had belonged to Gantvoort.

We couldn't get him to put his opinion of the Dexters in words, but that he disapproved of them was easily seen. Miss Dexter, he said, had called up on the telephone three times this night at about eight o'clock, at nine, and at nine-thirty. She had asked for Mr. Leopold Gantvoort each

time, but she had left no message. Whipple was of the opinion that she was expecting Gantvoort, and he had not arrived.

He knew nothing, he said, of Emil Bonfils or of any threatening letters. Gantvoort had been out the previous night from eight until midnight. Whipple had not seen him closely enough when he came home to say whether he seemed excited or not. Gantvoort usually carried about a hundred dollars in his pockets.

"Is there anything that you know of that Gantvoort had on his person tonight which isn't among these things on the desk?" O'Gar asked.

"No, sir. Everything seems to be here—watch and chain, money, memorandum book, wallet, keys, handkerchiefs, fountain pen—everything that I know of."

"Did Charles Gantvoort go out tonight?"

"No, sir. He and Mrs. Gantvoort were at home all evening."

"Positive?"

Whipple thought a moment.

"Yes, sir, I'm fairly certain. But I know Mrs. Gantvoort wasn't out. To tell the truth, I didn't see Mr. Charles from about eight o'clock until he came downstairs with this gentleman"—pointing to me—"at eleven. But I'm fairly certain he was home all evening. I think Mrs. Gantvoort said he was."

Then O'Gar put another question—one that puzzled me at the time.

"What kind of collar buttons did Mr. Gantvoort wear?"

"You mean Mr. Leopold?"

"Yes."

"Plain gold ones, made all in one piece. They had a London jeweler's mark on them."

"Would you know them if you saw them?"

"Yes, sir."

We let Whipple go home then.

"Don't you think," I suggested when O'Gar and I were alone with this desk-load of evidence that didn't mean anything at all to me yet, "it's time you were loosening up and telling me what's what?"

"I guess so—listen! A man named Lagerquist,

a grocer, was driving through Golden Gate Park tonight, and passed a machine standing on a dark road, with its lights out. He thought there was something funny about the way the man in it was sitting at the wheel, so he told the first patrolman he met about it.

"The patrolman investigated and found Gantvoort sitting at the wheel—dead—with his head smashed in and this dingus"—putting one hand on the bloody typewriter—"on the seat beside him. That was at a quarter of ten. The doc says Gantvoort was killed—his skull crushed—with this typewriter.

"The dead man's pockets, we found, had all been turned inside out; and all this stuff on the desk, except this new wallet, was scattered about in the car—some of it on the floor and some on the seats. This money was there too—nearly a hundred dollars of it. Among the papers was this."

He handed me a sheet of white paper upon which the following had been typewritten:

> *L. F. G.—*
>
> *I want what is mine. 6,000 miles and 21 years are not enough to hide you from the victim of your treachery. I mean to have what you stole.*
>
> *E. B.*

"L. F. G. could be Leopold F. Gantvoort," I said. "And E. B. could be Emil Bonfils. Twenty-one years is the time from 1902 to 1923, and 6,000 miles is, roughly, the distance between Paris and San Francisco."

I laid the letter down and picked up the jewel case. It was a black imitation leather one, lined with white satin, and unmarked in any way.

Then I examined the cartridges. There were two of them, S. W. .45-caliber, and deep crosses had been cut in their soft noses—an old trick that makes the bullet spread out like a saucer when it hits.

"These in the car, too?"

"Yep—and this."

From a vest pocket O'Gar produced a short tuft of blond hair—hairs between an inch and two inches in length. They had been cut off, not pulled out by the roots.

"Any more?"

There seemed to be an endless stream of things.

He picked up the new wallet from the desk—the one that both Whipple and Charles Gantvoort had said did not belong to the dead man—and slid it over to me.

"That was found in the road, three or four feet from the car."

It was of a cheap quality, and had neither manufacturer's name nor owner's initials on it. In it were two ten-dollar bills, three small newspaper clippings, and a typewritten list of six names and addresses, headed by Gantvoort's.

The three clippings were apparently from the Personal columns of three different newspapers—the type wasn't the same—and they read:

> *GEORGE—*
> *Everything is fixed. Don't wait too long.*
>
> *D. D. D.*
>
> *R. H. T.—*
> *They do not answer.*
>
> *FLO.*
>
> *CAPPY.—*
> *Twelve on the dot and look sharp.*
> *BINGO.*

The names and addresses on the typewritten list, under Gantvoort's, were:

Quincy Heathcote, 1223 S. Jason Street, Denver; B. D. Thornton, 96 Hughes Circle, Dallas; Luther G. Randall, 615 Columbia Street, Portsmouth; J. H. Boyd Willis, 4544 Harvard Street, Boston; Hannah Hindmarsh, 218 E. 79th Street, Cleveland.

"What else?" I asked when I had studied these.

The detective-sergeant's supply hadn't been exhausted yet.

"The dead man's collar buttons—both front and back—had been taken out, though his collar and tie were still in place. And his left shoe was gone. We hunted high and low all around, but didn't find either shoe or collar buttons."

"Is that all?"

I was prepared for anything now.

"What the hell do you want?" he growled. "Ain't that enough?"

"How about fingerprints?"

"Nothing stirring! All we found belonged to the dead man."

"How about the machine he was found in?"

"A coupe belonging to a Doctor Wallace Girargo. He phoned in at six this evening that it had been stolen from near the corner of McAllister and Polk Streets. We're checking up on him—but I think he's all right."

The things that Whipple and Charles Gantvoort had identified as belonging to the dead man told us nothing. We went over them carefully, but to no advantage. The memoranda book contained many entries, but they all seemed totally foreign to the murder. The letters were quite as irrelevant.

The serial number of the typewriter with which the murder had been committed had been removed, we found—apparently filed out of the frame.

"Well, what do you think?" O'Gar asked when we had given up our examination of our clews and sat back burning tobacco.

"I think we want to find Monsieur Emil Bonfils."

"It wouldn't hurt to do that," he grunted. "I guess our best bet is to get in touch with these five people on the list with Gantvoort's name. Suppose that's a murder list? That this Bonfils is out to get all of them?"

"Maybe. We'll get hold of them anyway. Maybe we'll find that some of them have already been killed. But whether they have been killed or are to be killed or not, it's a cinch they have some connection with this affair. I'll get off a batch of telegrams to the agency's branches, having the names on the list taken care of. I'll try to have the three clippings traced, too."

O'Gar looked at his watch and yawned.

"It's after four. What say we knock off and get some sleep? I'll leave word for the department's expert to compare the typewriter with that letter signed E. B. and with that list to see if they were written on it. I guess they were, but we'll make sure. I'll have the park searched all around where we found Gantvoort as soon as it gets light enough to see, and maybe the missing shoe and the collar buttons will be found. And I'll have a couple of the boys out calling on all the typewriter shops in the city to see if they can get a line on this one."

I stopped at the nearest telegraph office and got off a wad of messages. Then I went home to dream of nothing even remotely connected with crime or the detecting business.

CHAPTER III

"A SLEEK KITTEN THAT DAME!"

At eleven o'clock that same morning, when, brisk and fresh with five hours' sleep under my belt, I arrived at the police detective bureau, I found O'Gar slumped down at his desk, staring dazedly at a black shoe, half a dozen collar buttons, a rusty flat key, and a rumpled newspaper—all lined up before him.

"What's all this? Souvenir of your wedding?"

"Might as well be." His voice was heavy with disgust. "Listen to this: one of the porters of the Seamen's National Bank found a package in the vestibule when he started cleaning up this morning. It was this shoe—Gantvoort's missing one—wrapped in this sheet of a five-day-old *Philadelphia Record*, and with these collar buttons and this old key in it. The heel of the shoe, you'll notice, has been pried off, and is still missing. Whipple identifies it all right, as well as two of the collar buttons, but he never saw the key before. These other four collar buttons are new, and common gold-rolled ones. The key don't look like it had had much use for a long time. What do you make of all that?"

I couldn't make anything out of it.

"How did the porter happen to turn the stuff in?"

"Oh, the whole story was in the morning papers—all about the missing shoe and collar buttons and all."

"What did you learn about the typewriter?" I asked.

"The letter and the list were written with it, right enough; but we haven't been able to find where it came from yet. We checked up the doc who owns the coupe, and he's in the clear. We accounted for all his time last night. Lagerquist, the grocer who found Gantvoort, seems to be all right, too. What did you do?"

"Haven't had any answers to the wires I sent last night. I dropped in at the agency on my way down this morning, and got four operatives out covering the hotels and looking up all the people named Bonfils they can find—there are two or three families by that name listed in the directory. Also I sent our New York branch a wire to have the steamship records searched to see if an Emil Bonfils had arrived recently; and I put a cable through to our Paris correspondent to see what he could dig up over there."

"I guess we ought to see Gantvoort's lawyer—Abernathy—and that Dexter woman before we do anything else," the detective-sergeant said.

"I guess so," I agreed, "let's tackle the lawyer first. He's the most important one, the way things now stand."

Murray Abernathy, attorney-at-law, was a long, stringy, slow-spoken old gentleman who still clung to starched-bosom shirts. He was too full of what he thought were professional ethics to give us as much help as we had expected; but by letting him talk—letting him ramble along in his own way—we did get a little information from him. What we got amounted to this:

The dead man and Creda Dexter had intended being married the coming Wednesday.

His son and her brother were both opposed to the marriage, it seemed, so Gantvoort and the woman had planned to be married secretly in Oakland, and catch a boat for the Orient that same afternoon; figuring that by the time their lengthy honeymoon was over they could return to a son and brother who had become resigned to the marriage.

A new will had been drawn up, leaving half of Gantvoort's estate to his new wife and half to his son and daughter-in-law. But the new will had not been signed yet, and Creda Dexter knew it had not been signed. She knew—and this was one of the few points upon which Abernathy would make a positive statement—that under the old will, still in force, everything went to Charles Gantvoort and his wife.

The Gantvoort estate, we estimated from Abernathy's roundabout statements and allusions, amounted to about a million and a half in cash value. The attorney had never heard of Emil Bonfils, he said, and had never heard of any threats or attempts at murder directed toward the dead man. He knew nothing—or would tell us nothing—that threw any light upon the nature of the thing that the threatening letter had accused the dead man of stealing.

From Abernathy's office we went to Creda Dexter's apartment, in a new and expensively elegant building only a few minutes' walk from the Gantvoort residence.

Creda Dexter was a small woman in her early twenties. The first thing you noticed about her were her eyes. They were large and deep and the color of amber, and their pupils were never at rest. Continuously they changed size, expanded and contracted—slowly at times, suddenly at others—ranging incessantly from the size of pinheads to an extent that threatened to blot out the amber irises.

With the eyes for a guide, you discovered that she was pronouncedly feline throughout. Her every movement was the slow, smooth, sure one of a cat; and the contours of her rather pretty face, the shape of her mouth, her small nose, the set of her eyes, the swelling of her brows, were all cat-like. And the effect was heightened by the way she wore her hair, which was thick and tawny.

"Mr. Gantvoort and I," she told us after the preliminary explanations had been disposed of, "were to have been married the day after tomorrow. His son and daughter-in-law were both opposed to the marriage, as was my brother Madden. They all seemed to think that the difference between our ages was too great. So to avoid any unpleasantness, we had planned to be married quietly and then go abroad for a year or more, feeling sure that they would all have forgotten their grievances by the time we returned.

"That was why Mr. Gantvoort persuaded Madden to go to New York. He had some business there—something to do with the disposal of his interest in a steel mill—so he used it as an excuse to get Madden out of the way until we were off on our wedding trip. Madden lived here with me, and it would have been nearly impossible for me to have made any preparations for the trip without him seeing them."

"Was Mr. Gantvoort here last night?" I asked her.

"No. I expected him—we were going out. He usually walked over—it's only a few blocks. When eight o'clock came and he hadn't arrived, I telephoned his house, and Whipple told me that he had left nearly an hour before. I called up again, twice, after that. Then, this morning, I called up again before I had seen the papers, and I was told that he—"

She broke off with a catch in her voice—the only sign of sorrow she displayed throughout the interview. The impression of her we had received from Charles Gantvoort and Whipple had prepared us for a more or less elaborate display of grief on her part. But she disappointed us. There was nothing crude about her work—she didn't even turn on the tears for us.

"Was Mr. Gantvoort here night before last?"

"Yes. He came over at a little after eight and stayed until nearly twelve. We didn't go out."

"Did he walk over and back?"

"Yes, so far as I know."

"Did he ever say anything to you about his life being threatened?"

"No."

She shook her head decisively.

"Do you know Emil Bonfils?"

"No."

"Ever hear Mr. Gantvoort speak of him?"

"No."

"At what hotel is your brother staying in New York?"

The restless black pupils spread out abruptly, as if they were about to overflow into the white areas of her eyes. That was the first clear indication of fear I had seen. But, outside of those tell-tale pupils, her composure was undisturbed.

"I don't know."

"When did he leave San Francisco?"

"Thursday—four days ago."

O'Gar and I walked six or seven blocks in thoughtful silence after we left Creda Dexter's apartment, and then he spoke.

"A sleek kitten—that dame! Rub her the right way, and she'll purr pretty. Rub her the wrong way—and look out for the claws!"

"What did that flash of her eyes when I asked about her brother tell you?" I asked.

"Something—but I don't know what! It wouldn't hurt to look him up and see if he's really in New York. If he is there today it's a cinch he wasn't here last night—even the mail planes take twenty-six or twenty-eight hours for the trip."

"We'll do that," I agreed. "It looks like this Creda Dexter wasn't any too sure that her brother wasn't in on the killing. And there's nothing to show that Bonfils didn't have help. I can't figure Creda being in on the murder, though. She knew the new will hadn't been signed. There'd be no sense in her working herself out of that three-quarters of a million berries."

We sent a lengthy telegram to the Continental's New York branch, and then dropped in at the agency to see if any replies had come to the wires I had got off the night before.

They had.

None of the people whose names appeared on

the typewritten list with Gantvoort's had been found; not the least trace had been found of any of them. Two of the addresses given were altogether wrong. There were no houses with those numbers on those streets—and there never had been.

CHAPTER IV

"MAYBE THAT AIN'T SO FOOLISH!"

What was left of the afternoon, O'Gar and I spent going over the street between Gantvoort's house on Russian Hill and the building in which the Dexters lived. We questioned everyone we could find—man, woman and child—who lived, worked, or played along any of the three routes the dead man could have taken.

We found nobody who had heard the shot that had been fired by Bonfils on the night before the murder. We found nobody who had seen anything suspicious on the night of the murder. Nobody who remembered having seen him picked up in a coupe.

Then we called at Gantvoort's house and questioned Charles Gantvoort again, his wife, and all the servants—and we learned nothing. So far as they knew, nothing belonging to the dead man was missing—nothing small enough to be concealed in the heel of a shoe.

The shoes he had worn the night he was killed were one of three pairs made in New York for him two months before. He could have removed the heel of the left one, hollowed it out sufficiently to hide a small object in it, and then nailed it on again; though Whipple insisted that he would have noticed the effects of any tampering with the shoe unless it had been done by an expert repairman.

This field exhausted, we returned to the agency. A telegram had just come from the New York branch, saying that none of the steamship companies' records showed the arrival of an Emil Bonfils from either England, France, or Germany within the past six months.

The operatives who had been searching the city for Bonfils had all come in empty-handed. They had found and investigated eleven persons named Bonfils in San Francisco, Oakland, Berkeley, and Alameda. Their investigations had definitely cleared all eleven. None of these Bonfilses knew an Emil Bonfils. Combing the hotels had yielded nothing.

O'Gar and I went to dinner together—a quiet, grouchy sort of meal during which we didn't speak six words apiece—and then came back to the agency to find that another wire had come in from New York.

Madden Dexter arrived McAlpin Hotel this morning with Power of Attorney to sell Gantvoort interest in B. F. and F. Iron Corporation. Denies knowledge of Emil Bonfils or of murder. Expects to finish business and leave for San Francisco tomorrow.

I let the sheet of paper upon which I had decoded the telegram slide out of my fingers, and we sat listlessly facing each other across my desk, looking vacantly each at the other, listening to the clatter of charwomen's buckets in the corridor.

"It's a funny one," O'Gar said softly to himself at last.

I nodded. It was.

"We got nine clews," he spoke again presently, "and none of them have got us a damned thing.

"Number one: the dead man called up you people and told you that he had been threatened and shot at by an Emil Bonfils that he'd had a run-in with in Paris a long time ago.

"Number two: the typewriter he was killed with and that the letter and list were written on. We're still trying to trace it, but with no breaks so far. What the hell kind of a weapon was that, anyway? It looks like this fellow Bonfils got hot and hit Gantvoort with the first thing he put his hand on. But what was the typewriter doing in a stolen car? And why were the numbers filed off it?"

I shook my head to signify that I couldn't guess the answer, and O'Gar went on enumerating our clews.

"Number three: the threatening letter, fitting in with what Gantvoort had said over the phone that afternoon.

"Number four: those two bullets with the crosses in their snoots.

"Number five: the jewel case.

"Number six: that bunch of yellow hair.

"Number seven: the fact that the dead man's shoe and collar buttons were carried away.

"Number eight: the wallet, with two ten-dollar bills, three clippings, and the list in it, found in the road.

"Number nine: finding the shoe next day, wrapped up in a five-day-old Philadelphia paper, and with the missing collar buttons, four more, and a rusty key in it.

"That's the list. If they mean anything at all, they mean that Emil Bonfils whoever he is—was flimflammed out of something by Gantvoort in Paris in 1902, and that Bonfils came to get it back. He picked Gantvoort up last night in a stolen car, bringing his typewriter with him—for God knows what reason! Gantvoort put up an argument, so Bonfils bashed in his noodle with the typewriter, and then went through his pockets, apparently not taking anything. He decided that what he was looking for was in Gantvoort's left shoe, so he took the shoe away with him. And then—but there's no sense to the collar button trick, or the phoney list, or—"

"Yes there is!" I cut in, sitting up, wide awake now. "That's our tenth clew—the one we're going to follow from now on. That list was, except for Gantvoort's name and address, a fake. Our people would have found at least one of the five people whose names were on it if it had been on the level. But they didn't find the least trace of any of them. And two of the addresses were of street numbers that didn't exist!

"That list was faked up, put in the wallet with the clippings and twenty dollars—to make the play stronger—and planted in the road near the car to throw us off-track. And if that's so, then it's a hundred to one that the rest of the things were cooked up too.

"From now on I'm considering all those nine lovely clews as nine bum steers. And I'm going just exactly contrary to them. I'm looking for a man whose name isn't Emil Bonfils, and whose initials aren't either E or B; who isn't French, and who wasn't in Paris in 1902. A man who hasn't light hair, doesn't carry a .45-caliber pistol, and has no interest in Personal advertisements in newspapers. A man who didn't kill Gantvoort to recover anything that could have been hidden in a shoe or on a collar button. That's the sort of a guy I'm hunting for now!"

The detective-sergeant screwed up his little green eyes reflectively and scratched his head.

"Maybe that ain't so foolish!" he said. "You might be right at that. Suppose you are—what then? That Dexter kitten didn't do it—it cost her three-quarters of a million. Her brother didn't do it—he's in New York. And, besides, you don't croak a guy just because you think he's too old to marry your sister. Charles Gantvoort? He and his wife are the only ones who make any money out of the old man dying before the new will was signed. We have only their word for it that Charles was home that night. The servants didn't see him between eight and eleven. You were there, and you didn't see him until eleven. But me and you both believe him when he says he *was* home all that evening. And neither of us think he bumped the old man off—though of course he might. Who then?"

"This Creda Dexter," I suggested, "was marrying Gantvoort for his money, wasn't she? You don't think she was in love with him, do you?"

"No. I figure, from what I saw of her, that she was in love with the million and a half."

"All right," I went on. "Now she isn't exactly homely—not by a long shot. Do you reckon Gantvoort was the only man who ever fell for her?"

"I got you! I got you!" O'Gar exclaimed. "You mean there might have been some young fellow in the running who didn't have any million and a half behind him, and who didn't take kindly to being nosed out by a man who did. Maybe—maybe."

"Well, suppose we bury all this stuff we've been working on and try out that angle."

"Suits me," he said. "Starting in the morning, then, we spend our time hunting for Gantvoort's rival for the paw of this Dexter kitten."

CHAPTER V

"MEET MR. SMITH"

Right or wrong, that's what we did. We stowed all those lovely clews away in a drawer, locked the drawer, and forgot them. Then we set out to find Creda Dexter's masculine acquaintances and sift them for the murderer.

But it wasn't as simple as it sounded.

All our digging into her past failed to bring to light one man who could be considered a suitor. She and her brother had been in San Francisco three years. We traced them back the length of that period, from apartment to apartment. We questioned everyone we could find who even knew her by sight. And nobody could tell us of a single man who had shown an interest in her besides Gantvoort. Nobody, apparently, had ever seen her with any man except Gantvoort or her brother.

All of which, while not getting us ahead, at least convinced us that we were on the right trail. There must have been, we argued, at least one man in her life in those three years besides Gantvoort. She wasn't—unless we were very much mistaken—the sort of woman who would discourage masculine attention; and she was certainly endowed by nature to attract it. And if there was another man, then the very fact that he had been kept so thoroughly under cover strengthened the probability of him having been mixed up in Gantvoort's death.

We were unsuccessful in learning where the Dexters had lived before they came to San Francisco, but we weren't so very interested in their earlier life. Of course it was possible that some old-time lover had come upon the scene again recently; but in that case it should have been easier to find the recent connection than the old one.

There was no doubt, our explorations showed, that Gantvoort's son had been correct in thinking the Dexters were fortune hunters. All their activities pointed to that, although there seemed to be nothing downright criminal in their pasts.

I went up against Creda Dexter again, spending an entire afternoon in her apartment, banging away with question after question, all directed toward her former love affairs. Who had she thrown over for Gantvoort and his million and a half? And the answer was always *nobody*—an answer that I didn't choose to believe.

We had Creda Dexter shadowed night and day—and it carried us ahead not an inch. Perhaps she suspected that she was being watched. Anyway, she seldom left her apartment, and then on only the most innocent of errands. We had her apartment watched whether she was in it or not. Nobody visited it. We tapped her telephone—and all our listening-in netted us nothing. We had her mail covered—and she didn't receive a single letter, not even an advertisement.

Meanwhile, we had learned where the three clippings found in the wallet had come from—from the Personal columns of a New York, a Chicago, and a Portland newspaper. The one in the Portland paper had appeared two days before the murder, the Chicago one four days before, and the New York one five days before. All three of those papers would have been on the San Francisco newsstands the day of the murder—ready to be purchased and cut out by anyone who was looking for material to confuse detectives with.

The agency's Paris correspondent had found no less than six Emil Bonfilses—all bloomers* so

_____

* Australian for mistakes

far as our job was concerned—and had a line on three more.

But O'Gar and I weren't worrying over Emil Bonfils any more—that angle was dead and buried. We were plugging away at our new task—the finding of Gantvoort's rival.

Thus the days passed, and thus the matter stood when Madden Dexter was due to arrive home from New York.

Our New York branch had kept an eye on him until he left that city, and had advised us of his departure, so I knew what train he was coming on. I wanted to put a few questions to him before his sister saw him. He could tell me what I wanted to know, and he might be willing to if I could get to him before his sister had an opportunity to shut him up.

If I had known him by sight I could have picked him up when he left his train at Oakland, but I didn't know him; and I didn't want to carry Charles Gantvoort or anyone else along with me to pick him out for me.

So I went up to Sacramento that morning, and boarded his train there. I put my card in an envelope and gave it to a messenger boy in the station. Then I followed the boy through the train, while he called out:

"Mr. Dexter! Mr. Dexter!"

In the last car—the observation-club car—a slender, dark-haired man in well-made tweeds turned from watching the station platform through a window and held out his hand to the boy.

I studied him while he nervously tore open the envelope and read my card. His chin trembled slightly just now, emphasizing the weakness of a face that couldn't have been strong at its best. Between twenty-five and thirty, I placed him; with his hair parted in the middle and slicked down; large, too-expressive brown eyes; small well-shaped nose; neat brown mustache; very red, soft lips—that type.

I dropped into the vacant chair beside him when he looked up from the card.

"You are Mr. Dexter?"

"Yes," he said. "I suppose it's about Mr. Gantvoort's death that you want to see me?"

"Uh-huh. I wanted to ask you a few questions, and since I happened to be in Sacramento, I thought that by riding back on the train with you I could ask them without taking up too much of your time."

"If there's anything I can tell you," he assured me, "I'll be only too glad to do it. But I told the New York detectives all I knew, and they didn't seem to find it of much value."

"Well, the situation has changed some since you left New York." I watched his face closely as I spoke. "What we thought of no value then may be just what we want now."

I paused while he moistened his lips and avoided my eyes. He may not know anything, I thought, but he's certainly jumpy. I let him wait a few minutes while I pretended deep thoughtfulness. If I played him right, I was confident I could turn him inside out. He didn't seem to be made of very tough material.

We were sitting with our heads close together, so that the four or five other passengers in the car wouldn't overhear our talk; and that position was in my favor. One of the things that every detective knows is that it's often easy to get information—even a confession—out of a feeble nature simply by putting your face close to his and talking in a loud tone. I couldn't talk loud here, but the closeness of our faces was by itself an advantage.

"Of the men with whom your sister was acquainted," I came out with it at last, "who, outside of Mr. Gantvoort, was the most attentive?"

He swallowed audibly, looked out of the window, fleetingly at me, and then out of the window again.

"Really, I couldn't say."

"All right. Let's get at it this way. Suppose we check off one by one all the men who were interested in her and in whom she was interested."

He continued to stare out of the window.

"Who's first?" I pressed him.

His gaze flickered around to meet mine for a second, with a sort of timid desperation in his eyes.

"I know it sounds foolish, but I, her brother, couldn't give you the name of even one man in whom Creda was interested before she met Gantvoort. She never, so far as I know, had the slightest feeling for any man before she met him. Of course it is possible that there may have been someone that I didn't know anything about, but—"

It did sound foolish, right enough! The Creda Dexter I had talked to—a sleek kitten, as O'Gar had put it—didn't impress me as being at all likely to go very long without having at least one man in tow. This pretty little guy in front of me was lying. There couldn't be any other explanation.

I went at him tooth and nail. But when he reached Oakland early that night he was still sticking to his original statement—that Gantvoort was the only one of his sister's suitors that he knew anything about. And I knew that I had blundered, had underrated Madden Dexter, had played my hand wrong in trying to shake him down too quickly—in driving too directly at the point I was interested in. He was either a lot stronger than I had figured him, or his interest in concealing Gantvoort's murderer was much greater than I had thought it would be.

But I had this much: if Dexter was lying—and there couldn't be much doubt of that—then Gantvoort *had* had a rival, and Madden Dexter believed or knew that this rival had killed Gantvoort.

When we left the train at Oakland I knew I was licked, that he wasn't going to tell me what I wanted to know—not this night, anyway. But I clung to him, stuck at his side when we boarded the ferry for San Francisco, in spite of the obviousness of his desire to get away from me. There's always a chance of something unexpected happening; so I continued to ply him with questions as our boat left the slip.

Presently a man came toward where we were sitting—a big burly man in a light overcoat, carrying a black bag.

"Hello, Madden!" he greeted my companion, striding over to him with outstretched hand. "Just got in and was trying to remember your phone number," he said, setting down his bag, as they shook hands warmly.

Madden Dexter turned to me.

"I want you to meet Mr. Smith," he told me, and then gave my name to the big man, adding, "he's with the Continental Detective Agency here."

That tag—clearly a warning for Smith's benefit—brought me to my feet, all watchfulness. But the ferry was crowded—a hundred persons were within sight of us, all around us. I relaxed, smiled pleasantly, and shook hands with Smith. Whoever Smith was, and whatever connection he might have with the murder—and if he hadn't any, why should Dexter have been in such a hurry to tip him off to my identity?—he couldn't do anything here. The crowd around us was all to my advantage.

That was my second mistake of the day.

Smith's left hand had gone into his overcoat pocket—or rather, through one of those vertical slits that certain styles of overcoats have so that inside pockets may be reached without unbuttoning the overcoat. His hand had gone through that slit, and his coat had fallen away far enough for me to see a snub-nosed automatic in his hand—shielded from everyone's sight but mine—pointing at my waist-line.

"Shall we go on deck?" Smith asked—and it was an order.

I hesitated. I didn't like to leave all these people who were so blindly standing and sitting around us. But Smith's face wasn't the face of a cautious man. He had the look of one who might easily disregard the presence of a hundred witnesses.

I turned around and walked through the crowd. His right hand lay familiarly on my shoulder as he walked behind me; his left hand held his gun, under the overcoat, against my spine.

The deck was deserted. A heavy fog, wet as

rain,—the fog of San Francisco Bay's winter nights,—lay over boat and water, and had driven everyone else inside. It hung about us, thick and impenetrable; I couldn't see so far as the end of the boat, in spite of the lights glowing overhead.

I stopped.

Smith prodded me in the back.

"Farther away, where we can talk," he rumbled in my ear.

I went on until I reached the rail.

The entire back of my head burned with sudden fire . . . tiny points of light glittered in the blackness before me . . . grew larger . . . came rushing toward me. . . .

CHAPTER VI

"THOSE DAMNED HORNS!"

Semi-consciousness! I found myself mechanically keeping afloat somehow and trying to get out of my overcoat. The back of my head throbbed devilishly. My eyes burned. I felt heavy and logged, as if I had swallowed gallons of water.

The fog hung low and thick on the water—there was nothing else to be seen anywhere. By the time I had freed myself of the encumbering overcoat my head had cleared somewhat, but with returning consciousness came increased pain.

A light glimmered mistily off to my left, and then vanished. From out of the misty blanket, from every direction, in a dozen different keys, from near and far, fog-horns sounded. I stopped swimming and floated on my back, trying to determine my whereabouts.

After a while I picked out the moaning, evenly spaced blasts of the Alcatraz siren. But they told me nothing. They came to me out of the fog without direction—seemed to beat down upon me from straight above.

I was somewhere in San Francisco Bay, and that was all I knew, though I suspected the current was sweeping me out toward the Golden Gate.

A little while passed, and I knew that I had left the path of the Oakland ferries—no boat had passed close to me for some time. I was glad to be out of that track. In this fog a boat was a lot more likely to run me down than to pick me up.

The water was chilling me, so I turned over and began swimming, just vigorously enough to keep my blood circulating while I saved my strength until I had a definite goal to try for.

A horn began to repeat its roaring note nearer and nearer, and presently the lights of the boat upon which it was fixed came into sight. One of the Sausalito ferries, I thought.

It came quite close to me, and I halloed until I was breathless and my throat was raw. But the boat's siren, crying its warning, drowned my shouts.

The boat went on and the fog closed in behind it.

The current was stronger now, and my attempts to attract the attention of the Sausalito ferry had left me weaker. I floated, letting the water sweep me where it would, resting.

Another light appeared ahead of me suddenly—hung there for an instant—disappeared.

I began to yell, and worked my arms and legs madly, trying to drive myself through the water to where it had been.

I never saw it again.

Weariness settled upon me, and a sense of futility. The water was no longer cold. I was warm with a comfortable, soothing numbness. My head stopped throbbing; there was no feeling at all in it now. No lights, now, but the sound of fog-horns . . . fog-horns . . . fog-horns ahead of me, behind me, to either side; annoying me, irritating me.

But for the moaning horns I would have ceased all effort. They had become the only disagreeable detail of my situation—the water was pleasant, fatigue was pleasant. But the horns tormented me. I cursed them petulantly and decided to swim until I could no longer hear them, and then, in the quiet of the friendly fog, go to sleep. . . .

Now and then I would doze, to be goaded into wakefulness by the wailing voice of a siren.

"Those damned horns! Those damned horns!" I complained aloud, again and again.

One of them, I found presently, was bearing down upon me from behind, growing louder and stronger. I turned and waited. Lights, dim and steaming, came into view.

With exaggerated caution to avoid making the least splash, I swam off to one side. When this nuisance was past I could go to sleep. I sniggered softly to myself as the lights drew abreast, feeling a foolish triumph in my cleverness in eluding the boat. Those damned horns. . . .

Life—the hunger for life—all at once surged back into my being.

I screamed at the passing boat, and with every iota of my being struggled toward it. Between strokes I tilted up my head and screamed. . . .

CHAPTER VII

"YOU HAVE A LOT OF FUN, DON'T YOU?"

When I returned to consciousness for the second time that evening, I was lying on my back on a baggage truck, which was moving. Men and women were crowding around, walking beside the truck, staring at me with curious eyes.

I sat up.

"Where are we?" I asked.

A little red-faced man in uniform answered my question.

"Just landing in Sausalito. Lay still. We'll take you over to the hospital."

I looked around.

"How long before this boat goes back to San Francisco?"

"Leaves right away."

I slid off the truck and started back aboard the boat.

"I'm going with it," I said.

Half an hour later, shivering and shaking in my wet clothes, keeping my mouth clamped tight so that my teeth wouldn't sound like a dice-

game, I climbed into a taxi at the Ferry Building and went to my flat.

There, I swallowed half a pint of whisky, rubbed myself with a coarse towel until my skin was sore, and, except for an enormous weariness and a worse headache, I felt almost human again.

I reached O'Gar by phone, asked him to come up to my flat right away, and then called up Charles Gantvoort.

"Have you seen Madden Dexter yet?" I asked him.

"No, but I talked to him over the phone. He called me up as soon as he got in. I asked him to meet me in Mr. Abernathy's office in the morning, so we could go over that business he transacted for father."

"Can you call him up now and tell him that you have been called out of town—will have to leave early in the morning—and that you'd like to run over to his apartment and see him tonight?"

"Why yes, if you wish."

"Good! Do that. I'll call for you in a little while and go over to see him with you."

"What is—"

"I'll tell you about it when I see you," I cut him off.

O'Gar arrived as I was finishing dressing.

"So he told you something?" he asked, knowing of my plan to meet Dexter on the train and question him.

"Yes," I said with sour sarcasm, "but I came near forgetting what it was. I grilled him all the way from Sacramento to Oakland, and couldn't get a whisper out of him. On the ferry coming over he introduces me to a man he calls Mr. Smith, and he tells Mr. Smith that I'm a gumshoe. This, mind you, all happens in the middle of a crowded ferry! Mr. Smith puts a gun in my belly, marches me out on deck, raps me across the back of the head, and dumps me into the bay."

"You have a lot of fun, don't you?" O'Gar grinned, and then wrinkled his forehead. "Looks like Smith would be the man we want then—

the buddy who turned the Gantvoort trick. But what the hell did he want to give himself away by chucking you overboard for?"

"Too hard for me," I confessed, while trying to find which of my hats and caps would sit least heavily upon my bruised head. "Dexter knew I was hunting for one of his sister's former lovers, of course. And he must have thought I knew a whole lot more than I do, or he wouldn't have made that raw play—tipping my mitt to Smith right in front of me.

"It may be that after Dexter lost his head and made that break on the ferry, Smith figured that I'd be on to him soon, if not right away; and so he'd take a desperate chance on putting me out of the way. But we'll know all about it in a little while," I said, as we went down to the waiting taxi and set out for Gantvoort's.

"You ain't counting on Smith being in sight, are you?" the detective-sergeant asked.

"No. He'll be holed up somewhere until he sees how things are going. But Madden Dexter will have to be out in the open to protect himself. He has an alibi, so he's in the clear so far as the actual killing is concerned. And with me supposed to be dead, the more he stays in the open, the safer he is. But it's a cinch that he knows what this is all about, though he wasn't necessarily involved in it. As near as I could see, he didn't go out on deck with Smith and me tonight. Anyway he'll be home. And this time he's going to talk—he's going to tell his little story!"

Charles Gantvoort was standing on his front steps when we reached his house. He climbed into our taxi and we headed for the Dexters' apartment. We didn't have time to answer any of the questions that Gantvoort was firing at us with every turning of the wheels.

"He's home and expecting you?" I asked him. "Yes."

Then we left the taxi and went into the apartment building.

"Mr. Gantvoort to see Mr. Dexter," he told the Philippine boy at the switchboard.

The boy spoke into the phone.

"Go right up," he told us.

At the Dexters' door I stepped past Gantvoort and pressed the button.

Creda Dexter opened the door. Her amber eyes widened and her smile faded as I stepped past her into the apartment.

I walked swiftly down the little hallway and turned into the first room through whose open door a light showed.

And came face to face with Smith!

We were both surprised, but his astonishment was a lot more profound than mine. Neither of us had expected to see the other; but I had known he was still alive, while he had every reason for thinking me at the bottom of the bay.

I took advantage of his greater bewilderment to the extent of two steps toward him before he went into action.

One of his hands swept down.

I threw my right fist at his face—threw it with every ounce of my 180 pounds behind it, re-enforced by the memory of every second I had spent in the water and every throb of my battered head.

His hand, already darting down for his pistol, came back up too late to fend off my punch.

Something clicked in my hand as it smashed into his face, and my hand went numb.

But he went down—and lay where he fell.

I jumped across his body to a door on the opposite side of the room, pulling my gun loose with my left hand.

"Dexter's somewhere around!" I called over my shoulder to O'Gar, who with Gantvoort and Creda, was coming through the door by which I had entered. "Keep your eyes open!"

I dashed through the four other rooms of the apartment, pulling closet doors open, looking everywhere—and I found nobody.

Then I returned to where Creda Dexter was trying to revive Smith, with the assistance of O'Gar and Gantvoort.

The detective-sergeant looked over his shoulder at me.

"Who do you think this joker is?" he asked.

"My friend Mr. Smith."

"Gantvoort says he's Madden Dexter."

I looked at Charles Gantvoort, who nodded his head.

"This is Madden Dexter," he said.

CHAPTER VIII

"I HOPE YOU SWING!"

We worked upon Dexter for nearly ten minutes before he opened his eyes.

As soon as he sat up we began to shoot questions and accusations at him, hoping to get a confession out of him before he recovered from his shakiness—but he wasn't that shaky.

All we could get out of him was:

"Take me in if you want to. If I've got anything to say I'll say it to my lawyer, and to nobody else."

Creda Dexter, who had stepped back after her brother came to, and was standing a little way off, watching us, suddenly came forward and caught me by the arm.

"What have you got on him?" she demanded, imperatively.

"I wouldn't want to say," I countered, "but I don't mind telling you this much. We're going to give him a chance in a nice modern court-room to prove that he didn't kill Leopold Gantvoort."

"He was in New York!"

"He was not! He had a friend who went to New York as Madden Dexter and looked after Gantvoort's business under that name. But if this is the real Madden Dexter then the closest he got to New York was when he met his friend on the ferry to get from him the papers connected with the B. F. & F. Iron Corporation transaction; and learned that I had stumbled upon the truth about his alibi—even if I didn't know it myself at the time."

She jerked around to face her brother.

"Is that on the level?" she asked him.

He sneered at her, and went on feeling with the fingers of one hand the spot on his jaw where my fist had landed.

"I'll say all I've got to say to my lawyer," he repeated.

"You will?" she shot back at him. "Well, I'll say what I've got to say right now!"

She flung around to face me again.

"Madden is not my brother at all! My name is Ives. Madden and I met in St. Louis about four years ago, drifted around together for a year or so, and then came to Frisco. He was a con man—still is. He made Mr. Gantvoort's acquaintance six or seven months ago, and was getting him all ribbed up to unload a fake invention on him. He brought him here a couple of times, and introduced me to him as his sister. We usually posed as brother and sister.

"Then, after Mr. Gantvoort had been here a couple times, Madden decided to change his game. He thought Mr. Gantvoort liked me, and that we could get more money out of him by working a fancy sort of badger-game on him. I was to lead the old man on until I had him wrapped around my finger—until we had him tied up so tight he couldn't get away—had something on him—something good and strong. Then we were going to shake him down for plenty of money.

"Everything went along fine for a while. He fell for me—fell hard. And finally he asked me to marry him. We had never figured on that. Blackmail was our game. But when he asked me to marry him I tried to call Madden off. I admit the old man's money had something to do with it—it influenced me—but I had come to like him a little for himself. He was mighty fine in lots of ways—nicer than anybody I had ever known.

"So I told Madden all about it, and suggested that we drop the other plan, and that I marry Gantvoort. I promised to see that Madden was kept supplied with money—I knew I could get whatever I wanted from Mr. Gantvoort. And I was on the level with Madden. I liked Mr. Gantvoort, but Madden had found him and brought him around to me; and so I wasn't going to run out on Madden. I was willing to do all I could for him.

"But Madden wouldn't hear of it. He'd have got more money in the long run by doing as I suggested—but he wanted his little handful right away. And to make him more unreasonable he got one of his jealous streaks. He beat me one night!

"That settled it. I made up my mind to ditch him. I told Mr. Gantvoort that my brother was bitterly opposed to our marrying, and he could see that Madden was carrying a grouch. So he arranged to send Madden East on that steel business, to get him out of the way until we were off on our wedding trip. And we thought Madden was completely deceived—but I should have known that he would see through our scheme. We planned to be gone about a year, and by that time I thought Madden would have forgotten me—or I'd be fixed to handle him if he tried to make any trouble.

"As soon as I heard that Mr. Gantvoort had been killed I had a hunch that Madden had done it. But then it seemed like a certainty that he was in New York the next day, and I thought I had done him an injustice. And I was glad he was out of it. But now—"

She whirled around to her erstwhile confederate.

"Now I hope you swing, you big sap!"

She spun around to me again. No sleek kitten, this, but a furious, spitting cat, with claws and teeth bared.

"What kind of looking fellow was the one who went to New York for him?"

I described the man I had talked to on the train.

"Evan Felter," she said, after a moment of thought. "He used to work with Madden. You'll probably find him hiding in Los Angeles. Put the screws on him and he'll spill all he knows—he's a weak sister! The chances are he didn't know what Madden's game was until it was all over."

"How do you like that?" she spat at Madden Dexter. "How do you like that for a starter? You messed up my little party, did you? Well, I'm going to spend every minute of my time from now until they pop you off helping them pop you!"

And she did, too—with her assistance it was no trick at all to gather up the rest of the evidence we needed to hang him. And I don't believe her enjoyment of her three-quarters of a million dollars is spoiled a bit by any qualms over what she did to Madden. She's a very respectable woman *now*, and glad to be free of the con-man.

BLACK MASK, JANUARY 1, 1924

FROM THE AUTHOR OF "THE TENTH CLEW"

Thanks for the check for "The Tenth Clew."

And I want to plead guilty to a bit of cowardice in connection with the story. The original of *Creda Dexter* didn't resemble a kitten at all. She looked exactly like a bull-pup—and she was pretty in the bargain!

Except for her eyes, I never succeeded in determining just what was responsible for the resemblance, but it was a very real one.

When, however, it came to actually putting her down on paper, my nerve failed me. "Nobody will believe you if you write a thing like that," I told myself. "They'll think you're trying to spoof them." So, for the sake of plausibility, I lied about her!

Sincerely,
DASHIELL HAMMETT
San Francisco

BLACK MASK, FEBRUARY 1, 1924

Night Shots

BY DASHIELL HAMMETT

Mr. Hammett's nameless detective is lured into a sweet little domestic mess with an outside mystery; as usual, he walks into a lot of excitement, not all of which comes from the muzzle of a gun.

I

THE HOUSE WAS of red brick, large and square, with a green slate roof, whose wide overhang gave the building an appearance of being too squat for its two stories; and it stood on a grassy hill, well away from the county road, upon which it turned its back to look down on the Mokelumne River.

The Ford that I had hired to bring me out from Knownburg carried me into the grounds through a high steel-meshed gate, followed the circling gravel drive, and set me down within a foot of the screen porch that ran all the way around the house's first floor.

"There's Exon's son-in-law now," the driver told me as he pocketed the bill I had given him, and prepared to drive away.

I turned to see a tall, loose-jointed man of thirty or so coming across the porch toward me—a carelessly dressed man, with a mop of rumpled brown hair over a handsome sunburned face. There was a hint of cruelty in the lips that were smiling lazily just now, and more than a hint of recklessness in his narrow gray eyes.

"Mr. Gallaway?" I asked as he came down the steps.

"Yes." His voice was a drawling baritone. "You are—"

"From the Continental Detective Agency's San Francisco branch," I finished for him.

He nodded, and held the screen-door open for me.

"Just leave your bag there. I'll have it taken up to your room."

He guided me into the house and—after I had

assured him that I had already eaten luncheon—gave me a soft chair and an excellent cigar. He sprawled on his spine in an armchair opposite me—all loose-jointed angles sticking out of it in every direction—and blew smoke at the ceiling for several thoughtful minutes.

"First off," he began presently, his words coming out languidly, "I may as well tell you that I don't expect very much in the way of results. I sent for you more for the soothing effect of your presence on the household than because I expect you to do anything. I don't believe there's anything to do. However, I'm not a detective. I may be wrong. You may find out all sorts of more or less important things. If you do—fine! But I don't insist upon it."

I didn't say anything, though this beginning wasn't much to my taste. He smoked in silence for a moment, and then went on:

"My father-in-law, Talbert Exon, is a man of fifty-seven, and ordinarily a tough, hard, active, and fiery old devil. But just now he's recovering from a rather serious attack of pneumonia, which has taken most of the starch out of him. He hasn't been able to leave his bed yet, and I understand that Dr. Rench hopes to keep him on his back for another week at the very least.

"The old man has a room on the second floor—the front, right-hand corner room—just over where we are sitting. His nurse, Miss Caywood, occupies the next room, and there is a connecting door between. My room is the other front one, just across the hall from the old man's; and my wife's bedroom is next to mine—across the hall from the nurse's. I'll show you around later; I just want to make the situation clear to you first.

"Last night, or rather this morning, at about half-past one, somebody shot at Exon while he was sleeping—and missed. The bullet went into the frame of the door that leads to his nurse's room, about six inches above his body as he lay in bed. The course the bullet took in the woodwork would indicate that it had been fired from one of the windows—either through it or from just inside."

"Exon woke up, of course, but he saw nobody. The rest of us—my wife, Miss Caywood, the Figgs, and myself—were also awakened by the shot. We all rushed into his room, and we saw nothing either. There's no doubt that whoever fired it left by the window. Otherwise some of us would have seen him—we came from every other direction. However, we found nobody on the grounds, and no traces of anybody. That, I think, is all."

"Who are the Figgs, and who else is there on the place besides you and your wife, Mr. Exon, and his nurse?"

"The Figgs are Adam and Emma; she is the housekeeper and he is a sort of handy-man about the place. Their room is in the extreme rear, on the second floor. Besides them, there is Gong Lim, the cook, who sleeps in a little room near the kitchen, and the three farm hands. Joe Natara and Felipe Fadelia are Italians, and have been here for possibly more than two years; Jesus Mesa, a Mexican, has been here a year or longer. The farm hands sleep in a little house near the barns. I think—if my opinion is of any value—that none of these people had anything to do with the shooting."

"Did you dig the bullet out of the door-frame?"

"Yes. Shand, the deputy sheriff at Knownburg, dug it out. He says it is a .38-caliber bullet."

"Any guns of that caliber in the house?"

"No. A .22 and my .44—which I keep in the car—are the only pistols on the place. Then there are two shotguns and a .30-30 rifle. Shand made a thorough search, and found nothing else in the way of firearms."

"What does Mr. Exon say?"

"Not much of anything, except that if we'll put a gun in bed with him he'll manage to take care of himself without bothering any policemen or detectives. I don't know whether he knows who shot at him or not—he's a close-mouthed old devil. From what I know of him, I imagine there are quite a few men who would think themselves justified in killing him. He was, I understand, far from being a lily in his youth—or in his mature years either, for that matter."

"Anything definite you know, or are you guessing?"

Gallaway grinned at me—a mocking grin that I was to see often before I was through with this Exon affair.

"Both," he drawled. "I know that his life has been rather more than sprinkled with swindled partners and betrayed friends; and that he saved himself from prison at least once by turning state's evidence and sending his associates there. And I know that his wife died under rather peculiar circumstances while heavily insured, and that he was for some time held on suspicion of having murdered her, but was finally released because of a lack of evidence against him. Those, I understand, are fair samples of the old boy's normal behavior; so there may be any number of people gunning for him."

"Suppose you give me a list of all the names you know of enemies he's made, and I'll have them checked up, and see what we can find that way."

He raised an indolent hand in protest.

"The names I could give you would be only a few in many, and it might take you months to check up those few. It isn't my intention to go to all that trouble and expense. As I told you, I'm not insisting upon results. My wife is very nervous, and for some peculiar reason she seems to like the old man. So, to soothe her, I agreed to employ a private detective when she asked me to. My idea is that you hang around for a couple of days, until things quiet down and she feels safe again. Meanwhile, if you should stumble upon anything—go to it! If you don't—well and good."

My face must have shown something of what I was thinking, for his eyes twinkled and he chuckled banteringly.

"Don't, please," he drawled, "get the idea that you aren't to find my father-in-law's would-be assassin if you wish to. You're to have a free hand. Go as far as you like; except that I want you to be around the place as much as possible,

so my wife will see you and feel that we are being adequately protected. Beyond that, I don't care what you do. You can apprehend criminals by the carload. As you may have gathered by now, I'm not exactly in love with my wife's father; and he's no more fond of me. To be frank, if hating weren't such an effort—if it didn't require so much energy—I think I should hate the old devil. But if you want to, and can, catch the man who shot at him, I'd be glad to have you do it. But—"

"All right," I said. "I don't like this job much; but since I'm up here I'll take it on. But, remember, I'm trying all the time."

"Sincerity and earnestness," he showed his teeth in a sardonic smile as we got to our feet, "are very praiseworthy traits."

"So I hear," I growled shortly. "Now let's take a look at Mr. Exon's room."

Gallaway's wife and the nurse were with the invalid, but I examined the room before I asked the occupants any questions.

It was a large room, with three wide windows, opening over the porch; and two doors, one of which gave to the hall, and the other to the adjoining room, occupied by the nurse. This door stood open, with a green Japanese screen across it; and, I was told, was left that way at night, so that the nurse could hear readily if her patient was restless or if he wanted attention.

A man standing on the slate roof of the porch, I found, could have easily leaned across one of the window-sills (if he did not care to step over it into the room) and fired at the man in the bed. To get from the ground to the porch roof would have required but little effort; and the descent would be still easier—he could slide down the roof, let himself go feet-first over the edge, checking his speed with hands and arms spread out on the slate, and drop down to the gravel drive. No trick at all, either coming or going. The windows were unscreened.

The sick man's bed stood just beside the connecting doorway between his room and the nurse's, which, when he was lying down, placed him between the doorway and the window from which the shot had been fired. Outside, within long rifle range, there was no building, tree, or eminence of any character from which the bullet that had been dug out of the door-frame could have been fired.

I turned from the room to the occupants, questioning the invalid first. He had been a raw-boned man of considerable size in his health, but now he was wasted and stringy and dead-white. His face was thin and hollow; small beady eyes crowded together against the thin bridge of his nose; his mouth was a colorless gash above a bony projecting chin.

His statement was a marvel of petulant conciseness.

"The shot woke me. I didn't see anything. I don't know anything. I've got a million enemies, most of whose names I can't remember. That's all I can tell you."

He jerked this out crossly, turned his face away, closed his eyes, and refused to speak again.

Mrs. Gallaway and the nurse followed me into the latter's room, where I questioned them. They were of as opposite type as you could find anywhere; and between them there was a certain coolness, an unmistakable hostility which I was able to account for later in the day.

Mrs. Gallaway was perhaps five years older than her husband; dark, strikingly beautiful in a statuesque way, with a worried look in her dark eyes that was particularly noticeable when those eyes rested on her husband. There was no doubt that she was very much in love with him, and the anxiety that showed in her eyes at times—the pains she took to please him in each slight thing during my stay at the Exon house—convinced me that she struggled always with a fear that she would not be able to hold him, that she was about to lose him.

Mrs. Gallaway could add nothing to what her husband had told me. She had been awakened by the shot, had run to her father's room, had seen nothing—knew nothing—suspected nothing.

The nurse—Barbra Caywood was her name—told the same story, in almost the same words. She had jumped out of bed when awak-ened by the shot, pushed the screen away from the connecting doorway, and rushed into her patient's room. She was the first one to arrive there, and she had seen nothing but the old man sitting up in bed, roaring and shaking his feeble fists at the window.

This Barbra Caywood was a girl of twenty-one or two, and just the sort that a man would pick to help him get well. A girl of a little under the average height, with an erect figure wherein slimness and roundness got an even break under the stiff white of her uniform; with soft golden hair above a face that was certainly made to be looked at. But she was businesslike and had an air of efficiency, for all her prettiness.

From the nurse's room, Gallaway led me to the kitchen, where I questioned the Chinese cook. Gong Lim was a sad-faced Oriental whose ever-present smile somehow made him look more gloomy than ever; and he bowed and smiled and yes-yes'd me from start to finish, and told me nothing.

Adam and Emma Figg—thin and stout, respectively, and both rheumatic—entertained a wide variety of suspicions, directed at the cook and the farm hands, individually and collectively, flitting momentarily from one to the other. They had nothing upon which to base these suspicions, however, except their firm belief that nearly all crimes of violence were committed by foreigners; which, while enough for them, didn't satisfy me.

The farm hands—two smiling middle-aged and heavily mustached Italians, and a soft-eyed Mexican youth—I found in one of the fields. I talked to them for nearly two hours, and I left with a reasonable amount of assurance that neither of the three had had any part in the shooting.

II

Dr. Rench had just come down from a visit to his patient when Gallaway and I returned from the fields. He was a little wizened old man with mild manners and eyes, and a wonderful growth of hair on head, brows, cheeks, lips, chin, and nostrils.

The excitement, he said, had retarded Exon's recovery somewhat, but he did not think the setback would be serious. The invalid's temperature had gone up a little, but he seemed to be improving now.

I followed Dr. Rench out to his machine after he left the others, for a few questions I wanted to put to him in privacy; but the questions might as well have gone unasked for all the good they did me. He could tell me nothing of any value. The nurse, Barbra Caywood, had been secured, he said, from San Francisco, through the usual channels, which made it seem unlikely that she had worked her way into the Exon house for any hidden purpose which might have some connection with the attempt upon Exon's life.

Returning from my talk with the doctor, I came upon Hilary Gallaway and the nurse in the hall, near the foot of the stairs. His arm was resting lightly across her shoulders, and he was smiling down at her. Just as I came through the door, she twisted away, so that his arm slid off, laughed elfishly up into his face, and went on up the stairs.

I did not know whether she had seen me approaching before she eluded the encircling arm or not; nor did I know how long the arm had been there; and both of those questions would make a difference in how their positions were to be construed.

Hilary Gallaway was certainly not a man to allow a girl as pretty as the nurse to lack attention, and he was just as certainly attractive enough in himself to make his advances not too unflattering. Nor did Barbra Caywood impress me as being a girl who would dislike his admiration. But, at that, it was more than likely that there was nothing very serious between them; nothing more than a playful sort of flirtation.

But, no matter what the situation might be in that quarter, it didn't have any direct bearing upon the shooting—none that I could see, any-

way. But I understood now the strained relations between the nurse and Gallaway's wife.

Gallaway was grinning quizzically at me while I was chasing these thoughts around in my head.

"Nobody's safe with a detective around," he complained.

I grinned back at him. That was the only sort of an answer you could give this bird.

After dinner, Gallaway drove me to Knownburg in his roadster, and set me down on the door-step of the deputy sheriff's house. He offered to drive me back to the Exon house when I had finished my investigations in town, but I did not know how long those investigations would take, so I told him I would hire a car when I was ready to return.

Shand, the deputy sheriff, was a big, slow-spoken, slow-thinking, blond man of thirty or so—just the type best fitted for a deputy sheriff job in a San Joaquin County town—and he balanced a fat blond child on each knee while he talked to me.

"I went out to Exon's as soon as Gallaway called me up," he said. "About four-thirty in the morning, I reckon it was when I got there. I didn't find nothing. There weren't no marks on the porch roof, but that don't mean nothing. I tried climbing up and down it myself, and I didn't leave no marks neither. The ground around the house is too firm for footprints to be followed. I found a few, but they didn't lead nowhere; and everybody had run all over the place before I got there, so I couldn't tell who they belonged to.

"Far's I can learn, there ain't been no suspicious characters in the neighborhood lately. The only folks around here who have got any grudge against the old man are the Deemses—Exon beat 'em in a law suit a couple years back—but all of them—the father and both the boys—were at home when the shooting was done."

"How long has Exon been living here?"

"Four—five years, I reckon. Came in 1918 or '19."

"Nothing at all to work on, then?"

He shifted one of the kids around to keep from having an eye jabbed by a stubby finger, and shook his head.

"Nothing I know about."

"What do you know about the Exon family?" I asked.

Shand scratched his head thoughtfully and frowned.

"I reckon it's Hilary Gallaway you're meaning," he said slowly. "I thought of that. The Gallaways showed up here a couple of years after her father had bought the place, and Hilary seems to spend most of his evenings up in Ady's back room, teaching the boys how to play poker. I hear he's fitted to teach them a lot. I don't know, myself. Ady runs a quiet game, so I let 'em alone. But naturally I don't never set in, myself. I just stay away so I won't see nothing.

"Outside of being a card-hound, and drinking pretty heavy, and making a lot of trips to the city, where he's supposed to have a girl on the string, I don't know nothing much about Hilary. But it's no secret that him and the old man don't hit it off together very well. And then Hilary's room is just across the hall from Exon's, and their windows open out on the porch roof just a little apart. But I don't know—"

Shand confirmed what Gallaway had told me about the bullet being .38-caliber; about the absence of any pistol of that caliber on the premises; and about the lack of any reason for suspecting the farm hands or servants.

I put in the next couple hours talking to whomever I could find to talk to in Knownburg; and I learned nothing worth putting down on paper. Then I got a car and driver from the garage, and was driven out to Exon's.

Gallaway had not yet returned from town. His wife and Barbra Caywood were just about to sit down to a light luncheon before retiring, so I joined them. Exon, the nurse, said, was asleep, and had spent a quiet evening. We talked for a while—until about half-past twelve—and then went to our rooms.

My room was next to the nurse's, on the same side of the hall that divided the second story in half. I sat down and wrote my report for the day, smoked a cigar, and then—the house being quiet by this time—put a gun and a flashlight in my pockets, went downstairs, and let myself out of the kitchen door.

The moon was just coming up, lighting the grounds vaguely, except for the shadows cast by house, outbuildings, and the several clumps of shrubbery. Keeping in these shadows as much as possible, I explored the grounds, finding everything as it should be.

The lack of any evidence to the contrary pointed to last night's shot having been fired— either accidentally, or in fright at some fancied move of Exon's—by a burglar, who had been entering the sick man's room through a window. If that were so, then there wasn't one chance in a thousand of anything happening tonight. But I felt restless and ill at ease, nevertheless— possibly a result of my failure to learn the least thing of importance all day.

Gallaway's roadster was not in the garage. He had not returned from Knownburg. Beneath the farm hands' window I paused until snores in three distinct keys told me that they were all safely abed.

After an hour of this snooping around, I returned to the house. The luminous dial of my watch registered 2:35 as I stopped outside the Chinese cook's door to listen to his regular breathing.

Upstairs, I paused at the door of the Figgs' room, until my ear told me that they were sleeping. At Mrs. Gallaway's door I had to wait several minutes before she sighed and turned in bed. Barbra Caywood was breathing deeply and strongly, with the regularity of a young animal whose sleep is without disturbing dreams. The invalid's breath came to me with the evenness of slumber and the rasping of the pneumonia convalescent.

This listening tour completed, I returned to my room.

Still feeling wide-awake and restless, I pulled a chair up to a window, and sat looking at the moonlight on the river—which twisted just below the house so as to be visible from this side—smoking another cigar, and turning things over in my mind—to no great advantage.

Outside there was no sound.

Suddenly down the hall came the heavy explosion of a gun being fired indoors!

I threw myself across the room, out into the hall.

A woman's voice filled the house with its shriek—high, frenzied.

Barbra Caywood's door was unlocked when I reached it. I slammed it open. By the light of the moonbeams that slanted past her window, I saw her sitting upright in the center of her bed. She wasn't beautiful now. Her face was distorted, twisted with terror. The scream was just dying in her throat.

All this I got in the flash of time that it took me to put a running foot across her sill.

Then another shot crashed out—in Exon's room.

The girl's face jerked up—so abruptly that it seemed her neck must snap—she clutched both hands to her breast—and fell face-down among the bedclothes.

I don't know whether I went through, over, or around the screen that stood in the connecting doorway. I was circling Exon's bed. He lay on the floor on his side, facing a window. I jumped over him—leaned out the window.

In the yard that was bright now under the moon, nothing moved. There was no sound of flight.

Presently, while my eyes still searched the surrounding country, the farm hands, in their underwear, came running bare-footed from the direction of their quarters. I called down to them, stationing them at points of vantage.

Meanwhile, behind me, Gong Lim and Adam Figg had put Exon back in his bed, while Mrs. Gallaway and Emma Figg tried to check the blood that spurted from a hole in Barbra Caywood's side.

I sent Adam Figg to the telephone, to wake the doctor and the deputy sheriff, and then I hurried down to the grounds.

Stepping out of the door, I came face to face with Hilary Gallaway, coming from the direction of the garage. His face was flushed, and his breath was eloquent of the refreshments that had accompanied the game in Ady's back room; but his step was steady enough, and his smile was as lazy as ever. He had apparently arrived while I was sending Figg to the phone and running downstairs—otherwise I would have heard his car.

"What's the excitement?" he asked.

"Same as last night! Meet anybody on the road? Or see anybody leaving here?"

"No."

"All right. Get in that bus of yours, and burn up the road in the other direction. Stop anybody you meet going away from here or who looks wrong! Got a gun?"

He spun on his heel with nothing of indolence.

"One in my car," he called over his shoulder, as he broke into a run.

The farm hands still at their posts, I combed the grounds from east to west and from north to south. I realized that I was spoiling my chance of finding footprints when it would be light enough to see them; but I was banking on the man I wanted still being close at hand. And then Shand had told me that the ground was unfavorable for tracing prints, anyway.

On the gravel drive in front of the house I found the pistol from which the shots had been fired—a cheap .38-caliber revolver, slightly rusty, smelling freshly of burnt powder, with three empty shells and three that had not been fired in it.

Besides that I found nothing. The murderer—from what I had seen of the hole in the girl's side, I called him that—had vanished completely.

Shand and Dr. Rench arrived together, just as I was finishing my fruitless search. A little later, Hilary Gallaway came back—empty-handed.

III

Breakfast that morning was a melancholy meal, except to Hilary Gallaway. He refrained from jesting openly about the night's excitement; but his eyes twinkled whenever they met mine, and I knew he thought it a tremendously good joke for the shooting to have taken place right under my nose. During his wife's presence at the table, however, he was almost grave, as if not to offend her.

Mrs. Gallaway left the table shortly, and Dr. Rench joined us. He said that both of his patients were in as good shape as could be expected, and he thought both would recover.

The bullet had barely grazed the girl's ribs and breast bone, going through the flesh and muscles of her chest, in on the right side and out again on the left. Except for the shock and the loss of blood, she was not in danger, although she was still unconscious.

Exon was sleeping, the doctor said; so Shand and I crept up into his room to examine it. The first bullet had gone into the door-frame, about four inches above the one that had been fired the night before. The second bullet had pierced the Japanese screen, and, after passing through the girl, had lodged in the plaster of the wall. We dug out both bullets—they were of .38-caliber. Both had been apparently fired from the vicinity of one of the windows—either just inside or just outside.

Shand and I grilled the Chinese cook, the farm hands, and the Figgs, unmercifully that day. Detectives are only human—or at least this one is—and I don't mind confessing that some of my humiliation and chagrin was worked off on these people. But they came through it standing up—there was nothing to fix the shooting on any of them.

And all day long that damned Hilary Gallaway followed me from pillar to post, with a mocking glint in his eyes that said plainer than words, "I'm the logical suspect. Why don't you put me through your little third degree?" But I grinned back, and asked him nothing.

Shand had to go to town that afternoon. He called me up on the telephone later, and told me that Gallaway had left Knownburg early enough that morning to have arrived home fully half an hour before the shooting, if he had driven at his usual fast pace.

The day passed—too rapidly—and I found myself dreading the coming of night. Two nights in succession Exon's life had been attempted—and now the third night was coming.

At dinner Hilary Gallaway announced that he was going to stay home this evening. Knownburg, he said, was tame in comparison; and he grinned at me.

Dr. Rench left after the meal, saying that he would return as soon as possible, but that he had two patients on the other side of town whom he must visit. Barbra Caywood had returned to consciousness, but had been extremely hysterical, and the doctor had given her an opiate. She was asleep now. Exon was resting easily except for a high temperature.

I went up to Exon's room for a few minutes after the meal, and tried him out with a gentle question or two. But he refused to answer them, and he was too sick for me to press him.

He asked how the girl was.

"The doc says she's in no particular danger. Just loss of blood and shock. If she doesn't rip her bandages off and bleed to death in one of her hysterical spells, he says, he'll have her on her feet in a couple weeks."

Mrs. Gallaway came in then, and I went downstairs again, where I was seized by Gallaway, who insisted with bantering gravity that I tell him about some of the mysteries I had solved. He was enjoying my discomfort to the limit. He kidded me for about an hour, and had me burning up inside; but I managed to grin back with a fair pretense of indifference.

When his wife joined us presently—saying that both of the invalids were sleeping—I made my escape from her tormenting husband, saying that I had some writing to do. But I didn't go to my room.

Instead, I crept stealthily into the girl's room,

crossed to a clothespress that I had noted earlier in the day, and planted myself in it. By leaving the door open the least fraction of an inch, I could see through the connecting doorway—from which the screen had been removed—across Exon's bed, and out of the window from which three bullets had already come, and the Lord only knew what else might come.

Time passed, and I was stiff from standing still. But I had expected that—had felt it before on somewhat similar occasions—and I knew it would pass. But whether it did or not, I meant to stay here until something happened—if it was only the rising of the sun. Nothing else was going to be pulled off in this corner of the house without my being in on it!

Twice Mrs. Gallaway came up to look at her father and the nurse. Each time I shut my closet door entirely as soon as I heard her tip-toeing steps in the hall, I was hiding from *everybody*.

She had just gone from her second visit, when, before I had time to open my door again, I heard a faint rustling, and a soft padding on the floor. Not knowing what it was or where it was, I was afraid to push the door open.

In my narrow hiding-place I stood still and waited.

The padding was recognizable now—quiet footsteps, coming nearer. They passed not far from my clothespress door.

I waited.

An almost inaudible rustling. A pause. The softest and faintest of tearing sounds.

I came out of the closet—my gun in my hand.

Standing beside the girl's bed, leaning over her unconscious form, was old Talbert Exon, his face flushed with fever, his night shirt hanging limply around his wasted legs. One of his hands still rested upon the bedclothes he had turned down from her body. The other hand held a narrow strip of adhesive tape, with which her bandages had been fixed in place, and which he had just torn off.

He snarled at me, and both his hands went toward the girl's bandages.

The crazy, feverish glare of his eyes told me that the threat of the gun in my hand meant nothing to him. I jumped to his side, plucked his hands aside, picked him up in my arms, and carried him—kicking, clawing and swearing—back to his bed.

Then I called the others.

IV

Hilary Gallaway, Shand—who had come out from town again—and I sat over coffee and cigarettes in the kitchen, while the rest of the household helped Dr. Rench battle for Exon's life. The old man had gone through enough excitement in the last three days to kill a healthy man, let alone a pneumonia convalescent.

"But why should the old devil want to kill her?" Gallaway asked me.

"Search me," I confessed, a little testily perhaps. "I don't know why he wanted to kill her, but it's a cinch that he did. The gun was found just about where he could have thrown it when he heard me coming. I was in the girl's room when she was shot, and I got to Exon's window without wasting much time, and I saw nothing. You, yourself, driving home from Knownburg, and arriving here right after the shooting, didn't see anybody leave by the road; and I'll take an oath that nobody could have left in any other direction without either one of the farm hands or me seeing them.

"And then, tonight, I told Exon that the girl would recover if she didn't tear off her bandages; which, while true enough, gave him the idea that she had been trying to tear them off. And from that he built up a plan of tearing them off himself—knowing that she had been given an opiate, perhaps—and thinking that everybody would believe she had torn them off herself. And he was putting that plan in execution—had torn off one piece of tape—when I stopped him. He shot her intentionally, and that's flat. Maybe I couldn't prove it in court without knowing why;

but I know he did. But the doc says he'll hardly live to be tried; he killed himself trying to kill the girl."

"Maybe you're right," and Gallaway's mocking grin flashed at me, "but you're a hell of a detective just the same. Why didn't you suspect me?"

"I did," I grinned back, "but not enough."

"Why not? You may be making a mistake," he drawled. "You know my room is just across the hall from his, and I could have left my window, crept across the porch, fired at him, and then run back to my room, on that first night.

"And on the second night—when you were here—you ought to know that I left Knownburg in plenty of time to have come out here, parked my car down the road a bit, fired those two shots, crept around in the shadow of the house, ran back to my car, and then come driving innocently up to the garage. You should know also that my reputation isn't any too good—that I'm supposed to be a bad egg; and you do know that I don't like the old man. And for a motive, there is the fact that my wife is Exon's only heir. What more do you want? I hope," he raised his eyebrows in burlesqued pain, "that you don't think I have any moral scruples against a well-placed murder now and then."

I laughed.

"I don't."

"Well, then?"

"If Exon had been killed that first night, and I had come up here, you'd be doing your joking behind bars long before this. And if he'd been killed the second night, even, I might have grabbed you. But I don't figure you as a man who'd bungle so easy a job—not twice, anyway. You wouldn't have missed, and then run away, leaving him alive."

He reached over for my hand and shook it gravely.

"It is comforting to have one's few virtues appreciated."

Before Talbert Exon died he sent for me. He wanted to die, he said, with his curiosity appeased; and so we traded information. I told him how I had come to suspect him—just about what I had told his son-in-law—and he told me why he had tried to kill Barbra Caywood.

Fourteen years ago he had killed his wife; not for the insurance, as he had been suspected of doing, but in a fit of jealousy. However, he had so thoroughly covered up the proofs of his guilt that he had never been brought to trial; but the murder had weighed upon him, to the extent of becoming an obsession.

He knew that he would never give himself away consciously—he was too shrewd for that—and he knew that proof of his guilt could never be found. But there was always the chance that some time, in delirium, in his sleep, or when drunk, he might tell enough to bring him to the gallows.

He thought upon this angle too often, until it became a morbid fear that always hounded him. He had given up drinking—that was easy—but there was no way of guarding against the other things.

And one of them, he said, had finally happened. He had got pneumonia, and for a week he had been out of his head, and he had talked. Coming out of that week's delirium, he had questioned the nurse. She had given him vague answers, would not tell him what he had talked about, what he had said. And then, in unguarded moments, he had discovered that her eyes rested upon him with loathing—with intense repulsion.

He knew then that he had babbled of his wife's murder; and he set about laying plans for removing the nurse before she repeated what she had heard. For so long as she remained in his house, he counted himself safe. She would not tell strangers, and it might be that for a while she would not tell anyone. Professional ethics would keep her quiet, perhaps; but he could not let her leave his house with her knowledge of his secret.

Daily and in secret, he had tested his strength, until he knew himself strong enough to walk about the room a little, and to hold a revolver steady. His bed was fortunately placed for his purpose—directly in line with one of the windows, the connecting door, and the girl's bed. In an old bond-box in his closet—and nobody but he had ever seen the things in that box—was a revolver; a revolver that could not possibly be traced to him.

On the first night, he had taken this gun out, stepped back from his bed a little, and fired a bullet into the door-frame. Then he had jumped back into bed, concealing the gun under the blankets—where none thought to look for it—until he could return it to its box.

That was all the preparation he had needed. He had established an attempted murder directed against himself; and he had shown that a bullet fired at him could easily go near—and therefore through—the connecting doorway.

On the second night, he had waited until the house had seemed quiet. Then he had peeped through one of the cracks in the Japanese screen at the girl, whom he could see in the reflected light from the moon. He had found, though, that when he stepped far enough back from the screen for it to escape powder marks, he could not see the girl, not while she was lying down. So he had fired first into the door-frame—near the previous night's bullet—to awaken her.

She had sat up in bed immediately, screaming, and he had shot her. He had intended firing another shot into her body—to make sure of her death—but my approach had made that impossible, and had made concealment of the gun impossible; so, with what strength he had left, he had thrown the revolver out of the window.

He died that afternoon, and I returned to San Francisco.

But that was not quite the end of the story.

In the ordinary course of business, the agency's bookkeeping department sent Gallaway a bill for my services. With the check that he sent by return mail, he enclosed a letter to me, from which I quote a paragraph:

I don't want to let you miss the cream of the whole affair. The lovely Caywood, when she recovered, denied that Exon had talked of murder or any other crime during his delirium. The cause of the distaste with which she might have looked at him afterward, and the reason she would not tell him what he had said, was that his entire conversation during that week of delirium had consisted of an uninterrupted stream of obscenities and blasphemies, which seem to have shocked the girl through and through.

BLACK MASK, MARCH 1, 1924

Zigzags of Treachery

BY DASHIELL HAMMETT

Here is a detective story which we think will please all comers. It is a happy combination of deduction and swift action.

I

"ALL I KNOW about Dr. Estep's death," I said, "is the stuff in the papers."

Vance Richmond's lean gray face took on an expression of distaste.

"The newspapers aren't always either thorough or accurate. I'll give you the salient points as I know them; though I suppose you'll want to go over the ground for yourself, and get your information first-hand."

I nodded, and the attorney went on, shaping each word precisely with his thin lips before giving it sound.

"Dr. Estep came to San Francisco in '98 or '99—a young man of twenty-five, just through qualifying for his license. He opened an office here, and, as you probably know, became in time a rather excellent surgeon. He married two or three years after he came here. There were no children. He and his wife seem to have been a bit happier together than the average.

"Of his life before coming to San Francisco, nothing is known. He told his wife briefly that he had been born and raised in Parkersburg, W. Va., but that his home life had been so unpleasant that he was trying to forget it, and that he did not like to talk—or even think—about it. Bear that in mind.

"Two weeks ago—on the third of the month—a woman came to his office, in the afternoon. His office was in his residence on Pine Street. Lucy Coe, who was Dr. Estep's nurse and assistant, showed the woman into his office, and then went back to her own desk in the reception room."

"She didn't hear anything the doctor said to the woman, but through the closed door she heard the woman's voice now and then—a high and anguished voice, apparently pleading. Most of the words were lost upon the nurse, but she heard one coherent sentence. 'Please! Please!' she heard the woman cry, 'Don't turn me away!' The woman was with Dr. Estep for about fifteen minutes, and left sobbing into a handkerchief. Dr. Estep said nothing about the caller either to his nurse or to his wife, who didn't learn of it until after his death.

"The next day, toward evening, while the nurse was putting on her hat and coat preparatory to leaving for home, Dr. Estep came out of his office, with his hat on and a letter in his hand. The nurse saw that his face was pale—'white as my uniform,' she says—and he walked with the care of one who takes pains to keep from staggering.

"She asked him if he was ill. 'Oh, it's nothing!' he told her. 'I'll be all right in a very few minutes.' Then he went on out. The nurse left the house just behind him, and saw him drop the letter he had carried into the mail box on the corner, after which he returned to the house.

"Mrs. Estep, coming downstairs ten minutes later,—it couldn't have been any later than that,—heard, just as she reached the first floor, the sound of a shot from her husband's office. She rushed into it, meeting nobody. Her husband stood by his desk, swaying, with a hole in his right temple and a smoking revolver in his hand. Just as she reached him and put her arms around him, he fell across the desk—dead."

"Anybody else—any of the servants, for instance—able to say that Mrs. Estep didn't go to the office until after the shot?" I asked.

The attorney shook his head sharply.

"No, damn it! That's where the rub comes in!"

His voice, after this one flare of feeling, resumed its level, incisive tone, and he went on with his tale.

"The next day's papers had accounts of Dr. Estep's death, and late that morning the woman who had called upon him the day before his death came to the house. She is Dr. Estep's first wife—which is to say, his legal wife! There seems to be no reason—not the slightest—for doubting it, as much as I'd like to. They were married in Philadelphia in '96. She has a certified copy of the marriage record. I had the matter investigated in Philadelphia, and it's a certain fact that Dr. Estep and this woman—Edna Fife was her maiden name—were really married.

"She says that Estep, after living with her in Philadelphia for two years, deserted her. That would have been in '98, or just before he came to San Francisco. She has sufficient proof of her identity—that she really is the Edna Fife who married him; and my agents in the East found positive proof that Estep had practiced for two years in Philadelphia.

"And here is another point. I told you that Estep had said he was born and raised in Parkersburg. I had inquiries made there, but found nothing to show that he had ever lived there, and found ample to show that he had never lived at the address he had given his wife. There is, then, nothing for us to believe except that his talk of an unhappy early life was a ruse to ward off embarrassing questions."

"Did you do anything toward finding out whether the doctor and his first wife had ever been divorced?" I asked.

"I'm having that taken care of now, but I hardly expect to learn that they had. That would be too crude. To get on with my story: This woman—the first Mrs. Estep—said that she had just recently learned her husband's whereabouts, and had come to see him in an attempt to effect a reconciliation. When she called upon him the afternoon before his death, he asked for a little time to make up his mind what he should do. He promised to give her his decision in two days. My personal opinion, after talking to the woman several times, is that she had learned that he had accumulated some money, and that her interest was more in getting the money than in getting him. But that, of course, is neither here nor there.

"At first the authorities accepted the natural explanation of the doctor's death—suicide. But after the first wife's appearance, the second wife—my client—was arrested and charged with murder.

"The police theory is that after his first wife's visit, Dr. Estep told his second wife the whole story; and that she, brooding over the knowledge that he had deceived her, that she was not his wife at all, finally worked herself up into a rage, went to the office after his nurse had left for the day, and shot him with the revolver that she knew he always kept in his desk.

"I don't know, of course, just what evidence the prosecution has, but from the newspapers I gather that the case against her will be built upon her finger prints on the revolver with which he was killed; an upset inkwell on his desk; splashes of ink on the dress she wore; and an inky print of her hand on a torn newspaper on his desk.

"Unfortunately, but perfectly naturally, one of the first things she did was to take the revolver out of her husband's hand. That accounts for her prints on it. He fell—as I told you—just as she put her arms around him, and, though her memory isn't very clear on this point, the probabilities are that he dragged her with him when he fell across the desk. That accounts for the upset inkwell, the torn paper, and the splashes of ink. But the prosecution will try to persuade the jury that those things all happened before the shooting—that they are proofs of a struggle."

"Not so bad," I gave my opinion.

"Or pretty damned bad—depending on how you look at it. And this is the worst time imaginable for a thing like this to come up! Within the past few months there have been no less than five widely-advertised murders of men by women who were supposed to have been betrayed, or deceived, or one thing or another.

"Not one of those five women was convicted. As a result, we have the press, the public, and even the pulpit, howling for a stricter enforcement of justice. The newspapers are lined up against Mrs. Estep as strongly as their fear of libel suits will permit. The woman's clubs are lined up against her. Everybody is clamoring for an example to be made of her.

"Then, as if all that isn't enough, the Prosecuting Attorney has lost his last two big cases, and he'll be out for blood this time—election day isn't far off."

The calm, even, precise voice was gone now. In its place was a passionate eloquence.

"I don't know what you think," Richmond cried. "You're a detective. This is an old story to you. You're more or less callous, I suppose, and skeptical of innocence in general. But I *know* that Mrs. Estep didn't kill her husband. I don't say it because she's my client! I was Dr. Estep's attorney, and his friend, and if I thought Mrs. Estep guilty, I'd do everything in my power to help convict her. But I know as well as I know anything that she didn't kill him—couldn't have killed him.

"She's innocent. But I know too that if I go into court with no defense beyond what I now have, she'll be convicted! There has been too much leniency shown feminine criminals, public sentiment says. The pendulum will swing the other way—Mrs. Estep, if convicted, will get the limit. I'm putting it up to you! Can you save her?"

"Our best mark is the letter he mailed just before he died," I said, ignoring everything he said that didn't have to do with the facts of the case. "It's good betting that when a man writes and mails a letter and then shoots himself, that the letter isn't altogether unconnected with the suicide. Did you ask the first wife about the letter?"

"I did, and she denies having received one."

"That wasn't right. If the doctor had been driven to suicide by her appearance, then according to all the rules there are, the letter should have been addressed to her. He might have written one to his second wife, but he would hardly have mailed *it*.

"Would she have any reason for lying about it?"

"Yes," the lawyer said slowly, "I think she would. His will leaves everything to the second wife. The first wife, being the only legal wife, will have no difficulty in breaking that will, of course; but if it is shown that the second wife had no knowledge of the first one's existence—that she really believed herself to be Dr. Estep's legal wife—then I think that she will receive at least a portion of the estate. I don't think any court would, under the circumstances, take everything away from her. But if she should be found guilty of murdering Dr. Estep, then no consideration will be shown her, and the first wife will get every penny."

"Did he leave enough to make half of it, say, worth sending an innocent person to the gallows for?"

"He left about half a million, roughly; $250,000 isn't a mean inducement."

"Do you think it would be enough for the first wife—from what you have seen of her?"

"Candidly, I do. She didn't impress me as being a person of many very active scruples."

"Where does this first wife live?" I asked.

"She's staying at the Montgomery Hotel now. Her home is in Louisville, I believe. I don't think you will gain anything by talking to her, however. She has retained Somerset, Somerset, and Quill to represent her—a very reputable firm, by the way—and she'll refer you to them. They will tell you nothing. But if there's anything dishonest about her affairs—such as the concealing of Dr. Estep's letter—I'm confident that Somerset, Somerset and Quill know nothing of it."

"Can I talk to the second Mrs. Estep—your client?"

"Not at present, I'm afraid; though perhaps in a day or two. She is on the verge of collapse just now. She has always been delicate; and the shock of her husband's death, followed by her own arrest and imprisonment, has been too much for her. She's in the city jail, you know, held without bail. I've tried to have her transferred to the prisoner's ward of the City Hospital, even; but the authorities seem to think that her illness is simply a ruse. I'm worried about her. She's really in a critical condition."

His voice was losing its calmness again, so I picked up my hat, said something about starting to work at once, and went out. I don't like eloquence: if it isn't effective enough to pierce your hide, it's tiresome; and if it is effective enough, then it muddles your thoughts.

II

I spent the next couple of hours questioning the Estep servants, to no great advantage. None of them had been near the front of the house at the time of the shooting, and none had seen Mrs. Estep immediately prior to her husband's death.

After a lot of hunting, I located Lucy Coe, the nurse, in an apartment on Vallejo Street. She was a small, brisk, business-like woman of thirty or so. She repeated what Vance Richmond had told me, and could add nothing to it.

That cleaned up the Estep end of the job; and I set out for the Montgomery Hotel, satisfied that my only hope for success—barring miracles, which usually don't happen—lay in finding the letter that I believed Dr. Estep had written to his first wife.

My drag with the Montgomery Hotel management was pretty strong—strong enough to get me anything I wanted that wasn't too far outside the law. So as soon as I got there, I hunted up Stacey, one of the assistant managers.

"This Mrs. Estep who's registered here," I asked, "what do you know about her?"

"Nothing, myself, but if you'll wait a few minutes I'll see what I can learn."

The assistant manager was gone about ten minutes.

"No one seems to know much about her," he told me when he came back. "I've questioned the telephone girls, bell-boys, maids, clerks, and the house detective; but none of them could tell me much.

"She registered from Louisville, on the second of the month. She has never stopped here before, and she seems unfamiliar with the city—

asks quite a few questions about how to get around. The mail clerks don't remember handling any mail for her, nor do the girls on the switchboard have any record of phone calls for her.

"She keeps regular hours—usually goes out at ten or later in the morning, and gets in before midnight. She doesn't seem to have any callers or friends."

"Will you have her mail watched—let me know what postmarks and return addresses are on any letters she gets?"

"Certainly."

"And have the girls on the switchboard put their ears up against any talking she does over the wire?"

"Yes."

"Is she in her room now?"

"No, she went out a little while ago."

"Fine! I'd like to go up and take a look at her stuff."

Stacey looked sharply at me, and cleared his throat.

"Is it as—ah—important as all that? I want to give you all the assistance I can, but—"

"It's this important," I assured him, "that another woman's life depends on what I can learn about this one."

"All right!" he said. "I'll tell the clerk to let us know if she comes in before we are through; and we'll go right up."

The woman's room held two valises and a trunk, all unlocked, and containing not the least thing of importance—no letters—nothing. So little, in fact, that I was more than half convinced that she had expected her things to be searched.

Downstairs again, I planted myself in a comfortable chair within sight of the key rack, and waited for a view of this first Mrs. Estep.

She came in at 11:15 that night. A large woman of forty-five or fifty, well dressed, and carrying herself with an air of assurance. Her face was a little too hard as to mouth and chin, but not enough to be ugly. A capable looking woman—a woman who would get what she went after.

III

Eight o'clock was striking as I went into the Montgomery lobby the next morning and picked out a chair, this time, within eye-range of the elevators.

At 10:30 Mrs. Estep left the hotel, with me in her wake. Her denial that a letter from her husband, written immediately before his death, had come to her didn't fit in with the possibilities as I saw them. And a good motto for the detective business is, "When in doubt—shadow 'em."

After eating breakfast at a restaurant on O'Farrell Street, she turned toward the shopping district; and for a long, long time—though I suppose it was a lot shorter than it seemed to me—she led me through the most densely packed portions of the most crowded department stores she could find.

She didn't buy anything, but she did a lot of thorough looking, with me muddling along behind her, trying to act like a little fat guy on an errand for his wife; while stout women bumped me and thin ones prodded me and all sorts got in my way and walked on my feet.

Finally, after I had sweated off a couple of pounds, she left the shopping district, and cut up through Union Square, walking along casually, as if out for a stroll.

Three-quarters way through, she turned abruptly, and retraced her steps, looking sharply at everyone she passed. I was on a bench, reading a stray page from a day-old newspaper, when she went by. She walked on down Post Street to Kearny, stopping every now and then to look—or to pretend to look—in store windows; while I ambled along sometimes beside her, sometimes almost by her side, and sometimes in front.

She was trying to check up the people around her, trying to determine whether she was being followed or not. But here, in the busy part of town, that gave me no cause for worry. On a less crowded street it might have been different, though not necessarily so.

There are four rules for shadowing: Keep

behind your subject as much as possible; never try to hide from him; act in a natural manner no matter what happens; and never meet his eye. Obey them, and, except in unusual circumstances, shadowing is the easiest thing that a sleuth has to do.

Assured, after a while, that no one was following her, Mrs. Estep turned back toward Powell Street, and got into a taxicab at the St. Francis stand. I picked out a modest touring car from the rank of hire-cars along the Geary Street side of Union Square, and set out after her.

Our route was out Post Street to Laguna, where the taxi presently swung into the curb and stopped. The woman got out, paid the driver, and went up the steps of an apartment building. With idling engine my own car had come to rest against the opposite curb in the block above.

As the taxicab disappeared around a corner, Mrs. Estep came out of the apartment building doorway, went back to the sidewalk, and started down Laguna Street.

"Pass her," I told my chauffeur, and we drew down upon her.

As we came abreast, she went up the front steps of another building, and this time she rang a bell. These steps belonged to a building apparently occupied by four flats, each with its separate door, and the button she had pressed belonged to the right-hand second-story flat.

Under cover of my car's rear curtains, I kept my eye on the doorway while my driver found a convenient place to park in the next block.

I kept my eye on the vestibule until 5:35 P.M., when she came out, walked to the Sutter Street car line, returned to the Montgomery, and went to her room.

I called up the Old Man—the Continental Detective Agency's San Francisco manager—and asked him to detail an operative to learn who and what were the occupants of the Laguna Street flat.

That night Mrs. Estep ate dinner at her hotel, and went to a show afterward, and she displayed no interest in possible shadowers. She

went to her room at a little after eleven, and I knocked off for the day.

IV

The following morning I turned the woman over to Dick Foley, and went back to the agency to wait for Bob Teale, the operative who had investigated the Laguna Street flat. He came in at a little after ten.

"A guy named Jacob Ledwich lives there," Bob said. "He's a crook of some sort, but I don't know just what. He and 'Wop' Healey are friendly, so he must be a crook! 'Porky' Grout says he's an ex-bunco man who is in with a gambling ring now; but 'Porky' would tell you a bishop was a safe-ripper* if he thought it would mean five bucks for himself.

"This Ledwich goes out mostly at night, and he seems to be pretty prosperous. Probably a high-class worker of some sort. He's got a Buick—license number 645-221—that he keeps in a garage around the corner from his flat. But he doesn't seem to use the car much."

"What sort of looking fellow is he?"

"A big guy—six feet or better—and he'll weigh a couple hundred easy. He's got a funny mug on him. It's broad and heavy around the cheeks and jaw, but his mouth is a little one that looks like it was made for a smaller man. He's no youngster—middle-aged."

"Suppose you tail him around for a day or two, Bob, and see what he's up to. Try to get a room or apartment in the neighborhood—a place that you can cover his front door from."

V

Vance Richmond's lean face lighted up as soon as I mentioned Ledwich's name to him.

"Yes!" he exclaimed. "He was a friend, or at

_____
* one who breaks into safes

least an acquaintance, of Dr. Estep's. I met him once—a large man with a peculiarly inadequate mouth. I dropped in to see the doctor one day, and Ledwich was in the office. Dr. Estep introduced us."

"What do you know about him?"

"Nothing."

"Don't you know whether he was intimate with the doctor, or just a casual acquaintance?"

"No. For all I know, he might have been a friend, a patient, or almost anything. The doctor never spoke of him to me, and nothing passed between them while I was there that afternoon. I simply gave the doctor some information he had asked for and left. Why?"

"Dr. Estep's first wife—after going to a lot of trouble to see that she wasn't followed—connected with Ledwich yesterday afternoon. And from what we can learn, he seems to be a crook of some sort."

"What would that indicate?"

"I'm not sure what it means, but I can do a lot of guessing. Ledwich knew both the doctor and the doctor's first wife; then it's not a bad bet that *she* knew where her husband was all the time. If she did, then it's another good bet that she was getting money from him right along. Can you check up his accounts and see whether he was passing out any money that can't be otherwise accounted for?"

The attorney shook his head.

"No, his accounts are in rather bad shape, carelessly kept. He must have had more than a little difficulty with his income tax statements."

"I see. To get back to my guesses: If she knew where he was all the time, and was getting money from him, then why did his first wife finally come to see her husband? Perhaps because—"

"I think I can help you there," Richmond interrupted. "A fortunate investment in lumber nearly doubled Dr. Estep's wealth two or three months ago."

"That's it, then! She learned of it through Ledwich. She demanded, either through Ledwich, or by letter, a rather large share of it—

more than the doctor was willing to give. When he refused, she came to see him in person, to demand the money under threat—we'll say—of instant exposure. He thought she was in earnest. Either he couldn't raise the money she demanded, or he was tired of leading a double life. Anyway, he thought it all over, and decided to commit suicide. This is all a guess, or a series of guesses—but it sounds reasonable to me."

"To me, too," the attorney said. "What are you going to do now?"

"I'm still having both of them shadowed—there's no other way of tackling them just now. I'm having the woman looked up in Louisville. But, you understand, I might dig up a whole flock of things on them, and when I got through still be as far as ever from finding the letter Dr. Estep wrote before he died.

"There are plenty of reasons for thinking that the woman destroyed the letter—that would have been her wisest play. But if I can get enough on her, even at that, I can squeeze her into admitting that the letter was written, and that it said something about suicide—if it did. And that will be enough to spring your client. How is she today—any better?"

His thin face lost the animation that had come to it during our discussion of Ledwich, and became bleak.

"She went completely to pieces last night, and was removed to the hospital, where she should have been taken in the first place. To tell you the truth, if she isn't liberated soon, she won't need our help. I've done my utmost to have her released on bail—pulled every wire I know—but there's little likelihood of success in that direction.

"Knowing that she is a prisoner—charged with murdering her husband—is killing her. She isn't young, and she has always been subject to nervous disorders. The bare shock of her husband's death was enough to prostrate her—but now—You've *got* to get her out—and quickly!"

He was striding up and down his office, his voice throbbing with feeling. I left quickly.

VI

From the attorney's office, I returned to the agency, where I was told that Bob Teale had phoned in the address of a furnished apartment he had rented on Laguna Street. I hopped on a street car, and went up to take a look at it.

But I didn't get that far.

Walking down Laguna Street, after leaving the car, I spied Bob Teale coming toward me. Between Bob and me—also coming toward me—was a big man whom I recognized as Jacob Ledwich: a big man with a big red face around a tiny mouth.

I walked on down the street, passing both Ledwich and Bob, without paying any apparent attention to either. At the next corner I stopped to roll a cigarette, and steal a look at the pair.

And then I came to life!

Ledwich had stopped at a vestibule cigar stand up the street to make a purchase. Bob Teale, knowing his stuff, had passed him and was walking steadily up the street.

He was figuring that Ledwich had either come out for the purpose of buying cigars or cigarettes, and would return to his flat with them; or that after making his purchase the big man would proceed to the car line, where, in either event, Bob would wait.

But as Ledwich had stopped before the cigar stand, a man across the street had stepped suddenly into a doorway, and stood there, back in the shadows. This man, I now remembered, had been on the opposite side of the street from Bob and Ledwich, and walking in the same direction.

He, too, was following Ledwich.

By the time Ledwich had finished his business at the stand, Bob had reached Sutter Street, the nearest car line. Ledwich started up the street in that direction. The man in the doorway stepped out and went after him. I followed that one.

A ferry-bound car came down Sutter Street just as I reached the corner. Ledwich and I got aboard together. The mysterious stranger fumbled with a shoe-string several pavements from the corner until the car was moving again, and then he likewise made a dash for it.

He stood beside me on the rear platform, hiding behind a large man in overalls, past whose shoulder he now and then peeped at Ledwich. Bob had gone to the corner above, and was already seated when Ledwich, this amateur detective,—there was no doubting his amateur status,—and I got on the car.

I sized up the amateur while he strained his neck peeping at Ledwich. He was small, this sleuth, and scrawny and frail. His most noticeable feature was his nose—a limp organ that twitched nervously all the time. His clothes were old and shabby, and he himself was somewhere in his fifties.

After studying him for a few minutes, I decided that he hadn't tumbled to Bob Teale's part in the game. His attention had been too firmly fixed upon Ledwich, and the distance had been too short thus far for him to discover that Bob was also tailing the big man.

So when the seat beside Bob was vacated presently, I chucked my cigarette away, went into the car, and sat down, my back toward the little man with the twitching nose.

"Drop off after a couple of blocks and go back to the apartment. Don't shadow Ledwich any more until I tell you. Just watch his place. There's a bird following him, and I want to see what he's up to," I told Bob in an undertone.

He grunted that he understood, and, after a few minutes, left the car.

At Stockton Street, Ledwich got off, the man with the twitching nose behind him, and me in the rear. In that formation we paraded around town all afternoon.

The big man had business in a number of pool rooms, cigar stores, and soft drink parlors—most of which I knew for places where you can get a bet down on any horse that's running in North America, whether at Tanforan, Tijuana, or Timonium.

Just what Ledwich did in these places, I didn't learn. I was bringing up the rear of the procession, and my interest was centered upon the mysterious little stranger. He didn't enter any of the places behind Ledwich, but loitered in their neighborhoods until Ledwich reappeared.

He had a rather strenuous time of it— laboring mightily to keep out of Ledwich's sight, and only succeeding because we were downtown, where you can get away with almost any sort of shadowing. He certainly made a lot of work for himself, dodging here and there.

After a while, Ledwich shook him.

The big man came out of a cigar store with another man. They got into an automobile that was standing beside the curb, and drove away; leaving my man standing on the edge of the sidewalk twitching his nose in chagrin. There was a taxi stand just around the corner, but he either didn't know it or didn't have enough money to pay the fare.

I expected him to return to Laguna Street then, but he didn't. He led me down Kearny Street to Portsmouth Street, where he stretched himself out on the grass, face down, lit a black pipe, and lay looking dejectedly at the Stevenson monument, probably without seeing it.

I sprawled on a comfortable piece of sod some distance away—between a Chinese woman with two perfectly round children and an ancient Portuguese in a gaily checkered suit—and we let the afternoon go by.

When the sun had gone low enough for the ground to become chilly, the little man got up, shook himself, and went back up Kearny Street to a cheap lunch-room, where he ate meagerly. Then he entered a hotel a few doors away, took a key from the row of hooks, and vanished down a dark corridor.

Running through the register, I found that the key he had taken belonged to a room whose occupant was "John Boyd, St. Louis, Mo.," and that he had arrived the day before.

This hotel wasn't of the sort where it is safe to make inquiries, so I went down to the street again, and came to rest on the least conspicuous nearby corner.

Twilight came, and the street and shop lights were turned on. It got dark. The night traffic of

Kearny Street went up and down past me: Filipino boys in their too-dapper clothes, bound for the inevitable black-jack game; gaudy women still heavy-eyed from their day's sleep; plain clothes men on their way to headquarters, to report before going off duty; Chinese going to or from Chinatown; sailors in pairs, looking for action of any sort; hungry people making for the Italian and French restaurants; worried people going into the bail bond broker's office on the corner to arrange for the release of friends and relatives whom the police had nabbed; Italians on their homeward journeys from work; odds and ends of furtive-looking citizens on various shady errands.

Midnight came, and no John Boyd, and I called it a day, and went home.

Before going to bed, I talked with Dick Foley over the wire. He said that Mrs. Estep had done nothing of any importance all day, and had received neither mail nor phone calls. I told him to stop shadowing her until I solved John Boyd's game.

I was afraid Boyd might turn his attention to the woman, and I didn't want him to discover that she was being shadowed. I had already instructed Bob Teale to simply watch Ledwich's flat—to see when he came in and went out, and with whom—and now I told Dick to do the same with the woman.

My guess on this Boyd person was that he and the woman were working together—that she had him watching Ledwich for her, so that the big man couldn't double-cross her. But that was only a guess—and I don't gamble too much on my guesses.

VII

The next morning I dressed myself up in an army shirt and shoes, an old faded cap, and a suit that wasn't downright ragged, but was shabby enough not to stand out too noticeably beside John Boyd's old clothes.

It was a little after nine o'clock when Boyd

left his hotel and had breakfast at the grease-joint where he had eaten the night before. Then he went up to Laguna Street, picked himself a corner, and waited for Jacob Ledwich.

He did a lot of waiting. He waited all day; because Ledwich didn't show until after dark. But the little man was well-stocked with patience—I'll say that for him. He fidgeted, and stood on one foot and then the other, and even tried sitting on the curb for awhile, but he stuck it out.

I took it easy, myself. The furnished apartment Bob Teale had rented to watch Ledwich's flat from was a ground floor one, across the street, and just a little above the corner where Boyd waited. So we could watch him and the flat with one eye.

Bob and I sat and smoked and talked all day, taking turns watching the fidgeting man on the corner and Ledwich's door.

Night had just definitely settled when Ledwich came out and started up toward the car line. I slid out into the street, and our parade was under way again—Ledwich leading, Boyd following him, and we following *him*.

Half a block of this, and I got an idea!

I'm not what you'd call a brilliant thinker—such results as I get are usually the fruits of patience, industry, and unimaginative plugging, helped out now and then, maybe, by a little luck—but I do have my flashes of intelligence. And this was one of them.

Ledwich was about a block ahead of me; Boyd half that distance. Speeding up, I passed Boyd, and caught up with Ledwich. Then I slackened my pace so as to walk beside him, though with no appearance from the rear of having any interest in him.

"Jake," I said, without turning my head, "there's a guy following you!"

The big man almost spoiled my little scheme by stopping dead still, but he caught himself in time, and, taking his cue from me, kept walking.

"Who the hell are you?" he growled.

"Don't get funny!" I snapped back, still looking and walking ahead. "It ain't my funeral. But

I was coming up the street when you came out, and I seen this guy duck behind a pole until you was past, and then follow you up."

That got him.

"You sure?"

"Sure! All you got to do to prove it is turn the next corner and wait."

I was two or three steps ahead of him by this time, I turned the corner, and halted, with my back against the brick building front. Ledwich took up the same position at my side.

"Want any help?" I grinned at him—a reckless sort of grin, unless my acting was poor.

"No."

His little lumpy mouth was set ugly, and his blue eyes were hard as pebbles.

I flicked the tail of my coat aside to show him the butt of my gun.

"Want to borrow the rod?" I asked.

"No."

He was trying to figure me out, and small wonder.

"Don't mind if I stick around to see the fun, do you?" I asked, mockingly.

There wasn't time for him to answer that. Boyd had quickened his steps, and now he came hurrying around the corner, his nose twitching like a tracking dog's.

Ledwich stepped into the middle of the sidewalk, so suddenly that the little man thudded into him with a grunt. For a moment they stared at each other, and there was recognition between them.

Ledwich shot one big hand out and clamped the other by a shoulder.

"What are you snooping around me for, you rat? Didn't I tell you to keep away from Frisco?"

"Aw, Jake!" Boyd begged. "I didn't mean no harm. I just thought that—"

Ledwich silenced him with a shake that clicked his mouth shut, and turned to me.

"A friend of mine," he sneered.

His eyes grew suspicious and hard again, and ran up and down me from cap to shoes.

"How'd you know my name?" he demanded.

"A famous man like you?" I asked, in burlesque astonishment.

"Never mind the comedy!" He took a threatening step toward me. "How'd you know my name?"

"None of your damned business," I snapped.

My attitude seemed to reassure him. His face became less suspicious.

"Well," he said slowly, "I owe you something for this trick, and—How are you fixed?"

"I have been dirtier." Dirty is Pacific Coast argot for prosperous.

He looked speculatively from me to Boyd, and back.

"Know 'The Circle'?" he asked me.

I nodded. The underworld calls "Wop" Healey's joint "The Circle."

"If you'll meet me there tomorrow night, maybe I can put a piece of change your way."

"Nothing stirring!" I shook my head with emphasis. "I ain't circulating that prominent these days."

A fat chance I'd have of meeting him there! "Wop" Healey and half his customers knew me as a detective. So there was nothing to do but to try to get the impression over that I was a crook who had reasons for wanting to keep away from the more notorious hang-outs for a while. Apparently it got over. He thought a while, and then gave me his Laguna Street number.

"Drop in this time tomorrow and maybe I'll have a proposition to make you—if you've got the guts."

"I'll think it over," I said noncommittally, and turned as if to go down the street.

"Just a minute," he called, and I faced him again. "What's your name?"

"Wisher," I said, "Shine, if you want a front one."

"Shine Wisher," he repeated. "I don't remember ever hearing it before."

It would have surprised me if he had—I had made it up only about fifteen minutes before.

"You needn't yell it," I said sourly, "so that everybody in the burg *will* remember hearing it."

And with that I left him, not at all dissatisfied with myself. By tipping him off to Boyd, I had put him under obligations to me, and had led him to accept me, at least tentatively, as a fellow crook. And by making no apparent effort to gain his good graces, I had strengthened my hand that much more.

I had a date with him for the next day, when I was to be given a chance to earn—illegally, no doubt—"a piece of change."

There was a chance that this proposition he had in view for me had nothing to do with the Estep affair, but then again it might; and whether it did or not, I had my entering wedge at least a little way into Jake Ledwich's business.

I strolled around for about half an hour, and then went back to Bob Teale's apartment.

"Ledwich come back?"

"Yes," Bob said, "with that little guy of yours. They went in about half an hour ago."

"Good! Haven't seen a woman go in?"

"No."

I expected to see the first Mrs. Estep arrive sometime during the evening, but she didn't. Bob and I sat around and talked and watched Ledwich's doorway, and the hours passed.

At one o'clock Ledwich came out alone.

"I'm going to tail him, just for luck," Bob said, and caught up his cap.

Ledwich vanished around a corner, and then Bob passed out of sight behind him.

Five minutes later Bob was with me again.

"He's getting his machine out of the garage."

I jumped for the telephone and put in a rush order for a fast touring car.

Bob, at the window, called out, "Here he is!"

I joined Bob in time to see Ledwich going into his vestibule. His car stood in front of the house. A very few minutes, and Boyd and Ledwich came out together. Boyd was leaning heavily on Ledwich, who was supporting the little man with an arm across his back. We couldn't see their faces in the dark, but the little man was plainly either sick, drunk, or drugged!

Ledwich helped his companion into the touring car. The red tail-lights laughed back at us for a few blocks, and then disappeared. The automobile I had ordered arrived twenty minutes later, so we sent it back unused.

At a little after three that morning, Ledwich, alone and afoot, returned from the direction of his garage. He had been gone exactly two hours.

VIII

Neither Bob nor I went home that night, but slept in the Laguna Street apartment.

Bob went down to the corner grocer's to get what we needed for breakfast in the morning, and he brought a morning paper back with him.

I cooked breakfast while he divided his attention between Ledwich's front door and the newspaper.

"Hey!" he called suddenly, "look here!"

I ran out of the kitchen with a handful of bacon.

"What is it?"

"Listen! 'Park murder mystery!'" he read. "'Early this morning the body of an unidentified man was found near a driveway in Golden Gate Park. His neck had been broken, according to the police; who say that the absence of any considerable bruises on the body, as well as the orderly condition of the clothes and the ground nearby, show that he did not come to his death through falling, or being struck by an automobile. It is believed that he was killed and then carried to the Park in an automobile, to be left there.'"

"Boyd!" I said.

"I bet you!" Bob agreed.

And at the morgue a very little while later, we learned that we were correct. The dead man was John Boyd.

"He was dead when Ledwich brought him out of the house," Bob said.

I nodded.

"He was! He was a little man, and it wouldn't have been much of a stunt for a big bruiser like Ledwich to have dragged him along with one arm the short distance from the door to the curb,

pretending to be holding him up, like you do with a drunk. Let's go over to the Hall of Justice and see what the police have got on it—if anything."

At the detective bureau we hunted up O'Gar, the detective-sergeant in charge of the Homicide Detail, and a good man to work with.

"This dead man found in the park," I asked, "know anything about him?"

O'Gar pushed back his village constable's hat—a big black hat with a floppy brim that belongs in vaudeville—scratched his bullet-head, and scowled at me as if he thought I had a joke up my sleeve.

"Not a damned thing except that he's dead!" he said at last.

"How'd you like to know who he was last seen with?"

"It wouldn't hinder me any in finding out who bumped him off, and that's a fact."

"How do you like the sound of this?" I asked. "His name was John Boyd and he was living at a hotel down in the next block. The last person he was seen with was a guy who is tied up with Dr. Estep's first wife. You know—the Dr. Estep whose second wife is the woman you people are trying to prove a murder on. Does that sound interesting?"

"It does," he said. "Where do we go first?"

"This Ledwich—he's the fellow who was last seen with Boyd—is going to be a hard bird to shake down. We better try to crack the woman first—the first Mrs. Estep. There's a chance that Boyd was a pal of hers, and in that case when she finds out that Ledwich rubbed him out, she may open up and spill the works to us.

"On the other hand, if she and Ledwich are stacked up against Boyd together, then we might as well get her safely placed before we tie into him. I don't want to pull him before night, anyway. I got a date with him, and I want to try to rope him first."

Bob Teale made for the door.

"I'm going up and keep my eye on him until you're ready for him," he called over his shoulder.

"Good," I said. "Don't let him get out of town on us. If he tries to blow have him chucked in the can."

In the lobby of the Montgomery Hotel, O'Gar and I talked to Dick Foley first. He told us that the woman was still in her room—had had her breakfast sent up. She had received neither letters, telegrams, or phone calls since we began to watch her.

I got hold of Stacey again.

"We're going up to talk to this Estep woman, and maybe we'll take her away with us. Will you send up a maid to find out whether she's up and dressed yet? We don't want to announce ourselves ahead of time, and we don't want to burst in on her while she's in bed, or only partly dressed."

He kept us waiting about fifteen minutes, and then told us that Mrs. Estep was up and dressed.

We went up to her room, taking the maid with us.

The maid rapped on the door.

"What is it?" an irritable voice demanded.

"The maid; I want to—"

The key turned on the inside, and an angry Mrs. Estep jerked the door open. O'Gar and I advanced, O'Gar flashing his "buzzer."*

"From headquarters," he said. "We want to talk to you."

O'Gar's foot was where she couldn't slam the door on us, and we were both walking ahead, so there was nothing for her to do but to retreat into the room, admitting us—which she did with no pretense of graciousness.

We closed the door, and then I threw our big load at her.

"Mrs. Estep, why did Jake Ledwich kill John Boyd?"

The expressions ran over her face like this: Alarm at Ledwich's name, fear at the word "kill," but the name John Boyd brought only bewilderment.

"Why did what?" she stammered meaninglessly, to gain time.

_____

* badge

"Exactly," I said. "Why did Jake kill him last night in his flat, and then take him in the park and leave him?"

Another set of expressions: Increased bewilderment until I had almost finished the sentence, and then the sudden understanding of something, followed by the inevitable groping for poise. These things weren't as plain as billboards, you understand, but they were there to be read by anyone who had ever played poker—either with cards or people.

What I got out of them was that Boyd hadn't been working with or for her, and that, though she knew Ledwich had killed somebody at some time, it wasn't Boyd and it wasn't last night. Who, then? And when? Dr. Estep? Hardly! There wasn't a chance in the world that—if he had been murdered—anybody except his wife had done it—his second wife. No possible reading of the evidence could bring any other answer.

Who, then, had Ledwich killed before Boyd? Was he a wholesale murderer?

These things are flitting through my head in flashes and odd scraps while Mrs. Estep is saying:

"This is absurd! The idea of your coming up here and—"

She talked for five minutes straight, the words fairly sizzling from between her hard lips; but the words themselves didn't mean anything. She was talking for time—talking while she tried to hit upon the safest attitude to assume.

And before we could head her off, she had hit upon it—silence!

We got not another word out of her; and that is the only way in the world to beat the grilling game. The average suspect tries to talk himself out of being arrested; and it doesn't matter how shrewd a man is, or how good a liar, if he'll talk to you, and you play your cards right, you can hook him—can make him help you convict him. But if he won't talk you can't do a thing with him.

And that's how it was with this woman. She refused to pay any attention to our questions—she wouldn't speak, nod, grunt, or wave an arm in reply. She gave us a fine assortment of facial expressions, true enough, but we wanted verbal information—and we got none.

We weren't easily licked, however. Three beautiful hours of it we gave her without rest. We stormed, cajoled, threatened, and at times I think we danced; but it was no go. So in the end we took her away with us. We didn't have anything on her, but we couldn't afford to have her running around loose until we nailed Ledwich.

At the Hall of Justice we didn't book her; but simply held her as a material witness, putting her in an office with a matron and one of O'Gar's men, who were to see what they could do with her while we went after Ledwich. We had had her frisked as soon as she reached the Hall, of course; and, as we expected, she hadn't a thing of importance on her.

O'Gar and I went back to the Montgomery and gave her room a thorough overhauling—and found nothing.

"Are you sure you know what you're talking about?" the detective-sergeant asked as we left the hotel. "It's going to be a pretty joke on somebody if you're mistaken."

I let that go by without an answer.

"I'll meet you at 6:30," I said, "and we'll go up against Ledwich."

He grunted an approval, and I set out for Vance Richmond's office.

IX

The attorney sprang up from his desk as soon as his stenographer admitted me. His face was leaner and grayer than ever; its lines had deepened, and there was a hollowness around his eyes.

"You've *got* to do something!" he cried huskily. "I have just come from the hospital. Mrs. Estep is on the point of death! A day more of this—two days at the most—and she will—"

I interrupted him, and swiftly gave him an account of the day's happenings, and what I expected, or hoped, to make out of them. But he received the news without brightening, and shook his head hopelessly.

"But don't you see," he exclaimed when I had finished, "that that won't do? I know you can find proof of her innocence in time. I'm not complaining—you've done all that could be expected, and more! But all that's no good! I've got to have—well—a miracle, perhaps.

"Suppose that you do finally get the truth out of Ledwich and the first Mrs. Estep or it comes out during their trials for Boyd's murder? Or that you even get to the bottom of the matter in three or four days? That will be too late! If I can go to Mrs. Estep and tell her she's free now, she may pull herself together, and come through. But another day of imprisonment—two days, or perhaps even two hours—and she won't need anybody to clear her. Death will have done it! I tell you, she's—"

I left Vance Richmond abruptly again. This lawyer was bound upon getting me worked up; and I like my jobs to be simply jobs—emotions are nuisances during business hours.

X

At a quarter to seven that evening, while O'Gar remained down the street, I rang Jacob Ledwich's bell. As I had stayed with Bob Teale in our apartment the previous night, I was still wearing the clothes in which I had made Ledwich's acquaintance as Shine Wisher.

Ledwich opened the door.

"Hello, Wisher!" he said without enthusiasm, and led me upstairs.

His flat consisted of four rooms, I found, running the full length and half the breadth of the building, with both front and rear exits. It was furnished with the ordinary none-too-spotless appointments of the typical moderately priced furnished flat—alike the world over.

In his front room we sat down and talked and smoked and sized one another up. He seemed a little nervous. I thought he would have been just as well satisfied if I had forgotten to show up.

"About this job you mentioned?" I asked presently.

"Sorry," he said, moistening his little lumpy mouth, "but it's all off." And then he added, obviously as an afterthought, "for the present, at least."

I guessed from that that my job was to have taken care of Boyd—but Boyd had been taken care of for good.

He brought out some whisky after a while, and we talked over it for some time, to no purpose whatever. He was trying not to appear too anxious to get rid of me, and I was cautiously feeling him out.

Piecing together things he let fall here and there, I came to the conclusion that he was a former con man who had fallen into an easier game of late years. That was in line, too, with what "Porky" Grout had told Bob Teale.

I talked about myself with the evasiveness that would have been natural to a crook in my situation; and made one or two carefully planned slips that would lead him to believe that I had been tied up with the "Jimmy the Riveter" hold-up mob, most of whom were doing long hitches at Walla Walla then.

He offered to lend me enough money to tide me over until I could get on my feet again. I told him I didn't need chicken feed so much as a chance to pick up some real jack.

The evening was going along, and we were getting nowhere.

"Jake," I said casually—outwardly casual, that is, "you took a big chance putting that guy out of the way like you did last night."

I meant to stir things up, and I succeeded.

His face went crazy.

A gun came out of his coat.

Firing from my pocket, I shot it out of his hand.

"Now behave!" I ordered.

He sat rubbing his benumbed hand and staring with wide eyes at the smouldering hole in my coat.

Looks like a great stunt—this shooting a gun out of a man's hand, but it's a thing that happens now and then. A man who is a fair shot (and that is exactly what I am—no more, no less), natu-rally and automatically shoots pretty close to the spot upon which his eyes are focused. When a man goes for his gun in front of you, you shoot at *him*—not at any particular part of him. There isn't time for that—you shoot at *him*. However, you are more than likely to be looking at his gun, and in that case it isn't altogether surprising if your bullet should hit his gun—as mine had done. But it looks impressive.

I beat out the fire around the bullet-hole in my coat, crossed the room to where his revolver had been knocked, and picked it up. I started to eject the bullets from it, but, instead, I snapped it shut again and stuck it in my pocket. Then I returned to my chair, opposite him.

"A man oughtn't to act like that," I kidded him, "he's likely to hurt somebody."

His little mouth curled up at me.

"An elbow, huh?" putting all the contempt he could in his voice; and somehow any synonym for detective seems able to hold a lot of contempt.

I might have tried to talk myself back into the Wisher role. It could have been done, but I doubted that it would be worth it; so I nodded my confession.

His brain was working now, and the passion left his face, while he sat rubbing his right hand, and his little mouth and eyes began to screw themselves up calculatingly.

I kept quiet, waiting to see what the outcome of his thinking would be. I knew he was trying to figure out just what my place in this game was. Since, to his knowledge, I had come into it no later than the previous evening, then the Boyd murder hadn't brought me in. That would leave the Estep affair—unless he was tied up in a lot of other crooked stuff that I didn't know anything about.

"You're not a city dick, are you?" he asked finally; and his voice was on the verge of friendliness now: the voice of one who wants to persuade you of something, or sell you something.

The truth, I thought, wouldn't hurt.

"No," I said, "I'm with the Continental."

He hitched his chair a little closer to the muzzle of my automatic.

"What are you after, then? Where do you come in on it?"

I tried the truth again.

"The second Mrs. Estep. She didn't kill her husband."

"You're trying to dig up enough dope to spring her?"

"Yes."

I waved him back as he tried to hitch his chair still nearer.

"How do you expect to do it?" he asked, his voice going lower and more confidential with each word.

I took still another flier at the truth.

"He wrote a letter before he died."

"Well?"

But I called a halt for the time.

"Just that," I said.

He leaned back in his chair, and his eyes and mouth grew small in thought again.

"What's your interest in the man who died last night?" he asked slowly.

"It's something on you," I said, truthfully again. "It doesn't do the second Mrs. Estep any direct good, maybe; but you and the first wife are stacked up together against her. Anything, therefore, that hurts you two will help her, somehow. I admit I'm wandering around in the dark; but I'm going ahead wherever I see a point of light—and I'll come through to daylight in the end. Nailing you for Boyd's murder is one point of light."

He leaned forward suddenly, his eyes and mouth popping open as far as they would go.

"You'll come out all right," he said very softly, "if you use a little judgment."

"What's that supposed to mean?"

"Do you think," he asked, still very softly, "that you can nail me for Boyd's murder—that you can convict me of murder?"

"I do."

But I wasn't any too sure. In the first place, though we were morally certain of it, neither Bob Teale nor I could swear that the man who had got in the machine with Ledwich was John Boyd.

We knew it was, of course, but the point is

that it had been too dark for us to see his face. And, again, in the dark, we had thought him alive; it wasn't until later that we knew he had been dead when he came down the steps.

Little things, those, but a private detective on the witness stand—unless he is absolutely sure of every detail—has an unpleasant and ineffectual time of it.

"I do," I repeated, thinking these things over, "and I'm satisfied to go to the bat with what I've got on you and what I can collect between now and the time you and your accomplice go to trial."

"Accomplice?" he said, not very surprised. "That would be Edna. I suppose you've already grabbed her?"

"Yes."

He laughed.

"You'll have one sweet time getting anything out of her. In the first place, she doesn't know much, and in the second—well, I suppose you've tried, and have found out what a helpful sort she is! So don't try the old gag of pretending that she has talked!"

"I'm not pretending anything."

Silence between us for a few seconds, and then—

"I'm going to make you a proposition," he said. "You can take it or leave it. The note Dr. Estep wrote before he died was to me, and it is positive proof that he committed suicide. Give me a chance to get away—just a chance—a half-hour start—and I'll give you my word of honor to send you the letter."

"I know I can trust you," I said sarcastically.

"I'll trust you, then!" he shot back at me. "I'll turn the note over to you if you'll give me your word that I'm to have half an hour's start."

"For what?" I demanded. "Why shouldn't I take both you and the note?"

"If you can get them! But do I look like the kind of sap who would leave the note where it would be found? Do you think it's here in the room maybe?"

I didn't, but neither did I think that because he had hidden it, it couldn't be found.

"I can't think of any reason why I should bargain with you," I told him. "I've got you cold, and that's enough."

"If I can show you that your only chance of freeing the second Mrs. Estep is through my voluntary assistance, will you bargain with me?"

"Maybe—I'll listen to your persuasion, anyway."

"All right," he said, "I'm going to come clean with you. But most of the things I'm going to tell you can't be proven in court without my help; and if you turn my offer down I'll have plenty of evidence to convince the jury that these things are all false, that I never said them, and that you are trying to frame me."

That part was plausible enough. I've testified before juries all the way from the City of Washington to the State of Washington, and I've never seen one yet that wasn't anxious to believe that a private detective is a double-crossing specialist who goes around with a cold deck in one pocket, a complete forger's outfit in another, and who counts that day lost in which he railroads no innocent to the hoosegow.

XI

"There was once a young doctor in a town a long way from here," Ledwich began. "He got mixed up in a scandal—a pretty rotten one—and escaped the pen only by the skin of his teeth. The state medical board revoked his license.

"In a large city not far away, this young doc, one night when he was drunk,—as he usually was in those days,—told his troubles to a man he had met in a dive. The friend was a resourceful sort; and he offered, for a price, to fix the doc up with a fake diploma, so he could set up in practice in some other state.

"The young doctor took him up, and the friend got the diploma for him. The doc was the man you know as Dr. Estep, and I was the friend. The real Dr. Estep was found dead in the park this morning!"

That was news—if true!

"You see," the big man went on, "when I offered to get the phoney diploma for the young doc—whose real name doesn't matter—I had in mind a forged one. Nowadays they're easy to get—there's a regular business in them,—but twenty-five years ago, while you could manage it, they were hard to get. While I was trying to get one, I ran across a woman I used to work with—Edna Fife. That's the woman you know as the first Mrs. Estep.

"Edna had married a doctor—the real Dr. Humbert Estep. He was a hell of a doctor, though; and after starving with him in Philadelphia for a couple of years, she made him close up his office, and she went back to the bunko game,[*] taking him with her. She was good at it, I'm telling you—a real cleaner[†]—and, keeping him under her thumb all the time, she made him a pretty good worker himself.

"It was shortly after that that I met her, and when she told me all this, I offered to buy her husband's medical diploma and other credentials. I don't know whether he wanted to sell them or not—but he did what she told him, and I got the papers.

"I turned them over to the young doc, who came to San Francisco and opened an office under the name of Humbert Estep. The real Esteps promised not to use that name any more—not much of an inconvenience for them, as they changed names every time they changed addresses.

"I kept in touch with the young doctor, of course, getting my regular rake-off from him. I had him by the neck, and I wasn't foolish enough to pass up any easy money. After a year or so, I learned that he had pulled himself together and was making good. So I jumped on a train and came to San Francisco. He was doing fine; so I camped here, where I could keep my eye on him and watch out for my own interests.

"He got married about then, and, between his practice and his investments, he began to

---

* swindle
† the one who takes all the money

accumulate a roll. But he tightened up on me—damn him! He wouldn't be bled. I got a regular percentage of what he made, and that was all.

"For nearly twenty-five years I got it—but not a nickel over the percentage. He knew I wouldn't kill the goose that laid the golden eggs, so no matter how much I threatened to expose him, he sat tight, and I couldn't budge him. I got my regular cut, and not a nickel more.

"That went along, as I say, for years. I was getting a living out of him, but I wan't getting any big money. A few months ago I learned that he had cleaned up heavily in a lumber deal so I made up my mind to take him for what he had.

"During all these years I had got to know the doc pretty well. You do when you're bleeding a man—you get a pretty fair idea of what goes on in his head, and what he's most likely to do if certain things should happen. So I knew the doc pretty well.

"I knew for instance, that he had never told his wife the truth about his past; that he had stalled her with some lie about being born in West Virginia. That was fine—for me! Then I knew that he kept a gun in his desk, and I knew why. It was kept there for the purpose of killing himself if the truth ever came out about his diploma. He figured that if, at the first hint of exposure, he wiped himself out, the authorities, out of respect for the good reputation he had built up, would hush things up.

"And his wife—even if she herself learned the truth—would be spared the shame of a public scandal. I can't see myself dying just to spare some woman's feeling, but the doc was a funny guy in some ways—and he was nutty about his wife.

"That's the way I had him figured out, and that's the way things turned out.

"My plan might sound complicated, but it was simple enough. I got hold of the real Estep—it took a lot of hunting, but I found them at last. I brought the woman to San Francisco, and told the man to stay away.

"Everything would have gone fine if he had

done what I told him; but he was afraid that Edna and I were going to double-cross him, so he came here to keep an eye on us. But I didn't know that until you put the finger on him for me.

"I brought Edna here and, without telling her any more than she had to know, drilled her until she was letter-perfect in her part.

"A couple days before she came I had gone to see the doc, and had demanded a hundred thousand cool smacks. He laughed at me, and I left, pretending to be as hot as hell.

"As soon as Edna arrived, I sent her to call on him. She asked him to perform an illegal operation on her daughter. He, of course, refused. Then she pleaded with him, loud enough for the nurse or whoever else was in the reception-room to hear. And when she raised her voice she was careful to stick to words that could be interpreted the way we wanted them to. She ran off her end to perfection, leaving in tears.

"Then I sprung my other trick! I had a fellow—a fellow who's a whiz at that kind of stuff—make me a plate: an imitation of newspaper printing. It was all worded like the real article, and said that the state authorities were investigating information that a prominent surgeon in San Francisco was practicing under a license secured by false credentials. This plate measured four and an eighth by six and three-quarter inches. If you'll look at the first inside page of the *Evening Times* any day in the week you'll see a photograph just that size.

"On the day after Edna's call, I bought a copy of the first edition of the *Times*—on the street at ten in the morning. I had this scratcher[*] friend of mine remove the photograph with acid, and print this fake article in its place.

"That evening I substituted a 'home edition' outer sheet for the one that had come with the paper we had cooked up, and made a switch as soon as the doc's newsboy made his delivery. There was nothing to that part of it. The kid just tossed the paper into the vestibule. It's simply

---

[*] forger

a case of duck into the doorway, trade papers, and go on, leaving the loaded one for the doc to read."

I was trying not to look too interested, but my ears were cocked for every word. At the start, I had been prepared for a string of lies. But I knew now that he was telling me the truth! Every syllable was a boast; he was half-drunk with appreciation of his own cleverness—the cleverness with which he had planned and carried out his program of treachery and murder.

I knew that he was telling the truth, and I suspected that he was telling more of it than he had intended. He was fairly bloated with vanity—the vanity that fills the crook almost invariably after a little success, and makes him ripe for the pen.

His eyes glistened, and his little mouth smiled triumphantly around the words that continued to roll out of it.

"The doc read the paper, all right—and shot himself. But first he wrote and mailed a note—to me. I didn't figure on his wife's being accused of killing him. That was plain luck.

"I figured that the fake piece in the paper would be overlooked in the excitement. Edna would then go forward, claiming to be his first wife; and his shooting himself after her first call, with what the nurse had overheard, would make his death seem a confession that Edna *was* his wife.

"I was sure that she would stand up under any sort of an investigation. Nobody knew anything about the doc's real past; except what he had told them, which would be found false.

"Edna had really married a Dr. Humbert Estep in Philadelphia in '96; and the twenty-seven years that had passed since then would do a lot to hide the fact that that Dr. Humbert Estep wasn't this Dr. Humbert Estep.

"All I wanted to do was convince the doc's real wife and her lawyers that she wasn't really his wife at all. And we did that! Everybody took it for granted that Edna was the legal wife.

"The next play would have been for Edna and the real wife to have reached some sort of an agreement about the estate, whereby Edna would have got the bulk—or at least half—of it; and nothing would have been made public.

"If worst came to worst, we were prepared to go to court. We were sitting pretty! But I'd have been satisfied with half the estate. It would have come to a few hundred thousand at the least, and that would have been plenty for me—even deducting the twenty thousand I had promised Edna.

"But when the police grabbed the doc's wife and charged her with his murder, I saw my way into the whole roll. All I had to do was sit tight and wait until they convicted her. Then the court would turn the entire pile over to Edna.

"I had the only evidence that would free the doc's wife: the note he had written me. But I couldn't—even if I had wanted to—have turned it in without exposing my hand. When he read that fake piece in the paper, he tore it out, wrote his message to me across the face of it, and sent it to me. So the note is a dead give-away. However, I didn't have any intention of publishing it, anyhow.

"Up to this point everything had gone like a dream. All I had to do was wait until it was time to cash in on my brains. And that's the time that the real Humbert Estep picked out to mess up the works.

"He shaved his mustache off, put on some old clothes, and came snooping around to see that Edna and I didn't run out on him. As if he could have stopped us! After you put the finger on him for me, I brought him up here.

"I intended salving him along until I could find a place to keep him until all the cards had been played. That's what I was going to hire you for—to take care of him.

"But we got to talking, and wrangling, and I had to knock him down. He didn't get up, and I found that he was dead. His neck was broken. There was nothing to do but take him out to the park and leave him.

"I didn't tell Edna. She didn't have a lot of use for him, as far as I could see, but you can't tell how women will take things. Anyhow, she'll stick, now that it's done. She's on the up and up all the time. And if she should talk, she can't do a lot of damage. She only knows her own part of the lay.

"All this long-winded story is so you'll know just exactly what you're up against. Maybe you think you can dig up the proof of these things I have told you. You can this far. You can prove that Edna wasn't the doc's wife. You can prove that I've been blackmailing him. But you can't prove that the doc's wife didn't *believe* that Edna was his real wife! It's her word against Edna's and mine.

"We'll swear that we had convinced her of it, which will give her a motive. You can't prove that the phoney news article I told you about ever existed. It'll sound like a hop-head's dream to a jury.

"You can't tie last night's murder on me— I've got an alibi that will knock your hat off! I can prove that I left here with a friend of mine who was drunk, and that I took him to his hotel and put him to bed, with the help of a night clerk and a bellboy. And what have you got against that? The word of two private detectives. Who'll believe you?

"You can convict me of conspiracy to defraud, or something—maybe. But, regardless of that, you can't free Mrs. Estep without my help.

"Turn me loose and I'll give you the letter the doc wrote me. It's the goods, right enough! In his own handwriting, written across the face of the fake newspaper story—which ought to fit the torn place in the paper that the police are supposed to be holding—and he wrote that he was going to kill himself, in words almost that plain."

That would turn the trick—there was no doubt of it. And I believed Ledwich's story. The more I thought it over the better I liked it. It fit into the facts everywhere. But I wasn't enthusiastic about giving this big crook his liberty.

"Don't make me laugh!" I said. "I'm going to put you away and free Mrs. Estep—both."

"Go ahead and try it! You're up against it without the letter; and you don't think a man with brains enough to plan a job like this one would be foolish enough to leave the note where it could be found, do you?"

I wasn't especially impressed with the difficulty of convicting this Ledwich and freeing the dead man's widow. His scheme—that cold-blooded zigzag of treachery for everybody he had dealt with, including his latest accomplice, Edna Estep—wasn't as airtight as he thought it. A week in which to run out a few lines in the East, and— But a week was just what I didn't have!

Vance Richmond's words were running through my head: "But another day of imprisonment—two days, or perhaps even two hours—and she won't need anybody to clear her. Death will have done it!"

If I was going to do Mrs. Estep any good, I had to move quick. Law or no law, her life was in my fat hands. This man before me—his eyes bright and hopeful now and his mouth anxiously pursed—was thief, blackmailer, double-crosser, and at least twice a murderer. I hated to let him walk out. But there was the woman dying in a hospital. . . .

XII

Keeping my eye on Ledwich, I went to the telephone, and got Vance Richmond on the wire at his residence.

"How is Mrs. Estep?" I asked.

"Weaker! I talked with the doctor half an hour ago, and he says—"

I cut in on him; I didn't want to listen to the details.

"Get over to the hospital, and be where I can reach you by phone. I may have news for you before the night is over."

"What—Is there a chance? Are you—"

I didn't promise him anything. I hung up the receiver and spoke to Ledwich. "I'll do this much for you. Slip me the note, and I'll give you your gun and put you out the back door. There's a bull on the corner out front, and I can't take you past him."

He was on his feet, beaming.

"Your word on it?" he demanded.

"Yes—get going!"

He went past me to the phone, gave a number (which I made a note of), and then spoke hurriedly into the instrument.

"This is Shuler. Put a boy in a taxi with that envelope I gave you to hold for me, and send him out here right away."

He gave his address, said "Yes" twice and hung up.

There was nothing surprising about his unquestioning acceptance of my word. He couldn't afford to doubt that I'd play fair with him. And, also, all successful bunko men come in time to believe that the world—except for themselves—is populated by a race of human sheep who may be trusted to conduct themselves with true sheep-like docility.

Ten minutes later the door-bell rang. We answered it together, and Ledwich took a large envelope from a messenger boy, while I memorized the number on the boy's cap. Then we went back to the front room.

Ledwich slit the envelope and passed its contents to me: a piece of rough-torn newspaper. Across the face of the fake article he had told me about was written a message in a jerky hand.

I wouldn't have suspected you, Ledwich, of such profound stupidity. My last thought will be—this bullet that ends my life also ends your years of leisure. You'll have to go to work now.

ESTEP.

The doctor had died game!

I took the envelope from the big man, put the death note in it, and put them in my pocket. Then I went to a front window, flattening a cheek against the glass until I could see O'Gar, dimly outlined in the night, patiently standing where I had left him hours before.

"The city dick is still on the corner," I told Ledwich. "Here's your gat"*—holding out the gun I had shot from his fingers a little while back—"take it, and blow through the back door. Remember, that's all I'm offering you—the gun and a fair start. If you play square with me, I'll not do anything to help find you—unless I have to keep myself in the clear."

"Fair enough!"

He grabbed the gun, broke it to see that it was still loaded, and wheeled toward the rear of the flat. At the door he pulled up, hesitated, and faced me again. I kept him covered with my automatic.

"Will you do me one favor I didn't put in the bargain?" he asked.

"What is it?"

"That note of the doc's is in an envelope with my handwriting and maybe my fingerprints on it. Let me put it in a fresh envelope, will you? I don't want to leave any broader trail behind than I have to."

With my left hand—my right being busy with the gun—I fumbled for the envelope and tossed it to him. He took a plain envelope from the table, wiped it carefully with his handkerchief, put the note in it, taking care not to touch it with the balls of his fingers, and passed it back to me; and I put it in my pocket.

I had a hard time to keep from grinning in his face.

That fumbling with the handkerchief told me that the envelope in my pocket was empty, that the death-note was in Ledwich's possession—though I hadn't seen it pass there. He had worked one of his bunko tricks upon me.

"Beat it!" I snapped, to keep from laughing in his face.

He spun on his heel. His feet pounded against the floor. A door slammed in the rear.

I tore into the envelope he had given me. I needed to be sure he had double-crossed me.

The envelope was empty.

Our agreement was wiped out.

I sprang to the front window, threw it

_____

* gun

wide open, and leaned out. O'Gar saw me immediately—clearer than I could see him. I swung my arm in a wide gesture toward the rear of the house. O'Gar set out for the alley on the run. I dashed back through Ledwich's flat to the kitchen, and stuck my head out of an already open window.

I could see Ledwich against the white-washed fence—throwing the back gate open, plunging through it into the alley.

O'Gar's squat bulk appeared under a light at the end of the alley.

Ledwich's revolver was in his hand. O'Gar's wasn't—not quite.

Ledwich's gun swung up—the hammer clicked.

O'Gar's gun coughed fire.

Ledwich fell with a slow revolving motion over against the white fence, gasped once or twice, and went down in a pile.

I walked slowly down the stairs to join O'Gar; slowly, because it isn't a nice thing to look at a man you've deliberately sent to his death. Not even if it's the surest way of saving an innocent life, and if the man who dies is a Jake Ledwich—altogether treacherous.

"Howcome?" O'Gar asked, when I came into the alley, where he stood looking down at the dead man.

"He got out on me," I said simply.

"He must've."

I stooped and searched the dead man's pockets until I found the suicide note, still crumpled in the handkerchief. O'Gar was examining the dead man's revolver.

"Lookit!" he exclaimed. "Maybe this ain't my lucky day! He snapped at me once, and his gun missed fire. No wonder! Somebody must've been using an ax on it—the firing pin's broke clean off!"

"Is that so?" I asked; just as if I hadn't discovered, when I first picked the revolver up, that the bullet which had knocked it out of Ledwich's hand had made it harmless.

BLACK MASK, MARCH 1, 1924

FROM THE AUTHOR OF "ZIGZAGS OF TREACHERY"

I'll have another story riding your way in a day or two; one for the customers who don't like their sleuths to do too much brain-work.

The four rules for shadowing that I gave in "Zigzags" are the first and last words on the subject. There are no other tricks to learn. Follow them, and, once you get the hang of it, shadowing is the easiest of detective work, except, perhaps, to an extremely nervous man. You simply saunter along somewhere within sight of your subject; and, barring bad breaks, the only thing that can make you lose him is over-anxiety on your own part.

Even a clever criminal may be shadowed for weeks without suspecting it. I know one operative who shadowed a forger—a wily old hand—for more than three months without arousing his suspicion. I myself trailed one for six weeks, riding trains and making half a dozen small towns with him; and I'm not exactly inconspicuous—standing an inch or so over six feet.

Another thing: a detective may shadow a man for days and in the end have but the haziest idea of the man's features. Tricks of carriage, ways of wearing clothes, general outline, individual mannerisms—all as seen from the rear—are much more important to the shadow than faces. They can be recognized at a greater distance, and do not necessitate getting in front of his subject at any time.

Back—and it's only a couple years back—in the days before I decided that there was more fun in writing about manhunting than in that hunting, I wasn't especially fond of shadowing, though I had plenty of it to do. But I worked under one superintendent who needed only the flimsiest of excuses to desert his desk and get out on the street behind some suspect.

Sincerely,
DASHIELL HAMMETT
San Francisco, Cal.

BLACK MASK, APRIL 1, 1924

One Hour

BY DASHIELL HAMMETT

(Author of "The Tenth Clew")

Like all of Mr. Hammett's detective stories, this tale starts with a very ordinary police case, and just as you think you have it all figured out, it takes several unexpected turns and ends up with a bang.

CHAPTER I

"THIS IS MR. CHROSTWAITE," Vance Richmond said.

Chrostwaite, wedged between the arms of one of the attorney's large chairs, grunted what was perhaps meant for an acknowledgment of the introduction. I grunted back at him, and found myself a chair.

He was a big balloon of a man—this Chrostwaite—in a green plaid suit that didn't make him look any smaller than he was. His tie was a gaudy thing, mostly of yellow, with a big diamond set in the center of it, and there were more stones on his pudgy hands. Spongy fat blurred his features, making it impossible for his round purplish face to ever hold any other expression than the discontented hoggishness that was habitual to it. He reeked of gin.

"Mr. Chrostwaite is the Pacific Coast agent for the Mutual Fire Extinguisher Manufacturing Company," Vance Richmond began, as soon as I had got myself seated. "His office is on Kearny Street, near California. Yesterday, at about two-forty-five in the afternoon, he went to his office, leaving his machine—a Hudson touring car—standing in front, with the engine running. Ten minutes later, he came out. The car was gone."

I looked at Chrostwaite. He was looking at his fat knees, showing not the least interest in what his attorney was saying. I looked quickly back at Vance Richmond; his clean gray face and lean figure were downright beautiful beside his bloated client.

"A man named Newhouse," the lawyer was saying, "who was the proprietor of a printing establishment on California Street, just around the corner from Mr. Chrostwaite's office, was run down and killed by Mr. Chrostwaite's car at the corner of Clay and Kearny Streets, five minutes after Mr. Chrostwaite had left the car to go into his office. The police found the car shortly afterward, only a block away from the scene of the accident—on Montgomery near Clay.

"The thing is fairly obvious. Some one stole the car immediately after Mr. Chrostwaite left it; and in driving rapidly away, ran down Newhouse; and then, in fright, abandoned the car. But here is Mr. Chrostwaite's position; three nights ago, while driving perhaps a little recklessly out—"

"Drunk," Chrostwaite said, not looking up from his plaid knees; and though his voice was hoarse, husky—it was the hoarseness of a whisky-burnt throat—there was no emotion in his voice.

"While driving perhaps a little recklessly out Van Ness Avenue," Vance Richmond went on, ignoring the interruption, "Mr. Chrostwaite knocked a pedestrian down. The man wasn't badly hurt, and he is being compensated very generously for his injuries. But we are to appear in court next Monday to face a charge of reckless driving, and I am afraid that this accident of yesterday, in which the printer was killed, may hurt us.

"No one thinks that Mr. Chrostwaite was in his car when it killed the printer—we have a world of evidence that he wasn't. But I am afraid that the printer's death may be made a weapon against us when we appear on the Van Ness Avenue charge. Being an attorney, I know just how much capital the prosecuting attorney—if he so chooses—can make out of the really insignificant fact that the same car that knocked down the man on Van Ness Avenue killed another man yesterday. And, being an attorney, I know how likely the prosecuting attorney is to so choose. And he can handle it in such a way that we will be given little or no opportunity to tell our side.

"The worst that can happen, of course, is that, instead of the usual fine, Mr. Chrostwaite will be sent to the city jail for thirty or sixty days. That is bad enough, however, and that is what we wish to—"

Chrostwaite spoke again, still regarding his knees.

"Damned nuisance!" he said.

"That is what we wish to avoid," the attorney continued. "We are willing to pay a stiff fine, and expect to, for the accident on Van Ness Avenue was clearly Mr. Chrostwaite's fault. But we—"

"Drunk as a lord!" Chrostwaite said.

"But we don't want to have this other accident, with which we had nothing to do, given a false weight in connection with the slighter accident. What we want, then, is to find the man or men who stole the car and ran down John Newhouse. If they are apprehended before we go to court, we won't be in danger of suffering for their act. Think you can find them before Monday?"

"I'll try," I promised; "though it isn't—"

The human balloon interrupted me by heaving himself to his feet, fumbling with his fat jeweled fingers for his watch.

"Three o'clock," he said. "Got a game of golf for three-thirty." He picked up his hat and gloves from the desk. "Find 'em, will you? Damned nuisance going to jail!"

And he waddled out.

CHAPTER II

From the attorney's office, I went down to the Hall of Justice, and, after hunting around a few minutes, found a policeman who had arrived at the corner of Clay and Kearny Streets a few seconds after Newhouse had been knocked down.

"I was just leaving the Hall when I seen a bus scoot around the corner at Clay Street," this patrolman—a big sandy-haired man named

Coffee—told me. "Then I seen people gathering around, so I went up there and found this John Newhouse stretched out. He was already dead. Half a dozen people had seen him hit, and one of 'em had got the license number of the car that done it. We found the car standing empty just around the corner on Montgomery Street, pointing north. They was two fellows in the car when it hit Newhouse, but nobody saw what they looked like. Nobody was in it when we found it."

"In what direction was Newhouse walking?"

"North along Kearny Street, and he was about three-quarters across Clay when he was knocked. The car was coming north on Kearny, too, and turned east on Clay. It mightn't have been all the fault of the fellows in the car—according to them that seen the accident. Newhouse was walking across the street looking at a piece of paper in his hand. I found a piece of foreign money—paper money—in his hand, and I guess that's what he was looking at. The lieutenant tells me it was Dutch money—a hundred-florin note, he says."

"Found out anything about the men in the car?"

"Nothing! We lined up everybody we could find in the neighborhood of California and Kearny Streets—where the car was stolen from—and around Clay and Montgomery Streets—where it was left at. But nobody remembered seeing the fellows getting in it or getting out of it. The man that owns the car wasn't driving it—it was stole all right, I guess. At first I thought maybe they was something shady about the accident. This John Newhouse had a two- or three-day-old black eye on him. But we run that out and found that he had a attack of heart trouble or something a couple days ago, and fell, fetching his eye up against a chair. He'd been home sick for three days—just left his house half an hour or so before the accident."

"Where'd he live?"

"On Sacramento Street—way out. I got his address here somewhere."

He turned over the pages of a grimy memo-randa book, and I got the dead man's house number, and the names and addresses of the witnesses to the accident that Coffee had questioned.

That exhausted the policeman's information, so I left him.

CHAPTER III

My next play was to canvass the vicinity of where the car had been stolen and where it had been deserted, and then interview the witnesses. The fact that the police had fruitlessly gone over this ground made it unlikely that I would find anything of value; but I couldn't skip these things on that account. Ninety-nine per cent of detective work is a patient collecting of details—and your details must be got as nearly first-hand as possible, regardless of who else has worked the territory before you.

Before starting on this angle, however, I decided to run around to the dead man's printing establishment—only three blocks from the Hall of Justice—and see if any of his employees had heard anything that might help me.

Newhouse's establishment occupied the ground floor of a small building on California, between Kearny and Montgomery. A small office was partitioned off in front, with a connecting doorway leading to the press-room in the rear.

The only occupant of the small office, when I came in from the street, was a short, stocky, worried-looking blond man of forty or thereabouts, who sat at the desk in his shirt-sleeves, checking off figures in a ledger, against others on a batch of papers before him.

I introduced myself, telling him that I was a Continental Detective Agency operative, interested in Newhouse's death. He told me his name was Ben Soules, and that he was Newhouse's foreman. We shook hands, and then he waved me to a chair across the desk; pushed back the papers and book upon which he had been working, and scratched his head disgustedly with the pencil in his hand.

"This is awful!" he said. "What with one thing and another, we're heels over head in work, and I got to fool with these books that I don't know anything at all about, and—"

He broke off to pick up the telephone, which had jingled.

"Yes. . . . This is Soules. . . . We're working on them now . . . I'll give 'em to you by Monday noon at the least. . . . I know we promised them for yesterday, but . . . I know! I know! But the boss's death set us back. Explain that to Mr. Chrostwaite. And . . . And I'll promise you that we'll give them to you Monday morning, sure!"

Soules slapped the receiver irritably on its hook and looked at me.

"You'd think that since it was his own car that killed the boss, he'd have decency enough not to squawk over the delay!"

"Chrostwaite?"

"Yes—that was one of his clerks. We're printing some leaflets for him—promised to have 'em ready yesterday—but between the boss's death and having a couple new hands to break in, we're behind with everything. I been here eight years, and this is the first time we ever fell down on an order—and every damned customer is yelling his head off. If we were like most printers they'd be used to waiting; but we've been too good to them. But this Chrostwaite! You'd think he'd have some decency, seeing that his car killed the boss!"

I nodded sympathetically, slid a cigar across the desk, and waited until it was burning in Soules' mouth before I asked:

"You said something about having a couple new hands to break in. How come?"

"Yes. Mr. Newhouse fired two of our printers last week—Fincher and Key. He found that they belonged to the I. W. W., so he gave them their time."

"Any trouble with them, or anything against them except that they were Wobblies?"

"No—they were pretty good workers."

"Any trouble with them after he fired them?" I asked.

"No real trouble, though they were pretty hot. They made red speeches all over the place before they left."

"Remember what day that was?"

"Wednesday of last week, I think. Yes, Wednesday, because I hired two new men on Thursday."

"How many men do you work?"

"Three, besides myself."

"Was Mr. Newhouse sick very often?"

"Not sick enough to stay away very often, though every now and then his heart would go back on him, and he'd have to stay in bed for a week or ten days. He wasn't what you could call real well at any time. He never did anything but the office work—I run the shop."

"When was he taken sick this last time?"

"Mrs. Newhouse called up Tuesday morning and said he had had another spell, and wouldn't be down for a few days. He came in yesterday—which was Thursday—for about ten minutes in the afternoon, and said he would be back on the job this morning. He was killed just after he left."

"How did he look—very sick?"

"Not so bad. He never looked well, of course, but I couldn't see much difference from usual yesterday. This last spell hadn't been as bad as most, I reckon—he was usually laid up for a week or more."

"Did he say where he was going when he left? The reason I ask is that, living out on Sacramento Street, he would naturally have taken a car at that street if he had been going home, whereas he was run down on Clay Street."

"He said he was going up to Portsmouth Square to sit in the sun for half an hour or so. He had been cooped up indoors for two or three days, he said, and he wanted some sunshine before he went back home."

"He had a piece of foreign money in his hand when he was hit. Know anything about it?"

"Yes. He got it here. One of our customers—a man named Van Pelt—came in to pay for some work we had done yesterday afternoon while the boss was here. When Van Pelt pulled out his wallet to pay his bill, this piece of Holland money—I don't know what you call it—was among the bills. I think he said it was worth something like thirty-eight dollars. Anyway, the boss took it, giving Van Pelt his change. The boss said he wanted to show the Holland money to his boys—and he could have it changed back into American money later."

"Who is this Van Pelt?"

"He's a Hollander—is planning to open a tobacco importing business here in a month or two. I don't know much about him outside of that."

"Where's his home, or office?"

"His office is on Bush Street, near Sansome."

"Did he know that Newhouse had been sick?"

"I don't think so. The boss didn't look much different from usual."

"What's this Van Pelt's full name?"

"Hendrik Van Pelt."

"What does he look like?"

Before Soules could answer, three evenly spaced buzzes sounded above the rattle and whirring of the presses in the back of the shop.

I slid the muzzle of my gun—I had been holding it in my lap for five minutes—far enough over the edge of the desk for Ben Soules to see it.

"Put both of your hands on top of the desk," I said.

He put them there.

The press-room door was directly behind him, so that, facing him across the desk, I could look over his shoulder at it. His stocky body served to screen my gun from the view of whoever came through the door, in response to Soules' signal.

I didn't have long to wait.

Three men—black with ink—came to the door, and through it into the little office. They strolled in careless and casual, laughing and joking to one another.

But one of them licked his lips as he stepped through the door. Another's eyes showed white circles all around the irises. The third was the best actor—but he held his shoulders a trifle too stiffly to fit his otherwise careless carriage.

"Stop right there!" I barked at them when the last one was inside the office—and I brought my gun up where they could see it.

They stopped as if they had all been mounted on the same pair of legs.

I kicked my chair back, and stood up.

I didn't like my position at all. The office was entirely too small for me. I had a gun, true enough, and whatever weapons may have been distributed among these other men were out of sight. But these four men were too close to me; and a gun isn't a thing of miracles. It's a mechanical contraption that is capable of just so much and no more.

If these men decided to jump me, I could down just one of them before the other three were upon me. I knew it, and they knew it.

"Put your hands up," I ordered, "and turn around!"

None of them moved to obey. One of the inked men grinned wickedly; Soules shook his head slowly; the other two stood and looked at me.

I was more or less stumped. You can't shoot a man just because he refuses to obey an order—even if he is a criminal. If they had turned around for me, I could have lined them up against the wall, and, being behind them, have held them safe while I used the telephone.

But that hadn't worked.

My next thought was to back across the office to the street door, keeping them covered, and then either stand in the door and yell for help, or take them into the street, where I could handle them. But I put that thought away as quickly as it came to me.

These four men were going to jump me—there was no doubt of that. All that was needed was a spark of any sort to explode them into action. They were standing stiff-legged and tense, waiting for some move on my part. If I took a step backward—the battle would be on.

We were close enough for any of the four to have reached out and touched me. One of them I could shoot before I was smothered—one out of four. That meant that each of them had only one chance out of four of being the victim—low enough odds for any but the most cowardly of men.

I grinned what was supposed to be a confident grin—because I was up against it hard—and reached for the telephone: I had to do something! Then I cursed myself! I had merely changed the signal for the onslaught. It would come now when I picked up the receiver.

But I couldn't back down again—that, too, would be a signal—I had to go through with it.

The perspiration trickled across my temples from under my hat as I drew the phone closer with my left hand.

The street door opened! An exclamation of surprise came from behind me.

I spoke rapidly, without taking my eyes from the four men in front of me.

"Quick! The phone! The police!"

With the arrival of this unknown person—one of Newhouse's customers, probably—I figured I had the edge again. Even if he took no active part beyond calling the police in, the enemy would have to split to take care of him—and that would give me a chance to pot at least two of them before I was knocked over. Two out of four—each of them had an even chance of being dropped—which *is* enough to give even a nervy man cause for thinking a bit before he jumps.

"Hurry!" I urged the newcomer.

"Yes! Yes!" he said—and in the blurred sound of the "s" there was evidence of foreign birth.

Keyed up as I was, I didn't need any more warning than that.

I threw myself sidewise—a blind tumbling away from the spot where I stood. But I wasn't quite quick enough.

The blow that came from behind didn't hit me fairly, but I got enough of it to fold up my legs as if the knees were hinged with paper—and I slammed into a heap on the floor. . . .

Something dark crashed toward me. I caught it with both hands. It may have been a foot kicking at my face. I wrung it as a washerwoman wrings a towel.

Down my spine ran jar after jar. Perhaps somebody was beating me over the head. I don't know. My head wasn't alive. The blow that had knocked me down had numbed me all over. My eyes were no good. Shadows swam to and fro in front of them—that was all. I struck, gouged, tore at the shadows. Sometimes I found nothing. Sometimes I found things that felt like parts of bodies. Then I would hammer at them, tear at them. My gun was gone.

My hearing was no better than my sight—or not so good. There wasn't a sound in the world. I moved in a silence that was more complete than any silence I had ever known. I was a ghost fighting ghosts.

I found presently that my feet were under me again, though some squirming thing was on my back, and kept me from standing upright. A hot, damp thing like a hand was across my face.

I put my teeth into it. I snapped my head back as far as it would go. Maybe it smashed into the face it was meant for. I don't know. Anyhow the squirming thing was no longer on my back.

Dimly I realized that I was being buffeted about by blows that I was too numb to feel. Ceaselessly, with head and shoulders and elbows and fists and knees and feet, I struck at the shadows that were around me. . . .

Suddenly I could see again—not clearly—but the shadows were taking on colors; and my ears came back a little, so that grunts and growls and curses and the impact of blows sounded in them. My straining gaze rested upon a brass cuspidor six inches or so in front of my eyes. I knew then that I was down on the floor again.

As I twisted about to hurl a foot into a soft body above me, something that was like a burn, but wasn't a burn, ran down one leg—a knife. The sting of it brought consciousness back into me with a rush.

I grabbed the brass cuspidor and used it to club a way to my feet—to club a clear space in front of me. Men were hurling themselves upon me. I swung the cuspidor high and flung it over their heads, through the frosted glass door into California Street.

Then we fought some more.

But you can't throw a brass cuspidor through a glass door into California Street between Montgomery and Kearny without attracting attention—it's too near the heart of daytime San Francisco. So presently—when I was on the floor again with six or eight hundred pounds of flesh hammering my face into the boards—we were pulled apart, and I was dug out of the bottom of the pile by a squad of policemen.

Big sandy-haired Coffee was one of them, but it took a lot of arguing to convince him that I was the Continental operative who had talked to him a little while before.

"Man! Man!" he said, when I finally convinced him. "Them lads sure—God! have worked you over! You got a face on you like a wet geranium!"

I didn't laugh. It wasn't funny.

I looked out of the one eye, which was working just now, at the five men lined up across the office—Soules, the three inky printers, and the man with the blurred "s," who had started the slaughter by tapping me on the back of the head.

He was a rather tall man of thirty or so, with a round ruddy face that wore a few bruises now. He had been, apparently, rather well-dressed in expensive black clothing, but he was torn and ragged now. I knew who he was without asking—Hendrik Van Pelt.

"Well, man, what's the answer?" Coffee was asking me.

By holding one side of my jaw firmly with one hand I found that I could talk without too much pain.

"This is the crowd that ran down Newhouse," I said, "and it wasn't an accident. I wouldn't mind having a few more of the details myself, but I was jumped before I got around to all of them. Newhouse had a hundred-florin note in his hand when he was run down, and he was walking in the direction of police headquarters—was only half a block away from the Hall of Justice.

"Soules tells me that Newhouse said he was going up to Portsmouth Square to sit in the sun. But Soules didn't seem to know that Newhouse was wearing a black eye—the one you told me you had investigated. If Soules didn't see the shiner, then it's a good bet that Soules didn't see Newhouse's face that day!

"Newhouse was walking from his printing shop toward police headquarters with a piece of foreign paper money in his hand—remember that!

"He had frequent spells of sickness, which, according to friend Soules, always before kept him at home for a week or ten days at a time. This time he was laid up for only two and a half days.

"Soules tells me that the shop is three days behind with its orders, and he says that's the first time in eight years they've ever been behind. He blames Newhouse's death—which only happened yesterday. Apparently, Newhouse's previous sick spells never delayed things—why should this last spell?

"Two printers were fired last week, and two new ones hired the very next day—pretty quick work. The car with which Newhouse was run down was taken from just around the corner, and was deserted within quick walking distance of the shop. It was left facing north, which is pretty good evidence that its occupants went south after they got out. Ordinary car thieves wouldn't have circled back in the direction from which they came.

"Here's my guess: This Van Pelt is a Dutchman, and he had some plates for phoney hundred-florin notes. He hunted around until he found a printer who would go in with him. He found Soules, the foreman of a shop whose proprietor was now and then at home for a week or more at a time with a bad heart. One of the printers under Soules was willing to go in with them. Maybe the other two turned the offer down. Maybe Soules didn't ask them at all. Anyhow, they were discharged, and two friends of Soules were given their places.

"Our friends then got everything ready, and waited for Newhouse's heart to flop again. It did—Monday night. As soon as his wife called up next morning and said he was sick, these birds started running off their counterfeits. That's why they fell behind with their regular work. But this spell of Newhouse's was lighter than usual. He was up and moving around within two days, and yesterday afternoon he came down here for a few minutes.

"He must have walked in while all of our friends were extremely busy in some far corner. He must have spotted some of the phoney money, immediately sized up the situation, grabbed one bill to show the police, and started out for police headquarters—no doubt thinking he had not been seen by our friends here.

"They must have got a glimpse of him as he was leaving, however. Two of them followed him out. They couldn't, afoot, safely knock him over within a block or two of the Hall of Justice. But, turning the corner, they found Chrostwaite's car standing there with idling engine. That solved their getaway problem. They got in the car and went on after Newhouse. I suppose the original plan was to shoot him—but he crossed Clay Street with his eyes fastened upon the phoney money in his hand. That gave them a golden chance. They piled the car into him. It was sure death, they knew—his bum heart would finish the job if the actual collision didn't kill him. Then they deserted the car and came back here.

"There are a lot of loose ends to be gathered in—but this pipe-dream I've just told you fits in with all the facts we know—and I'll bet a month's salary I'm not far off anywhere. There ought to be a three-day crop of Dutch notes cached somewhere! You people—"

I suppose I'd have gone on talking forever—in the giddy, head-swimming intoxication of utter exhaustion that filled me—if the big sandy-haired patrolman hadn't shut me off by putting a big hand across my mouth.

"Be quiet, man," he said, lifting me out of the chair, and spreading me flat on my back on the desk. "I'll have an ambulance here in a second for you."

The office was swirling around in front of my one open eye—the yellow ceiling swung down toward me, rose again, disappeared, came back in odd shapes. I turned my head to one side to avoid it, and my glance rested upon the white dial of a spinning clock.

Presently the dial came to rest, and I read it—four o'clock.

I remembered that Chrostwaite had broken up our conference in Vance Richmond's office at three, and I had started to work.

"One full hour!" I tried to tell Coffee before I went to sleep.

The police wound up the job while I was lying on my back in bed. In Van Pelt's office on Bush Street they found a great bale of hundred-florin notes. Van Pelt, they learned, had considerable reputation in Europe as a high-class counterfeiter. One of the printers came through, stating that Van Pelt and Soules were the two who followed Newhouse out of the shop, and killed him.

THE CODY YEARS

Introduction

THE CODY YEARS: 1924–1926

THE CHARACTER OF *Black Mask* and of Hammett's fiction changed abruptly when Philip C. Cody, described by H. L. Mencken as "a mild and pleasant fellow who was almost stone deaf," succeeded Sutton as editor. Cody was spread as thinly as his predecessor with regard to his editorial duties. He was vice president and general manager of Warner Publications, a growing concern that included *Field and Stream*, *Black Mask*, and other pulps, as well as a short-lived book club started in 1925. Cody had doubled as circulation manager of *Black Mask*, and he brought to the editor's chair a sense of marketing that Sutton lacked. Cody transformed *Black Mask* into a magazine that offered increased emphasis on action-packed crime fiction, enlivened by violence and punctuated with sexual titillation. He nurtured a small stable of favorite writers and encouraged them to write stories of substantial length.

The effect on Hammett was immediately clear. His stories more than doubled in length after "One Hour," a story that the editors of this collection assume to have been accepted by Sutton though it was published in the April 1, 1924, *Black Mask*, the first that carried Cody's name as editor. With two exceptions ("The Tenth Clew" at 11,419 words and "Zigzags of Treachery" at 14,521 words), Hammett's Op stories for Sutton averaged just under 6,000 words apiece. The ten Op stories published by Cody between April 1924 and March 1926 averaged about 14,000 words each. And the Op got meaner. During the course of the nine Op stories written for Sutton, the Op usually didn't carry a gun, and he was not directly involved in any lethal activity. Hammett's first story for Cody features six murders, three of which are committed with cause by the Op. During the rest of Cody's tenure, Hammett's stories average some six dead bodies each. The Op was turning blood simple. The plots become more complicated; the women more seductive and dangerous; the crooks more professional. Dramatic confrontation rather than simple description increasingly served to advance the plot. Notably in "The Girl with the Silver Eyes" (June 1924), the first of a handful of stories in which the Op struggles to overcome a dangerous attraction to a beautiful woman, Hammett's Op begins to reveal his emotions. And Hammett's settings began to exhibit an international flair, as in "The Golden

Horseshoe" (November 1924), "The Gutting of Couffignal" (December 1925), and "The Creeping Siamese" (March 1926).

Cody may have been the boss, but his vision was implemented by associate editor Harry C. North, who had served under Sutton, as well. North seems to have conducted an extensive editorial correspondence with his authors, and he minced no words in expressing his editorial opinion. Cody unleashed him. The communications with Hammett are lost, but North's style can be gleaned from his letters to Erle Stanley Gardner, who published more than one hundred stories in *Black Mask* between 1924 and 1943. That correspondence reveals North to be a man with a sharp editorial eye and firm opinions. His entire reply to an early submission by Gardner was "This stinks." His editorial principle was also simply stated. He advised Gardner: "If you could once appreciate the fact that the publisher of Black Mask is printing the magazine to make money and nothing else, perhaps you would be more nearly able to guess our needs."

Cody wasted no time asserting his authority, but he let North do the dirty work of rejecting two of Hammett's stories. The rejection must have taken place almost immediately after Cody took control, but the account of it did not appear until August 1924, four months after Cody's ascension, when he published Hammett's response to Harry North's rejection letter under the headline "Our Own Short Story Course":

We recently were obliged to reject two of Mr. Hammett's detective stories. We didn't like to do it, for Mr. Hammett and his Continental Detective Agency had become more or less fixtures in BLACK MASK. But in our opinion, the stories were not up to the standard of Mr. Hammett's own work—so they had to go back.

In returning the manuscripts, we enclosed the "Tragedy in One Act," referred to in the letter which follows. The "Tragedy" was simply a verbatim report of the discussion in this office, which led to the rejection of the stories.

We are printing Mr. Hammett's letter below; first, to show the difference between a good author and a poor one; and secondly, as a primary course in short story writing. We believe that authors—especially young authors, and also old authors who have fallen into the rut—can learn more about successful writing from the hundred or so words following, than they can possibly learn from several volumes of so-called short story instruction. Mr. Hammett has gone straight to the heart of the whole subject of writing—or of painting, singing, acting . . . or of just living for that matter. As the advertising gentry would say, here is the "Secret" of success.

I don't like that "tragedy in one act" at all; it's too damned true-to-life. The theatre, to amuse me, must be a bit artificial.

I don't think I shall send "Women, Politics, and Murder" back to you—not in time for the July issue anyway. The trouble is that this sleuth of mine has degenerated into a meal-ticket. I liked him at first and used to enjoy putting him through his tricks; but recently I have fallen into the habit of bringing him out and running him around whenever the landlord, or the butcher, or the grocer shows signs of nervousness.

There are men who can write like that, but I'm not one of them. If I stick to the stuff I want to write—the stuff I enjoy writing—I can make a go of it, but when I try to grind out a yarn because I think there's a market for it, then I flop.

Whenever, from now on, I get hold of a story that fits my sleuth, I shall put him to work, but I'm through with trying to run him on a schedule.

Possibly I could patch up "The Question's One Answer" and "Women, Politics, and Murder" enough to get by with them, but my frank opinion of them is that neither is worth the trouble. I have a liking for honest work, and honest work as I see it is work that is done for the worker's enjoyment as much as for the profit it will bring him. And henceforth that's my work.

I want to thank both you and Mr. Cody for jolting me into wakefulness. There's no telling how much good this will do me. And you may be sure that whenever you get a story from me hereafter,—frequently, I hope,—it will be one that I enjoyed writing.

DASHIELL HAMMETT
San Francisco, Cal.

Early in his tenure, Cody published "The House in Turk Street" (April 15, 1924) and "The Girl with the Silver Eyes" (June 1924), Hammett's first set of linked stories and the strongest fiction he had written to that point. Together these stories form a 25,000-word novelette and begin to treat the characters and themes Hammett perfected five years later in *The Maltese Falcon*. "Women, Politics and Murder" was published in the September 1924 *Black Mask* and "The Question's One Answer" was retitled "Who Killed Bob Teal?" and published in *True Detective Stories* in November 1924. Both of those initially rejected stories are included here.

Hammett didn't like Cody and North, but he needed the money they paid him. Two months after Cody became editor, Hammett's disability payment from the U.S. Veterans Bureau was discontinued due to his improving health. It is not known how much he was paid for his *Black Mask* stories, but the base rate is believed to have been a penny a word, though Mencken claimed to have paid a bit less. Other pulps were paying their star writers two cents a word by the mid-1920s and as much as three cents a word by the end of the decade. Because of his popularity, Hammett presumably commanded the top rate, but his income was limited by a schedule imposed by Cody, and generally observed, of no more than a story every other month. During Cody's tenure from April 1, 1924, until Hammett quit writing for him in March 1926, Hammett published fifteen stories in *Black Mask* of which ten featured the Op. If he made two cents a word under Cody, he earned about $4,500 in the two years he wrote for him, or an average of about $300 a story (about $4,000 in 2017 dollars). During that time he also published four stories (one of which was narrated by the Op) in other pulps, as well as a smattering of nonfiction and poems; those publications would have earned him no more than another $1,000. In September 1925, Hammett learned that his wife was pregnant with their second child. With another mouth to feed, Hammett asked Cody for more money, threatening to quit the magazine if he were denied. Gardner, an attorney, claimed he offered to take a cut in his own pay rate for Hammett's sake, but Cody refused to raise Hammett's rate on the grounds that it would be unfair to other *Black Mask* authors. The circumstances are unclear, but Hammett claimed Cody owed him $300, which Cody refused to pay. Hammett quit the magazine in anger early in 1926. His last story for Cody was "The Creeping Siamese" published in March.

RL

BLACK MASK, APRIL 15, 1924

The House in Turk Street

BY DASHIELL HAMMETT

Author of "The Tenth Clew," "One Hour," etc.

We wouldn't consider an issue complete without one of Mr. Hammett's stories in it, and after you've read this tale, you'll understand why.

I HAD BEEN TOLD that the man for whom I was hunting lived in a certain Turk Street block, but my informant hadn't been able to give me his house number. Thus it came about that late one rainy afternoon I was canvassing this certain block, ringing each bell, and reciting a myth that went like this:

"I'm from the law office of Wellington and Berkeley. One of our clients—an elderly lady—was thrown from the rear platform of a street car last week and severely injured. Among those who witnessed the accident, was a young man whose name we don't know. But we have been told that he lives in this neighborhood." Then I would describe the man I wanted, and wind up: "Do you know of anyone who looks like that?"

All down one side of the block the answers were:

"No," "No," "No."

I crossed the street and started to work the other side. The first house: "No."

The second: "No."

The third. The fourth.

The fifth—

No one came to the door in answer to my first ring. After a while, I rang again. I had just decided that no one was at home, when the knob turned slowly and a little old woman opened the door. She was a very fragile little old woman, with a piece of gray knitting in one hand, and faded eyes that twinkled pleasantly behind gold-rimmed spectacles. She wore a stiffly starched apron over a black dress and there was white lace at her throat.

"Good evening," she said in a thin friendly voice. "I hope you didn't mind waiting. I always have to peep out to see who's here before I open the door—an old woman's timidity."

She laughed with a little gurgling sound in her throat.

"Sorry to disturb you," I apologized. "But—"

"Won't you come in, please?"

"No; I just want a little information. I won't take much of your time."

"I wish you would come in," she said, and then added with mock severity, "I'm sure my tea is getting cold."

She took my damp hat and coat, and I followed her down a narrow hall to a dim room, where a man got up as we entered. He was old too, and stout, with a thin white beard that fell upon a white vest that was as stiffly starched as the woman's apron.

"Thomas," the little fragile woman told him; "this is Mr.—"

"Tracy," I said, because that was the name I had given the other residents of the block; but I came as near blushing when I said it, as I have in fifteen years. These folks weren't made to be lied to.

Their name, I learned, was Quarre; and they were an affectionate old couple. She called him "Thomas" every time she spoke to him, rolling the name around in her mouth as if she liked the taste of it. He called her "my dear" just as frequently, and twice he got up to adjust a cushion more comfortably to her frail back.

I had to drink a cup of tea with them and eat some little spiced cookies before I could get them to listen to a question. Then Mrs. Quarre made little sympathetic clicking sounds with her tongue and teeth, while I told about the elderly lady who had fallen off a street car. The old man rumbled in his beard that it was "a damn shame," and gave me a fat and oily cigar. I had to assure them that the fictitious elderly lady was being taken care of and was coming along nicely—I was afraid they were going to insist upon being taken to see her.

Finally I got away from the accident itself, and described the man I wanted. "Thomas,"

Mrs. Quarre said; "isn't that the young man who lives in the house with the railing—the one who always looks so worried?"

The old man stroked his snowy beard and pondered.

"But, my dear," he rumbled at last; "hasn't he got dark hair?"

She beamed upon her husband and then upon me.

"Thomas is *so* observant," she said with pride. "I had forgotten; but the young man I spoke of does have dark hair, so he couldn't be the one who saw the accident at all."

The old man then suggested that one who lived in the block below might be my man. They discussed this one at some length before they decided that he was too tall and too old. Mrs. Quarre suggested another. They discussed that one, and voted against him. Thomas offered a candidate; he was weighed and discarded. They chattered on:

"But don't you think, Thomas . . . Yes, my dear, but . . . Of course you're right, Thomas, but. . . ."

Two old folks enjoying a chance contact with the world that they had dropped out of.

Darkness settled. The old man turned on a light in a tall lamp that threw a soft yellow circle upon us, and left the rest of the room dim. The room was a large one, and heavy with the thick hangings and bulky horse-hair furniture of a generation ago. I burned the cigar the old man had given me, and slumped comfortably down in my chair, letting them run on, putting in a word or two whenever they turned to me. I didn't expect to get any information here; but I was comfortable, and the cigar was a good one. Time enough to go out into the drizzle when I had finished my smoke.

Something cold touched the nape of my neck.

"Stand up!"

I didn't stand up: I couldn't. I was paralyzed. I sat and blinked at the Quarres.

And looking at them, I knew that something cold *couldn't* be against the back of my neck; a harsh voice *couldn't* have ordered me to stand up. It wasn't possible!

Mrs. Quarre still sat primly upright against the cushions her husband had adjusted to her back; her eyes still twinkled with friendliness behind her glasses; her hands were still motionless in her lap, crossed at the wrists over the piece of knitting. The old man still stroked his white beard, and let cigar smoke drift unhurriedly from his nostrils.

They would go on talking about the young men in the neighborhood who might be the man I wanted. Nothing had happened. I had dozed.

"Get up!"

The cold thing against my neck jabbed deep into the flesh.

I stood up.

"Frisk him," the harsh voice came from behind.

The old man carefully laid his cigar down, came to me, and ran his hands over my body. Satisfied that I was unarmed, he emptied my pockets, dropping the contents upon the chair that I had just left.

Mrs. Quarre was pouring herself some more tea.

"Thomas," she said; "you've overlooked that little watch pocket in the trousers."

He found nothing there.

"That's all," he told the man behind me, and returned to his chair and cigar.

"Turn around, you!" the harsh voice ordered.

I turned and faced a tall, gaunt, raw-boned man of about my own age, which is thirty-five. He had an ugly face—hollow-cheeked, bony, and spattered with big pale freckles. His eyes were of a watery blue, and his nose and chin stuck out abruptly.

"Know me?" he asked.

"No."

"You're a liar!"

I didn't argue the point: he was holding a level gun in one big freckled hand.

"You're going to know me pretty well before you're through with me," this big ugly man threatened. "You're going to—"

"Hook!" a voice came from a portièred doorway—the doorway through which the ugly man had no doubt crept up behind me. "Hook, come here!"

The voice was feminine—young, clear, and musical.

"What do you want?" the ugly man called over his shoulder.

"*He's* here."

"All right!" He turned to Thomas Quarre. "Keep this joker safe."

From somewhere among his whiskers, his coat, and his stiff white vest, the old man brought out a big black revolver, which he handled with no signs of either weakness or unfamiliarity.

The ugly man swept up the things that had been taken from my pockets, and carried them through the portières with him.

Mrs. Quarre smiled brightly up at me.

"Do sit down, Mr. Tracy," she said.

I sat.

Through the portières a new voice came from the next room; a drawling baritone voice whose accent was unmistakably British; cultured British.

"What's up, Hook?" this voice was asking.

The harsh voice of the ugly man:

"Plenty's up, I'm telling you! They're onto us! I started out a while ago; and as soon as I got to the street, I seen a man I knowed on the other side. He was pointed out to me in Philly five-six years ago. I don't know his name, but I remembered his mug—he's a Continental Detective Agency man. I came back in right away, and me and Elvira watched him out of the window. He went to every house on the other side of the street, asking questions or something. Then he came over and started to give this side a whirl, and after a while he rings the bell. I tell the old woman and her husband to get him in, stall him along, and see what he says for himself. He's got a song and dance about looking for a guy what seen an old woman bumped by a street car—but that's the bunk! He's gunning for us. There ain't nothing else to it. I went in and stuck him up just now. I meant to wait till you come, but I was scared he'd get nervous and beat it. Here's his stuff if you want to give it the once-over."

The British voice:

"You shouldn't have shown yourself to him. The others could have taken care of him."

Hook:

"What's the diff? Chances is he knows us all anyway. But supposing he didn't, what diff does it make?"

The drawling British voice:

"It may make a deal of difference. It was stupid."

Hook, blustering:

"Stupid, huh? You're always bellyaching about other people being stupid. To hell with you, I say! If you don't like my style, to hell with you! Who does all the work? Who's the guy that swings all the jobs? Huh? Where—"

The young feminine voice:

"Now, Hook, for God's sake don't make that speech again. I've listened to it until I know it by heart!"

A rustle of papers, and the British voice:

"I say, Hook, you're correct about his being a detective. Here is an identification card among his things."

The Quarres were listening to the conversation in the next room with as much interest as I, but Thomas Quarre's eyes never left me, and his fat fingers never relaxed about the gun in his lap. His wife sipped tea, with her head cocked on one side in the listening attitude of a bird.

Except for the weapon in the old man's lap, there was not a thing to persuade the eye that melodrama was in the room; the Quarres were in every other detail still the pleasant old couple who had given me tea and expressed sympathy for the elderly lady who had been injured.

The feminine voice from the next room:

"Well, what's to be done? What's our play?"

Hook:

"That's easy to answer. We're going to knock this sleuth off, first thing!"

The feminine voice:

"And put our necks in the noose?"

Hook, scornfully:

"As if they ain't there if we don't! You don't think this guy ain't after us for the L.A. job, do you?"

The British voice:

"You're an ass, Hook, and a quite hopeless one. Suppose this chap is interested in the Los Angeles affair, as is probable; what then? He is a Continental operative. Is it likely that his organization doesn't know where he is? Don't you think they know he was coming up here? And don't they know as much about us—chances are—as he does? There's no use killing him. That would only make matters worse. The thing to do is to tie him up and leave him here. His associates will hardly come looking for him until tomorrow—and that will give us all night to manage our disappearance."

My gratitude went out to the British voice! Somebody was in my favor, at least to the extent of letting me live. I hadn't been feeling very cheerful these last few minutes. Somehow, the fact that I couldn't see these people who were deciding whether I was to live or die, made my plight seem all the more desperate. I felt better now, though far from gay; I had confidence in the drawling British voice; it was the voice of a man who habitually carries his point.

Hook, bellowing:

"Let me tell you something, brother: that guy's going to be knocked off! That's flat! I'm taking no chances. You can jaw all you want to about it, but I'm looking out for my own neck and it'll be a lot safer with that guy where he can't talk. That's flat. He's going to be knocked off!"

The feminine voice, disgustedly:

"Aw, Hook, be reasonable!"

The British voice, still drawling, but dead cold:

"There's no use reasoning with you, Hook, you've the instincts and the intellect of a troglodyte. There is only one sort of language that you understand; and I'm going to talk that language to you, my son. If you are tempted to do anything silly between now and the time of our departure, just say this to yourself two or three times: 'If he dies, I die. If he dies, I die.' Say it as if it were out of the Bible—because it's that true."

There followed a long space of silence, with a tenseness that made my not particularly sensitive scalp tingle. Beyond the portière, I knew, two men were matching glances in a battle of wills, which might any instant become a physical struggle, and my chances of living were tied up in that battle.

When, at last, a voice cut the silence, I jumped as if a gun had been fired; though the voice was low and smooth enough.

It was the British voice, confidently victorious, and I breathed again.

"We'll get the old people away first," the voice was saying. "You take charge of our guest, Hook. Tie him up neatly. But remember—no foolishness. Don't waste time questioning him—he'll lie. Tie him up while I get the bonds, and we'll be gone in less than half an hour."

The portières parted and Hook came into the room—a scowling Hook whose freckles had a greenish tinge against the sallowness of his face. He pointed a revolver at me, and spoke to the Quarres:

"He wants you."

They got up and went into the next room, and for a while an indistinguishable buzzing of whispers came from that room.

Hook, meanwhile, had stepped back to the doorway, still menacing me with his revolver; and pulled loose the plush ropes that were around the heavy curtains. Then he came around behind me, and tied me securely to the high-backed chair; my arms to the chair's arms, my legs to the chair's legs, my body to the chair's back and seat; and he wound up by gagging me with the corner of a cushion that was too well-stuffed for my comfort. The ugly man was unnecessarily rough throughout; but I was a lamb. He wanted an excuse for drilling me, and I wanted above all else that he should have no excuse.

As he finished lashing me into place, and stepped back to scowl at me, I heard the street door close softly, and then light footsteps ran back and forth overhead.

Hook looked in the direction of those footsteps, and his little watery blue eyes grew cunning.

"Elvira!" he called softly.

The portières bulged as if someone had touched them, and the musical feminine voice came through.

"What?"

"Come here."

"I'd better not. He wouldn't—"

"Damn him!" Hook flared up. "Come here!"

She came into the room and into the circle of light from the tall lamp; a girl in her early twenties, slender and lithe, and dressed for the street, except that she carried her hat in one hand. A white face beneath a bobbed mass of flame-colored hair. Smoke-gray eyes that were set too far apart for trustworthiness—though not for beauty—laughed at me; and her red mouth laughed at me, exposing the edges of little sharp animal-teeth. She was beautiful; as beautiful as the devil, and twice as dangerous.

She laughed at me—a fat man all trussed up with red plush rope, and with the corner of a green cushion in my mouth—and she turned to the ugly man.

"What do you want?"

He spoke in an undertone, with a furtive glance at the ceiling, above which soft steps still padded back and forth.

"What say we shake him?"

Her smoke-gray eyes lost their merriment and became hard and calculating.

"There's a hundred thousand he's holding—a third of it's mine. You don't think I'm going to take a Mickey Finn* on that, do you?"

"Course not! Supposing we get the hundred-grand?"

"How?"

---

* Get cheated out of. A Mickey Finn is a drugged drink.

"Leave it to me, kid; leave it to me! If I swing it, will you go with me? You know I'll be good to you."

She smiled contemptuously, I thought—but he seemed to like it.

"You're whooping right you'll be good to me," she said. "But listen, Hook: we couldn't get away with it—not unless you *get him*. I know him! I'm not running away with anything that belongs to him unless he is fixed so that he can't come after it."

Hook moistened his lips and looked around the room at nothing. Apparently he didn't like the thought of tangling with the owner of the British drawl. But his desire for the girl was too strong for his fear of the other man.

"I'll do it!" he blurted. "I'll get him! Do you mean it, kid? If I get him, you'll go with me?"

She held out her hand.

"It's a bet," she said, and he believed her.

His ugly face grew warm and red and utterly happy, and he took a deep breath and straight-ened his shoulders. In his place, I might have believed her myself—all of us have fallen for that sort of thing at one time or another—but sitting tied up on the side-lines, I knew that he'd have been better off playing with a gallon of nitro than with this baby. She was dangerous! There was a rough time ahead for this Hook!

"This is the lay*—" Hook began, and stopped, tongue-tied.

A step had sounded in the next room.

Immediately the British voice came through the portières, and there was an edge of exaspera-tion to the drawl now:

"This is really too much! I can't"—he said *reahly* and *cawnt*—"leave for a moment without having things done all wrong. Now just what got into you, Elvira, that you must go in and exhibit yourself to our detective friend?"

Fear flashed into her smoke-gray eyes, and out again, and she spoke airily:

"Don't be altogether yellow," she said. "Your

_____
* line or trick

precious neck can get along all right without so much guarding."

The portières parted, and I twisted my head around as far as I could get it for my first look at this man who was responsible for my still being alive. I saw a short fat man, hatted and coated for the street, and carrying a tan traveling bag in one hand.

Then his face came into the yellow circle of light, and I saw that it was a Chinese face. A short fat Chinese, immaculately clothed in gar-ments that were as British as his accent.

"It isn't a matter of color," he told the girl—and I understood now the full sting of her jibe; "it's simply a matter of ordinary wisdom."

His face was a round yellow mask, and his voice was the same emotionless drawl that I had heard before; but I knew that he was as surely under the girl's sway as the ugly man—or he wouldn't have let her taunt bring him into the room. But I doubted that she'd find this Angli-cized oriental as easily handled as Hook.

"There was no particular need," the Chinese was still talking, "for this chap to have seen any of us." He looked at me now for the first time, with little opaque eyes that were like two black seeds. "It's quite possible that he didn't know any of us, even by description. This showing ourselves to him is the most arrant sort of nonsense."

"Aw, hell, Tai!" Hook blustered. "Quit your bellyaching, will you? What's the diff? I'll knock him off, and that takes care of that!"

The Chinese set down his tan bag and shook his head.

"There will be no killing," he drawled, "or there will be quite a bit of killing. You don't mis-take my meaning, do you, Hook?"

Hook didn't. His Adam's apple ran up and down with the effort of his swallowing, and behind the cushion that was choking me, I thanked the yellow man again.

Then this red-haired she-devil put her spoon in the dish.

"Hook's always offering to do things that he has no intention of doing," she told the Chinese.

Hook's ugly face blazed red at this reminder of his promise to *get* the Chinese, and he swallowed again, and his eyes looked as if nothing would have suited him better than an opportunity to crawl under something. But the girl had him; her influence was stronger than his cowardice.

He suddenly stepped close to the Chinese, and from his advantage of a full head in height scowled down into the round yellow face that was as expressionless as a clock without hands.

"Tai," the ugly man snarled; "you're done. I'm sick and tired of all this dog you put on— acting like you was a king or something. I've took all the lip I'm going to take from a Chink! I'm going to—"

He faltered, and his words faded away into silence. Tai looked up at him with eyes that were as hard and black and inhuman as two pieces of coal. Hook's lips twitched and he flinched away a little.

I stopped sweating. The yellow man had won again. But I had forgotten the red-haired she-devil.

She laughed now—a mocking laugh that must have been like a knife to the ugly man.

A bellow came from deep in his chest, and he hurled one big fist into the round blank face of the yellow man.

The force of the punch carried Tai all the way across the room, and threw him on his side in one corner.

But he had twisted his body around to face the ugly man even as he went hurtling across the room—a gun was in his hand before he went down—and he was speaking before his legs had settled upon the floor—and his voice was a cultured British drawl.

"Later," he was saying; "we will settle this thing that is between us. Just now you will drop your pistol and stand very still while I get up."

Hook's revolver—only half out of his pocket when the oriental had covered him—thudded to the rug. He stood rigidly still while Tai got to his feet, and Hook's breath came out noisily, and each freckle stood ghastily out against the dirty scared white of his face.

I looked at the girl. There was contempt in the eyes with which she looked at Hook, but no disappointment.

Then I made a discovery: *something had changed in the room near her!*

I shut my eyes and tried to picture that part of the room as it had been before the two men had clashed. Opening my eyes suddenly, I had the answer.

On the table beside the girl had been a book and some magazines. They were gone now. Not two feet from the girl was the tan bag that Tai had brought into the room. Suppose the bag had held the bonds from the Los Angeles job that they had mentioned. It probably had. What then? It probably now held the book and magazines that had been on the table! The girl had stirred up the trouble between the two men to distract their attention while she made a switch. Where would the loot be, then? I didn't know, but I suspected that it was too bulky to be on the girl's slender person.

Just beyond the table was a couch, with a wide red cover that went all the way down to the floor. I looked from the couch to the girl. She was watching me, and her eyes twinkled with a flash of mirth as they met mine coming from the couch. The couch it was!

By now the Chinese had pocketed Hook's revolver, and was talking to him:

"If I hadn't a dislike for murder, and if I didn't think that you will perhaps be of some value to Elvira and me in effecting our departure, I should certainly relieve us of the handicap of your stupidity now. But I'll give you one more chance. I would suggest, however, that you think carefully before you give way to any more of your violent impulses." He turned to the girl. "Have you been putting foolish ideas in our Hook's head?"

She laughed.

"Nobody could put any kind in it."

"Perhaps you're right," he said, and then came over to test the lashings about my arms and body.

Finding them satisfactory, he picked up the

tan bag, and held out the gun he had taken from the ugly man a few minutes before.

"Here's your revolver, Hook, now try to be sensible. We may as well go now. The old man and his wife will do as they were told. They are on their way to a city that we needn't mention by name in front of our friend here, to wait for us and their share of the bonds. Needless to say, they will wait a long while—they are out of it now. But between ourselves there must be no more treachery. If we're to get clear, we must help each other."

According to the best dramatic rules, these folks should have made sarcastic speeches to me before they left, but they didn't. They passed me without even a farewell look, and went out of sight into the darkness of the hall.

Suddenly the Chinese was in the room again, running tiptoe—an open knife in one hand, a gun in the other. This was the man I had been thanking for saving my life!

He bent over me.

The knife moved on my right side, and the rope that held that arm slackened its grip. I breathed again, and my heart went back to beating.

"Hook will be back," Tai whispered, and was gone.

On the carpet, three feet in front of me, lay a revolver.

The street door closed, and I was alone in the house for a while.

You may believe that I spent that while struggling with the red plush ropes that bound me. Tai had cut one length, loosening my right arm somewhat and giving my body more play, but I was far from free. And his whispered "Hook will be back" was all the spur I needed to throw my strength against my bonds.

I understood now why the Chinese had insisted so strongly upon my life being spared. I was the weapon with which Hook was to be removed. The Chinese figured that Hook would make some excuse as soon as they reached the street, slip back into the house, knock me off, and rejoin his confederates. If he didn't do it on his own initiative, I suppose the Chinese would suggest it.

So he had put a gun within reach—in case I could get loose—and had loosened my ropes as much as he could, not to have me free before he himself got away.

This thinking was a side-issue. I didn't let it slow up my efforts to get loose. The *why* wasn't important to me just now—the important thing was to have that revolver in my hand when the ugly man came into this room again.

Just as the front door opened, I got my right arm completely free, and plucked the strangling cushion from my mouth. The rest of my body was still held by the ropes—held loosely—but held. There was no time for more.

I threw myself, chair and all, forward, breaking the fall with my free arm. The carpet was thick. I went down on my face, with the heavy chair atop me, all doubled up any which way; but my right arm was free of the tangle, and my right hand grasped the gun.

My left side—the wrong side—was toward the hall door. I twisted and squirmed and wrestled under the bulky piece of furniture that sat on my back.

An inch—two inches—six inches, I twisted. Another inch. Feet were at the hall door. Another inch.

The dim light hit upon a man hurrying into the room—a glint of metal in his hand.

I fired.

He caught both hands to his belly, bent double, and slid out across the carpet.

That was over. But that was far from being all. I wrenched at the plush ropes that held me, while my mind tried to sketch what lay ahead.

The girl had switched the bonds, hiding them under the couch—there was no question of that. She had intended coming back for them before I had time to get free. But Hook had come back first, and she would have to change her plan. What more likely than that she would now tell the Chinese that Hook had made the switch? What then? There was only one answer: Tai would come back for the bonds—both of them would come. Tai knew that I was armed now, but they had said that the bonds represented a hundred thousand dollars. That would be enough to bring them back!

I kicked the last rope loose and scrambled to the couch. The bonds were beneath it: four thick bundles of Liberty Bonds, done up with heavy rubber bands. I tucked them under one arm, and went over to the man who was dying near the door. His gun was under one of his legs, I pulled it out, stepped over him, and went into the dark hall.

Then I stopped to consider.

The girl and the Chinese would split to tackle me. One would come in the front door and the other in the rear. That would be the safest way for them to handle me. My play, obviously, was to wait just inside one of those doors for them. It would be foolish for me to leave the house. That's exactly what they would be expecting at first—and they would be lying in ambush.

Decidedly, my play was to lie low within sight of this front door and wait until one of them came through it—as one of them surely would, when they had tired of waiting for me to come out.

Toward the street door, the hall was lighted with the glow that filtered through the glass from the street lights. The stairway leading to the second-story threw a triangular shadow across part of the hall—a shadow that was black enough for any purpose. I crouched low in this three-cornered slice of night, and waited.

I had two guns: the one the Chinese had given me, and the one I had taken from Hook. I had fired one shot; that would leave me eleven still to use—unless one of the weapons had been used since it was loaded. I broke the gun Tai had given me, and in the dark ran my fingers across the back of the cylinder. My fingers touched *one* shell—under the hammer. Tai had taken no chances; he had given me one bullet—the bullet with which I had dropped Hook.

I put that gun down on the floor, and examined the one I had taken from Hook. It was *empty*. The Chinese had taken no chances at all!

He had emptied Hook's gun before returning it to him after their quarrel.

I was in a hole! Alone, unarmed, in a strange house that would presently hold two who were hunting me—and that one of them was a woman didn't soothe me any—she was none the less deadly on that account.

For a moment I was tempted to make a dash for it; the thought of being out in the street again was pleasant; but I put the idea away. That would be foolishness, and plenty of it. Then I remembered the bonds under my arm. They would have to be my weapon; and if they were to serve me, they would have to be concealed.

I slipped out of my triangular shadow and went up the stairs. Thanks to the street lights, the upstairs rooms were not too dark for me to move around. Around and around I went through the rooms, hunting for a place to hide the Liberty Bonds.

But when suddenly a window rattled, as if from the draught created by the opening of an outside door somewhere, I still had the loot in my hands.

There was nothing to do now but to chuck them out of a window and trust to luck. I grabbed a pillow from a bed, stripped off the white case, and dumped the bonds into it. Then I leaned out of an already open window and looked down into the night, searching for a desirable dumping place: I didn't want the bonds to land on an ash-can or a pile of bottles, or anything that would make a racket.

And, looking out of the window, I found a better hiding-place. The window opened into a narrow court, on the other side of which was a house of the same sort as the one I was in. That house was of the same height as this one, with a flat tin roof that sloped down the other way. The roof wasn't far from me—not too far to chuck the pillow-case. I chucked it. It disappeared over the edge of the roof and crackled softly on the tin.

If I had been a movie actor or something of the sort, I suppose I'd have followed the bonds; I suppose I'd have jumped from the sill, caught the edge of the roof with my fingers, swung a while, and then pulled myself up and away. But dangling in space doesn't appeal to me; I preferred to face the Chinese and the redhead.

Then I did another not at all heroic thing. I turned on all the lights in the room, lighted a cigarette (we all like to pose a little now and then), and sat down on the bed to await my capture. I might have stalked my enemies through the dark house, and possibly have nabbed them; but most likely I would simply have succeeded in getting myself shot. And I don't like to be shot.

The girl found me.

She came creeping up the hall, an automatic in each hand, hesitated for an instant outside the door, and then came in on the jump. And when she saw me sitting peacefully on the side of the bed, her eyes snapped scornfully at me, as if I had done something mean. I suppose she thought I should have given her an opportunity to put lead in me.

"I got him, Tai," she called, and the Chinese joined us.

"What did Hook do with the bonds?" he asked point blank.

I grinned into his round yellow face and led my ace.

"Why don't you ask the girl?"

His face showed nothing, but I imagined that his fat body stiffened a little within its fashionable British clothing. That encouraged me, and I went on with my little lie that was meant to stir things up.

"Haven't you rapped to it," I asked; "that they were fixing up to ditch you?"

"You dirty liar!" the girl screamed, and took a step toward me.

Tai halted her with an imperative gesture. He stared through her with his opaque black eyes, and as he stared the blood slid out of her face. She had this fat yellow man on her string, right enough, but he wasn't exactly a harmless toy.

"So that's how it is?" he said slowly, to no one in particular. "So that's how it is?" Then to me: "Where did they put the bonds?"

The girl went close to him and her words came out tumbling over each other:

"Here's the truth of it, Tai, so help me God! I switched the stuff myself. Hook wasn't in it. I was going to run out on both of you. I stuck them under the couch downstairs, but they're not there now. That's the God's truth!"

He was eager to believe her, and her words had the ring of truth to them. And I knew that—in love with her as he was—he'd more readily forgive her treachery with the bonds than he would forgive her for planning to run off with Hook; so I made haste to stir things up again. The old timer who said "*Divide to conquer*," or something of the sort, knew what he was talking about.

"Part of that is right enough," I said. "She did stick the bonds under the couch—but Hook was in on it. They fixed it up between them while you were upstairs. He was to pick a fight with you, and during the argument she was to make the switch, and that is exactly what they did."

I had him!

As she wheeled savagely toward me, he stuck the muzzle of an automatic in her side—a smart jab that checked the angry words she was hurling at me.

"I'll take your guns, Elvira," he said, and took them.

There was a purring deadliness in his voice that made her surrender them without a word.

"Where are the bonds now?" he asked me.

I grinned.

"I'm not with you, Tai. I'm against you."

He studied me with his little eyes that were like black seeds for a while, and I studied him; and I hoped that his studying was as fruitless as mine.

"I don't like violence," he said slowly, "and I believe you are a sensible person. Let us traffic, my friend."

"You name it," I suggested.

"Gladly! As a basis for our bargaining, we will stipulate that you have hidden the bonds where they cannot be found by anyone else; and that I have you completely in my power, as the shilling shockers[*] used to have it."

"Reasonable enough," I said, "go on."

"The situation, then, is what gamblers call a standoff. Neither of us has the advantage. As a detective, you want us; but we have you. As thieves, we want the bonds; but you have them. I offer you the girl in exchange for the bonds, and that seems to me an equitable offer. It will give me the bonds and a chance to get away. It will give you no small degree of success in your task as a detective. Hook is dead. You will have the girl. All that will remain is to find me and the bonds again—by no means a hopeless task. You will have turned a defeat into more than half of a victory, with an excellent chance to make it a complete one."

"How do I know that you'll give me the girl?" He shrugged.

"Naturally, there can be no guarantee. But, knowing that she planned to desert me for the swine who lies dead below, you can't imagine that my feelings for her are the most friendly. Too, if I take her with me, she will want a share in the loot."

I turned the lay-out over in my mind, and looked at it from this side and that and the other.

"This is the way it looks to me," I told him at last. "You aren't a killer. I'll come through alive no matter what happens. All right; why should I swap? You and the girl will be easier to find again than the bonds, and they are the most important part of the job anyway. I'll hold on to them, and take my chances on finding you folks again. Yes, I'm playing it safe."

And I meant it, for the time being, at least.

"No, I'm not a killer," he said, very softly; and he smiled the first smile I had seen on his face. It wasn't a pleasant smile: and there was something in it that made you want to shudder. "But I am other things, perhaps, of which you haven't thought. But this talking is to no purpose. Elvira!"

_____

[*] British pulp stories that sold for a shilling

The girl, who had been standing a little to one side, watching us, came obediently forward.

"You will find sheets in one of the bureau drawers," he told her. "Tear one or two of them into strips strong enough to tie up your friend securely."

The girl went to the bureau. I wrinkled my head, trying to find a not too disagreeable answer to the question in my mind. The answer that came first wasn't nice: *torture*.

Then a faint sound brought us all into tense motionlessness.

The room we were in had two doors: one leading into the hall, the other into another bedroom. It was through the hall door that the faint sound had come—the sound of creeping feet.

Swiftly, silently, Tai moved backward to a position from which he could watch the hall door without losing sight of the girl and me—and the gun poised like a live thing in his fat hand was all the warning we needed to make no noise.

The faint sound again, just outside the door.

The gun in Tai's hand seemed to quiver with eagerness.

Through the other door—the door that gave to the next room—popped Mrs. Quarre, an enormous cocked revolver in her thin hand.

"Let go it, you nasty heathen," she screeched.

Tai dropped his pistol before he turned to face her, and he held his hands up high—all of which was very wise.

Thomas Quarre came through the hall door then; he also held a cocked revolver—the mate of his wife's—though, in front of his bulk, his didn't look so enormously large.

I looked at the old woman again, and found little of the friendly fragile one who had poured tea and chatted about the neighbors. This was a witch if there ever was one—a witch of the blackest, most malignant sort. Her little faded eyes were sharp with ferocity, her withered lips were taut in a wolfish snarl, and her thin body fairly quivered with hate.

"I knew it," she was shrilling. "I told Tom as soon as we got far enough away to think things over. I knew it was a frame-up! I knew this supposed detective was a pal of yours! I knew it was just a scheme to beat Thomas and me out of our shares! Well, I'll show you, you yellow monkey! And the rest of you too! I'll show the whole caboodle of you! Where are them bonds? Where are they?"

The Chinese had recovered his poise, if he had ever lost it.

"Our stout friend can tell you perhaps," he said. "I was about to extract the information from him when you so—ah—dramatically arrived."

"Thomas, for goodness' sakes don't stand there dreaming," she snapped at her husband, who to all appearances was still the same mild old man who had given me an excellent cigar. "Tie up this Chinaman! I don't trust him an inch, and I won't feel easy until he's tied up. Tie him, up, and then we'll see what's to be done."

I got up from my seat on the side of the bed, and moved cautiously to a spot that I thought would be out of the line of fire if the thing I expected happened.

Tai had dropped the gun that had been in his hand, but he hadn't been searched. The Chinese are a thorough people; if one of them carries a gun at all, he usually carries two or three or more. (I remember picking up one in Oakland during the last tong war, who had five on him—one under each armpit, one on each hip, and one in his waistband.) One gun had been taken from Tai, and if they tried to truss him up without frisking him, there was likely to be fireworks. So I moved off to one side.

Fat Thomas Quarre went phlegmatically up to the Chinese to carry out his wife's orders—and bungled the job perfectly.

He put his bulk between Tai and the old woman's gun.

Tai's hands moved.

An automatic was in each.

Once more Tai ran true to racial form. When a Chinese shoots, he keeps on shooting until his gun is empty.

When I yanked Tai over backward by his fat throat, and slammed him to the floor, his guns were still barking metal; and they clicked empty as I got a knee on one of his arms. I didn't take any chances. I worked on his throat until his eyes and tongue told me that he was out of things for a while.

Then I looked around.

Thomas Quarre was huddled against the bed, plainly dead, with three round holes in his starched white vest—holes that were brown from the closeness of the gun that had put them there.

Across the room, Mrs. Quarre lay on her back. Her clothes had somehow settled in place around her fragile body, and death had given her once more the gentle friendly look she had worn when I first saw her. One thin hand was on her bosom, covering, I found later, the two bullet-holes that were there.

The red-haired girl Elvira was gone.

Presently Tai stirred, and, after taking another gun from his clothes, I helped him sit up. He stroked his bruised throat with one fat hand, and looked coolly around the room.

"So this is how it came out?" he said.

"Uh-huh!"

"Where's Elvira?"

"Got away—for the time being."

He shrugged.

"Well, you can call it a decidedly successful operation. The Quarres and Hook dead; the bonds and I in your hands."

"Not so bad," I admitted, "but will you do me a favor?"

"If I may."

"Tell me what the hell this is all about!"

"All about?" he asked.

"Exactly! From what you people have let me overhear, I gather that you pulled some sort of job in Los Angeles that netted you a hundred-thousand-dollars' worth of Liberty Bonds; but I can't remember any recent job of that size down there."

"Why, that's preposterous!" he said with what, for him, was almost wild-eyed amazement. "Preposterous! Of course you know all about it!"

"I do not! I was trying to find a young fellow named Fisher who left his Tacoma home in anger a week or two ago. His father wants him found on the quiet, so that he can come down and try to talk him into going home again. I was told that I might find Fisher in this block of Turk Street, and that's what brought me here."

He didn't believe me. He never believed me. He went to the gallows thinking me a liar.

When I got out into the street again (and Turk Street was a lovely place when I came free into it after my evening in that house!) I bought a newspaper that told me most of what I wanted to know.

A boy of twenty—a messenger in the employ of a Los Angeles stock and bond house—had disappeared two days before, while on his way to a bank with a wad of Liberty Bonds. That same night this boy and a slender girl with bobbed red hair had registered at a hotel in Fresno as *J. M. Riordan and wife*. The next morning the boy had been found in his room—murdered. The girl was gone. The bonds were gone.

That much the paper told me. During the next few days, digging up a little here and a little there, I succeeded in piecing together most of the story.

The Chinese—whose full name was Tai Choon Tau—had been the brains of the mob. Their game had been a variation of the always-reliable badger game. Tai selected the victims, and he must have been a good judge of humans, for he seems never to have picked a bloomer.* He would pick out some youth who was messenger or runner for a banker or broker—one who carried either cash or negotiable securities in large quantities around the city.

The girl Elvira would then *make* this lad, get

_____
* Australian for mistakes

him all fussed up over her—which shouldn't have been very hard for her—and then lead him gently around to running away with her and whatever he could grab in the way of his employer's bonds or currency.

Wherever they spent the first night of their flight, there Hook would appear—foaming at the mouth and loaded for bear. The girl would plead and tear her hair and so forth, trying to keep Hook—in his rôle of irate husband—from butchering the youth. Finally she would succeed, and in the end the youth would find himself without either girl or the fruits of his thievery.

Sometimes he had surrendered to the police. Two we found had committed suicide. The Los Angeles lad had been built of tougher stuff than the others. He had put up a fight, and Hook had had to kill him. You can measure the girl's skill in her end of the game by the fact that not one of the half dozen youths who had been trimmed had said the least thing to implicate her; and some of them had gone to great trouble to keep her out of it.

The house in Turk Street had been the mob's retreat, and, that it might be always a safe one, they had not worked their game in San Francisco. Hook and the girl were supposed by the neighbors to be the Quarres' son and daughter—and Tai was the Chinese cook. The Quarres' benign and respectable appearances had also come in handy when the mob had securities to be disposed of.

The Chinese went to the gallows. We threw out the widest and finest-meshed of drag-nets for the red-haired girl; and we turned up girls with bobbed red hair by the scores. But the girl Elvira was not among them.

I promised myself that some day. . . .

BLACK MASK, JUNE 1924

The Girl with the Silver Eyes

BY DASHIELL HAMMETT

(Author of "One Hour," "The House in Turk Street," etc.)

Mr. Hammett has written some lively and unusual tales about his realistic detective from the Continental Detective Agency, whose name has never been disclosed; but for action, shrewd detective-work, sheer interest, and surprise, his latest, herewith, surpasses them all.

COMPLETE DETECTIVE NOVELETTE

A BELL JANGLED ME into wakefulness. I rolled to the edge of my bed and reached for the telephone. The neat voice of the Old Man—the Continental Detective Agency's San Francisco manager—came to my ears:

"Sorry to disturb you, but you'll have to go up to the Glenton Apartments on Leavenworth Street. A man named Burke Pangburn, who lives there, phoned me a few minutes ago asking to have someone sent up to see him at once. He seemed rather excited. Will you take care of it? See what he wants."

I said I would and, yawning, stretching and cursing Pangburn—whoever he was—got my fat body out of pajamas and into street clothes.

The man who had disturbed my Sunday morning sleep—I found when I reached the Glenton—was a slim, white-faced person of about twenty-five, with big brown eyes that were red-rimmed just now from either sleeplessness or crying, or both. His long brown hair was rumpled when he opened the door to admit me; and he wore a mauve dressing-robe spotted with big jade parrots over wine-colored silk pajamas.

The room into which he led me resembled an auctioneer's establishment just before the sale—or maybe one of these alley tea-rooms. Fat blue vases, crooked red vases, lanky yellow vases, vases of various shapes and colors; marble statuettes, ebony statuettes, statuettes of any material; lanterns, lamps and candlesticks; draperies, hangings and rugs of all sorts; odds and ends of furniture that were all somehow queerly designed; peculiar pictures hung here and there in unexpected places. A hard room to feel comfortable in.

"My fiancée," he began immediately in a high-pitched voice that was within a notch of hysteria, "has disappeared! Something has happened to her! Foul play of some horrible sort! I want you to find her—to save her from this terrible thing that. . . ."

I followed him this far and then gave it up. A jumble of words came out of his mouth— "spirited away . . . mysterious something . . . lured into a trap"—but they were too disconnected for me to make anything out of them. So I stopped trying to understand him, and waited for him to babble himself empty of words.

I have heard ordinarily reasonable men, under stress of excitement, run on even more crazily than this wild-eyed youth; but his dress—the parroted robe and gay pajamas—and his surroundings—this deliriously furnished room—gave him too theatrical a setting; made his words sound utterly unreal.

He himself, when normal, should have been a rather nice-looking lad: his features were well spaced and, though his mouth and chin were a little uncertain, his broad forehead was good. But standing there listening to the occasional melodramatic phrase that I could pick out of the jumbled noises he was throwing at me, I thought that instead of parrots on his robe he should have had cuckoos.

Presently he ran out of language and was holding his long, thin hands out to me in an appealing gesture, saying,

"Will you?" over and over. "Will you? Will you?"

I nodded soothingly, and noticed that tears were on his thin cheeks.

"Suppose we begin at the beginning," I suggested, sitting down carefully on a carved bench affair that didn't look any too strong.

"Yes! Yes!" He was standing legs apart in front of me, running his fingers through his hair. "The beginning. I had a letter from her every day until—"

"That's not the beginning," I objected. "Who is she? What is she?"

"She's Jeanne Delano!" he exclaimed in surprise at my ignorance. "And she is my fiancée. And now she is gone, and I know that—"

The phrases *"victim of foul play," "into a trap"* and so on began to flow hysterically out again.

Finally I got him quieted down and, sandwiched in between occasional emotional outbursts, got a story out of him that amounted to this:

This Burke Pangburn was a poet. About two months before, he had received a note from a Jeanne Delano—forwarded from his publishers—praising his latest book of rhymes. Jeanne Delano happened to live in San Francisco, too, though she hadn't known that he did. He had answered her note, and had received another. After a little of this they met. If she really was as beautiful as he claimed, then he wasn't to be blamed for falling in love with her. But whether or not she was really beautiful, he thought she was, and he had fallen hard.

This Delano girl had been living in San Francisco for only a little while, and when the poet met her she was living alone in an Ashbury Avenue apartment. He did not know where she came from or anything about her former life. He suspected—from certain indefinite suggestions and peculiarities of conduct which he couldn't put in words—that there was a cloud of some sort hanging over the girl; that neither her past nor her present were free from difficulties. But he hadn't the least idea what those difficulties might be. He hadn't cared. He knew absolutely nothing about her, except that she was beautiful, and he loved her, and she had promised to marry him.

Then, on the third of the month—exactly twenty-one days before this Sunday morning— the girl had suddenly left San Francisco. He had received a note from her, by messenger.

This note, which he showed me after I had insisted point blank on seeing it, read:

Burkelove:

Have just received a wire, and must go East on next train. Tried to get you on the phone, but couldn't. Will write you as soon as I know what my address will be. If anything. (These two words were erased and could be read only with great difficulty.) *Love me until I'm back with you forever.*

Your Jeanne.

Nine days later he had received another letter from her, from Baltimore, Maryland. This one, which I had a still harder time getting a look at, read:

Dearest Poet:

It seems like two years since I have seen you, and I have a fear that it's going to be between one and two months before I see you again.

I can't tell you now, beloved, about what brought me here. There are things that can't be written. But as soon as I'm back with you, I shall tell you the whole wretched story.

If anything should happen—I mean to me—you'll go on loving me forever, won't you, beloved? But that's foolish. Nothing is going to happen. I'm just off the train, and tired from traveling.

Tomorrow I shall write you a long, long letter to make up for this.

My address here is 215 N. Stricker St. Please, Mister, at least one letter a day! Your own

Jeanne

For nine days he had had a letter from her each day—with two on Monday to make up for the none on Sunday—and then her letters had stopped. And the daily letters he had sent to the address she gave—215 N. Stricker Street—had begun to come back to him, marked "Not known."

He had sent a telegram, and the telegraph company had informed him that its Baltimore office had been unable to find a Jeanne Delano at the North Stricker Street address.

For three days he had waited, expecting hourly to hear from the girl, and no word had come. Then he had bought a ticket for Baltimore.

"But," he wound up, "I was afraid to go. I know she's in some sort of trouble—I can feel that—but I'm a silly poet. I can't deal with mysteries. Either I would find nothing at all or, if by luck I did stumble on the right track, the probabilities are that I would only muddle things; add fresh complications, perhaps endanger her life still further. I can't go blundering at it in that fashion, without knowing whether I am helping or harming her. It's a task for an expert in that sort of thing. So I thought of your agency. You'll be careful, won't you? It may be—I don't know—that she won't want assistance. It may be that you can help her without her knowing anything about it. You are accustomed to that sort of thing; you can do it, can't you?"

II

I turned the job over and over in my mind before answering him. The two great bugaboos of a reputable detective agency are the persons who bring in a crooked plan or a piece of divorce work all dressed up in the garb of a legitimate operation, and the irresponsible person who is laboring under wild and fanciful delusions—who wants a dream run out.

This poet—sitting opposite me now twining his long, white fingers nervously together—was, I thought, sincere; but I wasn't so sure of his sanity.

"Mr. Pangburn," I said after a while, "I'd like to handle this thing for you, but I'm not sure that I can. The Continental is rather strict, and, while I believe this thing is on the level, still I am only a hired man and have to go by the rules. Now if you could give us the endorsement of some firm or person of standing—a reputable lawyer, for instance, or any legally responsible party—we'd be glad to go ahead with the work. Otherwise, I am afraid—"

"But I know she's in danger!" he broke out. "I know that—And I can't be advertising her plight—airing her affairs—to everyone."

"I'm sorry, but I can't touch it unless you can give me some such endorsement." I stood up. "But you can find plenty of detective agencies that aren't so particular."

His mouth worked like a small boy's, and he caught his lower lip between his teeth. For a moment I thought he was going to burst into tears. But instead he said slowly:

"I dare say you are right. Suppose I refer you to my brother-in-law, Roy Axford. Will his word be sufficient?"

"Yes."

Roy Axford—R. F. Axford—was a mining man who had a finger in at least half of the big business enterprises of the Pacific Coast; and his word on anything was commonly considered good enough for anybody.

"If you can get in touch with him now," I said, "and arrange for me to see him today, I can get started without much delay."

Pangburn crossed the room and dug a telephone out from among a heap of his ornaments. Within a minute or two he was talking to someone whom he called "Rita."

"Is Roy home? . . . Will he be home this afternoon? . . . No, you can give him a message for me, though. . . . Tell him I'm sending a gentleman up to see him this afternoon on a personal matter—personal with me—and that I'll be very grateful if he'll do what I want. . . . Yes. . . . You'll find out, Rita. . . . It isn't a thing to talk about over the phone. . . . Yes, thanks!"

He pushed the telephone back into its hiding place and turned to me.

"He'll be at home until two o'clock. Tell him what I told you and if he seems doubtful, have him call me up. You'll have to tell him the whole thing; he doesn't know anything at all about Miss Delano."

"All right. Before I go, I want a description of her."

"She's beautiful!" he exclaimed. "The most beautiful woman in the world!"

That would look nice on a reward circular.

"That isn't exactly what I want," I told him. "How old is she?"

"Twenty-two."

"Height?"

"About five feet eight inches, or possibly nine."

"Slender, medium or plump?"

"She's inclined toward slenderness, but she—"

There was a note of enthusiasm in his voice that made me fear he was about to make a speech, so I cut him off with another question.

"What color hair?"

"Brown—so dark that it's almost black—and it's soft and thick and—"

"Yes, yes. Long or bobbed?"

"Long and thick and—"

"What color eyes?"

"You've seen shadows on polished silver when—"

I wrote down *gray eyes* and hurried on with the interrogation.

"Complexion?"

"Perfect!"

"Uh-huh. But is it light, or dark, or florid, or sallow, or what?"

"Fair."

"Face oval, or square, or long and thin, or what shape?"

"Oval."

"What shaped nose? Large, small, turned-up—"

"Small and regular!" There was a touch of indignation in his voice.

"How did she dress? Fashionably? And did she favor bright or quiet colors?"

"Beaut—" And then as I opened my mouth to head him off he came down to earth with:

"Very quietly—usually dark blues and browns."

"What jewelry did she wear?"

"I've never seen her wear any."

"Any scars, or moles?" The horrified look on his white face urged me on to give him a full shot. "Or warts, or deformities that you know?"

He was speechless, but he managed to shake his head.

"Have you a photograph of her?"

"Yes, I'll show you."

He bounded to his feet, wound his way through the room's excessive furnishings and out through a curtained doorway. Immediately he was back with a large photograph in a carved ivory frame. It was one of these artistic photographs—a thing of shadows and hazy outlines—not much good for identification purposes. She was beautiful—right enough—but that meant nothing; that's the purpose of an artistic photograph.

"This the only one you have?"

"Yes."

"I'll have to borrow it, but I'll get it back to you as soon as I have my copies made."

"No! No!" he protested against having his ladylove's face given to a lot of gumshoes. "That would be terrible!"

I finally got it, but it cost me more words than I like to waste on an incidental.

"I want to borrow a couple of her letters, or something in her writing, too," I said.

"For what?"

"To have photostatic copies made. Handwriting specimens come in handy—give you something to go over hotel registers with. Then, even if going under fictitious names, people now and then write notes and make memorandums."

We had another battle, out of which I came with three envelopes and two meaningless sheets of paper, all bearing the girl's angular writing.

"She have much money?" I asked, when the disputed photograph and handwriting specimens were safely tucked away in my pocket.

"I don't know. It's not the sort of thing that one would pry into. She wasn't poor; that is, she didn't have to practice any petty economies; but I haven't the faintest idea either as to the amount of her income or its source. She had an account at the Golden Gate Trust Company, but naturally I don't know anything about its size."

"Many friends here?"

"That's another thing I don't know. I think she knew a few people here, but I don't know who they were. You see, when we were together we never talked about anything but ourselves. You know what I mean: there was nothing we were interested in but each other. We were simply—"

"Can't you even make a guess at where she came from, who she was?"

"No. Those things didn't matter to me. She was Jeanne Delano, and that was enough for me."

"Did you and she ever have any financial interests in common? I mean, was there ever any transaction in money or other valuables in which both of you were interested?"

What I meant, of course, was had she got into him for a loan, or had she sold him something, or got money out of him in any other way.

He jumped to his feet, and his face went fog-gray. Then he sat down again—slumped down—and blushed scarlet.

"Pardon me," he said thickly. "You didn't know her, and of course you must look at the thing from all angles. No, there was nothing like that. I'm afraid you are going to waste time if you are going to work on the theory that she was an adventuress. There was nothing like that! She was a girl with something terrible hanging over her; something that called her to Baltimore suddenly; something that has taken her away from me. Money? What could money have to do with it? I love her!"

III

R. F. Axford received me in an office-like room in his Russian Hill residence: a big blond man, whose forty-eight or -nine years had not blurred the outlines of an athlete's body. A big, full-blooded man with the manner of one whose self-confidence is complete and not altogether unjustified.

"What's our Burke been up to now?" he asked amusedly when I told him who I was. His voice was a pleasant vibrant bass.

I didn't give him all the details.

"He was engaged to marry a Jeanne Delano, who went East about three weeks ago and then suddenly disappeared. He knows very little about her; thinks something has happened to her; and wants her found."

"Again?" His shrewd blue eyes twinkled. "And to a Jeanne this time! She's the fifth within a year, to my knowledge, and no doubt I missed one or two who were current while I was in Hawaii. But where do I come in?"

"I asked him for responsible endorsement. I think he's all right, but he isn't, in the strictest sense, a responsible person. He referred me to you."

"You're right about his not being, in the strictest sense, a responsible person." The big man screwed up his eyes and mouth in thought for a moment. Then: "Do you think that something has really happened to the girl? Or is Burke imagining things?"

"I don't know. I thought it was a dream at first. But in a couple of her letters there are hints that something was wrong."

"You might go ahead and find her then," Axford said. "I don't suppose any harm will come from letting him have his Jeanne back. It will at least give him something to think about for a while."

"I have your word for it then, Mr. Axford, that there will be no scandal or anything of the sort connected with the affair?"

"Assuredly! Burke is all right, you know. It's simply that he is spoiled. He has been in rather delicate health all his life; and then he has an income that suffices to keep him modestly, with a little over to bring out books of verse and buy doo-daws for his rooms. He takes himself a little too solemnly—is too much the poet—but he's sound at bottom."

"I'll go ahead with it, then," I said, getting up. "By the way, the girl has an account at the Golden Gate Trust Company, and I'd like to find out as much about it as possible, especially where her money came from. Clement, the cashier, is a model of caution when it comes to giving out information about depositors. If you could put in a word for me it would make my way smoother."

"Be glad to."

He wrote a couple of lines across the back of a card and gave it to me; and, promising to call on him if I needed further assistance, I left.

IV

I telephoned Pangburn that his brother-in-law had given the job his approval. I sent a wire to the agency's Baltimore branch, giving what information I had. Then I went up to Ashbury Avenue, to the apartment house in which the girl had lived.

The manager—an immense Mrs. Clute in rustling black—knew little, if any, more about the girl than Pangburn. The girl had lived there for two and a half months; she had had occasional callers, but Pangburn was the only one that the manager could describe to me. The girl had given up the apartment on the third of the month, saying that she had been called East, and she had asked the manager to hold her mail until she sent her new address. Ten days later Mrs. Clute had received a card from the girl instructing her to forward her mail to 215 N. Stricker Street, Baltimore, Maryland. There had been no mail to forward.

The single thing of importance that I learned at the apartment house was that the girl's two trunks had been taken away by a green transfer truck. Green was the color used by one of the city's largest transfer companies.

I went then to the office of this transfer company, and found a friendly clerk on duty. (A detective, if he is wise, takes pains to make and keep as many friends as possible among transfer company, express company and railroad employees.) I left the office with a memorandum of the transfer company's check numbers and the

Ferry baggage-room to which the two trunks had been taken.

At the Ferry Building, with this information, it didn't take me many minutes to learn that the trunks had been checked to Baltimore. I sent another wire to the Baltimore branch, giving the railroad check numbers.

Sunday was well into night by this time, so I knocked off and went home.

V

Half an hour before the Golden Gate Trust Company opened for business the next morning I was inside, talking to Clement, the cashier. All the traditional caution and conservatism of bankers rolled together wouldn't be one-two-three to the amount usually displayed by this plump, white-haired old man. But one look at Axford's card, with *"Please give the bearer all possible assistance"* inked across the back of it, made Clement even eager to help me.

"You have, or have had, an account here in the name of Jeanne Delano," I said. "I'd like to know as much as possible about it: to whom she drew checks, and to what amounts; but especially all you can tell me about where her money came from."

He stabbed one of the pearl buttons on his desk with a pink finger, and a lad with polished yellow hair oozed silently into the room. The cashier scribbled with a pencil on a piece of paper and gave it to the noiseless youth, who disappeared. Presently he was back, laying a handful of papers on the cashier's desk.

Clement looked through the papers and then up at me.

"Miss Delano was introduced here by Mr. Burke Pangburn on the sixth of last month, and opened an account with eight hundred and fifty dollars in cash. She made the following deposits after that: four hundred dollars on the tenth; two hundred and fifty on the twenty-first; three hundred on the twenty-sixth; two hundred on the thirtieth; and twenty thousand dollars on

the second of this month. All of these deposits except the last were made with cash. The last one was a check—which I have here."

He handed it to me: a Golden Gate Trust Company check.

PAY TO THE ORDER OF JEANNE DELANO,
TWENTY THOUSAND DOLLARS.
(SIGNED) BURKE PANGBURN.

It was dated the second of the month.

"Burke Pangburn!" I exclaimed, a little stupidly. "Was it usual for him to draw checks to that amount?"

"I think not. But we shall see."

He stabbed the pearl button again, ran his pencil across another slip of paper, and the youth with the polished yellow hair made a noiseless entrance, exit, entrance, and exit.

The cashier looked through the fresh batch of papers that had been brought to him.

"On the first of the month, Mr. Pangburn deposited twenty thousand dollars—a check against Mr. Axford's account here."

"Now how about Miss Delano's withdrawals?" I asked.

He picked up the papers that had to do with her account again.

"Her statement and canceled checks for last month haven't been delivered to her yet. Everything is here. A check for eighty-five dollars to the order of H. K. Clute on the fifteenth of last month; one 'to cash' for three hundred dollars on the twentieth, and another of the same kind for one hundred dollars on the twenty-fifth. Both of these checks were apparently cashed here by her. On the third of this month she closed out her account, with a check to her own order for twenty-one thousand, five hundred and fifteen dollars."

"And that check?"

"Was cashed here by her."

I lighted a cigarette, and let these figures drift around in my head. None of them—except those that were fixed to Pangburn's and Axford's signatures—seemed to be of any value to me.

The Clute check—the only one the girl had drawn in anyone else's favor—had almost certainly been for rent.

"This is the way of it," I summed up aloud. "On the first of the month, Pangburn deposited Axford's check for twenty thousand dollars. The next day he gave a check to that amount to Miss Delano, which she deposited. On the following day she closed her account, taking between twenty-one and twenty-two thousand dollars in currency."

"Exactly," the cashier said.

VI

Before going up to the Glenton Apartments to find out why Pangburn hadn't come clean with me about the twenty thousand dollars, I dropped in at the agency, to see if any word had come from Baltimore. One of the clerks had just finished decoding a telegram.

It read:

Baggage arrived Mt. Royal Station on eighth. Taken away same day. Unable to trace. 215 North Stricker Street is Baltimore Orphan Asylum.* Girl not known there. Continuing our efforts to find her.

The Old Man came in from luncheon as I was leaving. I went back into his office with him for a couple of minutes.

"Did you see Pangburn?" he asked.

"Yes. I'm working on his job now—but I think it's a bust."

"What is it?"

"Pangburn is R. F. Axford's brother-in-law. He met a girl a couple of months ago, and fell for her. She sizes up as a worker. He doesn't know anything about her. The first of the month he got twenty thousand dollars from his brother-in-law and passed it over to the girl. She blew,

telling him she had been called to Baltimore, and giving him a phoney address that turns out to be an orphan asylum. She sent her trunks to Baltimore, and sent him some letters from there—but a friend could have taken care of the baggage and could have remailed her letters for her. Of course, she would have needed a ticket to check the trunks on, but in a twenty-thousand-dollar game that would be a small expense. Pangburn held out on me; he didn't tell me a word about the money. Ashamed of being easy pickings, I reckon. I'm going to the bat with him on it now."

The Old Man smiled his mild smile that might mean anything, and I left.

VII

Ten minutes of ringing Pangburn's bell brought no answer. The elevator boy told me he thought Pangburn hadn't been in all night. I put a note in his box and went down to the railroad company's offices, where I arranged to be notified if an unused Baltimore–San Francisco ticket was turned in for redemption.

That done, I went up to the *Chronicle* office and searched the files for weather conditions during the past month, making a memorandum of four dates upon which it had rained steadily day and night. I carried my memorandum to the offices of the three largest taxicab companies.

That was a trick that had worked well for me before. The girl's apartment was some distance from the street car line, and I was counting upon her having gone out—or having had a caller—on one of those rainy dates. In either case, it was very likely that she—or her caller—had left in a taxi in preference to walking through the rain to the car line. The taxicab companies' daily records would show any calls from her address, and the fares' destinations.

The ideal trick, of course, would have been to have the records searched for the full extent of the girl's occupancy of the apartment; but no taxicab company would stand for having that

_____
* across the street from the house where Hammett grew up

amount of work thrust upon them, unless it was a matter of life and death. It was difficult enough for me to persuade them to turn clerks loose on the four days I had selected.

I called up Pangburn again after I left the last taxicab office, but he was not at home. I called up Axford's residence, thinking that the poet might have spent the night there, but was told that he had not.

Late that afternoon I got my copies of the girl's photograph and handwriting, and put one of each in the mail for Baltimore. Then I went around to the three taxicab companies' offices and got my reports. Two of them had nothing for me. The third's records showed two calls from the girl's apartment.

On one rainy afternoon a taxi had been called, and one passenger had been taken to the Glenton Apartments. That passenger, obviously, was either the girl or Pangburn. At half-past twelve one night another call had come in, and this passenger had been taken to the Marquis Hotel.

The driver who had answered this second call remembered it indistinctly when I questioned him, but he thought that his fare had been a man. I let the matter rest there for the time; the Marquis isn't a large hotel as San Francisco hotels go, but it is too large to make canvassing its guests for the one I wanted practicable.

I spent the evening trying to reach Pangburn, with no success. At eleven o'clock I called up Axford, and asked him if he had any idea where I might find his brother-in-law.

"Haven't seen him for several days," the millionaire said. "He was supposed to come up for dinner last night, but didn't. My wife tried to reach him by phone a couple times today, but couldn't."

VIII

The next morning I called Pangburn's apartment before I got out of bed, and got no answer. Then I telephoned Axford and made an appointment for ten o'clock at his office.

"I don't know what he's up to now," Axford said good-naturedly when I told him that Pangburn had apparently been away from his apartment since Sunday, "and I suppose there's small chance of guessing. Our Burke is nothing if not erratic. How are you progressing with your search for the damsel in distress?"

"Far enough to convince me that she isn't in a whole lot of distress. She got twenty thousand dollars from your brother-in-law the day before she vanished."

"Twenty thousand dollars from Burke? She must be a wonderful girl! But wherever did he get that much money?"

"From you."

Axford's muscular body straightened in his chair.

"From me?"

"Yes—your check."

"He did not."

There was nothing argumentative in his voice; it simply stated a fact.

"You didn't give him a check for twenty thousand dollars on the first of the month?"

"No."

"Then," I suggested, "perhaps we'd better take a run over to the Golden Gate Trust Company."

Ten minutes later we were in Clement's office.

"I'd like to see my cancelled checks," Axford told the cashier.

The youth with the polished yellow hair brought them in presently—a thick wad of them—and Axford ran rapidly through them until he found the one he wanted. He studied that one for a long while, and when he looked up at me he shook his head slowly but with finality.

"I've never seen it before."

Clement mopped his head with a white handkerchief, and tried to pretend that he wasn't burning up with curiosity and fears that his bank had been gypped.

The millionaire turned the check over and looked at the endorsement.

"Deposited by Burke," he said in the voice

of one who talks while he thinks of something entirely different, "on the first."

"Could we talk to the teller who took in the twenty-thousand-dollar check that Miss Delano deposited?" I asked Clement.

He pressed one of his desk's pearl buttons with a fumbling pink finger, and in a minute or two a little sallow man with a hairless head came in.

"Do you remember taking a check for twenty thousand from Miss Jeanne Delano a few weeks ago?" I asked him.

"Yes, sir! Yes, sir! Perfectly."

"Just what do you remember about it?"

"Well, sir, Miss Delano came to my window with Mr. Burke Pangburn. It was his check. I thought it was a large check for him to be drawing, but the bookkeepers said he had enough money in his account to cover it. They stood there—Miss Delano and Mr. Pangburn—talking and laughing while I entered the deposit in her book, and then they left, and that was all."

"This check," Axford said slowly, after the teller had gone back to his cage, "is a forgery. But I shall make it good, of course. That ends the matter, Mr. Clement, and there must be no more to-do about it."

"Certainly, Mr. Axford. Certainly."

Clement was all enormously relieved smiles and head-noddings, with this twenty-thousand-dollar load lifted from his bank's shoulders.

Axford and I left the bank then and got into his coupé, in which we had come from his office. But he did not immediately start the engine. He sat for a while staring at the traffic of Montgomery Street with unseeing eyes.

"I want you to find Burke," he said presently, and there was no emotion of any sort in his bass voice. "I want you to find him without risking the least whisper of scandal. If my wife knew of all this—She mustn't know. She thinks her brother is a choice morsel. I want you to find him for me. The girl doesn't matter any more, but I suppose that where you find one you will find the other. I'm not interested in the money,

and I don't want you to make any special attempt to recover that; it could hardly be done, I'm afraid, without publicity. I want you to find Burke before he does something else."

"If you want to avoid the wrong kind of publicity," I said, "your best bet is to spread the right kind first. Let's advertise him as missing, fill the papers up with his pictures and so forth. They'll play him up strong. He's your brother-in-law and he's a poet. We can say that he has been ill—you told me that he had been in delicate health all his life—and that we fear he has dropped dead somewhere or is suffering under some mental derangement. There will be no necessity of mentioning the girl or the money, and our explanation may keep people—especially your wife—from guessing the truth when the fact that he is missing leaks out. It's bound to leak out somehow."

He didn't like my idea at first, but I finally won him over.

We went up to Pangburn's apartment then, easily securing admittance on Axford's explanation that we had an engagement with him and would wait there for him. I went through the rooms inch by inch, prying into each hole and hollow and crack; reading everything that was written anywhere, even down to his manuscripts; and I found nothing that threw any light on his disappearance.

I helped myself to his photographs—pocketing five of the dozen or more that were there. Axford did not think that any of the poet's bags or trunks were missing from the packroom. I did not find his Golden Gate Trust Company deposit book.

I spent the rest of the day loading the newspapers up with what we wished them to have; and they gave my ex-client one grand spread: first-page stuff with photographs and all possible trimmings. Anyone in San Francisco who didn't know that Burke Pangburn—brother-in-law of R. F. Axford and author of *Sandpatches and Other Verse*—was missing, either couldn't read or wouldn't.

IX

This advertising brought results. By the following morning, reports were rolling in from all directions, from dozens of people who had seen the missing poet in dozens of places. A few of these reports looked promising—or at least possible—but the majority were ridiculous on their faces.

I came back to the agency from running out one that had—until run out—looked good, to find a note on my desk asking me to call up Axford.

"Can you come down to my office now?" he asked when I got him on the wire.

There was a lad of twenty-one or -two with Axford when I was ushered into his office: a narrow-chested, dandified lad of the sporting clerk type.

"This is Mr. Fall, one of my cmployees," Axford told me. "He says he saw Burke Sunday night."

"Where?" I asked Fall.

"Going into a roadhouse near Halfmoon Bay."

"Sure it was him?"

"Absolutely! I've seen him come in here to Mr. Axford's office to know him. It was him all right."

"How'd you come to see him?"

"I was coming up from further down the shore with some friends, and we stopped in at the roadhouse to get something to eat. As we were leaving, a car drovc up and Mr. Pangburn and a girl or woman—I didn't notice her particularly—got out and went inside. I didn't think anything of it until I saw in the paper last night that he hadn't been seen since Sunday. So then I thought to myself that—"

"What roadhouse was this?" I cut in, not being interested in his mental processes.

"The White Shack."

"About what time?"

"Somewhere between eleven-thirty and midnight, I guess."

"He see you?"

"No. I was already in our car when he drove up. I don't think he'd know me anyway."

"What did the woman look like?"

"I don't know. I didn't see her face, and I can't remember how she was dressed or even if she was short or tall."

That was all Fall could tell me.

We shooed him out of the office, and I used Axford's telephone to call up "Wop" Healey's dive in North Beach and leave word that when "Porky" Grout came in he was to call up "Jack." That was a standing arrangement by which I got word to Porky whenever I wanted to see him, without giving anybody a chance to tumble to the connection between us.

"Know the White Shack?" I asked Axford, when I was through phoning.

"I know where it is, but I don't know anything about it."

"Well, it's a tough hole. Run by 'Tin-Star' Joplin, an ex-yegg* who invested his winnings in the place when Prohibition made the roadhouse game good. He makes more money now than he ever heard of in his piking† safe-ripping days. Retailing liquor is a sideline with him; his real profit comes from acting as a relay station for the booze that comes through Halfmoon Bay for points beyond; and the dope is that half the booze put ashore by the Pacific rum fleet is put ashore in Halfmoon Bay.

"The White Shack is a tough hole, and it's no place for your brother-in-law to be hanging around. I can't go down there myself without stirring things up; Joplin and I are old friends. But I've got a man I can put in there for a few nights. Pangburn may be a regular visitor, or he may even be staying there. He wouldn't be the first one Joplin had ever let hide-out there. I'll put this man of mine in the place for a week, anyway, and see what he can find."

---

* burgler
† itinerant

"It's all in your hands," Axford said. "Find Burke without scandal—that's all I ask."

X

From Axford's office I went straight to my rooms, left the outer door unlocked, and sat down to wait for Porky Grout. I had waited an hour and a half when he pushed the door open and came in.

"'Lo! How's tricks?"

He swaggered to a chair, leaned back in it, put his feet on the table and reached for a pack of cigarettes that lay there.

That was Porky Grout. A pasty-faced man in his thirties, neither large nor small, always dressed flashily—even if sometimes dirtily—and trying to hide an enormous cowardice behind a swaggering carriage, a blustering habit of speech, and an exaggerated pretense of self-assurance.

But I had known him for three years; so now I crossed the room and pushed his feet roughly off the table, almost sending him over backward.

"What's the idea?" He came to his feet, crouching and snarling. "Where do you get that stuff? Do you want a smack in the—"

I took a step toward him. He sprang away, across the room.

"Aw, I didn't mean nothin'. I was only kiddin'!"

"Shut up and sit down," I advised him.

I had known this Porky Grout for three years, and had been using him for nearly that long, and I didn't know a single thing that could be said in his favor. He was a coward. He was a liar. He was a thief, and a hophead. He was a traitor to his kind and, if not watched, to his employers. A nice bird to deal with! But detecting is a hard business, and you use whatever tools come to hand. This Porky was an effective tool if handled right, which meant keeping your hand on his throat all the time and checking up every piece of information he brought in.

His cowardice was—for my purpose—his greatest asset. It was notorious throughout the criminal Coast; and though nobody—crook or not—could possibly think him a man to be trusted, nevertheless he was not actually distrusted. Most of his fellows thought him too much the coward to be dangerous; they thought he would be afraid to betray them; afraid of the summary vengeance that crookdom visits upon the squealer. But they didn't take into account Porky's gift for convincing himself that he was a lion-hearted fellow, when no danger was near. So he went freely where he desired and where I sent him, and brought me otherwise unobtainable bits of information upon matters in which I was interested.

For nearly three years I had used him with considerable success, paying him well, and keeping him under my heel. *Informant* was the polite word that designated him in my reports; the underworld has even less lovely names than the common *stool-pigeon* to denote his kind.

"I have a job for you," I told him, now that he was seated again, with his feet on the floor.

His loose mouth twitched up at the left corner, pushing that eye into a knowing squint.

"I thought so."

He always says something like that.

"I want you to go down to Halfmoon Bay and stick around Tin-Star Joplin's joint for a few nights. Here are two photos"—sliding one of Pangburn and one of the girl across the table. "Their names and descriptions are written on the backs. I want to know if either of them shows up down there, what they're doing, and where they're hanging out. It may be that Tin-Star is covering them up."

Porky was looking knowingly from one picture to the other.

"I think I know this guy," he said out of the corner of his mouth that twitches.

That's another thing about Porky. You can't mention a name or give a description that won't bring that same remark, even though you make them up.

"Here's some money." I slid some bills across the table. "If you're down there more than a couple of nights, I'll get some more to you. Keep in touch with me, either over this phone or the under-cover one at the office. And—remember this—lay off the stuff! If I come down there and find you all snowed up,* I promise that I'll tip Joplin off to you."

He had finished counting the money by now—there wasn't a whole lot to count—and he threw it contemptuously back on the table.

"Save that for newspapers," he sneered. "How am I goin' to get anywheres if I can't spend no money in the joint?"

"That's plenty for a couple of days' expenses; you'll probably knock back half of it. If you stay longer than a couple of days, I'll get more to you. And you get your pay when the job is done, and not before."

He shook his head and got up.

"I'm tired of pikin'† along with you. You can turn your own jobs. I'm through!"

"If you don't get down to Halfmoon Bay tonight, you *are* through," I assured him, letting him get out of the threat whatever he liked.

After a little while, of course, he took the money and left. The dispute over expense money was simply a preliminary that went with every job I sent him out on.

XI

After Porky had cleared out, I leaned back in my chair and burned half a dozen Fatimas over the job. The girl had gone first with the twenty thousand dollars, and then the poet had gone; and both had gone, whether permanently or not, to the White Shack. On its face, the job was an obvious affair. The girl had given Pangburn the *work* to the extent of having him forge a check against his brother-in-law's account; and then, after various moves whose value I couldn't determine at the time, they had gone into hiding together.

———————
* high on heroin
† walking

There were two loose ends to be taken care of. One of them—the finding of the confederate who had mailed the letters to Pangburn and who had taken care of the girl's baggage—was in the Baltimore branch's hands. The other was: Who had ridden in the taxicab that I had traced from the girl's apartment to the Marquis Hotel?

That might not have any bearing upon the job, or it might. Suppose I could find a connection between the Marquis Hotel and the White Shack. That would make a completed chain of some sort. I searched the back of the telephone directory and found the roadhouse number. Then I went up to the Marquis Hotel.

The girl on duty at the hotel switchboard, when I got there, was one with whom I had done business before.

"Who's been calling Halfmoon Bay numbers?" I asked her.

"My God!" She leaned back in her chair and ran a pink hand gently over the front of her rigidly waved red hair. "I got enough to do without remembering every call that goes through. This ain't a boarding-house. We have more'n one call a week."

"You don't have many Halfmoon Bay calls," I insisted, leaning an elbow on the counter and letting a folded five-spot peep out between the fingers of one hand. "You ought to remember any you've had lately."

"I'll see," she sighed, as if willing to do her best on a hopeless task.

She ran through her tickets.

"Here's one—from room 522, a couple weeks ago."

"What number was called?"

"Halfmoon Bay 51."

That was the roadhouse number. I passed over the five-spot.

"Is 522 a permanent guest?"

"Yes. Mr. Kilcourse. He's been here three or four months."

"What is he?"

"I don't know. A perfect gentleman, if you ask me."

"That's nice. What does he look like?"

"Tall and elegant."

"Be yourself," I pleaded. "What does he look like?"

"He's a young man, but his hair is turning gray. He's dark and handsome. Looks like a movie actor."

"Bull Montana?"* I asked, as I moved off toward the desk.

The key to 522 was in its place in the rack. I sat down where I could keep an eye on it. Perhaps an hour later a clerk took it out and gave it to a man who did look somewhat like an actor. He was a man of thirty or so, with dark skin, and dark hair that showed gray around the ears. He stood a good six feet of fashionably dressed slenderness.

Carrying the key, he disappeared into an elevator.

I called up the agency then and asked the Old Man to send Dick Foley over. Ten minutes later Dick arrived. He's a little shrimp of a Canadian—there isn't a hundred and ten pounds of him—who is the smoothest shadow I've ever seen, and I've seen most of them.

"I have a bird in here I want tailed," I told Dick. "His name is Kilcourse and he's in room 522. Stick around outside, and I'll give you the spot on him."

I went back to the lobby and waited some more.

At eight o'clock Kilcourse came down and left the hotel. I went after him for half a block— far enough to turn him over to Dick—and then went home, so that I would be within reach of a telephone if Porky Grout tried to get in touch with me. No call came from him that night.

XII

When I arrived at the agency the next morning, Dick was waiting for me.

"What luck?" I asked.

_____
* professional wrestler and silent-movie actor

"Damndest!" The little Canadian talks like a telegram when his peace of mind is disturbed, and just now he was decidedly peevish. "Took me two blocks. Shook me. Only taxi in sight."

"Think he made you?"

"No. Wise head. Playing safe."

"Try him again, then. Better have a car handy, in case he tries the same trick again."

My telephone jingled as Dick was going out. It was Porky Grout, talking over the agency's unlisted line.

"Turn up anything?" I asked.

"Plenty," he bragged.

"Good! Are you in town?"

"Yes."

"I'll meet you in my rooms in twenty minutes," I said.

The pasty-faced informant was fairly bloated with pride in himself when he came through the door I had left unlocked for him. His swagger was almost a cake-walk; and the side of his mouth that twitches was twisted into a knowing leer that would have fit a Solomon.

"I knocked it over for you, kid," he boasted. "Nothin' to it—for me! I went down there and talked to ever'body that knowed anything, seen ever'thing there was to see, and put the X-ray on the whole dump. I made a—"

"Uh-huh," I interrupted. "Congratulations and so forth. But just what did you turn up?"

"Now le'me tell you." He raised a dirty hand in a traffic-cop sort of gesture, and blew a stream of cigarette smoke at the ceiling. "Don't crowd me. I'll give you all the dope."

"Sure," I said. "I know. You're great, and I'm lucky to have you to knock off my jobs for me, and all that! But is Pangburn down there?"

"I'm gettin' around to that. I went down there and—"

"Did you see Pangburn?"

"As I was sayin', I went down there and—"

"Porky," I said, "I don't give a damn what you did! Did you see Pangburn?"

"Yes. I seen him."

"Fine! Now what did you see?"

"He's camping down there with Tin-Star. Him and the broad that you give me a picture of are both there. She's been there a month. I didn't see her, but one of the waiters told me about her. I seen Pangburn myself. They don't show themselves much—stick back in Tin-Star's part of the joint—where he lives—most of the time. Pangburn's been there since Sunday. I went down there and—"

"Learn who the girl is? Or anything about what they're up to?"

"No. I went down there and—"

"All right! *Went down there* again tonight. Call me up as soon as you know positively Pangburn is there—that he hasn't gone out. Don't make any mistakes. I don't want to come down there and scare them up on a false alarm. Use the agency's under-cover line, and just tell whoever answers that you won't be in town until late. That'll mean that Pangburn is there; and it'll let you call up from Joplin's without giving the play away."

"I got to have more dough," he said, as he got up. "It costs—"

"I'll file your application," I promised. "Now beat it, and let me hear from you tonight, the minute you're sure Pangburn is there."

Then I went up to Axford's office.

"I think I have a line on him," I told the millionaire. "I hope to have him where you can talk to him tonight. My man says he was at the White Shack last night, and is probably living there. If he's there tonight, I'll take you down, if you want."

"Why can't we go now?"

"No. The place is too dead in the daytime for my man to hang around without making himself conspicuous, and I don't want to take any chances on either you or me showing ourselves there until we're sure we're coming face to face with Pangburn."

"What do you want me to do then?"

"Have a fast car ready tonight, and be ready to start as soon as I get word to you."

"Righto. I'll be at home after five-thirty.

Phone me as soon as you're ready to go, and I'll pick you up."

XIII

At nine-thirty that evening I was sitting beside Axford on the front seat of a powerfully engined foreign car, and we were roaring down a road that led to Halfmoon Bay. Porky's telephone call had come.

Neither of us talked much during that ride, and the imported monster under us made it a rather short ride. Axford sat comfortable and relaxed at the wheel, but I noticed for the first time that he had a rather heavy jaw.

The White Shack is a large building, square-built, of imitation stone. It is set away back from the road, and is approached by two curving driveways, which, together, make a semi-circle whose diameter is the public road. The center of this semi-circle is occupied by sheds under which Joplin's patrons stow their cars, and here and there around the sheds are flower-beds and clumps of shrubbery.

We were still going at a fair clip when we turned into one end of this semi-circular driveway, and—

Axford slammed on his brakes, and the big machine threw us into the wind-shield as it jolted into an abrupt stop—barely in time to avoid smashing into a cluster of people who had suddenly loomed up before us.

In the glow from our headlights faces stood sharply out; white, horrified faces, furtive faces, faces that were callously curious. Below the faces, white arms and shoulders showed, and bright gowns and jewelry, against the duller background of masculine clothing.

This was the first impression I got, and then, by the time I had removed my face from the windshield, I realized that this cluster of people had a core, a thing about which it centered. I stood up, trying to look over the crowd's heads, but I could see nothing.

Jumping down to the driveway, I pushed through the crowd.

Face down on the white gravel a man sprawled—a thin man in dark clothes—and just above his collar, where the head and neck join, was a hole. I knelt to peer into his face.

Then I pushed through the crowd again, back to where Axford was just getting out of the car, the engine of which was still running.

"Pangburn is dead—shot!"

XIV

Methodically, Axford took off his gloves, folded them and put them in a pocket. Then he nodded his understanding of what I had told him, and walked toward where the crowd stood around the dead poet. I looked after him until he had vanished in the throng. Then I went winding through the outskirts of the crowd, hunting for Porky Grout.

I found him standing on the porch, leaning against a pillar. I passed where he could see me, and went on around to the side of the roadhouse that afforded most shadow.

In the shadows Porky joined me. The night wasn't cool, but his teeth were chattering.

"Who got him?" I demanded.

"I don't know," he whined, and that was the first thing of which I had ever known him to confess complete ignorance. "I was inside, keepin' an eye on the others."

"What others?"

"Tin-Star, and some guy I never seen before, and the broad. I didn't think the kid was going out. He didn't have no hat."

"What *do* you know about it?"

"A little while after I phoned you, the girl and Pangburn came out from Joplin's part of the joint and sat down at a table around on the other side of the porch, where it's fairly dark. They eat for a while and then this other guy comes over and sits down with 'em. I don't know his name, but I think I've saw him around town. He's a tall guy, all rung up in fancy rags."

That would be Kilcourse.

"They talk for a while and then Joplin joins 'em. They sit around the table laughin' and talkin' for maybe a quarter of an hour. Then Pangburn gets up and goes indoors. I got a table that I can watch 'em from, and the place is crowded, and I'm afraid I'll lose my table if I leave it, so I don't follow the kid. He ain't got no hat; I figure he ain't goin' nowhere. But he must of gone through the house and out front, because pretty soon there's a noise that I thought was a auto backfire, and then the sound of a car gettin' away quick. And then some guy squawks that there's a dead man outside. Ever'body runs out here, and it's Pangburn."

"You dead sure that Joplin, Kilcourse and the girl were all at the table when Pangburn was killed?"

"Absolutely," Porky said, "if this dark guy's name is Kilcourse."

"Where are they now?"

"Back in Joplin's hang-out. They went up there as soon as they seen Pangburn had been croaked."

I had no illusions about Porky. I knew he was capable of selling me out and furnishing the poet's murderer with an alibi. But there was this about it: if Joplin, Kilcourse or the girl had fixed him, and had fixed my informant, then it was hopeless for me to try to prove that they weren't on the rear porch when the shot was fired. Joplin had a crowd of hangers-on who would swear to anything he told them without batting an eye. There would be a dozen supposed witnesses to their presence on the rear porch.

Thus the only thing for me to do was to take it for granted that Porky was coming clean with me.

"Have you seen Dick Foley?" I asked, since Dick had been shadowing Kilcourse.

"No."

"Hunt around and see if you can find him. Tell him I've gone up to talk to Joplin, and tell him to come on up. Then you can stick around where I can get hold of you if I want you."

I went in through a French window, crossed

an empty dance-floor and went up the stairs that led to Tin-Star Joplin's living quarters in the rear second story. I knew the way, having been up there before. Joplin and I were old friends.

I was going up now to give him and his friends a shake-down on the off-chance that some good might come of it, though I knew that I had nothing on any of them. I could have tied something on the girl, of course, but not without advertising the fact that the dead poet had forged his brother-in-law's signature to a check. And that was no go.

"Come in," a heavy, familiar voice called when I rapped on Joplin's living-room door.

I pushed the door open and went in.

Tin-Star Joplin was standing in the middle of the floor: a big-bodied ex-yegg with inordinately thick shoulders and an expressionless horse face. Beyond him Kilcourse sat dangling one leg from the corner of a table, alertness hiding behind an amused half-smile on his handsome dark face. On the other side of a room a girl whom I knew for Jeanne Delano sat on the arm of a big leather chair. And the poet hadn't exaggerated when he told me she was beautiful.

"You!" Joplin grunted disgustedly as soon as he recognized me. "What the hell do *you* want?"

"What've you got?"

My mind wasn't on this sort of repartee, however; I was studying the girl. There was something vaguely familiar about her—but I couldn't place her. Perhaps I hadn't seen her before; perhaps much looking at the picture Pangburn had given me was responsible for my feeling of recognition. Pictures will do that.

Meanwhile, Joplin had said:

"Time to waste is one thing I ain't got."

And I had said:

"If you'd saved up all the time different judges have given you, you'd have plenty."

I had seen the girl somewhere before. She was a slender girl in a glistening blue gown that exhibited a generous spread of front, back and arms that were worth showing. She had a mass of dark brown hair above an oval face of the color that pink ought to be. Her eyes were wide-set

and of a gray shade that wasn't altogether unlike the shadows on polished silver that the poet had compared them to.

I studied the girl, and she looked back at me with level eyes, and still I couldn't place her. Kilcourse still sat dangling a leg from the table corner.

Joplin grew impatient.

"Will you stop gandering at the girl, and tell me what you want of me?" he growled.

The girl smiled then, a mocking smile that bared the edges of razor-sharp little animal teeth. And with the smile I knew her!

Her hair and skin had fooled me. The last time I had seen her—the only time I had seen her before—her face had been marble-white, and her hair had been short and the color of fire. She and an older woman and three men and I had played hide-and-seek one evening in a house in Turk Street over a matter of the murder of a bank messenger and the theft of a hundred thousand dollars' worth of Liberty Bonds. Through her intriguing three of her accomplices had died that evening, and the fourth—the Chinese—had eventually gone to the gallows at Folsom prison. Her name had been Elvira then, and since her escape from the house that night we had been fruitlessly hunting her from border to border, and beyond.

Recognition must have shown in my eyes in spite of the effort I made to keep them blank, for, swift as a snake, she had left the arm of the chair and was coming forward, her eyes more steel than silver.

I put my gun in sight.

Joplin took a half-step toward me.

"What's the idea?" he barked.

Kilcourse slid off the table, and one of his thin dark hands hovered over his necktie.

"This is the idea," I told them. "I want the girl for a murder a couple months back, and maybe—I'm not sure—for tonight's. Anyway, I'm—"

The snapping of a light-switch behind me, and the room went black.

I moved, not caring where I went so long as I

got away from where I had been when the lights went out.

My back touched a wall and I stopped, crouching low.

"Quick, kid!" A hoarse whisper that came from where I thought the door should be.

But both of the room's doors, I thought, were closed, and could hardly be opened without showing gray rectangles. People moved in the blackness, but none got between me and the lighter square of windows.

Something clicked softly in front of me—too thin a click for the cocking of a gun—but it could have been the opening of a spring-knife, and I remembered that Tin-Star Joplin had a fondness for that weapon.

"Let's go! Let's go!" A harsh whisper that cut through the dark like a blow.

Sounds of motion, muffled, indistinguishable . . . one sound not far away. . . .

Abruptly a strong hand clamped one of my shoulders, a hard-muscled body strained against me. I stabbed out with my gun, and heard a grunt.

The hand moved up my shoulder toward my throat.

I snapped up a knee, and heard another grunt.

A burning point ran down my side.

I stabbed again with my gun—pulled it back until the muzzle was clear of the soft obstacle that had stopped it, and squeezed the trigger.

The crash of the shot. Joplin's voice in my ear—a curiously matter-of-fact voice:

"God damn! That got me."

XV

I spun away from him then, toward where I saw the dim yellow of an open door. I had heard no sounds of departure. I had been too busy. But I knew that Joplin had tied into me while the others made their get-away.

Nobody was in sight as I jumped, slid, tumbled down the steps—any number at a time. A waiter got in my path as I plunged toward the dance-floor. I don't know whether his interference was intentional or not. I didn't ask. I slammed the flat of my gun in his face and went on. Once I jumped a leg that came out to trip me; and at the outer door I had to smear another face.

Then I was out in the semi-circular driveway, from one end of which a red tail-light was turning east into the county road.

While I sprinted for Axford's car I noticed that Pangburn's body had been removed. A few people still stood around the spot where he had lain, and they gaped at me now with open mouths.

The car was as Axford had left it, with idling engine. I swung it through a flower-bed and pointed it east on the public road. Five minutes later I picked up the red point of a tail-light again.

The car under me had more power than I would ever need, more than I would have known how to handle. I don't know how fast the one ahead was going, but I closed in as if it had been standing still.

A mile and a half, or perhaps two—

Suddenly a man was in the road ahead—a little beyond the reach of my lights. The lights caught him, and I saw that it was Porky Grout!

Porky Grout standing facing me in the middle of the road, the dull metal of an automatic in each hand.

The guns in his hands seemed to glow dimly red and then go dark in the glare of my headlights—glow and then go dark, like two bulbs in an automatic electric sign.

The windshield fell apart around me.

Porky Grout—the informant whose name was a synonym for cowardice the full length of the Pacific Coast—stood in the center of the road shooting at a metal comet that rushed down upon him. . . .

I didn't see the end.

I confess frankly that I shut my eyes when his set white face showed close over my radiator. The metal monster under me trembled—

not very much—and the road ahead was empty except for the fleeing red light. My windshield was gone. The wind tore at my uncovered hair and brought tears to my squinted-up eyes.

Presently I found that I was talking to myself, saying, "That was Porky. That was Porky." It was an amazing fact. It was no surprise that he had double-crossed me. That was to be expected. And for him to have crept up the stairs behind me and turned off the lights wasn't astonishing. But for him to have stood straight up and died—

An orange streak from the car ahead cut off my wonderment. The bullet didn't come near me—it isn't easy to shoot accurately from one moving car into another—but at the pace I was going it wouldn't be long before I was close enough for good shooting.

I turned on the searchlight above the dashboard. It didn't quite reach the car ahead, but it enabled me to see that the girl was driving, while Kilcourse sat screwed around beside her, facing me. The car was a yellow roadster.

I eased up a little. In a duel with Kilcourse here I would have been at a disadvantage, since I would have had to drive as well as shoot. My best play seemed to be to hold my distance until we reached a town, as we inevitably must. It wasn't midnight yet. There would be people on the streets of any town, and policemen. Then I could close in with a better chance of coming off on top.

A few miles of this and my prey tumbled to my plan. The yellow roadster slowed down, wavered, and came to rest with its length across the road. Kilcourse and the girl were out immediately and crouching in the road on the far side of their barricade.

I was tempted to dive pell-mell into them, but it was a weak temptation, and when its short life had passed I put on the brakes and stopped. Then I fiddled with my searchlight until it bore full upon the roadster.

A flash came from somewhere near the roadster's wheels, and the searchlight shook violently, but the glass wasn't touched. It would be their first target, of course, and . . .

Crouching in my car, waiting for the bullet that would smash the lense, I took off my shoes and overcoat.

The third bullet ruined the light.

I switched off the other lights, jumped to the road, and when I stopped running I was squatting down against the near side of the yellow roadster. As easy and safe a trick as can be imagined.

The girl and Kilcourse had been looking into the glare of a powerful light. When that light suddenly died, and the weaker ones around it went, too, they were left in pitch unseeing blackness, which must last for the minute or longer that their eyes would need to readjust themselves to the gray-black of the night. My stockinged feet had made no sound on the macadam road, and now there was only a roadster between us; and I knew it and they didn't.

From near the radiator Kilcourse spoke softly:

"I'm going to try to knock him off from the ditch. Take a shot at him now and then to keep him busy."

"I can't see him," the girl protested.

"Your eyes'll be all right in a second. Take a shot at the car anyway."

I moved toward the radiator as the girl's pistol barked at the empty touring car.

Kilcourse, on hands and knees, was working his way toward the ditch that ran along the south side of the road. I gathered my legs under me, intent upon a spring and a blow with my gun upon the back of his head. I didn't want to kill him, but I wanted to put him out of the way quick. I'd have the girl to take care of, and she was at least as dangerous as he.

As I tensed for the spring, Kilcourse, guided perhaps by some instinct of the hunted, turned his head and saw me—saw a threatening shadow.

Instead of jumping I fired.

I didn't look to see whether I had hit him or not. At that range there was little likelihood of missing. I bent double and slipped back to the rear of the roadster, keeping on my side of it.

Then I waited.

The girl did what I would perhaps have done in her place. She didn't shoot or move toward the place the shot had come from. She thought I had forestalled Kilcourse in using the ditch and that my next play would be to circle around behind her. To offset this, she moved around the rear of the roadster, so that she could ambush me from the side nearest Axford's car.

Thus it was that she came creeping around the corner and poked her delicately chiseled nose plunk into the muzzle of the gun that I held ready for her.

She gave a little scream.

Women aren't always reasonable: they are prone to disregard trifles like guns held upon them. So I grabbed her gun hand, which was fortunate for me. As my hand closed around the weapon, she pulled the trigger, catching a chunk of my forefinger between hammer and frame. I twisted the gun out of her hand; released my finger.

But she wasn't done yet.

With me standing there holding a gun not four inches from her body, she turned and bolted off toward where a clump of trees made a jet-black blot to the north.

When I recovered from my surprise at this amateurish procedure, I stuck both her gun and mine in my pockets, and set out after her, tearing the soles of my feet at every step.

She was trying to get over a wire fence when I caught her.

XVI

"Stop playing, will you?" I said crossly, as I set the fingers of my left hand around her wrist and started to lead her back to the roadster. "This is a serious business. Don't be so childish!"

"You are hurting my arm."

I knew I wasn't hurting her arm, and I knew this girl for the direct cause of four, or perhaps five, deaths; yet I loosened my grip on her wrist until it wasn't much more than a friendly clasp. She went back willingly enough to the roadster,

where, still holding her wrist, I switched on the lights.

Kilcourse lay just beneath the headlight's glare, huddled on his face, with one knee drawn up under him.

I put the girl squarely in the line of light.

"Now stand there," I said, "and behave. The first break you make, I'm going to shoot a leg out from under you," and I meant it.

I found Kilcourse's gun, pocketed it, and knelt beside him.

He was dead, with a bullet-hole above his collar-bone.

"Is he—" her mouth trembled.

"Yes."

She looked down at him, and shivered a little.

"Poor Fag," she whispered.

I've gone on record as saying that this girl was beautiful, and, standing there in the dazzling white of the headlights, she was more than that. She was a thing to start crazy thoughts even in the head of an unimaginative middle-aged thief-catcher. She was—

Anyhow, I suppose that is why I scowled at her and said:

"Yes, poor Fag, and poor Hook, and poor Tai, and poor kid of a Los Angeles bank messenger, and poor Burke," calling the roll, so far as I knew it, of men who had died loving her.

She didn't flare up. Her big gray eyes lifted, and she looked at me with a gaze that I couldn't fathom, and her lovely oval face under the mass of brown hair—which I knew was phoney—was sad.

"I suppose you do think—" she began.

But I had had enough of this; I was uncomfortable along the spine.

"Come on," I said. "We'll leave Kilcourse and the roadster here for the present."

She said nothing, but went with me to Axford's big machine, and sat in silence while I laced my shoes. I found a robe on the back seat and gave it to her.

"Better wrap this around your shoulders. The windshield is gone. It'll be cool."

She followed my suggestion without a word,

but when I had edged our vehicle around the rear of the roadster, and had straightened out in the road again, going east, she laid a hand on my arm.

"Aren't we going back to the White Shack?"

"No. Redwood City—the county jail."

A mile perhaps, during which, without looking at her, I knew she was studying my rather lumpy profile. Then her hand was on my forearm again and she was leaning toward me so that her breath was warm against my cheek.

"Will you stop for a minute? There's something—some things I want to tell you."

I brought the car to a halt in a cleared space of hard soil off to one side of the road, and screwed myself a little around in the seat to face her more directly.

"Before you start," I told her, "I want you to understand that we stay here for just so long as you talk about the Pangburn affair. When you get off on any other line—then we finish our trip to Redwood City."

"Aren't you even interested in the Los Angeles affair?"

"No. That's closed. You and Hook Riordan and Tai Choon Tau and the Quarres were equally responsible for the messenger's death, even if Hook did the actual killing. Hook and the Quarres passed out the night we had our party in Turk Street. Tai was hanged last month. Now I've got you. We had enough evidence to swing the Chinese, and we've even more against you. That is done—finished—completed. If you want to tell me anything about Pangburn's death, I'll listen. Otherwise—"

I reached for the self-starter.

A pressure of her fingers on my arm stopped me.

"I do want to tell you about it," she said earnestly. "I want you to know the truth about it. You'll take me to Redwood City, I know. Don't think that I expect—that I have any foolish hopes. But I'd like you to know the truth about this thing. I don't know why I should care especially what you think, but—"

Her voice dwindled off to nothing.

XVII

Then she began to talk very rapidly—as people talk when they fear interruptions before their stories are told—and she sat leaning slightly forward, so that her beautiful oval face was very close to mine.

"After I ran out of the Turk Street house that night—while you were struggling with Tai—my intention was to get away from San Francisco. I had a couple of thousand dollars, enough to carry me any place. Then I thought that going away would be what you people would expect me to do, and that the safest thing for me to do would be to stay right here. It isn't hard for a woman to change her appearance. I had bobbed red hair, white skin, and wore gay clothes. I simply dyed my hair, bought these transformations to make it look long, put color on my face, and bought some dark clothes. Then I took an apartment on Ashbury Avenue under the name of Jeanne Delano, and I was an altogether different person.

"But, while I knew I was perfectly safe from recognition anywhere, I felt more comfortable staying indoors for a while, and, to pass the time, I read a good deal. That's how I happened to run across Burke's book. Do you read poetry?"

I shook my head. An automobile going toward Halfmoon Bay came into sight just then—the first one we'd seen since we left the White Shack. She waited until it had passed before she went on, still talking rapidly.

"Burke wasn't a genius, of course, but there was something about some of his things that—something that got inside me. I wrote him a little note, telling him how much I had enjoyed these things, and sent it to his publishers. A few days later I had a note from Burke, and I learned that he lived in San Francisco. I hadn't known that.

"We exchanged several notes, and then he asked if he could call, and we met. I don't know whether I was in love with him or not, even at first. I did like him, and, between the ardor of his love for me and the flattery of having a fairly well-known poet for a suitor, I really thought that I loved him. I promised to marry him.

"I hadn't told him anything about myself, though now I know that it wouldn't have made any difference to him. But I was afraid to tell him the truth, and I wouldn't lie to him, so I told him nothing.

"Then Fag Kilcourse saw me one day on the street, and knew me in spite of my new hair, complexion and clothes. Fag hadn't much brains, but he had eyes that could see through anything. I don't blame Fag. He acted according to his code. He came up to my apartment, having followed me home; and I told him that I was going to marry Burke and be a respectable housewife. That was dumb of me. Fag was square. If I had told him that I was ribbing Burke up for a trimming, Fag would have let me alone, would have kept his hands off. But when I told him that I was through with the graft, had 'gone queer,' that made me his meat. You know how crooks are: everyone in the world is either a fellow crook or a prospective victim. So if I was no longer a crook, then Fag considered me fair game.

"He learned about Burke's family connections, and then he put it up to me—twenty thousand dollars, or he'd turn me up. He knew about the Los Angeles job, and he knew how badly I was wanted. I was up against it then. I knew I couldn't hide from Fag or run away from him. I told Burke I had to have twenty thousand dollars. I didn't think he had that much, but I thought he could get it. Three days later he gave me a check for it. I didn't know at the time how he had raised it, but it wouldn't have mattered if I had known. I had to have it.

"But that night he told me where he got the money; that he had forged his brother-in-law's signature. He told me because, after thinking it over, he was afraid that when the forgery was discovered I would be caught with him and considered equally guilty. I'm rotten in spots, but I wasn't rotten enough to let him put himself in the pen for me, without knowing what it was all about. I told him the whole story. He didn't bat an eye. He insisted that the money be paid Kilcourse, so that I would be safe, and began to plan for my further safety.

"Burke was confident that his brother-in-law wouldn't send him over for forgery, but, to be on the safe side, he insisted that I move and change my name again and lay low until we knew how Axford was going to take it. But that night, after he had gone, I made some plans of my own. I did like Burke—I liked him too much to let him be the goat without trying to save him, and I didn't have a great deal of faith in Axford's kindness. This was the second of the month. Barring accidents, Axford wouldn't discover the forgery until he got his cancelled checks early the following month. That gave me practically a month to work in.

"The next day I drew all my money out of the bank, and sent Burke a letter, saying that I had been called to Baltimore, and I laid a clear trail to Baltimore, with baggage and letters and all, which a pal there took care of for me. Then I went down to Joplin's and got him to put me up. I let Fag know I was there, and when he came down I told him I expected to have the money for him in a day or two.

"He came down nearly every day after that, and I stalled him from day to day, and each time it got easier. But my time was getting short. Pretty soon Burke's letters would be coming back from the phoney address I had given him, and I wanted to be on hand to keep him from doing anything foolish. And I didn't want to get in touch with him until I could give him the twenty thousand, so he could square the forgery before Axford learned of it from his cancelled checks.

"Fag was getting easier and easier to handle, but I still didn't have him where I wanted him. He wasn't willing to give up the twenty thousand dollars—which I was, of course, holding all this time—unless I'd promise to stick with him for good. And I still thought I was in love with Burke, and I didn't want to tie myself up with Fag, even for a little while.

"Then Burke saw me on the street one Sunday night. I was careless, and drove into the city in Joplin's roadster—the one back there. And, as luck would have it, Burke saw me. I told him the truth, the whole truth. And he told me that he had just hired a private detective to find me. He was like a child in some ways: it hadn't occurred to him that the sleuth would dig up anything about the money. But I knew the forged check would be found in a day or two at the most. I knew it!

"When I told Burke that he went to pieces. All his faith in his brother-in-law's forgiveness went. I couldn't leave him the way he was. He'd have babbled the whole thing to the first person he met. So I brought him back to Joplin's with me. My idea was to hold him there for a few days, until we could see how things were going. If nothing appeared in the papers about the check, then we could take it for granted that Axford had hushed the matter up, and Burke could go home and try to square himself. On the other hand, if the papers got the whole story, then Burke would have to look for a permanent hiding-place, and so would I.

"Tuesday evening's and Wednesday morning's papers were full of the news of his disappearance, but nothing was said about the check. That looked good, but we waited another day for good measure. Fag Kilcourse was in on the game by this time, of course, and I had had to pass over the twenty thousand dollars, but I still had hopes of getting it—or most of it—back, so I continued to string him along. I had a hard time keeping him off Burke, though, because he had begun to think he had some sort of right to me, and jealousy made him wicked. But I got Tin-Star to throw a scare into him, and I thought Burke was safe.

"Tonight one of Tin-Star's men came up and told us that a man named Porky Grout, who had been hanging around the place for a couple of nights, had made a couple of cracks that might mean he was interested in us. Grout was pointed out to me, and I took a chance on showing myself in the public part of the place, and sat at a table close to his. He was plain rat—as I guess you know—and in less than five minutes I had him at my table, and half an hour later I knew that he had tipped you off that Burke and I were in

the White Shack. He didn't tell me all this right out, but he told me more than enough for me to guess the rest.

"I went up and told the others. Fag was for killing both Grout and Burke right away. But I talked him out of it. That wouldn't help us any, and I had Grout where he would jump in the ocean for me. I thought I had Fag convinced, but—We finally decided that Burke and I would take the roadster and leave, and that when you got here Porky Grout was to pretend he was hopped up, and point out a man and a woman—any who happened to be handy—as the ones he had taken for us. I stopped to get a cloak and gloves, and Burke went on out to the car alone—and Fag shot him. I didn't know he was going to! I wouldn't have let him! Please believe that! I wasn't as much in love with Burke as I had thought, but please believe that after all he had done for me I wouldn't have let them hurt him!

"After that it was a case of stick with the others whether I liked it or not, and I stuck. We ribbed Grout to tell you that all three of us were on the back porch when Burke was killed, and we had any number of others primed with the same story. Then you came up and recognized me. Just my luck that it had to be you—the only detective in San Francisco who knew me!

"You know the rest: how Porky Grout came up behind you and turned off the lights, and Joplin held you while we ran for the car; and then, when you closed in on us, Grout offered to stand you off while we got clear, and now. . . ."

XVIII

Her voice died, and she shivered a little. The robe I had given her had fallen away from her white shoulders. Whether or not it was because she was so close against my shoulder, I shivered, too. And my fingers, fumbling in my pocket for a cigarette, brought it out twisted and mashed.

"That's all there is to the part you promised to listen to," she said softly, her face turned half away. "I wanted you to know. You're a hard man, but somehow I—"

I cleared my throat, and the hand that held the mangled cigarette was suddenly steady.

"Now don't be crude, sister," I said. "Your work has been too smooth so far to be spoiled by rough stuff now."

She laughed—a brief laugh that was bitter and reckless and just a little weary, and she thrust her face still closer to mine, and the gray eyes were soft and placid.

"Little fat detective whose name I don't know"—her voice had a tired huskiness in it, and a tired mockery—"you think I am playing a part, don't you? You think I am playing for liberty. Perhaps I am. I certainly would take it if it were offered me. But—Men have thought me beautiful, and I have played with them. Women are like that. Men have loved me and, doing what I liked with them, I have found men contemptible. And then comes this little fat detective whose name I don't know, and he acts as if I were a hag—an old squaw. Can I help then being piqued into some sort of feeling for him? Women are like that. Am I so homely that any man has a right to look at me without even interest? Am I ugly?"

I shook my head.

"You're quite pretty," I said, struggling to keep my voice as casual as the words.

"You beast!" she spat, and then her smile grew gentle again. "And yet it is because of that attitude that I sit here and turn myself inside out for you. If you were to take me in your arms and hold me close to the chest that I am already leaning against, and if you were to tell me that there is no jail ahead for me just now, I would be glad, of course. But, though for a while you might hold me, you would then be only one of the men with which I am familiar: men who love and are used and are succeeded by other men. But because you do none of these things, because you are a wooden block of a man, I find myself wanting you. Would I tell you this, little fat detective, if I were playing a game?"

I grunted noncommittally, and forcibly restrained my tongue from running out to moisten my dry lips.

"I'm going to this jail tonight if you are the same hard man who has goaded me into whining love into his uncaring ears, but before that, can't I have one whole-hearted assurance that you think me a little more than 'quite pretty'? Or at least a hint that if I were not a prisoner your pulse might beat a little faster when I touch you? I'm going to this jail for a long while—perhaps to the gallows. Can't I take my vanity there not quite in tatters to keep me company? Can't you do some slight thing to keep me from the afterthought of having bleated all this out to a man who was simply bored?"

Her lids had come down half over the silver-gray eyes; her head had tilted back so far that a little pulse showed throbbing in her white throat; her lips were motionless over slightly parted teeth, as the last word had left them. My fingers went deep into the soft white flesh of her shoulders. Her head went further back, her eyes closed, one hand came up to my shoulder.

"You're beautiful as all hell!" I shouted crazily into her face, and flung her against the door.

It seemed an hour that I fumbled with starter and gears before I had the car back in the road and thundering toward the San Mateo County jail. The girl had straightened herself up in the seat again, and sat huddled within the robe I had given her. I squinted straight ahead into the wind that tore at my hair and face, and the absence of the windshield took my thoughts back to Porky Grout.

Porky Grout, whose yellowness was notorious from Seattle to San Diego, standing rigidly in the path of a charging metal monster, with an inadequate pistol in each hand. She had done that to Porky Grout—this woman beside me! She had done that to Porky Grout, and he hadn't even been human! A slimy reptile whose highest thought had been a skinful of dope had gone grimly to death that she might get away—she—

this woman whose shoulders I had gripped, whose mouth had been close under mine!

I let the car out another notch, holding the road somehow.

We went through a town: a scurrying of pedestrians for safety, surprised faces staring at us, street lights glistening on the moisture the wind had whipped from my eyes. I passed blindly by the road I wanted, circled back to it, and we were out in the country again.

XIX

At the foot of a long, shallow hill I applied the brakes and we snapped to motionlessness.

I thrust my face close to the girl's.

"Furthermore, you are a liar!" I knew I was shouting foolishly, but I was powerless to lower my voice. "Pangburn never put Axford's name on that check. He never knew anything about it. You got in with him because you knew his brother-in-law was a millionaire. You pumped him, finding out everything he knew about his brother-in-law's account at the Golden Gate Trust. You stole Pangburn's bank book—it wasn't in his room when I searched it—and deposited the forged Axford check to his credit, knowing that under those circumstances the check wouldn't be questioned. The next day you took Pangburn into the bank, saying you were going to make a deposit. You took him in because with him standing beside you the check to which *his* signature had been forged wouldn't be questioned. You knew that, being a gentleman, he'd take pains not to see what you were depositing.

"Then you framed the Baltimore trip. He told the truth to me—the truth so far as he knew

it. Then you met him Sunday night—maybe accidentally, maybe not. Anyway, you took him down to Joplin's, giving him some wild yarn that he would swallow and that would persuade him to stay there for a few days. That wasn't hard, since he didn't know anything about either of the twenty-thousand-dollar checks. You and your pal Kilcourse knew that if Pangburn disappeared nobody would ever know that he hadn't forged the Axford check, and nobody would ever suspect that the second check was phoney. You'd have killed him quietly, but when Porky tipped you off that I was on my way down you had to move quick—so you shot him down. That's the truth of it!" I yelled.

All this while she had watched me with wide gray eyes that were calm and tender, but now they clouded a little and a pucker of pain drew her brows together.

I yanked my head away and got the car in motion.

Just before we swept into Redwood City one of her hands came up to my forearm, rested there for a second, patted the arm twice, and withdrew.

I didn't look at her, nor, I think, did she look at me, while she was being booked. She gave her name as Jeanne Delano, and refused to make any statement until she had seen an attorney. It all took a very few minutes.

As she was being led away, she stopped and asked if she might speak privately with me.

We went together to a far corner of the room.

She put her mouth close to my ear so that her breath was warm again on my cheek, as it had been in the car, and whispered the vilest epithet of which the English language is capable.

Then she walked out to her cell.

BLACK MASK, JUNE 1924

"THE GIRL WITH THE SILVER EYES"

Many thanks for the check for "The Girl with the Silver Eyes."

Taken in a lump, the story is pure fiction, but most of its details are based on things that I've either run into myself or got second hand from other detectives. For instance, *"Tin-Star" Joplin's* roadhouse is in California, though not near Halfmoon Bay, and he is exactly as I have set him down. *"Porky" Grout's* original died of tuberculosis in Butte, Montana, two or three years ago. (Some day I'm going to do a psychological study of a stool-pigeon. They're an interesting lot: almost without exception more cowardly even than the ordinary crook, yet they follow the most dangerous calling in the criminal world; for not only is their own world against them, but the detectives who use them seldom hesitate to sacrifice them if anything is gained thereby.) *Jeanne Delano* is partly real, but mostly "made up." (It may be that the Redwood City jail will fail to hold her.) *Fag Kilcourse* has perhaps a half a dozen originals: he isn't an unusual type.

I simply shook these people up together, added a few more to round out the cast of characters, and siced my little fat detective on 'em.

Sincerely yours,
DASHIELL HAMMETT.
San Francisco, Calif.

BLACK MASK, SEPTEMBER 1924

Women, Politics & Murder

BY DASHIELL HAMMETT

Mr. Hammett's San Francisco detective is on the job again, working on a mystery the solution of which is so simple that you'll be ashamed of yourself for not figuring it out. And take our word for it, you won't come within a thousand miles of the explanation—yet this is the most realistic and probable story in the issue.

A PLUMP MAID with bold green eyes and a loose, full-lipped mouth led me up two flights of steps and into an elaborately furnished boudoir, where a woman in black sat at a window. She was a thin woman of a little more than thirty, this murdered man's widow, and her face was white and haggard.

"You are from the Continental Detective Agency?" she asked before I was two steps inside the room.

"Yes."

"I want you to find my husband's murderer." Her voice was shrill, and her dark eyes had wild lights in them. "The police have done nothing. Four days, and they have done nothing. They say it was a robber, but they haven't found him. They haven't found anything!"

"But, Mrs. Gilmore," I began, not exactly tickled to death with this explosion, "you must—"

"I know! I know!" she broke in. "But they have done nothing, I tell you—nothing. I don't believe they've made the slightest effort. I don't believe they want to find h-him!"

"Him?" I asked, because she had started to say *her*. "You think it was a man?"

She bit her lip and looked away from me, out of the window to where San Francisco Bay, the distance making toys of its boats, was blue under the early afternoon sun.

"I don't know," she said hesitantly; "it might have—"

Her face spun toward me—a twitching face—and it seemed impossible that anyone could talk so fast, hurl words out so rapidly one after the other.

"I'll tell you. You can judge for yourself. Bernard wasn't faithful to me. There was a woman who calls herself Cara Kenbrook. She wasn't the first. But I learned about her last month. We quarreled. Bernard promised to give her up. Maybe he didn't. But if he did, I wouldn't put it past her—A woman like that would do anything—anything. And down in my heart I really believe she did it!"

"And you think the police don't want to arrest her?"

"I didn't mean exactly that. I'm all unstrung, and likely to say anything. Bernard was mixed up in politics, you know; and if the police found, or thought, that politics had anything to do with his death, they might—I don't know just what I mean. I'm a nervous, broken woman, and full of crazy notions." She stretched a thin hand out to me. "Straighten this tangle out for me! Find the person who killed Bernard!"

I nodded with empty assurance, still not any too pleased with my client.

"Do you know this Kenbrook woman?" I asked.

"I've seen her on the street, and that's enough to know what sort of person she is!"

"Did you tell the police about her?"

"No-o." She looked out of the window again, and then, as I waited, she added, defensively:

"The police detectives who came to see me acted as if they thought I might have killed Bernard. I was afraid to tell them that I had cause for jealousy. Maybe I shouldn't have kept quiet about that woman, but I didn't think she had done it until afterward, when the police failed to find the murderer. Then I began to think she had done it; but I couldn't make myself go to the police and tell them that I had withheld information. I knew what they'd think. So I—You can twist it around so it'll look as if I hadn't known about the woman, can't you?"

"Possibly. Now as I understand it, your husband was shot on Pine Street, between Leavenworth and Jones, at about three o'clock Tuesday morning. That right?"

"Yes."

"Where was he going?"

"Coming home, I suppose; but I don't know where he had been. Nobody knows. The police haven't found out, if they have tried. He told me Monday evening that he had a business engagement. He was a building contractor, you know. He went out at about half-past eleven, saying he would probably be gone four or five hours."

"Wasn't that an unusual hour to be keeping a business engagement?"

"Not for Bernard. He often had men come to the house at midnight."

"Can you make any guess at all where he was going that night?"

She shook her head with emphasis.

"No. I knew nothing at all about his business affairs, and even the men in his office don't seem to know where he went that night."

That wasn't unlikely. Most of the B. F. Gilmore Construction Company's work had been on city and state contracts, and it isn't altogether unheard-of for secret conferences to go with that kind of work. Your politician-contractor doesn't always move in the open.

"How about enemies?" I asked.

"I don't know anybody that hated him enough to kill him."

"Where does this Kenbrook woman live, do you know?"

"Yes—in the Garford Apartments on Bush Street."

"Nothing you've forgotten to tell me, is there?" I asked, stressing the *me* a little.

"No, I've told you everything I know—every single thing."

CHAPTER II

Walking over to California Street, I shook down my memory for what I had heard here and there of Bernard Gilmore. I could remember a few things—the opposition papers had been in the habit of exposing him every election year—but none of them got me anywhere. I had known him by sight: a boisterous, red-faced man who had hammered his way up from hod-carrier to the ownership of a half-a-million-dollar business and a pretty place in local politics. "A roughneck with a manicure," somebody had called him; a man with a lot of enemies and more friends; a big, good-natured, hard-hitting rowdy.

Odds and ends of a dozen graft scandals in which he had been mixed up, without anybody ever really getting anything on him, flitted through my head as I rode downtown on the too-small outside seat of a cable-car. Then there had been some talk of a bootlegging syndicate of which he was supposed to be the head. . . .

I left the car at Kearny Street and walked over to the Hall of Justice. In the detectives' assembly-room I found O'Gar, the detective-sergeant in charge of the Homicide Detail: a squat man of fifty who goes in for wide-brimmed hats of the movie-sheriff sort, but whose little blue eyes and bullet head aren't handicapped by the trick headgear.

"I want some dope on the Gilmore killing," I told him.

"So do I," he came back. "But if you'll come along I'll tell you what little I know while I'm eating. I ain't had lunch yet."

Safe from eavesdroppers in the clatter of a Sutter Street lunchroom, the detective-sergeant leaned over his clam chowder and told me what he knew about the murder, which wasn't much.

"One of the boys, Kelly, was walking his beat early Tuesday morning, coming down the Jones Street hill from California Street to Pine. It was about three o'clock—no fog or nothing—a clear night. Kelly's within maybe twenty feet of Pine Street when he hears a shot. He whisks around the corner, and there's a man dying on the north sidewalk of Pine Street, halfway between Jones and Leavenworth. Nobody else is in sight. Kelly runs up to the man and finds it's Gilmore. Gilmore dies before he can say a word. The doctors say he was knocked down and then shot; because there's a bruise on his forehead, and the bullet slanted upward in his chest. See what I mean? He was lying on his back when the bullet

hit him, with his feet pointing toward the gun it came from. It was a .38."

"Any money on him?"

O'Gar fed himself two spoons of chowder and nodded.

"Six hundred smacks, a coupla diamonds and a watch. Nothing touched."

"What was he doing on Pine Street at that time in the morning?"

"Damned if I know, brother. Chances are he was going home, but we can't find out where he'd been. Don't even know what direction he was walking in when he was knocked over. He was lying across the sidewalk with his feet to the curb; but that don't mean nothing—he could of turned around three or four times after he was hit."

"All apartment buildings in that block, aren't there?"

"Uh-huh. There's an alley or two running off from the south side; but Kelly says he could see the mouths of both alleys when the shot was fired—before he turned the corner—and nobody got away through them."

"Reckon somebody who lives in that block did the shooting?" I asked.

O'Gar tilted his bowl, scooped up the last drops of the chowder, put them in his mouth, and grunted.

"Maybe. But we got nothing to show that Gilmore knew anybody in that block."

"Many people gather around afterward?"

"A few. There's always people on the street to come running if anything happens. But Kelly says there wasn't anybody that looked wrong—just the ordinary night crowd. The boys gave the neighborhood a combing, but didn't turn up anything."

"Any cars around?"

"Kelly says there wasn't, that he didn't see any, and couldn't of missed seeing it if there'd been one."

"What do you think?" I asked.

He got to his feet, glaring at me.

"I don't think," he said disagreeably; "I'm a police detective."

I knew by that that somebody had been panning him for not finding the murderer.

"I have a line on a woman," I told him. "Want to come along and talk to her with me?"

"I want to," he growled, "but I can't. I got to be in court this afternoon—in half an hour."

CHAPTER III

In the vestibule of the Garford Apartments, I pressed the button tagged Miss Cara Kenbrook several times before the door clicked open. Then I mounted a flight of stairs and walked down a hall to her door. It was opened presently by a tall girl of twenty-three or -four in a black and white crepe dress.

"Miss Cara Kenbrook?"

"Yes."

I gave her a card—one of those that tell the truth about me.

"I'd like to ask you a few questions; may I come in?"

"Do."

Languidly she stepped aside for me to enter, closed the door behind me, and led me back into a living-room that was littered with newspapers, cigarettes in all stages of consumption from unlighted freshness to cold ash, and miscellaneous articles of feminine clothing. She made room for me on a chair by dumping off a pair of pink silk stockings and a hat, and herself sat on some magazines that occupied another chair.

"I'm interested in Bernard Gilmore's death," I said, watching her face.

It wasn't a beautiful face, although it should have been. Everything was there—perfect features; smooth, white skin; big, almost enormous, brown eyes—but the eyes were dead-dull, and the face was as empty of expression as a china door-knob, and what I said didn't change it.

"Bernard Gilmore," she said without interest. "Oh, yes."

"You and he were pretty close friends, weren't you?" I asked, puzzled by her blankness.

"We had been—yes."

"What do you mean by *had been?*"

She pushed back a lock of her short-cut brown hair with a lazy hand.

"I gave him the air last week," she said casually, as if speaking of something that had happened years ago.

"When was the last time you saw him?"

"Last week—Monday, I think—a week before he was killed."

"Was that the time when you broke off with him?"

"Yes."

"Have a row, or part friends?"

"Not exactly either. I just told him that I was through with him."

"How did he take it?"

"It didn't break his heart. I guess he'd heard the same thing before."

"Where were you the night he was killed?"

"At the Coffee Cup, eating and dancing with friends until about one o'clock. Then I came home and went to bed."

"Why did you split with Gilmore?"

"Couldn't stand his wife."

"Huh?"

"She was a nuisance." This without the faintest glint of either annoyance or humor. "She came here one night and raised a racket; so I told Bernie that if he couldn't keep her away from me he'd have to find another playmate."

"Have you any idea who might have killed him?" I asked.

"Not unless it was his wife—these excitable women are always doing silly things."

"If you had given her husband up, what reason would she have for killing him, do you think?"

"I'm sure I don't know," she replied with complete indifference. "But I'm not the only girl that Bernie ever looked at."

"Think there were others, do you? Know anything, or are you just guessing?"

"I don't know any names," she said, "but I'm not just guessing."

I let that go at that and switched back to Mrs. Gilmore, wondering if this girl could be full of dope.

"What happened the night his wife came here?"

"Nothing but that. She followed Bernie here, rang the bell, rushed past me when I opened the door, and began to cry and call Bernie names. Then she started on me, and I told him that if he didn't take her away I'd hurt her, so he took her home."

Admitting I was licked for the time, I got up and moved to the door. I couldn't do anything with this baby just now. I didn't think she was telling the whole truth, but on the other hand it wasn't reasonable to believe that anybody would lie so woodenly—with so little effort to be plausible.

"I may be back later," I said as she let me out.

"All right."

Her manner didn't even suggest that she hoped I wouldn't.

CHAPTER IV

From this unsatisfactory interview I went to the scene of the killing, only a few blocks away, to get a look at the neighborhood. I found the block just as I had remembered it and as O'Gar had described it: lined on both sides by apartment buildings, with two blind alleys—one of which was dignified with a name, Touchard Street—running from the south side.

The murder was four days old; I didn't waste any time snooping around the vicinity; but, after strolling the length of the block, boarded a Hyde Street car, transferred at California Street, and went up to see Mrs. Gilmore again. I was curious to know why she hadn't told me about her call on Cara Kenbrook.

The same plump maid who had admitted me earlier in the afternoon opened the door.

"Mrs. Gilmore is not at home," she said. "But I think she'll be back in half an hour or so."

"I'll wait," I decided.

The maid took me into the library, an immense room on the second floor, with barely enough books in it to give it that name. She switched on a light—the windows were too heavily curtained to let in much daylight—crossed to the door, stopped, moved over to straighten some books on a shelf, looked at me with a half-questioning, half-inviting look in her green eyes, started for the door again, and halted.

By that time I knew she wanted to say something, and needed encouragement. I leaned back in my chair and grinned at her, and decided I had made a mistake—the smile into which her slack lips curved held more coquetry than anything else. She came over to me, walking with an exaggerated swing of the hips, and stood close in front of me.

"What's your mind?" I asked.

"Suppose—suppose a person knew something that nobody else knew; what would it be worth to them?"

"That," I stalled, "would depend on how valuable it was."

"Suppose I knew who killed the boss?" She bent her face close down to mine, and spoke in a husky whisper. "What would that be worth?"

"The newspapers say that one of Gilmore's clubs has offered a thousand-dollar reward. You'd get that."

Her green eyes went greedy, and then suspicious.

"If *you* didn't."

I shrugged. I knew she'd go through with it—whatever it was—now; so I didn't even explain to her that the Continental doesn't touch rewards, and doesn't let its hired men touch them.

"I'll give you my word," I said; "but you'll have to use your own judgment about trusting me."

She licked her lips.

"You're a good fellow, I guess. I wouldn't tell the police, because I know they'd beat me out of the money. But you look like I can trust you." She leered into my face. "I used to have a gentleman friend who was the very image of you, and he was the grandest—"

"Better speak your piece before somebody comes in," I suggested.

She shot a look at the door, cleared her throat, licked her loose mouth again, and dropped on one knee beside my chair.

"I was coming home late Monday night—the night the boss was killed—and was standing in the shadows saying good night to my friend, when the boss came out of the house and walked down the street. And he had hardly got to the corner, when she—Mrs. Gilmore—came out, and went down the street after him. Not trying to catch up with him, you understand; but following him. What do you think of that?"

"What do *you* think of it?"

"*I* think that she finally woke up to the fact that all of her Bernie's dates didn't have anything to do with the building business."

"Do you know that they didn't?"

"Do I know it? I knew that man! He liked 'em—liked 'em all." She smiled into my face, a smile that suggested all evil. "I found *that* out soon after I first came here."

"Do you know when Mrs. Gilmore came back that night—what time?"

"Yes," she said; "at half-past three."

"Sure?"

"Absolutely! After I got undressed I got a blanket and sat at the head of the front stairs. My room's in the rear of the top floor. I wanted to see if they came home together, and if there was a fight. After she came in alone I went back to my room, and it was just twenty-five minutes to four then. I looked at my alarm clock."

"Did you see her when she came in?"

"Just the top of her head and shoulders when she turned toward her room at the landing."

"What's your name?" I asked.

"Lina Best."

"All right, Lina," I told her. "If this is the goods I'll see that you collect on it. Keep your eyes open, and if anything else turns up you can get in touch with me at the Continental office. Now you'd better beat it, so nobody will know we've had our heads together."

Alone in the library, I cocked an eye at the ceiling and considered the information Lina Best had given me. But I soon gave that up—no use trying to guess at things that will work out for themselves in a while. I found a book, and spent the next half-hour reading about a sweet young she-chump and a big strong he-chump and all their troubles.

Then Mrs. Gilmore came in, apparently straight from the street.

I got up and closed the doors behind her, while she watched me with wide eyes.

"Mrs. Gilmore," I said, when I faced her again, "why didn't you tell me that you followed your husband the night he was killed?"

"That's a lie!" she cried; but there was no truth in her voice. "That's a lie!"

"Don't you think you're making a mistake?" I urged. "Don't you think you'd better tell me the whole thing?"

She opened her mouth, but only a dry sobbing sound came out; and she began to sway with a hysterical rocking motion, the fingers of one black-gloved hand plucking at her lower lip, twisting and pulling it.

I stepped to her side and set her down in the chair I had been sitting in, making foolish clucking sounds—meant to soothe her—with my tongue. A disagreeable ten minutes—and gradually she pulled herself together; her eyes lost their glassiness, and she stopped clawing at her mouth.

"I did follow him." It was a hoarse whisper, barely audible.

Then she was out of the chair, kneeling, with arms held up to me, and her voice was a thin scream.

"But I didn't kill him! I didn't! Please believe that I didn't!"

I picked her up and put her back in the chair.

"I didn't say you did. Just tell me what did happen."

"I didn't believe him when he said he had a business engagement," she moaned. "I didn't trust him. He had lied to me before. I followed him to see if he went to that woman's rooms."

"Did he?"

"No. He went into an apartment house on Pine Street, in the block where he was killed. I don't know exactly which house it was—I was too far behind him to make sure. But I saw him go up the steps and into one—near the middle of the block."

"And then what did you do?"

"I waited, hiding in a dark doorway across the street. I knew the woman's apartment was on Bush Street, but I thought she might have moved, or be meeting him here. I waited a long time, shivering and trembling. It was chilly and I was frightened—afraid somebody would come into the vestibule where I was. But I made myself stay. I wanted to see if he came out alone, or if that woman came out. I had a right to do it—he had deceived me before.

"It was terrible, horrible—crouching there in the dark—cold and scared. Then—it must have been about half-past two—I couldn't stand it any longer. I decided to telephone the woman's apartment and find out if she were home. I went down to an all-night lunchroom on Ellis Street and called her up."

"Was she home?"

"No! I tried for fifteen minutes, or maybe longer, but nobody answered the phone. So I *knew* she was in that Pine Street building."

"And what did you do then?"

"I went back there, determined to wait until he came out. I walked up Jones Street. When I was between Bush and Pine I heard a shot. I thought it was a noise made by an automobile then, but now I know that it was the shot that killed Bernie.

"When I reached the corner of Pine and Jones, I could see a policeman bending over Bernie on the sidewalk, and I saw people gathering around. I didn't know then that it was Bernie lying on the sidewalk. In the dark and at that distance I couldn't even see whether it was a man or a woman.

"I was afraid that Bernard would come out to see what was going on, or look out of a window, and discover me; so I didn't go down that way. I was afraid to stay in the neighborhood now, for fear the police would ask me what I was doing loitering in the street at three in the morning—and have it come out that I had been following my husband. So I kept on walking up Jones Street, to California, and then straight home."

"And then what?" I led her on.

"Then I went to bed. I didn't go to sleep—lay there worrying over Bernie; but still not thinking it was he I had seen lying in the street. At nine o'clock that morning two police detectives came and told me Bernie had been killed. They questioned me so sharply that I was afraid to tell them the whole truth. If they had known I had reason for being jealous, and had followed my husband that night, they would have accused me of shooting him. And what could I have done? Everybody would have thought me guilty.

"So I didn't say anything about the woman. I thought they'd find the murderer, and then everything would be all right. I didn't think *she* had done it then, or I would have told you the whole thing the first time you were here. But four days went by without the police finding the murderer, and I began to think they suspected *me*! It was terrible! I couldn't go to them and confess that I had lied to them, and I was sure that the woman had killed him and that the police had failed to suspect her because I hadn't told them about her.

"So I employed you. But I was afraid to tell even you the whole truth. I thought that if I just told you there had been another woman and who she was, you could do the rest without having to know that I had followed Bernie that night. I was afraid *you* would think I had killed him, and would turn me over to the police if I told you everything. And now you *do* believe it! And you'll have me arrested! And they'll hang me! I know it! I know it!"

She began to rock crazily from side to side in her chair.

"Sh-h-h," I soothed her. "You're not arrested yet. Sh-h-h."

I didn't know what to make of her story. The trouble with these nervous, hysterical women is that you can't possibly tell when they're lying and when telling the truth unless you have outside evidence—half of the time they themselves don't know.

"When you heard the shot," I went on when she had quieted down a bit, "you were walking north on Jones, between Bush and Pine? You could see the corner of Pine and Jones?"

"Yes—clearly."

"See anybody?"

"No—not until I reached the corner and looked down Pine Street. Then I saw a policeman bending over Bernie, and two men walking toward them."

"Where were the two men?"

"On Pine Street east of Jones. They didn't have hats on—as if they had come out of a house when they heard the shot."

"Any automobiles in sight either before or after you heard the shot?"

"I didn't see or hear any."

"I have some more questions, Mrs. Gilmore," I said; "but I'm in a hurry now. Please don't go out until you hear from me again."

"I won't," she promised; "but—"

I didn't have any answers for anybody's questions, so I ducked my head and left the library.

Near the street door Lina Best appeared out of a shadow, her eyes bright and inquisitive.

"Stick around," I said without any meaning at all, stepped around her, and went on out into the street.

CHAPTER V

I returned then to the Garford Apartments, walking, because I had a lot of things to arrange in my mind before I faced Cara Kenbrook again. And, even though I walked slowly, they weren't all exactly filed in alphabetical order when I got there. She had changed the black and white dress for a plush-like gown of bright green, but her empty doll's face hadn't changed.

"Some more questions," I explained when she opened her door.

She admitted me without word or gesture, and led me back into the room where we had talked before.

"Miss Kenbrook," I asked, standing beside the chair she had offered me, "why did you tell me you were home in bed when Gilmore was killed?"

"Because it's so." Without the flicker of a lash.

"And you wouldn't answer the doorbell?"

I had to twist the facts to make my point. Mrs. Gilmore had phoned, but I couldn't afford to give this girl a chance to shunt the blame for her failure to answer off on central.

She hesitated for a split second.

"No—because I didn't hear it."

One cool article, this baby! I couldn't figure her. I didn't know then, and I don't know now, whether she was the owner of the world's best poker face or was just naturally stupid. But whichever she was, she was thoroughly and completely it!

I stopped trying to guess, and got on with my probing.

"And you wouldn't answer the phone either?"

"It didn't ring—or not enough to awaken me."

I chuckled—an artificial chuckle—because central could have been ringing the wrong number. However . . .

"Miss Kenbrook," I lied, "your phone rang at 2:30 and at 2:40 that morning. And your doorbell rang almost continually from about 2:50 until after 3:00."

"Perhaps," she said; "but I wonder who'd be trying to get me at that hour."

"You didn't hear either?"

"No."

"But you were here?"

"Yes—who was it?" carelessly.

"Get your hat," I bluffed, "and I'll show them to you down at headquarters."

She glanced down at the green gown and walked toward an open bedroom door.

"I suppose I'd better get a cloak, too," she said.

"Yes," I advised her; "and bring your toothbrush."

She turned around then and looked at me, and for a moment it seemed that some sort of expression—surprise maybe—was about to come into her big brown eyes; but none actually came. The eyes stayed dull and empty.

"You mean you're arresting me?"

"Not exactly. But if you stick to your story about being home in bed at 3:00 last Tuesday morning I can promise you you *will* be arrested. If I were you I'd think up another story while we're riding down to the Hall of Justice."

She left the doorway slowly and came back into the room, as far as a chair that stood between us, put her hands on its back, and leaned over it to look at me. For perhaps a minute neither of us spoke—just stood there staring at each other, while I tried to keep my face as expressionless as hers.

"Do you really think," she asked at last, "that I wasn't here when Bernie was killed?"

"I'm a busy man, Miss Kenbrook." I put all the certainty I could fake into my voice. "If you want to stick to your funny story, it's all right with me. But please don't expect me to stand here and argue about it. Get your hat and cloak."

She shrugged, and came around the chair on which she had been leaning.

"I suppose you *do* know something," she said, sitting down. "Well, it's tough on Stan, but women and children first."

My ears twitched at the name *Stan*, but I didn't interrupt her.

"I *was* in the Coffee Cup until one o'clock," she was saying, her voice still flat and emotionless. "And I *did* come home afterward. I'd been drinking *vino* all evening, and it always makes me blue. So after I came home I got to worrying over things. Since Bernie and I split finances haven't been so good. I took stock that night—or morning—and found only four dollars in my purse. The rent was due, and the world looked pretty damned blue.

"Half-lit on Dago wine as I was, I decided to run over and see Stan, tell him all my troubles, and make a touch. Stan is a good egg and he's always willing to go the limit for me. Sober, I wouldn't have gone to see him at three in the morning; but it seemed a perfectly sensible thing to do at the time.

"It's only a few minutes' walk from here to Stan's. I went down Bush Street to Leavenworth, and up Leavenworth to Pine. I was in the middle of that last block when Bernie was shot—I heard it. And when I turned the corner into Pine Street I saw a copper bending over a man on the pavement right in front of Stan's. I hesitated for a couple of minutes, standing in the shadow of a pole, until three or four men had gathered around the man on the sidewalk. Then I went over.

"It was Bernie. And just as I got there I heard the copper tell one of the men that he had been shot. It was an awful shock to me. You know how things like that will hit you!"

I nodded; though God knows there was nothing in this girl's face, manner, or voice to suggest shock. She might have been talking about the weather.

"Dumfounded, not knowing what to do," she went on, "I didn't even stop. I went on, passing as close to Bernie as I am to you now, and rang Stan's bell. He let me in. He had been half-undressed when I rang. His rooms are in the rear of the building, and he hadn't heard the shot, he said. He didn't know Bernie had been killed until I told him. It sort of knocked the wind out of him. He said Bernie had been there—in Stan's rooms—since midnight, and had just left.

"Stan asked me what I was doing there, and I told him my tale of woe. That was the first time Stan knew that Bernie and I were so thick. I met Bernie through Stan, but Stan didn't know we had got so chummy.

"Stan was worried for fear it would come out that Bernie had been to see him that night, because it would make a lot of trouble for him—some sort of shady deal they had on, I guess. So he didn't go out to see Bernie. That's about all there is to it. I got some money from Stan, and stayed in his rooms until the police had cleared out of the neighborhood; because neither of us wanted to get mixed up in anything. Then I came home. That's straight—on the level."

"Why didn't you get this off your chest before?" I demanded, knowing the answer.

It came.

"I was afraid. Suppose I told about Bernie throwing me down, and said I was close to him—a block or so away—when he was killed, and was half-full of vino? The first thing everybody would have said was that I had shot him! I'd lie about it still if I thought you'd believe me."

"So Bernie was the one who broke off, and not you?"

"Oh, yes," she said lightly.

CHAPTER VI

I lit a Fatima and breathed smoke in silence for a while, and the girl sat placidly watching me.

Here I had two women—neither normal. Mrs. Gilmore was hysterical, abnormally nervous. This girl was dull, subnormal. One was the dead man's wife; the other his mistress; and each with reason for believing she had been thrown down for the other. Liars, both; and both finally confessing that they had been near the scene of the crime at the time of the crime, though neither admitted seeing the other. Both, by their own accounts, had been at that time even further from normal than usual—Mrs. Gilmore filled with jealousy; Cara Kenbrook half-drunk.

What was the answer? Either could have killed Gilmore; but hardly both—unless they had formed some sort of crazy partnership, and in that event—

Suddenly all the facts I had gathered—true and false—clicked together in my head. I had the answer—the one simple, satisfying answer!

I grinned at the girl, and set about filling in the gaps in my solution.

"Who is Stan?" I asked.

"Stanley Tennant—he has something to do with the city."

Stanley Tennant. I knew him by reputation, a—

A key rattled in the hall door.

The hall door opened and closed, and a man's footsteps came toward the open doorway of the room in which we were. A tall, broad-shouldered man in tweeds filled the doorway—a ruddy-faced man of thirty-five or so, whose appearance of athletic blond wholesomeness was marred by close-set eyes of an indistinct blue.

Seeing me, he stopped—a step inside the room.

"Hello, Stan!" the girl said lightly. "This gentleman is from the Continental Detective Agency. I've just emptied myself to him about Bernie. Tried to stall him at first, but it was no good."

The man's vague eyes switched back and forth between the girl and me. Around the pale irises his eyeballs were pink.

He straightened his shoulders and smiled too jovially.

"And what conclusion have you come to?" he inquired.

The girl answered for me.

"I've already had *my* invitation to take a ride."

Tennant bent forward. With an unbroken swing of his arms, he swept a chair up from the floor into my face. Not much force behind it, but quick.

I went back against the wall, fending off the chair with both arms—threw it aside—and looked into the muzzle of a nickeled revolver.

A table drawer stood open—the drawer from which he had grabbed the gun while I was busy with the chair. The revolver, I noticed, was of .38 caliber.

"Now," his voice was thick, like a drunk's, "turn around."

I turned my back to him, felt a hand moving over my body, and my gun was taken away.

"All right," he said, and I faced him again.

He stepped back to the girl's side, still holding the nickel-plated revolver on me. My own gun wasn't in sight—in his pocket perhaps. He was breathing noisily, and his eyeballs had gone from pink to red. His face, too, was red, with veins bulging in the forehead.

"You know me?" he snapped.

"Yes, I know you. You're Stanley Tennant, assistant city engineer, and your record is none too lovely." I chattered away on the theory that conversation is always somehow to the advantage of the man who is looking into the gun. "You're supposed to be the lad who supplied the regiment of well-trained witnesses who turned last year's investigation of graft charges against the engineer's office into a comedy. Yes, Mr. Tennant, I know you. You're the answer to why Gilmore was so lucky in landing city contracts with bids only a few dollars beneath his competitors'. Yes, Mr. Tennant, I know you. You're the bright boy who—"

I had a lot more to tell him, but he cut me off.

"That will do out of you!" he yelled. "Unless you want me to knock a corner off your head with this gun."

Then he addressed the girl, not taking his eyes from me.

"Get up, Cara."

She got out of her chair and stood beside him. His gun was in his right hand, and that side was toward her. He moved around to the other side.

The fingers of his left hand hooked themselves inside of the girl's green gown where it was cut low over the swell of her breasts. His gun never wavered from me. He jerked his left hand, ripping her gown down to the waistline.

"*He* did that, Cara," Tennant said.

She nodded.

His fingers slid inside of the flesh-colored undergarment that was now exposed, and he tore that as he had torn the gown.

"*He* did that."

She nodded again.

His bloodshot eyes darted little measuring glances at her face—swift glances that never kept his eyes from me for the flash of time I would have needed to tie into him.

Then—eyes and gun on me—he smashed his left fist into the girl's blank white face.

One whimper—low and not drawn out—came from her as she went down in a huddle against the wall. Her face—well, there wasn't *much* change in it. She looked dumbly up at Tennant from where she had fallen.

"*He* did that," Tennant was saying.

She nodded, got up from the floor, and returned to her chair.

"Here's our story." The man talked rapidly, his eyes alert on me. "Gilmore was never in my rooms in his life, Cara, and neither were you. The night he was killed you were home shortly after one o'clock, and stayed there. You were sick—probably from the wine you had been drinking—and called a doctor. His name is Howard. I'll see that he's fixed. He got here at 2:30 and stayed until 3:30.

"Today, this gumshoe, learning that you had been intimate with Gilmore, came here to question you. He knew you hadn't killed Gilmore, but he made certain suggestions to you—you can play them up as strong as you like; maybe say that he's been annoying you for months—and when you turned him down he threatened to frame you.

"You refused to have anything to do with him, and he grabbed you, tearing your clothes, and bruising your face when you resisted. I happened to come along then, having an engagement with you, and heard you scream. Your front door was unlocked, so I rushed in, pulled this fellow away, and disarmed him. Then we held him until the police—whom we will phone for—came. Got that?"

"Yes, Stan."

"Good! Now listen: When the police get here this fellow will spill all he knows, of course, and the chances are that all three of us will be taken in. That's why I want you to know what's what right now. I ought to have enough pull to get you and me out on bail tonight, or, if worst comes to worst, to see that my lawyer gets to me tonight—so I can arrange for the witnesses we'll need. Also I ought to be able to fix it so our little fat friend will be held for a day or two, and not allowed to see anybody until late tomorrow—which will give us a good start on him. I don't know how much he knows, but between your story and the stories of a couple of other smart little ladies I have in mind, I'll fix him up with a rep that will keep any jury in the world from ever believing him about anything."

"How do you like that?" he asked me, triumphantly.

"You big clown," I laughed at him, "I think it's funny!"

But I didn't really think so. In spite of what I thought I knew about Gilmore's murder—in spite of my simple, satisfactory solution—something was crawling up my back, my knees felt jerky, and my hands were wet with sweat. I had had people try to frame me before—no detective stays in the business long without having it happen—but I had never got used to it. There's a peculiar deadliness about the thing—especially if you know how erratic juries can be—that makes your flesh crawl, no matter how safe your judgment tells you you are.

"Phone the police," Tennant told the girl; "and for God's sake keep your story straight!"

As he tried to impress that necessity on the girl his eyes left me.

I was perhaps five feet from him and his level gun.

A jump—not straight at him—off to one side—put me close.

The gun roared under my arm. I was surprised not to feel the bullet. It seemed that he *must* have hit me.

There wasn't a second shot.

I looped my right fist over as I jumped. It landed when I landed. It took him too high—up on the cheekbone—but it rocked him back a couple of steps.

I didn't know what had happened to his gun. It wasn't in his hand any more. I didn't stop to look for it. I was busy, crowding him back—not letting him set himself—staying close to him—driving at him with both hands.

He was a head taller than I, and had longer arms, but he wasn't any heavier or stronger. I suppose he hit me now and then as I hammered him across the room. He must have. But I didn't feel anything.

I worked him into a corner. Jammed him back in a corner with his legs cramped under him—which didn't give him much leverage to hit from. I got my left arm around his body, holding him where I wanted him. And I began to throw my right fist into him.

I liked that. His belly was flabby, and it got softer every time I hit it. I hit it often.

He was chopping at my face, but by digging my nose into his chest and holding it there I kept my beauty from being altogether ruined. Meanwhile I threw my right fist into him.

Then I became aware that Cara Kenbrook was moving around behind me; and I remembered the revolver that had fallen somewhere when I had charged Tennant. I didn't like that; but there was nothing I could do about it—except put more weight in my punches. My own gun, I thought, was in one of his pockets. But neither of us had time to hunt for it now.

Tennant's knees sagged the next time I hit him.

Once more, I said to myself, and then I'll step back, let him have one on the button, and watch him fall.

But I didn't get that far.

Something that I knew was the missing revolver struck me on the top of the head. An ineffectual blow—not clean enough to stun me—but it took the steam out of my punches.

Another.

They weren't hard, these taps, but to hurt a skull with a hunk of metal you don't have to hit it hard.

I tried to twist away from the next bump, and failed. Not only failed, but let Tennant wiggle away from me.

That was the end.

I wheeled on the girl just in time to take another rap on the head, and then one of Tennant's fists took me over the ear.

I went down in one of those falls that get pugs

called quitters—my eyes were open, my mind was alive, but my legs and arms wouldn't lift me up from the floor.

Tennant took my own gun out of a pocket, and with it held on me, sat down in a Morris chair, to gasp for the air I had pounded out of him. The girl sat in another chair; and I, finding I could manage it, sat up in the middle of the floor and looked at them.

Tennant spoke, still panting.

"This is fine—all the signs of a struggle we need to make our story good!"

"If they don't believe you were in a fight," I suggested sourly, pressing my aching head with both hands, "you can strip and show them your little tummy."

"And you can show them this!"

He leaned down and split my lip with a punch that spread me on my back.

Anger brought my legs to life. I got up on them. Tennant moved around behind the Morris chair. My black gun was steady in his hand.

"Go easy," he warned me. "My story will work if I have to kill you—maybe work better."

That was sense. I stood still.

"Phone the police, Cara," he ordered.

She went out of the room, closing the door behind her; and all I could hear of her talk was a broken murmur.

CHAPTER VII

Ten minutes later three uniformed policemen arrived. All three knew Tennant, and they treated him with respect. Tennant reeled off the story he and the girl had cooked up, with a few changes to take care of the shot that had been fired from the nickeled gun and our rough-house. She nodded her head vigorously whenever a policeman looked at her. Tennant turned both guns over to the white-haired sergeant in charge.

I didn't argue, didn't deny anything, but told the sergeant:

"I'm working with Detective-Sergeant O'Gar on a job. I want to talk to him over the phone and

then I want you to take all three of us down to the detective bureau."

Tennant objected to that, of course; not because he expected to gain anything, but on the off-chance that he might. The white-haired sergeant looked from one of us to the other in puzzlement. Me, with my skinned face and split lip; Tennant, with a red lump under one eye where my first wallop had landed; and the girl, with most of the clothes above the waistline ripped off and a bruised cheek.

"It has a queer look, this thing," the sergeant decided aloud; "and I shouldn't wonder but what the detective bureau was the place for the lot of you."

One of the patrolmen went into the hall with me, and I got O'Gar on the phone at his home. It was nearly ten o'clock by now, and he was preparing for bed.

"Cleaning up the Gilmore murder," I told him. "Meet me at the Hall. Will you get hold of Kelly, the patrolman who found Gilmore, and bring him down there? I want him to look at some people."

"I will that," O'Gar promised, and I hung up.

The "wagon" in which the three policemen had answered Cara Kenbrook's call carried us down to the Hall of Justice, where we all went into the captain of detectives' office. McTighe, a lieutenant, was on duty.

I knew McTighe, and we were on pretty good terms; but I wasn't an influence in local politics, and Tennant was. I don't mean that McTighe would have knowingly helped Tennant frame me; but with me stacked up against the assistant city engineer, I knew who would get the benefit of any doubt there might be.

My head was thumping and roaring just now, with knots all over it where the girl had beaned me. I sat down, kept quiet, and nursed my head while Tennant and Cara Kenbrook, with a lot of details that they had not wasted on the uniformed men, told their tale and showed their injuries.

Tennant was talking—describing the terrible scene that had met his eyes when, drawn by the girl's screams, he had rushed into her apartment—when O'Gar came into the office. He recognized Tennant with a lifted eyebrow, and came over to sit beside me.

"What the hell is all this?" he muttered.

"A lovely mess," I whispered back. "Listen—in that nickel gun on the desk there's an empty shell. Get it for me."

He scratched his head doubtfully, listened to the next few words of Tennant's yarn, glanced at me out of the corner of his eye, and then went over to the desk and picked up the revolver.

McTighe looked at him—a sharp, questioning look.

"Something on the Gilmore killing," the detective-sergeant said, breaking the gun.

The lieutenant started to speak, changed his mind, and O'Gar brought the shell over and handed it to me.

"Thanks," I said, putting it in my pocket. "Now listen to my friend there. It's a good act, if you like it."

Tennant was winding up his history.

". . . Naturally a man who tried a thing like that on an unprotected woman would be yellow; so it wasn't very hard to handle him after I got his gun away from him. I hit him a couple of times, and he quit—begging me to stop, getting down on his knees. Then we called the police."

McTighe looked at me with eyes that were cold and hard. Tennant had made a believer of him, and not only of him—the police-sergeant and his two men were glowering at me. I suspected that even O'Gar—with whom I had been through a dozen storms—would have been half-convinced if the engineer hadn't added the neat touches about my kneeling.

"Well, what have *you* got to say?" McTighe challenged me in a tone which suggested that it didn't make much difference what I said.

"I've got nothing to say about this dream," I said shortly. "I'm interested in the Gilmore murder—not in this stuff." I turned to O'Gar. "Is the patrolman here?"

The detective-sergeant went to the door, and called: "Oh, Kelly!"

Kelly came in—a big, straight-standing man, with iron-gray hair and an intelligent fat face.

"You found Gilmore's body?" I asked.

"I did."

I pointed at Cara Kenbrook.

"Ever see her before?"

His gray eyes studied her carefully.

"Not that I remember," he answered.

"Did she come up the street while you were looking at Gilmore, and go into the house he was lying in front of?"

"She did not."

I took out the empty shell O'Gar had got for me, and chucked it down on the desk in front of the patrolman.

"Kelly," I asked, "*why did you kill Gilmore?*"

Kelly's right hand went under his coat-tail at his hip.

I jumped for him.

Somebody grabbed me by the neck. Somebody else piled on my back. McTighe aimed a big fist at my face, but it missed. My legs had been suddenly kicked from under me, and I went down hard with men all over me.

When I was yanked to my feet again, big Kelly stood straight up by the desk, weighing his service revolver in his hand. His clear eyes met mine, and he laid the weapon on the desk. Then he unfastened his shield and put it with the gun.

"It was an accident," he said simply.

By this time the birds who had been man-handling me woke up to the fact that maybe they were missing part of the play—that maybe I wasn't a maniac. Hands dropped off me; and presently everybody was listening to Kelly.

He told his story with unhurried evenness, his eyes never wavering or clouding. A deliberate man, though unlucky.

"I was walkin' my beat that night, an' as I turned the corner of Jones into Pine I saw a man jump back from the steps of a buildin' into the vestibule. A burglar, I thought, an' cat-footed it down there. It was a dark vestibule, an' deep, an' I saw somethin' that looked like a man in it, but I wasn't sure.

"'Come out o' there!' I called, but there was no answer. I took my gun in my hand an' started up the steps. I saw him move just then, comin' out. An' then my foot slipped. It was worn smooth, the bottom step, an' my foot slipped. I fell forward, the gun went off, an' the bullet hit him. He had come out a ways by then, an' when the bullet hit him he toppled over frontwise, tumblin' down the steps onto the sidewalk.

"When I looked at him I saw it was Gilmore. I knew him to say 'howdy' to, an' he knew me—which is why he must o' ducked out of sight when he saw me comin' around the corner. He didn't want me to see him comin' out of a buildin' where I knew Mr. Tennant lived, I suppose, thinkin' I'd put two an' two together, an' maybe talk.

"I don't say that I did the right thing by lyin', but it didn't hurt anybody. It was an accident; but he was a man with a lot of friends up in high places, an'—accident or no—I stood a good chance of bein' broke, an' maybe sent over for a while. So I told my story the way you people know it. I couldn't say I'd seen anything suspicious without maybe puttin' the blame on some innocent party, an' I didn't want that. I'd made up my mind that if anybody was arrested for the murder, an' things looked bad for them, I'd come out an' say I'd done it. Home, you'll find a confession all written out—written out in case somethin' happened to me—so nobody else'd ever be blamed.

"That's why I had to say I'd never seen the lady here. I did see her—saw her go into the buildin' that night—the buildin' Gilmore had come out of. But I couldn't say so without makin' it look bad for her; so I lied. I could have thought up a better story if I'd had more time, I don't doubt; but I had to think quick. Anyways, I'm glad it's all over."

CHAPTER VIII

Kelly and the other uniformed policeman had left the office, which now held McTighe, O'Gar, Cara Kenbrook, Tennant and me. Tennant had crossed to my side, and was apologizing.

"I hope you'll let me square myself for this evening's work. But you know how it is when somebody you care for is in a jam. I'd have killed you if I had thought it would help Cara—on the level. Why didn't you tell us that you didn't suspect her?"

"But I did suspect the pair of you," I said. "It looked as if Kelly had to be the guilty one; but you people carried on so much that I began to feel doubtful. For a while it was funny—you thinking she had done it, and she thinking you had, though I suppose each had sworn to his or her innocence. But after a time it stopped being funny. You carried it too far."

"How did you rap to* Kelly?" O'Gar, at my shoulder, asked.

"Miss Kenbrook was walking north on Leavenworth—and was half-way between Bush and Pine—when the shot was fired. She saw nobody, no cars, until she rounded the corner. Mrs. Gilmore, walking north on Jones, was about the same distance away when *she* heard the shot, and she saw nobody until she reached Pine Street. If Kelly had been telling the truth, she would have seen him on Jones Street. He said he didn't turn the corner until after the shot was fired.

"Either of the women could have killed Gilmore, but hardly both; and I doubted that either could have shot him and got away without running into Kelly or the other. Suppose both of them were telling the truth—what then? Kelly must have been lying! He was the logical suspect anyway—the nearest known person to the murdered man when the shot was fired.

"To back all this up, he had let Miss Kenbrook go into the apartment building at 3:00 in the morning, in front of which a man had just been killed, without questioning her or mentioning her in his report. That looked as if he *knew*

_____

* figure out

who had done the killing. So I took a chance with the empty shell trick, it being a good bet that he would have thrown his away, and would think that—"

McTighe's heavy voice interrupted my explanation.

"How about this assault charge?" he asked, and had the decency to avoid my eye when I turned toward him with the others.

Tennant cleared his throat.

"Er—ah—in view of the way things have turned out, and knowing that Miss Kenbrook doesn't want the disagreeable publicity that would accompany an affair of this sort, why, I'd suggest that we drop the whole thing." He smiled brightly from McTighe to me. "You know nothing has gone on the records yet."

"Make the big heap play his hand out," O'Gar growled in my ear. "Don't let him drop it."

"Of course if Miss Kenbrook doesn't want to press the charge," McTighe was saying, watching me out of the tail of his eye, "I suppose—"

"If everybody understands that the whole thing was a plant," I said, "and if the policemen who heard the story are brought in here now and told by Tennant and Miss Kenbrook that it was all a lie—then I'm willing to let it go at that. Otherwise, I won't stand for a hush-up."

"You're a damned fool!" O'Gar whispered. "Put the screws on them!"

But I shook my head. I didn't see any sense in making a lot of trouble for myself just to make some for somebody else—and suppose Tennant *proved* his story . . .

So the policemen were found, and brought into the office again, and told the truth.

And presently Tennant, the girl, and I were walking together like three old friends through the corridors toward the door, Tennant still asking me to let him make amends for the evening's work.

"You've *got* to let me do something!" he insisted. "It's only right!"

His hand dipped into his coat, and came out with a thick bill-fold.

"Here," he said; "let me—"

We were going, at that happy moment, down the stone vestibule steps that led to Kearny Street—six or seven steps there are.

"No," I said; "let me—"

He was on the next to the top step, when I reached up and let go.

He settled in a rather limp pile at the bottom.

Leaving his empty-faced lady love to watch over him, I strolled up through Portsmouth Square toward a restaurant where the steaks come thick.

BLACK MASK, NOVEMBER 1924

The Golden Horseshoe

BY DASHIELL HAMMETT

Author of the San Francisco Detective Stories

In our recent voting contest for favorite BLACK MASK authors, Dashiell Hammett received thousands of votes because of his series of stories of the adventures of his San Francisco detective. He has created one of the most convincing and realistic characters in all detective fiction. The story, herewith, is one of his best to date. We know you'll enjoy it to the last word.

A COMPLETE NOVELETTE

"I HAVEN'T ANYTHING VERY EXCITING TO offer you this time," Vance Richmond said as we shook hands. "I want you to find a man for me—a man who is not a criminal."

There was an apology in his voice. The last couple of jobs this lean, gray-faced attorney had thrown my way had run to gun-play and other forms of rioting, and I suppose he thought anything less than that would put me to sleep. Was a time when he might have been right—when I was a young sprout of twenty or so, newly attached to the Continental Detective Agency. But the fifteen years that had slid by since then had dulled my appetite for rough stuff. I don't mean that I shuddered whenever I considered the possibility of some bird taking a poke at me; but I didn't call that day a total loss in which nobody tried to puncture my short, fat carcass.

"The man I want found," the lawyer went on, as we sat down, "is an English architect named Norman Ashcraft. He is a man of about thirty-seven, five feet ten inches tall, well built, and fair-skinned, with light hair and blue eyes. Four years ago he was a typical specimen of the clean-cut blond Britisher. He may not be like that now—those four years have been rather hard ones for him, I imagine.

"I want to find him for Mrs. Ashcraft, his wife. I know your agency's rule against meddling with family affairs, but I can assure you that no matter how things turn out there will be no divorce proceedings in which you will be involved.

"Here is the story. Four years ago the Ashcrafts were living together in England, in Bristol. It seems that Mrs. Ashcraft is of a very jealous disposition, and he was rather high-strung. Furthermore, he had only what money he earned at his profession, while she had inherited quite a bit from her parents. Ashcraft was rather foolishly sensitive about being the husband of a wealthy woman—was inclined to go out of his way to show that he was not dependent upon her money, that he wouldn't be influenced by it. Foolish, of course, but just the sort of attitude a man of his temperament would assume. One night she accused him of paying too much attention to another woman. They quarreled, and he packed up and left.

"She was repentant within a week—especially repentant since she had learned that her suspicion had had no foundation outside of her own jealousy—and she tried to find him. But he was gone. It became manifest that he had left England. She had him searched for in Europe, in Canada, in Australia, and in the United States. She succeeded in tracing him from Bristol to New York, and then to Detroit, where he had been arrested and fined for disturbing the peace in a drunken row of some sort. After that he dropped out of sight until he bobbed up in Seattle ten months later."

The attorney hunted through the papers on his desk and found a memorandum.

"On May 23, 1923, he shot and killed a burglar in his room in a hotel there. The Seattle police seem to have suspected that there was something funny about the shooting, but had nothing to hold Ashcraft on. The man he killed was undoubtedly a burglar. Then Ashcraft disappeared again, and nothing was heard of him until just about a year ago. Mrs. Ashcraft had advertisements inserted in the personal columns of papers in the principal American cities.

"One day she received a letter from him, from San Francisco. It was a very formal letter, and simply requested her to stop advertising. Although he was through with the name Norman Ashcraft, he wrote, he disliked seeing it published in every newspaper he read.

"She mailed a letter to him at the General Delivery window here, and used another advertisement to tell him about it. He answered it, rather caustically. She wrote him again, asking him to come home. He refused, though he seemed less bitter toward her. They exchanged several letters, and she learned that he had become a drug addict, and what was left of his pride would not let him return to her until he looked—and was at least somewhat like—his former self. She persuaded him to accept enough money from her to straighten himself out. She sent him this money each month, in care of General Delivery, here.

"Meanwhile she closed up her affairs in England—she had no close relatives to hold her there—and came to San Francisco, to be on hand when her husband was ready to return to her. A year has gone. She still sends him money each month. She still waits for him to come back to her. He has repeatedly refused to see her, and his letters are evasive—filled with accounts of the struggle he is having, making headway against the drug one month, slipping back the next.

"She suspects by now, of course, that he has no intention of ever coming back to her; that he does not intend giving up the drug; that he is simply using her as a source of income. I have urged her to discontinue the monthly allowance for a while. That would at least bring about an interview, I think, and she could learn definitely what to expect. But she will not do that. You see, she blames herself for his present condition. She thinks her foolish flare of jealousy is responsible for his plight, and she is afraid to do anything that might either hurt him or induce him to hurt himself further. Her mind is unchangeably made up in that respect. She wants him back, wants him straightened out; but if he will not come, then she is content to continue the payments for the rest of his life. But she wants to know what she is to expect. She wants to end this devilish uncertainty in which she has been living.

"What we want, then, is for you to find Ashcraft. We want to know whether there is any likelihood of his ever becoming a man again, or whether he is gone beyond redemption. There is your job. Find him, learn whatever you can about him, and then, after we know something, we will decide whether it is wiser to force an interview between them—in hopes that she will be able to influence him—or not."

"I'll try it," I said. "When does Mrs. Ashcraft send him his monthly allowance?"

"On the first of each month."

"Today is the twenty-eighth. That'll give me three days to wind up a job I have on hand. Got a photo of him?"

"Unfortunately, no. In her anger immediately after their row, Mrs. Ashcraft destroyed everything she had that would remind her of him. But I don't think a photograph would be of any great help at the post office. Without consulting me, Mrs. Ashcraft watched for her husband there on several occasions, and did not see him. It is more than likely that he has someone else call for his mail."

I got up and reached for my hat.

"See you around the second of the month," I said, as I left the office.

II

On the afternoon of the first, I went down to the post office and got hold of Lusk, the inspector in charge of the division at the time.

"I've got a line on a scratcher* from up north," I told Lusk, "who is supposed to be getting his mail at the window. Will you fix it up so I can get a spot on him?"

Post office inspectors are all tied up with rules and regulations that forbid their giving assistance to private detectives except on certain criminal matters. But a friendly inspector doesn't have to put you through the third degree. You lie to him—so that he will have an alibi in case there's a kick-back—and whether he thinks you're lying or not doesn't matter.

So presently I was downstairs again, loitering within sight of the A to D window, with the clerk at the window instructed to give me the office† when Ashcraft's mail was called for. There was no mail for him there at the time. Mrs. Ashcraft's letter would hardly get to the clerks that afternoon, but I was taking no chances. I stayed on the job until the windows closed at eight o'clock, and then went home.

At a few minutes after ten the next morning I got my action. One of the clerks gave me the signal. A small man in a blue suit and a soft gray hat was walking away from the window with an envelope in his hand. A man of perhaps forty years, though he looked older. His face was pasty, his feet dragged, and, although his clothes were fairly new, they needed brushing and pressing.

He came straight to the desk in front of which I stood fiddling with some papers. Out of the tail of my eye I saw that he had not opened the envelope in his hand—was not going to open it. He took a large envelope from his pocket, and I got just enough of a glimpse of its front to see that it was already stamped and addressed. I twisted my neck out of joint trying to read the address, but failed. He kept the addressed side against his body, put the letter he had got from the window in it, and licked the flap backward, so that there was no possible way for anybody to see the front of the envelope. Then he rubbed the flap down carefully and turned toward the mailing slots. I went after him. There was nothing to do but to pull the always reliable stumble.

I overtook him, stepped close and faked a fall on the marble floor, bumping into him, grabbing him as if to regain my balance. It went rotten. In the middle of my stunt my foot really did slip, and we went down on the floor like a pair of wrestlers, with him under me. To botch the trick thoroughly, he fell with the envelope pinned under him.

I scrambled up, yanked him to his feet, mumbled an apology and almost had to push him out of the way to beat him to the envelope that lay

---

* forger

† warning

face down on the floor. I had to turn it over as I handed it to him in order to get the address:

Mr. Edward Bohannon,
      Golden Horseshoe Cafe,
      Tijuana, Baja California,
  Mexico.

I had the address, but I had tipped my mitt. There was no way in God's world for this little man in blue to miss knowing that I had been trying to get that address.

I dusted myself off while he put his envelope through a slot. He didn't come back past me, but went on down toward the Mission Street exit. I couldn't let him get away with what he knew. I didn't want Ashcraft tipped off before I got to him. I would have to try another trick as ancient as the one the slippery floor had bungled for me. I set out after the little man again.

Just as I reached his side he turned his head to see if he was being followed.

"Hello, Micky!" I hailed him. "How's everything in Chi?"

"You got me wrong." He spoke out of the side of his gray-lipped mouth, not stopping. "I don't know nothin' about Chi."

His eyes were pale blue, with needlepoint pupils—the eyes of a heroin or morphine user.

"Quit stalling." I walked along at his side. We had left the building by this time and were going down Mission Street. "You fell off the rattler only this morning."

He stopped on the sidewalk and faced me.

"Me? Who do you think I am?"

"You're Micky Parker. The Dutchman gave us the rap that you were headed here. They got him—if you don't already know it."

"You're cuckoo," he sneered. "I don't know what the hell you're talkin' about!"

That was nothing—neither did I. I raised my right hand in my overcoat pocket.

"Now I'll tell one," I growled at him. "And keep your hands away from your clothes or I'll let the guts out of you."

He flinched away from my bulging pocket.

"Hey, listen, brother!" he begged. "You got me wrong—on the level. My name ain't Micky Parker, an' I ain't been in Chi in six years. I been here in Frisco for a solid year, an' that's the truth."

"You got to show me."

"I can do it," he exclaimed, all eagerness. "You come down the drag* with me, an' I'll show you. My name's Ryan, an' I been livin' aroun' the corner here on Sixth Street for six or eight months."

"Ryan?" I asked.

"Yes—John Ryan."

I chalked that up against him. Of course there have been Ryans christened John, but not enough of them to account for the number of times that name appears in criminal records. I don't suppose there are three old-time yeggs† in the country who haven't used the name at least once; it's the John Smith of yeggdom.

This particular John Ryan led me around to a house on Sixth Street, where the landlady—a rough-hewn woman of fifty, with bare arms that were haired and muscled like the village smithy's—assured me that her tenant had to her positive knowledge been in San Francisco for months, and that she remembered seeing him at least once a day for a couple of weeks back. If I had been really suspicious that this Ryan was my mythical Micky Parker from Chicago, I wouldn't have taken the woman's word for it, but as it was I pretended to be satisfied.

That seemed to be all right then. Mr. Ryan had been led astray, had been convinced that I had mistaken him for another crook, and that I was not interested in the Ashcraft letter. I would be safe—reasonably safe—in letting the situation go as it stood. But loose ends worry me. And you can't always count on people doing and thinking what you want. This bird was a hophead, and he had given me a phoney-sounding name, so . . .

"What do you do for a living?" I asked him.

---

* street
† burglars

"I ain't been doin' nothin' for a coupla months," he pattered, "but I expec' to open a lunch room with a fella nex' week."

"Let's go up to your room," I suggested. "I want to talk to you."

He wasn't enthusiastic, but he took me up. He had two rooms and a kitchen on the third floor. They were dirty, foul-smelling rooms. I dangled a leg from the corner of a table and waved him into a squeaky rocking chair in front of me. His pasty face and dopey eyes were uneasy.

"Where's Ashcraft?" I threw at him. He jerked, and then looked at the floor.

"I don't know what you're talkin' about," he mumbled.

"You'd better figure it out," I advised him, "or there's a nice cool cell down in the booby-hutch that will be wrapped around you."

"You ain't got nothin' on me."

"What of that? How'd you like to do a thirty or a sixty on a vag charge?"

"Vag, hell!" he snarled, looking up at me. "I got five hundred smacks in my kick. Does that look like you can vag me?"

I grinned down at him.

"You know better than that, Ryan. A pocketful of money'll get you nothing in California. You've got no job. You can't show where your money comes from. You're made to order for the vag law."

I had this bird figured as a dope peddler. If he was—or was anything else off color that might come to light when he was vagged—the chances were that he would be willing to sell Ashcraft out to save himself; especially since, so far as I knew, Ashcraft wasn't on the wrong side of the criminal law.

"If I were you," I went on while he stared at the floor and thought, "I'd be a nice, obliging fellow and do my talking now. You're—"

He twisted sidewise in his chair and one of his hands went behind him.

I kicked him out of his chair.

The table slipped under me or I would have stretched him. As it was, the foot that I aimed at his jaw took him on the chest and carried him over backward, with the rocking-chair piled on top of him. I pulled the chair off and took his gun—a cheap nickel-plated .32. Then I went back to my seat on the corner of the table.

He had only that one flash of fight in him. He got up sniveling.

"I'll tell you. I don't want no trouble, an' it ain't nothin' to me. I didn't know there was nothin' wrong. This Ashcraft told me he was jus' stringin' his wife along. He give me ten bucks a throw to get his letter ever' month an' send it to him in Tijuana. I knowed him here, an' when he went south six months ago—he's got a girl down there—I promised I'd do it for him. I knowed it was money—he said it was his 'alimony'—but I didn't know there was nothin' wrong."

"What sort of a hombre is this Ashcraft? What's his graft?"

"I don't know. He could be a con man—he's got a good front. He's a Englishman, an' mostly goes by the name of Ed Bohannon. He hits the hop.* I don't use it myself"—that was a good one—"but you know how it is in a burg like this, a man runs into all kinds of people. I don't know nothin' about what he's up to. I jus' send the money ever' month an' get my ten."

That was all I could get out of him. He couldn't—or wouldn't—tell me where Ashcraft had lived in San Francisco or who he had mobbed up with. However, I had learned that Bohannon was Ashcraft, and not another go-between, and that was something.

Ryan squawked his head off when he found that I was going to vag him anyway. For a moment it looked like I would have to kick him loose from his backbone again.

"You said you'd spring me if I talked," he wailed.

"I did not. But if I had—when a gent flashes a rod on me I figure it cancels any agreement we might have had. Come on."

I couldn't afford to let him run around loose until I got in touch with Ashcraft. He would have been sending a telegram before I was

_____

* narcotics: opium, morphine, or heroin

three blocks away, and my quarry would be on his merry way to points north, east, south and west.

It was a good hunch I played in nabbing Ryan. When he was fingerprinted at the Hall of Justice he turned out to be one Fred Rooney, alias "Jamocha," a peddler and smuggler who had crushed out of the Federal Prison at Leavenworth, leaving eight years of a tenner still unserved.

"Will you sew him up for a couple of days?" I asked the captain of the city jail. "I've got work to do that will go smoother if he can't get any word out for a while."

"Sure," the captain promised. "The federal people won't take him off our hands for two or three days. I'll keep him air-tight till then."

III

From the jail I went up to Vance Richmond's office and turned my news over to him.

"Ashcraft is getting his mail in Tijuana. He's living down there under the name of Ed Bohannon, and maybe has a woman there. I've just thrown one of his friends—the one who handled the mail and an escaped con—in the cooler."

"Was that necessary?" Richmond asked. "We don't want to work any hardships. We're really trying to help Ashcraft, you know."

"I could have spared this bird," I admitted. "But what for? He was all wrong. If Ashcraft can be brought back to his wife, he's better off with some of his shady friends out of the way. If he can't, what's the difference? Anyway, we've got one line on him safely stowed away where we can find it when we want it."

The attorney shrugged, and reached for the telephone.

He called a number. "Is Mrs. Ashcraft there? . . . This is Mr. Richmond. . . . No, we haven't exactly found him, but I think we know where he is. . . . Yes. . . . In about fifteen minutes."

He put down the telephone and stood up.

"We'll run up to Mrs. Ashcraft's house and see her."

Fifteen minutes later we were getting out of Richmond's car in Jackson Street near Gough. The house was a three-story white stone building, set behind a carefully sodded little lawn with an iron railing around it.

Mrs. Ashcraft received us in a drawing-room on the second floor. A tall woman of less than thirty, slimly beautiful in a gray dress. Clear was the word that best fits her; it described the blue of her eyes, the pink-white of her skin, and the light brown of her hair.

Richmond introduced me to her, and then I told her what I had learned, omitting the part about the woman in Tijuana. Nor did I tell her that the chances were her husband was a crook nowadays.

"Mr. Ashcraft is in Tijuana, I have been told. He left San Francisco about six months ago. His mail is being forwarded to him in care of a cafe there, under the name of Edward Bohannon."

Her eyes lighted up happily, but she didn't throw a fit. She wasn't that sort. She addressed the attorney.

"Shall I go down? Or will you?"

Richmond shook his head.

"Neither. You certainly shouldn't go, and I cannot—not at present. I must be in Eureka by the day after tomorrow, and shall have to spend several days there." He turned to me. "You'll have to go. You can no doubt handle it better than I could. You will know what to do and how to do it. There are no definite instructions I can give you. Your course will have to depend on Mr. Ashcraft's attitude and condition. Mrs. Ashcraft doesn't wish to force herself on him, but neither does she wish to leave anything undone that might help him."

Mrs. Ashcraft held a strong, slender hand out to me.

"You will do whatever you think wisest."

It was partly a question, partly an expression of confidence.

"I will," I promised.

I liked this Mrs. Ashcraft.

IV

Tijuana hadn't changed much in the two years I had been away. Still the same six or seven hundred feet of dusty and dingy street running between two almost solid rows of saloons,—perhaps thirty-five of them to a row,—with dirtier side streets taking care of the dives that couldn't find room on the main street.

The automobile that had brought me down from San Diego dumped me into the center of the town early in the afternoon, and the day's business was just getting under way. That is, there were only two or three drunks wandering around among the dogs and loafing Mexicans in the street, although there was already a bustle of potential drunks moving from one saloon to the next. But this was nothing like the crowd that would be here the following week, when the season's racing started.

In the middle of the next block I saw a big gilded horseshoe. I went down the street and into the saloon behind the sign. It was a fair sample of the local joint. A bar on your left as you came in, running half the length of the building, with three or four slot machines on one end. Across from the bar, against the right-hand wall, a dance floor that ran from the front wall to a raised platform, where a greasy orchestra was now preparing to go to work. Behind the orchestra was a row of low stalls or booths, with open fronts and a table and two benches apiece. Opposite them, in the space between the bar and the rear of the building, a man with a hair-lip was shaking pills out of a keno goose.[*]

It was early in the day, and there were only a few buyers present, so the girls whose business it is to speed the sale of drinks charged down on me in a flock.

"Buy me a drink? Let's have a little drink? Buy a drink, honey?"

I shooed them away—no easy job—and caught a bartender's eye. He was a beefy, red-faced Irishman, with sorrel hair plastered down in two curls that hid what little forehead he had.

"I want to see Ed Bohannon," I told him confidentially.

He turned blank fish-green eyes on me.

"I don't know no Ed Bohannon."

Taking out a piece of paper and a pencil I scribbled, *Jamocha is copped*, and slid the paper over to the bartender.

"If a man who says he's Ed Bohannon asks for that, will you give it to him?"

"I guess so."

"Good," I said. "I'll hang around a while."

I walked down the room and sat at a table in one of the stalls. A lanky girl who had done something to her hair that made it purple was camped beside me before I had settled in my seat.

"Buy me a little drink?" she asked.

The face she made at me was probably meant for a smile. Whatever it was, it beat me. I was afraid she'd do it again, so I surrendered.

"Yes," I said, and ordered a bottle of beer for myself from the waiter who was already hanging over my shoulder.

The beer wasn't bad, for green beer, but at four bits a bottle it wasn't anything to write home about. This Tijuana happens to be in Mexico—by about a mile—but it's an American town, run by Americans, who sell American artificial booze at American prices. If you know your way around the United States you can find lots of places—especially near the Canadian line—where good booze can be bought for less than you are soaked for poison in Tijuana.

The purple-haired woman at my side downed her shot of whiskey, and was opening her mouth to suggest that we have another drink,—hustlers down there don't waste any time at all,—when a voice spoke from behind me.

"Cora, Frank wants you."

Cora scowled, looking over my shoulder.

Then she made that damned face at me again, said "All right, Kewpie. Will you take care of my friend here?" and left me.

Kewpie slid into the seat beside me. She was

---

[*] a globe from which Keno balls are shaken

a little chunky girl of perhaps eighteen—not a day more than that. Just a kid. Her short hair was brown and curly over a round, boyish face with laughing, impudent eyes. Rather a cute little trick.

I bought her a drink and got another bottle of beer.

"What's on your mind?" I asked her.

"Hooch." She grinned at me—a grin that was as boyish as the straight look of her brown eyes. "Gallons of it."

"And besides that?"

I knew this switching of girls on me hadn't been purposeless.

"I hear you're looking for a friend of mine," Kewpie said.

"That might be. What friends have you got?"

"Well, there's Ed Bohannon for one. You know Ed?"

I shook my head.

"No—not yet."

"But you're looking for him?"

"Uh-huh."

"Maybe I could tell you how to find him, if I knew you were all right."

"It doesn't make any difference to me," I said carelessly. "I've a few more minutes to waste, and if he doesn't show up by then it's all one to me."

She cuddled against my shoulder.

"What's the racket? Maybe I could get word to Ed."

I stuck a cigarette in her mouth, one in my own, and lit them.

"Let it go," I bluffed. "This Ed of yours seems to be as exclusive as all hell. Well, it's no skin off *my* face. I'll buy you another drink and then trot along."

She jumped up.

"Wait a minute. I'll see if I can get him. What's your name?"

"Parker will do as well as any other," I said, the name I had used on Ryan popping first into my mind.

"You wait," she called back as she moved toward the back door. "I think I can find him."

"I think so too," I agreed.

Ten minutes went by, and a man came to my table from the front of the establishment. He was a blond Englishman of less than forty, with all the marks of the gentleman gone to pot on him. Not altogether on the rocks yet, but you could see evidence of the downhill slide plainly in the dullness of his blue eyes, in the pouches under his eyes, in the blurred lines around his mouth and the mouth's looseness, and in the grayish tint of his skin. He was still fairly attractive in appearance—enough of his former wholesomeness remained for that.

He sat down facing me across the table.

"You're looking for me?"

There was only a hint of the Britisher in his accent.

"You're Ed Bohannon?"

He nodded.

"Jamocha was picked up a couple of days ago," I told him, "and ought to be riding back to the Kansas big house by now. He got word out for me to give you the rap. He knew I was heading this way."

"How did they come to get him?"

His blue eyes were suspicious on my face.

"Don't know," I said. "Maybe they picked him up on a circular."

He frowned at the table and traced a meaningless design with a finger in a puddle of beer. Then he looked sharply at me again.

"Did he tell you anything else?"

"*He* didn't tell me anything. He got word out to me by somebody's mouthpiece. I didn't see him."

"You're staying down here a while?"

"Yes, for two or three days," I said. "I've got something on the fire."

He stood up and smiled, and held out his hand.

"Thanks for the tip, Parker," he said. "If you'll take a walk with me I'll give you something real to drink."

I didn't have anything against that. He led me out of the Golden Horseshoe and down a side street to an adobe house set out where the town fringed off into the desert. In the front room he waved me to a chair and went into the next room.

"What do you fancy?" he called through the door. "Rye, gin, tequila, Scotch—"

"The last one wins," I interrupted his catalog.

He brought in a bottle of Black and White, a siphon and some glasses, and we settled down to drinking. When that bottle was empty there was another to take its place. We drank and talked, drank and talked, and each of us pretended to be drunker than he really was—though before long we were both as full as a pair of goats.

It was a drinking contest pure and simple. He was trying to drink me into a pulp—a pulp that would easily give up all of its secrets—and I was trying the same game on him. Neither of us made much progress. Neither he nor I was young enough in the world to blab much when we were drunk that wouldn't have come out if we had been sober. Few grown men do, unless they get to boasting, or are very skillfully handled. All that afternoon we faced each other over the table in the center of the room, drank and entertained each other.

"Y' know," he was saying somewhere along toward dark, "I've been a damn' ass. Got a wife—the nicesh woman in the worl'. Wantsh me t' come back to her, an' all tha' short of thing. Yet I hang around here, lappin' up this shtuff—hittin' the pipe—when I could be shomebody. Arc—architec', y' un'ershtand—good one, too. But I got in rut—got mixsh up with theshe people. C-can't sheem to break 'way. Goin' to, though—no spoofin'. Goin' back to li'l wife, nicesh woman in the worl'. Don't you shay anything t' Kewpie. She'd raishe hell 'f she knew I wash goin' t' shake her. Nishe girl, K-kewpie, but tough. S-shtick a bloomin' knife in me. Good job, too! But I'm goin' back to wife. Breakin' 'way from p-pipe an' ever'thing. Look at me. D' I look like a hop-head? Course not! Curin' m'self, tha's why. I'll show you—take a smoke now—show you I can take it or leave it alone."

Pulling himself dizzily up out of his chair, he wandered into the next room, bawling a song at the top of his voice:

"A dimber mort with a quarter-stone
    slum,
A-bubbin' of max with her cove—
A bingo fen in a crack-o'-dawn drum,*
A-waitin' for—"

He came staggering into the room again carrying an elaborate opium layout—all silver and ebony—on a silver tray. He put it on the table and flourished a pipe at me.

"Have a li'l rear on me, Parker."

I told him I'd stick to the Scotch.

"Give y' shot of C. 'f y'd rather have it," he invited me.

I declined the cocaine, so he sprawled himself comfortably on the floor beside the table, rolled and cooked a pill, and our party went on—with him smoking his hop and me punishing the liquor—each of us still talking for the other's benefit, and trying to get the other to talk for our own.

I was holding down a lovely package by the time Kewpie came in, at midnight.

"Looks like you folks are enjoying yourselves," she laughed, leaning down to kiss the Englishman's rumpled hair as she stepped over him.

She perched herself on the table and reached for the Scotch.

"Everything's lovely," I assured her, though probably I didn't say it that clear.

I was fighting a battle with myself just about then. I had an idea that I wanted to dance. Down in Yucatan, four or five months before—hunting for a lad who had done wrong by the bank that

---

* Cockney slang. Dimber mort is a pretty young woman. Quarter-stone possibly refers to a place where drugs are sold cheaply in small quantities. A slum is a squalid room. A-bubbin of max is drinking heavily. Her cove is her boyfriend. A bingo fen is a brandy-drinking whore. A crack-of-dawn drum is an all-night party.

employed him—I had seen some natives dance the *naual*. And that naual dance was the one thing in the world I wanted to do just then. (I was carrying a beautiful bun!) But I knew that if I sat still—as I had been sitting all evening—I could keep my cargo in hand, while it wasn't going to take much moving around to knock me over.

I don't remember whether I finally conquered the desire to dance or not. I remember Kewpie sitting on the table, grinning her boy's grin at me, and saying:

"You ought to stay oiled all the time, Shorty; it improves you."

I don't know whether I made any answer to that or not. Shortly afterward, I know, I spread myself beside the Englishman on the floor and went to sleep.

V

The next two days were pretty much like the first one. Ashcraft and I were together twenty-four hours each of the days, and usually the girl was with us, and the only time we weren't drinking was when we were sleeping off what we had been drinking. We spent most of those three days in either the adobe house or the Golden Horseshoe, but we found time to take in most of the other joints in town now and then. I had only a hazy idea of some of the things that went on around me, though I don't think I missed anything entirely. On the second day someone added a first name to the alias I had given the girl—and thereafter I was "Painless" Parker to Tijuana, and still am to some of them. I don't know who christened me, or why.

Ashcraft and I were as thick as thieves, on the surface, but neither of us ever lost his distrust of the other, no matter how drunk we got—and we got plenty drunk. He went up against his mud-pipe regularly. I don't think the girl used the stuff, but she had a pretty capacity for hard liquor. I would go to sleep not knowing whether I was going to wake up or not; but I had nothing on me to give me away, so I figured that I was safe unless I talked myself into a jam. I didn't worry much,—bedtime usually caught me in a state that made worry impossible.

Three days of this, and then, sobering up, I was riding back to San Francisco, making a list of what I knew and guessed about Norman Ashcraft, alias Ed Bohannon.

The list went something like this:

(1) He suspected, if he didn't know, that I had come down to see him on his wife's account: he had been too smooth and had entertained me too well for me to doubt that; (2) he apparently had decided to return to his wife, though there was no guarantee that he would actually do so; (3) he was not incurably addicted to drugs; he merely smoked opium and, regardless of what the Sunday supplements say, an opium smoker is little, if any, worse off than a tobacco smoker; (4) he might pull himself together under his wife's influence, but it was doubtful: physically he hadn't gone to the dogs, but he had had his taste of the gutter and seemed to like it; (5) the girl Kewpie was crazily in love with him, while he liked her, but wasn't turning himself inside out over her.

A good night's sleep on the train between Los Angeles and San Francisco set me down in the Third and Townsend Street station with nearly normal head and stomach and not too many kinks in my nerves. I put away a breakfast that was composed of more food than I had eaten in three days, and went up to Vance Richmond's office.

"Mr. Richmond is still in Eureka," his stenographer told me. "I don't expect him back until the first of the week."

"Can you get him on the phone for me?"

She could, and did.

Without mentioning any names, I told the attorney what I knew and guessed.

"I see," he said. "Suppose you go out to Mrs. A's house and tell her. I will write her tonight, and I probably shall be back in the city by the day after tomorrow. I think we can safely delay action until then."

I caught a street car, transferred at Van Ness Avenue, and went out to Mrs. Ashcraft's house. Nothing happened when I rang the bell. I rang it several times before I noticed that there were two morning newspapers in the vestibule. I looked at the dates—this morning's and yesterday morning's.

An old man in faded overalls was watering the lawn next door.

"Do you know if the people who live here have gone away?" I called to him.

"I don't guess so. The back door's open, I seen this mornin'."

He returned his attention to his hose, and then stopped to scratch his chin.

"They may of gone," he said slowly. "Come to think on it, I ain't seen any of 'em for—I don't remember seein' any of 'em yesterday."

I left the front steps and went around the house, climbed the low fence in back and went up the back steps. The kitchen door stood about a foot open. Nobody was visible in the kitchen, but there was a sound of running water.

I knocked on the door with my knuckles, loudly. There was no answering sound. I pushed the door open and went in. The sound of water came from the sink. I looked in the sink.

Under a thin stream of water running from one of the faucets lay a carving knife with nearly a foot of keen blade. The knife was clean, but the back of the porcelain sink—where water had splashed with only small, scattered drops—was freckled with red-brown spots. I scraped one of them with a finger-nail—dried blood.

Except for the sink, I could see nothing out of order in the kitchen. I opened a pantry door. Everything seemed all right there. Across the room another door led to the front of the house. I opened the door and went into a passageway. Not enough light came from the kitchen to illuminate the passageway. I fumbled in the dusk for the light-button that I knew should be there. I stepped on something soft.

Pulling my foot back, I felt in my pocket for matches, and struck one. In front of me, his head and shoulders on the floor, his hips and legs on the lower steps of a flight of stairs, lay a Filipino boy in his underclothes.

He was dead. One eye was cut, and his throat was gashed straight across, close up under his chin. I could see the killing without even shutting my eyes. At the top of the stairs—the killer's left hand dashing into the Filipino's face—thumb-nail gouging into eye—pushing the brown face back—tightening the brown throat for the knife's edge—the slash—and the shove down the steps.

The light from my second match showed me the button. I clicked on the lights, buttoned my coat, and went up the steps. Dried blood darkened them here and there, and at the second-floor landing the wall paper was stained with a big blot. At the head of the stairs I found another light-button, and pressed it.

I walked down the hall, poked my head into two rooms that seemed in order, and then turned a corner—and pulled up with a jerk, barely in time to miss stumbling over a woman who lay there.

She was huddled on the floor, face down, with knees drawn up under her and both hands clasped to her stomach. She wore a nightgown, and her hair was in a braid down her back.

I put a finger on the back of her neck. Stone-cold.

Kneeling on the floor—to avoid the necessity of turning her over—I looked at her face. She was the maid who had admitted Richmond and me four days ago.

I stood up again and looked around. The maid's head was almost touching a closed door. I stepped around her and pushed the door open. A bedroom, and not the maid's. It was an expensively dainty bedroom in cream and gray, with French prints on the walls. Nothing in the room was disarranged except the bed. The bed clothes were rumpled and tangled, and piled high in the center of the bed—in a pile that was too large. . . .

Leaning over the bed, I began to draw the covers off. The second piece came away stained with blood. I yanked the rest off.

Mrs. Ashcraft was dead there.

Her body was drawn up in a little heap, from which her head hung crookedly, dangling from a neck that had been cut clean through to the bone. Her face was marked with four deep scratches from temple to chin. One sleeve had been torn from the jacket of her blue silk pajamas. Bedding and pajamas were soggy with the blood that the clothing piled over her had kept from drying.

I put the blanket over her again, edged past the dead woman in the hall, and went down the front stairs, switching on more lights, hunting for the telephone. Near the foot of the stairs I found it. I called the police detective bureau first, and then Vance Richmond's office.

"Get word to Mr. Richmond that Mrs. Ashcraft has been murdered," I told his stenographer. "I'm at her house, and he can get in touch with me here any time during the next two or three hours."

Then I went out of the front door and sat on the top step, smoking a cigarette while I waited for the police.

I felt rotten. I've seen dead people in larger quantities than three in my time, and I've seen some that were hacked up pretty badly; but this thing had fallen on me while my nerves were ragged from three days of boozing.

The police automobile swung around the corner and began disgorging men before I had finished my first cigarette. O'Gar, the detective sergeant in charge of the Homicide Detail, was the first man up the steps.

"Hullo," he greeted me. "What have you got hold of this time?"

I was glad to see him. This squat, bullet-headed sergeant is as good a man as the department has, and he and I have always been lucky when we tied up together.

"I found three bodies in there before I quit looking," I told him as I led him indoors. "Maybe a regular detective like you—with a badge and everything—can find more."

"You didn't do bad—for a lad," he said.

My wooziness had passed. I was eager to get to work. These people lying dead around the house were merely counters in a game again—or almost. I remembered the feel of Mrs. Ashcraft's slim hand in mine, but I stuck that memory in the back of my mind. You hear now and then of detectives who have not become callous, who have not lost what you might call the human touch. I always feel sorry for them, and wonder why they don't chuck their jobs and find another line of work that wouldn't be so hard on their emotions. A sleuth who doesn't grow a tough shell is in for a gay life—day in and day out poking his nose into one kind of woe or another.

I showed the Filipino to O'Gar first, and then the two women. We didn't find any more. Detail work occupied all of us—O'Gar, the eight men under him, and me—for the next few hours. The house had to be gone over from roof to cellar. The neighbors had to be grilled. The employment agencies through which the servants had been hired had to be examined. Relatives and friends of the Filipino and the maid had to be traced and questioned. Newsboys, mail carriers, grocers' delivery men, laundrymen, had to be found, questioned and, when necessary, investigated.

When the bulk of the reports were in, O'Gar and I sneaked away from the others—especially away from the newspaper men, who were all over the place by now—and locked ourselves in the library.

"Night before last, huh? Wednesday night?" O'Gar grunted when we were comfortable in a couple of leather chairs, burning tobacco.

I nodded. The report of the doctor who had examined the bodies, the presence of the two newspapers in the vestibule, and the fact that neither neighbor, grocer nor butcher had seen any of them since Wednesday, combined to make Wednesday night—or early Thursday morning—the correct date.

"I'd say the killer cracked the back door," O'Gar went on, staring at the ceiling through smoke, "picked up the carving knife in the kitchen, and went upstairs. Maybe he went straight to Mrs. Ashcraft's room—maybe not. But after a bit he went in there. The torn sleeve and the scratches on her face mean that there was a tussle. The Filipino and the maid heard the noise—heard her scream maybe—and rushed to her room to find out what was the matter. The maid most likely got there just as the killer was coming out—and got hers. I guess the Filipino saw him then and ran. The killer caught him at the head of the back stairs—and finished him. Then he went down to the kitchen, washed his hands, dropped the knife, and blew."

"So far, so good," I agreed; "but I notice you skip lightly over the question of who he was and why he killed."

He pushed his hat back and scratched his bullet head.

"Don't crowd me," he rumbled; "I'll get around to that. There seem to be just three guesses to take your pick from. We know that nobody else lived in the house outside of the three that were killed. So the killer was either a maniac who did the job for the fun of it, a burglar who was discovered and ran wild, or somebody who had a reason for bumping off Mrs. Ashcraft, and then had to kill the two servants when they discovered him.

"Taking the knife from the kitchen would make the burglar guess look like a bum one. And, besides, we're pretty sure nothing was stolen. A good prowler would bring his own weapon with him if he wanted one. But the hell of it is that there are a lot of bum prowlers in the world—half-wits who would be likely to pick up a knife in the kitchen, go to pieces when the house woke up, slash everybody in sight, and then beat it without turning anything over.

"So it could have been a prowler; but my personal guess is that the job was done by somebody who wanted to wipe out Mrs. Ashcraft."

"Not so bad," I applauded. "Now listen to this: Mrs. Ashcraft has a husband in Tijuana, a mild sort of hop-head who is mixed up with a bunch of thugs. She was trying to persuade him to come back to her. He has a girl down there who is young, goofy over him, and a bad actor—one tough youngster. He was planning to run out on the girl and come back home."

"So-o-o?" O'Gar said softly.

"But," I continued, "I was with both him and the girl, in Tijuana, night before last—when this killing was done."

"So-o?"

A knock on the door interrupted our talk. It was a policeman to tell me that I was wanted on the phone. I went down to the first floor, and Vance Richmond's voice came over the wire.

"What is it? Miss Henry delivered your message, but she couldn't give me any details."

I told him the whole thing.

"I'll leave for the city tonight," he said when I had finished. "You go ahead and do whatever you want. You're to have a free hand."

"Right," I replied. "I'll probably be out of town when you get back. You can reach me through the agency if you want to get in touch with me. I'm going to wire Ashcraft to come up—in your name."

After Richmond had hung up, I called the city jail and asked the captain if John Ryan, alias Fred Rooney, alias Jamocha, was still there.

"No. Federal officers left for Leavenworth with him and two other prisoners yesterday morning."

Up in the library again, I told O'Gar hurriedly:

"I'm catching the evening train south, betting my marbles that the job was made in Tijuana. I'm wiring Ashcraft to come up. I want to get him away from the Mexican town for a day or two, and if he's up here you can keep an eye on him. I'll give you a description of him, and you can pick him up at Vance Richmond's office. He'll probably connect there first thing."

Half an hour of the little time I had left I spent writing and sending three telegrams. The first was to Ashcraft.

Edward Bohannon,
Golden Horseshoe Cafe,
Tijuana, Mexico.

Mrs. Ashcraft is dead. Can you come immediately?

Vance Richmond

The other two were in code. One went to the Continental Detective Agency's Kansas City branch, asking that an operative be sent to Leavenworth to question Jamocha. The other requested the Los Angeles branch to have a man meet me in San Diego the next day.

Then I dashed out to my rooms for a bagful of clean clothes, and went to sleep riding south again.

VI

San Diego was gay and packed when I got off the train early the next afternoon—filled with the crowd that the first Saturday of the racing season across the border had drawn. Movie folk from Los Angeles, farmers from the Imperial Valley, sailors from the Pacific Fleet, gamblers, tourists, grifters, and even regular people, from everywhere. I lunched, registered and left my bag at a hotel, and went up to the U.S. Grant Hotel to pick up the Los Angeles operative I had wired for.

I found him in the lobby—a freckle-faced youngster of twenty-two or so, whose bright gray eyes were busy just now with a racing program, which he held in a hand that had a finger bandaged with adhesive tape. I passed him and stopped at the cigar stand, where I bought a package of cigarettes and straightened out an imaginary dent in my hat. Then I went out to the street again. The bandaged finger and the business with the hat were our introductions. Somebody invented those tricks back before the Civil War, but they still worked smoothly, so their antiquity was no reason for discarding them.

I strolled up Fourth Street, getting away from Broadway—San Diego's main stem—and the operative caught up with me. His name was Gorman, and he turned out to be a pretty good lad. I gave him the lay.

"You're to go down to Tijuana and take a plant on the Golden Horseshoe Café. There's a little chunk of a girl hustling drinks in there—short curly brown hair; brown eyes; round face; rather large red mouth; square shoulders. You can't miss her; she's a nice-looking kid of about eighteen, called Kewpie. She's the target for your eye. Keep away from her. Don't try to rope her. I'll give you an hour's start. Then I'm coming down to talk to her. I want to know what she does right after I leave, and what she does for the next few days. You can get in touch with me at the"—I gave him the name of my hotel and my room number—"each night. Don't give me a tumble anywhere else. I'll most likely be in and out of the Golden Horseshoe often."

We parted, and I went down to the plaza and sat on a bench under the palms for an hour. Then I went up to the corner and fought for a seat on a Tijuana stage.

Fifteen or more miles of dusty riding—packed five in a seat meant for three—a momentary halt at the Immigration Station on the line, and I was climbing out of the stage at the entrance to the race track. The ponies had been running for some time, but the turnstiles were still spinning a steady stream of customers into the track. I turned my back on the gate and went over to the row of jitneys in front of the Monte Carlo—the big wooden casino—got into one, and was driven over to the Old Town.

The Old Town had a deserted look. Nearly everybody was over watching the dogs do their stuff. Gorman's freckled face showed over a drink of mescal when I entered the Golden Horseshoe. I hoped he had a good constitution. He needed one if he was going to do his sleuthing on a distilled cactus diet.

The welcome I got from the Horseshoers was just like a homecoming. Even the bartender with the plastered-down curls gave me a grin.

"Where's Kewpie?" I asked.

"Brother-in-lawing,* Ed?" a big Swede girl leered at me. "I'll see if I can find her for you."

Kewpie came through the back door just then.

"Hello, Painless!" She climbed all over me, hugging me, rubbing her face against mine, and

_____
* checking up on her

the Lord knows what all. "Down for another swell souse?"

"No," I said, leading her back toward the stalls. "Business this time. Where's Ed?"

"Up north. His wife kicked off and he's gone to collect the remains."

"That makes you sorry?"

She showed her big white teeth in a boy's smile of pure happiness.

"You bet! It's tough on me that papa has come into a lot of sugar."

I looked at her out of the corner of my eyes—a glance that was supposed to be wise.

"And you think Ed's going to bring the jack back to you?"

Her eyes snapped darkly at me.

"What's eating you?" she demanded.

I smiled knowingly.

"One of two things is going to happen," I predicted. "Ed's going to ditch you—he was figuring on that, anyway—or he's going to need every brownie he can scrape up to keep his neck from being—"

"You God-damned liar!"

Her right shoulder was to me, touching my left. Her left hand flashed down under her short skirt. I pushed her shoulder forward, twisting her body sharply away from me. The knife her left hand had whipped up from her leg jabbed deep into the underside of the table. A thick-bladed knife, I noticed, balanced for accurate throwing.

She kicked backward, driving one of her sharp heels into my ankle. I slid my left arm around behind her and pinned her elbow to her side just as she freed the knife from the table.

"What th' hell's all 'is?"

I looked up.

Across the table a man stood glaring at me— legs apart, fists on hips. He was a big man, and ugly. A tall, raw-boned man with wide shoulders, out of which a long, skinny yellow neck rose to support a little round head. His eyes were black shoe-buttons stuck close together at the top of a little mashed nose. His mouth looked as if it had been torn in his face, and it was stretched in a snarl now, baring a double row of crooked brown teeth.

"Where d' yuh get 'at stuff?" this lovely person roared at me.

He was too tough to reason with.

"If you're a waiter," I told him, "bring me a bottle of beer and something for the kid. If you're not a waiter—sneak."

He leaned over the table and I gathered my feet in. It looked like I was going to need them to move around on.

"I'll bring yuh a—"

The girl wriggled out of my hands and shut him up.

"Mine's liquor," she said sharply.

He snarled, looked from one of us to the other, showed me his dirty teeth again, and wandered away.

"Who's your friend?"

"You'll do well to lay off him," she advised me, not answering my question.

Then she slid her knife back in its hiding place under her skirt and twisted around to face me.

"Now what's all this about Ed being in trouble?"

"You read about the killing in the papers?"

"Yes."

"You oughtn't need a map, then," I said. "Ed's only out is to put the job on you. But I doubt if he can get away with that. If he can't, he's nailed."

"You're crazy!" she exclaimed. "You weren't too drunk to know that both of us were here with you when the killing was done."

"I'm not crazy enough to think that proves anything," I corrected her. "But I am crazy enough to expect to go back to San Francisco wearing the killer on my wrist."

She laughed at me. I laughed back and stood up.

"See you some more," I said as I strolled toward the door.

I returned to San Diego and sent a wire to Los Angeles, asking for another operative. Then I got something to eat and spent the evening lying across the bed in my hotel room smoking and scheming and waiting for Gorman.

It was late when he arrived, and he smelled of mescal from San Diego to St. Louis and back, but his head seemed level enough.

"Looked like I was going to have to shoot you loose from the place for a moment," he grinned. "Between the twist flashing the pick and the big guy loosening a sap in his pocket, it looked like action was coming."

"You let me alone," I ordered. "Your job is to see what goes on, and that's all. If I get carved, you can mention it in your report, but that's your limit. What did you turn up?"

"After you blew, the girl and the big guy put their noodles together. They seemed kind of agitated—all agog, you might say. He slid out, so I dropped the girl and slid along behind him. He came to town and got a wire off. I couldn't crowd him close enough to see who it was to. Then he went back to the joint. Things were normal when I knocked off."

"Who is the big guy? Did you learn?"

"He's no sweet dream, from what I hear. 'Gooseneck' Flinn is the name on his calling cards. He's bouncer and general utility man for the joint. I saw him in action against a couple of gobs,* and he's nobody's meat—as pretty a double throw-out as I've ever seen."

So this Gooseneck party was the Golden Horseshoe's clean-up man, and he hadn't been in sight during my three-day spree? I couldn't possibly have been so drunk that I'd forget his ugliness. And it had been on one of those three days that Mrs. Ashcraft and her servants had been killed.

"I wired your office for another op," I told Gorman. "He's to connect with you. Turn the girl over to him, and you camp on Gooseneck's trail. I think we're going to hang three killings on him, so watch your step. I'll be in to stir things up a little more tomorrow; but remember, no matter what happens, everybody plays his own game. Don't ball things up trying to help me."

_____
* loudmouths, sailors

"Aye, aye, Cap," and he went off to get some sleep.

The next afternoon I spent at the race track, fooling around with the bangtails while I waited for night. The track was jammed with the usual Sunday crowd. I ran into any number of old acquaintances, some of them on my side of the game, some on the other, and some neutral. One of the second lot was "Trick-hat" Schultz. At our last meeting—a copper was leading him out of a Philadelphia court room toward a fifteen-year bit—he had promised to open me up from my eyebrows to my ankles the next time he saw me. He greeted me this afternoon with an eight-inch smile, bought me a shot of what they sell for gin under the grandstand, and gave me a tip on a horse named Beeswax. I'm not foolish enough to play anybody's tips, so I didn't play this one. Beeswax ran so far ahead of the others that it looked like he and his competitors were in separate races, and he paid twenty-something to one. So Trick-hat had his revenge after all.

After the last race, I got something to eat at the Sunset Inn, and then drifted over to the big casino—the other end of the same building. A thousand or more people of all sorts were jostling one another there, fighting to go up against poker, craps, chuck-a-luck, wheels of fortune, roulette and twenty-one with whatever money the race track had left or given them. I didn't buck any of the games. My playtime was over. I walked around through the crowd looking for my men.

I spotted the first one—a sunburned man who was plainly a farm hand in his Sunday clothes. He was pushing toward the door, and his face held that peculiar emptiness which belongs to the gambler who has gone broke before the end of the game. It's a look of regret that is not so much for the loss of the money as for the necessity of quitting.

I got between the farm hand and the door.

"Clean you?" I asked sympathetically when he reached me.

A sheepish sort of nod.

"How'd you like to pick up five bucks for a few minutes' work?" I tempted him.

He would like it, but what was the work?

"I want you to go over to the Old Town with me and look at a man. Then you get your pay. There are no strings to it."

That didn't exactly satisfy him, but five bucks are five bucks; and he could drop out any time he didn't like the looks of things. He decided to try it.

I put the farm hand over by a door, and went after another—a little, plump man with round, optimistic eyes and a weak mouth. He was willing to earn five dollars in the simple and easy manner I had outlined. The next man I braced was a little too timid to take a chance on a blind game. Then I got a Filipino—glorious in a fawn-colored suit, with a coat split to the neck and pants whose belled bottoms would have held a keg apiece—and a stocky young Greek who was probably either a waiter or a barber.

Four men were enough. My quartet pleased me immensely. They didn't look too intelligent for my purpose, and they didn't look like thugs or sharpers.* I put them in a jitney and took them over to the Old Town.

"Now this is it," I coached them when we had arrived. "I'm going into the Golden Horseshoe Café, around the corner. Give me two or three minutes, and then come in and buy yourselves a drink." I gave the farm hand a five-dollar bill. "You pay for the drinks with that—it isn't part of your wages. There's a tall, broad-shouldered man with a long, yellow neck and a small ugly face in there. You can't miss him. I want you all to take a good look at him without letting him get wise. When you're sure you'd know him again anywhere, give me the nod, and come back here and you get your money. Be careful when you give me the nod. I don't want anybody in there to find out that you know me."

It sounded queer to them, but there was the promise of five dollars apiece, and there were the games back in the casino, where five dollars might buy a man into a streak of luck that—write the rest of it yourself. They asked

_____
* cheating gamblers

questions, which I refused to answer, but they stuck.

Gooseneck was behind the bar, helping out the bartenders, when I entered the place. They needed help. The joint bulged with customers. The dance floor looked like a mob scene. Thirsts were lined up four deep at the bar. A shotgun wouldn't have sounded above the din: men and women laughing, roaring and cursing; bottles and glasses rattling and banging; and louder and more disagreeable than any of those noises was the noise of the sweating orchestra. Turmoil, uproar, stink—a Tijuana joint on Sunday night.

I couldn't find Gorman's freckled face in the crowd, but I picked out the hatchet-sharp white face of Hooper, another Los Angeles operative, who, I knew then, had been sent down in response to my second telegram. Kewpie was farther down the bar, drinking with a little man whose meek face had the devil-may-care expression of a model husband on a tear. She nodded at me, but didn't leave her client.

Gooseneck gave me a scowl and the bottle of beer I had ordered. Presently my four hired men came in. They did their parts beautifully!

First they peered through the smoke, looking from face to face, and hastily avoiding eyes that met theirs. A little of this, and one of them, the Filipino, saw the man I had described, behind the bar. He jumped a foot in the excitement of his discovery, and then, finding Gooseneck glaring at him, turned his back and fidgeted. The three others spotted Gooseneck now, and sneaked looks at him that were as conspicuously furtive as a set of false whiskers. Gooseneck glowered at them.

The Filipino turned around, looked at me, ducked his head sharply, and bolted for the street. The three who were left shot their drinks down their gullets and tried to catch my eye. I was reading a sign high on the wall behind the bar:

ONLY GENUINE PRE–WAR AMERICAN AND BRIT-ISH WHISKEYS SERVED HERE

I was trying to count how many lies could be found in those nine words, and had reached four, with promise of more, when one of my confederates, the Greek, cleared his throat with the noise of a gasoline engine's backfire. Gooseneck was edging down the bar, a bungstarter* in one hand, his face purple.

I looked at my assistants. Their nods wouldn't have been so terrible had they come one at a time; but they were taking no chances on my looking away again before they could get their reports in. The three heads bobbed together—a signal that nobody within twenty feet could, or did, miss—and they scooted out of the door, away from the long-necked man and his bungstarter.

I emptied my glass of beer, sauntered out of the saloon and around the corner. They were clustered where I had told them to wait.

"We'd know him! We'd know him!" they chorused.

"That's fine," I praised them. "You did great. I think you're all natural-born gumshoes. Here's your pay. Now if I were you boys, I think I'd sort of avoid that place after this; because, in spite of the clever way you covered yourselves up—and you did nobly!—he might possibly suspect something. There's no use taking chances, anyway."

They grabbed their wages and were gone before I had finished my speech. I returned to the Golden Horseshoe—to be on hand in case one of them should decide to sell me out and come back there to spill the deal to Gooseneck.

Kewpie had left her model husband, and met me at the door. She stuck an arm through mine and led me toward the rear of the building. I noticed that Gooseneck was gone from behind the bar. I wondered if he was out gunning for my four ex-employees.

"Business looks good," I chattered as we pushed through the crowd. "You know, I had a tip on Beeswax this afternoon, and wouldn't play the pup."† I made two or three more aimless cracks of that sort—just because I knew the girl's mind was full of something else. She paid no attention to anything I said.

But when we had dropped down in front of a vacant table, she asked:

"Who were your friends?"

"What friends?"

"The four jobbies who were at the bar when you were there a few minutes ago."

"Too hard for me, sister." I shook my head. "There were slews of men there. Oh, yes! I know who you mean! Those four gents who seemed kind of smitten with Gooseneck's looks. I wonder what attracted them to him—besides his beauty."

She grabbed my arm with both hands.

"So help me God, Painless," she swore, "if you tie anything on Ed, I'll kill you!"

Her brown eyes were big and damp. She was a hard and wise little baby—had rubbed the world's sharp corners with both shoulders—but she was only a kid, and she was worried sick over this man of hers. However, the business of a sleuth is to catch criminals, not to sympathize with their ladyloves.

I patted her hands.

"I could give you some good advice," I said as I stood up, "but you wouldn't listen to it, so I'll save my breath. It won't do any harm to tell you to keep an eye on Gooseneck, though—he's shifty."

There wasn't any special meaning to that speech, except that it might tangle things up a little more. One way of finding what's at the bottom of either a cup of coffee or a situation is to keep stirring it up until whatever is on the bottom comes to the surface. I had been playing that system thus far on this affair.

Hooper came into my room in the San Diego hotel at a little before two the next morning.

"Gooseneck disappeared, with Gorman tailing him, immediately after your first visit," he said. "After your second visit, the girl went around to a 'dobe house on the edge of town, and she was still there when I knocked off. The place was dark."

Gorman didn't show up.

---

* mallet to loosen the bung of a cask
† play innocent

VII

A bell-hop with a telegram roused me at ten o'clock in the morning. The telegram was from Mexicali:

DROVE HERE LAST NIGHT HOLED UP WITH
FRIENDS SENT TWO WIRES.
GORMAN.

That was good news. The long-necked man had fallen for my play, had taken my four busted gamblers for four witnesses, had taken their nods for identifications. Gooseneck was the lad who had done the actual killing, and Gooseneck was in flight.

I had shed my pajamas and was reaching for my union suit when the boy came back with another wire. This one was from O'Gar, through the agency:

ASHCRAFT DISAPPEARED YESTERDAY

I used the telephone to get Hooper out of bed.
"Get down to Tijuana," I told him. "Stick up the house where you left the girl last night, unless you run across her at the Golden Horse-shoe. Stay there until she shows. Stay with her until she connects with a big blond Englishman, and then switch to him. He's a man of less than forty, tall, with blue eyes and yellow hair. Don't let him shake you—he's the big boy in this party just now. I'll be down. If the Englishman and I stay together and the girl leaves, take her, but otherwise stick to him."

I dressed, put down some breakfast and caught a stage for the Mexican town. The boy driving the stage made fair time, but you would have thought we were standing still to see a maroon roadster pass us near Palm City. Ashcraft was driving the roadster.

The roadster was empty, standing in front of the adobe house, when I saw it again. Up in the next block, Hooper was doing an imitation of a drunk, talking to two Indians in the uniforms of the Mexican Army.

I knocked on the door of the adobe house. Kewpie's voice: "Who is it?"
"Me—Painless. Just heard that Ed is back."
"Oh!" she exclaimed. A pause. "Come in."
I pushed the door open and went in. The Englishman sat tilted back in a chair, his right elbow on the table, his right hand in his coat pocket—if there was a gun in that pocket it was pointing at me.
"Hello," he said. "I hear you've been making guesses about me."
"Call 'em anything you like." I pushed a chair over to within a couple of feet of him, and sat down. "But don't let's kid each other. You had Gooseneck knock your wife off so you could get what she had. The mistake you made was in picking a sap like Gooseneck to do the turn—a sap who went on a killing spree and then lost his nerve. Going to read and write[*] just because three or four witnesses put the finger on him! And only going as far as Mexicali! That's a fine place to pick! I suppose he was so scared that the five- or six-hour ride over the hills seemed like a trip to the end of the world!"
The man's face told me nothing. He eased himself around in his chair an inch or two, which would have brought the gun in his pocket—if a gun *was* there—in line with my thick middle. The girl was somewhere behind me, fidgeting around. I was afraid of her. She was crazily in love with this man in front of me, and I had seen the blade she wore on one leg. I imagined her fingers itching for it now. The man and his gun didn't worry me much. He was not rattle-brained, and he wasn't likely to bump me off either in panic or for the fun of it.
I kept my chin going.
"You aren't a sap, Ed, and neither am I. I want to take you riding north with bracelets on, but I'm in no hurry. What I mean is, I'm not going to stand up and trade lead with you. This is all in my daily grind. It isn't a matter of life or death with me. If I can't take you today, I'm willing to wait until tomorrow. I'll get you in the

_____

[*] going into seclusion; going to jail

end, unless somebody beats me to you—and that won't break my heart. There's a rod between my vest and my belly. If you'll have Kewpie get it out, we'll be all set for the talk I want to make."

He nodded slowly, not taking his eyes from me. The girl came close to my back. One of her hands came over my shoulder, went under my vest, and my old black gun left me. Before she stepped away she laid the point of her knife against the nape of my neck for an instant—a gentle reminder. I managed not to squirm or jump.

"Good," I said when she gave my gun to the Englishman, who pocketed it with his left hand. "Now here's my proposition. You and Kewpie ride across the border with me—so we won't have to fool with extradition papers—and I'll have you locked up. We'll do our fighting in court. I'm not absolutely certain that I can tie the killings on either of you, and if I flop, you'll be free. If I make the grade—as I hope to—you'll swing, of course. But there's always a good chance of beating the courts—especially if you're guilty—and that's the only chance you have that's worth a damn.

"What's the sense of scooting? Spending the rest of your life dodging bulls? Only to be nabbed finally—or bumped off trying to get away? You'll maybe save your neck, but what of the money your wife left? That money is what you are in the game for—it's what you had your wife killed for. Stand trial and you've a chance to collect it. Run—and you kiss it good-by. Are you going to ditch it—throw it away just because your cat's-paw bungled the deal? Or are you going to stick to the finish—win everything or lose everything?"

A lot of these boys who make cracks about not being taken alive have been wooed into peaceful surrender with that kind of talk. But my game just now was to persuade Ed and his girl to bolt. If they let me throw them in the can I might be able to convict one of them, but my chances weren't any too large. It depended on how things turned out later. It depended on whether I could prove that Gooseneck had been in San Fran-

cisco on the night of the killings, and I imagined that he would be well supplied with all sorts of proof to the contrary. We had not been able to find a single finger-print of the killer's in Mrs. Ashcraft's house. And if I *could* convince a jury that he was in San Francisco at the time, then I would have to show that he had done the killing. And after that I would have the toughest part of the job still ahead of me—to prove that he had done the killing for one of these two, and not on his own account. I had an idea that when we picked Gooseneck up and put the screws to him he would talk. But that was only an idea.

What I was working for was to make this pair dust out. I didn't care where they went or what they did, so long as they scooted. I'd trust to luck and my own head to get profit out of their scrambling—I was still trying to stir things up.

The Englishman was thinking hard. I knew I had him worried, chiefly through what I had said about Gooseneck Flinn. If I had pulled the moth-eaten stuff—said that Gooseneck had been picked up and had squealed—this Englishman would have put me down as a liar; but the little I had said was bothering him.

He bit his lip and frowned. Then he shook himself and chuckled.

"You're balmy, Painless," he said. "But you—"

I don't know what he was going to say—whether I was going to win or lose.

The front door slammed open, and Gooseneck Flinn came into the room.

His clothes were white with dust. His face was thrust forward to the full length of his long, yellow neck.

His shoe-button eyes focused on me. His hands turned over. That's all you could see. They simply turned over—and there was a heavy revolver in each.

"Your paws on the table, Ed," he snarled.

Ed's gun—if that is what he had in his pocket—was blocked from a shot at the man in the doorway by a corner of the table. He took his hand out of his pocket, empty, and laid both palms down on the table-top.

"Stay where y'r at!" Gooseneck barked at the girl.

She was standing on the other side of the room. The knife with which she had pricked the back of my neck was not in sight.

Gooseneck glared at me for nearly a minute, but when he spoke it was to Ed and Kewpie.

"So this is what y' wired me to come back for, huh? A trap! Me the goat for yur! I'll be y'r goat! I'm goin' to speak my piece, an' then I'm goin' out o' here if I have to smoke my way through the whole damn' Mex army! I killed y'r wife all right—an' her help, too. Killed 'em for the thousand bucks—"

The girl took a step toward him, screaming:

"Shut up, damn you!"

Her mouth was twisting and working like a child's, and there was water in her eyes.

"Shut up, yourself!" Gooseneck roared back at her, and his thumb raised the hammer of the gun that threatened her. "I'm doin' the talkin'. I killed her for—"

Kewpie bent forward. Her left hand went under the hem of her skirt. The hand came up—empty. The flash from Gooseneck's gun lit on a flying steel blade.

The girl spun back across the room—hammered back by the bullets that tore through her chest. Her back hit the wall. She pitched forward to the floor.

Gooseneck stopped shooting and tried to speak. The brown haft of the girl's knife stuck out of his yellow throat. He couldn't get his words past the blade. He dropped one gun and tried to take hold of the protruding haft. Halfway up to it his hand came, and dropped. He went down slowly—to his knees—hands and knees—rolled over on his side—and lay still.

I jumped for the Englishman. The revolver Gooseneck had dropped turned under my foot, spilling me sidewise. My hand brushed the Englishman's coat, but he twisted away from me, and got his guns out.

His eyes were hard and cold and his mouth was shut until you could hardly see the slit of it. He backed slowly across the floor, while I lay still where I had tumbled. He didn't make a speech. A moment of hesitation in the doorway. The door jerked open and shut. He was gone.

I scooped up the gun that had thrown me, sprang to Gooseneck's side, tore the other gun out of his dead hand, and plunged into the street. The maroon roadster was trailing a cloud of dust into the desert behind it. Thirty feet from me stood a dirt-caked black touring car. That would be the one in which Gooseneck had driven back from Mexicali.

I jumped for it, climbed in, brought it to life, and pointed it at the dust-cloud ahead.

VIII

The car under me, I discovered, was surprisingly well engined for its battered looks—its motor was so good that I knew it was a border-runner's car. I nursed it along, not pushing it. There were still four or five hours of daylight left, and while there was any light at all I couldn't miss the cloud of dust from the fleeing roadster.

I didn't know whether we were following a road or not. Sometimes the ground under me looked like one, but mostly it didn't differ much from the rest of the desert. For half an hour or more the dust-cloud ahead and I held our respective positions, and then I found that I was gaining.

The going was roughening. Any road that we might originally have been using had petered out. I opened up a little, though the jars it cost me were vicious. But if I was going to avoid playing Indian among the rocks and cactus, I would have to get within striking distance of my man before he deserted his car and started a game of hide and seek on foot. I'm a city man. I have done my share of work in the open spaces, but I don't like it. My taste in playgrounds runs more to alleys, backyards and cellars than to canyons, mesas and arroyos.

I missed a boulder that would have smashed me up—missed it by a hair—and looked ahead again to see that the maroon roadster was no longer stirring up the grit. It had stopped.

The roadster was empty. I kept on.

From behind the roadster a pistol snapped at me, three times. It would have taken good shooting to plug me at that instant. I was bounding and bouncing around in my seat like a pellet of quicksilver in a nervous man's palm.

He fired again from the shelter of his car, and then dashed for a narrow arroyo—a sharp-edged, ten-foot crack in the earth—off to the left. On the brink, he wheeled to snap another cap at me—and jumped down out of sight.

I twisted the wheel in my hands, jammed on the brakes and slid the black touring car to the spot where I had seen him last. The edge of the arroyo was crumbling under my front wheels. I released the brake. Tumbled out. Shoved.

The car plunged down into the gully after him.

Sprawled on my belly, one of Gooseneck's guns in each hand, I wormed my head over the edge. On all fours, the Englishman was scrambling out of the way of the car. The car was mangled, but still sputtering. One of the man's fists was bunched around a gun—mine.

"Drop it and stand up, Ed!" I yelled.

Snake-quick, he flung himself around in a sitting position on the arroyo bottom, swung his gun up—and I smashed his forearm with my second shot.

He was holding the wounded arm with his left hand when I slid down beside him, picked up the gun he had dropped, and frisked him to see if he had any more.

He grinned at me.

"You know," he drawled, "I fancy your true name isn't Painless Parker at all. You don't act like it."

Twisting a handkerchief into a tourniquet of a sort, I knotted it around his wounded arm, which was bleeding.

"Let's go upstairs and talk," I suggested, and helped him up the steep side of the gully.

We climbed into his roadster.

"Out of gas," he said. "We've got a nice walk ahead of us."

"We'll get a lift. I had a man watching your house, and another one shadowing Gooseneck. They'll be coming out after me, I reckon. Meanwhile, we have time for a nice heart-to-heart talk."

"Go ahead, talk your head off," he invited; "but don't expect me to add much to the conversation. You've got nothing on me." (I'd like to have a dollar, or even a nickel, for every time I've heard that remark!) "You saw Kewpie bump Gooseneck off to keep him from peaching* on her."

"So that's your play?" I inquired. "The girl hired Gooseneck to kill your wife—out of jealousy—when she learned that you were planning to shake her and return to your own world?"

"Exactly."

"Not bad, Ed, but there's one rough spot in it."

"Yes?"

"Yes," I repeated. "You are not Ashcraft!"

He jumped, and then laughed.

"Now your enthusiasm is getting the better of your judgment," he kidded me. "Could I have deceived another man's wife? Don't you think her lawyer, Richmond, made me prove my identity?"

"Well, I'll tell you, Ed, I think I'm a smarter baby than either of them. Suppose you had a lot of stuff that belonged to Ashcraft—papers, letters, things in his handwriting? If you were even a fair hand with a pen, you could have fooled his wife. She thought her husband had had four tough years and had become a hophead. That would account for irregularities in his writing. And I don't imagine you ever got very familiar in your letters—not enough so to risk any missteps. As for the lawyer—his making you identify yourself was only a matter of form. It never occurred to him that you weren't Ashcraft. Identification is easy, anyway. Give me a week and I'll prove that I'm the Sultan of Turkey."

He shook his head sadly.

———————————

* informing

"That comes from riding around in the sun." I went on.

"At first your game was to bleed Mrs. Ashcraft for an allowance—to take the cure. But after she closed out her affairs in England and came here, you decided to wipe her out and take everything. You knew she was an orphan and had no close relatives to come butting in. You knew it wasn't likely that there were many people in America who could say you were not Ashcraft. Now if you want to you can do your stalling for just as long as it takes us to send a photograph of you to England—to be shown to the people that knew him there. But you understand that you will do your stalling in the can, so I don't see what it will get you."

"Where do you think Ashcraft would be while I was spending his money?"

There were only two possible guesses. I took the more reasonable one.

"Dead."

I imagined his mouth tightened a little, so I took another shot, and added:

"Up north."

That got to him, though he didn't get excited. But his eyes became thoughtful behind his smile. The United States is all "up north" from Tijuana, but it was even betting that he thought I meant Seattle, where the last record of Ashcraft had come from.

"You may be right, of course," he drawled. "But even at that, I don't see just how you expect to hang me. Can you prove that Kewpie didn't think I was Ashcraft? Can you prove that she knew why Mrs. Ashcraft was sending me money? Can you prove that she knew anything about my game? I rather think not. There are still any number of reasons for her to have been jealous of this other woman.

"I'll do my bit for fraud, Painless, but you're not going to swing me. The only two who could possibly tie anything on me are dead behind us. Maybe one of them told you something. What of it? You know damned well that you won't be allowed to testify to it in court. What someone who is now dead may have told you—unless the person it affects was present—isn't evidence, and you know it."

"You may get away with it," I admitted. "Juries are funny, and I don't mind telling you that I'd be happier if I knew a few things about those murders that I don't know. Do you mind telling me about the ins and outs of your switch with Ashcraft—in Seattle?"

He squinted his blue eyes at me.

"You're a puzzling chap, Painless," he said. "I can't tell whether you know everything, or are just sharp-shooting." He puckered his lips and then shrugged. "I'll tell you. It won't matter greatly. I'm due to go over for this impersonation, so a confession to a little additional larceny won't matter."

IX

"The hotel-sneak* used to be my lay,"† the Englishman said after a pause. "I came to the States after England and the Continent got uncomfortable. I was rather good at it. I had the proper manner—the front. I could do the gentleman without sweating over it, you know. In fact there was a day, not so long ago, when I wasn't 'Liverpool Ed.' But you don't want to hear me brag about the select blood that flows through these veins.

"To get back to our knitting‡: I had rather a successful tour on my first American voyage. I visited most of the better hotels between New York and Seattle, and profited nicely. Then, one night in a Seattle hotel, I worked the tarrel§ and put myself into a room on the fourth floor. I had hardly closed the door behind me before another key was rattling in it. The room was night-dark. I risked a flash from my light, picked out a closet door, and got behind it just in time.

"The clothes closet was empty; rather a

---

* stealing from hotel rooms
† job
‡ story
§ possibly typo for barrel—meaning picked the lock

stroke of luck, since there was nothing in it for the room's occupant to come for. He—it was a man—had switched on the lights by then.

"He began pacing the floor. He paced it for three solid hours—up and down, up and down, up and down—while I stood behind the closet door with my gun in my hand, in case he should pull it open. For three solid hours he paced that damned floor. Then he sat down and I heard a pen scratching on paper. Ten minutes of that and he was back at his pacing; but he kept it up for only a few minutes this time. I heard the latches of a valise click. And a shot!

"I bounded out of my retreat. He was stretched on the floor, with a hole in the side of his head. A bad break for me, and no mistake! I could hear excited voices in the corridor. I stepped over the dead chap, found the letter he had been writing on the writing-desk. It was addressed to Mrs. Norman Ashcraft, at a Wine Street number in Bristol, England. I tore it open. He had written that he was going to kill himself, and it was signed Norman. I felt better. A murder couldn't be made out of it.

"Nevertheless, I was here in this room with a flashlight, skeleton keys, and a gun—to say nothing of a handful of jewelry that I had picked up on the next floor. Somebody was knocking on the door.

"'Get the police!' I called through the door, playing for time.

"Then I turned to the man who had let me in for all this. I would have pegged him for a fellow Britisher even if I hadn't seen the address on his letter. There are thousands of us on the same order—blond, fairly tall, well set up. I took the only chance there was. His hat and topcoat were on a chair where he had tossed them. I put them on and dropped my hat beside him. Kneeling, I emptied his pockets, and my own, gave him all my stuff, pouched all of his. Then I traded guns with him and opened the door.

"What I had in mind was that the first arrivals might not know him by sight, or not well enough to recognize him immediately. That would give me several seconds to arrange my disappearance

in. But when I opened the door I found that my idea wouldn't work out as I had planned. The house detective was there, and a policeman, and I knew I was licked. There would be little chance of sneaking away from them. But I played my hand out. I told them I had come up to my room and found this chap on the floor going through my belongings. I had seized him, and in the struggle had shot him.

"Minutes went by like hours, and nobody denounced me. People were calling me Mr. Ashcraft. My impersonation was succeeding. It had me gasping then, but after I learned more about Ashcraft it wasn't so surprising. He had arrived at the hotel only that afternoon, and no one had seen him except in his hat and coat—the hat and coat I was wearing. We were of the same size and type—typical blond Englishmen.

"Then I got another surprise. When the detective examined the dead man's clothes he found that the maker's labels had been ripped out. When I got a look at his diary, later, I found the explanation of that. He had been tossing mental coins with himself, alternating between a determination to kill himself, and another to change his name and make a new place for himself in the world—putting his old life behind him. It was while he was considering the second plan that he had removed the markers from all of his clothing.

"But I didn't know that while I stood there among those people. All I knew was that miracles were happening. I met the miracles half-way, not turning a hair, accepting everything as a matter of course. I think the police smelled something wrong, but they couldn't put their hands on it. There was the dead man on the floor, with a prowler's outfit in his pockets, a pocketful of stolen jewelry, and the labels gone from his clothes—a burglar's trick. And there I was—a well-to-do Englishman whom the hotel people recognized as the room's rightful occupant.

"I had to talk small just then, but after I went through the dead man's stuff I knew him inside and outside, backward and forward. He had nearly a bushel of papers, and a diary that had everything he had ever done or thought in it. I put in the first night studying those things—memorizing them—and practicing his signature. Among the other things I had taken from his pockets were fifteen hundred dollars' worth of traveler's checks, and I wanted to be able to get them cashed in the morning.

"I stayed in Seattle for three days—as Norman Ashcraft. I had tumbled into something rich and I wasn't going to throw it away. The letter to his wife would keep me from being charged with murder if anything slipped, and I knew I was safer seeing the thing through than running. When the excitement had quieted down I packed up and came down to San Francisco, resuming my own name—Edward Bohannon. But I held on to all of Ashcraft's property, because I had learned from it that his wife had money, and I knew I could get some of it if I played my cards right.

"She saved me the trouble of figuring out a deal for myself. I ran across one of her advertisements in the *Examiner*, answered it, and—here we are."

I looked toward Tijuana. A cloud of yellow dust showed in a notch between two low hills. That would be the machine in which Gorman and Hooper were tracking me. Hooper would have seen me set out after the Englishman, would have waited for Gorman to arrive in the car in which he had followed Gooseneck from Mexicali—Gorman would have had to stay some distance in the rear—and then both of the operatives would have picked up my trail.

I turned to the Englishman.

"But you didn't have Mrs. Ashcraft killed?"

He shook his head.

"You'll never prove it."

"Maybe not," I admitted.

I took a package of cigarettes out of my pocket and put two of them on the seat between us.

"Suppose we play a game. This is just for my own satisfaction. It won't tie anybody to anything—won't prove anything. If you did a certain thing, pick up the cigarette that is nearer me. If you didn't do that thing, pick up the one nearer you. Will you play?"

"No, I won't," he said emphatically. "I don't like your game. But I do want a cigarette."

He reached out his uninjured arm and picked up the cigarette nearer *me*.

"Thanks, Ed," I said. "Now I hate to tell you this, but I'm going to swing you."

"You're balmy, my son."

"You're thinking of the San Francisco job, Ed," I explained. "I'm talking about Seattle. You, a hotel sneak-thief, were discovered in a room with a man who had just died with a bullet in his head. What do you think a jury will make out of that, Ed?"

He laughed at me. And then something went wrong with the laugh. It faded into a sickly grin.

"Of course you did," I said. "When you started to work out your plan to inherit all of Mrs. Ashcraft's wealth by having her killed, the first thing you did was to destroy that suicide letter of her husband's. No matter how carefully you guarded it, there was always a chance that somebody would stumble into it and knock your game on the head. It had served its purpose—you wouldn't need it. It would be foolish to take a chance on it turning up.

"I can't put you up for the murders you engineered in San Francisco; but I can sock you with the one you didn't do in Seattle—so justice won't be cheated. You're going to Seattle, Ed, to hang for Ashcraft's suicide."

And he did.

TRUE DETECTIVE MAGAZINE, NOVEMBER 1924

Who Killed Bob Teal?

BY DASHIELL HAMMETT

of the Continental Detective Agency

Operative Teal went out to shadow a thief, who didn't even know he was suspected. Seven hours after Teal left his agency's office, he was found— shot to death. Whose hand cut him down?

"TEAL WAS KILLED LAST NIGHT."

The Old Man—the Continental Detective Agency's San Francisco manager—spoke without looking at me. His voice was as mild as his smile, and gave no indication of the turmoil that was seething in his mind.

If I kept quiet, waiting for the Old Man to go on, it wasn't because the news didn't mean anything to me. I had been fond of Bob Teal—we all had. He had come to the agency fresh from college two years before; and if ever a man had the makings of a crack detective in him, this slender, broad-shouldered lad had. Two years is little enough time in which to pick up the first principles of sleuthing, but Bob Teal, with his quick eye, cool nerve, balanced head, and whole-hearted interest in the work, was already well along the way to expertness. I had an almost fatherly interest in him, since I had given him most of his early training.

The Old Man didn't look at me as he went on. He was talking to the open window at his elbow.

"He was shot with a .32, twice, through the heart. He was shot behind a row of signboards on the vacant lot on the northwest corner of Hyde and Eddy Streets, at about ten last night. His body was found by a patrolman a little after eleven. The gun was found about fifteen feet away. I have seen him and I have gone over the ground myself. The rain last night wiped out any leads the ground may have held, but from the condition of Teal's clothing and the position in which he was found, I would say that there was no struggle, and that he was shot where he was found, and not carried there afterward. He was lying behind the signboards, about thirty feet from the sidewalk, and his hands were empty. The gun was held close enough to him to singe the breast of his coat. Apparently no one either saw or heard the shooting. The rain and wind would have kept pedestrians off the street, and would have deadened the reports of a .32, which are not especially loud, anyway."

The Old Man's pencil began to tap the desk, its gentle clicking setting my nerves on edge. Presently it stopped, and the Old Man went on:

"Teal was shadowing a Herbert Whitacre—had been shadowing him for three days. Whitacre is one of the partners in the firm Ogburn & Whitacre, farm-development engineers. They have options on a large area of land in several of the new irrigation districts. Ogburn handles the sales end, while Whitacre looks after the rest of the business, including the bookkeeping.

"Last week Ogburn discovered that his partner had been making false entries. The books show certain payments made on the land, and Ogburn learned that these payments had not been made. He estimates that the amount of Whitacre's thefts may be anywhere from $150,000 to $250,000. He came in to see me three days ago and told me all this, and wanted to have Whitacre shadowed in an endeavor to learn what he has done with the stolen money. Their firm is still a partnership, and a partner cannot be prosecuted for stealing from the partnership, of course. Thus, Ogburn could not have his partner arrested, but he hoped to find the money, and then recover it through civil action. Also he was afraid that Whitacre might disappear.

"I sent Teal out to shadow Whitacre, who supposedly didn't know that his partner suspected him. Now I am sending you out to find Whitacre. I'm determined to find him and convict him if I have to let all regular business go and put every man I have on this job for a year. You can get Teal's reports from the clerks. Keep in touch with me."

All that, from the Old Man, was more than an ordinary man's oath written in blood.

In the clerical office I got the two reports Bob had turned in. There was none for the last day, of course, as he would not have written that until after he had quit work for the night. The first of these two reports had already been copied and a copy sent to Ogburn; a typist was working on the other now.

In his reports Bob had described Whitacre as a man of about thirty-seven, with brown hair and eyes, a nervous manner, a smooth-shaven, medium-complexioned face, and rather small feet. He was about five feet eight inches tall, weighed about a hundred and fifty pounds, and dressed fashionably, though quietly. He lived with his wife in an apartment on Gough Street. They had no children. Ogburn had given Bob a description of Mrs. Whitacre: a short, plump, blond woman of something less than thirty.

Those who remember this affair will know that the city, the detective agency, and the people involved all had names different from the ones I have given them. But they will know also that I have kept the facts true. Names of some sort are essential to clearness, and when the use of the real names might cause embarrassment, or pain even, pseudonyms are the most satisfactory alternative.

In shadowing Whitacre, Bob had learned nothing that seemed to be of any value in finding the stolen money. Whitacre had gone about his usual business, apparently, and Bob had seen him do nothing downright suspicious. But Whitacre had seemed very nervous, had often stopped to look around, obviously suspecting that he was being shadowed without being sure of it. On several occasions Bob had had to drop him to avoid being recognized. On one of these occasions, while waiting in the vicinity of Whitacre's residence for him to return, Bob had seen Mrs. Whitacre—or a woman who fit the description Ogburn had given—leave in a taxicab. Bob had not tried to follow her, but he had made a memorandum of the taxi's license number.

These two reports read and practically memorized, I left the agency and went down to Ogburn & Whitacre's suite in the Packard Building. A stenographer ushered me into a tastefully furnished office, where Ogburn sat at a desk signing mail. He offered me a chair. I introduced myself to him: a medium-sized man of perhaps thirty-five, with sleek brown hair and the cleft chin that is associated in my mind with orators, lawyers, and salesmen.

"Oh, yes!" he said, pushing aside the mail, his mobile, intelligent face lighting up. "Has Mr. Teal found anything?"

"Mr. Teal was shot and killed last night."

He looked at me blankly for a moment out of wide brown eyes, and then repeated: "Killed?"

"Yes," I replied, and told him what little I knew about it.

"You don't think—" he began when I had finished, and then stopped. "You don't think Herb would have done that?"

"What do you think?"

"I don't think Herb would commit murder! He's been jumpy the last few days, and I was beginning to think he suspected I had discovered his thefts, but I don't believe he would have gone that far, even if he knew Mr. Teal was following him. I honestly don't!"

"Suppose," I suggested, "that sometime yesterday Teal found where he had put the stolen money, and then Whitacre learned that Teal knew it. Don't you think that under those circumstances Whitacre might have killed him?"

"Perhaps," he said slowly, "but I'd hate to think so. In a moment of panic Herb might—but I really don't think he would."

"When did you see him last?"

"Yesterday. We were here in the office together most of the day. He left for home a few minutes before six. But I talked with him over the phone later. He called me up at home at a little after seven, and said he was coming down to see me, wanted to tell me something. I thought he was going to confess his dishonesty, and that maybe we would be able to straighten out this miserable affair. But he didn't show up; changed his mind, I suppose. His wife called up at about ten. She wanted him to bring something from downtown when he went home, but of course he was not there. I staid in all evening waiting for him, but he didn't—"

He stuttered, stopped talking, and his face drained white.

"My God. I'm wiped out!" he said faintly, as if the thought of his own position had just come to him. "Herb gone, money gone, three years' work gone for nothing! And I'm legally responsible for every cent he stole. God!"

He looked at me with eyes that pleaded for a contradiction, but I couldn't do anything except assure him that everything possible would be done to find both Whitacre and the money. I left him trying frantically to get his attorney on the telephone.

From Ogburn's office I went up to Whitacre's apartment. As I turned the corner below into Gough Street I saw a big, hulking man going up the apartment house steps, and recognized him as George Dean. Hurrying to join him, I regretted that he had been assigned to the job instead of some other member of the Police Detective Homicide Detail. Dean isn't a bad sort, but he isn't so satisfactory to work with as some of the others; that is, you can never be sure that he isn't holding out some important detail so that George Dean would shine as the clever sleuth in the end. Working with a man of that sort, you're bound to fall into the same habit—which doesn't make for teamwork.

I arrived in the vestibule as Dean pressed Whitacre's bell-button.

"Hello," I said. "You in on this?"

"Uh-huh. What d'you know?"

"Nothing. I just got it."

The front door clicked open, and we went together up to the Whitacre's apartment on the third floor. A plump, blond woman in a light blue house-dress opened the apartment door. She was rather pretty in a thick-featured, stolid way.

"Mrs. Whitacre?" Dean inquired.

"Yes."

"Is Mr. Whitacre in?"

"No. He went to Los Angeles this morning," she said, and her face was truthful.

"Know where we can get in touch with him there?"

"Perhaps at the Ambassador, but I think he'll be back by to-morrow or the next day."

Dean showed her his badge.

"We want to ask you a few questions," he told her, and with no appearance of astonishment she opened the door wide for us to enter. She led us into a blue and cream living-room, where we found a chair apiece. She sat facing us on a big blue settle.

"Where was your husband last night?" Dean asked.

"Home. Why?" Her round blue eyes were faintly curious.

"Home all night?"

"Yes, it was a rotten rainy night. Why?" She looked from Dean to me.

Dean's glance met mine, and I nodded an answer to the question that I read there.

"Mrs. Whitacre," he said bluntly, "I have a warrant for your husband's arrest."

"A warrant? For what?"

"Murder."

"Murder?" It was a stifled scream.

"Exactly, an' last night."

"But—but I told you he was—"

"And Ogburn told me," I interrupted leaning forward, "that you called up his apartment last night, asking if your husband was there."

She looked at me blankly for a dozen sec-

onds; and then she laughed, the clear laugh of one who has been the victim of some slight joke.

"You win," she said, and there was neither shame nor humiliation in either face or voice. "Now listen"—the amusement had left her—"I don't know what Herb has done, or how I stand, and I oughtn't to talk until I see a lawyer. But I like to dodge all the trouble I can. If you folks will tell me what's what, on your word of honor, I'll maybe tell you what I know, if anything. What I mean is, if talking will make things any easier for me, if you can show me it will, maybe I'll talk—provided I know anything."

That seemed fair enough, if a little surprising. Apparently this plump woman who could lie with every semblance of candor, and laugh when she was tripped up, wasn't interested in anything much beyond her own comfort.

"You tell it," Dean said to me.

I shot it out all in a lump.

"Your husband had been cooking the books for some time, and got into his partner for something like $200,000 before Ogburn got wise to it. Then he had your husband shadowed, trying to find the money. Last night your husband took the man who was shadowing him over on a lot and shot him."

Her face puckered thoughtfully. Mechanically she reached for a package of a popular brand of cigarettes that lay on a table behind the settle, and proffered them to Dean and me. We shook our heads. She put a cigarette in her mouth, scratched a match on the sole of her slipper, lit the cigarette, and stared at the burning end. Finally she shrugged, her face cleared, and she looked up at us.

"I'm going to talk," she said. "I never got any of the money, and I'd be a chump to make a goat of myself for Herb. He was all right, but if he's run out and left me flat, there's no use of me making a lot of trouble for myself over it. Here goes: I'm not Mrs. Whitacre, except on the register. My name is Mae Landis. Maybe there is a real Mrs. Whitacre, and maybe not. I don't know. Herb and I have been living together here for over a year.

"About a month ago he began to get jumpy, nervous, even worse than usual. He said he had business worries. Then a couple of days ago I discovered that his pistol was gone from the drawer where it had been kept ever since we came here, and that he was carrying it. I asked him: 'What's the idea?' He said he thought he was being followed, and asked me if I'd seen anybody hanging around the neighborhood as if watching our place. I told him no; I thought he was nutty.

"Night before last he told me that he was in trouble, and might have to go away, and that he couldn't take me with him, but would give me enough money to take care of me for a while. He seemed excited, packed his bags so they'd be ready if he needed them in a hurry, and burned up all his photos and a lot of letters and papers. His bags are still in the bedroom, if you want to go through them. When he didn't come home last night I had a hunch that he had beat it without his bags and without saying a word to me, much less giving me any money—leaving me with only twenty dollars to my name and not even much that I could hock, and with the rent due in four days."

"When did you see him last?"

"About eight o'clock last night. He told me he was going down to Mr. Ogburn's apartment to talk some business over with him, but he didn't go there. I know that. I ran out of cigarettes—I like Elixir Russians, and I can't get them uptown here—so I called up Mr. Ogburn's to ask Herb to bring some home with him when he came, and Mr. Ogburn said he hadn't been there."

"How long have you known Whitacre?" I asked.

"Couple of years. I guess. I think I met him first at one of the Beach resorts."

"Has he got any people?"

———

"Not that I know of. I don't know a whole lot about him. Oh, yes! I do know that he served three years in prison in Oregon for forgery. He told me that one night when he was lushed up. He served them under the name of Barber, or Barbee, or something like that. He said he was walking the straight and narrow now."

Dean produced a small automatic pistol, fairly new-looking in spite of the mud that clung to it, and handed it to the woman.

"Ever see that?"

She nodded her blond head.

"Yep! That's Herb's, or its twin."

Dean pocketed the gun again, and we stood up.

"Where do I stand now?" she asked. "You're not going to lock me up as a witness or anything, are you?"

"Not just now," Dean assured her. "Stick around where we can find you if we want you, and you won't be bothered. Got any idea which direction Whitacre'd be likely to go in?"

"No."

"We'd like to give the place the once-over. Mind?"

"Go ahead," she invited. "Take it apart if you want to. I'm coming all the way with you people."

We very nearly did take the place apart, but we found not a thing of value. Whitacre, when he had burned the things that might have given him away, had made a clean job of it.

"Did he ever have any pictures taken by a professional photographer?" I asked just before we left.

"Not that I know of."

"Will you let us know if you hear anything or remember anything else that might help?"

"Sure," she said heartily; "sure."

Dean and I rode down in the elevator in silence, and walked out into Gough Street.

"What do you think of all that?" I asked when we were outside.

"She's a lil,* huh?" He grinned. "I wonder how much she knows. She identified the gun an' gave us that dope about the forgery sentence up north, but we'd of found out them things anyway. If she was wise she'd tell us everything she knew we'd find out, an' that would make her other stuff go over stronger. Think she's dumb or wise?"

"We won't guess," I said. "We'll slap a shadow on her and cover her mail. I have the number of a taxi she used a couple days ago. We'll look that up too."

At a corner drug store I telephoned the Old Man, asking him to detail a couple of the boys to keep Mae Landis and her apartment under surveillance night and day; also to have the Post Office Department let us know if she got any mail that might have been addressed by Whitacre. I told the Old Man I would see Ogburn and get some specimens of the fugitive's writing for comparison with the woman's mail.

Then Dean and I set about tracing the taxi in which Bob Teal had seen the woman ride away. Half an hour in the taxi company's office gave us the information that she had been driven to a number on Greenwich Street. We went to the Greenwich Street address.

It was a ramshackle building, divided into apartments or flats of a dismal and dingy sort. We found the landlady in the basement: a gaunt woman in soiled gray, with a hard, thin-lipped mouth and pale, suspicious eyes. She was rocking vigorously in a creaking chair and sewing on a pair of overalls, while three dirty kids tussled with a mongrel puppy up and down the room.

Dean showed his badge, and told her that we wanted to speak to her in privacy. She got up to chase the kids and their dog out, and then stood with hands on hips facing us.

"Well, what do you want?" she demanded sourly.

---

* the sense is "She's something, huh?"

"Want to get a line on your tenants," Dean said. "Tell us about them."

"Tell you about them?" She had a voice that would have been harsh enough even if she hadn't been in such a peevish mood. "What do you think I got to say about 'em? What do you think I am? I'm a woman that minds her own business! Nobody can't say that I don't run a respectable—"

This was getting us nowhere.

"Who lives in number one?" I asked.

"The Auds—two old folks and their grandchildren. If you know anything against them, it's more'n them that has lived with 'em for ten years does!"

"Who lives in number two?"

"Mrs. Codman and her boys, Frank and Fred. They been here three years, and—"

I carried her from apartment to apartment, until finally we reached a second-floor one that didn't bring quite so harsh an indictment of my stupidity for suspecting its occupants of whatever it was that I suspected them of.

"The Quirks live there." She merely glowered now, whereas she had had a snippy manner before. "And they're decent people, if you ask me!"

"How long have they been here?"

"Six months or more."

"What does he do for a living?"

"I don't know." Sullenly: "Travels maybe."

"How many in the family?"

"Just him and her, and they're nice quiet people, too."

"What does he look like?"

"Like an ordinary man. I ain't a detective. I don't go 'round snoopin' into folks' faces to see what they look like, and prying into their business. I ain't—"

"How old a man is he?"

"Maybe between thirty-five and forty, if he ain't younger or older."

"Large or small?"

"He ain't as short as you, and he ain't as tall as this feller with you," glaring scornfully from my short stoutness to Dean's big bulk, "and he ain't as fat as neither of you."

"Mustache?"

"No."

"Light hair?"

"No." Triumphantly: "Dark."

"Dark eyes, too?"

"I guess so."

Dean, standing off to one side, looked over the woman's shoulder at me. His lips framed the name: "Whitacre."

"Now how about Mrs. Quirk—what does she look like?" I went on.

"She's got light hair, is short and chunky, and maybe under thirty."

Dean and I nodded our satisfaction at each other; that sounded like Mae Landis, right enough.

"Are they home much?" I continued.

"I don't know," the gaunt woman snarled sullenly, and I knew she did know, so I waited, looking at her, and presently she added grudgingly: I think they're away a lot, but I ain't sure."

"I know," I ventured, "they are home very seldom, and then only in the daytime—and you know it."

She didn't deny it, so I asked: "Are they in now?"

"I don't think so, but they might be."

"Let's take a look at the joint, I suggested to Dean.

He nodded and told the woman: "Take us up to their apartment an' unlock the door for us."

"I won't!" she said with sharp emphasis. "You got no right goin' into folks' homes unless you got a search-warrant. You got one?"

"We got nothin'," Dean grinned at her, "but we can get plenty if you want to put us to the trouble. You run this house; you can go into any of the flats any time you want, an' you can take us

in. Take us up, an' we'll lay off you: but if you're going to put us to a lot of trouble, then you'll take your chances of bein' tied up with the Quirks, an' maybe sharin' a cell with 'em. Think that over."

She thought it over, and then, grumbling and growling with each step, took us up to the Quirks' apartment. She made sure they weren't at home, then admitted us.

The apartment consisted of three rooms, a bath, and a kitchen, furnished in the shabby fashion that the ramshackle exterior of the building had prepared us for. In these rooms we found a few articles of masculine and feminine clothing, toilet accessories, and so on. But the place had none of the marks of a permanent abode; there were no pictures, no cushions, none of the dozens of odds and ends of personal belongings that are usually found in homes. The kitchen had the appearance of long disuse; the interiors of the coffee, tea, spice, and flour containers were clean.

Two things we found that meant something: A handful of Elixer Russian cigarettes on a table; and a new box of .32 cartridges—ten of which were missing—in a dresser drawer.

All through our searching the landlady hovered over us, her pale eyes sharp and curious; but now we chased her out, telling her that, law or no law, we were taking charge of the apartment.

"This was or is a hide-out for Whitacre and his woman all right," Dean said when we were alone. "The only question is whether he intended to lay low here or whether it was just a place where he made preparations for his getaway. I reckon the best thing is to have the Captain put a man in here night and day until we turn up Brother Whitacre."

"That's safest," I agreed, and he went to the telephone in the front room to arrange it.

After Dean was through phoning, I called up the Old Man to see if anything new had developed.

"Nothing new," he told me. "How are you coming along?"

"Nicely. Maybe I'll have news for you this evening."

"Did you get those specimens of Whitacre's writing from Ogburn? Or shall I have someone else take care of it?"

"I'll get them this evening," I promised.

I wasted ten minutes trying to reach Ogburn at his office before I looked at my watch and saw that it was after six o'clock. I found his residence listed in the telephone directory, and called him there.

"Have you anything in Whitacre's writing at home?" I asked. "I want to get a couple of samples—would like to get them this evening, though if necessary I can wait until to-morrow."

"I think I have some of his letters here. If you come over now I'll give them to you."

"Be with you in fifteen minutes," I told him.

"I'm going down to Ogburn's," I told Dean, "to get some of Whitacre's scribbling while you're waiting for your man to come from Headquarters to take charge of this place. I'll meet you at the States as soon as you can get away. We'll eat there, and make our plans for the night."

"Uh-huh," he grunted, making himself comfortable in one chair, with his feet on another, as I let myself out.

Ogburn was dressing when I reached his apartment, and had his collar and tie in his hand when he came to the door to let me in.

"I found quite a few of Herb's letters," he said as we walked back to his bedroom.

I looked through the fifteen or more letters that lay on a table, selecting the ones I wanted, while Ogburn went on with his dressing.

"How are you progressing?" he asked presently.

"So-so. Heard anything that might help?"

"No, but just a few minutes ago I happened to remember that Herb used to go over to the Mills Building quite frequently. I've seen him going in and out often, but never thought anything of it. I don't know whether it is of any importance or—"

I jumped out of my chair.

"That does it!" I cried. "Can I use your phone?"

"Certainly. It's in the hallway, near the door." He looked at me in surprise. "It's a slot phone; have you a nickel in change?"

"Yes." I was going through the bedroom door.

"The switch is near the door," he called after me, "if you want a light. Do you think—"

But I didn't stop to listen to his questions. I was making for the telephone, searching my pockets for a nickel. And, fumbling hurriedly with the nickel, I muffed it—not entirely by accident, for I had a hunch that I wanted to work out. The nickel rolled away down the carpeted hallway. I switched on the light, recovered the nickel, and called the "Quirks'" number. I'm glad I played that hunch.

Dean was still there.

"That joint's dead," I sang. "Take the landlady down to Headquarters, and grab the Landis woman, too. I'll meet you there—at Headquarters."

"You mean it?" he rumbled.

"Almost," I said, and hung up the receiver.

I switched off the hall light and, whistling a little tune to myself, walked back to the room where I had left Ogburn. The door was not quite closed. I walked straight up to it, kicked it open with one foot, and jumped back, hugging the wall.

Two shots—so close together that they were almost one—crashed.

Flat against the wall, I pounded my feet against the floor and wainscot, and let out a medley of shrieks and groans that would have done credit to a carnival wild-man.

A moment later Ogburn appeared in the doorway, a revolver in his hand, his face wolfish. He was determined to kill me. It was my life or his, so—

I slammed my gun down on the sleek, brown top of his head.

When he opened his eyes, two policemen were lifting him into the back of a patrol-wagon.

I found Dean in the detectives' assembly-room in the Hall of Justice.

"The landlady identifies Mae Landis as Mrs. Quirk," he said. "Now what?"

"Where is she now?"

"One of the policewomen is holding both of them in the Captain's office."

"Ogburn is over in the Pawnshop Detail office," I told him. "Let's take the landlady in for a look at him."

Ogburn sat leaning forward, holding his head in his hands and staring sullenly at the feet of the uniformed man who guarded him, when we took the gaunt landlady in to see him.

"Ever see him before?" I asked her.

"Yes"—reluctantly—"that's Mr. Quirk."

Ogburn didn't look up, and he paid not the least attention to any of us.

After we had told the landlady that she could go home, Dean led me back to a far corner of the assembly-room, where we could talk without disturbance.

"Now spill it!" he burst out. "How come all the startling developments, as the newspaper boys call 'em?"

"Well, first-off, I knew that the question *Who killed Bob Teal?* could have only one answer. Bob wasn't a boob! He might possibly have let a man he was trailing lure him behind a row of billboards on a dark night, but he would have gone prepared for trouble. He wouldn't have died with empty hands, from a gun that was close enough to scorch his coat. The murderer *had* to be somebody Bob trusted, so it couldn't be Whitacre. Now Bob was a conscientious sort of lad, and he wouldn't have stopped shadowing Whitacre to go over and talk with some friend. There was only one man who could have persuaded him to drop Whitacre for a while, and that one man was the one he was working for—Ogburn.

"If I hadn't known Bob, I might have thought he had hidden behind the billboards to watch Whitacre; but Bob wasn't an amateur. He knew better than to pull any of that spectacular gumshoe stuff. So there was nothing to it but Ogburn!

"With that to go on, the rest was ducksoup. All the stuff Mae Landis gave us—identifying the gun as Whitacre's, and giving Ogburn an alibi by saying she had talked to him on the phone at ten o'clock—only convinced me that she and Ogburn were working together. When the landlady described 'Quirk' for us, I was fairly certain of it. Her description would fit either Whitacre or Ogburn, but there was no sense to Whitacre's having the apartment on Greenwich Street, while if Ogburn and the Landis woman were thick, they'd need a meeting-place of some sort. The rest of the box of cartridges there helped some too.

"Then to-night I put on a little act in Ogburn's apartment, chasing a nickel along the floor and finding traces of dried mud that had escaped the cleaning-up he no doubt gave the carpet and clothes after he came home from walking through the lot in the rain. We'll let the experts decide whether it *could* be mud from the lot on which Bob was killed, and the jury can decide whether it *is*.

"There are a few more odds and ends—like the gun. The Landis woman said Whitacre had had it for more than a year, but in spite of being muddy it looks fairly new to me. We'll send the serial number to the factory, and find when it was turned out.

"For motive, just now all I'm sure of is the woman, which should be enough. But I think that when Ogburn & Whitacre's books are audited, and their finances sifted, we'll find something there. What I'm banking on strong is that Whitacre will come in, now that he is cleared of the murder charge."

And that is exactly what happened.

Next day Herbert Whitacre walked into Police Headquarters at Sacramento and surrendered.

Neither Ogburn nor Mae Landis ever told what they knew, but with Whitacre's testimony, supported by what we were able to pick up here and there, we went into court when the time came and convinced the jury that the facts were these:

Ogburn and Whitacre had opened their farm development business as a plain swindle. They had options on a lot of land, and they planned to sell as many shares in their enterprise as possible before the time came to exercise their options. Then they intended packing up their bags and disappearing. Whitacre hadn't much nerve, and he had a clear remembrance of the three years he had served in prison for forgery; so, to bolster his courage, Ogburn had told his partner that he had a friend in the Post Office Department in Washington, D.C., who would tip him off the instant any official suspicion was aroused.

The two partners made a neat little pile out of their venture, Ogburn taking charge of the money until the time came for the split-up. Meanwhile Ogburn and Mae Landis—Whitacre's supposed wife—had become intimate, and had rented the apartment on Greenwich Street, meeting there afternoons when Whitacre was busy at the office, and when Ogburn was supposed to be out hunting fresh victims. In this apartment Ogburn and the woman had hatched their little scheme, whereby they were to get rid of Whitacre, keep all the loot, and clear Ogburn of criminal complicity in the affairs of Ogburn & Whitacre.

Ogburn had come into the Continental Office and told his little tale of his partner's dishonesty, engaging Bob Teal to shadow him. Then he had told Whitacre that he had received a tip from his friend in Washington that an investigation was about to be made. The two partners planned to leave town on their separate ways the following week. The next night Mae Landis told Whitacre she had seen a man loitering in the neighborhood, apparently watching the building in which they lived. Whitacre—thinking Bob a Post Office Inspector—had gone completely to pieces, and it had taken the combined efforts of the woman and his partner—apparently working separately—to keep him from bolting immediately. They had persuaded him to stick it out another few days.

On the night of the murder, Ogburn, pretending skepticism of Whitacre's story about being followed, had met Whitacre for the purpose of learning if he really was being shadowed. They had walked the streets in the rain for an hour. Then Ogburn, convinced, had announced his intention of going back and talking to the supposed Post Office Inspector, to see if he could be bribed. Whitacre had refused to accompany his partner, but had agreed to wait for him in a dark doorway.

Ogburn had taken Bob Teal over behind the billboards on some pretext, and had murdered him. Then he had hurried back to his partner, crying: "My God! He grabbed me and I shot him. We'll have to leave!"

Whitacre, in blind panic, had left San Francisco without stopping for his bags or even notifying Mae Landis. Ogburn was supposed to leave by another route. They were to meet in Oklahoma City ten days later, where Ogburn—after getting the loot out of the Los Angeles banks, where he had deposited it under various names—was to give Whitacre his share, and then they were to part for good.

In Sacramento next day Whitacre had read the newspapers, and had understood what had been done to him. He had done all the bookkeeping; all the false entries in Ogburn & Whitacre's books were in his writing. Mae Landis had revealed his former criminal record, and had fastened the ownership of the gun—really Ogburn's—upon him. He was framed completely! He hadn't a chance of clearing himself.

He had known that his story would sound like a far-fetched and flimsy lie; he had a criminal record. For him to have surrendered and told the truth would have been merely to get himself laughed at.

As it turned out, Ogburn went to the gallows, Mae Landis is now serving a fifteen-year sentence, and Whitacre, in return for his testimony and restitution of the loot, was not prosecuted for his share in the land swindle.

BLACK MASK, JANUARY 1925

Mike or Alec or Rufus

BY DASHIELL HAMMETT

(Author of "The Girl with the Silver Eyes," etc.)

Mr. Hammett and his hard-boiled sleuth are too well known to BLACK MASK readers to need much of an introduction. That the following story is as interesting and surprising as any which Mr. Hammett has yet written, is all we need to say to arouse your interest.

I DON'T KNOW whether Jacob Coplin was tall or short. All of him I ever got a look at was his round head—naked scalp and wrinkled face, both of them the color and texture of Manila paper—propped up on white pillows in a big four-poster bed. The rest of him was buried under a thick pile of bedding.

Besides he and I in the room that first time, there were his wife, a roly-poly woman with lines in a plump white face like scratches in ivory; his daughter Phyllis, a smart little Jewess of the popular-member-of-the-younger-set type; and the maid who had opened the door for me, a big-boned blonde girl in apron and cap.

I had introduced myself as a representative of the North American Casualty Company's San Francisco office, which I was in a way. There was no immediate profit in admitting I was a Conti-nental Detective Agency sleuth, just now in the casualty company's hire, so I held back that part.

"I want a list of the stuff you lost," I told Coplin; "but first—"

"Stuff?" Coplin's yellow sphere of a skull bobbed off the pillows, and he wailed to the ceiling: "A hundred thousand dollars if a nickel, and he calls it *stuff*!"

Mrs. Coplin pushed her husband's head down on the pillows again with a short-fingered fat hand.

"Now, Jakie, don'd ged excited," she soothed him.

Phyllis Coplin's dark eyes twinkled, and she winked one of them at me.

The man in bed turned his face to me again, smiled a bit shamefacedly, and chuckled.

"Well, if you people want to call your seventy-five-thousand-dollar loss *stuff*, I guess I can stand it for twenty-five thousand."

"So it adds up to a hundred thousand?" I asked.

"Yes. None of them were insured to their full value, and some weren't insured at all."

That was very usual. I don't remember ever having anybody admit that anything stolen from them was insured to the hilt—always it was half, or, at most, three-quarters covered by the policy.

"Suppose you tell me exactly what happened," I suggested, and added, to head off another speech that usually comes: "I know you've already told the police the whole thing, but I'll have to have it from you."

"Well, we were getting dressed to go to the Bauers' last night. I brought my wife's and daughter's jewelry—the valuable pieces—home with me from the safe-deposit box. I had just got my coat on, and had called to them to hurry up with their dressing when the door-bell rang."

"What time was this?"

"Just about half past eight. I went out of this room into the sitting-room across the passageway, and was putting some cigars in my case when Hilda"—nodding at the blonde maid—"came walking into the room, backwards. I started to ask her if she had gone crazy, walking around backwards, when I saw the robber. He—"

"Just a moment." I turned to the maid. "What happened when you answered the bell?"

"Why, I opened the door, of course, and this man was standing there, and he had a revolver in his hand, and he stuck it against my—my stomach, and pushed me back into the room where Mr. Coplin was, and he shot Mr. Coplin, and—"

"When I saw him and the revolver in his hand," Coplin took the story away from his servant; "it gave me a fright, sort of, and I let my cigar case slip out of my hand. Trying to catch it again—no sense in ruining good cigars even if you are being robbed—he must have thought I was trying to get a gun or something. Anyway he shot me in the leg. My wife and Phyllis came

running in when they heard the shot, and he pointed the revolver at them, took all their jewels, and had them empty my pockets. Then he made them drag me back into Phyllis's room, into the closet, and he locked us all in there. And, mind you, he don't say a word all this time, not a word—just makes motions with his gun and his left hand."

"How bad did he bang your leg?"

"Depends on whether you want to believe me or the doctor. He says it's nothing much. Just a scratch, he says, but it's my leg that's shot, not his!"

"Did he say anything when you opened the door?" I asked the maid.

"No, sir."

"Did any of you hear him say anything while he was here?"

None of them had.

"What happened after he locked you in the closet?"

"Nothing that we knew about," Coplin said; "until McBirney and a policeman came and let us out."

"Who's McBirney?"

"The janitor."

"How'd he happen along with a policeman?"

"He heard the shot, and came upstairs just as the robber was starting down after leaving here. The robber turned around and ran upstairs, then, into an apartment on the seventh floor, and stayed there—keeping the woman who lives there, a Miss Eveleth, quiet with his revolver—until he got a chance to sneak out and get away. He knocked her unconscious before he left, and—and that's all. McBirney called the police right after he saw the robber, but they got here too late to be any good."

"How long were you in the closet?"

"Ten minutes—maybe fifteen."

"What sort of looking man was the robber?"

"Short and thin and—"

"How short?"

"About your height, or maybe shorter."

"About five feet five or six, say? What would he weigh?"

"Oh, I don't know—maybe a hundred and fifteen or twenty. He was kind of puny."

"How old?"

"Not more than twenty-two or three."

"Oh, Papa," Phyllis objected; "he was thirty, or near it!"

"What do you think?" I asked Mrs. Coplin.

"Twendy-five, I'll say."

"And you?" to the maid.

"I don't know exactly, sir; but he wasn't very old."

"Light or dark?"

"He was light," Coplin said. "He needed a shave, and his beard was yellowish."

"More of a light brown," Phyllis amended.

"Maybe, but it was light."

"What color eyes?"

"I don't know. He had a cap pulled down over them. They looked dark, but that might have been because they were in the shadow."

"How would you describe the part of his face you could see?"

"Pale, and kind of weak looking—small chin. But you couldn't see much of his face: he had his coat collar turned up and his cap pulled down."

"How was he dressed?"

"A blue cap pulled down over his eyes, a blue suit, black shoes, and black gloves—silk ones."

"Shabby or neat?"

"Kind of cheap looking clothes, needing pressing, awfully wrinkled."

"What sort of gun?"

Phyllis Coplin put in her word ahead of her father.

"Papa and Hilda keep calling it a revolver, but it was an automatic—a .38."

"Would you folks know him if you saw him again?"

"Yes," they agreed.

I cleared a space on the bedside table and got out a pencil and sheet of paper.

"I want a list of what he got, with as thorough a description of each piece as possible, and the price you paid for it, where you bought it, and when."

I got the list half an hour later.

"Do you know the number of Miss Eveleth's apartment?" I asked as I reached for my hat.

"702, two floors above."

I went up there and rang the bell. The door was opened by a girl of twenty-something, whose nose was hidden under adhesive tape. She had nice clear hazel eyes, dark hair, and outdoor athletics written all over her.

"Miss Eveleth?"

"Yes."

"I'm from the insurance company that insured the Coplin's jewelry, and I'm looking for information about the robbery."

She touched her bandaged nose and smiled ruefully.

"This is some of my information."

"How did it happen?"

"A penalty of femininity—I forgot to mind my own business. But what you want, I suppose, is what I know about the scoundrel. The doorbell rang a few minutes before nine last night, and when I opened the door he was here. As soon as I got the door open he jabbed a pistol at me, and said:

"'Inside, kid!'

"I let him in with no hesitancy at all: I was quite instantaneous about it, and he kicked the door to behind him.

"'Where's the fire-escape?' he asked.

"The fire-escape doesn't come to any of my windows, and I told him so, but he wouldn't take my word for it. He drove me ahead of him to each of the windows; but of course he didn't find his fire-escape, and he got peevish about it, as if it were my fault. I didn't like some of the things he called me, and he was such a little half-portion of a man, so I tried to take him in hand. But—well, man is still the dominant male so far as I'm concerned. In plain American, he busted me in the nose and left me where I fell. I was dazed, though not quite all the way out, and when I got up he had gone. I ran out into the corridor then, and found some policemen on the stairs. I sobbed out my pathetic little tale to them, and they told me of the Coplin robbery. Two of them came back here with me and searched the apartment. I hadn't seen him actually leave, and they thought he might be foxy enough or desperate enough to jump into a closet and stay there until the coast was clear. But they didn't find him here."

"How long do you think it was after he knocked you down that you ran out into the corridor?"

"Oh, it couldn't have been five minutes. Perhaps only half that time."

"What did Mr. Robber look like?"

"Small, not quite so large as I; with a couple of days' growth of light hair on his face; dressed in shabby blue clothes, with black cloth gloves."

"How old?"

"Not very. His beard was thin, patchy, and he had a boyish face."

"Notice his eyes?"

"Blue. His hair, where it showed under the edge of his cap was a very light yellow, almost white."

"What sort of voice?"

"Very deep bass, though he may have been putting that on."

"Know him if you'd see him again?"

"Yes, indeed!" She put a gentle finger on her bandaged nose. "My nose would know, as the ads say, anyway!"

From Miss Eveleth's apartment I went down to the office on the first floor, where I found McBirney, the janitor, and his wife, who managed the apartment building. She was a scrawny little woman with the angular mouth and nose of a nagger; he was big, broad-shouldered; with sandy hair and mustache; good-humored, shiftless red face; and genial eyes of a pale and watery blue.

He drawled out what he knew of the looting.

"I was a-fixin' a spigot on the fourth floor when I heard the shot. I went up to see what was the matter, an' just as I got far enough up the front stairs to see the Coplins' door, the fella came out. We seen each other at the same time, an' he aims his gun at me. There's a lot o' things I might of done, but what I did do was to duck down an' get my head out o' range. I heard him run upstairs, an' I got up just in time to see him make the turn between the fifth and sixth floors.

"I didn't go after him. I didn't have a gun or nothin', an' I figured we had him cooped. A man could get out o' this buildin' to the roof of the next from the fourth floor, an' maybe from the fifth, but not from any above that; an' the Coplins' apartment is on the fifth. I figured we had this fella. I could stand in front of the elevator an' watch both the front an' back stairs; an' I rang for the elevator, an' told Ambrose, the elevator-boy, to give the alarm an' run outside an' keep his eye on the fire-escape until the police came.

"The missus came up with my gun in a minute or two, an' told me that Martinez—Ambrose's brother, who takes care of the switchboard an' the front door—was callin' the police. I could see both stairs plain, an' the fella didn't come down them; an' it wasn't more'n a few minutes before the police—a whole pack of 'em—came from the Richmond Station. Then we let the Coplins out of the closet where they were, an' started to search the buildin'. An' then Miss Eveleth came runnin' down the stairs, her face an' dress all bloody an' told about him bein' in her apartment; so we were pretty sure we'd land him. But we didn't. We searched every apartment in the buildin', but didn't find hide nor hair of him."

"Of course you didn't!" Mrs. McBirney said unpleasantly. "But if you had—"

"I know," the janitor said with the indulgent air of one who has learned to take his pannings as an ordinary part of married life; "if I'd been a hero an' grabbed him, an' got myself all mussed up. Well, I ain't foolish like old man Coplin, gettin' himself plugged in the foot, or Blanche Eveleth, gettin' her nose busted. I'm a sensible man that knows when he's licked; an' I ain't jumpin' at no guns!"

"No! You're not doing anything that—"

This Mr. and Mrs. stuff wasn't getting me

anywhere, so I cut in with a question to the woman.

"Who is the newest tenant you have?"

"Mr. and Mrs. Jerald; they came the day before yesterday."

"What apartment?"

"704—next door to Miss Eveleth."

"Who are these Jeralds?"

"They come from Boston. He told me he came out here to open a branch of a manufacturing company. He's a man of at least fifty, thin and dyspeptic looking."

"Just him and his wife?"

"Yes. She's poorly too—been in a sanatorium for a year or two."

"Who's the next newest tenant?"

"Mr. Heaton, in 535. He's been here a couple of weeks; but he's down in Los Angeles right now. He went away three days ago, and said he would be gone for ten or twelve days."

"What does he look like, and what does he do?"

"He's with a theatrical agency, and he's kind of fat and red-faced."

"Who's the next newest?"

"Miss Eveleth. She's been here about a month."

"And the next?"

"The Wageners, in 923. They've been here going on two months."

"What are they?"

"He's a retired real estate agent. The others are his wife and son Jack—a boy of maybe nineteen. I see him with Phyllis Coplin a lot."

"How long have the Coplins been here?"

"It'll be two years next month."

I turned from Mrs. McBirney to her husband.

"Did the police search all these people's apartments?"

"Yeah," he said. "We went into every room, every alcove an' every closet from cellar to roof."

"Did you get a good look at the robber?"

"Yeah. There's a light in the hall outside of the Coplins' door, an' it was shinin' full on his face when I saw him."

"Could he have been one of your tenants?"

"No, he couldn't."

"Know him if you saw him again?"

"You bet."

"What did he look like?"

"A little runt; a light-complected youngster of twenty-three or four in an old blue suit."

"Can I get hold of Ambrose and Martinez—the elevator and door boys who were on duty last night—now?"

The janitor looked at his watch.

"Yeah. They ought to be on the job now. They come on at two."

I went out into the lobby and found them together, matching nickels. They were brothers: slim, bright-eyed Filipino boys. They didn't add much to my dope.

Ambrose had come down to the lobby and told his brother to call the police as soon as McBirney had given him his orders, and then he had beat it out the back door to take a plant on the fire-escapes. The fire-escapes ran down the back and one side wall. By standing a little off from the corner of those walls, the Filipino had been able to keep his eyes on both of them, as well as on the back door.

There was plenty of illumination, he said, and he could see both fire-escapes all the way to the roof, and he had seen nobody on them.

Martinez had given the police a rap on the phone, and had then watched the front door and the foot of the front stairs. He had seen nothing.

Neither of them had seen anyone in the building either before or after the Coplins were turned for their jewels who fit the robber's description.

I had just finished questioning the Filipinos when the street door opened and two men came in. I knew one of them: Bill Garren, a police detective on the Pawn Shop Detail. The other was a small blond youth all flossy in pleated pants, short, square-shouldered coat, and patent-leather shoes with fawn spats to match his hat and gloves. His face wore a sullen pout. He didn't seem to like being with Garren.

"What are you up to around here?" the detective hailed me.

"The Coplin doings for the insurance company," I explained.

"Getting anywhere?" he wanted to know.

"About ready to make a pinch," I said, not altogether in earnest and not altogether joking.

"The more the merrier," he grinned. "I've already made mine." Nodding at the dressy youth. "Come on upstairs with us."

The three of us got into the elevator, and Ambrose carried us to the fifth floor. Before pressing the Coplins' bell, Garren gave me what he had.

"This lad tried to soak* a ring in a Third Street shop a little while ago—an emerald and diamond ring that looks like one of the Coplin lot. He's doing the clam† now; he hasn't said a word—yet. I'm going to show him to these people; then I'm going to take him down to the Hall of Justice and get words out of him—words that fit together in nice sentences and everything!"

The prisoner looked sullenly at the floor and paid no attention to this threat. Garren rang the bell, and the maid Hilda opened the door. Her eyes widened when she saw the dressy boy, but she didn't say anything as she led us into the sitting-room, where Mrs. Coplin and her daughter were. They looked up at us.

"Hello, Jack!" Phyllis greeted the prisoner.

"'Lo, Phyl," he mumbled, not looking at her.

"Among friends, huh? Well, what's the answer?" Garren demanded of the girl.

She put her chin in the air, and although her face turned red, she looked haughtily at the police detective.

"Would you mind removing your hat?" she asked.

Bill isn't a bad bimbo,‡ but he hasn't any meekness. He answered her by tilting his hat over one eye and turning to her mother.

"Ever see this lad before?"

"Why, cerdainly!" Mrs. Coplin exclaimed. "Thad's Mr. Wagener who lives upsdairs."

---

* pawn
† refusing to talk
‡ guy

"Well," said Bill; "Mr. Wagener was picked up in a hock-shop trying to get rid of this ring." He fished a gaudy green and white ring from his pocket. "Know it?"

"Cerdainly!" Mrs. Coplin said, looking at the ring. "Id belongs to my Phyllis, and the robber—" Her mouth dropped open as she began to understand. "How could Mr. Wagener—?"

"Yes, how?" Bill repeated.

The girl stepped between Garren and me, turning her back on him to face me.

"I can explain everything," she announced.

That sounded too much like a movie sub-title to be very promising, but—

"Go ahead," I encouraged her.

"I found that ring in the passageway near the front door after the excitement was over. The robber must have dropped it. I didn't say anything to Papa and Mama about it, because I thought nobody would ever know the difference, and it was insured, so I thought I might as well sell it and be that much money in. I asked Jack last night if he could sell it for me, and he said he knew just how to go about it. He didn't have anything to do with it outside of that; but I did think he'd have sense enough not to try to pawn it right away!"

She looked scornfully at her accomplice.

"See what you've done!" she accused him.

He fidgeted and pouted at his feet.

"Ha! Ha! Ha!" Bill Garren said sourly. "That's a nifty! Did you ever hear the one about the two Irishmen that got in the Y.W.C.A. by mistake?"

She didn't say whether she had heard it or not.

"Mrs. Coplin," I asked; "making allowances for the different clothes, and the unshaven face, could this lad have been the robber?"

She shook her head with emphasis.

"No! He could nod be id!"

"Set your prize down, Bill," I suggested; "and let's go over in a corner and whisper things at each other."

"Right."

He dragged a heavy chair to the center of

the floor, sat Wagener on it, anchored him there with handcuffs,—not exactly necessary, but Bill was grouchy at not getting his prisoner identified as the robber,—and then he and I stepped out into the passageway. We could keep an eye on the sitting-room from there without having our low-voiced conversation overheard.

"This is simple!" I whispered into his big red ear. "There are only five ways to figure the lay. First: Wagener stole the stuff for the Coplins. Second: the Coplins framed the robbery themselves, and got Wagener to peddle it. Third: Wagener and the girl engineered the deal without the old folks being in on it. Fourth: Wagener pulled it on his own hook and the girl is covering him up. Fifth: she told us the truth. None of them explain why your little playmate should have been dumb enough to flash the ring downtown this morning; but that can't be explained by any system. Which of the five do you favor?"

"I like 'em all," he grumbled. "But what I like most is that I've got this baby right—got him trying to pass a hot ring. That suits me fine. You do the guessing. I don't ask for any more than I've got."

That wasn't so foolish.

"It doesn't irritate me any either," I agreed. "The way it stands the insurance company can welch on the policies; but I'd like to smoke it out a little further, far enough to put away anybody who has been trying to run a hooligan on the North American. We'll clean up all we can on this kid, stow him in the can, and then see what further damage we can do."

"All right," Garren said. "Suppose you get hold of the janitor and that Eveleth woman while I'm showing the boy to old man Coplin, and getting the maid's opinion."

I nodded and went out into the corridor, leaving the door unlocked behind me. I took the elevator to the seventh floor, and told Ambrose to get hold of McBirney and send him to the Coplins' apartment. Then I rang Blanche Eveleth's bell.

"Can you come downstairs for a minute or two?" I asked her. "We've a prize who might be your friend of last night."

"Will I?" She started toward the stairs with me. "And if he's the right one, can I pay him back for my battered beauty?"

"You can," I promised. "Go as far as you like, so you don't maul him too badly to stand trial."

I took her into the Coplins' apartment without ringing the bell, and found everybody in Jacob Coplin's bedroom. A look at Garren's glum face told me that neither the old man nor the maid had given him a nod on the prisoner.

I put the finger on Jack Wagener. Disappointment came into Blanche Eveleth's eyes.

"You're wrong," she said. "That's not he."

Garren scowled at her. It was a pipe* that if the Coplins were tied up with young Wagener, they wouldn't identify him as the robber. Bill had been counting on that identification coming from the two outsiders,—Blanche Eveleth and the janitor,—and now one of them had flopped.

The other one rang the bell just then, and the maid brought him into the room.

I pointed at Jack Wagener, who stood beside Garren, staring sullenly at the floor.

"Know him, McBirney?"

"Yeah. Mr. Wagener's son Jack."

"Is he the man who shooed you away with a gun last night?"

McBirney's watery eyes popped in surprise.

"No," he said with decision, and began to look doubtful.

"In an old suit, cap pulled down, needing a shave—could it have been him?"

"No-o-o," the janitor drawled; "I don't think so, though it—You know, now that I come to think about it, there was something familiar about that fella, an' maybe—By cracky, I think maybe you're right—though I couldn't exactly say for sure."

"That'll do!" Garren grunted in disgust.

An identification of the sort the janitor was giving isn't worth a damn one way or the other. Even positive and immediate identifications

---

* cinch

aren't always the goods. A lot of people who don't know any better—and some who do, or should—have given circumstantial evidence a bad name. It is misleading sometimes. But for genuine, undiluted, pre-war untrustworthiness, it can't come within gunshot of human testimony. Take any man you like—unless he is the one in a hundred thousand with a mind trained to keep things straight, and not always even then—get him excited, show him something, give him a few hours to think it over and talk it over, and then ask him about it. It's dollars to marks that you'll have a hard time finding any connection between what he saw and what he says he saw. Like this McBirney—another hour, and he'd be ready to gamble his life on Jack Wagener's being the robber.

Garren wrapped his fingers around the boy's arm and started for the door.

"Where to, Bill?" I asked.

"Up to talk to his people. Coming along?"

"Stick around a while," I invited. "I'm going to put on a party. But first, tell me, did the coppers who came here when the alarm was turned in do a good job?"

"I didn't see it," the police detective said. "I didn't get here until the fireworks were pretty well over, but I understand the boys did all that could be expected of them."

I turned to Jacob Coplin. I did my talking to him chiefly because we—his wife and daughter, the maid, the janitor, Blanche Eveleth, Garren and his prisoner, and I—were grouped around the old man's bed, and by looking at him I could get at least a one-eyed view of everybody else.

"Somebody has been kidding me somewhere," I began my speech. "If all the things I've been told about this job are right, then so is Prohibition. Your stories don't fit together, not even almost. Take the bird who stuck you up. He seems to have been pretty well acquainted with your affairs. It might be luck that he hit your apartment at a time when all of your jewelry was on hand, instead of another apartment, or your apartment at another time. But I don't like luck. I'd rather figure that he knew what he was doing.

He nicked you for your pretties, and then he galloped up to Miss Eveleth's apartment. He may have been about to go downstairs when he ran into McBirney, or he may not. Anyway, he went upstairs, into Miss Eveleth's apartment, looking for a fire-escape. Funny, huh? He knew enough about the place to make a push-over out of the stick-up, but he didn't know there were no fire-escapes on Miss Eveleth's side of the building.

"He didn't speak to you or to McBirney, but he talked to Miss Eveleth, in a bass voice. A very, very deep voice. Funny, huh? From Miss Eveleth's apartment he vanished with every exit watched. The police must have been here before he left her apartment, and they would have blocked the outlets first thing, whether McBirney and Ambrose had already done that or not. But he got away. Funny, huh? He wore a wrinkled suit, which might have been taken from a bundle just before he went to work, and he was a small man. Miss Eveleth isn't a small woman, but she would be a small man. A guy with a suspicious disposition would almost think Blanche Eveleth was the robber."

Jacob Coplin, his wife, young Wagener, the janitor and the maid were gaping at me. Garren was sizing up the Eveleth girl with narrowed eyes, while she glared white-hot at me. Phyllis Coplin was looking at me with a contemptuous sort of pity for my feeble-mindedness.

Bill Garren finished his inspection of the girl and nodded slowly.

"She could get away with it," he gave his opinion; "indoors and if she kept her mouth shut."

"Exactly," I said.

"Exactly my eye!" Phyllis Coplin exploded. "Do you two correspondence-school detectives think we wouldn't know the difference between a man and a woman dressed in man's clothes? He had a day or two's growth of hair on his face—real hair, if you know what I mean. Do you think he could have fooled us with false whiskers? This happened, you know; it's not in a play!"

The others stopped gaping, and heads bobbed up and down.

"Phyllis is right," Jacob Coplin backed up his offspring; "he was a man—no woman dressed like one."

His wife, the maid, and the janitor nodded vigorous indorsements.

But I'm a bullheaded sort of bird when it comes to going where the evidence leads. I spun to face Blanche Eveleth.

"Can you add anything to the occasion?" I asked her.

She smiled very sweetly at me and shook her head.

"All right, bum," I said. "You're pinched. Let's go."

Then it seemed she could add something to the occasion. She had something to say, quite a few things to say, and they were all about me. They weren't nice things. In anger her voice was shrill, and just now she was madder than you'd think anybody could get on short notice. I was sorry for that. This job had run along peacefully and gently so far, hadn't been marred by any rough stuff, had been almost ladylike in every particular; and I had hoped it would go that way to the end. But the more she screamed at me the nastier she got. She didn't have any words I hadn't heard before, but she fitted them together in combinations that were new to me. I stood as much of it as I could.

Then I knocked her over with a punch in the mouth.

"Here! Here!" Bill Garren yelled, grabbing my arm.

"Save your strength, Bill," I advised him, shaking his hand off and going over to yank the Eveleth person up from the floor. "Your gallantry does you credit, and all the like of that, but I think you'll find Blanche's real name is Mike or Alec or Rufus."

I hauled her or him—which ever you like—to his or her feet and asked it:

"Feel like telling us about it?"

For answer I got a snarl.

"All right," I said to the others; "in the absence of authoritative information I'll give you my dope. If Blanche Eveleth could have been the robber except for the beard and the difficulty of a woman passing for a man, why couldn't the robber have been Blanche Eveleth before and after the robbery by using a—what do you call it—strong depilatory on his face, and a wig? It's hard for a woman to masquerade as a man, but there are lots of men who can get away with the feminine rôle. Couldn't this bird, after renting his apartment as Blanche Eveleth and getting everything lined up, have stayed in his apartment for a couple of days letting his beard grow? Come down and knock the job over? Beat it upstairs, get the hair off his face, and get into his female rig in, say, fifteen minutes? My guess is that he could. And he had fifteen minutes. I don't know about the smashed nose. Maybe he stumbled going up the stairs and had to twist his plans to account for it; or maybe he smacked himself intentionally."

My guesses weren't far off, though his name was Fred—Frederick Agnew Rudd. He was known in Toronto, having done a stretch in the Ontario Reformatory as a boy of nineteen, caught shop-lifting in his she-makeup. He wouldn't come through, and we never turned up his gun or the blue suit, cap, and black gloves, although we found a cavity in his mattress where he had stuffed them out of the police's sight until later that night, when he could get rid of them. The Coplin sparklers came to light piece by piece when we had plumbers take apart the drains and radiators in apartment 702.

BLACK MASK, MARCH 1925

The Whosis Kid

BY DASHIELL HAMMETT

We have talked so many times of Mr. Hammett's "shrewd, canny sleuth," his "hard-boiled detective," etc., that we're at the end of our rope for words to introduce him to new readers. . . . Well, he is a shrewd, canny, hard-boiled sleuth, and this is an exciting tale.

A COMPLETE DETECTIVE NOVELETTE

IT STARTED IN BOSTON, back in 1917. I ran into Lew Maher on the Tremont street sidewalk of the Touraine Hotel one afternoon, and we stopped to swap a few minutes' gossip in the snow.

I was telling him something or other when he cut in with:

"Sneak a look at this kid coming up the street. The one with the dark cap."

Looking, I saw a gangling youth of eighteen or so; pasty and pimply face, sullen mouth, dull hazel eyes, thick, shapeless nose. He passed the city sleuth and me without attention, and I noticed his ears. They weren't the battered ears of a pug, and they weren't conspicuously deformed, but their rims curved in and out in a peculiar crinkled fashion.

At the corner he went out of sight, turning down Boylston street toward Washington.

"There's a lad that will make a name for his-self if he ain't nabbed or rocked off* too soon," Lew predicted. "Better put him on your list. The Whosis Kid. You'll be looking for him some one of these days."

"What's his racket?"

"Stick-up, gunman. He's got the makings of a good one. He can shoot, and he's plain crazy. He ain't hampered by nothing like imagination or fear of consequences. I wish he was. It's these careful, sensible birds that are easiest caught. I'd swear the Kid was in on a coupla jobs that were turned in Brookline last month. But I can't fit

_____

* arrested

him to 'em. I'm going to clamp him some day, though—and that's a promise."

Lew never kept his promise. A prowler killed him in an Audubon Road residence a month later.

A week or two after this conversation I left the Boston branch of the Continental Detective Agency to try army life. When the war was over I returned to the agency payroll in Chicago, stayed there for a couple of years, and got transferred to San Francisco.

So, all in all, it was nearly eight years later that I found myself sitting behind the Whosis Kid's crinkled ears at the Dreamland Rink.

Friday night is fight night at the Steiner Street house. This particular one was my first idle evening in several weeks. I had gone up to the rink, fitted myself to a hard wooden chair not too far from the ring, and settled down to watch the boys throw gloves at one another. The show was about a quarter done when I picked out this pair of odd and somehow familiar ears two rows ahead of me.

I didn't place them right away. I couldn't see their owner's face. He was watching Kid Cipriani and Bunny Keogh assault each other. I missed most of that fight. But during the brief wait before the next pair of boys went on, the Whosis Kid turned his head to say something to the man beside him. I saw his face and knew him.

He hadn't changed much, and he hadn't improved any. His eyes were duller and his mouth more wickedly sullen than I had remembered them. His face was as pasty as ever, if not so pimply.

He was directly between me and the ring. Now that I knew him, I didn't have to pass up the rest of the card. I could watch the boys over his head without being afraid he would get out on me.

So far as I knew, the Whosis Kid wasn't wanted anywhere—not by the Continental, anyway—and if he had been a pickpocket, or a con man, or a member of any of the criminal trades in which we are only occasionally interested, I would have let him alone. But stick-ups are always in demand. The Continental's most important clients are insurance companies of one sort or another, and robbery policies make up a good percentage of the insurance business these days.

When the Whosis Kid left in the middle of the main event—along with nearly half of the spectators, not caring what happened to either of the muscle-bound heavies who were putting on a room-mate act in the ring—I went with him.

He was alone. It was the simplest sort of shadowing. The streets were filled with departing fight fans. The Kid walked down to Fillmore street, took on a stack of wheats, bacon and coffee at a lunch room, and caught a No. 22 car.

He—and likewise I—transferred to a No. 5 car at McAllister street, dropped off at Polk, walked north one block, turned back west for a block and a fraction, and went up the front stairs of a dingy light-housekeeping room establishment that occupied the second and third floors over a repair shop on the south side of Golden Gate avenue, between Van Ness and Franklin.

That put a wrinkle in my forehead. If he had left the street car at either Van Ness or Franklin, he would have saved himself a block of walking. He had ridden down to Polk and walked back. For the exercise, maybe.

I loafed across the street for a short while, to see what—if anything—happened to the front windows. None that had been dark before the Kid went in lighted up now. Apparently he didn't have a front room—unless he was a very cautious young man. I knew he hadn't tumbled to my shadowing. There wasn't a chance of that. Conditions had been too favorable to me.

The front of the building giving me no information, I strolled down Van Ness avenue to look at the rear. The building ran through to Redwood street, a narrow back street that split the block in half. Four back windows were lighted, but they told me nothing. There was a back door. It seemed to belong to the repair shop. I doubted that the occupants of the upstairs rooms could use it.

On my way home to my bed and alarm clock,

I dropped in at the office, to leave a note for the Old Man:

Tailing the Whosis Kid, stick-up, 25–27, 135, 5 foot 11 inches, sallow, br. hair, hzl. eyes, thick nose, crooked ears. Origin Boston. Anything on him? Will be vicinity Golden Gate and Van Ness.

CHAPTER II

Eight o'clock the next morning found me a block below the house in which the Kid had gone, waiting for him to appear. A steady, soaking rain was falling, but I didn't mind that. I was closed up inside a black coupé, a type of car whose tamely respectable appearance makes it the ideal one for city work. This part of Golden Gate avenue is lined with automobile repair shops, second-hand automobile dealers, and the like. There are always dozens of cars standing idle to the block. Although I stayed there all day, I didn't have to worry over my being too noticeable.

That was just as well. For nine solid, end-to-end hours I sat there and listened to the rain on the roof, and waited for the Whosis Kid, with not a glimpse of him, and nothing to eat except Fatimas. I wasn't any too sure he hadn't slipped me. I didn't know that he lived in this place I was watching. He could have gone to his home after I had gone to mine. However, in this detective business pessimistic guesses of that sort are always bothering you, if you let them. I stayed parked, with my eye on the dingy door into which my meat had gone the night before.

At a little after five that evening, Tommy Howd, our pug-nosed office boy, found me and gave me a memorandum from the Old Man:

Whosis Kid known to Boston branch as robbery-suspect, but have nothing definite on him. Real name believed to be Arthur Cory or Carey. May have been implicated in Tunnicliffe jewelry robbery in Boston last month.

Employee killed, $60,000 unset stones taken. No description of two bandits. Boston branch thinks this angle worth running out. They authorize surveillance.

After I had read this memorandum, I gave it back to the boy,—there's no wisdom in carrying around a pocketful of stuff relating to your job,—and asked him:

"Will you call up the Old Man and ask him to send somebody up to relieve me while I get a bite of food? I haven't chewed since breakfast."

"Swell chance!" Tommy said. "Everybody's busy. Hasn't been an op in all day. I don't see why you fellas don't carry a hunk or two of chocolate in your pockets to—"

"You've been reading about Arctic explorers," I accused him. "If a man's starving he'll eat anything, but when he's just ordinarily hungry he doesn't want to clutter up his stomach with a lot of candy. Scout around and see if you can pick me up a couple of sandwiches and a bottle of milk."

He scowled at me, and then his fourteen-year-old face grew cunning.

"I tell you what," he suggested. "You tell me what this fella looks like, and which building he's in, and I'll watch while you go get a decent meal. Huh? Steak, and French fried potatoes, and pie, and coffee."

Tommy has dreams of being left on the job in some such circumstance, of having everything break for him while he's there, and of rounding up regiments of desperadoes all by himself. I don't think he'd muff a good chance at that, and I'd be willing to give him a whack at it. But the Old Man would scalp me if he knew I turned a child loose among a lot of thugs.

So I shook my head.

"This guy wears four guns and carries an ax, Tommy. He'd eat you up."

"Aw, applesauce! You ops are all the time trying to make out nobody else could do your work. These crooks can't be such tough mugs—or they wouldn't let you catch 'em!"

There was some truth in that, so I put Tommy out of the coupé into the rain.

"One tongue sandwich, one ham, one bottle of milk. And make it sudden."

But I wasn't there when he came back with the food. He had barely gone out of sight when the Whosis Kid, his overcoat collar turned up against the rain that was driving down in close-packed earnest just now, came out of the rooming-house doorway.

He turned south on Van Ness.

When the coupé got me to the corner he was not in sight. He couldn't have reached McAllister street. Unless he had gone into a building, Redwood street—the narrow one that split the block—was my best bet. I drove up Golden Gate avenue another block, turned south, and reached the corner of Franklin and Redwood just in time to see my man ducking into the back door of an apartment building that fronted on McAllister street.

I drove on slowly, thinking.

The building in which the Kid had spent the night and this building into which he had just gone had their rears on the same back street, on opposite sides, a little more than half a block apart. If the Kid's room was in the rear of his building, and he had a pair of strong glasses, he could keep a pretty sharp eye on all the windows—and probably much of the interiors—of the rooms on that side of the McAllister street building.

Last night he had ridden a block out of his way. Having seen him sneak into the back door just now, my guess was that he had not wished to leave the street car where he could be seen from this building. Either of his more convenient points of departure from the car would have been in sight of this building. This would add up to the fact that the Kid was watching someone in this building, and did not want them to be watching him.

He had now gone calling through the back door. That wasn't difficult to explain. The front door was locked, but the back door—as in most

large buildings—probably was open all day. Unless the Kid ran into a janitor or someone of the sort, he could get in with no trouble. The Kid's call was furtive, whether his host was at home or not.

I didn't know what it was all about, but that didn't bother me especially. My immediate problem was to get to the best place from which to pick up the Kid when he came out.

If he left by the back door, the next block of Redwood street—between Franklin and Gough—was the place for me and my coupé. But he hadn't promised me he would leave that way. It was more likely that he would use the front door. He would attract less attention walking boldly out the front of the building than sneaking out the back. My best bet was the corner of McAllister and Van Ness. From there I could watch the front door as well as one end of Redwood street.

I slid the coupé down to that corner and waited.

Half an hour passed. Three quarters.

The Whosis Kid came down the front steps and walked toward me, buttoning his overcoat and turning up the collar as he walked, his head bent against the slant of the rain.

A curtained black Cadillac touring car came from behind me, a car I thought had been parked down near the City Hall when I took my plant here.

It curved around my coupé, slid with chainless recklessness in to the curb, skidded out again, picking up speed somehow on the wet paving.

A curtain whipped loose in the rain.

Out of the opening came pale fire-streaks. The bitter voice of a small-caliber pistol. Seven times.

The Whosis Kid's wet hat floated off his head—a slow balloon-like rising.

There was nothing slow about the Kid's moving.

Plunging, in a twisting swirl of coat-skirts, he flung into a shop vestibule.

The Cadillac reached the next corner, made a dizzy sliding turn, and was gone up Franklin street. I pointed the coupé at it.

Passing the vestibule into which the Kid had plunged, I got a one-eyed view of him, on his knees, still trying to get a dark gun untangled from his overcoat. Excited faces were in the doorway behind him. There was no excitement in the street. People are too accustomed to automobile noises nowadays to pay much attention to the racket of anything less than a six-inch gun.

By the time I reached Franklin street, the Cadillac had gained another block on me. It was spinning to the left, up Eddy street.

I paralleled it on Turk street, and saw it again when I reached the two open blocks of Jefferson Square. Its speed was decreasing. Five or six blocks further, and it crossed ahead of me—on Steiner street—close enough for me to read the license plate. Its pace was moderate now. Confident that they had made a clean getaway, its occupants didn't want to get in trouble through speeding. I slid into their wake, three blocks behind.

Not having been in sight during the early blocks of the flight, I wasn't afraid that they would suspect my interest in them now.

Out on Haight street near the park panhandle, the Cadillac stopped to discharge a passenger. A small man—short and slender—with cream-white face around dark eyes and a tiny black mustache. There was something foreign in the cut of his dark coat and the shape of his gray hat. He carried a walking-stick.

The Cadillac went on out Haight street without giving me a look at the other occupants. Tossing a mental nickel, I stuck to the man afoot. The chances always are against you being able to trace a suspicious car by its license number, but there is a slim chance.

My man went into a drug store on the corner and used the telephone. I don't know what else he did in there, if anything. Presently a taxicab arrived. He got in and was driven to the Marquis Hotel. A clerk gave him the key to room 761. I dropped him when he stepped into an elevator.

CHAPTER III

At the Marquis I am among friends.

I found Duran, the house copper, on the mezzanine floor, and asked him:

"Who is 761?"

Duran is a white-haired old-timer who looks, talks, and acts like the president of an exceptionally strong bank. He used to be captain of detectives in one of the larger Middle Western cities. Once he tried too hard to get a confession out of a safe-ripper, and killed him. The newspapers didn't like Duran. They used that accident to howl him out of his job.

"761?" he repeated in his grandfatherly manner. "That is Mr. Maurois, I believe. Are you especially interested in him?"

"I have hopes," I admitted. "What do you know about him?"

"Not a great deal. He has been here perhaps two weeks. We shall go down and see what we can learn."

We went to the desk, the switchboard, the captain of bell-hops, and upstairs to question a couple of chambermaids. The occupant of 761 had arrived two weeks ago, had registered as *Edouard Maurois, Dijon, France*, had frequent telephone calls, no mail, no visitors, kept irregular hours and tipped freely. Whatever business he was in or had was not known to the hotel people.

"What is the occasion of your interest in him, if I may ask?" Duran inquired after we had accumulated these facts. He talks like that.

"I don't exactly know yet," I replied truthfully. "He just connected with a bird who is wrong, but this Maurois may be all right himself. I'll give you a rap the minute I get anything solid on him."

I couldn't afford to tell Duran I had seen his guest snapping caps at a gunman under the eves of the City Hall in daylight. The Marquis Hotel goes in for respectability. They would have shoved the Frenchman out in the streets. It wouldn't help me to have him scared up.

"Please do," Duran said. "You owe us something for our help, you know, so please don't withhold any information that might save us unpleasant notoriety."

"I won't," I promised. "Now will you do me another favor? I haven't had my teeth in anything except my mouth since seven-thirty this morning. Will you keep an eye on the elevators, and let me know if Maurois goes out? I'll be in the grill, near the door."

"Certainly."

On my way to the grillroom I stopped at the telephone booths and called up the office. I gave the night office man the Cadillac's license number.

"Look it up on the list and see whom it belongs to."

The answer was: "H. J. Paterson, San Pablo, issued for a Buick roadster."

That about wound up that angle. We could look up Paterson, but it was safe betting it wouldn't get us anything. License plates, once they get started in crooked ways, are about as easy to trace as Liberty Bonds.

All day I had been building up hunger. I took it into the grillroom and turned it loose. Between bites I turned the day's events over in my mind. I didn't think hard enough to spoil my appetite. There wasn't that much to think about.

The Whosis Kid lived in a joint from which some of the McAllister street apartments could be watched. He visited the apartment building furtively. Leaving, he was shot at, from a car that must have been waiting somewhere in the vicinity. Had the Frenchman's companion in the Cadillac—or his companions, if more than one—been the occupant of the apartment the Kid had visited? Had they expected him to visit it? Had they tricked him into visiting it, planning to shoot him down as he was leaving? Or were they watching the front while the Kid watched the rear? If so, had either known that the other was watching? And who lived there?

I couldn't answer any of these riddles. All I knew was that the Frenchman and his companions didn't seem to like the Whosis Kid.

Even the sort of meal I put away doesn't take forever to eat. When I finished it, I went out to the lobby again.

Passing the switchboard, one of the girls—the one whose red hair looks as if it had been poured into its waves and hardened—gave me a nod.

I stopped to see what she wanted.

"Your friend just had a call," she told me.

"You get it?"

"Yes. A man is waiting for him at Kearny and Broadway. Told him to hurry."

"How long ago?"

"None. They're just through talking."

"Any names?"

"No."

"Thanks."

I went on to where Duran was stalling with an eye on the elevators.

"Shown yet?" I asked.

"No."

"Good. The redhead on the switchboard just told me he had a phone call to meet a man at Kearny and Broadway. I think I'll beat him to it."

Around the corner from the hotel, I climbed into my coupé and drove down to the Frenchman's corner.

The Cadillac he had used that afternoon was already there, with a new license plate. I passed it and took a look at its one occupant—a thickset man of forty-something with a cap pulled low over his eyes. All I could see of his features was a wide mouth slanting over a heavy chin.

I put the coupé in a vacant space down the street a way. I didn't have to wait long for the Frenchman. He came around the corner afoot and got into the Cadillac. The man with the big chin drove. They went slowly up Broadway. I followed.

CHAPTER IV

We didn't go far, and when we came to rest again, the Cadillac was placed conveniently for its occupants to watch the Venetian Café, one of the gaudiest of the Italian restaurants that fill this part of town.

Two hours went by.

I had an idea that the Whosis Kid was eating at the Venetian. When he left, the fireworks would break out, continuing the celebration from where it had broken off that afternoon on McAllister street. I hoped the Kid's gun wouldn't get caught in his coat this time. But don't think I meant to give him a helping hand in his two-against-one fight.

This party had the shape of a war between gunmen. It would be a private one as far as I was concerned. My hope was that by hovering on the fringes until somebody won, I could pick up a little profit for the Continental, in the form of a wanted crook or two among the survivors.

My guess at the Frenchman's quarry was wrong. It wasn't the Whosis Kid. It was a man and a woman. I didn't see their faces. The light was behind them. They didn't waste any time between the Venetian's door and their taxicab.

The man was big—tall, wide, and thick. The woman looked small at his side. I couldn't go by that. Anything weighing less than a ton would have seemed tiny beside him.

As the taxicab pulled away from the café, the Cadillac went after it. I ran in the Cadillac's wake.

It was a short chase.

The taxicab turned into a dark block on the edge of Chinatown. The Cadillac jumped to its side, bearing it over to the curb.

A noise of brakes, shouting voices, broken glass. A woman's scream. Figures moving in the scant space between touring car and taxicab. Both cars rocking. Grunts. Thuds. Oaths.

A man's voice: "Hey! You can't do that! Nix! Nix!"

It was a stupid voice.

I had slowed down until the coupé was barely moving toward this tussle ahead. Peering through the rain and darkness, I tried to pick out a detail or so as I approached, but I could see little.

I was within twenty feet when the curbward door of the taxicab banged open. A woman bounced out. She landed on her knees on the sidewalk, jumped to her feet, and darted up the street.

Putting the coupé closer to the curb, I let the door swing open. My side windows were spattered with rain. I wanted to get a look at the woman when she passed. If she should take the open door for an invitation, I didn't mind talking to her.

She accepted the invitation, hurrying as directly to the car as if she had expected me to be waiting for her. Her face was a small oval above a fur collar.

"Help me!" she gasped. "Take me from here—quickly."

There was a suggestion of foreignness too slight to be called an accent.

"How about—?"

I shut my mouth. The thing she was jabbing me in the body with was a snub-nosed automatic.

"Sure! Get in," I urged her.

She bent her head to enter. I looped an arm over her neck, throwing her down across my lap. She squirmed and twisted—a small-boned, hard-fleshed body with strength in it.

I wrenched the gun out of her hand and pushed her back on the seat beside me.

Her fingers dug into my arms.

"Quick! Quick! Ah, please, quickly! Take me—"

"What about your friend?" I asked.

"Not him! He is of the others! Please, quickly!"

A man filled the open coupé door—the big-chinned man who had driven the Cadillac.

His hand seized the fur at the woman's throat.

She tried to scream—made the gurgling sound of a man with a slit throat. I smacked his chin with the gun I had taken from her.

He tried to fall into the coupé. I pushed him out.

Before his head had hit the sidewalk, I had the door closed, and was twisting the coupé around in the street.

We rode away. Two shots sounded just as we

turned the first corner. I don't know whether they were fired at us or not. I turned other corners. The Cadillac did not appear again.

So far, so good. I had started with the Whosis Kid, dropped him to take Maurois, and now let him go to see who this woman was. I didn't know what this confusion was all about, but I seemed to be learning *who* it was all about.

"Where to?" I asked presently.

"To home," she said, and gave me an address.

I pointed the coupé at it with no reluctance at all. It was the McAllister street apartments the Whosis Kid had visited earlier in the evening.

We didn't waste any time getting there. My companion might know it or might not, but I knew that all the other players in this game knew that address. I wanted to get there before the Frenchman and Big Chin.

Neither of us said anything during the ride. She crouched close to me, shivering. I was looking ahead, planning how I was to land an invitation into her apartment. I was sorry I hadn't held on to her gun. I had let it fall when I pushed Big Chin out of the car. It would have been an excuse for a later call if she didn't invite me in.

I needn't have worried. She didn't invite me. She insisted that I go in with her. She was scared stiff.

"You will not leave me?" she pleaded as we drove up McAllister street. "I am in complete terror. You cannot go from me! If you will not come in, I will stay with you."

I was willing enough to go in, but I didn't want to leave the coupé where it would advertise me.

"We'll ride around the corner and park the car," I told her, "and then I'll go in with you."

I drove around the block, with an eye in each direction for the Cadillac. Neither eye found it. I left the coupé on Franklin street and we returned to the McAllister street building.

She had me almost running through the rain that had lightened now to a drizzle.

The hand with which she tried to fit a key to the front door was a shaky, inaccurate hand.

I took the key and opened the door. We rode to the third floor in an automatic elevator, seeing no one. I unlocked the door to which she led me, near the rear of the building.

Holding my arm, with one hand, she reached inside and snapped on the lights in the passageway.

I didn't know what she was waiting for, until she cried:

"Frana! Frana! Ah, Frana!"

The muffled yapping of a small dog replied. The dog did not appear.

She grabbed me with both arms, trying to crawl up my damp coat-front.

"They are here!" she cried in the thin dry voice of utter terror. "They are here!"

CHAPTER V

"Is anybody supposed to be here?" I asked, putting her around to one side, where she wouldn't be between me and the two doors across the passageway.

"No! Just my little dog Frana, but—"

I slid my gun half out of my pocket and back again, to make sure it wouldn't catch if I needed it, and used my other hand to get rid of the woman's arms.

"You stay here. I'll see if you've got company."

Moving to the nearest door, I heard a seven-year-old voice—Lew Maher's—saying: *"He can shoot and he's plain crazy. He ain't hampered by nothing like imagination or fear of consequences."*

With my left hand I turned the first door's knob. With my left foot I kicked it open.

Nothing happened.

I put a hand around the frame, found the button, switched on the lights.

A sitting-room, all orderly.

Through an open door on the far side of the room came the muffled yapping of Frana. It was louder now and more excited. I moved to the doorway. What I could see of the next room, in the light from this, seemed peaceful and unoccupied enough. I went into it and switched on the lights.

The dog's voice came through a closed door. I crossed to it, pulled it open. A dark fluffy dog jumped snapping at my leg. I grabbed it where its fur was thickest and lifted it squirming and snarling. The light hit it. It was purple—purple as a grape! Dyed purple!

Carrying this yapping, yelping artificial hound a little away from my body with my left hand, I moved on to the next room—a bedroom. It was vacant. Its closet hid nobody. I found the kitchen and bathroom. Empty. No one was in the apartment. The purple pup had been imprisoned by the Whosis Kid earlier in the day.

Passing through the second room on my way back to the woman with her dog and my report, I saw a slitted envelope lying face-down on a table. I turned it over. The stationery of a fashionable store, it was addressed to Mrs. Inés Almad, here.

The party seemed to be getting international. Maurois was French; the Whosis Kid was Boston American; the dog had a Bohemian name (at least I remember nabbing a Czech forger a few months before whose first name was Frana); and Inés, I imagine, was either Spanish or Portuguese. I didn't know what Almad was, but she was undoubtedly foreign, and not, I thought, French.

I returned to her. She hadn't moved an inch.

"Everything seems to be all right," I told her. "The dog got himself caught in a closet."

"There is no one here?"

"No one."

She took the dog in both hands, kissing its fluffy stained head, crooning affectionate words to it in a language that made no sense to me.

"Do your friends—the people you had your row with tonight—know where you live?" I asked.

I knew they did. I wanted to see what she knew.

She dropped the dog as if she had forgotten it, and her brows puckered.

"I do not know that," she said slowly. "Yet it may be. If they do—"

She shuddered, spun on her heel, and pushed the hall door violently shut.

"They may have been here this afternoon," she went on. "Frana has made himself prisoner in closets before, but I fear everything. I am coward-like. But there is none here now?"

"No one," I assured her again.

We went into the sitting-room. I got my first good look at her when she shed her hat and dark cape.

She was a trifle under medium height, a dark-skinned woman of thirty in a vivid orange gown. She was dark as an Indian, with bare brown shoulders round and sloping, tiny feet and hands, her fingers heavy with rings. Her nose was thin and curved, her mouth full-lipped and red, her eyes—long and thickly lashed—were of an extraordinary narrowness. They were dark eyes, but nothing of their color could be seen through the thin slits that separated the lids. Two dark gleams through veiling lashes. Her black hair was disarranged just now in fluffy silk puffs. A rope of pearls hung down on her dark chest. Earrings of black iron—in a peculiar club-like design—swung beside her cheeks.

Altogether, she was an odd trick. But I wouldn't want to be quoted as saying that she wasn't beautiful—in a wild way.

She was shaking and shivering as she got rid of her hat and cloak. White teeth held her lower lip as she crossed the room to turn on an electric heater. I took advantage of this opportunity to shift my gun from my overcoat pocket to my pants. Then I took off the coat.

Leaving the room for a second, she returned with a brown-filled quart bottle and two tumblers on a bronze tray, which she put on a little table near the heater.

The first tumbler she filled to within half an inch of its rim. I stopped her when she had the other nearly half full.

"That'll do fine for me," I said.

It was brandy, and not at all hard to get down. She shot her tumblerful into her throat as if she needed it, shook her bare shoulders, and sighed in a satisfied way.

"You will think, certainly, I am lunatic," she smiled at me. "Flinging myself on you, a stranger in the street, demanding of you time and troubles."

"No," I lied seriously. "I think you're pretty level-headed for a woman who, no doubt, isn't used to this sort of stuff."

She was pulling a little upholstered bench closer to the electric heater, within reach of the table that held the brandy. She sat down now, with an inviting nod at the bench's empty half.

The purple dog jumped into her lap. She pushed it out. It started to return. She kicked it sharply in the side with the pointed toe of her slipper. It yelped and crawled under a chair across the room.

I avoided the window by going the long way around the room. The window was curtained, but not thickly enough to hide all of the room from the Whosis Kid—if he happened to be sitting at his window just now with a pair of field-glasses to his eyes.

"But I am not level-headed, really," the woman was saying as I dropped beside her. "I am coward-like, terribly. And even becoming accustomed—It is my husband, or he who was my husband. I should tell you. Your gallantry deserves the explanation, and I do not wish you should think a thing that is not so."

I tried to look trusting and credulous. I expected to disbelieve everything she said.

"He is most crazily jealous," she went on in her low-pitched, soft voice, with a peculiar way of saying words that just missed being marked enough to be called a foreign accent. "He is an old man, and incredibly wicked. These men he has sent to me! A woman there was once—tonight's men are not first. I don't know what—what they mean. To kill me, perhaps—to maim, to disfigure—I do not know."

"And the man in the taxi with you was one of them?" I asked. "I was driving down the street behind you when you were attacked, and I could see there was a man with you. He was one of them?"

"Yes! I did not know it, but it must have been

that he was. He does not defend me. A pretense, that is all."

"Ever try sicking the cops on this hubby of yours?"

"It is what?"

"Ever notify the police?"

"Yes, but"—she shrugged her brown shoulders—"I would as well have kept quiet, or better. In Buffalo it was, and they—they bound my husband to keep the peace, I think you call it. A thousand dollars! Poof! What is that to him in his jealousy? And I—I cannot stand the things the newspapers say—the jesting of them. I must leave Buffalo. Yes, once I do try sicking the cops on him. But not more."

"Buffalo?" I explored a little. "I lived there for a while—on Crescent avenue."

"Oh, yes. That is out by the Delaware Park."

That was right enough. But her knowing something about Buffalo didn't prove anything about the rest of her story.

CHAPTER VI

She poured more brandy. By speaking quick I held my drink down to a size suitable for a man who has work to do. Hers was as large as before. We drank, and she offered me cigarettes in a lacquered box—slender cigarettes, hand-rolled in black paper.

I didn't stay with mine long. It tasted, smelt and scorched like gunpowder.

"You don't like my cigarettes?"

"I'm an old-fashioned man," I apologized, rubbing its fire out in a bronze dish, fishing in my pocket for my own deck. "Tobacco's as far as I've got. What's in these fireworks?"

She laughed. She had a pleasant laugh, with a sort of coo in it.

"I am so very sorry. So many people do not like them. I have a Hindu incense mixed with the tobacco."

I didn't say anything to that. It was what you would expect of a woman who would dye her dog purple.

The dog moved under its chair just then, scratching the floor with its nails.

The brown woman was in my arms, in my lap, her arms wrapped around my neck. Close-up, opened by terror, her eyes weren't dark at all. They were gray-green. The blackness was in the shadow from her heavy lashes.

"It's only the dog," I assured her, sliding her back on her own part of the bench. "It's only the dog wriggling around under the chair."

"Ah!" she blew her breath out with enormous relief.

Then we had to have another shot of brandy.

"You see, I am most awfully the coward," she said when the third dose of liquor was in her. "But, ah, I have had so much trouble. It is a wonder that I am not insane."

I could have told her she wasn't far enough from it to do much bragging, but I nodded with what was meant for sympathy.

She lit another cigarette to replace the one she had dropped in her excitement. Her eyes became normal black slits again.

"I do not think it is nice"—there was a suggestion of a dimple in her brown cheek when she smiled like that—"that I throw myself into the arms of a man even whose name I do not know, or anything of him."

"That's easy to fix. My name is Young," I lied; "and I can let you have a case of Scotch at a price that will astonish you. I think maybe I could stand it if you call me Jerry. Most of the ladies I let sit in my lap do."

"Jerry Young," she repeated, as if to herself. "That is a nice name. And you are the bootlegger?"

"Not *the*," I corrected her; "just *a*. This is San Francisco."

The going got tough after that.

Everything else about this brown woman was all wrong, but her fright was real. She was scared stiff. And she didn't intend being left alone this night. She meant to keep me there—to massage any more chins that stuck themselves at her. Her idea—she being that sort—was that I would be most surely held with affection. So she must turn herself loose on me. She wasn't hampered by any pruderies or puritanisms at all.

I also have an idea. Mine is that when the last gong rings I'm going to be leading this baby and some of her playmates to the city prison. That is an excellent reason—among a dozen others I could think of—why I shouldn't get mushy with her.

I was willing enough to camp there with her until something happened. That apartment looked like the scene of the next action. But I had to cover up my own game. I couldn't let her know she was only a minor figure in it. I had to pretend there was nothing behind my willingness to stay but a desire to protect her. Another man might have got by with a chivalrous, knight-errant, protector-of-womanhood-without-personal-interest attitude. But I don't look, and can't easily act, like that kind of person. I had to hold her off without letting her guess that my interest wasn't personal. It was no cinch. She was too damned direct, and she had too much brandy in her.

I didn't kid myself that my beauty and personality were responsible for any of her warmth. I was a thick-armed male with big fists. She was in a jam. She spelled my name P-r-o-t-e-c-t-i-o-n. I was something to be put between her and trouble.

Another complication: I am neither young enough nor old enough to get feverish over every woman who doesn't make me think being blind isn't so bad. I'm at that middle point around forty where a man puts other feminine qualities—amiability, for one—above beauty on his list. This brown woman annoyed me. She was too sure of herself. Her work was rough. She was trying to handle me as if I were a farmer boy. But in spite of all this, I'm constructed mostly of human ingredients. This woman got more than a stand-off when faces and bodies were dealt. I didn't like her. I hoped to throw her in the can before I was through. But I'd be a liar if I didn't admit that she had me stirred up inside—between her cuddling against me, giving me the come-on, and the brandy I had drunk.

The going was tough—no fooling.

A couple of times I was tempted to bolt. Once I looked at my watch—2:06. She put a ring-heavy brown hand on the timepiece and pushed it down to my pocket.

"Please, Jerry!" the earnestness in her voice was real. "You cannot go. You cannot leave me here. I will not have it so. I will go also, through the streets following. You cannot leave me to be murdered here!"

I settled down again.

A few minutes later a bell rang sharply.

She went to pieces immediately. She piled over on me, strangling me with her bare arms. I pried them loose enough to let me talk.

"What bell is that?"

"The street door. Do not heed it."

I patted her shoulder.

"Be a good girl and answer it. Let's see who it is."

Her arms tightened.

"No! No! No! They have come!"

The bell rang again.

"Answer it," I insisted.

Her face was flat against my coat, her nose digging into my chest.

"No! No!"

"All right," I said. "I'll answer it myself."

I untangled myself from her, got up and went into the passageway. She followed me. I tried again to persuade her to do the talking. She would not, although she didn't object to my talking. I would have liked it better if whoever was downstairs didn't learn that the woman wasn't alone. But she was too stubborn in her refusal for me to do anything with her.

"Well?" I said into the speaking-tube.

"Who the hell are you?" a harsh, deep-chested voice asked.

"What do you want?"

"I want to talk to Inés."

"Speak your piece to me," I suggested, "and I'll tell her about it."

The woman, holding one of my arms, had an ear close to the tube.

"Billie, it is," she whispered. "Tell him that he goes away."

"You're to go away," I passed the message on.

"Yeah?" the voice grew harsher and deeper. "Will you open the door, or will I bust it in?"

There wasn't a bit of playfulness in the question. Without consulting the woman, I put a finger on the button that unlocks the street door.

"Welcome," I said into the tube.

"He's coming up," I explained to the woman. "Shall I stand behind the door and tap him on the skull when he comes in? Or do you want to talk to him first?"

"Do not strike him!" she exclaimed. "It is Billie."

That suited me. I hadn't intended putting the slug to him—not until I knew who and what he was, anyway. I had wanted to see what she would say.

CHAPTER VII

Billie wasn't long getting up to us. I opened the door when he rang, the woman standing beside me. He didn't wait for an invitation. He was through the doorway before I had the door half opened. He glared at me. There was plenty of him!

A big, red-faced, red-haired bale of a man—big in any direction you measured him—and none of him was fat. The skin was off his nose, one cheek was clawed, the other swollen. His hatless head was a tangled mass of red hair. One pocket had been ripped out of his coat, and a button dangled on the end of a six-inch ribbon of torn cloth.

This was the big heaver who had been in the taxicab with the woman.

"Who's this mutt?" he demanded, moving his big paws toward me.

I knew the woman was a goof. It wouldn't have surprised me if she had tried to feed me to the battered giant. But she didn't. She put a hand on one of his and soothed him.

"Do not be nasty, Billie. He is a friend. Without him I would not this night have escaped."

He scowled. Then his face straightened out and he caught her hand in both of his.

"So you got away it's all right," he said huskily. "I'd a done better if we'd been outside. There wasn't no room in that taxi for me to turn around. And one of them guys crowned me."

That was funny. This big clown was apologizing for getting mangled up protecting a woman who had scooted, leaving him to get out as well as he could.

The woman led him into the sitting-room, I tagging along behind. They sat on the bench. I picked out a chair that wasn't in line with the window the Whosis Kid ought to be watching.

"What did happen, Billie?" She touched his grooved cheek and skinned nose with her fingertips. "You are hurt."

He grinned with a sort of shamefaced delight. I saw that what I had taken for a swelling in one cheek was only a big hunk of chewing tobacco.

"I don't know all that happened," he said. "One of 'em crowned me, and I didn't wake up till a coupla hours afterwards. The taxi driver didn't give me no help in the fight, but he was a right guy and knowed where his money would come from. He didn't holler or nothing. He took me around to a doc that wouldn't squawk, and the doc straightened me out, and then I come up here."

"Did you see each one of those men?" she asked.

"Sure! I seen 'em, and felt 'em, and maybe tasted 'em."

"They were how many?"

"Just two of 'em. A little fella with a trick tickler,* and a husky with a big chin on him."

"There was no other? There was not a younger man, tall and thin?"

That could be the Whosis Kid. She thought he and the Frenchman were working together?

Billie shook his shaggy, banged-up head.

"Nope. They was only two of 'em."

She frowned and chewed her lip.

_____

* a beard

Billie looked sidewise at me—a look that said "Beat it."

The woman caught the glance. She twisted around on the bench to put a hand on his head.

"Poor Billie," she cooed; "his head most cruelly hurt saving me, and now, when he should be at his home giving it rest, I keep him here talking. You go, Billie, and when it is morning and your poor head is better, you will telephone to me?"

His red face got dark. He glowered at me.

Laughing, she slapped him lightly on the cheek that bulged around his cud of tobacco.

"Do not become jealous of Jerry. Jerry is enamored of one yellow and white lady somewhere, and to her he is most faithful. Not even the smallest liking has he for dark women." She smiled a challenge at me. "Is it not so, Jerry?"

"No," I denied. "And, besides, all women are dark."

Billie shifted his chew to the scratched cheek and bunched his shoulders.

"What the hell kind of a crack is that to be making?" he rumbled.

"That means nothing it should not, Billie," she laughed at him. "It is only an epigram."

"Yeah?" Billie was sour and truculent. I was beginning to think he didn't like me. "Well, tell your little fat friend to keep his smart wheezes to himself. I don't like 'em."

That was plain enough. Billie wanted an argument. The woman, who held him securely enough to have steered him off, simply laughed again. There was no profit in trying to find the reason behind any of her actions. She was a nut. Maybe she thought that since we weren't sociable enough for her to keep both on hand, she'd let us tangle, and hold on to the one who rubbed the other out of the picture.

Anyway, a row was coming. Ordinarily I am inclined to peace. The day is past when I'll fight for the fun of it. But I've been in too many rumpuses to mind them much. Usually nothing very bad happens to you, even if you lose. I wasn't going to back down just because this big stiff was meatier than I. I've always been lucky against the large sizes. He had been banged up earlier in the evening. That would cut down his steam some. I wanted to hang around this apartment a little longer, if it could be managed. If Billie wanted to tussle—and it looked as if he did—he could.

It was easy to meet him half-way: anything I said would be used against me.

I grinned at his red face, and suggested to the woman, solemnly:

"I think if you'd dip him in blueing he'd come out the same color as the other pup."

As silly as that was, it served. Billie reared up on his feet and curled his paws into fists.

"Me and you'll take a walk," he decided; "out where there's space enough."

I got up, pushed my chair back with a foot, and quoted "Red" Burns* to him: "If you're close enough, there's room enough."

He wasn't a man you had to talk to much. We went around and around.

It was fists at first. He started it by throwing his right at my head. I went in under it and gave him all I had in a right and left to the belly. He swallowed his chew of tobacco. But he didn't bend. Few big men are as strong as they look. Billie was.

He didn't know anything at all. His idea of a fight was to stand up and throw fists at your head—right, left, right, left. His fists were as large as wastebaskets. They wheezed through the air. But always at the head—the easiest part to get out of the way.

There was room enough for me to go in and out. I did that. I hammered his belly. I thumped his heart. I mauled his belly again. Every time I hit him he grew an inch, gained a pound and picked up another horsepower. I don't fool when I hit, but nothing I did to this human mountain—not even making him swallow his hunk of tobacco—had any visible effect on him.

I've always had a reasonable amount of pride in my ability to sock. It was disappointing to have this big heaver take the best I could give him without a grunt. But I wasn't discouraged.

_____

* a California boxer; he had two fights, 1923 and 1926

He couldn't stand it forever. I settled down to make a steady job of it.

Twice he clipped me. Once on the shoulder. A big fist spun me half around. He didn't know what to do next. He came in on the wrong side. I made him miss, and got clear. The other time he caught me on the forehead. A chair kept me from going down. The smack hurt me. It must have hurt him more. A skull is tougher than a knuckle. I got out of his way when he closed in, and let him have something to remember on the back of his neck.

The woman's dusky face showed over Billie's shoulder as he straightened up. Her eyes were shiny behind their heavy lashes, and her mouth was open to let white teeth gleam through.

Billie got tired of the boxing after that, and turned the set-to into a wrestling match, with trimmings. I would rather have kept on with the fists. But I couldn't help myself. It was his party. He grabbed one of my wrists, yanked, and we thudded chest to chest.

He didn't know any more about this than he had about that. He didn't have to. He was big enough and strong enough to play with me.

I was underneath when we tumbled down on the floor and began rolling around. I did my best. It wasn't anything. Three times I put a scissors on him. His body was too big for my short legs to clamp around. He chucked me off as if he were amusing the baby. There was no use at all in trying to do things to his legs. No hold known to man could have held them. His arms were almost as strong. I quit trying.

Nothing I knew was any good against this monster. He was out of my range. I was satisfied to spend all that was left of my strength trying to keep him from crippling me—and waiting for a chance to out-smart him.

He threw me around a lot. Then my chance came.

I was flat on my back, with everything but one or two of my most centrally located intestines squeezed out. Kneeling astride me, he brought his big hands up to my throat and fastened them there.

That's how much he didn't know!

You can't choke a man that way—not if his hands are loose and he knows a hand is stronger than a finger.

I laughed in his purple face and brought my own hands up. Each of them picked one of his little fingers out of my flesh. It wasn't a dream at that. I was all in, and he wasn't. But no man's little finger is stronger than another's hand. I twisted them back. They broke together.

He yelped. I grabbed the next—the ring fingers.

One of them snapped. The other was ready to pop when he let go.

Jerking up, I butted him in the face. I twisted from between his knees. We came on our feet together.

The doorbell rang.

CHAPTER VIII

Fight interest went out of the woman's face. Fear came in. Her fingers picked at her mouth.

"Ask who's there," I told her.

"Who—who is there?"

Her voice was flat and dry.

"Mrs. Keil," came from the corridor, the words sharp with indignation. "You will have to stop this noise immediately! The tenants are complaining—and no wonder! A pretty hour to be entertaining company and carrying on so!"

"The landlady," the dark woman whispered. Aloud: "I am sorry, Mrs. Keil. There will not be more noises."

Something like a sniff came through the door, and the sound of dimming footsteps.

Inés Almad frowned reproachfully at Billie.

"You should not have done this," she blamed him.

He looked humble, and at the floor, and at me. Looking at me, the purple began to flow back into his face.

"I'm sorry," he mumbled. "I told this fella we ought to take a walk. We'll do it now, and there won't be no more noise here."

"Billie!" her voice was sharp. She was reading the law to him. "You will go out and have attention for your hurts. If you have not won these fights, because of that am I to be left here alone to be murdered?"

The big man shuffled his feet, avoided her gaze and looked utterly miserable. But he shook his head stubbornly.

"I can't do it, Inés," he said. "Me and this guy has got to finish it. He busted my fingers, and I got to bust his jaw."

"Billie!"

She stamped one small foot and looked imperiously at him. He looked as if he'd like to roll over on his back and hold his paws in the air. But he stood his ground.

"I got to," he repeated. "There ain't no way out of it."

Anger left her face. She smiled very tenderly at him.

"Dear old Billie," she murmured, and crossed the room to a secretary in a corner.

When she turned, an automatic pistol was in her hand. Its one eye looked at Billie.

"Now, *lechón*,*" she purred, "go out!"

The red man wasn't a quick thinker. It took a full minute for him to realize that this woman he loved was driving him away with a gun. The big dummy might have known that his three broken fingers had disqualified him. It took another minute for him to get his legs in motion. He went toward the door in slow bewilderment, still only half believing this thing was really happening.

The woman followed him step by step. I went ahead to open the door.

I turned the knob. The door came in, pushing me back against the opposite wall.

In the doorway stood Edouard Maurois and the man I had swatted on the chin. Each had a gun.

I looked at Inés Almad, wondering what turn her craziness would take in the face of this situation. She wasn't so crazy as I had thought.

_____

* a sucking pig

Her scream and the thud of her gun on the floor sounded together.

"Ah!" the Frenchman was saying. "The gentlemen were leaving? May we detain them?"

The man with the big chin—it was larger than ever now with the marks of my tap—was less polite.

"Back up, you birds!" he ordered, stooping for the gun the woman had dropped.

I still was holding the doorknob. I rattled it a little as I took my hand away—enough to cover up the click of the lock as I pushed the button that left it unlatched. If I needed help, and it came, I wanted as few locks as possible between me and it.

Then—Billie, the woman and I walking backward—we all paraded into the sitting-room. Maurois and his companion both wore souvenirs of the row in the taxicab. One of the Frenchman's eyes was bruised and closed—a beautiful shiner. His clothes were rumpled and dirty. He wore them jauntily in spite of that, and he still had his walking stick, crooked under the arm that didn't hold his gun.

Big Chin held us with his own gun and the woman's while Maurois ran his hand over Billie's and my clothes, to see if we were armed. He found my gun and pocketed it. Billie had no weapons.

"Can I trouble you to step back against the wall?" Maurois asked when he was through.

We stepped back as if it was no trouble at all. I found my shoulder against one of the window curtains. I pressed it against the frame, and turned far enough to drag the curtain clear of a foot or more of pane.

If the Whosis Kid was watching, he should have had a clear view of the Frenchman—the man who had shot at him earlier in the evening. I was putting it up to the Kid. The corridor door was unlocked. If the Kid could get into the building—no great trick—he had a clear path. I didn't know where he fit in, but I wanted him to join us, and I hoped he wouldn't disappoint me. If everybody got together here, maybe whatever was going on would come out where I could see it and understand it.

Meanwhile, I kept as much of myself as possible out of the window. The Kid might decide to throw lead from across the alley.

Maurois was facing Inés. Big Chin's guns were on Billie and me.

"I do not *comprends* ze *anglais* ver' good," the Frenchman was mocking the woman. "So it is when you say you meet wit' me, I t'ink you say in New Orleans. I do not know you say San Francisc'. I am ver' sorry to make ze mistake. I am mos' sorry zat I keep you wait. But now I am here. You have ze share for me?"

"I have not." She held her hands out in an empty gesture. "The Kid took those—everything from me."

"What?" Maurois dropped his taunting smile and his vaudeville accent. His one open eye flashed angrily. "How could he, unless—?"

"He suspected us, Edouard." Her mouth trembled with earnestness. Her eyes pleaded for belief. She was lying. "He had me followed. The day after I am there he comes. He takes all. I am afraid to wait for you. I fear your unbelief. You would not—"

"*C'est incroyable!*" Maurois was very excited over it. "I was on the first train south after our—our theatricals. Could the Kid have been on that train without my knowing it? *Non!* And how else could he have reached you before I? You are playing with me, *ma petite* Inés. That you did join the Kid, I do not doubt. But not in New Orleans. You did not go there. You came here to San Francisco."

"Edouard!" she protested, fingering his sleeve with one brown hand, the other holding her throat as if she were having trouble getting the words out. "You cannot think that thing! Do not those weeks in Boston say it is not possible? For one like the Kid—or like any other—am I to betray you? You know me not more than to think I am like that?"

She was an actress. She was appealing, and pathetic, and anything else you like—including dangerous.

The Frenchman took his sleeve away from her and stepped back a step. White lines ringed his mouth below his tiny mustache, and his jaw muscles bulged. His one good eye was worried. She had got to him, though not quite enough to upset him altogether. But the game was young yet.

"I do not know what to think," he said slowly. "If I have been wrong—I must find the Kid first. Then I will learn the truth."

"You don't have to look no further, brother. I'm right among you!"

The Whosis Kid stood in the passageway door. A black revolver was in each of his hands. Their hammers were up.

CHAPTER IX

It was a pretty tableau.

There is the Whosis Kid in the door—a lean lad in his twenties, all the more wicked-looking because his face is weak and slack-jawed and dull-eyed. The cocked guns in his hands are pointing at everybody or at nobody, depending on how you look at them.

There is the brown woman, her cheeks pinched in her two fists, her eyes open until their green-grayishness shows. The fright I had seen in her face before was nothing to the fright that is there now.

There is the Frenchman—whirled doorward at the Kid's first word—his gun on the Kid, his cane still under his arm, his face a tense white blot.

There is Big Chin, his body twisted half around, his face over one shoulder to look at the door, with one of his guns following his face around.

There is Billie—a big, battered statue of a man who hasn't said a word since Inés Almad started to gun him out of the apartment.

And, last, here I am—not feeling so comfortable as I would home in bed, but not actually hysterical either. I wasn't altogether dissatisfied with the shape things were taking. Something was going to happen in these rooms. But I wasn't friendly enough to any present to care especially

what happened to whom. For myself, I counted on coming through all in one piece. Few men *get* killed. Most of those who meet sudden ends *get themselves* killed. I've had twenty years of experience at dodging that. I can count on being one of the survivors of whatever blow-up there is. And I hope to take most of the other survivors for a ride.

But right now the situation belonged to the men with guns—the Whosis Kid, Maurois and Big Chin.

The Kid spoke first. He had a whining voice that came disagreeably through his thick nose.

"This don't look nothing like Chi to me, but, anyways, we're all here."

"Chicago!" Maurois exclaimed. "You did not go to Chicago!"

The Kid sneered at him.

"Did you? Did she? What would I be going there for? You think me and her run out on you, don't you? Well, we would of if she hadn't put the two X's* to me the same as she done to you, and the same as the three of us done to the boob."

"That may be," the Frenchman replied; "but you do not expect me to believe that you and Inés are not friends? Didn't I see you leaving here this afternoon?"

"You seen me, all right," the Kid agreed; "but if my rod hadn't of got snagged in my flogger† you wouldn't have seen nothing else. But I ain't got nothing against you now. I thought you and her had ditched me, just as you think me and her done you. I know different now, from what I heard while I was getting in here. She twisted the pair of us, Frenchy, just like we twisted the boob. Ain't you got it yet?"

Maurois shook his head slowly.

What put an edge to this conversation was that both men were talking over their guns.

"Listen," the Kid asked impatiently. "We was to meet up in Chi for a three-way split, wasn't we?"

---

* cheated

† an instrument used to beat the bung stave of a cask; a blackjack here

The Frenchman nodded.

"But she tells me," the Kid went on, "she'll connect with me in St. Louis, counting you out; and she ribs you up to meet her in New Orleans, ducking me. And then she gyps the pair of us by running out here to Frisco with the stuff.

"We're a couple of suckers, Frenchy, and there ain't no use of us getting hot at each other. There's enough of it for a fat two-way cut. What I say is let's forget what's done, and me and you make it fifty-fifty. Understand, I ain't begging you. I'm making a proposition. If you don't like it, to hell with you! You know me. You never seen the day I wouldn't shoot it out with you or anybody else. Take your pick!"

The Frenchman didn't say anything for a while. He was converted, but he didn't want to weaken his hand by coming in too soon. I don't know whether he believed the Kid's words or not, but he believed the Kid's guns. You can get a bullet out of a cocked revolver a lot quicker than out of a hammerless automatic. The Kid had the bulge there. And the Kid had him licked because the Kid had the look of one who doesn't give a damn what happens next.

Finally Maurois looked a question at Big Chin. Big Chin moistened his lips, but said nothing.

Maurois looked at the Kid again, and nodded his head.

"You are right," he said. "We will do that."

"Good!" The Kid did not move from his door. "Now who are these plugs*?"

"These two"—Maurois nodded at Billie and me—"are friends of our Inés. This"—indicating Big Chin—"is a confrere of mine."

"You mean he's in with you? That's all right with me." The Kid spoke crisply. "But, you understand, his cut comes out of yours. I get half, and no trimming."

The Frenchman frowned, but he nodded in agreement.

"Half is yours, if we find it."

"Don't get no headache over that," the Kid advised him. "It's here and we'll get it."

_____
* slow horses; no good

He put one of his guns away and came into the room, the other gun hanging loosely at his side. When he walked across the room to face the woman, he managed it so that Big Chin and Maurois were never behind him.

"Where's the stuff?" he demanded.

Inés Almad wet her red mouth with her tongue and let her mouth droop a little and looked softly at the Kid, and made her play.

"One of us is as bad as are the others, Kid. We all—each of us tried to get for ourselves everything. You and Edouard have put aside what is past. Am I more wrong than you? I have them, true, but I have not them here. Until tomorrow will you wait? I will get them. We will divide them among us three, as it was to have been. Shall we not do that?"

"Not any!" The Kid's voice had finality in it.

"Is that just?" she pleaded, letting her chin quiver a bit. "Is there a treachery of which I am guilty that also you and Edouard are not? Do you—?"

"That ain't the idea at all," the Kid told her. "Me and Frenchy are in a fix where we got to work together to get anywhere. So we're together. With you it's different. We don't need you. We can take the stuff away from you. You're out! Where's the stuff?"

"Not here! Am I foolish sufficient to leave them here where so easily you could find them? You _do_ need my help to find them. Without me you cannot—"

"You're silly! I might flop for that if I didn't know you. But I know you're too damned greedy to let 'em get far away from you. And you're yellower than you're greedy. If you're smacked a couple of times, you'll kick in. And don't think I got any objections to smacking you over!"

She cowered back from his upraised hand.

The Frenchman spoke quickly.

"We should search the rooms first, Kid. If we don't find them there, then we can decide what to do next."

The Whosis Kid laughed sneeringly at Maurois.

"All right. But, get this, I'm not going out of

here without that stuff—not if I have to take this rat apart. My way's quicker, but we'll hunt first if you want to. Your con-whatever-you-call-him can keep these plugs tucked in while me and you upset the joint."

They went to work. The Kid put away his gun and brought out a long-bladed spring-knife. The Frenchman unscrewed the lower two-thirds of his cane, baring a foot and a half of sword-blade.

No cursory search, theirs. They took the room we were in first. They gutted it thoroughly, carved it to the bone. Furniture and pictures were taken apart. Upholstering gave up its stuffing. Floor coverings were cut. Suspicious lengths of wallpaper were scraped loose. They worked slowly. Neither would let the other get behind him. The Kid would not turn his back on Big Chin.

The sitting-room wrecked, they went into the next room, leaving the woman, Billie and me standing among the litter. Big Chin and his two guns watched over us.

As soon as the Frenchman and the Kid were out of sight, the woman tried her stuff out on our guardian. She had a lot of confidence in her power with men, I'll say that for her.

For a while she worked her eyes on Big Chin, and then, very softly:

"Can I—?"

"You can't!" Big Chin was loud and gruff. "Shut up!"

The Whosis Kid appeared at the door.

"If nobody don't say nothing maybe nobody won't get hurt," he snarled, and went back to his work.

The woman valued herself too highly to be easily discouraged. She didn't put anything in words again, but she looked things at Big Chin—things that had him sweating and blushing. He was a simple man. I didn't think she'd get anywhere. If there had been no one present but the two of them, she might have put Big Chin over the jumps; but he wouldn't be likely to let her get to him with a couple of birds standing there watching the show.

Once a sharp yelp told us that the purple Frana—who had fled rearward when Maurois and Big Chin arrived—had got in trouble with the searchers. There was only that one yelp, and it stopped with a suddenness that suggested trouble for the dog.

The two men spent nearly an hour in the other rooms. They didn't find anything. Their hands, when they joined us again, held nothing but the cutlery.

CHAPTER X

"I said to you it was not here," Inés told them triumphantly. "Now will you—?"

"You can't tell me nothing I'll believe." The Kid snapped his knife shut and dropped it in his pocket. "I still think it's here."

He caught her wrist, and held his other hand, palm up, under her nose.

"You can put 'em in my hand, or I'll take 'em."

"They are not here! I swear it!"

His mouth lifted at the corner in a savage grimace.

"Liar!"

He twisted her arm roughly, forcing her to her knees. His free hand went to the shoulder-strap of her orange gown.

"I'll damn soon find out," he promised.

Billie came to life.

"Hey!" he protested, his chest heaving in and out. "You can't do that!"

"Wait, Kid!" Maurois—putting his sword-cane together again—called. "Let us see if there is not another way."

The Whosis Kid let go of the woman and took three slow steps back from her. His eyes were dead circles without any color you could name—the dull eyes of the man whose nerves quit functioning in the face of excitement. His bony hands pushed his coat aside a little and rested where his vest bulged over the sharp corners of his hip-bones.

"Let's me and you get this right, Frenchy,"

he said in his whining voice. "Are you with me or her?"

"You, most certainly, but—"

"All right. Then *be* with me! Don't be trying to gum every play I make. I'm going to frisk this dolly, and don't think I ain't. What are you going to do about it?"

The Frenchman pursed his mouth until his little black mustache snuggled against the tip of his nose. He puckered his eyebrows and looked thoughtfully out of his one good eye. But he wasn't going to do anything at all about it, and he knew he wasn't. Finally he shrugged.

"You are right," he surrendered. "She should be searched."

The Kid grunted contemptuous disgust at him and went toward the woman again.

She sprang away from him, to me. Her arms clamped around my neck in the habit they seemed to have.

"Jerry!" she screamed in my face. "You will not allow him! Jerry, please not!"

I didn't say anything.

I didn't think it was exactly genteel of the Kid to frisk her, but there were several reasons why I didn't try to stop him. First, I didn't want to do anything to delay the unearthing of this "stuff" there had been so much talk about. Second, I'm no Galahad. This woman had picked her playmates, and was largely responsible for this angle of their game. If they played rough, she'd have to make the best of it. And, a good strong third, Big Chin was prodding me in the side with a gun-muzzle to remind me that I couldn't do anything if I wanted to—except get myself slaughtered.

The Kid dragged Inés away. I let her go.

He pulled her over to what was left of the bench by the electric heater, and called the Frenchman there with a jerk of his head.

"You hold her while I go through her," he said.

She filled her lungs with air. Before she could turn it loose in a shriek, the Kid's long fingers had fit themselves to her throat.

"One chirp out of you and I'll tie a knot in your neck," he threatened.

She let the air wheeze out of her nose.

Billie shuffled his feet. I turned my head to look at him. He was puffing through his mouth. Sweat polished his forehead under his matted red hair. I hoped he wasn't going to turn his wolf loose until the "stuff" came to the surface. If he would wait a while I might join him.

He wouldn't wait. He went into action when—Maurois holding her—the Kid started to undress the woman.

He took a step toward them. Big Chin tried to wave him back with a gun. Billie didn't even see it. His eyes were red on the three by the bench.

"Hey, you can't do that!" he rumbled. "You can't do that!"

"No?" The Kid looked up from his work. "Watch me."

"Billie!" the woman urged the big man on in his foolishness.

Billie charged.

Big Chin let him go, playing safe by swinging both guns on me. The Whosis Kid slid out of the plunging giant's path. Maurois hurled the girl straight at Billie—and got his gun out.

Billie and Inés thumped together in a swaying tangle.

The Kid spun behind the big man. One of the Kid's hands came out of his pocket with the spring-knife. The knife clicked open as Billie regained his balance.

The Kid jumped close.

He knew knives. None of your clumsy downward strokes with the blade sticking out the bottom of his fist.

Thumb and crooked forefinger guided blade. He struck upward. Under Billie's shoulder. Once. Deep.

Billie pitched forward, smashing the woman to the floor under him. He rolled off her and was dead on his back among the furniture-stuffing. Dead, he seemed larger than ever, seemed to fill the room.

The Whosis Kid wiped his knife clean on a piece of carpet, snapped it shut, and dropped it back in his pocket. He did this with his left hand.

His right was close to his hip. He did not look at the knife. His eyes were on Maurois.

But if he expected the Frenchman to squawk, he was disappointed. Maurois' little mustache twitched, and his face was white and strained, but:

"We'd better hurry with what we have to do, and get out of here," he suggested.

The woman sat up beside the dead man, whimpering. Her face was ashy under her dark skin. She was licked. A shaking hand fumbled beneath her clothes. It brought out a little flat silk bag.

Maurois—nearer than the Kid—took it. It was sewed too securely for his fingers to open. He held it while the Kid ripped it with his knife. The Frenchman poured part of the contents out in one cupped hand.

Diamonds. Pearls. A few colored stones among them.

CHAPTER XI

Big Chin blew his breath out in a faint whistle. His eyes were bright on the sparkling stones. So were the eyes of Maurois, the woman, and the Kid.

Big Chin's inattention was a temptation. I could reach his jaw. I could knock him over. The strength Billie had mauled out of me had nearly all come back by now. I could knock Big Chin over and have at least one of his guns by the time the Kid and Maurois got set. It was time for me to do something. I had let these comedians run the show long enough. The stuff had come to light. If I let the party break up there was no telling when, if ever, I could round up these folks again.

But I put the temptation away and made myself wait a bit longer. No use going off half-cocked. With a gun in my hand, facing the Kid and Maurois, I still would have less than an even break. That's not enough. The idea in this detective business is to catch crooks, not to put on heroics.

Maurois was pouring the stones back in the bag when I looked at him again. He started to put the bag in his pocket. The Whosis Kid stopped him with a hand on his arm.

"I'll pack 'em."

Maurois' eyebrows went up.

"There's two of you and one of me," the Kid explained. "I trust you, and all the like of that, but just the same I'm carrying my own share."

"But—"

The doorbell interrupted Maurois' protest.

The Kid spun to the girl.

"You do the talking—and no wise breaks!"

She got up from the floor and went to the passageway.

"Who is there?" she called.

The landlady's voice, stern and wrathful:

"Another sound, Mrs. Almad, and I shall call the police. This is disgraceful!"

I wondered what she would have thought if she had opened the unlocked door and taken a look at her apartment—furniture whittled and gutted; a dead man—the noise of whose dying had brought her up here this second time—lying in the middle of the litter.

I wondered—I took a chance.

"Aw, go jump down the sewer!" I told her.

A gasp, and we heard no more from her. I hoped she was speeding her injured feelings to the telephone. I might need the police she had mentioned.

The Kid's gun was out. For a while it was a toss-up. I would lie down beside Billie, or I wouldn't. If I could have been knifed quietly, I would have gone. But nobody was behind me. The Kid knew I wouldn't stand still and quiet while he carved me. He didn't want any more racket than necessary, now that the jewels were on hand.

"Keep your clam shut or I'll shut it for you!" was the worst I got out of it.

The Kid turned to the Frenchman again. The Frenchman had used the time spent in this side-play to pocket the gems.

"Either we divvy here and now, or I carry the stuff," the Kid announced. "There's two of you to see I don't take a Micky Finn on you."

"But, Kid, we cannot stay here! Is not the landlady even now calling the police? We will go elsewhere to divide. Why cannot you trust me when you are with me?"

Two steps put the Kid between the door and both Maurois and Big Chin. One of the Kid's hands held the gun he had flashed on me. The other was conveniently placed to his other gun.

"Nothing stirring!" he said through his nose. "My cut of them stones don't go out of here in nobody else's kick. If you want to split 'em here, good enough. If you don't, I'll do the carrying. That's flat!"

"But the police!"

"You worry about them. I'm taking one thing at a time, and it's the stones right now."

A vein came out blue in the Frenchman's forehead. His small body was rigid. He was trying to collect enough courage to swap shots with the Kid. He knew, and the Kid knew, that one of them was going to have all the stuff when the curtain came down. They had started off by double-crossing each other. They weren't likely to change their habits. One would have the stones in the end. The other would have nothing—except maybe a burial.

Big Chin didn't count. He was too simple a thug to last long in his present company. If he had known anything, he would have used one of his guns on each of them right now. Instead, he continued to cover me, trying to watch them out of the tail of his eye.

The woman stood near the door, where she had gone to talk to the landlady. She was staring at the Frenchman and the Kid. I wasted precious minutes that seemed to run into hours trying to catch her eye. I finally got it.

I looked at the light-switch, only a foot from her. I looked at her. I looked at the switch again. At her. At the switch.

She got me. Her hand crept sidewise along the wall.

I looked at the two principal players in this button-button game.

The Kid's eyes were dead—and deadly—circles. Maurois' one open eye was watery. He

couldn't make the grade. He put a hand in his pocket and brought out the silk bag.

The woman's brown finger topped the light-button. God knows she was nothing to gamble on, but I had no choice. I had to be in motion when the lights went. Big Chin would pump metal. I had to trust Inés not to balk. If she did, my name was Denis.[*]

Her nail whitened.

I went for Maurois.

Darkness—streaked with orange and blue—filled with noise.

My arms had Maurois. We crashed down on dead Billie. I twisted around, kicking the Frenchman's face. Loosened one arm. Caught one of his. His other hand gouged at my face. That told me the bag was in the one I held. Clawing fingers tore my mouth. I put my teeth in them and kept them there. One of my knees was on his face. I put my weight on it. My teeth still held his hand. Both of my hands were free to get the bag.

Not nice, this work, but effective.

The room was the inside of a black drum on which a giant was beating the long roll. Four guns worked together in a prolonged throbbing roar.

Maurois' fingernails dug into my tongue. I had to open my mouth—let his hand escape. One of my hands found the bag. He wouldn't let go. I screwed his thumb. He cried out. I had the bag.

I tried to leave him then. He grabbed my legs. I kicked at him—missed. He shuddered twice—and stopped moving. A flying bullet had hit him, I took it. Rolling over to the floor, snuggling close to him, I ran a hand over him. A hard bulge came under my hand. I put my hand in his pocket and took back my gun.

On hands and knees—one fist around my gun, the other clutching the silk sack of jewels—I turned to where the door to the next room should have been. A foot wrong, I corrected my course. As I went through the door, the racket in the room behind me stopped.

_____

* nautical term for a pig; an insulting name

CHAPTER XII

Huddled close to the wall inside the door, I stowed the silk bag away, and regretted that I hadn't stayed plastered to the floor behind the Frenchman. This room was dark. It hadn't been dark when the woman switched off the sitting-room lights. Every room in the apartment had been lighted then. All were dark now. Not knowing who had darkened them, I didn't like it.

No sounds came from the room I had quit.

The rustle of gently falling rain came from an open window that I couldn't see, off to one side.

Another sound came from behind me. The muffled tattoo of teeth on teeth.

That cheered me. Inés the scary, of course. She had left the sitting-room in the dark and put out the rest of the lights. Maybe nobody else was behind me.

Breathing quietly through wide-open mouth, I waited. I couldn't hunt for the woman in the dark without making noises. Maurois and the Kid had strewn furniture and parts of furniture everywhere. I wished I knew if she was holding a gun. I didn't want to have her spraying me.

Not knowing, I waited where I was.

Her teeth clicked on for minutes.

Something moved in the sitting-room. A gun thundered.

"Inés!" I hissed toward the chattering teeth.

No answer. Furniture scraped in the sitting-room. Two guns went off together. A groaning broke out.

"I've got the stuff," I whispered under cover of the groaning.

That brought an answer.

"Jerry! Ah, come here to me!"

The groans went on, but fainter, in the other room. I crawled toward the woman's voice. I went on hands and knees, bumping as carefully as possible against things. I couldn't see anything. Midway, I put a hand down on a soggy bundle of fur—the late purple Frana. I went on.

Inés touched my shoulder with an eager hand.

"Give them to me," were her first words.

I grinned at her in the dark, patted her hand, found her head, and put my mouth to her ear.

"Let's get back in the bedroom," I breathed, paying no attention to her request for the loot. "The Kid will be coming." I didn't doubt that he had bested Big Chin. "We can handle him better in the bedroom."

I wanted to receive him in a room with only one door.

She led me—both of us on hands and knees—to the bedroom. I did what thinking seemed necessary as we crawled. The Kid couldn't know yet how the Frenchman and I had come out. If he guessed, he would guess that the Frenchman had survived. He would be likely to put me in the chump class with Billie, and think the Frenchman could handle me. The chances were that he had got Big Chin, and knew it by now. It was black as black in the sitting-room, but he must know by now that he was the only living thing there.

He blocked the only exit from the apartment. He would think, then, that Inés and Maurois were still alive in it, with the spoils. What would he do about it? There was no pretense of partnership now. That had gone with the lights. The Kid was after the stones. The Kid was after them alone.

I'm no wizard at guessing the other guy's next move. But my idea was that the Kid would be on his way after us, soon. He knew—he must know—that the police were coming; but I had him doped as crazy enough to disregard the police until they appeared. He'd figure that there would be only a couple of them—prepared for nothing more violent than a drinking-party. He could handle them—or he would think he could. Meanwhile, he would come after the stones.

The woman and I reached the bedroom, the room farthest back in the apartment, a room with only one door. I heard her fumbling with the door, trying to close it. I couldn't see, but I got my foot in the way.

"Leave it open," I whispered.

I didn't want to shut the Kid out. I wanted to take him in.

On my belly, I crawled back to the door, felt for my watch, and propped it on the sill, in the angle between door and frame. I wriggled back from it until I was six or eight feet away, looking diagonally across the open doorway at the watch's luminous dial.

The phosphorescent numbers could not be seen from the other side of the door. They faced me. Anybody who came through the door—unless he jumped—must, if only for a split-second, put some part of himself between me and the watch.

On my belly, my gun cocked, its butt steady on the floor, I waited for the faint light to be blotted out.

I waited a time. Pessimism: perhaps he wasn't coming; perhaps I would have to go after him; perhaps he would run out, and I would lose him after all my trouble.

Inés, beside me, breathed quaveringly in my ear, and shivered.

"Don't touch me," I growled at her as she tried to cuddle against me.

She was shaking my arm.

Glass broke in the next room.

Silence.

The luminous patches on the watch burnt my eyes. I couldn't afford to blink. A foot could pass the dial while I was blinking. I couldn't afford to blink, but I had to blink. I blinked. I couldn't tell whether something had passed the watch or not. I had to blink again. Tried to hold my eyes stiffly opened. Failed. I almost shot at the third blink. I could have sworn something had gone between me and the watch.

The Kid, whatever he was up to, made no sound.

The dark woman began to sob beside me. Throat noises that could guide bullets.

I lumped her with my eyes and cursed the lot—not aloud, but from the heart.

My eyes smarted. Moisture filmed them. I blinked it away, losing sight of the watch for precious instants. The butt of my gun was slimy with my hand's sweat. I was thoroughly uncomfortable, inside and out.

Gunpowder burned at my face.

A screaming maniac of a woman was crawling all over me.

My bullet hit nothing lower than the ceiling.

I flung, maybe kicked, the woman off, and snaked backward. She moaned somewhere to one side. I couldn't see the Kid—couldn't hear him. The watch was visible again, farther away. A rustling.

The watch vanished.

I fired at it.

Two points of light near the floor gave out fire and thunder.

My gun-barrel as close to the floor as I could hold it, I fired between those points. Twice.

Twin flames struck at me again.

My right hand went numb. My left took the gun. I sped two more bullets on their way. That left one in my gun.

I don't know what I did with it. My head filled up with funny notions. There wasn't any room. There wasn't any darkness. There wasn't anything. . . .

I opened my eyes in dim light. I was on my back. Beside me the dark woman knelt, shivering and sniffling. Her hands were busy—in my clothes.

One of them came out of my vest with the jewel-bag.

Coming to life, I grabbed her arm. She squealed as if I were a stirring corpse. I got the bag again.

"Give them back, Jerry," she wailed, trying frantically to pull my fingers loose. "They are my things. Give them!"

Sitting up, I looked around.

Beside me lay a shattered bedside lamp, whose fall—caused by carelessness with my feet, or one of the Kid's bullets—had KO'd me. Across the room, face down, arms spread in a crucified posture, the Whosis Kid sprawled. He was dead.

From the front of the apartment—almost indistinguishable from the throbbing in my head—came the pounding of heavy blows. The police were kicking down the unlocked door.

The woman went quiet. I whipped my head around. The knife stung my cheek—put a slit in the lapel of my coat. I took it away from her.

There was no sense to this. The police were already here. I humored her, pretending a sudden coming to full consciousness.

"Oh, it's you!" I said. "Here they are."

I handed her the silk bag of jewels just as the first policeman came into the room.

CHAPTER XIII

I didn't see Inés again before she was taken back East to be hit with a life-sentence in the Massachusetts big house. Neither of the policemen who crashed into her apartment that night knew me. The woman and I were separated before I ran into anyone who did know me, which gave me an opportunity to arrange that she would not be tipped off to my identity. The most difficult part of the performance was to keep myself out of the newspapers, since I had to tell the coroner's jury about the deaths of Billie, Big Chin, Maurois and the Whosis Kid. But I managed it. So far as I know, the dark woman still thinks I am Jerry Young, the bootlegger.

The Old Man talked to her before she left San Francisco. Fitting together what he got from her and what the Boston branch got, the history runs like this:

A Boston jeweler named Tunnicliffe had a trusted employee named Binder. Binder fell in with a dark woman named Inés Almad. The dark woman, in turn, had a couple of shifty friends—a Frenchman named Maurois, and a native of Boston whose name was either Carey or Cory, but who was better known as the Whosis Kid. Out of that sort of combination almost anything was more than likely to come.

What came was a scheme. The faithful Binder—part of whose duties it was to open the shop in the morning and close it at night—was to pick out the richest of the unset stones bought for the holiday trade, carry them off with him one evening, and turn them over to Inés. She was to turn them into money.

To cover up Binder's theft, the Whosis Kid and the Frenchman were to rob the jeweler's shop immediately after the door was opened the following morning. Binder and the porter—who would not notice the absence of the most valuable pieces from the stock—would be the only ones in the shop. The robbers would take whatever they could get. In addition to their pickings, they were to be paid two hundred and fifty dollars apiece, and in case either was caught later, Binder could be counted on not to identify them.

That was the scheme as Binder knew it. There were angles he didn't suspect.

Between Inés, Maurois and the Kid there was another agreement. She was to leave for Chicago with the stones as soon as Binder gave them to her, and wait there for Maurois and the Kid. She and the Frenchman would have been satisfied to run off and let Binder hold the sack. The Whosis Kid insisted that the hold-up go through as planned, and that the foolish Binder be killed. Binder knew too much about them, the Kid said, and he would squawk his head off as soon as he learned he had been double-crossed.

The Kid had his way, and he had shot Binder.

Then had come the sweet mess of quadruple and sextuple crossing that had led all three into calamity: the woman's private agreements with the Kid and Maurois—to meet one in St. Louis and the other in New Orleans—and her flight alone with the loot to San Francisco.

Billie was an innocent bystander—or almost. A lumber-handler Inés had run into somewhere, and picked up as a sort of cushion against the rough spots along the rocky road she traveled.

BLACK MASK, MAY 1925

The Scorched Face

BY DASHIELL HAMMETT

(Author of "The Whosis Kid," etc.)

Here's another realistic detective tale by Mr. Hammett, formerly of the Pinkerton's. It has a ring of truth in it that makes you forget that you are only reading and not actually following the San Francisco sleuth around.

A NOVELETTE OF THE CONTINENTAL SLEUTH

"WE EXPECTED THEM home yesterday," Alfred Banbrock wound up his story. "When they had not come by this morning, my wife telephoned Mrs. Walden. Mrs. Walden said they had not been down there—had not been expected, in fact."

"On the face of it, then," I suggested, "it seems that your daughters went away of their own accord, and are staying away on their own accord?"

Banbrock nodded gravely. Tired muscles sagged in his fleshy face.

"It would seem so," he agreed. "That is why I came to your agency for help instead of going to the police."

"Have they ever disappeared before?"

"No. If you read the papers and magazines, you've no doubt seen hints that the younger generation is given to irregularity. My daughters came and went pretty much as they pleased. But, though I can't say I ever knew what they were up to, we always knew where they were in a general way."

"Can you think of any reason for their going away like this?"

He shook his weary head.

"Any recent quarrels?" I probed.

"N—" He changed it to: "Yes—although I didn't attach any importance to it, and wouldn't have recalled it if you hadn't jogged my memory. It was Thursday evening—the evening before they went away."

"And it was about—?"

"Money, of course. We never disagreed over anything else. I gave each of my daughters an adequate allowance—perhaps a very liberal one. Nor did I keep them strictly within it. There were few months in which they didn't exceed it. Thursday evening they asked for an amount of money even more than usual in excess of what two girls should need. I wouldn't give it to them, though I finally did give them a somewhat smaller amount. We didn't exactly quarrel—not in the strict sense of the word—but there was a certain lack of friendliness between us."

"And it was after this disagreement that they said they were going down to Mrs. Walden's, in Monterey, for the week-end?"

"Possibly. I'm not sure of that point. I don't think I heard of it until the next morning, but they may have told my wife before that. I shall ask her if you wish."

"And you know of no other possible reason for their running away?"

"None. I can't think that our dispute over money—by no means an unusual one—had anything to do with it."

"What does their mother think?"

"Their mother is dead," Banbrock corrected me. "My wife is their stepmother. She is only two years older than Myra, my older daughter. She is as much at sea as I."

"Did your daughters and their stepmother get along all right together?"

"Yes! Yes! Excellently! If there was a division in the family, I usually found them standing together against me."

"Your daughters left Friday afternoon?"

"At noon, or a few minutes after. They were going to drive down."

"The car, of course, is still missing?"

"Naturally."

"What was it?"

"A Locomobile, with a special cabriolet body. Black."

"You can give me the license and engine numbers?"

"I think so."

He turned in his chair to the big roll-top desk that hid a quarter of one office wall, fumbled with papers in a compartment, and read the numbers over his shoulder to me. I put them on the back of an envelope.

"I'm going to have this car put on the police department list of stolen machines," I told him. "It can be done without mentioning your daughters. The police bulletin might find the car for us. That would help us find your daughters."

"Very well," he agreed, "if it can be done without disagreeable publicity. As I told you at first, I don't want any more advertising than is absolutely necessary—unless it becomes likely that harm has come to the girls."

I nodded understanding, and got up.

"I want to go out and talk to your wife," I said. "Is she home now?"

"Yes, I think so. I'll phone her and tell her you are coming."

II

In a big limestone fortress on top a hill in Sea Cliff, looking down on ocean and bay, I had my talk with Mrs. Banbrock. She was a tall dark girl of not more than twenty-two years, inclined to plumpness.

She couldn't tell me anything her husband hadn't at least mentioned, but she could give me finer details.

I got descriptions of the two girls:

Myra—20 years old; 5 feet 8 inches; 150 pounds; athletic; brisk, almost masculine manner and carriage; bobbed brown hair; brown eyes; medium complexion; square face, with large chin and short nose; scar over left ear, concealed by hair; fond of horses and all outdoor sports. When she left the house she wore a blue and green wool dress, small blue hat, short black seal coat, and black slippers.

Ruth—18 years; 5 feet 4 inches; 105 pounds; brown eyes; brown bobbed hair; medium complexion; small oval face; quiet, timid, inclined to lean on her more forceful sister. When last seen she had worn a tobacco-brown coat trimmed with brown fur over a gray silk dress, and a wide brown hat.

I got two photographs of each girl, and an additional snapshot of Myra standing in front of the cabriolet. I got a list of the things they had taken with them—such things as would naturally be taken on a week-end visit. What I valued most of what I got was a list of their friends, relatives, and other acquaintances, so far as Mrs. Banbrock knew them.

"Did they mention Mrs. Walden's invitation before their quarrel with Mr. Banbrock?" I asked, when I had my lists stowed away.

"I don't think so," Mrs. Banbrock said thoughtfully. "I didn't connect the two things at all. They didn't really quarrel with their father, you know. It wasn't harsh enough to be called a quarrel."

"Did you see them when they left?"

"Assuredly! They left at about half-past twelve Friday afternoon. They kissed me as usual when they went, and there was certainly nothing in their manner to suggest anything out of the ordinary."

"You've no idea at all where they might have gone?"

"None."

"Can't even make a guess?"

"I can't. Among the names and addresses I have given you are some of friends and relatives of the girls in other cities. They may have gone to one of those. Do you think we should—?"

"I'll take care of that," I promised. "Could you pick out one or two of them as the most likely places for the girls to have gone?"

She wouldn't try it.

"No," she said positively, "I could not."

From this interview I went back to the agency, and put the agency machinery in motion; arranging to have operatives from some of the Continental's other branches call on the out-of-town names on my list; having the missing Locomobile put on the police department list;

turning one photograph of each girl over to a photographer to be copied.

That done, I set out to talk to the persons on the list Mrs. Banbrock had given me. My first call was on a Constance Delee, in an apartment building on Post Street. I saw a maid. The maid said Miss Delee was out of town. She wouldn't tell me where her mistress was, or when she would be back.

From there I went up on Van Ness Avenue and found a Wayne Ferris in an automobile salesroom: a sleek-haired young man whose very nice manners and clothes completely hid anything else—brains for instance—he might have had. He was very willing to help me, and he knew nothing. It took him a long time to tell me so. A nice boy.

Another blank: "Mrs. Scott is in Honolulu."

In a real estate office on Montgomery Street I found my next one—another sleek, stylish, smooth-haired young man with nice manners and nice clothes. His name was Raymond Elwood. I would have thought him a no more distant relative of Ferris than cousin if I hadn't known that the world—especially the dancing, teaing world—was full of their sort. I learned nothing from him.

Then I drew some more blanks: "Out of town," "Shopping," "I don't know where you can find him."

I found one more of the Banbrock girls' friends before I called it a day. Her name was Mrs. Stewart Correll. She lived in Presidio Terrace, not far from the Banbrocks. She was a small woman, or girl, of about Mrs. Banbrock's age. A little fluffy blonde person with wide eyes of that particular blue which always looks honest and candid no matter what is going on behind it.

"I haven't seen either Ruth or Myra for two weeks or more," she said in answer to my question.

"At that time—the last time you saw them—did either say anything about going away?"

"No."

Her eyes were wide and frank. A little muscle twitched in her upper lip.

"And you've no idea where they might have gone?"

"No."

Her fingers were rolling her lace handkerchief into a little ball.

"Have you heard from them since you last saw them?"

"No."

She moistened her mouth before she said it.

"Will you give me the names and addresses of all the people you know who were also known by the Banbrock girls?"

"Why—? Is there—?"

"There's a chance that some of them may have seen them more recently than you," I explained. "Or may even have seen them since Friday."

Without enthusiasm, she gave me a dozen names. All were already on my list. Twice she hesitated as if about to speak a name she did not want to speak. Her eyes stayed on mine, wide and honest. Her fingers, no longer balling the handkerchief, picked at the cloth of her skirt.

I didn't pretend to believe her. But my feet weren't solidly enough on the ground for me to put her on the grill. I gave her a promise before I left, one that she could get a threat out of if she liked.

"Thanks, very much," I said. "I know it's hard to remember things exactly. If I run across anything that will help your memory, I'll be back to let you know about it."

"Wha—? Yes, do!" she said.

Walking away from the house, I turned my head to look back just before I passed out of sight. A curtain swung into place at a second-floor window. The street lights weren't bright enough for me to be sure the curtain had swung in front of a blonde head.

My watch told me it was nine-thirty: too late to line up any more of the girls' friends. I went home, wrote my report for the day, and turned in, thinking more about Mrs. Correll than about the girls.

She seemed worth an investigation.

III

Some telegraphic reports were in when I got to the office the next morning. None was of any value. Investigation of the names and addresses in other cities had revealed nothing. An investigation in Monterey had established reasonably—which is about as well as anything is ever established in the detecting business—that the girls had not been there recently; that the Locomobile had not been there.

The early editions of the afternoon papers were on the street when I went out to get some breakfast before taking up the grind where I had dropped it the previous night. I bought a paper to prop behind my grapefruit.

It spoiled my breakfast for me.

BANKER'S WIFE SUICIDE

Mrs. Stewart Correll, wife of the vice-president of the Golden Gate Trust Company, was found dead early this morning by her maid in her bedroom, in her home in Presidio Terrace. A bottle believed to have contained poison was on the floor beside the bed.

The dead woman's husband could give no reason for his wife's suicide. He said she had not seemed depressed or . . .

I gave my eggs and toast a quick play, put my coffee down in a lump, and got going.

At the Correll residence I had to do a lot of talking before I could get to Correll. He was a tall, slim man of less than thirty-five, with a sallow, nervous face and blue eyes that fidgeted.

"I'm sorry to disturb you at a time like this," I apologized when I had finally insisted my way into his presence. "I won't take up more of your time than necessary. I am an operative of the Continental Detective Agency. I have been trying to find Ruth and Myra Banbrock, who disappeared several days ago. You know them, I think."

"Yes," he said without interest. "I know them."

"You knew they had disappeared?"

"No." His eyes switched from a chair to a rug. "Why should I?"

"Have you seen either of them recently?" I asked, ignoring his question.

"Last week—Wednesday, I think. They were just leaving—standing at the door talking to my wife—when I came home from the bank."

"Didn't your wife say anything to you about their vanishing?"

"No. Really, I can't tell you anything about the Misses Banbrock. If you'll excuse me—"

"Just a moment longer," I said. "I wouldn't have bothered you if it hadn't been necessary. I was here last night, to question Mrs. Correll. She seemed nervous. My impression was that some of her answers to my questions were—uh—evasive. I want—"

He was up out of his chair. His face was red in front of mine.

"You!" he cried. "I can thank you for—"

"Now, Mr. Correll," I tried to quiet him, "there's no use—"

But he had himself all worked up.

"You drove my wife to her death," he accused me. "You killed her with your damned prying—with your bulldozing threats; with your—"

That was silly. I felt sorry for this young man whose wife had killed herself. Apart from that, I had work to do. I tightened the screws.

"We won't argue, Correll," I told him. "The point is that I came here to see if your wife could tell me anything about the Banbrocks. She told me less than the truth. Later, she committed suicide. I want to know why. Come through for me, and I'll do what I can to keep the papers and the public from linking her death with the girls' disappearance."

"Linking her death with their disappearance?" he exclaimed. "That's absurd!"

"Maybe—but the connection is there!" I hammered away at him. I felt sorry for him, but I had work to do. "It's there. If you'll give it to me, maybe it won't have to be advertised. I'm going to get it, though. You give it to me—or I'll go after it out in the open."

For a moment I thought he was going to take a poke at me. I wouldn't have blamed him. His body stiffened—then sagged, and he dropped back into his chair. His eyes fidgeted away from mine.

"There's nothing I can tell," he mumbled. "When her maid went to her room to call her this morning, she was dead. There was no message, no reason, nothing."

"Did you see her last night?"

"No. I was not home for dinner. I came in late and went straight to my own room, not wanting to disturb her. I hadn't seen her since I left the house that morning."

"Did she seem disturbed or worried then?"

"No."

"Why do you think she did it?"

"My God, man, I don't know! I've thought and thought, but I don't know!"

"Health?"

"She seemed well. She was never ill, never complained."

"Any recent quarrels?"

"We never quarreled—never in the year and a half we have been married!"

"Financial trouble?"

He shook his head without speaking or looking up from the floor.

"Any other worry?"

He shook his head again.

"Did the maid notice anything peculiar in her behavior last night?"

"Nothing."

"Have you looked through her things—for papers, letters?"

"Yes—and found nothing." He raised his head to look at me. "The only thing"—he spoke very slowly—"there was a little pile of ashes in the grate in her room, as if she had burned papers, or letters."

Correl held nothing more for me—nothing I could get out of him, anyway.

The girl at the front gate in Alfred Banbrock's Shoreman's Building suite told me he was *in conference.* I sent my name in. He came out of conference to take me into his private office. His tired face was full of questions.

I didn't keep him waiting for the answers. He was a grown man. I didn't edge around the bad news.

"Things have taken a bad break," I said as soon as we were locked in together. "I think we'll have to go to the police and newspapers for help. A Mrs. Correll, a friend of your daughters, lied to me when I questioned her yesterday. Last night she committed suicide."

"Irma Correll? Suicide?"

"You knew her?"

"Yes! Intimately! She was—that is, she was a close friend of my wife and daughters. She killed herself?"

"Yes. Poison. Last night. Where does she fit in with your daughters' disappearance?"

"Where?" he repeated. "I don't know. Must she fit in?"

"I think she must. She told me she hadn't seen your daughters for a couple of weeks. Her husband told me just now that they were talking to her when he came home from the bank last Wednesday afternoon. She seemed nervous when I questioned her. She killed herself shortly afterward. There's hardly a doubt that she fits in somewhere."

"And that means—?"

"That means," I finished for him, "that your daughters may be perfectly safe, but that we can't afford to gamble on that possibility."

"You think harm has come to them?"

"I don't think anything," I evaded, "except that with a death tied up closely with their going, we can't afford to play around."

Banbrock got his attorney on the phone—a pink-faced, white-haired old boy named Norwall, who had the reputation of knowing more about corporations than all the Morgans, but who hadn't the least idea as to what police procedure was all about—and told him to meet us at the Hall of Justice.

We spent an hour and a half there, getting the police turned loose on the affair, and giving the newspapers what we wanted them to have. That was plenty of dope on the girls, plenty of photographs and so forth; but nothing about the connection between them and Mrs. Correll. Of course we let the police in on that angle.

IV

After Banbrock and his attorney had gone away together, I went back to the detectives' assembly room to chew over the job with Pat Reddy, the police sleuth assigned to it.

Pat was the youngest member of the detective bureau—a big blond Irishman who went in for the spectacular in his lazy way.

A couple of years ago he was a new copper, pounding his feet in harness on a hillside beat. One night he tagged an automobile that was parked in front of a fireplug. The owner came out just then and gave him an argument. She was Althea Wallach, only and spoiled daughter of the owner of the Wallach Coffee Company—a slim, reckless youngster with hot eyes. She must have told Pat plenty. He took her over to the station and dumped her in a cell.

Old Wallach, so the story goes, showed up the next morning with a full head of steam and half the lawyers in San Francisco. But Pat made his charge stick, and the girl was fined. Old Wallach did everything but take a punch at Pat in the corridor afterward. Pat grinned his sleepy grin at the coffee importer, and drawled:

"You better lay off me—or I'll stop drinking your coffee."

That crack got into most of the newspapers in the country, and even into a Broadway show.

But Pat didn't stop with the snappy comeback. Three days later he and Althea Wallach went over to Alameda and got themselves married. I was in on that part. I happened to be on the ferry they took, and they dragged me along to see the deed done.

Old Wallach immediately disowned his daughter, but that didn't seem to worry anybody else. Pat went on pounding his beat, but, now that he was conspicuous, it wasn't long before his qualities were noticed. He was boosted into the detective bureau. Old Wallach relented before he died, and left Althea both of his millions.

Pat took the afternoon off to go to the funeral, and went back to work that night, catching a wagonload of gunmen. He kept on working. I don't know what his wife did with her money, but Pat didn't even improve the quality of his cigars—though he should have. He lived now in the Wallach mansion, true enough, and now and then on rainy mornings he would be driven down to the Hall in a Hispano-Suiza brougham; but there was no difference in him beyond that.

That was the big blond Irishman who sat across a desk from me in the assembly room and fumigated me with something shaped like a cigar.

He took the cigar-like thing out of his mouth presently, and spoke through the fumes.

"This Correll woman you think's tied up with the Banbrocks—she was stuck-up a couple of months back and nicked for eight hundred dollars. Know that?"

I hadn't known it.

"Lose anything besides cash?" I asked.

"No."

"You believe it?"

He grinned.

"That's the point," he said. "We didn't catch the bird who did it. With women who lose things that way—especially money—it's always a question whether it's a hold-up or a hold-out."

He teased some more poison-gas out of the cigar-thing, and added:

"The hold-up might have been on the level, though. What are you figuring on doing now?"

"Let's go up to the agency and see if anything new has turned up. Then I'd like to talk to Mrs. Banbrock again. Maybe she can tell us something about the Correll woman."

At the office I found that reports had come in on the rest of the out-of-town names and addresses. Apparently none of these people knew anything about the girls' whereabouts. Reddy

and I went on up to Sea Cliff to the Banbrock home.

Banbrock had telephoned the news of Mrs. Correll's death to his wife, and she had read the papers. She told us she could think of no reason for the suicide. She could imagine no possible connection between the suicide and her stepdaughters' vanishing.

"Mrs. Correll seemed as nearly contented and happy as usual the last time I saw her, two or three weeks ago," Mrs. Banbrock said. "Of course she was by nature inclined to be dissatisfied with things, but not to the extent of doing a thing like this."

"Do you know of any trouble between her and her husband?"

"No. So far as I know, they were happy, though—"

She broke off. Hesitancy, embarrassment showed in her dark eyes.

"Though?" I repeated.

"If I don't tell you now, you'll think I am hiding something," she said, flushing, and laughing a little laugh that held more nervousness than amusement. "It hasn't any bearing, but I was always just a little jealous of Irma. She and my husband were—well, everyone thought they would marry. That was a little before he and I married. I never let it show, and I dare say it was a foolish idea, but I always had a suspicion that Irma married Stewart more in pique than for any other reason, and that she was still fond of Alfred—Mr. Banbrock."

"Was there anything definite to make you think that?"

"No, nothing—really! I never thoroughly believed it. It was just a sort of vague feeling. Cattiness, no doubt, more than anything else."

It was getting along toward evening when Pat and I left the Banbrock house. Before we knocked off for the day, I called up the Old Man—the Continental's San Francisco branch manager, and therefore my boss—and asked him to sic an operative on Irma Correll's past.

I took a look at the morning papers—thanks to their custom of appearing almost as soon as the sun is out of sight—before I went to bed. They had given our job a good spread. All the facts except those having to do with the Correll angle were there, plus photographs, and the usual assortment of guesses and similar garbage.

The following morning I went after the friends of the missing girls to whom I had not yet talked. I found some of them, and got nothing of value from them. Late in the morning I telephoned the office to see if anything new had turned up.

It had.

"We've just had a call from the sheriff's office at Martinez," the Old Man told me. "An Italian grapegrower near Knob Valley picked up a charred photograph a couple of days ago, and recognized it as Ruth Banbrock when he saw her picture in this morning's paper. Will you get up there? A deputy sheriff and the Italian are waiting for you in the Knob Valley marshal's office."

"I'm on my way," I said.

At the ferry building I used the four minutes before my boat left trying to get Pat Reddy on the phone, with no success.

Knob Valley is a town of less than a thousand people, a dreary, dirty town in Contra Costa county. A San Francisco-Sacramento local set me down there while the afternoon was still young.

I knew the marshal slightly—Tom Orth. I found two men in the office with him. Orth introduced us. Abner Paget, a gawky man of forty-something, with a slack chin, scrawny face, and pale intelligent eyes, was the deputy sheriff. Gio Cereghino, the Italian grapegrower, was a small, nut-brown man with strong yellow teeth that showed in an everlasting smile under his black mustache, and soft brown eyes.

Paget showed me the photograph. A scorched piece of paper the size of a half-dollar, apparently all that had not been burned of the original picture. It was Ruth Banbrock's face. There was little room for doubting that. She had a peculiarly excited—almost drunken—look, and her eyes were larger than in the other pictures of her I had seen. But it was her face.

"He says he found it day 'fore yesterday," Paget explained dryly, nodding at the Italian. "The wind blew it against his foot when he was walkin' up a piece of road near his place. He picked it up an' stuck it in his pocket, he says, for no special reason, I guess, except maybe that guineas like pictures."

He paused to regard the Italian meditatively. The Italian nodded his head in vigorous affirmation.

"Anyways," the deputy sheriff went on, "he was in town this mornin', an' seen the pictures in the papers from Frisco. So he come in here an' told Tom about it. Tom an' me decided the best thing was to phone your agency—since the papers said you was workin' on it."

I looked at the Italian.

Paget, reading my mind, explained:

"Cereghino lives over in the hills. Got a grape-ranch there. Been around here five or six years, an' ain't killed nobody that I know of."

"Remember the place where you found the picture?" I asked the Italian.

His grin broadened under his mustache, and his head went up and down.

"For sure, I remember that place."

"Let's go there," I suggested to Paget.

"Right. Comin' along, Tom?"

The marshal said he couldn't. He had something to do in town. Cereghino, Paget and I went out and got into a dusty Ford that the deputy sheriff drove.

We rode for nearly an hour, along a county road that bent up the slope of Mount Diablo. After a while, at a word from the Italian, we left the county road for a dustier and ruttier one.

A mile of this one.

"This place," Cereghino said.

Paget stopped the Ford. We got out in a clearing. The trees and bushes that had crowded the road retreated here for twenty feet or so on either side, leaving a little dusty circle in the woods.

"About this place," the Italian was saying. "I think by this stump. But between that bend ahead and that one behind, I know for sure."

V

Paget was a countryman. I am not. I waited for him to move.

He looked around the clearing, slowly, standing still between the Italian and me. His pale eyes lighted presently. He went around the Ford to the far side of the clearing. Cereghino and I followed.

Near the fringe of brush at the edge of the clearing, the scrawny deputy stopped to grunt at the ground. The wheel-marks of an automobile were there. A car had turned around here.

Paget went on into the woods. The Italian kept close to his heels. I brought up the rear. Paget was following some sort of track. I couldn't see it, either because he and the Italian blotted it out ahead of me, or because I'm a shine Indian.*

We went back quite a way.

Paget stopped. The Italian stopped.

Paget said, "Uh-huh," as if he had found an expected thing.

The Italian said something with the name of God in it.

I trampled a bush, coming beside them to see what they saw.

I saw it.

At the base of a tree, on her side, her knees drawn up close to her body, a girl was dead.

She wasn't nice to see. Birds had been at her.

A tobacco-brown coat was half on, half off her shoulders. I knew she was Ruth Banbrock before I turned her over to look at the side of her face the ground had saved from the birds.

Cereghino stood watching me while I examined the girl. His face was mournful in a calm way. The deputy sheriff paid little attention to the body. He was off in the brush, moving around, looking at the ground.

He came back as I finished my examination.

"Shot," I told him, "once in the right temple. Before that, I think, there was a fight. There are marks on the arm that was under her body.

There's nothing on her—no jewelry, money—nothing."

"That goes," Paget said. "Two women got out of the car back in the clearin', an' came here. Could've been three women—if the others carried this one. Can't make out how many went back. One of 'em was larger than this one. There was a scuffle here. Find the gun?"

"No," I said.

"Neither did I. It went away in the car, then. There's what's left of a fire over there." He ducked his head to the left. "Paper an' rags burnt. Not enough left to do us any good. I reckon the photo Cereghino found blew away from the fire. Late Friday, I'd put it, or maybe Saturday mornin'. . . . No nearer than that."

I took the deputy sheriff's word for it. He seemed to know his stuff.

"Come here. I'll show you somethin'," he said, and led me over to a little black pile of ashes.

He hadn't anything to show me. He wanted to talk to me away from the Italian's ears.

"I think the guinea's all right," he said, "but I reckon I'd best hold him a while to make sure. This is some way from his place, an' he stuttered a little bit too much tellin' me how he happened to be passin' here. Course, that don't mean nothin' much. All these guineas peddle *vino*, an' I guess that's what brought him out this way. I'll hold him a day or two, anyways."

"Good," I agreed. "This is your country, and you know the people. Can you visit around and see what you can pick up? Whether anybody saw anything? Saw a Locomobile cabriolet? Or anything else? You can get more than I could."

"I'll do that," he promised.

"All right. Then I'll go back to San Francisco now. I suppose you'll want to camp here with the body?"

"Yeah. You drive the Ford back to Knob Valley, an' tell Tom what's what. He'll come or send out. I'll keep the guinea here with me."

Waiting for the next west-bound train out of Knob Valley, I got the office on the telephone.

---

* a black man passing as an Indian

The Old Man was out. I told my story to one of the office men and asked him to get the news to the Old Man as soon as he could.

Everybody was in the office when I got back to San Francisco. Alfred Banbrock, his face a pink-gray that was deader than solid gray could have been. His pink and white old lawyer. Pat Reddy, sprawled on his spine with his feet on another chair. The Old Man, with his gentle eyes behind gold spectacles and his mild smile, hiding the fact that fifty years of sleuthing had left him without any feelings at all on any subject. (Whitey Clayton used to say the Old Man could spit icicles in August.)

Nobody said anything when I came in. I said my say as briefly as possible.

"Then the other woman—the woman who killed Ruth was—?"

Banbrock didn't finish his question. Nobody answered it.

"We don't know what happened," I said after a while. "Your daughter and someone we don't know may have gone there. Your daughter may have been dead before she was taken there. She may have—"

"But Myra!" Banbrock was pulling at his collar with a finger inside. "Where is Myra?"

I couldn't answer that, nor could any of the others.

"You are going up to Knob Valley now?" I asked him.

"Yes, at once. You will come with me?"

I wasn't sorry I could not.

"No. There are things to be done here. I'll give you a note to the marshal. I want you to look carefully at the piece of your daughter's photograph the Italian found—to see if you remember it."

Banbrock and the lawyer left.

VI

Reddy lit one of his awful cigars. "We found the car," the Old Man said.

"Where?"

"In Sacramento. It was left in a garage there either late Friday night or early Saturday. Foley has gone up to investigate it. And Reddy has uncovered a new angle."

Pat nodded through his smoke.

"A hock-shop dealer came in this morning," Pat said, "and told us that Myra Banbrock and another girl came to his joint last week and hocked a lot of stuff. They gave him phoney names, but he swears one of them was Myra. He recognized her picture as soon as he saw it in the paper. Her companion wasn't Ruth. It was a little blonde."

"Mrs. Correll?"

"Uh-huh. The shark can't swear to that, but I think that's the answer. Some of the jewelry was Myra's, some Ruth's, and some we don't know. I mean we can't prove it belonged to Mrs. Correll—though we will."

"When did all this happen?"

"They soaked the stuff Monday before they went away."

"Have you seen Correll?"

"Uh-huh," Pat said. "I did a lot of talking to him, but the answers weren't worth much. He says he don't know whether any of her jewelry is gone or not, and doesn't care. It was hers, he says, and she could do anything she wanted with it. He was kind of disagreeable. I got along a little better with one of the maids. She says some of Mrs. Correll's pretties disappeared last week. Mrs. Correll said she had lent them to a friend. I'm going to show the stuff the hock-shop has to the maid tomorrow, to see if she can identify it. She didn't know anything else—except that Mrs. Correll was out of the picture for a while on Friday—the day the Banbrock girls went away."

"What do you mean, out of the picture?" I asked.

"She went out late in the morning and didn't show up until somewhere around three the next morning. She and Correll had a row over it, but she wouldn't tell him where she had been."

I liked that. It could mean something.

"And," Pat went on, "Correll has just remembered that his wife had an uncle who went crazy in Pittsburgh in 1902, and that she had a morbid fear of going crazy herself, and that she had often said she would kill herself if she thought she was going crazy. Wasn't it nice of him to remember those things at last? To account for her death?"

"It was," I agreed, "but it doesn't get us anywhere. It doesn't even prove that he knows anything. Now my guess is—"

"To hell with your guess," Pat said, getting up and pushing his hat in place. "Your guesses all sound like a lot of static to me. I'm going home, eat my dinner, read my Bible, and go to bed."

I suppose he did. Anyway, he left us.

We all might as well have spent the next three days in bed for all the profit that came out of our running around. No place we visited, nobody we questioned, added to our knowledge. We were in a blind alley.

We learned that the Locomobile was left in Sacramento by Myra Banbrock, and not by anyone else, but we didn't learn where she went afterward. We learned that some of the jewelry in the pawnshop was Mrs. Correll's. The Locomobile was brought back from Sacramento. Mrs. Correll was buried. Ruth Banbrock was buried. The newspapers found other mysteries. Reddy and I dug and dug, and all we brought up was dirt.

The following Monday brought me close to the end of my rope. There seemed nothing more to do but sit back and hope that the circulars with which we had plastered North America would bring results. Reddy had already been called off and put to running out fresher trails. I hung on because Banbrock wanted me to keep at it so long as there was the shadow of anything to keep at. But by Monday I had worked myself out.

Before going to Banbrock's office to tell him I was licked, I dropped in at the Hall of Justice to hold a wake over the job with Pat Reddy. He was crouched over his desk, writing a report on some other job.

"Hello!" he greeted me, pushing his report away and smearing it with ashes from his cigar. "How do the Banbrock doings?"

"They don't," I admitted. "It doesn't seem possible, with the stack-up what it is, that we should have come to a dead stop! It's there for us, if we can find it. The need of money before both the Banbrock and the Correll calamities: Mrs. Correll's suicide after I had questioned her about the girls; her burning things before she died and the burning of things immediately before or after Ruth Banbrock's death."

"Maybe the trouble is," Pat suggested, "that you're not such a good sleuth."

"Maybe."

We smoked in silence for a minute or two after that insult.

"You understand," Pat said presently, "there doesn't have to be any connection between the Banbrock death and disappearance and the Correll death."

"Maybe not. But there has to be a connection between the Banbrock death and the Banbrock disappearance. There was a connection—in a pawnshop—between the Banbrock and Correll actions before these things. If there is that connection, then—"

I broke off, all full of ideas.

"What's the matter?" Pat asked. "Swallow your gum?"

"Listen!" I let myself get almost enthusiastic. "We've got what happened to three women hooked up together. If we could tie up some more in the same string—I want the names and addresses of all the women and girls in San Francisco who have committed suicide, been murdered, or have disappeared within the past year."

"You think this is a wholesale deal?"

"I think the more we can tie up together, the more lines we'll have to run out. And they can't all lead nowhere. Let's get our list, Pat!"

We spent all the afternoon and most of the night getting it. Its size would have embarrassed the Chamber of Commerce. It looked like a hunk of the telephone book. Things happen in a city in a year. The section devoted to strayed wives and daughters was the largest; suicides next; and even the smallest division—murders—wasn't any too short.

We could check off most of the names against what the police department had already learned of them and their motives, weeding out those positively accounted for in a manner nowise connected with our present interest. The remainder we split into two classes; those of unlikely connection, and those of more possible connection. Even then, the second list was longer than I had expected, or hoped.

There were six suicides in it, three murders, and twenty-one disappearances.

Reddy had other work to do. I put the list in my pocket and went calling.

VII

For four days I ground at the list. I hunted, found, questioned, and investigated friends and relatives of the women and girls on my list. My questions all hit in the same direction. Had she been acquainted with Myra Banbrock? Ruth? Mrs. Correll? Had she been in need of money before her death or disappearance? Had she destroyed anything before her death or disappearance? Had she known any of the other women on my list?

Three times I drew yeses.

Sylvia Varney, a girl of twenty, who had killed herself on November 5th, had drawn six hundred dollars from the bank the week before her death. No one in her family could say what she had done with the money. A friend of Sylvia Varney's—Ada Youngman, a married woman of twenty-five or -six—had disappeared on December 2nd, and was still gone. The Varney girl had been at Mrs. Youngman's home an hour before she—the Varney girl—killed herself.

Mrs. Dorothy Sawdon, a young widow, had shot herself on the night of January 13th. No trace was found of either the money her husband had left her or the funds of a club whose trea-surer she was. A bulky letter her maid remembered having given her that afternoon was never found.

These three women's connection with the Banbrock-Correll affair was sketchy enough. None of them had done anything that isn't done by nine out of ten women who kill themselves or run away. But the troubles of all three had come to a head within the past few months—and all three were women of about the same financial and social position as Mrs. Correll and the Banbrocks.

Finishing my list with no fresh leads, I came back to these three.

I had the names and addresses of sixty-two friends of the Banbrock girls. I set about getting the same sort of catalogue on the three women I was trying to bring into the game. I didn't have to do all the digging myself. Fortunately, there were two or three operatives in the office with nothing else to do just then.

We got something.

Mrs. Sawdon had known Raymond Elwood. Sylvia Varney had known Raymond Elwood. There was nothing to show Mrs. Youngman had known him, but it was likely she had. She and the Varney girl had been thick.

I had already interviewed this Raymond Elwood in connection with the Banbrock girls, but had paid no especial attention to him. I had considered him just one of the sleek-headed, high-polished young men of whom there was quite a few listed.

I went back at him, all interest now. The results were promising.

He had, as I have said, a real estate office on Montgomery Street. We were unable to find a single client he had ever served, or any signs of one's existence. He had an apartment out in the Sunset District, where he lived alone. His local record seemed to go back no farther than ten months, though we couldn't find its definite starting point. Apparently he had no relatives in San Francisco. He belonged to a couple of fashionable clubs. He was vaguely supposed to be "well connected in the East." He spent money.

I couldn't shadow Elwood, having too recently interviewed him. Dick Foley did. Elwood was seldom in his office during the first three days Dick tailed him. He was seldom in the financial district. He visited his clubs, he danced and tead and so forth, and each of those three days he visited a house on Telegraph Hill.

The first afternoon Dick had him, Elwood went to the Telegraph Hill house with a tall fair girl from Burlingame. The second day—in the evening—with a plump young woman who came out of a house out on Broadway. The third evening with a very young girl who seemed to live in the same building as he.

Usually Elwood and his companion spent from three to four hours in the house on Telegraph Hill. Other people—all apparently well-to-do—went in and out of the house while it was under Dick's eye.

I climbed Telegraph Hill to give the house the up-and-down. It was a large house—a big frame house painted egg-yellow. It hung dizzily on a shoulder of the hill, a shoulder that was sharp where rock had been quarried away. The house seemed about to go ski-ing down on the roofs far below.

It had no immediate neighbors. The approach was screened by bushes and trees.

I gave that section of the hill a good strong play, calling at all the houses within shooting distance of the yellow one. Nobody knew anything about it, or about its occupants. The folks on the Hill aren't a curious lot—perhaps because most of them have something to hide on their own account.

My climbing uphill and downhill got me nothing until I succeeded in learning who owned the yellow house. The owner was an estate whose affairs were in the hands of the West Coast Trust Company.

I took my investigations to the trust company, with some satisfaction. The house had been leased eight months ago by Raymond Elwood, acting for a client named T. F. Maxwell.

We couldn't find Maxwell. We couldn't find anybody who knew Maxwell. We couldn't find any evidence that Maxwell was anything but a name.

One of the operatives went up to the yellow house on the hill, and rang the bell for half an hour with no result. We didn't try that again, not wanting to stir things up at this stage.

I made another trip up the hill, house-hunting. I couldn't find a place as near the yellow house as I would have liked, but I succeeded in renting a three-room flat from which the approach to it could be watched.

Dick and I camped in the flat—with Pat Reddy, when he wasn't off on other duties—and watched machines turn into the screened path that led to the egg-tinted house. Afternoon and night there were machines. Most of them carried women. We saw no one we could place as a resident of the house. Elwood came daily, once alone, the other time with women whose faces we couldn't see from our window.

We shadowed some of the visitors away. They were without exception reasonably well off financially, and some were socially prominent. We didn't go up against any of them with talk. Even a carefully planned pretext is as likely as not to tip your mitt when you're up against a blind game.

Three days of this—and our break came.

It was early evening, just dark. Pat Reddy had phoned that he had been up on a job for two days and a night, and was going to sleep the clock around. Dick and I were sitting at the window of our flat, watching automobiles turn toward the yellow house, writing down their license numbers as they passed through the blue-white patch of light an arc-lamp put in the road just beyond our window.

A woman came climbing the hill, afoot. She was a tall woman, strongly built. A dark veil, not thick enough to advertise the fact that she wore it to hide her features, nevertheless did hide them. Her way was up the hill, past our flat, on the other side of the roadway.

A night-wind from the Pacific was creaking

a grocer's sign down below, swaying the arc-light above. The wind caught the woman as she passed out of our building's sheltered area. Coat and skirts tangled. She put her back to the wind, a hand to her hat. Her veil whipped out straight from her face.

Her face was a face from a photograph—Myra Banbrock's face.

Dick made her with me.

"Our Baby!" he cried, bouncing to his feet.

"Wait," I said. "She's going into the joint on the edge of the hill. Let her go. We'll go after her when she's inside. That's our excuse for frisking the joint."

I went into the next room, where our telephone was, and called Pat Reddy's number.

"She didn't go in," Dick called from the window. "She went past the path."

"After her!" I ordered. "There's no sense to that! What's the matter with her?" I felt sort of indignant about it. "She's got to go in! Tail her. I'll find you after I get Pat."

Dick went.

Pat's wife answered the telephone. I told her who I was.

"Will you shake Pat out of the covers and send him up here? He knows where I am. Tell him I want him in a hurry."

"I will," she promised. "I'll have him there in ten minutes—wherever it is."

Outdoors, I went up the road, hunting for Dick and Myra Banbrock. Neither was in sight. Passing the bushes that masked the yellow house, I went on, circling down a stony path to the left. No sign of either.

I turned back in time to see Dick going into our flat. I followed.

"She's in," he said when I joined him. "She went up the road, cut across through some bushes, came back to the edge of the cliff, and slid feet-first through a cellar window."

That was nice. The crazier the people you are sleuthing act, as a rule, the nearer you are to an ending of your troubles.

Reddy arrived within a minute or two of the time his wife had promised. He came in buttoning his clothes.

"What the hell did you tell Althea?" he growled at me. "She gave me an overcoat to put over my pajamas, dumped the rest of my clothes in the car, and I had to get in them on the way over."

"I'll cry with you after awhile," I dismissed his troubles. "Myra Banbrock just went into the joint through a cellar window. Elwood has been there an hour. Let's knock it off."

Pat is deliberate.

"We ought to have papers, even at that," he stalled.

"Sure," I agreed, "but you can get them fixed up afterward. That's what you're here for. Contra Costa county wants her—maybe to try her for murder. That's all the excuse we need to get into the joint. We go there for her. If we happen to run into anything else—well and good."

Pat finished buttoning his vest.

"Oh, all right!" he said sourly. "Have it your way. But if you get me smashed for searching a house without authority, you'll have to give me a job with your law-breaking agency."

"I will." I turned to Foley. "You'll have to stay outside, Dick. Keep your eye on the get-away. Don't bother anybody else, but if the Banbrock girl gets out, stay behind her."

"I expected it," Dick howled. "Any time there's any fun I can count on being stuck off somewhere on a street corner!"

VIII

Pat Reddy and I went straight up the bush-hidden path to the yellow house's front door, and rang the bell.

A big black man in a red fez, red silk jacket over red-striped silk shirt, red zouave pants and red slippers, opened the door. He filled the opening, framed in the black of the hall behind him.

"Is Mr. Maxwell home?" I asked.

The black man shook his head and said words in a language I don't know.

"Mr. Elwood, then?"

Another shaking of the head. More strange language.

"Let's see whoever is home then," I insisted.

Out of the jumble of words that meant nothing to me, I picked three in garbled English, which I thought were "master," "not," and "home."

The door began to close. I put a foot against it. Pat flashed his buzzer.[*]

Though the black man had poor English, he had knowledge of police badges.

One of his feet stamped on the floor behind him. A gong boomed deafeningly in the rear of the house.

The black man bent his weight to the door.

My weight on the foot that blocked the door, I leaned sidewise, swaying to the negro.

Slamming from the hip, I put my fist in the middle of him.

Reddy hit the door and we went into the hall.

"'Fore God, Fat Shorty," the black man gasped in good black Virginian, "you done hurt me!"

Reddy and I went by him, down the hall whose bounds were lost in darkness.

The bottom of a flight of steps stopped my feet.

A gun went off upstairs. It seemed to point at us. We didn't get the bullets.

A babel of voices—women screaming, men shouting—came and went upstairs; came and went as if a door was being opened and shut.

"Up, my boy!" Reddy yelped in my ear.

We went up the stairs. We didn't find the man who had shot at us.

At the head of the stairs, a door was locked. Reddy's bulk forced it.

We came into a bluish light. A large room, all purple and gold. Confusion of overturned furniture and rumpled rugs. A gray slipper lay near a

_____
* badge

far door. A green silk gown was in the center of the floor. No person was there.

I raced Pat to the curtained door beyond the slipper. The door was not locked. Reddy yanked it wide.

A room with three girls and a man crouching in a corner, fear in their faces. Neither of them was Myra Banbrock, or Raymond Elwood, or anyone we knew.

Our glances went away from them after the first quick look.

The open door across the room grabbed our attention.

The door gave to a small room.

The room was chaos.

A small room, packed and tangled with bodies. Live bodies, seething, writhing. The room was a funnel into which men and women had been poured. They boiled noisily toward the one small window that was the funnel's outlet. Men and women, youths and girls, screaming, struggling, squirming, fighting. Some had no clothes.

"We'll get through and block the window!" Pat yelled in my ear.

"Like hell—" I began, but he was gone ahead into the confusion.

I went after him.

I didn't mean to block the window. I meant to save Pat from his foolishness. No five men could have fought through that boiling turmoil of maniacs. No ten men could have turned them from the window.

Pat—big as he is—was down when I got to him. A half dressed girl—a child—was driving at his face with sharp high-heels. Hands, feet, were tearing him apart.

I cleared him with a play of gun-barrel on shins and wrists—dragged him back.

"Myra's not there!" I yelled into his ear as I helped him up. "Elwood's not there!"

I wasn't sure, but I hadn't seen them, and I doubted that they would be in this mess. These savages, boiling again to the window, with no attention for us, whoever they were, weren't insiders. They were the mob, and the principals shouldn't be among them.

"We'll try the other rooms," I yelled again. "We don't want these."

Pat rubbed the back of his hand across his torn face and laughed.

"It's a cinch I don't want 'em any more," he said.

We went back to the head of the stairs the way we had come. We saw no one. The man and girls who had been in the next room were gone.

At the head of the stairs we paused. There was no noise behind us except the now fainter babel of the lunatics fighting for their exit.

A door shut sharply downstairs.

A body came out of nowhere, hit my back, flattened me to the landing.

The feel of silk was on my cheek. A brawny hand was fumbling at my throat.

I bent my wrist until my gun, upside down, lay against my cheek. Praying for my ear, I squeezed.

My cheek took fire. My head was a roaring thing, about to burst.

The silk slid away.

Pat hauled me upright.

We started down the stairs.

Swish!

A thing came past my face, stirring my bared hair.

A thousand pieces of glass, china, plaster, exploded upward at my feet.

I tilted head and gun together.

A negro's red-silk arms were still spread over the balustrade above.

I sent him two bullets. Pat sent him two.

The negro teetered over the rail.

He came down on us, arms out-flung—a dead man's swan-dive.

We scurried down the stairs from under him.

He shook the house when he landed, but we weren't watching him then.

The smooth sleek head of Raymond Elwood took our attention.

In the light from above, it showed for a fur-tive split-second around the newel-post at the foot of the stairs. Showed and vanished.

Pat Reddy, closer to the rail than I, went over it in a one-hand vault down into the blackness below.

I made the foot of the stairs in two jumps, jerked myself around with a hand on the newel, and plunged into the suddenly noisy dark of the hall.

A wall I couldn't see hit me. Caroming off the opposite wall, I spun into a room whose curtained grayness was the light of day after the hall.

IX

Pat Reddy stood with one hand on a chair-back, holding his belly with the other. His face was mouse-colored under its blood. His eyes were glass agonies. He had the look of a man who had been kicked.

The grin he tried failed. He nodded toward the rear of the house. I went back.

In a little passageway I found Raymond Elwood.

He was sobbing and pulling frantically at a locked door. His face was the hard white of utter terror.

I measured the distance between us.

He turned as I jumped.

I put everything I had in the downswing of my gun-barrel—

A ton of meat and bone crashed into my back.

I went over against the wall, breathless, giddy, sick.

Red-silk arms that ended in brown hands locked around me.

I wondered if there was a whole regiment of these gaudy negroes—or if I was colliding with the same one over and over.

This one didn't let me do much thinking.

He was big. He was strong. He didn't mean any good.

My gun-arm was flat at my side, straight down. I tried a shot at one of the negro's feet. Missed. Tried again. He moved his feet. I wriggled around, half facing him.

Elwood piled on my other side.

The negro bent me backward, folding my spine on itself like an accordion.

I fought to hold my knees stiff. Too much weight was hanging on me. My knees sagged. My body curved back.

Pat Reddy, swaying in the doorway, shone over the negro's shoulder like the Angel Gabriel.

Gray pain was in Pat's face, but his eyes were clear. His right hand held a gun. His left was getting a blackjack out of his hip pocket.

He swung the sap down on the negro's shaven skull.

The black man wheeled away from me, shaking his head.

Pat hit him once more before the negro closed with him—hit him full in the face, but couldn't beat him off.

Twisting my freed gun-hand up, I drilled Elwood neatly through the chest, and let him slide down me to the floor.

The negro had Pat against the wall, bothering him a lot. His broad red back was a target.

But I had used five of the six bullets in my gun. I had more in my pocket, but reloading takes time.

I stepped out of Elwood's feeble hands, and went to work with the flat of my gun on the negro. There was a roll of fat where his skull and neck fit together. The third time I hit it, he flopped, taking Pat with him.

I rolled him off. The blond police detective—not very blond now—got up.

At the other end of the passageway, an open door showed an empty kitchen.

Pat and I went to the door that Elwood had been playing with. It was a solid piece of carpentering, and neatly fastened.

Yoking ourselves together, we began to beat the door with our combined three hundred and seventy or eighty pounds.

It shook, but held. We hit it again. Wood we couldn't see tore.

Again.

The door popped away from us. We went through—down a flight of steps—rolling, snowballing down—until a cement floor stopped us.

Pat came back to life first.

"You're a hell of an acrobat," he said. "Get off my neck!"

I stood up. He stood up. We seemed to be dividing the evening between falling on the floor and getting up from the floor.

A light-switch was at my shoulder. I turned it on.

If I looked anything like Pat, we were a fine pair of nightmares. He was all raw meat and dirt, with not enough clothes left to hide much of either.

I didn't like his looks, so I looked around the basement in which we stood. To the rear was a furnace, coal-bins and a woodpile. To the front was a hallway and rooms, after the manner of the upstairs.

The first door we tried was locked, but not strongly. We smashed through it into a photographer's dark-room.

The second door was unlocked, and put us in a chemical laboratory: retorts, tubes, burners and a small still. There was a little round iron stove in the middle of the room. No one was there.

We went out into the hallway and to the third door, not so cheerfully. This cellar looked like a bloomer.[*] We were wasting our time here, when we should have stayed upstairs. I tried the door.

It was firm beyond trembling.

We smacked it with our weight, together, experimentally. It didn't shake.

"Wait."

Pat went to the woodpile in the rear and came back with an axe.

He swung the axe against the door, flaking out a hunk of wood. Silvery points of light spar-

_____

[*] Australian for mistakes

kled in the hole. The other side of the door was an iron or steel plate.

Pat put the axe down and leaned on the helve.

"You write the next prescription," he said.

I didn't have anything to suggest, except:

"I'll camp here. You beat it upstairs, and see if any of your coppers have shown up. This is a God-forsaken hole, but somebody may have sent in an alarm. See if you can find another way into this room—a window, maybe—or man-power enough to get us in through this door."

Pat turned toward the steps.

A sound stopped him—the clicking of bolts on the other side of the iron-lined door.

A jump put Pat on one side of the frame. A step put me on the other.

Slowly the door moved in. Too slowly.

I kicked it open.

Pat and I went into the room on top of my kick.

His shoulder hit the woman. I managed to catch her before she fell.

Pat took her gun. I steadied her back on her feet.

Her face was a pale blank square.

She was Myra Banbrock, but she now had none of the masculinity that had been in her photographs and description.

Steadying her with one arm—which also served to block her arms—I looked around the room.

A small cube of a room whose walls were brown-painted metal. On the floor lay a queer little dead man.

A little man in tight-fitting black velvet and silk. Black velvet blouse and breeches, black silk stockings and skull cap, black patent leather pumps. His face was small and old and bony, but smooth as stone, without line or wrinkle.

A hole was in his blouse, where it fit high under his chin. The hole bled very slowly. The floor around him showed it had been bleeding faster a little while ago.

Beyond him, a safe was open. Papers were on the floor in front of it, as if the safe had been tilted to spill them out.

The girl moved against my arm.

"You killed him?" I asked.

"Yes," too faint to have been heard a yard away.

"Why?"

She shook her short brown hair out of her eyes with a tired jerk of her head.

"Does it make any difference?" she asked. "I did kill him."

"It might make a difference," I told her, taking my arm away, and going over to shut the door. People talk more freely in a room with a closed door. "I happen to be in your father's employ. Mr. Reddy is a police detective. Of course, neither of us can smash any laws, but if you'll tell us what's what, maybe we can help you."

"My father's employ?" she questioned.

"Yes. When you and your sister disappeared, he engaged me to find you. We found your sister, and—"

Life came into her face and eyes and voice.

"I didn't kill Ruth!" she cried. "The papers lied! I didn't kill her! I didn't know she had the revolver. I didn't know it! We were going away to hide from—from everything. We stopped in the woods to burn the—those things. That's the first time I knew she had the revolver. We had talked about suicide at first, but I had persuaded her—thought I had persuaded her—not to. I tried to take the revolver away from her, but I couldn't. She shot herself while I was trying to get it away. I tried to stop her. I didn't kill her!"

This was getting somewhere.

"And then?" I encouraged her.

"And then I went to Sacramento and left the car there, and came back to San Francisco. Ruth told me she had written Raymond Elwood a letter. She told me that before I persuaded her not to kill herself—the first time. I tried to get the letter from Raymond. She had written him she was going to kill herself. I tried to get the letter, but Raymond said he had given it to Hador.

"So I came here this evening to get it. I had just found it when there was a lot of noise upstairs. Then Hador came in and found me. He bolted the door. And—and I shot him with the revolver that was in the safe. I—I shot him when he turned around, before he could say anything. It had to be that way, or I couldn't."

"You mean you shot him without being threatened or attacked by him?" Pat asked.

"Yes. I was afraid of him, afraid to let him speak. I hated him! I couldn't help it. It had to be that way. If he had talked I couldn't have shot him. He—he wouldn't have let me!"

"Who was this Hador?" I asked.

She looked away from Pat and me, at the walls, at the ceiling, at the queer little dead man on the floor.

X

"He was a—" She cleared her throat, and started again, staring down at her feet. "Raymond Elwood brought us here the first time. We thought it was funny. But Hador was a devil. He told you things and you believed them. You couldn't help it. He told you *everything* and you believed it. Perhaps we were drugged. There was always a warm bluish wine. It must have been drugged. We couldn't have done those things if it hadn't. Nobody would—He called himself a priest—a priest of Alzoa. He taught a freeing of the spirit from the flesh by—"

Her voice broke huskily. She shuddered.

"It was horrible!" she went on presently in the silence Pat and I had left for her. "But you believed him. That is the whole thing. You can't understand it unless you understand that. The things he taught could not be so. But he said they were, and you *believed* they were. Or maybe—I don't know—maybe you pretended you believed them, because you were crazy and drugs were in your blood. We came back again and again, for weeks, months, before the disgust that had to come drove us away.

"We stopped coming, Ruth and I—and Irma. And then we found out what he was. He demanded money, more money than we had been paying while we believed—or pretended

belief—in his cult. We couldn't give him the money he demanded. I told him we wouldn't. He sent us photographs—of us—taken during the—the times here. They were—*pictures—you—couldn't—explain*. And they were true! We knew them true! What could we do? He said he would send copies to our father, every friend, everyone we knew—unless we paid.

"What could we do—except pay? We got the money somehow. We gave him money—more—more—more. And then we had no more—could get no more. We didn't know what to do! There was nothing to do, except—Ruth and Irma wanted to kill themselves. I thought of that, too. But I persuaded Ruth not to. I said we'd go away. I'd take her away—keep her safe. And then—then—this!"

She stopped talking, went on staring at her feet.

I looked again at the little dead man on the floor, weird in his black cap and clothes. No more blood came from his throat.

It wasn't hard to put the pieces together. This dead Hador, self-ordained priest of something or other, staging orgies under the alias of religious ceremonies. Elwood, his confederate, bringing women of family and wealth to him. A room lighted for photography, with a concealed camera. Contributions from his converts so long as they were faithful to the cult. Blackmail—with the help of the photographs—afterward.

I looked from Hador to Pat Reddy. He was scowling at the dead man. No sound came from outside the room.

"You have the letter your sister wrote Elwood?" I asked the girl.

Her hand flashed to her bosom, and crinkled paper there.

"Yes."

"It says plainly she meant to kill herself?"

"Yes."

"That ought to square her with Contra Costa county," I said to Pat.

He nodded his battered head.

"It ought to," he agreed. "It's not likely that they could prove murder on her even without that letter. With it, they'll not take her into court. That's a safe bet. Another is that she won't have any trouble over this shooting. She'll come out of court free, and thanked in the bargain."

Myra Banbrock flinched away from Pat as if he had hit her in the face.

I was her father's hired man just now. I saw her side of the affair.

I lit a cigarette and studied what I could see of Pat's face through blood and grime. Pat is a right guy.

"Listen, Pat," I wheedled him, though with a voice that was as if I were not trying to wheedle him at all. "Miss Banbrock can go into court and come out free and thanked, as you say. But to do it, she's got to use everything she knows. She's got to have all the evidence there is. She's got to use all those photographs Hador took—or all we can find of them.

"Some of those pictures have sent women to suicide, Pat—at least two that we know. If Miss Banbrock goes into court, we've got to make the photographs of God knows how many other women public property. We've got to advertise things that will put Miss Banbrock—and you can't say how many other women and girls—in a position that at least two women have killed themselves to escape."

Pat scowled at me and rubbed his dirty chin with a dirtier thumb.

I took a deep breath and made my play.

"Pat, you and I came here to question Raymond Elwood, having traced him here. Maybe we suspected him of being tied up with the mob that knocked over the St. Louis bank last month. Maybe we suspected him of handling the stuff that was taken from the mail cars in that stick-up near Denver week before last. Anyway, we were after him, knowing that he had a lot of money that came from nowhere, and a real estate office that did no real estate business.

"We came here to question him in connection with one of these jobs I've mentioned. We were jumped by a couple of the shines upstairs when they found we were sleuths. The rest of it

grew out of that. This religious cult business was just something we ran into, and didn't interest us especially. So far as we knew, all these folks jumped us just through friendship for the man we were trying to question. Hador was one of them, and, tussling with you, you shot him with his own gun, which, of course, is the one Miss Banbrock found in the safe."

Reddy didn't seem to like my suggestion at all. The eyes with which he regarded me were decidedly sour.

"You're goofy," he accused me. "What'll that get anybody? That won't keep Miss Banbrock out of it. She's here, isn't she, and the rest of it will come out like thread off a spool."

"But Miss Banbrock *wasn't* here," I explained. "Maybe the upstairs is full of coppers by now. Maybe not. Anyway, you're going to take Miss Banbrock out of here and turn her over to Dick Foley, who will take her home. She's got nothing to do with this party. Tomorrow she, and her father's lawyer, and I, will all go up to Martinez and make a deal with the prosecuting attorney of Contra Costa county. We'll show him how Ruth killed herself. If somebody happens to connect the Elwood who I hope is dead upstairs with the Elwood who knew the girls and Mrs. Correll, what of it? If we keep out of court—as we'll do by convincing the Contra Costa people they can't possibly convict her of her sister's murder—we'll keep out of the newspapers—and out of trouble."

Pat hung fire, thumb still to chin.

"Remember," I urged him, "it's not only Miss Banbrock we're doing this for. It's a couple of dead ones, and a flock of live ones, who certainly got mixed up with Hador of their own accords, but who don't stop being human beings on that account."

Pat shook his head stubbornly.

"I'm sorry," I told the girl with faked hopelessness. "I've done all I can, but it's a lot to ask of Reddy. I don't know that I blame him for being afraid to take a chance on—"

Pat is Irish.

"Don't be so damned quick to fly off," he snapped at me, cutting short my hypocrisy. "But why do I have to be the one that shot this Hador? Why not you?"

I had him!

"Because," I explained, "you're a bull and I'm not. There'll be less chance of a slip-up if he was shot by a bona fide, star-wearing, flat-footed officer of the peace. I killed most of those birds upstairs. You ought to do something to show you were here."

That was only part of the truth. My idea was that if Pat took the credit, he couldn't very well ease himself out afterward, no matter what happened. Pat's a right guy, and I'd trust him anywhere—but you can trust a man just as easily if you have him sewed up.

Pat grumbled and shook his head, but:

"I'm ruining myself, I don't doubt," he growled, "but I'll do it, this once."

"Attaboy!" I went over to pick up the girl's hat from the corner in which it lay. "I'll wait here until you come back from turning her over to Dick." I gave the girl her hat and orders together. "You go to your home with the man Reddy turns you over to. Stay there until I come, which will be as soon as I can make it. Don't tell anybody anything, except that I told you to keep quiet. That includes your father. Tell him I told you not to tell him even where you saw me. Got it?"

"Yes, and I—"

Gratitude is nice to think about afterward, but it takes time when there's work to be done.

"Get going, Pat!"

They went.

XI

As soon as I was alone with the dead man I stepped over him and knelt in front of the safe, pushing letters and papers away, hunting for photographs. None was in sight. One compartment of the safe was locked.

I frisked the corpse. No key. The locked compartment wasn't very strong, but neither am I the best safe-burglar in the West. It took me a while to get into it.

What I wanted was there. A thick sheaf of negatives. A stack of prints—half a hundred of them.

I started to run through them, hunting for the Banbrock girls' pictures. I wanted to have them pocketed before Pat came back. I didn't know how much farther he would let me go.

Luck was against me—and the time I had wasted getting into the compartment. He was back before I had got past the sixth print in the stack. Those six had been—pretty bad.

"Well, that's done," Pat growled at me as he came into the room. "Dick's got her. Elwood is dead, and so is the only one of the negroes I saw upstairs. Everybody else seems to have beat it. No bulls have shown—so I put in a call for a wagonful."

I stood up, holding the sheaf of negatives in one hand, the prints in the other.

"What's all that?" he asked.

I went after him again.

"Photographs. You've just done me a big favor, Pat, and I'm not hoggish enough to ask another. But I'm going to put something in front of you, Pat. I'll give you the lay, and you can name it.

"These"—I waved the pictures at him—"are Hador's meal-tickets—the photos he was either collecting on or planning to collect on. They're photographs of people, Pat, mostly women and girls, and some of them are pretty rotten.

"If tomorrow's papers say that a flock of photos were found in this house after the fireworks, there's going to be a fat suicide-list in the next day's papers, and a fatter list of disappearances. If the papers say nothing about the photos, the lists may be a little smaller, but not much. Some of the people whose pictures are here know they are here. They will expect the police to come hunting for them. We know this much about the photographs—two women have killed themselves to get away from them. This is an armful of stuff that can dynamite a lot of people, Pat, and a lot of families—no matter which of those two ways the papers read.

"But, suppose, Pat, the papers say that just before you shot Hador he succeeded in burning a lot of pictures and papers, burning them beyond recognition. Isn't it likely, then, that there won't be any suicides? That some of the disappearances of recent months may clear themselves up? There she is, Pat—you name it."

Looking back, it seems to me I had come a lot nearer being eloquent than ever before in my life.

But Pat didn't applaud.

He cursed me. He cursed me thoroughly, bitterly, and with an amount of feeling that told me I had won another point in my little game.

He called me more things than I ever listened to before from a man who was built of meat and bone, and who therefore could be smacked.

When he was through, we carried the papers and photographs and a small book of addresses we found in the safe into the next room, and fed them to the little round iron stove there. The last of them was ash before we heard the police overhead.

"That's absolutely all!" Pat declared when we got up from our work. "Don't ever ask me to do anything else for you if you live to be a thousand."

"That's absolutely all," I echoed.

I LIKE Pat. He is a right guy. The sixth photograph in the stack had been of his wife—the coffee importer's reckless, hot-eyed daughter.

BLACK MASK, SEPTEMBER 1925

Corkscrew

BY DASHIELL HAMMETT

A STORY OF THE CONTINENTAL SLEUTH

BOILING LIKE A COFFEE POT before we were five miles out of Filmer, the automobile stage carried me south into the shimmering heat, blinding sunlight, and bitter white dust of the Arizona desert.

I was the only passenger. The driver felt as little like talking as I. All morning we rode through cactus-spiked, sage-studded oven-country, without conversation, except when the driver cursed the necessity of stopping to feed his clattering machine more water. The car crept through soft sifting sand; wound between steep-walled red mesas; dipped into dry arroyas where clumps of dusty mesquite were like white lace in the glare; and skirted sharp-edged barrancos.

All these things were hot. All of them tried to get rid of their heat by throwing it on the car. My fat melted in the heat. The heat dried my perspiration before I could feel its moisture. The dazzling light scorched my eyeballs; puckered my lids; cooked my mouth. Alkali stung my nose; was gritty between my teeth.

It was a nice ride! I understood why the natives were a hard lot. A morning like this would put any man in a mood to kill his brother, and would fry his brother into not caring whether he was killed.

The sun climbed up in the brazen sky. The higher it got, the larger and hotter it got. I wondered how much hotter it would have to get to explode the cartridges in the gun under my arm. Not that it mattered—if it got any hotter, we would all blow up anyway. Car, desert, chauffeur and I would all bang out of existence in one explosive flash. I didn't care if we did!

That was my frame of mind as we pushed up a long slope, topped a sharp ridge, and slid down into Corkscrew.

Corkscrew wouldn't have been impressive at any time. It especially wasn't this white-hot Sunday afternoon. One sandy street following the crooked edge of the Tirabuzon Cañon, from which, by translation, the town took its name. A town, it was called, but village would have been flattery: fifteen or eighteen shabby buildings slumped along the irregular street, with tumbledown shacks leaning against them, squatting close to them, and trying to sneak away from them.

That was Corkscrew. One look at it, and I believed all I had heard about it!

In the street, four dusty automobiles cooked. Between two buildings I could see a corral where half a dozen horses bunched their dejection under a shed. No person was in sight. Even the stage driver, carrying a limp and apparently empty mail sack, had vanished into a building labelled "Adderly's Emporium."

Gathering up my two gray-powdered bags, I climbed out and crossed the road to where a weather-washed sign, on which Cañon House was barely visible, hung over the door of a two-story, iron-roofed, adobe house.

I crossed the wide, unpainted and unpeopled porch, and pushed a door open with my foot, going into a dining-room, where a dozen men and a woman sat eating at oilcloth-covered tables. In one corner of the room, was a cashier's desk; and, on the wall behind it, a key-rack. Between rack and desk, a pudgy man whose few remaining hairs were the exact shade of his sallow skin, sat on a stool, and pretended he didn't see me.

"A room and a lot of water," I said, dropping my bags, and reaching for the glass that sat on top of a cooler in the corner.

"You can have your room," the sallow man growled, "but water won't do you no good. You

won't no sooner drink and wash, than you'll be thirsty and dirty all over again. Where in hell is that register?"

He couldn't find it, so he pushed an old envelope across the desk at me.

"Register on the back of that. Be with us a spell?"

"Most likely."

A chair upset behind me.

I turned around as a lanky man with enormous red ears reared himself upright with the help of his hands on the table—one of them flat in the plate of ham and eggs he had been eating.

"Ladiesh an' gentsh," he solemnly declaimed, "th' time hash came for yuh t' give up y'r evil waysh an' git out y'r knittin'. Th' law hash came to Orilla County!"

The drunk bowed to me, upset his ham and eggs, and sat down again. The other diners applauded with thump of knives and forks on tables and dishes.

I looked them over while they looked me over. A miscellaneous assortment: weather-beaten horsemen, clumsily muscled laborers, men with the pasty complexions of night workers. The one woman in the room didn't belong to Arizona. She was a thin girl of maybe twenty-five, with too-bright dark eyes, dark, short hair, and a sharp prettiness that was the mark of a larger settlement than this. You've seen her, or her sisters, in the larger cities, in the places that get going after the theaters let out.

The man with her was range country—a slim lad in the early twenties, not very tall, with pale blue eyes that were startling in so dark-tanned a face. His features were a bit too perfect in their clean-cut regularity.

"So you're the new deputy sheriff?" the sallow man questioned the back of my head.

Somebody had kept my secret right out in the open! There was no use trying to cover up.

"Yes." I hid my annoyance under a grin that took in him and the diners. "But I'll trade my star right now for that room and water we were talking about."

He took me through the dining-room and

upstairs to a board-walled room in the rear second floor, said, "This is it," and left me.

I did what I could with the water in a pitcher on the washstand to free myself from the white grime I had accumulated. Then I dug a gray shirt and a suit of whipcords out of my bags, and holstered my gun under my left shoulder, where it wouldn't be a secret.

In each side pocket of my coat I stowed a new .32 automatic—small, snub-nosed affairs that weren't much better than toys. Their smallness let me carry them where they'd be close to my hands without advertising the fact that the gun under my shoulder wasn't all my arsenal.

The dining-room was empty when I went downstairs again. The sallow pessimist who ran the place stuck his head out of a door.

"Any chance of getting something to eat?" I asked.

"Hardly any," jerking his head toward a sign that said:

"Meals 6 to 8 A.M., 12 to 2 and 5 to 7 P.M."

"You can grub up at the Jew's—if you ain't particular," he added sourly.

I went out, across the porch that was too hot for idlers, and into the street that was empty for the same reason. Huddled against the wall of a large one-story adobe building, which had Border Palace painted all across its front, I found the Jew's.

It was a small shack—three wooden walls stuck against the adobe wall of the Border Palace—jammed with a lunch counter, eight stools, a stove, a handful of cooking implements, half the flies in the world, an iron cot behind a half-drawn burlap curtain, and the proprietor. The interior had once been painted white. It was a smoky grease-color now, except where homemade signs said:

"Meals At All Hours. No Credit" and gave the prices of various foods. These signs were a fly-specked yellow-gray.

The proprietor wasn't a Jew—an Armenian or something of the sort, I thought. He was a small man, old, scrawny, dark-skinned, wrinkled and cheerful.

"You the new sheriff?" he asked, and when he grinned I saw he had no teeth.

"Deputy," I admitted, "and hungry. I'll eat anything you've got that won't bite back, and that won't take long to get ready."

"Sure!" He turned to his stove and began banging pans around. "We need sheriffs," he said over his shoulder. "Sure, we need them!"

"Somebody been picking on you?"

He showed his empty gums in another grin.

"Nobody pick on me—I tell you that!" He flourished a stringy hand at a sugar barrel under the shelves behind his counter. "I fix them decidedly!"

A shotgun butt stuck out of the barrel. I pulled it out: a double-barrel shotgun with the barrels sawed off short: a mean weapon close up.

I slid it back into its resting place as the old man began thumping dishes down in front of me.

II

The food inside me and a cigarette burning, I went out into the crooked street again. From the Border Palace came the clicking of pool balls. I followed the sound through the door.

In a large room, four men were leaning over a couple of pool tables, while five or six more watched them from chairs along the wall. On one side of the room was an oak bar, with nobody behind it. Through an open door in the rear came the sound of shuffling cards.

A big man whose paunch was dressed in a white vest, over a shirt in the bosom of which a diamond sparkled, came toward me; his triple-chinned red face expanding into the professionally jovial smile of a confidence man.

"I'm Bardell," he greeted me, stretching out a fat and shiny-nailed hand on which more diamonds glittered. "This is my joint. I'm glad to know you, sheriff! By God, we need you, and I hope you can spend a lot of your time here.

These waddies"*—and he chuckled, nodding at the pool players—"cut up rough on me sometimes, and I'm glad there's going to be somebody around who can handle them."

I let him pump my hand up and down.

"Let me make you known to the boys," he went on, turning with one arm across my shoulders. "These are Circle H. A. R. riders"—waving some of his rings at the pool players—"except this Milk River hombre, who, being a peeler,† kind of looks down on ordinary hands."

The Milk River hombre was the slender youth who had sat beside the girl in the Cañon House dining-room. His companions were young—though not quite so young as he—sun-marked, wind-marked, pigeontoed in high-heeled boots. Buck Small was sandy and pop-eyed; Smith was sandy and short; Dunne was a rangy Irishman.

The men watching the game were mostly laborers from the Orilla Colony, or hands from some of the smaller ranches in the neighborhood. There were two exceptions: Chick Orr, short, thick-bodied, heavy-armed, with the shapeless nose, battered ears, gold front teeth and gnarled hands of a pugilist; and Gyp Rainey, a slack-chinned, ratty individual whose whole front spelled cocaine.

Conducted by Bardell, I went into the back room to meet the poker players. There were only four of them. The other six card tables, the keno outfit, and the dice table were idle.

One of the players was the big-eared drunk who had made the welcoming speech at the hotel. Slim Vogel was the name. He was a Circle H. A. R. hand, as was Red Wheelan, who sat beside him. Both of them were full of hooch. The third player was a quiet, middle-aged man named Keefe. Number four was Mark Nisbet, a pale, slim man. Gambler was written all over him, from his heavy-lidded brown eyes to the slender sureness of his white fingers.

Nisbet and Vogel didn't seem to be getting along so good.

It was Nisbet's deal, and the pot had already been opened. Vogel, who had twice as many chips as anybody else, threw away two cards.

"I want both of 'em off'n th' top—this time!" and he didn't say it nicely.

Nisbet dealt the cards, with nothing in his appearance to show he had heard the crack. Red Wheelan took three cards. Keefe was out. Nisbet drew one. Wheelan bet. Nisbet stayed. Vogel raised. Wheelan stayed. Nisbet raised. Vogel bumped it again. Wheelan dropped out. Nisbet raised once more.

"I'm bettin' you took *your* draw off'n th' top, too," Vogel snarled across the table at Nisbet, and tilted the pot again.

Nisbet called. He had aces over kings. The cowpuncher had three nines.

Vogel laughed noisily as he raked in the chips.

"'F I could keep a sheriff behind you t' watch you all th' time, I'd do somethin' for myself!"

Nisbet pretended to be busy straightening his chips. I sympathized with him. He had played his hand rotten—but how else can you play against a drunk?

"How d'you like our little town?" Red Wheelan asked me.

"I haven't seen much of it yet," I stalled. "The hotel, the lunch-counter—they're all I've seen outside of here."

Wheelan laughed.

"So you met the Jew? That's Slim's friend!"

Everybody except Nisbet laughed, including Slim Vogel.

"Slim tried to beat the Jew out of two bits' worth of Java and sinkers‡ once. He says he forgot to pay for 'em, but it's more likely he sneaked out. Anyways, the next day, here comes the Jew, stirring dust into the ranch, a shotgun under his arm. He'd lugged that instrument of destruction fifteen miles across the desert, on foot, to collect his two bits. He collected, too! He took his little two bits away from Slim right there between the corral and the bunkhouse—at the cannon's mouth, as you might say!"

---

* cowboys; cattle rustlers
† specialist in breaking horses

---

‡ doughnut-like cake

Slim Vogel grinned ruefully and scratched one of his big ears.

"The old son-of-a-gun done came after me just like I was a damned thief! 'F he'd of been a man I'd of seen him in hell 'fore I'd of gave it to him. But what can y' do with an old buzzard that ain't even got no teeth to bite you with?"

His bleary eyes went back to the table, and the laughter went out of them. The laugh on his loose lips changed to a sneer.

"Let's play," he growled, glaring at Nisbet. "It's a honest man's deal this time!"

Bardell and I went back to the front of the building, where the cowboys were still knocking the balls around. I sat in one of the chairs against the wall, and let them talk around me. The conversation wasn't exactly fluent. Anybody could tell there was a stranger present.

My first job was to get over that.

"Got any idea," I asked nobody in particular, "where I could pick up a horse? One that can run pretty good, but that isn't too tricky for a bum rider to sit."

The Milk River hombre was playing the seven ball in a side pocket. He made the shot, and his pale eyes looked at the pocket into which the ball had gone for a couple of seconds before he straightened up. Lanky Dunne was looking fixedly at nothing, his mouth puckered a bit. Buck Small's pop-eyes were intent on the tip of his cue.

"You might get one at Echlin's stable," Milk River said slowly, meeting my gaze with guileless blue eyes; "though it ain't likely he's got anything that'll live long if you hurry it. I tell you what—Peery, out to the ranch, has got a buckskin that'd just fit you. He won't want to let him go, but if you took some real money along and flapped it in his face, maybe you could deal. He does need money."

"You're not steering me into a horse I can't handle, are you?" I asked.

The pale eyes went blank.

"I ain't steering you into nothing whatsomever, Mister," he said. "You asked for information. I give it to you. But I don't mind telling you

that anybody that can stay in a rocking chair can sit that buckskin."

"That's fine. I'll go out tomorrow."

Milk River put his cue down, frowning.

"Come to think of it, Peery's going down to the lower camp tomorrow. I tell you—if you got nothing else to do, we'll mosey out there right now. It's Sunday, and we'll be sure of catching him."

"Good," I said, and stood up.

"You boys going home?" Milk River asked his companions.

"Yeah," Smith spoke casually. "We gotta roll out early in the mornin', so I s'pose we'd ought to be shakin' along out there. I'll see if Slim an' Red are ready."

They weren't. Vogel's disagreeable voice came through the open door.

"I'm camped right here! I got this reptile on th' run, an' it's only a matter o' time 'fore he'll have t' take a chance on pullin' 'em off'n th' bottom t' save his hide. An' that's exac'ly what I'm awaitin' for! Th' first time he gets fancy, I'm goin' t' open him up from his Adam's apple plumb down to his ankles!"

Smith returned to us.

"Slim an' Red are gonna play 'em a while. They'll git a lift out when they git enough."

Milk River, Smith, Dunne, Small and I went out of the Border Palace.

III

Three steps from the door, a stooped, white-mustached man in a collarless stiff-bosomed shirt swooped down on me, as if he had been lying in wait.

"My name's Adderly," he introduced himself, holding out one hand toward me while flicking the other at Adderly's Emporium. "Got a minute or two to spare? I'd like to make you acquainted with some of the folks."

The Circle H. A. R. men were walking slowly toward one of the machines in the street.

"Can you wait a couple of minutes?" I called after them.

Milk River looked back over his shoulder.

"Yes. We got to gas and water the flivver. Take yor time."

Adderly led me toward his store, talking as he walked.

"Some of the better element is at my house—danged near all the better element. The folks who'll back you up if you'll put the fear of God in Corkscrew. We're tired and sick of this perpetual hell-raising."

We went through his store, across a yard, and into his house. There were a dozen or more people in his living-room.

The Reverend Dierks—a gangling, emaciated man with a tight mouth in a long, thin face—made a speech at me. He called me brother, he told me what a wicked place Corkscrew was, and he told me he and his friends were prepared to swear out warrants for the arrest of various men who had committed sixty-some crimes during the past two years.

He had a list of them, with names, dates, and hours, which he read to me. Everybody I had met that day—except those here—was on that list at least once, along with a lot of names I didn't know. The crimes ranged from murder to intoxication and the use of profane language.

"If you'll let me have that list, I'll study it," I promised.

He gave it to me, but he wasn't to be put off with promises.

"To refrain even for an hour from punishing wickedness is to be a partner to that wickedness, brother. You have been inside that house of sin operated by Bardell. You have heard the Sabbath desecrated with the sound of pool-balls. You have smelled the foul odor of illegal rum on men's breaths!

"Strike now, brother! Let it not be said that you condoned evil from your first day in Corkscrew! You have seen men whose garments did not conceal the deadly weapons under them! In that list is the black record of many months' unatoned sinfulness. Strike now, brother, for the Lord and righteousness! Go into those hells and do your duty as an officer of the law and a Christian!"

This was a minister; I didn't like to laugh.

I looked at the others. They were sitting—men and women—on the edges of their chairs. On their faces were the same expressions you see around a prize ring just before the gong rings.

Mrs. Echlin, the livery man's wife, an angular-faced, angular-bodied woman, caught my gaze with her pebble-hard eyes.

"And that brazen scarlet woman who calls herself Señora Gaia—and the three hussies who pretend they're her daughters! You ain't much of a deputy sheriff if you leave 'em in that house of theirs one night longer—to poison the manhood of Orilla County!"

The others nodded vigorously. Echlin's eyes had lit up at his wife's words, and he licked his lips as he nodded.

Miss Janey, school teacher, false-toothed, sour-faced, put in her part:

"And even worse than those—those creatures, is that Clio Landes! Worse, because at least those—those hussies"—she looked down, managed a blush, looked out of the corners of her eyes at the minister—"those hussies are at least openly what they are. While she—who knows how bad she really is?"

"I don't know about her," Adderly began, but his wife shut him up.

"I do!" she snapped. She was a large, mustached woman whose corsets made knobs and points in her shiny black dress. "Miss Janey is perfectly right. That woman is worse than the rest!"

"Is this Clio Landes person on your list?" I asked, not remembering it.

"No, brother, she is not," the Reverend Dierks said regretfully. "But only because she is more subtle than the others. Corkscrew would indeed be better without her—a woman of obviously low moral standards, with no visible means of support, associating with our worst element."

"I'm glad to have met you folks," I said as I

folded the list and put it in my pocket. "And I'm glad to know you'll back me up."

I edged toward the door, hoping to get away without much more talk. Not a chance. The Reverend Dierks followed me up.

"You will strike now, brother? You will carry God's war immediately into blind tiger and brothel and gambling hell?"

The others were on their feet now, closing in.

"I'll have to look things over first," I stalled.

"Brother, are you evading your duty? Are you procrastinating in the face of Satan? If you are the man I hope you are, you will march now, with the decent citizens of Corkscrew at your heels, to wipe from the face of our town the sin that blackens it!"

So that was it. I was to lead one of these vice-crusading mobs. I wondered how many of these crusaders would be standing behind me if one of the devil's representatives took a shot at me. The minister maybe—his thin face was grimly pugnacious. But I couldn't imagine what good he'd be in a row. The others would scatter at the first sign of trouble.

I stopped playing politics and said my say.

"I'm glad to have your support," I said, "but there isn't going to be any wholesale raiding—not for a while, anyway. Later, I'll try to get around to the bootleggers and gamblers and similar small fry, though I'm not foolish enough to think I can put them all out of business. Just now, so long as they don't cut up too rough, I don't expect to bother them. I haven't the time.

"This list you've given me—I'll do what I think ought to be done after I've examined it, but I'm not going to worry a lot over a batch of petty misdemeanors that happened a year ago. I'm starting from scratch. What happens from now on is what interests me. See you later."

And I left.

The cowboys' car was standing in front of the store when I came out.

"I've been meeting the better element," I explained as I found a place in it between Milk River and Buck Small.

Milk River's brown face wrinkled around his eyes.

"Then you know what kind of riff-raff we are," he said.

IV

Dunne driving, the car carried us out of Corkscrew at the street's southern end, and then west along the sandy and rocky bottom of a shallow draw. The sand was deep and the rocks were numerous; we didn't make very good time. An hour and a half of jolting, sweltering and smothering in this draw, and we climbed up out of it and crossed to a larger and greener draw, where the mesquite grew in small trees and bees zizzed among wild flowers.

Around a bend in this draw the Circle H. A. R. buildings sat. We got out of the automobile under a low shed, where another car already stood. A heavily muscled, heavily boned man came around a white-washed building toward us. His face was square and dark. His close-clipped mustache and deep-set small eyes were dark.

This, I learned, was Peery, who bossed the ranch for the owner, who lived in the East.

"He wants a nice, mild horse," Milk River told Peery, "and we thought maybe you might sell him that Rollo horse of yours. That's the nicest, mildest horse I ever heard tell of."

Peery tilted his high-crowned sombrero back on his head and rocked on his heels.

"What was you figuring on paying for this here horse?"

"If it suits me," I said, "I'm willing to pay what it takes to buy him."

"That ain't so bad," he said. "S'pose one of you boys dab a rope on that buckskin and bring him around for the gent to look at."

Smith and Dunne set out together, pretending they weren't going eagerly.

"Where's Red and Slim?" Peery asked.

"Stayin' in a while," Small told him. "Slim's a million ahead in a poker game."

Presently the two cowhands came back, riding, with the buckskin between them, already saddled and bridled. I noticed each of them had a rope on him. He was a loose-jointed pony of an unripe lemon color, with a sad, drooping, Roman-nosed head.

"There he is," Peery said. "Try him out and we'll talk dinero. I warn you, I ain't so damned anxious to get rid of him that I'll let him go for nothing. But you try him first—trot him down the draw a little ways and back. He's downright sweet."

I chucked away my cigarette and went over to the buckskin. He cocked one mournful eye at me, twitched one ear, and went on looking sadly at the ground. Dunne and Smith took their lines off him, and I got into the saddle.

Rollo stood still under me until the other horses had left his side.

Then he showed me what he had.

He went straight up in the air—and hung there long enough to turn around before he came down. He stood on his front feet and then on his hind ones, and then he got off all of them again.

I didn't like this, but it wasn't a surprise. I had known I was a lamb being led to the slaughter. This was the third time it had happened to me. I might as well get it over with. A city man in range country is bound to find himself sitting on a disagreeable bone sooner or later. I'm a city man. I can sit any street car or taxicab in the world, and I can even ride a horse if he'll coöperate. But when the horse doesn't want to stay under me—the horse wins.

Rollo was going to win. I wasn't foolish enough to waste strength fighting him.

So the next time he traded ends, I went away from him, holding myself limp, so the tumble wouldn't ruin me.

Smith had caught the yellow pony, and was holding its head, when I took my knees off my forehead and stood up.

Peery, squatting on his heels, was frowning at me. Milk River was looking at Rollo with what was supposed to be a look of utter amazement.

"Now whatever did you do to Rollo to make him act thataway?" Peery asked me.

"Maybe he was only fooling," I suggested. "I'll try him again."

Once more Rollo stood still and sad until I was securely up on him. Then he went into convulsions under me—convulsions that lasted until I piled on my neck and one shoulder in a clump of brush.

I stood up, rubbing my left shoulder, which had hit a rock. Smith was holding the buckskin. The faces of all five men were serious and solemn—too serious and solemn.

"Maybe he don't like you," Buck Small gave his opinion.

"Might be," I admitted as I climbed into the saddle for the third time.

The lemon-tinted devil was getting warmed up by now, was beginning to take pride in his work. He let me stay aboard longer than before, so he could slam me off harder.

I was sick when I hit the ground in front of Peery and Milk River. It took me a little while to get up, and I had to stand still for a moment, until I could feel the ground under my feet.

"Hold him a couple of seconds—" I began.

Peery's big frame stood in front of me.

"That's enough," he said. "I ain't going to have you killed on my hands."

I shook my head violently, trying to clear it, so I could see him better.

"Get out of my way," I growled. "I like this. I want more of it."

"You don't top my pony no more," he growled back at me. "He ain't used to playing so rough. You're liable to hurt him, falling off carelessly like that."

I tried to get past him. He barred my way with a thick arm. I drove my right fist at his dark face.

He went back, busy trying to keep his feet under him.

I went over and hoisted myself up on Rollo.

I had the buckskin's confidence by this time. We were old friends. He didn't mind showing me his secret stuff. He did things no horse could possibly do. Looking down, I was surprised not to see his kidneys and liver—because I knew damned well he was turning himself inside out.

I landed in the same clump of brush that had got me once before.

I couldn't see much when I got up—only the yellow of Rollo.

I heard Peery's bass voice, protesting to somebody:

"No, let the damned fool kill himself if he wants to."

I heaved myself wearily into the saddle again.

For a while I thought Rollo had had enough. He was a well-behaved animal under me. That was fine. I had ridden him at last.

Nonsense! He was fooling.

He put his nose in the sand. He put it in the sky. And, using his head for a base, he wagged his body as a puppy would wag its tail.

I went away from him—and stayed where I landed.

I didn't know whether I could have got up again if I had wanted to. But I didn't want to. I closed my eyes and rested. If I hadn't done what I had set out to do, I was willing to fail.

Small, Dunne and Milk River carried me indoors and spread me on a bunk.

"I don't think that horse would be much good to me," I told them. "Maybe I'd better look at another."

"You don't want to get discouraged like that," Small advised me.

"You better lay still and rest, fella," Milk River said. "You're liable to fall apart if you start moving around."

I took his advice.

V

When I woke up it was morning, and Milk River was prodding me with a finger.

"You figuring on getting up for breakfast, or would you like it brung to you?"

I moved cautiously until I found I was all in one piece.

"I can crawl that far."

He sat down on a bunk across the room and rolled a cigarette while I put on my shoes—the only things, except my hat, I hadn't slept in. He had something to say, so I gave him time, lacing my shoes slowly.

Presently he said it:

"I always had the idea that nobody that couldn't sit a horse some couldn't amount to nothing much. I ain't so sure now. You can't ride any, and never will. You don't seem to have the least notion what to do after you get in the middle of the animal! But, still and all, a hombre that'll let a bronc dirty him up three times and running and then ties into a gent who tries to keep him from making it permanent, ain't exactly hay wire."

He lit his cigarette, and broke the match in half.

"I got a sorrel horse you can have for a hundred dollars. He don't take no interest in handling cows, but he's all horse, and he ain't mean."

I went into my money-belt—slid five twenties over into his lap.

"Better look at him first," he objected.

"You've seen him," I yawned, standing up. "Where's that breakfast you were bragging about?"

Six men were eating in the chuck-shack when we came in. Three of them were hands I hadn't seen before. Neither Peery, Wheelan, nor Vogel was there. Milk River introduced me to the strangers as the high-diving deputy sheriff, and, between bites of the food the one-eyed Chinese cook put on the table, the meal was devoted almost exclusively to wise cracks about my riding ability.

That suited me. I was sore and stiff, but my bruises weren't wasted. I had bought myself a place of some sort in this desert community, and maybe even a friend or two. In less than a day I had accomplished what, by milder means, would have taken weeks, or months. These cowhands were kidding me just about as they would have kidded each other.

We were following the smoke of our cigarettes outdoors when running hoofs brought a swirl of dust up the draw.

Red Wheelan slid off his horse and staggered out of the sand-cloud.

"Slim's dead!" he said thickly.

Half a dozen voices shot questions at him. He stood swaying, trying to answer them. He was drunk as a lord!

"Nisbet shot him. I heard about it when I woke up this mornin'. He was shot early this mornin'—in front of Bardell's. I left 'em aroun' midnight last night, an' went down to Gaia's. I heard about it this mornin'. I went after Nisbet, but"—he looked down sheepishly at his empty belt—"Bardell took m' gun away."

He swayed again. I caught him, steadying him.

"Horses!" Peery bawled over my shoulder. "We're going to town!"

I let go of Wheelan and turned around.

"We're going to town," I repeated, "but no foolishness when we get there. This is my job, and if I want any help I'll tell you."

Peery's eyes met mine.

"Slim belonged to us," he said.

"And whoever killed Slim belongs to me," I said.

That was all on the subject, but I didn't think I had made the point stick.

VI

An hour later we were dismounting in front of the Border Palace, going indoors.

A long, thin, blanket-wrapped body lay on two tables that had been pushed together. Half the citizens of Corkscrew were there. Behind the bar, Chick Orr's battered face showed, hard and watchful. Gyp Rainey was sitting in a corner, rolling a cigarette with shaky fingers that sprinkled the floor with tobacco crumbs. Beside him, paying no attention to anything, not even looking up at our arrival, Mark Nisbet sat.

"By God, I'm glad to see you!" Bardell was telling me, his fat face not quite so red as it had been the day before. "This thing of having men killed at my front door has got to stop, and you're the man to stop it!"

I noticed that the Circle H. A. R. men had not followed me into the center of the room, but had stopped in a loose semi-circle just inside the street door.

I lifted a flap of the blanket and looked at the dead man. A small hole was in his forehead, over his right eye.

"Has a doctor seen him?" I asked.

"Yes," Bardell said. "Doc Haley saw him, but couldn't do anything. He must have been dead before he fell."

"Can you send for Haley?"

"I reckon I can." Bardell called to Gyp Rainey, "Run across the street and tell Doc Haley that the deputy sheriff wants to talk to him."

Gyp went gingerly through the cowboys grouped at the door and vanished.

I didn't like this public stuff. I'd rather do my questioning on the side. But to try that here would probably call for a showdown with Peery and his men, and I wasn't quite ready for that.

"What do you know about the killing, Bardell?" I began.

"Nothing," he said emphatically, and then went on to tell me what he knew. "Nisbet and I were in the back room, counting the day's receipts. Chick was straightening the bar up. Nobody else was in here. It was about half-past one this morning, maybe.

"We heard the shot—right out front, and all run out there, of course. Chick was closest, so he got there first. Slim was laying in the street—dead."

"And what happened after that?"

"Nothing. We brought him in here. Adderly and Doc Haley—who lives right across the street—and the Jew next door had heard the shot, too, and they came out and—and that's all there was to it."

I turned to Gyp.

He spit in a cuspidor and hunched his shoulders.

"Bardell's give it all to you."

"Didn't see anything before or after except what Bardell has said?"

"Nothin'."

"Don't know who shot him?"

"Nope."

I saw Adderly's white mustache near the front of the room, and I put him on the stand next. He couldn't contribute anything. He had heard the shot, had jumped out of bed, put on pants and shoes, and had arrived in time to see Chick kneeling beside the dead man. He hadn't seen anything Bardell hadn't mentioned.

Dr. Haley had not arrived by the time I was through with Adderly, and I wasn't ready to open on Nisbet yet. Nobody else there seemed to know anything.

"Be back in a minute," I said, and went through the cowboys at the door to the street.

The Jew was giving his joint a much-needed cleaning.

"Good work," I praised him; "it needed it."

He climbed down from the counter on which he had been standing to reach the ceiling. The walls and floor were already comparatively clean.

"I not think it was so dirty," he grinned, showing his empty gums, "but when the sheriff come in to eat and make faces at my place, what am I going to do but clean him up?"

"Know anything about the killing last night?"

"Sure, I know. I am in my bed, and I hear that shot. I jump out of my bed, grab that shotgun, and run to the door. There is that Slim Vogel in the street, and that Chick Orr on his knees alongside him. I stick my head out. There is Mr. Bardell and that Nisbet standing in their door.

"Mr. Bardell say, 'How is he, Chick?'

"That Chick Orr, he say, 'He's dead enough.'

"That Nisbet, he does not say anything, but he turn around and go back into the place. And then comes the doctor and Mr. Adderly, and I go out, and after the doctor looks at him and says he is dead, we carry him into Mr. Bardell's place and put him on those tables."

That was all the Jew knew. I returned to the Border Palace. Dr. Haley—a fussy little man whose nervous fingers played with his lips—was there.

The sound of the shot had awakened him, he said, but he had seen nothing beyond what the others had already told me. The bullet was a .38. Death had been instantaneous.

So much for that.

I sat on a corner of a pool table, facing Mark Nisbet. Feet shuffled on the floor behind me and I could feel tension making.

"What can you tell me, Nisbet?" I asked.

He didn't look up from the floor. No muscle moved in his face except those that shaped his mouth to his words.

"Nothing that is likely to help," he said, picking his words slowly and carefully. "You were in in the afternoon and saw Slim, Wheelan, Keefe and I playing. Well, the game went on like that. He won a lot of money—or he seemed to think it was a lot—as long as we played poker. But Keefe left before midnight, and Wheelan shortly after. Nobody else came in the game, so we were kind of short-handed for poker. We quit it and played some high-card. I cleaned Vogel—got his last nickel. It was about one o'clock when he left, say half an hour before he was shot."

"You and Vogel get along pretty well?"

The gambler's eyes switched up to mine, turned to the floor again.

"You know better than that. You heard him riding me ragged. Well, he kept that up—maybe was a little rawer toward the last."

"And you let him ride?"

"I did just that. I make my living out of cards, not out of picking fights."

"There was no trouble over the table, then?"

"I didn't say that. There was trouble. He made a break for his gun after I cleaned him."

"And you?"

"I shaded* him on the draw—took his gun—unloaded it—gave it back to him—told him to beat it. He went."

"No shooting in here?"

"Not a shot."

_____

* bested

"And you didn't see him again until after he had been killed?"

"That's right."

I got down from my perch on the table and walked over to Nisbet, holding out one hand.

"Let me look at your gun."

He slid it swiftly out of his clothes—butt-first—into my hand. A .38 S. & W., loaded in all six chambers.

"Don't lose it," I said as I handed it back to him, "I may want it later."

A roar from Peery turned me around. As I turned I let my hands go into my coat pockets to rest on the .32 toys.

Peery's right hand was near his neck, within striking distance of the gun I knew he had under his vest. Spread out behind him, his men were as ready for action as he. Their hands hovered close to the bulges that showed where their weapons were packed.

"Maybe that's a deputy sheriff's idea of what had ought to be done," Peery was bellowing, "but it ain't mine! That skunk killed Slim. Slim went out of here toting too much money. That skunk shot him down without even giving him a chance to go for his iron, and took his dirty money back. If you think we're going to stand for—"

"Maybe somebody's got some evidence I haven't heard," I cut in. "The way it stands, I haven't got enough to convict Nisbet, and I don't see any sense in arresting a man just because it looks as if he might have done a thing."

"Evidence be damned! Facts are facts, and you know this—"

"The first fact for you to study," I interrupted him again, "is that I'm running this show—running it my own way. Got anything against that?"

"Plenty!"

A worn .45 appeared in his fist. Guns blossomed in the hands of the men behind him.

I got between Peery's gun and Nisbet, feeling ashamed of the little popping noise my .32s were going to make compared with the roar of the guns facing me.

"What I'd like"—Milk River had stepped away from his fellows, and was leaning his elbows on the bar, facing them, a gun in each hand, a purring quality in his drawling voice—"would be for whosoever wants to swap lead with our high-diving deputy to wait his turn. One at a time is my idea. I don't like this idea of crowding him."

Peery's face went purple.

"What I don't like," he bellowed at the boy, "is a yellow puppy that'll throw down the men he rides with!"

Milk River's dark face flushed, but his voice was still a purring drawl.

"Mister jigger, what you don't like and what you do like are so damned similar to me that I can't tell 'em apart. And you don't want to forget that I ain't one of your rannies.* I got a contract to gentle some horses for you at ten dollars per gentle. Outside of that, you and yours are strangers to me."

The excitement was over. The action that had been brewing had been talked to death by now.

"Your contract expired just about a minute and a half ago," Peery was telling Milk River. "You can show up at the Circle H. A. R. just once more—that's when you come for whatever stuff you left behind you. You're through!"

He pushed his square-jawed face at me.

"And you needn't think all the bets are in!"

He spun on his heel, and his hands trailed him out to their horses.

VII

Milk River and I were sitting in my room in the Cañon House an hour later, talking. I had sent word to the county seat that the coroner had a job down here, and had found a place to stow Vogel's body until he came.

"Can you tell me who spread the grand news that I was a deputy sheriff?" I asked Milk River, who was making a cigarette while I lit one of the

_____

* top cowboys

Fatimas he had refused. "It was supposed to be a secret."

"Was it? Nobody would of thought it. Our Mr. Turney didn't do nothing else for two days but run around telling folks what was going to happen when the new deputy come. He sure laid out a reputation for you! According to his way of telling it, you was the toughest, hardest, strongest, fastest, sharpest, biggest, wisest and meanest man west of the Mississippi River."

"Who is this Turney?"

"You mean you don't know him? From the way he talked, I took it you and him ate off the same plate."

"Never even heard any rumors about him. Who is he?"

"He's the gent that bosses the Orilla County Company outfit up the way."

So my client's local manager was the boy who had tipped my mitt!

"Got anything special to do the next few days?" I asked.

"Nothing downright special."

"I've got a place on the payroll for a man who knows this country and can chaperon me around it."

He poured a mouthful of gray smoke at the ceiling.

"I'd have to know what the play was before I'd set in," he said slowly. "You ain't a regular deputy, and you don't belong in this country. It ain't none of my business, but I wouldn't want to tie in with a blind game."

That was sensible enough.

"I'll spread it out for you," I offered. "I'm a private detective—the San Francisco branch of the Continental Detective Agency. The stockholders of the Orilla Colony Company sent me down here. They've spent a lot of money irrigating and developing their land, and now they're about ready to start selling it.

"According to them, the combination of heat and water makes it ideal farm land—as good as the Imperial Valley. Nevertheless, there doesn't seem to be any great rush of customers. What's the matter, so the stockholders figure, is that you

original inhabitants of this end of the state are such a hard lot that peaceful farmers don't want to come among you.

"It's no secret from anybody that both borders of this United States are sprinkled with sections that are as lawless now as they ever were in the old days. There's too much money in running immigrants over the line, and it's too easy, not to have attracted a lot of gentlemen who don't care how they get their money. With only 450 immigration inspectors divided between the two borders, the government hasn't been able to do much. The official guess is that some 135,000 foreigners were run into the country last year through back and side doors. Compared to this graft, rum-running—even dope-running—is kid stuff!

"Because this end of Orilla County isn't railroaded or telephoned up, it has got to be one of the chief smuggling sections, and therefore, according to these men who hired me, full of assorted thugs. On another job a couple of months ago, I happened to run into a smuggling game, and knocked it over. The Orilla Colony people thought I could do the same thing for them down here. So hither I come to make this part of Arizona nice and lady-like.

"I stopped over at the county seat and got myself sworn in as deputy sheriff, in case the official standing came in handy. The sheriff said he didn't have a deputy down here and hadn't the money to hire one, so he was glad to sign me on. But we thought it was a secret—until I got here."

"I think you're going to have one hell of a lot of fun," Milk River grinned at me, "so I reckon I'll take that job you was offering. But I ain't going to be no deputy myself. I'll play around with you, but I don't want to tie myself up, so I'll have to enforce no laws I don't like. If you want to have me hanging around you sort of loose and individual-like, I'm with you."

"It's a bargain. Now what can you tell me that I ought to know?"

He blew more smoke at the ceiling.

"Well, you needn't bother none about the Circle H. A. R. They're plenty tough, but they ain't running nothing over the line."

"That's all right as far as it goes," I agreed, "but my job is to clean out trouble-makers, and from what I've seen of them they come under that heading."

"You're going to have one hell of a lot of fun," Milk River repeated. "Of course they're troublesome! But how could Peery raise cows down here if he didn't get hisself a crew that's a match for the gunmen your Orilla Colony people don't like? And you know how cowhands are. Set 'em down in a hard neighborhood and they're hell-bent on proving to everybody that they're just as tough as the next one—and tougher."

"I've nothing against them—if they behave. Now about these border-running folks?"

"I reckon Bardell's your big meat. Whether you'll ever get anything on him is another thing—something for you to work up a lather over. Next to him—Big 'Nacio. You ain't seen him yet? A big, black-whiskered Mex that's got a rancho down the cañon—four-five mile this side of the line. Anything that comes over the line comes through that rancho. But proving that's another item for you to beat your head about."

"He and Bardell work together?"

"Uh-huh—I reckon he works for Bardell. Another thing you got to include in your tally is that these foreign gents who buy their way across the line don't always—nor even mostly—wind up where they want to. It ain't nothing unusual these days to find some bones out in the desert beside what was a grave until the coyotes opened it. And the buzzards are getting fat! If the immigrant's got anything worth taking on him, or if a couple of government men happen to be nosing around, or if anything happens to make the smuggling gents nervous, they usually drop their customer and dig him in where he falls."

The racket of the dinner-bell downstairs cut off our conference at this point.

VIII

There were only eight or ten diners in the dining-room. None of Peery's men was there.

Milk River and I sat at a table back in one corner of the room. Our meal was about half eaten when the dark-eyed girl I had seen the previous day came in.

She came straight to our table. I stood up to learn her name was Clio Landes. She was the girl the better element wanted floated. She gave me a flashing smile, a strong, thin hand, and sat down.

"I hear you've lost your job again, you big bum," she laughed at Milk River.

I had known she didn't belong to Arizona. Her voice was New York.

"If that's all you heard, I'm still 'way ahead of you," Milk River grinned back at her. "I gone and got me another job—riding herd on law and order."

Something that could have been worry flashed into her dark eyes, and out again.

"You might just as well start looking for another hired man right away," she advised me. "He never kept a job longer than a few days in his life."

From the distance came the sound of a shot.

I went on eating.

Clio Landes said:

"Don't you coppers get excited over things like that?"

"The first rule," I told her, "is never to let anything interfere with your meals, if you can help it."

An overalled man came in from the street.

"Nisbet's been killed down in Bardell's!" he yelled.

To Bardell's Border Palace Milk River and I went, half the diners running ahead of us, with half the town.

We found Nisbet in the back room, stretched out on the floor, dead. A hole that a .45 could have made was in his chest, which the men around him had bared.

Bardell's fingers gripped my arm.

"Never give him a chance, the dogs!" he cried thickly. "Cold murder!"

"He say anything before he died?"

"No. He was dead when we got to him."

"Who shot him?"

"One of the Circle H. A. R., you can bet your neck on that!"

"Didn't anybody see it?"

"Nobody here admits they saw it."

"How did it happen?"

"Mark was out front. Me and Chick and five or six of these men were there. Mark came back here. Just as he stepped through the door—bang!"

Bardell shook his fist at the open window.

I crossed to the window and looked out. A five-foot strip of rocky ground lay between the building and the sharp edge of the Tirabuzon Cañon. A close-twisted rope was tight around a small knob of rock at the cañon's edge.

I pointed at the rope. Bardell swore savagely.

"If I'd of seen that we'd of got him! We didn't think anybody could get down there, and didn't look very close. We ran up and down the ledge, looking between buildings."

We went outside, where I lay on my belly and looked down into the cañon. The rope—one end fastened to the knob—ran straight down the rock wall for twenty feet, and disappeared among the trees and bushes of a narrow shelf that ran along the wall there. Once on that shelf, a man could find ample cover to shield his retreat.

"What do you think?" I asked Milk River, who lay beside me.

"A clean getaway."

I stood up, pulling up the rope. A rope such as any one of a hundred cowhands might have owned, in no way distinguishable from any other to my eyes. I handed it to Milk River.

"It don't mean nothing to me. Might be anybody's," he said.

"The ground tell you anything?"

He shook his head again.

"You go down into the cañon and see what you can pick up," I told him. "I'll ride out to the Circle H. A. R. If you don't find anything, ride out that way."

I went back indoors, for further questioning. Of the seven men who had been in Bardell's place at the time of the shooting, three seemed to be fairly trustworthy. The testimony of those three agreed with Bardell's in every detail.

"Didn't you say you were going out to see Peery?" Bardell asked.

"Yes."

"Chick, get horses! Me and you'll ride out there with the deputy, and as many of you other men as want to go. He'll need guns behind him!"

"Nothing doing!" I stopped Chick. "I'm going by myself. This posse stuff is out of my line."

Bardell scowled, but he nodded his head in agreement.

"You're running it," he said. "I'd like to go out there with you, but if you want to play it different, I'm gambling you're right."

IX

In the livery stable, where we had put our horses, I found Milk River saddling them, and we rode out of town together.

Half a mile out, we split. He turned to the left, down a trail that led into the cañon, calling over his shoulder to me:

"If you get through out there sooner than you think, you can maybe pick me up by following the draw the ranch-house is in down to the cañon. Don't be too hard on the boys!"

I turned into the draw that led toward the Circle H. A. R., the long-legged, long-bodied horse Milk River had sold me carrying me along easily and swiftly. It was too soon after midday for riding to be pleasant. Heat waves boiled out of the draw-bottom, the sun hurt my eyes, dust caked my throat. That same dust rose behind me in a cloud that advertised me to half the state, notwithstanding that I was riding below the landscape.

Crossing from this draw into the larger one the Circle H. A. R. occupied, I found Peery waiting for me.

He didn't say anything, didn't move a hand. He just sat his horse and watched me approach. Two .45s were holstered on his legs.

I came alongside and held out the lariat I had taken from the rear of the Border Palace. As I held it out I noticed that no rope decorated his saddle.

"Know anything about this?" I asked.

He looked at the rope, but made no move to take it.

"Looks like one of those things hombres use to drag steers around with."

"Can't fool you, can I?" I grunted. "Ever see this particular one before?"

He took a minute or more to think up an answer to that.

"Yeah," finally. "Fact is, I lost that same rope somewheres between here and town this morning."

"Know where I found it?"

"Don't hardly make no difference." He reached for it. "The main thing is you found it."

"It might make a difference," I said, moving the rope out of his reach. "I found it strung down the cañon wall, behind Bardell's, where you could slide down it after you potted Nisbet."

His hands went to his guns. I turned so he could see the shape of one of the pocketed automatics I was holding.

"Don't do anything you'll be sorry for," I advised him.

"Shall I gun this la-ad now?" Dunne's brogue rolled from behind me, "or will we wa-ait a bit?"

I looked around to see him standing behind a boulder, a .30-30 rifle held on me. Above other rocks, other heads and other weapons showed.

I took my hand out of my pocket and put it on my saddle horn.

Peery spoke past me to the others.

"He tells me Nisbet's been shot."

"Now ain't that provokin'?" Buck Small grieved. "I hope it didn't hurt him none."

"Dead," I supplied.

"Whoever could 'a' done th' like o' that?" Dunne wanted to know.

"It wasn't Santa Claus," I gave my opinion.

"Got anything else to tell me?" Peery demanded.

"Isn't that enough?"

"Yeah. Now if I was you, I'd ride right back to Corkscrew and go to bed."

"You mean you don't want to go back with me?"

"Not any. If you want to try and take me, now—"

I didn't want to try, and I said so.

"Then there's nothing keeping you here," he pointed out.

I grinned at him and his friends, pulled the sorrel around, and started back the way I had come.

A few miles down, I swung off to the south again, found the lower end of the Circle H. A. R. draw, and followed it down into the Tirabuzon Cañon. Then I started to work up toward the point where the rope had been let down.

The cañon deserved its name—a rough and stony, tree and bush-choked, winding gutter across the face of Arizona. But it was nicely green and cool compared to most of the rest of the State.

I hadn't gone far when I ran into Milk River, leading his horse toward me. He shook his head.

"Not a damned thing! I can cut sign with the rest of 'em, but there's too many rocky ridges here."

I dismounted. We sat under a tree and smoked some tobacco.

"How'd you come out?" he wanted to know.

"So-so. The rope is Peery's, but he didn't want to come along with me. I figure we can find him when we want him, so I didn't insist. It would have been kind of uncomfortable."

He looked at me out of the end of his pale eyes.

"A hombre might guess," he said slowly, "that you was playing the Circle H. A. R. against Bardell's crew, encouraging each side to eat up the other, and save you the trouble."

"You could be either right or wrong. Do you think that'd be a dumb play?"

"I don't know. I reckon not—if you're making it, and if you're sure you're strong enough to take hold when you have to."

X

Night was coming on when Milk River and I turned into Corkscrew's crooked street. It was too late for the Cañon House's dining-room, so we got down in front of the Jew's shack.

Chick Orr was standing in the Border Palace doorway. He turned his hammered mug to call something over his shoulder. Bardell appeared beside him, looked at me with a question in his eyes, and the pair of them stepped out into the street.

"What result?" Bardell asked.

"No visible ones."

"You didn't make the pinch?" Chick Orr demanded, incredulously.

"That's right. I invited a man to ride back with me, but he said no."

The ex-pug looked me up and down and spit on the ground at my feet.

"Ain't you a swell mornin'-glory?" he snarled. "I got a great mind to smack you down, you shine elbow,* you!"

"Go ahead," I invited him. "I don't mind skinning a knuckle on you."

His little eyes brightened. Stepping in, he let an open hand go at my face. I took my face out of the way, and turned my back, taking off coat and shoulder-holster.

"Hold these, Milk River. And make the spectators behave while I take this pork-and-beaner† for a romp."

Corkscrew came running as Chick and I faced each other. We were pretty much alike in size and age, but his fat was softer than mine, I thought. He had been a professional. I had battled around a little, but there was no doubt that he had me shaded on smartness. To offset that, his hands were lumpy and battered, while mine weren't. And he was—or had been—used to gloves, while bare knuckles was more in my line.

Popular belief has it that you can do more

damage with bare hands than with gloves, but, as usual, popular belief is wrong. The chief value of gloves is the protection they give your hands. Jaw-bones are tougher than finger-bones, and after you've pasted a tough face for a while with bare knuckles you find your hands aren't holding up very well, that you can't get the proper snap into your punches. If you don't believe me, look up the records. You'll find that knock-outs began to come quicker as soon as the boys in the profession began to pad their fists.

So I figured I hadn't anything to fear from this Chick Orr—or not a whole lot. I was in better shape, had stronger hands, and wasn't handicapped with boxing-glove training. I wasn't altogether right in my calculations.

He crouched, waiting for me to come to him. I went, trying to play the boob, faking a right swing for a lead.

Not so good! He stepped outside instead of in. The left I chucked at him went wide. He rapped me on the cheek-bone.

I stopped trying to out-smart him. His left hand played a three-note tune on my face before I could get in to him.

I smacked both hands into his body, and felt happy when the flesh folded softly around them. He got away quicker than I could follow, and shook me up with a sock on the jaw.

He left-handed me some more—in the eye, in the nose. His right scraped my forehead, and I was in again.

Left, right, left, I dug into his middle. He slashed me across the face with forearm and fist, and got clear.

He fed me some more lefts, splitting my lip, spreading my nose, stinging my face from forehead to chin. And when I finally got past that left hand I walked into a right uppercut that came up from his ankle to click on my jaw with a shock that threw me back half a dozen steps.

Keeping after me, he swarmed all over me. The evening air was full of fists. I pushed my feet into the ground and stopped the hurricane with a couple of pokes just above where his shirt ran into his pants.

---

* boxing slang for a series of flashy punches that do little damage
† down-and-outer

He copped me with his right again—but not so hard. I laughed at him, remembering that something had clicked in his hand when he landed that uppercut, and plowed into him, hammering at him with both hands.

He got away again—cut me up with his left. I smothered his left arm with my right, hung on to it, and whaled him with my own left, keeping them low. His right banged into me. I let it bang. It was dead.

He nailed me once more before the fight ended—with a high straight left that smoked as it came. I managed to keep my feet under me, and the rest of it wasn't so bad. He chopped me a lot more, but his steam was gone.

He went down after a while, from an accumulation of punches rather than from any especial one, and couldn't get up.

His face didn't have a mark on it that I was responsible for. Mine must have looked as if it had been run through a grinder.

"Maybe I ought to wash up before we eat," I said to Milk River as I took my coat and gun.

"Hell, yes!" he agreed, staring at my face.

A plump man in a Palm Beach suit got in front of me, taking my attention.

"I am Mr. Turney of the Orilla Colony Company," he introduced himself. "Am I to understand that you have not made an arrest since you have been here?"

This was the bird who had advertised me! I didn't like that, and I didn't like his round, aggressive face.

"Yes," I confessed.

"There have been two murders in two days," he ran on, "concerning which you have done nothing, though in each case the evidence seems clear enough. Do you think that is satisfactory? Do you think you are performing the duties for which you were employed?"

I didn't say anything.

"Let me tell you that it is not at all satisfactory," he supplied the answers to his own questions. "Neither is it satisfactory that you should have employed this man"—stabbing a plump finger in Milk River's direction—"who is notoriously one of the most lawless men in the county. I want you to understand clearly that unless there is a distinct improvement in your work—unless you show some disposition to do the things you were engaged to do—that engagement will be terminated!"

"Who'd you say you are?" I asked, when he had talked himself out.

"Mr. Turney, general superintendent of the Orilla Colony."

"So? Well, Mr. General Superintendent Turney, your owners forgot to tell me anything about you when they employed me. So I don't know you at all. Any time you've got anything to say to me, you turn it over to your owners, and if it's important enough, maybe they'll pass it on to me."

He puffed himself up.

"I shall certainly inform them that you have been extremely remiss in your duty, however proficient you may be in street brawls!"

"Will you put a postscript on for me," I called after him as he walked away. "Tell 'em I'm kind of busy just now and can't use any advice—no matter who it comes from."

Milk River and I went ten steps toward the Cañon House, and came face to face with the Reverend Dierks, Miss Janey, and old Adderly. None of them looked at me with anything you could call pleasure.

"You should be ashamed of yourself!" Miss Janey ground out between her false teeth. "Fighting in the street—you who are supposed to keep the peace!"

"As a deputy sheriff you're terrible," Adderly put in. "There's been more trouble here since you came than there ever was before!"

"I must say, brother, that I am deeply disappointed in your actions as a representative of the law!" was the minister's contribution.

I didn't like to say, "Go to hell!" to a group that included a minister and a woman, and I couldn't think of anything else, so, with Milk River making a poor job of holding in his laughter, I stepped around the better element, and we went on to the Cañon House.

Vickers, the sallow, pudgy proprietor, was at the door.

"If you think I got towels to mop up the blood from every hombre that gets himself beat up, you're mistaken," he growled at me. "And I don't want no sheets torn up for bandages, neither!"

"I never seen such a disagreeable cuss as you are," Milk River insisted as we climbed the stairs. "Seems like you can't get along with nobody. Don't you never make no friends?"

"Only with saps!"

I did what I could with water and adhesive tape to reclaim my face, but the result was a long way from beauty. Milk River sat on the bed and grinned and watched me.

"How does a fellow go about winning a fight he gets the worst of?" he inquired.

"It's a gift," was the only answer I could think up.

"You're a lot gifted. That Chick give you more gifts than a Christmas tree could hold."

XI

My patching finished, we went down to the Jew's for food. Three eaters were sitting at the counter. I had to exchange comments on the battle with them while I ate.

We were interrupted by the running of horses in the street. A dozen or more men went past the door, and we could hear them pulling up sharply, dismounting, in front of Bardell's.

Milk River leaned sidewise until his mouth was close to my ear.

"Big 'Nacio's crew from down the cañon. You better hold on tight, chief, or they'll shake the town from under you."

We finished our meal and went out to the street.

In the glow from the big lamp over Bardell's door a Mexican lounged against the wall. A big black-bearded man, his clothes gay with silver buttons, two white-handled guns holstered low on his thighs, the holsters tied down.

"Will you take the horses over to the stable?" I asked Milk River. "I'm going up and lie across the bed and grow strength again."

He looked at me curiously, and went over to where we had left the ponies.

I stopped in front of the bearded Mexican, and pointed with my cigarette at his guns.

"You're supposed to take those things off when you come to town," I said pleasantly. "Matter of fact, you're not supposed to bring 'em in at all, but I'm not inquisitive enough to look under a man's coat for them. You can't wear them out in the open, though."

Beard and mustache parted to show a smiling curve of yellow teeth.

"Mebbe if *el senor jerife* no lak t'ese t'ings, he lak try take t'em 'way?"

"No. *You* put 'em away."

His smile spread.

"I lak t'em here. I wear t'em here."

"You do what I tell you," I said, still pleasantly, and left him, going back to the Jew's shack.

Leaning over the counter, I picked the sawed-off shotgun out of its nest.

"Can I borrow this? I want to make a believer out of a guy."

"Yes, sir, sure! You help yourself!"

I cocked both barrels before I stepped outdoors.

The big Mexican wasn't in sight. I found him inside, telling his friends about it. Some of his friends were Mexican, some American, some God knows what. All wore guns. All had the look of thugs.

The big Mexican turned when his friends gaped past him at me. His hands dropped to his guns as he turned, but he didn't draw.

"I don't know what's in this cannon," I told the truth, centering the riot gun on the company, "maybe pieces of barbed wire and dynamite shavings. We'll find out if you birds don't start piling your guns on the bar right away—because I'll sure-God splash you with it!"

They piled their weapons on the bar. I didn't blame them. This thing in my hands would have mangled them plenty!

"After this, when you come to Corkscrew, put your guns out of sight."

Fat Bardell pushed through them, putting joviality back on his face.

"Will you tuck these guns away until your customers are ready to leave town?" I asked him.

"Yes! Yes! Be glad to!" he exclaimed when he had got over his surprise.

I returned the shotgun to its owner and went up to the Cañon House.

A door just a room or two from mine opened as I walked down the hall. Chick Orr came out, saying:

"Don't do nothin' I wouldn't do," over his shoulder.

I saw Clio Landes standing inside the door.

Chick turned from the door, saw me, and stopped, scowling at me.

"You can't fight worth a damn!" he said. "All you know is how to hit!"

"That's right."

He rubbed a swollen hand over his belly.

"I never could learn to take 'em down there. That's what beat me in the profesh."

I tried to look sympathetic, while he studied my face carefully.

"I messed you up, for a fact." His scowl curved up in a gold-toothed grin. The grin went away. The scowl came back. "Don't pick no more fights with me—I might hurt you!"

He poked me in the ribs with a thumb, and went on past me, down the stairs.

The girl's door was closed when I passed it. In my room, I dug out my fountain pen and paper, and had three words of my report written when a knock sounded on my door.

"Come in," I called, having left the door unlocked for Milk River.

Clio Landes pushed the door open.

"Busy?"

"No. Come in and make yourself comfortable. Milk River will be along in a few minutes."

I switched over to the bed, giving her my only chair.

"You're not foxing Milk River, are you?" she asked point-blank.

"No. I got nothing to hang on him. He's right so far as I'm concerned. Why?"

"Nothing, only I thought there might be a caper or two you were trying to cop him for. You're not fooling me, you know! These hicks think you're a bust, but I know different."

"Thanks for those few kind words. But don't be press-agenting my wisdom around. I've had enough advertising. What are you doing out here in the sticks?"

"Lunger!" She tapped her chest. "A croaker told me I'd last longer out here. Like a boob, I fell for it. Living out here isn't any different from dying in the big city."

"How long have you been away from the noise?"

"Three years—a couple up in Colorado, and then this hole. Seem like three centuries."

"I was back there on a job in April," I led her on, "for two or three weeks."

"You were?"

It was just as if I'd said I had been to heaven. She began to shoot questions at me: was this still so-and-so? Was that still thus?

We had quite a little gabfest, and I found I knew some of her friends. A couple of them were high-class swindlers, one was a bootleg magnate, and the rest were a mixture of bookies, conmen, and the like. When I was living in New York, back before the war, I had spent quite a few of my evenings in Dick Malloy's Briar Patch, a cabaret on Seventh Avenue, near where the Ringside opened later. This girl had been one of the Briar Patch's regular customers a few years after my time there.

I couldn't find out what her grift was. She talked a blend of thieves' slang and high-school English, and didn't say much about herself.

We were getting along fine when Milk River came in.

"My friends still in town?" I asked.

"Yes. I hear 'em bubbling around down in Bardell's. I hear you've been makin' yourself more unpopular."

"What now?"

"Your friends among the better element don't

seem to think a whole lot of that trick of yours of giving Big 'Nacio's guns, and his hombres', to Bardell to keep. The general opinion seems to be you took the guns out of their right hands and put 'em back in the left."

"I only took 'em to show that I could," I explained. "I didn't want 'em. They would have got more anyway. I think I'll go down and show myself to 'em. I won't be long."

The Border Palace was noisy and busy. None of Big 'Nacio's friends paid any attention to me. Bardell came across the room to tell me:

"I'm glad you backed the boys down. Saved me a lot of trouble, maybe."

I nodded and went out, around to the livery stable, where I found the night man hugging a little iron stove in the office.

"Got anybody who can ride to Filmer with a message tonight?"

"Maybe I can find somebody," he said without enthusiasm.

"Give him a good horse and send him up to the hotel as soon as you can," I requested.

I sat on the edge of the Cañon House porch until a long-legged lad of eighteen or so arrived on a pinto pony and asked for the deputy sheriff. I left the shadow I had been sitting in, and went down into the street, where I could talk to the boy without having an audience.

"Th' old man said yuh wanted to send somethin' to Filmer."

"Can you head out of here toward Filmer, and then cross over to the Circle H. A. R.?"

"Yes, suh, I c'n do that."

"Well, that's what I want. When you get there, tell Peery that Big 'Nacio and his men are in town, and might be riding that way before morning. And don't let the information get out to anybody else."

"I'll do jus' that, suh."

"This is yours, I'll pay the stable bill later." I slid a bill into his hand. "Get going."

Up in my room again, I found Milk River and the girl sitting around a bottle of liquor. I gave my oath of office the laugh to the extent of three drinks. We talked and smoked a while, and then the party broke up. Milk River told me he had the room next to mine.

I added another word to the report I had started, decided I needed sleep more than the client needed the report, and went to bed.

XII

Milk River's knuckles on the door brought me out of bed to shiver in the cold of five-something in the morning.

"This isn't a farm!" I grumbled at him as I let him in. "You're in the city now. You're supposed to sleep until the sun comes up."

"The eye of the law ain't never supposed to sleep," he grinned at me, his teeth clicking together, because he hadn't any more clothes on than I. "Fisher, who's got a ranch out that-away, sent a man in to tell you that there's a battle going on out at the Circle H. A. R. He hit my door instead of yours. Do we ride out that-away, chief?"

"We do. Hunt up some rifles, water, and the horses. I'll be down at the Jew's, ordering breakfast and getting some lunch wrapped up."

Forty minutes later Milk River and I were out of Corkscrew.

The morning warmed as we rode, the sun making long violet pictures on the desert, raising the dew in a softening mist. The mesquite was fragrant, and even the sand—which would be as nice as a dusty stove-top later—had a fresh, pleasant odor. There was nothing to hear but the creaking of leather, the occasional clink of metal, and the plop-plop of the horses' feet on hard ground, which changed to a shff-shff when we struck loose sand.

The battle seemed to be over, unless the battlers had run out of bullets and were going at it hand to hand.

Up over the ranch buildings, as we approached, three blue spots that were buzzards circled, and a moving animal showed against the sky for an instant on a distant ridge.

"A bronc that ought to have a rider and ain't," Milk River pronounced it.

Farther along, we passed a bullet-riddled Mexican sombrero, and then the sun sparkled on a handful of empty brass cartridges.

One of the ranch buildings was a charred black pile. Nearby another one of the men I had disarmed in Bardell's lay dead on his back.

A bandaged head poked around a building-corner, and its owner stepped out, his right arm in a sling, a revolver in his left. Behind him trotted the one-eyed Chinese cook, swinging a cleaver.

Milk River recognized the bandaged man.

"Howdy, Red! Been quarreling?"

"Some. We took all th' advantage we could of th' warnin' you sent out, an' when Big 'Nacio an' his herd showed up just 'fore daylight, we Injuned them all over the county. I stopped a couple o' slugs, so I stayed to home whilst th' rest o' th' boys followed 'em south. 'F you listen sharp, you can hear a pop now an' then."

"Do we follow 'em, or head 'em?" Milk River asked me.

"Can we head 'em?"

"Might. If Big 'Nacio's running, he'll circle back to his rancho along about dark. If we cut into the cañon and slide along down, maybe we can be there first. He won't make much speed having to fight off Peery and the boys as he goes."

"We'll try it."

Milk River leading, we went past the ranch buildings, and on down the draw, going into the cañon at the point where I had entered it the previous day. After a while the footing got better, and we made better time.

The sun climbed high enough to let its rays down on us, and the comparative coolness in which we had been riding went away. At noon we stopped to rest the horses, eat a couple of sandwiches, and smoke a bit. Then we went on.

Presently the sun passed, began to crawl down on our right, and shadows grew in the cañon. The welcome shade had reached the east wall when Milk River, in front, stopped.

"Around this next bend it is."

We dismounted, took a drink apiece, blew the sand off our rifles, and went forward afoot, toward a clump of bushes that covered the crooked cañon's next twist.

Beyond the bend, the floor of the cañon ran downhill into a round saucer. The saucer's sides sloped gently up to the desert floor. In the middle of the saucer, four low adobe buildings sat. In spite of their exposure to the desert sun, they looked somehow damp and dark. From one of them a thin plume of bluish smoke rose. Water ran out of a rock-bordered hole in one sloping cañon-wall, disappearing in a thin stream that curved behind one of the buildings.

No man, no animal was in sight.

"I'm going to prospect down there," Milk River said, handing me his hat and rifle.

"Right," I agreed. "I'll cover you, but if anything breaks, you'd better get out of the way. I'm not the most dependable rifle-shot in the world!"

For the first part of his trip Milk River had plenty of cover. He went ahead rapidly. The screening plants grew fewer. His pace fell off. Flat on the ground, he squirmed from clump to boulder, from hummock to bush.

Thirty feet from the nearest building, he ran out of places to hide. I thought he would scout the buildings from that point, and then come back. Instead, he jumped up and sprinted to the shelter of the nearest building.

Nothing happened. He crouched against the wall for several long minutes, and then began to work his way toward the rear.

A hatless Mexican came around the corner.

I couldn't make out his features, but I saw his body stiffen.

His hand went to his waist.

Milk River's gun flashed.

The Mexican dropped. The bright steel of his knife glittered high over Milk River's head, and rang when it landed on a stone.

Milk River went out of my sight around the building. When I saw him again he was charging at the black doorway of the second building.

Fire-streaks came out of the door to meet him.

I did what I could with the two rifles—laying a barrage ahead of him—pumping lead at the open door, as fast as I could get it out. I emptied the second rifle just as he got too close to the door for me to risk another shot.

Dropping the rifle, I ran back to my horse, and rode to my crazy assistant's assistance.

He didn't need any. It was all over when I arrived.

He was driving another Mexican and Gyp Rainey out of the building with the nozzles of his guns.

"This is the crop," he greeted me. "Leastways, I couldn't find no more."

"What are you doing here?" I asked Rainey.

But the hop-head didn't want to talk. He looked sullenly at the ground and made no reply.

"We'll tie 'em up," I decided, "and then look around."

Milk River did most of the tying, having had more experience with ropes.

He trussed them back to back on the ground, and we went exploring.

XIII

Except for plenty of guns of all sizes and more than plenty of ammunition to fit, we didn't find anything very exciting until we came to a heavy door—barred and padlocked—set half in the foundation of the principal building, half in the mound on which the building sat.

I found a broken piece of rusty pick, and knocked the padlock off with it. Then we took the bar off and swung the door open.

Men came eagerly toward us out of an unventilated, unlighted cellar. Seven men who talked a medley of languages as they came.

We used our guns to stop them.

Their jabbering went high, excited.

"Quiet!" I yelled at them.

They knew what I meant, even if they didn't understand the word. The babel stopped and we looked them over. All seven seemed to be foreigners—and a hard-looking gang of cut-

throats. A short Jap with a scar from ear to ear; three Slavs, one bearded, barrel-bodied, red-eyed, the other two bullet-headed, cunning-faced; a swarthy husky who was unmistakably a Greek; a bowlegged man whose probable nationality I couldn't guess; and a pale fat man whose china-blue eyes and puckered red mouth were probably Teutonic.

Milk River and I tried them out with English first, and then with what Spanish we could scrape up between us. Both attempts brought a lot of jabbering from them, but nothing in either of those languages.

"Got anything else?" I asked Milk River.

"Chinook is all that's left."

That wouldn't help much. I tried to remember some of the words we used to think were French in the A. E. F.[*]

Que désirez-vous? brought a bright smile to the fat face of the blue-eyed man.

I caught *Nous allons à les États-Unis* before the speed with which he threw the words at me confused me beyond recognizing anything else.

That was funny. Big 'Nacio hadn't let these birds know that they were already in the United States. I suppose he could manage them better if they thought they were still in Mexico.

Montrez-moi votre passe-port.

That brought a sputtering protest from Blue Eyes. They had been told no passports were necessary. It was because they had been refused passports that they were paying to be smuggled in.

Quand êtes-vous venu ici?

Hier meant yesterday, regardless of what the other things he put in his answer were. Big 'Nacio had come straight to Corkscrew after bringing these men across the border and sticking them in his cellar, then.

We locked the immigrants in their cellar again, putting Rainey and the Mexican in with them. Rainey howled like a wolf when I took his hypodermic needle and his coke away from him.

"Sneak up and take a look at the country,"

---

[*] American Expeditionary Forces

I told Milk River, "while I plant the man you killed."

By the time he came back I had the dead Mexican arranged to suit me: slumped down in a chair a little off from the front door of the principal building, his back against the wall, a sombrero tilted down over his face.

"There's dust kicking up some ways off," Milk River reported. "Wouldn't surprise me none if we got our company along towards dark."

Darkness had been solid for an hour when they came.

By then, fed and rested, we were ready for them. A light was burning in the house. Milk River was in there, tinkling a mandolin. Light came out of the open front door to show the dead Mexican dimly—a statue of a sleeper. Beyond him, around the corner except for my eyes and forehead, I lay close to the wall.

We could hear our company long before we could see them. Two horses—but they made enough noise for ten—coming lickety-split down to the lighted door.

Big 'Nacio, in front, was out of the saddle and had one foot in the doorway before his horse's front feet—thrown high by the violence with which the big man had pulled him up—hit the ground again. The second rider was close behind him.

The bearded man saw the corpse. He jumped at it, swinging his quirt, roaring:

"*Arriba, piojo!*"

The mandolin's tinkling stopped.

I scrambled up.

Big 'Nacio's whiskers went down in surprise.

His quirt caught a button of the dead man's clothes, tangled there, the loop on its other end holding one of Big 'Nacio's wrists.

His other hand went to his thigh.

My gun had been in my hand for an hour. I was close. I had leisure to pick my target. When his hand touched his gun-butt, I put a bullet through hand and thigh.

As he fell, I saw Milk River knock the second man down with a clout of gun-barrel on back of his head.

"Seems like we team-up pretty good," the sunburned boy said as he stooped to take the enemy's weapons from them.

The bearded man's bellowing oaths made conversation difficult.

"I'll put this one you beaned in the cooler," I said. "Watch 'Nacio, and we'll patch him up when I come back."

I dragged the unconscious man halfway to the cellar door before he came to. I goaded him the rest of the way with my gun, shooed him indoors, shooed the other prisoners away from the door, and closed and barred it again.

The bearded man had stopped howling when I returned.

"Anybody riding after you?" I asked, as I knelt beside him and began cutting his pants away with my pocket knife.

For answer to that I got a lot of information about myself, my habits, my ancestors. None of it happened to be the truth, but it was colorful.

"Maybe we'd better put a hobble on his tongue," Milk River suggested.

"No. Let him cry!" I spoke to the bearded man again. "If I were you, I'd answer that question. If it happens that the Circle H. A. R. riders trail you here and take us unawares, it's a gut that you're in for a lynching. *Ahorcar*, understand?"

He hadn't thought of that.

"*Sí, sí*. T'at Peery an' hees hombres. T'ey *seguir—mucho rapidez!*"

"Any of your men left, besides you and this other?"

"No! *Ningún!*"

"Suppose you build as much fire as you can out here in front while I'm stopping this egg's bleeding, Milk River."

The lad looked disappointed.

"Ain't we going to bushwack them waddies none?"

"Not unless we have to."

By the time I had put a couple of tourniquets on the Mexican, Milk River had a roaring fire lighting the buildings and most of the saucer in which they sat. I had intended stowing 'Nacio and Milk River indoors, in case I couldn't make

Peery talk sense. But there wasn't time. I had just started to explain my plan to Milk River when Peery's bass voice came from outside the ring of light.

"Put 'em up, everybody!"

XIV

"Easy!" I cautioned Milk River, and stood up. But I didn't raise my hands.

"The excitement's over," I called. "Come on down."

Ten minutes passed. Peery rode into the light. His square-jawed face was grime-streaked and grim. His horse was muddy lather all over. His guns were in his hands.

Behind him rode Dunne—as dirty, as grim, as ready with his firearms.

Nobody followed Dunne. The others were spread around us in the darkness, then.

Peery leaned over his pony's head to look at Big 'Nacio, who was lying breathlessly still on the ground.

"Dead?"

"No—a slug through hand and leg. I've got some of his friends under lock and key indoors."

Mad red rims showed around Peery's eyes in the firelight.

"You can keep the others," he said harshly. "This hombre will do us."

I didn't misunderstand him.

"I'm keeping all of them."

"I ain't got a damned bit of confidence in you," Peery growled down at me. "You ain't done nothing since you been here, and it ain't likely you ever will. I'm making sure that this Big 'Nacio's riding stops right here. I'm taking care of him myself."

"Nothing stirring!"

"How you figuring on keeping me from taking him?" he laughed viciously at me. "You don't think me and Irish are alone, do you? If you don't believe you're corralled, make a play!"

I believed him, but—

"That doesn't make any difference. If I were a grub-line rider, or a desert rat, or any lone guy with no connections, you'd rub me out quick enough. But I'm not, and you know I'm not. I'm counting on that. You've got to kill me to take 'Nacio. That's flat! I don't think you want him bad enough to go that far. Right or wrong, I'm playing it that way."

He stared at me for a while. Then his knees urged his horse toward the Mexican, 'Nacio sat up and began pleading with me to save him.

Slowly I raised my right hand to my shoulder-holstered gun.

"Drop it!" Peery ordered, both his guns close to my head.

I grinned at him, took my gun out slowly, slowly turned it until it was level between his two.

We held that pose long enough to work up a good sweat apiece. It wasn't restful!

A queer light flickered in his red-rimmed eyes.

I didn't guess what was coming until too late.

His left-hand gun swung away from me—exploded.

A hole opened in the top of Big 'Nacio's head. He pitched over on his side.

The grinning Milk River shot Peery out of the saddle.

I was under Peery's right-hand gun when it went off. I was scrambling under his rearing horse's feet.

Dunne's revolvers coughed.

"Inside!" I yelled to Milk River, and put two bullets into Dunne's pony.

Rifle bullets sang every which way across, around, under, over us.

Inside the lighted doorway Milk River hugged the floor, spouting fire and lead from both hands.

Dunne's horse was down. Dunne got up—caught both hands to his face—went down beside his horse.

Milk River turned off the fireworks long enough for me to dash over him into the house.

While I smashed the lamp chimney, blew out the flame, he slammed the door.

Bullets made music on door and wall.

"Did I do right, shooting that jigger*?" Milk River asked.

"Good work!" I lied.

There was no use bellyaching over what was done, but I hadn't wanted Peery dead. Dunne's death was unnecessary, too. The proper place for guns is after talk has failed, and I hadn't run out of words by any means when this brown-skinned lad had gone into action.

The bullets stopped punching holes in our door.

"The boys have got their heads together," Milk River guessed. "They can't have a hell of a lot of caps left if they've been snapping them at 'Nacio since early morning."

I found a white handkerchief in my pocket and began stuffing one corner in a rifle muzzle.

"What's for that?" Milk River asked.

"Talk." I moved to the door. "And you're to hold your hand until I'm through."

"I never seen such a hombre for making talk," he complained.

I opened the door a cautious crack. Nothing happened. I eased the rifle through the crack and waved it in the light of the still burning fire. Nothing happened. I opened the door and stepped out.

"Send somebody down to talk!" I yelled at the outer darkness.

A voice I didn't recognize cursed bitterly, and began a threat:

"We'll give yuh—"

It broke off in silence.

Metal glinted off to one side.

Buck Small, his bulging eyes dark-circled, a smear of blood on one cheek, came into the light.

"What are you people figuring on doing?" I asked.

He looked sullenly at me.

"We're figurin' on gettin' that Milk River party. We ain't got nothin' against you. You're

_____

* a lookout during a crime

doin' what you're paid to do. But Milk River hadn't ought of killed Peery!"

Milk River bounced stiff-legged out of the door.

"Any time you want any part of me, you pop-eyed this-and-that, all you got to do is name it!"

Small's hands curved toward his holstered guns.

"Cut it!" I growled at Milk River, getting in front of him, pushing him back to the door. "I've got work to do. I can't waste time watching you boys cut up. This is no time to be bragging about what a desperate guy you are!"

I finally got rid of him, and faced Small again.

"You boys want to take a tumble to yourselves, Buck. The wild and woolly days are over. You're in the clear so far. 'Nacio jumped you, and you did what was right when you massacred his riders all over the desert. But you've got no right to fool with my prisoners. Peery wouldn't understand that. And if we hadn't shot him, he'd have swung later!

"For Milk River's end of it: he doesn't owe you anything. He dropped Peery under your guns—dropped him with less than an even break! You people had the cards stacked against us. Milk River took a chance you or I wouldn't have taken. You've got nothing to howl about.

"I've got ten prisoners in there, and I've got a lot of guns, and stuff to put in 'em. If you make me do it, I'm going to deal out the guns to my prisoners and let 'em fight. I'd rather lose every damned one of them that way than let you take one of 'em away from me!

"All that you boys can get out of fighting us is a lot of grief—whether you win or lose. This end of Orilla County has been left to itself longer than most of the Southwest. But those days are over. Outside money has come into it; outside people are coming. You can't buck it! Men tried that in the old days, and failed. Will you talk it over with the others?"

"Yeah," and he went away in the darkness.

I went indoors.

"I think they'll be sensible," I told Milk

River, "but you can't tell. So maybe you better hunt around and see if you can find a way through the floor to our basement hoosegow, because I meant what I said about giving guns to our captives."

Twenty minutes later Buck Small was back.

"You win," he said. "We want to take Peery and Dunne with us."

XV

Nothing ever looked better to me than my bed in the Cañon House the next—Wednesday—night. My grandstand play with the yellow horse, my fight with Chick Orr, the unaccustomed riding I had been doing—these things had filled me fuller of aches than Orilla County was of sand.

Our ten prisoners were resting in an old outdoor store-room of Adderly's, guarded by volunteers from among the better element, under the supervision of Milk River. They would be safe there, I thought, until the immigration inspectors—to whom I had sent word—could come for them. Most of Big 'Nacio's men had been killed in the fight with the Circle H. A. R. hands, and I didn't think Bardell could collect men enough to try to open my prison.

The Circle H. A. R. riders would behave reasonably well from now on, I thought. There were two angles still open, but the end of my job in Corkscrew wasn't far away. So I wasn't dissatisfied with myself as I got stiffly out of my clothes and climbed into bed for the sleep I had earned.

Did I get it? No.

I was just comfortably bedded down when somebody began thumping on my door.

It was fussy little Dr. Haley.

"I was called into your temporary prison a few minutes ago to look at Rainey," the doctor said. "He tried to escape, and broke his arm in a fight with one of the guards. That isn't serious, but the man's condition is. He should be given some cocaine. I don't think it is safe to leave him without the drug any longer. I would have

given him an injection, but Milk River stopped me, saying you had given orders that nothing was to be done without instructions from you."

"Is he really in bad shape?"

"Yes."

"I'll go down and talk to him," I said, reluctantly starting to dress again. "I gave him a shot now and then on the way up from the rancho—enough to keep him from falling down on us. But I want to get some information out of him now, and he gets no more until he'll talk. Maybe he's ripe now."

We could hear Rainey's howling before we reached the jail.

Milk River was squatting on his heels outside the door, talking to one of the guards.

"He's going to throw a joe* on you, chief, if you don't give him a pill," Milk River told me. "I got him tied up now, so's he can't pull the splints off his arm. He's plumb crazy!"

The doctor and I went inside, the guard holding a lantern high at the door so we could see.

In one corner of the room, Gyp Rainey sat in the chair to which Milk River had tied him. Froth was in the corners of his mouth. He was writhing with cramps. The other prisoners were trying to get some sleep, their blankets spread on the floor as far from Rainey as they could get.

"For Christ's sake give me a shot!" Rainey whined at me.

"Give me a hand, Doctor, and we'll carry him out."

We lifted him, chair and all, and carried him outside.

"Now stop your bawling and listen to me," I ordered. "You shot Nisbet. I want the straight story of it. The straight story will bring you a shot, and nothing else will."

"I didn't kill him!" he screamed. "I didn't! Before God, I didn't!"

"That's a lie. You stole Peery's rope while the rest of us were in Bardell's place Monday

_____

* pass out

morning, talking over Slim's death. You tied the rope where it would look like the murderer had made a getaway down the cañon. Then you stood at the window until Nisbet came into the back room—and you shot him. Nobody went down that rope—or Milk River would have found some sign. Will you come through?"

He wouldn't. He screamed and cursed and pleaded and denied knowledge of the murder.

"Back you go!" I said.

Dr. Haley put a hand on my arm.

"I don't want you to think I am interfering, but I really must warn you that what you're doing is dangerous. It is my belief, and my duty to advise you, that you are endangering this man's life by refusing him some of the drug."

"I know it, Doctor, but I'll have to risk it. He's not so far gone, or he wouldn't be lying. When the sharp edge of the drug-hunger hits him, he'll talk!"

Gyp Rainey stowed away again, I went back to my room. But not to bed.

Clio Landes was waiting for me, sitting there—I had left the door unlocked—with a bottle of whisky. She was about three-quarters lit up—one of those melancholy lushes.

She was a poor, sick, lonely, homesick girl, far away from her world. She dosed herself with alcohol, remembered her dead parents, sad bits of her childhood and unfortunate slices of her past, and cried over them. She poured out all her hopes and fears to me—including her liking for Milk River, who was a good kid even if he had never been within two thousand miles of Forty-second Street and Broadway.

The talk always came back to that: New York, New York, New York.

It was close to four o'clock Thursday morning when the whisky finally answered my prayers, and she went to sleep on my shoulder.

I picked her up and carried her down the hall to her own room. Just as I reached her door, fat Bardell came up the stairs.

"More work for the sheriff," he commented jovially, and went on.

I took her slippers off, tucked her in bed, opened the window, and went out, locking the door behind me and chucking the key over the transom.

After that I slept.

XVI

The sun was high and the room was hot when I woke to the familiar sound of someone knocking on the door. This time it was one of the volunteer guards—the long-legged boy who had carried the warning to Peery Monday night.

"Gyp wants t' see yuh." The boy's face was haggard. "He wants yuh more'n I ever seen a man want anything."

Rainey was a wreck when I got to him.

"I killed him! I killed him!" he shrieked at me. "Bardell knowed the Circle H. A. R. would hit back f'r Slim's killin'. He made me kill Nisbet an' stack th' deal agin Peery so's it'd be up t' you t' go up agin 'em. He'd tried it before an' got th' worst of it!

"Gimme a shot! That's th' God's truth! I stoled th' rope, planted it, an' shot Nisbet wit' Bardell's gun when Bardell sent him back there! Th' gun's under th' tin-can dump in back o' Adderly's. Gimme th' shot! Gimme it!"

"Where's Milk River?" I asked the long-legged boy.

"Sleepin', I reckon. He left along about daylight."

"All right, Gyp! Hold it until the doc gets here. I'll send him right over!"

I found Dr. Haley in his house. A minute later he was carrying a charge over to the hypo.[*]

The Border Palace didn't open until noon. Its doors were locked. I went up the street to the Cañon House. Milk River came out just as I stepped up on the porch.

"Hello, young fellow," I greeted him. "Got any idea which room your friend Bardell reposes in?"

---

* drugs to the addict

He looked at me as if he had never seen me before.

"S'pose you find out for yourself. I'm through doing your chores. You can find yourself a new wet nurse, Mister, or you can go to hell!"

The odor of whisky came out with the words, but he wasn't drunk enough for that to be the whole explanation.

"What's the matter with you?" I asked.

"What's the matter is I think you're a lousy—"

I didn't let it get any farther than that.

His right hand whipped to his side as I stepped in.

I jammed him between the wall and my hip before he could draw, and got one of my hands on each of his arms.

"You may be a curly wolf* with your rod," I growled, shaking him, a lot more peeved than if he had been a stranger, "but if you try any of your monkey business on me, I'll turn you over my knee!"

Clio Landes' thin fingers dug into my arm.

"Stop it!" she cried. "Stop it! Why don't you behave?" to Milk River; and to me: "He's sore over something this morning. He doesn't mean what he says!"

I was sore myself.

"I mean what I said," I insisted.

But I took my hands off him, and went indoors. Inside the door I ran into sallow Vickers, who was hurrying to see what the rumpus was about.

"What room is Bardell's?"

"214. Why?"

I went on past him and upstairs.

My gun in one hand, I used the other to knock on Bardell's door.

"Who is it?" came through.

I told him.

"What do you want?"

I said I wanted to talk to him.

He kept me waiting for a couple of minutes

---

* formidable or belligerent man

before he opened. He was half-dressed. All his clothes below the waist were on. Above, he had a coat on over his undershirt, and one of his hands was in his coat pocket.

His eyes jumped big when they lit on my gun.

"You're arrested for Nisbet's murder!" I informed him. "Take your hand out of your pocket."

He tried to look as if he thought I was kidding him.

"For Nisbet's murder?"

"Uh-huh. Rainey came through. Take your hand out of your pocket."

"You're arresting me on the say-so of a hop-head?"

"Uh-huh. Take your hand out of your pocket."

"You're—"

"Take your hand out of your pocket."

His eyes moved from mine to look past my head, a flash of triumph burning in them.

I beat him to the first shot by a hairline, since he had wasted time waiting for me to fall for that ancient trick.

His bullet cut my neck.

Mine took him where his undershirt was tight over his fat chest.

He fell, tugging at his pocket, trying to get the gun out for another shot.

I could have jumped him, but he was going to die anyhow. That first bullet had got his lungs. I put another into him.

The hall filled with people.

"Get the doctor!" I called to them.

But Bardell didn't need him. He was dead before I had the words out of my mouth.

Chick Orr came through the crowd, into the room.

I stood up, sticking my gun back in its holster.

"I've got nothing on you, Chick, yet," I said slowly. "You know better than I do whether there is anything to get or not. If I were you, I'd drift out of Corkscrew without wasting too much time packing up."

The ex-pug squinted his eyes at me, rubbed his chin, and made a clucking sound in his mouth.

His gold teeth showed in a grin.

"'F anybody asks for me, you tell 'em I'm off on a tour," and he pushed out through the crowd again.

When the doctor came, I took him up the hall to my room, where he patched my neck. The wound wasn't much, but my neck is fleshy, and it bled a lot—all over me, in fact.

After he had finished, I got fresh clothes from my bag and undressed. But when I went to wash, I found the doctor had used all my water. Getting into coat, pants and shoes, I went down to the kitchen for more.

The hall was empty when I came upstairs again, except for Clio Landes.

She went past me without looking at me— deliberately not looking at me.

I washed, dressed, and strapped on my gun. One more angle to be cleaned up, and I would be through. I didn't think I'd need the .32 toys any more, so I put them away. One more angle, and I was done. I was pleased with the idea of getting away from Corkscrew. I didn't like the place, had never liked it, liked it less than ever since Milk River's break.

I was thinking about him when I stepped out of the hotel—to see him standing across the street.

I didn't give him a tumble, but turned toward the lower end of the street.

One step. A bullet kicked up dirt at my feet.

I stopped.

"Go for it, fat boy!" Milk River yelled. "It's me or you!"

I turned slowly to face him, looking for an out. But there wasn't any.

His eyes were insane-lighted slits. His face was a ghastly savage mask. He was beyond reasoning with.

"Put it away!" I ordered, though I knew the words were wasted.

"It's me or you!" he repeated, and put another bullet into the ground in front of me. "Warm your iron!"*

I stopped looking for an out. Blood thickened in my head, and things began to look queer. I could feel my neck thickening. I hoped I wasn't going to get too mad to shoot straight.

I went for my gun.

He gave me an even break.

His gun swung down to me as mine straightened to him.

We pulled triggers together.

Flame jumped at me.

I smacked the ground—my right side all numb.

He was staring at me—bewildered. I stopped staring at him, and looked at my gun—the gun that had only clicked when I pulled the trigger!

When I looked up again, he was coming toward me, slowly, his gun hanging at his side.

"Played it safe, huh?" I raised my gun so he could see the broken firing-pin. "Serves me right for leaving it on the bed when I went downstairs for water."

Milk River dropped his gun—grabbed mine.

Clio Landes came running from the hotel to him.

"You're not—?"

Milk River stuck my gun in her face.

"You done that?"

"I was afraid he—" she began.

"You——!"

With the back of an open hand, Milk River struck the girl's mouth.

He dropped down beside me, his face a boy's face. A tear fell hot on my hand.

"Chief, I didn't—"

"That's all right," I assured him, and I meant it.

I missed whatever else he said. The numbness was leaving my side, and the feeling that came in its place wasn't pleasant. Everything stirred inside me. . . .

---

* shoot your gun

XVII

I was in bed when I came to. Dr. Haley was doing disagreeable things to my side. Behind him, Milk River held a basin in unsteady hands.

"Milk River," I whispered, because that was the best I could do in the way of talk.

He bent his ear to me.

"Get the Jew. He killed Vogel. Careful—gun on him. Talk self-defense—maybe confess. Lock him up with others."

Sweet sleep again.

Night, dim lamplight was in the room when I opened my eyes again. Clio Landes sat beside my bed, staring at the floor, woebegone.

"Good evening," I managed.

I was sorry I had said anything.

She cried all over me and kept me busy assuring her she had been forgiven for the trickery with my gun. I don't know how many times I forgave her. It got to be a damned nuisance. No sooner would I say that everything was all right than she'd begin all over again to ask me to forgive her.

"I was so afraid you'd kill him, because he's only a kid, and somebody had told him a lot of things about you and me, and I knew how crazy he was, and he's only a kid, and I was so afraid you'd kill him," and so on and so on.

Half an hour of this had me woozy with fever.

"And now he won't talk to me, won't even look at me, won't let me come in here when he's here. And nothing will ever make things right again, and I was so afraid you'd kill him, because he's only a boy, and . . ."

I had to shut my eyes and pretend I had passed out to shut her up.

I must have slept some, because when I looked around again it was day, and Milk River was in the chair.

He stood up, not looking at me, his head hanging.

"I'll be moving on, Chief, now that you're coming around all right. I want you to know, though, that if I'd knowed what that—done to

your gun I wouldn't never have throwed down on you."

"What was the matter with you, anyhow?" I growled at him.

His face got beet-color and he shuffled his feet.

"Crazy, I reckon," he mumbled. "I had a couple of drinks, and then Bardell filled me full of stuff about you and her, and that you was playing me for a Chinaman.[*] And—and I just went plumb loco, I reckon."

"Any of it left in your system?"

"Hell, no, chief! I'd give a leg if none of it had never happened!"

"Then suppose you stop this foolishness and sit down and talk sense. Are you and the girl still on the outs?"

They were, most emphatically, most profanely.

"You're a big boob!" I told him. "She's a stranger out here, and homesick for her New York. I could talk her language and knew the people she knew. That's all there was—"

"But that ain't the big point, chief! Any woman that would pull a—"

"Bunk! It was a shabby trick, right enough. But a woman who'll pull a trick like that for you when you are in a jam is worth a million an ounce, and you'd know it if you had anything to know anything with. Now you run out and find this Clio person, and bring her back with you, and no nonsense!"

He pretended he was going reluctantly. But I heard her voice when he knocked on her door. And they let me lay there in my bed of pain for one solid hour before they remembered me. They came in walking so close together that they were stumbling over each other's feet.

"Now let's talk business," I grumbled. "What day is this?"

"Monday."

"Did you get the Jew?"

"I done that thing," Milk River said, divid-

_____

* playing me for a fool

ing the one chair with the girl. "He's over to the county seat now—went over with the others. He swallowed that self-defense bait, and told me all about it. How'd you ever figure it out, chief?"

"Figure what out?"

"That the Jew killed poor old Slim. He says Slim come in there that night, woke him up, ate a dollar and ten cents' worth of grub on him, and then dared him to try and collect. In the argument that follows, Slim goes for his gun, and the Jew gets scared and shoots him—after which Slim obligingly staggers out o' doors to die. I can see all that clear enough, but how'd you hit on it?"

"I oughtn't give away my professional secrets, but I will this once. The Jew was cleaning house when I went in to ask him for what he knew about the killing, and he had scrubbed his floor before he started on the ceiling. If that meant anything at all, it meant that he had had to scrub his floor, and was making the cleaning general to cover it up. So maybe Slim had bled some on that floor.

"Starting from that point, the rest came easily enough. Slim leaving the Border Palace in a wicked frame of mind, broke after his earlier winning, humiliated by Nisbet's triumph in the gun-pulling, soured further by the stuff he had been drinking all day. Red Wheelan had reminded him that afternoon of the time the Jew had followed him to the ranch to collect two bits.

What more likely than he'd carry his meanness into the Jew's shack? That Slim hadn't been shot with the shotgun didn't mean anything. I never had any faith in that shotgun from the first. If the Jew had been depending on that for his protection, he wouldn't have put it in plain sight, and under a shelf, where it wasn't easy to get out. I figured the shotgun was there for moral effect, and he'd have another one stowed out of sight for use.

"Another point you folks missed was that Nisbet seemed to be telling a straight story—not at all the sort of tale he'd have told if he were guilty. Bardell's and Chick's weren't so good, but the chances are they really thought Nisbet had killed Slim, and were trying to cover him up."

Milk River grinned at me, pulling the girl closer with the one arm that was around her.

"You ain't so downright dumb," he said. "Clio done warned me the first time she seen you that I'd best not try to run no sandies* on you."

A far-away look came into his pale eyes.

"Think of all them folks that were killed and maimed and jailed—all over a dollar and ten cents. It's a good thing Slim didn't eat five dollars' worth of grub. He'd of depopulated the State of Arizona complete!"

---

* Sandies are Scotsmen. Possibly a reference to parsimony.

BLACK MASK, NOVEMBER 1925

Dead Yellow Women

BY DASHIELL HAMMETT

SHE WAS SITTING STRAIGHT and stiff in one of the Old Man's chairs when he called me into his office—a tall girl of perhaps twenty-four, broad-shouldered, deep-bosomed, in mannish gray clothes. That she was Oriental showed only in the black shine of her bobbed hair, in the pale yellow of her unpowdered skin, and in the fold of her upper lids at the outer eye-corners, half hidden by the dark rims of her spectacles. But there was no slant to her eyes, her nose was almost aquiline, and she had more chin than Mongolians usually have. She was modern Chinese-American from the flat heels of her tan shoes to the crown of her untrimmed felt hat.

I knew her before the Old Man introduced me. The San Francisco papers had been full of her affairs for a couple of days. They had printed photographs and diagrams, interviews, edi-torials, and more or less expert opinions from various sources. They had gone back to 1912 to remember the stubborn fight of the local Chinese—mostly from Fokien and Kwangtung, where democratic ideas and hatred of Manchus go together—to have her father kept out of the United States, to which he had scooted when the Manchu rule flopped. The papers had recalled the excitement in Chinatown when Shan Fang was allowed to land—insulting placards had been hung in the streets, an unpleasant recep-tion had been planned.

But Shan Fang had fooled the Cantonese. Chinatown had never seen him. He had taken his daughter and his gold—presumably the accumulated profits of a life-time of provincial misrule—down to San Mateo County, where he had built what the papers described as a palace on the edge of the Pacific. There he had lived and died in a manner suitable to a *Ta Jen* and a millionaire.

So much for the father. For the daughter—this young woman who was coolly studying me as I sat down across the table from her: she had been ten-year-old Ai Ho, a very Chinese little girl, when her father had brought her to California. All that was Oriental of her now were the features I have mentioned and the money her father had left her. Her name, translated into English, had become Water Lily, and then, by another step, Lillian. It was as Lillian Shan that she had attended an eastern university, acquired several degrees, won a tennis championship of some sort in 1919, and published a book on the nature and significance of fetishes, whatever all that is or are.

Since her father's death, in 1921, she had lived with her four Chinese servants in the house on the shore, where she had written her first book and was now at work on another. A couple of weeks ago, she had found herself stumped, so she said—had run into a blind alley. There was, she said, a certain old cabalistic manuscript in the Arsenal Library in Paris that she believed would solve her troubles for her. So she had packed some clothes and, accompanied by her maid, a Chinese woman named Wang Ma, had taken a train for New York, leaving the three other servants to take care of the house during her absence. The decision to go to France for a look at the manuscript had been formed one morning—she was on the train before dark.

On the train between Chicago and New York, the key to the problem that had puzzled her suddenly popped into her head. Without pausing even for a night's rest in New York, she had turned around and headed back for San Francisco. At the ferry here she had tried to telephone her chauffeur to bring a car for her. No answer. A taxicab had carried her and her maid to her house. She rang the door-bell to no effect.

When her key was in the lock the door had been suddenly opened by a young Chinese man—a stranger to her. He had refused her admittance until she told him who she was. He mumbled an unintelligible explanation as she and the maid went into the hall.

Both of them were neatly bundled up in some curtains.

Two hours later Lillian Shan got herself loose—in a linen closet on the second floor. Switching on the light, she started to untie the maid. She stopped. Wang Ma was dead. The rope around her neck had been drawn too tight.

Lillian Shan went out into the empty house and telephoned the sheriff's office in Redwood City.

Two deputy sheriffs had come to the house, had listened to her story, had poked around, and had found another Chinese body—another strangled woman—buried in the cellar. Apparently she had been dead a week or a week and a half; the dampness of the ground made more positive dating impossible. Lillian Shan identified her as another of her servants—Wan Lan, the cook.

The other servants—Hoo Lun and Yin Hung—had vanished. Of the several hundred thousand dollars' worth of furnishings old Shan Fang had put into the house during his life, not a nickel's worth had been removed. There were no signs of a struggle. Everything was in order. The closest neighboring house was nearly half a mile away. The neighbors had seen nothing, knew nothing.

That's the story the newspapers had hung headlines over, and that's the story this girl, sitting very erect in her chair, speaking with businesslike briskness, shaping each word as exactly as if it were printed in black type, told the Old Man and me.

"I am not at all satisfied with the effort the San Mateo County authorities have made to apprehend the murderer or murderers," she wound up. "I wish to engage your agency."

The Old Man tapped the table with the point of his inevitable long yellow pencil and nodded at me.

"Have you any idea of your own on the murders, Miss Shan?" I asked.

"I have not."

"What do you know about the servants—the missing ones as well as the dead?"

"I really know little or nothing about them." She didn't seem very interested. "Wang Ma was the most recent of them to come to the house, and she has been with me for nearly seven years. My father employed them, and I suppose he knew something about them."

"Don't you know where they came from? Whether they have relatives? Whether they have friends? What they did when they weren't working?"

"No," she said. "I did not pry into their lives."

"The two who disappeared—what do they look like?"

"Hoo Lun is an old man, quite white-haired and thin and stooped. He did the housework. Yin Hung, who was my chauffeur and gardener, is younger, about thirty years old, I think. He is quite short, even for a Cantonese, but sturdy. His nose has been broken at some time and not set properly. It is very flat, with a pronounced bend in the bridge."

"Do you think this pair, or either of them, could have killed the women?"

"I do not think they did."

"The young Chinese—the stranger who let you in the house—what did he look like?"

"He was quite slender, and not more than twenty or twenty-one years old, with large gold fillings in his front teeth. I think he was quite dark."

"Will you tell me exactly why you are dissatisfied with what the sheriff is doing, Miss Shan?"

"In the first place, I am not sure they are competent. The ones I saw certainly did not impress me with their brilliance."

"And in the second place?"

"Really," she asked coldly, "is it necessary to go into all my mental processes?"

"It is."

She looked at the Old Man, who smiled at her with his polite, meaningless smile—a mask through which you can read nothing.

For a moment she hung fire. Then: "I don't think they are looking in very likely places. They seem to spend the greater part of their time in the vicinity of the house. It is absurd to think the murderers are going to return."

I turned that over in my mind.

"Miss Shan," I asked, "don't you think they suspect you?"

Her dark eyes burned through her glasses at me and, if possible, she made herself more rigidly straight in her chair.

"Preposterous!"

"That isn't the point," I insisted. "Do they?"

"I am not able to penetrate the police mind," she came back. "Do *you*?"

"I don't know anything about this job but what I've read and what you've just told me. I need more foundation than that to suspect anybody. But I can understand why the sheriff's office would be a little doubtful. You left in a hurry. They've got your word for why you went and why you came back, and your word is all. The woman found in the cellar could have been killed just before you left as well as just after. Wang Ma, who could have told things, is dead. The other servants are missing. Nothing was stolen. That's plenty to make the sheriff think about you!"

"Do you suspect me?" she asked again.

"No," I said truthfully. "But that proves nothing."

She spoke to the Old Man, with a chin-tilting motion, as if she were talking over my head.

"Do you wish to undertake this work for me?"

"We shall be very glad to do what we can," he said, and then to me, after they had talked terms and while she was writing a check, "you handle it. Use what men you need."

"I want to go out to the house first and look the place over," I said.

Lillian Shan was putting away her checkbook.

"Very well. I am returning home now. I will drive you down."

It was a restful ride. Neither the girl nor I

wasted energy on conversation. My client and I didn't seem to like each other very much. She drove well.

II

The Shan house was a big brownstone affair, set among sodded lawns. The place was hedged shoulder-high on three sides. The fourth boundary was the ocean, where it came in to make a notch in the shore-line between two small rocky points.

The house was full of hangings, rugs, pictures, and so on—a mixture of things American, European and Asiatic. I didn't spend much time inside. After a look at the linen-closet, at the still open cellar grave, and at the pale, thick-featured Danish woman who was taking care of the house until Lillian Shan could get a new corps of servants, I went outdoors again. I poked around the lawns for a few minutes, stuck my head in the garage, where two cars, besides the one in which we had come from town, stood, and then went off to waste the rest of the afternoon talking to the girl's neighbors. None of them knew anything. Since we were on opposite sides of the game, I didn't hunt up the sheriff's men.

By twilight I was back in the city, going into the apartment building in which I lived during my first year in San Francisco. I found the lad I wanted in his cubby-hole room, getting his small body into a cerise silk shirt that was something to look at. Cipriano was the bright-faced Filipino boy who looked after the building's front door in the daytime. At night, like all the Filipinos in San Francisco, he could be found down on Kearny Street, just below Chinatown, except when he was in a Chinese gambling-house passing his money over to the yellow brothers.

I had once, half-joking, promised to give the lad a fling at gumshoeing if the opportunity ever came. I thought I could use him now.

"Come in, sir!"

He was dragging a chair out of a corner for me, bowing and smiling. Whatever else the Spaniards do for the people they rule, they make them polite.

"What's doing in Chinatown these days?" I asked as he went on with his dressing.

He gave me a white-toothed smile.

"I take eleven bucks out of bean-game last night."

"And you're getting ready to take it back tonight?"

"Not all of 'em, sir! Five bucks I spend for this shirt."

"That's the stuff," I applauded his wisdom in investing part of his fan-tan profits. "What else is doing down there?"

"Nothing unusual, sir. You want to find something?"

"Yeah. Hear any talk about the killings down the country last week? The two Chinese women?"

"No, sir. Chinaboy don't talk much about things like that. Not like us Americans. I read about those things in newspapers, but I have not heard."

"Many strangers in Chinatown nowadays?"

"All the time there's strangers, sir. But I guess maybe some new Chinaboys are there. Maybe not, though."

"How would you like to do a little work for me?"

"Yes, sir! Yes, sir! Yes, sir!" He said it oftener than that, but that will give you the idea. While he was saying it he was down on his knees, dragging a valise from under the bed. Out of the valise he took a pair of brass knuckles and a shiny revolver.

"Here! I want some information. I don't want you to knock anybody off for me."

"I don't knock 'em," he assured me, stuffing his weapons in his hip pockets. "Just carry these—maybe I need 'em."

I let it go at that. If he wanted to make himself bow-legged carrying a ton of iron it was all right with me.

"Here's what I want. Two of the servants ducked out of the house down there." I described Yin Hung and Hoo Lun. "I want to find them. I want to find what anybody in Chinatown knows about the killings. I want to find who the dead women's friends and relatives are, where they came from, and the same thing for the two men. I want to know about those strange Chinese—where they hang out, where they sleep, what they're up to.

"Now, don't try to get all this in a night. You'll be doing fine if you get any of it in a week. Here's twenty dollars. Five of it is your night's pay. You can use the other to carry you around. Don't be foolish and poke your nose into a lot of grief. Take it easy and see what you can turn up for me. I'll drop in tomorrow."

From the Filipino's room I went to the office. Everybody except Fiske, the night man, was gone, but Fiske thought the Old Man would drop in for a few minutes later in the night.

I smoked, pretended to listen to Fiske's report on all the jokes that were at the Orpheum that week, and grouched over my job. I was too well known to get anything on the quiet in Chinatown. I wasn't sure Cipriano was going to be much help. I needed somebody who was in right down there.

This line of thinking brought me around to "Dummy" Uhl. Uhl was a dummerer* who had lost his store. Five years before, he had been sitting on the world. Any day on which his sad face, his package of pins, and his *I am deaf and dumb* sign didn't take twenty dollars out of the office buildings along his route was a rotten day. His big card was his ability to play the statue when skeptical people yelled or made sudden noises behind him. When the Dummy was right, a gun off beside his ear wouldn't make him twitch an eye-lid. But too much heroin broke his nerves until a whisper was enough to make him jump. He put away his pins and his sign—another man whose social life had ruined him.

Since then Dummy had become an errand boy for whoever would stake him to the price of his necessary nose-candy. He slept somewhere in Chinatown, and he didn't care especially how

he played the game. I had used him to get me some information on a window-smashing six months before. I decided to try him again.

I called "Loop" Pigatti's place—a dive down on Pacific Street, where Chinatown fringes into the Latin Quarter. Loop is a tough citizen, who runs a tough hole, and who minds his own business, which is making his dive show a profit. Everybody looks alike to Loop. Whether you're a yegg,† stool-pigeon, detective, or settlement worker, you get an even break out of Loop and nothing else. But you can be sure that, unless it's something that might hurt his business, anything you tell Loop will get no further. And anything he tells you is more than likely to be right.

He answered the phone himself.

"Can you get hold of Dummy Uhl for me?" I asked after I had told him who I was.

"Maybe."

"Thanks. I'd like to see him tonight."

"You got nothin' on him?"

"No, Loop, and I don't expect to. I want him to get something for me."

"All right. Where d'you want him?"

"Send him up to my joint. I'll wait there for him."

"If he'll come," Loop promised and hung up.

I left word with Fiske to have the Old Man call me up when he came in, and then I went up to my rooms to wait for my informant.

He came in a little after ten—a short, stocky, pasty-faced man of forty or so, with mouse-colored hair streaked with yellow-white.

"Loop says y'got sumpin' f'r me."

"Yes," I said, waving him to a chair, and closing the door. "I'm buying news."

He fumbled with his hat, started to spit on the floor, changed his mind, licked his lips, and looked up at me.

"What kind o' news? I don't know nothin'."

I was puzzled. The Dummy's yellowish eyes should have showed the pinpoint pupils of the heroin addict. They didn't. The pupils were normal. That didn't mean he was off the stuff—he

---

had put cocaine into them to distend them to normal. The puzzle was—why? He wasn't usually particular enough about his appearance to go to that trouble.

"Did you hear about the Chinese killings down the shore last week?" I asked him.

"No."

"Well," I said, paying no attention to the denial, "I'm hunting for the pair of yellow men who ducked out—Hoo Lun and Yin Hung. Know anything about them?"

"No."

"It's worth a couple of hundred dollars to you to find either of them for me. It's worth another couple hundred to find out about the killings for me. It's worth another to find the slim Chinese youngster with gold teeth who opened the door for the Shan girl and her maid."

"I don't know nothin' about them things," he said.

But he said it automatically while his mind was busy counting up the hundreds I had dangled before him. I suppose his dope-addled brains made the total somewhere in the thousands. He jumped up.

"I'll see what I c'n do. S'pose you slip me a hundred now, on account."

I didn't see that.

"You get it when you deliver."

We had to argue that point, but finally he went off grumbling and growling to get me my news.

I went back to the office. The Old Man hadn't come in yet. It was nearly midnight when he arrived.

"I'm using Dummy Uhl again," I told him, "and I've put a Filipino boy down there too. I've got another scheme, but I don't know anybody to handle it. I think if we offered the missing chauffeur and house-man jobs in some out-of-the-way place up the country, perhaps they'd fall for it. Do you know anybody who could pull it for us?"

"Exactly what have you in mind?"

"It must be somebody who has a house out in the country, the farther the better, the more

secluded the better. They would phone one of the Chinese employment offices that they needed three servants—cook, house-man, and chauffeur. We throw in the cook for good measure, to cover the game. It's got to be air-tight on the other end, and, if we're going to catch our fish, we have to give 'em time to investigate. So whoever does it must have some servants, and must put up a bluff—I mean in his own neighborhood—that they are leaving, and the servants must be in on it. And we've got to wait a couple of days, so our friends here will have time to investigate. I think we'd better use Fong Yick's employment agency, on Washington Street.

"Whoever does it could phone Fong Yick tomorrow morning, and say he'd be in Thursday morning to look the applicants over. This is Monday—that'll be long enough. Our helper gets at the employment office at ten Thursday morning. Miss Shan and I arrive in a taxicab ten minutes later, when he'll be in the middle of questioning the applicants. I'll slide out of the taxi into Fong Yick's, grab anybody that looks like one of our missing servants. Miss Shan will come in a minute or two behind me and check me up—so there won't be any false-arrest mix-ups."

The Old Man nodded approval.

"Very well," he said. "I think I can arrange it. I will let you know tomorrow."

I went home to bed. Thus ended the first day.

III

At nine the next morning, Tuesday, I was talking to Cipriano in the lobby of the apartment building that employs him. His eyes were black drops of ink in white saucers. He thought he had got something.

"Yes, sir! Strange Chinaboys are in town, some of them. They sleep in a house on Waverly Place—on the western side, four houses from the house of Jair Quon, where I sometimes play dice. And there is more—I talk to a white man who knows they are hatchet-men from Portland and Eureka and Sacramento. They are Hip Sing men—a tong war starts—pretty soon, maybe."

"Do these birds look like gunmen to you?"

Cipriano scratched his head.

"No, sir, maybe not. But a fellow can shoot sometimes if he don't look like it. This man tells me they are Hip Sing men."

"Who was this white man?"

"I don't know the name, but he lives there. A short man—snow-bird."

"Gray hair, yellowish eyes?"

"Yes, sir."

That, as likely as not, would be Dummy Uhl. One of my men was stringing the other. The tong stuff hadn't sounded right to me anyhow. Once in a while they mix things, but usually they are blamed for somebody else's crimes. Most wholesale killings in Chinatown are the result of family or clan feuds—such as the ones the "Four Brothers"* used to stage.

"This house where you think the strangers are living—know anything about it?"

"No, sir. But maybe you could go through there to the house of Chang Li Ching on other street—Spofford Alley."

"So? And who is this Chang Li Ching?"

"I don't know, sir. But he is there. Nobody sees him, but all Chinaboys say he is great man."

"So? And his house is in Spofford Alley?"

"Yes, sir, a house with red door and red steps. You find it easy, but better not fool with Chang Li Ching."

I didn't know whether that was advice or just a general remark.

"A big gun, huh?" I probed.

But my Filipino didn't really know anything about this Chang Li Ching. He was basing his opinion of the Chinese's greatness on the attitude of his fellow countrymen when they mentioned him.

"Learn anything about the two Chinese men?" I asked after I had fixed this point.

* powerful Chinese Tong active in New York City and in San Francisco

"No, sir, but I will—you bet!"

I praised him for what he had done, told him to try it again that night, and went back to my rooms to wait for Dummy Uhl, who had promised to come there at ten-thirty. It was not quite ten when I got there, so I used some of my spare time to call up the office. The Old Man said Dick Foley—our shadow ace—was idle, so I borrowed him. Then I fixed my gun and sat down to wait for my stool-pigeon.

He rang the bell at eleven o'clock. He came in frowning tremendously.

"I don't know what t' hell to make of it, kid," he spoke importantly over the cigarette he was rolling. "There's sumpin' makin' down there, an' that's a fact. Things ain't been anyways quiet since the Japs began buyin' stores in the Chink streets, an' maybe that's got sumpin' to do with it. But there ain't no strange Chinks in town—not a damn one! I got a hunch your men have gone down to L.A., but I expec' t' know f'r certain tonight. I got a Chink ribbed up t' get the dope; 'f I was you, I'd put a watch on the boats at San Pedro. Maybe those fellas'll swap papers wit' a coupla Chink sailors that'd like t' stay here."

"And there are no strangers in town?"

"Not any."

"Dummy," I said bitterly, "you're a liar, and you're a boob, and I've been playing you for a sucker. You were in on that killing, and so were your friends, and I'm going to throw you in the can, and your friends on top of you!"

I put my gun in sight, close to his scared-gray face.

"Keep yourself still while I do my phoning!"

Reaching for the telephone with my free hand, I kept one eye on the Dummy.

It wasn't enough. My gun was too close to him.

He yanked it out of my hand. I jumped for him.

The gun turned in his fingers. I grabbed it—too late. It went off, its muzzle less than a foot from where I'm thickest. Fire stung my body.

Clutching the gun with both hands I folded

down to the floor. Dummy went away from there, leaving the door open behind him.

One hand on my burning belly, I crossed to the window and waved an arm at Dick Foley, stalling on a corner down the street. Then I went to the bathroom and looked to my wound. A blank cartridge does hurt if you catch it close up!

My vest and shirt and union suit were ruined, and I had a nasty scorch on my body. I greased it, taped a cushion over it, changed my clothes, loaded the gun again, and went down to the office to wait for word from Dick. The first trick in the game looked like mine. Heroin or no heroin, Dummy Uhl would not have jumped me if my guess—based on the trouble he was taking to make his eyes look right and the lie he had sprung on me about there being no strangers in Chinatown—hadn't hit close to the mark.

Dick wasn't long in joining me.

"Good pickings!" he said when he came in. The little Canadian talks like a thrifty man's telegram. "Beat it for phone. Called Hotel Irvington. Booth—couldn't get anything but number. Ought to be enough. Then Chinatown. Dived in cellar west side Waverly Place. Couldn't stick close enough to spot place. Afraid to take chance hanging around. How do you like it?"

"I like it all right. Let's look up 'The Whistler's' record."

A file clerk got it for us—a bulky envelope the size of a brief case, crammed with memoranda, clippings and letters. The gentleman's biography, as we had it, ran like this:

Neil Conyers, alias The Whistler, was born in Philadelphia—out on Whiskey Hill—in 1883. In '94, at the age of eleven, he was picked up by the Washington police. He had gone there to join Coxey's Army.[*] They sent him home. In '98 he was arrested in his home town for stabbing another lad in a row over an election-night bonfire. This time he was released in his parents' custody. In 1901 the Philadelphia police

grabbed him again, charging him with being the head of the first organized automobile-stealing ring. He was released without trial, for lack of evidence. But the district attorney lost his job in the resultant scandal. In 1908 Conyers appeared on the Pacific Coast—at Seattle, Portland, San Francisco, and Los Angeles—in company with a con-man known as "Duster" Hughes. Hughes was shot and killed the following year by a man whom he'd swindled in a fake airplane manufacturing deal. Conyers was arrested on the same deal. Two juries disagreed and he was turned loose. In 1910 the Post Office Department's famous raid on get-rich-quick promoters caught him. Again there wasn't enough evidence against him to put him away. In 1915 the law scored on him for the first time. He went to San Quentin for buncoing some visitors to the Panama-Pacific International Exposition. He stayed there for three years. In 1919 he and a Jap named Hasegawa nicked the Japanese colony of Seattle for $20,000, Conyers posing as an American who had held a commission in the Japanese army during that late war. He had a counterfeit medal of the Order of the Rising Sun which the emperor was supposed to have pinned on him. When the game fell through, Hasegawa's family made good the $20,000—Conyers got out of it with a good profit and not even any disagreeable publicity. The thing had been hushed. He returned to San Francisco after that, bought the Hotel Irvington, and had been living there now for five years without anybody being able to add another word to his criminal record. He was up to something, but nobody could learn what. There wasn't a chance in the world of getting a detective into his hotel as a guest. Apparently the joint was always without vacant rooms. It was as exclusive as the Pacific-Union Club.

This, then, was the proprietor of the hotel Dummy Uhl had got on the phone before diving into his hole in Chinatown.

I had never seen Conyers. Neither had Dick. There were a couple of photographs in his envelope. One was the profile and full-face photograph of the local police, taken when he had

---

[*] followers of Jacob S. Coxey who marched on Washington, DC, in 1894 to protest government inaction following the financial panic of 1893

been picked up on the charge that led him to San Quentin. The other was a group picture: all rung up in evening clothes, with the phoney Japanese medal on his chest, he stood among half a dozen of the Seattle Japs he had trimmed—a flashlight picture taken while he was leading them to the slaughter.

These pictures showed him to be a big bird, fleshy, pompous-looking, with a heavy, square chin and shrewd eyes.

"Think you could pick him up?" I asked Dick.

"Sure."

"Suppose you go up there and see if you can get a room or apartment somewhere in the neighborhood—one you can watch the hotel from. Maybe you'll get a chance to tail him around now and then."

I put the pictures in my pocket, in case they'd come in handy, dumped the rest of the stuff back in its envelope, and went into the Old Man's office.

"I arranged that employment office stratagem," he said. "A Frank Paul, who has a ranch out beyond Martinez, will be in Fong Yick's establishment at ten Thursday morning, carrying out his part."

"That's fine! I'm going calling in Chinatown now. If you don't hear from me for a couple of days, will you ask the street-cleaners to watch what they're sweeping up?"

He said he would.

IV

San Francisco's Chinatown jumps out of the shopping district at California Street and runs north to the Latin Quarter—a strip two blocks wide by six long. Before the fire nearly twenty-five thousand Chinese lived in those dozen blocks. I don't suppose the population is a third of that now.

Grant Avenue, the main street and spine of this strip, is for most of its length a street of gaudy shops catering to the tourist trade and flashy chop-suey houses, where the racket of American jazz orchestras drowns the occasional squeak of a Chinese flute. Farther out, there isn't so much paint and gilt, and you can catch the proper Chinese smell of spices and vinegar and dried things. If you leave the main thoroughfares and show places and start poking around in alleys and dark corners, and nothing happens to you, the chances are you'll find some interesting things—though you won't like some of them.

However, I wasn't poking around as I turned off Grant Avenue at Clay Street, and went up to Spofford Alley, hunting for the house with red steps and red door, which Cipriano had said was Chang Li Ching's. I did pause for a few seconds to look up Waverly Place when I passed it. The Filipino had told me the strange Chinese were living there, and that he thought their house might lead through to Chang Li Ching's; and Dick Foley had shadowed Dummy Uhl there.

But I couldn't guess which was the important house. Four doors from Jair Quon's gambling house, Cipriano had said, but I didn't know where Jair Quon's was. Waverly Place was a picture of peace and quiet just now. A fat Chinese was stacking crates of green vegetables in front of a grocery. Half a dozen small yellow boys were playing at marbles in the middle of the street. On the other side, a blond young man in tweeds was climbing the six steps from a cellar to the street, a painted Chinese woman's face showing for an instant before she closed the door behind him. Up the street a truck was unloading rolls of paper in front of one of the Chinese newspaper plants. A shabby guide was bringing four sightseers out of the Temple of the Queen of Heaven—a joss house over the Sue Hing headquarters.*

I went on up to Spofford Alley and found my house with no difficulty at all. It was a shabby building with steps and door the color of dried blood, its windows solidly shuttered with thick, tight-nailed planking. What made it stand out

---

* headquarters of the Sue Hing Association, a Hui-guan, or benevolent society, founded in San Francisco at the end of the nineteenth century

from its neighbors was that its ground floor wasn't a shop or place of business. Purely residential buildings are rare in Chinatown: almost always the street floor is given to business, with the living quarters in cellar or upper stories.

I went up the three steps and tapped the red door with my knuckles.

Nothing happened.

I hit it again, harder. Still nothing. I tried it again, and this time was rewarded by the sounds of scraping and clicking inside.

At least two minutes of this scraping and clicking, and the door swung open—a bare four inches.

One slanting eye and a slice of wrinkled brown face looked out of the crack at me, above the heavy chain that held the door.

"Whata wan'?"

"I want to see Chang Li Ching."

"No savvy. Maybe closs stleet."

"Bunk! You fix your little door and run back and tell Chang Li Ching I want to see him."

"No can do! No savvy Chang."

"You tell him I'm here," I said, turning my back on the door. I sat down on the top step, and added, without looking around, "I'll wait."

While I got my cigarettes out there was silence behind me. Then the door closed softly and the scraping and clicking broke out behind it. I smoked a cigarette and another and let time go by, trying to look like I had all the patience there was. I hoped this yellow man wasn't going to make a chump of me by letting me sit there until I got tired of it.

Chinese passed up and down the alley, scuffling along in American shoes that can never be made to fit them. Some of them looked curiously at me, some gave me no attention at all. An hour went to waste, and a few minutes, and then the familiar scraping and clicking disturbed the door.

The chain rattled as the door swung open. I wouldn't turn my head.

"Go 'way! No catch 'em Chang!"

I said nothing. If he wasn't going to let me in

he would have let me sit there without further attention.

A pause.

"Whata wan'?"

"I want to see Chang Li Ching," I said without looking around.

Another pause, ended by the banging of the chain against the door-frame.

"All light."

I chucked my cigarette into the street, got up and stepped into the house. In the dimness I could make out a few pieces of cheap and battered furniture. I had to wait while the Chinese put four arm-thick bars across the door and padlocked them there. Then he nodded at me and scuffled across the floor, a small, bent man with hairless yellow head and a neck like a piece of rope.

Out of this room, he led me into another, darker still, into a hallway, and down a flight of rickety steps. The odors of musty clothing and damp earth were strong. We walked through the dark across a dirt floor for a while, turned to the left, and cement was under my feet. We turned twice more in the dark, and then climbed a flight of unplaned wooden steps into a hall that was fairly light with the glow from shaded electric lights.

In this hall my guide unlocked a door, and we crossed a room where cones of incense burned, and where, in the light of an oil lamp, little red tables with cups of tea stood in front of wooden panels, marked with Chinese characters in gold paint, which hung on the walls. A door on the opposite side of this room let us into pitch blackness, where I had to hold the tail of my guide's loose made-to-order blue coat.

So far he hadn't once looked back at me since our tour began, and neither of us had said anything. This running upstairs and downstairs, turning to the right and turning to the left, seemed harmless enough. If he got any fun out of confusing me, he was welcome. I was confused enough now, so far as the directions were concerned. I hadn't the least idea where I might be. But that didn't disturb me so much. If I was going to be cut down, a knowledge of my geographical position wouldn't make it any more pleasant. If I was going to come out all right, one place was still as good as another.

We did a lot more of the winding around, we did some stair-climbing and some stair-descending, and the rest of the foolishness. I figured I'd been indoors nearly half an hour by now, and I had seen nobody but my guide.

Then I saw something else.

We were going down a long, narrow hall that had brown-painted doors close together on either side. All these doors were closed—secretive-looking in the dim light. Abreast of one of them, a glint of dull metal caught my eye—a dark ring in the door's center.

I went to the floor.

Going down as if I'd been knocked, I missed the flash. But I heard the roar, smelled the powder.

My guide spun around, twisting out of one slipper. In each of his hands was an automatic as big as a coal scuttle. Even while trying to get my own gun out I wondered how so puny a man could have concealed so much machinery on him.

The big guns in the little man's hands flamed at me. Chinese-fashion, he was emptying them—crash! crash! crash!

I thought he was missing me until I had my finger tight on my trigger. Then I woke up in time to hold my fire.

He wasn't shooting at me. He was pouring metal into the door behind me—the door from which I had been shot at.

I rolled away from it, across the hall.

The scrawny little man stepped closer and finished his bombardment. His slugs shredded the wood as if it had been paper. His guns clicked empty.

The door swung open, pushed by the wreck of a man who was trying to hold himself up by clinging to the sliding panel in the door's center. Dummy Uhl—all the middle of him gone—

slid down to the floor and made more of a puddle than a pile there.

The hall filled with yellow men, black guns sticking out like briars in a blackberry patch.

I got up. My guide dropped his guns to his side and sang out a guttural solo. Chinese began to disappear through various doors, except four who began gathering up what twenty bullets had left of Dummy Uhl.

The stringy old boy tucked his empty guns away and came down the hall to me, one hand held out toward my gun.

"You give 'em," he said politely.

I gave 'em. He could have had my pants.

My gun stowed away in his shirt-bosom, he looked casually at what the four Chinese were carrying away, and then at me.

"No like 'em fella, huh?" he asked.

"Not so much," I admitted.

"All light. I take you."

Our two-man parade got under way again. The ring-around-the-rosy game went on for another flight of stairs and some right and left turns, and then my guide stopped before a door and scratched it with his finger-nails.

V

The door was opened by another Chinese. But this one was none of your Cantonese runts. He was a big meat-eating wrestler—bull-throated, mountain-shouldered, gorilla-armed, leather-skinned. The god that made him had plenty of material, and gave it time to harden.

Holding back the curtain that covered the door, he stepped to one side. I went in, and found his twin standing on the other side of the door.

The room was large and cubical, its doors and windows—if any—hidden behind velvet hangings of green and blue and silver. In a big black chair, elaborately carved, behind an inlaid black table, sat an old Chinese man. His face was round and plump and shrewd, with a straggle of thin white whiskers on his chin. A dark, close-fitting cap was on his head; a purple robe, tight around his neck, showed its sable lining at the bottom, where it had fallen back in a fold over his blue satin trousers.

He did not get up from his chair, but smiled mildly over his whiskers and bent his head almost to the tea things on the table.

"It was only the inability to believe that one of your excellency's heaven-born splendor would waste his costly time on so mean a clod that kept the least of your slaves from running down to prostrate himself at your noble feet as soon as he heard the Father of Detectives was at his unworthy door."

That came out smoothly in English that was a lot clearer than my own. I kept my face straight, waiting.

"If the Terror of Evildoers will honor one of my deplorable chairs by resting his divine body on it, I can assure him the chair shall be burned afterward, so no lesser being may use it. Or will the Prince of Thief-catchers permit me to send a servant to his palace for a chair worthy of him?"

I went slowly to a chair, trying to arrange words in my mind. This old joker was spoofing me with an exaggeration—a burlesque—of the well-known Chinese politeness. I'm not hard to get along with: I'll play anybody's game up to a certain point.

"It's only because I'm weak-kneed with awe of the mighty Chang Li Ching that I dare to sit down," I explained, letting myself down on the chair, and turning my head to notice that the giants who had stood beside the door were gone.

I had a hunch they had gone no farther than the other side of the velvet hangings that hid the door.

"If it were not that the King of Finders-out"—he was at it again—"knows everything, I should marvel that he had heard my lowly name."

"Heard it? Who hasn't?" I kidded back. "Isn't the word *change*, in English, derived from Chang? Change, meaning alter, is what happens to the wisest man's opinions after he has heard the wisdom of Chang Li Ching!" I tried to get away from this vaudeville stuff, which was a strain on my head. "Thanks for having your man save my life back there in the passage."

He spreads his hands out over the table.

"It was only because I feared the Emperor of Hawkshaws[*] would find the odor of such low blood distasteful to his elegant nostrils that the foul one who disturbed your excellency was struck down quickly. If I have erred, and you would have chosen that he be cut to pieces inch by inch, I can only offer to torture one of my sons in his place."

"Let the boy live," I said carelessly, and turned to business. "I wouldn't have bothered you except that I am so ignorant that only the help of your great wisdom could ever bring me up to normal."

"Does one ask the way of a blind man?" the old duffer asked, cocking his head to one side. "Can a star, however willing, help the moon? If it pleases the Grandfather of Bloodhounds to flatter Chang Li Ching into thinking he can add to the great one's knowledge, who is Chang to thwart his master by refusing to make himself ridiculous?"

I took that to mean he was willing to listen to my questions.

"What I'd like to know is, who killed Lillian Shan's servants, Wang Ma and Wan Lan?"

He played with a thin strand of his white beard, twisting it in a pale, small finger.

"Does the stag-hunter look at the hare?" he wanted to know. "And when so mighty a hunter pretends to concern himself with the death of servants, can Chang think anything except that it pleases the great one to conceal his real object? Yet it may be, because the dead were servants and not girdle-wearers, that the Lord of Snares thought the lowly Chang Li Ching, insignificant one of the Hundred Names, might have

---

[*] detectives, after the lead character in Gus Mager's comic strip *Hawkshawk the Detective* (1913–22, 1931–48), whose name had been appropriated from a sleuth in Tom Taylor's 1863 play, *The Ticket-of-Leave Man*

knowledge of them. Do not rats know the way of rats?"

He kept this stuff up for some minutes, while I sat and listened and studied his round, shrewd yellow mask of a face, and hoped that something clear would come of it all. Nothing did.

"My ignorance is even greater than I had arrogantly supposed," he brought his speech to an end. "This simple question you put is beyond the power of my muddled mind. I do not know who killed Wang Ma and Wan Lan."

I grinned at him, and put another question:

"Where can I find Hoo Lun and Yin Hung?"

"Again I must grovel in my ignorance," he murmured, "only consoling myself with the thought that the Master of Mysteries knows the answers to his questions, and is pleased to conceal his infallibly accomplished purpose from Chang."

And that was as far as I got.

There were more crazy compliments, more bowing and scraping, more assurances of eternal reverence and love, and then I was following my rope-necked guide through winding, dark halls, across dim rooms, and up and down rickety stairs again.

At the street door after he had taken down the bars—he slid my gun out of his shirt and handed it to me. I squelched the impulse to look at it then and there to see if anything had been done to it. Instead I stuck it in my pocket and stepped through the door.

"Thanks for the killing upstairs," I said.

The Chinese grunted, bowed, and closed the door.

I went up to Stockton Street, and turned toward the office, walking along slowly, punishing my brains.

First, there was Dummy Uhl's death to think over. Had it been arranged before-hand: to punish him for bungling that morning and, at the same time, to impress me? And how? And why? Or was it supposed to put me under obligations to the Chinese? And, if so, why? Or was it just one of those complicated tricks the Chinese like? I put the subject away and pointed my thoughts at the little plump yellow man in the purple robe.

I liked him. He had humor, brains, nerve, everything. To jam him in a cell would be a trick you'd want to write home about. He was my idea of a man worth working against.

But I didn't kid myself into thinking I had anything on him. Dummy Uhl had given me a connection between The Whistler's Hotel Irvington and Chang Li Ching. Dummy Uhl had gone into action when I accused him of being mixed up in the Shan killings. That much I had—and that was all, except that Chang had said nothing to show he wasn't interested in the Shan troubles.

In this light, the chances were that Dummy's death had not been a planned performance. It was more likely that he had seen me coming, had tried to wipe me out, and had been knocked off by my guide because he was interfering with the audience Chang had granted me. Dummy couldn't have had a very valuable life in the Chinese's eye—or in anybody else's.

I wasn't at all dissatisfied with the day's work so far. I hadn't done anything brilliant, but I had got a look at my destination, or thought I had. If I was butting my head against a stone wall, I at least knew where the wall was and had seen the man who owned it.

In the office, a message from Dick Foley was waiting for me. He had rented a front apartment up the street from the Irvington and had put in a couple of hours trailing The Whistler.

The Whistler had spent half an hour in "Big Fat" Thomson's place on Market Street, talking to the proprietor and some of the sure-thing gamblers who congregate there. Then he had taxi-cabbed out to an apartment house on O'Farrell Street—the Glenway—where he had rung one of the bells. Getting no answer, he had let himself into the building with a key. An hour later he had come out and returned to his hotel. Dick hadn't been able to determine which bell he had rung, or which apartment he had visited.

I got Lillian Shan on the telephone.

"Will you be in this evening?" I asked. "I've

something I want to go into with you, and I can't give it to you over the wire."

"I will be at home until seven-thirty."

"All right, I'll be down."

It was seven-fifteen when the car I had hired put me down at her front door. She opened the door for me. The Danish woman who was filling in until new servants were employed stayed there only in the daytime, returning to her own home—a mile back from the shore—at night.

The evening gown Lillian Shan wore was severe enough, but it suggested that if she would throw away her glasses and do something for herself, she might not be so unfeminine looking after all. She took me upstairs, to the library, where a clean-cut lad of twenty-something in evening clothes got up from a chair as we came in—a well-set-up boy with fair hair and skin.

His name, I learned when we were introduced, was Garthorne. The girl seemed willing enough to hold our conference in his presence. I wasn't. After I had done everything but insist point-blank on seeing her alone, she excused herself—calling him Jack—and took me out into another room.

By then I was a bit impatient.

"Who's that?" I demanded.

She put her eyebrows up for me.

"Mr. John Garthorne," she said.

"How well do you know him?"

"May I ask why you are so interested?"

"You may. Mr. John Garthorne is all wrong, I think."

"Wrong?"

I had another idea.

"Where does he live?"

She gave me an O'Farrell Street number.

"The Glenway Apartments?"

"I think so." She was looking at me without any affectation at all. "Will you please explain?"

"One more question and I will. Do you know a Chinese named Chang Li Ching?"

"No."

"All right. I'll tell you about Garthorne. So far I've run into two angles on this trouble of

yours. One of them has to do with this Chang Li Ching in Chinatown, and one with an ex-convict named Conyers. This John Garthorne was in Chinatown today. I saw him coming out of a cellar that probably connects with Chang Li Ching's house. The ex-convict Conyers visited the building where Garthorne lives, early this afternoon."

Her mouth popped open and then shut.

"That is absurd!" she snapped. "I have known Mr. Garthorne for some time, and—"

"Exactly how long?"

"A long—several months."

"Where'd you meet him?"

"Through a girl I knew at college."

"What does he do for a living?"

She stood stiff and silent.

"Listen, Miss Shan," I said. "Garthorne may be all right, but I've got to look him up. If he's in the clear there'll be no harm done. I want to know what you know about him."

I got it, little by little. He was, or she thought he was, the youngest son of a prominent Richmond, Virginia, family, in disgrace just now because of some sort of boyish prank. He had come to San Francisco four months ago, to wait until his father's anger cooled. Meanwhile his mother kept him in money, leaving him without the necessity of toiling during his exile. He had brought a letter of introduction from one of Lillian Shan's schoolmates. Lillian Shan had, I gathered, a lot of liking for him.

"You're going out with him tonight?" I asked when I had got this.

"Yes."

"In his car or yours?"

She frowned, but she answered my question.

"In his. We are going to drive down to Half Moon for dinner."

"I'll need a key, then, because I am coming back here after you have gone."

"You're what?"

"I'm coming back here. I'll ask you not to say anything about my more or less unworthy suspicions to him, but my honest opinion is that he's drawing you away for the evening. So if the engine breaks down on the way back, just pretend you see nothing unusual in it."

That worried her, but she wouldn't admit I might be right. I got the key, though, and then I told her of my employment agency scheme that needed her assistance, and she promised to be at the office at half past nine Thursday morning.

I didn't see Garthorne again before I left the house.

VI

In my hired car again, I had the driver take me to the nearest village, where I bought a plug of chewing tobacco, a flashlight, and a box of cartridges at the general store. My gun is a .38 Special, but I had to take the shorter, weaker cartridges, because the storekeeper didn't keep the specials in stock.

My purchases in my pocket, we started back toward the Shan house again. Two bends in the road this side of it, I stopped the car, paid the chauffeur, and sent him on his way, finishing the trip afoot.

The house was dark all around.

Letting myself in as quietly as possible, and going easy with the flashlight, I gave the interior a combing from cellar to roof. I was the only occupant. In the kitchen, I looted the icebox for a bite or two, which I washed down with milk. I could have used some coffee, but coffee is too fragrant.

The luncheon done, I made myself comfortable on a chair in the passageway between the kitchen and the rest of the house. On one side of the passageway, steps led down to the basement. On the other, steps led upstairs. With every door in the house except the outer ones open, the passageway was the center of things so far as hearing noises was concerned.

An hour went by—quietly except for the passing of cars on the road a hundred yards away and the washing of the Pacific down in the little cove. I chewed on my plug of tobacco—a substitute for cigarettes—and tried to count up the hours of my life I'd spent like this, sitting or standing around waiting for something to happen.

The telephone rang.

I let it ring. It might be Lillian Shan needing help, but I couldn't take a chance. It was too likely to be some egg trying to find out if anybody was in the house.

Another half hour went by with a breeze springing up from the ocean, rustling trees outside.

A noise came that was neither wind nor surf nor passing car.

Something clicked somewhere.

It was at a window, but I didn't know which. I got rid of my chew, got gun and flashlight out.

It sounded again, harshly.

Somebody was giving a window a strong play—too strong. The catch rattled, and something clicked against the pane. It was a stall. Whoever he was, he could have smashed the glass with less noise than he was making.

I stood up, but I didn't leave the passageway. The window noise was a fake to draw the attention of anyone who might be in the house. I turned my back on it, trying to see into the kitchen.

The kitchen was too black to see anything.

I saw nothing there. I heard nothing there.

Damp air blew on me from the kitchen.

That was something to worry about. I had company, and he was slicker than I. He could open doors or windows under my nose. That wasn't so good.

Weight on rubber heels, I backed away from my chair until the frame of the cellar door touched my shoulder. I wasn't sure I was going to like this party. I like an even break or better, and this didn't look like one.

So when a thin line of light danced out of the kitchen to hit the chair in the passageway, I was three steps cellar-ward, my back flat against the stair-wall.

The light fixed itself on the chair for a couple of seconds, and then began to dart around the passageway, through it into the room beyond. I could see nothing but the light.

Fresh sounds came to me—the purr of automobile engines close to the house on the road side, the soft padding of feet on the back porch, on the kitchen linoleum, quite a few feet. An odor came to me—an unmistakable odor—the smell of unwashed Chinese.

Then I lost track of these things. I had plenty to occupy me close up.

The proprietor of the flashlight was at the head of the cellar steps. I had ruined my eyes watching the light: I couldn't see him.

The first thin ray he sent downstairs missed me by an inch—which gave me time to make a map there in the dark. If he was of medium size, holding the light in his left hand, a gun in his right, and exposing as little of himself as possible—his noodle should have been a foot and a half above the beginning of the light-beam, the same distance behind it, six inches to the left—my left.

The light swung sideways and hit one of my legs.

I swung the barrel of my gun at the point I had marked X in the night.

His gun-fire cooked my cheek. One of his arms tried to take me with him. I twisted away and let him dive alone into the cellar, showing me a flash of gold teeth as he went past.

The house was full of "Ah yahs" and pattering feet.

I had to move—or I'd be pushed.

Downstairs might be a trap. I went up to the passageway again.

The passageway was solid and alive with stinking bodies. Hands and teeth began to take my clothes away from me. I knew damned well I had declared myself in on something!

I was one of a struggling, tearing, grunting and groaning mob of invisibles. An eddy of them swept me toward the kitchen. Hitting, kicking, butting, I went along.

A high-pitched voice was screaming Chinese orders.

My shoulder scraped the door-frame as I was carried into the kitchen, fighting as best I could against enemies I couldn't see, afraid to use the gun I still gripped.

I was only one part of the mad scramble. The flash of my gun might have made me the center of it. These lunatics were fighting panic now: I didn't want to show them something tangible to tear apart.

I went along with them, cracking everything that got in my way, and being cracked back. A bucket got between my feet.

I crashed down, upsetting my neighbors, rolled over a body, felt a foot on my face, squirmed from under it, and came to rest in a corner, still tangled up with the galvanized bucket.

Thank God for that bucket!

I wanted these people to go away. I didn't care who or what they were. If they'd depart in peace I'd forgive their sins.

I put my gun inside the bucket and squeezed the trigger. I got the worst of the racket, but there was enough to go around. It sounded like a crump* going off.

I cut loose in the bucket again, and had another idea. Two fingers of my left hand in my mouth, I whistled as shrill as I could while I emptied the gun.

It was a sweet racket!

When my gun had run out of bullets and my lungs out of air, I was alone. I was glad to be alone. I knew why men go off and live in caves by themselves. And I didn't blame them!

Sitting there alone in the dark, I reloaded my gun.

On hands and knees I found my way to the open kitchen door, and peeped out into the blackness that told me nothing. The surf made guzzling sounds in the cove. From the other side of the house came the noise of cars. I hoped it was my friends going away.

----

* artillery shell

I shut the door, locked it, and turned on the kitchen light.

The place wasn't as badly upset as I had expected. Some pans and dishes were down and a chair had been broken, and the place smelled of unwashed bodies. But that was all—except a blue cotton sleeve in the middle of the floor, a straw sandal near the passageway door, and a handful of short black hairs, a bit blood-smeared, beside the sandal.

In the cellar I did not find the man I had sent down there. An open door showed how he had left me. His flashlight was there, and my own, and some of his blood.

Upstairs again, I went through the front of the house. The front door was open. Rugs had been rumpled. A blue vase was broken on the floor. A table was pushed out of place, and a couple of chairs had been upset. I found an old and greasy brown felt hat that had neither sweat-band nor hat-band. I found a grimy photograph of President Coolidge—apparently cut from a Chinese newspaper—and six wheat-straw cigarette papers.

I found nothing upstairs to show that any of my guests had gone up there.

It was half past two in the morning when I heard a car drive up to the front door. I peeped out of Lillian Shan's bedroom window, on the second floor. She was saying good-night to Jack Garthorne.

I went back to the library to wait for her.

"Nothing happened?" were her first words, and they sounded more like a prayer than anything else.

"It did," I told her, "and I suppose you had your breakdown."

For a moment I thought she was going to lie to me, but she nodded, and dropped into a chair, not as erect as usual.

"I had a lot of company," I said, "but I can't say I found out much about them. The fact is, I bit off more than I could chew, and had to be satisfied with chasing them out."

"You didn't call the sheriff's office?" There

was something strange about the tone in which she put the question.

"No—I don't want Garthorne arrested yet."

That shook the dejection out of her. She was up, tall and straight in front of me, and cold.

"I'd rather not go into that again," she said.

That was all right with me, but:

"You didn't say anything to him, I hope."

"Say anything to him?" She seemed amazed. "Do you think I would insult him by repeating your guesses—your absurd guesses?"

"That's fine," I applauded her silence if not her opinion of my theories. "Now, I'm going to stay here tonight. There isn't a chance in a hundred of anything happening, but I'll play it safe."

She didn't seem very enthusiastic about that, but she finally went off to bed.

Nothing happened between then and sun-up, of course. I left the house as soon as daylight came and gave the grounds the once-over. Footprints were all over the place, from water's edge to driveway. Along the driveway some of the sod was cut where machines had been turned carelessly.

Borrowing one of the cars from the garage, I was back in San Francisco before the morning was far gone.

In the office, I asked the Old Man to put an operative behind Jack Garthorne; to have the old hat, flashlight, sandal and the rest of my souvenirs put under the microscope and searched for finger prints, foot prints, tooth-prints or what have you; and to have our Richmond branch look up the Garthornes. Then I went up to see my Filipino assistant.

He was gloomy.

"What's the matter?" I asked. "Somebody knock you over?"

"Oh, no, sir!" he protested. "But maybe I am not so good a detective. I try to follow one fella, and he turns a corner and he is gone."

"Who was he, and what was he up to?"

"I do not know, sir. There is four automobiles with men getting out of them into that cellar of which I tell you the strange Chinese live. After they are gone in, one man comes out. He wears his hat down over bandage on his upper face, and he walks away rapidly. I try to follow him, but he turns that corner, and where is he?"

"What time did all this happen?"

"Twelve o'clock, maybe."

"Could it have been later than that, or earlier?"

"Yes, sir."

My visitors, no doubt, and the man Cipriano had tried to shadow could have been the one I swatted. The Filipino hadn't thought to get the license numbers of the automobiles. He didn't know whether they had been driven by white men or Chinese, or even what make cars they were.

"You've done fine," I assured him. "Try it again tonight. Take it easy, and you'll get there."

From him I went to a telephone and called the Hall of Justice. Dummy Uhl's death had not been reported, I learned.

Twenty minutes later I was skinning my knuckles on Chang Li Ching's front door.

VII

The little old Chinese with the rope neck didn't open for me this time. Instead, a young Chinese with a smallpox-pitted face and a wide grin.

"You wanna see Chang Li Ching," he said before I could speak, and stepped back for me to enter.

I went in and waited while he replaced all the bars and locks. We went to Chang by a shorter route than before, but it was still far from direct. For a while I amused myself trying to map the route in my head as he went along, but it was too complicated, so I gave it up.

The velvet-hung room was empty when my guide showed me in, bowed, grinned, and left me. I sat down in a chair near the table and waited.

Chang Li Ching didn't put on the theatricals for me by materializing silently, or anything of the sort. I heard his soft slippers on the floor before he parted the hangings and came in. He was alone, his white whiskers ruffled in a smile that was grandfatherly.

"The Scatterer of Hordes honors my poor residence again," he greeted me, and went on at great length with the same sort of nonsense that I'd had to listen to on my first visit.

The Scatterer of Hordes part was cool enough—if it was a reference to last night's doings.

"Not knowing who he was until too late, I beaned one of your servants last night," I said when he had run out of flowers for the time. "I know there's nothing I can do to square myself for such a terrible act, but I hope you'll let me cut my throat and bleed to death in one of your garbage cans as a sort of apology."

A little sighing noise that could have been a smothered chuckle disturbed the old man's lips, and the purple cap twitched on his round head.

"The Disperser of Marauders knows all things," he murmured blandly, "even to the value of noise in driving away demons. If he says the man he struck was Chang Li Ching's servant, who is Chang to deny it?"

I tried him with my other barrel.

"I don't know much—not even why the police haven't yet heard of the death of the man who was killed here yesterday."

One of his hands made little curls in his white beard.

"I had not heard of the death," he said.

I could guess what was coming, but I wanted to take a look at it.

"You might ask the man who brought me here yesterday," I suggested.

Chang Li Ching picked up a little padded stick from the table and struck a tasseled gong that hung at his shoulder. Across the room the hangings parted to admit the pock-marked Chinese who had brought me in.

"Did death honor our hovel yesterday?" Chang asked in English.

"No, *Ta Jen*," the pock-marked one said.

"It was the nobleman who guided me here yesterday," I explained, "not this son of an emperor."

Chang imitated surprise.

"Who welcomed the King of Spies yesterday?" he asked the man at the door.

"I bring 'em, *Ta Jen*."

I grinned at the pock-marked man, he grinned back, and Chang smiled benevolently.

"An excellent jest," he said.

It was.

The pock-marked man bowed and started to duck back through the hangings. Loose shoes rattled on the boards behind him. He spun around. One of the big wrestlers I had seen the previous day loomed above him. The wrestler's eyes were bright with excitement, and grunted Chinese syllables poured out of his mouth. The pock-marked one talked back. Chang Li Ching silenced them with a sharp command. All this was in Chinese—out of my reach.

"Will the Grand Duke of Manhunters permit his servant to depart for a moment to attend to his distressing domestic affairs?"

"Sure."

Chang bowed with his hands together, and spoke to the wrestler.

"You will remain here to see that the great one is not disturbed and that any wishes he expresses are gratified."

The wrestler bowed and stood aside for Chang to pass through the door with the pock-marked man. The hangings swung over the door behind them.

I didn't waste any language on the man at the door, but got a cigarette going and waited for Chang to come back. The cigarette was half gone when a shot sounded in the building, not far away.

The giant at the door scowled.

Another shot sounded, and running feet thumped in the hall. The pock-marked man's face came through the hangings. He poured grunts at the wrestler. The wrestler scowled at me and protested. The other insisted.

The wrestler scowled at me again, rumbled, "You wait," and was gone with the other.

I finished my cigarette to the tune of muffled struggle-sounds that seemed to come from the floor below. There were two more shots, far apart. Feet ran past the door of the room I was in. Perhaps ten minutes had gone since I had been left alone.

I found I wasn't alone.

Across the room from the door, the hangings that covered the wall were disturbed. The blue, green and silver velvet bulged out an inch and settled back in place.

The disturbance happened the second time perhaps ten feet farther along the wall. No movement for a while, and then a tremor in the far corner.

Somebody was creeping along between hangings and wall.

I let them creep, still slumping in my chair with idle hands. If the bulge meant trouble, action on my part would only bring it that much quicker.

I traced the disturbance down the length of that wall and halfway across the other, to where I knew the door was. Then I lost it for some time. I had just decided that the creeper had gone through the door when the curtains opened and the creeper stepped out.

She wasn't four and a half feet high—a living ornament from somebody's shelf. Her face was a tiny oval of painted beauty, its perfection emphasized by the lacquer-black hair that was flat and glossy around her temples. Gold earrings swung beside her smooth cheeks, a jade butterfly was in her hair. A lavender jacket, glittering with white stones, covered her from under her chin to her knees. Lavender stockings showed under her short lavender trousers, and her bound-small feet were in slippers of the same color, shaped like kittens, with yellow stones for eyes and aigrettes for whiskers.

The point of all this our-young-ladies'-fashion stuff is that she was impossibly dainty. But there she was—neither a carving nor a painting, but a living small woman with fear in her black eyes and nervous, tiny fingers worrying the silk at her bosom.

Twice as she came toward me—hurrying with the awkward, quick step of the foot-bound Chinese woman—her head twisted around for a look at the hangings over the door.

I was on my feet by now, going to meet her.

Her English wasn't much. Most of what she babbled at me I missed, though I thought "yung hel-lup" might have been meant for "You help?"

I nodded, catching her under the elbows as she stumbled against me.

She gave me some more language that didn't make the situation any clearer—unless "sul-lay-vee gull" meant slave-girl and "tak-ka wah" meant take away.

"You want me to get you out of here?" I asked.

Her head, close under my chin, went up and down, and her red flower of a mouth shaped a smile that made all the other smiles I could remember look like leers.

She did some more talking. I got nothing out of it. Taking one of her elbows out of my hand, she pushed up her sleeve, baring a forearm that an artist had spent a life-time carving out of ivory. On it were five finger-shaped bruises ending in cuts where the nails had punctured the flesh.

She let the sleeve fall over it again, and gave me more words. They didn't mean anything to me, but they tinkled prettily.

"All right," I said, sliding my gun out. "If you want to go, we'll go."

Both her hands went to the gun, pushing it down, and she talked excitedly into my face, winding up with a flicking of one hand across her collar—a pantomime of a throat being cut.

I shook my head from side to side and urged her toward the door.

She balked, fright large in her eyes.

One of her hands went to my watch-pocket. I let her take the watch out.

She put the tiny tip of one pointed finger over the twelve and then circled the dial three times.

I thought I got that. Thirty-six hours from noon would be midnight of the following night—Thursday.

"Yes," I said.

She shot a look at the door and led me to the table where the tea things were. With a finger dipped in cold tea she began to draw on the table's inlaid top. Two parallel lines I took for a street. Another pair crossed them. The third pair crossed the second and paralleled the first.

"Waverly Place?" I guessed.

Her face bobbed up and down, delightedly.

On what I took for the east side of Waverly Place she drew a square—perhaps a house. In the square she set what could have been a rose. I frowned at that. She erased the rose and in its place put a crooked circle, adding dots. I thought I had it. The rose had been a cabbage. This thing was a potato. The square represented the grocery store I had noticed on Waverly Place. I nodded.

Her finger crossed the street and put a square on the other side, and her face turned up to mine, begging me to understand her.

"The house across the street from the grocer's," I said slowly, and then, as she tapped my watch-pocket, I added, "at midnight tomorrow."

I don't know how much of it she caught, but she nodded her little head until her earrings were swinging like crazy pendulums.

With a quick diving motion, she caught my right hand, kissed it, and with a tottering, hoppy run vanished behind the velvet curtains.

I used my handkerchief to wipe the map off the table and was smoking in my chair when Chang Li Ching returned some twenty minutes later.

I left shortly after that, as soon as we had traded a few dizzy compliments. The pock-marked man ushered me out.

At the office there was nothing new for me. Foley hadn't been able to shadow The Whistler the night before.

I went home for the sleep I had not got last night.

VIII

At ten minutes after ten the next morning Lillian Shan and I arrived at the front door of Fong Yick's employment agency on Washington Street.

"Give me just two minutes," I told her as I climbed out. "Then come in."

"Better keep your steam up," I suggested to the driver. "We might have to slide away in a hurry."

In Fong Yick's, a lanky, gray-haired man whom I thought was the Old Man's Frank Paul was talking around a chewed cigar to half a dozen Chinese. Across the battered counter a fat Chinese was watching them boredly through immense steel-rimmed spectacles.

I looked at the half-dozen. The third from me had a crooked nose—a short, squat man.

I pushed aside the others and reached for him.

I don't know what the stuff he tried on me was—jiu jitsu, maybe, or its Chinese equivalent. Anyhow, he crouched and moved his stiffly open hands trickily.

I took hold of him here and there, and presently had him by the nape of his neck, with one of his arms bent up behind him.

Another Chinese piled on my back. The lean, gray-haired man did something to his face, and the Chinese went over in a corner and stayed there.

That was the situation when Lillian Shan came in.

I shook the flat-nosed boy at her.

"Yin Hung!" she exclaimed.

"Hoo Lun isn't one of the others?" I asked, pointing to the spectators.

She shook her head emphatically, and began jabbering Chinese at my prisoner. He jabbered back, meeting her gaze.

"What are you going to do with him?" she asked me in a voice that wasn't quite right.

"Turn him over to the police to hold for the San Mateo sheriff. Can you get anything out of him?"

"No."

I began to push him toward the door. The steel-spectacled Chinese blocked the way, one hand behind him.

"No can do," he said.

I slammed Yin Hung into him. He went back against the wall.

"Get out!" I yelled at the girl.

The gray-haired man stopped two Chinese who dashed for the door, sent them the other way—back hard against the wall.

We left the place.

There was no excitement in the street. We climbed into the taxicab and drove the block and a half to the Hall of Justice, where I yanked my prisoner out. The rancher Paul said he wouldn't go in, that he had enjoyed the party, but now had some of his own business to look after. He went on up Kearny Street afoot.

Half-out of the taxicab, Lillian Shan changed her mind.

"Unless it's necessary," she said, "I'd rather not go in either. I'll wait here for you."

"Righto," and I pushed my captive across the sidewalk and up the steps.

Inside, an interesting situation developed.

The San Francisco police weren't especially interested in Yin Hung, though willing enough, of course, to hold him for the sheriff of San Mateo County.

Yin Hung pretended he didn't know any English, and I was curious to know what sort of story he had to tell, so I hunted around in the detectives' assembly room until I found Bill Thode of the Chinatown detail, who talks the language some.

He and Yin Hung jabbered at each other for some time.

Then Bill looked at me, laughed, bit off the end of a cigar, and leaned back in his chair.

"According to the way he tells it," Bill said, "that Wan Lan woman and Lillian Shan had a row. The next day Wan Lan's not anywheres around. The Shan girl and Wang Ma, her maid, say Wan Lan has left, but Hoo Lun tells this fellow he saw Wang Ma burning some of Wan Lan's clothes.

"So Hoo Lun and this fellow think something's wrong, and the next day they're damned sure of it, because this fellow misses a spade from his garden tools. He finds it again that night, and it's still wet with damp dirt, and he says no dirt was dug up anywheres around the place—not outside of the house anyways. So him and Hoo Lun put their heads together, didn't like the result, and decided they'd better dust out before they went wherever Wan Lan had gone. That's the message."

"Where is Hoo Lun now?"

"He says he don't know."

"So Lillian Shan and Wang Ma were still in the house when this pair left?" I asked. "They hadn't started for the East yet?"

"So he says."

"Has he got any idea why Wan Lan was killed?"

"Not that I've been able to get out of him."

"Thanks, Bill! You'll notify the sheriff that you're holding him?"

"Sure."

Of course Lillian Shan and the taxicab were gone when I came out of the Hall of Justice door.

I went back into the lobby and used one of the booths to phone the office. Still no report from Dick Foley—nothing of any value—and none from the operative who was trying to shadow Jack Garthorne. A wire had come from the Richmond branch. It was to the effect that the Garthornes were a wealthy and well-known local family, that young Jack was usually in trouble, that he had slugged a Prohibition agent during a cafe raid a few months ago, that his father had taken him out of his will and chased him from the house, but that his mother was believed to be sending him money.

That fit in with what the girl had told me.

A street car carried me to the garage where I had stuck the roadster I had borrowed from the girl's garage the previous morning. I drove around to Cipriano's apartment building. He had no news of any importance for me. He had spent the night hanging around Chinatown, but had picked up nothing.

I was a little inclined toward grouchiness as I turned the roadster west, driving out through Golden Gate Park to the Ocean Boulevard. The job wasn't getting along as snappily as I wanted it to.

I let the roadster slide down the boulevard at a good clip, and the salt air blew some of my kinks away.

A bony-faced man with pinkish mustache opened the door when I rang Lillian Shan's bell. I knew him—Tucker, a deputy sheriff.

"Hullo," he said. "What d'you want?"

"I'm hunting for her too."

"Keep on hunting," he grinned. "Don't let me stop you."

"Not here, huh?"

"Nope. The Swede woman that works for her says she was in and out half an hour before I got here, and I've been here about ten minutes now."

"Got a warrant for her?" I asked.

"You bet you! Her chauffeur squawked."

"Yes, I heard him," I said. "I'm the bright boy who gathered him in."

I spent five or ten minutes more talking to Tucker and then climbed in the roadster again.

"Will you give the agency a ring when you nab her?" I asked as I closed the door.

"You bet you."

I pointed the roadster at San Francisco again.

Just outside of Daly City a taxicab passed me, going south. Jack Garthorne's face looked through the window.

I snapped on the brakes and waved my arm. The taxicab turned and came back to me. Garthorne opened the door, but did not get out.

I got down into the road and went over to him.

"There's a deputy sheriff waiting in Miss Shan's house, if that's where you're headed."

His blue eyes jumped wide, and then narrowed as he looked suspiciously at me.

"Let's go over to the side of the road and have a little talk," I invited.

He got out of the taxicab and we crossed to a couple of comfortable-looking boulders on the other side.

"Where is Lil—Miss Shan?" he asked.

"Ask The Whistler," I suggested.

This blond kid wasn't so good. It took him a long time to get his gun out. I let him go through with it.

"What do you mean?" he demanded.

I hadn't meant anything. I had just wanted to see how the remark would hit him. I kept quiet.

"Has The Whistler got her?"

"I don't think so," I admitted, though I hated to do it. "But the point is that she has had to go in hiding to keep from being hanged for the murders The Whistler framed."

"Hanged?"

"Uh-huh. The deputy waiting in her house has a warrant for her—for murder."

He put away his gun and made gurgling noises in his throat.

"I'll go there! I'll tell everything I know!"

He started for his taxicab.

"Wait!" I called. "Maybe you'd better tell me what you know first. I'm working for her, you know."

He spun around and came back.

"Yes, that's right. You'll know what to do."

"Now what do you really know, if anything?" I asked when he was standing in front of me.

"I know the whole thing!" he cried. "About the deaths and the booze and—"

"Easy! Easy! There's no use wasting all that knowledge on the chauffeur."

He quieted down, and I began to pump him. I spent nearly an hour getting all of it.

IX

The history of his young life, as he told it to me, began with his departure from home after falling into disgrace through slugging the Prohi. He had come to San Francisco to wait until his father cooled off. Meanwhile his mother kept him in funds, but she didn't send him all the money a young fellow in a wild city could use.

That was the situation when he ran into The Whistler, who suggested that a chap with Gar-

thorne's front could pick up some easy money in the rum-running game if he did what he was told to do. Garthorne was willing enough. He didn't like Prohibition—it had caused most of his troubles. Rum-running sounded romantic to him—shots in the dark, signal lights off the starboard bow, and so on.

The Whistler, it seemed, had boats and booze and waiting customers, but his landing arrangements were out of whack. He had his eye on a little cove down the shore line that was an ideal spot to land hooch. It was neither too close nor too far from San Francisco. It was sheltered on either side by rocky points, and screened from the road by a large house and high hedges. Given the use of that house, his troubles would be over. He could land his hooch in the cove, run it into the house, repack it innocently there, put it through the front door into his automobiles, and shoot it to the thirsty city.

The house, he told Garthorne, belonged to a Chinese girl named Lillian Shan, who would neither sell nor rent it. Garthorne was to make her acquaintance—The Whistler was already supplied with a letter of introduction written by a former classmate of the girl's, a classmate who had fallen a lot since university days—and try to work himself in with her to a degree of intimacy that would permit him to make her an offer for the use of the house. That is, he was to find out if she was the sort of person who could be approached with a more or less frank offer of a share in the profits of The Whistler's game.

Garthorne had gone through with his part, or the first of it, and had become fairly intimate with the girl, when she suddenly left for the East, sending him a note saying she would be gone several months. That was fine for the rum-runners. Garthorne, calling at the house, the next day, had learned that Wang Ma had gone with her mistress, and that the three other servants had been left in charge of the house.

That was all Garthorne knew first-hand. He had not taken part in the landing of the booze, though he would have liked to. But The Whistler had ordered him to stay away, so that he could continue his original part when the girl returned.

The Whistler told Garthorne he had bought the help of the three Chinese servants, but that the woman, Wan Lan, had been killed by the two men in a fight over their shares of the money. Booze had been run through the house once during Lillian Shan's absence. Her unexpected return gummed things. The house still held some of the booze. They had to grab her and Wang Ma and stick them in a closet until they got the stuff away. The strangling of Wang Ma had been accidental—a rope tied too tight.

The worst complication, however, was that another cargo was scheduled to land in the cove the following Tuesday night, and there was no way of getting word out to the boat that the place was closed. The Whistler sent for our hero and ordered him to get the girl out of the way and keep her out of the way until at least two o'clock Wednesday morning.

Garthorne had invited her to drive down to Half Moon with him for dinner that night. She had accepted. He had faked engine trouble, and had kept her away from the house until two-thirty, and The Whistler had told him later that everything had gone through without a hitch.

After this I had to guess at what Garthorne was driving at—he stuttered and stammered and let his ideas rattle looser than ever. I think it added up to this: he hadn't thought much about the ethics of his play with the girl. She had no attraction for him—too severe and serious to seem really feminine. And he had not pretended—hadn't carried on what could possibly be called a flirtation with her. Then he suddenly woke up to the fact that she wasn't as indifferent as he. That had been a shock to him—one he couldn't stand. He had seen things straight for the first time. He had thought of it before as simply a wit-matching game. Affection made it different—even though the affection was all on one side.

"I told The Whistler I was through this afternoon," he finished.

"How did he like it?"

"Not a lot. In fact, I had to hit him."

"So? And what were you planning to do next?"

"I was going to see Miss Shan, tell her the truth, and then—then I thought I'd better lay low."

"I think you'd better. The Whistler might not like being hit."

"I won't hide now! I'll go give myself up and tell the truth."

"Forget it!" I advised him. "That's no good. You don't know enough to help her."

That wasn't exactly the truth, because he did know that the chauffeur and Hoo Lun had still been in the house the day after her departure for the East. But I didn't want him to get out of the game yet.

"If I were you," I went on, "I'd pick out a quiet hiding place and stay there until I can get word to you. Know a good place?"

"Yes," slowly. "I have a—a friend who will hide me—down near—near the Latin Quarter."

"Near the Latin Quarter?" That could be Chinatown. I did some sharp-shooting. "Waverly Place?"

He jumped.

"How did you know?"

"I'm a detective. I know everything. Ever hear of Chang Li Ching?"

"No."

I tried to keep from laughing into his puzzled face.

The first time I had seen this cut-up he was leaving a house in Waverly Place, with a Chinese woman's face showing dimly in the doorway behind him. The house had been across the street from a grocery. The Chinese girl with whom I had talked at Chang's had given me a slave-girl yarn and an invitation to that same house. Big-hearted Jack here had fallen for the same game, but he didn't know that the girl had anything to do with Chang Li Ching, didn't know that Chang existed, didn't know Chang and The Whistler were playmates. Now Jack is in trouble, and he's going to the girl to hide!

I didn't dislike this angle of the game. He

was walking into a trap, but that was nothing to me—or, rather, I hoped it was going to help me.

"What's your friend's name?" I asked.

He hesitated.

"What is the name of the tiny woman whose door is across the street from the grocery?" I made myself plain.

"Hsiu Hsiu."

"All right," I encouraged him in his foolishness. "You go there. That's an excellent hiding place. Now if I want to get a Chinese boy to you with a message, how will he find you?"

"There's a flight of steps to the left as you go in. He'll have to skip the second and third steps, because they are fitted with some sort of alarm. So is the handrail. On the second floor you turn to the left again. The hall is dark. The second door to the right—on the right-hand side of the hall—lets you into a room. On the other side of the room is a closet, with a door hidden behind old clothes. There are usually people in the room the door opens into, so he'll have to wait for a chance to get through it. This room has a little balcony outside that you can get to from either of the windows. The balcony's sides are solid, so if you crouch low you can't be seen from the street or from other houses. At the other end of the balcony there are two loose floor boards. You slide down under them into a little room between walls. The trap-door there will let you down into another just like it where I'll probably be. There's another way out of the bottom room, down a flight of steps, but I've never been that way."

A fine mess! It sounded like a child's game. But even with all this frosting on the cake our young chump hadn't tumbled. He took it seriously.

"So that's how it's done!" I said. "You'd better get there as soon as you can, and stay there until my messenger gets to you. You'll know him by the cast in one of his eyes, and maybe I'd better give him a password. Haphazard—that'll be the word. The street door—is it locked?"

"No. I've never found it locked. There are forty or fifty Chinamen—or perhaps a hundred—living in that building, so I don't suppose the door is ever locked."

"Good. Beat it now."

X

At 10:15 that night I was pushing open the door opposite the grocery in Waverly Place—an hour and three-quarters early for my date with Hsiu Hsiu. At 9:55 Dick Foley had phoned that The Whistler had gone into the red-painted door on Spofford Alley.

I found the interior dark, and closed the door softly, concentrating on the childish directions Garthorne had given me. That I knew they were silly didn't help me, since I didn't know any other route.

The stairs gave me some trouble, but I got over the second and third without touching the handrail, and went on up. I found the second door in the hall, the closet in the room behind it, and the door in the closet. Light came through the cracks around it. Listening, I heard nothing.

I pushed the door open—the room was empty. A smoking oil lamp stunk there. The nearest window made no sound as I raised it. That was inartistic—a squeak would have impressed Garthorne with his danger.

I crouched low on the balcony, in accordance with instructions, and found the loose floor-boards that opened up a black hole. Feet first, I went down in, slanting at an angle that made descent easy. It seemed to be a sort of slot cut diagonally through the wall. It was stuffy, and I don't like narrow holes. I went down swiftly, coming into a small room, long and narrow, as if placed inside a thick wall.

No light was there. My flashlight showed a room perhaps eighteen feet long by four wide, furnished with table, couch and two chairs. I looked under the one rug on the floor. The trap-door was there—a crude affair that didn't pretend it was part of the floor.

Flat on my belly, I put an ear to the trapdoor. No sound. I raised it a couple of inches. Darkness and a faint murmuring of voices. I pushed the trapdoor wide, let it down easily on the floor and stuck head and shoulders into the opening, discovering then that it was a double arrangement. Another door was below, fitting no doubt in the ceiling of the room below.

Cautiously I let myself down on it. It gave under my foot. I could have pulled myself up again, but since I had disturbed it I chose to keep going.

I put both feet on it. It swung down. I dropped into light. The door snapped up over my head. I grabbed Hsiu Hsiu and clapped a hand over her tiny mouth in time to keep her quiet.

"Hello," I said to the startled Garthorne; "this is my boy's evening off, so I came myself."

"Hello," he gasped.

This room, I saw, was a duplicate of the one from which I had dropped, another cupboard between walls, though this one had an unpainted wooden door at one end.

I handed Hsiu Hsiu to Garthorne.

"Keep her quiet," I ordered, "while—"

The clicking of the door's latch silenced me. I jumped to the wall on the hinged side of the door just as it swung open—the opener hidden from me by the door.

The door opened wide, but not much wider than Jack Garthorne's blue eyes, nor than this mouth. I let the door go back against the wall and stepped out behind my balanced gun.

The queen of something stood there!

She was a tall woman, straight-bodied and proud. A butterfly-shaped headdress decked with the loot of a dozen jewelry stores exaggerated her height. Her gown was amethyst filigreed with gold above, a living rainbow below. The clothes were nothing!

She was—maybe I can make it clear this way. Hsiu Hsiu was as perfect a bit of feminine beauty as could be imagined. She was perfect! Then comes this queen of something—and Hsiu Hsiu's beauty went away. She was a candle in the sun. She was still pretty—prettier than the woman in the doorway, if it came to that—but

you didn't pay any attention to her. Hsiu Hsiu was a pretty girl: this royal woman in the doorway was—I don't know the words.

"My God!" Garthorne was whispering harshly. "I never knew it!"

"What are you doing here?" I challenged the woman.

She didn't hear me. She was looking at Hsiu Hsiu as a tigress might look at an alley cat. Hsiu Hsiu was looking at her as an alley cat might look at a tigress. Sweat was on Garthorne's face and his mouth was the mouth of a sick man.

"What are you doing here?" I repeated, stepping closer to Lillian Shan.

"I am here where I belong," she said slowly, not taking her eyes from the slave-girl. "I have come back to my people."

That was a lot of bunk. I turned to the goggling Garthorne.

"Take Hsiu Hsiu to the upper room, and keep her quiet, if you have to strangle her. I want to talk to Miss Shan."

Still dazed, he pushed the table under the trapdoor, climbed up on it, hoisted himself through the ceiling, and reached down. Hsiu Hsiu kicked and scratched, but I heaved her up to him. Then I closed the door through which Lillian Shan had come, and faced her.

"How did you get here?" I demanded.

"I went home after I left you, knowing what Yin Hung would say, because he had told me in the employment office, and when I got home—When I got home I decided to come here where I belong."

"Nonsense!" I corrected her. "When you got home you found a message there from Chang Li Ching, asking you—ordering you to come here."

She looked at me, saying nothing.

"What did Chang want?"

"He thought perhaps he could help me," she said, "and so I stayed here."

More nonsense.

"Chang told you Garthorne was in danger—had split with The Whistler."

"The Whistler?"

"You made a bargain with Chang," I accused her, paying no attention to her question. The chances were she didn't know The Whistler by that name.

She shook her head, jiggling the ornaments on her headdress.

"There was no bargain," she said, holding my gaze too steadily.

I didn't believe her. I said so.

"You gave Chang your house—or the use of it—in exchange for his promise that"—the boob were the first words I thought of, but I changed them—"Garthorne would be saved from The Whistler, and that you would be saved from the law."

She drew herself up.

"I did," she said calmly.

I caught myself weakening. This woman who looked like the queen of something wasn't easy to handle the way I wanted to handle her. I made myself remember that I knew her when she was homely as hell in mannish clothes.

"You ought to be spanked!" I growled at her. "Haven't you had enough trouble without mixing yourself now with a flock of highbinders?* Did you see The Whistler?"

"There was a man up there," she said, "I don't know his name."

I hunted through my pocket and found the picture of him taken when he was sent to San Quentin.

"That is he," she told me when I showed it to her.

"A fine partner you picked," I raged. "What do you think his word on anything is worth?"

"I did not take his word for anything. I took Chang Li Ching's word."

"That's just as bad. They're mates. What was your bargain?"

She balked again, straight, stiff-necked and level-eyed. Because she was getting away from me with this Manchu princess stuff I got peevish.

_____
* Chinese thugs

"Don't be a chump all your life!" I pleaded. "You think you made a deal. They took you in! What do you think they're using your house for?"

She tried to look me down. I tried another angle of attack.

"Here, you don't mind who you make bargains with. Make one with me. I'm still one prison sentence ahead of The Whistler, so if his word is any good at all, mine ought to be highly valuable. You tell me what the deal was. If it's half-way decent, I'll promise you to crawl out of here and forget it. If you don't tell me, I'm going to empty a gun out of the first window I can find. And you'd be surprised how many cops a shot will draw in this part of town, and how fast it'll draw them."

The threat took some of the color out of her face.

"If I tell, you will promise to do nothing?"

"You missed part of it," I reminded her. "If I think the deal is half-way on the level I'll keep quiet."

She bit her lips and let her fingers twist together, and then it came.

"Chang Li Ching is one of the leaders of the anti-Japanese movement in China. Since the death of Sun Wen—or Sun Yat-Sen, as he is called in the south of China and here—the Japanese have increased their hold on the Chinese government until it is greater than it ever was. It is Sun Wen's work that Chang Li Ching and his friends are carrying on.

"With their own government against them, their immediate necessity is to arm enough patriots to resist Japanese aggression when the time comes. That is what my house is used for. Rifles and ammunition are loaded into boats there and sent out to ships lying far offshore. This man you call The Whistler is the owner of the ships that carry the arms to China."

"And the death of the servants?" I asked.

"Wan Lan was a spy for the Chinese government—for the Japanese. Wang Ma's death was an accident, I think, though she, too, was suspected of being a spy. To a patriot, the death of traitors is a necessary thing, you can understand that? Your people are like that too when your country is in danger."

"Garthorne told me a rum-running story," I said. "How about it?"

"He believed it," she said, smiling softly at the trapdoor through which he had gone. "They told him that, because they did not know him well enough to trust him. That is why they would not let him help in the loading."

One of her hands came out to rest on my arm.

"You will go away and keep silent?" she pleaded. "These things are against the law of your country, but would you not break another country's laws to save your own country's life? Have not four hundred million people the right to fight an alien race that would exploit them? Since the day of Taou-kwang my country has been the plaything of more aggressive nations. Is any price too great for patriotic Chinese to pay to end that period of dishonor? You will not put yourself in the way of my people's liberty?"

"I hope they win," I said, "but you've been tricked. The only guns that have gone through your house have gone through in pockets! It would take a year to get a shipload through there. Maybe Chang is running guns to China. It's likely. But they don't go through your place.

"The night I was there coolies went through—coming in, not going out. They came from the beach, and they left in machines. Maybe The Whistler is running the guns over for Chang and bringing coolies back. He can get anything from a thousand dollars up for each one he lands. That's about the how of it. He runs the guns over for Chang, and brings his own stuff—coolies and no doubt some opium—back, getting his big profit on the return trip. There wouldn't be enough money in the guns to interest him.

"The guns would be loaded at a pier, all regular, masquerading as something else. Your house is used for the return. Chang may or may not be tied up with the coolie and opium game, but it's a cinch he'll let The Whistler do whatever he likes if only The Whistler will run his guns across. So, you see, you have been gypped!"

"But—"

"But nothing! You're helping Chang by taking part in the coolie traffic. And, my guess is, your servants were killed, not because they were spies, but because they wouldn't sell you out."

She was white-faced and unsteady on her feet. I didn't let her recover.

"Do you think Chang trusts The Whistler? Did they seem friendly?"

I knew he couldn't trust him, but I wanted something specific.

"No-o-o," she said slowly. "There was some talk about a missing boat."

That was good.

"They still together?"

"Yes."

"How do I get there?"

"Down these steps, across the cellar—straight across—and up two flights of steps on the other side. They were in a room to the right of the second-floor landing."

Thank God I had a direct set of instructions for once!

I jumped up on the table and rapped on the ceiling.

"Come on down, Garthorne, and bring your chaperon."

"Don't either of you budge out of here until I'm back," I told the boob and Lillian Shan when we were all together again. "I'm going to take Hsiu Hsiu with me. Come on, sister, I want you to talk to any bad men I meet. We go to see Chang Li Ching, you understand?" I made faces. "One yell out of you, and—" I put my fingers around her collar and pressed them lightly.

She giggled, which spoiled the effect a little.

"To Chang," I ordered, and, holding her by one shoulder, urged her toward the door.

We went down into the dark cellar, across it, found the other stairs, and started to climb them. Our progress was slow. The girl's bound feet weren't made for fast walking.

A dim light burned on the first floor, where we had to turn to go up to the second floor. We had just made the turn when footsteps sounded behind us.

I lifted the girl up two steps, out of the light, and crouched beside her, holding her still. Four Chinese in wrinkled street clothes came down the first-floor hall, passed our stairs without a glance, and started on.

Hsiu Hsiu opened her red flower of a mouth and let out a squeal that could have been heard over in Oakland.

I cursed, turned her loose, and started up the steps. The four Chinese came after me. On the landing ahead one of Chang's big wrestlers appeared—a foot of thin steel in his paw. I looked back.

Hsiu Hsiu sat on the bottom step, her head over her shoulder, experimenting with different sorts of yells and screams, enjoyment all over her laughing doll's face. One of the climbing yellow men was loosening an automatic.

My legs pushed me on up toward the man-eater at the head of the steps.

When he crouched close above me I let him have it.

My bullet cut the gullet out of him.

I patted his face with my gun as he tumbled down past me.

A hand caught one of my ankles.

Clinging to the railing, I drove my other foot back. Something stopped my foot. Nothing stopped me.

A bullet flaked some of the ceiling down as I made the head of the stairs and jumped for the door to the right.

Pulling it open, I plunged in.

The other of the big man-eaters caught me—caught my plunging hundred and eighty-some pounds as a boy would catch a rubber ball.

Across the room, Chang Li Ching ran plump fingers through his thin whiskers and smiled at me. Beside him, a man I knew for The Whistler started up from his chair, his beefy face twitching.

"The Prince of Hunters is welcome," Chang said, and added something in Chinese to the man-eater who held me.

The man-eater set me down on my feet, and turned to shut the door on my pursuers.

The Whistler sat down again, his red-veined eyes shifty on me, his bloated face empty of enjoyment.

I tucked my gun inside my clothes before I started across the room toward Chang. And crossing the room, I noticed something.

Behind The Whistler's chair the velvet hangings bulged just the least bit, not enough to have been noticed by anyone who hadn't seen them bulge before. So Chang didn't trust his confederate at all!

"I have something I want you to see," I told the old Chinese when I was standing in front of him, or, rather, in front of the table that was in front of him.

"That eye is privileged indeed which may gaze on anything brought by the Father of Avengers."

"I have heard," I said, as I put my hand in my pocket, "that all that starts for China doesn't get there."

The Whistler jumped up from his chair again, his mouth a snarl, his face a dirty pink. Chang Li Ching looked at him, and he sat down again.

I brought out the photograph of The Whistler standing in a group of Japs, the medal of the Order of the Rising Sun on his chest. Hoping Chang had not heard of the swindle and would not know the medal for a counterfeit, I dropped the photograph on the table.

The Whistler craned his neck, but could not see the picture.

Chang Li Ching looked at it for a long moment over his clasped hands, his old eyes shrewd and kindly, his face gentle. No muscle in his face moved. Nothing changed in his eyes.

The nails of his right hand slowly cut a red gash across the back of the clasped left hand.

"It is true," he said softly, "that one acquires wisdom in the company of the wise."

He unclasped his hands, picked up the photograph, and held it out to the beefy man. The Whistler seized it. His face drained gray, his eyes bulged out.

"Why, that's—" he began, and stopped, let the photograph drop to his lap, and slumped down in an attitude of defeat.

That puzzled me. I had expected to argue with him, to convince Chang that the medal was not the fake it was.

"You may have what you wish in payment for this," Chang Li Ching was saying to me.

"I want Lillian Shan and Garthorne cleared, and I want your fat friend here, and I want anybody else who was in on the killings."

Chang's eyes closed for a moment—the first sign of weariness I had seen on his round face.

"You may have them," he said.

"The bargain you made with Miss Shan is all off, of course," I pointed out. "I may need a little evidence to make sure I can hang this baby," nodding at The Whistler.

Chang smiled dreamily.

"That, I am regretful, is not possible."

"Why—?" I began, and stopped.

There was no bulge in the velvet curtain behind The Whistler now, I saw. One of the chair legs glistened in the light. A red pool spread on the floor under him. I didn't have to see his back to know he was beyond hanging.

"That's different," I said, kicking a chair over to the table. "Now we'll talk business."

I sat down and we went into conference.

XI

Two days later everything was cleared up to the satisfaction of police, press and public. The Whistler had been found in a dark street, hours dead from a cut in his back, killed in a bootlegging war, I heard. Hoo Lun was found. The gold-toothed Chinese who had opened the door for Lillian Shan was found. Five others were found. These seven, with Yin Hung, the chauffeur, eventually drew a life sentence apiece. They were The Whistler's men, and Chang sacrificed them without batting an eye. They had as little proof of Chang's complicity as I had, so they couldn't hit back, even if they knew that Chang had given me most of my evidence against them.

Nobody but the girl, Chang and I knew anything about Garthorne's part, so he was out, with liberty to spend most of his time at the girl's house.

I had no proof that I could tie on Chang, couldn't get any. Regardless of his patriotism, I'd have given my right eye to put the old boy away. That would have been something to write home about. But there hadn't been a chance of nailing him, so I had had to be content with making a bargain whereby he turned everything over to me except himself and his friends.

I don't know what happened to Hsiu Hsiu, the squealing slave-girl. She deserved to come through all right. I might have gone back to Chang's to ask about her, but I stayed away. Chang had learned that the medal in the photo was a trick one. I had a note from him:

Greetings and Great Love to the Unveiler of Secrets:

One whose patriotic fervor and inherent stupidity combined to blind him, so that he broke a valuable tool, trusts that the fortunes of worldly traffic will not again ever place his feeble wits in opposition to the irresistible will and dazzling intellect of the Emperor of Untanglers.

You can take that any way you like. But I know the man who wrote it, and I don't mind admitting that I've stopped eating in Chinese restaurants, and that if I never have to visit Chinatown again it'll be soon enough.

BLACK MASK, DECEMBER 1925

The Gutting of Couffignal

BY DASHIELL HAMMETT

WEDGE-SHAPED COUFFIGNAL is not a large island, and not far from the mainland, to which it is linked by a wooden bridge. Its western shore is a high, straight cliff that jumps abruptly up out of San Pablo Bay. From the top of this cliff the island slopes eastward, down to a smooth pebble beach that runs into the water again, where there are piers and a clubhouse and moored pleasure boats.

Couffignal's main street, paralleling the beach, has the usual bank, hotel, moving-picture theater, and stores. But it differs from most main streets of its size in that it is more carefully arranged and preserved. There are trees and hedges and strips of lawn on it, and no glaring signs. The buildings seem to belong beside one another, as if they had been designed by the same architect, and in the stores you will find goods of a quality to match the best city stores.

The intersecting streets—running between rows of neat cottages near the foot of the slope—become winding hedged roads as they climb toward the cliff. The higher these roads get, the farther apart and larger are the houses they lead to. The occupants of these higher houses are the owners and rulers of the island. Most of them are well-fed old gentlemen who, the profits they took from the world with both hands in their younger days now stowed away at safe percentages, have bought into the island colony so they may spend what is left of their lives nursing their livers and improving their golf among their kind. They admit to the island only as many storekeepers, working-people, and similar riffraff as are needed to keep them comfortably served.

That is Couffignal.

It was some time after midnight. I was sitting in a second-story room in Couffignal's largest house, surrounded by wedding presents whose value would add up to something between fifty and a hundred thousand dollars.

Of all the work that comes to a private detective (except divorce work, which the Continental Detective Agency doesn't handle) I like weddings as little as any. Usually I manage to avoid them, but this time I hadn't been able to. Dick Foley, who had been slated for the job, had been handed a black eye by an unfriendly pickpocket the day before. That let Dick out and me in. I had come up to Couffignal—a two-hour ride from San Francisco by ferry and auto stage— that morning, and would return the next.

This had been neither better nor worse than the usual wedding detail. The ceremony had been performed in a little stone church down the hill. Then the house had begun to fill with reception guests. They had kept it filled to overflowing until some time after the bride and groom had sneaked off to their eastern train.

The world had been well represented. There had been an admiral and an earl or two from England; an ex-president of a South American country; a Danish baron; a tall young Russian princess surrounded by lesser titles, including a fat, bald, jovial and black-bearded Russian general who had talked to me for a solid hour about prize fights, in which he had a lot of interest, but not so much knowledge as was possible; an ambassador from one of the Central European countries; a justice of the Supreme Court; and a mob of people whose prominence and near-prominence didn't carry labels.

In theory, a detective guarding wedding presents is supposed to make himself indistinguishable from the other guests. In practice, it never works out that way. He has to spend most of his time within sight of the booty, so he's easily spotted. Besides that, eight or ten people I recognized among the guests were clients or former clients of the agency, and so knew me. However, being known doesn't make so much difference as you might think, and everything had gone off smoothly.

A couple of the groom's friends, warmed by wine and the necessity of maintaining their reputations as cut-ups, had tried to smuggle some of the gifts out of the room where they were displayed and hide them in the piano. But I had been expecting that familiar trick, and blocked it before it had gone far enough to embarrass anybody.

Shortly after dark a wind smelling of rain began to pile storm clouds up over the bay. Those guests who lived at a distance, especially those who had water to cross, hurried off for their homes. Those who lived on the island stayed until the first raindrops began to patter down. Then they left.

The Hendrixson house quieted down. Musicians and extra servants left. The weary house servants began to disappear in the direction of their bedrooms. I found some sandwiches, a couple of books and a comfortable armchair, and took them up to the room where the presents were now hidden under gray-white sheeting.

Keith Hendrixson, the bride's grandfather— she was an orphan—put his head in at the door.

"Have you everything you need for your comfort?" he asked.

"Yes, thanks."

He said good night and went off to bed—a tall old man, slim as a boy.

The wind and the rain were hard at it when I went downstairs to give the lower windows and doors the up-and-down. Everything on the first floor was tight and secure, everything in the cellar. I went upstairs again.

Pulling my chair over by a floor lamp, I put sandwiches, books, ash-tray, gun and flashlight on a small table beside it. Then I switched off the other lights, set fire to a Fatima, sat down, wriggled my spine comfortably into the chair's padding, picked up one of the books, and prepared to make a night of it.

The book was called *The Lord of the Sea*,

and had to do with a strong, tough and violent fellow named Hogarth, whose modest plan was to hold the world in one hand. There were plots and counterplots, kidnappings, murders, prison-breakings, forgeries and burglaries, diamonds large as hats and floating forts larger than Couffignal. It sounds dizzy here, but in the book it was as real as a dime.

Hogarth was still going strong when the lights went out.

II

In the dark, I got rid of the glowing end of my cigarette by grinding it in one of the sandwiches. Putting the book down, I picked up gun and flashlight, and moved away from the chair.

Listening for noises was no good. The storm was making hundreds of them. What I needed to know was why the lights had gone off. All the other lights in the house had been turned off some time ago. So the darkness of the hall told me nothing.

I waited. My job was to watch the presents. Nobody had touched them yet. There was nothing to get excited about.

Minutes went by, perhaps ten of them.

The floor swayed under my feet. The windows rattled with a violence beyond the strength of the storm. The dull boom of a heavy explosion blotted out the sounds of wind and falling water. The blast was not close at hand, but not far enough away to be off the island.

Crossing to the window, peering through the wet glass, I could see nothing. I should have seen a few misty lights far down the hill. Not being able to see them settled one point. The lights had gone out all over Couffignal, not only in the Hendrixson house.

That was better. The storm could have put the lighting system out of whack, could have been responsible for the explosion—maybe.

Staring through the black window, I had an impression of great excitement down the hill, of movement in the night. But all was too far away for me to have seen or heard even had there been lights, and all too vague to say what was moving. The impression was strong but worthless. It didn't lead anywhere. I told myself I was getting feeble-minded, and turned away from the window.

Another blast spun me back to it. This explosion sounded nearer than the first, maybe because it was stronger. Peering through the glass again, I still saw nothing. And still had the impression of things that were big moving down there.

Bare feet pattered in the hall. A voice was anxiously calling my name. Turning from the window again, I pocketed my gun and snapped on the flashlight. Keith Hendrixson, in pajamas and bathrobe, looking thinner and older than anybody could be, came into the room.

"Is it—"

"I don't think it's an earthquake," I said, since that is the first calamity your Californian thinks of. "The lights went off a little while ago. There have been a couple of explosions down the hill since the—"

I stopped. Three shots, close together, had sounded. Rifle-shots, but of the sort that only the heaviest of rifles could make. Then, sharp and small in the storm, came the report of a far-away pistol.

"What is it?" Hendrixson demanded.

"Shooting."

More feet were pattering in the halls, some bare, some shod. Excited voices whispered questions and exclamations. The butler, a solemn, solid block of a man, partly dressed, and carrying a lighted five-pronged candlestick, came in.

"Very good, Brophy," Hendrixson said as the butler put the candlestick on the table beside my sandwiches. "Will you try to learn what is the matter?"

"I have tried, sir. The telephone seems to be out of order, sir. Shall I send Oliver down to the village?"

"No-o. I don't suppose it's that serious. Do you think it is anything serious?" he asked me.

I said I didn't think so, but I was paying more

attention to the outside than to him. I had heard a thin screaming that could have come from a distant woman, and a volley of small-arms shots. The racket of the storm muffled these shots, but when the heavier firing we had heard before broke out again, it was clear enough.

To have opened the window would have been to let in gallons of water without helping us to hear much clearer. I stood with an ear tilted to the pane, trying to arrive at some idea of what was happening outside.

Another sound took my attention from the window—the ringing of the doorbell. It rang loudly and persistently.

Hendrixson looked at me. I nodded.

"See who it is, Brophy," he said.

The butler went solemnly away, and came back even more solemnly.

"Princess Zhukovski," he announced.

She came running into the room—the tall Russian girl I had seen at the reception. Her eyes were wide and dark with excitement. Her face was very white and wet. Water ran in streams down her blue waterproof cape, the hood of which covered her dark hair.

"Oh, Mr. Hendrixson!" She had caught one of his hands in both of hers. Her voice, with nothing foreign in its accents, was the voice of one who is excited over a delightful surprise. "The bank is being robbed, and the—what do you call him?—marshal of police has been killed!"

"What's that?" the old man exclaimed, jumping awkwardly, because water from her cape had dripped down on one of his bare feet. "Weegan killed? And the bank robbed?"

"Yes! Isn't it terrible?" She said it as if she were saying wonderful. "When the first explosion woke us, the general sent Ignati down to find out what was the matter, and he got down there just in time to see the bank blown up. Listen!"

We listened, and heard a wild outbreak of mixed gun-fire.

"That will be the general arriving!" she said. "He'll enjoy himself most wonderfully. As soon

as Ignati returned with the news, the general armed every male in the household from Aleksandr Sergyeevich to Ivan the cook, and led them out happier than he's been since he took his division to East Prussia in 1914."

"And the duchess?" Hendrixson asked.

"He left her at home with me, of course, and I furtively crept out and away from her while she was trying for the first time in her life to put water in a samovar. This is not the night for one to stay at home!"

"H-m-m," Hendrixson said, his mind obviously not on her words. "And the bank!"

He looked at me. I said nothing. The racket of another volley came to us.

"Could you do anything down there?" he asked.

"Maybe, but—" I nodded at the presents under their covers.

"Oh, those!" the old man said. "I'm as much interested in the bank as in them; and, besides, we will be here."

"All right!" I was willing enough to carry my curiosity down the hill. "I'll go down. You'd better have the butler stay in here, and plant the chauffeur inside the front door. Better give them guns if you have any. Is there a raincoat I can borrow? I brought only a light overcoat with me."

Brophy found a yellow slicker that fit me. I put it on, stowed gun and flashlight conveniently under it, and found my hat while Brophy was getting and loading an automatic pistol for himself and a rifle for Oliver, the mulatto chauffeur.

Hendrixson and the princess followed me downstairs. At the door I found she wasn't exactly following me—she was going with me.

"But, Sonya!" the old man protested.

"I'm not going to be foolish, though I'd like to," she promised him. "But I'm going back to my Irinia Androvana, who will perhaps have the samovar watered by now."

"That's a sensible girl!" Hendrixson said, and let us out into the rain and the wind.

It wasn't weather to talk in. In silence we turned downhill between two rows of hedging, with the storm driving at our backs. At the first break in the hedge I stopped, nodding toward the black blot a house made.

"That is your—"

Her laugh cut me short. She caught my arm and began to urge me down the road again.

"I only told Mr. Hendrixson that so he would not worry," she explained. "You do not think I am not going down to see the sights."

III

She was tall. I am short and thick. I had to look up to see her face—to see as much of it as the rain-gray night would let me see.

"You'll be soaked to the hide, running around in this rain," I objected.

"What of that? I am dressed for it."

She raised a foot to show me a heavy waterproof boot and a woolen-stockinged leg.

"There's no telling what we'll run into down there, and I've got work to do," I insisted. "I can't be looking out for you."

"I can look out for myself."

She pushed her cape aside to show me a square automatic pistol in one hand.

"You'll be in my way."

"I will not," she retorted. "You'll probably find I can help you. I'm as strong as you, and quicker, and I can shoot."

The reports of scattered shooting had punctuated our argument, but now the sound of heavier firing silenced the dozen objections to her company that I could still think of. After all, I could slip away from her in the dark if she became too much of a nuisance.

"Have it your own way," I growled, "but don't expect anything from me."

"You're so kind," she murmured as we got under way again, hurrying now, with the wind at our backs speeding us along.

Occasionally dark figures moved on the road ahead of us, but too far away to be recognizable. Presently a man passed us, running uphill—a tall man whose nightshirt hung out of his trou-

sers, down below his coat, identifying him as a resident.

"They've finished the bank and are at Medcraft's!" he yelled as he went by.

"Medcraft is the jeweler," the girl informed me.

The sloping under our feet grew less sharp. The houses—dark but with faces vaguely visible here and there at windows—came closer together. Below, the flash of a gun could be seen now and then—orange streaks in the rain.

Our road put us into the lower end of the main street just as a staccato rat-ta-tat broke out.

I pushed the girl into the nearest doorway, and jumped in after her.

Bullets ripped through walls with the sound of hail tapping on leaves.

That was the thing I had taken for an exceptionally heavy rifle—a machine gun.

The girl had fallen back in a corner, all tangled up with something. I helped her up. The something was a boy of seventeen or so, with one leg and a crutch.

"It's the boy who delivers papers," Princess Zhukovski said, "and you've hurt him with your clumsiness."

The boy shook his head, grinning as he got up.

"No'm, I ain't hurt none, but you kind of scared me, jumping on me like that."

She had to stop and explain that she hadn't jumped on him, that she had been pushed into him by me, and that she was sorry and so was I.

"What's happening?" I asked the newsboy when I could get a word in.

"Everything," he boasted, as if some of the credit were his. "There must be a hundred of them, and they've blowed the bank wide open, and now some of 'em is in Medcraft's, and I guess they'll blow that up, too. And they killed Tom Weegan. They got a machine gun on a car in the middle of the street. That's it shooting now."

"Where's everybody—all the merry villagers?"

"Most of 'em are up behind the Hall. They

can't do nothing, though, because the machine gun won't let 'em get near enough to see what they're shooting at, and that smart Bill Vincent told me to clear out, 'cause I've only got one leg, as if I couldn't shoot as good as the next one, if I only had something to shoot with!"

"That wasn't right of them," I sympathized. "But you can do something for me. You can stick here and keep your eye on this end of the street, so I'll know if they leave in this direction."

"You're not just saying that so I'll stay here out of the way, are you?"

"No," I lied. "I need somebody to watch. I was going to leave the princess here, but you'll do better."

"Yes," she backed me up, catching the idea. "This gentleman is a detective, and if you do what he asks you'll be helping more than if you were up with the others."

The machine gun was still firing, but not in our direction now.

"I'm going across the street," I told the girl. "If you—"

"Aren't you going to join the others?"

"No. If I can get around behind the bandits while they're busy with the others, maybe I can turn a trick."

"Watch sharp now!" I ordered the boy, and the princess and I made a dash for the opposite sidewalk.

We reached it without drawing lead, sidled along a building for a few yards, and turned into an alley. From the alley's other end came the smell and wash and the dull blackness of the bay.

While we moved down this alley I composed a scheme by which I hoped to get rid of my companion, sending her off on a safe wild-goose chase. But I didn't get a chance to try it out.

The big figure of a man loomed ahead of us.

Stepping in front of the girl, I went on toward him. Under my slicker I held my gun on the middle of him.

He stood still. He was larger than he had looked at first. A big, slope-shouldered, barrel-bodied husky. His hands were empty. I spot-ted the flashlight on his face for a split second. A flat-cheeked, thick-featured face, with high cheek-bones and a lot of ruggedness in it.

"Ignati!" the girl exclaimed over my shoulder.

He began to talk what I suppose was Russian to the girl. She laughed and replied. He shook his big head stubbornly, insisting on something. She stamped her foot and spoke sharply. He shook his head again and addressed me.

"General Pleshskev, he tell me bring Princess Sonya to home."

His English was almost as hard to understand as his Russian. His tone puzzled me. It was as if he was explaining some absolutely necessary thing that he didn't want to be blamed for, but that nevertheless he was going to do.

While the girl was speaking to him again, I guessed the answer. This big Ignati had been sent out by the general to bring the girl home, and he was going to obey his orders if he had to carry her. He was trying to avoid trouble with me by explaining the situation.

"Take her," I said, stepping aside.

The girl scowled at me, laughed.

"Very well, Ignati," she said in English, "I shall go home," and she turned on her heel and went back up the alley, the big man close behind her.

Glad to be alone, I wasted no time in moving in the opposite direction until the pebbles of the beach were under my feet. The pebbles ground harshly under my heels. I moved back to more silent ground and began to work my way as swiftly as I could up the shore toward the center of action.

The machine gun barked on. Smaller guns snapped. Three concussions, close together— bombs, hand grenades, my ears and my memory told me.

The stormy sky glared pink over a roof ahead of me and to the left. The boom of the blast beat my ear-drums. Fragments I couldn't see fell around me. That, I thought, would be the jeweler's safe blowing apart.

I crept on up the shore line. The machine

gun went silent. Lighter guns snapped, snapped, snapped. Another grenade went off. A man's voice shrieked pure terror.

Risking the crunch of pebbles, I turned down to the water's edge again. I had seen no dark shape on the water that could have been a boat. There had been boats moored along this beach in the afternoon. With my feet in the water of the bay I still saw no boat. The storm could have scattered them, but I didn't think it had. The island's western height shielded this shore. The wind was strong here, but not violent.

My feet sometimes on the edge of the pebbles, sometimes in the water, I went on up the shore line. Now I saw a boat. A gently bobbing black shape ahead. No light was on it. Nothing I could see moved on it. It was the only boat on that shore. That made it important.

Foot by foot, I approached.

A shadow moved between me and the dark rear of a building. I froze. The shadow, man-size, moved again, in the direction from which I was coming.

Waiting, I didn't know how nearly invisible, or how plain, I might be against my background. I couldn't risk giving myself away by trying to improve my position.

Twenty feet from me the shadow suddenly stopped.

I was seen. My gun was on the shadow.

"Come on," I called softly. "Keep coming. Let's see who you are."

The shadow hesitated, left the shelter of the building, drew nearer. I couldn't risk the flashlight. I made out dimly a handsome face, boyishly reckless, one cheek dark-stained.

"Oh, how d'you do?" the face's owner said in a musical baritone voice. "You were at the reception this afternoon."

"Yes."

"Have you seen Princess Zhukovski? You know her?"

"She went home with Ignati ten minutes or so ago."

"Excellent!" He wiped his stained cheek with a stained handkerchief, and turned to look at the boat. "That's Hendrixson's boat," he whispered. "They've got it and they've cast the others off."

"That would mean they are going to leave by water."

"Yes," he agreed, "unless—Shall we have a try at it?"

"You mean jump it?"

"Why not?" he asked. "There can't be very many aboard. God knows there are enough of them ashore. You're armed. I've a pistol."

"We'll size it up first," I decided, "so we'll know what we're jumping."

"That is wisdom," he said, and led the way back to the shelter of the buildings.

Hugging the rear walls of the buildings, we stole toward the boat.

The boat grew clearer in the night. A craft perhaps forty-five feet long, its stern to the shore, rising and falling beside a small pier. Across the stern something protruded. Something I couldn't quite make out. Leather soles scuffled now and then on the wooden deck. Presently a dark head and shoulders showed over the puzzling thing in the stern.

The Russian lad's eyes were better than mine.

"Masked," he breathed in my ear. "Something like a stocking over his head and face."

The masked man was motionless where he stood. We were motionless where we stood.

"Could you hit him from here?" the lad asked.

"Maybe, but night and rain aren't a good combination for sharpshooting. Our best bet is to sneak as close as we can, and start shooting when he spots us."

"That is wisdom," he agreed.

Discovery came with our first step forward. The man in the boat grunted. The lad at my side jumped forward. I recognized the thing in the boat's stern just in time to throw out a leg and trip the young Russian. He tumbled down, all sprawled out on the pebbles. I dropped behind him.

The machine gun in the boat's stern poured metal over our heads.

IV

"No good rushing that!" I said. "Roll out of it!"

I set the example by revolving toward the back of the building we had just left.

The man at the gun sprinkled the beach, but sprinkled it at random, his eyes no doubt spoiled for night-seeing by the flash of his gun.

Around the corner of the building, we sat up.

"You saved my life by tripping me," the lad said coolly.

"Yes. I wonder if they've moved the machine gun from the street, or if—"

The answer to that came immediately. The machine gun in the street mingled its vicious voice with the drumming of the one in the boat.

"A pair of them!" I complained. "Know anything about the layout?"

"I don't think there are more than ten or twelve of them," he said, "although it is not easy to count in the dark. The few I have seen are completely masked—like the man in the boat. They seem to have disconnected the telephone and light lines first and then to have destroyed the bridge. We attacked them while they were looting the bank, but in front they had a machine gun mounted in an automobile, and we were not equipped to combat on equal terms."

"Where are the islanders now?"

"Scattered, and most of them in hiding, I fancy, unless General Pleshskev has succeeded in rallying them again."

I frowned and beat my brains together. You can't fight machine guns and hand grenades with peaceful villagers and retired capitalists. No matter how well led and armed they are, you can't do anything with them. For that matter, how could anybody do much against a game of that toughness?

"Suppose you stick here and keep your eye on the boat," I suggested. "I'll scout around and see what's doing further up, and if I can get a few good men together, I'll try to jump the boat again, probably from the other side. But we can't count on that. The get-away will be by boat. We can count on that, and try to block it. If you lie down you can watch the boat around the corner of the building without making much of a target of yourself. I wouldn't do anything to attract attention until the break for the boat comes. Then you can do all the shooting you want."

"Excellent!" he said. "You'll probably find most of the islanders up behind the church. You can get to it by going straight up the hill until you come to an iron fence, and then follow that to the right."

"Right."

I moved off in the direction he had indicated.

At the main street I stopped to look around before venturing across. Everything was quiet there. The only man I could see was spread out face-down on the sidewalk near me.

On hands and knees I crawled to his side. He was dead. I didn't stop to examine him further, but sprang up and streaked for the other side of the street.

Nothing tried to stop me. In a doorway, flat against a wall, I peeped out. The wind had stopped. The rain was no longer a driving deluge, but a steady down-pouring of small drops. Couffignal's main street, to my senses, was a deserted street.

I wondered if the retreat to the boat had already started. On the sidewalk, walking swiftly toward the bank, I heard the answer to that guess.

High up on the slope, almost up to the edge of the cliff, by the sound, a machine gun began to hurl out its stream of bullets.

Mixed with the racket of the machine gun were the sounds of smaller arms, and a grenade or two.

At the first crossing, I left the main street and began to run up the hill. Men were running toward me. Two of them passed, paying no attention to my shouted, "What's up now?"

The third man stopped because I grabbed him—a fat man whose breath bubbled, and whose face was fish-belly white.

"They've moved the car with the machine gun on it up behind us," he gasped when I had shouted my question into his ear again.

"What are you doing without a gun?" I asked.

"I—I dropped it."

"Where's General Pleshskev?"

"Back there somewhere. He's trying to capture the car, but he'll never do it. It's suicide! Why don't help come?"

Other men had passed us, running downhill, as we talked. I let the white-faced man go, and stopped four men who weren't running so fast as the others.

"What's happening now?" I questioned them.

"They's going through the houses up the hill," a sharp-featured man with a small mustache and a rifle said.

"Has anybody got word off the island yet?" I asked.

"Can't," another informed me. "They blew up the bridge first thing."

"Can't anybody swim?"

"Not in that wind. Young Catlan tried it and was lucky to get out again with a couple of broken ribs."

"The wind's gone down," I pointed out.

The sharp-featured man gave his rifle to one of the others and took off his coat.

"I'll try it," he promised.

"Good! Wake up the whole country, and get word through to the San Francisco police boat and to the Mare Island Navy Yard. They'll lend a hand if you tell 'em the bandits have machine guns. Tell 'em the bandits have an armed boat waiting to leave in. It's Hendrixson's."

The volunteer swimmer left.

"A boat?" two of the men asked together.

"Yes. With a machine gun on it. If we're going to do anything, it'll have to be now, while we're between them and their get-away. Get every man and every gun you can find down there. Tackle the boat from the roofs if you can. When the bandits' car comes down there, pour it into it. You'll do better from the buildings than from the street."

The three men went on downhill. I went uphill, toward the crackling of firearms ahead. The machine gun was working irregularly. It would pour out its rat-tat-tat for a second or so, and then stop for a couple of seconds. The answering fire was thin, ragged.

I met more men, learned from them that the general, with less than a dozen men, was still fighting the car. I repeated the advice I had given the other men. My informants went down to join them. I went on up.

A hundred yards farther along, what was left of the general's dozen broke out of the night, around and past me, flying downhill, with bullets hailing after them.

The road was no place for mortal man. I stumbled over two bodies, scratched myself in a dozen places getting over a hedge. On soft, wet sod I continued my uphill journey.

The machine gun on the hill stopped its clattering. The one in the boat was still at work.

The one ahead opened again, firing too high for anything near at hand to be its target. It was helping its fellow below, spraying the main street.

Before I could get closer it had stopped. I heard the car's motor racing. The car moved toward me.

Rolling into the hedge, I lay there, straining my eyes through the spaces between the stems. I had six bullets in a gun that hadn't yet been fired on this night that had seen tons of powder burned.

When I saw wheels on the lighter face of the road, I emptied my gun, holding it low.

The car went on.

I sprang out of my hiding-place.

The car was suddenly gone from the empty road.

There was a grinding sound. A crash. The noise of metal folding on itself. The tinkle of glass.

I raced toward those sounds.

V

Out of a black pile where an engine sputtered, a black figure leaped—to dash off across the soggy lawn. I cut after it, hoping that the others in the wreck were down for keeps.

I was less than fifteen feet behind the fleeing man when he cleared a hedge. I'm no sprinter, but neither was he. The wet grass made slippery going.

He stumbled while I was vaulting the hedge. When we straightened out again I was not more than ten feet behind him.

Once I clicked my gun at him, forgetting I had emptied it. Six cartridges were wrapped in a piece of paper in my vest pocket, but this was no time for loading.

I was tempted to chuck the empty gun at his head. But that was too chancy.

A building loomed ahead. My fugitive bore off to the right, to clear the corner.

To the left a heavy shotgun went off.

The running man disappeared around the house-corner.

"Sweet God!" General Pleshskev's mellow voice complained. "That with a shotgun I should miss all of a man at the distance!"

"Go round the other way!" I yelled, plunging around the corner after my quarry.

His feet thudded ahead. I could not see him. The general puffed around from the other side of the house.

"You have him?"

"No."

In front of us was a stone-faced bank, on top of which ran a path. On either side of us was a high and solid hedge.

"But, my friend," the general protested. "How could he have—?"

A pale triangle showed on the path above—a triangle that could have been a bit of shirt showing above the opening of a vest.

"Stay here and talk!" I whispered to the general, and crept forward.

"It must be that he has gone the other way," the general carried out my instructions, rambling on as if I were standing beside him, "because if he had come my way I should have seen him, and if he had raised himself over either of the hedges

or the embankment, one of us would surely have seen him against . . ."

He talked on and on while I gained the shelter of the bank on which the path sat, while I found places for my toes in the rough stone facing.

The man on the road, trying to make himself small with his back in a bush, was looking at the talking general. He saw me when I had my feet on the path.

He jumped, and one hand went up.

I jumped, with both hands out.

A stone, turning under my foot, threw me sidewise, twisting my ankle, but saving my head from the bullet he sent at it.

My outflung left arm caught his legs as I spilled down. He came over on top of me. I kicked him once, caught his gun-arm, and had just decided to bite it when the general puffed up over the edge of the path and prodded the man off me with the muzzle of the shotgun.

When it came my turn to stand up, I found it not so good. My twisted ankle didn't like to support its share of my hundred-and-eighty-some pounds. Putting most of my weight on the other leg, I turned my flashlight on the prisoner.

"Hello, Flippo!" I exclaimed.

"Hello!" he said without joy in the recognition.

He was a roly-poly Italian youth of twenty-three or -four. I had helped send him to San Quentin four years ago for his part in a payroll stick-up. He had been out on parole for several months now.

"The prison board isn't going to like this," I told him.

"You got me wrong," he pleaded. "I ain't been doing a thing. I was up here to see some friends. And when this thing busted loose I had to hide, because I got a record, and if I'm picked up I'll be railroaded for it. And now you got me, and you think I'm in on it!"

"You're a mind reader," I assured him, and asked the general: "Where can we pack this bird away for a while, under lock and key?"

"In my house there is a lumber-room with a strong door and not a window."

"That'll do it. March, Flippo!"

General Pleshskev collared the youth, while I limped along behind them, examining Flippo's gun, which was loaded except for the one shot he had fired at me, and reloading my own.

We had caught our prisoner on the Russian's grounds, so we didn't have far to go.

The general knocked on the door and called out something in his language. Bolts clicked and grated, and the door was swung open by a heavily mustached Russian servant. Behind him the princess and a stalwart older woman stood.

We went in while the general was telling his household about the capture, and took the captive up to the lumber-room. I frisked him for his pocket-knife and matches—he had nothing else that could help him get out—locked him in and braced the door solidly with a length of board. Then we went downstairs again.

"You are injured!" the princess, seeing me limp across the floor, cried.

"Only a twisted ankle," I said. "But it does bother me some. Is there any adhesive tape around?"

"Yes," and she spoke to the mustached servant, who went out of the room and presently returned, carrying rolls of gauze and tape and a basin of steaming water.

"If you'll sit down," the princess said, taking these things from the servant.

But I shook my head and reached for the adhesive tape.

"I want cold water, because I've got to go out in the wet again. If you'll show me the bathroom, I can fix myself up in no time."

We had to argue about that, but I finally got to the bathroom, where I ran cold water on my foot and ankle, and strapped it with adhesive tape, as tight as I could without stopping the circulation altogether. Getting my wet shoe on again was a job, but when I was through I had two firm legs under me, even if one of them did hurt some.

When I rejoined the others I noticed that the sound of firing no longer came up the hill, and that the patter of rain was lighter, and a gray streak of coming daylight showed under a drawn blind.

I was buttoning my slicker when the knocker rang on the front door. Russian words came through, and the young Russian I had met on the beach came in.

"Aleksandr, you're—" the stalwart older woman screamed when she saw the blood on his cheek, and fainted.

He paid no attention to her at all, as if he was used to having her faint.

"They've gone in the boat," he told me while the girl and two men servants gathered up the woman and laid her on an ottoman.

"How many?" I asked.

"I counted ten, and I don't think I missed more than one or two, if any."

"The men I sent down there couldn't stop them?"

He shrugged.

"What would you? It takes a strong stomach to face a machine gun. Your men had been cleared out of the buildings almost before they arrived."

The woman who had fainted had revived by now and was pouring anxious questions in Russian at the lad. The princess was getting into her blue cape. The woman stopped questioning the lad and asked her something.

"It's all over," the princess said. "I am going to view the ruins."

That suggestion appealed to everybody. Five minutes later all of us, including the servants, were on our way downhill. Behind us, around us, in front of us, were other people going downhill, hurrying along in the drizzle that was very gentle now, their faces tired and excited in the bleak morning light.

Halfway down, a woman ran out of a cross-path and began to tell me something. I recognized her as one of Hendrixson's maids.

I caught some of her words.

"Presents gone. . . . Mr. Brophy murdered. . . . Oliver. . . ."

VI

"I'll be down later," I told the others, and set out after the maid.

She was running back to the Hendrixson house. I couldn't run, couldn't even walk fast. She and Hendrixson and more of his servants were standing on the front porch when I arrived.

"They killed Oliver and Brophy," the old man said.

"How?"

"We were in the back of the house, the rear second story, watching the flashes of the shooting down in the village. Oliver was down here, just inside the front door, and Brophy in the room with the presents. We heard a shot in there, and immediately a man appeared in the doorway of our room, threatening us with two pistols, making us stay there for perhaps ten minutes. Then he shut and locked the door and went away. We broke the door down—and found Brophy and Oliver dead."

"Let's look at them."

The chauffeur was just inside the front door. He lay on his back, with his brown throat cut straight across the front, almost back to the vertebrae. His rifle was under him. I pulled it out and examined it. It had not been fired.

Upstairs, the butler Brophy was huddled against a leg of one of the tables on which the presents had been spread. His gun was gone. I turned him over, straightened him out, and found a bullet-hole in his chest. Around the hole his coat was charred in a large area.

Most of the presents were still here. But the most valuable pieces were gone. The others were in disorder, lying around any which way, their covers pulled off.

"What did the one you saw look like?" I asked.

"I didn't see him very well," Hendrixson said. "There was no light in our room. He was simply a dark figure against the candle burning in the hall. A large man in a black rubber raincoat, with some sort of black mask that covered his whole head and face, with small eyeholes."

"No hat?"

"No, just the mask over his entire face and head."

As we went downstairs again I gave Hendrixson a brief account of what I had seen and heard and done since I had left him. There wasn't enough of it to make a long tale.

"Do you think you can get information about the others from the one you caught?" he asked, as I prepared to go out.

"No. But I expect to bag them just the same."

Couffignal's main street was jammed with people when I limped into it again. A detachment of Marines from Mare Island was there, and men from a San Francisco police boat. Excited citizens in all degrees of partial nakedness boiled around them. A hundred voices were talking at once, recounting their personal adventures and braveries and losses and what they had seen. Such words as machine gun, bomb, bandit, car, shot, dynamite, and killed sounded again and again, in every variety of voice and tone.

The bank had been completely wrecked by the charge that had blown the vault. The jewelry store was another ruin. A grocer's across the street was serving as a field hospital. Two doctors were toiling there, patching up damaged villagers.

I recognized a familiar face under a uniform cap—Sergeant Roche of the harbor police—and pushed through the crowd to him.

"Just get here?" he asked as we shook hands. "Or were you in on it?"

"In on it."

"What do you know?"

"Everything."

"Who ever heard of a private detective that didn't," he joshed as I led him out of the mob.

"Did you people run into an empty boat out

in the bay?" I asked when we were away from audiences.

"Empty boats have been floating around the bay all night," he said.

I hadn't thought of that.

"Where's your boat now?" I asked him.

"Out trying to pick up the bandits. I stayed with a couple of men to lend a hand here."

"You're in luck," I told him. "Now sneak a look across the street. See the stout old boy with the black whiskers? Standing in front of the druggist's."

General Pleshskev stood there, with the woman who had fainted, the young Russian whose bloody cheek had made her faint, and a pale, plump man of forty-something who had been with them at the reception. A little to one side stood big Ignati, the two menservants I had seen at the house, and another who was obviously one of them. They were chatting together and watching the excited antics of a red-faced property-owner who was telling a curt lieutenant of Marines that it was his own personal private automobile that the bandits had stolen to mount their machine gun on, and what he thought should be done about it.

"Yes," said Roche, "I see your fellow with the whiskers."

"Well, he's your meat. The woman and two men with him are also your meat. And those four Russians standing to the left are some more of it. There's another missing, but I'll take care of that one. Pass the word to the lieutenant, and you can round up those babies without giving them a chance to fight back. They think they're safe as angels."

"Sure, are you?" the sergeant asked.

"Don't be silly!" I growled, as if I had never made a mistake in my life.

I had been standing on my one good prop. When I put my weight on the other to turn away from the sergeant, it stung me all the way to the hip. I pushed my back teeth together and began to work painfully through the crowd to the other side of the street.

The princess didn't seem to be among those present. My idea was that, next to the general, she was the most important member of the push. If she was at their house, and not yet suspicious, I figured I could get close enough to yank her in without a riot.

Walking was hell. My temperature rose. Sweat rolled out on me.

"Mister, they didn't none of 'em come down that way."

The one-legged newsboy was standing at my elbow. I greeted him as if he were my pay-check.

"Come on with me," I said, taking his arm. "You did fine down there, and now I want you to do something else for me."

Half a block from the main street I led him up on the porch of a small yellow cottage. The front door stood open, left that way when the occupants ran down to welcome police and Marines, no doubt. Just inside the door, beside a hall rack, was a wicker porch chair. I committed unlawful entry to the extent of dragging that chair out on the porch.

"Sit down, son," I urged the boy.

He sat, looking up at me with puzzled freckled face. I took a firm grip on his crutch and pulled it out of his hand.

"Here's five bucks for rental," I said, "and if I lose it I'll buy you one of ivory and gold."

And I put the crutch under my arm and began to propel myself up the hill.

It was my first experience with a crutch. I didn't break any records. But it was a lot better than tottering along on an unassisted bum ankle.

The hill was longer and steeper than some mountains I've seen, but the gravel walk to the Russians' house was finally under my feet.

I was still some dozen feet from the porch when Princess Zhukovski opened the door.

VII

"Oh!" she exclaimed, and then, recovering from her surprise, "your ankle is worse!"

She ran down the steps to help me climb them. As she came I noticed that something heavy was sagging and swinging in the right-hand pocket of her gray flannel jacket.

With one hand under my elbow, the other arm across my back, she helped me up the steps and across the porch. That assured me she didn't think I had tumbled to the game. If she had, she wouldn't have trusted herself within reach of my hands. Why, I wondered, had she come back to the house after starting downhill with the others?

While I was wondering we went into the house, where she planted me in a large and soft leather chair.

"You must certainly be starving after your strenuous night," she said. "I will see if—"

"No, sit down." I nodded at a chair facing mine. "I want to talk to you."

She sat down, clasping her slender white hands in her lap. In neither face nor pose was there any sign of nervousness, not even of curiosity. And that was overdoing it.

"Where have you cached the plunder?" I asked.

The whiteness of her face was nothing to go by. It had been white as marble since I had first seen her. The darkness of her eyes was as natural. Nothing happened to her other features. Her voice was smoothly cool.

"I am sorry," she said. "The question doesn't convey anything to me."

"Here's the point," I explained. "I'm charging you with complicity in the gutting of Couffignal, and in the murders that went with it. And I'm asking you where the loot has been hidden."

Slowly she stood up, raised her chin, and looked at least a mile down at me.

"How dare you? How dare you speak so to me, a Zhukovski!"

"I don't care if you're one of the Smith Brothers!" Leaning forward, I had pushed my twisted ankle against a leg of the chair, and the resulting agony didn't improve my disposition. "For the purpose of this talk you are a thief and a murderer."

Her strong slender body became the body of a lean crouching animal. Her white face became the face of an enraged animal. One hand—claw now—swept to the heavy pocket of her jacket.

Then, before I could have batted an eye—though my life seemed to depend on my not batting it—the wild animal had vanished. Out of it—and now I know where the writers of the old fairy stories got their ideas—rose the princess again, cool and straight and tall.

She sat down, crossed her ankles, put an elbow on an arm of her chair, propped her chin on the back of that hand, and looked curiously into my face.

"However," she murmured, "did you chance to arrive at so strange and fanciful a theory?"

"It wasn't chance, and it's neither strange nor fanciful," I said. "Maybe it'll save time and trouble if I show you part of the score against you. Then you'll know how you stand and won't waste your brains pleading innocence."

"I should be grateful," she smiled, "very!"

I tucked my crutch in between one knee and the arm of my chair, so my hands would be free to check off my points on my fingers.

"First—whoever planned the job knew the island—not fairly well, but every inch of it. There's no need to argue about that. Second—the car on which the machine gun was mounted was local property, stolen from the owner here. So was the boat in which the bandits were supposed to have escaped. Bandits from the outside would have needed a car or a boat to bring their machine guns, explosives, and grenades here and there doesn't seem to be any reason why they shouldn't have used that car or boat instead of stealing a fresh one. Third—there wasn't the least hint of the professional bandit touch on this job. If you ask me, it was a military job from beginning to end. And the worst safe-burglar in the world could have got into both the bank vault and the jeweler's safe without wrecking the buildings. Fourth—bandits from the outside wouldn't have destroyed the bridge. They might have blocked it, but they wouldn't have destroyed it. They'd have saved it in case

344

they had to make their get-away in that direction. Fifth—bandits figuring on a get-away by boat would have cut the job short, wouldn't have spread it over the whole night. Enough racket was made here to wake up California all the way from Sacramento to Los Angeles. What you people did was to send one man out in the boat, shooting, and he didn't go far. As soon as he was at a safe distance, he went overboard, and swam back to the island. Big Ignati could have done it without turning a hair."

That exhausted my right hand. I switched over, counting on my left.

"Sixth—I met one of your party, the lad, down on the beach, and he was coming from the boat. He suggested that we jump it. We were shot at, but the man behind the gun was playing with us. He could have wiped us out in a second if he had been in earnest, but he shot over our heads. Seventh—that same lad is the only man on the island, so far as I know, who saw the departing bandits. Eighth—all of your people that I ran into were especially nice to me, the general even spending an hour talking to me at the reception this afternoon. That's a distinctive amateur crook trait. Ninth—after the machine gun car had been wrecked I chased its occupant. I lost him around this house. The Italian boy I picked up wasn't him. He couldn't have climbed up on the path without my seeing him. But he could have run around to the general's side of the house and vanished indoors there. The general liked him, and would have helped him. I know that, because the general performed a downright miracle by missing him at some six feet with a shotgun. Tenth—you called at Hendrixson's house for no other purpose than to get me away from there."

That finished the left hand. I went back to the right.

"Eleventh—Hendrixson's two servants were killed by someone they knew and trusted. Both were killed at close quarters and without firing a shot. I'd say you got Oliver to let you into the house, and were talking to him when one of your men cut his throat from behind. Then you went upstairs and probably shot the unsuspecting Brophy yourself. He wouldn't have been on his guard against you. Twelfth—but that ought to be enough, and I'm getting a sore throat from listing them."

She took her chin off her hand, took a fat white cigarette out of a thin black case, and held it in her mouth while I put a match to the end of it. She took a long pull at it—a draw that accounted for a third of its length—and blew the smoke down at her knees.

"That would be enough," she said when all these things had been done, "if it were not that you yourself know it was impossible for us to have been so engaged. Did you not see us—did not everyone see us—time and time again?"

"That's easy!" I argued. "With a couple of machine guns, a trunkful of grenades, knowing the island from top to bottom, in the darkness and in a storm, against bewildered civilians—it was duck soup. There are nine of you that I know of, including two women. Any five of you could have carried on the work, once it was started, while the others took turns appearing here and there, establishing alibis. And that is what you did. You took turns slipping out to alibi yourselves. Everywhere I went I ran into one of you. And the general! That whiskered old joker running around leading the simple citizens to battle! I'll bet he led 'em plenty! They're lucky there are any of 'em alive this morning!"

She finished her cigarette with another inhalation, dropped the stub on the rug, ground out the light with one foot, sighed wearily, put her hands on her hips, and asked:

"And now what?"

"Now I want to know where you have stowed the plunder."

The readiness of her answer surprised me.

"Under the garage, in a cellar we dug secretly there some months ago."

I didn't believe that, of course, but it turned out to be the truth.

I didn't have anything else to say. When I fumbled with my borrowed crutch, preparing to get up, she raised a hand and spoke gently:

"Wait a moment, please. I have something to suggest."

Half standing, I leaned toward her, stretching out one hand until it was close to her side.

"I want the gun," I said.

She nodded, and sat still while I plucked it from her pocket, put it in one of my own, and sat down again.

VIII

"You said a little while ago that you didn't care who I was," she began immediately. "But I want you to know. There are so many of us Russians who once were somebodies and who now are nobodies that I won't bore you with the repetition of a tale the world has grown tired of hearing. But you must remember that this weary tale is real to us who are its subjects. However, we fled from Russia with what we could carry of our property, which fortunately was enough to keep us in bearable comfort for a few years.

"In London we opened a Russian restaurant, but London was suddenly full of Russian restaurants, and ours became, instead of a means of livelihood, a source of loss. We tried teaching music and languages, and so on. In short, we hit on all the means of earning our living that other Russian exiles hit upon, and so always found ourselves in overcrowded, and thus unprofitable, fields. But what else did we know—could we do?

"I promised not to bore you. Well, always our capital shrank, and always the day approached on which we should be shabby and hungry, the day when we should become familiar to readers of your Sunday papers—charwomen who had been princesses, dukes who now were butlers. There was no place for us in the world. Outcasts easily become outlaws. Why not? Could it be said that we owed the world any fealty? Had not the world sat idly by and seen us despoiled of place and property and country?

"We planned it before we had heard of Couffignal. We could find a small settlement of the wealthy, sufficiently isolated, and, after establishing ourselves there, we would plunder it. Couffignal, when we found it, seemed to be the ideal place. We leased this house for six months, having just enough capital remaining to do that and to live properly here while our plans matured. Here we spent four months establishing ourselves, collecting our arms and our explosives, mapping our offensive, waiting for a favorable night. Last night seemed to be that night, and we had provided, we thought, against every eventuality. But we had not, of course, provided against your presence and your genius. They were simply others of the unforeseen misfortunes to which we seem eternally condemned."

She stopped, and fell to studying me with mournful large eyes that made me feel like fidgeting.

"It's no good calling me a genius," I objected. "The truth is you people botched your job from beginning to end. Your general would get a big laugh out of a man without military training who tried to lead an army. But here are you people with absolutely no criminal experience trying to swing a trick that needed the highest sort of criminal skill. Look at how you all played around with me! Amateur stuff! A professional crook with any intelligence would have either let me alone or knocked me off. No wonder you flopped! As for the rest of it—your troubles—I can't do anything about them."

"Why?" very softly. "Why can't you?"

"Why should I?" I made it blunt.

"No one else knows what you know." She bent forward to put a white hand on my knee. "There is wealth in that cellar beneath the garage. You may have whatever you ask."

I shook my head.

"You aren't a fool!" she protested. "You know—"

"Let me straighten this out for you," I interrupted. "We'll disregard whatever honesty I happen to have, sense of loyalty to employers, and so on. You might doubt them, so we'll throw them out. Now I'm a detective because I happen to like the work. It pays me a fair salary, but I could find other jobs that would pay more. Even a hundred dollars more a month would be twelve hundred a year. Say twenty-five or thirty thousand dollars in the years between now and my sixtieth birthday.

"Now I pass up that twenty-five or thirty thousand of honest gain because I like being a detective, like the work. And liking work makes you want to do it as well as you can. Otherwise there'd be no sense to it. That's the fix I am in. I don't know anything else, don't enjoy anything else, don't want to know or enjoy anything else. You can't weigh that against any sum of money. Money is good stuff. I haven't anything against it. But in the past eighteen years I've been getting my fun out of chasing crooks and tackling puzzles, my satisfaction out of catching crooks and solving riddles. It's the only kind of sport I know anything about, and I can't imagine a pleasanter future than twenty-some years more of it. I'm not going to blow that up!"

She shook her head slowly, lowering it, so that now her dark eyes looked up at me under the thin arcs of her brows.

"You speak only of money," she said. "I said you may have whatever you ask."

That was out. I don't know where these women get their ideas.

"You're still all twisted up," I said brusquely, standing now and adjusting my borrowed crutch. "You think I'm a man and you're a woman. That's wrong. I'm a manhunter and you're something that has been running in front of me. There's nothing human about it. You might just as well expect a hound to play tiddly-winks with the fox he's caught. We're wasting time anyway. I've been thinking the police or Marines might come up here and save me a walk. You've been waiting for your mob to come back and grab me. I could have told you they were being arrested when I left them."

That shook her. She had stood up. Now she

fell back a step, putting a hand behind her for steadiness, on her chair. An exclamation I didn't understand popped out of her mouth. Russian, I thought, but the next moment I knew it had been Italian.

"Put your hands up."

It was Flippo's husky voice. Flippo stood in the doorway, holding an automatic.

IX

I raised my hands as high as I could without dropping my supporting crutch, meanwhile cursing myself for having been too careless, or too vain, to keep a gun in my hand while I talked to the girl.

So this was why she had come back to the house. If she freed the Italian, she had thought, we would have no reason for suspecting that he hadn't been in on the robbery, and so we would look for the bandits among his friends. A prisoner, of course, he might have persuaded us of his innocence. She had given him the gun so he could either shoot his way clear, or, what would help her as much, get himself killed trying.

While I was arranging these thoughts in my head, Flippo had come up behind me. His empty hand passed over my body, taking away my own gun, his, and the one I had taken from the girl.

"A bargain, Flippo," I said when he had moved away from me, a little to one side, where he made one corner of a triangle whose other corners were the girl and I. "You're out on parole, with some years still to be served. I picked you up with a gun on you. That's plenty to send you back to the big house. I know you weren't in on this job. My idea is that you were up here on a smaller one of your own, but I can't prove that and don't want to. Walk out of here, alone and neutral, and I'll forget I saw you."

Little thoughtful lines grooved the boy's round, dark face.

The princess took a step toward him.

"You heard the offer I just now made him?" she asked. "Well, I make that offer to you, if you will kill him."

The thoughtful lines in the boy's face deepened.

"There's your choice, Flippo," I summed up for him. "All I can give you is freedom from San Quentin. The princess can give you a fat cut of the profits in a busted caper, with a good chance to get yourself hanged."

The girl, remembering her advantage over me, went at him hot and heavy in Italian, a language in which I know only four words. Two of them are profane and the other two obscene. I said all four.

The boy was weakening. If he had been ten years older, he'd have taken my offer and thanked me for it. But he was young and she—now that I thought of it—was beautiful. The answer wasn't hard to guess.

"But not to bump him off," he said to her, in English, for my benefit. "We'll lock him up in there where I was at."

I suspected Flippo hadn't any great prejudice against murder. It was just that he thought this one unnecessary, unless he was kidding me to make the killing easier.

The girl wasn't satisfied with his suggestion. She poured more hot Italian at him. Her game looked sure-fire, but it had a flaw. She couldn't persuade him that his chances of getting any of the loot away were good. She had to depend on her charms to swing him. And that meant she had to hold his eye.

He wasn't far from me.

She came close to him. She was singing, chanting, crooning Italian syllables into his round face.

She had him.

He shrugged. His whole face said yes. He turned—

I knocked him on the noodle with my borrowed crutch.

The crutch splintered apart. Flippo's knees bent. He stretched up to his full height. He fell on his face on the floor. He lay there, dead-still, except for a thin worm of blood that crawled out of his hair to the rug.

A step, a tumble, a foot or so of hand-and-knee scrambling put me within reach of Flippo's gun.

The girl, jumping out of my path, was halfway to the door when I sat up with the gun in my hand.

"Stop!" I ordered.

"I shan't," she said, but she did, for the time at least. "I am going out."

"You are going out when I take you."

She laughed, a pleasant laugh, low and confident.

"I'm going out before that," she insisted good-naturedly.

I shook my head.

"How do you purpose stopping me?" she asked.

"I don't think I'll have to," I told her. "You've got too much sense to try to run while I'm holding a gun on you."

She laughed again, an amused ripple.

"I've got too much sense to stay," she corrected me. "Your crutch is broken, and you're lame. You can't catch me by running after me, then. You pretend you'll shoot me, but I don't believe you. You'd shoot me if I attacked you, of course, but I shan't do that. I shall simply walk out, and you know you won't shoot me for that. You'll wish you could, but you won't. You'll see."

Her face turned over her shoulder, her dark eyes twinkling at me, she took a step toward the door.

"Better not count on that!" I threatened.

For answer to that she gave me a cooing laugh. And took another step.

"Stop, you idiot!" I bawled at her.

Her face laughed over her shoulder at me. She walked without haste to the door, her short skirt of gray flannel shaping itself to the calf of each gray wool-stockinged leg as its mate stepped forward.

Sweat greased the gun in my hand.

When her right foot was on the doorsill, a little chuckling sound came from her throat.

"Adieu!" she said softly.

And I put a bullet in the calf of her left leg.

She sat down—plump! Utter surprise stretched her white face. It was too soon for pain.

I had never shot a woman before. I felt queer about it.

"You ought to have known I'd do it!" My voice sounded harsh and savage and like a stranger's in my ears. "Didn't I steal a crutch from a cripple?"

BLACK MASK, MARCH 1926

Creeping Siamese

BY DASHIELL HAMMETT

STANDING BESIDE the cashier's desk in the front office of the Continental Detective Agency's San Francisco branch, I was watching Porter check up my expense account when the man came in. He was a tall man, raw-boned, hard-faced. Gray clothes bagged loosely from his wide shoulders. In the late afternoon sunlight that came through partially drawn blinds, his skin showed the color of new tan shoes.

He opened the door briskly, and then hesitated, standing in the doorway, holding the door open, turning the knob back and forth with one bony hand. There was no indecision in his face. It was ugly and grim, and its expression was the expression of a man who is remembering something disagreeable.

Tommy Howd, our freckled and snub-nosed office boy, got up from his desk and went to the rail that divided the office.

"Do you—?" Tommy began, and jumped back.

The man had let go the doorknob. He crossed his long arms over his chest, each hand gripping a shoulder. His mouth stretched wide in a yawn that had nothing to do with relaxation. His mouth clicked shut. His lips snarled back from clenched yellow teeth.

"Hell!" he grunted, full of disgust, and pitched down on the floor.

I heaved myself over the rail, stepped across his body, and went out into the corridor.

Four doors away, Agnes Braden, a plump woman of thirty-something who runs a public stenographic establishment, was going into her office.

350

"Miss Braden!" I called, and she turned, waiting for me to come up. "Did you see the man who just came in our office?"

"Yes." Curiosity put lights in her green eyes. "A tall man who came up in the elevator with me. Why?"

"Was he alone?"

"Yes. That is, he and I were the only ones who got off at this floor. Why?"

"Did you see anybody close to him?"

"No, though I didn't notice him in the elevator. Why?"

"Did he act funny?"

"Not that I noticed. Why?"

"Thanks. I'll drop in and tell you about it later."

I made a circuit of the corridors on our floor, finding nothing.

The raw-boned man was still on the floor when I returned to the office, but he had been turned over on his back. He was as dead as I had thought. The Old Man, who had been examining him, straightened up as I came in. Porter was at the telephone, trying to get the police. Tommy Howd's eyes were blue half-dollars in a white face.

"Nothing in the corridors," I told the Old Man. "He came up in the elevator with Agnes Braden. She says he was alone, and she saw nobody close to him."

"Quite so." The Old Man's voice and smile were as pleasantly polite as if the corpse at his feet had been a part of the pattern in the carpet. Fifty years of sleuthing have left him with no more emotion than a pawnbroker. "He seems to have been stabbed in the left breast, a rather large wound that was staunched with this piece of silk"—one of his feet poked at a rumpled ball of red cloth on the floor—"which seems to be a sarong."

Today is never Tuesday to the Old Man: it *seems* to be Tuesday.

"On his person," he went on, "I have found some nine hundred dollars in bills of various denominations, and some silver; a gold watch and a pocket knife of English manufacture; a

Japanese silver coin, 50 *sen*; tobacco, pipe and matches; a Southern Pacific timetable; two handkerchiefs without laundry marks; a pencil and several sheets of blank paper; four two-cent stamps; and a key labeled *Hotel Montgomery, Room 540*.

"His clothes seem to be new. No doubt we shall learn something from them when we make a more thorough examination, which I do not care to make until the police come. Meanwhile, you had better go to the Montgomery and see what you can learn there."

In the Hotel Montgomery's lobby the first man I ran into was the one I wanted: Pederson, the house copper, a blond-mustached ex-bartender who doesn't know any more about gumshoeing than I do about saxophones, but who does know people and how to handle them, which is what his job calls for.

"Hullo!" he greeted me. "What's the score?"

"Six to one, Seattle, end of the fourth. Who's in 540, Pete?"

"They're not playing in Seattle, you chump! Portland! A man that hasn't got enough civic spirit to know where his team—"

"Stop it, Pete! I've got no time to be fooling with your childish pastimes. A man just dropped dead in our joint with one of your room-keys in his pocket—540."

Civic spirit went blooey in Pederson's face.

"540?" He stared at the ceiling. "That would be that fellow Rounds. Dropped dead, you say?"

"Dead. Tumbled down in the middle of the floor with a knife-cut in him. Who is this Rounds?"

"I couldn't tell you much off-hand. A big bony man with leathery skin. I wouldn't have noticed him excepting he was such a sour looking body."

"That's the bird. Let's look him up."

At the desk we learned that the man had arrived the day before, registering as H. R. Rounds, New York, and telling the clerk he expects to leave within three days. There was no record of mail or telephone calls for him.

Nobody knew when he had gone out, since he had not left his key at the desk. Neither elevator boys nor bell-hops could tell us anything.

His room didn't add much to our knowledge. His baggage consisted of one pigskin bag, battered and scarred, and covered with the marks of labels that had been scraped off. It was locked, but traveling bags locks don't amount to much. This one held us up about five minutes.

Rounds' clothes—some in the bag, some in the closet—were neither many nor expensive, but they were all new. The washable stuff was without laundry marks. Everything was of popular makes, widely advertised brands that could be bought in any city in the country. There wasn't a piece of paper with anything written on it. There wasn't an identifying tag. There wasn't anything in the room to tell where Rounds had come from or why.

Pederson was peevish about it.

"I guess if he hadn't got killed he'd of beat us out of a week's bill! These guys that don't carry anything to identify 'em, and that don't leave their keys at the desk when they go out, ain't to be trusted too much!"

We had just finished our search when a bell-hop brought Detective Sergeant O'Gar, of the police department Homicide Detail, into the room.

"Been down to the agency?" I asked him.

"Yeah, just came from there."

"What's new?"

O'Gar pushed back his wide-brimmed black village-constable's hat and scratched his bullet head.

"Not a heap. The doc says he was opened with a blade at least six inches long by a couple wide, and that he couldn't of lived two hours after he got the blade—most likely not more'n one. We didn't find any news on him. What've you got here?"

"His name is Rounds. He registered here yesterday from New York. His stuff is new, and there's nothing on any of it to tell us anything except that he didn't want to leave a trail. No letters, no memoranda, nothing. No blood, no signs of a row, in the room."

O'Gar turned to Pederson.

"Any brown men been around the hotel? Hindus or the like?"

"Not that I saw," the house copper said. "I'll find out for you."

"Then the red silk was a sarong?" I asked.

"And an expensive one," the detective sergeant said. "I saw a lot of 'em the four years I was soldiering on the islands, but I never saw as good a one as that."

"Who wears them?"

"Men and women in the Philippines, Borneo, Java, Sumatra, Malay Peninsula, parts of India."

"Is it your idea that whoever did the carving advertised himself by running around in the streets in a red petticoat?"

"Don't try to be funny!" he growled at me. "They're often enough twisted or folded up into sashes or girdles. And how do I know he was knifed in the street? For that matter, how do I know he wasn't cut down in your joint?"

"We always bury our victims without saying anything about 'em. Let's go down and give Pete a hand in the search for your brown men."

That angle was empty. Any brown men who had snooped around the hotel had been too good at it to be caught.

I telephoned the Old Man, telling him what I had learned—which didn't cost me much breath—and O'Gar and I spent the rest of the evening sharp-shooting around without ever getting on the target once. We questioned taxi-cab drivers, questioned the three Roundses listed in the telephone book, and our ignorance was as complete when we were through as when we started.

The morning papers, on the streets at a little after eight o'clock that evening, had the story as we knew it.

At eleven o'clock O'Gar and I called it a night, separating in the direction of our respective beds.

We didn't stay apart long.

II

I opened my eyes sitting on the side of my bed in the dim light of a moon that was just coming up, with the ringing telephone in my hand.

O'Gar's voice: "1856 Broadway! On the hump!"

"1856 Broadway," I repeated, and he hung up.

I finished waking up while I phoned for a taxicab, and then wrestled my clothes on. My watch told me it was 12:55 A.M. as I went downstairs. I hadn't been fifteen minutes in bed.

1856 Broadway was a three-story house set behind a pocket-size lawn in a row of like houses behind like lawns. The others were dark. 1856 shed light from every window, and from the open front door. A policeman stood in the vestibule.

"Hello, Mac! O'Gar here?"

"Just went in."

I walked into a brown and buff reception hall, and saw the detective sergeant going up the wide stairs.

"What's up?" I asked as I joined him.

"Don't know."

On the second floor we turned to the left, going into a library or sitting room that stretched across the front of the house.

A man in pajamas and bathrobe sat on a davenport there, with one bared leg stretched out on a chair in front of him. I recognized him when he nodded to me: Austin Richter, owner of a Market Street moving picture theater. He was a round-faced man of forty-five or so, partly bald, for whom the agency had done some work a year or so before in connection with a ticket-seller who had departed without turning in the day's receipts.

In front of Richter a thin white-haired man with doctor written all over him stood looking at Richter's leg, which was wrapped in a bandage just below the knee. Beside the doctor, a tall woman in a fur-trimmed dressing-gown stood, a roll of gauze and a pair of scissors in her hands. A husky police corporal was writing in a notebook at a long narrow table, a thick hickory walking stick laying on the bright blue table cover at his elbow.

All of them looked around at us as we came into the room. The corporal got up and came over to us.

"I knew you were handling the Rounds job, sergeant, so I thought I'd best get word to you as soon as I heard they was brown men mixed up in this."

"Good work, Flynn," O'Gar said. "What happened here?"

"Burglary, or maybe only attempted burglary. They was four of them—crashed the kitchen door."

Richter was sitting up very straight, and his blue eyes were suddenly excited, as were the brown eyes of the woman.

"I beg your pardon," he said, "but is there—you mentioned brown men in connection with another affair—is there another?"

O'Gar looked at me.

"You haven't seen the morning papers?" I asked the theater owner.

"No."

"Well, a man came into the Continental office late this afternoon, with a stab in his chest, and died there. Pressed against the wound, as if to stop the bleeding, was a sarong, which is where we got the brown men idea."

"His name?"

"Rounds, H. R. Rounds."

The name brought no recognition into Richter's eyes.

"A tall man, thin, with dark skin?" he asked. "In a gray suit?"

"All of that."

Richter twisted around to look at the woman.

"Molloy!" he exclaimed.

"Molloy!" she exclaimed.

"So you know him?"

Their faces came back toward me.

"Yes. He was here this afternoon. He left—"

Richter stopped, to turn to the woman again, questioningly.

"Yes, Austin," she said, putting gauze and scissors on the table, and sitting down beside him on the davenport. "Tell them."

He patted her hand and looked up at me again with the expression of a man who has seen a nice spot on which to lay down a heavy load.

"Sit down. It isn't a long story, but sit down."

We found ourselves chairs.

"Molloy—Sam Molloy—that is his name, or the name I have always known him by. He came here this afternoon. He'd either called up the theater or gone there, and they had told him I was home. I hadn't seen him for three years. We could see—both my wife and I—that there was something the matter with him when he came in.

"When I asked him, he said he'd been stabbed, by a Siamese, on his way here. He didn't seem to think the wound amounted to much, or pretended he didn't. He wouldn't let us fix it for him, or look at it. He said he'd go to a doctor after he left, after he'd got rid of the thing. That was what he had come to me for. He wanted me to hide it, to take care of it until he came for it again.

"He didn't talk much. He was in a hurry, and suffering. I didn't ask him any questions. I couldn't refuse him anything. I couldn't question him even though he as good as told us that it was illegal as well as dangerous. He saved our lives once—more than my wife's life—down in Mexico, where we first knew him. That was in 1916. We were caught down there during the Villa troubles. Molloy was running guns over the border, and he had enough influence with the bandits to have us released when it looked as if we were done for.

"So this time, when he wanted me to do something for him, I couldn't ask him about it. I said, 'Yes,' and he gave me the package. It wasn't a large package: about the size of—well—a loaf of bread, perhaps, but quite heavy for its size. It was wrapped in brown paper. We unwrapped it after he had gone, that is, we took the paper off. But the inner wrapping was of canvas, tied with silk cord, and sealed, so we didn't open that. We put it upstairs in the pack room, under a pile of old magazines.

"Then, at about a quarter to twelve tonight—I had only been in bed a few minutes, and hadn't gone to sleep yet—I heard a noise in here. I don't own a gun, and there's nothing you could properly call a weapon in the house, but that walking stick"—indicating the hickory stick on the table—"was in a closet in our bedroom. So I got that and came in here to see what the noise was.

"Right outside the bedroom door I ran into a man. I could see him better than he could see me, because this door was open and he showed against the window. He was between me and it, and the moonlight showed him fairly clear. I hit him with the stick, but didn't knock him down. He turned and ran in here. Foolishly, not thinking that he might not be alone, I ran after him. Another man shot me in the leg just as I came through the door.

"I fell, of course. While I was getting up, two of them came in with my wife between them. There were four of them. They were medium-sized men, brown-skinned, but not so dark. I took it for granted that they were Siamese, because Molloy had spoken of Siamese. They turned on the lights here, and one of them, who seemed to be the leader, asked me:

"'Where is it?'

"His accent was pretty bad, but you could understand his words good enough. Of course I knew they were after what Molloy had left, but I pretended I didn't. They told me, or rather the leader did, that he knew it had been left here, but they called Molloy by another name—Dawson. I said I didn't know any Dawson, and nothing had been left here, and I tried to get them to tell me what they expected to find. They wouldn't, though—they just called it '*it.*'

"They talked among themselves, but of course I couldn't make out a word of what they were saying, and then three of them went out, leaving one here to guard us. He had a Luger pistol. We could hear the others moving around the house. The search must have lasted an hour. Then the one I took for the leader came in, and said something to our guard. Both of them looked quite elated.

"'It is not wise if you will leave this room for many minutes,' the leader said to me, and they left us—both of them—closing the door behind them.

"I knew they were going, but I couldn't walk on this leg. From what the doctor says, I'll be lucky if I walk on it inside of a couple of months. I didn't want my wife to go out, and perhaps run into one of them before they'd got away, but she insisted on going. She found they'd gone, and she phoned the police, and then ran up to the pack room and found Molloy's package was gone."

"And this Molloy didn't give you any hint at all as to what was in the package?" O'Gar asked when Richter had finished.

"Not a word, except that it was something the Siamese were after."

"Did he know the Siamese who stabbed him?" I asked.

"I think so," Richter said slowly, "though I am not sure he said he did."

"Do you remember his words?"

"Not exactly, I'm afraid."

"I think I remember them," Mrs. Richter said. "My husband, Mr. Richter, asked him, 'What's the matter, Molloy? Are you hurt, or sick?'

"Molloy gave a little laugh, putting a hand on his chest, and said, 'Nothing much. I run into a Siamese who was looking for me on my way here, and got careless and let him scratch me. But I kept my little bundle!' And he laughed again, and patted the package."

"Did he say anything else about the Siamese?"

"Not directly," she replied, "though he did tell us to watch out for any Asiatics we saw around the neighborhood. He said he wouldn't leave the package if he thought it would make trouble for us, but that there was always a chance that something would go wrong, and we'd better be careful. And he told my husband"—nodding at Richter—"that the Siamese had been dogging him for months, but now that he had a safe place for the package he was going to 'take them for a walk and forget to bring them back.' That was the way he put it."

"How much do you know about Molloy?"

"Not a great deal, I'm afraid," Richter took up the answering again. "He liked to talk about the places he had been and the things he had seen, but you couldn't get a word out of him about his own affairs. We met him first in Mexico, as I have told you, in 1916. After he saved us down there and got us away, we didn't see him again for nearly four years. He rang the bell one night, and came in for an hour or two. He was on his way to China, he said, and had a lot of business to attend to before he left the next day.

"Some months later I had a letter from him, from the Queen's Hotel in Kandy, asking me to send him a list of the importers and exporters in San Francisco. He wrote me a letter thanking me for the list, and I didn't hear from him again until he came to San Francisco for a week, about a year later. That was in 1921, I think.

"He was here for another week about a year after that, telling us that he had been in Brazil, but, as usual, not saying what he had been doing there. Some months later I had a letter from him, from Chicago, saying he would be here the following week. However, he didn't come. Instead, some time later, he wrote from Vladivostok, saying he hadn't been able to make it. Today was the first we'd heard of him since then."

"Where's his home? His people?"

"He always says he has neither. I've an idea he was born in England, though I don't know that he ever said so, or what made me think so."

"Got any more questions?" I asked O'Gar.

"No. Let's give the place the eye, and see if the Siamese left any leads behind 'em."

The eye we gave the house was thorough. We didn't split the territory between us, but went over everything together—everything from roof to cellar—every nook, drawer, corner.

The cellar did most for us: it was there, in the cold furnace, that we found the handful of black buttons and the fire-darkened garter clasps. But the upper floors hadn't been altogether worthless: in one room we had found the crumpled sales slip of an Oakland store, marked *1 table cover*; and in another room we had found no garters.

"Of course it's none of my business," I told Richter when O'Gar and I joined the others again, "but I think maybe if you plead self-defense you might get away with it."

He tried to jump up from the davenport, but his shot leg failed him.

The woman got up slowly.

"And maybe that would leave an out for you," O'Gar told her. "Why don't you try to persuade him?"

"Or maybe it would be better if you plead the self-defense," I suggested to her. "You could say that Richter ran to your help when your husband grabbed you, that your husband shot him and was turning his gun on you when you stabbed him. That would sound smooth enough."

"My husband?"

"Uh-huh, Mrs. Rounds-Molloy-Dawson. Your late husband, anyway."

Richter got his mouth far enough closed to get words out of it.

"What is the meaning of this damned nonsense?" he demanded.

"Them's harsh words to come from a fellow like you," O'Gar growled at him. "If this is nonsense, what do you make of that yarn you told us about creeping Siamese and mysterious bundles, and God knows what all?"

"Don't be too hard on him," I told O'Gar. "Being around movies all the time has poisoned his idea of what sounds plausible. If it hadn't, he'd have known better than to see a Siamese in the moonlight at 11:45, when the moon was just coming up at somewhere around 12:45, when you phoned me."

Richter stood up on his one good leg.

The husky police corporal stepped close to him.

"Hadn't I better frisk him, sergeant?"

O'Gar shook his bullet head.

"Waste of time. He's got nothing on him. They cleaned the place of weapons. The chances are the lady dropped them in the bay when she rode over to Oakland to get a table cover to take the place of the sarong her husband carried away with him."

That shook the pair of them. Richter pretended he hadn't gulped, and the woman had a fight of it before she could make her eyes stay still on mine.

O'Gar struck while the iron was hot by bringing the buttons and garters clasps we had salvaged out of his pocket, and letting them trickle from one hand to another. That used up the last bit of the facts we had.

I threw a lie at them.

"Never me to knock the press, but you don't want to put too much confidence in what the papers say. For instance, a fellow might say a few pregnant words before he died, and the papers might say he didn't. A thing like that would confuse things."

The woman reared up her head and looked at O'Gar.

"May I speak to Austin alone?" she asked. "I don't mean out of your sight."

The detective sergeant scratched his head and looked at me. This letting your victims go into conference is always a ticklish business: they may decide to come clean, and then again, they may frame up a new out. On the other hand, if you don't let them, the chances are they get stubborn on you, and you can't get anything out of them. One way was as risky as another. I grinned at O'Gar and refused to make a suggestion. He could decide for himself, and, if he was wrong, I'd have him to dump the blame on. He scowled at me, and then nodded to the woman.

"You can go over into that corner and whisper together for a couple of minutes," he said, "but no foolishness."

She gave Richter the hickory stick, took his other arm, helped him hobble to a far corner, pulled a chair over there for him. He sat with his back to us. She stood behind him, leaning over his shoulder, so that both their faces were hidden from us.

O'Gar came closer to me.

"What do you think?" he muttered.

"I think they'll come through."

"That shot of yours about being Molloy's wife hit center. I missed that one. How'd you make it?"

"When she was telling us what Molloy had said about the Siamese she took pains both times she said 'my husband' to show that she meant Richter."

"So? Well—"

The whispering in the far corner had been getting louder, so that the s's had become sharp hisses. Now a clear emphatic sentence came from Richter's mouth.

"I'll be damned if I will!"

Both of them looked furtively over their shoulders, and they lowered their voices again, but not for long. The woman was apparently trying to persuade him to do something. He kept shaking his head. He put a hand on her arm. She pushed it away, and kept on whispering.

He said aloud, deliberately:

"Go ahead, if you want to be a fool. It's your neck. I didn't put the knife in him."

She jumped away from him, her eyes black blazes in a white face. O'Gar and I moved softly toward them.

"You rat!" she spat at Richter, and spun to face us.

"I killed him!" she cried. "This thing in the chair tried to and—"

Richter swung the hickory stick.

I jumped for it—missed—crashed into the back of his chair. Hickory stick, Richter, chair, and I sprawled together on the floor. The corporal helped me up. He and I picked Richter up and put him on the davenport again.

The woman's story poured out of her angry mouth:

"His name wasn't Molloy. It was Lange, Sam Lange. I married him in Providence in 1913 and went to China with him—to Canton, where he had a position with a steamship line. We didn't stay there long, because he got into some trouble through being mixed up in the revolution that year. After that we drifted around, mostly around Asia.

"We met this thing"—she pointed at the now sullenly quiet Richter—"in Singapore, in 1919, I think—right after the World War was over. His name is Holley, and Scotland Yard can tell you something about him. He had a proposition. He knew of a gem-bed in upper Burma, one of many that were hidden from the British when they took the country. He knew the natives who were working it, knew where they were hiding their gems.

"My husband went in with him, with two other men that were killed. They looted the natives' cache, and got away with a whole sackful of sapphires, topazes and even a few rubies. The two other men were killed by the natives and my husband was badly wounded.

"We didn't think he could live. We were hiding in a hut near the Yunnan border. Holley persuaded me to take the gems and run away with them. It looked as if Sam was done for, and if we stayed there long we'd be caught. I can't say that I was crazy about Sam anyway; he wasn't the kind you would be, after living with him for a while.

"So Holley and I took it and lit out. We had to use a lot of the stones to buy our way through Yunnan and Kwangsi and Kwangtung, but we made it. We got to San Francisco with enough to buy this house and the movie theater, and we've been here since. We've been honest since we came here, but I don't suppose that means anything. We had enough money to keep us comfortable.

"Today Sam showed up. We hadn't heard of him since we left him on his back in Burma. He said he'd been caught and jailed for three years. Then he'd got away, and had spent the other three hunting for us. He was that kind. He didn't want me back, but he did want money. He wanted everything we had. Holley lost his nerve. Instead of bargaining with Sam, he lost his head and tried to shoot him.

"Sam took his gun away from him and shot

him in the leg. In the scuffle Sam had dropped a knife—a kris, I think. I picked it up, but he grabbed me just as I got it. I don't know how it happened. All I saw was Sam staggering back, holding his chest with both hands—and the kris shining red in my hand.

"Sam had dropped his gun. Holley got it and was all for shooting Sam, but I wouldn't let him. It happened in this room. I don't remember whether I gave Sam the sarong we used for a cover on the table or not. Anyway, he tried to stop the blood with it. He went away then, while I kept Holley from shooting him.

"I knew Sam wouldn't go to the police, but I didn't know what he'd do. And I knew he was hurt bad. If he dropped dead somewhere, the chances are he'd be traced here. I watched from a window as he went down the street, and nobody seemed to pay any attention to him, but he looked so conspicuously wounded to me that I thought everybody would be sure to remember him if it got into the papers that he had been found dead somewhere.

"Holley was even more scared than I. We couldn't run away, because he had a shot leg. So we made up that Siamese story, and I went over to Oakland, and bought the table cover to take the place of the sarong. We had some guns and even a few oriental knives and swords here. I wrapped them up in paper, breaking the swords, and dropped them off the ferry when I went to Oakland.

"When the morning papers came out we read what had happened, and then we went ahead with what we had planned. We burned the suit Holley had worn when he was shot, and his garters—because the pants had a bullet-hole in them, and the bullet had cut one garter. We fixed a hole in his pajama-leg, unbandaged his leg,—I had fixed it as well as I could,—and washed away the clotted blood until it began to bleed again. Then I gave the alarm."

She raised both hands in a gesture of finality and made a clucking sound with her tongue.

"And there you are," she said.

"You got anything to say?" I asked Holley, who was staring at his bandaged leg.

"To my lawyer," he said without looking up.

O'Gar spoke to the corporal.

"The wagon, Flynn."

Ten minutes later we were in the street, helping Holley and the woman into a police car.

Around the corner on the other side of the street came three brown-skinned men, apparently Malay sailors. The one in the middle seemed to be drunk, and the other two were supporting him. One of them had a package that could have held a bottle under his arm.

O'Gar looked from them to me and laughed.

"We wouldn't be doing a thing to those babies right now if we had fallen for that yarn, would we?" he whispered.

"Shut up, you, you big heap!" I growled back, nodding at Holley, who was in the car by now. "If that bird sees them he'll identify 'em as his Siamese, and God knows what a jury would make of it!"

We made the puzzled driver twist the car six blocks out of his way to be sure we'd miss the brown men. It was worth it, because nothing interfered with the twenty years apiece that Holley and Mrs. Lange drew.

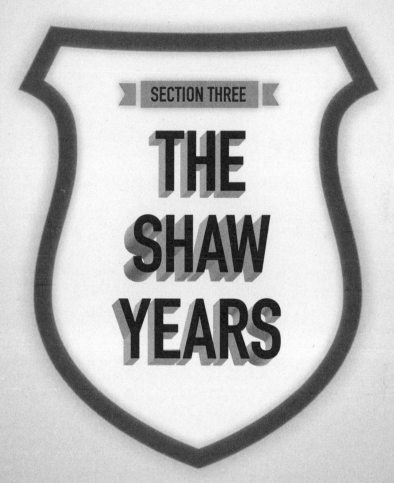

SECTION THREE

THE SHAW YEARS

Introduction

THE SHAW YEARS: 1926–1930

DASHIELL HAMMETT SERVED his apprenticeship under editors Sutton and Cody, but by the end of 1925 he had outgrown them. When Cody refused his demand for more money, Hammett angrily broke off relations with him, and in March 1926 he took a job as advertising manager at Samuels Jewelers in San Francisco, "The House of Lucky Wedding Rings." The pay was $350 per month (about $50,000 per year in 2017 dollars), double his monthly income from writing for the pulps. It was his first full-time job in at least three years and, more likely, since he left the army. At Samuels he impressed his boss with his energy and ingenuity, working from eight to six, six days a week—but it was too much. Five months later, on July 20, he was found collapsed in his office, lying in a pool of blood. His younger daughter, Josephine, was not quite two months old. Eight weeks later, Samuels wrote a notarized letter to the Veterans Bureau certifying that Hammett had resigned his position due to ill health. His earnings, now reduced to disability payments, dropped to $80 per month, plus payment for some part-time work he did for Samuels. Moreover, the Veterans Bureau nurses insisted that Hammett live apart from his wife and children, which meant two rent payments. Within three months, he took rooms at 891 Post Street (the model for Sam Spade's apartment in *The Maltese Falcon*), and Jose and the girls stayed first in an apartment in San Francisco, then across San Francisco Bay in Fairfax. In desperation, Hammett tried to revive his advertising career from his apartment, publishing how-to articles in the trade journal *Western Advertising*.

Meanwhile, a shake-up was materializing at *Black Mask*. Circulation was decreasing sharply, and Cody, whose attentions were divided among other Pro-Distributors projects, needed a new editor to revitalize the magazine. The successful applicant was a fifty-one-year-old aspiring mystery writer who had submitted his first story to *Black Mask* in summer 1926. Joseph Thompson Shaw was a most unlikely candidate to edit a pulp detective-fiction magazine. He was a graduate of Bowdoin College, where he was a member of the editorial board for the school literary magazine. He was a four-time national sabers champion. He had worked as a journalist at the *New York World*, as a clerk at G. P. Putnam's publishing company, and as editor of *American Textile Jour-*

nal before embarking on a successful career in the textile business. Then he opened his own office to sell securities on the stock exchange. He wrote a history of the textile industry, *From Wool to Cloth* (Boston: American Woolen Company, 1904), and a travel book, *Spain of to-Day* (New York: Grafton, 1909). During World War I he served as a captain in the army and after the war as an officer in the American Relief Administration in France, and as director of the Bureau for Children's Relief in Czechoslovakia. And he was socially connected. In February 1925, the *Brooklyn Daily Eagle* noted that he was a member of the Pinehurst Country Club in Brooklyn, where he was frequently seen taking tea and dancing with his wife after polo and golf matches. Shaw's first mystery story (presumably his first fiction), "Makings," was published in the December 1926 issue of *Black Mask*, the month after he took over from Cody as editor.

Shaw was the first full-time editor of *Black Mask* since Hammett started writing for it, and he took his job seriously. Though he had no experience in pulp-magazine publishing, he was an excellent businessman and a superb promoter. His primary goal was to separate *Black Mask* from the rest of the pulp-fiction field by virtue of the quality of its fiction, detective fiction. Upon assuming the editor's chair, he read through back issues of the magazine to identify the authors he wished to cultivate. He chose four, whom he called his "backfield," employing a football metaphor: Erle Stanley Gardner, J. Paul Suter, Carroll John Daly, and Hammett, his favorite among them; for the line he named "a splendid nucleus" in Tom Curry, Raoul Whitfield, and Frederick Nebel. In the introduction to a 1946 anthology of stories from *Black Mask*, Shaw recalled his first days as editor:

> We meditated on the possibility of creating a new type of detective story differing from that accredited to the Chaldeans and employed more recently by Gaborieau, Poe, Conan Doyle—in fact universally by detective story writers; that is, the deduc-

tive type, the cross-word puzzle sort, lacking—deliberately—all other human emotional values. . . .

So we wrote to Dashiell Hammett. His response was immediate and most enthusiastic: *That is exactly what I've been thinking about and working toward. As I see it, the approach I have in mind has never been attempted. The field is unscratched and wide open.* . . .

We felt obligated to stipulate our boundaries. We wanted simplicity for the sake of clarity, plausibility, and belief. We wanted action, but we held that action is meaningless unless it involves recognizable human character in three-dimensional form.

Hammett's enthusiasm was amplified by Shaw's check for $300, the money Hammett felt Cody owed him from earlier in the year. Shaw also passed along what he represented as lavish praise from Cody and Gardner. By February 1927, Hammett was back in the fold. He responded with his most accomplished short fiction to date, "The Big Knock-Over," the linked story "$106,000 Blood Money," and "The Main Death," all Op stories and his only submissions to *Black Mask* for the next year, totaling just under 45,000 words (for a total income of more than $1,000). They are also his most violent.

Little is known of the particulars of Shaw's editorial method, but his authors revered him. In 1958, Lester Dent wrote to English professor Philip Durham about his experience as a *Black Mask* author: He called Shaw "the personification of English culture." "His writers regarded Captain Shaw with—if any writer ever truly gave an editor such—reverence. . . . Here was an editor who thought his writers were truly great . . . could breathe this pride of his into a writer." He went on: "You will hear it said Joseph Shaw told his writers what to write and how, demanded they do 'Black Mask' style. That was not true. He demanded nothing of the sort. He did demand that every word mean something—he must be able to hardly touch your piece with a blue pencil. And he didn't rewrite himself—if there was one paragraph off, you got it back to redo."

With "The Big Knock-Over," Hammett's writing took on a new energy. The language was sharper than before; the plotting was more interesting; the dialogue was surer; and the dramatic scenes were more vivid. There was more action than in Hammett's earlier stories, and the action was linked to real-life crime, as Shaw reminded readers in his introductory blurb, which mentioned the Illinois gang wars and a recent mail-truck robbery in Elizabeth, New Jersey, that netted more than $800,000 and eventually left six people dead: "Mr. Hammett pictures a daring action that is almost stunning in its scope and effectiveness—yet can anyone be sure that it isn't likely to occur?" The Op's comment in "The Gutting of Couffignal" about M. P. Shiel's *The Lord of the Sea* well describes Hammett's first stories for Shaw: "There were plots and counterplots, kidnappings, murders, prison-breakings, forgeries and burglaries, diamonds large as hats . . . It sounds dizzy here, but in the book it was as real as a dime." Readers agreed.

The star of Shaw's backfield produced, and the new editorial formula worked. In May 1927, Shaw announced that the circulation of *Black Mask* had increased 60 percent: "BECAUSE IT'S GOT THE STUFF! The stories in it are the best of their kind that can possibly be gotten, written by men who not only know how to write, but know what they are writing about."

Unlike his predecessors, Shaw nurtured his authors' careers, and he took a special interest in Hammett's. It seems likely that he arranged for Hammett to become the mystery-fiction reviewer for the *Saturday Review of Literature* in January 1927. Cofounded in 1924 and edited by Yale English professor Henry Seidel Canby, who also chaired the editorial board of the newly formed Book-of-the-Month Club, the *Saturday Review* was regarded as the most influential literary magazine in the United States. Hammett did not then have the cachet to land that job, but Shaw, a fledgling literary agent as well as an editor, had the social and business connections to recommend his star writer. Book reviewing was significant to Hammett's literary development in two ways. Not only did that job give him national exposure in a respected literary venue, it forced him to articulate his editorial standards, an effort that showed in the increased care he took with his own stories and his growing confidence that he could make detective fiction—which he regarded as subliterary in the hands of its most popular practitioners—respectable.

Hammett believed that detective fiction should accurately reflect the work of professionals in the field and the world they operated in. He gained his experience in the years when real-life detectives worked hand in hand with municipal police forces and were usually better trained with superior resources at hand. Pinkerton's, Hammett's agency, had the first national fingerprint file, and its operatives drew on far better national records than most any police force in the nation at that time. Pinkerton's detectives worked for hire to track down crooks of all descriptions, who could move freely from jurisdiction to jurisdiction to avoid the grasp of local police departments. Hammett was contemptuous of writers who carelessly imagined a profession that he took most seriously. He began one review with the anecdote about the only fellow operative he knew who read mystery fiction: "When I'm through my day's gumshoeing I like to relax; I like to get my mind on something that's altogether different from the daily grind; so I read detective stories."

While Hammett's later stories had an element of the sensationalism demanded by Cody in the violent confrontations between the Op and his prey, they also captured the professional methods of the working detective, and increasingly during Shaw's watch, Hammett depicted the emotional toll police work exacted from the dedicated op.

RL

BLACK MASK, FEBRUARY 1927

The Big Knock-Over

BY DASHIELL HAMMETT

Before they actually do it, one is inclined to say it isn't done. But the gang warfare in Illinois, the big mail-truck holdup in Jersey found bandits using airplanes, bombs and machine guns. And now Mr. Hammett pictures a daring action that is almost stunning in its scope and effectiveness—yet can anyone be sure that it isn't likely to occur?

I FOUND PADDY the Mex in Jean Larrouy's dive.

Paddy—an amiable con man who looked like the King of Spain—showed me his big white teeth in a smile, pushed a chair out for me with one foot, and told the girl who shared his table:

"Nellie, meet the biggest-hearted dick in San Francisco. This little fat guy will do anything for anybody, if only he can send 'em over for life in the end." He turned to me, waving his cigar at the girl: "Nellie Wade, and you can't get anything on her. She don't have to work—her old man's a bootlegger."

She was a slim girl in blue—white skin, long green eyes, short chestnut hair. Her sullen face livened into beauty when she put a hand across the table to me, and we both laughed at Paddy.

"Five years?" she asked.

"Six," I corrected.

"Damn!" said Paddy, grinning and hailing a waiter. "Some day I'm going to fool a sleuth."

So far he had fooled all of them—he had never slept in a hoosegow.

I looked at the girl again. Six years before, this Angel Grace Cardigan had buncoed half a dozen Philadelphia boys out of plenty. Dan Morey and I had nailed her, but none of her victims would go to the bat against her, so she had been turned loose. She was a kid of nineteen then, but already a smooth grifter.

In the middle of the floor one of Larrouy's girls began to sing "Tell Me What You Want and I'll Tell You What You Get." Paddy the Mex tipped a gin bottle over the glasses of gingerale the waiter had brought. We drank and I gave Paddy a piece of paper with a name and address penciled on it.

"Itchy Maker asked me to slip you that," I explained. "I saw him in the Folsom big house yesterday. It's his mother, he says, and he wants you to look her up and see if she wants anything. What he means, I suppose, is that you're to give her his cut from the last trick you and he turned."

"You hurt my feelings," Paddy said, pocketing the paper and bringing out the gin again.

I downed the second gin-gingerale and gathered in my feet, preparing to rise and trot along home. At that moment four of Larrouy's clients came in from the street. Recognition of one of them kept me in my chair. He was tall and slender and all dolled up in what the well-dressed man should wear. Sharp-eyed, sharp-faced, with lips thin as knife-edges under a small pointed mustache—Bluepoint Vance. I wondered what he was doing three thousand miles away from his New York hunting-grounds.

While I wondered I put the back of my head to him, pretending interest in the singer, who was now giving the customers "I Want to Be a Bum." Beyond her, back in a corner, I spotted another familiar face that belonged in another city—Happy Jim Hacker, round and rosy Detroit gunman, twice sentenced to death and twice pardoned.

When I faced front again, Bluepoint Vance and his three companions had come to rest two tables away. His back was to us. I sized up his playmates.

Facing Vance sat a wide-shouldered young giant with red hair, blue eyes and a ruddy face that was good-looking in a tough, savage way. On his left was a shifty-eyed dark girl in a floppy hat. She was talking to Vance. The red-haired giant's attention was all taken by the fourth member of the party, on his right. She deserved it.

She was neither tall nor short, thin nor plump. She wore a black Russian tunic affair, green-trimmed and hung with silver dinguses. A black fur coat was spread over the chair behind her. She was probably twenty. Her eyes were blue, her mouth red, her teeth white, the hair-ends showing under her black-green-and-silver turban were brown, and she had a nose. Without getting steamed up over the details, she was nice. I said so. Paddy the Mex agreed with a "That's what," and Angel Grace suggested that I go over and tell Red O'Leary I thought her nice.

"Red O'Leary the big bird?" I asked, sliding down in my seat so I could stretch a foot under the table between Paddy and Angel Grace. "Who's his nice girl friend?"

"Nancy Regan, and the other one's Sylvia Yount."

"And the slicker with his back to us?" I probed.

Paddy's foot, hunting the girl's under the table, bumped mine.

"Don't kick me, Paddy," I pleaded. "I'll be good. Anyway, I'm not going to stay here to be bruised. I'm going home."

I swapped so-longs with them and moved toward the street, keeping my back to Bluepoint Vance.

At the door I had to step aside to let two men come in. Both knew me, but neither gave me a tumble—Sheeny Holmes (not the old-timer who staged the Moose Jaw looting back in the buggy-riding days) and Denny Burke, Baltimore's King of Frog Island. A good pair—neither of them would think of taking a life unless assured of profit and political protection.

Outside, I turned down toward Kearny Street, strolling along, thinking that Larrouy's joint had been full of crooks this one night, and that there seemed to be more than a sprinkling of prominent visitors in our midst. A shadow in a doorway interrupted my brain-work.

The shadow said, "Ps-s-s-s! Ps-s-s-s!"

Stopping, I examined the shadow until I saw it was Beno, a hophead newsie who had given me a tip now and then in the past—some good, some phoney.

"I'm sleepy," I growled as I joined Beno and

his arm-load of newspapers in the doorway, "and I've heard the story about the Mormon who stuttered, so if that's what's on your mind, say so, and I'll keep going."

"I don't know nothin' about no Mormons," he protested, "but I know somethin' else."

"Well?"

"'S all right for you to say 'Well,' but what I want to know is, what am I gonna get out of it?"

"Flop in the nice doorway and go shut-eye," I advised him, moving toward the street again. "You'll be all right when you wake up."

"Hey! Listen, I got somethin' for you. Hones' to Gawd!"

"Well?"

"Listen!" He came close, whispering. "There's a caper rigged for the Seaman's National. I don't know what's the racket, but it's real. Hones' to Gawd! I ain't stringin' you. I can't give you no monickers. You know I would if I knowed 'em. Hones' to Gawd! Gimme ten bucks. It's worth that to you, ain't it? This is straight dope—hones' to Gawd!"

"Yeah, straight from the nose-candy!"

"No! Hones' to Gawd! I—"

"What *is* the caper, then?"

"I don't know. All I got was that the Seaman's is gonna be nicked. Hones' to—"

"Where'd you get it?"

Beno shook his head. I put a silver dollar in his hand.

"Get another shot and think up the rest of it," I told him, "and if it's amusing enough I'll give you the other nine bucks."

I walked on down to the corner, screwing up my forehead over Beno's tale. By itself, it sounded like what it probably was—a yarn designed to get a dollar out of a trusting gumshoe. But it wasn't altogether by itself. Larrouy's—just one drum* in a city that had a number—had been heavy with grifters† who were threats against life and property. It was worth a look-see, especially

---

* a place of business, especially where you get reliable information
† cons

since the insurance company covering the Seaman's National Bank was a Continental Detective Agency client.

Around the corner, twenty feet or so along Kearny Street, I stopped.

From the street I had just quit came two bangs—the reports of a heavy pistol. I went back the way I had come. As I rounded the corner I saw men gathering in a group up the street. A young Armenian—a dapper boy of nineteen or twenty—passed me, going the other way, sauntering along, hands in pockets, softly whistling "Broken-hearted Sue."

I joined the group—now becoming a crowd—around Beno. Beno was dead, blood from two holes in his chest staining the crumpled newspapers under him.

I went up to Larrouy's and looked in. Red O'Leary, Bluepoint Vance, Nancy Regan, Sylvia Yount, Paddy the Mex, Angel Grace, Denny Burke, Sheeny Holmes, Happy Jim Hacker—not one of them was there.

Returning to Beno's vicinity, I loitered with my back to a wall while the police arrived, asked questions, learned nothing, found no witnesses, and departed, taking what was left of the newsie with them.

I went home and to bed.

II

In the morning I spent an hour in the agency file-room, digging through the gallery and records. We didn't have anything on Red O'Leary, Denny Burke, Nancy Regan, Sylvia Yount, and only some guesses on Paddy the Mex. Nor were there any open jobs definitely chalked against Angel Grace, Bluepoint Vance, Sheeny Holmes and Happy Jim Hacker, but their photos were there. At ten o'clock—bank opening time—I set out for the Seaman's National, carrying these photos and Beno's tip.

The Continental Detective Agency's San Francisco office is located in a Market Street office building. The Seaman's National Bank occupies the ground floor of a tall gray building in Montgomery Street, San Francisco's financial center. Ordinarily, since I don't like even seven blocks of unnecessary walking, I would have taken a street car. But there was some sort of traffic jam on Market Street, so I set out afoot, turning off along Grant Avenue.

A few blocks of walking, and I began to see that something was wrong with the part of town I was heading for. Noises for one thing—roaring, rattling, explosive noises. At Sutter Street a man passed me, holding his face with both hands and groaning as he tried to push a dislocated jaw back in place. His cheek was scraped red.

I went down Sutter Street. Traffic was in a tangle that reached to Montgomery Street. Excited, bare-headed men were running around. The explosive noises were clearer. An automobile full of policemen went down past me, going as fast as traffic would let it. An ambulance came up the street, clanging its gong, taking to the sidewalks where the traffic tangle was worst.

I crossed Kearny Street on the trot. Down the other side of the street two patrolmen were running. One had his gun out. The explosive noises were a drumming chorus ahead.

Rounding into Montgomery Street, I found few sightseers ahead of me. The middle of the street was filled with trucks, touring cars, taxis—deserted there. Up in the next block—between Bush and Pine Streets—hell was on a holiday.

The holiday spirit was gayest in the middle of the block, where the Seaman's National Bank and the Golden Gate Trust Company faced each other across the street.

For the next six hours I was busier than a flea on a fat woman.

III

Late that afternoon I took a recess from blood-hounding and went up to the office for a pow-wow with the Old Man. He was leaning back in his chair, staring out the window, tapping on his desk with the customary long yellow pencil.

A tall, plump man in his seventies, this boss of mine, with a white-mustached, baby-pink grandfatherly face, mild blue eyes behind rimless spectacles, and no more warmth in him than a hangman's rope. Fifty years of crook-hunting for the Continental had emptied him of everything except brains and a soft-spoken, gently smiling shell of politeness that was the same whether things went good or bad—and meant as little at one time as another. We who worked under him were proud of his cold-bloodedness. We used to boast that he could spit icicles in July, and we called him Pontius Pilate among ourselves, because he smiled politely when he sent us out to be crucified on suicidal jobs.

He turned from the window as I came in, nodded me to a chair, and smoothed his mustache with the pencil. On his desk the afternoon papers screamed the news of the Seaman's National Bank and Golden Gate Trust Company double-looting in five colors.

"What is the situation?" he asked, as one would ask about the weather.

"The situation is a pip," I told him. "There were a hundred and fifty crooks in the push if there was one. I saw a hundred myself—or think I did—and there were slews of them that I didn't see—planted where they could jump out and bite when fresh teeth were needed. They bit, too. They bushwacked the police and made a merry wreck out of 'em—going and coming. They hit the two banks at ten sharp—took over the whole block—chased away the reasonable people—dropped the others. The actual looting was duck soup to a mob of that size. Twenty or thirty of 'em to each of the banks while the others held the street. Nothing to it but wrap up the spoils and take 'em home.

"There's a highly indignant business men's meeting down there now—wild-eyed stockbrokers up on their hind legs yelling for the chief of police's heart's blood. The police didn't do any miracles, that's a cinch, but no police department is equipped to handle a trick of that size—no matter how well they think they are. The whole thing lasted less than twenty minutes. There were, say, a hundred and fifty thugs in on it, loaded for bear, every play mapped to the inch. How are you going to get enough coppers down there, size up the racket, plan your battle, and put it over in that little time? It's easy enough to say the police should look ahead—should have a dose for every emergency—but these same birds who are yelling, 'Rotten,' down there now would be the first to squawk, 'Robbery,' if their taxes were boosted a couple of cents to buy more policemen and equipment.

"But the police fell down—there's no question about that—and there will be a lot of beefy necks feel the ax. The armored cars were no good, the grenading was about fifty-fifty, since the bandits knew how to play that game, too. But the real disgrace of the party was the police machine-guns. The bankers and brokers are saying they were fixed. Whether they were deliberately tampered with, or were only carelessly taken care of, is anybody's guess, but only one of the damned things would shoot, and it not very well.

"The getaway was north on Montgomery to Columbus. Along Columbus the parade melted, a few cars at a time, into side streets. The police ran into an ambush between Washington and Jackson, and by the time they had shot their way through it the bandit cars had scattered all over the city. A lot of 'em have been picked up since then—empty.

"All the returns aren't in yet, but right now the score stands something like this: The haul will run God only knows how far into the millions—easily the richest pickings ever got with civilian guns. Sixteen coppers were knocked off, and three times that many wounded. Twelve innocent spectators, bank clerks, and the like, were killed and about as many banged around. There are two dead and five shot-ups who might be either thugs or spectators that got too close. The bandits lost seven dead that we know of, and thirty-one prisoners, most of them bleeding somewhere.

"One of the dead was Fat Boy Clarke. Remember him? He shot his way out of a Des Moines courtroom three or four years ago. Well, in his pocket we found a piece of paper, a map of Montgomery Street between Pine and Bush, the block of the looting. On the back of the map were typed instructions, telling him exactly what to do and when to do it. An X on the map showed him where he was to park the car in which he arrived with his seven men, and there was a circle where he was to stand with them, keeping an eye on things in general and on the windows and roofs of the buildings across the street in particular. Figures 1, 2, 3, 4, 5, 6, 7, 8 on the map marked doorways, steps, a deep window, and so on, that were to be used for shelter if shots had to be traded with those windows and roofs. Clarke was to pay no attention to the Bush Street end of the block, but if the police charged the Pine Street end he was to move his men up there, distributing them among points marked a, b, c, d, e, f, g, and h. (His body was found on the spot marked a.) Every five minutes during the looting he was to send a man to an automobile standing in the street at a point marked on the map with a star, to see if there were any new instructions. He was to tell his men that if he were shot down one of them must report to the car, and a new leader would be given them. When the signal for the getaway was given, he was to send one of his men to the car in which he had come. If it was still in commission, this man was to drive it, not passing the car ahead of him. If it was out of whack, the man was to report to the star-marked car for instructions how to get a new one. I suppose they counted on finding enough parked cars to take care of this end. While Clarke waited for his car he and his men were to throw as much lead as possible at every target in their district, and none of them was to board the car until it came abreast of them. Then they were to drive out Montgomery to Columbus to—blank.

"Get that?" I asked. "Here are a hundred and fifty gunmen, split into groups under group-leaders, with maps and schedules showing what each man is to do, showing the fire-plug he's to kneel behind, the brick he's to stand on, where he's to spit—everything but the name and address of the policeman he's to shoot! It's just as well Beno couldn't give me the details—I'd have written it off as a hop-head's dream!"

"Very interesting," the Old Man said, smiling blandly.

"The Fat Boy's was the only timetable we found," I went on with my history. "I saw a few friends among the killed and caught, and the police are still identifying others. Some are local talent, but most of 'em seem to be imported stock. Detroit, Chi, New York, St. Louis, Denver, Portland, L.A., Philly, Baltimore—all seem to have sent delegates. As soon as the police get through identifying them I'll make out a list.

"Of those who weren't caught, Bluepoint Vance seems to be the main squeeze. He was in the car that directed operations. I don't know who else was there with him. The Shivering Kid was in on the festivities, and I think Alphabet Shorty McCoy, though I didn't get a good look at him. Sergeant Bender told me he spotted Toots Salda and Darby M'Laughlin in the push, and Morgan saw the Did-and-Dat Kid. That's a good cross-section of the layout— gunmen, swindlers, hijackers from all over Rand-McNally.

"The Hall of Justice has been a slaughter-house all afternoon. The police haven't killed any of their guests—none that I know of—but they're sure-God making believers out of them. Newspaper writers who like to sob over what they call the third degree should be down there now. After being knocked around a bit, some of the guests have talked. But the hell of it is they don't know a whole lot. They know some names—Denny Burke, Toby the Lugs, Old Pete Best, Fat Boy Clarke and Paddy the Mex were named—and that helps some, but all the smacking power in the police force arm can't bring out anything else.

"The racket seems to have been organized like this: Denny Burke, for instance, is known as a shifty worker in Baltimore. Well, Denny talks to eight or ten likely boys, one at a time. 'How'd you like to pick up a piece of change out on the Coast?' he asks them. 'Doing what?' the candidate wants to know. 'Doing what you're told,' the King of Frog Island says. 'You know me. I'm telling you this is the fattest picking ever rigged, a kick in the pants to go through—air-tight. Everybody in on it will come home lousy with cush*—and they'll all come home if they don't dog it. That's all I'm spilling. If you don't like it—forget it.'

"And these birds did know Denny, and if he said the job was good that was enough for them. So they put in with him. He told them nothing. He saw that they had guns, gave 'em each a ticket to San Francisco and twenty bucks, and told them where to meet him here. Last night he collected them and told them they went to work this morning. By that time they had moved around the town enough to see that it was bubbling over with visiting talent, including such moguls as Toots Salda, Bluepoint Vance and the Shivering Kid. So this morning they went forth eagerly with the King of Frog Island at their head to do their stuff.

"The other talkers tell varieties of the same tale. The police found room in their crowded jail to stick in a few stool-pigeons. Since few of the bandits knew very many of the others, the stools had an easy time of it, but the only thing they could add to what we've got is that the prisoners are looking for a wholesale delivery tonight. They seem to think their mob will crash the prison and turn 'em loose. That's probably a lot of chewing-gum, but anyway this time the police will be ready.

"That's the situation as it stands now. The police are sweeping the streets, picking up everybody who needs a shave or can't show a certificate of attendance signed by his parson, with special attention to outward bound trains, boats and automobiles. I sent Jack Counihan and Dick Foley down North Beach way to play the joints and see if they can pick up anything."

"Do you think Bluepoint Vance was the actual directing intelligence in this robbery?" the Old Man asked.

_____

* money

"I hope so—we know him."

The Old Man turned his chair so his mild eyes could stare out the window again, and he tapped his desk reflectively with the pencil.

"I'm afraid not," he said in a gently apologetic tone. "Vance is a shrewd, resourceful and determined criminal, but his weakness is one common to his type. His abilities are all for present action and not for planning ahead. He has executed some large operations, but I've always thought I saw in them some other mind at work behind him."

I couldn't quarrel with that. If the Old Man said something was so, then it probably was, because he was one of these cautious babies who'll look out of the window at a cloudburst and say, "It seems to be raining," on the off-chance that somebody's pouring water off the roof.

"And who is this arch-gonif?"* I asked.

"You'll probably know that before I do," he said, smiling benignantly.

IV

I went back to the Hall and helped boil more prisoners in oil until around eight o'clock, when my appetite reminded me I hadn't eaten since breakfast. I attended to that, and then turned down toward Larrouy's, ambling along leisurely, so the exercise wouldn't interfere with my digestion. I spent three-quarters of an hour in Larrouy's, and didn't see anybody who interested me especially. A few gents I knew were present, but they weren't anxious to associate with me—it's not always healthy in criminal circles to be seen wagging your chin with a sleuth right after a job has been turned.

Not getting anything there, I moved up the street to Wop Healy's—another hole. My reception was the same here—I was given a table and let alone. Healy's orchestra was giving "Don't You Cheat" all they had, while those custom-

___
* thief

ers who felt athletic were romping it out on the dance-floor. One of the dancers was Jack Counihan, his arms full of a big olive-skinned girl with a pleasant, thick-featured, stupid face.

Jack was a tall, slender lad of twenty-three or four who had drifted into the Continental's employ a few months before. It was the first job he'd ever had, and he wouldn't have had it if his father hadn't insisted that if sonny wanted to keep his fingers in the family till he'd have to get over the notion that squeezing through a college graduation was enough work for one lifetime. So Jack came to the agency. He thought gum-shoeing would be fun. In spite of the fact that he'd rather catch the wrong man than wear the wrong necktie, he was a promising young thief-catcher. A likable youngster, well-muscled for all his slimness, smooth-haired, with a gentleman's face and a gentleman's manner, nervy, quick with head and hands, full of the don't-give-a-damn gaiety that belonged to his youthfulness. He was jingle-brained, of course, and needed holding, but I would rather work with him than with a lot of old-timers I knew.

Half an hour passed with nothing to interest me.

Then a boy came into Healy's from the street—a small kid, gaudily dressed, very pressed in the pants-legs, very shiny in the shoes, with an impudent sallow face of pronounced cast. This was the boy I had seen sauntering down Broadway a moment after Beno had been rubbed out.

Leaning back in my chair so that a woman's wide-hatted head was between us, I watched the young Armenian wind between tables to one in a far corner, where three men sat. He spoke to them—off-hand—perhaps a dozen words—and moved away to another table where a snub-nosed, black-haired man sat alone. The boy dropped into the chair facing snub-nose, spoke a few words, sneered at snub-nose's questions, and ordered a drink. When his glass was empty he crossed the room to speak to a lean, buzzard-faced man, and then went out of Healy's.

I followed him out, passing the table where

Jack sat with the girl, catching his eye. Outside, I saw the young Armenian half a block away. Jack Counihan caught up with me, passed me. With a Fatima in my mouth I called to him:

"Got a match, brother?"

While I lighted my cigarette with a match from the box he gave me I spoke behind my hands:

"The goose in the glad rags*—tail him. I'll string behind you. I don't know him, but if he blipped Beno off for talking to me last night, he knows me. On his heels!"

Jack pocketed his matches and went after the boy. I gave Jack a lead and then followed him. And then an interesting thing happened.

The street was fairly well filled with people, mostly men, some walking, some loafing on corners and in front of soft-drink parlors. As the young Armenian reached the corner of an alley where there was a light, two men came up and spoke to him, moving a little apart so that he was between them. The boy would have kept walking apparently paying no attention to them, but one checked him by stretching an arm out in front of him. The other man took his right hand out of his pocket and flourished it in the boy's face so that the nickel plated knuckles on it twinkled in the light. The boy ducked swiftly under threatening hand and outstretched arm, and went on across the alley, walking, and not even looking over his shoulder at the two men who were now closing on his back.

Just before they reached him another reached them—a broad-backed, long-armed, ape-built man I had not seen before. His gorilla's paws went out together. Each caught a man. By the napes of their necks he yanked them away from the boy's back, shook them till their hats fell off, smacked their skulls together with a crack that was like a broom-handle breaking, and dragged their rag-limp bodies out of sight up the alley. While this was happening the boy walked jauntily down the street, without a backward glance.

When the skull-cracker came out of the alley

I saw his face in the light—a dark-skinned, heavily-lined face, broad and flat, with jaw-muscles bulging like abscesses under his ears. He spit, hitched his pants, and swaggered down the street after the boy.

The boy went into Larrouy's. The skull-cracker followed him in. The boy came out, and in his rear—perhaps twenty feet behind—the skull-cracker rolled. Jack had tailed them into Larrouy's while I had held up the outside.

"Still carrying messages?" I asked.

"Yes. He spoke to five men in there. He's got plenty of body-guard, hasn't he?"

"Yeah," I agreed. "And you be damned careful you don't get between them. If they split, I'll shadow the skull-cracker, you keep the goose."

We separated and moved after our game. They took us to all the hangouts in San Francisco, to cabarets, grease-joints,† pool-rooms, saloons, flop-houses, hook-shops,‡ gambling-joints and what have you. Everywhere the kid found men to speak his dozen words to, and between calls he found them on street-corners.

I would have liked to get behind some of these birds, but I didn't want to leave Jack alone with the boy and his bodyguard—they seemed to mean too much. And I couldn't stick Jack on one of the others, because it wasn't safe for me to hang too close to the Armenian boy. So we played the game as we had started it, shadowing our pair from hole to hole, while night got on toward morning.

It was a few minutes past midnight when they came out of a small hotel up on Kearny Street, and for the first time since we had seen them they walked together, side by side, up to Green Street, where they turned east along the side of Telegraph Hill. Half a block of this, and they climbed the front steps of a ramshackle furnished-room house and disappeared inside. I joined Jack Counihan on the corner where he had stopped.

"The greetings have all been delivered,"

---

* a Jewish dandy

† cheap diners
‡ brothels

I guessed, "or he wouldn't have called in his bodyguard. If there's nothing stirring within the next half hour I'm going to beat it. You'll have to take a plant on the joint till morning."

Twenty minutes later the skull-cracker came out of the house and walked down the street.

"I'll take him," I said. "You stick to the other baby."

The skull-cracker took ten or twelve steps from the house and stopped. He looked back at the house, raising his face to look at the upper stories. Then Jack and I could hear what had stopped him. Up in the house a man was screaming. It wasn't much of a scream in volume. Even now, when it had increased in strength, it barely reached our ears. But in it—in that one wailing voice—everything that fears death seemed to cry out its fear. I heard Jack's teeth click. I've got horny skin all over what's left of my soul, but just the same my forehead twitched. The scream was so damned weak for what it said.

The skull-cracker moved. Five gliding strides carried him back to the house. He didn't touch one of the six or seven front steps. He went from pavement to vestibule in a spring no monkey could have beaten for swiftness, ease or silence. One minute, two minutes, three minutes, and the screaming stopped. Three more minutes and the skull-cracker was leaving the house again. He paused on the sidewalk to spit and hitch his pants. Then he swaggered off down the street.

"He's your meat, Jack," I said. "I'm going to call on the boy. He won't recognize me now."

V

The street-door of the rooming-house was not only unlocked but wide open. I went through it into a hallway, where a dim light burning upstairs outlined a flight of steps. I climbed them and turned toward the front of the house. The scream had come from the front—either this floor or the third. There was a fair likelihood of the skull-cracker having left the room-door unlocked, just as he had not paused to close the street-door.

I had no luck on the second floor, but the third knob I cautiously tried on the third floor turned in my hand and let its door edge back from the frame. In front of this crack I waited a moment, listening to nothing but a throbbing snore somewhere far down the hallway. I put a palm against the door and eased it open another foot. No sound. The room was black as an honest politician's prospects. I slid my hand across the frame, across a few inches of wallpaper, found a light button, pressed it. Two globes in the center of the room threw their weak yellow light on the shabby room and on the young Armenian who lay dead across the bed.

I went into the room, closed the door and stepped over to the bed. The boy's eyes were wide and bulging. One of his temples was bruised. His throat gaped with a red slit that ran actually from ear to ear. Around the slit, in the few spots not washed red, his thin neck showed dark bruises. The skull-cracker had dropped the boy with a poke in the temple and had choked him until he thought him dead. But the kid had revived enough to scream—not enough to keep from screaming. The skull-cracker had returned to finish the job with a knife. Three streaks on the bed-clothes showed where the knife had been cleaned.

The lining of the boy's pockets stuck out. The skull-cracker had turned them out. I went through his clothes, but with no better luck than I expected—the killer had taken everything. The room gave me nothing—a few clothes, but not a thing out of which information could be squeezed.

My prying done, I stood in the center of the floor scratching my chin and considering. In the hall a floor-board creaked. Three backward steps on my rubber heels put me in the musty closet, dragging the door all but half an inch shut behind me.

Knuckles rattled on the room door as I slid my gun off my hip. The knuckles rattled again and a feminine voice said, "Kid, oh, Kid!"

Neither knuckles nor voice was loud. The lock clicked as the knob was turned. The door opened and framed the shifty-eyed girl who had been called Sylvia Yount by Angel Grace.

Her eyes lost their shiftiness for surprise when they settled on the boy.

"Holy hell!" she gasped, and was gone.

I was half out of the closet when I heard her tip-toeing back. In my hole again, I waited, my eye to the crack. She came in swiftly, closed the door silently, and went to lean over the dead boy. Her hands moved over him, exploring the pockets whose linings I had put back in place.

"Damn such luck!" she said aloud when the unprofitable frisking was over, and went out of the house.

I gave her time to reach the sidewalk. She was headed toward Kearny Street when I left the house. I shadowed her down Kearny to Broadway, up Broadway to Larrouy's. Larrouy's was busy, especially near the door, with customers going and coming. I was within five feet of the girl when she stopped a waiter and asked, in a whisper that was excited enough to carry, "Is Red here?"

The waiter shook his head.

"Ain't been in tonight."

The girl went out of the dive, hurrying along on clicking heels to a hotel in Stockton Street.

While I looked through the glass front, she went to the desk and spoke to the clerk. He shook his head. She spoke again and he gave her paper and envelope, on which she scribbled with the pen beside the register. Before I had to leave for a safer position from which to cover her exit, I saw which pigeon-hole the note went into.

From the hotel the girl went by street-car to Market and Powell Streets, and then walked up Powell to O'Farrell, where a fat-faced young man in gray overcoat and gray hat left the curb to link arms with her and lead her to a taxi stand up O'Farrell Street. I let them go, making a note of the taxi number—the fat-faced man looked more like a customer than a pal.

It was a little shy of two in the morning when I turned back into Market Street and went up

to the office. Fiske, who holds down the agency at night, said Jack Counihan had not reported, nothing else had come in. I told him to rouse me an operative, and in ten or fifteen minutes he succeeded in getting Mickey Linehan out of bed and on the wire.

"Listen, Mickey," I said, "I've got the nicest corner picked out for you to stand on the rest of the night. So pin on your diapers and toddle down there, will you?"

In between his grumbling and cursing I gave him the name and number of the Stockton Street hotel, described Red O'Leary, and told him which pigeon-hole the note had been put in.

"It mightn't be Red's home, but the chance is worth covering," I wound up. "If you pick him up, try not to lose him before I can get somebody down there to take him off your hands."

I hung up during the outburst of profanity this insult brought.

The Hall of Justice was busy when I reached it, though nobody had tried to shake the upstairs prison loose yet. Fresh lots of suspicious characters were being brought in every few minutes. Policemen in and out of uniform were everywhere. The detective bureau was a bee-hive.

Trading information with the police detectives, I told them about the Armenian boy. We were making up a party to visit the remains when the captain's door opened and Lieutenant Duff came into the assembly room.

"*Allez! Oop!*" he said, pointing a thick finger at O'Gar, Tully, Reeder, Hunt and me. "There's a thing worth looking at in Fillmore."

We followed him out to an automobile.

VI

A gray frame house in Fillmore Street was our destination. A lot of people stood in the street looking at the house. A police-wagon stood in front of it, and police uniforms were indoors and out.

A red-mustached corporal saluted Duff and led us into the house, explaining as we went,

"'Twas the neighbors give us the rumble, complaining of the fighting, and when we got here, faith, there weren't no fight left in nobody."

All the house held was fourteen dead men.

Eleven of them had been poisoned—overdoses of knockout drops in their booze, the doctors said. The other three had been shot, at intervals along the hall. From the looks of the remains, they had drunk a toast—a loaded one—and those who hadn't drunk, whether because of temperance or suspicious natures, had been gunned as they tried to get away.

The identity of the bodies gave us an idea of what their toast had been. They were all thieves—they had drunk their poison to the day's looting.

We didn't know all the dead men then, but all of us knew some of them, and the records told us who the others were later. The completed list read like *Who's Who in Crookdom*.

There was the Dis-and-Dat Kid, who had crushed out of Leavenworth only two months before; Sheeny Holmes; Snohomish Whitey, supposed to have died a hero in France in 1919; L. A. Slim, from Denver, sockless and underwearless as usual, with a thousand-dollar bill sewed in each shoulder of his coat; Spider Girrucci wearing a steel-mesh vest under his shirt and a scar from crown to chin where his brother had carved him years ago; Old Pete Best, once a congressman; Nigger Vojan, who once won $175,000 in a Chicago crap-game—*Abacadbra* tattooed on him in three places; Alphabet Shorty McCoy; Tom Brooks, Alphabet Shorty's brother-in-law, who invented the Richmond *razzle-dazzle*, and bought three hotels with the profits; Red Cudahy, who stuck up a Union Pacific train in 1924; Denny Burke; Bull McGonickle, still pale from fifteen years in Joliet; Toby the Lugs, Bull's running-mate, who used to brag about picking President Wilson's pocket in a Washington vaudeville theater; and Paddy the Mex.

Duff looked them over and whistled.

"A few more tricks like this," he said, "and we'll all be out of jobs. There won't be any grifters left to protect the taxpayers from."

"I'm glad you like it," I told him. "Me—I'd hate like hell to be a San Francisco copper the next few days."

"Why especially?"

"Look at this—one grand piece of double-crossing. This village of ours is full of mean lads who are waiting right now for these stiffs to bring 'em their cut of the stick-up. What do you think's going to happen when the word gets out that there's not going to be any gravy for the mob? There are going to be a hundred and more stranded thugs busy raising getaway dough. There'll be three burglaries to a block and a stick-up to every corner until the carfare's raised. God bless you, my son, you're going to sweat for your wages!"

Duff shrugged his thick shoulders and stepped over bodies to get to the telephone. When he was through I called the agency.

"Jack Counihan called a couple of minutes ago," Fiske told me, and gave me an Army Street address. "He says he put his man in there, with company."

I phoned for a taxi, and then told Duff, "I'm going to run out for a while. I'll give you a ring here if there's anything to the angle, or if there isn't. You'll wait?"

"If you're not too long."

I got rid of my taxicab two blocks from the address Fiske had given me, and walked down Army Street to find Jack Counihan planted on a dark corner.

"I got a bad break," was what he welcomed me with. "While I was phoning from the lunch-room up the street some of my people ran out on me."

"Yeah? What's the dope?"

"Well, after that apey chap left the Green Street house he trolleyed to a house in Fillmore Street, and—"

"What number?"

The number Jack gave was that of the death-house I had just left.

"In the next ten or fifteen minutes just about that many other chaps went into the same house. Most of them came afoot, singly or in pairs.

Then two cars came up together, with nine men in them—I counted them. They went into the house, leaving their machines in front. A taxi came past a little later, and I stopped it, in case my chap should motor away.

"Nothing happened for at least half an hour after the nine chaps went in. Then everybody in the house seemed to become demonstrative—there was a quantity of yelling and shooting. It lasted long enough to awaken the whole neighborhood. When it stopped, ten men—I counted them—ran out of the house, got into the two cars, and drove away. My man was one of them.

"My faithful taxi and I cried *Yoicks** after them, and they brought us here, going into that house down the street in front of which one of their motors still stands. After half an hour or so I thought I'd better report, so, leaving my taxi around the corner—where it's still running up expenses—I went up to yon all-night caravansary and phoned Fiske. And when I came back, one of the cars was gone—and I, woe is me!—don't know who went with it. Am I rotten?"

"Sure! You should have taken their cars along to the phone with you. Watch the one that's left while I collect a strong-arm squad."

I went up to the lunch room and phoned Duff, telling him where I was, and:

"If you bring your gang along maybe there'll be profit in it. A couple of carloads of folks who were in Fillmore Street and didn't stay there came here, and part of 'em may still be here, if you make it sudden."

Duff brought his four detectives and a dozen uniformed men with him. We hit the house front and back. No time was wasted ringing the bell. We simply tore down the doors and went in. Everything inside was black until flashlights lit it up. There was no resistance. Ordinarily the six men we found in there would have damned near ruined us in spite of our outnumbering them. But they were too dead for that.

We looked at one another sort of open-mouthed.

---

* a call to urge on a hound

"This is getting monotonous," Duff complained, biting off a hunk of tobacco. "Everybody's work is pretty much the same thing over and over, but I'm tired of walking into roomfuls of butchered crooks."

The catalog here had fewer names than the other, but they were bigger names. The Shivering Kid was here—nobody would collect all the reward money piled up on him now; Darby M'Laughlin, his horn-rimmed glasses crooked on his nose, ten thousand dollars' worth of diamonds on fingers and tie; Happy Jim Hacker; Donkey Marr, the last of the bow-legged Marrs, killers all, father and five sons; Toots Salda, the strongest man in crookdom, who had once picked up and run away with two Savannah coppers to whom he was handcuffed; and Rumdum Smith, who killed Lefty Read in Chi in 1916—a rosary wrapped around his left wrist.

No gentlemanly poisoning here—these boys had been mowed down with a .30-30 rifle fitted with a clumsy but effective home-made silencer. The rifle lay on the kitchen table. A door connected the kitchen with the dining-room. Directly opposite that door, double doors—wide open—opened into the room in which the dead thieves lay. They were all close to the front wall, lying as if they had been lined up against the wall to be knocked off.

The gray-papered wall was spattered with blood, punctured with holes where a couple of bullets had gone all the way through. Jack Counihan's young eyes picked out a stain on the paper that wasn't accidental. It was close to the floor, beside the Shivering Kid, and the Kid's right hand was stained with blood. He had written on the wall before he died—with fingers dipped in his own and Toots Salda's blood. The letters in the words showed breaks and gaps where his fingers had run dry, and the letters were crooked and straggly, because he must have written them in the dark.

By filling in the gaps, allowing for the kinks, and guessing where there weren't any indications to guide us, we got two words: *Big Flora*.

"They don't mean anything to me," Duff

said, "but it's a name and most of the names we have belong to dead men now, so it's time we were adding to our list."

"What do you make of it?" asked bullet-headed O'Gar, detective-sergeant in the Homicide Detail, looking at the bodies. "Their pals got the drop on them, lined them against the wall, and the sharpshooter in the kitchen shot 'em down—bing-bing-bing-bing-bing-bing?"

"It reads that way," the rest of us agreed.

"Ten of 'em came here from Fillmore Street," I said. "Six stayed here. Four went to another house—where part of 'em are now cutting down the other part. All that's necessary is to trail the corpses from house to house until there's only one man left—and he's bound to play it through by croaking himself, leaving the loot to be recovered in the original packages. I hope you folks don't have to stay up all night to find the remains of that last thug. Come on, Jack, let's go home for some sleep."

VII

It was exactly 5 A.M. when I separated the sheets and crawled into my bed. I was asleep before the last draw of smoke from my good-night Fatima was out of my lungs. The telephone woke me at 5:15.

Fiske was talking: "Mickey Linehan just phoned that your Red O'Leary came home to roost half an hour ago."

"Have him booked," I said, and was asleep again by 5:17.

With the help of the alarm clock I rolled out of bed at nine, breakfasted, and went down to the detective bureau to see how the police had made out with the redhead. Not so good.

"He's got us stopped," the captain told me. "He's got alibis for the time of the looting and for last night's doings. And we can't even vag the son-of-a-gun. He's got means of support. He's salesman for Humperdickel's Universal Encyclopædiac Dictionary of Useful and Valuable Knowledge, or something like it. He started

peddling these pamphlets the day before the knock-over, and at the time it was happening he was ringing doorbells and asking folks to buy his durned books. Anyway, he's got three witnesses that say so. Last night, he was in a hotel from eleven to four-thirty this morning, playing cards, and he's got witnesses. We didn't find a durned thing on him or in his room."

I borrowed the captain's phone to call Jack Counihan's house.

"Could you identify any of the men you saw in the cars last night?" I asked when he had been stirred out of bed.

"No. It was dark and they moved too fast. I could barely make sure of my chap."

"Can't, huh?" the captain said. "Well, I can hold him twenty-four hours without laying charges, and I'll do that, but I'll have to spring him then unless you can dig up something."

"Suppose you turn him loose now," I suggested after thinking through my cigarette for a few minutes. "He's got himself all alibied up, so there's no reason why he should hide out on us. We'll let him alone all day—give him time to make sure he isn't being tailed—and then we'll get behind him tonight and stay behind him. Any dope on Big Flora?"

"No. That kid that was killed in Green Street was Bernie Bernheimer, alias the Motsa Kid. I guess he was a dip—he ran with dips—but he wasn't very—"

The buzz of the phone interrupted him. He said, "Hello, yes," and "Just a minute," into the instrument, and slid it across the desk to me.

A feminine voice: "This is Grace Cardigan. I called your agency and they told me where to get you. I've got to see you. Can you meet me now?"

"Where are you?"

"In the telephone station on Powell Street."

"I'll be there in fifteen minutes," I said.

Calling the agency, I got hold of Dick Foley and asked him to meet me at Ellis and Market right away. Then I gave the captain back his phone, said "See you later," and went uptown to keep my dates.

Dick Foley was on his corner when I got there. He was a swarthy little Canadian who stood nearly five feet in his high-heeled shoes, weighed a hundred pounds minus, talked like a Scotchman's telegram, and could have shadowed a drop of salt water from the Golden Gate to Hong Kong without ever losing sight of it.

"You know Angel Grace Cardigan?" I asked him.

He saved a word by shaking his head, no.

"I'm going to meet her in the telephone station. When I'm through, stay behind her. She's smart, and she'll be looking for you, so it won't be duck soup, but do what you can."

Dick's mouth went down at the corners and one of his rare long-winded streaks hit him.

"Harder they look, easier they are," he said.

He trailed along behind me while I went up to the station. Angel Grace was standing in the doorway. Her face was more sullen than I had ever seen it, and therefore less beautiful—except her green eyes, which held too much fire for sullenness. A rolled newspaper was in one of her hands. She neither spoke, smiled nor nodded.

"We'll go to Charley's, where we can talk," I said, guiding her down past Dick Foley.

Not a murmur did I get out of her until we were seated cross-table in the restaurant booth, and the waiter had gone off with our orders. Then she spread the newspaper out on the table with shaking hands.

"Is this on the level?" she demanded.

I looked at the story her shaking finger tapped—an account of the Fillmore and Army Street findings, but a cagey account. A glance showed that no names had been given, that the police had censored the story quite a bit. While I pretended to read I wondered whether it would be to my advantage to tell the girl the story was a fake. But I couldn't see any clear profit in that, so I saved my soul a lie.

"Practically straight," I admitted.

"You were there?"

She had pushed the paper aside to the floor and was leaning over the table.

"With the police."

"Was—?" Her voice broke huskily. Her white fingers wadded the tablecloth in two little bunches half-way between us. She cleared her throat. "Who was—?" was as far as she got this time.

A pause. I waited. Her eyes went down, but not before I had seen water dulling the fire in them. During the pause the waiter came in, put our food down, went away.

"You know what I want to ask," she said presently, her voice low, choked. "Was he? Was he? For God's sake tell me!"

I weighed them—truth against lie, lie against truth. Once more truth triumphed.

"Paddy the Mex was shot—killed—in the Fillmore Street house," I said.

The pupils of her eyes shrank to pinpoints—spread again until they almost covered the green irises. She made no sound. Her face was empty. She picked up a fork and lifted a forkful of salad to her mouth—another. Reaching across the table, I took the fork out of her hand.

"You're only spilling it on your clothes," I growled. "You can't eat without opening your mouth to put the food in."

She put her hands across the table, reaching for mine, trembling, holding my hand with fingers that twitched so that the nails scratched me.

"You're not lying to me?" she half sobbed, half chattered. "You're on the square! You were white to me that time in Philly! Paddy always said you were one white dick! You're not tricking me?"

"Straight up," I assured her. "Paddy meant a lot to you?"

She nodded dully, pulling herself together, sinking back in a sort of stupor.

"The way's open to even up for him," I suggested.

"You mean—?"

"Talk."

She stared at me blankly for a long while, as if she was trying to get some meaning out of what I had said. I read the answer in her eyes before she put it in words.

"I wish to God I could! But I'm Paper-box-

John Cardigan's daughter. It isn't in me to turn anybody up. You're on the wrong side. I can't go over. I wish I could. But there's too much Cardigan in me. I'll be hoping every minute that you nail them, and nail them dead right, but—"

"Your sentiments are noble, or words to that effect," I sneered at her. "Who do you think you are—Joan of Arc? Would your brother Frank be in stir now if his partner, Johnny the Plumber, hadn't put the finger on him for the Great Falls bulls? Come to life, dearie! You're a thief among thieves, and those who don't double-cross get crossed. Who rubbed your Paddy the Mex out? Pals! But you mustn't slap back at 'em because it wouldn't be clubby. My God!"

My speech only thickened the sullenness in her face.

"I'm going to slap back," she said, "but I can't, can't split. I can't, I tell you. If you were a gun, I'd—Anyway, what help I get will be on my side of the game. Let it go at that, won't you? I know how you feel about it, but—Will you tell me who besides—who else was—was found in those houses?"

"Oh, sure!" I snarled. "I'll tell you everything. I'll let you pump me dry. But you mustn't give me any hints, because it might not be in keeping with the ethics of your highly honorable profession!"

Being a woman, she ignored all this, repeating, "Who else?"

"Nothing stirring. But I will do this—I'll tell you a couple who weren't there—Big Flora and Red O'Leary."

Her dopiness was gone. She studied my face with green eyes that were dark and savage.

"Was Bluepoint Vance?" she demanded.

"What do you guess?" I replied.

She studied my face for a moment longer and then stood up.

"Thanks for what you've told me," she said, "and for meeting me like this. I do hope you win."

She went out to be shadowed by Dick Foley. I ate my lunch.

VIII

At four o'clock that afternoon Jack Counihan and I brought our hired automobile to rest within sight of the front door of the Stockton Street hotel.

"He cleared himself with the police, so there's no reason why he should have moved, maybe," I told Jack, "and I'd rather not monkey with the hotel people, not knowing them. If he doesn't show by late we'll have to go up against them then."

We settled down to cigarettes, guesses on who'd be the next heavyweight champion and when, the possibilities of Prohibition being either abolished or practiced, where to get good gin and what to do with it, the injustice of the new agency ruling that for purposes of expense accounts Oakland was not to be considered out of town, and similar exciting topics, which carried us from four o'clock to ten minutes past nine.

At 9:10 Red O'Leary came out of the hotel.

"God is good," said Jack as he jumped out of the machine to do the footwork while I stirred the motor.

The fire-topped giant didn't take us far. Larrouy's front door gobbled him. By the time I had parked the car and gone into the dive, both O'Leary and Jack had found seats. Jack's table was on the edge of the dance-floor. O'Leary's was on the other side of the establishment, against the wall, near a corner. A fat blond couple were leaving the table back in that corner when I came in, so I persuaded the waiter who was guiding me to a table to make it that one.

O'Leary's face was three-quarters turned away from me. He was watching the front door, watching it with an earnestness that turned suddenly to happiness when a girl appeared there. She was the girl Angel Grace had called Nancy Regan. I have already said she was nice. Well, she was. And the cocky little blue hat that hid all her hair didn't handicap her niceness any tonight.

The redhead scrambled to his feet and pushed

a waiter and a couple of customers out of his way as he went to meet her. As reward for his eagerness he got some profanity that he didn't seem to hear and a blue-eyed, white-toothed smile that was—well—nice. He brought her back to his table and put her in a chair facing me, while he sat very much facing her.

His voice was a baritone rumble out of which my snooping ears could pick no words. He seemed to be telling her a lot, and she listened as if she liked it.

"But, Reddy, dear, you shouldn't," she said once. Her voice—I know other words, but we'll stick to this one—was nice. Outside of the music in it, it had quality. Whoever this gunman's moll was, she either had had a good start in life or had learned her stuff well. Now and then, when the orchestra came up for air, I would catch a few words, but they didn't tell me anything except that neither she nor her rowdy playmate had anything against the other.

The joint had been nearly empty when she came in. By ten o'clock it was fairly crowded, and ten o'clock is early for Larrouy's customers. I began to pay less attention to Red's girl—even if she was nice—and more to my other neighbors. It struck me that there weren't many women in sight. Checking up on that, I found damned few women in proportion to the men. Men—rat-faced men, hatchet-faced men, square-jawed men, slack-chinned men, pale men, ruddy men, dark men, bull-necked men, scrawny men, funny-looking men, tough-looking men, ordinary men—sitting two to a table, four to a table, more coming in—and damned few women.

These men talked to one another, as if they weren't much interested in what they were saying. They looked casually around the joint, with eyes that were blankest when they came to O'Leary. And always those casual—bored—glances did rest on O'Leary for a second or two.

I returned my attention to O'Leary and Nancy Regan. He was sitting a little more erect in his chair than he had been, but it was an easy, supple erectness, and though his shoulders had hunched a bit, there was no stiffness in them.

She said something to him. He laughed, turning his face toward the center of the room, so that he seemed to be laughing not only at what she had said, but also at these men who sat around him, waiting. It was a hearty laugh, young and careless.

The girl looked surprised for a moment, as if something in the laugh puzzled her, then she went on with whatever she was telling him. She didn't know she was sitting on dynamite, I decided. O'Leary knew. Every inch of him, every gesture, said, "I'm big, strong, young, tough and redheaded. When you boys want to do your stuff I'll be here."

Time slid by. Few couples danced. Jean Larrouy went around with dark worry in his round face. His joint was full of customers, but he would rather have had it empty.

By eleven o'clock I stood up and beckoned to Jack Counihan. He came over, we shook hands, exchanged *How's everythings* and *Getting muches*, and he sat at my table.

"What is happening?" he asked under cover of the orchestra's din. "I can't see anything, but there is something in the air. Or am I being hysterical?"

"You will be presently. The wolves are gathering, and Red O'Leary's the lamb. You could pick a tenderer one if you had a free hand, maybe. But these bimbos once helped pluck a bank, and when pay-day came there wasn't anything in their envelopes, not even any envelopes. The word got out that maybe Red knew how-come. Hence this. They're waiting now—maybe for somebody—maybe till they get enough hooch in them."

"And we sit here because it's the nearest table to the target for all these fellows' bullets when the blooming lid blows off?" Jack inquired. "Let's move over to Red's table. It's still nearer, and I rather like the appearance of the girl with him."

"Don't be impatient, you'll have your fun," I promised him. "There's no sense in having this O'Leary killed. If they bargain with him in a gentlemanly way, we'll lay off. But if they start heaving things at him, you and I are going to pry him and his girl friend loose."

"Well spoken, my hearty!" He grinned, whitening around the mouth. "Are there any details, or do we just simply and unostentatiously pry 'em loose?"

"See the door behind me, to the right? When the pop-off comes, I'm going back there and open it up. You hold the line midway between. When I yelp, you give Red whatever help he needs to get back there."

"Aye, aye!" He looked around the room at the assembled plug-uglies, moistened his lips, and looked at the hand holding his cigarette, a quivering hand. "I hope you won't think I'm in a funk," he said. "But I'm not an antique murderer like you. I get a reaction out of this prospective slaughtering."

"Reaction, my eye," I said. "You're scared stiff. But no nonsense, mind! If you try to make a vaudeville act out of it I'll ruin whatever these guerrillas leave of you. You do what you're told, and nothing else. If you get any bright ideas, save 'em to tell me about afterward."

"Oh, my conduct will be most exemplary!" he assured me.

IX

It was nearly midnight when what the wolves waited for came. The last pretense of indifference went out of faces that had been gradually taking on tenseness. Chairs and feet scraped as men pushed themselves back a little from their tables. Muscles flexed bodies into readiness for action. Tongues licked lips and eyes looked eagerly at the front door.

Bluepoint Vance was coming into the room. He came alone, nodding to acquaintances on this side and that, carrying his tall body gracefully, easily, in its well-cut clothing. His sharp-featured face was smilingly self-confident. He came without haste and without delay to Red O'Leary's table. I couldn't see Red's face, but muscles thickened the back of his neck. The girl

smiled cordially at Vance and gave him her hand. It was naturally done. She didn't know anything.

Vance turned his smile from Nancy Regan to the red-haired giant—a smile that was a trifle cat-to-mousey.

"How's everything, Red?" he asked.

"Everything suits me," bluntly.

The orchestra had stopped playing. Larrouy, standing by the street door, was mopping his forehead with a handkerchief. At the table to my right, a barrel-chested, broken-nosed bruiser in a widely striped suit was breathing heavily between his gold teeth, his watery gray eyes bulging at O'Leary, Vance and Nancy. He was in no way conspicuous—there were too many others holding the same pose.

Bluepoint Vance turned his head, called to a waiter: "Bring me a chair."

The chair was brought and put at the unoccupied side of the table, facing the wall. Vance sat down, slumping back in the chair, leaning indolently toward Red, his left arm hooked over the chair-back, his right hand holding a cigarette.

"Well, Red," he said when he was thus installed, "have you got any news for me?"

His voice was suave, but loud enough for those at nearby tables to hear.

"Not a word." O'Leary's voice made no pretense of friendliness, nor of caution.

"What, no spinach?" Vance's thin-lipped smile spread, and his dark eyes had a mirthful but not pleasant glitter. "Nobody gave you anything to give me?"

"No," said O'Leary, emphatically.

"My goodness!" said Vance, the smile in his eyes and mouth deepening, and getting still less pleasant. "That's ingratitude! Will you help me collect, Red?"

"No."

I was disgusted with this redhead—half-minded to let him go under when the storm broke. Why couldn't he have stalled his way out—fixed up a fancy tale that Bluepoint would have had to half-way accept? But no—this O'Leary boy was so damned childishly proud of his toughness that he had to make a show of it when he should have been using his bean. If it had been only his own carcass that was due for a beating, it would have been all right. But it wasn't all right that Jack and I should have to suffer. This big chump was too valuable to lose. We'd have to get ourselves all battered up saving him from the rewards of his own pig-headedness. There was no justice in it.

"I've got a lot of money coming to me, Red." Vance spoke lazily, tauntingly. "And I need that money." He drew on his cigarette, casually blew the smoke into the redhead's face, and drawled, "Why, do you know the laundry charges twenty-six cents just for doing a pair of pajamas? I need money."

"Sleep in your underclothes," said O'Leary.

Vance laughed. Nancy Regan smiled, but in a bewildered way. She didn't seem to know what it was all about, but she couldn't help knowing that it was about something.

O'Leary leaned forward and spoke deliberately, loud enough for any to hear:

"Bluepoint, I've got nothing to give you—now or ever. And that goes for anybody else that's interested. If you or them think I owe you something—try and get it. To hell with you, Bluepoint Vance! If you don't like it you've got friends here. Call 'em on!"

What a prime young idiot! Nothing would suit him but an ambulance—and I must be dragged along with him.

Vance grinned evilly, his eyes glittering into O'Leary's face.

"You'd like that, Red?"

O'Leary hunched his big shoulders and let them drop.

"I don't mind a fight," he said. "But I'd like to get Nancy out of it." He turned to her. "Better run along, honey, I'm going to be busy."

She started to say something, but Vance was talking to her. His words were lightly spoken, and he made no objection to her going. The substance of what he told her was that she was going to be lonely without Red. But he went intimately into the details of that loneliness.

Red O'Leary's right hand rested on the table.

It went up to Vance's mouth. The hand was a fist when it got there. A wallop of that sort is awkward to deliver. The body can't give it much. It has to depend on the arm muscles, and not on the best of those. Yet Bluepoint Vance was driven out of his chair and across to the next table.

Larrouy's chairs went empty. The shindig was on.

"On your toes," I growled at Jack Counihan, and, doing my best to look like the nervous little fat man I was, I ran toward the back door, passing men who were moving not yet swiftly toward O'Leary. I must have looked the part of a scared trouble-dodger, because nobody stopped me, and I reached the door before the pack had closed on Red. The door was closed, but not locked. I wheeled with my back to it, black-jack in right hand, gun in left. Men were in front of me, but their backs were to me.

O'Leary was towering in front of his table, his tough red face full of bring-on-your-hell, his big body balanced on the balls of his feet. Between us, Jack Counihan stood, his face turned to me, his mouth twitching in a nervous grin, his eyes dancing with delight. Bluepoint Vance was on his feet again. Blood trickled from his thin lips, down his chin. His eyes were cool. They looked at Red O'Leary with the businesslike look of a logger sizing up the tree he's going to bring down. Vance's mob watched Vance.

"Red!" I bawled into the silence. "This way, Red!"

Faces spun to me—every face in the joint—millions of them.

"Come on, Red!" Jack Counihan yelped, taking a step forward, his gun out.

Bluepoint Vance's hand flashed to the V of his coat. Jack's gun snapped at him. Bluepoint had thrown himself down before the boy's trigger was yanked. The bullet went wide, but Vance's draw was gummed.

Red scooped the girl up with his left arm. A big automatic blossomed in his right fist. I didn't pay much attention to him after that. I was busy.

Larrouy's home was pregnant with weapons—guns, knives, saps, knucks, club-swung chairs and bottles, miscellaneous implements of destruction. Men brought their weapons over to mingle with me. The game was to nudge me away from my door. O'Leary would have liked it. But I was no fire-haired young rowdy. I was pushing forty, and I was twenty pounds overweight. I had the liking for ease that goes with that age and weight. Little ease I got.

A squint-eyed Portuguese slashed at my neck with a knife that spoiled my necktie. I caught him over the ear with the side of my gun before he could get away, saw the ear tear loose. A grinning kid of twenty went down for my legs—football stuff. I felt his teeth in the knee I pumped up, and felt them break. A pock-marked mulatto pushed a gun-barrel over the shoulder of the man in front of him. My blackjack crunched the arm of the man in front. He winced sidewise as the mulatto pulled the trigger—and had the side of his face blown away.

I fired twice—once when a gun was leveled within a foot of my middle, once when I discovered a man standing on a table not far off taking careful aim at my head. For the rest I trusted to my arms and legs, and saved bullets. The night was young and I had only a dozen pills—six in the gun, six my pocket.

It was a swell bag of nails. Swing right, swing left, kick, swing right, swing left, kick. Don't hesitate, don't look for targets. God will see that there's always a mug there for your gun or blackjack to sock, a belly for your foot.

A bottle came through and found my forehead. My hat saved me some, but the crack didn't do me any good. I swayed and broke a nose where I should have smashed a skull. The room seemed stuffy, poorly ventilated. Somebody ought to tell Larrouy about it. How do you like that lead-and-leather pat on the temple, blondy? This rat on my left is getting too close. I'll draw him in by bending to the right to poke the mulatto, and then I'll lean back into him and let him have it. Not bad! But I can't keep this up all night. Where are Red and Jack? Standing off watching me?

Somebody socked me in the shoulder with something—a piano from the feel of it. A bleary-eyed Greek put his face where I couldn't miss it. Another thrown bottle took my hat and part of my scalp. Red O'Leary and Jack Counihan smashed through, dragging the girl between them.

X

While Jack put the girl through the door, Red and I cleared a little space in front of us. He was good at that. When he chucked them back they went back. I didn't dog it on him, but I did let him get all the exercise he wanted.

"All right!" Jack called.

Red and I went through the door, slammed it shut. It wouldn't hold even if locked. O'Leary sent three slugs through it to give the boys something to think about, and our retreat got under way.

We were in a narrow passageway lighted by a fairly bright light. At the other end was a closed door. Halfway down, to the right, steps led up.

"Straight ahead?" asked Jack, who was in front.

O'Leary said, "Yes." And I said, "No. Vance will have that blocked by now if the bulls haven't. Upstairs—the roof."

We reached the stairs. The door behind us burst open. The light went out. The door at the other end of the passage slammed open. No light came through either door. Vance would want light. Larrouy must have pulled the switch, trying to keep his dump from being torn to toothpicks.

Tumult boiled in the dark passage as we climbed the stairs by the touch system. Whoever had come through the back door was mixing it with those who had followed us—mixing it with blows, curses and an occasional shot. More power to them! We climbed, Jack leading, the girl next, then me, and last of all, O'Leary.

Jack was gallantly reading road-signs to the

girl: "Careful of the landing, half a turn to the left now, put your right hand on the wall and—"

"Shut up!" I growled at him. "It's better to have her falling down than to have everybody in the drum fall on us."

We reached the second floor. It was black as black. There were three stories to the building.

"I've mislaid the blooming stairs," Jack complained.

We poked around in the dark, hunting for the flight that should lead up toward our roof. We didn't find it. The riot downstairs was quieting. Vance's voice was telling his push that they were mixing it with each other, asking where we had gone. Nobody seemed to know. We didn't know, either.

"Come on," I grumbled, leading the way down the dark hall toward the back of the building. "We've got to go somewhere."

There was still noise downstairs, but no more fighting. Men were talking about getting lights. I stumbled into a door at the end of the hall, pushed it open. A room with two windows through which came a pale glow from the street lights. It seemed brilliant after the hall. My little flock followed me in and we closed the door.

Red O'Leary was across the room, his noodle to an open window.

"Back street," he whispered. "No way down unless we drop."

"Anybody in sight?" I asked.

"Don't see any."

I looked around the room—bed, couple of chairs, chest of drawers, and a table.

"The table will go through the window," I said. "We'll chuck it as far as we can and hope the racket will lead 'em out there before they decide to look up here."

Red and the girl were assuring each other that each was still all in one piece. He broke away from her to help me with the table. We balanced it, swung it, let it go. It did nicely, crashing into the wall of the building opposite, dropping down into a backyard to clang and clatter on a pile of

tin, or a collection of garbage cans, or something beautifully noisy. You couldn't have heard it more than a block and a half away.

We got away from the window as men bubbled out of Larrouy's back door.

The girl, unable to find any wounds on O'Leary, had turned to Jack Counihan. He had a cut cheek. She was monkeying with it and a handkerchief.

"When you finish that," Jack was telling her, "I'm going out and get one on the other side."

"I'll never finish if you keep talking—you jiggle your cheek."

"That's a swell idea," he exclaimed. "San Francisco is the second largest city in California. Sacramento is the state capital. Do you like geography? Shall I tell you about Java? I've never been there, but I drink their coffee. If—"

"Silly!" she said, laughing. "If you don't hold still I'll stop now."

"Not so good," he said. "I'll be still."

She wasn't doing anything except wiping blood off his cheek, blood that had better been let dry there. When she finished this perfectly useless surgery, she took her hand away slowly, surveying the hardly noticeable results with pride. As her hand came on a level with his mouth, Jack jerked his head forward to kiss the tip of one passing finger.

"Silly!" she said again, snatching her hand away.

"Lay off that," said Red O'Leary, "or I'll knock you off."

"Pull in your neck," said Jack Counihan.

"Reddy!" the girl cried, too late.

The O'Leary right looped out. Jack took the punch on the button, and went to sleep on the floor. The big redhead spun on the balls of his feet to loom over me.

"Got anything to say?" he asked.

I grinned down at Jack, up at Red.

"I'm ashamed of him," I said. "Letting himself be stopped by a palooka who leads with his right."

"You want to try it?"

"Reddy! Reddy!" the girl pleaded, but no-body was listening to her.

"If you'll lead with your right," I said.

"I will," he promised, and did.

I grandstanded, slipping my head out of the way, laying a forefinger on his chin.

"That could have been a knuckle," I said.

"Yes? This one is."

I managed to get under his left, taking the forearm across the back of my neck. But that about played out the acrobatics. It looked as if I would have to see what I could do to him, if any. The girl grabbed his arm and hung on.

"Reddy, darling, haven't you had enough fighting for one night? Can't you be sensible, even if you are Irish?"

I was tempted to paste the big chaw while his playmate had him tied up.

He laughed down at her, ducked his head to kiss her mouth, and grinned at me.

"There's always some other time," he said good-naturedly.

XI

"We'd better get out of here if we can," I said. "You've made too much rumpus for it to be safe."

"Don't get it up in your neck, little man," he told me. "Hold on to my coat-tails and I'll pull you out."

The big tramp. If it hadn't been for Jack and me he wouldn't have had any coat-tail by now.

We moved to the door, listened there, heard nothing.

"The stairs to the third floor must be up front," I whispered. "We'll try for them now."

We opened the door carefully. Enough light went past us into the hall to show a promise of emptiness. We crept down the hall, Red and I each holding one of the girl's hands. I hoped Jack would come out all right, but he had put himself to sleep, and I had troubles of my own.

I hadn't known that Larrouy's was large enough to have two miles of hallway. It did. It

was an even mile in the darkness to the head of the stairs we had come up. We didn't pause there to listen to the voices below. At the end of the next mile O'Leary's foot found the bottom step of the flight leading up.

Just then a yell broke out at the head of the other flight.

"All up—they're up here!"

A white light beamed up on the yeller, and a brogue addressed him from below: "Come on down, ye windbag."

"The police," Nancy Regan whispered, and we hustled up our new-found steps to the third floor.

More darkness, just like that we'd left. We stood still at the top of the stairs. We didn't seem to have any company.

"The roof," I said. "We'll risk matches."

Back in a corner our feeble match-light found us a ladder nailed to the wall, leading to a trap in the ceiling. As little later as possible we were on Larrouy's roof, the trap closed behind us.

"All silk so far," said O'Leary, "and if Vance's rats and the bulls will play a couple of seconds longer—bingavast."*

I led the way across the roofs. We dropped ten feet to the next building, climbed a bit to the next, and found on the other side of it a fire-escape that ran down to a narrow court with an opening into the back street.

"This ought to do it," I said, and went down.

The girl came behind me, and then Red. The court into which we dropped was empty—a nar-row cement passage between buildings. The bot-tom of the fire-escape creaked as it hinged down under my weight, but the noise didn't stir any-thing. It was dark in the court, but not black.

"When we hit the street, we split," O'Leary told me, without a word of gratitude for my help—the help he didn't seem to know he had needed. "You roll your hoop, we'll roll ours."

"Uh-huh," I agreed, chasing my brains around in my skull. "I'll scout the alley first."

Carefully I picked my way down to the end of

---

* Get out of here! Gypsy root.

the court and risked the top of my hatless head to peep into the back street. It was quiet, but up at the corner, a quarter of a block above, two loafers seemed to be loafing attentively. They weren't coppers. I stepped out into the back street and beckoned them down. They couldn't recognize me at that distance, in that light, and there was no reason why they shouldn't think me one of Vance's crew, if they belonged to him.

As they came toward me I stepped back into the court and hissed for Red. He wasn't a boy you had to call twice to a row. He got to me just as they arrived. I took one. He took the other.

Because I wanted a disturbance, I had to work like a mule to get it. These bimbos were a couple of lollipops for fair. There wouldn't have been an ounce of fight in a ton of them. The one I had didn't know what to make of my roughing him around. He had a gun, but he managed to drop it first thing, and in the wrestling it got kicked out of reach. He hung on while I sweated ink jockeying him around into position. The darkness helped, but even at that it was no cinch to pretend he was putting up a battle while I worked him around behind O'Leary, who wasn't having any trouble at all with his man.

Finally I made it. I was behind O'Leary, who had his man pinned against the wall with one hand, preparing to sock him again with the other. I clamped my left hand on my playmate's wrist, twisted him to his knees, got my gun out, and shot O'Leary in the back, just below the right shoulder.

Red swayed, jamming his man into the wall. I beaned mine with the gun-butt.

"Did he get you, Red?" I asked, steadying him with an arm, knocking his prisoner across the noodle.

"Yeah."

"Nancy," I called.

She ran to us.

"Take his other side," I told her. "Keep on your feet, Red, and we'll make the sneak O.K."

The bullet was too freshly in him to slow him up yet, though his right arm was out of commission. We ran down the back street to the corner.

We had pursuers before we made it. Curious faces looked at us in the street. A policeman a block away began to move our way. The girl helping O'Leary on one side, me on the other, we ran half a block away from the copper, to where I had left the automobile Jack and I had used. The street was active by the time I got the machinery grinding and the girl had Red stowed safely in the back seat. The copper sent a yell and a high bullet after us. We left the neighborhood.

I didn't have any special destination yet, so, after the necessary first burst of speed, I slowed up a little, went around lots of corners, and brought the bus to rest in a dark street beyond Van Ness Avenue.

Red was drooping in one corner of the back, the girl holding him up, when I screwed around in my seat to look at them.

"Where to?" I asked.

"A hospital, a doctor, something!" the girl cried. "He's dying!"

I didn't believe that. If he was, it was his own fault. If he had had enough gratitude to take me along with him as a friend I wouldn't have had to shoot him so I could go along as nurse.

"Where to, Red?" I asked him, prodding his knee with a finger.

He spoke thickly, giving me the address of the Stockton Street hotel.

"That's no good," I objected. "Everybody in town knows you bunk there, and if you go back, it's lights out for yours. Where to?"

"Hotel," he repeated.

I got up, knelt on the seat, and leaned back to work on him. He was weak. He couldn't have much resistance left. Bulldozing a man who might after all be dying wasn't gentlemanly, but I had invested a lot of trouble in this egg, trying to get him to lead me to his friends, and I wasn't going to quit in the stretch. For a while it looked as if he wasn't weak enough yet, as if I'd have to shoot him again. But the girl sided with me, and between us we finally convinced him that his only safe bet was to go somewhere where he could hide while he got the right kind of care. We didn't actually convince him—we wore him out and he gave in because he was too weak to argue longer. He gave me an address out by Holly Park.

Hoping for the best, I pointed the machine thither.

XII

The house was a small one in a row of small houses. We took the big boy out of the car and between us to the door. He could just about make it with our help. The street was dark. No light showed from the house. I rang the bell.

Nothing happened. I rang again, and then once more.

"Who is it?" a harsh voice demanded from the inside.

"Red's been hurt," I said.

Silence for a while. Then the door opened half a foot. Through the opening a light came from the interior, enough light to show the flat face and bulging jaw-muscles of the skull-cracker who had been the Motsa Kid's guardian and executioner.

"What the hell?" he asked.

"Red was jumped. They got him," I explained, pushing the limp giant forward.

We didn't crash the gate that way. The skull-cracker held the door as it was.

"You'll wait," he said, and shut the door in our faces. His voice sounded from within, "Flora." That was all right—Red had brought us to the right place.

When he opened the door again he opened it all the way, and Nancy Regan and I took our burden into the hall. Beside the skull-cracker stood a woman in a low-cut black silk gown—Big Flora, I supposed.

She stood at least five feet ten in her high-heeled slippers. They were small slippers, and I noticed that her ringless hands were small. The rest of her wasn't. She was broad-shouldered, deep-bosomed, thick-armed, with a pink throat which, for all its smoothness, was muscled like a wrestler's. She was about my age—close to

forty—with very curly and very yellow bobbed hair, very pink skin, and a handsome, brutal face. Her deep-set eyes were gray, her thick lips were well-shaped, her nose was just broad enough and curved enough to give her a look of strength, and she had chin enough to support it. From forehead to throat her pink skin was underlaid with smooth, thick, strong muscles.

This Big Flora was no toy. She had the look and the poise of a woman who could have managed the looting and the double-crossing afterward. Unless her face and body lied, she had all the strength of physique, mind and will that would be needed, and some to spare. She was made of stronger stuff than either the ape-built bruiser at her side or the red-haired giant I was holding.

"Well?" she asked, when the door had been closed behind us. Her voice was deep but not masculine—a voice that went well with her looks.

"Vance ganged him in Larrouy's. He took one in the back," I said.

"Who are you?"

"Get him to bed," I stalled. "We've got all night to talk."

She turned, snapping her fingers. A shabby little old man darted out of a door toward the rear. His brown eyes were very scary.

"Get to hell upstairs," she ordered. "Fix the bed, get hot water and towels."

The little old man scrambled up the stairs like a rheumatic rabbit.

The skull-cracker took the girl's side of Red, and he and I carried the giant up to a room where the little man was scurrying around with basins and cloth. Flora and Nancy Regan followed us. We spread the wounded man face-down on the bed and stripped him. Blood still ran from the bullet-hole. He was unconscious.

Nancy Regan went to pieces.

"He's dying! He's dying! Get a doctor! Oh, Reddy, dearest—"

"Shut up!" said Big Flora. "The damned fool ought to croak—going to Larrouy's tonight!" She caught the little man by the shoulder and threw him at the door. "Zonite and more water," she called after him. "Give me your knife, Pogy."

The ape-built man took from his pocket a spring-knife with a long blade that had been sharpened until it was narrow and thin. This is the knife, I thought, that cut the Motsa Kid's throat.

With it, Big Flora cut the bullet out of Red O'Leary's back.

The ape-built Pogy kept Nancy Regan over in a corner of the room while the operating was done. The little scared man knelt beside the bed, handing the woman what she asked for, mopping up Red's blood as it ran from the wound.

I stood beside Flora, smoking cigarettes from the pack she had given me. When she raised her head, I would transfer the cigarette from my mouth to hers. She would fill her lungs with a draw that ate half the cigarette and nod. I would take the cigarette from her mouth. She would blow out the smoke and bend to her work again. I would light another cigarette from what was left of that one, and be ready for her next smoke.

Her bare arms were blood to the elbows. Her face was damp with sweat. It was a gory mess, and it took time. But when she straightened up for the last smoke, the bullet was out of Red, the bleeding had stopped, and he was bandaged.

"Thank God that's over," I said, lighting one of my own cigarettes. "Those pills you smoke are terrible."

The little scared man was cleaning up. Nancy Regan had fainted in a chair across the room, and nobody was paying any attention to her.

"Keep your eye on this gent, Pogy," Big Flora told the skull-cracker, nodding at me, "while I wash up."

I went over to the girl, rubbed her hands, put some water on her face, and got her awake.

"The bullet's out. Red's sleeping. He'll be picking fights again within a week," I told her.

She jumped up and ran over to the bed.

Flora came in. She had washed and had changed her blood-stained black gown for a green kimono affair, which gaped here and there to show a lot of orchid-colored underthings.

"Talk," she commanded, standing in front of me. "Who, what and why?"

"I'm Percy Maguire," I said, as if this name, which I had just thought up, explained everything.

"That's the who," she said, as if my phoney alias explained nothing. "Now what's the what and why?"

The ape-built Pogy, standing on one side, looked me up and down. I'm short and lumpy. My face doesn't scare children, but it's a more or less truthful witness to a life that hasn't been overburdened with refinement and gentility. The evening's entertainment had decorated me with bruises and scratches, and had done things to what was left of my clothes.

"Percy," he echoed, showing wide-spaced yellow teeth in a grin. "My Gawd, brother, your folks must of been color-blind!"

"That's the what and why," I insisted to the woman, paying no attention to the wheeze from the zoo. "I'm Percy Maguire, and I want my hundred and fifty thousand dollars."

The muscles in her brows came down over her eyes.

"You've got a hundred and fifty thousand dollars, have you?"

I nodded up into her handsome brutal face.

"Yeah," I said. "That's what I came for."

"Oh, you haven't got them? You want them?"

"Listen, sister, I want my dough." I had to get tough if this play was to go over. "This swapping *Oh-have-yous* and *Yes-I-haves* don't get me anything but a thirst. We were in the big knock-over, see? And after that, when we find the pay-off's a bust, I said to the kid I was training with, 'Never mind, Kid, we'll get our whack. Just follow Percy.' And then Bluepoint comes to me and asks me to throw in with him, and I said, 'Sure!' and me and the kid throw in with him until we all come across Red in the dump tonight. Then I told the kid, 'These coffee-and-doughnut[*] guns are going to rub Red out, and that won't get us anything. We'll take him away from 'em and

_____

[*] small-time

387

make him steer us to where Big Flora's sitting on the jack. We ought to be good for a hundred and fifty grand apiece, now that there's damned few in on it. After we get that, if we want to bump Red off, all right. But business before pleasure, and a hundred and fifty thou is business.' So we did. We opened an out for the big boy when he didn't have any. The kid got mushy with the broad along the road and got knocked for a loop. That was all right with me. If she was worth a hundred and fifty grand to him—fair enough. I came on with Red. I pulled the big tramp out after he stopped the slug. By rights I ought to collect the kid's dib, too—making three hundred thou for me—but give me the hundred and fifty I started out for and we'll call it even-steven."

I thought this hocus ought to stick. Of course I wasn't counting on her ever giving me any money, but if the rank and file of the mob hadn't known these people, why should these people know everybody in the mob?

Flora spoke to Pogy:

"Get that damned heap away from the front door."

I felt better when he went out. She wouldn't have sent him out to move the car if she had meant to do anything to me right away.

"Got any food in the joint?" I asked, making myself at home.

She went to the head of the steps and yelled down, "Get something for us to eat."

Red was still unconscious. Nancy Regan sat beside him, holding one of his hands. Her face was drained white. Big Flora came into the room again, looked at the invalid, put a hand on his forehead, felt his pulse.

"Come on downstairs," she said.

"I—I'd rather stay here, if I may," Nancy Regan said. Voice and eyes showed utter terror of Flora.

The big woman, saying nothing, went downstairs. I followed her to the kitchen, where the little man was working on ham and eggs at the range. The window and back door, I saw, were reinforced with heavy planking and braced with timbers nailed to the floor. The clock over the sink said 2:50 A.M.

Flora brought out a quart of liquor and poured drinks for herself and me. We sat at the table and while we waited for our food she cursed Red O'Leary and Nancy Regan, because he had got himself disabled keeping a date with her at a time when Flora needed his strength most. She cursed them individually, as a pair, and was making it a racial matter by cursing all the Irish when the little man gave us our ham and eggs.

We had finished the solids and were stirring hooch in our second cups of coffee when Pogy came back. He had news.

"There's a couple of mugs hanging around the corner that I don't much like."

"Bulls or—?" Flora asked.

"Or," he said.

Flora began to curse Red and Nancy again. But she had pretty well played that line out already. She turned to me.

"What the hell did you bring them here for?" she demanded. "Leaving a mile-wide trail behind you! Why didn't you let the lousy bum die where he got his dose?"

"I brought him here for my hundred and fifty grand. Slip it to me and I'll be on my way. You don't owe me anything else. I don't owe you anything. Give me my rhino* instead of lip and I'll pull my freight."

"Like hell you will," said Pogy.

The woman looked at me under lowered brows and drank her coffee.

XIII

Fifteen minutes later the shabby little old man came running into the kitchen, saying he had heard feet on the roof. His faded brown eyes were dull as an ox's with fright, and his withered lips writhed under his straggly yellow-white mustache.

———————————

* money

Flora profanely called him a this-and-that kind of old one-thing-and-another and chased him upstairs again. She got up from the table and pulled the green kimono tight around her big body.

"You're here," she told me, "and you'll put in with us. There's no other way. Got a rod?"

I admitted I had a gun but shook my head at the rest of it.

"This is not my wake—yet," I said. "It'll take one hundred and fifty thousand berries, spot cash, paid in the hand, to buy Percy in on it."

I wanted to know if the loot was on the premises.

Nancy Regan's tearful voice came from the stairs:

"No, no, darling! Please, please, go back to bed! You'll kill yourself, Reddy, dear!"

Red O'Leary strode into the kitchen. He was naked except for a pair of gray pants and his bandage. His eyes were feverish and happy. His dry lips were stretched in a grin. He had a gun in his left hand. His right arm hung useless. Behind him trotted Nancy. She stopped pleading and shrank behind him when she saw Big Flora.

"Ring the gong, and let's go," the half-naked redhead laughed. "Vance is in our street."

Flora went over to him, put her fingers on his wrist, held them there a couple of seconds, and nodded:

"You crazy son-of-a-gun," she said in a tone that was more like maternal pride than anything else. "You're good for a fight right now. And a damned good thing, too, because you're going to get it."

Red laughed—a triumphant laugh that boasted of his toughness—then his eyes turned to me. Laughter went out of them and a puzzled look drew them narrow.

"Hello," he said. "I dreamed about you, but I can't remember what it was. It was—Wait. I'll get it in a minute. It was—By God! I dreamed it was you that plugged me!"

Flora smiled at me, the first time I had seen her smile, and she spoke quickly:

"Take him, Pogy!"

I twisted obliquely out of my chair.

Pogy's fist took me in the temple. Staggering across the room, struggling to keep my feet, I thought of the bruise on the dead Motsa Kid's temple.

Pogy was on me when the wall bumped me upright.

I put a fist—spat!—in his flat nose. Blood squirted, but his hairy paws gripped me. I tucked my chin in, ground the top of my head into his face. The scent Big Flora used came strong to me. Her silk clothes brushed against me. With both hands full of my hair she pulled my head back, stretching my neck for Pogy. He took hold of it with his paws. I quit. He didn't throttle me any more than was necessary, but it was bad enough.

Flora frisked me for gun and blackjack.

".38 special," she named the caliber of the gun. "I dug a .38 special bullet out of you, Red." The words came faintly to me through the roaring in my ears.

The little old man's voice was chattering in the kitchen. I couldn't make out anything he said. Pogy's hands went away from me. I put my own hands to my throat. It was hell not to have any pressure at all there. The blackness went slowly away from my eyes, leaving a lot of little purple clouds that floated around and around. Presently I could sit up on the floor. I knew by that I had been lying down on it.

The purple clouds shrank until I could see past them enough to know there were only three of us in the room now. Cringing in a chair, back in a corner, was Nancy Regan. On another chair, beside the door, a black pistol in his hand, sat the scared little old man. His eyes were desperately frightened. Gun and hand shook at me. I tried to ask him to either stop shaking or move his gun away from me, but I couldn't get any words out yet.

Upstairs, guns boomed, their reports exaggerated by the smallness of the house.

The little man winced.

"Let me get out," he whispered with unexpected abruptness, "and I will give you everything. I will! Everything—if you will let me get out of this house!"

This feeble ray of light where there hadn't been a dot gave me back the use of my vocal apparatus.

"Talk turkey," I managed to say.

"I will give you those upstairs—that she-devil. I will give you the money. I will give you all—if you will let me go out. I am old. I am sick. I cannot live in prison. What have I to do with robberies? Nothing. Is it my fault that she-devil—? You have seen it here. I am a slave—I who am near the end of my life. Abuse, cursings, beatings—and those are not enough. Now I must go to prison because that she-devil is a she-devil. I am an old man who cannot live in prisons. You let me go out. You do me that kindness. I will give you that she-devil—those other devils—the money they stole. That I will do!"

Thus this panic-stricken little old man, squirming and fidgeting on his chair.

"How can I get you out?" I asked, getting up from the floor, my eye on his gun. If I could get to him while we talked. . . .

"How not? You are a friend of the police—that I know. The police are here now—waiting for daylight before they come into this house. I myself with my old eyes saw them take that Bluepoint Vance. You can take me out past your friends, the police. You do what I ask, and I will give you those devils and their moneys."

"Sounds good," I said, taking a careless step toward him. "But can I just stroll out of here when I want to?"

"No! No!" he said, paying no attention to the second step I took toward him. "But first I will give you those three devils. I will give them to you alive but without power. And their money. That I will do, and then you will take me out—and this girl here." He nodded suddenly at Nancy, whose white face, still nice in spite of its terror, was mostly wide eyes just now. "She, too, has nothing to do with those devils' crimes. She must go with me."

I wondered what this old rabbit thought he could do. I frowned exceedingly thoughtful while I took still another step toward him.

"Make no mistake," he whispered earnestly. "When that she-devil comes back into this room you will die—she will kill you certainly."

Three more steps and I would be close enough to take hold of him and his gun.

Footsteps were in the hall. Too late for a jump.

"Yes?" he hissed desperately.

I nodded a split-second before Big Flora came through the door.

XIV

She was dressed for action in a pair of blue pants that were probably Pogy's, beaded moccasins, a silk waist. A ribbon held her curly yellow hair back from her face. She had a gun in one hand, one in each hip pocket.

The one in her hand swung up.

"You're done," she told me, quite matter-of-fact.

My newly acquired confederate whined, "Wait, wait, Flora! Not here like this, please! Let me take him into the cellar."

She scowled at him, shrugging her silken shoulders.

"Make it quick," she said. "It'll be light in another half-hour."

I felt too much like crying to laugh at them. Was I supposed to think this woman would let the rabbit change her plans? I suppose I must have put some value on the old gink's help, or I wouldn't have been so disappointed when this little comedy told me it was a frame-up. But any hole they worked me into couldn't be any worse than the one I was in.

So I went ahead of the old man into the hall, opened the door he indicated, switched on the basement light, and went down the rough steps.

Close behind me he was whispering, "I'll first show you the moneys, and then I will give to you those devils. And you will not forget your promise? I and that girl shall go out through the police?"

"Oh, yes," I assured the old joker.

He came up beside me, sticking a gun-butt in my hand.

"Hide it," he hissed, and, when I had pocketed that one, gave me another, producing them with his free hand from under his coat.

Then he actually showed me the loot. It was still in the boxes and bags in which it had been carried from the banks. He insisted on opening some of them to show me the money—green bundles belted with the bank's yellow wrappers. The boxes and bags were stacked in a small brick cell that was fitted with a padlocked door, to which he had the key.

He closed the door when we were through looking, but he did not lock it, and he led me back part of the way we had come.

"That, as you see, is the money," he said. "Now for those. You will stand here, hiding behind these boxes."

A partition divided the cellar in half. It was pierced by a doorway that had no door. The place the old man told me to hide was close beside this doorway, between the partition and four packing cases. Hiding there, I would be to the right of, and a little behind, anyone who came downstairs and walked through the cellar toward the cell that held the money. That is, I would be in that position when they went to go through the doorway in the partition.

The old man was fumbling beneath one of the boxes. He brought out an eighteen-inch length of lead pipe stuffed in a similar length of black garden hose. He gave this to me as he explained everything.

"They will come down here one at a time. When they are about to go through this door, you will know what to do with this. And then you will have them, and I will have your promise. Is it not so?"

"Oh, yes," I said, all up in the air.

He went upstairs. I crouched behind the boxes, examining the guns he had given me—and I'm damned if I could find anything wrong

with them. They were loaded and they seemed to be in working order. That finishing touch completely balled me up. I didn't know whether I was in a cellar or a balloon.

When Red O'Leary, still naked except for pants and bandage, came into the cellar, I had to shake my head violently to clear it in time to bat him across the back of the noodle as his first bare foot stepped through the doorway. He sprawled down on his face.

The old man scurried down the steps, full of grins.

"Hurry! Hurry!" he panted, helping me drag the redhead back into the money cell. Then he produced two pieces of cord and tied the giant hand and foot.

"Hurry!" he panted again as he left me to run upstairs, while I went back to my hiding-place and hefted the lead-pipe, wondering if Flora had shot me and I was now enjoying the rewards of my virtue—in a heaven where I could enjoy myself forever and ever socking folks who had been rough with me down below.

The ape-built skull-cracker came down, reached the door. I cracked his skull. The little man came scurrying. We dragged Pogy to the cell, tied him up.

"Hurry!" panted the old gink, dancing up and down in his excitement. "That she-devil next—and strike hard!"

He scrambled upstairs and I could hear his feet pattering overhead.

I got rid of some of my bewilderment, making room for a little intelligence in my skull. This foolishness we were up to wasn't so. It couldn't be happening. Nothing ever worked out just that way. You didn't stand in corners and knock down people one after the other like a machine, while a scrawny little bozo up at the other end fed them to you. It was too damned silly! I had enough!

I passed up my hiding place, put down the pipe and found another spot to crouch in, under some shelves, near the steps. I hunkered down there with a gun in each fist. This game I was playing in was—it had to be—gummy around the edges. I wasn't going to stay put any longer.

Flora came down the steps. Two steps behind her the little man trotted.

Flora had a gun in each hand. Her gray eyes were everywhere. Her head was down like an animal's coming to a fight. Her nostrils quivered. Her body, coming down neither slowly nor swiftly, was balanced like a dancer's. If I live to a million I'll never forget the picture this handsome brutal woman made coming down those unplaned cellar stairs. She was a beautiful fight-bred animal going to a fight.

She saw me as I straightened.

"Drop 'em!" I said, but I knew she wouldn't.

The little man flicked a limp brown blackjack out of his sleeve and knocked her behind the ear just as she swung her left gun on me.

I jumped over and caught her before she hit the cement.

"Now, you see!" the old man said gleefully. "You have the money and you have them. And now you will get me and that girl out."

"First we'll stow this with the others," I said.

After he had helped me do that I told him to lock the cell door. He did, and I took the key with one hand, his neck with the other. He squirmed like a snake while I ran my other hand over his clothes, removing the blackjack and a gun, and finding a money-belt around his waist.

"Take it off," I ordered. "You don't carry anything out with you."

His fingers worked with the buckle, dragged the belt from under his clothes, let it fall on the floor. It was padded fat.

Still holding his neck, I took him upstairs, where the girl still sat frozen on the kitchen chair. It took a stiff hooker of whisky and a lot of words to thaw her into understanding that she was going out with the old man and that she wasn't to say a word to anybody, especially not to the police.

"Where's Reddy?" she asked when color had come back into her face—which had even at the worst never lost its niceness—and thoughts to her head.

I told her he was all right, and promised her he would be in a hospital before the morning was over. She didn't ask anything else. I shooed her upstairs for her hat and coat, went with the old man while he got his hat, and then put the pair of them in the front ground-floor room.

"Stay here till I come for you," I said, and I locked the door and pocketed the key when I went out.

XV

The front door and the front window on the ground floor had been planked and braced like the rear ones. I didn't like to risk opening them, even though it was fairly light by now. So I went upstairs, fashioned a flag of truce out of a pillow-slip and a bed-slat, hung it out a window, waited until a heavy voice said, "All right, speak your piece," and then I showed myself and told the police I'd let them in.

It took five minutes' work with a hatchet to pry the front door loose. The chief of police, the captain of detectives, and half the force were waiting on the front steps and pavement when I got the door open. I took them to the cellar and turned Big Flora, Pogy and Red O'Leary over to them, with the money. Flora and Pogy were awake, but not talking.

While the dignitaries were crowded around the spoils I went upstairs. The house was full of police sleuths. I swapped greetings with them as I went through to the room where I had left Nancy Regan and the old gink. Lieutenant Duff was trying the locked door, while O'Gar and Hunt stood behind him.

I grinned at Duff and gave him the key.

He opened the door, looked at the old man and the girl—mostly at her—and then at me. They were standing in the center of the room. The old man's faded eyes were miserably worried, the girl's blue ones darkly anxious. Anxiety didn't ruin her looks a bit.

"If that's yours I don't blame you for locking it up," O'Gar muttered in my ear.

"You can run along now," I told the two in the room. "Get all the sleep you need before you report for duty again."

They nodded and went out of the house.

"That's how your agency evens up?" Duff said. "The she-employees make up in looks for the ugliness of the he's."

Dick Foley came into the hall.

"How's your end?" I asked.

"Finis. The Angel led me to Vance. He led here. I led the bulls here. They got him—got her."

Two shots crashed in the street.

We went to the door and saw excitement in a police car down the street. We went down there. Bluepoint Vance, handcuffs on his wrists, was writhing half on the seat, half on the floor.

"We were holding him here in the car, Houston and me," a hard-mouthed plain-clothes man explained to Duff. "He made a break, grabbed Houston's gat with both hands. I had to drill him—twice. The cap'll raise hell! He specially wanted him kept here to put up against the others. But God knows I wouldn't of shot him if it hadn't been him or Houston!"

Duff called the plain-clothesman a damned clumsy mick as they lifted Vance up on the seat. Bluepoint's tortured eyes focused on me.

"I—know—you?" he asked painfully. "Continental—New—York?"

"Yes," I said.

"Couldn't—place—you—Larrouy's—with—Red."

He stopped to cough blood.

"Got—Red?"

"Yeah," I told him. "Got Red, Flora, Pogy and the cush."

"But—not—Papa—dop—oul—os."

"Papa does what?" I asked impatiently, a shiver along my spine.

He pulled himself up on the seat.

"Papadopoulos," he repeated, with an agonizing summoning of the little strength left in him. "I tried—shoot him—saw him—walk 'way—with girl—bull—too damn quick—wish . . ."

His words ran out. He shuddered. Death wasn't a sixteenth of an inch behind his eyes. A white-coated intern tried to get past me into the car. I pushed him out of the way and leaned in, taking Vance by the shoulders. The back of my neck was ice. My stomach was empty.

"Listen, Bluepoint," I yelled in his face, "Papadopoulos? Little old man? Brains of the push?"

"Yes," Vance said, and the last live blood in him came out with the word.

I let him drop back on the seat and walked away.

Of course! How had I missed it? The little old scoundrel—if he hadn't, for all his scariness, been the works, how could he have so neatly turned the others over to me one at a time? They had been absolutely cornered. It was be killed fighting, or surrender and be hanged. They had no other way out. The police had Vance, who could and would tell them that the little buzzard was the headman—there wasn't even a chance for him beating the courts with his age, his weakness and his mask of being driven around by the others.

And there I had been—with no choice but to accept his offer. Otherwise lights out for me. I had been putty in his hands, his accomplices had been putty. He had slipped the cross over on them as they had helped him slip it over on the others—and I had sent him safely away.

Now I could turn the city upside down for him—my promise had been only to get him out of the house—but . . .

What a life!

BLACK MASK, MAY 1927

$106,000 Blood Money

BY DASHIELL HAMMETT

THE BIG KNOCK-OVER told of the looting of two banks by a large band of crooks gathered from all parts of the country for that purpose. Following the successful getaway with the plunder, a number of well-known members of the underworld of various cities are found murdered. These men were seen before the holdup and were suspected leaders of small groups participating in it. It becomes evident that the division of spoils is to be made among a few rather than between many. Murder succeeds murder, as the Continental detective narrows his search for the unknown head of the huge plot. In the end he finds him, only to let him escape, as the price of his own life, without knowing him to be the man he was after. $106,000 BLOOD MONEY is a sequel to THE BIG KNOCK-OVER.

"I'M TOM-TOM CAREY," he said, drawling the words.

I nodded at the chair beside my desk and weighed him in while he moved to it. Tall, wide-shouldered, thick-chested, thin-bellied, he would add up to say a hundred and ninety pounds. His swarthy face was hard as a fist, but there was nothing ill-humored in it. It was the face of a man of forty-something who lived life raw and thrived on it. His blue clothes were good and he wore them well.

In the chair, he twisted brown paper around a charge of Bull Durham and finished introducing himself:

"I'm Paddy the Mex's brother."

I thought maybe he was telling the truth. Paddy had been like this fellow in coloring and manner.

"That would make your real name Carrera," I suggested.

"Yes," he was lighting his cigarette. "Alfredo Estanislao Cristobal Carrera, if you want all the details."

I asked him how to spell Estanislao, wrote the name down on a slip of paper, adding alias *Tom-Tom Carey*, rang for Tommy Howd, and told him to have the file clerk see if we had anything on it.

"While your people are opening graves I'll tell you why I'm here," the swarthy man drawled through smoke when Tommy had gone away with the paper.

"Tough—Paddy being knocked off like that," I said.

"He was too damned trusting to live long," his brother explained. "This is the kind of hombre he was—the last time I saw him was four years ago, here in San Francisco. I'd come in from an expedition down to—never mind where. Anyway I was flat. Instead of pearls all I'd got out of the trip was a bullet-crease over my hip. Paddy was dirty with fifteen thousand or so he'd just nicked somebody for. The afternoon I saw him he had a date that he was leery of toting so much money to. So he gives me the fifteen thousand to hold for him till that night."

Tom-Tom Carey blew out smoke and smiled softly past me at a memory.

"That's the kind of hombre he was," he went on. "He'd trust even his own brother. I went to Sacramento that afternoon and caught a train east. A girl in Pittsburgh helped me spend the fifteen thousand. Her name was Laurel. She liked rye whisky with milk for a chaser. I used to drink it with her till I was all curdled inside, and I've never had any appetite for *schmierkäse*[*] since. So there's a hundred thousand dollars reward on this Papadopoulos, is there?"

"And six. The insurance companies put up a hundred thousand, the bankers' association five, and the city a thousand."

Tom-Tom Carey chucked the remains of his cigarette in the cuspidor and began to assemble another one.

"Suppose I hand him to you?" he asked. "How many ways will the money have to go?"

"None of it will stop here," I assured him.

_____
[*] a soft white cheese made from strained curds of milk

"The Continental Detective Agency doesn't touch reward money—and won't let its hired men. If any of the police are in on the pinch they'll want a share."

"But if they aren't, it's all mine?"

"If you turn him in without help, or without any help except ours."

"I'll do that." The words were casual. "So much for the arrest. Now for the conviction part. If you get him, are you sure you can nail him to the cross?"

"I ought to be, but he'll have to go up against a jury—and that means anything can happen."

The muscular brown hand holding the brown cigarette made a careless gesture.

"Then maybe I'd better get a confession out of him before I drag him in," he said off-hand.

"It would be safer that way," I agreed. "You ought to let that holster down an inch or two. It brings the gunbutt too high. The bulge shows when you sit down."

"Uh-huh. You mean the one on the left shoulder. I took it away from a fellow after I lost mine. Strap's too short. I'll get another one this afternoon."

Tommy came in with a folder labeled, *Carey, Tom-Tom, 1361-C*. It held some newspaper clippings, the oldest dated ten years back, the youngest eight months. I read them through, passing each one to the swarthy man as I finished it. Tom-Tom Carey was written down in them as soldier of fortune, gun-runner, seal poacher, smuggler and pirate. But it was all alleged, supposed and suspected. He had been captured variously but never convicted of anything.

"They don't treat me right," he complained placidly when we were through reading. "For instance, stealing that Chinese gunboat wasn't my fault. I was forced to do it—I was the one that was double-crossed. After they'd got the stuff aboard they wouldn't pay for it. I couldn't unload it. I couldn't do anything but take gunboat and all. The insurance companies must want this Papadopoulos plenty to hang a hundred thousand on him."

"Cheap enough if it lands him," I said.

"Maybe he's not all the newspapers picture him as, but he's more than a handful. He gathered a whole damned army of strong-arm men here, took over a block in the center of the financial district, looted the two biggest banks in the city, fought off the whole police department, made his getaway, ditched the army, used some of his lieutenants to bump off some more of them,—that's where your brother Paddy got his,—then, with the help of Pogy Reeve, Big Flora Brace and Red O'Leary, wiped out the rest of his lieutenants. And remember, these lieutenants weren't schoolboys—they were slick grifters like Bluepoint Vance and the Shivering Kid and Darby M'Laughlin—birds who knew their what's what."

"Uh-huh." Carey was unimpressed. "But it was a bust just the same. You got all the loot back, and he just managed to get away himself."

"A bad break for him," I explained. "Red O'Leary broke out with a complication of love and vanity. You can't chalk that against Papadopoulos. Don't get the idea he's half-smart. He's dangerous, and I don't blame the insurance companies for thinking they'll sleep better if they're sure he's not out where he can frame some more tricks against their policy-holding banks."

"Don't know much about this Papadopoulos, do you?"

"No." I told the truth. "And nobody does. The hundred thousand offer made rats out of half the crooks in the country. They're as hot after him as we—not only because of the reward but because of his wholesale double-crossing. And they know just as little about him as we do—that he's had his fingers in a dozen or more jobs, that he was the brains behind Bluepoint Vance's bond tricks, and that his enemies have a habit of dying young. But nobody knows where he came from, or where he lives when he's home. Don't think I'm touting him as a Napoleon or a Sunday-supplement master mind—but he's a shifty, tricky old boy. As you say, I don't know much about him—but there are lots of people I don't know much about."

Tom-Tom Carey nodded to show he understood the last part and began making his third cigarette.

"I was in Nogales when Angel Grace Cardigan got word to me that Paddy had been done in," he said. "That was nearly a month ago. She seemed to think I'd romp up here pronto—but it was no skin off my face. I let it sleep. But last week I read in a newspaper about all this reward money being posted on the hombre she blamed for Paddy's rub-out. That made it different—a hundred thousand dollars different. So I shipped up here, talked to her, and then came in to make sure there'll be nothing between me and the blood money when I put the loop on this Papadoodle."

"Angel Grace sent you to me?" I inquired.

"Uh-huh—only she don't know it. She dragged you into the story—said you were a friend of Paddy's, a good guy for a sleuth, and hungry as hell for this Papadoodle. So I thought you'd be the gent for me to see."

"When did you leave Nogales?"

"Tuesday—last week."

"That," I said, prodding my memory, "was the day after Newhall was killed across the border."

The swarthy man nodded. Nothing changed in his face.

"How far from Nogales was that?" I asked.

"He was gunned down near Oquitoa—that's somewhere around sixty miles southwest of Nogales. You interested?"

"No—except I was wondering about your leaving the place where he was killed the day after he was killed, and coming up where he had lived. Did you know him?"

"He was pointed out to me in Nogales as a San Francisco millionaire going with a party to look at some mining property in Mexico. I was figuring on maybe selling him something later, but the Mexican patriots got him before I did."

"And so you came north?"

"Uh-huh. The hubbub kind of spoiled things for me. I had a nice little business in—call it supplies—to and fro across the line. This

Newhall killing turned the spotlight on that part of the country. So I thought I'd come up and collect that hundred thousand and give things a chance to settle down there. Honest, brother, I haven't killed a millionaire in weeks, if that's what's worrying you."

"That's good. Now, as I get it, you're counting on landing Papadopoulos. Angel Grace sent for you, thinking you'd run him down just to even up for Paddy's killing, but it's the money you want, so you figure on playing with me as well as the Angel. That right?"

"Check."

"You know what'll happen if she learns you're stringing along with me?"

"Uh-huh. She'll chuck a convulsion—kind of balmy on the subject of keeping clear of the police, isn't she?"

"She is—somebody told her something about honor among thieves once and she's never got over it. Her brother's doing a hitch up north now—Johnny the Plumber sold him out. Her man Paddy was mowed down by his pals. Did either of those things wake her up? Not a chance. She'd rather have Papadopoulos go free than join forces with us."

"That's all right," Tom-Tom Carey assured me. "She thinks I'm the loyal brother—Paddy couldn't have told her much about me—and I'll handle her. You having her shadowed?"

I said: "Yes—ever since she was turned loose. She was picked up the same day Flora and Pogy and Red were grabbed, but we hadn't anything on her except that she had been Paddy's lady-love, so I had her sprung. How much dope did you get out of her?"

"Descriptions of Papadoodle and Nancy Regan, and that's all. She don't know any more about them than I do. Where does this Regan girl fit in?"

"Hardly any, except that she might lead us to Papadopoulos. She was Red's girl. It was keeping a date with her that he upset the game. When Papadopoulos wriggled out he took the girl with him. I don't know why. She wasn't in on the stick-ups."

Tom-Tom Carey finished making and lighting his fifth cigarette and stood up.

"Are we teamed?" he asked as he picked up his hat.

"If you turn in Papadopoulos I'll see that you get every nickel you're entitled to," I replied. "And I'll give you a clear field—I won't handicap you with too much of an attempt to keep my eyes on your actions."

He said that was fair enough, told me he was stopping at a hotel in Ellis Street, and went away.

II

Calling the late Taylor Newhall's office on the phone, I was told that if I wanted any information about his affairs I should try his country residence, some miles south of San Francisco. I tried it. A ministerial voice that said it belonged to the butler told me that Newhall's attorney, Franklin Ellert, was the person I should see. I went over to Ellert's office.

He was a nervous, irritable old man with a lisp and eyes that stuck out with blood pressure.

"Is there any reason," I asked point-blank, "for supposing that Newhall's murder was anything more than a Mexican bandit outburst? Is it likely that he was killed purposely, and not resisting capture?"

Lawyers don't like to be questioned. This one sputtered and made faces at me and let his eyes stick out still further and, of course, didn't give me an answer.

"How? How?" he snapped disagreeably. "Exthplain your meaning, thir!"

He glared at me and then at the desk, pushing papers around with excited hands, as if he were hunting for a police whistle. I told my story—told him about Tom-Tom Carey.

Ellert sputtered some more, demanded, "What the devil do you mean?" and made a complete jumble of the papers on his desk.

"I don't mean anything," I growled back. "I'm just telling you what was said."

"Yeth! Yeth! I know!" He stopped glaring at

me and his voice was less peevish. "But there ith abtholutely no reathon for thuthpecting anything of the thort. None at all, thir, none at all!"

"Maybe you're right." I turned to the door. "But I'll poke into it a little anyway."

"Wait! Wait!" He scrambled out of his chair and ran around the desk to me. "I think you are mithtaken, but if you are going to invethtigate it I would like to know what you dithcover. Perhapth you'd better charge me with your regular fee for whatever ith done, and keep me informed of your progreth. Thatithfactory?"

I said it was, came back to his desk and began to question him. There was, as the lawyer had said, nothing in Newhall's affairs to stir us up. The dead man was several times a millionaire, with most of his money in mines. He had inherited nearly half his money. There was no shady practice, no claim-jumping, no trickery in his past, no enemies. He was a widower with one daughter. She had everything she wanted while he lived, and she and her father had been very fond of one another. He had gone to Mexico with a party of mining men from New York who expected to sell him some property there. They had been attacked by bandits, had driven them off, but Newhall and a geologist named Parker had been killed during the fight.

Back in the office, I wrote a telegram to our Los Angeles branch, asking that an operative be sent to Nogales to pry into Newhall's killing and Tom-Tom Carey's affairs. The clerk to whom I gave it to be coded and sent told me the Old Man wanted to see me. I went into his office and was introduced to a short, rolly-polly man named Hook.

"Mr. Hook," the Old Man said, "is the proprietor of a restaurant in Sausalito. Last Monday he employed a waitress named Nelly Riley. She told him she had come from Los Angeles. Her description, as Mr. Hook gives it, is quite similar to the description you and Counihan have given of Nancy Regan. Isn't it?" he asked the fat man.

"Absolutely. It's exactly what I read in the papers. She's five feet five inches tall, about,

and medium in size, and she's got blue eyes and brown hair, and she's around twenty-one or two, and she's got looks, and the thing that counts most is she's high-hat as the devil—she don't think nothin's good enough for her. Why, when I tried to be a little sociable she told me to keep my 'dirty paws' to myself. And then I found out she didn't know hardly nothing about Los Angeles, though she claimed to have lived there two or three years. I bet you she's the girl, all right," and he went on talking about how much reward money he ought to get.

"Are you going back there now?" I asked him.

"Pretty soon. I got to stop and see about some dishes. Then I'm going back."

"This girl will be working?"

"Yes."

"Then we'll send a man over with you—one who knows Nancy Regan."

I called Jack Counihan in from the operatives' room and introduced him to Hook. They arranged to meet in half an hour at the ferry and Hook waddled out.

"This Nelly Riley won't be Nancy Regan," I said. "But we can't afford to pass up even a hundred to one chance."

I told Jack and the Old Man about Tom-Tom Carey and my visit to Ellert's office. The Old Man listened with his usual polite attentiveness. Young Counihan—only four months in the man-hunting business—listened with wide eyes.

"You'd better run along now and meet Hook," I said when I had finished, leaving the Old Man's office with Jack. "And if she should be Nancy Regan—grab her and hang on." We were out of the Old Man's hearing, so I added, "And for God's sake don't let your youthful gallantry lead you to a poke in the jaw this time. Pretend you're grown up."

The boy blushed, said, "Go to hell!" adjusted his necktie, and set off to meet Hook.

I had some reports to write. After I had finished them I put my feet on my desk, made cavities in a package of Fatimas, and thought about Tom-Tom Carey until six o'clock. Then I went down to the States for my abalone chowder and minute steak and home to change clothes before going out Sea Cliff way to sit in a poker game.

The telephone interrupted my dressing. Jack Counihan was on the other end.

"I'm in Sausalito. The girl wasn't Nancy, but I've got hold of something else. I'm not sure how to handle it. Can you come over?"

"Is it important enough to cut a poker game for?"

"Yes, it's—I think it's big." He was excited. "I wish you would come over. I really think it's a lead."

"Where are you?"

"At the ferry there. Not the Golden Gate, the other."

"All right. I'll catch the first boat."

III

An hour later I walked off the boat in Sausalito. Jack Counihan pushed through the crowd and began talking:

"Coming down here on my way back—"

"Hold it till we get out of the mob," I advised him. "It must be tremendous—the eastern point of your collar is bent."

He mechanically repaired this defect in his otherwise immaculate costuming while we walked to the street, but he was too intent on whatever was on his mind to smile.

"Up this way," he said, guiding me around a corner. "Hook's lunch-room is on the corner. You can take a look at the girl if you like. She's of the same size and complexion as Nancy Regan, but that is all. She's a tough little job who probably was fired for dropping her chewing gum in the soup the last place she worked."

"All right. That lets her out. Now what's on your mind?"

"After I saw her I started back to the ferry. A boat came in while I was still a couple of blocks away. Two men who must have come in on it came up the street. They were Greeks, rather young, tough, though ordinarily I shouldn't have paid much attention to them. But, since

Papadopoulos is a Greek, we have been interested in them, of course, so I looked at these chaps. They were arguing about something as they walked, not talking loud, but scowling at one another. As they passed me the chap on the gutter side said to the other, 'I tell him it's been twenty-nine days.'

"Twenty-nine days. I counted back and it's just twenty-nine days since we started hunting for Papadopoulos. He is a Greek and these chaps were Greeks. When I had finished counting I turned around and began to follow them. They took me all the way through the town and up a hill on the fringe. They went to a little cottage—it couldn't have more than three rooms—set back in a clearing in the woods by itself. There was a 'For Sale' sign on it, and no curtains in the windows, no sign of occupancy—but on the ground behind the back door there was a wet place, as if a bucket or pan of water had been thrown out.

"I stayed in the bushes until it got a little darker. Then I went closer. I could hear people inside, but I couldn't see anything through the windows. They're boarded up. After a while the two chaps I had followed came out, saying something in a language I couldn't understand to whoever was in the cottage. The cottage door stayed open until the two men had gone out of sight down the path—so I couldn't have followed them without being seen by whoever was at the door.

"Then the door was closed and I could hear people moving around inside—or perhaps only one person—and could smell cooking, and some smoke came out of the chimney. I waited and waited and nothing more happened and I thought I had better get in touch with you."

"Sounds interesting," I agreed.

We were passing under a street light. Jack stopped me with a hand on my arm and fished something out of his overcoat pocket.

"Look!" He held it out to me. A charred piece of blue cloth. It could have been the remains of a woman's hat that had been three-quarters burned. I looked at it under the street light and then used my flashlight to examine it more closely.

"I picked it up behind the cottage while I was nosing around," Jack said, "and—"

"And Nancy Regan wore a hat of that shade the night she and Papadopoulos vanished," I finished for him. "On to the cottage."

We left the street lights behind, climbed the hill, dipped down into a little valley, turned into a winding sandy path, left that to cut across sod between trees to a dirt road, trod half a mile of that, and then Jack led the way along a narrow path that wound through a black tangle of bushes and small trees. I hoped he knew where he was going.

"Almost there," he whispered to me.

A man jumped out of the bushes and took me by the neck.

My hands were in my overcoat pockets—one holding the flashlight, the other my gun.

I pushed the muzzle of the pocketed gun toward the man—pulled the trigger.

The shot ruined seventy-five dollars' worth of overcoat for me. But it took the man away from my neck.

That was lucky. Another man was on my back.

I tried to twist away from him—didn't altogether make it—felt the edge of a knife along my spine.

That wasn't so lucky—but it was better than getting the point.

I butted back at his face—missed—kept twisting and squirming while I brought my hands out of my pockets and clawed at him.

The blade of his knife came flat against my cheek. I caught the hand that held it and let myself go—down backward—him under.

He said: "Uh!"

I rolled over, got hands and knees on the ground, was grazed by a fist, scrambled up.

Fingers dragged at my ankle.

My behavior was ungentlemanly. I kicked the fingers away—found the man's body—kicked it twice—hard.

Jack's voice whispered my name. I couldn't see him in the blackness, nor could I see the man I had shot.

"All right here," I told Jack. "How did you come out?"

"Top-hole. Is that all of it?"

"Don't know, but I'm going to risk a peek at what I've got."

Tilting my flashlight down at the man under my foot, I snapped it on. A thin blond man, his face blood-smeared, his pink-rimmed eyes jerking as he tried to play 'possum in the glare.

"Come out of it!" I ordered.

A heavy gun went off back in the bush—another, lighter one. The bullets ripped through the foliage.

I switched off the light, bent to the man on the ground, knocked him on the top of the head with my gun.

"Crouch down low," I whispered to Jack.

The smaller gun snapped again, twice. It was ahead, to the left.

I put my mouth to Jack's ear.

"We're going to that damned cottage whether anybody likes it or no. Keep low and don't do any shooting unless you can see what you're shooting at. Go ahead."

Bending as close to the ground as I could, I followed Jack up the path. The position stretched the slash in my back—a scalding pain from between my shoulders almost to my waist. I could feel blood trickling down over my hips—or thought I could.

The going was too dark for stealthiness. Things crackled under our feet, rustled against our shoulders. Our friends in the bush used their guns. Luckily, the sound of twigs breaking and leaves rustling in pitch blackness isn't the best of targets. Bullets zipped here and there, but we didn't stop any of them. Neither did we shoot back.

We halted where the end of the bush left the night a weaker gray.

"That's it," Jack said about a square shape ahead.

"On the jump," I grunted and lit out for the dark cottage.

Jack's long slim legs kept him easily at my side as we raced across the clearing.

A man-shape oozed from behind the blot of the building and his gun began to blink at us. The shots came so close together that they sounded like one long stuttering bang.

Pulling the youngster with me, I flopped, flat to the ground except where a ragged-edged empty tin-can held my face up.

From the other side of the building another gun coughed. From a tree-stem to the right, a third.

Jack and I began to burn powder back at them.

A bullet kicked my mouth full of dirt and pebbles. I spit mud and cautioned Jack:

"You're shooting too high. Hold it low and pull easy."

A hump showed in the house's dark profile. I sent a bullet at it.

A man's voice yelled: "Ow—ooh!" and then, lower but very bitter, "Oh, damn you—damn you!"

For a warm couple of seconds bullets spattered all around us. Then there was not a sound to spoil the night's quietness.

When the silence had lasted five minutes, I got myself up on hands and knees and began to move forward, Jack following. The ground wasn't made for that sort of work. Ten feet of it was enough. We stood up and walked the rest of the way to the building.

"Wait," I whispered, and leaving Jack at one corner of the building, I circled it, seeing nobody, hearing nothing but the sounds I made.

We tried the front door. It was locked but rickety.

Bumping it open with my shoulder, I went indoors—flashlight and gun in my fists.

The shack was empty.

Nobody—no furnishings—no traces of either in the two bare rooms—nothing but bare wooden walls, bare floor, bare ceiling, with a stove-pipe connected to nothing sticking through it.

Jack and I stood in the middle of the floor, looked at the emptiness, and cursed the dump from back door to front for being empty. We hadn't quite finished when feet sounded outside, a white light beamed on the open doorway, and a cracked voice said:

"Hey! You can come out one at a time—kind of easy like!"

"Who says so?" I asked, snapping off the flashlight, moving over close to a side wall.

"A whole goldurned flock of deputy sheriffs," the voice answered.

"Couldn't you push one of 'em in and let us get a look at him?" I asked. "I've been choked and carved and shot at tonight until I haven't got much faith left in anybody's word."

A lanky, knock-kneed man with a thin leathery face appeared in the doorway. He showed me a buzzer,* I fished out my credentials, and the other deputies came in. There were three of them in all.

"We were driving down the road bound for a little job near the point when we heard the shooting," the lanky one explained. "What's up?"

I told him.

"This shack's been empty a long while," he said when I had finished. "Anybody could have camped in it easy enough. Think it was that Papadopoulos, huh? We'll kind of look around for him and his friends—especial since there's that nice reward money."

We searched the woods and found nobody. The man I had knocked down and the man I had shot were both gone.

Jack and I rode back to Sausalito with the deputies. I hunted up a doctor there and had my back bandaged. He said the cut was long but shallow. Then we returned to San Francisco and separated in the direction of our homes.

And thus ended the day's doings.

_____

* badge

IV

Here is something that happened next morning. I didn't see it. I heard about it a little before noon and read about it in the papers that afternoon. I didn't know then that I had any personal interest in it, but later I did—so I'll put it in here where it happened.

At ten o'clock that morning, into busy Market Street, staggered a man who was naked from the top of his battered head to the soles of his blood-stained feet. From his bare chest and sides and back, little ribbons of flesh hung down, dripping blood. His left arm was broken in two places. The left side of his bald head was smashed in. An hour later he died in the emergency hospital—without having said a word to anyone, with the same vacant, distant look in his eyes.

The police easily ran back the trail of blood drops. They ended with a red smear in an alley beside a small hotel just off Market Street. In the hotel, the police found the room from which the man had jumped, fallen, or been thrown. The bed was soggy with blood. On it were torn and twisted sheets that had been knotted and used rope-wise. There was also a towel that had been used as a gag.

The evidence read that the naked man had been gagged, trussed up and worked on with a knife. The doctors said the ribbons of flesh had been cut loose, not torn or clawed. After the knife-user had gone away, the naked man had worked free of his bonds, and, probably crazed by pain, had either jumped or fallen out of the window. The fall had crushed his skull and broken his arm, but he had managed to walk a block and a half in that condition.

The hotel management said the man had been there two days. He was registered as H. F. Barrows, City. He had a black Gladstone bag in which, besides clothes, shaving implements and so on, the police found a box of .38 cartridges, a black handkerchief with eye-holes cut in it, four skeleton keys, a small jimmy, and a quantity of morphine, with a needle and the rest of the kit. Elsewhere in the room they found the rest of his clothes, a .38 revolver and two quarts of liquor. They didn't find a cent.

The supposition was that Barrows had been a burglar, and that he had been tied up, tortured and robbed, probably by pals, between eight and nine that morning. Nobody knew anything about him. Nobody had seen his visitor or visitors. The room next to his on the left was unoccupied. The occupant of the room on the other side had left for his work in a furniture factory before seven o'clock.

While this was happening I was at the office, sitting forward in my chair to spare my back, reading reports, all of which told how operatives attached to various Continental Detective Agency branches had continued to fail to turn up any indications of the past, present, or future whereabouts of Papadopoulos and Nancy Regan. There was nothing novel about these reports—I had been reading similar ones for three weeks.

The Old Man and I went out to luncheon together, and I told him about the previous night's adventures in Sausalito while we ate. His grandfatherly face was as attentive as always, and his smile as politely interested, but when I was half through my story he turned his mild blue eyes from my face to his salad and he stared at his salad until I had finished talking. Then, still not looking up, he said he was sorry I had been cut. I thanked him and we ate a while.

Finally he looked at me. The mildness and courtesy he habitually wore over his cold-bloodedness were in face and eyes and voice as he said:

"This first indication that Papadopoulos is still alive came immediately after Tom-Tom Carey's arrival."

It was my turn to shift my eyes.

I looked at the roll I was breaking while I said: "Yes."

That afternoon a phone call came in from a woman out in the Mission who had seen some highly mysterious happenings and was sure they had something to do with the well-advertised bank robberies. So I went out to see her and spent most of the afternoon learning that half of her happenings were imaginary and the other half were the efforts of a jealous wife to get the low-down on her husband.

It was nearly six o'clock when I returned to the agency. A few minutes later Dick Foley called me on the phone. His teeth were chattering until I could hardly get the words.

"C-c-canyoug-g-get-t-townt-t-tooth-ar-r-rbr-r-spittle?"

"What?" I asked, and he said the same thing again, or worse. But by this time I had guessed that he was asking me if I could get down to the Harbor Hospital.

I told him I could in ten minutes, and with the help of a taxi I did.

V

The little Canadian operative met me at the hospital door. His clothes and hair were dripping wet, but he had had a shot of whisky and his teeth had stopped chattering.

"Damned fool jumped in bay!" he barked as if it were my fault.

"Angel Grace?"

"Who else was I shadowing? Got on Oakland ferry. Moved off by self by rail. Thought she was going to throw something over. Kept eye on her. Bingo! She jumps." Dick sneezed. "I was goofy enough to jump after her. Held her up. Were fished out. In there," nodding his wet head toward the interior of the hospital.

"What happened before she took the ferry?"

"Nothing. Been in joint all day. Straight out to ferry."

"How about yesterday?"

"Apartment all day. Out at night with man. Roadhouse. Home at four. Bad break. Couldn't tail him off."

"What did he look like?"

The man Dick described was Tom-Tom Carey.

"Good," I said. "You'd better beat it home for a hot bath and some dry rags."

I went in to see the near-suicide.

She was lying on her back on a cot, staring at the ceiling. Her face was pale, but it always was, and her green eyes were no more sullen than usual. Except that her short hair was dark with dampness she didn't look as if anything out of the ordinary had happened.

"You think of the funniest things to do," I said when I was beside the bed.

She jumped and her face jerked around to me, startled. Then she recognized me and smiled—a smile that brought into her face the attractiveness that habitual sullenness kept out.

"You have to keep in practice—sneaking up on people?" she asked. "Who told you I was here?"

"Everybody knows it. Your pictures are all over the front pages of the newspapers, with your life history and what you said to the Prince of Wales."

She stopped smiling and looked steadily at me.

"I got it!" she exclaimed after a few seconds. "That runt who came in after me was one of your ops—tailing me. Wasn't he?"

"I didn't know anybody had to go in after you," I answered. "I thought you came ashore after you had finished your swim. Didn't you want to land?"

She wouldn't smile. Her eyes began to look at something horrible.

"Oh! Why didn't they let me alone?" she wailed, shuddering. "It's a rotten thing, living."

I sat down on a small chair beside the white bed and patted the lump her shoulder made in the sheets.

"What was it?" I was surprised at the fatherly tone I achieved. "What did you want to die for, Angel?"

Words that wanted to be said were shiny in her eyes, tugged at muscles in her face, shaped her lips—but that was all. The words she said came out listlessly, but with a reluctant sort of finality. They were:

"No. You're law. I'm thief. I'm staying on my side of the fence. Nobody can say—"

"All right! All right!" I surrendered. "But for

God's sake don't make me listen to another of those ethical arguments. Is there anything I can do for you?"

"Thanks, no."

"There's nothing you want to tell me?"

She shook her head.

"You're all right now?"

"Yes. I was being shadowed, wasn't I? Or you wouldn't have known about it so soon."

"I'm a detective—I know everything. Be a good girl."

From the hospital I went up to the Hall of Justice, to the police detective bureau. Lieutenant Duff was holding down the captain's desk. I told him about the Angel's dive.

"Got any idea what she was up to?" he wanted to know when I had finished.

"She's too far off center to figure. I want her vagged."

"Yeah? I thought you wanted her loose so you could catch her."

"That's about played out now. I'd like to try throwing her in the can for thirty days. Big Flora is in waiting trial. The Angel knows Flora was one of the troupe that rubbed out her Paddy. Maybe Flora don't know the Angel. Let's see what will come of mixing the two babies for a month."

"Can do," Duff agreed. "This Angel's got no visible means of support, and it's a cinch she's got no business running around jumping in people's bays. I'll put the word through."

From the Hall of Justice I went up to the Ellis Street hotel at which Tom-Tom Carey had told me he was registered. He was out. I left word that I would be back in an hour, and used that hour to eat. When I returned to the hotel the tall swarthy man was sitting in the lobby. He took me up to his room and set out gin, orange juice and cigars.

"Seen Angel Grace?" I asked.

"Yes, last night. We did the dumps."

"Seen her today?"

"No."

"She jumped in the bay this afternoon."

"The hell she did." He seemed moderately surprised. "And then?"

"She was fished out. She's O.K."

The shadow in his eyes could have been some slight disappointment.

"She's a funny sort of kid," he remarked. "I wouldn't say Paddy didn't show good taste when he picked her, but she's a queer one!"

"How's the Papadopoulos hunt progressing?"

"It is. But you oughtn't have split on your word. You half-way promised you wouldn't have me shadowed."

"I'm not the big boss," I apologized. "Sometimes what I want don't fit in with what the headman wants. This shouldn't bother you much—you can shake him, can't you?"

"Uh-huh. That's what I've been doing. But it's a damned nuisance jumping in and out of taxis and back doors."

We talked and drank a few minutes longer, and then I left Carey's room and hotel, and went to a drug-store telephone booth, where I called Dick Foley's home, and gave Dick the swarthy man's description and address.

"I don't want you to tail Carey, Dick. I want you to find out who is trying to tail him—and that shadower is the bird you're to stick to. The morning will be time enough to start—get yourself dried out."

And that was the end of that day.

VI

I woke to a disagreeable rainy morning. Maybe it was the weather, maybe I'd been too frisky the day before, anyway the slit in my back was like a foot-long boil. I phoned Dr. Canova, who lived on the floor below me, and had him look at the cut before he left for his downtown office. He rebandaged it and told me to take life easy for a couple of days. It felt better after he had fooled with it, but I phoned the agency and told the Old Man that unless something exciting broke I was going to stay on sick-call all day.

I spent the day propped up in front of the gas-log, reading, and smoking cigarettes that wouldn't burn right on account of the weather. That night I used the phone to organize a poker game, in which I got very little action one way or the other. In the end I was fifteen dollars ahead, which was just about five dollars less than enough to pay for the booze my guests had drunk on me.

My back was better the following day, and so was the day. I went down to the agency. There was a memorandum on my desk saying Duff had phoned that Angel Grace Cardigan had been vagged—thirty days in the city prison. There was a familiar pile of reports from various branches on their operatives' inability to pick up anything on Papadopoulos and Nancy Regan. I was running through these when Dick Foley came in.

"Made him," he reported. "Thirty or thirty-two. Five, six. Hundred, thirty. Sandy hair, complexion. Blue eye. Thin face, some skin off. Rat. Lives dump in Seventh Street."

"What did he do?"

"Tailed Carey one block. Carey shook him. Hunted for Carey till two in morning. Didn't find him. Went home. Take him again?"

"Go up to his flophouse and find out who he is."

The little Canadian was gone half an hour.

"Sam Arlie," he said when he returned. "Been there six months. Supposed to be barber—when he's working—if ever."

"I've got two guesses about this Arlie," I told Dick. "The first is that he's the gink who carved me in Sausalito the other night. The second is that something's going to happen to him."

It was against Dick's rules to waste words, so he said nothing.

I called Tom-Tom Carey's hotel and got the swarthy man on the wire.

"Come over," I invited him. "I've got some news for you."

"As soon as I'm dressed and breakfasted," he promised.

"When Carey leaves here you're to go along behind him," I told Dick after I had hung up. "If Arlie connects with him now, maybe there'll be something doing. Try to see it."

Then I phoned the detective bureau and made a date with Sergeant Hunt to visit Angel Grace Cardigan's apartment. After that I busied myself with paper work until Tommy came in to announce the swarthy man from Nogales.

"The jobbie* who's tailing you," I informed him when he had sat down and begun work on a cigarette, "is a barber named Arlie," and I told him where Arlie lived.

"Yes. A slim-faced, sandy lad?"

I gave him the description Dick had given me.

"That's the hombre," Tom-Tom Carey said. "Know anything else about him?"

"No."

"You had Angel Grace vagged."

It was neither an accusation nor a question, so I didn't answer it.

"It's just as well," the tall man went on. "I'd have had to send her away. She was bound to gum things with her foolishness when I got ready to swing the loop."

"That'll be soon?"

"That all depends on how it happens." He stood up, yawned and shook his wide shoulders. "But nobody would starve to death if they decided not to eat any more till I'd got him. I oughtn't have accused you of having me shadowed."

"It didn't spoil my day."

Tom-Tom Carey said, "So long," and sauntered out.

I rode down to the Hall of Justice, picked up Hunt, and we went to the Bush Street apartment house in which Angel Grace Cardigan had lived. The manager—a highly scented fat woman with a hard mouth and soft eyes—already knew her tenant was in the cooler. She willingly took us up to the girl's rooms.

The Angel wasn't a good housekeeper. Things were clean enough, but upset. The kitchen sink was full of dirty dishes. The folding bed was worse than loosely made up. Clothes and odds and ends of feminine equipment hung over everything from bathroom to kitchen.

---

* character

We got rid of the landlady and raked the place over thoroughly. We came away knowing all there was to know about the girl's wardrobe, and a lot about her personal habits. But we didn't find anything pointing Papadopoulos-ward.

No report came in on the Carey-Arlie combination that afternoon or evening, though I expected to hear from Dick every minute.

At three o'clock in the morning my bedside phone took my ear out of the pillows. The voice that came over the wire was the Canadian op's.

"Exit Arlie," he said.

"R.I.P.?"

"Yep."

"How?"

"Lead."

"Our lad's?"

"Yep."

"Keep till morning?"

"Yep."

"See you at the office," and I went back to sleep.

VII

When I arrived at the agency at nine o'clock, one of the clerks had just finished decoding a night letter from the Los Angeles operative who had been sent over to Nogales. It was a long telegram, and meaty.

It said that Tom-Tom Carey was well known along the border. For some six months he had been engaged in over-the-line traffic—guns going south, booze, and probably dope and immigrants, coming north. Just before leaving there the previous week he had made inquiries concerning one Hank Barrows. This Hank Barrows' description fit the H. F. Barrows who had been cut into ribbons, who had fallen out the hotel window and died.

The Los Angeles operative hadn't been able to get much of a line on Barrows, except that he hailed from San Francisco, had been on the border only a few days, and had apparently returned to San Francisco. The operative had turned up

nothing new on the Newhall killing—the signs still read that he had been killed resisting capture by Mexican patriots.

Dick Foley came into my office while I was reading this news. When I had finished he gave me his contribution to the history of Tom-Tom Carey.

"Tailed him out of here. To hotel. Arlie on corner. Eight o'clock, Carey out. Garage. Hire car without driver. Back hotel. Checked out. Two bags. Out through park. Arlie after him in flivver. My boat after Arlie. Down boulevard. Off cross-road. Dark. Lonely. Arlie steps on gas. Closes in. Bang! Carey stops. Two guns going. Exit Arlie. Carey back to city. Hotel Marquis. Registers George F. Danby, San Diego. Room 622."

"Did Tom-Tom frisk Arlie after he dropped him?"

"No. Didn't touch him."

"So? Take Mickey Linehan with you. Don't let Carey get out of your sight. I'll get somebody up to relieve you and Mickey late tonight, if I can, but he's got to be shadowed twenty-four hours a day until—" I didn't know what came after that so I stopped talking.

I took Dick's story into the Old Man's office and told it to him, winding up:

"Arlie shot first, according to Foley, so Carey gets a self-defense on it, but we're getting action at last and I don't want to do anything to slow it up. So I'd like to keep what we know about this shooting quiet for a couple of days. It won't increase our friendship any with the county sheriff if he finds out what we're doing, but I think it's worth it."

"If you wish," the Old Man agreed, reaching for his ringing phone.

He spoke into the instrument and passed it on to me. Detective-sergeant Hunt was talking:

"Flora Brace and Grace Cardigan crushed out just before daylight. The chances are they—"

I wasn't in a humor for details.

"A clean sneak?" I asked.

"Not a lead on 'em so far, but—"

"I'll get the details when I see you. Thanks," and I hung up.

"Angel Grace and Big Flora have escaped from the city prison," I passed the news on to the Old Man.

He smiled courteously, as if at something that didn't especially concern him.

"You were congratulating yourself on getting action," he murmured.

I turned my scowl to a grin, mumbled, "Well, maybe," went back to my office and telephoned Franklin Ellert. The lisping attorney said he would be glad to see me, so I went over to his office.

"And now, what progreth have you made?" he asked eagerly when I was seated beside his desk.

"Some. A man named Barrows was also in Nogales when Newhall was killed, and also came to San Francisco right after. Carey followed Barrows up here. Did you read about the man found walking the streets naked, all cut up?"

"Yeth."

"That was Barrows. Then another man comes into the game—a barber named Arlie. He was spying on Carey. Last night, in a lonely road south of here, Arlie shot at Carey. Carey killed him."

The old lawyer's eyes came out another inch.

"What road?" he gasped.

"You want the exact location?"

"Yeth!"

I pulled his phone over, called the agency, had Dick's report read to me, gave the attorney the information he wanted.

It had an effect on him. He hopped out of his chair. Sweat was shiny along the ridges wrinkles made in his face.

"Mith Newhall ith down there alone! That plath ith only half a mile from her houth!"

I frowned and beat my brains together, but I couldn't make anything out of it.

"Suppose I put a man down there to look after her?" I suggested.

"Exthellent!" His worried face cleared until there weren't more than fifty or sixty wrinkles in it. "The would prefer to thtay there during

her firth grief over her fatherth death. You will thend a capable man?"

"The Rock of Gibraltar is a leaf in the breeze beside him. Give me a note for him to take down. Andrew MacElroy is his name."

While the lawyer scribbled the note I used his phone again to call the agency, to tell the operator to get hold of Andy and tell him I wanted him. I ate lunch before I returned to the agency. Andy was waiting when I got there.

Andy MacElroy was a big boulder of a man— not very tall, but thick and hard of head and body. A glum, grim man with no more imagination than an adding machine. I'm not even sure he could read. But I was sure that when Andy was told to do something, he did it and nothing else. He didn't know enough not to.

I gave him the lawyer's note to Miss Newhall, told him where to go and what to do, and Miss Newhall's troubles were off my mind.

Three times that afternoon I heard from Dick Foley and Mickey Linehan. Tom-Tom Carey wasn't doing anything very exciting, though he had bought two boxes of .44 cartridges in a Market Street sporting goods establishment.

The afternoon papers carried photographs of Big Flora Brace and Angel Grace Cardigan, with a story of their escape. The story was as far from the probable facts as newspaper stories generally are. On another page was an account of the discovery of the dead barber in the lonely road. He had been shot in the head and in the chest, four times in all. The county officials' opinion was that he had been killed resisting a stick-up, and that the bandits had fled without robbing him.

At five o'clock Tommy Howd came to my door.

"That guy Carey wants to see you again," the freckle-faced boy said.

"Shoot him in."

The swarthy man sauntered in, said "Howdy," sat down, and made a brown cigarette.

"Got anything special on for tonight?" he asked when he was smoking.

"Nothing I can't put aside for something better. Giving a party?"

THE BIG BOOK OF THE CONTINENTAL OP

"Uh-huh. I had thought of it. A kind of surprise party for Papadoodle. Want to go along?"

It was my turn to say, "Uh-huh."

"I'll pick you up at eleven—Van Ness and Geary," he drawled. "But this has got to be a kind of tight party—just you and me—and him."

"No. There's one more who'll have to be in on it. I'll bring him along."

"I don't like that." Tom-Tom Carey shook his head slowly, frowning amiably over his cigarette. "You sleuths oughtn't out-number me. It ought to be one and one."

"You won't be out-numbered," I explained. "This jobbie I'm bringing won't be on my side more than yours. And it'll pay you to keep as sharp an eye on him as I do—and to see he don't get behind either of us if we can help it."

"Then what do you want to lug him along for?"

"Wheels within wheels," I grinned.

The swarthy man frowned again, less amiably now.

"The hundred and six thousand reward money—I'm not figuring on sharing that with anybody."

"Right enough," I agreed. "Nobody I bring along will declare themselves in on it."

"I'll take your word for it." He stood up. "And we've got to watch this hombre, huh?"

"If we want everything to go all right."

"Suppose he gets in the way—cuts up on us. Can we put it to him, or do we just say, 'Naughty! Naughty!'?"

"He'll have to take his own chances."

"Fair enough." His hard face was good-natured again as he moved toward the door. "Eleven o'clock at Van Ness and Geary."

VIII

I went back into the operatives' room, where Jack Counihan was slumped down in a chair reading a magazine.

"I hope you've thought up something for me

to do," he greeted me. "I'm getting bed-sores from sitting around."

"Patience, son, patience—that's what you've got to learn if you're ever going to be a detective. Why when I was a child of your age, just starting in with the agency, I was lucky—"

"Don't start that," he begged. Then his good-looking young face got earnest. "I don't see why you keep me cooped up here. I'm the only one besides you who really got a good look at Nancy Regan. I should think you would have me out hunting for her."

"I told the Old Man the same thing," I sympathized. "But he is afraid to risk something happening to you. He says in all his fifty years of gumshoeing he's never seen such a handsome op, besides being a fashion plate and a social butterfly and the heir to millions. His idea is we ought to keep you as a sort of show piece, and not let you—"

"Go to hell!" Jack said, all red in the face.

"But I persuaded him to let me take the cotton packing off you tonight," I continued. "So meet me at Van Ness and Geary before eleven o'clock."

"Action?" He was all eagerness.

"Maybe."

"What are we going to do?"

"Bring your little pop-gun along." An idea came into my head and I worded it. "You'd better be all dressed up—evening duds."

"Dinner coat?"

"No—the limit—everything but the high hat. Now for your behavior: you're not supposed to be an op. I'm not sure just what you're supposed to be, but it doesn't make any difference. Tom-Tom Carey will be along. You act as if you were neither my friend nor his—as if you didn't trust either of us. We'll be cagey with you. If anything is asked that you don't know the answer to—you fall back on hostility. But don't crowd Carey too far. Got it?"

"I—I think so." He spoke slowly, screwing up his forehead. "I'm to act as if I was going along on the same business as you, but that outside of that we weren't friends. As if I wasn't willing to trust you. That it?"

"Very much. Watch yourself. You'll be swimming in nitroglycerine all the way."

"What is up? Be a good chap and give me some idea."

I grinned up at him. He was a lot taller than I.

"I could," I admitted, "but I'm afraid it would scare you off. So I'd better tell you nothing. Be happy while you can. Eat a good dinner. Lots of condemned folks seem to eat hearty breakfasts of ham and eggs just before they parade out to the rope. Maybe you wouldn't want 'em for dinner, but—"

At five minutes to eleven that night, Tom-Tom Carey brought a black touring car to the corner where Jack and I stood waiting in a fog that was like a damp fur coat.

"Climb in," he ordered as we came to the curb.

I opened the front door and motioned Jack in. He rang up the curtain on his little act, looking coldly at me and opening the rear door.

"I'm going to sit back here," he said bluntly.

"Not a bad idea," and I climbed in beside him.

Carey twisted around in his seat and he and Jack stared at each other for a while. I said nothing, did not introduce them. When the swarthy man had finished sizing the youngster up, he looked from the boy's collar and tie—all of his evening clothes not hidden by his overcoat—to me, grinned, and drawled:

"Your friend's a waiter, huh?"

I laughed, because the indignation that darkened the boy's face and popped his mouth open was natural, not part of his acting. I pushed my foot against his. He closed his mouth, said nothing, looked at Tom-Tom Carey and me as if we were specimens of some lower form of animal life.

I grinned back at Carey and asked, "Are we waiting for anything?"

He said we weren't, left off staring at Jack, and put the machine in motion. He drove us out

through the park, down the boulevard. Traffic going our way and the other loomed out of and faded into the fog-thick night. Presently we left the city behind, and ran out of the fog into clear moonlight. I didn't look at any of the machines running behind us, but I knew that in one of them Dick Foley and Mickey Linehan should be riding.

Tom-Tom Carey swung our car off the boulevard, into a road that was smooth and well made, but not much traveled.

"Wasn't a man killed down along here somewhere last night?" I asked.

Carey nodded his head without turning it, and, when we had gone another quarter-mile, said: "Right here."

We rode a little slower now, and Carey turned off his lights. In the road that was half moon-silver, half shadow-gray, the machine barely crept along for perhaps a mile. We stopped in the shade of tall shrubs that darkened a spot of the road.

"All ashore that's going ashore," Tom-Tom Carey said, and got out of the car.

Jack and I followed him. Carey took off his overcoat and threw it into the machine.

"The place is just around the bend, back from the road," he told us. "Damn this moon! I was counting on fog."

I said nothing, nor did Jack. The boy's face was white and excited.

"We'll bee-line it," Carey said, leading the way across the road to a high wire fence.

He went over the fence first, then Jack, then—the sound of someone coming along the road from ahead stopped me. Signalling silence to the two men on the other side of the fence, I made myself small beside a bush. The coming steps were light, quick, feminine.

A girl came into the moonlight just ahead. She was a girl of twenty-something, neither tall nor short, thin nor plump. She was short-skirted, bare-haired, sweatered. Terror was in her white face, in the carriage of her hurrying figure—but something else was there too—more beauty than a middle-aged sleuth was used to seeing.

When she saw Carey's automobile bulking in the shadow, she stopped abruptly, with a gasp that was almost a cry.

I walked forward, saying:

"Hello, Nancy Regan."

This time the gasp was a cry.

"Oh! Oh!" Then, unless the moonlight was playing tricks, she recognized me and terror began to go away from her. She put both hands out to me, with relief in the gesture.

"Well?" A bearish grumble came from the big boulder of a man who had appeared out of the darkness behind her. "What's all this?"

"Hello, Andy," I greeted the boulder.

"Hullo," MacElroy echoed and stood still.

Andy always did what he was told to do. He had been told to take care of Miss Newhall. I looked at the girl and then at him again.

"Is this Miss Newhall?" I asked.

"Yeah," he rumbled. "I came down like you said, but she told me she didn't want me—wouldn't let me in the house. But you hadn't said anything about coming back. So I just camped outside, moseying around, keeping my eyes on things. And when I seen her shinnying out a window a little while ago, I just went on along behind her to take care of her, like you said I was to do."

Tom-Tom Carey and Jack Counihan came back into the road, crossed it to us. The swarthy man had an automatic in one hand. The girl's eyes were glued on mine. She paid no attention to the others.

"What is it all about?" I asked her.

"I don't know," she babbled, her hands holding on to mine, her face close to mine. "Yes, I'm Ann Newhall. I didn't know. I thought it was fun. And then when I found out it wasn't I couldn't get out of it."

Tom-Tom Carey grunted and stirred impatiently. Jack Counihan was staring down the road. Andy MacElroy stood stolid in the road, waiting to be told what to do next. The girl never once looked from me to any of these others.

"How did you get in with them?" I demanded. "Talk fast."

IX

I had told the girl to talk fast. She did. For twenty minutes she stood there and turned out words in a chattering stream that had no breaks except where I cut in to keep her from straying from the path I wanted her to follow. It was jumbled, almost incoherent in spots, and not always plausible, but the notion stayed with me throughout that she was trying to tell the truth—most of the time.

And not for a fraction of a second did she turn her gaze from my eyes. It was as if she was afraid to look anywhere else.

This millionaire's daughter had, two months before, been one of a party of four young people returning late at night from some sort of social affair down the coast. Somebody suggested that they stop at a roadhouse along their way—a particularly tough joint. Its toughness was its attraction, of course—toughness was more or less of a novelty to them. They got a first-hand view of it that night, for, nobody knew just how, they found themselves taking part in a row before they had been ten minutes in the dump.

The girl's escort had shamed her by showing an unreasonable amount of cowardice. He had let Red O'Leary turn him over his knee and spank him—and had done nothing about it afterward. The other youth in the party had been not much braver. The girl, insulted by this meekness, had walked across to the red-haired giant who had wrecked her escort, and she had spoken to him loud enough for everybody to hear:

"Will you please take me home?"

Red O'Leary was glad to do it. She left him a block or two from her city house. She told him her name was Nancy Regan. He probably doubted it, but he never asked her any questions, pried into her affairs. In spite of the difference in their worlds, a genuine companionship had grown up between them. She liked him. He was so gloriously a roughneck that she saw him as a romantic figure. He was in love with her, knew she was miles above him, and so she had no trouble making him behave so far as she was concerned.

They met often. He took her to all the rowdy holes in the bay district, introduced her to yeggs,* gunmen, swindlers, told her wild tales of criminal adventuring. She knew he was a crook, knew he was tied up in the Seamen's National and Golden Gate Trust jobs when they broke. But she saw it all as a sort of theatrical spectacle. She didn't see it as it was.

She woke up the night they were in Larrouy's and were jumped by the crooks that Red had helped Papadopoulos and the others double-cross. But it was too late then for her to wriggle clear. She was blown along with Red to Papadopoulos' hangout after I had shot the big lad. She saw then what her romantic figures really were—what she had mixed herself with.

When Papadopoulos escaped, taking her with him, she was wide awake, cured, through forever with her dangerous trifling with outlaws. So she thought. She thought Papadopoulos was the little, scary old man he seemed to be—Flora's slave, a harmless old duffer too near the grave to have any evil in him. He had been whining and terrified. He begged her not to forsake him, pleaded with her while tears ran down his withered cheeks, begging her to hide him from Flora. She took him to her country house and let him fool around in the garden, safe from prying eyes. She had no idea that he had known who she was all along, had guided her into suggesting this arrangement.

Even when the newspapers said he had been the commander-in-chief of the thug army, when the hundred and six thousand dollar reward was offered for his arrest, she believed in his innocence. He convinced her that Flora and Red had simply put the blame for the whole thing on him

---

* burglars

so they could get off with lighter sentences. He was such a frightened old gink—who wouldn't have believed him?

Then her father's death in Mexico had come and grief had occupied her mind to the exclusion of most other things until this day, when Big Flora and another girl—probably Angel Grace Cardigan—had come to the house. She had been deathly afraid of Big Flora when she had seen her before. She was more afraid now. And she soon learned that Papadopoulos was not Flora's slave but her master. She saw the old buzzard as he really was. But that wasn't the end of her awakening.

Angel Grace had suddenly tried to kill Papadopoulos. Flora had overpowered her. Grace, defiant, had told them she was Paddy's girl. Then she had screamed at Ann Newhall:

"And you, you damned fool, don't you know they killed your father? Don't you know——?"

Big Flora's fingers, around Angel Grace's throat, stopped her words. Flora tied up the Angel and turned to the Newhall girl.

"You're in it," she said brusquely. "You're in it up to your neck. You'll play along with us, or else—Here's how it stands, dearie. The old man and I are both due to step off if we're caught. And you'll do the dance with us. I'll see to that. Do what you're told, and we'll all come through all right. Get funny, and I'll beat holy hell out of you."

The girl didn't remember much after that. She had a dim recollection of going to the door and telling Andy she didn't want his services. She did this mechanically, not even needing to be prompted by the big blonde woman who stood close behind her. Later, in the same fearful daze, she had gone out her bedroom window, down the vine-covered side of the porch, and away from the house, running along the road, not going anywhere, just escaping.

That was what I learned from the girl. She didn't tell me all of it. She told me very little of it in those words. But that is the story I got by combining her words, her manner of telling them, her facial expressions, with what I already knew, and what I could guess.

And not once while she talked had her eyes turned from mine. Not once had she shown that she knew there were other men standing in the road with us. She stared into my face with a desperate fixity, as if she was afraid not to, and her hands held mine as if she might sink through the ground if she let go.

"How about your servants?" I asked.

"There aren't any there now."

"Papadopoulos persuaded you to get rid of them?"

"Yes—several days ago."

"Then Papadopoulos, Flora and Angel Grace are alone in the house now?"

"Yes."

"They know you ducked?"

"I don't know. I don't think they do. I had been in my room some time. I don't think they suspected I'd dare do anything but what they told me."

It annoyed me to find I was staring into the girl's eyes as fixedly as she into mine, and that when I wanted to take my gaze away it wasn't easily done. I jerked my eyes away from her, took my hands away.

"The rest of it you can tell me later," I growled, and turned to give Andy MacElroy his orders. "You stay here with Miss Newhall until we get back from the house. Make yourselves comfortable in the car."

The girl put a hand on my arm.

"Am I—? Are you—?"

"We're going to turn you over to the police, yes," I assured her.

"No! No!"

"Don't be childish," I begged. "You can't run around with a mob of cutthroats, get yourself tied up in a flock of crimes, and then when you're tripped say, 'Excuse it, please,' and go free. If you tell the whole story in court—including the parts you haven't told me—the chances are you'll get off. But there's no way in God's world for you to escape arrest. Come

on," I told Jack and Tom-Tom Carey. "We've got to shake it up if we want to find our folks at home."

Looking back as I climbed the fence, I saw that Andy had put the girl in the car and was getting in himself.

"Just a moment," I called to Jack and Carey, who were already starting across the field.

"Thought of something else to kill time," the swarthy man complained.

I went back across the road to the car and spoke quickly and softly to Andy:

"Dick Foley and Mickey Linehan should be hanging around the neighborhood. As soon as we're out of sight, hunt 'em up. Turn Miss Newhall over to Dick. Tell him to take her with him and beat it for a phone—rouse the sheriff. Tell Dick he's to turn the girl over to the sheriff, to hold for the San Francisco police. Tell him he's not to give her up to anybody else—not even to me. Got it?"

"Got it."

"All right. After you've told him that and have given him the girl, then you bring Mickey Linehan to the Newhall house as fast as you can make it. We'll likely need all the help we can get as soon as we can get it."

"Got you," Andy said.

X

"What are you up to?" Tom-Tom Carey asked suspiciously when I rejoined Jack and him.

"Detective business."

"I ought to have come down and turned the trick all by myself," he grumbled. "You haven't done a damned thing but waste time since we started."

"I'm not the one that's wasting it now."

He snorted and set out across the field again, Jack and I following him. At the end of the field there was another fence to be climbed. Then we came over a little wooded ridge and the Newhall house lay before us—a large white house, glistening in the moonlight, with yellow rectangulars where blinds were down over the windows of lighted rooms. The lighted rooms were on the ground floor. The upper floor was dark. Everything was quiet.

"Damn the moonlight!" Tom-Tom Carey repeated, bringing another automatic out of his clothes, so that he now had one in each hand.

Jack started to take his gun out, looked at me, saw I was letting mine rest, let his slide back in his pocket.

Tom-Tom Carey's face was a dark stone mask—slits for eyes, slit for mouth—the grim mask of a manhunter, a mankiller. He was breathing softly, his big chest moving gently. Beside him, Jack Counihan looked like an excited school-boy. His face was ghastly, his eyes all stretched out of shape, and he was breathing like a tire-pump. But his grin was genuine, for all the nervousness in it.

"We'll cross to the house on this side," I whispered. "Then one of us can take the front, one the back, and the other can wait till he sees where he's needed most. Right?"

"Right," the swarthy one agreed.

"Wait!" Jack exclaimed. "The girl came down the vines from an upper window. What's the matter with my going up that way? I'm lighter than either of you. If they haven't missed her, the window would still be open. Give me ten minutes to find the window, get through it, and get myself placed. Then when you attack I'll be there behind them. How's that?" he demanded applause.

"And what if they grab you as soon as you light?" I objected.

"Suppose they do. I can make enough racket for you to hear. You can gallop to the attack while they're busy with me. That'll be just as good."

"Blue hell!" Tom-Tom Carey barked. "What good's all that? The other way's best. One of us at the front door, one at the back, kick 'em in and go in shooting."

"If this new one works, it'll be better," I gave my opinion. "If you want to jump in the furnace,

Jack, I won't stop you. I won't cheat you out of your heroics."

"No!" the swarthy man snarled. "Nothing doing!"

"Yes," I contradicted him. "We'll try it. Better take twenty minutes, Jack. That won't give you any time to waste."

He looked at his watch and I at mine, and he turned toward the house.

Tom-Tom Carey, scowling darkly, stood in his way. I cursed and got between the swarthy man and the boy. Jack went around my back and hurried away across the too-bright space between us and the house.

"Keep your feet on the ground," I told Carey. "There are a lot of things to this game you don't know anything about."

"Too damned many!" he snarled, but he let the boy go.

There was no open second-story window on our side of the building. Jack rounded the rear of the house and went out of sight.

A faint rustling sounded behind us. Carey and I spun together. His guns went up. I stretched out an arm across them, pushing them down.

"Don't have a hemorrhage," I cautioned him. "This is just another of the things you don't know about."

The rustling had stopped.

"All right," I called softly.

Mickey Linehan and Andy MacElroy came out of the tree-shadows.

Tom-Tom Carey stuck his face so close to mine that I'd have been scratched if he had forgotten to shave that day.

"You double-crossing—"

"Behave! Behave! A man of your age!" I admonished him. "None of these boys want any of your blood money."

"I don't like this gang stuff," he snarled. "We—"

"We're going to need all the help we can get," I interrupted, looking at my watch. I told the two operatives: "We're going to close in on the house now. Four of us ought to be able to wrap it up snug. You know Papadopoulos, Big Flora and Angel Grace by description. They're in there. Don't take any chances with them—Flora and Papadopoulos are dynamite. Jack Counihan is trying to ease inside now. You two look after the back of the joint. Carey and I will take the front. We'll make the play. You see that nobody leaks out on us. Forward march!"

The swarthy man and I headed for the front porch—a wide porch, grown over with vines on the side, yellowly illuminated now by the light that came through four curtained French windows.

We hadn't taken our first steps across the porch when one of these tall windows moved—opened.

The first thing I saw was Jack Counihan's back.

He was pushing the casement open with a hand and foot, not turning his head.

Beyond the boy—facing him across the brightly lighted room—stood a man and a woman. The man was old, small, scrawny, wrinkled, pitifully frightened—Papadopoulos. I saw he had shaved off his straggly white mustache. The woman was tall, full-bodied, pink-fleshed and yellow-haired—a she-athlete of forty with clear gray eyes set deep in a handsome brutal face—Big Flora Brace. They stood very still, side by side, watching the muzzle of Jack Counihan's gun.

While I stood in front of the window looking at this scene, Tom-Tom Carey, his two guns up, stepped past me, going through the tall window to the boy's side. I did not follow him into the room.

Papadopoulos' scary brown eyes darted to the swarthy man's face. Flora's gray ones moved there deliberately, and then looked past him to me.

"Hold it, everybody!" I ordered, and moved away from the window, to the side of the porch where the vines were thinnest.

Leaning out between the vines, so my face was clear in the moonlight, I looked down the side of the building. A shadow in the shadow of the garage could have been a man. I put an arm out in the moonlight and beckoned. The shadow came toward me—Mickey Linehan. Andy MacElroy's head peeped around the back of the house. I beckoned again and he followed Mickey.

I returned to the open window.

Papadopoulos and Flora—a rabbit and a lioness—stood looking at the guns of Carey and Jack. They looked again at me when I appeared, and a smile began to curve the woman's full lips.

Mickey and Andy came up and stood beside me. The woman's smile died grimly.

"Carey," I said, "you and Jack stay as is. Mickey, Andy, go in and take hold of our gifts from God."

When the two operatives stepped through the window—things happened.

Papadopoulos screamed.

Big Flora lunged against him, knocking him at the back door.

"Go! Go!" she roared.

Stumbling, staggering, he scrambled across the room.

Flora had a pair of guns—sprung suddenly into her hands. Her big body seemed to fill the room, as if by willpower she had become a giantess. She charged—straight at the guns Jack and Carey held—blotting the back door and the fleeing man from their fire.

A blur to one side was Andy MacElroy moving.

I had a hand on Jack's gun-arm.

"Don't shoot," I muttered in his ear.

Flora's guns thundered together. But she was tumbling. Andy had crashed into her. Had thrown himself at her legs as a man would throw a boulder.

When Flora tumbled, Tom-Tom Carey stopped waiting.

His first bullet was sent so close past her that it clipped her curled yellow hair. But it went past—caught Papadopoulos just as he went through the door. The bullet took him low in the back—smeared him out on the floor.

Carey fired again—again—again—into the prone body.

"It's no use," I growled. "You can't make him any deader."

He chuckled and lowered his guns.

"Four into a hundred and six." All his ill-humor, his grimness was gone. "That's twenty-six thousand, five hundred dollars each of those slugs was worth to me."

Andy and Mickey had wrestled Flora into submission and were hauling her up off the floor.

I looked from them back to the swarthy man, muttering, "It's not all over yet."

"No?" He seemed surprised. "What next?"

"Stay awake and let your conscience guide you," I replied, and turned to the Counihan youngster. "Come along Jack."

I led the way out through the window and across the porch, where I leaned against the railing. Jack followed and stood in front of me, his gun still in his hand, his face white and tired from nervous tension. Looking over his shoulder, I could see the room we had just quit. Andy and Mickey had Flora sitting between them on a sofa. Carey stood a little to one side, looking curiously at Jack and me. We were in the middle of the band of light that came through the open window. We could see inside—except that Jack's back was that way—and could be seen from there, but our talk couldn't be overheard unless we made it loud.

All that was as I wanted it.

"Now tell me about it," I ordered Jack.

XI

"Well, I found the open window," the boy began.

"I know all that part," I cut in. "You came in and told your friends—Papadopoulos and Flora—about the girl's escape, and that Carey and I were coming. You advised them to make out you had captured them single-handed. That would draw Carey and me in. With you unsuspected behind us, it would be easy for the three of you to grab the two of us. After that you could

stroll down the road and tell Andy I had sent you for the girl. That was a good scheme—except that you didn't know I had Dick and Mickey up my sleeve, didn't know I wouldn't let you get behind me. But all that isn't what I want to know. I want to know why you sold us out—and what you think you're going to do now."

"Are you crazy?" His young face was bewildered, his young eyes horrified. "Or is this some—?"

"Sure, I'm crazy," I confessed. "Wasn't I crazy enough to let you lead me into that trap in Sausalito? But I wasn't too crazy to figure it out afterward. I wasn't too crazy to see that Ann Newhall was afraid to look at you. I'm not crazy enough to think you could have captured Papadopoulos and Flora unless they wanted you to. I'm crazy—but in moderation."

Jack laughed—a reckless young laugh, but too shrill. His eyes didn't laugh with mouth and voice. While he was laughing his eyes looked from me to the gun in his hand and back to me.

"Talk, Jack," I pleaded huskily, putting a hand on his shoulder. "For God's sake why did you do it?"

The boy shut his eyes, gulped, and his shoulders twitched. When his eyes opened they were hard and glittering and full of merry hell.

"The worst part of it," he said harshly, moving his shoulder from under my hand, "is that I wasn't a very good crook, was I? I didn't succeed in deluding you."

I said nothing.

"I suppose you've earned your right to the story," he went on after a little pause. His voice was consciously monotonous, as if he was deliberately keeping out of it every tone or accent that might seem to express emotion. He was too young to talk naturally. "I met Ann Newhall three weeks ago, in my own home. She had gone to school with my sisters, though I had never met her before. We knew each other at once, of course—I knew she was Nancy Regan, she knew I was a Continental operative.

"So we went off by ourselves and talked things over. Then she took me to see Papadopoulos. I liked the old boy and he liked me. He showed me how we together could accumulate unheard-of piles of wealth. So there you are. The prospect of all that money completely devastated my morals. I told him about Carey as soon as I had heard from you, and I led you into that trap, as you say. He thought it would be better if you stopped bothering us before you found the connection between Newhall and Papadopoulos.

"After that failure, he wanted me to try again, but I refused to have a hand in any more fiascos. There's nothing sillier than a murder that doesn't come off. Ann Newhall is quite innocent of everything except folly. I don't think she has the slightest suspicion that I have had any part in the dirty work beyond refraining from having everybody arrested. That, my dear Sherlock, about concludes the confession."

I had listened to the boy's story with a great show of sympathetic attentiveness. Now I scowled at him and spoke accusingly, but still not without friendliness.

"Stop spoofing! The money Papadopoulos showed you didn't buy you. You met the girl and were too soft to turn her in. But your vanity—your pride in looking at yourself as a pretty cold proposition—wouldn't let you admit it even to yourself. You had to have a hard-boiled front. So you were meat to Papadopoulos' grinder. He gave you a part you could play to yourself—a super-gentleman-crook, a master-mind, a desperate suave villain, and all that kind of romantic garbage. That's the way you went, my son. You went as far as possible beyond what was needed to save the girl from the hoosegow—just to show the world, but chiefly yourself, that you were not acting through sentimentality, but according to your own reckless desires. There you are. Look at yourself."

Whatever he saw in himself—what I had seen or something else—his face slowly reddened, and he wouldn't look at me. He looked past me at the distant road.

I looked into the lighted room beyond him.

Tom-Tom Carey had advanced to the center of the floor, where he stood watching us. I jerked a corner of my mouth at him—a warning.

"Well," the boy began again, but he didn't know what to say after that. He shuffled his feet and kept his eyes from my face.

I stood up straight and got rid of the last trace of my hypocritical sympathy.

"Give me your gun, you lousy rat!" I snarled at him.

He jumped back as if I had hit him. Craziness writhed in his face. He jerked his gun chest-high.

Tom-Tom Carey saw the gun go up. The swarthy man fired twice. Jack Counihan was dead at my feet.

Mickey Linehan fired once. Carey was down on the floor, bleeding from the temple.

I stepped over Jack's body, went into the room, knelt beside the swarthy man. He squirmed, tried to say something, died before he could get it out. I waited until my face was straight before I stood up.

Big Flora was studying me with narrowed gray eyes. I stared back at her.

"I don't get it all yet," she said slowly, "but if you—"

"Where's Angel Grace?" I interrupted.

"Tied to the kitchen table," she informed me, and went on with her thinking aloud. "You've dealt a hand that—"

"Yeah," I said sourly, "I'm another Papadopoulos."

Her big body suddenly quivered. Pain clouded her handsome brutal face. Two tears came out of her lower eye-lids.

I'm damned if she hadn't loved the old scoundrel!

XII

It was after eight in the morning when I got back to the city. I ate breakfast and then went up to the agency, where I found the Old Man going through his morning mail.

"It's all over," I told him. "Papadopoulos knew Nancy Regan was Taylor Newhall's heiress. When he needed a hiding-place after the bank jobs flopped, he got her to take him down to the Newhall country place. He had two holds on her. She pitied him as a misused old duffer, and she was—even if innocently—an accomplice after the fact in the stick-ups.

"Pretty soon Papa Newhall had to go to Mexico on business. Papadopoulos saw a chance to make something. If Newhall was knocked off, the girl would have millions—and the old thief knew he could take them away from her. He sent Barrows down to the border to buy the murder from some Mexican bandits. Barrows put it over, but talked too much. He told a girl in Nogales that he had to go back 'to Frisco to collect plenty from an old Greek,' and then he'd return and buy her the world. The girl passed the news on to Tom-Tom Carey. Carey put a lot of twos together and got at least a dozen for an answer. He followed Barrows up here.

"Angel Grace was with him the morning he called on Barrows here—to find out if his 'old Greek' really was Papadopoulos, and where he could be found. Barrows was too full of morphine to listen to reason. He was so dope-deadened that even after the dark man began to reason with a knife-blade he had to whittle Barrows all up before he began to feel hurt. The carving sickened Angel Grace. She left, after vainly trying to stop Carey. And when she read in the afternoon papers what a finished job he had made of it, she tried to commit suicide, to stop the images from crawling around in her head.

"Carey got all the information Barrows had, but Barrows didn't know where Papadopoulos was hiding. Papadopoulos learned of Carey's arrival—you know how he learned. He sent Arlie to stop Carey. Carey wouldn't give the barber a chance—until the swarthy man began to suspect Papadopoulos might be at the Newhall place. He drove down there, letting Arlie follow. As soon as Arlie discovered his destination, Arlie closed in, hell-bent on stopping Carey at any cost. That was what Carey wanted. He gunned Arlie, came back to town, got hold of me, and took me down to help wind things up.

"Meanwhile, Angel Grace, in the cooler, had made friends with Big Flora. She knew Flora but Flora didn't know her. Papadopoulos had arranged a crush-out for Flora. It's always easier for two to escape than one. Flora took the Angel along, took her to Papadopoulos. The Angel went for him, but Flora knocked her for a loop.

"Flora, Angel Grace and Ann Newhall, alias Nancy Regan, are in the county jail," I wound up. "Papadopoulos, Tom-Tom Carey and Jack Counihan are dead."

I stopped talking and lighted a cigarette, taking my time, watching cigarette and match carefully throughout the operation. The Old Man picked up a letter, put it down without reading it, picked up another.

"They were killed in course of making the arrests?" His mild voice held nothing but its usual unfathomable politeness.

"Yes. Carey killed Papadopoulos. A little later he shot Jack. Mickey—not knowing—not knowing anything except that the dark man was shooting at Jack and me—we were standing apart talking—shot and killed Carey." The words twisted around my tongue, wouldn't come out straight. "Neither Mickey nor Andy know that Jack—Nobody but you and I know exactly what the thing—exactly what Jack was doing. Flora Brace and Ann Newhall did know, but if we say he was acting on orders all the time, nobody can deny it."

The Old Man nodded his grandfatherly face and smiled, but for the first time in the years I had known him I knew what he was thinking. He was thinking that if Jack had come through alive we would have had the nasty choice between letting him go free or giving the agency a black-eye by advertising the fact that one of our operatives was a crook.

I threw away my cigarette and stood up. The Old Man stood also, and held out a hand to me.

"Thank you," he said.

I took his hand, and I understood him, but I didn't have anything I wanted to confess—even by silence.

"It happened that way," I said deliberately. "I played the cards so we would get the benefit of the breaks—but it just happened that way."

He nodded, smiling benignantly.

"I'm going to take a couple of weeks off," I said from the door.

I felt tired, washed out.

This story is a sequel to THE BIG KNOCK-OVER which appeared in February BLACK MASK. If you missed reading it, send a request to the Editor for a free copy of that issue.

THE MAIN DEATH

BY DASHIELL HAMMETT

In the JUNE issue of BLACK MASK

After an enforced absence from literary work, Mr. Hammett is once more in the lineup of BLACK MASK regular contributors, and, judging from the many enthusiastic comments on The Big Knock-Over, his popularity is greater than ever. In The Main Death—which, by the way, is a short story—he is at his cleverest and best. By its surprise development, its subtleties, its wonderfully clear picturization, its easy, swift movement to the climax, this tale will delight every lover of the short story. It is a gem—a model of what the short story can be.

BLACK MASK, JUNE 1927

The Main Death

BY DASHIELL HAMMETT

A curious tangle of a robbery, a mysterious killing and jealousy.

THE CAPTAIN TOLD ME Hacken and Begg were handling the job. I caught them leaving the detectives' assembly room. Begg was a freck-led heavyweight, as friendly as a Saint Bernard puppy, but less intelligent. Lanky detective-sergeant Hacken, not so playful, carried the team's brains behind his worried hatchet face.

"In a hurry?" I inquired.

"Always in a hurry when we're quitting for the day," Begg said, his freckles climbing up his face to make room for his grin.

"What do you want?" Hacken asked.

"I want the low-down on the Main doings—if any."

"You going to work on it?"

"Yes," I said, "for Main's boss—Gungen."

"Then you can tell us something. Why'd he have the twenty thou in cash?"

"Tell you in the morning," I promised. "I haven't seen Gungen yet. Got a date with him tonight."

While we talked we had gone into the assembly room, with its school-room arrangement of desks and benches. Half a dozen police detectives were scattered among them, doing reports. We three sat around Hacken's desk and the lanky detective-sergeant talked:

"Main got home from Los Angeles at eight, Sunday night, with twenty thousand in his wallet. He'd gone down there to sell something for Gungen. You find out why he had that much in cash. He told his wife he had driven up from L.A. with a friend—no name. She went to bed around ten-thirty, leaving him reading. He had the money—two hundred hundred-dollar bills—in a brown wallet.

419

"So far, so good. He's in the living-room reading. She's in the bedroom sleeping. Just the two of them in the apartment. A racket wakes her. She jumps out of bed, runs into the living-room. There's Main wrestling with a couple of men. One's tall and husky. The other's little—kind of girlish built. Both have got black handkerchiefs over their mugs and caps pulled down.

"When Mrs. Main shows, the little one breaks away from Main and sticks her up. Puts a gun in Mrs. Main's face and tells her to behave. Main and the other guy are still scuffling. Main has got his gun in his hand, but the thug has him by the wrist, trying to twist it. He makes it pretty soon—Main drops the rod. The thug flashes his own, holding Main off while he bends down to pick up the one that fell.

"When the man stoops, Main piles on him. He manages to knock the fellow's gun out of his hand, but by that time the fellow had got the one on the floor—the one Main had dropped. They're heaped up there for a couple of seconds. Mrs. Main can't see what's happening. Then bang! Main's falling away, his vest burning where the shot had set fire to it, a bullet in his heart, his gun smoking in the masked guy's fist. Mrs. Main passes out.

"When she comes to there's nobody in the apartment but herself and her dead husband. His wallet's gone, and so is his gun. She was unconscious for about half an hour. We know that, because other people heard the shot and could give us the time—even if they didn't know where it come from.

"The Mains' apartment is on the sixth floor. It's an eight-story building. Next door to it, on the corner of Eighteenth Avenue, is a two-story building—grocery downstairs, grocer's flat upstairs. Behind these buildings runs a narrow back street—an alley. All right.

"Kinney—the patrolman on that beat—was walking down Eighteenth Avenue. He heard the shot. It was clear to him, because the Mains' apartment is on that side of the building—the side overlooking the grocer's—but Kinney couldn't place it right away. He wasted time scouting around up the street. By the time he got down as far as the alley in his hunting, the birds had flown. Kinney found signs of 'em though—they had dropped a gun in the alley—the gun they'd taken from Main and shot him with. But Kinney didn't see 'em—didn't see anybody who might have been them.

"Now, from a hall window of the apartment house's third floor to the roof of the grocer's building is easy going. Anybody but a cripple could make it—in or out—and the window's never locked. From the grocer's roof to the back street is almost as easy. There's a cast iron pipe, a deep window, a door with heavy hinges sticking out—a regular ladder up and down that back wall. Begg and I did it without working up a sweat. The pair could have gone in that way. We know they left that way. On the grocer's roof we found Main's wallet—empty, of course—and a handkerchief. The wallet had metal corners. The handkerchief had caught on one of 'em, and went with it when the crooks tossed it away."

"Main's handkerchief?"

"A woman's—with an E in one corner."

"Mrs. Main's?"

"Her name is Agnes," Hacken said. "We showed her the wallet, the gun, and the handkerchief. She identified the first two as her husband's, but the handkerchief was a new one on her. However, she could give us the name of the perfume on it—*Dèsir du Cœur*. And—with it for a guide—she said the smaller of the masked pair could have been a woman. She had already described him as kind of girlish built."

"Any fingerprints, or the like?" I asked.

"No. Phels went over the apartment, the window, the roof, the wallet and the gun. Not a smear."

"Mrs. Main identify 'em?"

"She says she'd know the little one. Maybe she would."

"Got anything on the who?"

"Not yet," the lanky detective-sergeant said as we moved toward the door.

In the street I left the police sleuths and set out for Bruno Gungen's home in Westwood Park.

The dealer in rare and antique jewelry was a little bit of a man and a fancy one. His dinner jacket was corset-tight around his waist, padded high and sharp at the shoulders. Hair, mustache and spade-shaped goatee were dyed black and greased until they were as shiny as his pointed pink finger-nails. I wouldn't bet a cent that the color in his fifty-year-old cheeks wasn't rouge.

He came out of the depths of a leather library chair to give me a soft, warm hand that was no larger than a child's, bowing and smiling at me with his head tilted to one side.

Then he introduced me to his wife, who bowed without getting up from her seat at the table. Apparently she was a little more than a third of his age. She couldn't have been a day over nineteen, and she looked more like sixteen. She was as small as he, with a dimpled olive-skinned face, round brown eyes, a plump painted mouth and the general air of an expensive doll in a toy-store window.

Bruno Gungen explained to her at some length that I was connected with the Continental Detective Agency, and that he had employed me to help the police find Jeffrey Main's murderers and recover the stolen twenty thousand dollars.

She murmured, "Oh, yes!" in a tone that said she was not the least bit interested, and stood up, saying, "Then I'll leave you to—"

"No, no, my dear!" Her husband was waving his pink fingers at her. "I would have no secrets from you."

His ridiculous little face jerked around to me, cocked itself sidewise, and he asked, with a little giggle:

"Is not that so? That between husband and wife there should be no secrets?"

I pretended I agreed with him.

"You, I know, my dear," he addressed his wife, who had sat down again, "are as much interested in this as I, for did we not have an equal affection for dear Jeffrey? Is it not so?"

She repeated, "Oh, yes!" with the same lack of interest.

Her husband turned to me and said, "Now?" encouragingly.

"I've seen the police," I told him. "Is there anything you can add to their story? Anything new? Anything you didn't tell them?"

He whisked his face around toward his wife.

"Is there, Enid, dear?"

"I know of nothing," she replied.

He giggled and made a delighted face at me.

"That is it," he said. "We know of nothing."

"He came back to San Francisco eight o'clock Sunday night—three hours before he was killed and robbed—with twenty thousand dollars in hundred-dollar bills. What was he doing with it?"

"It was the proceeds of a sale to a customer," Bruno Gungen explained. "Mr. Nathaniel Ogilvie, of Los Angeles."

"But why cash?"

The little man's painted face screwed itself up into a shrewd leer.

"A bit of hanky-panky," he confessed complacently, "a trick of the trade, as one says. You know the genus collector? Ah, there is a study for you! Observe. I obtain a golden tiara of early Grecian workmanship, or let me be correct—purporting to be of early Grecian workmanship, purporting also to have been found in Southern Russia, near Odessa. Whether there is any truth in either of these suppositions I do not know, but certainly the tiara is a thing of beauty."

He giggled.

"Now I have a client, a Mr. Nathaniel Ogilvie, of Los Angeles, who has an appetite for curios of the sort—a very devil of a *cacoethes carpendi*.[*] The value of these items, you will comprehend, is exactly what one can get for them—no more, little less. This tiara—now ten thousand dollars is the least I could have expected for it, if sold

_____

[*] uncontrollable urge

as one sells an ordinary article of the sort. But can one call a golden cap made long ago for some forgotten Scythian king an ordinary article of any sort? No! No! So, swaddled in cotton, intricately packed, Jeffrey carries this tiara to Los Angeles to show our Mr. Ogilvie.

"In what manner the tiara came into our hands Jeffrey will not say. But he will hint at devious intrigues, smuggling, a little of violence and lawlessness here and there, the necessity for secrecy. For your true collector, there is the bait! Nothing is anything to him except as it is difficultly come by. Jeffrey will not lie. No! *Mon Dieu*, that would be dishonest, despicable! But he will suggest much, and he will refuse, oh, so emphatically! to take a check for the tiara. No check, my dear sir! Nothing which may be traced! Cash moneys!

"Hanky-panky, as you see. But where is the harm? Mr. Ogilvie is certainly going to buy the tiara, and our little deceit simply heightens his pleasure in his purchase. He will enjoy its possession so much the more. Besides, who is to say that this tiara is not authentic? If it is, then these things Jeffrey suggests are indubitably true. Mr. Ogilvie does buy it, for twenty thousand dollars, and that is why poor Jeffrey had in his possession so much cash money."

He flourished a pink hand at me, nodded his dyed head vigorously, and finished with:

"*Voilà!* That is it!"

"Did you hear from Main after he got back?" I asked.

The dealer smiled as if my question tickled him, turning his head so that the smile was directed at his wife.

"Did we, Enid, darling?" he passed on the question.

She pouted and shrugged her shoulders indifferently.

"The first we knew he had returned," Gungen interpreted these gestures to me, "was Monday morning, when we heard of his death. Is it not so, my dove?"

His dove murmured, "Yes," and left her chair, saying, "You'll excuse me? I have a letter to write."

"Certainly, my dear," Gungen told her as he and I stood up.

She passed close to him on her way to the door. His small nose twitched over his dyed mustache and he rolled his eyes in a caricature of ecstasy.

"What a delightful scent, my precious!" he exclaimed. "What a heavenly odor! What a song to the nostrils! Has it a name, my love?"

"Yes," she said, pausing in the doorway, not looking back.

"And it is?"

"*Désir du Cœur*," she replied over her shoulder as she left us.

Bruno Gungen looked at me and giggled.

I sat down again and asked him what he knew about Jeffrey Main.

"Everything, no less," he assured me. "For a dozen years, since he was a boy of eighteen he has been my right eye, my right hand."

"Well, what sort of man was he?"

Bruno Gungen showed me his pink palms side by side.

"What sort is any man?" he asked over them.

That didn't mean anything to me, so I kept quiet, waiting.

"I shall tell you," the little man began presently. "Jeffrey had the eye and the taste for this traffic of mine. No man living save myself alone has a judgment in these matters which I would prefer to Jeffrey's. And, honest, mind you! Let nothing I say mislead you on that point. Never a lock have I to which Jeffrey had not also the key, and might have it forever, if he had lived so long.

"But there is a but. In his private life, rascal is a word that only does him justice. He drank, he gambled, he loved, he spent—dear God, how he spent! He was, in this drinking and gaming and loving and spending, a most promiscuous fellow, beyond doubt. With moderation he had nothing to do. Of the moneys he got by inheritance, of the fifty thousand dollars or more his wife had when they were married, there is no remainder.

Fortunately, he was well insured—else his wife would have been left penniless. Oh, he was a true Heliogabalus,* that fellow!"

Bruno Gungen went down to the front door with me when I left. I said, "Good night," and walked down the gravel path to where I had left my car. The night was clear, dark, moonless. High hedges were black walls on both sides of the Gungen place. To the left there was a barely noticeable hole in the blackness—a dark-gray hole—oval—the size of a face.

I got into my car, stirred up the engine and drove away. Into the first cross-street I turned, parked the machine, and started back toward Gungen's afoot. I was curious about that face-size oval.

When I reached the corner, I saw a woman coming toward me from the direction of Gungen's. I was in the shadow of a wall. Cautiously, I backed away from the corner until I came to a gate with brick buttresses sticking out. I made myself flat between them.

The woman crossed the street, went on up the driveway, toward the car line. I couldn't make out anything about her, except that she was a woman. Maybe she was coming from Gungen's grounds, maybe not. Maybe it was her face I had seen against the hedge, maybe not. It was a heads or tails proposition. I guessed yes and tailed her up the drive.

Her destination was a drug store on the car line. Her business there was with the telephone. She spent ten minutes at it. I didn't go into the store to try for an earful, but stayed on the other side of the street, contenting myself with a good look at her.

She was a girl of about twenty-five, medium in height, chunky in build, with pale gray eyes that had little pouches under them, a thick nose and a prominent lower lip. She had no hat over her brown hair. Her body was wrapped in a long blue cape.

From the drug store I shadowed her back to the Gungen house. She went in the back door. A servant, probably, but not the maid who had opened the door for me earlier in the evening.

I returned to my car, drove back to town, to the office.

"Is Dick Foley working on anything?" I asked Fiske, who sits on the Continental Detective Agency's affairs at night.

"No. Did you ever hear the story about the fellow who had his neck operated on?"

With the slightest encouragement, Fiske is good for a dozen stories without a stop, so I said:

"Yes. Get hold of Dick and tell him I've got a shadow job out Westwood Park way for him to start on in the morning."

I gave Fiske—to be passed on to Dick—Gungen's address and a description of the girl who had done the phoning from the drug store. Then I assured the night man that I had also heard the story about the pickaninny named Opium, and likewise the one about what the old man said to his wife on their golden wedding anniversary. Before he could try me with another, I escaped to my own office, where I composed and coded a telegram to our Los Angeles branch, asking that Main's recent visit to that city be dug into.

The next morning Hacken and Begg dropped in to see me and I gave them Gungen's version of why the twenty thousand had been in cash. The police detectives told me a stool-pigeon had brought them word that Bunky Dahl—a local guerrilla who did a moderate business in hijacking—had been flashing a roll since about the time of Main's death.

"We haven't picked him up yet," Hacken said. "Haven't been able to place him, but we've got a line on his girl. Course, he might have got his dough somewhere else."

At ten o'clock that morning I had to go over to Oakland to testify against a couple of flimflammers who had sold bushels of stock in a sleight-of-hand rubber manufacturing business. When

---

* emperor of Rome, 218–22, with a lust for luxury

I got back to the agency, at six that evening, I found a wire from Los Angeles on my desk.

Jeffrey Main, the wire told me, had finished his business with Ogilvie Saturday afternoon, had checked out of his hotel immediately, and had left on the Owl that evening, which would have put him in San Francisco early Sunday morning. The hundred-dollar bills with which Ogilvie had paid for the tiara had been new ones, consecutively numbered, and Ogilvie's bank had given the Los Angeles operative the numbers.

Before I quit for the day, I phoned Hacken, gave him these numbers, as well as the other dope in the telegram.

"Haven't found Dahl yet," he told me.

Dick Foley's report came in the next morning. The girl had left the Gungen house at 9:15 the previous night, had gone to the corner of Miramar Avenue and Southwood Drive, where a man was waiting for her in a Buick coupe. Dick described him: Age about 30; height about five feet ten; slender, weight about 140; medium complexion; brown hair and eyes; long, thin face with pointed chin; brown hat, suit and shoes and gray overcoat.

The girl got into the car with him and they drove out to the beach, along the Great Highway for a little while, and then back to Miramar and Southwood, where the girl got out. She seemed to be going back to the house, so Dick let her go and tailed the man in the Buick down to the Futurity Apartments in Mason Street.

The man stayed in there for half an hour or so and then came out with another man and two women. This second man was of about the same age as the first, about five feet eight inches tall, would weigh about a hundred and seventy pounds, had brown hair and eyes, a dark complexion, a flat, broad face with high cheek bones, and wore a blue suit, gray hat, tan overcoat, black shoes, and a pear-shaped pearl tie-pin.

One of the women was about twenty-two years old, small, slender and blonde. The other was probably three or four years older, red-haired, medium in height and build, with a turned-up nose.

The quartet had got in the car and gone to the Algerian Café, where they had stayed until a little after one in the morning. Then they had returned to the Futurity Apartments. At half-past three the two men had left, driving the Buick to a garage in Post Street, and then walking to the Mars Hotel.

When I had finished reading this I called Mickey Linehan in from the operatives' room, gave him the report and instructions:

"Find out who these folks are."

Mickey went out. My phone rang.

Bruno Gungen: "Good morning. May you have something to tell me today?"

"Maybe," I said. "You're downtown?"

"Yes, in my shop. I shall be here until four."

"Right. I'll be in to see you this afternoon."

At noon Mickey Linehan returned. "The first bloke," he reported, "the one Dick saw with the girl, is named Benjamin Weel. He owns the Buick and lives in the Mars—room 410. He's a salesman, though it's not known what of. The other man is a friend of his who has been staying with him for a couple of days. I couldn't get anything on him. He's not registered. The two women in the Futurity are a couple of hustlers. They live in apartment 303. The larger one goes by the name of Mrs. Effie Roberts. The little blonde is Violet Evarts."

"Wait," I told Mickey, and went back into the file room, to the index-card drawers.

I ran through the W's—*Weel, Benjamin, alias Coughing Ben, 36,312W.*

The contents of folder No. 36,312W told me that Coughing Ben Weel had been arrested in Amador County in 1916 on a highgrading[*] charge and had been sent to San Quentin for three years. In 1922 he had been picked up again in Los Angeles and charged with trying to blackmail a movie actress, but the case

_____

* stealing processed gold ore

had fallen through. His description fit the one Dick had given of the man in the Buick. His photograph—a copy of the one taken by the Los Angeles police in '22—showed a sharp-featured young man with a chin like a wedge.

I took the photo back to my office and showed it to Mickey.

"This is Weel five years ago. Follow him around a while."

When the operative had gone I called the police detective bureau. Neither Hacken nor Begg was in. I got hold of Lewis, in the identification department.

"What does Bunky Dahl look like?" I asked him.

"Wait a minute," Lewis said, and then: "32, 67½, 174, medium, brown, brown, broad flat face with prominent cheek-bones, gold bridge work in lower left jaw, brown mole under right ear, deformed little toe on right foot."

"Have you a picture of him to spare?"

"Sure."

"Thanks, I'll send a boy down for it."

I told Tommy Howd to go down and get it, and then went out for some food. After luncheon I went up to Gungen's establishment in Post Street. The little dealer was gaudier than ever this afternoon in a black coat that was even more padded in the shoulders and tighter in the waist than his dinner coat had been the other night, striped gray pants, a vest that leaned toward magenta, and a billowy satin tie wonderfully embroidered with gold thread.

We went back through his store, up a narrow flight of stairs to a small cube of an office on the mezzanine floor.

"And now you have to tell me?" he asked when we were seated, with the door closed.

"I've got more to ask than tell. First, who is the girl with the thick nose, the thick lower lip, and the pouches under gray eyes, who lives in your house?"

"That is one Rose Rubury." His little painted face was wrinkled in a satisfied smile. "She is my dear wife's maid."

"She goes riding with an ex-convict."

"She does?" He stroked his dyed goatee with a pink hand, highly pleased. "Well, she is my dear wife's maid, that she is."

"Main didn't drive up from Los Angeles with a friend, as he told his wife. He came up on the train Saturday night—so he was in town twelve hours before he showed up at home."

Bruno Gungen giggled, cocking his delighted face to one side.

"Ah!" he tittered. "We progress! We progress! Is it not so?"

"Maybe. Do you remember if this Rose Rubury was in the house on Sunday night—say from eleven to twelve?"

"I do remember. She was. I know it certainly. My dear wife was not feeling well that night. My darling had gone out early that Sunday morning, saying she was going to drive out into the country with some friends—what friends I do not know. But she came home at eight o'clock that night complaining of a distressing headache. I was quite frightened by her appearance, so that I went often to see how she was, and thus it happens that I know her maid was in the house all of that night, until one o'clock, at least."

"Did the police show you the handkerchief they found with Main's wallet?"

"Yes." He squirmed on the edge of his chair, his face like the face of a kid looking at a Christmas tree.

"You're sure it's your wife's?"

His giggle interfered with his speech, so he said, "Yes," by shaking his head up and down until the goatee seemed to be a black whisk-broom brushing his tie.

"She could have left it at the Mains' some time when she was visiting Mrs. Main," I suggested.

"That is not possible," he corrected me eagerly. "My darling and Mrs. Main are not acquainted."

"But your wife and Main were acquainted?"

He giggled and brushed his tie with his whisker again.

"How well acquainted?"

He shrugged his padded shoulders up to his ears.

"I know not," he said merrily. "I employ a detective."

"Yeah?" I scowled at him. "You employ this one to find out who killed and robbed Main—and for nothing else. If you think you're employing him to dig up your family secrets, you're as wrong as Prohibition."

"But why? But why?" He was flustered. "Have I not the right to know? There will be no trouble over it, no scandal, no divorce suing, of that be assured. Even Jeffrey is dead, so it is what one calls ancient history. While he lived I knew nothing, was blind. After he died I saw certain things. For my own satisfaction—that is all, I beg you to believe—I should like to know with certainty."

"You won't get it out of me," I said bluntly. "I don't know anything about it except what you've told me, and you can't hire me to go further into it. Besides, if you're not going to do anything about it, why don't you keep your hands off—let it sleep?"

"No, no, my friend." He had recovered his bright-eyed cheerfulness. "I am not an old man, but I am fifty-two. My dear wife is eighteen, and a truly lovely person." He giggled. "This thing happened. May it not happen again? And would it not be the part of husbandly wisdom to have—shall I say—a hold on her? A rein? A check? Or if it never happen again, still might not one's dear wife be the more docile for certain information which her husband possesses?"

"It's your business." I stood up, laughing. "But I don't want any part of it."

"Ah, do not let us quarrel!" He jumped up and took one of my hands in his. "If you will not, you will not. But there remains the criminal aspect of the situation—the aspect that has engaged you thus far. You will not forsake that? You will fulfil your engagement there? Surely?"

"Suppose—just suppose—it should turn out that your wife had a hand in Main's death. What then?"

"That"—he shrugged, holding his hands out, palms up—"would be a matter for the law."

"Good enough. I'll stick—if you understand that you're entitled to no information except what touches your 'criminal aspect.'"

"Excellent! And if it so happens you cannot separate my darling from that—"

I nodded. He grabbed my hand again, patting it. I took it away from him and returned to the agency.

A memorandum on my desk asked me to phone detective-sergeant Hacken. I did.

"Bunky Dahl wasn't in on the Main job," the hatchet-faced man told me. "He and a pal named Coughing Ben Weel were putting on a party in a roadhouse near Vallejo that night. They were there from around ten until they were thrown out after two in the morning for starting a row. It's on the up-and-up. The guy that gave it to me is right—and I got a check-up on it from two others."

I thanked Hacken and phoned Gungen's residence, asking for Mrs. Gungen, asking her if she would see me if I came out there.

"Oh, yes," she said. It seemed to be her favorite expression, though the way she said it didn't express anything.

Putting the photos of Dahl and Weel in my pocket, I got a taxi and set out for Westwood Park. Using Fatima-smoke on my brains while I rode, I concocted a wonderful series of lies to be told my client's wife—a series that I thought would get me the information I wanted.

A hundred and fifty yards or so up the drive from the house I saw Dick Foley's car standing.

A thin, pasty-faced maid opened the Gungens' door and took me into a sitting room on the second floor, where Mrs. Gungen put down a copy of *The Sun Also Rises* and waved a cigarette at a nearby chair. She was very much the expensive doll this afternoon in a Persian orange dress, sitting with one foot tucked under her in a brocaded chair.

Looking at her while I lighted a cigarette, remembering my first interview with her and her husband, and my second one with him, I decided to chuck the tale-of-woe I had spent my ride building.

"You've a maid—Rose Rubury," I began. "I don't want her to hear what's said."

She said, "Very well," without the least sign of surprise, added, "Excuse me a moment," and left her chair and the room.

Presently she was back, sitting down with both feet tucked under her now.

"She will be away for at least half an hour."

"That will be long enough. This Rose is friendly with an ex-convict named Weel."

The doll face frowned, and the plump painted lips pressed themselves together. I waited, giving her time to say something. She didn't say it. I took Weel's and Dahl's pictures out and held them out to her.

"The thin-faced one is your Rose's friend. The other's a pal of his—also a crook."

She took the photographs with a tiny hand that was as steady as mine, and looked at them carefully. Her mouth became smaller and tighter, her brown eyes darker. Then, slowly, her face cleared, she murmured, "Oh, yes," and returned the pictures to me.

"When I told your husband about it"—I spoke deliberately—"he said, 'She's my wife's maid,' and laughed."

Enid Gungen said nothing.

"Well?" I asked. "What did he mean by that?"

"How should I know?" she sighed.

"You know your handkerchief was found with Main's empty wallet." I dropped this in a by-the-way tone, pretending to be chiefly occupied putting cigarette ash in a jasper tray that was carved in the form of a lidless coffin.

"Oh, yes," she said wearily, "I've been told that."

"How do you think it happened?"

"I can't imagine."

"I can," I said, "but I'd rather know positively. Mrs. Gungen, it would save a lot of time if we could talk plain language."

"Why not?" she asked listlessly. "You are in my husband's confidence, have his permission to question me. If it happens to be humiliating to me—well, after all, I am only his wife. And it is hardly likely that any new indignities either of you can devise will be worse than those to which I have already submitted."

I grunted at this theatrical speech and went ahead.

"Mrs. Gungen, I'm only interested in learning who robbed and killed Main. Anything that points in that direction is valuable to me, but only in so far as it points in that direction. Do you understand what I mean?"

"Certainly," she said. "I understand you are in my husband's employ."

That got us nowhere. I tried again:

"What impression do you suppose I got the other evening, when I was here?"

"I can't imagine."

"Please try."

"Doubtless"—she smiled faintly—"you got the impression that my husband thought I had been Jeffrey's mistress."

"Well?"

"Are you"—her dimples showed; she seemed amused—"asking me if I really was his mistress?"

"No—though of course I'd like to know."

"Naturally you would," she said pleasantly.

"What impression did you get that evening?" I asked.

"I?" She wrinkled her forehead. "Oh, that my husband had hired you to prove that I had been Jeffrey's mistress." She repeated the word mistress as if she liked the shape of it in her mouth.

"You were wrong."

"Knowing my husband, I find that hard to believe."

"Knowing myself, I'm sure of it," I insisted. "There's no uncertainty about it between your husband and me, Mrs. Gungen. It is understood that my job is to find who stole and killed—nothing else."

"Really?" It was a polite ending of an argument of which she had grown tired.

"You're tying my hands," I complained,

standing up, pretending I wasn't watching her carefully. "I can't do anything now but grab this Rose Rubury and the two men and see what I can squeeze out of them. You said the girl would be back in half an hour?"

She looked at me steadily with her round brown eyes.

"She should be back in a few minutes. You're going to question her?"

"But not here," I informed her. "I'll take her down to the Hall of Justice and have the men picked up. Can I use your phone?"

"Certainly. It's in the next room." She crossed to open the door for me.

I called Davenport 20 and asked for the detective bureau.

Mrs. Gungen, standing in the sitting room, said, so softly I could barely hear it:

"Wait."

Holding the phone, I turned to look through the door at her. She was pinching her red mouth between thumb and finger, frowning. I didn't put down the phone until she took the hand from her mouth and held it out toward me. Then I went back into the sitting-room.

I was on top. I kept my mouth shut. It was up to her to make the plunge. She studied my face for a minute or more before she began:

"I won't pretend I trust you." She spoke hesitantly, half as if to herself. "You're working for my husband, and even the money would not interest him so much as whatever I had done. It's a choice of evils—certain on the one hand, more than probable on the other."

She stopped talking and rubbed her hands together. Her round eyes were becoming indecisive. If she wasn't helped along she was going to balk.

"There's only the two of us," I urged her. "You can deny everything afterward. It's my word against yours. If you don't tell me—I know now I can get it from the others. Your calling me from the phone lets me know that. You think I'll tell your husband everything. Well, if I have to fry it out of the others, he'll probably read it all in the papers. Your one chance is to trust me. It's

not as slim a chance as you think. Anyway, it's up to you."

A half-minute of silence.

"Suppose," she whispered, "I should pay you to—"

"What for? If I'm going to tell your husband, I could take your money and still tell him, couldn't I?"

Her red mouth curved, her dimples appeared and her eyes brightened.

"That is reassuring," she said. "I shall tell you. Jeffrey came back from Los Angeles early so we could have the day together in a little apartment we kept. In the afternoon two men came in—with a key. They had revolvers. They robbed Jeffrey of the money. That was what they had come for. They seemed to know all about it and about us. They called us by name, and taunted us with threats of the story they would tell if we had them arrested.

"We couldn't do anything after they had gone. It was a ridiculously hopeless plight they had put us in. There wasn't anything we could do—since we couldn't possibly replace the money. Jeffrey couldn't even pretend he had lost it or had been robbed of it while he was alone. His secret early return to San Francisco would have been sure to throw suspicion on him. Jeffrey lost his head. He wanted me to run away with him. Then he wanted to go to my husband and tell him the truth. I wouldn't permit either course—they were equally foolish.

"We left the apartment, separating, a little after seven. We weren't, the truth is, on the best of terms by then. He wasn't—now that we were in trouble—as—No, I shouldn't say that."

She stopped and stood looking at me with a placid doll's face that seemed to have got rid of all its troubles by simply passing them to me.

"The pictures I showed you are the two men?" I asked.

"Yes."

"This maid of yours knew about you and Main? Knew about the apartment? Knew about his trip to Los Angeles and his plan to return early with the cash?"

"I can't say she did. But she certainly could have learned most of it by spying and eavesdropping and looking through my—I had a note from Jeffrey telling me about the Los Angeles trip, making the appointment for Sunday morning. Perhaps she could have seen it. I'm careless."

"I'm going now," I said. "Sit tight till you hear from me. And don't scare up the maid."

"Remember, I've told you nothing," she reminded me as she followed me to the sitting-room door.

From the Gungen house I went direct to the Mars Hotel. Mickey Linehan was sitting behind a newspaper in a corner of the lobby.

"They in?" I asked him.

"Yep."

"Let's go up and see them."

Mickey rattled his knuckles on door number 410. A metallic voice asked: "Who's there?"

"Package," Mickey replied in what was meant for a boy's voice.

A slender man with a pointed chin opened the door. I gave him a card. He didn't invite us into the room, but he didn't try to keep us out when we walked in.

"You're Weel?" I addressed him while Mickey closed the door behind us, and then, not waiting for him to say yes, I turned to the broad-faced man sitting on the bed. "And you're Dahl?"

Weel spoke to Dahl, in a casual, metallic voice:

"A couple of gumshoes."

The man on the bed looked at us and grinned. I was in a hurry.

"I want the dough you took from Main," I announced.

They sneered together, as if they had been practicing.

I brought out my gun.

Weel laughed harshly.

"Get your hat, Bunky," he chuckled. "We're being taken into custody."

"You've got the wrong idea," I explained.

"This isn't a pinch. It's a stick-up. Up go the hands!"

Dahl's hands went up quick. Weel hesitated until Mickey prodded him in the ribs with the nose of a .38-special.

"Frisk 'em," I ordered Mickey.

He went through Weel's clothes, taking a gun, some papers, some loose money, and a money-belt that was fat. Then he did the same for Dahl.

"Count it," I told him.

Mickey emptied the belts, spit on his fingers and went to work.

"Nineteen thousand, one hundred and twenty-six dollars and sixty-two cents," he reported when he was through.

With the hand that didn't hold my gun, I felt in my pocket for the slip on which I had written the numbers of the hundred-dollar bills Main had got from Ogilvie. I held the slip out to Mickey.

"See if the hundreds check against this."

He took the slip, looked, said, "They do."

"Good—pouch the money and the guns and see if you can turn up any more in the room."

Coughing Ben Weel had got his breath by now.

"Look here!" he protested. "You can't pull this, fellow! Where do you think you are? You can't get away with this!"

"I can try," I assured him. "I suppose you're going to yell, *Police*! Like hell you are! The only squawk you've got coming is at your own dumbness in thinking because your squeeze on the woman was tight enough to keep her from having you copped, you didn't have to worry about anything. I'm playing the same game you played with her and Main—only mine's better, because you can't get tough afterward without facing stir. Now shut up!"

"No more jack," Mickey said. "Nothing but four postage stamps."

"Take 'em along," I told him. "That's practically eight cents. Now we'll go."

"Hey, leave us a couple of bucks," Weel begged.

"Didn't I tell you to shut up?" I snarled at

him, backing to the door, which Mickey was opening.

The hall was empty. Mickey stood in it, holding his gun on Weel and Dahl while I backed out of the room and switched the key from the inside to the outside. Then I slammed the door, twisted the key, pocketed it, and we went downstairs and out of the hotel.

Mickey's car was around the corner. In it, we transferred our spoils—except the guns—from his pockets to mine. Then he got out and went back to the agency. I turned the car toward the building in which Jeffrey Main had been killed.

Mrs. Main was a tall girl of less than twenty-five, with curled brown hair, heavily-lashed gray-blue eyes, and a warm, full-featured face. Her ample body was dressed in black from throat to feet.

She read my card, nodded at my explanation that Gungen had employed me to look into her husband's death, and took me into a gray and white living room.

"This is the room?" I asked.

"Yes." She had a pleasant, slightly husky voice.

I crossed to the window and looked down on the grocer's roof, and on the half of the back street that was visible. I was still in a hurry.

"Mrs. Main," I said as I turned, trying to soften the abruptness of my words by keeping my voice low, "after your husband was dead, you threw the gun out the window. Then you stuck the handkerchief to the corner of the wallet and threw that. Being lighter than the gun, it didn't go all the way to the alley, but fell on the roof. Why did you put the handkerchief—?"

Without a sound she fainted.

I caught her before she reached the floor, carried her to a sofa, found Cologne and smelling salts, applied them.

"Do you know whose handkerchief it was?" I asked when she was awake and sitting up.

She shook her head from left to right.

"Then why did you take that trouble?"

"It was in his pocket. I didn't know what else

to do with it. I thought the police would ask about it. I didn't want anything to start them asking questions."

"Why did you tell the robbery story?"

No answer.

"The insurance?" I suggested.

She jerked up her head, cried defiantly:

"Yes! He had gone through his own money and mine. And then he had to—to do a thing like that. He—"

I interrupted her complaint:

"He left a note, I hope—something that will be evidence." Evidence that she hadn't killed him, I meant.

"Yes." She fumbled in the bosom of her black dress.

"Good," I said, standing. "The first thing in the morning, take that note down to your lawyer and tell him the whole story."

I mumbled something sympathetic and made my escape.

Night was coming down when I rang the Gungens' bell for the second time that day. The pasty-faced maid who opened the door told me Mr. Gungen was at home. She led me upstairs.

Rose Rubury was coming down the stairs. She stopped on the landing to let us pass. I halted in front of her while my guide went on toward the library.

"You're done, Rose," I told the girl on the landing. "I'll give you ten minutes to clear out. No word to anybody. If you don't like that—you'll get a chance to see if you like the inside of the can."

"Well—the idea!"

"The racket's flopped." I put a hand into a pocket and showed her one wad of the money I had got at the Mars Hotel. "I've just come from visiting Coughing Ben and Bunky."

That impressed her. She turned and scurried up the stairs.

Bruno Gungen came to the library door, searching for me. He looked curiously from the girl—now running up the steps to the third story—to me. A question was twisting the little man's lips, but I headed it off with a statement:

"It's done."

"Bravo!" he exclaimed as we went into the library. "You hear that, my darling? It is done!"

His darling, sitting by the table, where she had sat the other night, smiled with no expression in her doll's face, and murmured, "Oh, yes," with no expression in her words.

I went to the table and emptied my pockets of money.

"Nineteen thousand, one hundred and twenty-six dollars and seventy cents, including the stamps," I announced. "The other eight hundred and seventy-three dollars and thirty cents is gone."

"Ah!" Bruno Gungen stroked his spade-shaped black beard with a trembling pink hand and pried into my face with hard bright eyes. "And where did you find it? By all means sit down and tell us the tale. We are famished with eagerness for it, eh, my love?"

His love yawned, "Oh, yes!"

"There isn't much story," I said. "To recover the money I had to make a bargain, promising silence. Main was robbed Sunday afternoon. But it happens that we couldn't convict the robbers if we had them. The only person who could identify them—won't."

"But who killed Jeffrey?" The little man was pawing my chest with both pink hands. "Who killed him that night?"

"Suicide. Despair at being robbed under circumstances he couldn't explain."

"Preposterous!" My client didn't like the suicide.

"Mrs. Main was awakened by the shot. Suicide would have canceled his insurance—would

have left her penniless. She threw the gun and wallet out the window, hid the note he left, and framed the robber story."

"But the handkerchief!" Gungen screamed. He was all worked up.

"That doesn't mean anything," I assured him solemnly, "except that Main—you said he was promiscuous—had probably been fooling with your wife's maid, and that she—like a lot of maids—helped herself to your wife's belongings."

He puffed up his rouged cheeks, and stamped his feet, fairly dancing. His indignation was as funny as the statement that caused it.

"We shall see!" He spun on his heel and ran out of the room, repeating over and over, "We shall see!"

Enid Gungen held a hand out to me. Her doll face was all curves and dimples.

"I thank you," she whispered.

"I don't know what for," I growled, not taking the hand. "I've got it jumbled so anything like proof is out of the question. But he can't help knowing—didn't I practically tell him?"

"Oh, that!" She put it behind her with a toss of her small head. "I'm quite able to look out for myself so long as he has no definite proof."

I believed her.

Bruno Gungen came fluttering back into the library, frothing at the mouth, tearing his dyed goatee, raging that Rose Rubury was not to be found in the house.

The next morning Dick Foley told me the maid had joined Weel and Dahl and had left for Portland with them.

MYSTERY STORIES, JANUARY 1928

This King Business

A COMPLETE NOVELETTE

BY DASHIELL HAMMETT

The desire to rule is inherent in the breasts of most of us, notwithstanding the number of thrones that have toppled in the past decade. Mr. Hammett tells us of the strange series of events which led an American youth to seek kingship in "the Powder Magazine of Europe"—the Balkans. The consequences were—to put it mildly—exciting.

CHAPTER I

"YES"—AND "NO"

The train from Belgrade set me down in Stefania, capital of Muravia, in early afternoon—a rotten afternoon. Cold wind blew cold rain in my face and down my neck as I left the square granite barn of a railroad station to climb into a taxicab.

English meant nothing to the chauffeur, nor French. Good German might have failed. Mine wasn't good. It was a hodgepodge of grunts and gargles. This chauffeur was the first person who had ever pretended to understand it. I suspected him of guessing, and I expected to be taken to some distant suburban point. Maybe he was a good guesser. Anyhow, he took me to the Hotel of the Republic.

The hotel was a new six-story affair, very proud of its elevators, American plumbing, private baths, and other modern tricks. After I had washed and changed clothes I went down to the café for luncheon. Then, supplied with minute instructions in English, French, and sign-language by a highly uniformed head porter, I turned up my raincoat collar and crossed the muddy plaza to call on Roy Scanlan, United States *chargé d'affaires* in this youngest and smallest of the Balkan States.

He was a pudgy man of thirty, with smooth hair already far along the gray route, a nervous, flabby face, plump white hands that twitched, and very nice clothes. He shook hands with me, patted me into a chair, barely glanced at my letter of introduction, and stared at my necktie while saying:

"So you're a private detective from San Francisco?"

"Yes."

"And?"

"Lionel Grantham."

"Surely not!"

"Yes."

"But he's—" The diplomat realized he was looking into my eyes, hurriedly switched his gaze to my hair, and forgot what he had started to say.

"But he's what?" I prodded him.

"Oh!"—with a vague upward motion of head and eyebrows—"not that sort."

"How long has he been here?" I asked.

"Two months. Possibly three or three and a half or more."

"You know him well?"

"Oh, no! By sight, of course, and to talk to. He and I are the only Americans here, so we're fairly well acquainted."

"Know what he's doing here?"

"No, I don't. He just happened to stop here in his travels, I imagine, unless, of course, he's here for some special reason. No doubt there's a girl in it—she is General Radnjak's daughter—though I don't think so."

"How does he spend his time?"

"I really haven't any idea. He lives at the Hotel of the Republic, is quite a favorite among our foreign colony, rides a bit, lives the usual life of a young man of family and wealth."

"Mixed up with anybody who isn't all he ought to be?"

"Not that I know of, except that I've seen him with Mahmoud and Einarson. They are certainly scoundrels, though they may not be."

"Who are they?"

"Nubar Mahmoud is private secretary to Doctor Semich, the President. Colonel Einarson is an Icelander, just now virtually the head of the army. I know nothing about either of them."

"Except that they are scoundrels?"

The *chargé d'affaires* wrinkled his round white forehead in pain and gave me a reproachful glance.

"Not at all," he said. "Now, may I ask, of what is Grantham suspected?"

"Nothing."

"Then?"

"Seven months ago, on his twenty-first birthday, this Lionel Grantham got hold of the money his father had left him—a nice wad. Till then the boy had had a tough time of it. His mother had, and has, highly developed middle-class notions of refinement. His father had been a genuine aristocrat in the old manner—a hard-souled, soft-spoken individual who got what he wanted by simply taking it; with a liking for old wine and young women, and plenty of both, and for cards and dice and running horses—and fights, whether he was in them or watching them.

"While he lived the boy had a he-raising. Mrs. Grantham thought her husband's tastes low, but he was a man who had things his own way. Besides, the Grantham blood was the best in America. She was a woman to be impressed by that. Eleven years ago—when Lionel was a kid of ten—the old man died. Mrs. Grantham swapped the family roulette wheel for a box of dominoes and began to convert the kid into a patent leather Galahad.

"I've never seen him, but I'm told the job wasn't a success. However, she kept him bundled up for eleven years, not even letting him escape to college. So it went until the day when he was legally of age and in possession of his share of his father's estate. That morning he kisses Mamma and tells her casually that he's off for a little run around the world—alone. Mamma does and says all that might be expected of her, but it's no good. The Grantham blood is up. Lionel promises to drop her a post-card now and then, and departs.

"He seems to have behaved fairly well during his wandering. I suppose just being free gave him all the excitement he needed. But a few weeks ago the trust company that handles his affairs got instructions from him to turn some railroad bonds into cash and ship the money to him in care of a Belgrade bank. The amount was large—over the three million mark—so the trust company told Mrs. Grantham about it. She chucked a fit. She had been getting letters from him—from Paris, without a word said about Belgrade.

"Mamma was all for dashing over to Europe at once. Her brother, Senator Walbourn, talked her out of it. He did some cabling, and learned that Lionel was neither in Paris nor in Belgrade, unless he was hiding. Mrs. Grantham packed her trunks and made reservations. The Senator headed her off again, convincing her that the lad would resent her interference, telling her the best thing was to investigate on the quiet. He brought the job to the agency. I went to Paris, learned that a friend of Lionel's there was relaying his mail, and that Lionel was here in Stefania. On the way down I stopped off in Belgrade and learned that the money was being sent here to him—most of it already has been. So here I am."

Scanlan smiled happily.

"There's nothing I can do," he said. "Grantham is of age, and it's his money."

"Right," I agreed, "and I'm in the same fix. All I can do is poke around, find out what he's up to, try to save his dough if he's being gypped. Can't you give me even a guess at the answer? Three million dollars—what could he put it into?"

"I don't know." The *chargé d'affaires* fidgeted uncomfortably. "There's no business here that amounts to anything. It's purely an agricultural country, split up among small land-owners— ten, fifteen, twenty acre farms. There's his association with Einarson and Mahmoud, though. They'd certainly rob him if they got the chance. I'm positive they're robbing him. But I don't think they would. Perhaps he isn't acquainted with them. It's probably a woman."

"Well, whom should I see? I'm handicapped by not knowing the country, not knowing the language. To whom can I take my story and get help?"

"I don't know," he said gloomily. Then his face brightened. "Go to Vasilije Djudakovich. He is Minister of Police. He is the man for you! He can help you, and you may trust him. He has a digestion instead of a brain. He'll not understand a thing you tell him. Yes, Djudakovich is your man!"

"Thanks," I said, and staggered out into the muddy street.

CHAPTER II

ROMAINE

I found the Minister of Police's offices in the Administration Building, a gloomy concrete pile next to the Executive Residence at the head of the plaza. In French that was even worse than my German, a thin, white-whiskered clerk, who looked like a consumptive Santa Claus, told me His Excellency was not in. Looking solemn, lowering my voice to a whisper, I repeated that I had come from the United States *chargé d'affaires*. This hocus-pocus seemed to impress Saint Nicholas. He nodded understandingly and shuffled out of the room. Presently he was back, bowing at the door, asking me to follow him.

I tailed him along a dim corridor to a wide door marked "15." He opened it, bowed me through it, wheezed, "*Asseyez-vous, s'il vous plaît*," closed the door and left me. I was in an office, a large, square one. Everything in it was large. The four windows were double-size. The chairs were young benches, except the leather one at the desk, which could have been the rear half of a touring car. A couple of men could have slept on the desk. Twenty could have eaten at the table.

A door opposite the one through which I had come opened, and a girl came in, closing the door behind her, shutting out a throbbing purr, as of some heavy machine, that had sounded through.

"I'm Romaine Frankl," she said in English, "His Excellency's secretary. Will you tell me what you wish?"

She might have been any age from twenty to thirty, something less than five feet in height, slim without boniness, with curly hair as near black as brown can get, black-lashed eyes whose gray irises had black rims, a small, delicate-featured face, and a voice that seemed too soft and faint to carry as well as it did. She wore a red woolen dress that had no shape except that which her body gave it, and when she moved—to walk or raise a hand—it was as if it cost her no energy—as if some one else were moving her.

"I'd like to see him," I said while I was accumulating this data.

"Later, certainly," she promised, "but it's impossible now." She turned, with her peculiar effortless grace, back to the door, opening it so that the throbbing purr sounded in the room again. "Hear?" she said. "He's taking his nap."

She shut the door against His Excellency's snoring and floated across the room to climb up in the immense leather chair at the desk.

"Do sit down," she said, wriggling a tiny forefinger at a chair beside the desk. "It will save time if you will tell me your business, because, unless you speak our tongue, I'll have to interpret your message to His Excellency."

I told her about Lionel Grantham and my interest in him, in practically the same words I had used on Scanlan, winding up:

"You see, there's nothing I can do except try to learn what the boy's up to and give him a hand if he needs it. I can't go to him—he's too much Grantham, I'm afraid, to take kindly to what he'd think was nurse-maid stuff. Mr. Scanlan advised me to come to the Minister of Police."

"You were fortunate." She looked as if she wanted to make a joke about my country's representative but weren't sure how I'd take it. "Your *chargé d'affaires* is not always easy to understand."

"Once you get the hang of it, it's not hard," I said. "You just throw out all his statements that have *no's* or *not's* or *nothing's* or *don't's* in them."

"That's it! That's it, exactly!" She leaned toward me, laughing. "I've always known there was some key to it, but nobody's been able to find it before. You've solved our national problem."

"For reward, then, I should be given all the information you have about Grantham."

"You should, but I'll have to speak to His Excellency first. He'll wake presently."

"You can tell me unofficially what you think of Grantham. You know him?"

"Yes. He's charming. A nice boy, delightfully naïf, inexperienced, but really charming."

"Who are his friends here?"

She shook her head and said:

"No more of that until His Excellency wakes. You're from San Francisco? I remember the funny little street cars, and the fog, and the salad right after the soup, and Coffee Dan's."*

"You've been there?"

"Twice. I was in the United States for a year and half, in vaudeville, bringing rabbits out of hats."

We were still talking about that half an hour later when the door opened and the Minister of Police came in.

The over-size furniture immediately shrank to normal, the girl became a midget, and I felt like somebody's little boy.

This Vasilije Djudakovich stood nearly seven feet tall, and that was nothing to his girth. Maybe he wouldn't weigh more than five hundred pounds, but, looking at him, it was hard to think except in terms of tons. He was a blond-haired, blond-bearded mountain of meat in a black frock coat. He wore a necktie, so I suppose he had a collar, but it was hidden all the way around by the red rolls of his neck. His white vest was the size and shape of a hoop-skirt, and in spite of that it strained at the buttons. His eyes were almost invisible between the cushions

---

* A cabaret popular with elite customers. It operated at the corner of Powell and O'Farrell Streets after the 1906 earthquake.

of flesh around them, and were shaded into a colorless darkness, like water in a deep well. His mouth was a fat red oval among the yellow hairs of his whiskers and mustache. He came into the room slowly, ponderously, and I was surprised that the floor didn't creak nor the room tremble.

Romaine Frankl was watching me attentively as she slid out of the big leather chair and introduced me to the Minister. He gave me a fat, sleepy smile and a hand that had the general appearance of a naked baby, and let himself down slowly into the chair the girl had quit. Planted there, he lowered his head until it rested on the pillows of his several chins, and then he seemed to go to sleep.

I drew up another chair for the girl. She took another sharp look at me—she seemed to be hunting for something in my face—and began to talk to him in what I suppose was the native lingo. She talked rapidly for about twenty minutes, while he gave no sign that he was listening or that he was even awake.

When she was through, he said: "*Da*." He spoke dreamily, but there was a volume to the syllable that could have come from no place smaller than his gigantic belly.

The girl turned to me, smiling.

"His Excellency will be glad to give you every possible assistance. Officially, of course, he does not care to interfere in the affairs of a visitor from another country, but he realizes the importance of keeping Mr. Grantham from being victimized while here. If you will return tomorrow afternoon, at, say, three o'clock . . ."

I promised to do that, thanked her, shook hands with the mountain again, and went out into the rain.

CHAPTER III

SHADOWING

Back at the hotel, I had no trouble learning that Lionel Grantham occupied a suite on the sixth floor and was in it at that time. I had his photograph in my pocket and his description in my head. I spent what was left of the afternoon and the early evening waiting for a look at him. At a little after seven I got it.

He stepped out of the elevator, a tall, flat-backed boy with a supple body that tapered from broad shoulders to narrow hips, carried erectly on long, muscular legs—the sort of frame that tailors like. His pink, regular-featured, really handsome face wore an expression of aloof superiority that was too marked to be anything else than a cover for youthful self-consciousness.

Lighting a cigarette, he passed into the street. The rain had stopped, though clouds overhead promised more shortly. He turned down the street afoot. So did I.

We went to a much gilded restaurant two blocks from the hotel, where a gypsy orchestra played on a little balcony stuck insecurely high on one wall. All the waiters and half the diners seemed to know the boy. He bowed and smiled to this side and that as he walked down to a table near the far end, where two men were waiting for him.

One of them was tall and thick-bodied, with bushy dark hair and a flowing dark mustache. His florid, short-nosed face wore the expression of a man who doesn't mind a fight now and then. This one was dressed in a green and gold military uniform, with high boots of the shiniest black leather. His companion was in evening clothes, a plump, swarthy man of medium height, with oily black hair and a suave, oval face.

While young Grantham joined this pair I found a table some distance from them for myself. I ordered dinner and looked around at my neighbors. There was a sprinkling of uniforms in the room, some dress coats and evening gowns, but most of the diners were in ordinary daytime clothes. I saw a couple of faces that were probably British, a Greek or two, a few Turks. The food was good and so was my appetite. I was smoking a cigarette over a tiny cup of syrupy coffee when Grantham and the big florid officer got up and went away.

I couldn't have got my bill and paid it in time to follow them, without raising a disturbance, so I let them go. Then I settled for my meal and waited until the dark, plump man they had left behind called for his check. I was in the street a minute or more ahead of him, standing, looking up toward the dimly electric-lighted plaza with what was meant for the expression of a tourist who didn't quite know where to go next.

He passed me, going up the muddy street with the soft, careful-where-you-put-your-foot tread of a cat.

A soldier—a bony man in sheepskin coat and cap, with a gray mustache bristling over gray, sneering lips—stepped out of a dark doorway and stopped the swarthy man with whining words.

The swarthy man lifted hands and shoulders in a gesture that held both anger and surprise.

The soldier whined again, but the sneer on his gray mouth became more pronounced. The plump man's voice was low, sharp, angry, but he moved a hand from pocket to soldier, and the brown of Muravian paper money showed in the hand. The soldier pocketed the money, raised a hand in a salute, and went across the street.

When the swarthy man had stopped staring after the soldier, I moved toward the corner around which sheepskin coat and cap had vanished. My soldier was a block and a half down the street, striding along with bowed head. He was in a hurry. I got plenty of exercise keeping up with him. Presently the city began to thin out. The thinner it got, the less I liked this expedition. Shadowing is at its best in daytime, downtown in a familiar large city. This was shadowing at its worst.

He led me out of the city along a cement road bordered by few houses. I stayed as far back as I could, so he was a faint, blurred shadow ahead. He turned a sharp bend in the road. I hustled toward the bend, intending to drop back again as soon as I had rounded it. Speeding, I nearly gummed the works.

The soldier suddenly appeared around the curve, coming toward me.

A little behind me, a small pile of lumber on the roadside was the only cover within a hundred feet. I stretched my short legs thither.

Irregularly piled boards made a shallow cavity in one end of the pile, almost large enough to hold me. On my knees in the mud, I huddled into that cavity.

The soldier came into sight through a chink between boards. Bright metal gleamed in one of his hands. A knife, I thought. But when he halted in front of my shelter I saw it was a revolver of the old-style nickel-plated sort.

He stood still, looking at my shelter, looking up the road and down the road. He grunted, came toward me. Slivers stung my cheek as I rubbed myself flatter against the timber-ends. My gun was with my blackjack—in my Gladstone bag, in my room in my hotel. A fine place to have them now! The soldier's gun was bright in his hand.

Rain began to patter on boards and ground. The soldier turned up the collar of his coat as he came. Nobody ever did anything I liked more. A man stalking another wouldn't have done that. He didn't know I was there. He was hunting a hiding place for himself. The game was even. If he found me, he had the gun, but I had seen him first.

His sheepskin coat rasped against the wood as he went by me, bending low as he passed my corner for the back of the pile, so close to me that the same raindrops seemed to be hitting both of us. I undid my fists after that. I couldn't see him, but I could hear him breathing, scratching himself, even humming.

A couple of weeks went by.

The mud I was kneeling in soaked through my pants-legs, wetting my knees and shins. The rough wood filed skin off my face every time I breathed. My mouth was as dry as my knees were wet, because I was breathing through it for silence.

An automobile came around the bend, headed for the city. I heard the soldier grunt softly, heard the click of his gun as he cocked it. The car came abreast, went on. The soldier blew out his breath and started scratching himself and humming again.

Another couple of weeks passed.

Men's voices came through the rain, barely audible, louder, quite clear. Four soldiers in sheepskin coats and hats walked down the road the way we had come, their voices presently shrinking into silence as they disappeared around the curve.

In the distance an automobile horn barked two ugly notes. The soldier grunted—a grunt that said clearly: "Here it is." His feet slopped in the mud, and the lumber pile creaked under his weight. I couldn't see what he was up to.

White light danced around the bend in the road, and an automobile came into view—a high-powered car going cityward with a speed that paid no attention to the wet slipperiness of the road. Rain and night and speed blurred its two occupants, who were in the front seat.

Over my head a heavy revolver roared. The soldier was working. The speeding car swayed crazily along the wet cement, its brakes screaming.

When the sixth shot told me the nickel-plated gun was probably empty, I jumped out of my hollow.

The soldier was leaning over the lumber pile, his gun still pointing at the skidding car while he peered through the rain.

He turned as I saw him, swung the gun around to me, snarled an order I couldn't understand. I was betting the gun was empty. I raised both hands high over my head, made an astonished face, and kicked him in the belly.

He folded over on me, wrapping himself around my leg. We both went down. I was underneath, but his head was against my thigh. His cap fell off. I caught his hair with both hands and yanked myself into a sitting position. His teeth went into my leg. I called him disagreeable things and put my thumbs in the hollows under his ears. It didn't take much pressure to teach him that he oughtn't to bite people. When

he lifted his face to howl, I put my right fist in it, pulling him into the punch with my left hand in his hair. It was a nice solid sock.

I pushed him off my leg, got up, took a handful of his coat collar, and dragged him out into the road.

CHAPTER IV

INTRODUCTIONS

White light poured over us. Squinting into it, I saw the automobile standing down the road, its spotlight turned on me and my sparring partner. A big man in green and gold came into the light—the florid officer who had been one of Grantham's companions in the restaurant. An automatic was in one of his hands.

He strode over to us, stiff-legged in his high boots, ignored the soldier on the ground, and examined me carefully with sharp little dark eyes.

"British?" he asked.

"American."

He bit a corner of his mustache and said meaninglessly:

"Yes, that is better."

His English was guttural, with a German accent.

Lionel Grantham came from the car to us. His face wasn't as pink as it had been.

"What is it?" he asked the officer, but he looked at me.

"I don't know," I said. "I took a stroll after dinner and got mixed up on my directions. Finding myself out here, I decided I was headed the wrong way. When I turned around to go back I saw this fellow duck behind the lumber pile. He had a gun in his hand. I took him for a stick-up, so I played Indian on him. Just as I got to him he jumped up and began spraying you people. I reached him in time to spoil his aim. Friend of yours?"

"You're an American," the boy said. "I'm Lionel Grantham. This is Colonel Einarson. We're very grateful to you." He screwed up his forehead and looked at Einarson. "What do you think of it?"

The officer shrugged his shoulders, growled, "One of my children—we'll see," and kicked the ribs of the man on the ground.

The kick brought the soldier to life. He sat up, rolled over on hands and knees, and began a broken, long-winded entreaty, plucking at the Colonel's tunic with dirty hands.

"Ach!" Einarson knocked the hands down with a tap of pistol barrel across knuckles, looked with disgust at the muddy marks on his tunic, and growled an order.

The soldier jumped to his feet, stood at attention, got another order, did an about-face, and marched to the automobile. Colonel Einarson strode stiff-legged behind him, holding his automatic to the man's back. Grantham put a hand on my arm.

"Come along," he said. "We'll thank you properly and get better acquainted after we've taken care of this fellow."

Colonel Einarson got into the driver's seat, with the soldier beside him. Grantham waited while I found the soldier's revolver. Then we got into the rear seat. The officer looked doubtfully at me out of his eye-corners, but said nothing. He drove the car back the way it had come. He liked speed, and we hadn't far to go. By the time we were settled in our seats the car was whisking us through a gateway in a high stone wall, with a sentry on each side presenting arms. We did a sliding half-circle into a branching driveway and jerked to a stand-still in front of a square white-washed building.

Einarson prodded the soldier out ahead of him. Grantham and I got out. To the left, a row of long, low buildings showed pale gray in the rain—barracks. The door of the square, white building was opened by a bearded orderly in green. We went in. Einarson pushed his prisoner across the small reception hall and through the open door of a bedroom. Grantham and I followed them in. The orderly stopped in the door-way, traded some words with Einarson, and went away, closing the door.

The room we were in looked like a cell, except that there were no bars over the one small window. It was a narrow room, with bare, white-washed walls and ceiling. The wooden floor, scrubbed with lye until it was almost as white as the walls, was bare. For furniture there was a black iron cot, three folding chairs of wood and canvas, and an unpainted chest of drawers, with comb, brush, and a few papers on top. That was all.

"Be seated, gentlemen," Einarson said, indicating the camp chairs. "We'll get at this thing now."

The boy and I sat down. The officer laid his pistol on the top of the chest of drawers, rested one elbow beside the pistol, took a corner of his mustache in one big red hand, and addressed the soldier. His voice was kindly, paternal. The soldier, standing rigidly upright in the middle of the floor, replied, whining, his eyes focused on the officer's with a blank, in-turned look.

They talked for five minutes or more. Impatience grew in the Colonel's voice and manner. The soldier kept his blank abjectness. Einarson ground his teeth together and looked angrily at the boy and me.

"This pig!" he exclaimed, and began to bellow at the soldier.

Sweat sprang out on the soldier's gray face, and he cringed out of his military stiffness. Einarson stopped bellowing at him and yelled two words at the door. It opened and the bearded orderly came in with a short, thick, leather whip. At a nod from Einarson, he put the whip beside the automatic on the top of the chest of drawers and went out.

The soldier whimpered. Einarson spoke curtly to him. The soldier shuddered, began to unfasten his coat with shaking fingers, pleading all the while with whining, stuttering words. He took off his coat, his green blouse, his gray undershirt, letting them fall on the floor, and stood there, his hairy, not exactly clean body naked from the waist up. He worked his fingers together and cried.

Einarson grunted a word. The soldier stiffened at attention, hands at sides, facing us, his left side to Einarson.

Slowly Colonel Einarson removed his own belt, unbuttoned his tunic, took it off, folded it carefully, and laid it on the cot. Beneath it he wore a white cotton shirt. He rolled the sleeves up above his elbows and picked up the whip.

"This pig!" he said again.

Lionel Grantham stirred uneasily on his chair. His face was white, his eyes dark.

CHAPTER V

A FLOGGING

Leaning his left elbow on the chest of drawers again, playing with his mustache-end with his left hand, standing indolently cross-legged, Einarson began to flog the soldier. His right arm raised the whip, brought the lash whistling down to the soldier's back, raised it again, brought it down again. It was especially nasty because he was not hurrying himself, not exerting himself. He meant to flog the man until he got what he wanted, and he was saving his strength so that he could keep it up as long as necessary.

With the first blow the terror went out of the soldier's eyes. They dulled sullenly and his lips stopped twitching. He stood woodenly under the beating, staring over Grantham's head. The officer's face had also become expressionless. Anger was gone. He showed no pleasure in his work, not even that of relieving his feelings. His air was the air of a stoker shoveling coal, of a carpenter sawing a board, of a stenographer typing a letter. Here was a job to be done in a workmanlike manner, without haste or excitement or wasted effort, without either enthusiasm or repulsion. It was nasty, but it taught me respect for this Colonel Einarson.

Lionel Grantham sat on the edge of his folding chair, staring at the soldier with white-ringed eyes. I offered the boy a cigarette, making an unnecessarily complicated operation out of lighting it and my own—to break up his score-keeping. He had been counting the strokes, and that wasn't good for him.

The whip curved up, swished down, cracked on the naked back—up, down, up, down. Einarson's florid face took on the damp glow of moderate exercise. The soldier's gray face was a lump of putty. He was facing Grantham and me. We couldn't see the marks of the whip.

Grantham said something to himself in a whisper. Then he gasped:

"I can't stand this!"

Einarson didn't look around from his work.

"Don't stop it now," I muttered. "We've gone this far."

The boy got up unsteadily and went to the window, opened it and stood looking out into the rainy night. Einarson paid no attention to him. He was putting more weight into the whipping now, standing with his feet far apart, leaning forward a little, his left hand on his hip, his right carrying the whip up and down with increasing swiftness.

The soldier swayed and a sob shook his hairy chest. The whip cut—cut—cut. I looked at my watch. Einarson had been at it for forty minutes, and looked good for the rest of the night.

The soldier moaned and turned toward the officer. Einarson did not break the rhythm of his stroke. The lash cut the man's shoulder. I caught a glimpse of his back—raw meat. Einarson spoke sharply. The soldier jerked himself to attention again, his left side to the officer. The whip went on with its work—up, down, up, down, up, down.

The soldier flung himself on hands and knees at Einarson's feet and began to pour out sob-broken words. Einarson looked down at him, listening carefully, holding the lash of the whip in his left hand, the butt still in his right. When the man had finished, Einarson asked questions, got answers, nodded, and the soldier stood up. Einarson put a friendly hand on the man's shoulder, turned him around, looked at his mangled red back, and said something in a sympathetic tone. Then he called the orderly in and gave him some orders. The soldier, moaning as he bent, picked up his discarded clothes and followed the orderly out of the bedroom.

Einarson tossed the whip up on top of the chest of drawers and crossed to the bed to pick up his tunic. A leather pocketbook slid from an inside pocket to the floor. When he recovered it, a soiled newspaper clipping slipped out and floated across to my feet. I picked it up and gave it back to him—a photograph of a man, the Shah of Persia, according to the French caption under it.

"That pig!" he said—meaning the soldier, not the Shah—as he put on his tunic and buttoned it. "He has a son, also until last week of my troops. This son drinks too much of wine. I reprimand him. He is insolent. What kind of army is it without discipline? Pigs! I knock this pig down, and he produces a knife. Ach! What kind of army is it where a soldier may attack his officers with knives? After I—personally, you comprehend—have finished with this swine, I have him court-martialed and sentenced to twenty years in the prison. This elder pig, his father, does not like that. So he will shoot me to-night. Ach! What kind of army is that?"

Lionel Grantham came away from his window. His young face was haggard. His young eyes were ashamed of the haggardness of his face.

Colonel Einarson made me a stiff bow and a formal speech of thanks for spoiling the soldier's aim—which I hadn't—and saving his life. Then the conversation turned to my presence in Muravia. I told them briefly that I had held a captain's commission in the military intelligence department during the war. That much was the truth, and that was all the truth I gave them. After the war—so my fairy tale went—I had decided to stay in Europe, had taken my discharge there and had drifted around, doing

odd jobs at one place and another. I was vague, trying to give them the impression that those odd jobs had not always, or usually, been ladylike. I gave them more definite—though still highly imaginary—details of my recent employment with a French syndicate, admitting that I had come to this corner of the world because I thought it better not to be seen in Western Europe for a year or so.

"Nothing I could be jailed for," I said, "but things could be made uncomfortable for me. So I roamed over into *Mitteleuropa*, learned that I might find a connection in Belgrade, got there to find it a false alarm, and came on down here. I may pick up something here. I've got a date with the Minister of Police to-morrow. I think I can show him where he can use me."

"The gross Djudakovich!" Einarson said with frank contempt. "You find him to your liking?"

"No work, no eat," I said.

"Einarson," Grantham began quickly, hesitated, said: "Couldn't we—don't you think—" and didn't finish.

The Colonel frowned at him, saw I had noticed the frown, cleared his throat, and addressed me in a gruffly hearty tone:

"Perhaps it would be well if you did not too speedily engage yourself to this fat minister. It may be—there is a possibility that we know of another field where your talents might find employment more to your taste—and profit."

I let the matter stand there, saying neither yes nor no.

CHAPTER VI

CARDS ON THE TABLE

We returned to the city in the officer's car. He and Grantham sat in the rear. I sat beside the soldier who drove. The boy and I got out at our hotel. Einarson said good night and was driven away as if he were in a hurry.

"It's early," Grantham said as we went indoors. "Come up to my room."

I stopped at my own room to wash off the mud I'd gathered around the lumber stack and to change my clothes, and then went up with him. He had three rooms on the top floor, overlooking the plaza.

He set out a bottle of whisky, a syphon, lemons, cigars and cigarettes, and we drank, smoked, and talked. Fifteen or twenty minutes of the talk came from no deeper than the mouth on either side—comments on the night's excitement, our opinions of Stefania, and so on. Each of us had something to say to the other. Each was weighing the other in before he said it.

I decided to put mine over first.

"Colonel Einarson was spoofing us to-night," I said.

"Spoofing?" The boy sat up straight, blinking.

"His soldier shot for money, not revenge."

"You mean—?" His mouth stayed open.

"I mean the little dark man you ate with gave the soldier money."

"Mahmoud! Why, that's—You are sure?"

"I saw it."

He looked at his feet, yanking his gaze away from mine as if he didn't want me to see that he thought I was lying.

"The soldier may have lied to Einarson," he said presently, still trying to keep me from knowing he thought me the liar. "I can understand some of the language, as spoken by the educated Muravians, but not the country dialect the soldier talked, so I don't know what he said, but he may have lied, you know."

"Not a chance," I said. "I'd bet my pants he told the truth."

He continued to stare at his outstretched feet, fighting to hold his face cool and calm. Part of what he was thinking slipped out in words:

"Of course, I owe you a tremendous debt for saving us from—"

"You don't. You owe that to the soldier's bad aim. I didn't jump him till his gun was empty."

"But—" His young eyes were wide before mine, and if I had pulled a machine gun out of my cuff he wouldn't have been surprised. He

suspected me of everything on the blotter. I cursed myself for overplaying my hand. There was nothing to do now but spread the cards.

"Listen, Grantham. Most of what I told you and Einarson about myself is the bunk. Your uncle, Senator Walbourn, sent me down here. You were supposed to be in Paris. A lot of your dough was being shipped to Belgrade. The Senator was leery of the racket, didn't know whether you were playing a game or somebody was putting over a fast one. I went to Belgrade, traced you here, and came here, to run into what I ran into. I've traced the money to you, have talked to you. That's all I was hired to do. My job's done—unless there's anything I can do for you now."

"Not a thing," he said very calmly. "Thanks, just the same." He stood up, yawning. "Perhaps I'll see you again before you leave for the United States."

"Yeah." It was easy for me to make my voice match his in indifference: I hadn't a cargo of rage to hide. "Good night."

I went down to my room, got into bed, and, not having anything to think about, went to sleep.

CHAPTER VII

LIONEL'S PLANS

I slept till late the next morning and then had breakfast in my room. I was in the middle of it when knuckles tapped my door. A stocky man in a wrinkled gray uniform, set off with a short, thick sword, came in, saluted, gave me a square white envelope, looked hungrily at the American cigarettes on my table, smiled and took one when I offered them, saluted again, and went out.

The square envelope had my name written on it in a small, very plain and round, but not childish, handwriting. Inside was a note from the same pen:

The Minister of Police regrets that departmental affairs prevent his receiving you this afternoon.

It was signed "Romaine Frankl," and had a postscript:

If it's convenient for you to call on me after nine this evening, perhaps I can save you some time.

R. F.

Below this an address was written.

I put the note in my pocket and called: "Come in," to another set of knocking knuckles.

Lionel Grantham entered.

His face was pale and set.

"Good morning," I said, making it cheerfully casual, as if I attached no importance to last night's rumpus. "Had breakfast yet? Sit down, and—"

"Oh, yes, thanks. I've eaten." His handsome red face was reddening. "About last night—I was—"

"Forget it! Nobody likes to have his business pried into."

"That's good of you," he said, twisting his hat in his hands. He cleared his throat. "You said you'd—ah—do—ah—help me if I wished."

"Yeah. I will. Sit down."

He sat down, coughed, ran his tongue over his lips.

"You haven't said anything to any one about last night's affair with the soldier?"

"No," I said.

"Will you not say anything about it?"

"Why?"

He looked at the remains of my breakfast and didn't answer. I lit a cigarette to go with my coffee and waited. He stirred uneasily in his chair and, without looking up, asked:

"You know Mahmoud was killed last night?"

"The man in the restaurant with you and Einarson?"

"Yes. He was shot down in front of his house a little after midnight."

"Einarson?"

The boy jumped.

"No!" he cried. "Why do you say that?"

"Einarson knew Mahmoud had paid the soldier to wipe him out, so he plugged Mahmoud, or had him plugged. Did you tell him what I told you last night?"

"No." He blushed. "It's embarrassing to have one's family sending guardians after one."

I made a guess:

"He told you to offer me the job he spoke of last night, and to caution me against talking about the soldier. Didn't he?"

"Y-e-s."

"Well, go ahead and offer."

"But he doesn't know you're—"

"What are you going to do, then?" I asked. "If you don't make me the offer, you'll have to tell him why."

"Oh, Lord, what a mess!" he said wearily, putting elbows on knees, face between palms, looking at me with the harried eyes of a boy finding life too complicated.

He was ripe for talk. I grinned at him, finished my coffee, and waited.

"You know I'm not going to be led home by an ear," he said with a sudden burst of rather childish defiance.

"You know I'm not going to try to take you," I soothed him.

We had some more silence after that. I smoked while he held his head and worried. After a while he squirmed in his chair, sat stiffly upright, and his face turned perfectly crimson from hair to collar.

"I'm going to ask for your help," he said, pretending he didn't know he was blushing. "I'm going to tell you the whole foolish thing. If you laugh, I'll—You won't laugh, will you?"

"If it's funny I probably will, but that needn't keep me from helping you."

"Yes, do laugh! It's silly! You ought to laugh!" He took a deep breath. "Did you ever—did you ever think you'd like to be a"—he stopped, looked at me with a desperate sort of shyness, pulled himself together, and almost shouted the last word—"king?"

"Maybe. I've thought of a lot of things I'd like to be, and that might be one of 'em."

"I met Mahmoud at an embassy ball in Constantinople," he dashed into the story, dropping his words quickly as if glad to get rid of them. "He was President Semich's secretary. We got quite friendly, though I wasn't especially fond of him. He persuaded me to come here with him, and introduced me to Colonel Einarson. Then they—there's really no doubt that the country is wretchedly governed. I wouldn't have gone into it if that hadn't been so.

"A revolution was being prepared. The man who was to lead it had just died. It was handicapped, too, by a lack of money. Believe this—it wasn't all vanity that made me go into it. I believed—I still believe—that it would have been—will be—for the good of the country. The offer they made me was that if I would finance the revolution I could be—could be king.

"Now wait! The Lord knows it's bad enough, but don't think it sillier than it is. The money I have would go a long way in this small, impoverished country. Then, with an American ruler, it would be easier—it ought to be—for the country to borrow in America or England. Then there's the political angle. Muravia is surrounded by four countries, any one of which is strong enough to annex it if it wants. Even Albania, now that it is a protégé of Italy's. Muravia has stayed independent so far only because of the jealousy among its stronger neighbors and because it hasn't a seaport. But with the balance shifting—with Greece, Italy, and Albania allied against Jugoslavia for control of the Balkans—it's only a matter of time before something will happen here, as it now stands.

"But with an American ruler—and if loans in America and England were arranged, so we had their capital invested here—there would be a change in the situation. Muravia would be in a stronger position, would have at least some slight claim on the friendship of stronger powers. That would be enough to make the neighbors cautious.

"Albania, shortly after the war, thought of the same thing, and offered its crown to one of the wealthy American Bonapartes. He didn't want it. He was an older man and had already made his career. I did want my chance when it came. There were"—some of the embarrassment that had left him during his talking returned—"there were kings back in the Grantham lines. We trace our descent from James the Fourth, of Scotland. I wanted—it was nice to think of carrying the line back to a crown.

"We weren't planning a violent revolution. Einarson holds the army. We simply had to use the army to force the Deputies—those who were not already with us—to change the form of government and elect me king. My descent would make it easier than if the candidate were one who hadn't royal blood in him. It would give me a certain standing in spite—in spite of my being young, and—and the people really want a king, especially the peasants. They don't think they're really entitled to call themselves a nation without one. A president means nothing to them—he's simply an ordinary man like themselves. So, you see, I—It was—Go ahead, laugh! You've heard enough to know how silly it is!" His voice was high-pitched, screechy. "Laugh! Why don't you laugh?"

"What for?" I asked. "It's crazy, God knows, but not silly. Your judgment was gummy, but your nerve's all right. You've been talking as if this were all dead and buried. Has it flopped?"

"No, it hasn't," he said slowly, frowning, "but I keep thinking it has. Mahmoud's death shouldn't change the situation, yet I've a feeling it's all over."

"Much of your money sunk?"

"I don't mind that. But—well—suppose the American newspapers get hold of the story, and they probably will. You know how ridiculous they could make it. And then the others who'll know about it—my mother and uncle and the trust company. I won't pretend I'm not ashamed to face them. And then—" His face got red and shiny. "And then Valeska—Miss Radnjak—her father was to have led the revolution. He did lead it—until he was murdered. She is—I never could be good enough for her." He said this in a peculiarly idiotic tone of awe. "But I've hoped that perhaps by carrying on her father's work, and if I had something besides mere money to offer her—if I had done something—made a place for myself—perhaps she'd—you know."

I said: "Uh-huh."

"What shall I do?" he asked earnestly. "I can't run away. I've got to see it through for her, and to keep my own self-respect. But I've got that feeling that it's all over. You offered to help me. Help me. Tell me what I ought to do!"

"You'll do what I tell you—if I promise to bring you through with a clean face?" I asked, just as if steering millionaire descendants of Scotch kings through Balkan plots were an old story to me, merely part of the day's work.

"Yes!"

"What's the next thing on the revolutionary program?"

"There's a meeting to-night. I'm to bring you."

"What time?"

"Midnight."

"I'll meet you here at eleven-thirty. How much am I supposed to know?"

"I was to tell you about the plot, and to offer you whatever inducements were necessary to bring you in. There was no definite arrangement as to how much or how little I was to tell you."

CHAPTER VIII

AN ENLIGHTENING INTERVIEW

At nine-thirty that night a cab set me down in front of the address the Minister of Police's secretary had given in her note. It was a small two-story house in a badly paved street on the city's eastern edge. A middle-aged woman in very clean, stiffly starched, ill-fitting clothes opened the door for me. Before I could speak, Romaine Frankl, in a sleeveless pink satin gown, floated into sight behind the woman, smiling, holding out a small hand to me.

"I didn't know you'd come," she said.

"Why?" I asked, with a great show of surprise at the notion that any man would ignore an invitation from her, while the servant closed the door and took my coat and hat.

We were standing in a dull-rose-papered room, finished and carpeted with oriental richness. There was one discordant note in the room—an immense leather chair.

"We'll go upstairs," the girl said, and addressed the servant with words that meant nothing to me, except the name Marya. "Or would you"—she turned to me and English again—"prefer beer to wine?"

I said I wouldn't, and we went upstairs, the girl climbing ahead of me with her effortless appearance of being carried. She took me into a black, white, and gray room that was very daintily furnished with as few pieces as possible, its otherwise perfect feminine atmosphere spoiled by the presence of another of the big padded chairs.

The girl sat on a gray divan, pushing away a stack of French and Austrian magazines to make a place for me beside her. Through an open door I could see the painted foot of a Spanish bed, a short stretch of purple counterpane, and half of a purple-curtained window.

"His Excellency was very sorry," the girl began, and stopped.

I was looking—not staring—at the big leather chair. I knew she had stopped because I was looking at it, so I wouldn't take my eyes away.

"Vasilije," she said, more distinctly than was really necessary, "was very sorry he had to postpone this afternoon's appointment. The assassination of the President's secretary—you heard of it?—made us put everything else aside for the moment."

"Oh, yes, that fellow Mahmoud—" slowly shifting my eyes from the leather chair to her. "Found out who killed him?"

Her black-ringed, black-centered eyes seemed to study me from a distance while she shook her head, jiggling the nearly black curls.

"Probably Einarson," I said.

"You haven't been idle." Her lower lids lifted when she smiled, giving her eyes a twinkling effect.

The servant Marya came in with wine and fruit, put them on a small table beside the divan, and went away. The girl poured wine and offered me cigarettes in a silver box. I passed them up for one of my own. She smoked a king-size Egyptian cigarette—big as a cigar. It accentuated the smallness of her face and hand—which is probably why she favored that size.

"What sort of revolution is this they've sold my boy?" I asked.

"It was a very nice one until it died."

"How come it died?"

"It—do you know anything about our history?"

"No."

"Well, Muravia came into existence after the war as a result of the fear and jealousy of four countries. The nine or ten thousand square miles that make this country aren't very valuable land. There's little here that any of those four countries especially wanted, but no three of them would agree to let the fourth have it. The only way to settle the thing was to make a separate country out of it. That was done in 1923.

"Doctor Semich was elected the first president, for a ten-year term. He is not a statesman, not a politician, and never will be. But since he was the only Muravian who had ever been heard of outside his own town, it was thought that his election would give the new country some prestige. Besides, it was a fitting honor for Muravia's only great man. He was not meant to be anything but a figure-head. The real governing was to be done by General Danilo Radnjak, who was elected vice-president, which, here, is more than equivalent to Prime Minister. General Radnjak was a capable man. The army worshiped him, the peasants trusted him, and our *bourgeoisie* knew him to be honest, conservative, intelligent, and as good a business administrator as a military one.

"Doctor Semich is a very mild, elderly scholar with no knowledge whatever of worldly affairs. You can understand him from this—he is easily the greatest of living bacteriologists, but he'll tell you, if you are on intimate terms with him, that he doesn't believe in the value of bacteriology at all. 'Mankind must learn to live with bacteria as with friends,' he'll say. 'Our bodies must adapt themselves to diseases, so there will be little difference between having tuberculosis, for example, or not having it. That way lies victory. This making war on bacteria is a futile business. Futile but interesting. So we do it. Our poking around in laboratories is perfectly useless—but it amuses us.'

"Now when this delightful old dreamer was honored by his countrymen with the presidency, he took it in the worst possible way. He determined to show his appreciation by locking up his laboratory and applying himself heart and soul to running the government. Nobody expected or wanted that. Radnjak was to have been the government. For a while he did control the situation, and everything went well enough.

"But Mahmoud had designs of his own. He was Doctor Semich's secretary, and he was trusted. He began calling the President's attentions to various trespasses of Radnjak's on the presidential powers. Radnjak, in an attempt to keep Mahmoud from control, made a terrible mistake. He went to Doctor Semich and told him frankly and honestly that no one expected him, the President, to give all his time to executive business, and that it had been the intention of his countrymen to give him the honor of being the first president rather than the duties.

"Radnjak had played into Mahmoud's

hands—the secretary became the actual government. Doctor Semich was now thoroughly convinced that Radnjak was trying to steal his authority, and from that day on Radnjak's hands were tied. Doctor Semich insisted on handling every governmental detail himself, which meant that Mahmoud handled it, because the President knows as little about statesmanship today as he did when he took office. Complaints—no matter who made them—did no good. Doctor Semich considered every dissatisfied citizen a fellow-conspirator of Radnjak's. The more Mahmoud was criticized in the Chamber of Deputies, the more faith Doctor Semich had in him. Last year the situation became intolerable, and the revolution began to form.

"Radnjak headed it, of course, and at least ninety percent of the influential men in Muravia were in it. The attitude of people as a whole, it is difficult to judge. They are mostly peasants, small land-owners, who ask only to be let alone. But there's no doubt they'd rather have a king than a president, so the form was to be changed to please them. The army, which worshiped Radnjak, was in it. The revolution matured slowly. General Radnjak was a cautious, careful man, and, as this is not a wealthy country, there was not much money available.

"Two months before the date set for the outbreak, Radnjak was assassinated. And the revolution went to pieces, split up into half a dozen factions. There was no other man strong enough to hold them together. Some of these groups still meet and conspire, but they are without general influence, without real purpose. And this is the revolution that has been sold Lionel Grantham. We'll have more information in a day or two, but what we've learned so far is that Mahmoud, who spent a month's vacation in Constantinople, brought Grantham back here with him and joined forces with Einarson to swindle the boy.

"Mahmoud was very much out of the revolution, of course, since it was aimed at him. But Einarson had been in it with his superior, Radnjak. Since Radnjak's death Einarson has succeeded in transferring to himself much of the allegiance that the soldiers gave the dead general. They do not love the Icelander as they did Radnjak, but Einarson is spectacular, theatrical—has all the qualities that simple men like to see in their leaders. So Einarson had the army and could get enough of the late revolution's machinery in his hands to impress Grantham. For money he'd do it. So he and Mahmoud put on a show for your boy. They used Valeska Radnjak, the general's daughter, too. She, I think, was also a dupe. I've heard that the boy and she are planning to be king and queen. How much did he invest in this little farce?"

"Maybe as much as three million American dollars."

Romaine Frankl whistled softly and poured more wine.

CHAPTER IX

CONJECTURES

"How did the Minister of Police stand, when the revolution was alive?" I asked.

"Vasilije," she told me, sipping wine between phrases, "is a peculiar man, an original. He is interested in nothing except his comfort. Comfort to him means enormous amounts of food and drink and at least sixteen hours of sleep each day, and not having to move around much during his eight waking hours. Outside of that he cares for nothing. To guard his comfort he has made the police department a model one. They've got to do their work smoothly and neatly. If they don't, crimes will go unpunished, people will complain, and those complaints might disturb His Excellency. He might even have to shorten his afternoon nap to attend a conference or meeting. That wouldn't do. So he insists on an organization that will keep crime down to a minimum, and catch the perpetrators of that minimum. And he gets it."

"Catch Radnjak's assassin?"

"Killed resisting arrest ten minutes after the murder."

"One of Mahmoud's men?"

The girl emptied her glass, frowning at me, her lifted lower lids putting a twinkle in the frown.

"You're not so bad," she said slowly, "but now it's my turn to ask: Why did you say Einarson killed Mahmoud?"

"Einarson knew Mahmoud had tried to have him and Grantham shot earlier in the evening."

"Really?"

"I saw a soldier take money from Mahmoud, ambush Einarson and Grantham, and miss 'em with six shots."

She clicked a finger-nail against her teeth.

"That's not like Mahmoud," she objected, "to be seen paying for his murders."

"Probably not," I agreed. "But suppose his hired man decided he wanted more pay, or maybe he'd only been paid part of his wages. What better way to collect than to pop out and ask for it in the street a few minutes before he was scheduled to turn the trick?"

She nodded, and spoke as if thinking aloud:

"Then they've got all they expect to get from Grantham, and each was trying to hog it by removing the other."

"Where you go wrong," I told her, "is in thinking that the revolution is dead."

"But Mahmoud wouldn't, for three million dollars, conspire to remove himself from power."

"Right! Mahmoud thought he was putting on a show for the boy. When he learned it wasn't a show—learned Einarson was in earnest—he tried to have him knocked off."

"Perhaps." She shrugged her smooth bare shoulders. "But now you're guessing."

"Yes? Einarson carries a picture of the Shah of Persia. It's worn, as if he handled it a lot. The Shah of Persia is a Russian soldier who went in there after the war, worked himself up until he had the army in his hands, became dictator, then Shah. Correct me if I'm wrong. Einarson

is an Icelandic soldier who came in here after the war and has worked himself up until he's got the army in his hands. If he carries the Shah's picture and looks at it often enough to have it shabby from handling, does it mean he hopes to follow his example? Or doesn't it?"

Romaine Frankl got up and roamed around the room, moving a chair two inches here, adjusting an ornament there, shaking out the folds of a window-curtain, pretending a picture wasn't quite straight on the wall, moving from place to place with the appearance of being carried—a graceful small girl in pink satin.

She stopped in front of a mirror, moved a little to one side so she could see my reflection in it, and fluffed her curls while saying:

"Very well, Einarson wants a revolution. What will your boy do?"

"What I tell him."

"What will you tell him?"

"Whatever pays best. I want to take him home with all his money."

She left the mirror and came over to me, rumpled my hair, kissed my mouth, and sat on my knees, holding my face between small warm hands.

"Give me a revolution, nice man!" Her eyes were black with excitement, her voice throaty, her mouth laughing, her body trembling. "I detest Einarson. Use him and break him for me. But give me a revolution!"

I laughed, kissed her, and turned her around on my lap so her head would fit against my shoulder.

"We'll see," I promised. "I'm to meet the folks at midnight. Maybe I'll know then."

"You'll come back after the meeting?"

"Try to keep me away!"

CHAPTER X

EINARSON IN CONTROL

I got back to the hotel at eleven-thirty, loaded my hips with gun and blackjack, and went upstairs to Grantham's suite. He was alone, but said he expected Einarson. He seemed glad to see me.

"Tell me, did Mahmoud go to any of the meetings?" I asked.

"No. His part in the revolution was hidden even from most of those in it. There were reasons why he couldn't appear."

"There were. The chief one was that everybody knew he didn't want any revolts, didn't want anything but money."

Grantham chewed his lower lip and said: "Oh, Lord, what a mess!"

Colonel Einarson arrived, in a dinner coat, but very much the soldier, the man of action. His hand-clasp was stronger than it needed to be. His little dark eyes were hard and bright.

"You are ready, gentlemen?" he addressed the boy and me as if we were a multitude. "Excellent! We shall go now. There will be difficulties to-night. Mahmoud is dead. There will be those of our friends who will ask: 'Why now revolt?' Ach!" He yanked a corner of his flowing dark mustache. "I will answer that. Good souls, our confrères, but given to timidity. There is no timidity under capable leadership. You shall see!" And he yanked his mustache again. This military gent seemed to be feeling Napoleonic this evening. But I didn't write him off as a musical-comedy revolutionist—I remembered what he had done to the soldier.

We left the hotel, got into a machine, rode seven blocks, and went into a small hotel on a side street. The porter bowed to the belt when he opened the door for Einarson. Grantham and I followed the officer up a flight of stairs, down a dim hall. A fat, greasy man in his fifties came bowing and clucking to meet us. Einarson introduced him to me—the proprietor of the hotel. He took us into a low-ceilinged room where thirty or forty men got up from chairs and looked at us through tobacco smoke.

Einarson made a short, very formal speech which I couldn't understand, introducing me to

the gang. I ducked my head at them and found a seat beside Grantham. Einarson sat on his other side. Everybody else sat down again, in no especial order.

Colonel Einarson smoothed his mustache and began to talk to this one and that, shouting over the clamor of other voices when necessary. In an undertone, Lionel Grantham pointed out the more important conspirators to me—a dozen or more members of the Chamber of Deputies, a banker, a brother of the Minister of Finance (supposed to represent that official), half a dozen officers (all in civilian clothes tonight), three professors from the university, the president of a labor union, a newspaper publisher and his editor, the secretary of a students' club, a politician from out in the country, and a handful of small business men.

The banker, a white-bearded fat man of sixty, stood up and began a speech, staring intently at Einarson. He spoke deliberately, softly, but with a faintly defiant air. The Colonel didn't let him get far.

"Ach!" Einarson barked and reared up on his feet. None of the words he said meant anything to me, but they took the pinkness out of the banker's cheeks and brought uneasiness into the eyes around us.

"They want to call it off," Grantham whispered in my ear. "They won't go through with it now. I know they won't."

The meeting became rough. A lot of people were yelping at once, but nobody talked down Einarson's bellow. Everybody was standing up, either very red or very white in the face. Fists, fingers, and heads were shaking. The Minister of Finance's brother—a slender, elegantly dressed man with a long, intelligent face—took off his nose glasses so savagely that they broke in half, screamed words at Einarson, spun on his heel, and walked to the door.

He pulled it open and stopped.

The hall was full of green uniforms. Soldiers leaned against the wall, sat on their heels, stood in little groups. They hadn't guns—only bayonets in scabbards at their sides. The Minister of Finance's brother stood very still at the door, looking at the soldiers.

A brown-whiskered, dark-skinned, big man, in coarse clothes and heavy boots, glared with red-rimmed eyes from the soldiers to Einarson, and took two heavy steps toward the Colonel. This was the country politician. Einarson blew out his lips and stepped forward to meet him. Those who were between them got out of the way.

Einarson roared and the countryman roared. Einarson made the most noise, but the countryman wouldn't stop on that account.

Colonel Einarson said: "Ach!" and spat in the countryman's face.

The countryman staggered back a step and one of his paws went under his brown coat. I stepped around Einarson and shoved the muzzle of my gun in the countryman's ribs.

Einarson laughed, called two soldiers into the room. They took the countryman by the arms and led him out. Somebody closed the door. Everybody sat down. Einarson made another speech. Nobody interrupted him. The white-whiskered banker made another speech. The Minister of Finance's brother rose to say half a dozen polite words, staring near-sightedly at Einarson, holding half of his broken glasses in each slender hand. Grantham, at a word from Einarson, got up and talked. Everybody listened very respectfully.

Einarson spoke again. Everybody got excited. Everybody talked at once. It went on for a long time. Grantham explained to me that the revolution would start early Thursday morning—it was now early Wednesday morning—and that the details were now being arranged for the last time. I doubted that anybody was going to know anything about the details, with all this hubbub going on. They kept it up until half-past three. The last couple of hours I spent dozing in a chair, tilted back against the wall in a corner.

———

Grantham and I walked back to our hotel after the meeting. He told me we were to gather in the plaza at four o'clock the next morning. It would be daylight by six, and by then the government buildings, the President, most of the officials and Deputies who were not on our side, would be in our hands. A meeting of the Chamber of Deputies would be held under the eyes of Einarson's troops, and everything would be done as swiftly and regularly as possible.

I was to accompany Grantham as a sort of bodyguard, which meant, I imagined, that both of us were to be kept out of the way as much as possible. That was all right with me.

I left Grantham at the fifth floor, went to my room, ran cold water over my face and hands, and then left the hotel again. There was no chance of getting a cab at this hour, so I set out afoot for Romaine Frankl's house.

I had a little excitement on the way.

A wind was blowing in my face as I walked. I stopped and put my back to it to light a cigarette. A shadow down the street slid over into a building's shadow. I was being tailed, and not very skillfully. I finished lighting my cigarette and went on my way until I came to a sufficiently dark side street. Turning into it, I stopped in a street-level dark doorway.

A man came puffing around the corner. My first crack at him went wrong—the blackjack took him too far forward, on the cheek. The second one got him fairly behind the ear. I left him sleeping there and went on to Romaine Frankl's house.

CHAPTER XI

A ROMANTIC INTERLUDE

The servant Marya, in a woolly gray bathrobe, opened the door and sent me up to the black, white, and gray room, where the Minister's secretary, still in the pink gown, was propped up among cushions on the divan. A tray full of cigarette butts showed how she'd been spending her time.

"Well?" she asked as I moved her over to make a seat for myself beside her.

"Thursday morning at four we revolute."

"I knew you'd do it," she said, patting my hand.

"It did itself, though there were a few minutes when I could have stopped it by simply knocking our Colonel behind the ear and letting the rest of them tear him apart. That reminds me—somebody's hired man tried to follow me here tonight."

"What sort of a man?"

"Short, beefy, forty—just about my size and age."

"But he didn't succeed?"

"I slapped him flat and left him sleeping there."

She laughed and pulled my ear.

"That was Gopchek, our very best detective. He'll be furious."

"Well, don't sic any more of 'em on me. You can tell him I'm sorry I had to hit him twice, but it was his own fault. He shouldn't have jerked his head back the first time."

She laughed, then frowned, finally settling on an expression that held half of each.

"Tell me about the meeting," she commanded.

I told her what I knew. When I had finished she pulled my head down to kiss me, and held it down to whisper:

"You do trust me, don't you, dear?"

"Yeah. Just as much as you trust me."

"That's far from being enough," she said, pushing my face away with a hand flat against my nose.

Marya came in with a tray of food. We pulled the table around in front of the divan and ate.

"I don't quite understand you," Romaine said over a stalk of asparagus. "If you don't trust me why do you tell me things? As far as I know, you haven't done much lying to me. Why should you tell me the truth if you've no faith in me?"

"My susceptible nature," I explained. "I'm so overwhelmed by your beauty and charm and one thing and another that I can't refuse you anything."

"Don't!" she exclaimed, suddenly serious. "I've capitalized that beauty and charm in half the countries in the world. Don't say things like that to me ever again. It hurts, because—because—" She pushed her plate back, started to reach for a cigarette, stopped her hand in midair, and looked at me with disagreeable eyes. "I love you," she said.

I took the hand that was hanging in the air, kissed the palm of it, and asked:

"You love me more than any one else in the world?"

She pulled the hand away from me.

"Are you a bookkeeper?" she demanded. "Must you have amounts, weights, and measurements for everything?"

I grinned at her and tried to go on with my meal. I had been hungry. Now, though I had eaten only a couple of mouthfuls, my appetite was gone. I tried to pretend I still had the hunger I had lost, but it was no go. The food didn't want to be swallowed. I gave up the attempt and lighted a cigarette.

She used her left hand to fan away the smoke between us.

"You don't trust me," she insisted. "Then why do you put yourself in my hands?"

"Why not? You can make a flop of the revolution. That's nothing to me. It's not my party, and its failure needn't mean that I can't get the boy out of the country with his money."

"You don't mind a prison, an execution, perhaps?"

"I'll take my chances," I said. But what I was thinking was: if, after twenty years of scheming and slickering in big-time cities, I let myself get trapped in this hill village, I'd deserve all I got.

"And you've no feeling at all for me?"

"Don't be foolish." I waved my cigarette at my uneaten meal. "I haven't had anything to eat since eight o'clock last night."

She laughed, put a hand over my mouth, and said:

"I understand. You love me, but not enough to let me interfere with your plans. I don't like that. It's effeminate."

"You going to turn out for the revolution?" I asked.

"I'm not going to run through the streets throwing bombs, if that's what you mean."

"And Djudakovich?"

"He sleeps till eleven in the morning. If you start at four, you'll have seven hours before he's up." She said all this perfectly seriously. "Get it done in that time. Or he might decide to stop it."

"Yeah? I had a notion he wanted it."

"Vasilije wants nothing but peace and comfort."

"But listen, sweetheart," I protested. "If your Vasilije is any good at all, he can't help finding out about it ahead of time. Einarson and his army are the revolution. These bankers and deputies and the like that he's carrying with him to give the party a responsible look are a lot of movie conspirators. Look at 'em! They hold their meetings at midnight, and all that kind of foolishness. Now that they're actually signed up to something, they won't be able to keep from spreading the news. All day they'll be going around trembling and whispering together in odd corners."

"They've been doing that for months," she said. "Nobody pays any attention to them. And I promise you Vasilije shan't hear anything new. I won't tell him, and he never listens to anything any one else says."

"All right." I wasn't sure it was all right, but it might be. "Now this row is going through—if the army follows Einarson?"

"Yes, and the army will follow him."

"Then, after it's over, our real job begins?"

She rubbed a flake of cigarette ash into the table cloth with a small pointed finger, and said nothing.

"Einarson's got to be dumped," I continued.

"We'll have to kill him," she said thoughtfully. "You'd better do it yourself."

CHAPTER XII

THE NIGHT BEFORE

I saw Einarson and Grantham that evening, and spent several hours with them. The boy was fidgety, nervous, without confidence in the revolution's success, though he tried to pretend he was taking things as a matter of course. Einarson was full of words. He gave us every detail of the next day's plans. I was more interested in him than in what he was saying. He could put the revolution over, I thought, and I was willing to leave it to him. So while he talked I studied him, combing him over for weak spots.

I took him physically first—a tall, thick-bodied man in his prime, not as quick as he might have been, but strong and tough. He had an amply jawed, short-nosed, florid face that a fist wouldn't bother much. He wasn't fat, but he ate and drank too much to be hard-boiled, and your florid man can seldom stand much poking around the belt. So much for the gent's body.

Mentally, he wasn't a heavy-weight. His revolution was crude stuff. It would get over chiefly because there wasn't much opposition. He had plenty of will-power, I imagined, but I didn't put a big number on that. People who haven't much brains have to develop will-power to get anywhere. I didn't know whether he had guts or not, but before an audience I guessed he'd make a grand showing, and most of this act would be before an audience. Off in a dark corner I had an idea he would go watery. He believed in himself—absolutely. That's ninety percent of leadership, so there was no flaw in him there. He didn't trust me. He had taken me in because as things turned out it was easier to do so than to shut the door against me.

He kept on talking about his plans. There was nothing to talk about. He was going to bring his soldiers in town in the early morning and take over the government. That was all the plan that was needed. The rest of it was the lettuce around the dish, but this lettuce part was the only part we could discuss. It was dull.

At eleven o'clock Einarson stopped talking and left us, making this sort of speech:

"Until four o'clock, gentlemen, when Muravia's history begins." He put a hand on my shoulder and commanded me: "Guard His Majesty!"

I said, "Uh-huh," and immediately sent His Majesty to bed. He wasn't going to sleep, but he was too young to confess it, so he went off willingly enough. I got a taxi and went out to Romaine's.

She was like a child the night before a picnic. She kissed me and she kissed the servant Marya. She sat on my knees, beside me, on the floor, on all the chairs, changing her location every half-minute. She laughed and talked incessantly, about the revolution, about me, about herself, about anything at all. She nearly strangled herself trying to talk while swallowing wine. She lit her big cigarettes and forgot to smoke them, or forgot to stop smoking them until they scorched her lips. She sang lines from songs in half a dozen languages. She made puns and jokes and goofy rhymes.

I left at three o'clock. She went down to the door with me, pulled my head down to kiss my eyes and mouth.

"If anything goes wrong," she said, "come to the prison. We'll hold that until—"

"If it goes wrong enough I'll be brought there," I promised.

She wouldn't joke now.

"I'm going there now," she said. "I'm afraid Einarson's got my house on his list."

"Good idea," I said. "If you hit a bad spot get word to me."

I walked back to the hotel through the dark streets—the lights were turned off at midnight—without seeing a single other person, not even one of the gray-uniformed policemen. By the time I reached home rain was falling steadily.

In my room, I changed into heavier clothes and shoes, dug an extra gun—an automatic—out of my bag and hung it in a shoulder holster. Then I filled my pocket with enough ammunition to make me bow-legged, picked up hat and raincoat, and went upstairs to Lionel Grantham's suite.

"It's ten to four," I told him. "We might as well go down to the plaza. Better put a gun in your pocket."

He hadn't slept. His handsome young face was as cool and pink and composed as it had been the first time I saw him, though his eyes were brighter now.

He got into an overcoat, and we went downstairs.

CHAPTER XIII

PROGRESS GOES "BETUNE"

Rain drove into our faces as we went toward the center of the dark plaza. Other figures moved around us, though none came near. We halted at the foot of an iron statue of somebody on a horse.

A pale young man of extraordinary thinness came up and began to talk rapidly, gesturing with both hands, sniffing every now and then, as if he had a cold in his head. I couldn't understand a word he said.

The rumble of other voices began to compete with the patter of rain. The fat, white-whiskered face of the banker who had been at the meeting appeared suddenly out of the darkness and went back into it just as suddenly, as if he didn't want to be recognized. Men I hadn't seen before gathered around us, saluting Grantham with a sheepish sort of respect. A little man in a too big cape ran up and began to tell us something in a cracked, jerky voice. A thin, stooped man with glasses freckled by raindrops translated the little man's story into English for us:

"He says the artillery has betrayed us, and guns are being mounted in the government buildings to sweep the plaza at daybreak." There was an odd sort of hopefulness in his voice, and he added: "In that event, we can, naturally, do nothing."

"We can die," Lionel Grantham said gently.

There wasn't the least bit of sense to that crack. Nobody was here to die. They were all here because it was so unlikely that anybody would have to die, except perhaps a few of Einarson's soldiers. That's the sensible view of the boy's speech. But it's God's own truth that even I—a middle-aged detective who had forgotten what it was like to believe in fairies—felt suddenly warm inside my wet clothes. And if anybody had said to me: "This boy is a real king," I wouldn't have argued the point.

An abrupt hush came in the murmuring around us, leaving only the rustle of rain, and the tramp, tramp, tramp of orderly marching up the street—Einarson's men. Everybody commenced to talk at once, happily, expectantly, cheered by the approach of those whose part it was to do the heavy work.

An officer in a glistening slicker pushed through the crowd—a small, dapper boy with a too large sword. He saluted Grantham elaborately, and said in English, of which he seemed proud:

"Colonel Einarson's respects, Mister, and this progress goes betune."[*]

I wondered what the last word meant.

Grantham smiled and said: "Convey my thanks to Colonel Einarson."

The banker appeared again, bold enough now to join us. Others who had been at the meeting appeared. We made an inner group around the statue, with the mob around us—more easily seen now in the gray of early morning. I didn't see the countryman into whose face Einarson had spat.

The rain soaked us. We shifted our feet, shivered, and talked. Daylight came slowly, showing more and more who stood around us wet and curious-eyed. On the edge of the crowd

men burst into cheers. The rest of them took it up. They forgot their wet misery, laughed and danced, hugged and kissed one another. A bearded man in a leather coat came to us, bowed to Grantham, and explained that Einarson's own regiment could be seen occupying the Administration Building and the Executive Residence.

Day came fully. The mob around us opened to make way for an automobile that was surrounded by a squad of cavalrymen. It stopped in front of us. Colonel Einarson, holding a bare sword in his hand, stepped out of the car, saluted, and held the door open for Grantham and me. He followed us in, smelling of victory like a chorus girl of Coty.[†] The cavalrymen closed around the car again, and we were driven to the Administration Building, through a crowd that yelled and ran red-faced and happy after us. It was all quite theatrical.

CHAPTER XIV

CORONATION

"The city is ours," said Einarson, leaning forward in his seat, his sword's point on the car floor, his hands on its hilt. "The President, the Deputies, nearly every official of importance, is taken. Not a single shot fired, not a window broken!"

He was proud of his revolution, and I didn't blame him. I wasn't sure that he might not have brains, after all. He had had sense enough to park his civilian adherents in the plaza until his soldiers had done their work.

We got out at the Administration Building, walking up the steps between rows of infantrymen at present-arms, rain sparkling on their fixed bayonets. More green-uniformed soldiers

[*] possibly a reference to the Scottish Betunes listed in Burke's peerage, who came to France in the eleventh century and whose influence had waned by the eighteenth

[†] Perfumer François Coty was known for his sensuous packaging and his sybaritic lifestyle. In 1910, for example, he created a tester for Coty perfume that featured three art-nouveau-style female nudes dancing with one another, and he used his mistresses as models for his artistic ads.

presented arms along the corridors. We went into an elaborately furnished dining-room, where fifteen or twenty officers stood up to receive us. There were lots of speeches made. Everybody was triumphant. All through breakfast there was much talking. I didn't understand any of it. I attended to my eating.

After the meal we went to the Deputies' Chamber, a large, oval room with curved rows of benches and desks facing a raised platform. Besides three desks on the platform, some twenty chairs had been put there, facing the curved seats. Our breakfast party occupied these chairs. I noticed that Grantham and I were the only civilians on the platform. None of our fellow conspirators were there, except those who were in Einarson's army. I wasn't so fond of that.

Grantham sat in the first row of chairs, between Einarson and me. We looked down on the Deputies. There were perhaps a hundred of them distributed among the curved benches, split sharply in two groups. Half of them, on the right side of the room, were revolutionists. They stood up and hurrahed at us. The other half, on the left, were prisoners. Most of them seemed to have dressed hurriedly. They looked at us with uneasy eyes.

Around the room, shoulder to shoulder against the wall except on the platform and where the doors were, stood Einarson's soldiers.

An old man came in between two soldiers—a mild-eyed old gentleman, bald, stooped, with a wrinkled, clean-shaven, scholarly face.

"Doctor Semich," Grantham whispered.

The President's guards took him to the center one of the three desks on the platform. He paid no attention to us who were sitting on the platform, and he did not sit down.

A red-haired Deputy—one of the revolutionary party—got up and talked. His fellows cheered when he had finished. The President spoke—three words in a very dry, very calm voice, and left the platform to walk back the way he had come, the two soldiers accompanying him.

"Refused to resign," Grantham informed me.

The red-haired Deputy came up on the platform and took the center desk. The legislative machinery began to grind. Men talked briefly, apparently to the point—revolutionists. None of the prisoner Deputies rose. A vote was taken. A few of the in-wrongs didn't vote. Most of them seemed to vote with the ins.

"They've revoked the constitution," Grantham whispered.

The Deputies were hurrahing again—those who were there voluntarily. Einarson leaned over and mumbled to Grantham and me:

"That is as far as we may safely go to-day. It leaves all in our hands."

"Time to listen to a suggestion?" I asked.

"Yes."

"Will you excuse us a moment?" I said to Grantham, and got up and walked to one of the rear corners of the platform.

Einarson followed me, frowning suspiciously.

"Why not give Grantham his crown now?" I asked when we were standing in the corner, my right shoulder touching his left, half facing each other, half facing the corner, our backs to the officers who sat on the platform, the nearest less than ten feet away. "Push it through. You can do it. There'll be a howl, of course. To-morrow, as a concession to that howl, you'll make him abdicate. You'll get credit for that. You'll be fifty percent stronger with the people. Then you will be in a position to make it look as if the revolution was his party, and that you were the patriot who kept this newcomer from grabbing the throne. Meanwhile you'll be dictator, and whatever else you want to be when the time comes. See what I mean? Let him bear the brunt. You catch yours on the rebound."

He liked the idea, but he didn't like it to come from me. His little dark eyes pried into mine.

"Why should you suggest this?" he asked.

"What do you care? I promise you he'll abdicate within twenty-four hours."

He smiled under his mustache and raised his

head. I knew a major in the A.E.F.* who always raised his head like that when he was going to issue an unpleasant order. I spoke quickly:

"My raincoat—do you see it's folded over my left arm?"

He said nothing, but his eyelids crept together.

"You can't see my left hand," I went on.

His eyes were slits, but he said nothing.

"There's an automatic in it," I wound up.

"Well?" he asked contemptuously.

"Nothing—only—get funny, and I'll let your guts out."

"Ach!"—he didn't take me seriously—"and after that?"

"I don't know. Think it over carefully, Einarson. I've deliberately put myself in a position where I've got to go ahead if you don't give in. I can kill you before you do anything. I'm going to do it if you don't give Grantham his crown now. Understand? I've got to. Maybe—most likely—your boys would get me afterward, but you'd be dead. If I back down now, you'll certainly have me shot. So I can't back down. If neither of us backs down, we'll both take the leap. *I've* gone too far to weaken now. *You'll* have to give in. Think it over. I can't possibly be bluffing."

He thought it over. Some of the color washed out of his face, and a little rippling movement appeared in the flesh of his chin. I crowded him along by moving the raincoat enough to show him the muzzle of the gun that actually was there in my left hand. I had the big heaver†—he hadn't nerve enough to take a chance on dying in his hour of victory. A little earlier, a little later, I might have had to gun him. Now I had him.

He strode across the platform to the desk at which the redhead sat, drove the redhead away with a snarl and a gesture, leaned over the desk, and bellowed down into the chamber. I stood a little to one side of him, a little behind, close enough so no one could get between us.

No Deputy made a sound for a long minute after the Colonel's bellow had stopped. Then one of the anti-revolutionists jumped to his feet and yelped bitterly. Einarson pointed a long brown finger at him. Two soldiers left their places by the wall, took the Deputy roughly by neck and arms, and dragged him out. Another Deputy stood up, talked, and was removed. After the fifth drag-out everything was peaceful.

Einarson put a question and got a unanimous answer.

He turned to me, his gaze darting from my face to my raincoat and back, and said: "That is done."

"We'll have the coronation now," I commanded. "Any kind of ceremony, so it's short."

I missed most of the ceremony. I was busy keeping my hold on the florid officer, but finally Lionel Grantham was officially installed as Lionel the First, King of Muravia. Einarson and I congratulated him, or whatever it was, together. Then I took the officer aside.

"We're going to take a walk," I said. "No foolishness. Take me out a side door."

I had him now, almost without needing the gun. He would have to deal quietly with Grantham and me—kill us without any publicity—if he were to avoid being laughed at—this man who had let himself be stuck up and robbed of a throne in the middle of his army.

We went roundabout from the Administration Building to the Hotel of the Republic without meeting any one who knew us. The population was all in the plaza. We found the hotel deserted. I made him run the elevator to my floor, and herded him down the corridor to my room.

I tried the door, found it unlocked, let go the knob, and told him to go in. He pushed the door open and stopped.

Romaine Frankl was sitting cross-legged in the middle of my bed, sewing a button on one of my union suits.

---

* American Expeditionary Forces
† sigh of relief

CHAPTER XV

BARGAIN HUNTERS

I prodded Einarson into the room and closed the door. Romaine looked at him and at the automatic that was now uncovered in my hand. With burlesque disappointment she said:

"Oh, you haven't killed him yet!"

Colonel Einarson stiffened. He had an audience now—one that saw his humiliation. He was likely to do something. I'd have to handle him with gloves, or—maybe the other way was better. I kicked him on the ankle and snarled:

"Get over in the corner and sit down!"

He spun around to me. I jabbed the muzzle of the pistol in his face, grinding his lip between it and his teeth. When his head jerked back I slammed him in the belly with my other fist. He grabbed for air with a wide mouth. I pushed him over to a chair in one corner of the room.

Romaine laughed and shook a finger at me, saying:

"You're a rowdy!"

"What else can I do?" I protested, chiefly for my prisoner's benefit. "When somebody's watching him he gets notions that he's a hero. I stuck him up and made him crown the boy king. But this bird has still got the army, which is the government. I can't let go of him, or both Lionel the Once and I will gather lead. It hurts me more than it does him to have to knock him around, but I can't help myself. I've got to keep him sensible."

"You're doing wrong by him," she replied. "You've got no right to mistreat him. The only polite thing for you to do is to cut his throat in a gentlemanly manner."

"Ach!" Einarson's lungs were working again.

"Shut up," I yelled at him, "or I'll come over there and knock you double-jointed."

He glared at me, and I asked the girl: "What'll we do with him? I'd be glad to cut his throat, but the trouble is, his army might avenge him, and I'm not a fellow who likes to have anybody's army avenging on him."

"We'll give him to Vasilije," she said, swinging her feet over the side of the bed and standing up. "He'll know what to do."

"Where is he?"

"Upstairs in Grantham's suite, finishing his morning nap, I suppose."

Then she said lightly, casually, as if she hadn't been thinking seriously about it: "So you had the boy crowned?"

"I did. You want it for your Vasilije? Good! We want five million American dollars for our abdication. Grantham put in three to finance the doings, and he deserves a profit. He's been regularly elected by the Deputies. He's got no real backing here, but he can get support from the neighbors. Don't overlook that. There are a couple of countries not a million miles away that would gladly send in an army to support a legitimate king in exchange for whatever concessions they liked. But Lionel the First isn't unreasonable. He thinks it would be better for you to have a native ruler. All he asks is a decent provision from the government. Five million is low enough, and he'll abdicate to-morrow. Tell that to your Vasilije."

She went around me to avoid passing between my gun and its target, stood on tiptoe to kiss my ear, and said:

"You and your king are a couple of brigands. I'll be back in a few minutes."

She went out.

"Ten millions," Colonel Einarson said.

"I can't trust you now," I said. "You'd pay us off in front of a firing squad."

"You can trust this pig Djudakovich?"

"He's got no reason to hate us."

"He will when he's told of you and his Romaine."

I laughed.

"Besides, how can he be king? Ach! What is his promise to pay if he cannot become in a position to pay? Suppose even I am dead. What will he do with my army? Ach! You have seen the pig! What kind of king is he?"

"I don't know," I said truthfully. "I'm told he was a good Minister of Police because inefficiency would spoil his comfort. Maybe he'd be a good dictator or king for the same reason. I've seen him once. He's a bloated mountain, but there's nothing ridiculous about him. He weighs a ton, and moves without shaking the floor. I'd be afraid to try on him what I did to you."

This insult brought the soldier up on his feet, very tall and straight. His eyes burned at me while his mouth hardened in a thin line. He was going to make trouble for me before I was rid of him. I scowled at him and wondered what I should do next.

The door opened and Vasilije Djudakovich came in, followed by the girl. I grinned at the fat Minister. He nodded without smiling. His little dark eyes moved coldly from me to Einarson.

The girl said:

"The government will give Lionel the First a draft for four million dollars, American, on either a Vienna or Athens bank, in exchange for his abdication." She dropped her official tone and added: "That's every nickel I could get out of him."

"You and your Vasilije are a couple of rotten bargain hunters," I complained. "But we'll take it. We've got to have a special train to Saloniki—one that will put us across the border before the abdication goes into effect."

"That will be arranged," she promised.

"Good! Now to do all this your Vasilije has got to take the army away from Einarson. Can he do it?"

"Ach!" Colonel Einarson reared up his head, swelled his thick chest. "That is precisely what he has got to do!"

The fat man grumbled sleepily through his yellow beard. Romaine came over and put a hand on my arm.

"Vasilije wants a private talk with Einarson. Leave it to him. We'll go upstairs."

I agreed and offered Djudakovich my automatic. He paid no attention to the gun or to me. He was looking with a clammy sort of patience at the officer. I went out with the girl and closed the door. At the foot of the stairs I took her by the shoulders and turned her around.

"Can I trust your Vasilije?" I asked.

"Oh my dear, he could handle half a dozen Einarsons."

"I don't mean that. He won't try to gyp me?"

She frowned at me, asking: "Why should you start worrying about that now?"

"He doesn't seem to be exactly all broken out with friendliness."

She laughed, and twisted her face around to bite at one of my hands on her shoulders.

"He's got ideals," she explained. "He despises you and your king for a pair of adventurers who are making a profit out of his country's troubles. That's why he's so sniffy. But he'll keep his word."

Maybe he would, I thought, but he hadn't given me his word—the girl had.

"I'm going over to see His Majesty," I said. "I won't be long—then I'll join you up in his suite. What was the idea of the sewing act? I had no buttons off."

"You did," she contradicted me, rummaging in my pocket for cigarettes. "I pulled one off when one of our men told me you and Einarson were headed this way. I thought it would look domestic."

CHAPTER XVI

LIONEL REX

I found my king in a wine and gold drawing-room in the Executive Residence, surrounded by Muravia's socially and politically ambitious. Uniforms were still in the majority, but a sprinkling of civilians had finally got to him, along with their wives and daughters. He was too occupied to see me for a few minutes, so I stood around, looking the folks over. Particularly one—a tall girl in black, who stood apart from the others, at a window.

I noticed her first because she was beautiful in face and body, and then I studied her more closely because of the expression in the brown eyes with which she watched the new king. If ever anybody looked proud of anybody else, this girl did of Grantham. The way she stood there, alone, by the window, and looked at him—he would have had to be at least a combination of Apollo, Socrates, and Alexander to deserve half of it. Valeska Radnjak, I supposed.

I looked at the boy. His face was proud and flushed, and every two seconds turned toward the girl at the window while he listened to the jabbering of the worshipful group around him. I knew he wasn't any Apollo-Socrates-Alexander, but he managed to look the part. He had found a spot in the world that he liked. I was half sorry he couldn't hang on to it, but my regrets didn't keep me from deciding that I had wasted enough time.

I pushed through the crowd toward him. He recognized me with the eyes of a park sleeper being awakened from sweet dreams by a night-stick on his shoe-soles. He excused himself to the others and took me down a corridor to a room with stained glass windows and richly carved office furniture.

"This was Doctor Semich's office," he told me. "I shall—" He broke off and looked away from me.

"You'll be in Greece by to-morrow," I said bluntly.

He frowned at his feet, a stubborn frown.

"You ought to know you can't hold on," I argued. "You may think everything is going smoothly. If you do, you're deaf, dumb, and blind. I put you in with the muzzle of a gun against Einarson's liver. I've kept you in this long by kidnapping him. I've made a deal with Djudakovich—the only strong man I've seen here. It's up to him to handle Einarson. I can't hold him any longer. Djudakovich will make a

good dictator, and a good king later, if he wants it. He promises you four million dollars and a special train and safe-conduct to Saloniki. You go out with your head up. You've been a king. You've taken a country out of bad hands and put it into good—this fat guy is real. And you've made yourself a million profit."

Grantham looked at me and said:

"No. You go. I shall see it through. These people have trusted me, and I shall—"

"My God, that's old Doc Semich's line! These people haven't trusted you—not a bit of it. I'm the people who trusted you. I made you king, understand? I made you king so you could go home with your chin up—not so you could stay here and make an ass of yourself! I bought help with promises. One of them was that you'd get out within twenty-four hours. You've got to keep the promises I made in your name. The people trusted you, huh? You were crammed down their throats, my son! And I did the cramming! Now I'm going to uncram you. If it happens to be tough on your romance—if your Valeska won't take any price less than this lousy country's throne—that's—"

"That's enough." His voice came from some point at least fifty feet above me. "You shall have your abdication. I don't want the money. You will send word to me when the train is ready."

"Write the get-out now," I ordered.

He went over to the desk, found a sheet of paper, and with a steady hand wrote that in leaving Muravia he renounced his throne and all rights to it. He signed the paper *Lionel Rex* and gave it to me. I pocketed it and began sympathetically:

"I can understand your feelings, and I'm sorry that—"

He put his back to me and walked out of the room. I returned to the hotel.

At the fifth floor I left the elevator and walked softly to the door of my room. No sound came through. I tried the door, found it unlocked, and went in. Emptiness. Even my clothes and bags were gone. I went up to Grantham's suite.

Djudakovich, Romaine, Einarson, and half the police force were there.

CHAPTER XVII

MOB LAW

Colonel Einarson sat very erect in an armchair in the middle of the room. Dark hair and mustache bristled. His chin was out, muscles bulged everywhere in his florid face, his eyes were hot—he was in one of his finest scrapping moods. That came of giving him an audience.

I scowled at Djudakovich, who stood on wide-spread giant's legs with his back to a window. Why hadn't the fat fool known enough to keep Einarson off in a lonely corner, where he could be handled? Djudakovich looked sleepily at my scowl.

Romaine floated around and past the policeman who stood or sat everywhere in the room, and came to where I stood, just inside the door.

"Are your arrangements all made?" she asked.

"Got the abdication in my pocket."

"Give it to me."

"Not yet," I said. "First I've got to know that your Vasilije is as big as he looks. Einarson doesn't look squelched to me. Your fat boy ought to have known he'd blossom out in front of an audience."

"There's no telling what Vasilije is up to," she said lightly, "except that it will be adequate."

I wasn't as sure of that as she was. Djudakovich rumbled a question at her, and she gave him a quick answer. He rumbled some more—at the policemen. They began to go away from us, singly, in pairs, in groups. When the last one had gone the fat man pushed words out between his yellow whiskers at Einarson. Einarson stood up, chest out, shoulders back, grinning confidently under his flowing dark mustache.

"What now?" I asked the girl.

"Come along and you'll see," she said. Her breath came and went quickly, and the gray of her eyes was almost as dark as the black.

———

The four of us went downstairs and out the hotel's front door. The rain had stopped. In the plaza was gathered most of Stefania's population, thickest in front of the Administration Building and Executive Residence. Over their heads we could see the sheepskin caps of Einarson's regiment, still around those buildings as he had left them.

We—or at least Einarson—were recognized and cheered as we crossed the plaza. Einarson and Djudakovich went side by side in front, the soldier marching, the fat giant waddling. Romaine and I went close behind them. We headed straight for the Administration Building.

"What is he up to?" I asked irritably.

She patted my arm, smiled excitedly, and said:

"Wait and see."

There didn't seem to be anything else to do—except worry while I waited.

We arrived at the foot of the Administration Building's stone steps. Bayonets had an uncomfortably cold gleam in the early evening light as Einarson's troops presented arms. We climbed the steps. On the broad top step Einarson and Djudakovich turned to face soldiers and citizens below. The girl and I moved around behind the pair. Her teeth were chattering, her fingers were digging into my arm, but her lips and eyes were smiling recklessly.

The soldiers who were around the Executive Residence came to join those already before us, pushing back the citizens to make room. Another detachment came up. Einarson raised his hand, bawled a dozen words, growled at Djudakovich, and stepped back, giving the blond giant the center of the stage.

Djudakovich spoke, a drowsy, effortless roar that could have been heard as far as the hotel. As he spoke, he took a paper out of his pocket and held it before him. There was nothing theatrical in his voice or manner. He might have been talking about anything not too important. But—

looking at his audience, you'd have known it was important.

The soldiers had broken ranks to crowd nearer, faces were reddening, a bayoneted gun was shaken aloft here and there. Behind them the citizens were looking at one another with frightened faces, jostling each other, some trying to get nearer, some trying to get away.

Djudakovich talked on. The turmoil grew. A soldier pushed through his fellows and started up the steps, others at his heels. Angry voices raised cries.

Einarson cut in on the fat man's speech, stepping to the edge of the top step, bawling down at the upturned faces, with the voice of a man accustomed to being obeyed.

The soldiers on the steps tumbled down. Einarson bawled again. The broken ranks were slowly straightened, flourished guns were grounded. Einarson stood silent a moment, glowering at his troops, and then began an address. I couldn't understand his words any more than I had the fat man's, but there was no question about his impressiveness. And there was no doubt that the anger was going out of the faces below.

I looked at Romaine. She shivered and was no longer smiling. I looked at Djudakovich. He was as still and as emotionless as the mountain he resembled.

I wished I knew what it was all about, so I'd know whether it was wisest to shoot Einarson and duck through the apparently empty building behind us or not. I could guess that the paper in Djudakovich's hand had been evidence of some sort against the Colonel, evidence that would have stirred the soldiers to the point of attacking him if they hadn't been too accustomed to obeying him.

While I was wishing and guessing Einarson finished his address, stepped to one side, clicked his heels together, pointed a finger at Djudakovich, barked an order.

Down below, soldiers' faces were indecisive, shifty-eyed, but four of them stepped briskly out at their colonel's order and came up the steps. "So," I thought, "my fat candidate has lost! Well, he can have the firing squad. The back door for mine." My hand had been holding the gun in my coat pocket for a long time. I kept it there while I took a slow step back, drawing the girl with me.

"Move when I tell you," I muttered.

"Wait!" she gasped. "Look!"

The fat giant, sleepy-eyed as ever, put out an enormous paw and caught the wrist of Einarson's pointing hand. Pulled Einarson down. Let go the wrist and caught the Colonel's shoulder. Lifted him off his feet with that one hand that held his shoulder. Shook him at the soldiers below. Shook Einarson at them with one hand. Shook his piece of paper—whatever it was—at them with the other. And I'm damned if one seemed any more strain on his monstrous arms than the other!

While he shook them—man and paper—he roared sleepily, and when he had finished roaring he flung his two handfuls down to the wild-eyed ranks. Flung them with a gesture that said, *"Here is the man and here is the evidence against him. Do what you like."*

And the soldiers who had cringed back into ranks at Einarson's command when he stood tall and domineering above them, did what could have been expected when he was tossed down to them.

They tore him apart—actually—piece by piece. They dropped their guns and fought to get at him. Those farther away climbed over those nearer, smothering them, trampling them. They surged back and forth in front of the steps, an insane pack of men turned wolves, savagely struggling to destroy a man who must have died before he had been down half a minute.

I put the girl's hand off my arm and went to face Djudakovich.

"Muravia's yours," I said. "I don't want anything but our draft and train. Here's the abdication."

Romaine swiftly translated my words and then Djudakovich's:

"The train is ready now. The draft will be delivered there. Do you wish to go over for Grantham?"

"No. Send him down. How do I find the train?"

"I'll take you," she said. "We'll go through the building and out a side door."

One of Djudakovich's detectives sat at the wheel of a car in front of the hotel. Romaine and I got in it. Across the plaza tumult was still boiling. Neither of us said anything while the car whisked us through darkening streets. She sat as far from me as the width of the rear seat would let her.

Presently she asked very softly:

"And now you despise me?"

"No." I reached for her. "But I hate mobs, lynchings—they sicken me. No matter how wrong the man is, if a mob's against him, I'm for him. The only thing I ever pray to God for is a chance some day to squat down behind a machine gun with a lynching party in front of me. I had no use for Einarson, but I wouldn't have given him that! Well, what's done is done. What was the document?"

"A letter from Mahmoud. He had left it with a friend to be given to Vasilije if anything ever happened to him. He knew Einarson, it seems, and prepared his revenge. The letter confessed his—Mahmoud's—part in the assassination of General Radnjak, and said that Einarson was also implicated. The army worshiped Radnjak, and Einarson wanted the army."

"Your Vasilije could have used that to chase Einarson out—without feeding him to those wolves," I complained.

She shook her head and said:

"Vasilije was right. Bad as it was, that was the way to do it. It's over and settled forever, with Vasilije in power. An Einarson alive, an army not knowing he had killed their idol—too risky. Up to the end Einarson thought he had power enough to hold his troops, no matter what they knew. He—"

"All right—it's done. And I'm glad to be through with this king business. Kiss me."

She did, and whispered:

"When Vasilije dies—and he can't live long, the way he eats—I'm coming to San Francisco."

"You're a cold-blooded hussy," I said.

Lionel Grantham, ex-king of Muravia, was only five minutes behind us in reaching our train. He wasn't alone. Valeska Radnjak, looking as much like the queen of something as if she had been, was with him. She didn't seem to be all broken up over the loss of her throne.

The boy was pleasant and polite enough to me during our rattling trip to Saloniki, but obviously not very comfortable in my company. His bride-to-be didn't know anybody but the boy existed, unless she happened to find some one else directly in front of her. So I didn't wait for their wedding, but left Saloniki on a boat that pulled out a couple of hours after we arrived.

I left the draft with them, of course. They decided to take out Lionel's three millions and return the fourth to Muravia. And I went back to San Francisco to quarrel with my boss over what he thought were unnecessary five- and ten-dollar items in my expense account.

BLACK MASK, AUGUST 1929

Fly Paper

BY DASHIELL HAMMETT

The "Continental" detective tackles a killer.

IT WAS A WANDERING DAUGHTER JOB.

The Hambletons had been for several generations a wealthy and decently prominent New York family. There was nothing in the Hambleton history to account for Sue, the youngest member of the clan. She grew out of childhood with a kink that made her dislike the polished side of life, like the rough. By the time she was twenty-one, in 1926, she definitely preferred Tenth Avenue to Fifth, grifters to bankers, and Hymie the Riveter to the Honorable Cecil Windown, who had asked her to marry him.

The Hambletons tried to make Sue behave, but it was too late for that. She was legally of age. When she finally told them to go to hell and walked out on them there wasn't much they could do about it. Her father, Major Waldo Hambleton, had given up all the hopes he ever had of salvaging her, but he didn't want her to run into any grief that could be avoided. So he came into the Continental Detective Agency's New York office and asked to have an eye kept on her.

Hymie the Riveter was a Philadelphia racketeer who had moved north to the big city, carrying a Thompson submachine-gun wrapped in blue-checkered oil cloth, after a disagreement with his partners. New York wasn't so good a field as Philadelphia for machine-gun work. The Thompson lay idle for a year or so while Hymie made expenses with an automatic, preying on small-time crap games in Harlem.

Three or four months after Sue went to live with Hymie he made what looked like a promising connection with the first of the crew that came into New York from Chicago to organize the city on the western scale. But the boys from Chi didn't want Hymie; they wanted the Thompson. When he showed it to them, as the big item in his application for employment, they shot holes in the top of Hymie's head and went away with the gun.

Sue Hambleton buried Hymie, had a couple of lonely weeks in which she hocked a ring to eat, and then got a job as hostess in a speakeasy run by a Greek named Vassos.

One of Vassos' customers was Babe McCloor, two hundred and fifty pounds of hard Scotch-Irish-Indian bone and muscle, a black-haired, blue-eyed, swarthy giant who was resting up after doing a fifteen-year hitch in Leavenworth for ruining most of the smaller post offices between New Orleans and Omaha. Babe was keeping himself in drinking money while he rested by playing with pedestrians in dark streets.

Babe liked Sue. Vassos liked Sue. Sue liked Babe. Vassos didn't like that. Jealousy spoiled the Greek's judgment. He kept the speakeasy door locked one night when Babe wanted to come in. Babe came in, bringing pieces of the door with him. Vassos got his gun out, but couldn't shake Sue off his arm. He stopped trying when Babe hit him with the part of the door that had the brass knob on it. Babe and Sue went away from Vassos' together.

Up to that time the New York office had managed to keep in touch with Sue. She hadn't been kept under constant surveillance. Her father hadn't wanted that. It was simply a matter of sending a man around every week or so to see that she was still alive, to pick up whatever information he could from her friends and neighbors, without, of course, letting her know she was being tabbed. All that had been easy enough, but when she and Babe went away after wrecking the gin mill, they dropped completely out of sight.

After turning the city upside-down, the New York office sent a journal on the job to the other Continental branches throughout the country, giving the information above and enclosing photographs and descriptions of Sue and her new playmate. That was late in 1927.

We had enough copies of the photographs to go around, and for the next month or so whoever had a little idle time on his hands spent it looking through San Francisco and Oakland for the missing pair. We didn't find them. Operatives in other cities, doing the same thing, had the same luck.

Then, nearly a year later, a telegram came to us from the New York office. Decoded, it read:

Major Hambleton today received telegram from daughter in San Francisco quote Please wire me thousand dollars care apartment two hundred six number six hundred one Eddis Street stop I will come home if you will let me stop Please tell me if I can come but please please wire money anyway unquote Hambleton authorizes payment of money to her immediately stop Detail competent operative to call on her with money and to arrange for her return home stop If possible have man and woman operative accompany her here stop Hambleton wiring her stop Report immediately by wire.

II

The Old Man gave me the telegram and a check, saying:

"You know the situation. You'll know how to handle it."

I pretended I agreed with him, went down to the bank, swapped the check for a bundle of bills of several sizes, caught a street car, and went up to 601 Eddis Street, a fairly large apartment building on the corner of Larkin.

The name on Apartment 206's vestibule mail box was J. M. Wales.

I pushed 206's button. When the locked door buzzed off I went into the building, past the elevator to the stairs, and up a flight. 206 was just around the corner from the stairs.

The apartment door was opened by a tall, slim man of thirty-something in neat dark clothes. He had narrow dark eyes set in a long pale face. There was some gray in the dark hair brushed flat to his scalp.

"Miss Hambleton," I said.

"Uh—what about her?" His voice was smooth, but not too smooth to be agreeable.

"I'd like to see her."

His upper eyelids came down a little and the brows over them came a little closer together. He asked, "Is it—?" and stopped, watching me steadily.

I didn't say anything. Presently he finished his question:

"Something to do with a telegram?"

"Yeah."

His long face brightened immediately. He asked:

"You're from her father?"

"Yeah."

He stepped back and swung the door wide open, saying:

"Come in. Major Hambleton's wire came to her only a few minutes ago. He said someone would call."

We went through a small passageway into a sunny living-room that was cheaply furnished, but neat and clean enough.

"Sit down," the man said, pointing at a brown rocking chair.

I sat down. He sat on the burlap-covered sofa facing me. I looked around the room. I didn't see anything to show that a woman was living there.

He rubbed the long bridge of his nose with a longer forefinger and asked slowly:

"You brought the money?"

I said I'd feel more like talking with her there.

He looked at the finger with which he had been rubbing his nose, and then up at me, saying softly:

"But I'm her friend."

I said, "Yeah?" to that.

"Yes," he repeated. He frowned slightly, drawing back the corners of his thin-lipped mouth. "I've only asked whether you've brought the money."

I didn't say anything.

"The point is," he said quite reasonably, "that if you brought the money she doesn't expect you to hand it over to anybody except her. If you didn't bring it she doesn't want to see you. I don't think her mind can be changed about that. That's why I asked if you had brought it."

"I brought it."

He looked doubtfully at me. I showed him the money I had got from the bank. He jumped up briskly from the sofa.

"I'll have her here in a minute or two," he said over his shoulder as his long legs moved him toward the door. At the door he stopped to ask: "Do you know her? Or shall I have her bring means of identifying herself?"

"That would be best," I told him.

He went out, leaving the corridor door open.

III

In five minutes he was back with a slender blonde girl of twenty-three in pale green silk. The looseness of her small mouth and the puffiness around her blue eyes weren't yet pronounced enough to spoil her prettiness.

I stood up.

"This is Miss Hambleton," he said.

She gave me a swift glance and then lowered her eyes again, nervously playing with the strap of a handbag she held.

"You can identify yourself?" I asked.

"Sure," the man said. "Show them to him, Sue."

She opened the bag, brought out some papers and things, and held them up for me to take.

"Sit down, sit down," the man said as I took them.

They sat on the sofa. I sat in the rocking chair again and examined the things she had given me. There were two letters addressed to Sue Hambleton here, her father's telegram welcoming her home, a couple of receipted department store bills, an automobile driver's license, and a savings account pass book that showed a balance of less than ten dollars.

By the time I had finished my examination the girl's embarrassment was gone. She looked levelly at me, as did the man beside her. I felt in my pocket, found my copy of the photograph New York had sent us at the beginning of the hunt, and looked from it to her.

"Your mouth could have shrunk, maybe," I said, "but how could your nose have got that much longer?"

"If you don't like my nose," she said, "how'd you like to go to hell?" Her face had turned red.

"That's not the point. It's a swell nose, but it's not Sue's." I held the photograph out to her. "See for yourself."

She glared at the photograph and then at the man.

"What a smart guy you are," she told him.

He was watching me with dark eyes that had a brittle shine to them between narrow-drawn eyelids. He kept on watching me while he spoke to her out the side of his mouth, crisply:

"Pipe down."

She piped down. He sat and watched me. I sat and watched him. A clock ticked seconds away behind me. His eyes began shifting their focus from one of my eyes to the other. The girl sighed.

He said in a low voice: "Well?"

I said: "You're in a hole."

"What can you make out of it?" he asked casually.

"Conspiracy to defraud."

The girl jumped up and hit one of his shoulders angrily with the back of a hand, crying:

"What a smart guy you are, to get me in a jam like this. It was going to be duck soup—yeh! Eggs in the coffee—yeh! Now look at you. You haven't even got guts enough to tell this guy to go chase himself." She spun around to face me, pushing her red face down at me—I was still sitting in the rocker—snarling: "Well, what are you waiting for? Waiting to be kissed good-by? We don't owe you anything, do we? We didn't get any of your lousy money, did we? Outside, then. Take the air. Dangle."

"Stop it, sister," I growled. "You'll bust something."

The man said:

"For God's sake stop that bawling, Peggy, and give somebody else a chance." He addressed me: "Well, what do you want?"

"How'd you get into this?" I asked.

He spoke quickly, eagerly:

"A fellow named Kenny gave me that stuff and told me about this Sue Hambleton, and her old man having plenty. I thought I'd give it a whirl. I figured the old man would either wire the dough right off the reel or wouldn't send it at all. I didn't figure on this send-a-man stuff. Then when his wire came, saying he was sending a man to see her, I ought to have dropped it.

"But hell! Here was a man coming with a grand in cash. That was too good to let go of without a try. It looked like there still might be a chance of copping,* so I got Peggy to do Sue for me. If the man was coming today, it was a cinch he belonged out here on the Coast, and it was an even bet he wouldn't know Sue, would only have a description of her. From what Kenny had told me about her, I knew Peggy would come pretty close to fitting her description. I still don't see how you got that photograph. Television? I only wired the old man yesterday. I mailed a couple of letters to Sue, here, yesterday, so we'd have them with the other identification stuff to get the money from the telegraph company on."

"Kenny gave you the old man's address?"

"Sure he did."

"Did he give you Sue's?"

"No."

"How'd Kenny get hold of the stuff?"

"He didn't say."

"Where's Kenny now?"

"I don't know. He was on his way east, with something else on the fire, and couldn't fool with this. That's why he passed it on to me."

"Big-hearted Kenny," I said. "You know Sue Hambleton?"

_____

* getting the money

"No," emphatically. "I'd never even heard of her till Kenny told me."

"I don't like this Kenny," I said, "though without him your story's got some good points. Could you tell it leaving him out?"

He shook his head slowly from side to side, saying:

"It wouldn't be the way it happened."

"That's too bad. Conspiracies to defraud don't mean as much to me as finding Sue. I might have made a deal with you."

He shook his head again, but his eyes were thoughtful, and his lower lip moved up to overlap the upper a little.

The girl had stepped back so she could see both of us as we talked, turning her face, which showed she didn't like us, from one to the other as we spoke our pieces. Now she fastened her gaze on the man, and her eyes were growing angry again.

I got up on my feet, telling him:

"Suit yourself. But if you want to play it that way I'll have to take you both in."

He smiled with indrawn lips and stood up.

The girl thrust herself in between us, facing him.

"This is a swell time to be dummying up," she spit at him. "Pop off, you lightweight, or I will. You're crazy if you think I'm going to take the fall with you."

"Shut up," he said in his throat.

"Shut me up," she cried.

He tried to, with both hands. I reached over her shoulders and caught one of his wrists, knocked the other hand up.

She slid out from between us and ran around behind me, screaming:

"Joe does know her. He got the things from her. She's at the St. Martin on O'Farrell Street—her and Babe McCloor."

While I listened to this I had to pull my head aside to let Joe's right hook miss me, had got his left arm twisted behind him, had turned my hip to catch his knee, and had got the palm of my left hand under his chin. I was ready to give his

chin the Japanese tilt* when he stopped wrestling and grunted:

"Let me tell it."

"Hop to it," I consented, taking my hands away from him and stepping back.

He rubbed the wrist I had wrenched, scowling past me at the girl. He called her four unlovely names, the mildest of which was "a dumb twist," and told her:

"He was bluffing about throwing us in the can. You don't think old man Hambleton's hunting for newspaper space, do you?" That wasn't a bad guess.

He sat on the sofa again, still rubbing his wrist. The girl stayed on the other side of the room, laughing at him through her teeth.

I said: "All right, roll it out, one of you."

"You've got it all," he muttered. "I glaumed that stuff last week when I was visiting Babe, knowing the story and hating to see a promising layout like that go to waste."

"What's Babe doing now?" I asked.

"I don't know."

"Is he still puffing† them?"

"I don't know."

"Like hell you don't."

"I don't," he insisted. "If you know Babe you know you can't get anything out of him about what he's doing."

"How long have he and Sue been here?"

"About six months that I know of."

"Who's he mobbed up with?"

"I don't know. Any time Babe works with a mob he picks them up on the road and leaves them on the road."

"How's he fixed?"

"I don't know. There's always enough grub and liquor in the joint."

---

* Refers to a joke postcard with faux Japanese characters and the caption: "If you can't understand Japanese, tilt your head to the right." Read from the right are English letters that spell out: "You look really silly, asshole."

† blowing up safes, creating puffs of smoke

Half an hour of this convinced me that I wasn't going to get much information about my people here.

I went to the phone in the passageway and called the agency. The boy on the switchboard told me MacMan was in the operatives' room. I asked to have him sent up to me, and went back to the living-room. Joe and Peggy took their heads apart when I came in.

MacMan arrived in less than ten minutes. I let him in and told him:

"This fellow says his name's Joe Wales, and the girl's supposed to be Peggy Carroll who lives upstairs in 421. We've got them cold for conspiracy to defraud, but I've made a deal with them. I'm going out to look at it now. Stay here with them, in this room. Nobody goes in or out, and nobody but you gets to the phone. There's a fire-escape in front of the window. The window's locked now. I'd keep it that way. If the deal turns out O.K. we'll let them go, but if they cut up on you while I'm gone there's no reason why you can't knock them around as much as you want."

MacMan nodded his hard round head and pulled a chair out between them and the door. I picked up my hat.

Joe Wales called:

"Hey, you're not going to uncover me to Babe, are you? That's got to be part of the deal."

"Not unless I have to."

"I'd just as leave stand the rap," he said. "I'd be safer in jail."

"I'll give you the best break I can," I promised, "but you'll have to take what's dealt you."

IV

Walking over to the St. Martin—only half a dozen blocks from Wales's place—I decided to go up against McCloor and the girl as a Continental op who suspected Babe of being in on a branch bank stick-up in Alameda the previous week. He hadn't been in on it—if the bank people had described half-correctly the men who had robbed them—so it wasn't likely my supposed suspicions would frighten him much. Clearing himself, he might give me some information I could use. The chief thing I wanted, of course, was a look at the girl, so I could report to her father that I had seen her. There was no reason for supposing that she and Babe knew her father was trying to keep an eye on her. Babe had a record. It was natural enough for sleuths to drop in now and then and try to hang something on him.

The St. Martin was a small three-story apartment house of red brick between two taller hotels. The vestibule register showed, *R. K. McCloor, 313,* as Wales and Peggy had told me.

I pushed the bell button. Nothing happened. Nothing happened any of the four times I pushed it. I pushed the button labeled *Manager.*

The door clicked open. I went indoors. A beefy woman in a pink-striped cotton dress that needed pressing stood in an apartment doorway just inside the street door.

"Some people named McCloor live here?" I asked.

"Three-thirteen," she said.

"Been living here long?"

She pursed her fat mouth, looked intently at me, hesitated, but finally said: "Since last June."

"What do you know about them?"

She balked at that, raising her chin and her eyebrows.

I gave her my card. That was safe enough; it fit in with the pretext I intended using upstairs.

Her face, when she raised it from reading the card, was oily with curiosity.

"Come in here," she said in a husky whisper, backing through the doorway.

I followed her into her apartment. We sat on a Chesterfield and she whispered:

"What is it?"

"Maybe nothing." I kept my voice low, playing up to her theatricals. "He's done time for safe-burglary. I'm trying to get a line on him now, on the off chance that he might have been tied up in a recent job. I don't know that he was.

He may be going straight for all I know." I took his photograph—front and profile, taken at Leavenworth—out of my pocket. "This him?"

She seized it eagerly, nodded, said, "Yes, that's him, all right," turned it over to read the description on the back, and repeated, "Yes, that's him, all right."

"His wife is here with him?" I asked.

She nodded vigorously.

"I don't know her," I said. "What sort of looking girl is she?"

She described a girl who could have been Sue Hambleton. I couldn't show Sue's picture; that would have uncovered me if she and Babe heard about it.

I asked the woman what she knew about the McCloors. What she knew wasn't a great deal: paid their rent on time, kept irregular hours, had occasional drinking parties, quarreled a lot.

"Think they're in now?" I asked. "I got no answer on the bell."

"I don't know," she whispered. "I haven't seen either of them since night before last, when they had a fight."

"Much of a fight?"

"Not much worse than usual."

"Could you find out if they're in?" I asked.

She looked at me out of the ends of her eyes.

"I'm not going to make any trouble for you," I assured her. "But if they've blown I'd like to know it, and I reckon you would too."

"All right, I'll find out." She got up, patting a pocket in which keys jingled. "You wait here."

"I'll go as far as the third floor with you," I said, "and wait out of sight there."

"All right," she said reluctantly.

On the third floor, I remained by the elevator. She disappeared around a corner of the dim corridor, and presently a muffled electric bell rang. It rang three times. I heard her keys jingle and one of them grate in a lock. The lock clicked. I heard the doorknob rattle as she turned it.

Then a long moment of silence was ended by a scream that filled the corridor from wall to wall.

I jumped for the corner, swung around it, saw an open door ahead, went through it, and slammed the door shut behind me.

The scream had stopped.

I was in a small dark vestibule with three doors besides the one I had come through. One door was shut. One opened into a bathroom. I went to the other.

The fat manager stood just inside it, her round back to me. I pushed past her and saw what she was looking at.

Sue Hambleton, in pale yellow pajamas trimmed with black lace, was lying across a bed. She lay on her back. Her arms were stretched out over her head. One leg was bent under her, one stretched out so that its bare foot rested on the floor. That bare foot was whiter than a live foot could be. Her face was white as her foot, except for a mottled swollen area from the right eyebrow to the right cheek-bone and dark bruises on her throat.

"Phone the police," I told the woman, and began poking into corners, closets and drawers.

It was late afternoon when I returned to the agency. I asked the file clerk to see if we had anything on Joe Wales and Peggy Carroll, and then went into the Old Man's office.

He put down some reports he had been reading, gave me a nodded invitation to sit down, and asked:

"You've seen her?"

"Yeah. She's dead."

The Old Man said, "Indeed," as if I had said it was raining, and smiled with polite attentiveness while I told him about it—from the time I had rung Wales's bell until I had joined the fat manager in the dead girl's apartment.

"She had been knocked around some, was bruised on the face and neck," I wound up. "But that didn't kill her."

"You think she was murdered?" he asked, still smiling gently.

"I don't know. Doc Jordan says he thinks it

could have been arsenic. He's hunting for it in her now. We found a funny thing in the joint. Some thick sheets of dark gray paper were stuck in a book—*The Count of Monte Cristo*—wrapped in a month-old newspaper and wedged into a dark corner between the stove and the kitchen wall."

"Ah, arsenical fly paper," the Old Man murmured. "The Maybrick-Seddons trick.* Mashed in water, four to six grains of arsenic can be soaked out of a sheet—enough to kill two people."

I nodded, saying:

"I worked on one in Louisville in 1916. The mulatto janitor saw McCloor leaving at half-past nine yesterday morning. She was probably dead before that. Nobody's seen him since. Earlier in the morning the people in the next apartment had heard them talking, her groaning. But they had too many fights for the neighbors to pay much attention to that. The landlady told me they had a fight the night before that. The police are hunting for him."

"Did you tell the police who she was?"

"No. What do we do on that angle? We can't tell them about Wales without telling them all."

"I dare say the whole thing will have to come out," he said thoughtfully. "I'll wire New York."

I went out of his office. The file clerk gave me a couple of newspaper clippings. The first told me that, fifteen months ago, Joseph Wales, alias Holy Joe, had been arrested on the complaint of a farmer named Toomey that he had been taken for twenty-five hundred dollars on a phoney "Business Opportunity" by Wales and three

---

* Florence Maybrick was convicted in 1899 of the murder of her husband in Liverpool by poisoning his juice with arsenic. She was sentenced to death, but her death sentence was commuted and she was released in 1904 after five years in prison. Frederick Seddon murdered a boarder named Elizabeth with arsenic in London in 1911. His wife was shown to have purchased a large quantity of fly papers containing the poison. She was found innocent, and he was hanged on April 19, 1912.

other men. The second clipping said the case had been dropped when Toomey failed to appear against Wales in court—bought off in the customary manner by the return of part or all of his money. That was all our files held on Wales, and they had nothing on Peggy Carroll.

V

MacMan opened the door for me when I returned to Wales's apartment.

"Anything doing?" I asked him.

"Nothing—except they've been belly-aching a lot."

Wales came forward, asking eagerly:

"Satisfied now?"

The girl stood by the window, looking at me with anxious eyes.

I didn't say anything.

"Did you find her?" Wales asked, frowning. "She was where I told you?"

"Yeah," I said.

"Well, then." Part of his frown went away. "That lets Peggy and me out, doesn't—" He broke off, ran his tongue over his lower lip, put a hand to his chin, asked sharply: "You didn't give them the tip-off on me, did you?"

I shook my head, no.

He took his hand from his chin and asked irritably:

"What's the matter with you, then? What are you looking like that for?"

Behind him the girl spoke bitterly.

"I knew damned well it would be like this," she said. "I knew damned well we weren't going to get out of it. Oh, what a smart guy you are!"

"Take Peggy into the kitchen, and shut both doors," I told MacMan. "Holy Joe and I are going to have a real heart-to-heart talk."

The girl went out willingly, but when Mac-Man was closing the door she put her head in again to tell Wales:

"I hope he busts you in the nose if you try to hold out on him."

MacMan shut the door.

"Your playmate seems to think you know something," I said.

Wales scowled at the door and grumbled: "She's more help to me than a broken leg." He turned his face to me, trying to make it look frank and friendly. "What do you want? I came clean with you before. What's the matter now?"

"What do you guess?"

He pulled his lips in between his teeth.

"What do you want to make me guess for?" he demanded. "I'm willing to play ball with you. But what can I do if you won't tell me what you want? I can't see inside your head."

"You'd get a kick out of it if you could."

He shook his head wearily and walked back to the sofa, sitting down bent forward, his hands together between his knees.

"All right," he sighed. "Take your time about asking me. I'll wait for you."

I went over and stood in front of him. I took his chin between my left thumb and fingers, raising his head and bending my own down until our noses were almost touching. I said:

"Where you stumbled, Joe, was in sending the telegram right after the murder."

"He's dead?" It popped out before his eyes had even had time to grow round and wide.

The question threw me off balance. I had to wrestle with my forehead to keep it from wrinkling, and I put too much calmness in my voice when I asked:

"Is who dead?"

"Who? How do I know? Who do you mean?"

"Who did you think I meant?" I insisted.

"How do I know? Oh, all right! Old man Hambleton, Sue's father."

"That's right," I said, and took my hand away from his chin.

"And he was murdered, you say?" He hadn't moved his face an inch from the position into which I had lifted it. "How?"

"Arsenic—fly paper."

"Arsenic fly paper." He looked thoughtful. "That's a funny one."

"Yeah, very funny. Where'd you go about buying some if you wanted it?"

"Buying it? I don't know. I haven't seen any since I was a kid. Nobody uses fly paper here in San Francisco anyway. There aren't enough flies."

"Somebody used some here," I said, "on Sue."

"Sue?" He jumped so that the sofa squeaked under him.

"Yeah. Murdered yesterday morning— arsenical fly paper."

"Both of them?" he asked incredulously.

"Both of who?"

"Her and her father."

"Yeah."

He put his chin far down on his chest and rubbed the back of one hand with the palm of the other.

"Then I am in a hole," he said slowly.

"That's what," I cheerfully agreed. "Want to try talking yourself out of it?"

"Let me think."

I let him think, listening to the tick of the clock while he thought. Thinking brought drops of sweat out on his gray-white face. Presently he sat up straight, wiping his face with a fancily colored handkerchief.

"I'll talk," he said. "I've got to talk now. Sue was getting ready to ditch Babe. She and I were going away. She—Here, I'll show you."

He put his hand in his pocket and held out a folded sheet of thick notepaper to me. I took it and read:

Dear Joe:

I can't stand this much longer—we've simply got to go soon. Babe beat me again tonight. Please, if you really love me, let's make it soon.

Sue

The handwriting was a nervous woman's, tall, angular, and piled up.

"That's why I made the play for Hamble-ton's grand," he said. "I've been shatting on my uppers* for a couple of months, and when that letter came yesterday I just had to raise dough somehow to get her away. She wouldn't have stood for tapping her father though, so I tried to swing it without her knowing."

"When did you see her last?"

"Day before yesterday, the day she mailed that letter. Only I saw her in the afternoon—she was here—and she wrote it that night."

"Babe suspect what you were up to?"

"We didn't think he did. I don't know. He was jealous as hell all the time, whether he had any reason to be or not."

"How much reason did he have?"

Wales looked me straight in the eye and said: "Sue was a good kid."

I said: "Well, she's been murdered."

He didn't say anything.

Day was darkening into evening. I went to the door and pressed the light button. I didn't lose sight of Holy Joe Wales while I was doing it.

As I took my finger away from the button, something clicked at the window. The click was loud and sharp.

I looked at the window.

A man crouched there on the fire-escape, looking in through glass and lace curtain. He was a thick-featured dark man whose size identi-fied him as Babe McCloor. The muzzle of a big black automatic was touching the glass in front of him. He had tapped the glass with it to catch our attention.

He had our attention.

There wasn't anything for me to do just then. I stood there and looked at him. I couldn't tell whether he was looking at me or at Wales. I could see him clearly enough, but the lace cur-tain spoiled my view of details like that. I imag-ined he wasn't neglecting either of us, and I didn't imagine the lace curtain hid much from him. He was closer to the curtain than we, and I had turned on the room's lights.

_____
* completely broke

Wales, sitting dead still on the sofa, was look-ing at McCloor. Wales's face wore a peculiar, stiffly sullen expression. His eyes were sullen. He wasn't breathing.

McCloor flicked the nose of his pistol against the pane, and a triangular piece of glass fell out, tinkling apart on the floor. It didn't, I was afraid, make enough noise to alarm MacMan in the kitchen. There were two closed doors between here and there.

Wales looked at the broken pane and closed his eyes. He closed them slowly, little by little, exactly as if he were falling asleep. He kept his stiffly sul-len blank face turned straight to the window.

McCloor shot him three times.

The bullets knocked Wales down on the sofa, back against the wall. Wales's eyes popped open, bulging. His lips crawled back over his teeth, leaving them naked to the gums. His tongue came out. Then his head fell down and he didn't move any more.

When McCloor jumped away from the win-dow I jumped to it. While I was pushing the cur-tain aside, unlocking the window and raising it, I heard his feet land on the cement paving below.

MacMan flung the door open and came in, the girl at his heels.

"Take care of this," I ordered as I scrambled over the sill. "McCloor shot him."

VI

Wales's apartment was on the second floor. The fire-escape ended there with a counter-weighted iron ladder that a man's weight would swing down into a cement-paved court.

I went down as Babe McCloor had gone, swinging down on the ladder till within drop-ping distance of the court, and then letting go.

There was only one street exit to the court. I took it.

A startled looking, smallish man was stand-ing in the middle of the sidewalk close to the court, gaping at me as I dashed out.

I caught his arm, shook it.

"A big guy running." Maybe I yelled. "Where?"

He tried to say something, couldn't, and waved his arm at billboards standing across the front of a vacant lot on the other side of the street.

I forgot to say, "Thank you," in my hurry to get over there.

I got behind the billboards by crawling under them instead of going to either end, where there were openings. The lot was large enough and weedy enough to give cover to anybody who wanted to lie down and bushwhack a pursuer— even anybody as large as Babe McCloor.

While I considered that, I heard a dog barking at one corner of the lot. He could have been barking at a man who had run by. I ran to that corner of the lot. The dog was in a board-fenced backyard, at the corner of a narrow alley that ran from the lot to a street.

I chinned myself on the board fence, saw a wire-haired terrier alone in the yard, and ran down the alley while he was charging my part of the fence.

I put my gun back into my pocket before I left the alley for the street.

A small touring car was parked at the curb in front of a cigar store some fifteen feet from the alley. A policeman was talking to a slim dark-faced man in the cigar store doorway.

"The big fellow that come out of the alley a minute ago," I said. "Which way did he go?"

The policeman looked dumb. The slim man nodded his head down the street, said, "Down that way," and went on with his conversation.

I said, "Thanks," and went on down to the corner. There was a taxi phone there and two idle taxis. A block and a half below, a street car was going away.

"Did the big fellow who came down here a minute ago take a taxi or the street car?" I asked the two taxi chauffeurs who were leaning against one of the taxis.

The rattier looking one said:

"He didn't take a taxi."

I said:

"I'll take one. Catch that street car for me."

The street car was three blocks away before we got going. The street wasn't clear enough for me to see who got on and off it. We caught it when it stopped at Market Street.

"Follow along," I told the driver as I jumped out.

On the rear platform of the street car I looked through the glass. There were only eight or ten people aboard.

"There was a great big fellow got on at Hyde Street," I said to the conductor. "Where'd he get off?"

The conductor looked at the silver dollar I was turning over in my fingers and remembered that the big man got off at Taylor Street. That won the silver dollar.

I dropped off as the street car turned into Market Street. The taxi, close behind, slowed down, and its door swung open.

"Sixth and Mission," I said as I hopped in.

McCloor could have gone in any direction from Taylor Street. I had to guess. The best guess seemed to be that he would make for the other side of Market Street.

It was fairly dark by now. We had to go down to Fifth Street to get off Market, then over to Mission, and back up to Sixth. We got to Sixth Street without seeing McCloor. I couldn't see him on Sixth Street—either way from the crossing.

"On up to Ninth," I ordered, and while we rode told the driver what kind of man I was looking for.

We arrived at Ninth Street. No McCloor. I cursed and pushed my brains around.

The big man was a yegg. San Francisco was on fire for him. The yegg instinct would be to use a rattler to get away from trouble. The freight yards were in this end of town. Maybe he would be shifty enough to lie low instead of trying to powder. In that case, he probably hadn't crossed Market Street at all. If he stuck, there would still be a chance of picking him up tomorrow. If he was high-tailing, it was catch him now or not at all.

"Down to Harrison," I told the driver.

We went down to Harrison Street, and

down Harrison to Third, up Bryant to Eighth, down Brannan to Third again, and over to Townsend—and we didn't see Babe McCloor.

"That's tough, that is," the driver sympathized as we stopped across the street from the Southern Pacific passenger station.

"I'm going over and look around in the station," I said. "Keep your eyes open while I'm gone."

When I told the copper in the station my trouble he introduced me to a couple of plainclothes men who had been planted there to watch for McCloor. That had been done after Sue Hambleton's body was found. The shooting of Holy Joe Wales was news to them.

I went outside again and found my taxi in front of the door, its horn working over-time, but too asthmatically to be heard indoors. The ratty driver was excited.

"A guy like you said come up out of King Street just now and swung on a No. 16 car as it pulled away," he said.

"Going which way?"

"That-away," pointing southeast.

"Catch him," I said, jumping in.

The street car was out of sight around a bend in Third Street two blocks below. When we rounded the bend, the street car was slowing up, four blocks ahead. It hadn't slowed up very much when a man leaned far out and stepped off. He was a tall man, but didn't look tall on account of his shoulder spread. He didn't check his momentum, but used it to carry him across the sidewalk and out of sight.

We stopped where the man had left the car.

I gave the driver too much money and told him:

"Go back to Townsend Street and tell the copper in the station that I've chased Babe McCloor into the S. P. yards."

VII

I thought I was moving silently down between two strings of box cars, but I had gone less than twenty feet when a light flashed in my face and a sharp voice ordered:

"Stand still, you."

I stood still. Men came from between cars. One of them spoke my name, adding: "What are you doing here? Lost?" It was Harry Pebble, a police detective.

I stopped holding my breath and said:

"Hello, Harry. Looking for Babe?"

"Yes. We've been going over the rattlers."

"He's here. I just tailed him in from the street."

Pebble swore and snapped the light off.

"Watch, Harry," I advised. "Don't play with him. He's packing plenty of gun and he's cut down one boy tonight."

"I'll play with him," Pebble promised, and told one of the men with him to go over and warn those on the other side of the yard that McCloor was in, and then to ring for reinforcements.

"We'll just sit on the edge and hold him in till they come," he said.

That seemed a sensible way to play it. We spread out and waited. Once Pebble and I turned back a lanky bum who tried to slip into the yard between us, and one of the men below us picked up a shivering kid who was trying to slip out. Otherwise nothing happened until Lieutenant Duff arrived with a couple of carloads of coppers.

Most of our force went into a cordon around the yard. The rest of us went through the yard in small groups, working it over car by car. We picked up a few hoboes that Pebble and his men had missed earlier, but we didn't find McCloor.

We didn't find any trace of him until somebody stumbled over a railroad bull[*] huddled in the shadow of a gondola. It took a couple of minutes to bring him to, and he couldn't talk then. His jaw was broken. But when we asked if McCloor had slugged him, he nodded, and when we asked in which direction McCloor had been headed, he moved a feeble hand to the east.

We went over and searched the Santa Fe yards. We didn't find McCloor.

_____

[*] cop

VIII

I rode up to the Hall of Justice with Duff. Mac-Man was in the captain of detectives' office with three or four police sleuths.

"Wales die?" I asked.

"Yep."

"Say anything before he went?"

"He was gone before you were through the window."

"You held on to the girl?"

"She's here."

"She say anything?"

"We were waiting for you before we tapped her," detective-sergeant O'Gar said, "not knowing the angle on her."

"Let's have her in. I haven't had any dinner yet. How about the autopsy on Sue Hambleton?"

"Chronic arsenic poisoning."

"Chronic? That means it was fed to her little by little, and not in a lump?"

"Uh-huh. From what he found in her kidney, intestines, liver, stomach and blood, Jordan figures there was less than a grain of it in her. That wouldn't be enough to knock her off. But he says he found arsenic in the tips of her hair, and she'd have to be given some at least a month ago for it to have worked out that far."

"Any chance that it wasn't arsenic that killed her?"

"Not unless Jordan's a bum doctor."

A policewoman came in with Peggy Carroll.

The blonde girl was tired. Her eyelids, mouth corners and body drooped, and when I pushed a chair out toward her she sagged down in it.

O'Gar ducked his grizzled bullet head at me.

"Now, Peggy," I said, "tell us where you fit into this mess."

"I don't fit into it." She didn't look up. Her voice was tired. "Joe dragged me into it. He told you."

"You his girl?"

"If you want to call it that," she admitted.

"You jealous?"

"What," she asked, looking up at me, her face puzzled, "has that got to do with it?"

"Sue Hambleton was getting ready to go away with him when she was murdered."

The girl sat up straight in the chair and said deliberately:

"I swear to God I didn't know she was murdered."

"But you did know she was dead," I said positively.

"I didn't," she replied just as positively.

I nudged O'Gar with my elbow. He pushed his undershot jaw at her and barked:

"What are you trying to give us? You knew she was dead. How could you kill her without knowing it?"

While she looked at him I waved the others in. They crowded close around her and took up the chorus of the sergeant's song. She was barked, roared, and snarled at plenty in the next few minutes.

The instant she stopped trying to talk back to them I cut in again.

"Wait," I said, very earnestly. "Maybe she didn't kill her."

"The hell she didn't," O'Gar stormed, holding the center of the stage so the others could move away from the girl without their retreat seeming too artificial. "Do you mean to tell me this baby—"

"I didn't say she didn't," I remonstrated. "I said maybe she didn't."

"Then who did?"

I passed the question to the girl: "Who did?"

"Babe," she said immediately.

O'Gar snorted to make her think he didn't believe her.

I asked, as if I were honestly perplexed:

"How do you know that if you didn't know she was dead?"

"It stands to reason he did," she said. "Anybody can see that. He found out she was going away with Joe, so he killed her and then came to Joe's and killed him. That's just exactly what Babe would do when he found it out."

"Yeah? How long have *you* known they were going away together?"

"Since they decided to. Joe told me a month or two ago."

"And you didn't mind?"

"You've got this all wrong," she said. "Of course I didn't mind. I was being cut in on it. You know her father had the bees.* That's what Joe was after. She didn't mean anything to him but an in to the old man's pockets. And I was to get my dib. And you needn't think I was crazy enough about Joe or anybody else to step off in the air for them. Babe got next and fixed the pair of them. That's a cinch."

"Yeah? How do you figure Babe would kill her?"

"That guy? You don't think he'd—"

"I mean, how would he go about killing her?"

"Oh!" She shrugged. "With his hands, likely as not."

"Once he'd made up his mind to do it, he'd do it quick and violent?" I suggested.

"That would be Babe," she agreed.

"But you can't see him slow-poisoning her—spreading it out over a month?"

Worry came into the girl's blue eyes. She put her lower lip between her teeth, then said slowly:

"No, I can't see him doing it that way. Not Babe."

"Who can you see doing it that way?"

She opened her eyes wide, asking:

"You mean Joe?"

I didn't say anything.

"Joe might have," she said persuasively. "God only knows what he'd want to do it for, why he'd want to get rid of the kind of meal ticket she was going to be. But you couldn't always guess what he was getting at. He pulled plenty of dumb ones. He was too slick without being smart. If he was going to kill her, though, that would be about the way he'd go about it."

"Were he and Babe friendly?"

"No."

"Did he go to Babe's much?"

"Not at all that I know about. He was too

_____

* money

leary of Babe to take a chance on being caught there. That's why I moved upstairs, so Sue could come over to our place to see him."

"Then how could Joe have hidden the fly paper he poisoned her with in her apartment?"

"Fly paper!" Her bewilderment seemed honest enough.

"Show it to her," I told O'Gar.

He got a sheet from the desk and held it close to the girl's face.

She stared at it for a moment and then jumped up and grabbed my arm with both hands.

"I didn't know what it was," she said excitedly. "Joe had some a couple of months ago. He was looking at it when I came in. I asked him what it was for, and he smiled that wisenheimer smile of his and said, 'You make angels out of it,' and wrapped it up again and put it in his pocket. I didn't pay much attention to him: he was always fooling with some kind of tricks that were supposed to make him wealthy, but never did."

"Ever see it again?"

"No."

"Did you know Sue very well?"

"I didn't know her at all. I never even saw her. I used to keep out of the way so I wouldn't gum Joe's play with her."

"But you know Babe?"

"Yes, I've been on a couple of parties where he was. That's all I know him."

"Who killed Sue?"

"Joe," she said. "Didn't he have that paper you say she was killed with?"

"Why did he kill her?"

"I don't know. He pulled some awful dumb tricks sometimes."

"You didn't kill her?"

"No, no, no!"

I jerked the corner of my mouth at O'Gar.

"You're a liar," he bawled, shaking the fly paper in her face. "You killed her." The rest of the team closed in, throwing accusations at her. They kept it up until she was groggy and the policewoman beginning to look worried.

Then I said angrily:

"All right. Throw her in a cell and let her think it over." To her: "You know what you told Joe this afternoon: this is no time to dummy up. Do a lot of thinking tonight."

"Honest to God I didn't kill her," she said.

I turned my back to her. The policewoman took her away.

"Ho-hum," O'Gar yawned. "We gave her a pretty good ride at that, for a short one."

"Not bad," I agreed. "If anybody else looked likely, I'd say she didn't kill Sue. But if she's telling the truth, then Holy Joe did it. And why should he poison the goose that was going to lay nice yellow eggs for him? And how and why did he cache the poison in their apartment? Babe had the motive, but damned if he looks like a slow-poisoner to me. You can't tell, though; he and Holy Joe could even have been working together on it."

"Could," Duff said. "But it takes a lot of imagination to get that one down. Anyway you twist it, Peggy's our best bet so far. Go up against her again, hard, in the morning?"

"Yeah," I said. "And we've got to find Babe."

The others had had dinner. MacMan and I went out and got ours. When we returned to the detective bureau an hour later it was practically deserted of the regular operatives.

"All gone to Pier 42 on a tip that McCloor's there," Steve Ward told us.

"How long ago?"

"Ten minutes."

MacMan and I got a taxi and set out for Pier 42. We didn't get to Pier 42.

On First Street, half a block from the Embarcadero, the taxi suddenly shrieked and slid to a halt.

"What—?" I began, and saw a man standing in front of the machine. He was a big man with a big gun. "Babe," I grunted, and put my hand on MacMan's arm to keep him from getting his gun out.

"Take me to—" McCloor was saying to the frightened driver when he saw us. He came around to my side and pulled the door open, holding the gun on us.

He had no hat. His hair was wet, plastered to his head. Little streams of water trickled down from it. His clothes were dripping wet.

He looked surprised at us and ordered:

"Get out."

As we got out he growled at the driver:

"What the hell you got your flag up for if you had fares?"

The driver wasn't there. He had hopped out the other side and was scooting away down the street. McCloor cursed him and poked his gun at me, growling:

"Go on, beat it."

Apparently he hadn't recognized me. The light here wasn't good, and I had a hat on now. He had seen me for only a few seconds in Wales's room.

I stepped aside. MacMan moved to the other side.

McCloor took a backward step to keep us from getting him between us and started an angry word.

MacMan threw himself on McCloor's gun arm.

I socked McCloor's jaw with my fist. I might just as well have hit somebody else for all it seemed to bother him.

He swept me out of his way and pasted MacMan in the mouth. MacMan fell back till the taxi stopped him, spit out a tooth, and came back for more.

I was trying to climb up McCloor's left side.

MacMan came in on his right, failed to dodge a chop of the gun, caught it square on the top of the noodle, and went down hard. He stayed down.

I kicked McCloor's ankle, but couldn't get his foot from under him. I rammed my right fist into the small of his back and got a left-handful of his wet hair, swinging on it. He shook his head, dragging me off my feet.

He punched me in the side and I could feel my ribs and guts flattening together like leaves in a book.

I swung my fist against the back of his neck. That bothered him. He made a rumbling noise down in his chest, crunched my shoulder in his left hand, and chopped at me with the gun in his right.

I kicked him somewhere and punched his neck again.

Down the street, at the Embarcadero, a police whistle was blowing. Men were running up First Street toward us.

McCloor snorted like a locomotive and threw me away from him. I didn't want to go. I tried to hang on. He threw me away from him and ran up the street.

I scrambled up and ran after him, dragging my gun out.

At the first corner he stopped to squirt metal at me—three shots. I squirted one at him. None of the four connected.

He disappeared around the corner. I swung wide around it, to make him miss if he were flattened to the wall waiting for me. He wasn't. He was a hundred feet ahead, going into a space between two warehouses. I went in after him, and out after him at the other end, making better time with my hundred and ninety pounds than he was making with his two-fifty.

He crossed a street, turning up, away from the waterfront. There was a light on the corner. When I came into its glare he wheeled and leveled his gun at me. I didn't hear it click, but I knew it had when he threw it at me. The gun went past with a couple of feet to spare and raised hell against a door behind me.

McCloor turned and ran up the street. I ran up the street after him.

I put a bullet past him to let the others know where we were. At the next corner he started to turn to the left, changed his mind, and went straight on.

I sprinted, cutting the distance between us to forty or fifty feet, and yelped:

"Stop or I'll drop you."

He jumped sidewise into a narrow alley.

I passed it on the jump, saw he wasn't waiting for me, and went in. Enough light came in from the street to let us see each other and our surroundings. The alley was blind—walled on each side and at the other end by tall concrete buildings with steel-shuttered windows and doors.

McCloor faced me, less than twenty feet away. His jaw stuck out. His arms curved down free of his sides. His shoulders were bunched.

"Put them up," I ordered, holding my gun level.

"Get out of my way, little man," he grumbled, taking a stiff-legged step toward me. "I'll eat you up."

"Keep coming," I said, "and I'll put you down."

"Try it." He took another step, crouching a little. "I can still get to you *with* slugs in me."

"Not where I'll put them." I was wordy, trying to talk him into waiting till the others came up. I didn't want to have to kill him. We could have done that from the taxi. "I'm no Annie Oakley, but if I can't pop your kneecaps with two shots at this distance, you're welcome to me. And if you think smashed kneecaps are a lot of fun, give it a whirl."

"Hell with that," he said and charged.

I shot his right knee.

He lurched toward me.

I shot his left knee.

He tumbled down.

"You would have it," I complained.

He twisted around, and with his arms pushed himself into a sitting position facing me.

"I didn't think you had sense enough to do it," he said through his teeth.

IX

I talked to McCloor in the hospital. He lay on his back in bed with a couple of pillows slanting his head up. The skin was pale and tight around his mouth and eyes, but there was nothing else to show he was in pain.

"You sure devastated me, bo," he said when I came in.

"Sorry," I said, "but—"

"I ain't beefing. I asked for it."

"Why'd you kill Holy Joe?" I asked, off-hand, as I pulled a chair up beside the bed.

"Uh-uh—you're tooting the wrong ringer."

I laughed and told him I was the man in the room with Joe when it happened.

McCloor grinned and said:

"I thought I'd seen you somewheres before. So that's where it was. I didn't pay no attention to your mug, just so your hands didn't move."

"Why'd you kill him?"

He pursed his lips, screwed up his eyes at me, thought something over, and said:

"He killed a broad I knew."

"He killed Sue Hambleton?" I asked.

He studied my face a while before he replied: "Yep."

"How do you figure that out?"

"Hell," he said, "I don't have to. Sue told me. Give me a butt."

I gave him a cigarette, held a lighter under it, and objected:

"That doesn't exactly fit in with other things I know. Just what happened and what did she say? You might start back with the night you gave her the goog."*

He looked thoughtful, letting smoke sneak slowly out of his nose, then said:

"I hadn't ought to hit her in the eye, that's a fact. But, see, she had been out all afternoon and wouldn't tell me where she'd been, and we had a row over it. What's this—Thursday morning? That was Monday, then. After the row I went out and spent the night in a dump over on Army Street. I got home about seven the next morning. Sue was sick as hell, but she wouldn't let me get a croaker for her. That was kind of funny, because she was scared stiff."

McCloor scratched his head meditatively and suddenly drew in a great lungful of smoke, practically eating up the rest of the cigarette. He let the smoke leak out of mouth and nose together, looking dully through the cloud at me. Then he said bruskly:

"Well, she went under. But before she went she told me she'd been poisoned by Holy Joe."

"She say how he'd given it to her?"

McCloor shook his head.

"I'd been asking her what was the matter, and not getting anything out of her. Then she starts whining that she's poisoned. 'I'm poisoned, Babe,' she whines. 'Arsenic. That damned Holy Joe,' she says. Then she won't say anything else, and it's not a hell of a while after that that she kicks off."

"Yeah? Then what'd you do?"

"I went gunning for Holy Joe. I knew him but didn't know where he jungled up,† and didn't find out till yesterday. You was there when I came. You know about that. I had picked up a boiler‡ and parked it over on Turk Street, for the getaway. When I got back to it, there was a copper standing close to it. I figured he might have spotted it as a hot one and was waiting to see who came for it, so I let it alone, and caught a street car instead, and cut for the yards. Down there I ran into a whole flock of hammer and saws§ and had to go overboard in China Basin, swimming up to a pier, being ranked¶ again by a watchman there, swimming off to another, and finally getting through the line only to run into another bad break. I wouldn't of flagged that taxi if the *For Hire* flag hadn't been up."

"You knew Sue was planning to take a run-out on you with Joe?"

"I don't know it yet," he said. "I knew damned well she was cheating on me, but I didn't know who with."

---

* goose egg; black eye

† encamped
‡ a steam-engine car
§ guns and shotguns
¶ insulted; run off

"What would you have done if you had known that?" I asked.

"Me?" He grinned wolfishly. "Just what I did."

"Killed the pair of them," I said.

He rubbed his lower lip with a thumb and asked calmly:

"You think I killed Sue?"

"You did."

"Serves me right," he said. "I must be getting simple in my old age. What the hell am I doing barbering* with a lousy dick? That never got nobody nothing but grief. Well, you might just as well take it on the heel and toe† now, my lad. I'm through spitting."‡

And he was. I couldn't get another word out of him.

X

The Old Man sat listening to me, tapping his desk lightly with the point of a long yellow pencil, staring past me with mild blue, rimless-spectacled, eyes. When I had brought my story up to date, he asked pleasantly:

"How is MacMan?"

"He lost two teeth, but his skull wasn't cracked. He'll be out in a couple of days."

The Old Man nodded and asked:

"What remains to be done?"

"Nothing. We can put Peggy Carroll on the mat again, but it's not likely we'll squeeze much more out of her. Outside of that, the returns are pretty well all in."

"And what do you make of it?"

I squirmed in my chair and said: "Suicide."

The Old Man smiled at me, politely but skeptically.

"I don't like it either," I grumbled. "And I'm not ready to write it in a report yet. But that's

the only total that what we've got will add up to. That fly paper was hidden behind the kitchen stove. Nobody would be crazy enough to try to hide something from a woman in her own kitchen like that. But the woman might hide it there.

"According to Peggy, Holy Joe had the fly paper. If Sue hid it, she got it from him. For what? They were planning to go away together, and were only waiting till Joe, who was on the nut,§ raised enough dough. Maybe they were afraid of Babe, and had the poison there to slip him if he tumbled to their plan before they went. Maybe they meant to slip it to him before they went anyway.

"When I started talking to Holy Joe about murder, he thought Babe was the one who had been bumped off. He was surprised, maybe, but as if he was surprised that it had happened so soon. He was more surprised when he heard that Sue had died too, but even then he wasn't so surprised as when he saw McCloor alive at the window.

"She died cursing Holy Joe, and she knew she was poisoned, and she wouldn't let McCloor get a doctor. Can't that mean that she had turned against Joe, and had taken the poison herself instead of feeding it to Babe? The poison was hidden from Babe. But even if he found it, I can't figure him as a poisoner. He's too rough. Unless he caught her trying to poison him and made her swallow the stuff. But that doesn't account for the month-old arsenic in her hair."

"Does your suicide hypothesis take care of that?" the Old Man asked.

"It could," I said. "Don't be kicking holes in my theory. It's got enough as it stands. But, if she committed suicide this time, there's no reason why she couldn't have tried it once before—say after a quarrel with Joe a month ago—and failed to bring it off. That would have put the arsenic in her. There's no real proof that she took any between a month ago and day before yesterday."

* conversing
† walk away
‡ talking
§ had lost a lot of money

"No real proof," the Old Man protested mildly, "except the autopsy's finding—chronic poisoning."

I was never one to let experts' guesses stand in my way. I said:

"They base that on the small amount of arsenic they found in her remains—less than a fatal dose. And the amount they find in your stomach after you're dead depends on how much you vomit before you die."

The Old Man smiled benevolently at me and asked:

"But you're not, you say, ready to write this theory into a report? Meanwhile what do you propose doing?"

"If there's nothing else on tap, I'm going home, fumigate my brains with Fatimas, and try to get this thing straightened out in my head. I think I'll get a copy of *The Count of Monte Cristo* and run through it. I haven't read it since I was a kid. It looks like the book was wrapped up with the fly paper to make a bundle large enough to wedge tightly between the wall and stove, so it wouldn't fall down. But there might be something in the book. I'll see anyway."

"I did that last night," the Old Man murmured.

I asked: "And?"

He took a book from his desk drawer, opened it where a slip of paper marked a place, and held it out to me, one pink finger marking a paragraph.

"Suppose you were to take a millegramme of this poison the first day, two millegrammes the second day, and so on. Well, at the end of ten days you would have taken a centigramme: at the end of twenty days, increasing another millegramme, you would have taken three hundred centigrammes; that is to say, a dose you would

support without inconvenience, and which would be very dangerous for any other person who had not taken the same precautions as yourself. Well, then, at the end of the month, when drinking water from the same carafe, you would kill the person who had drunk this water, without your perceiving otherwise than from slight inconvenience that there was any poisonous substance mingled with the water."

"That does it," I said. "That does it. They were afraid to go away without killing Babe, too certain he'd come after them. She tried to make herself immune from arsenic poisoning by getting her body accustomed to it, taking steadily increasing doses, so when she slipped the big shot in Babe's food she could eat it with him without danger. She'd be taken sick, but wouldn't die, and the police couldn't hang his death on her because she too had eaten the poisoned food.

"That clicks. After the row Monday night, when she wrote Joe the note urging him to make the getaway soon, she tried to hurry up her immunity, and increased her preparatory doses too quickly, took too large a shot. That's why she cursed Joe at the end: it was his plan."

"Possibly she overdosed herself in an attempt to speed it along," the Old Man agreed, "but not necessarily. There are people who can cultivate an ability to take large doses of arsenic without trouble, but it seems to be a sort of natural gift with them, a matter of some constitutional peculiarity. Ordinarily, any one who tried it would do what Sue Hambleton did—slowly poison themselves until the cumulative effect was strong enough to cause death."

Babe McCloor was hanged, for killing Holy Joe Wales, six months later.

THE MALTESE FALCON

BY DASHIELL HAMMETT

Begins in the next issue—the September issue—of Black Mask, and we enthusiastically recommend it to all lovers of detective fiction and particularly those who are, as Mr. Herbert Asbury, the nationally known critic, says,* tired of conventional plots.

———————————

* Page iv includes the following, quoting Herbert Asbury in *The Bookman*, March 1929, p. 92:

The leading literary magazine of the country is The Bookman. Its criticisms of books are regarded as the last word. The Bookman said of "Red Harvest" that it is the liveliest detective story published in ten years, stating that "It is doubtful if even Ernest Hemingway has ever written more effective dialogue than may be found within the pages of this extraordinary tale. Those who begin to weary of the similarity of modern detective novels, with their clumsily involved plots and their artificial conversations and situations, will find their interest revived by this realistic, straightforward story, for it is concerned solely with fast and furious action and it introduces a detective who achieves his purpose without recourse to higher mathematics, necromancy or fanciful reasoning."

As all Black Mask Readers know, this magazine has been developing a new kind of detective story more in keeping with the times, more true to life than the wild, imaginative plot of earlier days and, therefore, of far more gripping interest to its readers.

Dashiell Hammett has been the leader in this development, and with publication of his Black Mask stories in book form, by a publisher of highest standing, is becoming recognized as the foremost writer of detective fiction of the present time.

THE MALTESE FALCON is too big a story to allow an adequate description of it—we can merely assure you that it is the best story of its kind we have ever seen in print and we only hope that you may have as much enjoyment from it as we, who are obliged to read so many millions of words a year, have had in our examination of it.

BLACK MASK, FEBRUARY 1930

The Farewell Murder

BY DASHIELL HAMMETT

The Continental Op is called in to protect a man and runs into plenty grief.

I WAS THE ONLY ONE who left the train at Farewell.

A man came through the rain from the passenger shed. He was a small man. His face was dark and flat. He wore a gray waterproof cap and a gray coat cut in military style.

He didn't look at me. He looked at the valise and Gladstone bag in my hands. He came forward quickly, walking with short, choppy steps.

He didn't say anything when he took the bags from me. I asked:

"Kavalov's?"

He had already turned his back to me and was carrying my bags towards a tan Stutz coach that stood in the roadway beside the gravel station platform. In answer to my question he bowed twice at the Stutz without looking around or checking his jerky half-trot.

I followed him to the car.

Three minutes of riding carried us through the village. We took a road that climbed westward into the hills. The road looked like a seal's back in the rain.

The flat-faced man was in a hurry. We purred over the road at a speed that soon carried us past the last of the cottages sprinkled up the hillside.

Presently we left the shiny black road for a paler one curving south to run along a hill's wooded crest. Now and then this road, for a hundred feet or more at a stretch, was turned into a tunnel by tall trees' heavily leafed boughs interlocking overhead.

Rain accumulated in fat drops on the boughs and came down to thump the Stutz's roof. The dullness of rainy early evening became almost the blackness of night inside these tunnels.

The flat-faced man switched on the lights, and increased our speed.

He sat rigidly erect at the wheel. I sat behind him. Above his military collar, among the hairs that were clipped short on the nape of his neck, globules of moisture made tiny shining points. The moisture could have been rain. It could have been sweat.

We were in the middle of one of the tunnels.

The flat-faced man's head jerked to the left, and he screamed:

"A-a-a-a-a-a!"

It was a long, quivering, high-pitched bleat, thin with terror.

I jumped up, bending forward to see what was the matter with him.

The car swerved and plunged ahead, throwing me back on the seat again.

Through the side window I caught a one-eyed glimpse of something dark lying in the road.

I twisted around to try the back window, less rain-bleared.

I saw a black man lying on his back in the road, near the left edge. His body was arched, as if its weight rested on his heels and the back of his head. A knife handle that couldn't have been less than six inches long stood straight up in the air from the left side of his chest.

By the time I had seen this much we had taken a curve and were out of the tunnel.

"Stop," I called to the flat-faced man.

He pretended he didn't hear me. The Stutz was a tan streak under us. I put a hand on the driver's shoulder.

His shoulder squirmed under my hand, and he screamed "A-a-a-a-a!" again as if the dead black man had him.

I reached past him and shut off the engine.

He took his hands from the wheel and clawed up at me. Noises came from his mouth, but they didn't make any words that I knew.

I got a hand on the wheel. I got my other forearm under his chin. I leaned over the back of his seat so that the weight of my upper body was on his head, mashing it down against the wheel.

Between this and that and the help of God,

the Stutz hadn't left the road when it stopped moving.

I got up off the flat-faced man's head and asked:

"What the hell's the matter with you?"

He looked at me with white eyes, shivered, and didn't say anything.

"Turn it around," I said. "We'll go back there."

He shook his head from side to side, desperately, and made some more of the mouth-noises that might have been words if I could have understood them.

"You know who that was?" I asked.

He shook his head.

"You do," I growled.

He shook his head.

By then I was beginning to suspect that no matter what I said to this fellow I'd get only head-shakes out of him.

I said:

"Get away from the wheel, then. I'm going to drive back there."

He opened the door and scrambled out.

"Come back here," I called.

He backed away, shaking his head.

I cursed him, slid in behind the wheel, said, "All right, wait here for me," and slammed the door.

He retreated backwards slowly, watching me with scared, whitish eyes while I backed and turned the coach.

I had to drive back farther than I had expected, something like a mile.

I didn't find the black man.

The tunnel was empty.

If I had known the exact spot in which he had been lying, I might have been able to find something to show how he had been removed. But I hadn't had time to pick out a landmark, and now any one of four or five places looked like the spot.

With the help of the coach's lamps I went over the left side of the road from one end of the tunnel to the other.

I didn't find any blood. I didn't find any footprints. I didn't find anything to show that anybody had been lying in the road. I didn't find anything.

It was too dark by now for me to try searching the woods.

I returned to where I had left the flat-faced man.

He was gone.

It looked, I thought, as if Mr. Kavalov might be right in thinking he needed a detective.

II

Half a mile beyond the place where the flat-faced man had deserted me, I stopped the Stutz in front of a grilled steel gate that blocked the road. The gate was padlocked on the inside. From either side of it tall hedging ran off into the woods. The upper part of a brown-roofed small house was visible over the hedge-top to the left.

I worked the Stutz's horn.

The racket brought a gawky boy of fifteen or sixteen to the other side of the gate. He had on bleached whipcord pants and a wildly striped sweater. He didn't come out to the middle of the road, but stood at one side, with one arm out of sight as if holding something that was hidden from me by the hedge.

"This Kavalov's?" I asked.

"Yes, sir," he said uneasily.

I waited for him to unlock the gate. He didn't unlock it. He stood there looking uneasily at the car and at me.

"Please, mister," I said, "can I come in?"

"What—who are you?"

"I'm the guy that Kavalov sent for. If I'm not going to be let in, tell me, so I can catch the six-fifty back to San Francisco."

The boy chewed his lip, said, "Wait till I see if I can find the key," and went out of sight behind the hedge.

He was gone long enough to have had a talk with somebody.

When he came back he unlocked the gate, swung it open, and said:

"It's all right, sir. They're expecting you."

When I had driven through the gate I could see lights on a hilltop a mile or so ahead and to the left.

"Is that the house?" I asked.

"Yes, sir. They're expecting you."

Close to where the boy had stood while talking to me through the gate, a double-barrel shotgun was propped up against the hedge.

I thanked the boy and drove on. The road wound gently uphill through farm land. Tall, slim trees had been planted at regular intervals on both sides of the road.

The road brought me at last to the front of a building that looked like a cross between a fort and a factory in the dusk. It was built of concrete. Take a flock of squat cones of various sizes, round off the points bluntly, mash them together with the largest one somewhere near the center, the others grouped around it in not too strict accordance with their sizes, adjust the whole collection to agree with the slopes of a hilltop, and you would have a model of the Kavalov house. The windows were steel-sashed. There weren't very many of them. No two were in line either vertically or horizontally. Some were lighted.

As I got out of the car, the narrow front door of this house opened.

A short, red-faced woman of fifty or so, with faded blonde hair wound around and around her head, came out. She wore a high-necked, tight-sleeved, gray woolen dress. When she smiled her mouth seemed wide as her hips.

She said:

"You're the gentleman from the city?"

"Yeah. I lost your chauffeur somewhere back on the road."

"Lord bless you," she said amiably, "that's all right."

A thin man with thin dark hair plastered down above a thin, worried face came past her to take my bags when I had lifted them out of the car. He carried them indoors.

The woman stood aside for me to enter, saying:

"Now I suppose you'll want to wash up a little bit before you go in to dinner, and they won't mind waiting for you the few minutes you'll take if you hurry."

I said, "Yeah, thanks," waited for her to get ahead of me again, and followed her up a curving flight of stairs that climbed along the inside of one of the cones that made up the building.

She took me to a second-story bedroom where the thin man was unpacking my bags.

"Martin will get you anything you need," she assured me from the doorway, "and when you're ready, just come on downstairs."

I said I would, and she went away. The thin man had finished unpacking by the time I had got out of coat, vest, collar and shirt. I told him there wasn't anything else I needed, washed up in the adjoining bathroom, put on a fresh shirt and collar, my vest and coat, and went downstairs.

The wide hall was empty. Voices came through an open doorway to the left.

One voice was a nasal whine. It complained:

"I will not have it. I will not put up with it. I am not a child, and I will not have it."

This voice's t's were a little too thick for t's, but not thick enough to be d's.

Another voice was a lively, but slightly harsh, barytone. It said cheerfully:

"What's the good of saying we won't put up with it, when we are putting up with it?"

The third voice was feminine, a soft voice, but flat and spiritless. It said:

"But perhaps he did kill him."

The whining voice said: "I do not care. I will not have it."

The barytone voice said, cheerfully as before: "Oh, won't you?"

A doorknob turned farther down the hall. I didn't want to be caught standing there listening. I advanced to the open doorway.

III

I was in the doorway of a low-ceilinged oval room furnished and decorated in gray, white and silver. Two men and a woman were there.

The older man—he was somewhere in his fifties—got up from a deep gray chair and bowed ceremoniously at me. He was a plump man of medium height, completely bald, dark-skinned and pale-eyed. He wore a wax-pointed gray mustache and a straggly gray imperial.

"Mr. Kavalov?" I asked.

"Yes, sir." His was the whining voice.

I told him who I was. He shook my hand and then introduced me to the others.

The woman was his daughter. She was probably thirty. She had her father's narrow, full-lipped mouth, but her eyes were dark, her nose was short and straight, and her skin was almost colorless. Her face had Asia in it. It was pretty, passive, unintelligent.

The man with the barytone voice was her husband. His name was Ringgo. He was six or seven years older than his wife, neither tall nor heavy, but well setup. His left arm was in splints and a sling. The knuckles of his right hand were darkly bruised. He had a lean, bony, quick-witted face, bright dark eyes with plenty of lines around them, and a good-natured hard mouth.

He gave me his bruised hand, wriggled his bandaged arm at me, grinned, and said:

"I'm sorry you missed this, but the future injuries are yours."

"How did it happen?" I asked.

Kavalov raised a plump hand.

"Time enough it is to go into that when we have eaten," he said. "Let us have our dinner first."

We went into a small green and brown dining-room where a small square table was set. I sat facing Ringgo across a silver basket of orchids that stood between tall silver candlesticks in the center of the table. Mrs. Ringgo sat to my right, Kavalov to my left. When Kavalov sat down I saw the shape of an automatic pistol in his hip pocket.

Two men servants waited on us. There was a lot of food and all of it was well turned out. We ate caviar, some sort of consommé, sand dabs, potatoes and cucumber jelly, roast lamb, corn and string beans, asparagus, wild duck and hominy cakes, artichoke-and-tomato salad, and orange ice. We drank white wine, claret, Burgundy, coffee and *crème de menthe*.

Kavalov ate and drank enormously. None of us skimped.

Kavalov was the first to disregard his own order that nothing be said about his troubles until after we had eaten. When he had finished his soup he put down his spoon and said:

"I am not a child. I will not be frightened."

He blinked pale, worried eyes defiantly at me, his lips pouting between mustache and imperial.

Ringgo grinned pleasantly at him. Mrs. Ringgo's face was as serene and inattentive as if nothing had been said.

"What is there to be frightened of?" I asked.

"Nothing," Kavalov said. "Nothing excepting a lot of idiotic and very pointless trickery and play-acting."

"You can call it anything you want to call it," a voice grumbled over my shoulder, "but I seen what I seen."

The voice belonged to one of the men who was waiting on the table, a sallow, youngish man with a narrow, slack-lipped face. He spoke with a subdued sort of stubbornness, and without looking up from the dish he was putting before me.

Since nobody else paid any attention to the servant's clearly audible remark, I turned my face to Kavalov again. He was trimming the edge of a sand dab with the side of his fork.

"What kind of trickery and play-acting?" I asked.

Kavalov put down his fork and rested his wrists on the edge of the table. He rubbed his lips together and leaned over his plate towards me.

"Supposing"—he wrinkled his forehead so that his bald scalp twitched forward—"you have done injury to a man ten years ago." He turned his wrists quickly, laying his hands palms-up on the white cloth. "You have done this injury in the ordinary business manner—you understand?— for profit. There is not anything personal concerned. You do not hardly know him. And then supposing he came to you after all those ten years and said to you: 'I have come to watch you

die.'" He turned his hands over, palms down. "Well, what would you think?"

"I wouldn't," I replied, "think I ought to hurry up my dying on his account."

The earnestness went out of his face, leaving it blank. He blinked at me for a moment and then began eating his fish. When he had chewed and swallowed the last piece of sand dab he looked up at me again. He shook his head slowly, drawing down the corners of his mouth.

"That was not a good answer," he said. He shrugged, and spread his fingers. "However, you will have to deal with this Captain Cat-and-mouse. It is for that I engaged you."

I nodded.

Ringgo smiled and patted his bandaged arm, saying:

"I wish you more luck with him than I had."

Mrs. Ringgo put out a hand and let the pointed fingertips touch her husband's wrist for a moment.

I asked Kavalov:

"This injury I was to suppose I had done: how serious was it?"

He pursed his lips, made little wavy motions with the fingers of his right hand, and said:

"Oh—ah—ruin."

"We can take it for granted, then, that your captain's really up to something?"

"Good God!" said Ringgo, dropping his fork. "I wouldn't like to think he'd broken my arm just in fun."

Behind me the sallow servant spoke to his mate:

"He wants to know if we think the captain's really up to something."

"I heard him," the other said gloomily. "A lot of help he's going to be to us."

Kavalov tapped his plate with a fork and made angry faces at the servants.

"Shut up," he said. "Where is the roast?" He pointed the fork at Mrs. Ringgo. "Her glass is empty." He looked at the fork. "See what care they take of my silver," he complained, holding it out to me. "It has not been cleaned decently in a month."

He put the fork down. He pushed back his plate to make room for his forearms on the table. He leaned over them, hunching his shoulders. He sighed. He frowned. He stared at me with pleading pale eyes.

"Listen," he whined. "Am I a fool? Would I send to San Francisco for a detective if I did not need a detective? Would I pay you what you are charging me, when I could get plenty good enough detectives for half of that, if I did not require the best detective I could secure? Would I require so expensive a one if I did not know this captain for a completely dangerous fellow?"

I didn't say anything. I sat still and looked attentive.

"Listen," he whined. "This is not April-foolery. This captain means to murder me. He came here to murder me. He will certainly murder me if somebody does not stop him from it."

"Just what has he done so far?" I asked.

"That is not it." Kavalov shook his bald head impatiently. "I do not ask you to undo anything that he has done. I ask you to keep him from killing me. What has he done so far? Well, he has terrorized my people most completely. He has broken Dolph's arm. He has done these things so far, if you must know."

"How long has this been going on? How long has he been here?"

"A week and two days."

"Did your chauffeur tell you about the black man we saw in the road?"

Kavalov pushed his lips together and nodded slowly.

"He wasn't there when I went back," I said.

He blew out his lips with a little puff and cried excitedly:

"I do not care anything about your black men and your roads. I care about not being murdered."

"Have you said anything to the sheriff's office?" I asked, trying to pretend I wasn't getting peevish.

"That I have done. But to what good? Has he threatened me? Well, he has told me he has come to watch me die. From him, the way he said it, that is a threat. But to your sheriff it is not a threat. He has terrorized my people. Have I proof that he has done that? The sheriff says I have not. What absurdity! Do I need proof? Don't I know? Must he leave fingerprints on the fright he causes? So it comes to this: the sheriff will keep an eye on him. 'An eye,' he said, mind you. Here I have twenty people, servants and farm hands, with forty eyes. And he comes and goes as he likes. An eye!"

"How about Ringgo's arm?" I asked.

Kavalov shook his head impatiently and began to cut up his lamb.

Ringgo said:

"There's nothing we can do about that. I hit him first." He looked at his bruised knuckles. "I didn't think he was that tough. Maybe I'm not as good as I used to be. Anyway, a dozen people saw me punch his jaw before he touched me. We performed at high noon in front of the post office."

"Who is this captain?"

"It's not him," the sallow servant said. "It's that black devil."

Ringgo said:

"Sherry's his name, Hugh Sherry. He was a captain in the British army when we knew him before—quartermasters department in Cairo. That was in 1917, all of twelve years ago. The commodore"—he nodded his head at his father-in-law—"was speculating in military supplies. Sherry should have been a line officer. He had no head for desk work. He wasn't timid enough. Somebody decided the commodore wouldn't have made so much money if Sherry hadn't been so careless. They knew Sherry hadn't made any money for himself. They cashiered Sherry at the same time they asked the commodore please to go away."

Kavalov looked up from his plate to explain:

"Business is like that in wartime. They wouldn't let me go away if I had done anything they could keep me there for."

"And now, twelve years after you had him

kicked out of the army in disgrace," I said, "he comes here, threatens to kill you, so you believe, and sets out to spread panic among your people. Is that it?"

"That is not it," Kavalov whined. "That is not it at all. I did not have him kicked out of any armies. I am a man of business. I take my profits where I find them. If somebody lets me take a profit that angers his employers, what is their anger to me? Second, I do not believe he means to kill me. I know that."

"I'm trying to get it straight in my mind."

"There is nothing to get straight. A man is going to murder me. I ask you not to let him do it. Is not that simple enough?"

"Simple enough," I agreed, and stopped trying to talk to him.

Kavalov and Ringgo were smoking cigars, Mrs. Ringgo and I cigarettes over *crème de menthe* when the red-faced blonde woman in gray wool came in.

She came in hurriedly. Her eyes were wide open and dark. She said:

"Anthony says there's a fire in the upper field."

Kavalov crunched his cigar between his teeth and looked pointedly at me.

I stood up, asking:

"How do I get there?"

"I'll show you the way," Ringgo said, leaving his chair.

"Dolph," his wife protested, "your arm."

He smiled gently at her and said:

"I'm not going to interfere. I'm only going along to see how an expert handles these things."

IV

I ran up to my room for hat, coat, flashlight and gun.

The Ringgos were standing at the front door when I started downstairs again.

He had put on a dark raincoat, buttoned tight over his injured arm, its left sleeve hanging empty. His right arm was around his wife.

Both of her bare arms were around his neck. She was bent far back, he far forward over her. Their mouths were together.

Retreating a little, I made more noise with my feet when I came into sight again. They were standing apart at the door, waiting for me. Ringgo was breathing heavily, as if he had been running. He opened the door.

Mrs. Ringgo addressed me:

"Please don't let my foolish husband be too reckless."

I said I wouldn't, and asked him:

"Worth while taking any of the servants or farm hands along?"

He shook his head.

"Those that aren't hiding would be as useless as those that are," he said. "They've all had it taken out of them."

He and I went out, leaving Mrs. Ringgo looking after us from the doorway. The rain had stopped for the time, but a black muddle overhead promised more presently.

Ringgo led me around the side of the house, along a narrow path that went downhill through shrubbery, past a group of small buildings in a shallow valley, and diagonally up another, lower, hill.

The path was soggy. At the top of the hill we left the path, going through a wire gate and across a stubbly field that was both gummy and slimy under our feet. We moved along swiftly. The gumminess of the ground, the sultriness of the night air, and our coats, made the going warm work.

When we had crossed this field we could see the fire, a spot of flickering orange beyond intervening trees. We climbed a low wire fence and wound through the trees.

A violent rustling broke out among the leaves overhead, starting at the left, ending with a solid thud against a tree trunk just to our right. Then something *plopped* on the soft ground under the tree.

Off to the left a voice laughed, a savage, hooting laugh.

The laughing voice couldn't have been far away. I went after it.

The fire was too small and too far away to be of much use to me: blackness was nearly perfect among the trees.

I stumbled over roots, bumped into trees, and found nothing. The flashlight would have helped the laugher more than me, so I kept it idle in my hand.

When I got tired of playing peekaboo with myself, I cut through the woods to the field on the other side, and went down to the fire.

The fire had been built in one end of the field, a dozen feet or less from the nearest tree. It had been built of dead twigs and broken branches that the rain had missed, and had nearly burnt itself out by the time I reached it.

Two small forked branches were stuck in the ground on opposite sides of the fire. Their forks held the ends of a length of green sapling. Spitted on the sapling, hanging over the fire, was an eighteen-inch-long carcass, headless, tailless, footless, skinless, and split down the front.

On the ground a few feet away lay an Airedale puppy's head, pelt, feet, tail, insides, and a lot of blood.

There were some dry sticks, broken in convenient lengths, beside the fire. I put them on as Ringgo came out of the woods to join me. He carried a stone the size of a grapefruit in his hand.

"Get a look at him?" he asked.

"No. He laughed and went."

He held out the stone to me, saying:

"This is what was chucked at us."

Drawn on the smooth gray stone, in red, were round blank eyes, a triangular nose, and a grinning, toothy mouth—a crude skull.

I scratched one of the red eyes with a fingernail, and said:

"Crayon."

Ringgo was staring at the carcass sizzling over the fire and at the trimmings on the ground.

"What do you make of that?" I asked.

He swallowed and said:

"Mickey was a damned good little dog."

"Yours?"

He nodded.

I went around with my flashlight on the ground. I found some footprints, such as they were.

"Anything?" Ringgo asked.

"Yeah." I showed him one of the prints. "Made with rags tied around his shoes. They're no good."

We turned to the fire again.

"This is another show," I said. "Whoever killed and cleaned the pup knew his stuff; knew it too well to think he could cook him decently like that. The outside will be burnt before the inside's even warm, and the way he's put on the spit he'd fall off if you tried to turn him."

Ringgo's scowl lightened a bit.

"That's a little better," he said. "Having him killed is rotten enough, but I'd hate to think of anybody eating Mickey, or even meaning to."

"They didn't," I assured him. "They were putting on a show. This the sort of thing that's been happening?"

"Yes."

"What's the sense of it?"

He glumly quoted Kavalov:

"Captain Cat-and-mouse."

I gave him a cigarette, took one myself, and lighted them with a stick from the fire.

He raised his face to the sky, said, "Raining again; let's go back to the house," but remained by the fire, staring at the cooking carcass. The stink of scorched meat hung thick around us.

"You don't take this very seriously yet, do you?" he asked presently, in a low, matter-of-fact voice.

"It's a funny layout."

"He's cracked," he said in the same low voice. "Try to see this. Honor meant something to him. That's why we had to trick him instead of bribing him, back in Cairo. Less than ten years of dishonor can crack a man like that. He'd go off and hide and brood. It would be either shoot himself when the blow fell—or that. I was like you at first." He kicked at the fire. "This is silly. But I can't laugh at it now, except when I'm around

Miriam and the commodore. When he first showed up I didn't have the slightest idea that I couldn't handle him. I had handled him all right in Cairo. When I discovered I couldn't handle him I lost my head a little. I went down and picked a row with him. Well, that was no good either. It's the silliness of this that makes it bad. In Cairo he was the kind of man who combs his hair before he shaves, so his mirror will show an orderly picture. Can you understand some of this?"

"I'll have to talk to him first," I said. "He's staying in the village?"

"He has a cottage on the hill above. It's the first one on the left after you turn into the main road." Ringgo dropped his cigarette into the fire and looked thoughtfully at me, biting his lower lip. "I don't know how you and the commodore are going to get along. You can't make jokes with him. He doesn't understand them, and he'll distrust you on that account."

"I'll try to be careful," I promised. "No good offering this Sherry money?"

"Hell, no," he said softly. "He's too cracked for that."

We took down the dog's carcass, kicked the fire apart, and trod it out in the mud before we returned to the house.

V

The country was fresh and bright under clear sunlight the next morning. A warm breeze was drying the ground and chasing raw-cotton clouds across the sky.

At ten o'clock I set out afoot for Captain Sherry's. I didn't have any trouble finding his house, a pinkish stuccoed bungalow with a terra cotta roof, reached from the road by a cobbled walk.

A white-clothed table with two places set stood on the tiled veranda that stretched across the front of the bungalow.

Before I could knock, the door was opened by a slim black man, not much more than a boy, in a white jacket. His features were thinner than most American negroes', aquiline, pleasantly intelligent.

"You're going to catch colds lying around in wet roads," I said, "if you don't get run over."

His mouth-ends ran towards his ears in a grin that showed me a lot of strong yellow teeth.

"Yes, sir," he said, buzzing his s's, rolling the r, bowing. "The *capitaine* have waited breakfast that you be with him. You do sit down, sir. I will call him."

"Not dog meat?"

His mouth-ends ran back and up again and he shook his head vigorously.

"No, sir." He held up his black hands and counted the fingers. "There is orange and kippers and kidneys grilled and eggs and marmalade and toast and tea or coffee. There is not dog meat."

"Fine," I said, and sat down in one of the wicker armchairs on the veranda.

I had time to light a cigarette before Captain Sherry came out.

He was a gaunt tall man of forty. Sandy hair, parted in the middle, was brushed flat to his small head, above a sunburned face. His eyes were gray, with lower lids as straight as ruler-edges. His mouth was another hard straight line under a close-clipped sandy mustache. Grooves like gashes ran from his nostrils past his mouth-corners. Other grooves, just as deep, ran down his cheeks to the sharp ridge of his jaw. He wore a gaily striped flannel bathrobe over sand-colored pajamas.

"Good morning," he said pleasantly, and gave me a semi-salute. He didn't offer to shake hands. "Don't get up. It will be some minutes before Marcus has breakfast ready. I slept late. I had a most abominable dream." His voice was a deliberately languid drawl. "I dreamed that Theodore Kavalov's throat had been cut from here to here." He put bony fingers under his ears. "It was an atrociously gory business. He bled and screamed horribly, the swine."

I grinned up at him, asking:

"And you didn't like that?"

"Oh, getting his throat cut was all to the

good, but he bled and screamed so filthily." He raised his nose and sniffed. "That's honeysuckle somewhere, isn't it?"

"Smells like it. Was it throat-cutting that you had in mind when you threatened him?"

"When I threatened him," he drawled. "My dear fellow, I did nothing of the sort. I was in Udja, a stinking Moroccan town close to the Algerian frontier, and one morning a voice spoke to me from an orange tree. It said: 'Go to Farewell, in California, in the States, and there you will see Theodore Kavalov die.' I thought that a capital idea. I thanked the voice, told Marcus to pack, and came here. As soon as I arrived I told Kavalov about it, thinking perhaps he would die then and I wouldn't be hung up here waiting. He didn't, though, and too late I regretted not having asked the voice for a definite date. I should hate having to waste months here."

"That's why you've been trying to hurry it up?" I asked.

"I beg your pardon?"

"*Schrecklichkeit*,"* I said, "rocky skulls, dog barbecues, vanishing corpses."

"I've been fifteen years in Africa," he said. "I've too much faith in voices that come from orange trees where no one is to try to give them a hand. You needn't fancy I've had anything to do with whatever has happened."

"Marcus?"

Sherry stroked his freshly shaven cheeks and replied:

"That's possible. He has an incorrigible bent for the ruder sort of African horse-play. I'll gladly cane him for any misbehavior of which you've reasonably definite proof."

"Let me catch him at it," I said, "and I'll do my own caning."

Sherry leaned forward and spoke in a cautious undertone:

"Be sure he suspects nothing till you've a firm grip on him. He's remarkably effective with either of his knives."

_____
* German term for frightfulness or horror, commonly associated with World War I atrocities

"I'll try to remember that. The voice didn't say anything about Ringgo?"

"There was no need. When the body dies, the hand is dead."

Black Marcus came out carrying food. We moved to the table and I started on my second breakfast.

Sherry wondered whether the voice that had spoken to him from the orange tree had also spoken to Kavalov. He had asked Kavalov, he said, but hadn't received a very satisfactory answer. He believed that voices which announced deaths to people's enemies usually also warned the one who was to die. "That is," he said, "the conventional way of doing it, I believe."

"I don't know," I said. "I'll try to find out for you. Maybe I ought to ask him what he dreamed last night, too."

"Did he look nightmarish this morning?"

"I don't know. I left before he was up."

Sherry's eyes became hot gray points.

"Do you mean," he asked, "that you've no idea what shape he's in this morning, whether he's alive or not, whether my dream was a true one or not?"

"Yeah."

The hard line of his mouth loosened into a slow delighted smile.

"By Jove," he said, "That's capital! I thought—you gave me the impression of knowing positively that there was nothing to my dream, that it was only a meaningless dream."

He clapped his hands sharply.

Black Marcus popped out of the door.

"Pack," Sherry ordered. "The bald one is finished. We're off."

Marcus bowed and backed grinning into the house.

"Hadn't you better wait to make sure?" I asked.

"But I am sure," he drawled, "as sure as when the voice spoke from the orange tree. There is nothing to wait for now: I have seen him die."

"In a dream."

"Was it a dream?" he asked carelessly.

When I left, ten or fifteen minutes later, Marcus was making noises indoors that sounded as if he actually was packing.

Sherry shook hands with me, saying:

"Awfully glad to have had you for breakfast. Perhaps we'll meet again if your work ever brings you to northern Africa. Remember me to Miriam and Dolph. I can't sincerely send condolences."

Out of sight of the bungalow, I left the road for a path along the hillside above, and explored the country for a higher spot from which Sherry's place could be spied on. I found a pip, a vacant ramshackle house on a jutting ridge off to the northeast. The whole of the bungalow's front, part of one side, and a good stretch of the cobbled walk, including its juncture with the road, could be seen from the vacant house's front porch. It was a rather long shot for naked eyes, but with field glasses it would be just about perfect, even to a screen of over-grown bushes in front.

When I got back to the Kavalov house Ringgo was propped up on gay cushions in a reed chair under a tree, with a book in his hand.

"What do you think of him?" he asked. "Is he cracked?"

"Not very. He wanted to be remembered to you and Mrs. Ringgo. How's the arm this morning?"

"Rotten. I must have let it get too damp last night. It gave me hell all night."

"Did you see Captain Cat-and-mouse?" Kavalov's whining voice came from behind me. "And did you find any satisfaction in that?"

I turned around. He was coming down the walk from the house. His face was more gray than brown this morning, but what I could see of his throat, above the v of a wing collar, was uncut enough.

"He was packing when I left," I said. "Going back to Africa."

VI

That day was Thursday. Nothing else happened that day.

Friday morning I was awakened by the noise of my bedroom door being opened violently.

Martin, the thin-faced valet, came dashing into my room and began shaking me by the shoulder, though I was sitting up by the time he reached my bedside.

His thin face was lemon-yellow and ugly with fear.

"It's happened," he babbled. "Oh, my God, it's happened!"

"What's happened?"

"It's happened. It's happened."

I pushed him aside and got out of bed. He turned suddenly and ran into my bathroom. I could hear him vomiting as I pushed my feet into slippers.

Kavalov's bedroom was three doors below mine, on the same side of the building.

The house was full of noises, excited voices, doors opening and shutting, though I couldn't see anybody.

I ran down to Kavalov's door. It was open.

Kavalov was in there, lying on a low Spanish bed. The bedclothes were thrown down across the foot.

Kavalov was lying on his back. His throat had been cut, a curving cut that paralleled the line of his jaw between points an inch under his ear lobes.

Where his blood had soaked into the blue pillow case and blue sheet it was purple as grape-juice. It was thick and sticky, already clotting.

Ringgo came in wearing a bathrobe like a cape.

"It's happened," I growled, using the valet's words.

Ringgo looked dully, miserably, at the bed and began cursing in a choked, muffled, voice.

The red-faced blonde woman—Louella Qually, the housekeeper—came in, screamed, pushed past us, and ran to the bed, still screaming. I caught her arm when she reached for the covers.

"Let things alone," I said.

"Cover him up. Cover him up, the poor man!" she cried.

I took her away from the bed. Four or five servants were in the room by now. I gave the housekeeper to a couple of them, telling them to take her out and quiet her down. She went away laughing and crying.

Ringgo was still staring at the bed.

"Where's Mrs. Ringgo?" I asked.

He didn't hear me. I tapped his good arm and repeated the question.

"She's in her room. She—she didn't have to see it to know what had happened."

"Hadn't you better look after her?"

He nodded, turned slowly, and went out.

The valet, still lemon-yellow, came in.

"I want everybody on the place, servants, farm hands, everybody downstairs in the front room," I told him. "Get them all there right away, and they're to stay there till the sheriff comes."

"Yes, sir," he said and went downstairs, the others following him.

I closed Kavalov's door and went across to the library, where I phoned the sheriff's office in the county seat. I talked to a deputy named Hilden. When I had told him my story he said the sheriff would be at the house within half an hour.

I went to my room and dressed. By the time I had finished, the valet came up to tell me that everybody was assembled in the front room—everybody except the Ringgos and Mrs. Ringgo's maid.

I was examining Kavalov's bedroom when the sheriff arrived. He was a white-haired man with mild blue eyes and a mild voice that came out indistinctly under a white mustache. He had brought three deputies, a doctor and a coroner with him.

"Ringgo and the valet can tell you more than I can," I said when we had shaken hands all around. "I'll be back as soon as I can make it. I'm going to Sherry's. Ringgo will tell you where he fits in."

In the garage I selected a muddy Chevrolet and drove to the bungalow. Its doors and windows were tight, and my knocking brought no answer.

I went back along the cobbled walk to the car, and rode down into Farewell. There I had no trouble learning that Sherry and Marcus had taken the two-ten train for Los Angeles the afternoon before, with three trunks and half a dozen bags that the village expressman had checked for them.

After sending a telegram to the agency's Los Angeles branch, I hunted up the man from whom Sherry had rented the bungalow.

He could tell me nothing about his tenants except that he was disappointed in their not staying even a full two weeks. Sherry had returned the keys with a brief note saying he had been called away unexpectedly.

I pocketed the note. Handwriting specimens are always convenient to have. Then I borrowed the keys to the bungalow and went back to it.

I didn't find anything of value there, except a lot of fingerprints that might possibly come in handy later. There was nothing there to tell me where my men had gone.

I returned to Kavalov's.

The sheriff had finished running the staff through the mill.

"Can't get a thing out of them," he said. "Nobody heard anything and nobody saw anything, from bedtime last night, till the valet opened the door to call him at eight o'clock this morning, and saw him dead like that. You know any more than that?"

"No. They tell you about Sherry?"

"Oh, yes. That's our meat, I guess, huh?"

"Yeah. He's supposed to have cleared out yesterday afternoon, with his black man, for Los Angeles. We ought to be able to find the work in that. What does the doctor say?"

"Says he was killed between three and four this morning, with a heavyish knife—one clean slash from left to right, like a left-handed man would do it."

"Maybe one clean cut," I agreed, "but not exactly a slash. Slower than that. A slash, if it curved, ought to curve up, away from the slasher, in the middle, and down towards him at the ends—just the opposite of what this does."

"Oh, all right. Is this Sherry a southpaw?"

"I don't know," I wondered if Marcus was. "Find the knife?"

"Nary hide nor hair of it. And what's more, we didn't find anything else, inside or out. Funny a fellow as scared as Kavalov was, from all accounts, didn't keep himself locked up tighter. His windows were open. Anybody could of got in them with a ladder. His door wasn't locked."

"There could be half a dozen reasons for that. He—"

One of the deputies, a big-shouldered blond man, came to the door and said:

"We found the knife."

The sheriff and I followed the deputy out of the house, around to the side on which Kavalov's room was situated. The knife's blade was buried in the ground, among some shrubs that bordered a path leading down to the farm hands' quarters.

The knife's wooden handle—painted red—slanted a little toward the house. A little blood was smeared on the blade, but the soft earth had cleaned off most. There was no blood on the painted handle, and nothing like a fingerprint.

There were no footprints in the soft ground near the knife. Apparently it had been tossed into the shrubbery.

"I guess that's all there is here for us," the sheriff said. "There's nothing much to show that anybody here had anything to do with it, or didn't. Now we'll look after this here Captain Sherry."

I went down to the village with him. At the post office we learned that Sherry had left a forwarding address: General Delivery, St. Louis, Mo. The postmaster said Sherry had received no mail during his stay in Farewell.

We went to the telegraph office, and were told that Sherry had neither received nor sent any telegrams. I sent one to the agency's St. Louis branch.

The rest of our poking around in the village brought us nothing—except we learned that most of the idlers in Farewell had seen Sherry and Marcus board the southbound two-ten train.

Before we returned to the Kavalov house a telegram came from the Los Angeles branch for me:

Sherry's trunks and bags in baggage room here not yet called for are keeping them under surveillance.

When we got back to the house I met Ringgo in the hall, and asked him:

"Is Sherry left-handed?"

He thought, and then shook his head. "I can't remember," he said. "He might be. I'll ask Miriam. Perhaps she'll know—women remember things like that."

When he came downstairs again he was nodding:

"He's very nearly ambidextrous, but uses his left hand more than his right. Why?"

"The doctor thinks it was done with a left hand. How is Mrs. Ringgo now?"

"I think the worst of the shock is over, thanks."

VII

Sherry's baggage remained uncalled for in the Los Angeles passenger station all day Saturday. Late that afternoon the sheriff made public the news that Sherry and the black were wanted for murder, and that night the sheriff and I took a train south.

Sunday morning, with a couple of men from the Los Angeles police department, we opened the baggage. We didn't find anything except legitimate clothing and personal belongings that told us nothing.

That trip paid no dividends.

I returned to San Francisco and had bales of circulars printed and distributed.

Two weeks went by, two weeks in which the circulars brought us nothing but the usual lot of false alarms.

Then the Spokane police picked up Sherry and Marcus in a Stevens Street rooming house.

Some unknown person had phoned the police that one Fred Williams living there had a mysterious black visitor nearly every day, and that their actions were very suspicious. The Spokane police had copies of our circular. They hardly needed the H. S. monograms on Fred Williams' cuff links and handkerchiefs to assure them that he was our man.

After a couple of hours of being grilled, Sherry admitted his identity, but denied having murdered Kavalov.

Two of the sheriff's men went north and brought the prisoners down to the county seat.

Sherry had shaved off his mustache. There was nothing in his face or voice to show that he was the least bit worried.

"I knew there was nothing more to wait for after my dream," he drawled, "so I went away. Then, when I heard the dream had come true, I knew you johnnies would be hot after me—as if one can help his dreams—and I—ah—sought seclusion."

He solemnly repeated his orange-tree-voice story to the sheriff and district attorney. The newspapers liked it.

He refused to map his route for us, to tell us how he had spent his time.

"No, no," he said. "Sorry, but I shouldn't do it. It may be I shall have to do it again some time, and it wouldn't do to reveal my methods."

He wouldn't tell us where he had spent the night of the murder. We were fairly certain that he had left the train before it reached Los Angeles, though the train crew had been able to tell us nothing.

"Sorry," he drawled. "But if you chaps don't know where I was, how do you know that I was where the murder was?"

We had even less luck with Marcus. His formula was:

"Not understand the English very good. Ask the *capitaine*. I don't know."

The district attorney spent a lot of time walking his office floor, biting his finger nails, and telling us fiercely that the case was going to fall apart if we couldn't prove that either Sherry or Marcus was within reach of the Kavalov house at, or shortly before or after, the time of the murder.

The sheriff was the only one of us who hadn't a sneaky feeling that Sherry's sleeves were loaded with assorted aces. The sheriff saw him already hanged.

Sherry got a lawyer, a slick looking pale man with hornrim glasses and a thin twitching mouth. His name was Schaeffer. He went around smiling to himself and at us.

When the district attorney had only thumb nails left and was starting to work on them, I borrowed a car from Ringgo and started following the railroad south, trying to learn where Sherry had left the train. We had mugged the pair, of course, so I carried their photographs with me.

I displayed those damned photographs at every railroad stop between Farewell and Los Angeles, at every village within twenty miles of the tracks on either side, and at most of the houses in between. And it got me nothing.

There was no evidence that Sherry and Marcus hadn't gone through to Los Angeles.

Their train would have put them there at ten-thirty that night. There was no train out of Los Angeles that would have carried them back to Farewell in time to kill Kavalov. There were two possibilities: an airplane could have carried them back in plenty of time; and an automobile might have been able to do it, though that didn't look reasonable.

I tried the airplane angle first, and couldn't find a flyer who had had a passenger that night. With the help of the Los Angeles police and some operatives from the Continental's Los Angeles branch, I had everybody who owned a plane—public or private—interviewed. All the answers were no.

We tried the less promising automobile angle. The larger taxicab and hire-car companies said, "No." Four privately owned cars had been reported stolen between ten and twelve o'clock that night. Two of them had been found in the city the next morning: they couldn't have made the trip to Farewell and back. One of the others had been picked up in San Diego the next day. That let that one out. The other was still loose, a Packard sedan. We got a printer working on postcard descriptions of it.

To reach all the small-fry taxi and hire-car owners was quite a job, and then there were the private car owners who might have hired out for one night. We went into the newspapers to cover these fields.

We didn't get any automobile information, but this new line of inquiry—trying to find traces of our men here a few hours before the murder—brought results of another kind.

At San Pedro (Los Angeles's seaport, twenty-five miles away) a negro had been arrested at one o'clock on the morning of the murder. The negro spoke English poorly, but had papers to prove that he was Pierre Tisano, a French sailor. He had been arrested on a drunk and disorderly charge.

The San Pedro police said that the photograph and description of the man we knew as Marcus fit the drunken sailor exactly.

That wasn't all the San Pedro police said.

Tisano had been arrested at one o'clock. At a little after two o'clock, a white man who gave his name as Henry Somerton had appeared and had tried to bail the negro out. The desk sergeant had told Somerton that nothing could be done till morning, and that, anyway, it would be better to let Tisano sleep off his jag before removing him. Somerton had readily agreed to that, had remained talking to the desk sergeant for more than half an hour, and had left at about three. At ten o'clock that morning he had reappeared to pay the black man's fine. They had gone away together.

The San Pedro police said that Sherry's photograph—without the mustache—and description were Henry Somerton's.

Henry Somerton's signature on the register of the hotel to which he had gone between his two visits to the police matched the handwriting in Sherry's note to the bungalow's owner.

It was pretty clear that Sherry and Marcus had been in San Pedro—a nine-hour train ride from Farewell—at the time that Kavalov was murdered.

Pretty clear isn't quite clear enough in a murder job: I carried the San Pedro desk sergeant north with me for a look at the two men.

"Them's them, all righty," he said.

VIII

The district attorney ate up the rest of his thumb nails.

The sheriff had the bewildered look of a child who had held a balloon in his hand, had heard a pop, and couldn't understand where the balloon had gone.

I pretended I was perfectly satisfied.

"Now we're back where we started," the district attorney wailed disagreeably, as if it was everybody's fault but his, "and with all those weeks wasted."

The sheriff didn't look at the district attorney, and didn't say anything.

I said:

"Oh, I wouldn't say that. We've made some progress."

"What?"

"We know that Sherry and the dinge have alibis."

The district attorney seemed to think I was trying to kid him. I didn't pay any attention to the faces he made at me, and asked:

"What are you going to do with them?"

"What can I do with them but turn them loose? This shoots the case to hell."

"It doesn't cost the county much to feed them," I suggested. "Why not hang on to them as long as you can, while we think it over? Something new may turn up, and you can always drop the case if nothing does. You don't think they're innocent, do you?"

He gave me a look that was heavy and sour with pity for my stupidity.

"They're guilty as hell, but what good's that to me if I can't get a conviction? And what's the good of saying I'll hold them? Damn it, man, you know as well as I do that all they've got to do now is ask for their release and any judge will hand it to them."

"Yeah," I agreed. "I'll bet you the best hat in San Francisco that they don't ask for it."

"What do you mean?"

"They want to stand trial," I said, "or they'd have sprung that alibi before we dug it up. I've an idea that they tipped off the Spokane police themselves. And I'll bet you that hat that you get no *habeas corpus* motions out of Schaeffer."

The district attorney peered suspiciously into my eyes.

"Do you know something that you're holding back?" he demanded.

"No, but you'll see I'm right."

I was right. Schaeffer went around smiling to himself and making no attempt to get his clients out of the county prison.

Three days later something new turned up.

A man named Archibald Weeks, who had a small chicken farm some ten miles south of the Kavalov place, came to see the district attorney. Weeks said he had seen Sherry on his—Weeks's—place early on the morning of the murder.

Weeks had been leaving for Iowa that morning to visit his parents. He had got up early to see that everything was in order before driving twenty miles to catch an early morning train.

At somewhere between half-past five and six o'clock he had gone to the shed where he kept his car, to see if it held enough gasoline for the trip.

A man ran out of the shed, vaulted the fence, and dashed away down the road. Weeks chased him for a short distance, but the other was too speedy for him. The man was too well-dressed for a hobo: Weeks supposed he had been trying to steal the car.

Since Weeks's trip east was a necessary one, and during his absence his wife would have only their two sons—one seventeen, one fifteen—there with her, he had thought it wisest not to frighten her by saying anything about the man he had surprised in the shed.

He had returned from Iowa the day before his appearance in the district attorney's office, and after hearing the details of the Kavalov murder, and seeing Sherry's picture in the papers, had recognized him as the man he had chased.

We showed him Sherry in person. He said Sherry was the man. Sherry said nothing.

With Weeks's evidence to refute the San Pedro police's, the district attorney let the case against Sherry come to trial. Marcus was held as a material witness, but there was nothing to weaken his San Pedro alibi, so he was not tried.

Weeks told his story straight and simply on the witness stand, and then, under cross-examination, blew up with a loud bang. He went to pieces completely.

He wasn't, he admitted in answer to Schaeffer's questions, quite as sure that Sherry was the man as he had been before. The man had certainly, the little he had seen of him, looked something like Sherry, but perhaps he had been a little hasty in saying positively that it was Sherry. He wasn't, now that he had had time to think it over, really sure that he had actually got a good look at the man's face in the dim morning light. Finally, all that Weeks would swear to was that he had seen a man who had seemed to look a little bit like Sherry.

It was funny as hell.

The district attorney, having no nails left, nibbled his finger-bones.

The jury said, "Not guilty."

Sherry was freed, forever in the clear so far as the Kavalov murder was concerned, no matter what might come to light later.

Marcus was released.

The district attorney wouldn't say good-bye to me when I left for San Francisco.

IX

Four days after Sherry's acquittal, Mrs. Ringgo was shown into my office.

She was in black. Her pretty, unintelligent, Oriental face was not placid. Worry was in it.

"Please, you won't tell Dolph I have come here?" were the first words she spoke.

"Of course not, if you say not," I promised and pulled a chair over for her.

She sat down and looked big-eyed at me, fidgeting with her gloves in her lap.

"He's so reckless," she said.

I nodded sympathetically, wondering what she was up to.

"And I'm so afraid," she added, twisting her gloves. Her chin trembled. Her lips formed words jerkily: "They've come back to the bungalow."

"Yeah?" I sat up straight. I knew who *they* were.

"They can't," she cried, "have come back for any reason except that they mean to murder Dolph as they did father. And he won't listen to me. He's so sure of himself. He laughs and calls me a foolish child, and tells me he can take care of himself. But he can't. Not, at least, with a broken arm. And they'll kill him as they killed father. I know it. I know it."

"Sherry hates your husband as much as he hated your father?"

"Yes. That's it. He does. Dolph was working for father, but Dolph's part in the—the business that led up to Hugh's trouble was more—more active than father's. Will you—will you keep them from killing Dolph? Will you?"

"Surely."

"And you mustn't let Dolph know," she insisted, "and if he does find out you're watching them, you mustn't tell him I got you to. He'd be angry with me. I asked him to send for you, but he—" She broke off, looking embarrassed: I supposed her husband had mentioned my lack of success in keeping Kavalov alive. "But he wouldn't."

"How long have they been back?"

"Since the day before yesterday."

"Any demonstrations?"

"You mean things like happened before? I don't know. Dolph would hide them from me."

"I'll be down tomorrow," I promised. "If you'll take my advice you'll tell your husband

that you've employed me, but I won't tell him if you don't."

"And you won't let them harm Dolph?"

I promised to do my best, took some money away from her, gave her a receipt, and bowed her out.

Shortly after dark that evening I reached Farewell.

X

The bungalow's windows were lighted when I passed it on my way uphill. I was tempted to get out of my coupé and do some snooping, but was afraid that I couldn't out-Indian Marcus on his own grounds, and so went on.

When I turned into the dirt road leading to the vacant house I had spotted on my first trip to Farewell, I switched off the coupé's lights and crept along by the light of a very white moon overhead.

Close to the vacant house I got the coupé off the path and at least partly hidden by bushes.

Then I went up on the rickety porch, located the bungalow, and began to adjust my field glasses to it.

I had them partly adjusted when the bungalow's front door opened, letting out a slice of yellow light and two people.

One of the people was a woman.

Another least turn of the set-screw and her face came clear in my eyes—Mrs. Ringgo.

She raised her coat collar around her face and hurried away down the cobbled walk. Sherry stood on the veranda looking after her.

When she reached the road she began running uphill, towards her house.

Sherry went indoors and shut the door.

I took the glasses away from my eyes and looked around for a place where I could sit. The only spot I could find where sitting wouldn't interfere with my view of the bungalow was the porch-rail. I made myself as comfortable as possible there, with a shoulder against the corner post, and prepared for an evening of watchful waiting.

Two hours and a half later a man turned into the cobbled walk from the road. He walked swiftly to the bungalow, with a cautious sort of swiftness, and he looked from side to side as he walked.

I suppose he knocked on the door.

The door opened, throwing a yellow glow on his face, Dolph Ringgo's face.

He went indoors. The door shut.

My watch-tower's fault was that the bungalow could only be reached from it roundabout by the path and road. There was no way of cutting cross-country.

I put away the field glasses, left the porch, and set out for the bungalow. I wasn't sure that I could find another good spot for the coupé, so I left it where it was and walked.

I was afraid to take a chance on the cobbled walk.

Twenty feet above it, I left the road and moved as silently as I could over sod and among trees, bushes and flowers. I knew the sort of folks I was playing with: I carried my gun in my hand.

All of the bungalow's windows on my side showed lights, but all the windows were closed and their blinds drawn. I didn't like the way the light that came through the blinds helped the moon illuminate the surrounding ground. That had been swell when I was up on the ridge getting cock-eyed squinting through glasses. It was sour now that I was trying to get close enough to do some profitable listening.

I stopped in the closest dark spot I could find—fifteen feet from the building—to think the situation over.

Crouching there, I heard something.

It wasn't in the right place. It wasn't what I wanted to hear. It was the sound of somebody coming down the walk towards the house.

I wasn't sure that I couldn't be seen from the path. I turned my head to make sure. And by turning my head I gave myself away.

Mrs. Ringgo jumped, stopped dead still in the path, and then cried:

"Is Dolph in there? Is he? Is he?"

I was trying to tell her that he was by nodding, but she made so much noise with her *Is he's* that I had to say "Yeah" out loud to make her hear.

I don't know whether the noise we made hurried things up indoors or not, but guns had started going off inside the bungalow.

You don't stop to count shots in circumstances like those, and anyway these were too blurred together for accurate score-keeping, but my impression was that at least fifty of them had been fired by the time I was bruising my shoulder on the front door.

Luckily, it was a California door. It went in the second time I hit it.

Inside was a reception hall opening through a wide arched doorway into a living-room. The air was hazy and the stink of burnt powder was sharp.

Sherry was on the polished floor by the arch, wriggling sidewise on one elbow and one knee, trying to reach a Luger that lay on an amber rug some four feet away. His upper teeth were sunk deep into his lower lip, and he was coughing little stomach coughs as he wriggled.

At the other end of the room, Ringgo was upright on his knees, steadily working the trigger of a black revolver in his good hand. The pistol was empty. It went snap, snap, snap, snap foolishly, but he kept on working the trigger. His broken arm was still in the splints, but had fallen out of the sling and was hanging down. His face was puffy and florid with blood. His eyes were wide and dull. The white bone handle of a knife stuck out of his back, just over one hip, its blade all the way in. He was clicking the empty pistol at Marcus.

The black boy was on his feet, feet far apart under bent knees. His left hand was spread wide over his chest, and the black fingers were shiny with blood. In his right hand he held a white bone-handled knife—its blade a foot long—held it, knife-fighter fashion, as you'd hold a sword. He was moving toward Ringgo, not directly, but from side to side, obliquely, closing in with shuffling steps, crouching, his hand turning the knife restlessly, but holding the point always towards Ringgo. Marcus's eyes were bulging and red-veined. His mouth was a wide grinning crescent. His tongue, far out, ran slowly around and around the outside of his lips. Saliva trickled down his chin.

He didn't see us. He didn't hear us. All of his world just then was the man on his knees, the man in whose back a knife—brother of the one in the black hand—was wedged.

Ringgo didn't see us. I don't suppose he even saw the black. He knelt there and persistently worked the trigger of his empty gun.

I jumped over Sherry and swung the barrel of my gun at the base of Marcus's skull. It hit. Marcus dropped.

Ringgo stopped working the gun and looked surprised at me.

"That's the idea; you've got to put bullets in them or they're no good," I told him, pulled the knife out of Marcus's hand, and went back to pick up the Luger that Sherry had stopped trying to get.

Mrs. Ringgo ran past me to her husband.

Sherry was lying on his back now. His eyes were closed.

He looked dead, and he had enough bullet holes in him to make death a good guess.

Hoping he wasn't dead, I knelt beside him—going around him so I could kneel facing Ringgo—and lifted his head up a little from the floor.

Sherry stirred then, but I couldn't tell whether he stirred because he was still alive or because he had just died.

"Sherry," I said sharply. "Sherry."

He didn't move. His eyelids didn't even twitch.

I raised the fingers of the hand that was holding up his head, making his head move just a trifle.

"Did Ringgo kill Kavalov?" I asked the dead or dying man.

Even if I hadn't known Ringgo was looking at me I could have felt his eyes on me.

"Did he, Sherry?" I barked into the still face.

The dead or dying man didn't move.

I cautiously moved my fingers again so that his dead or dying head nodded, twice.

Then I made his head jerk back, and let it gently down on the floor again.

"Well," I said, standing up and facing Ringgo, "I've got you at last."

XI

I've never been able to decide whether I would actually have gone on the witness stand and sworn that Sherry was alive when he nodded, and nodded voluntarily, if it had been necessary for me to do so to convict Ringgo.

I don't like perjury, but I knew Ringgo was guilty, and there I had him.

Fortunately, I didn't have to decide.

Ringgo believed Sherry had nodded, and then, when Marcus gave the show away, there was nothing much for Ringgo to do but try his luck with a plea of guilty.

We didn't have much trouble getting the story out of Marcus. Ringgo had killed his beloved *capitaine*. The black boy was easily persuaded that the law would give him his best revenge.

After Marcus had talked, Ringgo was willing to talk.

He stayed in the hospital until the day before his trial opened. The knife Marcus had planted in his back had permanently paralyzed one of his legs, though aside from that he recovered from the stabbing.

Marcus had three of Ringgo's bullets in him. The doctors fished two of them out, but were afraid to touch the third. It didn't seem to worry him. By the time he was shipped north to begin an indeterminate sentence in San Quentin for his part in the Kavalov murder he was apparently as sound as ever.

Ringgo was never completely convinced that I had ever suspected him before the last minute when I had come charging into the bungalow.

"Of course I had, right along," I defended my skill as a sleuth. That was while he was still in the hospital. "I didn't believe Sherry was cracked. He was one hard, sane-looking scoundrel. And I didn't believe he was the sort of man who'd be worried much over any disgrace that came his way. I was willing enough to believe that he was out for Kavalov's scalp, but only if there was some profit in it. That's why I went to sleep and let the old man's throat get cut. I figured Sherry was scaring him up—nothing more—to get him in shape for a big-money shake-down. Well, when I found out I had been wrong there I began to look around.

"So far as I knew, your wife was Kavalov's heir. From what I had seen, I imagined your wife was enough in love with you to be completely in your hands. All right, you, as the husband of his heir, seemed the one to profit most directly by Kavalov's death. You were the one who'd have control of his fortune when he died. Sherry could only profit by the murder if he was working with you."

"But didn't his breaking my arm puzzle you?"

"Sure. I could understand a phoney injury, but that seemed carrying it a little too far. But you made a mistake there that helped me. You were too careful to imitate a left-hand cut on Kavalov's throat; did it by standing by his head, facing his body when you cut him, instead of by his body, facing his head, and the curve of the slash gave you away. Throwing the knife out the window wasn't so good, either. How'd he happen to break your arm? An accident?"

"You can call it that. We had that supposed fight arranged to fit in with the rest of the play, and I thought it would be fun to really sock him. So I did. And he was tougher than I thought, tough enough to even up by snapping my arm. I suppose that's why he killed Mickey too. That wasn't on the schedule. On the level, did you suspect us of being in cahoots?"

I nodded.

"Sherry had worked the game up for you, had done everything possible to draw suspicion on himself, and then, the day before the

murder, had run off to build himself an alibi. There couldn't be any other answer to it: he had to be working with you. There it was, but I couldn't prove it. I couldn't prove it till you were trapped by the thing that made the whole game possible—your wife's love for you sent her to hire me to protect you. Isn't that one of the things they call ironies of life?"

Ringgo smiled ruefully and said:

"They should call it that. You know what Sherry was trying on me, don't you?"

"I can guess. That's why he insisted on standing trial."

"Exactly. The scheme was for him to dig out and keep going, with his alibi ready in case he was picked up, but staying uncaught as long as possible. The more time they wasted hunting him, the less likely they were to look elsewhere, and the colder the trail would be when they found he wasn't their man. He tricked me there. He had himself picked up, and his lawyer hired that Weeks fellow to egg the district attorney into not dropping the case. Sherry wanted to be tried and acquitted, so he'd be in the clear. Then he had me by the neck. He was legally cleared forever. I wasn't. He had me. He was supposed to get a hundred thousand dollars for his part. Kavalov had left Miriam something more than three million dollars. Sherry demanded one-half of it. Otherwise, he said, he'd go to the district attorney and make a complete confession. They couldn't do anything to him. He'd been acquitted. They'd hang me. That was sweet."

"You'd have been wise at that to have given it to him," I said.

"Maybe. Anyway I suppose I would have given it to him if Miriam hadn't upset things. There'd have been nothing else to do. But after she came back from hiring you she went to see Sherry, thinking she could talk him into going away. And he lets something drop that made her suspect I had a hand in her father's death, though she doesn't even now actually believe that I cut his throat.

"She said you were coming down the next

day. There was nothing for me to do but go down to Sherry's for a showdown that night, and have the whole thing settled before you came poking around. Well, that's what I did, though I didn't tell Miriam I was going. The showdown wasn't going along very well, too much tension, and when Sherry heard you outside he thought I had brought friends, and—fireworks."

"What ever got you into a game like that in the first place?" I asked. "You were sitting pretty enough as Kavalov's son-in-law, weren't you?"

"Yes, but it was tiresome being cooped up in that hole with him. He was young enough to live a long time. And he wasn't always easy to get along with. I'd no guarantee that he wouldn't get up on his ear and kick me out, or change his will, or anything of the sort.

"Then I ran across Sherry in San Francisco, and we got to talking it over, and this plan came out of it. Sherry had brains. On the deal back in Cairo that you know about, both he and I made plenty that Kavalov didn't know about. Well, I was a chump. But don't think I'm sorry that I killed Kavalov. I'm sorry I got caught. I'd done his dirty work since he picked me up as a kid of twenty, and all I'd got out of it was damned little except the hopes that since I'd married his daughter I'd probably get his money when he died—if he didn't do something else with it."

They hanged him.

From—
The Glass Key

BY DASHIELL HAMMETT

IN MARCH *BLACK MASK*

. . . Ned Beaumont was clipping the end of a pale spotted cigar. The shakiness of his hands was incongruous with the steadiness of his voice asking: "Was Taylor there?" He looked at Madvig without raising his head.

"Not for dinner. Why?"

Ned Beaumont stretched out crossed legs, leaned back in his chair, moved the hand holding his cigar in a careless arc, and said: "He's dead in a gutter up the street."

Madvig, unruffled, asked: "Is that so?"

Ned Beaumont leaned forward. Muscles tightened in his lean face.

The wrapper of his cigar broke between his fingers with a thin cracking sound. He asked irritably: "Did you understand what I said?"

Madvig nodded slowly.

"Well?"

"Well what?"

"He was killed."

"All right," Madvig said. "Do you want me to get hysterical about it?"

Ned Beaumont sat up straight in his chair and asked: "Shall I call the police?"

Madvig raised his eyebrows a little. "Don't they know it?"

Ned Beaumont, looking steadily at the blond man, replied: "There was nobody around when I saw him. I wanted to see you before I did anything. Is it all right for me to say I found him?"

Madvig's eyebrows came down over blank eyes. "Why not?"

Ned Beaumont rose, took two steps towards the telephone, halted and faced the blond man again. He spoke with slow emphasis: "His hat wasn't there."

"He won't need it now." Then Madvig drew his brows together and said: "You're a—damned fool, Ned."

Ned Beaumont said, "One of us is," and went to the telephone. . . .

BLACK MASK, NOVEMBER 1930

Death and Company

BY DASHIELL HAMMETT

The Continental Op turns in a Case.

THE OLD MAN introduced me to the other man in his office—his name was Chappell—and said: "Sit down."

I sat down.

Chappell was a man of forty-five or so, solidly built and dark-complexioned, but shaky and washed out by worry or grief or fear. His eyes were red-rimmed and their lower lids sagged, as did his lower lip. His hand, when I shook it, had been flabby and damp.

The Old Man picked up a piece of paper from his desk and held it out to me. I took it. It was a letter crudely printed in ink, all capital letters.

MARTIN CHAPPELL

DEAR SIR—

IF YOU EVER WANT TO SEE YOUR WIFE ALIVE AGAIN YOU WILL DO JUST WHAT YOU ARE TOLD AND THAT IS GO TO THE LOT ON THE CORNER OF TURK AND LARKIN ST. AT EXACTLY 12 TONIGHT AND PUT $5000 IN $100 BILLS UNDER THE PILE OF BRICKS BEHIND THE BILL BOARD. IF YOU DO NOT DO THIS OR IF YOU GO TO THE POLICE OR IF YOU TRY ANY TRICKS YOU WILL GET A LETTER TMORROW TELLING YOU WHERE

TO FIND HER CORPSE. WE MEAN BUSINESS.

DEATH & CO.

I put the letter back on the Old Man's desk.

He said: "Mrs. Chappell went to a matinée yesterday afternoon. She never returned home. Mr. Chappell received this in the mail this morning."

"She go alone?" I asked.

"I don't know," Chappell said. His voice was very tired. "She told me she was going when I left for the office in the morning, but she didn't say which show she was going to or if she was going with anybody."

"Who'd she usually go with?"

He shook his head hopelessly. "I can give you the names and addresses of all her closest friends, but I'm afraid that won't help. When she hadn't come home late last night I telephoned all of them—everybody I could think of—and none of them had seen her."

"Any idea who could have done this?" I asked.

Again he shook his head hopelessly.

"Any enemies? Anybody with a grudge against you, or against her? Think, even if it's an old grudge or seems pretty slight. There's something like that behind most kidnappings."

"I know of none," he said wearily. "I've tried to think of anybody I know or ever knew who might have done it, but I can't."

"What business are you in?"

He looked puzzled, but replied: "I've an advertising agency."

"How about discharged employees?"

"No, the only one I've ever discharged was John Hacker and he has a better job now with one of my competitors and we're on perfectly good terms."

I looked at the Old Man. He was listening attentively, but in his usual aloof manner, as if he had no personal interest in the job. I cleared my throat and said to Chappell: "Look here. I want to ask some questions that you'll probably think— well—brutal, but they're necessary. Right?"

He winced as if he knew what was coming, but nodded and said: "Right."

"Has Mrs. Chappell ever stayed away over night before?"

"No, not without my knowing where she was." His lips jerked a little. "I think I know what you are going to ask. I'd like—I'd rather not hear. I mean I know it's necessary, but, if I can, I think I'd rather try to tell you without your asking."

"I'd like that better too," I agreed. "I hope you don't think I'm getting any fun out of this."

"I know," he said. He took a deep breath and spoke rapidly, hurrying to get it over: "I've never had any reason to believe that she went anywhere that she didn't tell me about or had any friends she didn't tell me about. Is that"—his voice was pleading—"what you wanted to know?"

"Yes, thanks." I turned to the Old Man again. The only way to get anything out of him was to ask for it, so I said: "Well?"

He smiled courteously, like a well-satisfied blank wall, and murmured: "You have the essential facts now, I think. What do you advise?"

"Pay the money of course—first," I replied, and then complained: "It's a damned shame that's the only way to handle a kidnapping. These Death and Co. birds are pretty dumb, picking that spot for the pay-off. It would be duck soup to nab them there." I stopped complaining and asked Chappell: "You can manage the money all right?"

"Yes."

I addressed the Old Man: "Now about the police?"

Chappell began: "No, not the police! Won't they—?"

I interrupted him: "We've got to tell them, in case something goes wrong and to have them all set for action as soon as Mrs. Chappell is safely home again. We can persuade them to keep their hands off till then." I asked the Old Man: "Don't you think so?"

He nodded and reached for his telephone. "I think so. I'll have Lieutenant Fielding and perhaps someone from the District Attorney's office come up here and we'll lay the whole thing before them."

Fielding and an Assistant District Attorney named McPhee came up. At first they were all for making the Turk-and-Larkin-Street-brick-pile a midnight target for half the San Francisco police force, but we finally persuaded them to listen to reason. We dug up the history of kid-napping from Ross to Parker[*] and waved it in their faces and showed them that the statistics were on our side: more success and less grief had come from paying what was asked and going hunting afterwards than from trying to nail the kidnappers before the kidnapped were released.

At half past eleven o'clock that night Chappell left his house, alone, with five thousand dollars wrapped in a sheet of brown paper in his pocket. At twenty minutes past twelve he returned.

His face was yellowish and wet with perspira-tion and he was trembling.

"I put it there," he said difficultly. "I didn't see anybody."

I poured out a glass of his whiskey and gave it to him.

He walked the floor most of the night. I dozed in a sofa. Half a dozen times at least I heard him go to the street door to open it and look out. Detective-sergeants Muir and Callahan went to bed. They and I had planted ourselves there to get any information Mrs. Chappell could give us as soon as possible.

She did not come home.

At nine in the morning Callahan was called to the telephone. He came away from it scowling.

"Nobody's come for the dough yet," he told us.

_____
* Four-year-old Charlie Ross was kidnapped in Philadelphia in 1874; he was never found. That was reputedly the first abduction for ransom in Ameri-can history. Twelve-year-old Marion Parker was kid-napped and murdered in Los Angeles in December 1927.

Chappell's drawn face became wide-eyed and open-mouthed with horror. "You had the place watched?" he cried.

"Sure," Callahan said, "but in an all right way. We just had a couple of men stuck up in an apartment down the block with field-glasses. Nobody could tumble to that."

Chappell turned to me, horror deepening in his face. "What—?"

The door-bell rang.

Chappell ran to the door and presently came back excitedly tearing a special-delivery-stamped envelope open. Inside was another of the crudely printed letters.

MARTIN CHAPPELL

DEAR SIR—

WE GOT THE MONEY ALL RIGHT BUT HAVE GOT TO HAVE MORE TONIGHT THE SAME AMOUNT AT THE SAME TIME AND EVERY-THING ELSE THE SAME. THIS TIME WE WILL HONESTLY SEND YOUR WIFE HOME ALIVE IF YOU DO AS YOU ARE TOLD. IF YOU DO NOT OR SAY A WORD TO THE POLICE YOU KNOW WHAT TO EXPECT AND YOU BET YOU WILL GET IT.

DEATH & CO.

Callahan said: "What the hell?"

Muir growled: "Them —— at the window must be blind."

I looked at the postmark on the envelope. It was earlier that morning. I asked Chappell: "Well, what are you going to do?"

He swallowed and said: "I'll give them every cent I've got if it will bring Louise home safe."

At half past eleven o'clock that night Chappell left his house with another five thousand dollars.

When he returned the first thing he said was: "The money I took last night is really gone."

This night was much like the previous one except that he had less hopes of seeing Mrs. Chappell in the morning. Nobody said so, but all of us expected another letter in the morning asking for still another five thousand dollars.

Another special-delivery letter did come, but it read:

MARTIN CHAPPELL

DEAR SIR—

WE WARNED YOU TO KEEP THE POLICE OUT OF IT AND YOU DISOBEYED. TAKE YOUR POLICE TO APT. 313 AT 895 POST ST. AND YOU WILL FIND THE CORPSE WE PROMISED YOU IF YOU DISOBEYED.
DEATH & CO.

Callahan cursed and jumped for the telephone.

I put an arm around Chappell as he swayed, but he shook himself together and turned fiercely on me.

"You've killed her!" he cried.

"Hell with that," Muir barked. "Let's get going."

Muir, Chappell, and I went out to Chappell's car, which had stood two nights in front of the house. Callahan ran out to join us as we were moving away.

The Post Street address was only a ten-minute ride from Chappell's house the way we did it. It took a couple of more minutes to find the manager of the apartment house and to take her keys away from her. Then we went up and entered apartment 313.

A tall slender woman with curly red hair lay dead on the living-room floor. There was no question of her being dead: she had been dead long enough for discoloration to have got well under way. She was lying on her back. The tan flannel bathrobe—apparently a man's—she had

on had fallen open to show pinkish lingerie. She had on stockings and one slipper. The other slipper lay near her.

Her face and throat and what was visible of her body were covered with bruises. Her eyes were wide open and bulging, her tongue out: she had been beaten and then throttled.

More police detectives joined us and some policemen in uniform. We went into our routine.

The manager of the house told us the apartment had been occupied by a man named Harrison M. Rockfield. She described him: about thirty-five years old, six feet tall, blond hair, gray or blue eyes, slender, perhaps a hundred and sixty pounds, very agreeable personality, dressed well. She said he had been living there alone for three months. She knew nothing about his friends, she said, and had not seen Mrs. Chappell before. She had not seen Rockfield for two or three days but had thought nothing of it as she often went a week or so without seeing some tenants.

We found a plentiful supply of clothing in the apartment, some of which the manager positively identified as Rockfield's. The police department experts found a lot of masculine fingerprints that we hoped were his.

We couldn't find anybody in adjoining apartments who had heard the racket that must have been made by the murder.

We decided that Mrs. Chappell had probably been killed as soon as she was brought to the apartment—no later than the night of her disappearance, anyhow.

"But why?" Chappell demanded dumbfoundedly.

"Playing safe. You wouldn't know till after you'd come across. She wasn't feeble. It would be hard to keep her quiet in a place like this."

A detective came in with the package of hundred-dollar bills Chappell had placed under the brick-pile the previous night.

I went down to headquarters with Callahan to question the men stationed at a nearby apartment-window to watch the vacant lot. They swore up and down that nobody—"not as much as a rat"—could have approached the brick-pile without being seen by them. Callahan's answer to that was a bellowed "The Hell they couldn't—they did!"

I was called to the telephone. Chappell was on the wire. His voice was hoarse.

"The telephone was ringing when I got home," he said, "and it was him."

"Who?"

"Death and Co., he said. That's what he said, and he told me that it was my turn next. That's all he said. 'This is Death and Co., and it's your turn next.'"

"I'll be right out," I said. "Wait for me."

I told Callahan and the others what Chappell had told me.

Callahan scowled. "—," he said, "I guess we're up against another of those—damned nuts!"

Chappell was in a bad way when I arrived at his house. He was shivering as if with a chill and his eyes were almost idiotic in their fright.

"It's—it's not only that—that I'm afraid," he tried to explain. "I am—but it's—I'm not that afraid—but—but with Louise—and—it's the shock and all. I—"

"I know," I soothed him. "I know. And you haven't slept for a couple of days. Who's your doctor? I'm going to phone him."

He protested feebly, but finally gave me his doctor's name.

The telephone rang as I was going towards it. The call was for me, from Callahan.

"We've pegged the fingerprints," he said triumphantly. "They're Dick Moley's. Know him?"

"Sure," I said, "as well as you do."

Moley was a gambler, gunman, and grifter-in-general with a police record as long as his arm.

Callahan was saying cheerfully: "That's going to mean a fight when we find him, because you know how tough that—is. And he'll laugh while he's being tough."

"I know," I said.

I told Chappell what Callahan had told me. Rage came into his face and voice when he heard the name of the man accused of killing his wife.

"Ever hear of him?" I asked.

He shook his head and went on cursing Moley in a choked, husky voice.

I said: "Stop that. That's no good. I know where to find Moley."

His eyes opened wide. "Where?" he gasped.

"Want to go with me?"

"Do I?" he shouted. Weariness and sickness had dropped from him.

"Get your hat," I said, "and we'll go."

He ran upstairs for his hat and down with it.

He had a lot of questions as we went out and got into his car. I answered most of them with: "Wait, you'll see."

But in the car he went suddenly limp and slid down in his seat.

"What's the matter?" I asked.

"I can't," he mumbled. "I've got to—help me into the house—the doctor."

"Right," I said, and practically carried him into the house.

I spread him on a sofa, had a maid bring him water, and called his doctor's number. The doctor was not in.

When I asked him if there was any other particular doctor he wanted he said weakly: "No, I'm all right. Go after that—that man."

"All right," I said.

I went outside, got a taxicab, and sat in it.

Twenty minutes later a man went up Chappell's front steps and rang the bell. The man was Dick Moley, alias Harrison M. Rockfield.

He took me by surprise. I had been expecting Chappell to come out, not anyone to go in. He had vanished indoors and the door was shut by the time I got there.

I rang the bell savagely.

A heavy pistol roared inside, twice.

I smashed the glass out of the door with my gun and put my left hand in, feeling for the latch.

The heavy pistol roared again and a bullet

hurled splinters of glass into my cheek, but I found the latch and worked it.

I kicked the door back and fired once straight ahead at random. Something moved in the dark hallway then and without waiting to see what it was I fired again, and when something fell I fired at the sound.

A voice said: "Cut it out. That's enough. I've lost my gun."

It wasn't Chappell's voice. I was disappointed.

Near the foot of the stairs I found a light-switch and turned it on. Dick Moley was sitting on the floor at the other end of the hallway holding one leg.

"That damned fool maid got scared and locked this door," he complained, "or I'd've made it out back."

I went nearer and picked up his gun. "Get you anywhere but the leg?" I asked.

"No. I'd've been all right if I hadn't dropped the gun when it upset me."

"You've got a lot of ifs," I said. "I'll give you another one. You've got nothing to worry about but that bullet-hole if you didn't kill Chappell."

He laughed. "If he's not dead he must feel funny with those two .44s in his head."

"That was—damned dumb of you," I growled.

He didn't believe me. He said: "It was the best job I ever pulled."

"Yeah? Well, suppose I told you that I was only waiting for another move of his to pinch him for killing his wife?"

He opened his eyes at that.

"Yeah," I said, "and you have to walk in and mess things up. I hope to—they hang you for it." I knelt down beside him and began to slit his pants-leg with my pocket-knife.

"What'd you do? Go in hiding after you found her dead in your rooms because you knew a guy with your record would be out of luck, and then lose your head when you saw in the extras this afternoon what kind of a job he'd put up on you?"

"Yes," he said slowly, "though I'm not sure I lost my head. I've got a hunch I came pretty near giving the——————what he deserved."

"That's a swell hunch," I told him. "We were ready to grab him. The whole thing had looked phoney. Nobody had come for the money the first night, but it wasn't there the next day, so he said. Well, we only had his word for it that he had actually put it there and hadn't found it the next night. The next night, after he had been told the place was watched he left the money there, and then he wrote the note saying Death & Company knew he'd gone to the police. That wasn't public news, either. And then her being killed before anybody knew she was kidnapped. And then tying it to you when it was too dizzy—no, you are dizzy, or you wouldn't have pulled this one. Anyhow we had enough to figure he was wrong, and if you'd let him alone we'd have pulled him, put it in the papers, and waited for you to come forth and give us what we needed to clear you and swing him." I was twisting my necktie around his leg above the bullet-hole. "But that's too sensible for you. How long you been playing around with her?"

"A couple of months," he said, "only I wasn't playing. I meant it."

"How'd he happen to catch her there alone?"

He shook his head. "He must've followed her there that afternoon when she was supposed to be going to the theater. Maybe he waited out side until he saw me go out. I had to go downtown, but I wasn't gone an hour. She was already cold when I came back." He frowned. "I don't think she'd've answered the doorbell, though maybe—or maybe he'd had a duplicate made of the key she had."

Some policemen came in: the frightened maid had had sense enough to use the telephone.

"Do you think he planned it that way from the beginning?" Moley asked.

I didn't. I thought he had killed his wife in a jealous rage and later thought of the Death and Co. business.

BONUS

THE
UNFINISHED
OP

Commentary

DASHIELL HAMMETT'S PLAN for "Three Dimes" follows a familiar pattern. The Continental Op—characteristically wry and pragmatic—is working a routine job when he is drawn into a thorny criminal scheme perpetrated by colorful crooks operating in well-trod San Francisco territory. "Three Dimes" would have fit nicely into the Op's canon—one more adventure chalked up to Hammett's "little fat detective." But Hammett never completed the story. It exists only as a 1,367-word partial draft, preserved among an array of Hammett's papers entrusted by Lillian Hellman (after Hammett's death in 1961) to the Harry Ransom Center at the University of Texas at Austin.

The heading for Hammett's "Three Dimes" typescript is a simple title, appended with a one-word penciled note: "Unfinished?" While there is no date, or address to suggest a date, an accompanying half page of notes sketching characters and plot offers an inadvertent clue to time frame. Hammett typed his notes on the verso of a draft of "This King Business," the twenty-sixth of his twenty-eight Op tales, published in

Mystery Stories in January 1928, the same month in which the third of four installments of what would become his first novel, *Red Harvest*, was published in *Black Mask*.

Circumstantial evidence, then, locates "Three Dimes" among the last few of Hammett's Continental Op stories, probably alongside "The Main Death," "Fly Paper," and "The Farewell Murder," drafted in 1928 or 1929, a couple of years into Joseph Thompson Shaw's tenure as editor at *Black Mask*. If similar in length to those tales, it is perhaps one-tenth complete—a story rather than a novella. Hammett set aside the project for reasons about which we can only speculate, though clearly he was by then aspiring to longer, more sophisticated works. But we know, for hard fact, that he salted away both draft and notes for the Op's unfinished adventure in what is a strikingly sparse file of unfinished works. "Three Dimes," with whatever virtues and potentials inspired Hammett to preservation, is published here in print for the first time. His notes follow.

JMR

"THREE DIMES"

MCKAY & MACLEAN HAD a stationery store in San Francisco's Market Street. They had cash registers and a normally honest sales force, but, like most retailers, they didn't trust these two things blindly. Twice a year they got the agency to check up the sales force. About once a year we would catch somebody beating the damper.* The thief would be called into the partners' office and worked on. Usually he confessed, gave a more or less modest estimate of how much his stealing added up to in all, made that amount good, or promised to, and was fired. The sums were never large, and McKay & MacLean never worried the police with this petty larceny.

Dinky little jobs of that sort are not much fun for the operatives working on them, but detective agencies depend on them for bread and butter money: there are always plenty of them on tap, while murders, big swindles, kidnappings, and the rest of the showy crimes, are comparatively rare.

This time we nailed a boy of sixteen named Richard Allan. He was a tall stringy lad with wavy red hair, long-lashed blue eyes, girlish skin, and a pretty face that didn't show any character, good or bad. I hung a thirty-cent hold-out on him.

I had bought a box of writing paper for a dollar and a quarter, receiving my cash register receipt with it. Then I picked up a thirty-cent memoranda book from the counter rack, said,

---

* cheating the bank; stealing

514

"I'll take this too," handed him three dimes, put the book in my pocket, and walked out. That was the routine.

He had no change to make, nothing to wrap up, and I was gone, leaving him a clear field in which to do whatever he wanted to do with the thirty cents. The catch in it was that I had a receipt for a dollar and a quarter, with his letter on it, and that the cash register tape was similarly stamped. If the partners, after getting my report, didn't find his letter with a thirty-cent sale on the tape immediately after the dollar and a quarter one, they had him cold. If he pocketed the thirty cents, the only thing that could save him would be that the next sale he rang up happened also to be a thirty cent one.

Well, he did pocket my thirty cents, and no coincidences came to his rescue.

He was the only employee we trapped this time. I had landed him. It was my job to break him down, to make him confess he had been stealing regularly, and to try to find out how much.

The boy was selling a fountain pen to a girl when I went into the store a couple of mornings after my purchase. I went through to the rear of the store and climbed steps to the partners' office on the mezzanine.

McKay's bony face was solemn and full of righteousness. There was a grim glint in his never warm gray eyes. He had put on a black necktie. Plump MacLean, ten years younger than his partner, was nervous, uncomfortable, and very plainly on hand only because McKay had insisted that it was his duty to be on hand. I had heard them argue about it before.

"Shall we have the young man up now?" McKay asked after we had good-morninged each other. His voice had already taken on the tone in which he always made for-your-own-good-and-let-it-be-a-lesson-to-you speeches to his victims on these occasions.

I nodded. MacLean wet his lips and said wearily:

"Let's get it over with."

"Miss Carter," McKay told the stenographer, "will you ask Mr. Allan to come up?"

The girl went out of the office, and, when she returned, said that the boy would be up as soon as he had finished with a customer.

Ten minutes went by. McKay stared at a calendar with the look of a man thinking about what he was going to say. MacLean smoked cigarettes, fidgeted, and drew lopsided houses on his desk blotter.

McKay cleared his throat sternly and looked at the clock on the wall. Miss Carter stopped clattering her typewriter and went out. Presently she was back, frowning.

"Richard has gone out," she said. "Mr. Marrow says he went out as soon as the customer left, without his hat. He called to him, asking where he was going, but Richard didn't say anything, just went on out."

MacLean's face brightened, and he began drawing a girl's head on the blotter.

McKay said angrily that it was nonsense. The boy couldn't have gone out like that. His employees didn't go out without saying where they were going. He got up from his chair and marched out of the office.

MacLean grinned happily at me and said:

"Scared him away. A good job, too. Him and his undertaker's tie—going around looking like a cartoon of a Prohibitionist."

McKay was all steamed up when he returned from downstairs. The boy had skipped. McKay wanted me to gallop after him, catch him, and drag him back.

MacLean protested:

"Aw, let the kid alone, John. What do you want to hound him for?"

McKay didn't like the word *hound*. It made him indignant. The boy should be brought back, confronted with the proof of his crime, and made to realize its seriousness, all for his own good. It was the clear duty of both partners to do their utmost to turn the youth's feet from the pathway of crime, and both would be morally responsible for any further missteps he might make if, through weak sentimentality, they failed to do their duty toward him. McKay unloaded on us the sermon he had meant for the boy. MacLean maliciously stuck to the word *hound*, but he was no match for his partner. He hadn't McKay's stubborn certainty that what he thought right was right.

McKay gave me the Allan boy's address. He lived in a Sacramento Street apartment with his sister. I went up there. It was a smallish building across the street from the Pacific Union Club.* I pushed the button beside *408 Allan* in the vestibule directory. When I didn't get any answer I pushed one of the other buttons and the street door buzzed open. I went in, rode up to the fourth floor, found that 408 was the right-hand front apartment, tried its bell with no luck, and went downstairs again and out of the building. Huntington Square sits beside the Pacific Union Club grounds. I went over into the square, found a bench from which I could see both the street door of the apartment house and the windows of the Allans' apartment, and settled there. I spent the afternoon there. It was a pleasant enough afternoon except that too many children stumbled over my feet whenever I forgot to keep them

---

* exclusive private men's club located at Mason and California Streets in San Francisco

tucked under the bench. I didn't see Richard Allan.

II

At six-fifteen, the Allans' window blinds were drawn down—I couldn't see who did it—and a moment later lights were turned on behind them. I hadn't seen Richard Allan go in. I had seen half a dozen men, enter the building since five o'clock and three or four young women, any one of whom could have been the boy's sister.

By ten minutes after seven, when the Allans' lights went off, it was fairly dark.

Five minutes later one of the young women I had seen came out. She was a slender girl not a long way past twenty. Her green clothes were good and she knew how to wear them. She walked down the hill to Powell Street and boarded a cable car going down town. That's what I did. The boy hadn't come home. The chances were now that he wouldn't come home till late. Or, if he was badly frightened, he might not be coming home at all. He might have phoned his sister. She might be going to meet him. What I hoped was that she was going to dinner. I hoped she hadn't grabbed a bite during the hour she had been inside. Sitting in the park, smoking cigarettes and meditating had given me an appetite.

HAMMETT'S NOTES, UNDATED

THREE DIMES

Boy working in store suspected of knocking back. Op makes test on him with 30¢ buy and secures dope. Boy becomes panic striken when being shaken down, beats it, goes in hiding, is helped and used by gang of crooks who are staging big crime, op being drawn into it through his pursuit of boy.

McKay & Maclean's Stationery Store. Richard Allan. Celia Allan. Big Frank Stutz. Sterno Riley. The Indian Kid. Tommy Poole. Black Kate.

Op goes to store, checks boy, catches him with 30¢ purchase. Other Op's fail. Op returns two days later to grill boy. Boy recognizes him and, when proprietor sends for him, beats it. Next day proprietor phones agency that Celia had called up boy missing. Op sets out to find him.

Allan goes to Big Frank Stutz, who had been pointed out to him as con man, and asks him to help him. Big Frank pumps kid and frames a plan to use him.

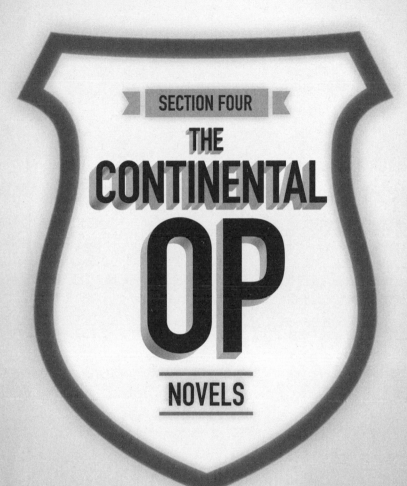

SECTION FOUR

THE
CONTINENTAL
OP
NOVELS

THE CLEANSING
OF POISONVILLE

Introduction

THE CLEANSING OF POISONVILLE

THE BEST IMPRESSION one can glean about Hammett's writing methods and editorial judgment comes from the correspondence that survives between him and Shaw and him and editors at Alfred A. Knopf, who published the novels in book form. There it is possible to get a sense of the guidance he was given by his publishers and his responses to it. Not until the end of the 1920s, when Hammett began to establish his reputation as a book author, did he feel empowered to assert himself fully as a writer. Shaw deserves credit for that. He gave Hammett the editorial freedom he required to write as he wished and, ultimately, to create what Hammett called "literature." In the pulp versions of his novels, Hammett was still bound by his earlier editors' insistence on violent action, and Shaw attempted to rationalize that tendency by pointing out that Hammett's novels mirrored the violence reported in daily newspapers. But the advice from the editors at Knopf to tone down the violence ultimately liberated him.

On June 1, 1927, Hammett wrote his wife:

Got home tonight to find a stack of letters from the Black Mask, one from Shaw telling me how good I am, one from Cody telling me

the same thing with further trimmings, and one from Gardner telling me the last dingus he read of mine [presumably "The Main Death"] was not only the best ever printed in the Black Mask, but the best he had ever read anywhere, and so on and so on and so on.

Overwhelmed by this applesauce I'm writing them to shoot me some dough and I'll do them some more shots-in-the-dark.

On the strength of that, I'm putting in an order for an Encyclopaedia Brittanica and some gin.

With this encouragement, Hammett began planning his foray into novel writing and book publication. The "shots in the dark" was "The Cleansing of Poisonville," and Hammett took his inspiration from the so-called copper wars in Butte and nearby Anaconda, Montana, that took place from the time of the Civil War until early in the twentieth century. Butte was by all accounts thoroughly corrupt, and the Copper Kings U.S. Senator William A. Clark and Marcus Daly fought bitterly for control of the mining interests in the area. Both owned local newspapers, both were politically influential, and both were enormously rich. Gambling, prostitution, and, during Prohibition, bootlegging were common. While Personville is clearly modeled on Butte, Hammett took liberties with his depiction of the city capturing it with fidelity, if not accuracy. There is no credible evidence that Hammett had personal experience in Butte or Anaconda, though his wife was raised in the area. He nonetheless created a strikingly credible hard-boiled novel of manners set in the area.

In mid-June 1927, he wrote his wife that "the story goeth slowly but nicely." Two weeks later, he reported that he had finished two thousand words that day, but he had hoped to finish five thousand. And on July 12, 1927, some six weeks after Hammett had begun his novel, which he called *The Cleansing of Poisonville*, Shaw responded to the first installment.

I have nothing but praise for POISONVILLE. In one of your recent letters you spoke of keeping your feet on the ground; the sense of reality which this tale gives is gripping. You can see the place, the scenes, the action, the faces and the character of the actors. Some of the parts are raw meat; but it is not thrown out in ragged chunks. It is served with a skill that preserves the virile strength of it and obliterates any suggestion of coarseness. I am going to say that I like this and, anticipating that the balance will be molded in the same spirit, I believe it will be a series to conjure with.

I am well aware that this sounds like enthusiasm. Reading your note that accompanied the story, I have been casting through my impression from first consideration, and I really do not see any important element to shun. This, of course, is the set-up. Naturally, as I wired, the following episodes will swing into quicker action. I suppose this would be more helpful if I should pick out one or two slants for constructive criticism. I shall read it over again more carefully in a few days and may then have something more to say. Just now I am satisfied that it holds well to the middle of the road.

"The Cleansing of Poisonville," the first installment of Hammett's four-part serialized novel, appeared in *Black Mask* in November 1927, one year after Shaw became editor. In February 1928, when the last monthly installment was published, Hammett sent what he called his "action-detective novel" to the editors at Alfred A. Knopf, who published Conrad Aiken, Willa Cather, H. L. Mencken, T. S. Eliot, and an array of classical literature. Since at least 1918, Knopf had maintained an imprint called the Borzoi Mysteries under the direction of Blanche Knopf, Alfred's wife, but little attention had been paid to that line until Hammett's novel arrived and Shaw later began feeding *Black Mask* authors to the firm.

On March 12, 1928, Hammett received the following letter:

Dear Mr. Hammett;

We have read POISONVILLE with a great deal of interest.

I would like to suggest some revisions, and I hope you won't object to them. Towards the middle of the book, the violence seems piled on too heavily; so many killings on a page I believe make the reader doubt the story, and instead of the continued suspense and feeling of horror, the interest slackens. One of our readers writes:

"I think that the best way to cut this would be to take Lew Yard out of the story entirely. He never figures personally, but even so, he is responsible for a good deal of violence that could be left out. This chiefly takes place in the shooting up of a roadhouse . . . and the blowing up of Yard's house. . . . Some rewriting would be necessary, but it seems to me that it could be very easily done by making Reno the head of this particular gang from the beginning. The roadhouse shooting is quite similar to several others that take place both before and after."

"Another episode that could be entirely cut is the dynamiting of the Police Sta-

tion. . . . If the Lew Yard material is cut, I should advise leaving this in. The brief shooting episode [a little later] could be cut profitably." and

"It should be possible to dispose of Pete in a less wholesale way than bombing him . . . although this is an exciting moment."

Of course you may have some ideas of your own regarding all this, and I certainly hope that you will not in any way resent our suggestions. There is no question whatever that we are keen about the mass, and with the necessary changes, I think that it would have a good chance. Won't you tell me something about your ideas for detective stories and whether you have any more under way?

Hoping that we will be able to get together on *POISONVILLE* (a hopeless title by the way) I am

Yours faithfully,
Mrs. Alfred A. Knopf

Hammett responded eight days later:

The middle of the book, as it now stands, undoubtedly is more than somewhat cluttered up with violence, and I am thoroughly willing to make whatever changes you consider necessary. But, if possible, I'd like to keep Lew Yard in the story, as most of the second half of the book hinges on Reno's break with him.

In the enclosed revised pages I have cut out the dynamiting of police headquarters. . . . ; have cut out the attack on Reno's house . . . , which shouldn't have been put in in the first place; and have changed the dynamiting of Yard's house . . . to simple shooting off stage. These changes will, I think, relieve the congestion quite a bit. If you think additional revision advisable please let me know. . . .

You will notice that I have left the bombing of Pete the Finn's establishment . . . as it was. Since both of the other dynamiting

episodes have been removed, I think this one might be retained, especially as it is further along in the story, not in the congested area.

Somehow I had got the idea the "Poisonville" was a pretty good title, and I was surprised at your considering it hopeless—sufficiently surprised to ask a couple of retail book sellers what they thought of it. They agreed with you, so I'm beginning to suspect which one of us is wrong. Here are the only new titles I have been able to think up so far.

THE POISONVILLE MURDERS,
THE SEVENTEENTH MURDER,
MURDER PLUS,
THE WILLSSON MATTER,
THE CITY OF DEATH,
THE CLEANSING OF
    POISONVILLE,
THE BLACK CITY,
RED HARVEST [√: this title is marked
    with a check, presumably at Knopf's
    office]

Maybe I'll be able to do better later, or maybe you can help me. The only prejudice I have in this connection is against the word "case" used where my sleuth would use "job" and, more officially, "matter" or "operation."

I've another book-length detective story—tentatively entitled The Dain Curse—*under way, using the same detective I used in this book, but not using him so violently. I hope to finish that next month. The first serial rights have been sold to* The Black Mask.

On April 9, Hammett returned a three-book contract to Knopf (which offered only a royalty, no advance), and in February 1929 they published *Red Harvest*—dedicated to Joseph Thompson Shaw—which received glowing reviews.

The novel that Hammett wrote for Shaw is significantly different from the one published by Alfred A. Knopf. There is hardly a paragraph in the *Black Mask* version that is not altered in the book, and there is evidence that many of the alterations came from Knopf copy editors. Hammett later complained that *The Dain Curse* "was edited to beat hell," and many of the editorial changes to *The Cleansing of Poisonville* seem uncharacteristic of Hammett, even a bit tin eared. At least one literary scholar, E. R. Hagemann, has declared the *Black Mask* novel superior to the book. In any event, it is fair to say that *The Cleansing of Poisonville* is significantly different from *Red Harvest*, and while the middle of the earlier iteration may be "cluttered up with violence," the language of *The Cleansing of Poisonville* is purer Hammett.

After the publication of *Red Harvest* in February 1929, Hammett began to attract interna-tional attention as an important new novelist whose modernist literary sensibility set him apart from the genre writers associated with the pulps. He was compared favorably to Ernest Hemingway by Herbert Asbury in the *Bookman*, and the *New Statesman* in London called him an author of "obvious intelligence." Moreover, he attracted the attention of Hollywood studio heads in need of talented writers who could handle dialogue to prepare scripts for the new talking movies, introduced commercially two years before *Red Harvest* was published. Hammett accommodated them, confiding to Blanche Knopf that he would concentrate on writing more fiction that could be adapted to the screen.

RL

BLACK MASK, NOVEMBER 1927

The Cleansing of Poisonville

BY DASHIELL HAMMETT

In recent years there have been too many examples where civic politics has degenerated into a business for profit. This story is the first, complete, episode in a series dealing with a city whose administrators have gone mad with power and lust of wealth. It is, also, to our minds, the ideal detective story—the new type of detective fiction which Black Mask is seeking to develop. You go along with the detective, meeting action with him, watching the development as the plot is unfolded, finding the clues as he finds them; and you have the feeling that you are living through the tense, exciting scenes rather than just reading a story. Poisonville is written by a master of his craft.

I FIRST HEARD PERSONVILLE called Poisonville in 1920, in the Big Ship* in Butte, by a red-haired mucker† named Hickey Dewey. But he also called his shirt a shoit, so I didn't think anything of what he had done to the city's name. Later, when I heard men who could manage their r's give it the same twist, I still didn't see anything in it but the meaningless sort of humor that used to make richardsnary the thieves' word

for dictionary. In 1927 I went to Personville and learned better.

Using one of the phones in the station, I called the *Herald*, asked for Donald Willsson, and told him I had arrived.

"Will you come out to my house at ten this evening?" He had a pleasantly crisp voice. "It's 2101 Mountain Boulevard. Take a Broadway car, get off at Laurel Avenue, and walk two blocks west."

I promised to do that. Then I went up to the Great Western Hotel, dumped my bags, and went out to look at the city.

It wasn't pretty. Most of its builders had

---

* a boarding house in Butte; also the nickname of the Anaconda Copper smelter

† a person who loads the waste from a mining operation

gone in for gaudiness. Maybe they had been successful at first. But since then the smelters, whose brick stacks stuck up tall against a gloomy mountain to the south, had yellow-smoked everything into a uniform dinginess. The result was an ugly city of 40,000 people, set in an ugly notch between two ugly mountains that had been all dirtied up by mining. Spread over this was a grimy sky that looked as if it had come out of the smelters' stacks.

The first policeman I saw needed a shave. The second had a couple of buttons off his shabby uniform. The third stood in the middle of Personville's main intersection—Broadway and Union Street—directing traffic with a cigar in one corner of his mouth. After that I stopped checking them up.

At nine-thirty I caught a Broadway car and followed the directions Donald Willsson had given me. His house was set in a hedged grass-plot on the corner. The maid who opened the door told me he wasn't home. While I was explaining that I had an appointment a slender blonde woman of something less than thirty, in green crepe, came to the door. When she smiled her blue eyes didn't lose their stoniness. I repeated my tale to her.

"My husband isn't in now." A barely noticeable accent slurred her s's. "But if he's expecting you he'll probably be home shortly."

She took me upstairs to a room on the Laurel Avenue side of the house, a square room with a lot of books in it. We sat in leather chairs, half facing each other, half facing a burning coal-grate, and she set about learning my business with her husband.

"Do you live in Personville?" she asked first.

"No—San Francisco."

"But this isn't your first visit?"

"Yes."

"Really? How do you like our city?"

"I haven't seen enough of it to know." That was a lie. I had. "I just got in this afternoon."

Her shiny eyes stopped prying while she said:

"I'm afraid you'll find it a dreary place." She shrugged and returned to her digging with: "I suppose all mining towns are like this. Are you engaged in mining?"

"Not just now."

She looked at the clock over the fire and said:

"It's inconsiderate of Donald to bring you out here and then keep you waiting, at this time of night, long after business hours."

I said that was all right.

"Though perhaps it isn't a business matter," she suggested.

I didn't say anything. She laughed—a brief laugh with something sharp in it.

"I'm ordinarily not curious about other people's affairs, really," she said gaily. "But you're so excessively secretive that you goad me on. You aren't a bootlegger, are you? Donald changes them so often."

I let her get whatever she could out of a grin. Downstairs a telephone bell rang. Mrs. Willsson stretched her green-slippered feet out toward the burning coal and pretended she hadn't heard the bell. I didn't know why she thought that necessary.

She began: "I'm afraid I'll ha—"and stopped to look at the maid in the doorway. The maid said Mrs. Willsson was wanted at the phone. She excused herself and followed the maid out. She didn't go downstairs, but spoke over an extension within earshot of my seat.

I heard: "Mrs. Willsson speaking . . . Yes . . . I beg your pardon? . . . Who? . . . Can't you speak a little louder? . . . *What?* . . . Yes . . . Yes . . . Who is this? . . . Hello! Hello!" The telephone hook rattled. Then her quick steps sounded down the hallway.

I set fire to a cigarette and stared at it until I heard her going downstairs. Then I went to a window, lifted the edge of the blind, and looked out at Laurel Avenue and at the small white garage that stood in the rear of the house on that side. Presently a slender woman in dark coat and hat came into sight, hurrying from house to garage. She drove away in a Buick coupé. It was Mrs. Willsson. I went back to my chair and waited.

Three quarters of an hour went by. At five

minutes past eleven automobile brakes screeched outside. Two minutes later Mrs. Willsson came into the room. She had taken off hat and coat. Her face was white, her eyes almost black.

"I'm awfully sorry." Her little tight-lipped mouth moved jerkily. "You've had all this waiting for nothing. My husband won't be home tonight."

I said I would get in touch with him at the *Herald* in the morning and went away— wondering why the green toe of her left slipper was dark and damp with something that could have been blood.

II

I walked over to Broadway and got into a street car. Three blocks north of my hotel I got off to see what the crowd was doing around a side entrance of the City Hall. Thirty or forty men and a sprinkling of women stood on the sidewalk looking at a door marked *Police Department*—a mixed crowd—men from mines and smelters still in their working clothes, gaudy boys from poolrooms and dance-halls, sleek men with cunning pale faces, men with the dull look of respectable fathers of families, a few just as respectable and dull women, and some ladies of the night.

On the edge of this congregation I stopped beside a square-set man in rumpled gray clothes. His face was grayish, too, even to the thick lips, though he didn't look much more than thirty—a broad, thick-featured face with intelligence in it. For color he depended on a red Windsor tie that blossomed over his gray flannel shirt.

"What's the rumpus?" I asked this fellow.

He looked at me carefully before he answered, as if to make sure that the information was going into safe hands. His eyes were as gray as his shirt, but not so soft.

"Don Willsson's gone to sit on the right hand of God—if God don't mind looking at the bullet holes in him."

"Who put them there?"

The gray man scratched the side of his neck and said: "Somebody with a gun."

I would have tried to find a less witty informant in the crowd if the red tie hadn't interested me.

"Sure. I'm a stranger in town," I said. "Hang the Punch and Judy* on me—That's what strangers are for."

"Mr. Donald Willsson, publisher of the *Morning* and *Evening Heralds*, son of the well-known Mr. Elihu Willsson," he recited in a rapid sing-song, "was found lying in Hurricane Street a little while ago, very dead, having been shot several places. Does that keep your feelings from being hurt?"

"Yeah. Thanks." I put out a finger and touched a loose end of his tie. "Mean anything? Or just wearing it?"

"I'm Bill Quint."

"The hell you are!" I exclaimed, trying to place the name. "By gad, I'm glad to meet you!"

I dug out my card case and ran through the collection of credentials I had picked up here and there by one means or another. The red card was the one I wanted. It identified me as Henry F. Brannan (a lie), member in good standing of Industrial Workers of the World, Seaman's No.—. I passed it to Bill Quint. He read it carefully, front and back, returned it to me, and looked me over from hat to shoes—not trustfully.

"He's not going to die again," he said. "Which way are you going?"

"Any."

We walked down the street together, turned a corner, strolled along—aimlessly so far as I knew.

"What brought you in here, if you're a sailor?" he asked casually.

"Where'd you get that idea?"

"There's the card."

"Yeah. I got another that proves I'm a timber-beast. If you want me to be a miner I'll get one for that tomorrow."

_____

* an unbelievable story

"No, you won't. I run 'em here."

"Suppose you got a wire from Chi?" I asked.

"To hell with Chi. I run 'em here. Drink?"

"Only when I can get it."

We went through a restaurant, up a flight of stairs, and into a narrow room with a long bar and a row of tables. Bill Quint nodded and said, "Hello," to some of the boys and girls at tables and bar and guided me into one of the booths that lined the opposite wall. We spent the next two hours drinking whiskey and talking.

The gray man didn't think I was a good Wobbly, didn't think I had any right to the red card I had shown him and the other one I had mentioned. As chief muckamuck of the I.W.W. in Personville he considered it his duty to find out how-come, and not to let himself be pumped about radical affairs while he was doing it. That was all right with me. I was more interested in Personville affairs. He didn't mind discussing them. They were something he could hide behind between casual pokings into my business with the red cards, my radical status.

What I got out of him amounted to this:

For forty years old Elihu Willsson had owned Personville heart, skin, guts and soul. He was president and majority stockholder of the Personville Mining Corporation, ditto of the First National Bank, owner of the *Morning Herald* and the *Evening Herald*, the city's only newspapers, and at least part owner of nearly every other enterprise of any importance in the city. Along with this other property he owned a United States Senator, a couple of Representatives and most of the State Legislature. Elihu Willsson was Personville, and he was almost the whole state.

Back in the war days, when the I.W.W. was blooming, they had lined up a lot of the Personville Mining Corporation's help. The help hadn't been pampered, and they used their new strength to demand the things they wanted. Old Elihu gave in to them and bided his time. In 1919 it came. Business was slack. He didn't care whether he had to shut down for a while or not. He cut wages, lengthened hours, generally kicked the help back into their old place.

Of course the help had yelled for action. Bill Quint had been sent out from Chicago to give it to them. He had been against a strike—a walkout. What he advised was the old sabotage racket, staying on the job and gumming things up from the inside. But the Personville crew wouldn't listen to him. They wanted to put themselves on the map, make labor history. So they struck.

The strike lasted eight months. Both sides bled plenty. The Wobblies had to do their own bleeding. Old Elihu could hire strike-breakers, gunmen, National Guardsmen and even parts of the regular army to do his. When the last skull had been cracked, the last rib kicked in, organized labor in Personville was a used firecracker.

But, said Bill Quint, old Elihu didn't know his Machiavelli. He had won the strike, but he had lost his hold on city and state affairs. To beat the Wobblies he had had to let his lieutenants run wild. When the fight was over he couldn't shake them off. Personville looked good to them and they took it over. Elihu was an enfeebled czar. He had given his city to his hired thugs, and now he wasn't strong enough to take it away from them. They had won his strike for him and now they took his city for their spoils. He couldn't openly break with them because he was responsible for all they had done during the strike. They had too much on him.

"They?" I asked. "Have they got names?"

"Uh-huh." Quint emptied his glass and pushed his hair out of his eyes. We were both fairly mellow by the time we had got this far. "The strongest of 'em is probably Pete the Finn. Then there's Lew Yard. He's got a loan joint down on Parker Street, does a lot of bail business, maybe handles hot stuff, and is pretty thick with Noonan, the chief of police. This kid Max Thaler has got a lot of friends, too. Little, slick dark guy with something wrong with his throat—a gambler. They call him Whisper because he does, which is a pretty good reason. Those three about help Elihu run his city, help him more than he wants. But he has to play with them or else."

"This fellow who was knocked off tonight—Elihu's son—where did he stand?"

"Where Papa put him, and he's where Papa put him now."

"You mean his old man had him—?"

"Maybe, at that, but it's not my guess. This Don just came home and began running the papers for the old man. It wasn't like old Elihu, even if he is getting along in years, to let anybody take his city away from him. But he had to be cagey. He brought the boy and his French wife home from Paris and used him as his monkey—a nice fatherly trick. Don starts a clean-up campaign in his papers—clear the city of vice and corruption, which means clear it of Pete and Lew and Max, if it goes far enough. See? The old man's using the boy to pry 'em loose. Well, I guess they got tired of being pried."

"I could find things wrong with that guess," I said.

"Uh-huh, you could find things wrong with everything in Poisonville. Had enough of this gut-paint?"

I said I had and we went down to the street. Bill Quint walked as far as my hotel with me. In front of it a beefy man with a look of a copper in civvies stood on the curb talking to a man in a Stutz touring car.

"That's Whisper in the car," Quint told me.

I looked past the beefy man and saw Thaler's profile, young, dark, small, with features as regular as if they had been cut with a die—pretty features.

"He's cute," I said.

"Uh-huh," the gray man agreed. "So's dynamite."

III

The *Morning Herald* gave two pages to Donald Willsson and his death. His picture showed a pleasant, intelligent face with curly hair, smiling

eyes and mouth, a cleft chin and a striped necktie. The story of his death was simple. At ten-thirty-five the previous night he had been shot four times with .32 pistol bullets in stomach, chest and back, in the eleven-hundred block of Hurricane Street and had been dead before anyone reached him.

Residents of the neighborhood who had looked out their windows after hearing the shooting had seen him lying on the sidewalk with a man and a woman bending over him. But the street was too dark for anyone to see anything or anybody clearly. The man and woman had disappeared before any of the neighbors had reached the street, and nobody knew exactly how or in what direction they had gone.

The police found that six shots had been fired at Willsson. The two that had missed him had hit a vacant house in front of which he had been shot. Tracing the course of the bullets from those two shots, the police had learned that the shooting had been done from a narrow alley across the street. Outside of that nobody knew anything.

Editorially, the *Morning Herald* gave a brief summary of the dead man's short career as a civic reformer and expressed its belief that he had been removed by some of the people who didn't want Personville cleaned up. The *Herald* said that the chief of police could best show his own innocence by speedily catching the murderer. The editorial was both blunt and bitter.

I finished it with my breakfast coffee, jumped a Broadway car, dropped off at Laurel Avenue, and turned down toward the dead man's house. I was half a block from it when something changed my mind.

A smallish young man in three shades of brown crossed the street ahead of me, showing a dark profile that was pretty—Max Thaler, alias Whisper. I reached the corner of Mountain Boulevard in time to catch the flash of his brown-covered rear leg vanishing into the late Donald Willsson's vestibule.

I went back to Broadway, found a drug store

with a phone booth in it, searched the directory for Elihu Willsson's residence number, called it, told somebody who claimed to be Elihu's secretary that I had been brought from San Francisco by Donald Willsson, that I knew something about his death, and that I wanted to see his father. When I made it emphatic enough I got an invitation to present myself.

The czar of Poisonville was propped up in bed when his secretary—a noiseless, slim, sharp-eyed man of forty—brought me into the bedroom.

The old man's head was small and almost perfectly round under its thick crop of close-cut white hair. His ears were too small and plastered too close to his head to spoil the spherical effect. His nose also was small, carrying down the curve of his bony forehead. Mouth and chin were straight lines chopping the sphere off. Below them a short thick neck ran down into white pajamas between square, meaty shoulders. One of his arms was outside the covers—a short, compact arm that ended in a thick-fingered, blunt, pink hand. His eyes were round, blue, small, and watery. But they looked as if they were hiding behind the watery film and under the bushy white eyebrows only until the time came to jump out and grab something. He wasn't the sort of man whose pocket you'd try to pick unless you had a lot of confidence in your fingers.

He ordered me into a bed-side chair with a two-inch jerk of his round head, chased the secretary away with another, and said:

"Now what is this about my son?" His voice was harsh. His chest had too much and his mouth not enough to do with his words for them to be very clear.

"I'm with the Continental Detective Agency's San Francisco branch," I told him. "We got a five hundred dollar check from your son and a letter asking that a man be sent over to do some work for him. I'm the man. I called him up when I got in yesterday afternoon. He told me to come to his house last night. I went there. He didn't show up. When I got downtown I learned he had been killed."

Elihu Willsson regarded me suspiciously and asked:

"Well, what of it?"

"While I was waiting your daughter-in-law got a phone message, went out, came back with what looked like blood on her shoe, and told me it was no use waiting, her husband wouldn't be home."

He sat straight up in bed and called Mrs. Willsson a flock of things. When he ran out of words of that sort he still had some breath left, so he used it to shout at me:

"Is she in jail?"

I said I didn't think so.

"What the hell are you waiting for, damn you?" was his response to that.

When a man, who is too old or too sick to be smacked, curses you, you can either curse back or laugh. I laughed and said:

"Evidence."

"Evidence! What do you want? You—"

"Don't be such a chump," I interrupted his bawling. "Why should she have killed him?"

"Because she's a French hussy! Because—"

The noiseless secretary's frightened face appeared at the door.

"Get out o' here!" the old man roared at it, and the face went.

"She jealous?" I asked before he could go on with his ranting. "And if you don't yell maybe I'll be able to hear you anyway. My deafness is a lot better since I've been eating yeast."

He put a fist on top of each hump his thighs made in the covers and pushed his square chin at me.

"Old as I am and sick as I am," he said very deliberately, "I've a mind to get up and kick you down the stairs—"

I paid no attention to that and repeated:

"Was she jealous?"

"She was," he said, not shouting now, "and she's domineering, and spoiled, and suspicious, and greedy, and mean, and unscrupulous, and deceitful, and selfish, and damned bad—altogether damned bad."

"Any reason for her jealousy?"

"I hope so," he said bitterly. "I'd hate to think a son of mine would be faithful to *her*. Though likely enough he was. He'd do things like that."

"But you don't know any reason why she should have killed him?"

"Don't know any?" He was bellowing again. "Haven't I just been telling you that—"

"Yeah. But none of that means anything. It's kind of childish."

The old man flung the covers back from his legs and started to get out of bed. Then he thought better of it, raised his red face, and roared:

"Stanley!"

The door slid open to let the secretary pop silently in.

"Throw this—out!" his master ordered, waving a fist at me.

The secretary turned to me. I shook my head and suggested: "Better get help."

He frowned. We were about the same age. He was weedy, nearly a head taller than I, but fifty pounds lighter. Some of my hundred and ninety pounds were fat, but not all of them. The secretary fidgeted, smiled apologetically, and ran out to follow my advice.

"What I was about to say," I told the old man. "I intended talking to your son's wife again this morning, but I saw Thaler go in there, so I put off my call."

Elihu Willsson carefully pulled the covers up over his legs again, leaned his head back on the pillows, screwed his eyes up at the ceiling, and said:

"Hm-m-m, so that's the way it is, is it?"

"Mean anything?"

"She killed him," he said emphatically. "That's what it means."

Feet made noises in the hall, huskier feet than the secretary's. I waited until they were just outside the door and then started a sentence:

"You were using your son to dig up dirt on—"

"Get out o' here!" the old man yelled at those in the doorway. "And keep that damned door closed!"

"Now what was I using my son for?" he demanded when we were alone again.

"To knife Thaler, Yard and the Finn."

"That's a lie. I gave the boy the papers. He did what he liked with them."

"You ought to explain that to the gang. They'd believe you—oh, yeah!"

"Whatever they believe, what I'm telling you is so."

"Well, what of it? Your son won't come back to life just because he was killed by mistake—if he was."

"That woman killed him!"

"Maybe."

"Damn you and your maybes! She did! If you're going to fool around with any other numbskull ideas you might just as well go back to Frisco now. You and your damned—"

"I'll go back to San Francisco when I'm ready," I said unpleasantly. "And it won't be just now. I'm at the Great Western Hotel. Don't bother me unless you want to talk sense for a change."

His curses followed me down the stairs. The secretary hovered around the bottom step, smiling apologetically.

"A fine old rowdy," I growled.

"A remarkably vital personality," the secretary murmured.

IV

From the old man's house I went down to the *Herald* and hunted up the murdered man's secretary. She was a small girl of nineteen or twenty with wide chestnut eyes, light brown hair and a pale pretty face. Her name was Lewis.

She said she hadn't known about the check and letter that had brought me from San Francisco.

"But then," she explained, "Mr. Willsson always liked to keep everything to himself as long as he could. It was—I—I don't think he trusted anybody here—completely."

"Not you?"

She flushed and said: "No. But of course he didn't know any of us very well. He had been here only such a short time."

"There must have been more to it than that," I protested.

"Well," she bit her lip and made a row of forefinger prints down the polished edge of the dead man's desk top, "his father wasn't—wasn't in sympathy with what he was doing, and his father really owned the papers, so I guess it was natural for Mr. Donald to think some of the employes might be more loyal to Mr. Elihu than to him."

"The old man wasn't in favor of the clean-up campaign? Then why did he stand for it, if the papers were his?"

She bent her head to study the fingerprints she had made, and her voice was so low that I had to lean closer to catch the words.

"It's—it's not easy to understand unless you know—The last time Mr. Elihu was taken sick he sent for Donald—Mr. Donald. Mr. Donald had lived in Europe most of his life, you know. Dr. Pride had told Mr. Elihu that he'd have to turn all his business affairs over to someone else, so he cabled his son to come home. But when he got here Mr. Elihu couldn't make up his mind to let go of everything. But he wanted Mr. Donald to stay, so he made him publisher of the papers. Mr. Donald liked that because he had been interested in journalism in Paris, and when he found out how terrible everything was here—in civic affairs and so on—he started that reform campaign. He didn't know—he had been away since he was a boy—and he didn't know—he didn't—"

"He didn't know his father was in it as deep as anybody else," I helped her along.

She squirmed a little over her examination of the fingerprints on the desk, nodded reluctantly, and went on:

"Mr. Elihu and he had a quarrel. Mr. Elihu told him to stop stirring things up, but Mr. Donald wouldn't. Maybe he would have if he had known—all there was to know. But I don't suppose it would ever have occurred to him that his father could have been really—deep in it. And Mr. Elihu wouldn't tell him. I guess it would be hard for a father to tell a son a thing like that. He threatened to take the papers away from him. But Mr. Donald said he'd start one of his own, and he said then he'd know his father had reasons for not wanting the light turned on Personville. He got terribly angry. I don't think Mr. Elihu was going to do anything, but he got sick again, and things went along like they did."

"Donald Willsson didn't confide in you?"

"No." It was almost a whisper.

"Then you learned all this—where?"

"I'm trying—trying to help you find the murderers," she said earnestly, looking at me with chestnut eyes that had pleas in them. "You've no right to—"

"Just now you'll help me most by telling me where you got this dope."

She stared at the desk again, chewing her lower lip. I waited. Presently she said:

"My father is Mr. Elihu's secretary."

"Thanks."

"But you mustn't think that we—"

"It's nothing to me," I assured her. "What was Willsson doing in Hurricane Street last night at a time when he had a date with me at his house?"

She said she didn't know. I asked her if she had been with him when he told me, over the phone, to come to his house at ten o'clock. She had.

"What did he do after that? Try to remember every least thing that was said and done from then until you left at the end of the day."

She leaned back in her chair, shut her eyes and wrinkled her forehead.

"You called up—if it was you he told to come to his house—around two o'clock. Mr. Donald dictated some letters after that—one to a paper mill, one to Senator Keefer about some changes in post office regulations and—Oh, yes! He went out for about twenty minutes, a little before three o'clock. But just before he went he wrote out a check."

"For whom?"

"I don't know, but I saw him writing it."

"Where's his check book? Carry it with him?"

"No, it's here." She jumped up, went around to the front of his desk and tried the center drawer. "Locked."

I joined her in front of the drawer, straightened out a wire clip, and with that and a blade of my knife fiddled the drawer open. The girl took out a thin flat First National Bank check book. The last used stub was marked $5,000. Nothing else. No name. No explanation.

"He went out with this check," I said, "and was gone twenty minutes. Long enough to get to the bank and back?"

"It wouldn't take him more than five minutes to get there."

"What else happened just before he wrote the check? Did he get any mail, any messages, any phone calls?"

"Let's see." She shut her eyes again. "He was dictating a letter and—Oh, how stupid of me! He did have a phone call, and he said, 'Yes, I can be there at ten, but I shall have to hurry away to keep an engagement.' Then again he said, 'Very well, at ten.' That was all he said except, 'Yes, yes,' several times."

"Man or woman he was talking to?"

"I don't know."

"Think. There'd be a difference in his tone."

She thought and said: "Then it was a woman."

"Did Willsson leave before you did in the evening?"

"No. He—I told you my father is Mr. Elihu's secretary. He and Mr. Donald had an engagement for that evening—something about the papers' finances. My father came in a little after five. They were going to dinner together after they left here, I think."

That's all the Lewis girl could give me. The rest of my pumping brought up nothing. We frisked the dead man's desk—nothing. I went up against the girl at the switchboard—nothing. I put in half an hour working on city editors and the like—nothing.

I went away from the *Herald* tickling my brains with the information I had got from the girl. Not a bad haul—if a fair share of it happened to be true.

V

In the First National Bank I got hold of an assistant cashier named Albury, a nice-looking blond youngster of twenty-five or so.

"I certified the check for Willsson," he said after I had unloaded my story. "It was drawn to the order of Dinah Brand—$5,000."

"Dinah Brand—know who she is?"

"Oh yes, I know her."

"Mind telling me what you know about her?"

"Not at all. I'd be glad to, but I'm already eight minutes overdue at a meeting with—"

"Suppose you had dinner with me this evening?"

"Glad to," he said.

"Seven, at the Great Western?"

"Righto."

"I'll run along then," I said, "but tell me, has she an account here?"

"Yes, and she deposited the check this morning. The police have it now."

"And where does she live?"

"1232 Hurricane Street."

I said, "Well, well!" and, "See you tonight," and went away.

My next stop was in the office of the chief of police in the City Hall. Noonan, the chief, was a fat man with twinkling greenish eyes set in a round, red, jovial face. When I told him what I was doing in his city he seemed glad of it, and gave me a hand-shake, a cigar and a comfortable chair.

"Now," he said when we were settled, "tell me who killed the man."

"His secret's safe with me."

"You and me both," the chief said cheerfully through smoke. "But what do you guess?"

"You know more about it than I do. Tell me what you know and I'll tell you what I guess."

"Fair enough. 'T won't take long to tell. Willsson got a $5,000 check in Dinah Brand's name certified yesterday afternoon. Last night he was shot and killed by bullets from a .32 pistol less than a block from her house. People that heard the shooting saw a man and a woman bending over the remains. Bright and early this morning the said Dinah Brand deposits the said check in the bank. Well?"

"Who is this Dinah Brand?"

The chief dumped the ash off his cigar in the center of his desk, flourished the cigar in his fat hand, and said:

"A soiled dove,* as the fellow says, a de luxe hustler, a big-league gold-digger."

"Gone up against her yet?"

"Nope. There's a couple of angles to be gathered in. So we're just keeping an eye on this baby and waiting. This I've told you is under the hat."

"Yeah. Now listen to this." And I told him what I had seen and heard while waiting in Donald Willsson's house the previous night.

When I had finished the chief bunched his fat mouth, whistled softly, and exclaimed:

"Man, that's an interesting thing you've been telling me. So it was blood on her slipper, was it? And she said her husband wouldn't be home, did she?"

"That's what I took it for," I replied to the first question, and, "Yeah," to the second.

"And have you talked to her since then?" he asked.

"No. I was up that way this morning, but a young fellow named Thaler went into the house ahead of me, so I put off my visit."

"Grease us twice!† Are you telling me the Whisper was there?" His greenish eyes glittered happily.

"Yeah."

He threw his cigar on the floor, stood up, planted his fat hands on the desk top and leaned over them toward me, oozing delight from every pore.

* a prostitute
† Cockney rhyming slang for Jesus Christ

"Man, man, you've done something!" he purred. "Dinah Brand is this Whisper's woman! Let's me and you just go out and kind of talk to the widow."

VI

We climbed out of a police department touring car in front of Mrs. Willsson's. The chief stopped for a second with one foot on the bottom step to look at the black crepe hanging over the bell. Then he said: "Well, what's got to be done has got to be done," and we went up the steps.

Mrs. Willsson wasn't anxious to see us, but people usually see the chief of police if he insists. This one did. We were taken upstairs to where our lady sat in the library. She was dressed in black. Her blue eyes had frost in them.

Noonan and I took turns mumbling condolences, and then he began:

"We just wanted to ask you a couple of questions. For instance, like where'd you go last night?"

She looked disagreeably at me, then back to the chief, frowned, and spoke haughtily:

"May I ask why I am being questioned in this manner?"

I wondered how many times I had heard that question asked while the chief, disregarding it, went on amiably:

"And then there was something about one of your shoes being stained. The right one, or maybe the left. Anyway it was one or the other."

A muscle began to twitch in her upper lip.

"Was that all?" the chief asked me. Before I could reply he made a clucking noise with his tongue and turned his genial face to the woman again. "I almost forgot—there was a matter of how you knew your husband wouldn't be home."

She rose a little unsteadily, holding the back of her chair with one hand.

"Under the circumstances, I'm sure you'll excuse—"

"'S all right." The chief made a big-hearted

gesture with one beefy paw. "We don't want to bother you. Just where you went, and about the shoe, and how you knew he wouldn't be home. And, come to think of it, there's another—what Thaler wanted here this afternoon."

The woman sat down again, very rigidly. The chief looked at her—a tender smile making funny curves and lines in his fat face. After a little while her shoulders began to relax, her chin went lower, a curve came into her back. I moved a chair over to face her and sat in it.

"You'll have to tell us, Mrs. Willsson," I said, making it as gravely sympathetic as I could. "It's all hopelessly muddled without these things explained."

Her body jerked stiff and straight in the chair again, and if her eyes were half so hard as they looked you could have cut diamonds with them.

"Do you think I have anything to conceal?" She turned each word out very precisely, except that the slight foreign accent slurred the "s" sound. "I did go out. The stain was blood. I knew my husband was dead. Thaler came to see me about my husband's death. Are your questions answered now?"

"Not fully." I shook my head. "We knew all that. Please, Mrs. Willsson, this is as distasteful to us as to you. Won't you help us get it over with?"

"Very well!" Her blue eyes looked cold defiance into mine. She took a deep breath and spat out words like rain pattering on a tin roof. "While we were waiting for Donald I had a phone call. It was a man who wouldn't give his name. He said Donald had gone to the house of a woman named Dinah Brand with a five-thousand-dollar check. He gave me her address. I drove out there and waited down the street in the machine until Donald came out.

"While I was waiting I saw Thaler, whom I knew by sight. He went to that woman's house, but did not go in. He went away. Then Donald came out and walked down the street. I intended to drive home before he could get there. I had just started the engine when I heard the shots, and I saw Donald fall. I ran over to him. He was

dead. I was frantic. Then Thaler came. He said if I was found there they would say I had killed him. He made me hurry back to the car and drive home. Is that enough?"

"Practically," Noonan assured her. "What did Thaler say this afternoon?"

"He urged me not to say anything." Her voice had suddenly become very small and flat. "He said either of us would be suspected if anyone knew we were there, because Donald had been killed coming from that woman's house after giving her money."

"Where did the shots come from?"

"I don't know. I saw nothing—except when I looked up—Donald falling."

"Did Thaler fire them?"

"No," she said quickly, and then mouth and eyes spread. She put a hand to her breast. "I don't know. I didn't think so, and he said he didn't. I don't know where he was. I don't know why I thought he hadn't."

"What do you think now?"

"He—he may have."

The chief winked at me, an athletic sort of wink in which all his facial muscles took part, and cast back a little farther:

"And you don't know who called you up?"

"He wouldn't give his name."

"Didn't recognize his voice?"

"No."

"What kind of voice was it?"

"He spoke in an undertone, as if afraid of being overheard. I had trouble understanding him."

"He whispered?" The chief's mouth hung open as the last sound had left it, and his greenish eyes sparkled greedily between their pads of fat.

"Yes—a hoarse whisper."

The chief shut his mouth with a click, opened it again to say persuasively:

"You've heard Thaler talk. . . ."

She raised her head and looked at the chief.

"It was he!" she cried. "It was he!"

Noonan turned his broad back on her and beckoned me over to a window.

"We'll take her down to the Hall and have her go over it again with the Prosecuting Attorney and a stenog," he muttered triumphantly.

"All right." I looked at my watch. "But I've got a date for seven. I'm going to run along. I'll see you in the morning, or you can get me at the Great Western if anything turns up."

"Well, be good," he said.

VII

The assistant cashier, young Albury, was sitting in the lobby when I reached the hotel. We went up to my room, had some ice-water brought, used its ice to put chill in Scotch, lemon-juice and grenadine, and then went down to the dining-room.

"Now tell me about the lady," I said when we were working on the soup.

"Have you seen her yet?" he asked.

"Not yet."

"But you've heard something about her?"

"Only that she's an expert in her line."

"She is," he agreed. "You'll go see her, of course. You'll be disappointed at first. Then, without being able to say how or when it happened, you'll find you've forgotten your disappointment, and the first thing you know you'll be telling her your life's history, and all your troubles and hopes." He laughed with boyish ruefulness. "And then you're caught—absolutely caught."

"Thanks for the warning. How'd you come by the information?" He grinned shamefacedly across his suspended soup spoon and confessed:

"Bought it."

"Then I suppose you paid plenty. I hear the lady likes dinero."

"She's money-mad, all right, but somehow you don't mind it. She's so thoroughly mercenary, so frankly greedy, that there's nothing disagreeable about it. You'll understand what I mean when you get to know her."

"Maybe. Mind telling me how you came to part with her?"

"No, I don't mind. I spent it all, that's how."

"Cold-blooded like that?"

His face flushed a little. He nodded.

"You seemed to have taken it well, anyway," I said.

"There's nothing else to do." The flush in his pleasant young face deepened and he spoke hesitantly. "And it happens I owe her a lot for it. She—I'm going to tell you this—I want you to see this side of her. I had a little money. After that was gone—you must remember I'm not very old and I was head over heels—there was the bank's money. I had—You don't care whether I had actually done anything or just thinking about it. Anyhow, she found it out. I never could hide anything from her. And that was the end."

"She gave you the air?"

"Yes, she did. So if it hadn't been for her you might have been hunting for me now. I owe her that!" He wrinkled his forehead earnestly. "You won't say anything about this—you know what I mean. I just wanted you to know that she had her good side, too."

"Maybe she has. Or maybe it was that she didn't think she'd get enough to pay for the chance of being caught in a jam."

He turned that over in his mind for a minute and shook his head.

"How about Dan Rolff?" he objected.

"Who's he?"

"A down-and-outer—t. b. He's supposed to be her brother, or half-brother, or something of the sort. He lives there. She keeps him. She's not in love with him or anything of the sort. She just found him somewhere and took him in."

"Mark up one for her. Any more?"

"There was that radical chap she used to play with. It's a cinch she never got much money out of him."

"What radical chap was this?"

"The chap who came here in 1919 to run the strike—Quint."

"So he's *still* on her list?"

"That's supposed to be the reason he stayed after the strike was over."

"So he's *still* on her list?"

"No. She told me she was afraid of him—he had threatened to kill her."

"Has she had everybody in town on her string at one time or another?" I asked.

"Everybody she wanted," he said, and he said it seriously.

"Well, what about her and Donald Willsson?"

"I don't know a thing about that—absolutely nothing. He had never issued any checks to her before, that I know of."

"Then he was probably recent?"

"Probably—but why did he have the check certified?"

I didn't know. I could have made some guesses, but none that I wanted to put into words. During the rest of the dinner we talked back and forth over the ground we had already covered, and I picked up nothing else of any value. At eight-thirty young Albury ran off to keep a date.

Bill Quint had told me he was living in the Miners' Hotel in Forest Street. I walked down that way and was lucky enough to run into him in the street half a block or so from the hotel.

"Hello," I hailed him, "I was just coming down to see you."

He stopped in front of me, looked me up and down, growled, "So you're a lousy gumshoe," pursed his gray lips, and by forcing breath out through them made a noise like a rag tearing.

"That's the bunk!" I complained. "I come all the way down here to rope you and you're smarted up!"*

"What'd you want to know this time?" he demanded.

"I'll save my breath. You'd only lie to me. So long."

I walked back to Broadway, found a taxi, and told the driver to take me to 1232 Hurricane Street.

_____
* wise to me

VIII

My destination was a gray frame cottage with an iron picket fence around it. When I rang the bell the door was opened by a very thin man with a very tired face that had no color in it except a red spot the size of a half-dollar high on each cheek. This, I thought, is the lunger, Dan Rolff.

"I'd like to see Miss Brand," I told him.

"What name shall I tell her?" His voice was a sick man's voice, also an educated man's.

"It wouldn't mean anything to her. I want to see her about Willsson's death."

He looked at me with level, tired, dark eyes and said: "Yes?"

"I'm from the San Francisco office of the Continental Detective Agency. We're interested in the murder."

"That's nice of you," he said ironically. "Come in."

I went in—into a ground-floor room where a young woman sat at a table with a lot of papers on it. The room was disorderly, cluttered up. There were too many pieces of furniture in it, and none of them seemed to be in its proper place.

"Dinah," the lunger introduced me, "this gentleman has come from San Francisco to inquire into the late Mr. Willsson's demise on behalf of the Continental Detective Agency."

The young woman got up from the table, kicked a couple of newspapers out of her way, and came toward me with one hand out.

She was a couple of inches taller than I, which would make her about five feet eight, with a broad-shouldered, full-breasted, round-hipped body and big muscular legs. The hand she gave me was soft, warm, strong. Her face was the face of a girl of twenty-five, already beginning to show signs of wear. Little lines ran across the corners of her big ripe mouth. Other lines made nets around her thick-lashed eyes. They were large eyes, blue, and a bit blood-shot. Her coarse brown hair needed trimming and was parted crookedly. Her upper lip had been rouged higher on one side than the other. She wore a dress of a particularly unbecoming wine color, and it gaped here and there down one side, where she had neglected to snap the fasteners, or they had popped open. There was a run in the front of her left stocking.

This was Dinah Brand, Poisonville's Cleopatra, if there was any truth in what I had been told.

"His father sent for you, of course," she said as she moved a pair of lizard-skin slippers and a cup and saucer off a chair to make room for me. Her voice was soft, lazy.

I told her the truth:

"Donald Willsson sent for me. I was waiting to see him when he was out being killed."

"Don't go away, Dan," she called to Rolff. He came back into the room. She returned to her place at the table. He sat on the opposite side, leaning his thin face on a thinner hand, staring at me without interest. She drew her brows together, making two creases between them, and asked: "You mean he knew someone was going to try to kill him?"

"I don't know," I admitted. "He didn't say what he wanted—maybe just help in the clean-up."

"But do you—?"

I made a complaint:

"It's no fun being a sleuth when somebody steals your stuff—does all the asking."

"I like to find out what's going on," she said, with a little laugh gurgling down in her throat.

"I'm that way, too," I replied. "For instance, I'd like to know why you made him have the check certified."

Very casually, Dan Rolff shifted in his chair, leaning back, lowering his thin hands out of sight below the table's edge.

"So you found out about that?" She crossed left leg over right and looked down. Her eyes focused on the run in her stocking. "I'm going to stop wearing 'em! I paid five bucks for these socks yesterday. Now look at the damned things! Every day—runs! runs! runs!"

"It's no secret," I said. "I mean the check, not the runs. Noonan's got it."

She looked at Rolff, who stopped watching me long enough to nod once.

"If you talked my language," she drawled, looking at me through narrowed lashes, "maybe I could give you some help."

"Maybe I could talk it if I knew what it was."

"Money," she explained. "The more the better. I like it."

I got proverbial:

"Money saved is money earned. I can save you trouble and dough."

"I can save my own. What I need is more."

"Giving it to lawyers isn't saving it."

"That doesn't mean anything to me," she said.

"The police haven't told or asked you anything about the check?"

She shook her head no.

"I thought not," I said. "Noonan's figuring on hanging the rap on you as well as Whisper."

"Don't scare me," she lisped, "I'm only a child."

"Noonan knows that Thaler knew Willsson brought the check here, that Thaler came while he was here but didn't get in, that Thaler was hanging around the neighborhood when Willsson was shot, and that Thaler and a woman were seen bending over the dead man."

The girl picked a pencil up from the table and thoughtfully scratched her cheek with it. It made little black lines over the rouge. Rolff's eyes had suddenly lost their weariness. They were bright, feverish, fixed on mine. He leaned forward, but kept his hands out of sight below the table.

"Those things," he said softly, "concern Thaler, not Miss Brand."

"Thaler and Miss Brand are not strangers," I pointed out. "Willsson brought a five-thousand-dollar check here and was killed leaving. That way, Miss Brand might have had trouble cashing it—if Willsson hadn't been thoughtful enough to have it certified."

"Say!" the girl objected, "if I'd been going to kill him I'd have done it in here where nobody could have seen it! Or waited till he got out of sight of the house! What kind of dumb onion do you take me for?"

"I'm not altogether satisfied you killed him," I assured her. "I'm just telling you the fat chief means to hang it on you."

"What are *you* trying to do?"

"Learn who killed him—not who might have or could have—who did."

"I could give you some help," she said, "but there'd have to be something in it for me."

"Safety," I reminded her, but she shook her head.

"I mean it would have to get me something in a financial way," she went into details. "It'd be worth something to you, and you ought to pay, even if not a lot."

"Can't be done." I grinned at her. "Forget your bank-roll for once and go in for charity. Pretend I'm Bill Quint."

Dan Rolff started up from his chair, his lips white as the rest of his face, his eyes burning. He sat down again when the girl laughed, a lazy, good-natured laugh.

"He thinks I didn't make any profit out of Bill, Dan!" She leaned forward and put a hand on my knee. "Listen, old timer. Suppose you knew far enough ahead that a company's employes were going to strike, and when, and then far enough ahead when they were going to call the strike off. Could you take that information and some capital to the stock market and do yourself some good playing with the company's stock? You bet you could!" she wound up triumphantly. "So don't go round thinking Billy boy didn't pay his way."

"Well, you've been spoiled. I'm not going to make you worse."

"What's the use of being so tight?" she demanded. "It's not like it had to come out of your own pocket. You've got an expense account to charge it to, haven't you?"

I said nothing. She frowned at me, at the run in her stocking, and at Rolff. Then she said to him:

"Maybe he'd loosen up if he had a drink."

The thin man got up and went out of the room.

IX

Dinah Brand pouted at me, prodded my shin with her toe, and explained:

"It's not so much the money. It's the principle of the thing. If a girl's got something that's worth something to somebody, she's a boob if she doesn't collect."

I grinned.

"Why don't you be a good guy?" she coaxed.

Dan Rolff came in with a siphon, a bottle of gin, some lemons, and a bowl of cracked ice. We had a drink apiece. The lunger went away. The girl and I wrangled over the money question while we had more drinks. I kept trying to bring the talk around to Thaler and Willsson. She kept bringing it back to the money she deserved. It went on like that until the gin-bottle was empty. My watch said it was a quarter after one.

She chewed a piece of lemon peel and said for the thirtieth or fortieth time:

"It won't come out of *your* pocket. What do you care?"

"It's not the money," I assured her. "It's the principle of the thing."

She made a face at me and set her glass where she thought the table was. She was eight inches wrong. I don't remember whether the glass broke when it hit the floor, or what happened to it. But I do remember that I took her missing the table for my cue to launch another attack.

"Another thing," I opened up, "I'm not dead sure I really need what you can tell me. I'd like to have it, but maybe I can get along without it."

"It'll be nice if you can," she replied, "but don't forget I'm the last person who saw him alive, besides the murderers."

Neither of us was talking as clear as it looks here.

"You're mistaken, my dear," I said. "His wife saw him come out, walk away and get shot."

"His wife?"

"Yeah. She was sitting in a machine across the street."

"How did she know he was here?"

"She says Thaler phoned her that Willsson

was coming here—or had come—with a five-thousand-dollar check."

"You're trying to kid me. Max couldn't have known it!"

"I'm telling you what she told Noonan and me."

The girl spit what was left of the lemon peel out on the floor, further disarranged her hair by running her fingers through it, wiped her mouth on the back of her hand, and then slapped the table.

"All right, Mr. Knowitall, I'm going to play with you! You can think it's not going to cost you anything, but I'll get mine before we're through. You think I won't?" she challenged me, peering at me as if I were a block distant.

This was no time to start an argument, so I said, "I hope you do." I think I said it three or four times, very earnestly.

"I will. Now listen to me. You're drunk and I'm drunk, and I'm just drunk enough to tell the truth. I'll tell you anything you want to know. That's the kind of girl I am. If I like a person I'll tell 'em anything they want to know. Just ask me! Go ahead, ask me!"

I did: "What did Willsson give you five thousand dollars for?"

"For fun!" She leaned back and laughed heartily. Then: "Listen to this, old darling, it's a humdinger and I want you to get it the first time. Donald was hunting for scandal on the home talent. I had some stuff stuck away, some affidavits and things that I thought might be good for some jack some day. I'm a girl that likes to pick up a piece of change when she can. So I put these affidavits and things away in the old sock.

"So when this Donald began putting the boys on the pan for hunching, I let him know that I had some dirt on them, and it was for sale. He came to bargain and I gave him enough of a look at some of them to let him know they were good. And they *were* good! Then we talked how much. He wasn't as tight as you—nobody ever was—but he was a little bit close. So the deal hung fire, till yesterday.

"Then I gave him the rush—phoned him and told him I had another customer for the stuff, and that if he wanted it he could have it by showing up at ten that night with five thousand smacks—either cash or a certified check. That was hooey, but he fell for it. He was a nice boy in his way, but he didn't know much. You want to know why it had to be cash or a certified check, huh? All right, I'll tell you. I'll tell you anything you want to know. That's the kind of girl I am. Always was."

She went on for five or more minutes telling me in detail just exactly what and which sort of girl she was and always had been, and why. I finally cut in:

"I knew you were regular as soon as I saw you. A good girl, I told myself, a good girl. Now why did it have to be cash or a certified check?"

She shut one eye, waggled a forefinger at me, and said:

"So he couldn't stop payment. Because he couldn't use the stuff I sold him. It would have put his old man in jail along with the rest of 'em." She thumped my knee and laughed hilariously. "A good one, huh? The stuff I sold him would have nailed old Elihu tighter than anybody else!"

I laughed with her while I fought to keep my head above the gin I had guzzled.

"Who else would it nail?"

"The whole damned gang of 'em." She waved a hand in the air. "Max and Lew Yard and Noonan and Pete the Finn and old Elihu—the whole blooming crew!"

"Did Max know what you were doing?"

"Of course not—nobody knew but Willsson and me."

"Sure of that?"

"Sure I'm sure. You don't think I was going to brag about it ahead of time, do you?"

"Who do you think knows about it now?"

"I don't care," she said. "It was only a joke on him. That's all I meant it for."

"Yeah. But the gents whose secrets you sold won't see anything funny in it. Noonan's trying to hang the killing on you and Thaler. That means he found the stuff in Willsson's pocket.

The rest of the gang already thought that old Elihu was using his son to chase them out of the city with that clean-up campaign, didn't they?"

"Yes, sir!" she said. "And I'm another one that thinks it!"

"You're probably wrong, but that doesn't matter. Now if Noonan found your stuff in young Willsson's pocket, and found out about the check, why shouldn't he add 'em up to mean that you and Thaler had gone over to old Elihu's side. See? That's why he's pointing the rap at you and Thaler."

"I don't care what he thinks," she said obstinately. "It was only a joke. That's all I meant it for. Willsson would have found out he couldn't use the stuff without hurting the old man. It was only a joke—that's all it was."

"That's good. You can go to the gallows with a clear conscience. Just what was this stuff you sold him?"

But she had gone stubborn on me.

"I've told you enough," she said. "I've told you too much."

"Haven't you seen Thaler since the murder?"

"No. But Max didn't kill him, even if he was around."

"Why?"

"Lots of reasons. First place, Max wouldn't have done it himself. He'd have had somebody else do it, and he'd have been off some place else with an alibi nobody could shake. Second place, Max packs a .38, and anybody he sent on the job would have had that much gun or more. What kind of a gunman would use a .32?"

"Then who did kill him?"

"I've told you all I know. And remember, it's going to cost you something before you're through. I'm going to cash in somewhere."

"I hope you do," I said as I stood up. "You deserve it. You've practically cleaned up the job for me."

"You mean you know who killed him?"

"Yes, thanks, though there are a couple of things I'll have to cover before I make the pinch."

"Who? Who?" She stood up, suddenly almost sober, tugging at my lapels. "Who did it? Tell me!"

"No, I won't do that."

She let go my lapels, put her hands behind her, and laughed in my face.

"All right. Try to figure out which part of what I've told you is true."

I thought Albury had been right when he said that after you had been with this girl a while you forgot to be disappointed in her. I said:

"Thanks for the part that is, anyway. Don't let Noonan job you, and if Max means anything to you you ought to pass him the tip. And thanks for the gin."

X

It must have been close to two o'clock of a crisp morning when I said, "Goodnight," to Dinah Brand at her door and started to foot it downtown to my hotel. The first half a block of the distance went very nicely. Then somebody shot at me—twice.

I dived into a dark doorway.

I wasn't exactly sober, but my head was clear enough for me to know that it was close to my present location that Donald Willsson had died the previous night, and that the present shooter had a heavier gun than a .32.

I wasn't exactly drunk, but I had too much gin in me for effective gun-fighting in the dark with somebody I couldn't see.

I crowded myself back into a corner of my dark vestibule and wondered what I ought to do about it. My foot upset a milk-bottle. A window was lifted squeakily down the street. The two things clicked together in my mind.

I picked up the milk-bottle, swung it underhand, let it go at the front of the house across the street. It smashed through the glass of a second-story window. That was capital!

I put a hand around the front of my crouching-place, found a bell-button, pushed it. Behind me the bell made a jangling clamor in the house.

I made a megaphone of my hands, pointed it at the street, and bellowed:

"Help! Help! Police! Help! Help!"

Windows began to go up along the street. In the house whose doorway I occupied a man's voice, shrill with fright, whined: "Go away from there! Go away, or I'll call the police!"

I thought that a swell idea.

"Do that," I encouraged him, "and the fire department and the public health service."

The whining voice made no reply. On hands and knees I peeped out into the street. The occupants of most of the houses seemed to be looking out, up and down the street, hunting for a repetition of last night's murder. That was fine! I didn't think anybody wanted my life badly enough to assassinate me in front of all these witnesses.

I jumped up, trotted down the front steps, waved my hand gratefully at the audience, and went away from the neighborhood. I turned most of the corners I came to, making sure that nobody turned them after me. Presently I got lost, but I kept on turning corners. After a while I found myself down in Union Street, four or five blocks from my hotel. I got back to it without anything happening to me.

With my key the night clerk gave me a memorandum that asked me to call Poplar 605. I knew the number, had called it earlier, it was Elihu Willsson's.

"How long has it been here?" I asked.

"Since a little after one o'clock."

That sounded urgent. I went back to a booth and put in the call. The secretary answered, and told me the old man desired my company at once. I promised to hustle, asked the night clerk to get me a taxi, and went up to my room for a couple of shots of Scotch. I would rather have been cold sober. But I wasn't, and if the night held more work for me I didn't want it to catch me in the raggedy condition that sobering-up brings. Two snifters revived me a lot. I poured more of the King George into a flask, pocketed it, and went down to the taxi.

Elihu Willsson's house was lighted from top to bottom. The secretary opened the door before I could get my finger on the button. His thin body was shivering in pale blue pajamas and dark blue bathrobe. His face was full of excitement.

"Hurry!" he begged. "Mr. Willsson is waiting." His dark eyes had something horrified in them. "And please, will you try to persuade him to let us remove the body!"

I nodded and followed him up to the old man's bedroom. He was in bed as before, but now a black automatic pistol lay on the covers under one of his hands.

As soon as I appeared he took his head off the pillows, leaned forward, and barked at me:

"Have you got as much guts as you've got gall?"

His face was an unhealthy dark red. The film was gone from his eyes. They were hard and hot.

I let his question wait while I looked at the corpse on the floor between door and bed. A short thick-set man in brown, half on his side, half on his back, with dead eyes staring at the ceiling from under the visor of a gray cap. A piece of his jaw had been knocked off. His chin was tilted to show where another bullet had gone through tie and collar to make a hole in his neck. One hand was bent under him. The other still held a blackjack as big as a milk bottle. There was a lot of blood.

I looked up from this mess at the old man again. His grin was both vicious and idiotic.

"You're a great talker," he said. "I know that. A two-fisted, you-be-damned man with your words! But have you got anything else? Have you got the guts to match your gall? Or is it just the gab you've got?"

There was no use trying to get along with the old boy. I scowled and reminded him:

"Didn't I tell you not to bother me unless you wanted to talk sense for a change?"

"You did, my boy!" There was a foolish sort of triumph in his sneer. "And I'll talk you your sense. I want a man to clean this pig-sty of a Personville for me, to smoke out the big rats and the little ones. It's a man's job. Are you a man?"

"What's the use of getting poetic about it?" I growled. "If you've got an honest job to be done, and want to pay an honest price for it, maybe I'll take it. But a lot of howling about smoking rats and pig-pens doesn't mean anything."

"All right. I want Personville emptied of crooks and grafters. Is that plain enough language for you?"

"You didn't want that last week," I said. "Why do you want it this week?"

"Nobody that ever lived can tell Elihu Willsson where he's got to get on and where he's got to get off," he blustered at the top of his voice. "That's why!" He turned loose a cloud of profanity. "While they keep their places I let 'em alone. But when they begin to think Personville belongs to them, and that they can tell me what I've got to do, then it's time to show them, the—, who Personville does belong to. I built this city with my own hands, and I'll keep it or I'll wipe it off the side of the mountain." More cursing. "I'll show them what they'll get out of their threats!" He pointed at the dead body on the floor. "I'll show 'em there's still a sting in the old man!"

I wished I was sober. The old man's clowning puzzled me. I couldn't put my finger on the something under it.

"Was he from your friends?" I asked, nodding at the corpse.

"I only talked to him with this," he boasted, patting the gun on the bed, "but I reckon he was."

"How did it happen?"

"It happened simple enough. I heard the door opening, and I switched on the light, and there he was, and I shot him, and there he is."

"What time?"

"It was about one o'clock."

"And you've let him lie there all this time?"

"Yes, that I have!" The old man laughed savagely and began blustering again: "Does the sight of a dead man turn your stomach? Or is it his ghost you're afraid of?"

I looked at him and laughed. I had it. The old boy was scared—scared stiff. That's why he blustered. That's why he hadn't let them take the corpse away. He wanted it there to look at, to keep panic away—visible proof of his ability to defend himself. Now I knew where I stood.

"You really want the burg cleaned up?" I asked.

"I said I did and I do."

"I'll have to have an absolutely free hand—no favors to anybody—handle the job as I please. And I'll have to have a ten-thousand-dollar retainer to cover expenses and service charges."

"Ten-thousand-dollar retainer! Why in hell should I pay that much money to a man I don't know from Adam, a man who's done nothing I know of but talk?"

"Be serious. When I say, 'Me,' I mean the Continental Detective Agency."

"You do, do you? Well, if I know your Continental Detective Agency, then they ought to know me, and they ought to know I'm good for—"

"That's not the idea! These people you want taken to the cleaners were your friends last week. Maybe they will be again next week. I don't care about that. But we're not going to play politics for you. We're not starting a job and having it blow up on us. If you really want the burg ventilated you'll plank down enough cash to pay for a complete job. Any that's left over will be returned. That's the way it'll have to be. Take it or leave it."

"I'll damned well leave it," he bawled.

He let me get half-way down the stairs before he yelled for me. I went back.

"I'm an old man," he grumbled. "If I was ten years younger, I'd—" He glared at me and worked his lips together. "I'll give you your damned check."

"And a free hand?"

"And a free hand."

"We'll get it done now. Where's your secretary?"

Willsson pushed a button on his bedside table and the secretary silently appeared from wherever he had been hiding. I told him:

"Mr. Willsson wants to draw a ten-thousand-dollar check to the order of the Continental Detective Agency. Also he wants to write a letter to them, saying that the ten thousand dollars are to be used in investigating crime and so forth in Personville, and giving the agency full power to conduct the investigation as they see fit."

The secretary looked questioningly at the old man, who scowled and nodded his round white head.

"But first," I told the secretary as he moved to the door, "you'd better phone the police that we've a dead burglar here. And call Mr. Willsson's doctor."

The old man flared up:

"I don't want any damned doctors!"

"You're going to have a nice shot in the arm so you can sleep," I promised him, stepping over the corpse to take the black gun from the bed.

He said he wouldn't, making a long and profane story of it. He was still going strong when the secretary returned with the check and a typed letter. The old man gave up his cursing long enough to put a shaky signature on each. I had them folded in my pocket when the police arrived.

XI

The first copper into the room was the chief himself, fat Noonan. He nodded amiably at Willsson, shook hands with me, and looked at the dead man with twinkling green eyes.

"Well, well," he said. "It's a good job he did, whoever did it—Yakima Shorty. And will you look at the sap he's toting?" He kicked the big blackjack out of the dead man's hand. "Big enough to sink a battleship. You drop him?" he asked me.

"No, Mr. Willsson."

"Well, that certainly is fine," he congratulated the old man. "You saved a lot of people a lot of troubles, including me. Pack him out, boys," he said to the four men behind him.

The two in uniform picked Yakima Shorty's remains up by legs and armpits and went away

with him, while one of the others gathered up the blackjack and a flashlight that had been under the body.

"If everybody did that to their prowlers, it would certainly be fine," the chief babbled on. He produced three cigars, stuck one at me, threw one over on old Elihu's bed, and put the other in his own mouth. "I was just wondering where I could get hold of you," he told me as we lighted up. "I got a little job ahead that I thought maybe you'd like to be in on." He put his mouth close to my ear and whispered: "Going to pick up Whisper. Want to go along?"

"I do."

"I thought you would. Hello, Doc!" He shook hands with a man the secretary had just ushered in—a little plump man with a tired round face and eyes that still had sleep in them.

The doctor went over to the bed, where one of Noonan's men was asking Willsson all about the shooting. I followed the secretary out into the hallway and asked him:

"Any men in the house besides you?"

"Yes—a chauffeur, the gardener, and the Chinese cook."

"Let one of 'em stay in the old man's room tonight. I don't think you'll have any more excitement, but no matter what happens don't leave the old man alone. And don't leave him alone with Noonan or any of Noonan's men."

The secretary's mouth and eyes popped wide.

"What time did you leave Donald Willsson the night he was killed?" I asked.

"At precisely ten minutes after nine." He seemed to have been expecting the question.

"You were with him from five o'clock till then?"

"From about a quarter after five. We went over some financial statements and that sort of thing in his office until seven o'clock. Then we went to Bayard's and finished our business over our dinners. He left at ten minutes after nine, saying he had an engagement."

"What else did he say about this engagement?"

"Not a thing."

"Didn't give you any hint of where he was going, who he was going to meet?"

"He only said he had an engagement."

"And you didn't know anything about it?"

"No. Why? Did you think I did?"

"I thought he might have said something." I switched back to tonight's doings: "What visitors did Willsson have today—not counting the one he shot?"

"You'll have to pardon me." The secretary shifted his feet, smiling apologetically. "I can't tell you that without Mr. Willsson's permission. I'm sorry."

"Weren't some of the local powers here—say, Lew Yard, Pete the Finn, and—?"

The secretary shook his head, repeating: "I'm sorry."

I gave it up, said, "We won't fight about it," and started back toward the bedroom door. The doctor came trotting out, buttoning his overcoat.

"He will sleep now," he said hurriedly. "Someone should stay with him. I shall be in early in the morning." And he ran down the stairs.

I went into the bedroom. The chief and the man who had questioned Willsson were standing beside his bed. The chief grinned as if he were glad to see me. The other man scowled. Willsson was lying on his back, staring at the ceiling.

"That's about all there is here," Noonan said cheerfully. "What say we mosey along?"

I agreed and said, "Goodnight," to the old man. He said, "Goodnight," without looking at me. The secretary came in with a tall sunburned young man who looked like a chauffeur. The chief, the other sleuth and I went downstairs and out to a black touring car at the curb. The other man—Noonan called him McGraw—drove. The chief and I sat in the back seat.

"We'll make the pinch along about daylight," the chief explained to me as we rode. "Whisper's got a joint over on King Street. He generally leaves there about daylight. We could crash the place, but that'd mean gun-play, and it's just as well to take it easy. So we'll pick him up when he leaves."

I wondered if he meant to pick him up or pick him off. I asked:

"You've got enough on him to make the rap stick?"

"Enough?" He laughed good-naturedly. "If what the Willsson dame gave us ain't enough to swing him I'm a pickpocket."

I thought of a couple of wise-crack answers to that, but kept them to myself.

Our ride lasted half an hour. The chief didn't ask any questions about my progress, about what I had done since I left him with Mrs. Willsson. That was clumsy. He had told me he was keeping an eye on Dinah Brand. I had been shot at leaving her house. My guess was that I had been shot at by one of Noonan's bulls. Otherwise, how-come none of the men he had watching the house had come to my rescue? The chief's silence now made my guess look better—just as too many questions would have made it look better. I wondered why he was getting careless.

While I was wondering our machine came to rest under a line of trees in a dark street. We got out and walked down to the corner. A burly man in a gray overcoat, with a gray hat pulled far down over his eyes, came to meet us.

"Whisper phoned Donohoe that he's in his joint and going to stay there," the burly man told the chief. "If you think you can pull him out, he says, try it."

Noonan chuckled, scratched an earlobe, and asked pleasantly:

"How many would you say was in there with him?"

"Fifty, anyhow."

"Aw, now! There wouldn't be that many this time of morning."

"The hell there wouldn't!" the burly man snarled. "They've been drifting in since midnight."

"Is that so? A leak somewhere. Maybe you oughtn't to have let 'em in."

"Maybe I oughtn't!" The burly man was mad. "But I did what you told me. You said to let anybody go in or out that wants to, but when Whisper showed to—"

"To arrest him," the chief said.

"Well, yes," the burly man agreed, and looked savagely at me.

More men joined us and we held a talk-fest. Everybody was in bad humor except the chief. He seemed to enjoy it all. I didn't know why.

Whisper's joint was a three-story brick building in the middle of the block, between two two-story buildings. The ground floor of his joint was occupied by a cigar store that served as entrance and cover for the gambling establishment upstairs. Inside, if the burly man's information was to be depended on, Whisper had collected half a hundred friends, presumably loaded for a fight. Outside, Noonan's force was spread around the building, in the street in front, in the alley in back, and on adjoining roofs.

"Well, boys," the chief said amiably after the talk had gone around in circles for a while, "I don't reckon Whisper wants trouble any more than we do, or he'd have tried to shoot his way out before this, if he's got *that* many with him, though I don't mind saying I don't think he has—not *that* many."

The burly man said: "The hell he ain't!"

"So if he don't want trouble," Noonan went on, "maybe talking might do some good. You run over, Nick, and see if you can't argue him into being peaceable."

The burly man said: "The hell I will!"

"Phone him then," the chief suggested.

The burly Nick growled, "That's more like it," and went away. When he came back he looked completely satisfied with his message.

"He says," he reported, "'Go to hell!'"

"Get the rest of the boys down here," Noonan said cheerfully. "We'll knock it over as soon as it gets light."

XII

The burly Nick and I went around with the chief while he placed his men. I didn't think much of them—a shabby, shifty-eyed lot with no enthusiasm for the job ahead of them.

The sky became a faded gray. The chief, Nick and I had stopped in a plumber's doorway diagonally across the street from our target. Whisper's joint was dark, blank, with the cigar store blinds down over window and door, all upper windows curtained.

"I hate to start this without giving Whisper a chance," Noonan said. "He's not a bad kid. But there's no use o' me trying to talk to him. He never did like me much."

He looked at me. I said nothing.

"You wouldn't want to make a stab at it?" he asked.

"I'll try it."

"That's fine of you! I'll appreciate that, if you will. You just see if you can't talk him into coming along peaceable. You know what to say—for his own good and all that—like it is."

"Yeah," I said, and started across the street toward the cigar store, taking pains to let my hands be seen swinging empty at my sides.

Day was still a little way off. The street was the color of smoke. My feet seemed to be making a lot of noise on the paving. I stopped in front of the door and knocked the glass with a knuckle, not heavily. The green blind down inside the door made a mirror of the glass. In it I saw two men moving up the other side of the street.

No sound came from inside. I knocked louder, then slid my hand down to rattle the knob.

Advice came from indoors:

"Get away from there while you're able."

It was a muffled voice, but probably not Thaler's because it wasn't a whisper.

"I want to talk to Thaler," I said.

"Go talk to the fat—that sent you!"

"I'm not talking for Noonan. Is Thaler where he can hear me?"

A pause. Then the muffled voice, "Yes."

"Listen, Thaler: I'm the Continental op who tipped Dinah Brand off that the chief was framing you. I want five minutes' talk with you. I've got nothing to do with Noonan except to queer his game if I can. I'm alone. I'll drop my gun in the street if you say so. Let me in."

I waited. It depended on whether the girl had got to him with the story of my call. I waited what seemed a long time. Then the muffled voice came:

"When we open, come in quick! And no stunts!"

"All set!" I said.

The latch clicked.

I plunged in with the door.

Across the street a dozen guns emptied themselves. Glass shot from door and windows tinkled everywhere.

Somebody tripped me. As I fell I twisted around to face the door. My gun was in my hand before I hit the floor.

Fear gave me three brains and half a dozen eyes. These birds couldn't help thinking I was taking part in a trick of Noonan's.

Across the street the burly Nick had stepped out of a doorway to pump lead at us with both hands.

I steadied my gun-hand wrist on the floor. The detective's burly body showed over the front sight. I squeezed.

Nick stopped shooting. He put both hands tight to his belly and piled down on his face.

Hands on my ankles dragged me back. The floor scraped pieces off my chin. The door slammed shut. Some comedian said:

"Uh-huh, people don't like you."

"I wasn't in on that," I said earnestly through the racket.

A husky whisper came through the darkness:

"Dropping Big Nick squares you. Hank, you and Slats keep an eye on things down here. The rest of us might as well go upstairs."

We went back through another room, into a passageway, up a flight of carpeted stairs, and into a large room that held a green-topped table banked for crap-shooting. This room was lighted, and had no windows.

There were five of us. Thaler sat down and lighted a cigarette—a small, dark young man with a face that was pretty in a chorus-man way until you took another look at the thin, hard mouth. An angular blond kid of hardly more than twenty, in tweeds, sprawled on his back on a couch and blew cigarette smoke at the ceiling. Another boy, just as blond and just as young, but not so angular, was busy straightening his tie, smoothing down his yellow hair. A thin-faced man of thirty, with little or no chin under a wide, loose mouth, wandered up and down the room humming *Rosy Cheeks* and looking bored.

The gunfire had stopped.

"How long is Noonan going to keep this up?" Thaler asked. His voice was a hoarse whisper, but there was no great amount of emotion in it—just a little annoyance.

"He's after you this trip," I gave my opinion. "He means to see it through." Thaler smiled a thin, contemptuous smile.

"Maybe he thinks so now, but the longer he thinks it over the smaller his chance of hanging a one-legged rap like that on me will look."

"He's not figuring on proving anything in court."

"What, then?"

"You're to be knocked off resisting arrest or trying to escape. He won't need much of a case after that."

The thin lips twisted themselves into another contemptuous smile. This lad didn't seem to think much of the fat man's deadliness.

"He's getting tough in his old age. Any time he rubs me out I deserve rubbing. What's he got against you?"

"I'm getting to be a nuisance around town, too."

"Too bad," Thaler said. "Dinah told me you were a pretty good guy—except kind of Scotch with the roll."[*]

"I had a nice visit. Will you tell me what you know about Donald Willsson's killing?"

"Sure," he said coolly. "His wife turned the trick."

"You saw her?"

"Saw her the next second—with the rod[†] in her hand."

_____

[*] stingy

[†] gun

"That's no good to me, Thaler. And it's no good to you. If you've got it rigged right maybe it would work in court, but you're never going to tell it there. If Noonan takes you at all he'll take you stiff. Give me low-down. I only need your angle to clean up the job."

He leaned forward, his dark eyes seeming to draw together.

"Are you that hot?"

"With your story I'll be ready to make the pinch—if I can get out."

He dropped his cigarette on the floor, mashed it under his foot, lighted another, and studied its red end.

"Mrs. Willsson said it was me that phoned her about the check?" he asked.

"She said that after Noonan had persuaded her. But she believes it now—maybe."

He put some smoke in and out of his lungs, brushed a flake or two of ash off his black suit with a hand that was very small and very manicured, nodded to himself, and said:

"A man phoned me that night. I don't know who he was. Said Willsson had gone to Dinah's with a check for five grand. What the hell did I care? But, see, it was funny that somebody I didn't know phoned me about it. So I went around. Dan stalled me away from the door. That was all right. But still it was funny that guy phoned me. I went up and took a plant in a doorway. I saw Mrs. Willsson's car down the street, but didn't know it was her in it then.

"Willsson came out and walked down the street. I didn't see the shots, but I heard 'em. Then this woman jumps out of the car and runs over to him. I knew she hadn't done the shooting. I ought to have beat it. But curiosity got me. When I saw it was Mrs. Willsson I went over. That was a bull,* see? So I had to make an out for myself, in case something slipped. I strung the woman. That's all there was to it—on the level."

"Thanks," I said. "That's what I came for. Now the trick is to get out of here without being mowed down by Noonan's crew."

_____
* cop

"No trick at all," Thaler assured me. "We go any time we want to."

"Well, I'm ready now. And if I were you, I'd go, too. You don't think much of Noonan, but he might pull something. And if you'll take a sneak and hide out till noon his frame-up will be a wash-out."

"Yeah?"

"Yeah."

Thaler put a hand in his pants pocket and dragged out a fat roll of bills. He counted off a hundred or two, some fifties, twenties, tens, and held them out to the chinless man.

"Buy us a getaway, Jerry," he ordered. "And you don't have to give anybody any more dough than they're used to."

Jerry took the sheaf of bills, picked up a hat from the table, and strolled out. Half an hour later he strolled in again and returned part of the sheaf to Thaler, saying casually:

"We wait in the kitchen until we get the office."

We went down to the kitchen. It was dark there. More men joined us.

Presently something hit the door.

Jerry opened it and we went down three steps into the back yard. It was almost full daylight. There were ten of us in the party.

"This all?" I asked Thaler.

He nodded.

"Nick said there were fifty of you."

"Fifty to stand off that crummy force?" he asked scornfully.

A copper in uniform held the back gate open for us, muttering nervously:

"Hurry it up a little, boys, please!"

I was willing to oblige him, but everybody else ignored the request. We crossed the alley, were beckoned through another gate by a beefy man in brown, passed through a house, out into the next street, and climbed into a touring car that stood at the curb.

One of the blond boys drove. He knew what speed was.

"I want to be dropped off near the Great Western," I said.

The blond driver looked at Whisper, who nodded. We turned the next corner, and five minutes later I got out in front of my hotel.

"See you later," Thaler said, and the car slid away. The last I saw of it was its police department license plate vanishing around a corner.

XIII

It was half-past five. I went up Broadway to where an unlighted electric sign said Hotel Windom, mounted a flight of steps to the second floor office, left a call for ten o'clock, was shown into a shabby room, moved some of the Scotch from my flask to my stomach, and took Elihu Willsson's ten-thousand-dollar check and my gun to bed with me.

When my call roused me I dressed, went up to the First National Bank, found young Albury, and asked him to certify the old man's check for me. He kept me waiting a while, so I supposed he phoned Willsson's residence to find out if the check was on the up-and-up. Finally he brought it back to me, properly scribbled on.

I sponged an envelope, put Willsson's letter and check in it, addressed it to the agency in San Francisco, stuck a stamp on it and went out to drop it in the mail-box on the corner.

Then I returned to the bank and said to the boy:

"Now, sonny, tell me why you killed him."

"Cock Robin or President Lincoln?" he asked, smiling.

"You're not going to admit off-hand that you killed Willsson?"

"I don't want to be disagreeable," he laughed, "but I'd rather not."

"That makes it bad," I complained. "We can't stand here and talk very long without being interrupted. Who's the stout party with the cheaters* coming this way?"

The boy's face pinkened, and he said: "Mr. Dutton, the cashier."

_____
* eyeglasses

"Introduce me."

The boy looked uncomfortable, but he called the cashier's name. Dutton—a large man with a smooth pink face, a fringe of white hair around an almost totally bald pink head, and rimless nose-glasses—came over to us. The assistant cashier mumbled the introduction. I shook Dutton's hand without losing sight of the boy.

"I was just saying," I addressed Dutton, "that we ought to have a more private place for our talk. He probably won't confess till I've worked on him a while, and I don't want everybody in the bank to hear me yelling at him."

"Confess?" The cashier's tongue showed between his lips.

"Sure." I kept my voice and manner bland, mimicking Noonan. "Didn't you know that Albury is the fellow who killed Donald Willsson?"

A polite smile at what he thought a foolish joke started in back of the cashier's glasses—changed to puzzlement when he looked at his assistant. The boy was rouge-red and the grin he was forcing his mouth into was a terrible thing.

Dutton cleared his throat and said heartily:

"It's a splendid morning. Splendid weather."

"But isn't there a private room where we can talk?" I insisted.

Dutton jumped nervously and questioned the boy:

"What—what is this?"

Young Albury mumbled something unintelligible.

"If there isn't," I said, "I'll have to take him down to the City Hall."

Dutton caught his glasses as they slid down his nose, jammed them back in place, sputtered:

"Come back here!"

We followed him down the length of the lobby, through a gate, and into an office whose door was marked _President_. Old Elihu's office. Nobody was there. I motioned Albury into one chair and picked another for myself. The cashier fidgeted with his back against the desk, facing us.

"Now, sir, will you explain this," he said, but

his words weren't as impressive as they were meant to be.

"We'll get around to that, I hope," I told him and turned to Albury. "You're the only person I've run across who knew Dinah Brand intimately, and who knew about the check in time to phone Mrs. Willsson and Thaler. You were in love with Dinah and were given the gate.* Willsson was shot with a .32. Banks like that caliber. I'm going to have a gun-sharp compare the bank's guns with the bullets taken out of Willsson. Maybe the gun you used wasn't a bank gun. I think it was. Maybe you didn't put it back. Then there'll be one missing, but I think you returned it to its place next morning."

The boy had his control back. He looked boldly at me and said nothing. That wouldn't do.

"I know you were nuts about this girl," I said, "because you confessed to me that it was only because she refused to be tangled up in it that you didn't help yourself to—"

"Don't! Please don't!" The boy's face was sick white. My murderer didn't like being labeled *Thief* in front of his boss.

I looked at the boy, making myself sneer until his eyes went down. Then I let him have the other barrel:

"You know you killed him. You know if you used a bank gun—and if you put it back. If you did, you're nailed right now, without an out. An expert with a microscope and a micrometer can prove absolutely that a certain bullet was fired from a certain gun. And an expert is going to look at the bank guns. If you didn't use a bank gun, I'm going to nail you anyhow. If you did, you're nailed *now*!

"All right. I don't have to tell you whether you've got a chance or not. *You know!* But here's something. Noonan is framing Thaler for the job. He can't convict him, but the frame-up is strong enough that if Thaler is killed resisting arrest, the chief will be in the clear. That's what he means to do. Thaler stood off the whole force all night in his King Street joint. He's standing

---

* she broke off the relationship

them off now, unless they've got to him. The first copper that gets to him—exit Thaler. If you figure you've got a chance to beat your rap—and you want to let Thaler be killed for you—that's your business. But if you know you haven't got a chance—and you haven't if the gun can be found—and God's sake give Thaler one by clearing him!"

"I'd like—" Albury didn't look up and his voice was as an old man's. "You'll find the gun in Harper's cage. I didn't—" He looked up, saw Dutton, and stopped.

I scowled at the cashier and asked him:

"Will you get the gun?"

He ran out as if he was glad to go.

"I didn't mean to kill him," the boy said. "I don't think I did—though I took the gun with me. I *was*—what did you say?—nuts about Dinah. It was worse some days than others. The day Willsson came in with the check was one of the bad ones. All I could think about was that I lost her because I had no more money, and he was taking five thousand dollars to her. I watched her house that night and saw him go in. I had the gun in my pocket and was afraid of what I might do.

"Believe me when I say I didn't want to do anything. But it was one of the bad days, and I couldn't think straight—couldn't think of anything except that I had lost her because my money was gone, and he had taken five thousand dollars to her. And there was the bank gun in my pocket, and I was afraid of what I might do.

"I knew Willsson's wife was jealous—everybody knew that. I thought if I called her up and told her—I don't know what I thought then, but I went and called her up. And then I called Thaler. I didn't know whether he was—I only knew I had heard that he and Dinah—were—you know—so I called him up. Then I went back and watched her house again. I saw Mrs. Willsson come, and then Thaler, and saw them both stay watching the house. I was glad of that.

"Then Willsson came out and walked down the street. I looked up at where Mrs. Willsson and Thaler were. Neither did anything, and he was walking away. I knew then why I had wanted them there. I had thought that maybe they would do something, and I wouldn't have to. But they didn't do anything. And he was walking down the street—away. Maybe if one of them had gone over and said something to him, or even followed him, I wouldn't have done anything. But they didn't. I remember taking the gun out of my pocket. I don't remember anything else until I was running up the alley. When I got home I found the gun was empty—all the cartridges had been fired. I cleaned it and reloaded it and put it back in the paying teller's cage the next morning."

"Well," I said, "you're certainly a swell actor. Nobody would have guessed you were still in love with the girl from the way you talked to me about her."

He winced.

"That wasn't acting," he said slowly. "After—after I was in danger—facing the gallows—she—she didn't seem so—so important. I couldn't understand why I had—you know—and that spoiled the whole thing—made it—and me—cheap."

XIV

I took Albury and the gun down to the City Hall in a taxicab. In the chief's office we found one of the men who had been along on the storming party last night—a red-faced lieutenant named Biddle. He goggled* at me with fishy blue eyes, but asked no questions about my part in last night's doings.

Biddle called in the Prosecuting Attorney. The boy was repeating his story to these officials when the chief of police arrived, looking as if he had just crawled out of bed.

"Well, it certainly is fine to see you!" Noonan pumped my hand up and down while patting my back jovially with his other hand. "You had a narrow one last night—the rats! I was sure

_____
* stared

they'd got you till we kicked in the doors and found the place empty. Tell me how those son-of-a-guns got out of there!"

"One of your men let them out the back door and sent them away in a department car. They took me along so I couldn't tip you off."

"One of my men did that?" He didn't seem very surprised. "Well, well! If I line 'em up in front of you, will you pick him out for me?"

"Sure."

"Fine! Now what's all this?" nodding his fat face at Albury, the Prosecuting Attorney and Biddle.

I told him briefly. He chuckled and said:

"Well, well, I did Whisper an injustice. I'll have to hunt him up and square myself. So you landed the boy? That certainly is fine! Congratulations and thanks!" He grabbed my hand and pumped it up and down again. "You'll not be leaving our city now, will you?"

"Not for a while."

"That's fine!" he assured me.

I hung around the office a little longer and then went out for breakfast-and-lunch. After that I treated myself to a shave and a hair-cut, hunted up a telegraph office, wired the agency to send Dick Foley and Mickey Linehan to join me, and then went over to my hotel.

There was another telephone memorandum in my box. Elihu Willsson's number. I called it and was invited out by the secretary.

The old man, wrapped in blankets, was sitting in an armchair at a sunny window. He held out his stubby hand to me and thanked me for catching his son's murderer. I made some more or less appropriate reply.

"The check I gave you last night," he said, "is only fair pay for the work you've done."

"Your son's check more than covered that," I protested.

"Then call mine a reward or bonus."

"We've got a rule against taking rewards or bonuses."

His face began to redden.

"Well, damn it—"

"You haven't forgotten that your check was

to cover the expense of investigating crime and corruption in Personville, have you?"

"That was damned nonsense!" he snorted. "We were excited last night. That's off."

"Not with me."

He exploded. First a string of profanity. Then:

"It's my money and I won't have it used for any such damned silliness. If you won't take it for what you've done, give it back to me! I'll stop payment on—"

"Stop yelling at me. You can't stop payment, because it's been certified. We made a bargain. You and your playmates each thought the other was trying to double-cross them. I suppose as soon as the word got out that your son had been killed by Albury you made peace again— deciding that there hadn't been any double-crossing. I expected something like that. That's why I got you sewed up. And you are sewed up.

"I've got ten thousand dollars of your money to work with and I'm going to use it to open Personville up from Adam's Apple to ankles. Your fat chief of police tried to assassinate me twice last night. That's at least once too many. Now I'm going to have my fun. I'll see that my reports are mailed to you regularly. I hope you enjoy reading them."

And I went out of the house with his curses sizzling around my head.

CRIME WANTED—MALE OR FEMALE, relates the further adventures of the Continental detective in THE CLEANSING OF POISON-VILLE, by Dashiell Hammett.

CRIME WANTED is packed with action and is told as only Mr. Hammett can tell a story.

It will appear in the next issue of BLACK MASK—the DECEMBER number.

BLACK MASK, DECEMBER 1927

Crime Wanted—
Male or Female

BY DASHIELL HAMMETT

The grim adventures of the Continental detective in The Cleansing of Poisonville.

I HAD JUST DECIDED in favor of a pounded rumps steak with mushrooms when I heard myself being paged. The boy took me to one of the lobby booths. Dinah Brand's lazy voice came out of the receiver:

"Max wants to see you. Can you run up tonight?"

"Your place?"

"Yes."

I promised to be there in an hour, and went back to the hotel dining-room and my meal. When that was through I went up to my room— front, fifth floor. I unlocked the door and went in, snapping on the light.

A bullet kissed a hole in the door-frame close to my noodle. The report sounded outside. I moved across the floor, out of line with the window. There were more reports. More bullets made more holes in door, door-frame and wall.

In a safe and far corner I took off a shoe. The shooter had to be on the roof of a four-story office building across the street, I knew—a roof a little above the level of my window. The roof would be dark. My light was on. I chucked my shoe at it. The globe popped apart, giving me darkness. But the shooting had already stopped.

Pieces of the broken globe and of the bullet-punctured window-panes bit into my shoeless foot as I crept over to the window. I knelt with one eye in one of its lower corners. The roof across the street was dark and too high for me to see beyond its rim. Ten minutes of this one-eyed peeping got me nothing except a kink in my neck.

I went to the phone and asked the girl to send up the house copper. I waited for him in the bathroom, sitting on the side of the tub, picking fragments of glass out of my stocking-sole.

The hotel detective was a portly, white-mustached man with the round, undeveloped forehead of a child. He wore a too-small hat on the back of his head to show the forehead. His name was Keever. He got too excited over the shooting.

The hotel manager came in, a plump man with carefully controlled face, voice and manner. He didn't get excited at all. He struck the this-is-unheard-of-but-not-really-serious-of-course attitude of a street fakir whose mechanical din-gus flops during a demonstration.

We risked light, getting a new globe for the bedroom socket, and added up the bullet-holes. There were ten of them. Policemen under Detective Sergeant McGraw—a flat-faced, big man I had met before—came, went, and returned to report no luck in picking up any traces of my gunman. Noonan, chief of police, phoned. He talked to McGraw and then to me.

"I just this minute heard of the shooting," he told me. "Now who do you reckon would be after you like that?"

"I couldn't guess," I lied.

"None of 'em touched you?"

"None."

"Well, that certainly is fine!" he said heartily. "And we'll nail that baby, whoever he is, you can bet your life on that! Would you like me to leave a couple of the boys with you—just to see nothing else happens?"

"No, thanks."

"You can have 'em if you want 'em," he insisted.

"No, thanks."

He made me promise to come over to the City Hall the next day to see him, told me the Person-ville police department was at my disposal, gave me to understand that if anything happened to me his whole life would be spoiled, and I finally got rid of him.

The police detail went away. I had my stuff moved into another room—one that bullets couldn't be so easily funneled into. The manager pretended he wasn't disappointed in my not leaving his hotel.

Then I changed clothes and set out for Hurricane Street, to keep my date with the whispering gambler and his gold-greedy ladylove.

II

Dinah Brand opened the door for me. Her big ripe mouth was rouged evenly this night, but her brown hair still needed trimming, was parted haphazardly, and there were spots down the front of her orange silk dress.

"So you're still alive," she said. "Well, I suppose nothing can be done about it. Come on in."

We went into her cluttered-up living-room. Dan Rolff and Max Thaler were playing pinocle there. Rolff nodded to me. The fever-spots were bright on the cheek-bones of his thin, tired, sickman's face. Thaler stood up to shake my hand—a small, dapper young man with hard, narrow lips that kept his dark face from being merely pretty.

His hoarse, whispering voice said:

"I hear you've declared war on Poisonville."

"Don't blame me. I've got a client who wants the burg cleaned up."

"Wanted—not wants," he corrected me as we sat down. "Why don't you chuck it?"

I made a speech:

"No. I don't like the way Poisonville's treated me, I got my chance now and I'm going to even up. If you people had let me alone while I was clearing up Donald Willsson's murder, I'd have been riding back to San Francisco now. But you didn't—especially that fat chief of police, Noonan, didn't. He's tried for my scalp three times in two days, and I'm disagreeable when I'm picked on. So when I got old Elihu Willsson in a corner—scared stiff that the rest of you were going to wipe him out—I tied him up with a contract to clean house, and got a ten-grand certified check out of him.

"Now that he knows his son was bumped off by one of Miss Brand's boy friends and that the rest of you weren't double-crossing him, he wants to call the deal off. Well, he can't! Now that your little family of Poisonville bosses is reunited—everybody trusting everybody else like they used to before Donald Willsson was killed and you all began suspecting each other of backcarving—you want me to go away and let you alone. Well, I won't!

"Yesterday I was the one who wanted to be let alone. All I was interested in was finding young Willsson's murderer. Did you let me alone? Like hell! You were afraid I'd turn up things you didn't want turned up—so you tried your best to run me ragged. Now it's my turn. I've got ten thousand dollars of old Elihu's money to spend and I'm going to spend it turning up the things you don't want turned up. It's my turn to run somebody ragged, and that's what I'm going to do. Poisonville's ripe for the cleaners. It's a job I like and I'm going to it!"

"While you last," the gambler added.

"Yeah," I agreed. "I was reading in the paper this morning about a fellow choking to death eating a chocolate eclair in bed."

"That sounds good," Dinah Brand said, "but it wasn't in this morning's paper."

She had sprawled her big body down in an armchair. She lighted a cigarette and threw the match out of sight under the Chesterfield. The sick man had gathered up the cards and was shuffling them over and over, aimlessly. Thaler frowned at me and said:

"But Willsson's willing for you to keep the ten grand. Why don't you let it go at that?"

"I've got a mean disposition. Being shot at makes me mad."

"That won't get you anything—except a box. I'm for you. You kept Noonan from framing me. That's why I'm telling you—forget it and go back to Frisco."

"I'm for you," I said. "That's why I'm telling

you—split with the gang. They tried to double-cross you once. Now you're back with 'em. But it'll happen again. Anyway, they're slated for the chute. Break with 'em, Thaler."

He shook his head and replied:

"I'm sitting too pretty. Both my joints are taking in plenty. I'm able to look out for myself."

"Maybe, but you know the racket's too good to last long. You've had your pickings. Now it's get-away day. If ever a burg was ripe for a shake-up this one is."

"I don't know where you get that stuff," he objected. "Just because some bright light nick-names Personville Poisonville don't mean anything. It's a swift town, maybe, but there are tougher ones."

"But no crookeder ones."

"You've got a lot of words," he said, "but what of it? Suppose it is the kind of camp you think? Suppose you're set on cracking it? And suppose you live long enough to make your play? Just where are you figuring on getting the dope you need to bust it open?"

"Honest to Gawd," Dinah Brand complained, yawning, "you sound like a couple of school-kids arguing over who's got the biggest father! He's going to advertise in the *Herald—Crime Wanted—Male or Female*. Isn't there anything to drink in the dump, Dan?"

The lunger got up from the table and went out. Thaler said:

"You can't buck the game. I'd like to see you do it. If I thought you could, I'd be with you. You know how I stand with Noonan—the rat! But you can't make it. Chuck it!"

"No—he's had three tries at me in two days. Now I'm going to have mine."

"You're wrong. Law of averages against you. He's chief of police. He can have you shot at from now till Prohibition. Don't make any difference how bad the shooting is—one of 'em will get into you some time. Law of averages."

"Maybe. But you can still lose. The Continental's got more ops."

"That'll do you a lot of good. Chuck it!"

"No."

"I told you he was too damned pig-headed to listen to reason," the girl said.

"All right." Thaler shrugged. "You're supposed to know what you're doing. Going to the fights tomorrow night?"

I said I thought I would. Dan Rolff came in with gin and trimmings. We had a couple of drinks apiece. We talked about the fights and nothing more was said of me versus Poisonville. Thaler apparently had washed his hands of me, but he didn't seem annoyed at my stubbornness. He even gave me a tip on the next night's main event—suggesting that any bet would be good if its maker remembered that Kid Cooper would probably knock Ike Bush out in the sixth round. He seemed to know what he was talking about, and it didn't seem to be news to the others.

I left a little after eleven, returning to the hotel by taxi, without anything happening.

III

I woke up next morning with an idea in my skull. Personville had only some 40,000 inhabitants. It shouldn't be hard to spread news. Ten o'clock found me out spreading it. I did my spreading on street-corners, in poolrooms, cigar stores, soft-drink speakeasies—wherever I found a man or two loafing. My spreading technique was something like this:

"Got a match? . . . Thanks. . . . Going to the fights tonight? . . . I hear Ike Bush takes a dive in the sixth. . . . It ought to be straight—I got it from Whisper. . . . Yeah, they all are."

Folks like inside stuff, and anything that had Thaler's name to it was very inside in Poisonville. The news spread nicely. Half the men I gave it to worked as hard as I passing it on to others, just to show they knew what was what. When I started my Paul Revereing 7 to 4 was being offered that Ike Bush would win, 2 to 3 that he'd win by a knockout, in the joints where bets were taken. By two o'clock the best that any

would give was even money, and by half-past three Kid Cooper was a 2 to 1 favorite.

I made my last stop a lunch-counter, where I tossed the news out to a waiter and a couple of customers while wrapping myself around a hot beef sandwich. When I went out I found a man waiting by the door for me. He had bowed legs and a long, sharp jaw, like a hog's. He nodded and walked down the street beside me, chewing a toothpick, squinting sidewise into my face. At the corner he said:

"I know for a fact that ain't so."

"What?" I asked.

"About Ike Bush flopping. I know for a fact it ain't so."

"Then it oughtn't bother you any. But the wise money's going 2 to 1 on Cooper, and he's not that good unless Bush lets him be."

The hog jaw spit out the mangled toothpick and snapped yellow teeth at me.

"He told me his own self that Cooper was a set-up for him, last night, and he wouldn't do nothing like that—not to me."

"Friend of yours?"

"Not exactly, but he knows I—Hey, listen! Did Whisper tell you that? On the level?"

"On the level."

He cursed bitterly. "And I put my last thirty-five bucks in the world down on that—on his say-so. Me—that could send him over for—" He broke off and stood staring down the street.

"Could send him over for what?" I asked.

"Plenty," he said. "Nothing."

I had a suggestion.

"If you've got something on him, maybe we ought to talk it over. I wouldn't mind seeing Bush win, myself. If what you've got on him is any good, what's the matter with putting it up to him?"

He looked at me, at the sidewalk, fumbled in his vest pocket for a toothpick that had a second-hand look, put it in his mouth, and mumbled:

"Who are you?"

I gave him a name—something like Hunter or Hunt or Huntington—and asked him his. He said it was MacSwain—and I could ask anybody in town if it wasn't right. I said I believed him and asked:

"What do you say? Will we put the squeeze to Bush?"

Little hard lights came into his mud-colored eyes and died.

"No," he gulped. "I ain't that kind of fellow. I never—"

"You never did anything but let people gyp you," I finished for him. "You don't have to go up against him. Give me the dope and I'll make the play—if it's any good."

He thought that over, licking his lips, letting the toothpick fall down to stick on his coat-front.

"If I give it to you, you won't let on about me having any part in it?" he asked. "I belong here and I wouldn't stand a chance if it got out. And you won't turn him up? You'll just use it to make him fight?"

"Right."

He grabbed my hand excitedly and demanded: "Honest to Gawd?"

"Honest to God."

"Mind, I'm trusting you! He was in on the Keystone Trust knock-over in Philly two years ago, when Scissors Haggerty's mob croaked two messengers. He didn't do the killing, but he was in on the caper. His real moniker is Al Kennedy. He used to scrap around Philly. The bulls got the rest of 'em, but he made the sneak. They're still looking for him. That's why he's sticking out here in the bushes. That's why he won't let 'em put his mug on any cards or in any papers. That's why he's a pork-and-beaner* when he's as good as any of 'em. See? This Ike Bush is Al Kennedy that the Philly bulls want for the Keystone trick. See? He was in on—"

"I see, I see," I stopped the merry-go-round. "The next thing is to get to see him. How will we do that?"

"He flops at the Maxwell, on Union Street. I guess maybe he'd be there now, resting up for the mill."

"Resting for what? He don't know he's going to fight yet. We'll give it a try, though."

"We! We! Where do you get that *we* at? You swore you'd keep me covered!"

"Yea, I remember that now. What kind of looking bird is he?"

"A black-headed kid, kind of slim, with one tin ear† and eyebrows that run straight across. I don't know that you can make him like it."

"Leave that to me. Where'll I see you afterward?"

"I'll be hanging around Murry's. Mind you don't drag me in it—you promised."

IV

The Maxwell was one of the dozens of hotels along Union Street with narrow front doors between stores and shabby flights of steps leading up to second-story offices. The office was a wide place in the hall, with a key- and mail-rack behind a wooden counter that needed paint just as badly. A brass bell and a dirty day-book register were on the counter. Nobody was there.

I had to run back eight pages in the book before I found *Ike Bush, Salt Lake City, 214*. The pigeon-hole that had that number was empty. I climbed another flight of stairs and knocked on a door that had it. Nothing came of that. I tried it two or three times more and then turned back to the stairs. Somebody was coming up.

I stood at the top waiting for a look at him. There was just light enough to see by. He was a slim, muscular lad in army shirt, blue suit, gray cap. Black eyebrows made a straight line over his eyes.

I nodded at him and said, "Hello!"

He nodded without stopping or saying anything.

"Win tonight?" I asked.

"Hope so," he said shortly, passing me.

I let him go a couple of steps more toward his room and then told him:

---

* down-and-out

† cauliflower ear

"So do I. I'd hate to have to ship you back to Philly, Al."

He took another step, turned around very slowly, rested one shoulder against the wall, let his eyes get sleepy, and grunted: "Huh?"

"If you were smacked down in the sixth or any other round by a palooka like Kid Cooper it'd make me peevish," I said. "Don't do it, Al. You don't want to go back to Philly."

The youngster put his chin down in his neck and came back to me. When he was within an arm's length he stopped, letting his left side turn a bit to the front. His hands were hanging loose. Mine were in my overcoat pockets.

He said "Huh?" again.

I said: "Try to remember that—if Ike Bush don't turn in a win tonight, Al Kennedy will be riding East in the morning."

He lifted his left shoulder an inch or two. I moved the gun around in my overcoat pocket, enough. He grumbled:

"Where do you get that stuff about me not winning?"

"Just something I heard. I didn't think there was anything in it—except maybe a ducat* back to Philly."

"I ought to bust your jaw, you fat crook!"

"Now's the time to do it. Because if you win tonight you're not likely to see me again. If you lose you'll see me all right, but your wrists won't be loose."

I found MacSwain in Murry's, a poolroom in Broadway.

"Did you get to him?" he asked.

"I think it's fixed—if he don't blow town, or say something to his backers, or just pay no attention to me, or—"

MacSwain developed a lot of nervousness.

"You better damn sight be careful," he warned me hurriedly. "They might try to put you out the way. He—I got to see a fellow down the street," and he deserted me.

Personville's prize-fighting was done in a big wooden ex-casino in what had once been an amusement park on the edge of town. When I got there at eight-thirty most of the population seemed to be on hand, packed tight in close rows of folding chairs on the main floor, packed still tighter on benches in two dinky balconies. Smoke. Stink. Noise. Heat.

My seat was in the third row, ringside. Moving down to it, I discovered Dan Rolff sitting in an aisle seat not far away, with Dinah Brand beside him. She had had her hair trimmed at last, and marcelled, and looked like a lot of money in a big gray fur coat.

"Get down on Cooper?" she asked after we had swapped hellos.

"No. You playing him heavy?"

"Not as heavy as I'd have liked to. We held off, thinking the odds would get better, but they went to hell."

"Yeah," I said. "Everybody in town seems to know Bush is going to dive. I saw a hundred berries put on Cooper at four to one a couple of minutes ago." I leaned past Rolff and put my mouth close to where the gray fur collar hid the girl's ear. "The dive is off. Better copper† your bets while there's time."

Her big bloodshot eyes went wide and dark with curiosity, anxiety, greed, suspicion.

"You mean it?" she asked huskily.

"Yeah."

She chewed her reddened lips, frowned, asked: "Where'd you get it?"

I wouldn't say. She chewed her mouth some more, asked: "Is Max on?"

"I haven't seen him since I left your place. Is he here?"

"I suppose so," she said absentmindedly, a distant look in her eyes. Her lips moved as if she was counting to herself.

I said: "Take it or leave it, but it's a gut."‡

<hr>

* ticket

<hr>

† from the dice game craps; bet the shooter will lose

‡ the money staked by principal bettors

She opened her bag and dragged out a roll of bills the size of a coffee-can. Part of the roll she pushed at Rolff.

"Here, Dan, slap it on Bush. You've got an hour anyway to look for the best odds."

Rolff took the money and went off on his errand. I took his seat. She put a hand on my forearm and said:

"God help you if you've made me drop that dough!"

I pretended the idea was ridiculous, pretended I was absolutely sure Bush was going to win. The preliminary bouts got going—four-round affairs between assorted hams. I kept an eye out for Thaler, but didn't spot him. The girl fidgeted beside me, paying little attention to the preliminaries, dividing her time between asking me where I had got my information and threatening me with hell-fire and damnation if it turned out to be a bust.

The semi-final was on when Rolff came back and gave the girl a handful of tickets. She was straining her eyes over them when I left for my own seat. Without looking up she called after me: "Wait outside for us when it's over."

Kid Cooper climbed into the ring while I was squeezing through to my seat. He was a ruddy, straw-haired, solid-built boy with a dented face and too much meat around the top of his lavender trunks. Ike Bush, alias Al Kennedy, came through the ropes in the opposite corner. His body looked better—slim, nicely ridged, snaky—but his face was pale and worried.

They were introduced, went into the center of the ring with referee and seconds for the usual instructions, returned to their corners shedding bathrobes, stretched on the ropes, the gong rang, and the scrap was on.

Cooper was a clumsy bum. He had nothing but a pair of wide swings that might have hurt if they landed—but anybody with two feet could have kept away from them. Bush had class— nimble legs, a smooth, fast left hand, and a right that got away quick. It would have been murder to put Cooper in the ring with him, if he had been trying. But he wasn't. That is, he wasn't

trying to win. He had a sweet job on his hands trying not to.

Cooper waddled flat-footed around the ring throwing his wide swings at everything from the lights to the cornerposts. His system was simply to turn 'em loose and let 'em take their chances. Bush moved in and out, putting a glove on the ruddy boy whenever he wanted to, but not putting anything behind the glove.

The customers were booing before the first round was over. The second round was just as bad. I didn't feel so good, myself. Bush didn't seem to have been much influenced by our little conversation. Out of the corner of my eye I could see Dinah Brand trying to catch my attention. She looked hot. I took care not to have my attention caught.

The room-mate act in the ring was continued in the third round, to the tune of yelled Throw-'em-outs, Why-don't-you-kiss-hims and Make-'em-fights from the seats. The pugs' waltz brought them around to the corner nearest me just as the booing broke off for a moment. I made a megaphone of my hands and bawled:

"Back to Philly, Al!"

Bush's back was to me. He wrestled Cooper around, shoving him into the ropes, so he— Bush—faced my way.

From somewhere far back in another part of the house another voice yelled: "Back to Philly, Al!" MacSwain, I supposed. A drunk down the line raised a puffy face and bawled the same thing, laughing as if it were a swell joke. A couple of other birds took up the cry for no reason at all.

Bush's eyes jerked from side to side under the black bar of his eyebrows. One of Cooper's wild mitts clouted the slim boy on the side of the jaw and piled him at the referee's feet.

The referee counted five in two seconds, but the gong cut him off. I looked over at Dinah Brand and laughed. What else was there to do? She looked at me and didn't laugh. Her face was sick as Dan Rolff's, but madder.

Bush's handlers had dragged him to his stool and were rubbing him up, not working very hard at it. He opened his eyes and watched his feet. The gong was tapped.

Cooper paddled out hitching up his trunks. Bush waited until the bum was in the middle of the ring, and then came to him, fast. Bush's left glove went down, out—practically out of sight in Cooper's belly.

Cooper said, "Ugh!" and backed away, folding up. Bush straightened him with a right-hand poke in the chin, and sank the left again. Cooper said, "Ugh" again and had trouble with his knees. Bush cuffed him once on each side of his head, cocked his right, carefully pushed Cooper's face into position with a long left, and threw his right hand straight from under his jaw to Cooper's.

Everybody in the house felt the punch. Cooper hit the floor, bounced, and settled there. It took the referee half a minute to count ten seconds. It would have been just the same if he had taken half an hour. Kid Cooper was out.

When the referee had finally stalled through the count he raised Bush's hand. Neither of them looked happy.

A twinkle of light, high up, caught my eye. A short silvery streak slanted down from one of the small balconies. A woman shrieked. The silvery streak ended its flashing slant in the ring—with a sound that was partly a snap, partly a thud.

Ike Bush took his arm out of the referee's hand and pitched down on top of Kid Cooper. A black knife-handle stuck out of the nape of Bush's neck.

V

Half an hour later, when I left the building, Dinah Brand was sitting at the wheel of a pale blue little Marmon, talking to Max Thaler, who stood in the road. The girl's square chin was tilted up. Her big red mouth was brutal around the words it shaped, and the lines that crossed its ends were deep, hard. Her eyes were heavily lashed dark slits. The gambler looked as unpleasant as she. His pretty face was yellow and tough

as oak, and when it was his turn to talk his lips curled paper-thin. It seemed to be a nice family party. I wouldn't have joined it if the girl hadn't seen me and called:

"My Gawd, I thought you were never coming!"

I went over to the car. Thaler looked across the hood at me with no friendliness at all.

"Last night I advised you to get out of town." His whisper was harsher than anybody's shout could have been. "Now I'm telling you."

"Thanks, just the same," I said.

The girl swung the door open and I got in beside her. While she was stirring up the engine Thaler said to her:

"This isn't the first time you've sold me out. It's the last."

As we slid away she turned her head back over her shoulder and sang:

"To hell, my love, with you!"

We rode into town rapidly.

"Is Bush dead?" she asked as she twisted the car into Broadway.

"Decidedly. When they turned him over the point of the knife was sticking out in front."

"He ought to have known better than to double-cross them. Let's get something to eat. I'm almost eleven hundred ahead on the night's doings, so if the boy friend doesn't like it, it's just too bad. How'd you come out?"

"Didn't bet. So your Max didn't like it?"

"Didn't bet?" she cried, stopping the car violently in front of a Chinese restaurant. "What kind of an ass are you, anyway? Who ever heard of anybody not betting when they had a thing like that sewed up?"

"I wasn't very sure it was sewed up. So Max didn't like the way things came out?"

"You guessed it! He must have dropped a couple of thousand. And then he got sore with me because I had sense enough to switch over and get in on the pickings. Well, to hell with him, the little tin-horn runt!"

Her eyes were shiny—because they were wet. She jabbed them with a wadded handkerchief as we got out of the car.

"My Gawd I'm hungry!" she said, dragging me across the sidewalk to the restaurant door. "Will you buy me a ton of *chow mein*?"

She didn't eat a ton of it, but she did pretty well, putting away a heaping dish of her own and half of mine. Then we got back into the Marmon and rode out to her house.

Dan Rolff was in the dining-room. A brown bottle with no label and a water glass stood on the table in front of him. He sat straight up in a chair, staring at the bottle with eye-pupils the size of pin-heads. The room smelled of laudanum.

Dinah Brand slid her fur coat off, letting it fall half on a chair, half on the floor, and snapped her fingers at Rolff, saying impatiently:

"Did you collect?"

Without looking up from the bottle, he took a wad of paper money out of his inside coat pocket and dropped it on the table. The girl grabbed it, counted the bills twice, smacked her lips, and stuffed the money in her bag.

She went out to the kitchen and began chopping ice. I sat down and lighted a cigarette. Rolff stared at his bottle. He and I never seemed to have much to say to one another. Presently the girl brought in some gin, lemon-juice, seltzer and ice. We drank and she told the sick man:

"Max is sore as hell. He heard you'd been running around putting last-minute money on Bush, and the little monkey thinks I double-crossed him. What did I have to do with it? All I did was what any sensible person would have done—get in on the win. I didn't have any more to do with it than a baby, did I?" she asked me.

"No."

"Of course not. What's the matter with Max is he's afraid his gang will think he was in on it too—that Dan was putting down his dough as well as mine. Well, that's his trouble. He can go climb trees for all I care, the lousy little runt! Another little drink would be all right."

She poured another for herself and me. Rolff hadn't touched his first one. He said, still staring at the brown bottle:

"You can hardly expect him to be hilarious over it."

The girl scowled and said disagreeably:

"I can expect anything I want. And he's got no right to talk to me the way he did. He doesn't own me! Maybe he thinks he does. But I'll show him he doesn't!" She emptied her glass, banged it down on the table, and twisted around in her chair to face me. "Is that on the level about you having ten grands from Elihu Willsson to clean up Personville?"

"Yeah."

Her bloodshot eyes glistened hungrily.

"And if I help you will I get some of the ten—"

"You can't do that, Dinah!" Rolff's voice was thick, but gently firm, as if he were talking to a child. "That would be utterly filthy."

The girl turned her face slowly around toward him, and her mouth began to take on the look it had worn while she talked to Thaler.

"I *am* going to do it," she said. "That makes me utterly filthy, does it?"

He didn't say anything, didn't look up from the bottle. Her face got red, hard, cruel, her voice soft, cooing:

"It's just too bad that a gentleman of your purity, even if he is a little bit consumptive, has to associate with a filthy bum like me."

"That can be remedied," he said slowly, getting up. He was laudanumed to the scalp.

Dinah Brand jumped out of her chair and ran around the table. He watched her with no expression in his thin face—only weariness. She put her face close to his and demanded:

"So I'm too utterly filthy for you now, am I?"

He said evenly:

"I said to betray your friends to this chap would be utterly filthy, and it would."

She seized one of his thin wrists and twisted it until he was on his knees. Her other hand, open, beat his hollow cheeks, half a dozen times on each side, rocking his head from side to side. He could have put up his free arm to cover his face, but didn't. She let go his wrist, turned her back on him and reached for gin and seltzer. She was smiling to herself. I didn't like the smile.

He got up on his feet, blinking. His wrist was

dark where she had gripped it, his face bruised. He steadied himself and looked at me with dull eyes.

Without any change in face or eyes he put a hand under his coat, brought out a black automatic and fired at me. But he was too shaky for either speed or accuracy. I had time to toss my glass at him. The glass hit his shoulder. His bullet went somewhere overhead. Before he got the next one out I had jumped—was close to him—close enough to knock the gun down. The second slug went into the floor. I socked him in the jaw. He fell away from me and lay still where he fell.

I turned around. Dinah Brand was getting ready to bat me over the head with the seltzer bottle—a heavy glass siphon that would have made pulp of my skull.

"Don't!" I yelped.

"You didn't have to bust him like that!" she snarled.

"Well, it's done. You'd better get him straightened out."

She put down the siphon and I helped her carry him up to his bed-room. When he began moving his eyes I left her to finish the work and went down to the dining-room again. She joined me there fifteen or twenty minutes later.

"He's all right," she said. "But you could have handled him without that."

"I know, but I did it for him. You know why he took the shot at me?"

"So I'd have nobody to sell Max out to?"

"No. Because I'd seen you maul him around."

"That doesn't make sense to me," she said. "I was the one that did it."

"Sure, but he's probably in love with you, and besides, this isn't the first time you've done it—he acted like he knew there was no use matching muscle with you. But you can't expect him to enjoy having another man see you slap his face."

"I used to think I knew men," she complained, "but, by Gawd, I don't! They're lunatics, all of 'em!"

"So I poked him to give him back some of his self-respect. You know—treated him like a he-man instead of a down-and-outer who could be spanked by girls."

"Anything you say," she sighed. "I give it up. We ought to have a drink."

VI

We had the drink and I said:

"Before the excitement broke loose you were saying you'd work with me if there was a share of the Willsson money in it for you. There is."

"How much?"

"Whatever you earn. Whatever what you do is worth."

"That's kind of uncertain."

"So's your help, so far as I know."

"Is it? I can give you the stuff, loads of it, brother, and don't think I can't. I'm a girl who knows her Poisonville." She looked down at her gray-stockinged knees, waved one leg at me, and exclaimed indignantly: "Look at that! Another run! Did you ever see anything to beat it? Honest to Gawd, I'm going bare-footed!"

"Your legs are too big," I told her. "They put too much strain on the material."

"That'll do out of you! What's your idea of how to go about purifying our village?"

"You weren't far off yesterday when you said I was going to advertise—*Crime Wanted—Male or Female*. If I haven't been lied to, Thaler, Pete the Finn, Lew Yard and Noonan are the four men who've made Poisonville the sweet mess it is. Old Elihu Willsson comes in for his share of the blame, too, but it's not all his fault. He has to play with the others whether he wants to or not and, besides, he's my client—even if he doesn't want to be now—so I'd like to go easy on him. Well, my scheme is simply to dig up anything that looks like it might implicate one or more of those four and run it out. If they're as crooked as I think they are, sooner or later I'll land 'em."

"Is that what you were up to when you uncooked the fight?"

"That was only an experiment—just to see what would happen."

"So that's the way you scientific detectives work! Good Gawd! For a fat, middle-aged, hard-boiled, pig-headed guy, you've got the vaguest way of doing things I ever heard of!"

"Plans are all right sometimes," I said. "And sometimes just stirring things up is all right—if you're tough enough to survive, and keep your eyes open so you'll see what you want when it comes to the top."

"That ought to be good for another drink," she said.

We had it. She put her glass down, licked her lips and said:

"If stirring things up is your system, I've got a swell spoon for you, old darling. Did you ever hear of Noonan's brother Tim—the one that committed suicide out at Mock Lake a couple of years ago?"

"No."

"You wouldn't have heard much good. Anyway, he didn't commit suicide. Max killed him."

"Yeah?"

"Yeah. For Gawd's sake, wake up! This I'm giving you is real. Noonan was like a father to the kid. He'll be after Max like nobody's business if you take the proof to him. That's what you want, isn't it—split 'em?"

"We've got proof, have we?"

"There are two people that got to Tim before he died, and he told 'em Max had done it. They're both in town, though one of 'em isn't going to live a lot longer. How's that?"

She looked as if she was telling the truth, though with women—especially blue-eyed women—that doesn't always mean anything.

"Sounds all right so far," I said. "Let's listen to the rest of it. I like details and things."

"You'll get 'em. You ever been out to Mock Lake? Well, it's our summer resort, thirty miles up the canyon road. It's a dump, but it's cool in summer, so it gets a good play. This was summer a year ago—the last week-end in August. I was out there with a fellow named Holly. He's back in England now, but you don't care about that, because he hasn't anything to do with it. He was a funny sort of an old woman—used to wear white silk socks inside out so the loose threads wouldn't hurt his feet. I got a letter from him last week. It's around here somewhere, but that doesn't make any difference.

"We were up there, and Max was up there with a girl he used to play around with. She's in the hospital now—City Hospital—dying of Bright's disease or something. She's all swelled up now, but she was a classy-looking kid then—a slender blonde. I liked her, except that she got too gay when she had a few drinks. Tim Noonan was crazy about her, but she couldn't see anybody but Max that summer. Tim wouldn't let her alone. He was a big, good-looking Irishman, but a sap and a cheap crook that only got by because his brother was chief of police. Wherever Myrtle went, he'd pop up sooner or later. She didn't like to say anything to Max about it—not wanting Max to get in wrong with Noonan—the chief.

"So Tim showed up at Mock Lake this Saturday. Myrtle and Max were just by themselves. Holly and I were with a crowd, but I saw Myrtle to talk to and she told me she had got a note from Tim, asking her to meet him for fifteen minutes that night in one of the little arbor things on the hotel grounds. He said if she didn't he was going to kill himself. That was a laugh for us—the big false alarm! I tried to talk her out of meeting him, but she said she was going to give him a mouthful.

"That night we were all dancing in the hotel. Max was there for a while and then I didn't see him any more. Myrtle was dancing with a fellow named Rutgers—a lawyer here in town. After a while she left him and passed me, going out one of the side doors. She winked when she passed, so I knew she was going out to meet Tim. She'd just got out when I heard the shot. Nobody else paid any attention to it, if they heard it. I suppose I wouldn't have either if it hadn't been that I knew about Myrtle and Tim and the note.

"I told Holly I wanted to see Myrtle, and went out after her. I must have been at least five minutes behind her. When I got outside there were lights down by one of the arbors, and people. I went down there and—This talking is thirsty work!"

I poured a couple of shots of gin. She went into the kitchen for another siphon and more ice. We mixed them up, wet our mouths, and she settled down to her tale again.

"Well, there was Tim Noonan, dead, with a hole in his temple and his gun laying beside him. There were, say, a dozen people standing around—hotel people, guests, one of Noonan's bulls—a dick named MacSwain. As soon as Myrtle saw me she grabbed me and took me away from the crowd, back in the dark.

"'Max killed him!' she said. 'What'll I do?'

"I asked her all about it, and she told me she had seen the flash of the gun and she thought Tim had killed himself after all. But when she ran down to him he was rolling around, moaning. 'He didn't have to kill me over her. I'd have—' She couldn't make out the rest of it. He was pitching and rolling around, bleeding from the head. Myrtle was afraid right way that Max had done it, but she had to know for sure. So she knelt down and tried to pick up Tim's head, asking, 'Who did it, Tim?'

"He was almost gone, but before he passed out he got strength enough to tell her, 'Max!'

"She kept asking me, 'What'll I do?' I asked her if anybody else had heard him, and she said the dick had. He had come running up while she was trying to lift Tim's head. She didn't think anybody else had been close enough to hear, but the dick had.

"I didn't want Max to get in a jam over killing a mutt like Tim Noonan. Max didn't mean anything to me then, but I liked him, and I didn't like any of the Noonans. I knew the dick—MacSwain. He had been a pretty good guy—was straight as ace, deuce, trey, four, five till he got on the force. Then he went the way of the rest of 'em. Graft and booze. I knew his wife. She stood as much of it as she could and then left him. So, knowing this dick, I told Myrtle I thought we could fix things. A little jack would ruin MacSwain's memory, or if he didn't like that Max could have him bumped off. She

had Tim's note threatening suicide. If the dick would play along, the hole in Tim's temple from his own gun and the note would smooth everything over pretty.

"I left Myrtle in the bushes and went out to look for Max. He wasn't around. There weren't very many people there, and I could hear the hotel orchestra still playing dance music. There were even people strolling along the slope between the hotel and the arbors, not knowing anything had happened. I couldn't find Max, so I went back to Myrtle. She was all worked up over another idea. She didn't want Max to know that she knew he had killed Tim. She was afraid of him. She was afraid that if she and Max ever broke off he'd put her out of the way if he knew she had enough on him to swing him. I know how she felt. I got the same notion later, and kept just as quiet as she did. So we figured that if it could be fixed without his knowing about it—so much the better.

"I didn't want to be in it either. So Myrtle went back alone to the crowd around Tim and got hold of MacSwain. She took him off a little way and made the deal with him. She had some dough on her. She gave him two hundred smacks and a diamond ring that had cost a thousand. I thought he'd come back for more, later. But he didn't. He shot square with her. With the help of the letter he put over the suicide. Noonan knew there was something fishy about the layout, and I think he suspected Max of being tied up in it. But Max had an air-tight alibi—trust the boy for that—and I think even Noonan finally gave up that notion, but he never believed it all happened the way it was made to look. He broke MacSwain—kicked him off the force.

"Max and Myrtle slid apart a little while after that—no row or anything—they just slid apart. I don't think she ever felt easy around him again, though so far as I know he never suspected her of knowing anything. She's got Bright's disease or something now, I told you, and hasn't got long to live. I think she'd not so much mind telling the truth if she was asked. MacSwain's still hanging around town. I don't suppose he'd mind talking either if there was something in it for him. Anyway, those two have got the stuff on Max—and wouldn't Noonan eat it up! Is that good enough to give your stirring-up a start? Let's have a little drink."

VII

We had the drink, and I asked:

"Couldn't it have been suicide? With Tim Noonan getting a last-minute bright idea to stick it on Max?"

"That four-flusher* shoot himself! Not a chance! Besides, he was right-handed and was shot in the side of his left temple—an awkward place to shoot himself. That's what made Noonan leery. But if Tim had wanted to go in for acrobatics he could have plugged himself there, so they had to let it go at that."

"How about Myrtle? Could she have shot him?"

"Noonan didn't overlook that one, either. But she couldn't have been a third the distance down the slope when the shot was fired. Tim had powder marks on his forehead, and he hadn't been shot and rolled down. Myrtle's out. Max."

"But he had an alibi?"

"Sure. He was in the hotel bar, on the other side of the building, all the time. He had four men who said so. As I remember, they said it openly and often, long before anybody asked them. It happens there were other men in the bar who didn't remember his being there, but these four remembered all right—they'd remember anything Max wanted remembered."

Her eyes got large and then narrowed to two black-fringed slits. She leaned toward me, upsetting her glass with an elbow.

"Here's something that might help," she exclaimed. "Peak Murry was one of the four. He and Max are on the outs now. Peak might tell it straight. He's got a pool-room on Broadway."

"This MacSwain—does he happen to be named Bob? A bow-legged man with a long jaw like a hog's?"

"Yes—you know him?"

"By sight. What does he do now?"

"A small-time grifter.† What do you think of the stack-up?"

"Not bad. Maybe I can do something with it."

"Then let's talk scratch."

I grinned at the greed in her eyes, and said:

"Not just yet, sister. We'll have to wait and see how it works out before we start scattering pennies around."

She called me a damned nickel-nurser and reached for the gin.

"No more for me," I told her, looking at my watch. "It's getting along toward five A.M. and I'm in for a busy day scouting up these people you've been telling me about."

She decided she was hungry again. It took her half an hour or more to get waffles, ham and coffee off the stove. It took us another while to move them from table to stomachs and to smoke some cigarettes over extra cups of the coffee. It was after six when I left.

"If you don't mind," I said, "I'll leave by the back door. What with Noonan and Thaler not liking me, and the number of times I've already had to dodge lead in this burg, I'd like to be as little conspicuous as possible."

"Get a taxi."

"Too showy. And I need air and exercise now that there's no chance of getting any sleep."

She let me out the back door. Everything was quiet in the morning light. I went through her yard, into the alley, down it for a couple of blocks, over into one of the streets paralleling Broadway, down it, and over to my hotel and a tub of cold water.

The cold water braced me up, and I had needed it. At forty I could get along without sleep, but not comfortably. After I had dressed I sat down and composed a document:

---

* braggart and cheat

† swindler

Just before he died Tim Noonan told me he had been shot by Max Thaler. Detective Bob MacSwain heard him tell me. I gave MacSwain $200 and a diamond ring worth $1000 to keep quiet and make it look like suicide.

With this document in my pocket I went downstairs, had another breakfast that was chiefly coffee, and went up to the City Hospital. Visiting hours were in the afternoon, but by flourishing my Continental Detective Agency credentials and giving everybody to understand that an hour's delay might cause hundreds of deaths, or words to that effect, I got to see Myrtle Jennison.

She was in a ward on the third floor, alone. The other four beds were empty. She could have been a girl of twenty-five or a woman of fifty-five. Her face was a bloated, spotty mask. Lifeless yellow hair was gathered in two stringy braids that lay on the pillow beside her. I waited until the nurse who had brought me in was gone. Then I held my document out to the invalid and said:

"Will you sign this, please, Miss Jennison?"

She looked at me with unpleasant eyes that were shaded into no particular color by the pads of flesh around them, then at the document, and finally brought a shapeless, fat white hand from under the covers to take it. She pretended it took her nearly five minutes to read the forty-one words I had written. She let it fall down on the covers and asked:

"Where'd you get that?" Her voice was tinny, irritable.

"Dinah Brand told me."

She licked her swollen lips and asked eagerly:

"Has she broken off with Max?"

"Not that I know of," I lied. "I imagine she just wants to have this on hand in case it should come in handy."

"And get her fool throat slit. Give me a pencil."

I gave her my fountain pen and held my note-book under the document to stiffen it while she scribbled her signature at the bottom, and to have it in my hands as soon as she had finished. While I fanned the paper dry she said:

"If that's what she wants it's all right with me. What do I care what anybody does any more? I'm done. Hell with 'em all!" She sniggered evilly.

"Thanks very much for this, Miss Jennison."

"That's all right. It's nothing to me any more. Only"—her puffy chin quivered—"it's hell to die ugly as this."

VIII

I went out to hunt for MacSwain. Neither city directory nor telephone book told me anything. I did the pool-rooms, cigar stores, speak-easies, looking around first, then asking cautious questions. That got me nothing. I walked the streets, looking for bowed legs. That got me nothing. I decided to go back to my hotel, take a nap, and resume the hunt that night.

In a far corner of the lobby a man stopped hiding behind a newspaper and came out to meet me. He had bowed legs, a hog jaw, and was MacSwain. I nodded carelessly at him and walked on to the elevator. He followed me, mumbling:

"Hey, you got a minute?"

"Yeah." I stopped, pretending indifference.

"Let's get out of sight then."

I took him up to my room. He straddled a chair and put a match in his mouth. I sat on the side of the bed and waited for him to say something. He chewed his match a while and began:

"I'm going to come clean with you, brother. I'm—"

"You are?" I asked. "You mean you're going to tell me you knew who I was when you braced me yesterday? And you weren't a friend of Bush's? And you didn't have any money down on him then? And you knew who he was because you used to be a bull? And you thought if you could get me to put it to him you could clean up a little dough playing him?"

"I'll be damned if I was going to come through with that much," he said, "but you've got it about right, so I'll put a yes to it."

"Did you clean up?"

"I win myself six hundred iron men."* He pushed his hat back and scratched his forehead with the chewed end of his match. "And then I lose myself six hundred and forty iron men in a crap game. What do you think of that? I pick up six hundred berries like shooting fish—and have to bum four bits for breakfast!"

I said it was a tough break but that was the kind of world we lived in.

He said "Uh-huh," put the match back in his mouth, ground it some more, and added: "That's why I thought I'd come and see you. I used to be in the racket myself, and—"

"What did Noonan put the skids under† you for?"

"Skids? What skids? I quit! I come into a piece of change when my wife got killed in an automobile accident—insurance— ten grand— and I quit."

"I heard he kicked you off the force the time his brother shot himself."

"You heard wrong. It was just after that— maybe a week—but I quit, and you can ask him if I didn't."

"It's not that much to me. Go on telling me why you came to see me."

"I'm busted—flat. I know you're a Continental op and I got a pretty good idea what you're up to here. I'm pretty close to a lot that's going on in this burg. There's things I could do for you, knowing the ropes both ways, being a ex-dick myself."

"You want to stool-pigeon for me."

He looked me straight in the eye and said evenly:

"There's no sense in a man picking out the worst name he can find for everything."

"All right, MacSwain. I'll give you something

to do." I took out Myrtle Jennison's document and passed it to him. "Tell me about that."

He read it through carefully, his lips framing the words, the match jumping up and down in his mouth. He got up, put the paper on the bed beside me, and scowled down at it.

"There's something I'll have to find out first," he said, very seriously. "I'll be back in a little while and give you the whole story."

I laughed.

"Don't be silly," I told him. "You know I'm not going to let you walk out on me."

"I don't know that." He shook his head, still very serious. "Neither do you. All you know is whether you're going to try to stop me."

"The answer's yeah," I said while I considered that he was fairly hard and strong, six or seven years younger than I, twenty or thirty pounds lighter.

He stood at the foot of the bed and looked at me with solemn eyes. I sat on the side of the bed and looked at him with whatever sort of eyes I had at the time. We did this for nearly three minutes. I used part of the time measuring the distance between us, figuring out how, by throwing my body back on the bed and turning on my hip, I could get my heels in his face if he jumped me. He was too close for me to pull the gat. I had just finished this mental map-making when he spoke:

"That lousy ring wasn't worth no grand. I did swell to get two centuries‡ for it."

"Sit down," I suggested, "and tell me about it."

He wouldn't. He shook his head and stood where he was, within reach of me.

"Then tell me about it without sitting down."

He shook his head again and said:

"First I want to know what you're going to do about it.

"Cop§ Whisper."

"I don't mean that. I mean with me."

"You'll have to go over to the Hall with me."

"Won't!"

"Why not? You're only a witness."

"That's right. I'm only a witness that Noonan can hang a bribe-taking rap and a perjury rap, or both, on. And he'll be tickled simple to have the chance, damn him!"

The jaw-wagging didn't seem to be getting us anywhere. I said:

"That's too bad. But you're going to see him just the same."

"Try and take me."

I sat up straighter and slid my right hand back to my hip. He grabbed at me. I threw my body back on the bed, did the hip-swing, swung my feet at him. It was a good trick, only it didn't work. In his hurry to get at me he bumped the bed aside just enough to spill me off on the floor. I landed all sprawled out on my back. I kept dragging at my gun while I tried to roll under the bed. Missing me, his lunge carried him over the low footboard, over the side of the bed. He came down beside me, on the back of his neck, his body somersaulting over. I put the muzzle of my gun in his left eye and said:

"You're making a swell pair of clowns out of us! Be still while I get up or I'll make an opening in your head for brains to leak in."

I got up, found and pocketed my document, and let him get up.

"Knock the dents out of your hat and put your necktie back in front," I ordered after I had run a hand over his clothes and found nothing that felt like a weapon, "so you won't disgrace me going through the street. And you can suit yourself about whether you want to remember this gat is in my overcoat pocket, with a hand on it."

He straightened his hat and tie and said:

"Hey, listen! I'm in this, I guess, and cutting up won't get me nothing. Suppose I come clean when we get up there? Could you forget about the tussle? See—maybe it'd be smoother for me if they thought I come along without being dragged."

"O.K."

"Thanks, brother."

IX

We went over to the City Hall. Noonan was out eating. We had to wait half an hour for him. When he came in he greeted me with the usual hearty *How are you? That certainly is fine!* and the rest of it. Then his fat face and greenish eyes lost their geniality for sourness as he looked at MacSwain.

"Let's go inside," I said, and the chief led the way back to his private office. He pulled a chair over to his desk for me and then sat in his own, ignoring the ex-dick.

I gave Noonan the document. He gave it one glance, bounced out of his chair, and smashed a fist the size of a cantaloup into MacSwain's face.

The punch carried MacSwain across the room until a wall stopped him. The wall creaked under the strain, and a framed photograph of Noonan and some other city dignitaries welcoming somebody in spats dropped down to the floor with the hit man. The fat chief waddled over, picked up the picture and beat it into splinters on MacSwain's head and shoulders.

Noonan came back to his desk, puffing, smiling, saying cheerfully to me: "That fellow's a rat if there ever was one."

MacSwain sat up and looked around, bleeding from nose, mouth and head.

Noonan roared at him: "Come here, you——!"

MacSwain said, "Yes, chief!" scrambled up and ran over to the desk.

Noonan said: "Come through or I'll kill you!"

MacSwain said: "Yes, chief! It was like she says in the letter, only that rock wasn't worth no grand. But she give me it and the two centuries to keep my mouth shut, because I got there just when she asks him, 'Who did it, Tim?' and he says, 'Max!' He says it kind of loud and sharp, like he wanted to get it out before he died, because he died right then, almost before he'd got it out. That's the way it was, chief, only that rock wasn't worth no—"

"Damn the rock!" Noonan barked. "And stop bleeding on my rug!"

MacSwain fumbled in his pocket for a dirty handkerchief, mopped his nose and mouth with it, and jabbered on:

"And that's the way it was, chief. Everything else was like I said at the time, only I didn't say anything about hearing him say Max done it. I know I hadn't ought to—"

"Shut up!" Noonan yelled, and pressed one of the buttons on his desk. A uniformed copper came in. The chief jerked a thumb at MacSwain and said: "Take this—down cellar and let the wrecking crew work a while on him before you lock him up."

MacSwain started a desperate plea, "Aw, chief!" but the copper took him away before he could get any further.

Noonan stuck a cigar at me, tapped the document with another and asked:

"Where is this broad?"

"In the pogy*—dying. You'll have the cuter† get a stiff‡ out of her? That's not so good, legally—I framed it for effect. Another thing: I hear that Peak Murry and Whisper aren't playmates any more. Wasn't Murry one of his alibis? How about going up against him?"

The chief nodded, picked up one of his phones, said "McGraw" and then: "Get hold of Peak Murry. Have him come in. And have Tony Agosti picked up. That knife-throwing."

He put the phone down, stood up, made a lot of cigar smoke, and spoke through it:

"I haven't always been on the up-and-up with you." I thought that was putting it mildly, but I didn't say anything, while he went on: "You know your way around. You know what these

---

* normally jail; in this case a hospital
† prosecutor
‡ correspondence passed to a prison warden for delivery

jobs are. There's this one and that one that's got to be listened to. Just because a man's chief of police don't mean he's chief. Maybe you're a lot of trouble to somebody that can be a lot of trouble to me. Don't make any difference if I think you're a good guy. I got to play with them that play with me. See what I mean?"

I wagged my head to show that I did.

"That's the way it was," he said. "But no more. This is something else—a new deal. When the old woman kicked off, Tim was just a lad. There was only the two of us, and the old woman said to me, 'Take care of him, John.' And I said I would. And then Whisper murders him on account of that tramp!" He reached down and took my hand. "See what I'm getting at? That's a year and a half ago, and you give me my first chance to hang it on him. I'm telling you there's no man in Personville with a voice big enough to talk you down—not after today."

That made me happy, and I said so. We held a mutual admiration meeting until a lanky man with an extremely upturned nose in the middle of a round and freckled face was ushered in. It was Peak Murry.

"We were just wondering about the time when Tim died," the chief said when Murry had been given a chair and a cigar, "where Whisper was. You were out to the Lake that night, weren't you?"

"Yep!" Murry said, and the end of his nose seemed to get sharper and higher.

"With Whisper?"

"I wasn't with him all the time."

"Were you with him at the time of the shooting?"

"Nope."

The chief's greenish eyes got smaller and brighter. He asked softly:

"Know where he was?"

"Nope."

The chief sighed in a thoroughly satisfied way and leaned back in his chair.

"Damn it, Peak, you said before that you were with him in the bar!"

"Yep, I did," the lanky man admitted. "But

that don't mean nothing except that he asked me to and I didn't mind helping out a friend."

"Meaning you don't mind standing a perjury rap?"

"Don't kid me!" Murry spit emphatically at the cuspidor. "I didn't say nothing in no court rooms."

"How about Jerry and George Kelly and O'Brien?" the chief asked. "Did they say they were with him just because he asked 'em to?"

"O'Brien did. I don't know nothing about the others. I was going out of the bar when I run into Whisper, Jerry and Kelly, and went back to have a snifter with them. Kelly told me Tim had been knocked off. Then Whisper says, 'It never hurts anybody to have an alibi. We were here all the time, weren't we?' and he looks at O'Brien, who's behind the bar. O'Brien says, 'Sure you was!' and when Whisper looks at me I say the same thing. That was then. But I don't know no reason why I've got to cover him up nowadays."

"And Kelly said Tim had been knocked off? Didn't say he'd been found dead?"

"Nope. Knocked off was the words he used."

The chief said: "Thanks, Peak. You oughtn't to have done like you did, but what's done is done. How are the kids?"

Peak said they were doing fine, only the baby wasn't quite as fat as he would have liked to have him. Noonan had an assistant prosecuting attorney—a young fellow named Dart—come in with a stenographer. Peak repeated his story to them, waited until it had been typed, swore to it and signed it. Then he went away.

The rest of them set out for the City Hospital to get Myrtle Jennison's statement. I didn't go along. I saw another chance to get the nap Mac-Swain had robbed me of. So I told the chief I'd see him later, and went over to the hotel.

X

I had my vest unbuttoned when the phone rang.

It was Dinah Brand, complaining that she had been trying to get me since ten o'clock.

"Have you done anything on what I told you about?" she asked.

"I've been looking the ground over. It looks pretty good. I think maybe I'll crack it this afternoon."

"No! Hold off till I see you! Can you come up now?"

I looked at the vacant white bed, and said "Yes" without much enthusiasm.

Another tub of cold water did me so little good that I nearly fell asleep in it. Dan Rolff let me in when I rang the girl's bell. He looked and acted as if nothing out of the ordinary had happened the night before. Dinah Brand came into the hall to help me off with my overcoat. She had on a tan woolen dress with a two-inch tear in one shoulder seam.

She and I went into the living-room. She sat on the Chesterfield beside me and said:

"I'm going to ask you to do something for me. You like me enough, don't you?"

I admitted it. She counted the knuckles of my left hand with a warm forefinger and explained:

"I want you to not do anything more about what I told you last night. Now wait a minute! Wait till I get through! Dan was right. I oughtn't sell Max out like that—it *would* be utterly filthy. Besides, it's Noonan you chiefly want, isn't it? Well, if you'll be a nice darling and lay off Max this time I'll give you enough on Noonan to swing him. You'd like that better, wouldn't you? And you like me too much to take advantage of me by using the information I gave you when I was mad at what Max had said, don't you?"

"What is this dirt on Noonan?" I asked.

She kneaded my biceps, and murmured: "You promise?"

"Not yet."

She pouted at me and said:

"I'm off Max for life—on the level. You've got no right to make me turn rat."

"What about Noonan?"

"Promise first."

"No."

She dug her fingers into my arm and asked sharply:

"You've already gone to Noonan?"

"Yeah."

She let go my arm, frowned, shrugged and said gloomily: "Well, how can I help it?"

I stood up, and a voice said: "Sit down!"

It was a hoarse, whispering voice. I knew it belonged to Thaler before I turned to see him standing in the dining-room doorway, a big rod in one of his little hands. A red-faced man with a scarred cheek stood behind him. The other doorway—opening to the hall—filled up as I sat down. An almost chinless man with a wide, loose mouth in a thin, pimply face came a step through it. He had a couple of guns. An angular blond kid looked over his shoulder. I had met this pair before, in Whisper's King Street joint. The chinless one was called Jerry—probably the Jerry of the alibi party.

Dinah Brand got up from the Chesterfield, put her back to Thaler and addressed me. Her voice was husky with rage.

"This is none of my doing. He came here by himself, said he was sorry for what he said last night, and showed me how he and I could make ourselves a lot of money by turning Noonan up for you. Now I know it was a plant. He was to wait upstairs while I put it to you. I didn't know anything about these others."

Jerry's casual voice drawled:

"If I shoot a pin* from under her she'll sure sit down and maybe shut up. O.K.?"

I couldn't see Whisper. The girl was between us. He said: "Not now. Where's Dan?"

The blond kid said: "Up on the bathroom floor. I had to sap him."

Dinah Brand turned around to face Thaler. Stocking seams made s's up the ample backs of her legs. She said:

"Max Thaler, you're a lousy little—"

He whispered, very deliberately: "Shut . . . up . . . and . . . get . . . out . . . of . . . the . . . way."

She surprised me by doing both, and she kept quiet while he spoke to me:

"So you and Noonan are trying to paste his brother's death on me?"

"It don't need pasting. It's a natural."

He curved his thin lips at me and said: "You're as crooked as he is."

I said: "You know better. When he tried to frame you for Donald Willsson's killing I played your side. This time he's got you copped to rights."†

Dinah Brand flared up again, waving her arms in the middle of the room, storming:

"Get out of here, the whole lot of you! Why should I give a damn about your troubles? Get out!"

The blond kid who had sapped Rolff squeezed past Jerry and came grinning into the room. He caught one of the girl's flourished arms and bent it behind her. She twisted toward him, socked him in the belly with her other fist. It was a very respectable wallop—man-size. It broke his grip on her arm, sent him back a couple of long steps.

The kid gulped in a wide mouthful of air, whisked a blackjack from his hip, and stepped in again. His grin was gone. Jerry laughed what little chin he had out of sight. Thaler whispered harshly: "Lay off!" The kid didn't hear him. He was snarling things at the girl. She watched him with a face hard as a silver dollar. She was standing one-legged, her weight on her left foot. I guessed blondy was going to stop a kick when he closed in.

The kid feinted a grab with his empty left hand—started the blackjack at her face. Thaler whispered "Lay off!" again, and fired.

The bullet smacked blondy under the right eye, spun him around and dropped him backwards into Dinah Brand's arms.

This looked like the time, if there was to be any. In the excitement I had got a hand on my hip. I dragged the gun out and snapped a cap at Thaler, trying for his shoulder. That was wrong. If I'd tried for a bull's-eye I'd have winged him. Chinless Jerry hadn't laughed himself blind. He

_____

* leg

† has the evidence to arrest you

beat me to the shot. His bullet burnt my wrist, throwing me off the target. But, missing Thaler, my slug crumpled the red-faced man behind him.

I didn't know how bad my wrist was nicked, so I shifted the gun to my left hand. Jerry took another try at me.

The girl spoiled it by heaving the corpse at him. The dead yellow head banged into his knees. I jumped for him while he was off balance.

The jump took me out of the way of Thaler's bullet. It also tumbled Jerry out into the hall. I was all tangled up with him. He wasn't very tough to handle. But I had to work quick. There was Thaler to consider.

I socked Jerry twice, kicked him a couple of times, butted him once and was hunting for a place to bite when he went limp under me. I poked him again where his chin should have been—just to make sure he wasn't faking—and went away on hands and knees—down the hall a bit, out of line with the door.

Then I sat on my heels against the wall, held my gun level at Thaler's part of the premises, and waited. I couldn't hear anything for the moment except the blood singing in my head.

Dinah Brand stepped out of the door I had tumbled through, looked at Jerry, at me, smiled with her tongue between her teeth, beckoned with a jerk of her head, and returned to the living-room.

I followed her in, cautiously.

Whisper stood in the center of the floor. His hands were empty and so was his face. Except for his vicious little mouth, he looked like something displaying suits in a clothing-store window. Dan Rolff stood behind him with a gun-muzzle tilted to the little gambler's left kidney. Rolff's face was mostly blood. A piece of his scalp dangled over his forehead. The blond kid had sapped him plenty.

I grinned at Thaler and said: "Well, this is nice," before I saw that Rolff had another gun—centered on my chubby middle. That wasn't so nice. But my own gun was reasonably level, so I didn't have much worse than an even break.

Rolff said: "Drop your pistol!"

I looked at Dinah—looked puzzled, I suppose. She shrugged and told me:

"It seems to be Dan's party."

"Yeah. Well, somebody ought to tell him that I don't like to play this way."

Rolff repeated: "Drop your pistol!"

"I'll be damned if I will! I've shed twenty pounds trying to nab this baby. I got twenty more I'm willing to spend doing the same thing."

Rolff said: "I'm not interested in what is between you two, and I have no intention of giving either of you into the other's hands. You shall—"

Dinah Brand had wandered across the room. When she was behind Rolff I interrupted his speech by telling her:

"If you upset him now you're sure of making two friends—Noonan and me. You can't trust Whisper any more, no matter what happens, so there's no use helping *him*."

She laughed and said:

"Talk money, darling."

"Dinah!" Rolff protested. He was caught. She was behind him and he knew she was strong enough to handle him. He couldn't look away from me unless he shot me first, and even then, unless he wanted to shoot her, too, he'd still be at her mercy.

"A hundred dollars," I bid.

"My Gawd!" she exclaimed, "I've actually got a cash offer out of you at last! But you ought to do a little better than that."

"Two hundred."

"You're getting positively reckless. But I still can't hear you."

"Try," I said. "It's worth that to me not to have to try to shoot Rolff's gat out of his hand, but no more than that."

"You've got a good start. Don't weaken. One more bid."

"Two hundred dollars and ten cents, and that's all."

"You big bum!" she said. "I won't do it."

"Fair enough!" I made a face at Thaler and told him: "When what happens happens be damned sure you keep still."

Dinah cried:

"Wait! Are you really going to start something?"

"I'm going to take Thaler out with me—regardless."

"Two hundred and a dime?"

"Yeah."

"Dinah!" Rolff called again. "You won't—"

But she laughed, came close to his back and wound her strong arms around him. I shoved the gambler aside, kept him covered while I used my wounded right hand to yank Rolff's weapons away. Dinah turned Rolff loose.

He took two steps toward the dining-room door, said calmly, "There is no—" and collapsed on the floor.

Dinah gave a cry and ran to him. I pushed Thaler out into the hall, past the still sleeping Jerry, and to the alcove beneath the front stairs, where I had seen a phone. I called Noonan, told him I had Thaler, and where.

"Grease us twice!" he said. "Don't kill him till I get there!"

XI

The news of Whisper's capture spread quickly. When Noonan, the half a dozen coppers he had brought along, and I took the gambler and the now conscious Jerry out of the police car and into the City Hall there were at least a hundred men standing around watching us. All of them didn't look pleased. Noonan's coppers—not a good lot at best—moved around with whitish, drawn faces. But Noonan was the most triumphant guy west of the Mississippi.

Even the bad luck he had trying to third-degree Whisper couldn't spoil his happiness. Whisper stood up under everything they gave him. He would talk to his lawyer, he said, and not to anybody else, and he stuck to it. As much as Noonan hated him, I noticed that here was a prisoner he didn't give the works—didn't turn him over to the wrecking crew. Whisper had killed the chief's brother, and the chief hated his

guts, but Whisper was still somebody in Personville, and not a tramp like MacSwain.

Noonan finally got tired of playing with his prisoner and sent him up—the prison was on the top floor of the City Hall—to be stowed away till morning.

I lighted another of Noonan's cigars and glanced through the detailed statement he had got from the woman in the hospital. There was nothing in it that I hadn't heard from Dinah or MacSwain. The chief wanted me to come out to his house to dinner, but I lied out of it, pretending that my wrist—now bandaged—was bothering me. It was really nothing more than a bruise and a burn.

While we were talking about that a couple of plain-clothes men came in with the red-faced bird who had been hit by the slug I had missed Whisper with. It had broken a rib for him, and he had taken a back-door sneak while the rest of us were busy. Noonan's men had picked him up in a doctor's office. The chief failed to get any information out of him, and sent him off to the hospital.

I got up and prepared to leave, saying: "It was the Brand girl who gave me the tip-off on this. That's why I asked you to keep her and Rolff out of it."

The chief grabbed my left hand for the fifth or sixth time in the past couple of hours.

"If you want her taken care of that's enough for me," he assured me. "But if she had a hand in turning that—up, you can tell her any time she wants anything from me all she's got to do is name it."

I said I'd tell her that, and went over to my hotel, thinking about that neat white bed again. But it was nearly eight o'clock, and my stomach needed attention. I went into the dining-room and had that fixed. A leather chair tempted me into stopping in the lobby while I burnt up a cigar. That led to conversation with a traveling railroad auditor from Denver who knew a man I knew in St. Louis. Then there was a lot of shooting in the street.

We went to the door and decided the fireworks were up near the City Hall. I shook the auditor and moved up that way. I had done two-thirds of the distance when an automobile came down the street toward me, coming like a bat out of hell, leaking gunfire from the rear.

I backed into an alley entrance and slid my own gun loose. An arc-light brightened two faces in the front of the car. The driver's meant nothing to me. The upper part of the other's was hidden by a pulled-down hat. The lower part was Whisper's.

Across the street was the entrance to another block of alley, lighted at the far end. Between me and the light somebody moved just as Whisper's car roared past. The somebody had dodged from behind one shadow that might have been an ash-can to another. What took my eyes away from Whisper, and kept me from taking a shot at him, was that the legs of the somebody in the alley had a bowed look.

A load of coppers buzzed past, throwing lead at the first car. I skipped across the street and into the section of the alley which held a man who might have bowed legs. It was a fair bet he wasn't heeled* if he was my man. I played it that way, moving straight up the slimy middle of the alley, looking into shadows with eyes, ears and nose.

Three-quarters of a block of it—and a shadow broke away from another shadow—a man going hell-bent away from me.

"Stop!" I bawled, pounding my feet after him. "Stop, or I'll plug you, MacSwain!"

He ran half a dozen strides farther and stopped, turning.

"Oh, it's you," he said, as if it made any difference who took him back to the hoosegow.

"Yeah," I confessed. "What are all you people doing wandering around outside?"

"I don't know. Somebody dynamited the floor out of the can. I dropped down through the hole with the rest of 'em. There was some mugs standing off the bulls. I made the back-trotters†

with one bunch, and then we split, and I was figuring on cutting across and making the hills. I didn't have nothing to do with it. I just went along when she blew open."

"Whisper was pinched this afternoon," I told him.

"Hell, then that's it! Noonan had ought to know he'd never keep that guy screwed up‡— not in this burg."

We were still standing where MacSwain had stopped running, in the alley.

"You know what he was pinched for?" I asked.

"Uh-huh—for killing Tim."

"You know who killed Tim."

"Huh? Sure he did!"

"You did."

"Huh? What's the matter? You simple?"

"There's a gun in my left hand," I cautioned him.

"But look here—didn't he tell the broad that Whisper done it? What's the matter with you?"

"He didn't say *Whisper*. I've heard women call Thaler *Max*, but I've never heard a man here call him anything but *Whisper*. Tim didn't say *Max*. He said *MacS*—the first part of *MacSwain*—and died before he could finish it. Don't forget about the gun."

"What would I have killed him for? He was after Whisper's—"

"I haven't got around to the motive yet," I admitted, "but let's see. You and your wife had busted up. Tim seems to have been a ladies' man. Maybe there's something there. I'll have to look it up. What started me thinking was that you never tried to get any more dough out of the girl. I reckon you had sense enough to know what luck you'd played in and to let it alone."

"Cut it out!" he begged. "You know there ain't no sense to it. What would I have hung around afterwards for? I'd have been out getting an alibi, like Whisper!"

"Why? You were a bull then—close by was

---

the place for you—to see the job was handled right."

"You know damned well it don't hang together—don't make no sense. Cut it out, for God's sake!"

"I don't mind how goofy it is," I said. "It's something to put to Noonan when we go back. He's likely all broken up over Whisper's crushout. This'll take his mind off it."

MacSwain got down on his knees in the muddy alley and cried: "Oh, God, no! He'd croak me with his hands!"

"Get up and stop yelling!" I growled. "Now will you give it to me straight?"

He whined: "He'd croak me with his hands!"

"All right. Suit yourself. If you won't talk, I will—to Noonan. If you'll come clean with me I'll give you my word that I'll do what I can to keep it to myself while you're where Noonan can get at you."

"You mean it?" he asked eagerly, and then started sniveling again: "How do I know you'll do what you say?"

I risked a little truth on him:

"You said you had some idea of what I was doing in Personville. Then you can see that it's my play to keep Noonan and Whisper split. Letting Noonan think Whisper croaked Tim will keep 'em split. But suit yourself. If you don't want to play with me, come on, we'll play with Noonan."

He spent a few more minutes hemming and hawing, but he was too afraid of the chief to hold out on me, and the story finally came out:

"I don't know how much you know, but it was like you said. My wife fell for Tim. That's what made a bum out of me. You can ask anybody if I wasn't a good guy before that. It got me in a bad way, see? I couldn't stop being in love with her, and I wanted her to do whatever she wanted to do, even if it wasn't what I wanted. Can you understand that? And mostly what she wanted was tough on me. But I couldn't do anything else, see? So I had to let her move out and put in divorce papers, so she could marry him, thinking he meant to.

"Pretty soon I begin hearing that he's chasing this Myrtle Jennison. I couldn't go that. I had given him his chance with Helen, fair and square. She wanted him and I didn't stand in the way. Now he was giving her the air for this Myrtle. I wasn't going to stand for that. He had to keep his bargain with Helen. She wasn't no trollop. It was accidental, though, running into him at the Lake that Saturday. I kept my eye on him till I seen him go down by them summer houses. Then I went after him. That looked like a good quiet place to have it out with him.

"I guess maybe we'd both had a little too much hooch. Anyway, we had it hot and heavy. When it got too hot for him he pulled the gun. He was yellow! I grabbed it, and in the tussle it went off. I swear to God I didn't shoot him, excepting like that. It went off while the both of us had hold of it. I ran away, back in some bushes. I had seen the hole it knocked in his head and I knew he was croaked. But when I got in the bushes I could hear him still moaning and talking. There was people coming—especially a broad running down from the hotel—that Myrtle Jennison.

"I wanted to go back and hear what he said, so I'd know where I stood, but I was afraid to be the first one there. So I had to wait till the girl got to him, listening all the time to his moaning and talking, but too far away to make it out. When she got to him I ran over and got there just as he died trying to say my name. I didn't think about that being Whisper's name till she came and propositioned me with the suicide letter and the two centuries and the rock. I'd just been stalling around, pretending to get the job lined up—being on the force then—and trying to find out how I stood. Then she makes that play and I know I'm sitting pretty. And that's the way it went till you started digging it up again."

He slopped his feet up and down in the mud and added: "Next week my wife was killed—an accident. Uh-huh, accident. She drove the Ford square in front of Number 6 where it comes down the long grade from Tanner and stopped it there. But what the hell do you or anybody else care about that?"

"Keep your mouth shut when we get up to the Hall," I said, "and I'll keep my promise."

He went back meekly—three blocks of walking without either of us saying anything. Noonan was trotting up and down his office floor, cursing the half-dozen bulls who stood around wishing they were somewhere else.

"I found this walking around loose," I said, pushing MacSwain forward.

Noonan knocked MacSwain down, kicked him, and told one of the coppers to take him away. I slipped out without saying good-night and walked back to the hotel.

Off to the north some guns popped. A group of three men passed me, shifty-eyed, walking pigeon-toed. Down the street a little farther another man moved all the way over to the curb to give me plenty of room. I didn't know him and don't suppose he knew me. A lone shot sounded not far away. As I reached the hotel a battered black touring car went down the street, crammed to the curtains with men, hitting fifty at least.

I grinned after it. Poisonville was beginning to boil out under the lid. And I felt so much like a native that even the memory of my part in the boiling—of the frame-up I had engineered—didn't keep me from getting twelve solid hours of sleep.

THE CLEANSING OF POISONVILLE

is not a serial, but in reality is a series of adventures of the Continental detective who is drawn into a fight for life with the crooked bosses of a city, who have gone mad with the power of their own corruption. Outside of their gripping interest, these stories are remarkable if only for the fact that their manner of telling points the way to a new type of detective fiction, which in BLACK MASK is coming to take the place of the old, worn-out formula sort of gruesome-murder-and-clever-solution detective story. The first of these adventures appeared in November BLACK MASK. Any reader who missed that number may have it by sending ten cents with his name and address to the Editor, 578 Madison Avenue, New York City.

DYNAMITE, the third adventure in The Cleansing of Poisonville, by Dashiell Hammett, is probably one of the most exciting detective-action tales ever told. It appears in JANUARY BLACK MASK.

BLACK MASK, JANUARY 1928

Dynamite

BY DASHIELL HAMMETT

The Cleansing of Poisonville.

MICKEY LINEHAN USED the telephone to wake me at noon.

"We're here," he told me. "Where's the reception committee?"

"Probably stopped to get a rope. Check your bags and come up to the hotel. Room 537. Don't advertise your visit."

I was dressed when they arrived.

Mickey Linehan was a big slob with sagging shoulders and a shapeless body that seemed to be coming apart at all its joints. His ears stuck out like red wings, and his round red face usually wore the meaningless smirk of a half-wit. Dick Foley was a boy-sized Canadian with a sharp, irritable face. He wore high heels to increase his height, perfumed his handkerchiefs, and saved all the words he could. They were both good operatives.

"What did the Old Man tell you about the job?" I asked when we had settled into seats.

"He didn't seem to know much," Mickey said. "Said you'd wired for help, and that he hadn't got any reports from you for a couple of days."

"The chances are he won't for a couple more. Know anything about this Personville?"

Dick shook his head. Mickey said:

"Only that people call it Poisonville as if they meant it."

"Here's the way it stacks up," I said. "Old Elihu Willsson owns the Personville Mining Corporation, the First National Bank, the newspapers—practically the whole city and a fair slice of the state. He used to run it as well as own it—by himself. Now he's got help—more than he wants. A few years back, when he had a strike and other troubles on his hands, he needed help. Now his helpers have got him by the neck. He has to play along with them whether he likes it or not.

"There seem to be four of these helpers who count. Pete the Finn, who is Poisonville's boot-leg king; Lew Yard; Max Thaler, alias Whis-per, who runs a couple of gambling joints; and Noonan, chief of police. I'm told Lew Yard is head man and fence for the burg's grifters. I don't know much about him or Pete the Finn. I've been too busy to look 'em over.

"Elihu Willsson is old and sick. His doc-tor told him he'd have to give up handling his affairs. So Elihu brought his son Donald home from Paris. But when the son gets here the old man can't make up his mind to pass everything over to him. He compromised by giving the boy the newspapers to play with. Donald seems to have been a pretty nice boy, but he wasn't a wise head. It didn't take him long to find out that Personville wasn't exactly a paradise of righ-teousness, but he didn't tumble to the fact that his old man was in the mud as deep as the rest.

"The youngster starts a reform campaign in his—or really his father's—papers. Papa tries to reason with him, but he doesn't want to admit that he's tied up with the town's choicest thugs. So he doesn't make much headway. Papa's confederates—knowing he'd shake 'em off if he could—begin to think he's using Donald to do it. I don't think he was—but he might have been at that. Anyway, everybody suspects everybody else all around.

"That's the way it stood last week when we got a check from Donald and a letter asking that an op be sent here to do some work for him. I was the op. I got here Monday. Donald was shot and killed before I saw him. He was killed right after buying some graft evidence from a Dinah Brand, who was Max Thaler's girl. It comes out afterwards that he couldn't have used what she sold him—or so she thought. She was gypping him. But—with everybody watching everybody else—Lew Yard, Pete the Finn and Noonan got the idea that Thaler and old Elihu were double-crossing them. They hit back by trying to frame Thaler for the killing, and trying to knock off Elihu.

"That was none of my business, then. All I wanted was to nail Donald's murderer. But these people wouldn't let me alone. They were afraid I'd dig up stuff they didn't want dug up. See, they thought the boy's killing was part of the double-crossing. They ran me ragged for a couple of days, until this thing of being shot at by coppers got on my nerves. Elihu, scared stiff that his ex-friends were going to wipe him out, sent for me. He wanted *them* wiped out. I was sore enough by then to be glad of the chance.

"I took advantage of his fright to get a certi-fied check out of him, and a letter that was as good as a contract, so he couldn't call the job off if he and the others patched up their quarrel. It was a good thing I did. When I landed Donald's murderer—a boy named Albury, ex-boy-friend of Dinah Brand's—everybody found out that the killing had nothing to do with politics, was just the result of crazy jealousy.

"Elihu, Thaler, Yard, Pete and Noonan immediately fell on each other's necks and kissed their differences away. Elihu tried to call me off. But I had him sewed up too tight for that. He couldn't block me without raising more stink than he wanted. Since then it's been me versus Poisonville. I had—"

The telephone bell interrupted me. Dinah Brand's lazy voice:

"Hello! How's the wrist?"

"Only a scratch. What do you think of the crush-out?"

"It's not my fault," she said. "I did my part. If Noonan couldn't hold him, it's just too bad. I'm coming downtown to buy a hat this after-noon. I thought I'd drop in and see you for a couple of minutes if you're going to be there."

"What time?"

"Oh, around three."

"Right. I'll expect you, and I'll have that two hundred berries and a dime I owe you."

"Do," she said. "That's what I'm coming in for. Cheerio!"

I went back to my seat on the bed and my story:

"I had kept Thaler from being framed for Donald's murder. That gave me a good stand-in with him. But I had to blow it. This girl of his—Dinah Brand, that was her on the phone—is a money-hungry baby with some local knowledge I could use. So I tried my hand at splitting her and Thaler. He had a fight fixed Thursday night. A pug who called himself Ike Bush was to lay down to another named Kid Cooper.

"With the help of an ex-bull named Mac-Swain I unfixed it, making Bush win, letting the girl in on it in time to switch her bets. It stirred things up plenty. Bush won but got a knife through his neck before he could get out of the ring. Thaler accused the girl of selling him out. She got mad and tipped me off to where I could dig up proof that Thaler killed Noonan's brother a year and a half ago.

"That was what I wanted—something to set the boys against one another. I took the dope to Noonan. Later, the girl helped me turn Thaler in to him. That's where I got this bandaged wrist—we fireworked each other. Last night Thaler's friends dynamited him out of the hoosegow. I don't know whether Noonan has caught him again or not. I haven't been out yet today. I hope he hasn't. I imagine Lew Yard and Pete the Finn will try to make the chief lay off of Thaler. I don't know what he'll do. He's shifty as hell and he does want his revenge for brother Tim's bump-off.

"The tricky part of it is that Thaler didn't kill Noonan's brother. The ex-copper MacSwain, who helped me uncook the fight, did it. He's in the can now, held as a witness or something. He got away during the crush-out last night. I caught him. He came through to me on the murder. I took him back to jail, but promised him I wouldn't crack the rap on him while he was in Noonan's hands. The chief would kill him in a second. With a fair trial I think MacSwain will beat his case—self-defense. That, gents, is what's what and who's who in Poisonville today."

Mickey Linehan whistled, said:

"Maybe the Old Man wouldn't crucify you if he knew what you've been doing! No wonder you're afraid to send in reports!"

"If it works out the way I want it, there'll be no reason for reporting all the details," I said. "It's all right for our Continental Detective Agency to have its rules and regulations, but when you're out on a job you do it the best way you can. The work's got to be done. And anybody that brings any ethics to Poisonville is going to get 'em rusty. But a report is no place for the dirty details. Don't you birds be sending any to San Francisco without letting me see them first."

"Fair enough," Mickey agreed. "What kind of crimes have you got for us to pull?"

"I want you to go after Pete the Finn. Dick will take Lew Yard. You'll both have to play it the way I've played. Do what you can when you can. I could buy more dope on them from Dinah Brand. But the way it stands now there's no use taking anybody into court no matter what you've got on 'em. They own the courts. Evidence won't do. What we've got to have is dynamite. If we can smash things up enough—break the combination—they'll have their knives in each other's backs, doing our work for us. The break between Noonan and Thaler is a starter. I'm afraid it'll sag on us if we don't help it along."

"How about your client, old Elihu?" Mickey asked. "What are you going to do with him?"

"Maybe ruin him. Maybe club him into backing us up. I don't care. You'd better stay at the Hotel Person, Mickey, and Dick can go to the National. Keep apart and for God's sake burn the job up before the Old Man gets hep! Make notes of these, so you'll know 'em when and if you run across 'em."

I gave them names, descriptions and addresses—when I had them—of Elihu Willsson; Stanley Lewis, his secretary; Dinah Brand; Dan Rolff, her tubercular boy-friend; Chief of Police Noonan; Max Thaler, alias Whisper; and his right-hand man, the chinless Jerry.

"Now go to it," I said. "And don't kid yourselves that there's any law in Poisonville except what you make for yourself."

Mickey said:

"You'd be surprised how many laws I can get along without."

Dick said: "So long."

They departed. I went down to the café for breakfast, then over to the City Hall to see the fat chief of police.

II

His greenish eyes were bleary—as if they hadn't been sleeping—and his fleshy face had lost some of its color. But he pumped my hand up and down as enthusiastically as ever, and the usual cordiality was in his voice and manner.

"Any line on Whisper?" I asked when we had finished the glad-handing.

"I think I've got something." He looked at the clock on the wall and then at his phone. "I'm expecting a word any minute now. Sit down."

"Who else got away?"

"Jerry Hooper and Tony Agosti are the only others still out. We picked up all the rest. Jerry is Whisper's right bower,[*] and the wop's one of the mob, too. He's the bozo that put the knife in Ike Bush the night of the fights."

"Any more of Whisper's mob in?"

"No—we just had the three of 'em. Except Buck Wallace, the fellow you potted. He's in the hospital."

Noonan looked at the wall-clock again, then at his watch. It was exactly two o'clock. He turned to the phone. It rang. He grabbed it, said:

"Noonan speaking . . . Yes . . . Yes . . . Yes . . . Right."

He pushed the phone back and played a tune on the row of pearl buttons on his desk. The office filled up with coppers.

"Cedar Hill Inn," he said. "You follow me out with your detail, Bates. Terry, you shoot out

---

[*] from the card game euchre: highest ranking gang member

Broadway and hit the dump from behind. Pick up the boys on traffic duty as you go along. It's likely we'll need everybody we can get. Duffy, take yours out Union Street and around by the old mine road. McGraw will hold headquarters down. Get hold of everybody you can and send 'em after us. Jump!"

He grabbed his hat and went after them, calling over his shoulder to me:

"Come on, man! This is the kill!"

I followed him down to the department garage, where the engines of half a dozen police cars were roaring. The chief sat beside his driver. I sat in the rear of his car with four of his bulls.

Men climbed into other cars. Machine-guns were unwrapped. Armloads of rifles, riot-guns were distributed. Packages of ammunition were dumped into cars.

We got away first—off with a jump that clicked our teeth together. We missed the garage doorway by half an inch, chased a couple of pedestrians diagonally across the sidewalk, bounced off the curb into the roadway, missed a truck as narrowly as we had missed the door, and dashed out King Street with our siren wide open. Panicky automobiles darted right and left—regardless of traffic rules—to let us through. It was a lot of fun.

I looked back, saw another police car following us, another turning into Broadway. Noonan chewed a cold cigar and told the driver:

"Give her a bit more, Pat."

Pat twisted us around a frightened woman's coupé, put us through a slot between street car and laundry wagon—a slot too narrow for us to slide through if our car hadn't been so smoothly enameled—and said:

"All right, but the brakes ain't good."

"That's nice!" the gray-mustached dick on my left said. He didn't sound sincere.

Out of the center of the city there wasn't so much traffic to bother us, but the streets were rougher. It was a nice half-hour's ride, with everybody getting a chance to sit on everybody else's lap. The last ten minutes of it was over an uneven road that had hills enough to keep us from forgetting what Pat had said about the brakes.

We wound up at a gate topped by a shabby electric sign that had said *Cedar Hill Inn* before it lost its globes. The roadhouse—twenty feet behind the gate—was a squat wooden building painted a moldy green and chiefly surrounded by rubbish. Front door and windows were closed, blank.

We followed Noonan out of the car. The machine that had been trailing us came into sight around a bend in the road, slid to rest beside ours, unloaded its cargo of men and artillery.

Noonan ordered this and that.

A couple of coppers went around each side of the building. A couple more, including a machine-gunner, remained at the gate. The rest of us walked through tin cans, bottles and ancient newspaper to the front of the house.

The gray-mustached detective who had sat beside me in the car carried a red axe. We stepped up on the porch.

Noise and a slice of fire came out from under a window-sill.

The gray-mustached detective fell down, hiding the axe under his corpse.

The rest of us ran away.

I ran with Noonan. We hid in the ditch on the Inn side of the road. It was deep enough, and banked high enough, to let us stand almost erect without being targets.

The chief was excited.

"What luck!" he said happily. "He's here! By God, he's here!"

"That shot came from *under* the sill," I said. "A machine-gun ought to be able to spoil that trick."

"Spoil it?" he asked cheerfully. "We'll sieve the dump! Duffy ought to be pulling up on the other road by now, and Terry Shane won't be more than a minute or two behind him. Hey, Donner!" he called to a man who was peeping around a boulder. "Swing around back and tell Duffy and Shane to start closing in as soon as they come, letting fly with all they got. Where's Kimble?"

The peeper jerked a thumb toward a tree on his far side. We could see only the upper part of it from our ditch.

"Tell him to set up his mill and start popping," Noonan ordered. "Low, across the front ought to do it like cutting cheese."

The peeper disappeared. Noonan went up and down the ditch, risking his noodle over the top now and then for a look around, once in a while gesturing or calling to his men. He came back, sat on his heels beside me, gave me a cigar and lighted one for himself.

"It'll do," he said complacently. "Whisper won't have a chance in the world."

The machine-gun by the tree fired, haltingly, experimentally, half a dozen shots. Noonan grinned and let a ring of cigar smoke drift out of his fat mouth.

The machine-gun got down to business, grinding out metal like the busy little death-factory it was. Noonan blew another smoke ring and said:

"That's exactly what'll do it."

Farther away another machine-gun began, then others. Irregularly, rifles, pistols, shotguns joined in. Noonan nodded approvingly and said:

"Five minutes of that ought to do things."

I agreed that it ought. We leaned against the clay bank and smoked until the five minutes were up. I suggested a look at the remains, if any. I gave him a boost up the bank and climbed up after him. The roadhouse was as bleak and empty-looking as at first, but more battered. No shots came from it. Plenty were going into it.

"What do you think?" Noonan asked.

"If there's a cellar, there might be a mouse alive in it."

"Well, we could finish him afterward."

He took a whistle out of his pocket and made a lot of noise. He waved his fat arms and the gunfire began to dwindle. We had to wait a while for the word to go all the way around.

Then we crashed the door.

The first floor was ankle-deep with booze that was still gurgling from bullet holes in the stacked-up cases and barrels that filled most of the house. Dizzy from the fumes of spilled hooch, we waded around until we found four dead bodies and no live ones. The four were swarthy, foreign-looking men in laborers' clothes. Two of them were practically shot to pieces.

Noonan said: "Leave 'em here and get out."

His voice was cheerful, but in a flashlight's glow his greenish eyes showed white-ringed with fear.

We went out gladly, though I did hesitate long enough to pocket an unbroken bottle labeled *Dewar*.

At the gate a khaki-dressed copper was tumbling off a motorcycle. He yelled at us:

"The First National Bank has been stuck up!"

Noonan cursed savagely, bawled:

"He's foxed us, damn him! Back to town, everybody!"

Everybody except us who had ridden with the chief beat it for the machines. Two of them carried the dead dectective with them.

Noonan looked at me out of his eye-corners and said:

"This is a tough one, no fooling."

I said, "Well," shrugged, and sauntered out to his automobile, where the driver was sitting at the wheel. I stood with my back to the house, talking to Pat. I don't remember what we talked about. Presently Noonan and the other detectives joined us.

Only a little flame showed through the open roadhouse door before we had passed out of sight around the bend in the road.

III

There was a mob around the First National Bank. We pushed through it to the door, where we found McGraw, a raw-boned, sour police captain.

"Was six of 'em, masked," he reported to the chief as we went inside. "They hit it about two-thirty. Five of 'em got away clean with the jack.* The watchman here dropped one of 'em—Jerry Hooper. He's over on the bench—cold. We got the roads blocked, and I wired around, if it ain't too late. Last seen of 'em was when they made the turn into King Street—in a black Lincoln."

We went over for a look at dead Jerry, lying on one of the lobby benches with a shabby robe over him.

The bullet had gone in under his left shoulder-blade.

The bank watchman, a harmless looking old duffer, pushed up his chest and told us all about it:

"There wasn't no chance to do nothing at first. They was in 'fore anybody knew anything. And maybe they didn't work fast! Right down the line, scooping it up. No chance to do anything then. But I says to myself, 'All right, young fellows, you've got it all your way now, but wait till you try to leave!' And I was as good as my word, you bet! I runs right to the door after 'em and cuts loose with the old firearm. I got that fellow just as he was stepping in the car. I bet you I would have got more of 'em if I had more bullets, because it's kind of hard shooting like that, standing in the door, and I bet you—"

Noonan stopped the monologue by patting the old boy's back hard enough to empty his lungs, telling him, "That certainly was fine of you."

McGraw drew the blanket over the dead man again and growled:

"No identifications. But if Jerry was there it's a cinch it was Whisper's caper."

The chief nodded happily and said:

"Well, I'll leave it in your hands, Mac. Going to poke around here or down to the Hall with me?" he asked me.

"Neither. I've got a date and I want to get into dry shoes."

Dinah Brand's blue little Marmon was stand-

---

* loot

ing in front of the hotel. I didn't see her. I went up to my room, leaving the door unlocked. I had got my hat and overcoat off when she came in without knocking.

"My Gawd, you keep a boozy smelling room," she said.

"It's my shoes. Noonan took me wading in rum."

She crossed to the window, opened it, sat on the sill and asked:

"What was that for?"

"He thought he was going to find your Max out in a dump called Cedar Hill Inn. So we went out, shot the joint silly, murdered some dagoes, spilled gallons of liquor, and left the place burning."

"Cedar Hill Inn? I thought it had been closed up for a year or more?"

"It looked it, but it was somebody's warehouse."

"But you didn't find Max there?" she asked.

"While we were there he seems to have been knocking over Elihu Willsson's First National Bank."

"I saw that!" she said. "I had just come out of Bengren's—the store two doors away. I had just got in my car when I saw a big guy backing out of the bank, carrying a sack and a gun, and with a black swipe over his face."

"Was Max with them?"

"No—he wouldn't be. He'd send Jerry and the boys. That's what he has them for. Jerry was there. I knew him as soon as he stepped out, in spite of the rag. Four of 'em came out of the bank, running down to the car at the curb. Jerry and another fellow were in the car. When the four came across the sidewalk Jerry jumped out and went to meet them. That's when the shooting started and Jerry dropped. The others jumped in the car and beat it. How about that dough you owe me?"

I counted out ten twenty-dollar bills and a dime. She left the window to come for the money.

"That's for pulling Dan off so you could cop

Max," she said when she had stowed it in the bottom of her bag. "Now how about what I was to get for showing you where you could get the dope on him for killing Tim?"

"You'll have to wait till he's indicted. How do I know the dope's any good?"

She frowned and said:

"What do you do with all the money you don't spend?" Her face brightened. "You know where Max is now?"

"No."

"What's it worth to know?"

"Not much."

"I'll tell you for five hundred bucks."

"I wouldn't want to take advantage of you that way."

"I'll tell you for three hundred bucks."

I shook my head.

"A hundred and fifty," she said.

"I don't want him. I don't care where he is."

"A hundred."

"Why don't you peddle the news to Noonan?" I asked.

"Yes—and try to collect. Do you only perfume yourself with hooch, or is there any for drinking purposes?"

"Here's a bottle of Dewar that I picked up at Cedar Hill this afternoon. There's a bottle of King George in my bag. What's your choice?"

She voted for King George. We had a drink apiece, straight, and I said:

"Sit down and play with it while I get into clean clothes."

When I came out of the bathroom twenty-five minutes later she was sitting at the secretary, smoking a cigarette and studying a memoranda book that had been in the side pocket of my Gladstone bag.

"I guess these are the expenses you've charged up on some other cases," she said without looking up. "I'm damned if I can see why you can't be a little bit liberal with me, then! Look. Here's a six-hundred-dollar item marked *Inf*. That's information bought from somebody, isn't it? And here's a hundred and fifty below it—*Top*—whatever that is. And here's another day when you spent nearly a thousand dollars."

"They must be telephone numbers," I said, taking the book from her. "Where were you raised? Fanning my baggage!"

"I was raised in a convent," she told me. "I won the good behavior medal every year I was there. I thought little girls who put extra spoons of sugar in their chocolate went to hell for gluttony. I didn't even know there was such a thing as profanity till I was eighteen. The first time I heard any I damned near fainted." She spit on the rug in front of her, tilted back in the chair, put her feet on my bed, and asked: "And what do you think of that?"

I pushed her feet off the bed and said:

"I was raised in a waterfront saloon. Keep your saliva off my floor or I'll toss you out on your neck."

"Let's have another drink first. Listen. What'll you give me for the inside story of how the boys got themselves a quarter of a million building the city hall three years ago?"

"That doesn't click with me. Try another."

"Then how about why the first Mrs. Lew Yard was sent to the insane asylum?"

"No."

"King, our district attorney, eight thousand dollars in debt four years ago, now the owner of a couple of downtown blocks. I can't give you the whole thing, but I can show you where to start digging—say, a hundred dollars' worth?"

"Keep trying," I encouraged her.

"No. You don't want to buy anything. You're just hoping you'll pick up something for nothing. This isn't bad Scotch. Where'd you get it?"

"Brought it from San Francisco with me."

"Well, what's the idea of not wanting any of this information I offered? Think you can get it cheaper?"

"Uh-uh! Information's not much good to me now. I need dynamite—something to blow 'em apart."

She laughed and jumped up, her big eyes hot.

"I've got one of Lew Yard's cards. Suppose we sent the bottle of Dewar you copped to Pete with the cards. Wouldn't he take that as a declaration of war? Think Noonan had pulled it under orders from Lew?"

I considered it and said:

"No, I don't think it would fool him. Besides, I'd rather have him and Lew both against the chief just now."

She pouted and said:

"You're just hard to get along with. You think you know it all. Take me out tonight? I've got a new dress and hat that will knock 'em all cock-eyed."

"Yeah."

"Come up for me around eight." She patted my cheek with a warm soft hand, said "Ta-Ta," and went out as the telephone began jingling.

IV

"The chief wants to know if you can drop in and see him for a little minute," said a bass voice.

"Tell him I'm on my way."

"I'll do that."

I stalled a few minutes, giving Dinah Brand time to get away from the hotel, and then went up to the City Hall. A pock-marked sergeant, one of the three men in the chief's outer office, told me Noonan was in the Identification Bureau on the second floor.

"He sent for me," I said. "Shall I wait here or go up?"

The sergeant said:

"If he sent for you, maybe you'd—"

The door of the chief's private office came over and smashed the sergeant.

Blasting red heat quivered out of the doorway. The building rocked. Things flew around. Noise paralyzed eardrums, giving the effect of total silence.

I sat cross-legged in a corner, with a shoe in my lap. It wasn't my shoe. It was high, black and police-size. It was empty but fully laced. I put it aside and stood up, moving slowly, taking stock of myself. My back was sore. My hands were smeared with dirt and blood. A warm trickle itched on one of my cheeks. There didn't seem anything seriously the matter with me.

The air was thick with dust, smoke, and the stink of burnt chemicals. Fragments of metal, wood, plaster, clothing and glass were all over everything. None of the windows had any glass in it.

I lifted the door off the pock-marked sergeant, and was sorry I had. He hadn't any face.

The chief's secretary was huddled behind the desk, arms over head. I pulled him out flat on the floor. He was battered a lot on one side and quite still, but not dead.

Across the room the third man was stirring, on his back, taking his feet out of his chair-seat. One of his feet was in a white stocking, with no shoe. I went back to where I had dropped the shoe, picked it up, and had carried it to him before I realized what a damned silly thing that was to do.

There were a lot of men in the room and they did a lot of talking and moving around. None of it meant much to me yet.

I went to the door of the chief's private office. His room looked as if the wrath of God had hit it. The center of the floor was gone—a hole a horse could have fallen through. Around the edge of the hole the rug smouldered. The mahogany desk was a lot of splinters scattered around. The iron swivel of the chief's chair was imbedded in the plaster high up in a wall. Part of a man was lying where the bookcase had been. His hips and legs weren't there. The wickerwork waste basket had tilted on its side but was otherwise unharmed.

"Who's that?" I asked, pointing at the mangled man.

"Biddle. For God's sake, what happened?"

I was conscious enough now to recognize McGraw's voice, and Noonan's big face when he came puffing in.

"Well, well," the chief exclaimed good-naturedly, "somebody's certainly been doing something to us!"

"Did you have anybody phone me to come over?" I asked him.

"No, sir!"

"Somebody did."

"They did, did they?" He smacked his fat lips apart, shut one eye, said, "Uh-huh! And I reckon it was that same baby. I was up in Identification. Somebody gets me on the phone and asks me to hold the line. I'm holding it when I hear this racket. See it? They send you over. Then they call me up, thinking that if I answer the phone it shows I'm in my office—see? They got us together where a bomb chucked through my window will do a lot of good. They pull it fast, so we won't have much time for thinking after you find I didn't phone you. The window's too high for 'em to see in. Get it?"

I said I did. I suggested we try to do something about it. Noonan gave McGraw a flock of orders, then asked me:

"You all right?"

"Except that my back's sore and I've a damned rotten headache."

"Well, I certainly am glad it's no worse than that," he assured me, patting my shoulder. "We'll go back in—"

I moved away from his patting hand and said:

"I'm going over to my room to lie down a while."

"Better let the doc have a look at you."

"No, rest is all I need."

I went back to the hotel. One of my eyes was swollen. There were metal slivers in my left cheek. They weren't hard to get out. Cold water made my face feel human again. A bellhop fetched ammonia for my headache. I spread myself on the bed.

I was feeling a lot spryer half an hour later, when Mickey Linehan phoned.

"My bird and Dick's were together at your client's house this afternoon," he said. "Mine's been generally busy as hell, though I don't know what it's all about yet. Anything new?"

"No. Things are breaking pretty good, though."

I sprawled on the bed again until seven-thirty. Then I dressed, loaded my pockets with my gun and a pint flask of Scotch, and went up to Dinah Brand's house in Hurricane Street.

V

"Now what have you been up to?" she asked when she got a look at my face.

"Up to City Hall. Somebody tossed a package of dynamite in Noonan's window."

"Kill the big sap?" she asked hopefully.

I said it hadn't and gave her the details. She wrinkled her forehead and suggested:

"Sounds a little like something he rigged himself."

"Yeah, I noticed that, too."

"That's more than you've done to my new dress," she complained, backing off and revolving. "Do you like it?"

I said I did. She explained that the color was rose beige, and that the dinguses on the side were something or other, winding up:

"And you really think I look good in it?"

"You always look charming. Lew Yard and Pete the Finn went calling on Elihu this afternoon."

She made a face at me and said:

"You don't give a damn about my dress. What did they do there?"

"A pow-wow, I suppose."

She looked at me through her lashes and asked:

"Don't you really know where Max is?"

Then I did. There was no use admitting I hadn't known before. I said:

"At Willsson's, probably, but I haven't been interested enough to make sure."

"That's goofy of you. He's got reasons for not liking you and me. Take mama's advice and nail him quick—if you like living and like having mama live, too."

I laughed and said:

"You don't know the worst of it. Max didn't kill Noonan's brother. Tim didn't say *Max*. He tried to say *MacSwain* and died before he could finish."

She grabbed my shoulders and tried to shake my hundred and ninety pounds. She was nearly strong enough to do it.

"Damn you!" Her breath was hot in my face. Her face was white as her teeth. Rouge stood out sharply like red labels pasted on her mouth and cheeks. "If you've framed him and made me frame him you've got to kill him—now! You've—"

I don't like being manhandled, even by young women who look like something out of mythology when they're steamed up. I took her hands off my shoulders and said:

"Stop bellyaching. You're still alive."

"Yes—still. But I know Max better than you do. And I know how much chance anybody that frames him has of staying alive. It would be bad enough if we had got him right, but—"

"Don't make such a fuss over it. I've framed my millions and nothing's happened to me. Get your hat and coat and we'll feed. You'll feel better then."

"You're crazy if you think I'm going out. Not with that—"

"Stop it, sister! If he's that bad he's just as likely to get you here as any place else. So what difference does it make?"

"It makes a—You know what you're going to do? You're going to stay here till Max is put out of the way. It's your fault and you've got to look out for me. Dan's still in the hospital. You've got to stay here!"

"I can't," I said. "I've got work to do. You're all burnt up over nothing. He's probably forgotten all about you by now. Get your hat and coat. I'm hungry."

She put her face close to mine again and her eyes looked as if they had found something horrible in mine.

"Oh, you're rotten!" she said. "You don't

give a damn what happens to me! You're using me as you used the others—that dynamite you wanted! I trusted you!"

"You're dynamite, all right," I agreed, "but the rest of it's kind of foolish. You look a lot better when you're happy. Your features are heavy. Anger makes 'em downright brutal. I'm hungry, sister."

"Well, you'll eat right here," she said emphatically. "You're not going to get me outside after dark."

She meant it. She swapped the rose beige dress for an apron and took inventory of the icebox. There were potatoes, lettuce, canned soup and half a fruit cake. I went out and got a couple of steaks, rolls, asparagus and tomatoes.

When I came back she was mixing gin, vermouth and orange bitters in a quart shaker—not leaving a whole lot of space for them to move around in.

"Did you see anything?" she asked.

I sneered at her in a friendly way. We carried the cocktails into the dining-room and played bottoms-up while the meal cooked. The drinks cheered her a lot. By the time we sat down to the food she had almost forgotten her fright. She wasn't a very good cook, but we ate as if she were.

We put a couple of gin-and-seltzers in on top the dinner. She decided she wanted to go places and do things. No lousy little runt could keep her cooped up, because she had been as square with him as anybody could until he got nasty over nothing, and if he didn't like it he could go climb trees, and we'd go out to the Silver Arrow where she had meant to take me, because she had promised Reno she'd show up at his party, and anybody who thought she wouldn't was crazy as a pet cuckoo, and what did I think of that?

"Who's Reno?" I asked while she tied herself tighter in the apron by pulling the strings the wrong way.

"Reno Starkey. You'll like him. He's a right guy. I promised him I'd come to his celebration, and that's just what I'll do."

"What's he celebrating?"

"What the hell's the matter with this apron? Sprung this afternoon."

"Turn around and I'll unwind you. What was he in for? Stand still."

"Blowing a safe six or seven months ago—Aigren's, the jeweler. Reno, Put Collings, Blackie Whalen, Hank O'Marra, and a little lame guy called Step-and-a-half. They had plenty of cover—Lew Yard—but the jewelers' association dicks tied the job to 'em last week. So Noonan had to go through the motions. Doesn't mean anything. They got out on bail at five o'clock this afternoon, and that's the last anybody will hear about it. Reno's used to it. He was already out on bail for three or four other capers. Suppose you mix another little drink while I'm inserting myself in my dress."

VI

The Silver Arrow was half-way between Personville and Mock Lake. "It's not a bad dump," Dinah Brand told me as her little Marmon carried us toward it. "Polly deVoto is a good scout and anything she sells you is good, except maybe the Bourbon. You'll like her. She's a good scout. Anything you do out there's all right so long as you don't get noisy. She won't stand for a racket—not that kind. There it is. See the red and blue lights through the trees."

We rode out of the woods into full view of the roadhouse—a very electric-lighted imitation castle set close to the road.

"What do you mean she doesn't like noise?" I asked, listening to the chorus of pistols singing *Bang-bang-bang*.

"Something up," the girl muttered, stopping the car.

Two men dragging a woman between them ran out the roadhouse's front door, ran away into the darkness. A man sprinted out a side door, away. The guns were still talking. I didn't see any flashes.

Another man came out and disappeared around the back.

A man leaned far out a front second-story window, a black gun in his hand. Dinah Brand blew her breath out sharply.

From a hedge by the road a flash pointed briefly up at the man in the window. His gun flashed downward. He leaned farther out. No second flash came from the hedge.

The man in the window put a leg over the sill—bent—hung by his hands—dropped. Our car jerked forward.

The man who had dropped from the window was gathering himself up slowly on hands and knees. Dinah Brand put her face in front of mine and screamed:

"Reno!"

The man jumped up, his face to us. He made the road in three leaps—as we got to him.

Dinah had the Marmon wide open before Reno's feet were on the running-board beside me. I wrapped my arms around him and damn near dislocated them holding him on. He made it as tough as he could for me by leaning out to try for a shot at the guns that were tossing lead all around us.

Then it was all over. We were out of range, sight and sound of the Silver Arrow, speeding away from Personville.

Reno turned around and did his own holding on. I took my arms in and found that all the joints still worked. Dinah was busy with the car.

Reno said: "Thanks, kid. I needed pulling out."

"That's all right," she told him. "So this is the kind of party you throw?"

"We had guests that wasn't invited. You know the Tanner road?"

"Yes."

"Take it. It'll put us over to Mountain Boulevard and we can get back to town thataway."

The girl nodded, slowed up a little, and asked:

"Who were the uninvited guests?"

"Some guerrillas that don't know enough to lay off o' me."

"Do I know them?" she asked, too casually, as she turned the car into a narrower and rougher road.

"Let it alone, kid," Reno said. "Better get as much out of the heap as it's got."

She prodded another fifteen miles an hour out of the Marmon. She had plenty to do now holding the car on the road, and Reno had plenty holding himself on the car. Neither of them made any more conversation until the road brought us into one that had more and better paving. Then he asked:

"So you paid Whisper off?"

"Um-hmm."

"They're saying you turned rat on him."

"They would. What do you think?"

"Ditching him was all right. But throwing in with a dick and cracking the works to him is kind of sour. Damned sour, if you ask me."

He looked at me while he said it. He was a man of thirty-four or five, fairly tall, broad and heavy without fat. His eyes were large, brown, dull and set far apart in a long, slightly sallow horse-face. It was a humorless face, stolid but somehow not unpleasant. I looked at him and said nothing.

The girl said:

"If that's the way you—"

"Look out!" he barked.

We had rounded a curve. A long black car was drawn straight across the road in front of us—a barricade.

Bullets flew around us. Reno and I threw bullets around while the girl made a polo pony of the little Marmon.

She twisted it over to the left of the road, let the left wheels ride the bank high, crossed the road again with Reno's and my weight on the inside, got the right bank under the left wheels just as our side of the car began to lift in spite of our weight, slid us down in the road with our backs to the enemy, and took us out of the neighborhood by the time we had emptied our guns.

A lot of people had done a lot of shooting, but so far as we could tell nobody's bullets had hurt anybody.

Reno, holding to the door with his elbows while he pushed another clip into his automatic, said:

"Nice work, kid. You handle the bus like you meant it."

Dinah asked, "Where now?"

"Far away first. Just follow the road. We'll have to figure it out. Looks like they got the burg closed up on us. Keep your foot on it."

We put ten or twelve more miles between Personville and us. We passed a few cars, saw nothing to show we were being chased.

A short bridge rumbled under us. Reno said, "Take the right-hand branch at the top of the hill."

We took it, a dirt road that wound between trees down the side of a rock-ridged hill. Here ten miles an hour was fast going. After five minutes of this creeping Reno ordered a halt. We heard nothing, saw nothing during the half-hour we sat in the darkness. Then Reno said:

"There's an empty shack a mile or two down the way. We'll camp there, huh? There's no use trying to crash the city line again tonight."

Dinah said she would rather do anything than be shot at again. I said it was all right with me, though I'd rather have found some way back to Personville.

We followed the dirt track cautiously until our headlights settled on a small clapboard building that badly needed the paint it had never got.

"Is this it?" Dinah asked.

"Uh-huh. Stay here till I look it over," Reno said, leaving us.

He appeared in the beam of our lights at the shack door. He fumbled with keys at the padlock, got it off, opened the door, went in. Presently he came to the door and called:

"All right. Come in and make yourselves to home."

Dinah switched off the engine and got out.

"Is there a flashlight in the car?" I asked.

She said, "Yes," gave it to me, yawned, "My Gawd, I'm tired! I hope you haven't lost that flask."

The shack was a one-room affair that held an army cot covered with brown blankets, a deal table with a deck of cards and some poker chips on it, a brown iron stove, four chairs, an oil lamp, dishes, pots and pans, three shelves with canned food on them, a pile of firewood and a wheelbarrow.

Reno was lighting the lamp when we came in. He said:

"Not so lousy. I'll hide the heap and then we'll be all set till daylight."

Dinah went over to the cot, turned back the blankets, reported:

"Maybe there's things in it, but anyway it's not alive with them. Now give me that drink."

I took the top off the flask and passed it to her while Reno went outside to hide the car. When she had finished with the flask I took a shot at it. The purr of the Marmon's engine grew fainter. I opened the door and looked out. Down-hill, through trees and bushes, I could see broken flashes of white light going away. When I lost them for good I returned indoors and asked the girl:

"Have you ever had to walk back before?"

"What?"

"Reno has gone with the car."

"The dirty tramp! Thank God he left me where there's a bed, anyway!"

"That'll get you nothing."

"No?"

"No. Reno had the key to this dump. Ten to one the birds after him know about it. That's why he ditched us here. We're supposed to argue with them—hold them off his trail a while."

She got up wearily from the cot, cursed Reno, me, all men from Adam down, said disagreeably:

"You know everything. What do we do next?"

"Find a comfortable spot not too near, not too far, and wait to see what happens."

"I'm going to take the blankets."

"Maybe one won't be missed, but if you take more than that you'll tip our mitts."

"Damn your mitts," she grumbled, but she took only one blanket.

I blew out the lamp, padlocked the door

behind us, and with the help of the flashlight picked a way through the undergrowth.

On the hillside above the shack we found a little hollow from which road and shack could be not too dimly seen through foliage thick enough to hide us unless we showed a light.

I spread the blanket there and we settled down. The girl leaned against my shoulder and complained that the ground was damp, that she was cold in spite of her fur coat, that she had a cramp in her leg, that she wanted a cigarette. I gave her another drink from the flask. That bought me ten minutes of peace. Then she said:

"I'm catching cold. By the time anybody comes, if they do, I'll be sneezing and coughing loud enough to be heard in the city."

"Just once," I told her. "Then you'll be strangled."

"There's a mouse or something crawling under the blanket."

"Probably only a snake."

"Are you married?"

"Aw, don't start that!"

"Then you are?"

"No."

"I'll bet your wife's glad of it."

I was trying to find a comeback for that wisecrack when a distant light gleamed up the road. It vanished as I sh-h-hed the girl.

"What is it?" she asked.

"A light. It's gone now. Our visitors have left their car and are finishing the trip afoot."

A lot of time went by. The girl shivered with her cheek warm against mine. We heard footsteps, saw dark figures moving on the road and around the shack, without being sure whether we did or didn't.

A flashlight ended our doubt by putting a bright circle on the shack's door.

A heavy voice said:

"We'll let the broad come out."

There was a half-minute of silence while they waited for a reply from indoors. Then the same heavy voice demanded: "Coming?" More silence.

Gunfire—a familiar sound tonight—broke the silence. Something hammered boards.

"Come on!" I whispered to the girl. "We'll have a try at their car while they're making their noise."

"No, let them alone," she said, pulling my arm down as I started up. "I've had enough of it for one night. We're all right here."

"Come on!" I insisted.

She said, "I won't," and she wouldn't, and presently, while we argued, it was too late. The boys below had kicked in the door, found the joint empty, and were bellowing for their car. It came, took six or eight men aboard, and followed Reno's track down-hill.

"We might as well move in again," I said. "It's not likely they'll be back this way again tonight."

"I hope to Gawd there's still some Scotch left," she said as I helped her to her feet.

VII

The shack's supply of canned goods didn't include any solids that tempted us for breakfast. We made a meal off of coffee made with very stale water from a galvanized bucket.

A mile of walking brought us to a farm house where there was a kid who didn't mind earning a few dollars by driving us to town in the family Ford. He had a lot of questions, to which we gave him phony answers or none. He set us down in front of a little restaurant in upper King Street, where we ate quantities of waffles and fried ham.

A taxicab put us at Dinah's door a little before nine o'clock. I searched the place for her, from roof to cellar, and found neither visitors nor signs of visitors.

"When will you be back?" she asked as she went to the door with me.

"I'll try to pop in between now and midnight, if only for a few minutes. Where does Lew Yard live?"

"1622 Painter Street. Painter's three blocks

over. 1622's four blocks up. What are you going to do there?" Before I could answer she put her hands on my arm and begged: "Get Max, will you! Honest to Gawd, I'm afraid of him!"

"Maybe I'll sic Noonan on him a little later. It depends on how things work out."

She called me a damned rotten double-crossing something or other who didn't care what happened to her so long as his dirty work got done.

I went over to Painter Street. 1622 was a red brick house with a garage under the front porch. A block up the street I found Dick Foley sitting in a hired drive-yourself Buick. I got in beside him, asking:

"What's doing?"

The little Canadian said:

"Spot four—office to Willsson's—Mickey—five—home—busy—kept plant—off three-seven—Lewis maybe eight-thirty—still there."

That was supposed to inform me that he had started shadowing Lew Yard at four the previous afternoon, had tailed him to Willsson's house, where Mickey had gone behind Pete the Finn, had tailed him away at five, to his home, had seen people going in and out of the house but had not shadowed any of them, had watched the house until three in the morning, had returned to the job at seven, had seen a man who answered Stanley Lewis' description go into Yard's house at eight-thirty, and had not seen him come out.

"We'll wait for a look at him," I said. "Then you'll have to drop Yard and take a plant on Willsson's. I hear Thaler is staying there."

While we waited I told Dick what had happened to me since I last saw him.

It made him talkative.

"You asked for dynamite," he said, almost smiling. "Nice burg."

"Yeah. There they are!" Two men, hatted and overcoated, were coming down Yard's porch steps. One of them was a slim man of forty. "That's Willsson's secretary, right enough," I said. "The other's Yard?"

"Yes."

At that distance all I could make out was that he was tall, gaunt, and had white hair. He unlocked the garage door, opened it, and Lewis followed him in.

"We might as well see where they go before we drop them," I decided.

Dick put the Buick's engine in motion.

The bottom of Lew Yard's house blew apart, sifting bricks and mortar all over the street.

"More dynamite," Dick said.

I jumped out of the car and told him:

"Beat it! Go up and keep your eye on Willsson's."

The neighbors were all out by then. The dynamited house was half-hidden by a cloud of dust. A policeman was running up the street toward it. Other people were following his example.

The dust cleared a little. The upper part of the house toppled forward, sprawled down lazily over the blasted garage, burying it.

I hung around the fringes of the gathering crowd until a squad of coppers, a couple of loads of firemen arrived, failed to find anybody alive in the ruins, and began digging for corpses. Then I went down to my hotel.

There was a letter from the Old Man:

"Send by return mail full explanation of present operation and of circumstances under which you accepted it, with your daily reports to date."

I put the letter in my pocket and hoped things would keep breaking fast. To send him the information he wanted at that time would have been the same as handing in my resignation. I bent a fresh collar around my neck and trotted over to the City Hall.

The chief of police had moved across the corridor from the dynamited office, to one that had no windows for anybody to chuck things through.

"Hullo," he said. "I was hoping you'd show up. Tried to get you at your hotel, but they said you hadn't been in. How's the head? And the back? That certainly is fine!"

He didn't look well this morning, but under his glad-handing he seemed, for a change, genuinely glad to see me.

"Been out to view Lew Yard's remains?" I asked.

"No. To tell the truth, I'm getting sick of this killing. It—it's getting to me, on my nerves, I mean. Was Lew there?"

"Yeah," I said, surprised, "and Stanley Lewis, Willsson's secretary."

"Sure of that?" he asked, not looking at me.

"I saw them come out of the house, go into the garage—then the blow-up. Didn't they find them?"

"Not yet. Mrs. Yard and the servant girl were found, both dead, but the last I heard they hadn't got to the bottom of the ruins yet, so I thought maybe there was a chance that Lew hadn't been home. Was the explosion in the garage?"

"Yeah. My guess is that a bundle of dynamite was hooked up to his starter. Think it's the same party that had a try at us yesterday?"

"God knows," he said wearily. "It's so damned easy to get hold of a fistful of dynamite in these mining towns that everybody starts tossing it around as soon as trouble breaks."

"Who do you think tossed yesterday's batch? Pete the Finn—because we shot up his warehouse?"

Noonan winced and said:

"God knows!"

I considered his low spirits and asked:

"Anybody knocked off in the battle at the Silver Arrow last night?"

"Three."

"Who are they?"

"A pair of yeggs*—Blackie Whalen and Put Collings—that only got out on bail around five yesterday evening, and Dutch Jake, gunman."

"What was it all about?"

"Just a roughhouse, I guess. It seems Blackie and Put and the others that got out with them

_____

* burglars

were celebrating with a lot of friends, and it wound up in smoke."

"All of 'em Lew Yard's men?"

"I don't know anything about that yet."

I got up, said, "Oh, all right," and started for the door.

"Hey, wait," he called. "Don't run off like that. I guess they were."

I came back to my chair. Noonan watched the top of his desk. His face was gray, flabby, damp—like fresh putty.

"Thaler's staying at Willsson's," I told him.

He jerked his head up. His eyes darkened. Then his mouth twitched, and he let his head sag again. His eyes faded.

"I can't go through with it," he mumbled. "I'm sick of this killing. I can't stand any more of this."

"Sick enough to give up the idea of evening the score for Tim's killing—if it'll make peace?" I asked.

"I am."

"That's what started it," I said. "If you're willing to call that off, it ought to be possible to stop it all."

He raised his face and looked at me with eyes that were almost childishly hopeful.

"Tell the others how you feel about it," I went on. "They ought to be as sick of it as you are. Have a get-together with 'em and make peace."

"They'd think I was up to some kind of trick," he objected.

"Have your meeting at Willsson's. Thaler's there now. You'd be the one who risked tricks going there. Are you afraid of that?"

He frowned and asked:

"Will you go with me?"

"Sure, if you want me."

"Thanks," he said. "I—I'll try."

VIII

All the other delegates to the peace conference were on hand when Noonan and I arrived at Elihu Willsson's home at the appointed time, nine o'clock that night. Everybody nodded to us, but the greetings didn't go any farther than that.

Pete the Finn was the only one I hadn't met before. The bootleg king was a big-boned man of fifty, with a completely bald head. His forehead was small, his jaws enormous—wide, heavy, bulging with muscles.

We sat around Willsson's library table.

Old Elihu sat at the head. The short-clipped hair on his round, pink skull was like silver in the light. His round blue eyes were hard, domineering, under their tangled white brows. Mouth and chin were horizontal lines.

On his right sat Pete the Finn, watching everything with tiny black eyes that never moved. Reno Starkey sat next to the bootlegger. Reno's sallow horseface was as stolidly dull as his eyes.

Max Thaler was tilted back in a chair on Willsson's left. The little gambler's carefully pressed pants-legs were crossed carelessly. A cigarette hung from one corner of the thin, tight-lipped mouth that kept his delicately molded dark face from being the face of a wax-model. I sat next to Thaler. Noonan sat on my other side.

Elihu Willsson opened the meeting.

He said things couldn't go on the way they were going. We were all sensible men, reasonable men, grown men, who had been in the world long enough to know that no matter who a man was he couldn't have everything his own way all the time. Compromises were things everybody had to make sometimes. To get what he wanted a man had to give up something that somebody else wanted. He said he was sure that what we all wanted most just now was to stop this senseless killing. He said he was sure that everything could be frankly discussed and settled in an hour without turning Personville into a slaughterhouse.

It wasn't a bad speech.

When it was over there was a moment of silence. Thaler looked at Noonan, as if he expected something of him. The rest of us did the same. Noonan's face turned red and he spoke huskily:

"Whisper, I'll forget you killed Tim!" He stood up and held out a beefy hand. "Here's my hand on it."

Thaler's thin lip-corners curved scornfully.

"Your——of a brother needed killing, but I didn't kill him," he whispered coldly.

Red became purple in the chief's face. I said loudly:

"Wait, Noonan! We're doing this wrong. We're not going to get anywhere unless everybody comes clean. Be on the up-and-up or we'll be worse off than if we hadn't got together. Mac-Swain killed Tim." I added a lie for the final touch: "And you know it!"

He stared at me with astonished eyes. He gaped. He couldn't understand what I had done to him.

I looked at the others, tried to look virtuous as hell, asked:

"That's settled, isn't it? Let's get the rest of the kicks squared." I addressed Pete the Finn: "How do you feel about yesterday's accident to your warehouse? And the four men?"

"One hell of an accident!" he growled.

I explained:

"Noonan didn't know you were using the joint. He went there thinking it empty, just to clear the way for a job in town. Your men shot first and he really thought he had run into Thaler's hiding place. Then when he found he'd been stepping in your puddle he lost his head and touched the place off."

Thaler was watching me with a hard little smile around eyes and mouth. Reno Starkey was all dull stolidity. Elihu Willsson was leaning toward me, his old eyes sharp and wary. I couldn't afford to look at Noonan. I was in a good spot if I played my hand right, but it was easy to go wrong.

"The men, they get paid for taking chances," Pete the Finn rumbled. "For the other—twenty-five grand will make it right."

"All right, Pete. Twenty-five thousand. All right," Noonan agreed. "I'll give you the check tomorrow."

I had to fight to keep from laughing at the

quickness and eagerness with which he surrendered. He was licked now, I knew, broken, willing to do anything to save his fat neck. I could look at him safely. He wouldn't look at me. He sat down and looked at nobody. He was busy trying to look as if he didn't expect to be murdered before he got away from these enemies to whom I had betrayed him. In a way it was pitiful. But a pitiful fat brute is more disgusting than pitiful. I went back to my work, turning to Elihu Willsson.

"Do you want to squawk about your bank being knocked over, or do you like it?"

Before he could answer, Max Thaler touched my arm and suggested:

"We could tell better who's entitled to squawk if you'd spill the story first, maybe."

I was glad to.

"Noonan wanted to nail you, Thaler, but he either got word or expected it from Lew Yard and Willsson to let you alone. So he thought if he had the bank stuck up, framing you for it, your backers would ditch you. Yard, I understand, was supposed to put his O.K. on all the capers in town. You'd be going over into his territory, and gypping Willsson. That was supposed to make them mad enough that they'd help him cop you. He didn't know you were staying there.

"Reno and his mob were in jail. Reno was Yard's pup, but he didn't mind crossing his headman. He already had an idea that he was about ready to take the city away from Lew. Noonan fakes a tip that you're at Cedar Hill, and takes all the bulls he can't trust out there with him, even cleaning the traffic cops out of Broadway, so Reno would have no interference. McGraw and the bulls that are in it with Noonan let Reno and his mob sneak out of the can, pull the job, and duck back in. Nice alibi. Then they get sprung on bail a couple of hours later.

"It looks as if Lew tumbled to the trick. He sent Dutch Jake and some other boys out to the Silver Arrow to teach Reno and his mob not to take things in their own hands like that. But Reno got clear, got back to the city. It was either him or Lew then, so he made sure who it would

be by prying himself into Lew's garage, attaching some dynamite to Lew's car. Reno seems to have had the dope, because I notice that right now he's holding down a seat that would have been Lew's if Lew hadn't been blown to hell."

Everybody was sitting very still, as if to call attention to the fact that they weren't doing anything. Nobody had any friends. It was no time for careless motions.

Thaler whispered very softly:

"Didn't you skip some of it?"

"You mean about Jerry?" I went on being the life of the party: "I was coming back to that. I don't know why he didn't escape when you did, how Noonan came to recapture him; but he did catch him. I don't know whether Jerry went along willingly on the stick-up or not. But he was dropped and left in front of the bank because he was your pal and his being killed there was supposed to tie the job to you. He was kept in the car until the get-away was on. Then he was put out, and was shot in the back. He was facing the bank, with his back to the car. Dinah Brand saw it."

Thaler nodded to me, looked at Reno Starkey, whispered:

"Well?"

Reno looked with dull eyes at Thaler and asked calmly:

"What of it?"

Thaler stood up, said to Willsson and Pete the Finn: "Deal me out." To me: "Thanks." He walked to the door.

Pete the Finn stood up, leaning on the table with bony hands, speaking from deep in his chest:

"Whisper!" And when Thaler had stopped and turned to face him: "I'm telling you this. That damned gun-work is out. All of you understand it. You've got no brains to know what is best for yourselves. So I'll tell you. This busting the town open is no good for business. I won't have it. You'll be nice boys or I'll show you what playing with guns and dynamite is. I've got me an army of young fellows that know what to do on either end of the gun. I got to have 'em in my racket. If I got to use 'em on you I'll use 'em on you. Be good. If you think any of you or all of you can get together mobs that'll stop my young fellows—just don't pay attention to what I tell you. That's all—if you're going to fight I'll give you something to fight."

Pete the Finn sat down. Thaler looked thoughtful for a moment and went out without saying or showing what he had thought.

His going made the others impatient. None wanted to remain until some earlier departer had time to accumulate a few guns in the neighborhood.

In a very few minutes Elihu Willsson and I were the only occupants of his library.

IX

We sat and looked at one another. Presently he said:

"How would you like to be chief of police?"

"Not at all. I'm a rotten errand boy."

"I don't mean with this bunch—after we clean them out."

"And get another just like 'em?"

"Damn you," he snarled, "it wouldn't hurt to take a nicer tone to a man old enough to be your father!"

"Who curses me and hides behind his age," I added.

Anger brought a vein out blue in his forehead. Then he laughed.

"You're a damned nasty talking lad," he said, "but I can't say you haven't done what I paid you to do."

"A swell lot of help I got out of you!"

"Did you need wet-nursing? I gave you the money and turned you loose. What more do you want?"

"You old pirate," I said, "I blackmailed you into it! And you played against me all the way, until tonight, when even you can see they're hell-bent on blasting each other out of the game. Now you're talking about what you did for me!"

"Pirate!" he repeated. "Son, if I hadn't been a pirate I'd be working for the Anaconda Copper Company today—straw boss—and there'd be no Personville Mining Corporation. You're a damned little woolly lamb, yourself, I suppose. I believe that after what you've done to Personville, what you did to this friendly gathering just now."

"I was had, son, where the hair was short. There were things I didn't like, worse things that I didn't know about until this night. But I was caught, and what could I do but bide my time? And don't think I wasn't doing that. Why since that damned Whisper Thaler has been here I've been a prisoner in my own home—understand—a damned hostage!"

"Tough! Where do you stand now?" I demanded. "Are you behind me?"

"If you win."

I got up and said: "I hope to God you get caught with them!"

He said: "I reckon you do, but I won't." He squinted his eyes merrily at me. "I'm financing you. Doesn't that show I mean well? Don't be too hard on me, son, I kind of—"

I said: "Go to hell!" and walked out.

Dick Foley in his hired Buick was at the next corner. I had him drive me over to within a block of Dinah Brand's house and walked the rest of the way.

"You look tired," she said when I followed her into the living-room. "Been working?"

"Yeah. Attending a peace conference out of which at least a dozen murders ought to grow."

The phone rang. She answered it and called me.

Reno Starkey's voice:

"I thought maybe you'd like to hear about Noonan being shot to hell and gone in front of his house tonight just as he was getting out of his heap. You never saw anybody that was deader. Must have had thirty bullets in him."

"Thanks."

Dinah's big blue eyes asked questions.

"First fruits of the peace conference, plucked by Whisper Thaler," I told her. "Where's the gin?"

THE 19TH MURDER

BY DASHIELL HAMMETT

A Complete Novelette

The fourth and concluding adventure of the Continental detective in "The Cleansing of Poisonville," a dramatic and intensely exciting climax to one of the greatest stories of politics and crime ever written.

IN FEBRUARY BLACK MASK.

BLACK MASK, FEBRUARY 1928

The 19th Murder

BY DASHIELL HAMMETT

The Continental detective cleans up.

"RENO STARKEY, wasn't it?" Dinah Brand asked as I put the phone down.

"Yeah. He thought I'd like to hear about Poisonville being all out of police chiefs."

"You mean—?"

"Noonan was knocked off in front of his house tonight, according to Reno. Haven't you got any gin, or do you just like making me beg for it?"

"You know where it is. He owes his death to one of your cute little tricks!"

I went back into her kitchen, opened the top of the refrigerator and attacked the ice with an ice pick that had a six-inch awl-sharp blade set in a round blue and white handle. The girl stood in the doorway and asked questions. I didn't answer them while I put ice, gin, lemon juice and seltzer together in a couple of glasses.

"I hope to God the gin improves your disposition," she said as we carried the drinks into her dining-room. "What have you been doing? You look ghastly!"

I put my glass on the table, sat down in front of it, and complained:

"This damned town's getting me. If I don't get back to San Francisco soon I'll be going blood-simple like the natives. There's been what? Eighteen murders since I've been here. Donald Willsson, Ike Bush, the four wops and the dick out at Cedar Hill; Jerry Hooper, the pockmarked sergeant and Biddle when the chief's office was dynamited; Lew Yard, his wife and servant, and Stanley Lewis when Yard's joint was blown up; Dutch Jake, Blackie Whalen and Put Collings at the Silver Arrow last night, and now Noonan. An even dozen and a half of 'em, not counting the more or less necessary killings, like the blond kid Whisper got here, the prowler old Elihu got, and Big Nick, the bull I potted. A dozen and a half of 'em in a week, and more coming up!"

She frowned, said sharply:

"Don't look like that!"

I laughed and said:

"I've arranged a death or two in my time, when it was necessary. But this is the first time I've ever had the killing fever. It started right enough. When old Elihu Willsson ran out on me after hiring me to clean town, there was nothing I could do but set the boys against each other and have 'em wipe themselves out for me. Without Elihu's backing I couldn't have got anywhere fooling with courts and legal evidence. I had to do the job the best way I could, which meant stacking things so everybody—Pete the Finn, Whisper Thaler, Lew Yard and Noonan, especially—would think everybody else was double-crossing them. That couldn't lead any-where but to a lot of killings. How in hell could I help it? The job couldn't be swung any other way without Elihu's support."

"Well, you couldn't help it, so what's the use of making a fuss over it?" The girl's eyes were uneasy. "Drink your drink."

I drank half of it and felt the urge to talk some more.

"Play with enough murder, and it gets you one of two ways. It makes you sick, or you get to like it. It got Noonan the first way. I saw him this afternoon—after Yard was killed. He was green around the gills, all the stomach gone out of him, willing to do anything to make peace in Poisonville. I took him in, suggesting that he and the other survivors get together and patch up their differences. He fell for it after I'd promised to attend the peace conference with him.

"We had it tonight at Willsson's. Besides old Elihu, there were Pete the Finn, Whisper, Reno Starkey—who's making a play for the vacancy left by Yard—Noonan and me. It was a nice party. Pretending to try to clear away every-body's misunderstanding by coming clean all around, I stripped Noonan naked and threw

him to the wolves—him and Reno. I published the news that they had pulled the First National Bank stick-up, killing Jerry Hooper to pin the job on his friend Whisper.

"That broke up the peace conference. Whis-per got up and declared himself out. Before he left Pete the Finn made a speech at everybody, telling them where they stood. Pete said the quarreling was hurting his bootleg business and he wasn't going to stand for any more of it. He said anybody that started anything from then on could expect to have his army of booze guards turned loose on them. Whisper didn't look impressed."

"He wouldn't," the girl agreed.

"Whisper was the first man out, and he seems to have had time to collect some rods in front of Noonan's house by the time the chief reached home. The chief was shot down. Pete the Finn looks like a man who means what he says. Then he'll be out after Whisper. Reno was as much to blame as Noonan for Jerry Hooper's murder, so Whisper will be gunning for him. And, knowing it, Reno will be out to get Whisper first. Besides that, Reno will have a job on his hands stand-ing off those of the late Lew Yard's underlings who don't happen to want Reno for a boss. Any trouble Reno makes will bring Pete the Finn's beer-mob down on him, too. All in all, one swell dish."

Dinah Brand reached across the table, patted my hand, said:

"It's not your fault, darling. You say yourself there was nothing else you could do. Finish your drink and we'll have another."

"There was plenty else I could do," I con-tradicted her. "Old Elihu ran out on me at first simply because these birds had too much on him for him to risk a break with them unless he was sure he could wipe them out. He couldn't see how I was going to win, so he played with them. But he's not their brand of cutthroat, and besides, he thinks Personville is his own prop-erty, and doesn't take kindly to having them run it for him.

"I could have gone to him this afternoon

and showed him how I had them sewed up, had enough on them to ruin the whole lot. He'd have listened to reason. He'd have come over to my side, have given me the backing I needed to swing the play legally. I could have done that. But it's easier to have 'em killed off—easier and surer and—now that I'm feeling this way—more satisfying.

"Listen: I sat at Willsson's table tonight and played 'em like you play trout and got just as much fun out of it. Understand? I looked at Noonan and knew he couldn't live another day because of what I was doing to him, and I laughed and felt warm and happy inside. That's what this damned burg has done to me!"

She smiled too indulgently and spoke too softly:

"You exaggerate so, honey! They deserve all they get. I wish you wouldn't look like that. You make me feel creepy."

I laughed, picked up the glasses and went out into the kitchen for more gin. When I came back she frowned at me over anxious dark eyes and asked:

"What in the name of God did you bring the ice pick in for?"

"To show you how my mind's running. Yesterday, if I thought about it at all, it was as a good tool to pry off hunks of ice." I ran a finger down its half-foot of round steel blade to the needle point. "Not a bad thing to pin a man to his clothes with. That's the way I'm getting, on the level. There's a piece of copper wire lying out in the gutter in front of the house—thin and soft and just long enough to twist around a neck with enough ends to hold good. I had one hell of a time to keep from picking it up and putting it in my pocket, just in case—"

"You're crazy!"

"I told you I was going blood-simple."

"I don't like it. Put that thing back in the kitchen and sit down and be sensible."

I obeyed at least two-thirds of the order.

"The trouble with you is," she scolded, "your nerves are shot to hell. You've been through too much excitement the last few days. Keep it up

and you're going to have a nervous breakdown— the heebie-jeebies for fair."

I held up a hand with spread fingers. It was steady enough. She looked at it and said:

"That doesn't mean anything. It's inside you. Why don't you sneak off for a couple of days— rest? You've got things stirred up here enough to run themselves. Let's go down to Salt Lake. It'll do you good."

"Can't, sister. Somebody's got to stay here to count the dead. Besides, the whole program is arranged for the present combination of people and things. Our going out of town would change that. The chances are I'd have to do the job all over again."

"Nobody would have to know you were gone, and *I've* got nothing to do with it."

"Since when?"

She leaned forward, made her eyes small, asked:

"Now what are you getting at?"

"Nothing. Just wondering how you got to be a disinterested bystander all of a sudden. Forgotten that it was because of you Donald Willsson was killed and the whole thing started? Forgotten that the dope you gave me on Whisper after you broke with him kept the job from petering out in the middle?"

"You know just as well as I do that none of that was my fault," she said hotly. "It's all past anyhow. You're just dragging it up because you're in a hell of a frame of mind tonight and want to argue."

"It wasn't past last night, when you were scared stiff Whisper was going to kill you."

"Will you stop talking about killing!"

"Young Albury once told me that Bill Quint had threatened to kill you," I said.

"Stop it!"

"You seem to have a gift for arousing murderous notions in your boy friends. There's Albury waiting trial now for killing Donald Willsson because of you. There's Whisper, who's got you shivering in corners. I've got a private idea that Dan Rolff's going to have a try at you some day."

"Dan? You're crazy! Why, I—"

"Yeah. He was a lunger and down and out and you took him in. You gave him a home and all the laudanum he needed. You use him for errand boy. You've slapped his face in front of me and I've seen you knock him around in front of others. He's in love with you. One of these days you're going to wake up and find he's whittled your neck away."

"I'm glad one of us knows what you're talking about, if you do," she said as she carried our empty glasses through the kitchen door.

I lighted a cigarette and wondered why I felt the way I did, wondered if there was anything to this presentiment business or if my nerves were just ragged.

"The next best thing for you to do," the girl advised me when she returned with the full glasses, "is to get plastered and forget everything for a few hours. I put a double slug of gin in yours. You need it."

"It's not me," I said. "It's you. Every time I mention killing you jump on me. You're a woman. You think if nothing's said about it, none of the God knows how many people in town who might want to kill you will. That's silly. Nothing we say is going to make Whisper, for instance—"

"Please, please stop!" she begged, so softly that I had to watch her lips to make out the words. "I am silly. I am afraid of the words. I'm afraid of him. I—Oh, why didn't you put him out of the way when I asked you?"

"Sorry," I said, meaning it.

"Do you think he'll—?"

"I don't know," I told her, "and, as you say, there's no use talking about it. The thing to do is to drink—though there doesn't seem to be much authority to this gin."

"That's you, not the gin. Do you want an honest to God rear?"

"I'd drink nitroglycerine tonight."

"That's just about what you're going to get," she promised me.

She rattled bottles in the kitchen and brought me in a glass of what looked like the stuff we had been drinking. I sniffed at it and said:

"Some of Dan's laudanum, huh? He still in the hospital?"

"Yes. There's your nitroglycerine, mister, if that's what you want."

I put the doped gin down my throat. Presently I felt more comfortable. Time went by as we drank and talked in a world that was rosy, cheerful and full of friendship and peace on earth.

She stuck to gin. I tried that for a while, too, then had another gin and laudanum. It finished me up nicely. For a while I played a game, trying to hold my eyes open as if I were awake, even though I couldn't see a damned thing out of them. When the trick wouldn't fool her any more I gave it up.

The last I remembered was her helping me in to the living-room Chesterfield.

II

I dreamed I was sitting on a bench, facing the tumbling fountain in Harlem Park, Baltimore, beside a woman who wore a veil. I had come there with her. She was some one I knew well. But now I had suddenly forgotten who she was. I couldn't see her face because of the long black veil. I thought if I said something to her I would recognize her voice when she answered. But I was very embarrassed and it took me a long time to find anything to say. Finally I asked her if she knew a man named Carroll T. Harris. She spoke, but the roar and swish of the tumbling fountain drowned her voice, and I could hear nothing.

Fire engines went out Edmondson Avenue. She left me to run after them. As she ran she cried, "Fire! Fire!" I recognized her voice then, knew who she was—some one important to me. I ran after her, but it was too late. She and the fire engines were gone. I walked streets hunting for her—half the streets in the United States— Gay Street, Mount Royal Avenue in Baltimore, Colfax Avenue in Denver, Aetna Road, St. Clair Avenue in Cleveland, McKinney Avenue in Dallas, Lamartine, Cornell, Amory Streets in Boston, Berry Boulevard in Louisville, Lexington Avenue in New York—until I came to Victoria Street in Jacksonville, where I heard her voice again, though I still could not see her.

She was calling a name, not mine, one strange to me. I could hear her calling but no matter how fast I walked or in what direction, I could get no nearer the voice. It was the same distance from me in the street that runs past the Federal Building in El Paso as in Detroit's Grand Circus Park. Then the voice stopped. Discouraged, tired, I went into the lobby of the hotel that faces the railroad station in Rocky Mount, North Carolina, to rest. While I sat there a train came in. She got off it and came into the lobby, over to me, and began kissing me. I was very uncomfortable because everybody stood around looking at us and laughing.

That dream ended there.

I dreamed I was in a strange city, hunting for a man I hated. I had an open knife in my coat pocket and meant to kill him with it when I found him. It was Sunday morning. Church bells were ringing, crowds of people were in the streets, going to and from church. I walked almost as far as in the first dream, but always in this same strange city.

Then the man I was after yelled at me, and I saw him. He was a small brown man who wore an immense sombrero. He was standing on the steps of a tall building on the far side of a wide plaza, laughing at me. Between us the plaza was crowded with people, packed shoulder to shoulder. Keeping one hand on the open knife in my pocket, I ran toward the little brown man, running on the heads and shoulders of the people in the plaza. It was difficult running. I slipped and floundered. The heads and shoulders were of unequal heights and not evenly spaced.

The little brown man stood on the steps and laughed until I had almost reached him. Then he ran into the tall building. I chased him up miles of spiral stairway, always just an inch more than a hand's reach behind him. We came to the roof. He ran straight across to the edge and jumped just as one of my hands touched him. His shoul-

der slid out of my hand. My hand knocked his sombrero off. My fingers closed on his head, wrapping themselves around it. It was a smooth, hard, round head, no larger than a large egg.

Gripping his head with one hand, I tried to bring my knife out of my pocket with the other—and realized that I had gone off the edge of the roof with him. We dropped giddily down toward the millions of upturned faces in the plaza below—miles down. . . .

I opened my eyes in the dull light of morning sun filtered through drawn blinds. I was lying face down on the dining-room floor, my head resting on my left forearm. My right arm was stretched straight out. My right hand held the round blue-and-white handle of Dinah Brand's ice pick. The pick's six-inch needle-shaped blade was buried in the left side of Dinah Brand's bosom.

She was lying on her back—dead. Her long muscular legs were stretched out toward the kitchen door. There was, I noticed, a run in the front of her right stocking.

Very slowly and gently, as if I were afraid of awakening her, I let go the ice pick, withdrew my arm, and got up.

My eyes burned. My throat and mouth were hot, woolly. I went into the kitchen, found a bottle of gin, tilted it to my mouth, and kept it there until I had to breathe. The kitchen clock said 7:41.

With the gin in my belly, I returned to the dining-room, switched on the lights, and looked at the dead girl.

Not much blood was in sight—a spot the size of a silver dollar around the hole the ice pick made in her blue silk dress. There was a bruise on her right cheek, just under the cheek bone. Another bruise, finger-made, was on her right wrist. Her hands were empty. I moved her enough to look under her body. Nothing was there.

I examined the room. If anything had been changed in it since we sat drinking there the previous night I couldn't find it. I went back to the kitchen and found no recognizable changes.

The back door was locked, with no marks to show it had been tampered with. I went to the front door, failed to find any marks on it. I went through the house from roof to cellar, and learned nothing. The girl's jewelry—on her dressing-table—and four or five hundred dollars in paper money—in her handbag, on a bedroom chair—were undisturbed. The windows were all right.

In the dining-room again, I knelt beside the dead girl and used my handkerchief to wipe the ice pick handle clean of any prints my fingers might have left on it. I did the same to glasses, bottles, doors, light buttons, and the pieces of furniture I had touched, or was likely to have touched. Then I washed my hands, couldn't find any blood on my clothes, made sure I was leaving none of my property behind, and went to the front door. I opened it, wiped the inner knob, closed it behind me, wiped the outer knob, and went away.

[III]

From a drug store in upper Broadway I telephoned Dick Foley, at the National Hotel, and asked him to come over to my room in the Great Western. He arrived a few minutes after I had got there.

"Dinah Brand was killed in her house last night or early this morning," I told him, "stabbed with an ice pick. The police don't know it yet. I've told you enough about her for you to know there are any number of people who might have reasons for getting her. There are three I want looked up first. A red named Bill Quint, who threatened to kill her when she gave him the air some time ago, Whisper Thaler, and the lunger, Dan Rolff.

"Quint lives at the Miner's Hotel in Forest Street. He's a square-built man of thirty, broad, thick face, kind of grayish, even to the mouth. He goes in for flowing, red ties. You already have Whisper's and Rolff's descriptions. Rolff is, or was, in the hospital, getting over the effects of

being blackjacked. I don't know which hospital, but try the City first. Get hold of Mickey Linehan. He's still keeping his eye on Pete the Finn. Tell him to lay off that and give you a hand on this. Run those three down. See if you can learn where they were last night. And time means something."

The little Canadian operative had been watching me curiously while I talked. Now he started to say something, changed his mind, grunted "Righto," and departed.

I went out to look for Reno Starkey. After an hour of searching I located him, by telephone, in a Ronney Street rooming-house.

"By yourself?" he asked when I had said I wanted to see him.

"Yeah."

He said I could come out, and told me how to get there. I took a taxi. It was a dingy two-story house near the edge of town. A couple of men loitered in front of a grocer's on the corner above. Another pair sat on the low wooden steps of the house down at the other corner. None of the four was conspicuously refined in appearance.

When I rang the bell at the address Reno had given me, two men opened the door. They weren't so mild-looking either.

I was taken upstairs to a shabby room where Reno, collarless and in shirt-sleeves and vest, sat tilted back in a chair, with his feet on the window-sill.

He nodded his sallow horse face and said:

"Pull a chair over."

The men who had brought me up went away, closing the door. I sat down and said:

"I want an alibi. Dinah Brand was killed last night, after I left her. There's no chance of my being copped for it, but, with Noonan dead, I don't know how I'm hitched up with the police department. I don't want to give 'em any openings to even try to hang anything on me. If I've got to, I can prove where I was last night, but you can save me a hell of a lot of trouble if you will."

Reno looked at me with dull brown eyes and asked:

"Why pick on me?"

"You phoned me there. You're the only person who knows I was there the first part of the night. I'd have to fix it with you even if I got the alibi somewhere else, wouldn't I?"

He asked:

"You didn't croak her, did you?"

I said, "No," casually.

He stared out of the window for a little while before he spoke:

"You was at the Tanner House in Tanner. That's a little burg twenty-thirty miles up the hill. You went up there after the meeting bust, and stayed till morning. A guy named Ricker that hangs around Murry's with a hire heap drove you up and back. You ought to know what you was doing up there. Give me your sig and I'll have it put on the register."

"Thanks," I said as I unscrewed my fountain pen.

"Don't say 'em. I'm doing this because I need all the friends I can get. When the time comes that you sit in between me and Whisper and Pete I don't expect the sour end of it."

"You won't get it," I promised. "Who's going to be chief of police now?"

"McGraw's acting chief. He'll likely cinch it."

"How'll he play?"

"With Pete. Rough stuff will hurt his grift just like it does Pete's beer racket. It'll have to be hurt some. I'd be a swell palooka to sit still with a guy like Whisper on the loose. It's me or him. Think he croaked the broad?"

"He had reasons enough," I said as I gave him the slip of paper on which I had scribbled my name. "She double-crossed him, sold him out plenty."

"You and her was kind of—"

Somebody in the street whistled a bar from *I Left My Sugar Standing in the Rain*.

Reno dropped his feet to the floor and stood on them. He put his back to the wall beside the window, twisting his head over his shoulder so he could look down into the street without showing himself.

Through the window came the hum of big automobile engines tuned to the last fraction.

I got up and went to the other window, imitating Reno's position. It gave me a good view of the edge of the sidewalk in front just as a long black car that looked like a 1912 Pierce-Arrow halted there. The nose of another snuggled up behind it.

Men got out—not hiding their guns.

I looked at Reno. He was stolid as ever. Friends, I thought.

Reno stretched an arm across the window, high, and let it fall.

From the door and windows of a house that faced ours, across the street, a lot of guns were fired. More guns made more noise downstairs in our building. Some of the men who had got out of the cars below got back in them. The cars slid away from the curb, straightened themselves out, and roared off down the street with slugs sprinkling around them.

The shooting stopped.

I let Reno be first to put his head out the window. Nothing happened to it. I risked mine. Five men were lying on our sidewalk. Only two of them were squirming.

We pulled our heads in as the door of our room opened. A long-legged youngster of twenty-two or three, with a thin freckled face around reckless eyes, was shoving a .45 into a shoulder-holster as he came into the room.

"Whisper wasn't there?" Reno said.

"Nope. Just like you said—that little— wouldn't walk into the trap. He'd send the boys."

"We'll slide along." Reno picked up a coat and hat from a chair and followed the long-legged boy to the door, telling me, "You might as well go along with me and Hank."

I went along. Three other men joined us as we climbed, by way of chair and table, through a trap door to the roof. We crossed that roof and half a dozen others that were between the rooming-house and the lower cross street. We walked three roofs down the side street, and went through another trap door into a storeroom in one corner of a garage's second story.

We waited in the storeroom until long-legged Hank—I took him to be the Hank O'Marra who had been in on the First National stick-up with Reno—went out, staid ten minutes, and returned. Then we went downstairs one at a time and got into one of the dozen or more cars on the ground floor. There were only a couple of garage men in sight. They kept their backs to us while we were there.

"Where do you want to be dropped?" Reno asked me as we drove out of the garage.

"Any car line that'll take me down-town will do," I said, and asked him where I could reach him if I needed to.

"Know Peak Murry?" he asked.

"I've met him." He ran a pool room in Broadway, and was on the outs with Whisper.

"Anything you give him will get to me. That Tanner lay* is all set."

"Thanks," I said.

IV

Downtown, I went first to police headquarters. I found McGraw holding down the chief's desk. His blond-lashed eyes looked at me suspiciously and the lines in his leathery face were even deeper and sourer than usual.

"When'd you see Dinah Brand last?" he asked before the door was closed behind me. His voice rasped disagreeably through his bony nose.

"Ten-forty o'clock last night, or thereabout," I said. "Why?"

"Where?"

"1232 Hurricane Street—her house."

"How long were you there?"

"Five minutes, maybe ten."

"Why?"

"Why what?"

"Why didn't you stay any longer than that?"

"What," I asked, sitting down in the chair he hadn't offered me, "makes it any of your business?"

_____
* job

He glared at me while he filled his lungs so he could yell, "Murder!" in my face.

I laughed and said:

"You don't think *she* had anything to do with Noonan's killing!"

I wanted a cigarette, but cigarettes were too well known as first aids to the nervous for me to take a chance on one just then. McGraw was trying to look through my eyes. I let him look, having all sorts of confidence in my belief that, like a lot of people, I looked most honest when I was lying.

Presently he gave up the gimlet-eye posturing and asked:

"Why not?"

That was weak.

I said: "All right, why not?" indifferently, offered him a cigarette and took one myself. Then I added: "My guess is that Whisper did it."

"Was he there?" For once McGraw cheated his nose, snapping the words off his teeth.

"Was he where?"

"At Brand's!"

"No," I said, wrinkling my forehead. "Why should he have been there if he was off killing Noonan?"

"Damn Noonan!" the acting chief exclaimed irritably. "What do you keep dragging him in for?"

I tried to look at him as if I thought he was crazy. He said:

"Dinah Brand was murdered last night."

I said: "Yeh?"

"Now will you answer my questions?"

"Of course. I was at Willsson's with Noonan and the others. After I left there, around tenthirty, I dropped in at her house to tell her I had to go up to Tanner. I had half a date with her. I staid there about ten minutes—just long enough to have a drink. There was nobody else there, unless they were hiding. When was she killed? And how?"

McGraw told me he had sent a pair of his detectives—Shepp and Vanaman—to see the girl that morning, to see how much help she'd give the department in copping Whisper for Noonan's murder. The dicks got there at nine-thirty. The front door was ajar. Nobody answered their ringing. They went in and found the girl lying on her back in the dining-room, dead from a stab wound in her left breast.

The doctors said she had been stabbed at close to three o'clock that morning, with a pointed, round blade about half a foot long. Bureaus, closets, trunks, and so on showed signs of having been skilfully and thoroughly searched. There was no money in the girl's handbag and none elsewhere in the house. The jewel case on her dressing-table was empty, though two diamond rings had been left on her fingers. The weapon with which she had been killed was not found. The fingerprint experts hadn't turned up anything they could use. Neither doors nor windows seemed to have been forced. The kitchen looked as if the girl had been drinking with a guest or guests.

"Half a foot long, round, pointed," I repeated the weapon's description. "That sounds like her ice pick."

McGraw reached for the telephone and told somebody to send Shepp and Vanaman in. McGraw introduced us and asked them about the ice pick. They were positive it hadn't been there. They wouldn't have missed an article of that sort.

"Was it there last night?" McGraw asked me.

"Yeah. I stood beside her while she chipped off pieces of ice with it."

I described it. McGraw told the dicks to search the house again, and then to try to find the pick in the neighborhood.

"You knew her. What's your slant on it?" he asked me when the sleuths had gone.

"Too new for me to have one," I dodged the question. "Give me a couple of hours to chew it over. What do you think?"

He fell back into sourness, growling, "How the hell can I tell?"

But the fact that he let me go away without further questioning told me he had already made up his mind that Whisper was the murderer. I wondered if the little gambler was guilty—or if this was another of the wrong raps that Personville police chiefs liked to hang on him. It didn't seem to make much difference now. It was a gut he had—personally or by deputy—put Noonan down, and they could only hang him once anyway. That would be enough.

There were a lot of men in the corridors. Some of them were very young, quite a few were foreigners, most of them were every bit as tough-looking as any man should be. On my way to the street door I met Donner, a bow-legged bull who had been on a couple of expeditions with the dead chief and me.

"Hello," I greeted him. "What's the mob? Emptying the can* to make room for more?"

"Them's our new specials," he told me as if he didn't think much of them. "We're going to have a argumented force."

"Congratulations," I said and went on out.

I found Peak Murry sitting at his desk, behind the cigar-counter, in his pool room, talking to three men. I sat down on the other side of the room and watched a couple of kids knock the balls around. In a little while the lanky proprietor came over to me.

"If you see Reno sometime," I told him, "you might let him know that Pete the Finn's having his mob sworn in as special coppers."

"I might," Murry promised.

V

Mickey Linehan was sitting in the lobby when I got back to my hotel. He followed me up to my room and reported:

"Your Dan Rolff pulled a sneak from the pogy somewhere after midnight last night. The croakers† are kind of steamed up about it. Seems they were figuring on cutting a lot of little pieces of bone out of his brain this morning. But him and his duds were gone. We've got nothing on Whisper yet. Dick's out trying to place Bill

---

* jail
† doctors

Quint now. I hear there was some caps snapped[*] down Ronney Street today."

"Yeah. It oughtn't—"

The telephone bell rang.

A man's voice, carefully oratorical, spoke my name with a question mark after it.

I said: "Yes."

The voice said:

"Mr. Charles Proctor Dawn is speaking. I think you will find it well worth your while to appear at my office immediately."

"Yeah? Who are you?"

"Mr. Charles Proctor Dawn, attorney-at-law. My suite is in the Rutledge Block, 310 Green Street. I think you will find it well—"

"Mind telling me what it's all about?" I asked.

"There are affairs best not discussed over the telephone. I think you will find—"

"All right," I interrupted him again. "I'll be around to see you this afternoon if I'm not too busy."

"You will find it very, very advisable," he assured me.

I hung up on that. Mickey Linehan said:

"You were going to tell me about this morning's shooting."

I said:

"I wasn't. I started to say it oughtn't be hard to trace Rolff, running around with a fractured skull and probably a lot of bandages. Suppose you try it. I'd play Hurricane Street first, if I were you."

Mickey grinned all the way across his red comedian's face, said, "Don't tell me anything of what's going on—I'm only working with you," picked up his hat and left me.

I spread myself across the bed, smoked cigarettes end to end, and thought about last night, my frame of mind, my passing out, my dreams, and the situation into which I woke. The thinking was unpleasant enough to make me glad when it was interrupted.

Fingernails scratched on the outside of my door. I opened the door.

A man stood there, a stranger to me. He was young, thin, gaudily dressed, with heavy eyebrows and a small mustache that were coal-black against a very pale, nervous but not timid, face.

"I'm Ted Wright," he said, holding out a hand as if I were glad to meet him. "I guess you've heard Whisper talk about me."

I gave him my hand, let him in, closed the door, and asked:

"You're a friend of Whisper's?"

"You bet!" He held up two thin fingers pressed tightly together. "Me and him are just like that."

I didn't say anything. He looked around the room, smiling nervously, crossed to the open bathroom door, peeped in, came back to me, rubbed his lips with his tongue, and made his proposition:

"I'll knock him off for you for half a grand."

"Whisper?"

"Uh-huh. And it's dirt-cheap."

"Why do I want him killed?" I asked.

"He carved you all out of girls."

"Yeah?"

"You ain't dumb as that," Wright said.

A notion began crawling around in my noodle. To give it time I said:

"Sit down. This needs talking over."

"It don't need nothing," he said, looking at me sharply, not moving toward either chair. "You either want him knocked off or you don't."

"Then I don't."

He said something I couldn't catch—down in his throat—and turned toward the door. I got between him and it. He stood still, his eyes fidgeting. I said:

"So Whisper's dead?"

He stepped back and put a hand behind him.

I poked his jaw.

He got his legs crossed and went down.

I pulled him up by his wrists, yanked his face close to mine, growled:

"Come through. What's the racket?"

"I ain't done nothing to you."

"Let me catch you. Who got Whisper?"

"I don't know nothing a—"

I let go one of his wrists, slapped his face

---

[*] shots fired

with an open hand, caught his wrist again, and tried my luck at crunching both of them while I repeated:

"Who got Whisper?"

"Dan Rolff," he whined. "He walked right up to him and stuck him with the same skewer Whisper used on the twist. That's right!"

"How do you know it was the one Whisper killed the girl with?"

"Dan said so."

"What did Whisper say?"

"Nothing. He looked funny as all hell, standing there with the butt of the sticker sticking out his side. Then he flashes the rod and puts two slugs in Dan just like one, and the both of 'em go down together, cracking heads. Dan's all bloody through the bandages."

"Then?"

"Then I roll 'em over, and they're a pair of stiffs. Every word I'm telling you is right."

"Who else was there?"

"Nobody. Whisper was hiding out, with only me to go between him and the mob. He killed Noonan hisself, and he didn't want to trust nobody for a couple of days, nobody but me."

"So you, being a smart boy, thought you could go around to his enemies and pick up a piece or two of jack for killing him after he was dead?"

"I was clean, and this won't be no place for Whisper's friends after the news gets out he's croaked," Wright whined. "I had to raise a get-away stake."

"How'd you make out?"

"I got a century from Pete, and a century and a half from Peak Murry—for Reno—with a promise of more from both after I turned the trick," he said, the whine changing into boasting as he talked. "I bet you I could collect from McGraw, too—and I thought you'd kick in with something."

"They must be high in the air to put out dough on a game like that."

"I don't know," he said. "It ain't such a lousy one." He got humble again. "Give me a chance, brother. Don't gum it on me. I'll give you fifty bucks now and a split of whatever I get from McGraw if you'll keep your clam shut till I put it over and grab a rattler out."

"Nobody knows where Whisper is but you?"

"Nobody else, excepting Dan that's as dead as he is."

"Where are they?"

"It's the old Redman warehouse down on Porter Street. In the back, upstairs, Whisper had a room fixed up with a bed and stove and some grub. Give me a chance. Fifty bucks now and a cut on the rest."

I let go his arms and said:

"I don't want the dough, but go ahead. I'll lay off for a couple of hours, anyway. That ought to be long enough."

"Thanks, thanks, thanks!" And he hurried away from me.

I put on my hat and coat, went out, found Green Street and the Rutledge Block.

It was a wooden building a long while past any prime it might ever have had. Mr. Charles Proctor Dawn's establishment was on the second floor. There was no elevator. I climbed a worn and rickety flight of wooden stairs.

The lawyer had two rooms—both dingy, smelly and poorly lighted. I waited in the outer one while a clerk, who went well with the rooms, carried my name in to the lawyer. Half a minute later the clerk opened the door and beckoned me in.

Mr. Charles Proctor Dawn was a little fat man of fifty-something. He had prying triangular eyes of a very light color, a short, fleshy nose, and a fleshier mouth whose greediness was only partly hidden between a ragged gray mustache and a ragged gray Vandyke beard. His clothes were dark and unclean looking without actually being dirty.

He didn't get up from his desk, and throughout my visit he kept his right hand on the edge of a desk drawer that was some six inches open.

He said:

"Ah! my dear sir, I am extremely glad that you had the good judgment to follow my counsel."

His voice was even more oratorical than it had been over the wire.

I didn't say anything. He nodded his whiskers as if my not saying anything was another exhibition of good judgment. He said:

"I may say, in all justice, that you will find it the invariable part of sound judgment to follow the dictates of my counsel."

He knew a lot of sentences like that, and he didn't mind using them on me. Finally he got along to:

"Thus, that conduct which in a minor practitioner might seem irregular, becomes, when he who exercises it occupies such indisputable prominence in his community, simply that greater ethic which scorns the pettier conventionalities when confronted with an opportunity to serve mankind through one of its individual representatives. Therefore, my dear sir, I have not hesitated to summon you, to brush aside scornfully all trivial considerations of accepted precedent, to say to you frankly and candidly, my dear, sir, that your interests will best be served by retaining me as your legal representative."

I asked:

"What'll it cost?"

"That," he said loftily, "is of but secondary importance. However, it is a detail that has its place in our relationship, and must be arranged. We shall say, a thousand dollars now. Later, perhaps—" he ruffled his beard and didn't finish the sentence.

I said I hadn't, of course, that much money with me.

"Naturally, my dear sir! Naturally! But that is of no importance—none whatever. Any time will do for that—any time up to ten o'clock tomorrow morning."

"At ten tomorrow," I agreed. "Now I'd like to know why I need a legal representative."

He made an indignant face.

"My dear sir, it is no matter for jesting, I assure you!"

I explained that I hadn't been joking, that I really was puzzled.

He cleared his throat, frowned more or less majestically, said:

"It may well be, my dear sir, that you do not fully comprehend your peril, but it is indubitably preposterous that you should expect me to suppose that you are without any inkling of the difficulties—the legal difficulties, my dear sir—with which you are confronted. However, there is no time to go into that matter now. I have a pressing appointment with Judge Leffner. Tomorrow morning I shall be glad to go more thoroughly into every least ramification of the affair with you. Tomorrow at ten."

From this joker's office I went to Peak Murry's pool room, bought a bottle of Scotch, returned to my hotel for dinner, and went up to my room. I spent the evening drinking unpleasant Scotch, thinking unpleasant thoughts and waiting for reports that didn't come from Dick Foley and Mickey Linehan.

I went to sleep at midnight.

VI

I was half dressed at eight-thirty the next morning when Dick Foley came in. The little Canadian reported, in his word-saving manner, that Bill Quint had checked out of his hotel at noon the previous day, leaving no forwarding address. A train left for Ogden at twelve-fifty-five. Dick had wired the Continental's Salt Lake branch to send a man up there to trace Quint.

"I don't think we want Quint," I gave my opinion, "but we can't pass up any leads. My guess about him is that when he heard she had been killed he decided to duck—being a discarded lover who had threatened her. She gave him the air long ago. If he'd been going to do anything about it, he'd have gone into action before this."

Dick nodded and said:

"Gun-play out road last night—hijacking—four trucks of hooch nailed, burned."

That sounded like Reno Starkey's answer to the news that the big bootlegger's beer mob had been sworn in as special coppers.

As I finished dressing, Mickey Linehan arrived.

"Rolff was at the girl's house, all right," he reported. "The Greek grocer on the corner saw him come out around nine yesterday morning. The Greek thought he was drunk. He went down the street wobbling and talking to himself."

"How come the Greek didn't tell the coppers? Or did he?"

"Wasn't asked. A swell force this burg's got! Well, do we find him for 'em and turn him in with the job all sewed up?"

"Unless he left and came back for the ice pick later," I said, "Rolff didn't turn the trick. She was cut down at three in the morning. He wasn't there at eight-thirty, and the pick was still in her. It was—"

Dick Foley left his chair, stood in front of me, asked:

"How do you know?"

I didn't like the way he looked nor the way he spoke. I said:

"You know because I'm telling you."

Dick didn't say anything. Mickey, grinning his half-wit's grin, asked:

"What do we do next? Let's get the thing polished off."

"I've got a date for ten," I told them. "Hang around the hotel until I get back. Whisper and Rolff are dead, probably, so we won't have to hunt for them." I scowled at Dick and added: "I was told that. I didn't kill either of them."

The little Canadian nodded without lowering his steady eyes from mine.

I ate breakfast alone and set out for the lawyer's office.

Turning off King Street, I saw Hank O'Marra's freckled face in an automobile that was going up Green Street. He was sitting beside a man I didn't know. The long-legged youngster waved an arm at me and stopped the car. I went over to him. He said:

"Reno wants to see you."

"Where'll I find him?"

"Jump in."

"I can't go now," I explained. "Maybe not till late this afternoon."

"See Peak when you're ready."

I said I would.

O'Marra and his companion drove on up Green Street. I walked half a block south to the Rutledge Block.

With a foot on the first of the rickety steps that led up to the lawyer's floor, I stopped to look at something.

It was barely visible back in a dim corner of the first floor. It was a shoe. It was lying in a position that empty shoes don't lie in.

I took my foot off the step and went toward the shoe. Now I could see an ankle and the cuff of a black pants-leg above the shoe-top.

That prepared me for what I found.

I found Mr. Charles Proctor Dawn huddled among two brooms, a mop and a couple of buckets in a little alcove formed by the back of the stairs and a corner of the wall. His Vandyke beard was red with blood from a cut that ran diagonally across his forehead. His head was twisted sidewise and backward at an angle that was impossible without a broken neck.

I did what seemed necessary. Gingerly pulling one side of the dead man's coat out of the way, I emptied the inside pocket, transferring a black book and a sheaf of papers to my own coat. I couldn't get at any of his other pockets without moving him, so I passed them up.

Five minutes later I was going through a side door into my hotel. To avoid Dick and Mickey in the lobby I walked up to the mezzanine and took the elevator there.

In my room I sat down and examined my loot.

I took the book first—a small, imitation-leather-covered memoranda book of the sort that sells for not much money in any stationery store.

It held some fragmentary notes that meant nothing to me, and thirty or forty names and addresses that meant as little—with one exception:

Helen Albury
1229A Hurricane Street

That was interesting because, (1) a young man named Robert Albury was in jail, having confessed that he shot and killed Donald Willsson, my client's son, because he thought young Willsson had taken his place as Dinah Brand's lover, and (2) Dinah Brand had lived and had been murdered at 1232 Hurricane Street, across the street from 1229A.

I didn't find my name in the book. I put it aside and began unfolding and reading the papers I had taken from Dawn's pocket. Here, too, I had to wade through a lot that meant nothing to find anything that meant something.

This find was a group of four letters held together by a rubber band. The letters were in slitted envelopes that had postmarks dated a week apart, roughly. The latest was some six months old. The letters were addressed to Dinah Brand. The first wasn't so bad, for a love letter. The second was a bit goofier. The third and fourth were swell examples of how silly an ardent and unsuccessful wooer can be, especially if he's getting along in years. The letters were signed by Elihu Willsson.

I had found nothing to show definitely why Mr. Charles Proctor Dawn had thought he could blackmail me out of a thousand dollars, but I had found plenty to think about. I encouraged my brain with two Fatimas and then went down to join the two operatives in the lobby.

"Go out and see what you can dig up on a lawyer named Charles Proctor Dawn," I told Mickey. "He's got offices in Green Street. Stay away from them. Don't put in a lot of time on him. I just want a rough line."

I told Dick to give me five minutes start and then follow me out to the neighborhood of 1229A Hurricane Street.

I went out there. It was a two-story building almost directly opposite Dinah Brand's, divided into an upstairs and a downstairs flat, with a private entrance for each. 1229A was the upper flat. I rang the bell.

The door was opened by a thin girl of eighteen or nineteen, with dark eyes set close together in a shiny yellowish face under short-cut brown hair that looked damp.

She opened the door, made a choked, frightened sound in her throat, and backed away, holding both hands to her open mouth.

"You are Miss Helen Albury?" I asked.

She shook her head violently from side to side. There was no truthfulness in it. Her eyes were crazy.

I said:

"I'd like to come in and talk to you a few minutes," going in as I spoke, closing the door behind me.

She didn't say anything. She went up the stairs in front of me, her head bent over her shoulder so she could watch me with scary eyes.

We went into a scantily furnished living-room. Dinah Brand's house could be seen from the windows.

The girl stood in the middle of the room, her hands still to her mouth. I wasted time and words trying to convince her that I was harmless. It was no good. Everything I said seemed to increase her panic. It was a damned nuisance. I quit trying and got down to business.

"You are Robert Albury's sister."

No reply—nothing but the senseless look of utter fear. I said:

"After he was arrested for killing Willsson, you took this flat so you could watch her. What for?"

Not a word from her. I had to supply my own answer:

"Revenge. You blamed her for your brother's trouble. You watched for your chance. It came night before last. You sneaked into her house, found her drunk, stabbed her with the ice pick."

She didn't say anything. There was no change in the blankness of her frightened face. I said:

"Dawn helped you—engineered it for you. He wanted Elihu Willsson's letters. Who was the man he sent to do the actual killing? Who was he?"

No answer. No change in her expression. I thought I'd like to spank her. I said:

"I've given you your chance to talk. I'm willing to listen to your side of the story. But suit yourself."

She suited herself by keeping quiet. I went out of the flat not sure that she had understood a single word I had said.

At the corner I told Dick Foley:

"There's a girl in there—Helen Albury. She's about eighteen, five feet six, skinny, not more than a hundred, if that, eyes close together, yellowish skin, brown bobbed hair, straight, got on a gray suit now. Tail her. If she cuts up on you throw her in the can. Watch her—she's crazy as a pet cuckoo."

VII

I set out for Peak Murry's place to see what Reno wanted. Half a block from my destination I stepped into an office building doorway to look the situation over.

A police patrol wagon stood in front of Murry's pool room. Men were being led, dragged, carried from pool room to wagon. The leaders, draggers and carriers didn't look like regular policemen. They were Pete the Finn's boys, now special coppers, I supposed. Pete, with McGraw's help, evidently was making good on his threat to give Whisper and Reno all the war they wanted.

While I watched an ambulance arrived, was loaded, departed. I couldn't recognize anybody—or any bodies—from my post. When the height of the excitement was over I circled a couple of blocks and returned to my hotel.

Mickey Linehan was there, with information about Charles Proctor Dawn:

"He's the guy that the joke was wrote about: 'Is he a criminal lawyer?' 'Yes, very.' This fellow Albury that you nailed for the killing—some of his family hired Dawn to defend him. Albury wouldn't talk to him when he came to see him. This three-named shyster nearly went over himself last year on a blackmail rap—something

about a parson named Hill—but managed to wriggle out of it. Got some property out Ledbury Street, wherever that is. Want me to keep digging?"

"That's enough. We'll stick around till we hear from Dick."

Mickey yawned and said he was satisfied with that, never being one that had to run around a lot to keep his blood circulating, and asked if I knew we were getting nationally famous.

I asked him what he meant by that, if anything.

"I just saw Tommy Robins," he said. "The Consolidated Press sent him here to cover the doings. He tells me some of the other press associations and a big-city paper or two are sending in special correspondents—beginning to play our troubles up."

I was making one of my favorite complaints—that newspapers were good for nothing except to hash things up so nobody could unhash them—when I heard a boy chanting my name. For a dime he told me I was wanted on the phone. Dick Foley:

"She showed right away—to 310 Green Street—full of coppers—mouthpiece named Dawn killed—coppers took her to headquarters."

"Still there?"

"Yes. Chief's office."

"Stick and get anything you learn to me quick."

I went back to Mickey Linehan, gave him my room key and instructions:

"Camp in my room. Take anything that comes for me and pass it on. I'll be at the Shannon around the corner, registered J. W. Clark. Tell Dick and nobody."

Mickey asked, "What the hell?" got no answer, and moved his loose-jointed bulk toward the elevators.

I went around to the Shannon Hotel, registered my alias, paid my day's rent, and was taken to room 321.

An hour went by slowly before the phone bell rang.

Dick Foley said he was coming up to see me.

He arrived within five minutes. His sharp, worried face wasn't friendly. Neither was his voice. He said:

"Warrants out for you. Murder. Two counts—Brand and Dawn. I phoned. Mickey said he'd stick. Told me you were here. Police got him. Grilling him now."

"Yeah—I expected that."

"So did I!" he snapped.

I said, making myself drawl the words:

"You think I killed 'em, don't you, Dick?"

"If you didn't it's a good time to say so."

"Going to put the finger on me?" I asked.

He pulled his lips back over his teeth, his face white. I said:

"Go back to San Francisco, Dick. I've got enough to do without having to keep an eye on you."

He put his hat on very carefully and very carefully closed the door behind him when he went out.

At four o'clock I had some luncheon, cigarettes, and an *Evening Herald* brought up to me.

Dinah Brand's murder and the newer murder of Charles Proctor Dawn divided the newspaper's front page, with Helen Albury connecting them.

She was, I read, Robert Albury's sister, and she was, in spite of his confession, thoroughly convinced that her brother was not guilty of murder but the victim of a plot. She had retained Charles Proctor Dawn to defend him. (I could guess that the late Charles Proctor had hunted her up, and not she him.) The brother refused to have Dawn or any other lawyer or to repudiate his confession, but the girl (properly encouraged by Dawn, no doubt) hadn't given up the fight.

Finding a flat vacant across the street from Dinah Brand's house, Helen Albury had rented it and installed herself therein with a pair of field-glasses and one idea—to prove that Dinah and her associates were guilty of Donald Willsson's murder. It seems that I was one of the "associates." The paper called me "a man sup-posed to be a private detective from San Francisco, who has been in this city for several days, apparently on intimate terms with Max ('Whisper') Thaler, Daniel Rolff, Oliver ('Reno') Starkey and Dinah Brand." We were the plotters who had framed Robert Albury.

The night that Dinah Brand had been killed, Helen Albury, peeping through her window, had seen things that were very, very significant, according to the *Herald*, when considered in connection with the subsequent finding of Dinah's dead body. As soon as the girl heard of the murder, she took her important news to Charles Proctor Dawn. He, the police learned from his clerks, had immediately sent for me, and had been closeted with me that afternoon, and had told his clerks that I was to return the next morning at ten.

This morning I had not appeared to keep my appointment. At twenty-five minutes past ten the janitor of the Rutledge Block had found Charles Proctor Dawn's body in a corner behind the staircase, murdered. Valuable papers were gone from the dead man's pocket.

At the very minute that the body was being found I, it seems, was in Helen Albury's flat, having forced an entrance and was threatening her. After she succeeded in throwing me out, she hurried to Dawn's office, arriving while the police were there, telling them her story. Police sent to my hotel and had not found me there, but in my room they had found one Michael Linehan, who also represented himself to be a San Francisco private detective. Michael Linehan was being questioned by the police. Whisper, Reno, Rolff and I were being hunted by the police—on murder charges. Important developments were expected.

The whole thing was designed to tell the world that we "associates" were the poison in Poisonville, and the rest of the citizens angels.

Page two held an interesting half-column. Detectives Shepp and Vanaman, the discoverers of Dinah Brand's corpse, had mysteriously vanished. Foul play on the part of us "associates" was feared.

There was nothing in the paper about last night's hijacking, nothing about the raid on Peak Murry's.

After dark I went out.

VIII

I wanted to get in touch with Reno. From a drug store I telephoned Peak Murry's pool room.

"Is Peak there?" I asked.

"This is Peak," said a voice that didn't sound the least bit like his. "Who's talking?"

I said disgustedly, "This is Lillian Gish,"[*] hung up the receiver, and removed myself from the neighborhood.

I gave up the idea of finding Reno and decided to go calling on my client, old Elihu Willsson and try to blackjack him into good behavior with the love letters he had written Dinah Brand and I had stolen from Dawn's remains.

I walked, keeping to the darker side of the darkest streets. It was a fairly long walk for a man who sneers at exercise. By the time I reached Willsson's block I was in bad enough humor to be in good shape for the sort of interviews he and I usually had. But I wasn't to see him for another while.

I was two pavements from my destination when somebody "s s s sed" at me.

I probably didn't jump twenty feet.

"'S all right," a voice whispered.

It was dark. Peeping out under my bush—I was on one hand and my knee in somebody's front yard—I could make out the form of a man crouching close to a hedge, on my side of it.

My gun was in my hand. There was no special reason why I shouldn't take his word for it that it was all right.

I got up off my knees and went to him. When I got close enough I recognized him as one of the men who had let me into the Ronney Street rooming house the day before.

I sat on my heels beside him and asked:

"Where'll I find Reno? Hank O'Marra said he wants to see me."

"He does. Know where Kid McLeod's place is at?"

"No."

"It's on Martin Street above King—corner the alley. Ask for the Kid. Go back thataway three blocks and then down. You can't miss it."

I said I'd try not to, and left him crouching behind his hedge, waiting, I imagined, for a shot at Pete the Finn, Whisper, or any of Reno's other enemies that happened to come calling on old Elihu.

Following directions, I came to a soft drink and rummy[†] establishment with red and yellow paint all over it. Inside I asked for Kid McLeod. I was taken into a back room, where a fat man with a dirty collar, a lot of gold teeth and only one ear admitted he was McLeod.

"Reno sent for me," I said. "Where'll I find him?"

"And who does that make you?" he asked.

I told him who I was. He went away without saying anything. I waited ten minutes. He brought a boy back with him, a kid of fifteen or so with a vacant expression on a pimply red face.

"Go with Sonny," Kid McLeod told me.

I followed the boy out a side door, down two blocks of a back street, across a sandy lot, through a ragged back gate and up to the back door of a frame house.

The boy knocked on the door and was asked who he was.

"Sonny with a guy the Kid sent," he replied.

The door was opened. Sonny went away. I went into a kitchen where Reno Starkey and four other men—one of them was O'Marra—sat around a table that had a lot of beer on it. I noticed that two automatics hung on nails over the top of the doorframe through which I had come. They'd be handy if anybody in the house opened the door, found an enemy with a gun there, and was told to stick up his hands.

---

[*] silent-screen actress

[†] bootlegging

Reno gave me a glass of beer and led me through the dining-room into a front room. A man lay on his belly there, with one eye to the crack between the drawn blind and the bottom of the window.

"Go back and get some beer," Reno told him. He got up and went. We made ourselves comfortable in adjoining chairs.

"When I fixed up that Tanner alibi for you," Reno said, "I told you I was doing it because I needed all the friends I could get."

"You got one."

"Crack the alibi yet?" he asked.

"Not yet."

"It'll hold," he assured me, "unless they got too damned much on you. Think they have?" he asked with a grin.

I thought so. I said:

"No. McGraw's just feeling playful. That'll take care of itself. How's your end holding up?"

He emptied his glass, wiped his mouth on the back of his hand, and said:

"I'll make out. But that's what I wanted to see you for. Here's how she stacks up, see—Pete's throwed in with McGraw. That lines bulls and the beer mob up against me and Whisper. But hell! Me and Whisper are busier trying to put the chive* in each other than bucking the combine. That's a sour racket. While we're tangling, them bums will eat us up!"

I said I had been thinking the same thing. He went on:

"Whisper'll listen to you. Find him, will you? Put it up to him. Here's the proposish: He means to get me for knocking off Jerry Hooper. I mean to get him first. Let's forget that for a day or two. Nobody won't have to trust nobody else. He don't ever show in any of his jobs anyway. He just sends the boys. I'll do the same this time. We'll just put the mobs together to swing the job. We run 'em together, wipe out that damned Finn, and then after that we'll have plenty of time to go gunning for each other in peace.

"Put it to him cold. I don't want him to get

_____

* knife

any idea that I'm leery of him or any other guy. Tell him I say if we get Pete out the way we'll have more space to do our own scrapping in. Pete's holed-up down in Whiskeytown. I ain't got enough men to go down there and pull him out. Neither has Whisper. The two of us together have. Put it to him."

"Whisper," I said, "is dead."

Reno said, "Is that so?" as if he didn't exactly believe me.

"Dan Rolff killed him yesterday morning down in the old Redman warehouse; stuck him with the ice pick Whisper used on Dinah."

Reno asked:

"You *know* this? You're not just running off at the head, are you?"

"I know it," I exaggerated.

"Damned funny none of his mob act like he was gone," he said, but he was beginning to believe me.

"They don't know it. He was hiding out, with Ted Wright the only one that knew where. Ted knew it. He cashed in on it. He told me he got a hundred and fifty from you—from Peak Murry."

"I'd have given the big sap twice that much for the straight dope," Reno growled. He rubbed his chin, said, "Well, that settles the Whisper end."

I said: "No."

"What do you mean, no?"

"If his mob don't know where he is, let's tell 'em. They blasted him out of the can when Noonan copped him before. Think they'd try it again if the news got around that McGraw had picked him up?"

"Keep talking," Reno said.

"If his mob try to crack the hoosegow they'll give the department—including Pete's specials—something to do. While they're doing it, you could try your luck in Whiskeytown."

"Maybe," he said slowly, "maybe we'll try just that thing."

"It ought to work," I said, standing. "I'll see you—"

"Stick around. This is as good a spot for you

as any while the bulls are out for you. And we'll need a good guy like you on this party."

I didn't like that. I knew enough not to say so. I sat down again.

Reno got busy arranging the rumor. The telephone was worked overtime. The kitchen door was worked just as hard, letting men in and out. More men came in than went out. The house filled up with men, smoke and excitement.

IX

At half-past one Reno turned from answering a phone call and said:

"Let's take a ride."

He went upstairs. When he came down he carried a black valise. Most of the men had disappeared through the kitchen door by then. Reno gave me the valise, saying:

"Don't wrastle it around too much."

It was heavy.

The seven of us left in the house went out the front door and got into a curtained black touring car that had just pulled up to the curb. O'Marra was at the wheel. Reno sat beside him. I was squeezed in between men in the back seat, with the valise squeezed between my legs.

Another car came out of the first cross street and ran on ahead of us. A third followed us. Our speed hung around forty—fast enough to get us somewhere, not fast enough to get us a lot of attention. We had nearly finished the trip before we were bothered.

The action started in a block of one-story houses of the shack type, down in the southern part of the city. A man put his head out of a door, put his fingers in his mouth and whistled noisily.

Somebody in the car behind us shot him down.

At the next corner we ran through a volley of pistol bullets.

Reno turned around to tell me:

"If they pop the bag we'll all of us hit the moon. Get it open. We got to work fast when we get there."

I had the clasps loose by the time we came to rest at the curb in front of a dark three-story brick building.

The car in front had gone on to the next corner, passing out of sight around it. I looked back. The rear car was planted up the street, trading shots with the neighborhood.

Men crawled all over me, opening the valise, helping themselves to its contents—bombs made out of short sections of two-inch pipe, packed in sawdust in the bag. Bullets bit chunks out of the car's black curtains.

Reno reached back for one of the bombs, hopped out to the sidewalk, heaved the stuffed pipe at the brick building's door.

A sheet of flame, deafening noise, hunks of things pelting us while we tried to keep from being knocked over by the concussion—and there was no door to keep us out of the brick building.

A man ran forward, swung his arm, let a pipeful of hell go through the doorway. The shutters came off the downstairs windows, fire and glass flying behind them.

O'Marra, out in the middle of the street, bent far over, tossed a bomb to the roof. It didn't go off. O'Marra put one foot high in the air, clawed at his throat, fell solidly backward.

Gunfire sounded behind the brick building—a lot of it.

Another of our party went down under the slugs that were cutting at us from a frame house next to the brick one.

Reno cursed stolidly and said:

"Burn 'em out, Fat."

Fat spit on a bomb, ran around the back of our car, swung his arm. We picked ourselves up off the sidewalk, dodged flying things, and the frame house was all out of whack, with flames climbing up its torn edges.

"Any left?" Reno asked as we looked around, enjoying the feeling of not being shot at.

"Here's the last one," Fat said, holding out a bomb.

Fire was dancing inside the upper windows of the brick house. Reno nodded at it, took the bomb from Fat and ordered:

"Back up. They'll be coming out."

We moved away from the front of the house.

A heavy voice indoors yelled:

"Reno!"

Reno slipped into the shadow of our car before he called back:

"Well?"

"We're done. We're coming out. Don't shoot."

Reno asked:

"Who's we're?"

"This is Pete," the heavy voice said. "There's four of us left."

"You come first," Reno ordered, "with your mitts on the top of your head. The others come out one at a time, same way, after you. And half a minute apart is close enough. Come on."

Pete the Finn appeared in the blasted doorway, his hands holding the bald top of his head. In the glare from the burning next-door house we could see that his face was cut, his clothes torn.

Stepping over wreckage, the bootlegger came down the steps to the sidewalk.

Reno called him a lousy fish-eater* and shot him four times in face and body.

Pete went down. A man behind me laughed. Reno hurled the remaining bomb through the doorway. We scrambled into our car. Reno took the wheel. The engine was dead—a bullet had got to it.

Reno worked the horn while the rest of us jumped out.

The machine that had stopped at the corner behind came for us. I looked up and down the street that was bright with the glow from two burning buildings. There were faces at windows, but whoever besides us was in the street had taken to cover. Not far away fire-bells sounded.

The other machine slowed down for us to climb in. It was already full. We packed it in layers, with the overflow hanging to the running-boards.

We bumped over dead O'Marra's legs and

_____

* a Catholic

headed for home. We covered one block with safety if not comfort. After that we had neither.

A limousine turned into the street ahead of us, came halfway to us, put its side to us and stopped. Out of the side—gunfire.

Another car came around the limousine and charged us. Out of it—gunfire.

We did our best, but we were too amalgamated for good fighting. You can't shoot straight holding a man in your lap, another hanging on your shoulder, while a third does his shooting from an inch or two behind your ear.

Our other car—which had been around at the rear of the brick building—came up and gave us a hand. But by then two more cars had joined the opposition. Thaler's mob's attack on the jail was over, one way or the other, apparently, and Pete's army—sent to help there—had returned in time to spoil our getaway. It looked like a sweet mess.

I leaned over a burning gun and yelled in Reno's ear:

"This is the bunk! Let's us extras get out and do our fighting in the street.

He thought it a good idea and gave orders:

"Pile out, some of you birds, and take 'em from the pavements!"

I was the first man down, with my eye on a dark alley entrance.

Fat followed me to it. In my shelter I turned on him and growled:

"Pick your own hole. There's a cellarway that looks good."

He agreeably trotted off toward it and was shot down at his third step.

I explored my alley. It was only twenty feet long and ended against a high board fence with a locked gate. A garbage can helped me over the gate into a brick-paved yard. The side fence of that yard led me into another, and from there I got into another, where a fox terrier raised hell at me. I kicked it out of the way, made the opposite fence, untangled myself from some clothesline, crossed two more yards, got yelled at from a window, had a bottle thrown at me and dropped into a cobble-stoned back street.

The shooting was behind me, but not far enough. I did all I could to remedy that. I must have walked as many streets as I did in my dreams the night Dinah was killed.

My watch said it was 3:30 A.M. when I looked at it on Elihu Willsson's front steps.

X

I had to push my client's doorbell a lot before I got any play on it.

Finally the door was opened by the tall, sun-burned chauffeur. He was dressed in undershirt and pants, and had a piece of billiard cue in one fist.

"What do you want?" he demanded, and then, when he got another look at me: "Oh, it's you! Well, what do you want?"

"I want to see Mr. Willsson."

"At four o'clock in the morning! Go on with you!" and he started to close the door.

I put a foot against it. He looked from my foot to my face, hefted the piece of billiard cue and asked:

"You after getting your kneecap cracked?"

"I'm not playing," I insisted. "I've got to see the old man. Tell him."

"I don't have to tell him. He told me no later than this afternoon that if you came around he didn't want to see you."

"Yeah?" I took the four love letters out of my pocket, found the first and least idiotic of them, held it out to the chauffeur, and said: "Give him that and tell him I'm sitting on the steps with the rest of 'em. Tell him I'll sit here five minutes and then carry 'em to Tommy Robins of the Consolidated Press."

The chauffeur scowled at the letter, said: "To hell with Tommy Robins and his blind aunt!" took the letter and closed the door. Four minutes later he opened the door and said: "Come in, you!"

I followed him upstairs to old Elihu's bedroom. My client sat up in bed with his love letter crushed in one round, pink fist, its envelope in the other. His short white hair bristled all over the top of his round head. His round eyes were as much red as blue. The parallel lines of mouth and chin almost touched. He was in a lovely humor. As soon as he saw me he shouted:

"So after all your brave talking you had to come back to the old pirate to have your neck saved, did you?"

I said I didn't anything of the sort. I said if he was going to talk like a sap he ought to lower his voice so the people in Los Angeles wouldn't learn what a sap he was.

The old boy let his voice out another notch, bellowing:

"Because you've stolen a letter or two that don't belong to you, you needn't—"

I put fingers in my ears. It didn't shut out the noise, but it insulted him into cutting the bellows short. I took the fingers out and said:

"Send the flunkey away so we can talk. You won't need him. I'm not going to hurt you."

He said, "Get out!" to the chauffeur. The chauffeur, looking at me without fondness, left us, closing the door behind him.

Old Elihu gave me the rush act, demanding that I surrender the rest of the letters immediately, wanting to know loudly and profanely where I got them, what I was doing with them, threatening me with this, that and the other, but mostly cursing me.

I didn't give them to him. I said:

"I took 'em from the man you hired to recover 'em. Tough on you that he had to kill the girl."

Enough red went out of the old man's face to leave it normally pink. He worked his lips over his teeth, screwed his eyes up at me, said:

"Is that the way you're playing it?"

His voice came comparatively quiet from his chest. He had settled down to fight.

I pulled a chair over by the bed, sat, put as much amusement as I could in a grin, and said:

"That's one way."

He watched me, worked his lips, said nothing. I said:

"You're the damndest client I ever had! What do you do? You hire me to clean town, change your mind and run out on me, work against me until I begin to look like a winner, then get on the fence, and now when you think I'm licked you don't even want to let me in the house. Lucky for me I happened to pick up those letters!"

He said: "Blackmail."

I laughed and said:

"Listen who's naming it! All right, call it that." I leaned forward to tap the edge of the bed with a forefinger. "I'm not licked, old top. I've won. You came crying to me that four naughty men had taken your little city away from you and were playing with it as they damned pleased. Pete the Finn, Lew Yard, Whisper Thaler and Noonan. Where are they now?

"Yard died Tuesday morning, Noonan Tuesday night, Whisper Wednesday morning, and the Finn a little while ago. I'm giving your city back to you whether you want it or not. If that's blackmail—O.K. Now here's what you're going to do. You're going to get hold of your mayor—I suppose the lousy burg's got one—and you and he are going to get the governor on the phone— Keep quiet till I get through!

"You're going to have the governor turn out the national guard—martial law for Poisonville. I've been told that the governor and the mayor are both pieces of your property, and will do what you tell 'em. That's what you're going to tell 'em! I don't know how various ruckuses around town came out tonight, but I know the big leaders are dead. The ones that had too much on you for you to talk back to 'em. There are plenty of substitutes working like hell to get into the dead men's shoes. The more the better. They'll make it easier for the white-collar soldiers to take hold while everything's disorganized. And none of the substitutes are likely to know enough about you to do much damage.

"There it is. It can be done. It's got to be done. Then you'll have your city back, all nice and clean and ready to go to the dogs again. If you don't do it, I'm going to turn these love letters of yours over to the newspaper buzzards— not to your *Herald* crew, but to the special men

from the press associations. I got the letters from Dawn. You'll have a lot of fun proving you didn't hire him to recover them, and that he didn't have to kill the girl to get 'em. But the fun you'll have is nothing to the fun people will have reading them. They're hot! I haven't laughed so much over anything since the hogs ate my kid brother!"

I stopped talking.

He was shaking, but not from fear. His face was purple again. He opened his mouth and roared:

"Publish them and be damned!"

I took them out of my pocket, dropped them on his bed, got up from my chair, put on my hat, and said:

"I'd give my right leg to be able to believe that the girl was killed by somebody you sent to get the letters. By God, I'd like to top off the clean-up by sending you to the gallows!"

He didn't touch the letters. He said:

"You told me the truth about Thaler and Pete?"

"Yeah. But what difference does it make? You'll only be pushed around by somebody else instead of them."

He threw the bed clothes aside and swung his stocky, pajamaed legs and bare pink feet over the edge of the bed.

"Have you got the guts," he barked, "to take the chief of police job I offered you before?"

"No. I lost my guts out fighting your fights while you were hiding in bed thinking up new ways of disowning me. Find some other wet nurse."

He glared at me. Then shrewd wrinkles came around his eyes. He said:

"You're afraid to take the job. You *did* kill the girl."

I left him as I had left him the last time, saying, "Go to hell!" and walking out.

The tall chauffeur, still toting his billiard cue, still regarding me without fondness, met me on the ground floor and took me to the door, looking as if he hoped I'd start something. I didn't. He slammed the door after me.

XI

The street was gray with the beginning of daylight. Up the street a black coupé stood under some trees. I couldn't see if any one was in it. I played safe by walking in the opposite direction. The coupé moved after me.

There's nothing in running down streets with automobiles in pursuit. I stopped, facing this one. It came on. I took my hand away from my side when I saw Mickey Linehan's red face through the windshield. He swung the door open for me to get in beside him.

"I thought you might come up here," he said as I got in, "but I was a second or two too late. I was too far away to get your eye when you went in."

"How'd you make out with the police?" I asked. "Better keep driving while we talk."

"I didn't know anything, couldn't guess anything, didn't have any idea what you were working on, just happened to hit town and meet you. Old friends—that line. They were still trying to get more out of me when the riot broke. They had me in one of the little offices across from the assembly room. When the circus cut loose I back-doored 'em."

"How'd the circus wind up?"

"The coppers shot hell out of 'em. They'd got the tip-off half an hour before and had the whole neighborhood packed with specials. Seems to have been a juicy row while it lasted—no duck soup for the bulls at that. Whisper's mob, I hear."

"Yeah. Reno and Pete the Finn tangled tonight. Hear anything about it?"

"Only that they'd tangled."

"Reno killed Pete and ran into an ambush in the get away. I don't know what happened after that. Seen Dick?"

"I went up to his hotel and was told he'd checked out to catch the evening train."

"I told him to go back to San Francisco," I explained. "He seemed to think I'd killed Dinah Brand. He was getting on my nerves with it."

"Well?"

"You mean, did I kill her? I don't know. I'm trying to find out. Want to follow Dick back to the coast, or you want to keep riding with me?"

Mickey said:

"Don't get so swelled up over one lousy murder. That's likely to happen to anybody. But what the hell? You didn't lift her dough and pretties!"

"Neither did the killer. They were still there after eight, when I left. Dan Rolff was in and out between then and nine. He wouldn't have taken them. The—I've got it! The coppers that found the body—Shepp and Vanaman—got there at nine-thirty. Besides the jewelry and the money, some letters old Willsson had written the girl were—must have been—taken. I found them later in Dawn's pocket. The two coppers disappeared just about then. See it?

"When they found the girl dead they looted the joint before turning in the alarm. Old Willsson being wealthy, the letters looked good to them, so they took them along with the other valuables and turned the letters over to the shyster to peddle back to Elihu for them. Dawn was killed before he had done anything on that end. I took the letters. Shepp and Vanaman—whether they did or didn't know the letters weren't found in the dead man's possession—got cold feet. They were afraid the letters would be traced to them. They had the money and jewelry. They beat it."

"Sounds fair enough," Mickey agreed, "but it doesn't seem to put any fingers on any murderers."

"It clears things up some. We'll try to clear up another point. See if you can find Porter Street and an old warehouse called Redman. The way I got it—Rolff killed Whisper there—walked up to him and stabbed him with the ice pick he'd found in the girl's corpse. If he did it that way, then Whisper didn't kill her, or he'd have been expecting something of the sort, and would have dropped Rolff before the lunger got to him. I'd like to look at Whisper's remains and check up on it."

"Porter's over beyond King," Mickey said. "We'll try the southern end first. It's nearer and more likely to have warehouses. Where do you set this Rolff guy?"

"Out. My notion is that he left the hospital, spent the night God knows where, showed up at the girl's house in the morning, after I'd left, let himself in with his key—he lived there, you know—found her, decided Whisper had killed her, took the sticker out of her and went hunting Whisper. She had bruises on her cheek and arm. He wasn't strong enough to manhandle her, even without his fractured skull."

"So? And where do you get the idea that you might have—"

"Stop it!" I growled as we turned into Porter Street, "and let's find the warehouse."

We rode down the street, jerking our eyes around, hunting for buildings that looked like deserted warehouses. It was light enough now to see well.

Presently I spotted a big, square, rusty-red building set in the middle of a weedy lot. Disuse stuck out all over building and lot. It was a likely candidate.

"Pull up at the next corner," I said. "That looks like the dump. You stick with the heap while I scout it."

I walked two extra blocks so I could come into the lot behind the building. I crossed the lot carefully, not sneaking, but not making any noises I could avoid.

I tried the back door cautiously. It was locked, of course. I moved around to a window, tried to look in, couldn't because of gloom and dirt, tried the window, couldn't budge it.

I went to the next window—with the same luck. I rounded the corner of the building and began working my way along the north side. The first window had me beaten. The second went up slowly with my push—and didn't make much noise doing it.

Across the inside of the window frame, from top to bottom, boards were nailed. They looked solid and strong from where I stood.

I cursed them and remembered hopefully that the window hadn't made much noise when

I raised it. I climbed up on the sill, put a hand against the boards, tried them gently.

They gave.

I put more weight behind my hand. The boards went away from the left side of the frame, showing me a row of shiny nail points. I pushed them back farther, looked past them, saw nothing but darkness, heard nothing.

With my gun in my right fist, I stepped over the sill, down into the building. Another step to the left put me out of the window's gray light. I switched my gun to my left hand while I used my right to push the boards back over the window.

A full minute of breathless listening got me nothing. Holding my gun-arm tight to my side I began exploring the joint. Nothing but the floor came under my feet as I inch-by-inched them forward. My groping left hand felt nothing until it touched a rough wall. I seemed to have crossed a room that was empty.

I moved along the wall, hunting for a door. Half a dozen of my undersized steps brought me to one. I leaned an ear against it. No sound.

I found the knob, turned it softly, eased the door back.

Something swished.

I did four things at the same time: let go the knob, jumped, pulled trigger, and had my left arm hit with something as hard and heavy as a tombstone.

The flare of my gun showed me nothing. (Most of the things people see in the dark by gunfire are imaginary.) Not knowing what else to do, I fired again, and once more.

An old man's voice pleaded:

"Don't do that, partner! You don't have to do that!"

I said:

"Strike a light."

A match spluttered on the floor, kindled, put flickering yellow light on a time-battered face. It was the useless, characterless sort of old face that goes well with a park bench. He was sitting on the floor, his stringy legs sprawled far apart. He didn't seem hurt anywhere. A table-leg lay beside him.

"Get up and make a light," I ordered, "and keep matches burning till you've done it."

"What are you doing here?" I asked when a candle was burning.

I didn't need his answer. One end of the room was filled with wooden cases piled six-high, branded *Perfection Maple Syrup*. While the old man explained that as God was his keeper he didn't know nothing about it, that all he knew was that a man named Keeler had two days ago hired him as night watchman, and if anything was wrong he was as innocent as innocence. I pulled part of the top off one case. The bottles inside had Canadian Club labels that looked like they had been printed with rubber stamps.

I left the cases, drove the old man with his candle in front of me, and searched the building. As I expected, I found nothing to show that this was the warehouse Whisper had occupied.

By the time we returned to the room that held the liquor my left arm was strong enough to lift a bottle. I put it in my pocket and advised the old man:

"Better clear out. You were hired to take the place of some of the guards that Pete the Finn turned into special coppers. Pete's dead. His racket's gone blooey."

When I climbed out the window the old man was standing in front of the cases, looking at them with greedy eyes while he counted on his fingers.

XII

"Well?" Mickey asked when I returned to him and his hired coupé.

I took out the bottle of anything but Canadian Club, pulled the cork, passed it to him, and then put a shot into my own system.

He asked, "Well?" again.

I said:

"Let's try to find the old Redman warehouse."

He said:

"You're going to ruin yourself some time tell-ing people too much," and urged the car down the street.

Three blocks farther on we saw a faded sign—*Redman & Co*. The building under it was long, low, narrow, with corrugated iron roof and few windows.

"We'll leave the boat around the corner," I said. "And you'll go with me. I didn't have a lot of fun by myself last time."

When we climbed out of the coupé, an alley ahead promised a path to the warehouse's rear. We took it. A few people were wandering around the streets, but it was still too early for the factories that filled most of this part of town to have come to life.

At the rear of the warehouse we found something interesting. The back door was closed. Its edge, and the edge of the frame, close to the knob, were scarred. Somebody had worked there with a jimmy.

Mickey tried the door. It was unlocked. Six inches at a time, with pauses between, he pushed it far enough back to let us squeeze in.

When it was open that far we could hear a voice inside. We couldn't hear what it said. All we could hear was the faint rumble of a distant man's voice—with a suggestion of quarrelsomeness in it.

Mickey pointed a thumb at the door's scar and whispered:

"Not coppers."

I went in, keeping my weight on my rubber heels. Mickey followed, his breath hot down the back of my neck.

Ted Wright had told me Whisper's hiding place was in the back, upstairs. I twisted my face around to Mickey and asked:

"Flashlight?"

He put it in my left hand. I put my gun in my right. We crept forward.

The door, still a foot open, let in enough light to show us the way across the room to a doorless doorway. The other side of the doorway was dark. I flicked the light across darkness, found a door, shut off the light and went forward. The next squirt of light showed us steps leading up.

We went up them as if we were afraid they would break under our feet. The rumbling voice had stopped. There was something else in the air. I didn't know what. Maybe a voice not quite loud enough to be heard—if that means anything.

I had counted nine steps when a voice spoke clearly above us:

It said:

"Sure, I killed her, the—!"

A gun said something—the same thing four times—roaring like a 16-inch rifle under the iron roof.

The first voice said: "All right."

By that time Mickey and I had put the rest of the steps behind us, had shoved a door out of the way, and were trying to pull Reno Starkey's hands away from Whisper's throat.

It was a tough job and a useless one. Whisper was dead.

Reno recognized me and let his hands relax. His eyes were as dull, his sallow face as stolid as ever.

Mickey spread the dead gambler on a cot that stood in one end of the room. The room, apparently once an office, had two windows. In their light I could see a body stowed under the cot—Dan Rolff. A Colt's service automatic lay in the center of the floor.

Reno bent his shoulders, swaying.

"Hurt?" I asked.

"He put all four in me," he said calmly, bending to press both forearms against his lower body.

"Get a doc!" I told Mickey.

"No good," Reno said. "I got no more belly left than Peter Collins."*

I pulled a folding-chair over and sat him down on it as Mickey ran out, so he could lean forward and hold himself together.

"Did you know he wasn't croaked?" he asked, nodding at Whisper.

"No. I gave it to you the way I got it from Ted Wright."

"Ted left too soon," he said. "I was leery of

_____
* prison slang; nobody

something like that—came to make sure. He trapped me pretty—played dead on me till I was under the gun. Game at that, damn him! Dead but wouldn't lay down—bandaging self—waiting all by hisself." He smiled, the first smile I'd ever seen him use. "But he's just meat now, and not much of it."

His voice was thickening. A little red puddle had formed under the edge of the chair. I was afraid to touch him. Only his arms and his bent-forward position were holding him together.

He stared at the puddle and asked:

"How the hell did you figure out that you didn't croak the girl?"

"I didn't know whether I killed her or not," I said, "till just now. The best I could do was hope I hadn't. I had you pegged for it, but couldn't be sure. I was all laudanumed up that night. I had a couple of dreams, with bells ringing, and voices calling and me trying to find people. I got an idea that they mightn't have been straight dreams so much as hop-head nightmares stirred up by things that were happening around me at the time.

"When I woke up and found her dead, the lights were out. I couldn't have turned 'em out if I had killed her and kept my fist on the ice pick. You knew I was there the first part of the night. When I went to you for the alibi, you gave it to me right off the reel, without any bargaining or questions. That got me thinking. Then Dawn tried to blackmail me after he had heard Helen Albury's story. The police, after hearing her story, tied you, Whisper, Rolff and me together. I found Dawn killed after meeting O'Marra half a block away. It looked like the shyster had tried the same game on you as on me. That—and the police tying us all together—started me suspecting that the Albury girl had as much on the rest of you as on me. What she had on me, of course, was that she'd seen me go in or out or both. There were good reasons for counting Whisper and Rolff out. That left you the best prospect. But the why's still got me puzzled."

"I bet you," he said, watching the red puddle grow on the floor. He spoke slower, turned out his words more deliberately, as talking became more difficult. He meant to die as he had lived—inside the same hard-boiled, stolid shell. Talking could be torture, but he wouldn't bat an eye, wouldn't stop talking on that account. "It was her own damned fault. She calls me up—tells me Whisper's coming to see her—says if I get there first I can bushwhack him. I'd like that—I go over there—stick around—he don't show.

"I get tired of waiting—hit her door—ask how come. She takes me in—tells me there's nobody there. I get leery—she swears she's alone—we go back in kitchen. Knowing what she is—I'm getting the idea that me and not Whisper is the one being trapped."

Reno stopped as Mickey came in. Mickey said he had phoned for an ambulance.

Reno continued his story:

"Later I find out Whisper did phone her he was coming—got there before me—you were hopped—she was afraid to let him in—he went away. She don't tell me that—afraid I'd go—she's scared—you're hopped she wants protection if he comes back. I don't know none of that. I'm leery I've walked into something. Think I'll take hold of her slap the truth out of her. Try it. She grabs the ice pick—screams. When she screams, I hear man's feet hitting floor. The trap's sprung, I think. I don't mean to be the only one hurt. Twist pick out of her hand—stick it in her. You gallop out of the dark living-room—coked to the edges—charging at the whole world with both eyes shut.

"She tumbles into you. You go down—roll round till your hand hits the butt of the pick. You go to sleep there—peaceful as she is. I see it then—what I've done. But hell, she's croaked! Nothing to do about it. I switch off the lights and go home. When you come—"

A tired-looking ambulance crew—Personville gave them plenty of work those days—brought a litter into the room, cutting off the story.

I took Mickey over into a corner and muttered in his ear:

"The job's yours. I'm going to duck. I ought to be in the clear now, but I know my Poisonville too well to take chances. I'll drive the coupé to some way station where I can catch a train for Ogden. I'll be at the Roosevelt, registered as P. F. King. Stay with the job and let me know when it's best to either take my own name again or buy a ticket to Honduras."

I spent most of my two-day wait in Ogden fixing up my reports so they wouldn't sound as if I had broken as many laws, rules and bones as I had.

On the third night Mickey arrived. He told me that Reno was dead, that I was no longer officially a criminal, and that Poisonville, under martial law, was developing into a sweet-smelling and thornless bed of roses.

We went back to San Francisco. The trouble I'd taken to make my reports read harmlessly didn't keep the Old Man from giving me merry hell.

THE DAIN CURSE

Introduction

THE DAIN CURSE

IN SUMMER 1928, Hammett was in desperate need of money. His second daughter, Josephine, was two years old, and the cost of supporting two households was more than he could handle. He was writing at a furious pace, working part-time in advertising for Samuels, and investigating the possibility of a career as a screenwriter. He was beginning to make a reasonable income as a writer, but his expenses were mounting as well. Encouraged by the sale of *The Cleansing of Poisonville*, Hammett set to work immediately on *The Dain Curse*. He completed that sixty-five-thousand-word novel in three months and mailed it to Knopf on June 29, 1928, seven months before the first of four installments was published in *Black Mask*. The novel was, as he admitted to his Knopf editor Harry Block, "a group of connected stories."

Block, who took over editing duties from Mrs. Knopf, wrote on July 10, "THE DAIN CURSE has been given several readings, and we shall certainly want to publish it." He added, "I don't think, though, that as it stands now it quite measures up to the standard you set for yourself with RED HARVEST." He complained that the novel "falls too definitely into three sections,"

and he asked for a stronger "connecting thread" between the murders in the three sections of the book. He thought there were too many characters, and he noted that "for anyone so attractive, Gabrielle is singularly repulsive." Hammett responded immediately to that point:

> "Without the deformities her mental kinks would be too slightly justified: without those stigmata to brood over from childhood she could hardly have got her mind so completely addled."
>
> Then, too, some of the oddities I gave her seem very serious to me. There's something personal in that, of course. My ears are practically lobeless, the upper joints of my thumbs don't work, and I barely missed having only four toes on my left foot. So far as I know, nobody has ever noticed any of these things unless I pointed them out, and I honestly can't trace my deficiencies in sex appeal to any of them.
>
> My last argument is that I tried to make her slightly repulsive at first, and then to lure the reader into sympathy with her, step by step, more or less against his will. (Repulsive

isn't the right word: suspect, objectionable, distasteful.) And I don't think I gave her so bad a break as Dinah Brand, at that.

Hammett revised the manuscript, mostly along the lines of Block's suggestions, but not enough to suit. On November 22, Block sent the revised manuscript back, asking Hammett to "Please go over it again. . . . The book is an excellent one as it stands but while there is a chance to make it better, I don't think we can disregard it." Block asked for the final draft by April 1, 1929, so it could be published in the fall. The book appeared on July 19, 1929. Hammett later called it "a silly story."

Hammett's final Op stories, "The Farewell Murder" (February 1930) and "Death and Company" (November 1930), marked the end of his tenure at *Black Mask*. Then he was done with the Op. He had begun *The Maltese Falcon* in fall 1928 with higher aspirations and a more sophisticated approach to his fiction. That novel, featuring private detective Sam Spade, was serialized in five parts in *Black Mask* from September 1929 to February 1930. *The Glass Key*, featuring a political fixer named Ned Beaumont but no detective, appeared in four parts in *Black Mask* from March to June 1930. By then Hammett was a literary celebrity without financial cares. He received a $25,000 advance from Knopf for book publication of *The Glass Key* (1931), equivalent to some $400,000 in 2017 dollars, and he was earning money from the movies as well.

The reputations of Hammett and the magazine that nurtured his talent rose together, and by 1930 each had altered the course of English-language literature. *Black Mask* had grown in circulation to one hundred thousand copies a month, and it was grudgingly respected as the unquestioned king of the pulps, beginning to show its influence in the mainstream development of tough-guy literature. Hammett, already regarded as the master of the hard-boiled detective story, was being recognized as a major force in what arguably can be called America's most talented literary generation, the generation of Ernest Hemingway, F. Scott Fitzgerald, William Faulkner, and John Dos Passos. Hammett did not regard the Op stories, early or late, as his best work—he reserved that distinction for *The Maltese Falcon* (serialized in *Black Mask* from September 1928 to January 1929) and *The Glass Key* (serialized in *Black Mask* from March to June 1930)—but there is no question that he used these stories to test characters, plots, and dialogue he used in his novels. His genius shines through in every one, and ultimately they made him rich.

In 1929, Hammett moved to New York, where he was the toast of the town; wrote his last novel, *The Thin Man* (1934); and turned to other interests.

RL

BLACK MASK, OCTOBER 1928

Black Lives

THE DAIN CURSE

BY DASHIELL HAMMETT

Author of "The Cleansing of Poisonville" and other stories of the "Continental" detective.

IT WAS A DIAMOND, all right, sparkling in the grass half a dozen feet from the blue brick walk. It was small—not more than a quarter of a carat—and unmounted. I put it in my pocket and began examining the lawn as thoroughly as I could without going at it on hands and knees.

I had covered a couple of square yards of sod when the Leggetts' front door opened. A woman stepped out on the broad stone top step and looked down at me with good-natured curiosity.

She was a woman of about my age—forty— with darkish blonde hair, a pleasant, plump face, and dimpled pink cheeks. She had on a lavender-flowered white house dress.

I called off my search for the time and went up to her, asking:

"Is Mr. Leggett in?"

"Yes." Her voice was as pleasant and placid as her face. She smiled from me to the lawn. "You'␣re another detective, aren't you?"

I admitted it. She led me up to a green, orange and chocolate room on the second floor, put me in a brocaded chair, and told me she would call her husband from his laboratory.

While I waited for him I looked around the room, deciding that the dull orange rug under my feet was probably both genuinely Oriental and genuinely ancient, that the carved walnut furniture hadn't been ground out by machinery, and that the Japanese prints on the walls hadn't been selected by a puritan.

Edgar Leggett came in, saying:

"I'm sorry to have kept you waiting, but I was at a point at which I couldn't stop. Have you learned something?"

His voice was unexpectedly harsh, metallic,

though friendly enough. He was a dark-skinned, erect man of forty-five or so, medium in height, muscularly slender. He would have been handsome if his brown face hadn't been so deeply marked with lines of pain or of bitterness—sharp, hard lines across his forehead, from his nostrils down across his mouth-corners. Dark hair, worn rather long, curled above and around his broad grooved forehead. Red-brown eyes of abnormal brightness looked out through horn-rimmed spectacles. His nose was long, thin and high-bridged. His lips were thin, sharp and nimble over a small but bony chin. Black and white clothes, carefully made, carefully pressed and laundered, carefully worn, finished the picture.

He was as unusual, and as striking, in appearance as his wife—who had followed him into the room—was wholesomely normal.

"Not yet," I answered his question. "I'm not a police detective—Continental Agency, for the insurance company, and I've just started."

"The insurance company?" he repeated, surprised.

"Yes—North American Surety. Did—"

"Surely," he said quickly, smiling, stopping my words with a flourish of one of his hands. It was a long, thin, dark hand with over-developed finger-tips, ugly as most highly trained hands are. "Surely, they would have been insured. I hadn't thought of that. The diamonds did not belong to me, you know. They were Halstead & Beauchamp's."

"I didn't know that. The insurance company gave us no details. You had them from Halstead & Beauchamp on approval?"

"No. I was using them for experimental purposes. Last year I devised a method by which color could be introduced into glass after its manufacture. Halstead became interested in the possibility of the same method being adapted to precious stones, especially in improving the color of off-shade diamonds, removing yellowish and brownish tints, emphasizing blues. He asked me to attempt it, and supplied me with the stones on which to work. These are the diamonds the burglar got."

"How long had you had them, and how many were there?"

"Five weeks, I think, and there were eight of them, none especially valuable. The largest weighed only a trifle more than half a carat, the smallest only a quarter, and all but two were of poor color."

"Then you hadn't succeeded?"

"Not yet," he admitted readily. "This was a much more delicate matter than staining glass, and on more obdurate material. I had, frankly, made not the slightest progress."

"Where were the diamonds kept?"

"They were locked up last night, though quite often I had left them lying out in the open, considering them as subjects for my experiments rather than as valuables. But last night they were locked in a cabinet drawer in the laboratory. I put them there several days ago, after my last unsuccessful experiment."

"Who knew about your experiments?"

"Anyone, everyone—there was no necessity for secrecy."

"Now, about the burglary?" I said.

"We heard nothing last night. This morning we found our front door open, the cabinet drawer forced, and the diamonds gone. The police found marks on the kitchen door, and say he came in that way and left by the front door."

"The front door was ajar when I came downstairs this morning, at half-past seven," said Mrs. Leggett. She was sitting beside her husband, her hands folded in her lap. "I went upstairs again and awakened Edgar, and we searched the house and found the diamonds gone."

"What else was taken?"

"Nothing else seems to have been touched."

"How about your servants?"

"We've only one," she said, "Minnie Hershey, a negress. She doesn't sleep here, and I'm sure she had nothing to do with it. She has been with us for two years, and I'm sure of her honesty."

I said I'd like to talk to Minnie, and Mrs. Leggett called her in. The servant was a small, wiry mulatto of twenty-something, with the straight black hair and the brown features of an Indian. She was very polite and very insistent that she had nothing to do with the theft of the diamonds, and had known nothing about it until she arrived at the house at eight-thirty this morning. She gave me her home address, a Geary Street number.

"The police questioned her this morning," Mrs. Leggett told me after the girl had gone out. "They don't think she had anything to do with it. They think it was the man I saw—the one Gabrielle saw three nights ago."

I asked for more details.

"When I opened the bedroom windows last night, about midnight, just before going to bed, I saw a man standing up on the corner. I can't say, even now, that there was anything very suspicious-looking about him. He was simply standing there as if waiting for someone, and, though he was looking down this way, there was nothing about him to make me think he might have been watching this house or any other. He was a man past forty, I should say, rather short and broad, somewhat of your build. But he had a bristly brown mustache and was pale. And he wore a brown soft hat and a brown—or dark—overcoat."

"Somebody else had seen him three nights before?" I asked.

"Yes, Gabrielle, my daughter. Coming home late one night, he passed her a pavement or two up the street. She was in an automobile and he was walking. She thought she had seen him come from our steps, but she wasn't sure, and she thought nothing more of it until after the burglary."

"Is she home now? I'd like to talk to her."

Mrs. Leggett went out to get her. I asked Leggett:

"Were the diamonds loose?"

"They were unset, of course, and in small manila envelopes—Halstead & Beauchamp's—each in its own, with a number and the weight of the stone written on it in pencil. The envelopes were taken, too."

Mrs. Leggett returned with her daughter, a girl of twenty or less, in a sleeveless white silk dress; a girl of medium height who looked slenderer than she really was. I stood up to be introduced to her and then asked her about the man she had seen coming from the house the other night.

"I'm not positive that he came from the house," she replied, "or from the lawn." Her manner was a bit petulant, as if being questioned was distasteful. "I thought he might have, but I only saw him walking up the street."

"This was Saturday night?"

"Yes—that is, Sunday morning."

"What time?" I asked, studying her as we talked. Her hair was as curly as, and no longer than, her father's, but of a much lighter brown. Of her features, only her green-brown eyes were large, forehead, mouth and teeth were unusually small. There was a barely noticeable hollowness at cheeks and eyes. She had a pointed chin and extremely white, smooth skin. Her expression was sullen: I couldn't tell whether it was habitual or simply in resentment of my prying.

"Three o'clock or after," she said impatiently.

"Were you alone?"

"Hardly. Eric Collinson brought me home."

I asked her where I could find Eric Collinson. She frowned, hesitated, and said that he was employed by Spear, Hoover & Camp, stock brokers, that she had a putrid headache, and that she hoped I would excuse her now as she knew I couldn't have any more questions to ask.

Without waiting for my answer, she turned and went out of the room. Her ears, I noticed, were without lobes and peculiarly pointed at the tops.

Leggett and his wife took me up to the laboratory, a large room that occupied most of the third story. Charts were hung here and there between the windows on the white-washed walls. The wooden floor was uncovered. An X-ray machine—or something similar—four or five smaller machines, a small forge, a large sink, a large zinc table, some smaller porcelain ones, stands, racks of glassware, siphon-shaped metal tanks—that sort of stuff filled the room.

The cabinet from which the diamonds had been taken was a green-painted steel affair of six drawers, all locking together. The second drawer from the top—the one the diamonds had been in—was open. Its edge was dented where a jimmy or chisel had been forced between it and the frame. The other drawers were still locked.

From the laboratory we went downstairs, through a room where the mulatto girl was walking around behind a vacuum cleaner, and into the kitchen. The back door and its frame were marked much as the cabinet had been, the same tool apparently having been used on it.

When I had finished looking at the door I took the diamond I had found out of my pocket and showed it to the Leggetts, asking:

"Is this one of them?"

Leggett picked it up with forefinger and thumb, held it up to the light, turned it from side to side, and said:

"Yes. It has that cloudy spot down at the culet. Where did you get it?"

"Out front, in the grass. I saw it when I came up the walk."

"Ah, where our burglar dropped it in his hurried departure."

I said I doubted it.

Leggett pulled his brows together, looked at me with smaller eyes, asking harshly:

"What do you mean?"

"I think it was planted there," I explained. "Your burglar knew exactly which drawer to go to, and he didn't waste any time on anything else. Somebody who—"

Mrs. Leggett put a hand on my forearm and said earnestly:

"No, no. You're thinking of Minnie. You are mistaken, I assure you. She—"

Minnie came to the door, still holding the vacuum cleaner, and began to cry that she was an honest girl, and nobody had any right to accuse her of anything, and they could search her and her room if they wanted to, and just because she was a colored girl was no reason, and so on and so on. Not all of it could be made out, because the vacuum cleaner was still humming in her

hand and she sobbed while she talked. Tears ran down her cheeks.

Mrs. Leggett went to her, patted her shoulder, saying: "There, there, don't cry. I know you hadn't anything to do with it. Nobody thinks you had. There, there." Presently she got the girl's tears turned off and sent her upstairs.

Leggett sat on a corner of the kitchen table and asked: "You suspect someone in this house?"

"Somebody who's been in it."

"Whom?"

"Nobody yet."

"That"—he smiled, showing white teeth almost as small as his daughter's—"means everybody—all of us."

"Let's go out and look at the lawn," I suggested. "If we find any more diamonds I'll admit I'm mistaken about this one being planted."

Half-way through the house, as we went toward the front door, we met Minnie Hershey, in a tan coat and violet hat, coming to say "Good-bye" to her mistress.

She wouldn't, she said tearfully, work anywhere where anybody thought she had stolen anything. She was just as honest as anybody else, and more than some, and just as much entitled to respect, and if she couldn't get it in one place she could in another, because she knew places where people wouldn't accuse her of being a th-thief after she had worked for them for two long years without ever taking so much as a slice of bread.

Mrs. Leggett pleaded with her, reasoned with her, scolded her, and commanded her, but none of it was any good. The brown girl's mind was made up. She went away. Mrs. Leggett looked at me as severely as her pleasant face would let her, and said reprovingly: "Now see what you've done."

I said I was sorry, and Leggett and I went out to search the lawn. We didn't find any more diamonds.

II

Leaving Leggett's, I put in a couple of hours canvassing the neighborhood, trying to place the man Mrs. and Miss Leggett had seen. I didn't have any luck on him, but I picked up news of another suspicious character.

A Mrs. Priestly—a pale semi-invalid who lived three doors below the Leggetts—gave me the first news of him. She often sat at a front window in the dark at night, when she couldn't sleep, looking into the street. On two nights she had seen this man.

The first time had been a week ago. He had passed up and down the other side of the street five or six times, at intervals of fifteen or twenty minutes, with his face turned as if he was watching something on Mrs. Priestly's—and the Leggetts'—side of the street. She thought it was between eleven and twelve o'clock when she had seen him the first time, and perhaps one o'clock the last. Several nights later—Saturday night—she had seen him again, not walking, this time, but standing on the corner below, looking up the street, at a little after midnight. He went away after she had watched him for half an hour, down the street, and she had not seen him again.

She said he was a fairly tall man of medium build, young, she thought, and he walked with his head thrust out in front. The street was too dark for her to describe his clothes.

Mrs. Priestly knew all the Leggetts by sight, but said she knew very little about them, except that the daughter was supposed to be a trifle wild. They seemed to be nice people, but kept to themselves. He had moved into the house in 1921, alone except for the housekeeper, a Mrs. Begg, who, Mrs. Priestly understood, was now keeping house for a family named Freemander in Berkeley. Mrs. Leggett and Gabrielle had not come to live with Leggett until 1923.

Mrs. Priestly said she had not been at her window the previous night, and she had not seen the man Mrs. Leggett and her daughter had seen.

A man named Warren Darley, who lived on the opposite side of the street from the Leggetts, but down near the corner on which Mrs. Priestly had seen her man, had, when locking up the house one night, surprised a man—apparently the same one Mrs. Priestly had seen—in his vestibule. Darley was not at home when I called, but Mrs. Darley, after telling me this much, got her husband on the phone for me.

Darley said the man had been standing in the vestibule, either hiding from or watching someone in the street. As soon as Darley opened the door the man ran away, paying no attention to Darley's "What are you doing there?" Darley said he was a man of thirty-five or six, fairly well dressed in dark clothes, and with a very long, thin and sharp nose.

That was all I could get out of the neighbors. I went downtown, to the Montgomery Street offices of Spear, Hoover & Camp, and asked for Eric Collinson.

He was young, blond, tall, broad, sunburned and immaculate, with the good-looking dumb face of one who would know everything about polo, or shooting, or flying, or stocks and bonds, or whatever interested him, and nothing about anything else. We sat on a broad leather seat in the customers' room, now, after market hours, empty except for a weedy boy juggling numbers on the board. I told Collinson about the burglary and asked him about the man he and Miss Leggett had seen Saturday night.

"Ordinary looking chap—short, chunky. You think he took them?"

"Was he coming from the Leggetts' house?"

"From the lawn, yes. Jumpy looking chap. I thought he'd been snooping around. That's why I suggested going after him. Gaby wouldn't have it. Probably a friend of papa's. He goes in for odd eggs."

"Wasn't that late for a visitor to be leaving? What time was it?"

"Midnight, I dare say," but he didn't look at me while he said it.

"Midnight?" I asked sharply.

"That's the word. Time when the graves give up their dead and ghosts walk."

"Miss Leggett said it was after three o'clock."

"You see how it is?" he asked, blandly triumphant, as if he had just demonstrated something we had been arguing about. "Half blind and won't wear glasses for fear of losing beauty. Always doing things like that. Plays abominable bridge—takes deuces for aces. Probably a quarter after twelve. Looks at the clock and gets the hands mixed."

I said, "That's too bad. Thanks," and went around the corner to see Archie Little, junior partner of the Brenderman-Little Company, investment bankers.

I asked Archie what he knew about Collinson. He said there was nothing to know about him, except that his old man was the lumber Collinson and Eric was Princeton and stocks and bonds, a nice boy.

"Maybe he is," I agreed, "but he just lied to me."

"Ts, ts, ts!" Archie shook his sleek head, grinning. "Isn't that like a sleuth? You must have had the wrong fellow. Somebody's impersonating him. The Chevalier Bayard* doesn't lie, and, besides, lying requires imagination. You've— Wait! Was there a woman involved in your question?"

I nodded.

"You're correct, then," Archie assured me. "I apologize. The Chevalier Bayard always lies when there's a woman involved, even if it's unnecessary and puts her to a lot of trouble. It's one of the conventions of Bayardism— something to do with guarding her honor and the like. Is she young? Do I know her? I make a point of knowing all the women people lie about."

I thanked him instead of answering his questions and went up to the Geary Street jewelry store of Halstead & Beauchamp.

Halstead was a suave, pale, bald, fat man with vague eyes and a too-tight collar. I told him what I was doing and asked him if he knew Leggett very well.

"I know him as an occasional customer, and by reputation as a scientist. Why do you ask?"

---

* French soldier (1473–1524); "the knight without fear and beyond reproach"

"The burglary looks phoney."

"Preposterous! That is, it's preposterous if you think a man of his caliber would have anything to do with it. A servant, of course, that is possible, but not Leggett. He is a scientist, and he is, unless our credit department has been misinformed, which I think unlikely, if not wealthy, at least of sufficient means to prevent suspicion falling on him. I happen to know that he has at present with the Seamen's National Bank a balance in excess of ten thousand dollars."

"What were the diamonds worth?"

"Not more than fifteen hundred dollars at retail."

"That would be seven hundred at cost?"

"Well," smiling, "eight-fifty would be closer."

"How did you come to give him the diamonds?"

"I knew him as a customer, and then, when Fitzstephan told me of his work with glass, it occurred to me that the same sort of treatment applied to diamonds might be of great value. So I persuaded Leggett to try it."

"What Fitzstephan?" I asked.

"Owen, the novelist."

"I've met him," I said, "but I didn't know he was on the Coast. Have you his address?"

Halstead gave it to me—a Nob Hill apartment building.

From the jeweler's I went out to the vicinity of the Geary Street address Minnie Hershey had given me. It was a negro neighborhood, which made the getting of reasonably accurate information even more difficult than it always is.

What I got added up to this: The girl had lived in San Francisco for four or five years, coming from Winchester, Virginia. For the last half-year she had been living in a flat at her present address, with a negro called Rhino Tingley. One informant told me Tingley's first name was Ed, another Bill, but both descriptions agreed; he was young, big, black, and could readily be recognized by his scarred chin and his tie pin, pearls grouped to make a cluster of grapes; he was rather shiftless, depending for his living on Minnie and pool, but not bad except when he got mad—then he was a holy terror.

I was told that I could get a look at him the early part of almost any evening in either Bunny Mack's barber shop or Big-foot Gerber's cigar store. I learned where these establishments were located, and then went downtown again, to the police detective bureau in the Hall of Justice.

Nobody was in the Pawnshop Detail office. I crossed the corridor and asked Lieutenant Duff whether any one had been assigned to the Leggett job.

"See O'Gar," he said.

I went into the assembly room, looking for O'Gar and wondering what he—a detective-sergeant attached to the Homicide Detail—had to do with it. Neither O'Gar nor his partner, Pat Reddy, was in. I smoked a cigarette, worried about homicide men being mixed up in my job, and decided to phone Leggett and see if anything had happened out there.

"Have any of the police detectives been in to see you since I left?" I asked when Leggett's harsh voice was in my ear.

"No, but the police called up a little while ago and asked my wife and daughter to come to a house in Golden Gate Avenue to see if they could identify a man who had been killed there. They left a few minutes ago. I didn't accompany them, since I hadn't seen the supposed burglar."

"What was the address?"

He didn't remember the exact number, but he knew the block, one near Van Ness Avenue. I thanked him and went out there.

A uniformed policeman standing in the doorway of a small apartment house guided me to my goal when I reached the designated block. I asked him if O'Gar was there, and where.

"Three-ten," he said.

I went up in a rickety elevator. When I got out of it on the third floor I came face to face with Mrs. Leggett and her daughter, leaving.

"Now I hope you're satisfied that Minnie had nothing to do with it," Mrs. Leggett said chidingly.

"Was he the man you saw?"

"Yes. And the envelopes the diamonds were in are there."

I turned to Gabrielle Leggett and said:

"Eric Collinson insists that it was only midnight, or a few minutes after, that you got home, and saw the man, Saturday night."

"Eric," she said irritably, walking past me to enter the elevator, "is an ass."

Her mother, following her into the elevator, reprimanded her amiably: "Now, dear!"

I closed the door for them and walked down the hall to a doorway where Pat Reddy stood talking to a couple of reporters, said "Hello" to them, squeezed past them into a short passageway, and went through that to a shabbily furnished room where a dead man lay on a wall bed.

Phels of the Identification Bureau looked up from his magnifying glass to nod at me, and then went on examining the edge of a mission table that stood against one wall. O'Gar pulled his head and shoulders in the open window and growled:

"So we got to put up with you again?"

He was a burly, hard-faced, stolid man of fifty who wore wide-brimmed soft black hats of the movie village-constable sort. There were a lot of shrewd ideas in his grizzled bullet head and he was comfortable to work with.

I looked at the corpse—a man of forty or so, with a heavy face, short hair touched with gray, a scrubby dark mustache, thick shoulders and stocky arms and legs. There was a bullet-hole just above his navel, and another high in the left side of his chest.

"It's a man," O'Gar informed me as I put the blanket over him again. "He's dead."

"What else did somebody tell you?" I asked.

"Looks like him and another bimbo nicked Leggett for the ice and then the other bimbo decided to take a one-way split. The envelopes are here"—O'Gar took them out of his pocket and ruffled them with his thumb—"but the stuff ain't. Neither is the gun the two slugs came out of. It went down the fire-escape with Mr. X a little while back. People saw him go down, but they lost him when he cut through the alley. Tall guy with a long nose. This one"—O'Gar pointed at the bed with the envelopes—"has been here a week. Name of Louis Upton. New York labels. We don't know him. Nobody in the dump's ever seen him with anybody else. Nobody will say they know Mr. X."

Pat Reddy, a big, jovial youngster, with almost enough brains to make up for his lack of experience, came in. I told him and O'Gar what I had turned up on the diamond job so far.

"Long-nose and this bird taking turns watching Leggett's," Reddy suggested when I was through.

"Maybe," I admitted, "but there was an inside angle to the job."

"How about the yellow girl?"

"I'm going out for a look at her man tonight. You people are trying New York on this Upton?"

"Practically," O'Gar said.

III

At the Nob Hill address that Halstead had given me I told the boy at the switchboard my name, wondering if Fitzstephan would remember it. I had run into him five years ago, in New York City, where I had been digging dirt on a chain of fake mediums who had taken a coal-and-ice dealer's widow for a hundred thousand dollars. Fitzstephan was combing the same field for literary material, and, becoming acquainted, we had pooled forces. He knew the ghost racket inside and out. With his help I had cleaned up my job in a week or two. We kept up a fairly intimate friendship for a couple of months after that, until I left New York for the West.

At that time he had been in his early thirties—a long, lean, sorrel-haired man with sleepy gray eyes, a wide, humorous mouth, and carelessly worn clothes. He pretended to be lazier

than he was, would rather talk than do anything else, and had a lot of what seemed to be accurate information and original ideas on any subject that happened to come up, so long as it was out of the ordinary.

"Mr. Fitzstephan says to come right up, sir," the boy said.

His apartment was on the sixth floor. He was standing at its door when I got out of the elevator.

"By God!" he said, holding out a lean hand, "it is you."

"None other."

We went into a room where half a dozen bookcases and four tables left little room for anything else. Magazines and books in various languages, papers, clippings, proof sheets, were scattered everywhere—all exactly as it had been in his New York rooms.

We sat down, found places for our feet between table-legs, and accounted, more or less roughly, for our lives since we had last seen one another. He had been in San Francisco a little less than a year. He liked the city, he said, but he wouldn't oppose any movement to give the West back to the Indians.

"How's the literary grift go?" I asked.

He looked at me sharply, demanded:

"You haven't been reading me?"

"No. Where'd you get that idea?"

"There was something in your tone, something proprietary, as in the voice of one who had bought an author for two dollars and a half. I haven't met it often enough to be used to it. Good God! Remember once I offered to give you a set of my books?"

"You were drunk," I said.

"On sherry—Elsa Donne's sherry. Remember Elsa? She showed us a picture she had just finished and you said it was pretty. Whoops, wasn't she furious! You said it so vapidly, and sincerely. Remember? She put us out, but I had already got tight on her sherry, and so had you. But you weren't plastered enough to accept the books."

"I was afraid I'd read them and understand

them," I explained, "and then you'd have felt insulted."

A Chinese boy brought us cold white wine. Fitzstephan said:

"It's queer we should have been in the same city for a year without running into one another. How did you finally come across me?"

"Watt Halstead gave me your address, after he'd told me you knew Edgar Leggett."

A gleam pushed through the sleepiness in the novelist's gray eyes.

"Leggett's been up to something?" he drawled, sitting a little higher in his chair.

"Why do you say that?"

"I didn't say it." He sank back lazily in his chair, but the gleam was still in his eyes. "I asked it. Come—out with it. I'm a novelist. My business is with souls and what goes on in them. What's Leggett been up to?"

"We don't do it that way. We trade information. How long have you known him?"

"Nearly a year. I met him soon after I came here, I think at Marquard's—the sculptor, not the restaurant. He interested me. There's something obscure in him, something dark and inviting. Physically ascetic—neither smoking nor drinking—eating meagerly, a vegetarian, sleeping only four hours a night, I'm told. Mentally sensual—does that mean anything?—to the point of decadence. You think I like the fantastic—you should know him. His friends—he hasn't any. His choice in companions are those who have the most outlandish ideas to offer—the wildest, most maniac, brutal, degenerate, abnormal. Marquard, with his insane figures that are not figures but boundaries of the portions of space which are the real figures; Denbar Curt, with his algebraism; crazy Laura Joines; Farnham—"

"And you," I put in, "with your explanations and descriptions that explain and describe nothing. I hope you don't suppose that what you've said so far means anything to me."

"I remember you now; you were always like that." He grinned at me, running long fingers through his sorrel hair. "Tell me what's up while I try to find one-syllable words to use on you."

I told him about the diamonds, and about the dead man. He looked very disappointed.

"That's trivial, sordid," he complained. "I've been thinking of Leggett in terms of Dumas, and you bring me a piece of gimcrackery out of O. Henry. You've let me down—you and your shabby diamonds. But"—his eyes brightened again—"they may lead to something. Leggett may or may not be a criminal, but there's more to him than a two-penny insurance swindle."

"You mean," I asked sarcastically, "that he's one of these master minds? So you've been reading newspapers? What do you think he is? King of the bootleggers? Chief of an international crime syndicate? A white slave magnate? Head of a dope ring? Or maybe queen of the counterfeiters in disguise?"

"Don't be an idiot. He's got brains, that man, and there's something black in him. There's something he doesn't want to think about. I've told you that he revels in all that's dizziest in thought, yet he's intellectually as cold as a fish, but with a bitter-dry coldness. He's neurotic, yet he doesn't even smoke. He keeps his body sensitive and fit and ready—for what?—while he drugs his mind against memory with the wildest of intellectual lunacies, with ideas that belong to the mad. Yet the man is cold and sane.

"There's only one explanation: there's darkness in his past that he wants to forget. But why shouldn't he anesthetize his mind through his body, by sensuality if not by drugs? There's still only one explanation; the darkness in his past is not dead, and he must keep himself fit to cope with it should it come into the present."

"All right. What is it?"

"If I don't know—and I don't—it isn't because I haven't tried to learn; but try getting information out of Leggett some time. I don't believe that's his name."

"No?"

"No," Fitzstephan said, "he's French. I'd risk anything on it. He told me once that he came from Atlanta, but he's French in outlook, in quality of mind, in everything but admission."

"What of the rest of the family? The daughter's cuckoo, isn't she?"

"I wonder." Fitzstephan looked queerly at me. "Are you saying that carelessly, or do you really think she's off?"

"I don't know, but she's odd. She's got animal ears and almost no forehead, and her eyes change from green to brown. An uncomfortable sort of person."

"If you're cataloging her physical peculiarities you can add that her upper thumb joints—between metacarpal bones and first phalanx—don't work."

"I'm not. In your snooping around have you been able to pry into any of her affairs?"

"Are you—who make your living snooping and prying—sneering at my curiosity about people and my attempts to satisfy it?"

"We're different," I said. "I do mine with the object of putting people in jail, and I get paid for it, though not as much as I should."

"That's not different," he said. "I do mine with the object of putting people in books, and I get paid for it, and not as much as I should. Gabrielle hates her father. He worships her."

"How come the hate?"

Fitzstephan shrugged his lean shoulders; said:

"I don't know. Perhaps because he worships her."

"There's no sense to that," I growled. "You're just being literary. How about Mrs. Leggett?"

"You've never eaten one of her meals, I suppose? You'd have no doubts about her if you had. None but a serene sane soul ever achieved such cooking. I've often wondered what she thinks of the weird pair that is her husband and daughter, or if she simply accepts them as they are without being aware of their weirdness. I rather suppose she does."

"All this is well enough in its way," I said, "but you still haven't told me anything definite about them. Come on, loosen up."

"I've told you," he insisted, "everything I know. And that's the thing, my son. You know what a—in your words—a snooper and prier—I

am. Well, if, after a year of it, I know no more about a man who interests me than I do about Leggett, isn't that the most conclusive sort of evidence that he's hiding something, and that he is a hider of no mean sort?"

"Is it? I don't know. But I know I've wasted enough time here learning nothing that anybody can be jailed for."

It was a little after five o'clock when I left Fitzstephan's apartment. I stopped at a restaurant for some food, and then went out for a look at Minnie Hershey's man, Rhino Tingley.

I found him in Big-foot Gerber's cigar store, rolling a fat cigar around in his mouth, telling something to the other negroes—four of them in the place.

". . . says to him, 'Nigger, you talking yourself out of skin,' and I reaches out my hand for him, and, 'fore Gawd, there wasn't none of him there excepting his footprints in the cement pavement, eight feet apart and leading home."

Buying a package of cigarettes, I weighed him in while he talked. He was a chocolate man of not more than thirty years, close to six feet tall, and weighing two hundred pounds plus, with big yellow-balled pop eyes, a broad nose, a big mouth, and a ragged black scar running from his lower lip down behind his blue and white striped collar. His clothes were new enough to look new, and he wore them sportily. His voice was a heavy bass, and when he laughed with his audience after he had finished his story the glass of the showcases shook.

I went out of the store while they were laughing, heard his laughter stop short behind me, resisted the temptation to look back, and moved down in the direction of the building where he and Minnie lived. He came abreast of me when I was half a block from the flats.

I said nothing while we took seven steps. Then he said:

"You the man that been inquiring around about me?"

The sour odor of Italian red wine came thick enough to be seen.

I considered and replied:

"Yeah."

"What you got to do with me?" he asked, not disagreeably, but as if he wanted to know.

On the other side of the street, Gabrielle Leggett, in brown coat, brown and yellow hat, came out of Minnie's building and walked up the street, not turning her head toward us. She walked swiftly and her lower lip was between her teeth.

I looked at the negro. He was looking at me. There was nothing in his face to show that he had seen Gabrielle Leggett or that the sight of her meant anything to him. I said:

"You've got nothing to hide, have you? What do you care who asks about you?"

"All the same, I'm the party to come to if he wants to know about me. You the man that got Minnie fired?"

"She wasn't fired. She quit."

"Minnie don't have to take nobody's lip. She—"

"Let's go over and talk to her," I suggested, leading the way across the street. At the door he went ahead, up a flight of steps, down a dark hall to a door that he opened with one of the twenty or more keys on his ring.

Minnie Hershey, in a pink kimono trimmed with yellow ostrich feathers that looked like little dead ferns, came out of the bedroom to meet us in the living-room. Her eyes got big when she saw me.

Rhino Tingley said: "You know this gentleman, Minnie?"

Minnie said: "Yes."

I said: "You shouldn't have left Leggetts' that way. Nobody thinks you had anything to do with the diamonds. What did Miss Leggett want here?"

"There been no Miss Leggetts here," she told me. "I don't know what you talking about."

"She came out just as we were coming in."

"Oh, *Miss* Leggett! I thought you said *Mrs.* Leggett. I beg your pardon. Yes, sir. Miss Gabrielle was sure enough here. She wanted to know if I wouldn't come back. She thinks a powerful lot of me, Miss Gabrielle does."

That, I thought, is a lie.

"That," I said, "is what you ought to do. It was foolish—leaving like that." Rhino Tingley took the cigar out of his mouth and pointed it at the girl. "You away from them," he boomed, "and you stay away from them. You don't have to take nothing from nobody." He put a hand in his pants pocket, lugged out a thick bundle of paper money, thumped it down on the table, and rumbled: "What for you have to work for folks?"

He was talking to the girl, but looking at me, grinning, gold teeth shining. The bundle of money was on the table close to me. I picked it up, counted it—eleven hundred and sixty-five dollars—and dropped it on the table again. Rhino, still grinning, returned it to his pocket.

The girl looked at the man, said scornfully, "Lead him around, vino," and turned to me again, her small face tense, anxious to be believed, saying:

"Rhino got that money in a crapgame, mister. Hope to die if he didn't."

I assured her that I believed every word she said, again advised her to go back to the Leggetts, and departed.

Downtown, in an Owl drug store, I looked in the Berkeley section of the telephone directory, found only one Freemander listed, and called it. Mrs. Begg was there, and she told me she could see me if I came over right away. I caught the next ferry. The Freemander house was set off a road that wound uphill toward the University of California.

Mrs. Begg was a scrawny, big-boned woman with not much gray hair packed close around a bony skull, hard gray eyes, and hard, capable hands. She was sour and severe, but plain-spoken enough to let us talk turkey without a lot of hemming and hawing.

I told her about the theft of the diamonds and my belief that the burglar had been helped, at least with information, by someone who knew the Leggett household, and added:

"Mrs. Priestly told me you had been Leggett's housekeeper a few years ago, and thought you could help me."

Mrs. Begg said she doubted if she could tell me anything that would help me, but she was willing to do all she could, being an honest woman and having nothing to conceal from anybody. Once she started, she told me a great deal, damned near talking me earless. Throwing out the stuff that didn't interest me, I came away with the following information:

In the spring of 1921 Mrs. Begg had been hired by Leggett, through an agency, as housekeeper. At first she had a girl to help her, but there wasn't work enough for both, so, at her suggestion, the girl was let go. Leggett was a man of simple tastes, and spent most of his time on the top floor, where he had his laboratory and bedroom. He seldom used the rest of the house except when he had friends in for an evening. Mrs. Begg didn't like his friends, though she could tell me nothing much about them except that "the way they talked was a shame and a disgrace."

Edgar Leggett was as nice a man as a person could want to know, she said, only so secretive that he made a person nervous. She was never allowed to go up on the top floor, and the doors were kept locked. Once a month he would have a Jap in to clean up under his supervision. Well, she supposed he had a lot of scientific secrets, and maybe dangerous chemicals, that he didn't want people poking into, but just the same it made a person uneasy.

She didn't know anything about her employer, and knew her place better than to ask him. In August, 1923—it was a rainy morning, she remembered—a woman and a girl of fifteen with a lot of suitcases arrived at the house. She let them in and the woman asked for Mr. Leggett. Mrs. Begg went up to the laboratory and told him, and he came down. Never in all her born days had she seen such a surprised man as he was when he saw them. He turned absolutely white and she thought he was going to fall down, he shook so bad.

She didn't know what Leggett said to the woman and girl, because they all jabbered in some foreign language, though the lot of them could talk as good English as anybody else, and

better than most. She went about her work. Pretty soon Leggett came out to the kitchen and told her the visitors were a Mrs. Dain, his sister-in-law, and her daughter Gabrielle, neither of whom he had seen for ten years, and that they were going to stay with him. Mrs. Dain later told the housekeeper that they were English but had been living in New York for several years. Mrs. Begg said she liked Mrs. Dain, who was a sensible woman and a real housewife, but Gabrielle was a tartar.

With Mrs. Dain's arrival, and with her ability as a housekeeper, there was no longer any place in the household for Mrs. Begg. They had been very liberal with her, she said, helping her find a new place and giving her a generous bonus when she left. She had seen none of them since, but in the *Examiner* a week later—she was the sort of woman who keeps a careful watch on marriages, deaths and births—she saw that a marriage license had been issued to Edgar Leggett and Alice Dain.

IV

When I arrived at the agency at nine the next morning, Eric Collinson was sitting in the outer office. His sunburned face was dingy without pinkness, and he had neglected to put stick-em on his hair.

"Do you know anything about Miss Leggett?" he asked, jumping up and striding toward me as soon as I appeared in the doorway. "She wasn't home last night, and she's not home yet. Her father wouldn't say he didn't know where she was, but I'm sure he didn't. He told me not to worry, but how can I help worrying? Do you know anything about it?"

I said I didn't, told him I had seen her leaving Minnie Hershey's, gave him the mulatto's address, and suggested that he see if he could learn anything from her. He jammed his hat on his head and hurried out of the office.

Getting O'Gar on the phone, I asked if he had heard from New York.

"Uh-huh. Upton—that's his right name—was once a private detective, till '23, when him and a fellow named Harry Ruppert were sent over to Sing Sing for fixing a jury. They were sprung last month. How'd you make out with the dinges?"

"Her man—a big smoke called Rhino Tingley—is toting an eleven-hundred-buck roll. He says he won it in a crap-game. It's more than he could have got for the diamonds, but maybe the diamonds aren't the big item in this job. Suppose you have Rhino looked up."

O'Gar said he would and hung up.

I wired our New York branch for additional dope on Upton and Ruppert, and then trotted up to the County Clerk's office, in the City Hall, and dug into the August and September, 1923, marriage licenses. I found the applications I wanted, dated August 26. Edgar Leggett had stated that he was born in Atlanta, Georgia, on March 6, 1883, and that this was his second marriage. Alice Dain had given London as her birthplace, October 22, 1888, as the date, and had stated that she had never been married before.

That clicked with my opinion that Gabrielle, if not the daughter of both, was more likely the man's than the woman's.

When I got back to the agency, Eric Collinson, his yellow hair still further disarranged, confronted me again.

"I saw Minnie," he said excitedly, "and she wouldn't tell me anything. She said Gaby was there last night to ask her to come back to work, but that's all she knows about her. But she—she was wearing an emerald ring which I'm positive is Gaby's."

"Did you ask her about it?"

"Who? Minnie? No. How could I? It would have been—you know."

"That's right," I agreed, "we must always be polite. Why did you lie to me about the time you and Miss Leggett got home the other night?"

His face got stupider than ever with embarrassment.

"That was silly of me," he stammered, "but I didn't—I was afraid you'd—I thought that—"

He wasn't getting anywhere. I suggested:

"You thought that was too late for her to be out and didn't want me to get wrong notions about her?"

"Yes, that's it."

I thought of Little's *Chevalier Bayard*, hid my grin, and shooed Collinson out.

In the operatives' room Mickey Linehan—big, loose-hung, red-faced—and Al Mason—slim, dark, sleek—were swapping lies about the times they had been shot at, each pretending to have been more frightened than the other. I told them who was who in my diamond job, and sent Al out to keep an eye on the Leggetts, Mickey to see how Minnie and Rhino were behaving.

Mrs. Leggett, a worried shadow on her pleasant face, opened the door when I rang her bell an hour later. We went up to the green, orange and chocolate room, where we were joined by her husband.

I passed on to them the information about Upton that O'Gar had got from New York, and told them I had wired for additional information on Harry Ruppert.

"Some of your neighbors saw a man who was not Upton loitering around, and the same man was seen running down the fire-escape from Upton's room. There's no reason why he couldn't have been Ruppert."

Nothing changed in the scientist's too bright red-brown eyes. They held interest and nothing else. No muscle flickered in his face.

I asked "Is Miss Leggett in?"

"No," he replied.

"When will she be?"

"Probably not for several days."

"Where can I find her?" I asked, turning to Mrs. Leggett. "I've some questions to ask her."

Mrs. Leggett avoided my gaze, looking at her husband. His metallic voice answered my question:

"We don't know, exactly. Friends of hers, a Mr. and Mrs. Harper, drove up from Los Angeles and asked her to go with them on their trip up in the mountains. I don't know which route

they are taking, and doubt if they had any definite plans."

I didn't believe that. I asked questions about
the Harpers. Edgar Leggett admitted knowing very little about them. Mrs. Harper's given
name was Carmel, he said, and everybody called
the man Bud, but he, Leggett, didn't know
either his first name or his initials. Nor did he
know their Los Angeles address. He thought
they had a house somewhere near Pasadena, but
he wasn't sure.

While he told me all this nonsense, his wife
sat staring at the floor, lifting her blue eyes now
and then to look swiftly, pleadingly, at her husband.

"Don't you know more about them than
that?" I asked her.

"N-no," she said weakly, darting a timid look
at her husband's face, while he, paying no attention to her, stared levelly at me.

"When did they leave?" I asked.

"Early this morning," Leggett told me.
"They were staying at one of the hotels—I don't
know which—and Gabrielle spent the night
with them, so they could make an early start."

I had enough of the Harpers.

"Did any of you have any dealings with
Upton before this affair?" I asked.

"No."

There were other questions to which I would
have liked answers, but the sort of replies he
gave me answered nothing. I was tempted to
tell him what I thought of him, but there was no
profit in that. I stood up.

He got on his feet, smiled apologetically, and
said:

"I'm sorry to have caused the insurance
company all this trouble and expense. After all,
the diamonds were probably lost because of my
carelessness in not safeguarding them. I should
like your opinion; do you really think I should
accept the responsibility for the loss and make
it good?"

"I think you should," I replied, "but it won't
stop the investigation."

Mrs. Leggett put her handkerchief to her
mouth quickly. Leggett said calmly:

"Thanks. I'll have to think it over."

On my way back to the agency I dropped in
on Owen Fitzstephan for a half-hour visit. He
was writing, he told me, an article for the *Psy-
chopathological Review*, or something of the sort,
condemning the hypothesis of an unconscious
or subconscious mind as a snare and delusion, a
pitfall for the unwary and a set of false whiskers
for the charlatan, a gap in psychology's roof that
made it impossible, or nearly, for the sound scientist to smoke out such faddists as, for example,
the psychoanalyst and the behaviorist. He went
on like that for ten minutes or more before he
came back to the United States with:

"How are you getting along with the problem
of the elusive diamonds?"

"This way and that way," I said, and told him
all I had done and learned so far.

"You've certainly," he complimented me
when I had finished, "got it all as tangled and
confused as possible."

"It'll be worse before it's better," I predicted.
"I'd like to have ten minutes alone with Mrs.
Leggett. Away from her husband, I imagine
things could be got out of her. Could you do
anything with her?"

"I'll try. Suppose I go out there tomorrow
afternoon, to borrow a book—Waite's *Rosy
Cross** will do it. They know I'm interested in
that sort of stuff. He will be working in the laboratory and I'll insist on not disturbing him, and
perhaps I can get something from her, though
it'll have to be in a casual, offhand way."

I thanked him, returned to the agency, and
spent most of the afternoon putting my findings
on paper and trying to fit them together in some
sort of order. Eric Collinson phoned twice to
ask if I had found his Gabrielle. Neither Mickey
Linehan nor Al Mason sent in any report. At six
o'clock I called it a day.

---

* *The Brotherhood of the Rosy Cross* by Arthur
Edward Waite (1924)

V

The following day brought happenings.

Early in the morning there was a telegram from our New York branch. Decoded, it read:

Louis Upton formerly proprietor detective agency here stop *arrested September first one nine two three for bribing two jurors in Sexton murder trial* stop *Upton attempted to save self by implicating Harry Ruppert operative in his employ* stop *Upton and Ruppert convicted and sent to Sing Sing* stop *released February six this year* stop *Ruppert in New York following week hunting for Upton* stop *threatened to kill him for framing him on bribery charge* stop *Ruppert thirty two years five feet eleven inches one hundred fifty pounds brown hair and eyes sallow complexion thin face long sharp nose walks with slight stoop and chin out* stop *mailing photographs.*

That placed Harry Ruppert; he was undoubtedly the man Mrs. Priestly and Darley had seen, and the man who had been seen leaving Upton's room.

My phone rang. Detective-sergeant O'Gar:

"That nigger Rhino Tingley of yours was picked up last night in a hock shop, trying to unload some jewelry, pretty good junk. We haven't been able to crack him yet—just got him identified this morning. I sent the stuff out to Leggett's, thinking maybe they'd know something about it, but they didn't."

"Try Halstead & Beauchamp," I suggested. "Tell them you think the stuff is Gabrielle Leggett's, but don't tell them the Leggetts have said 'no.'"

Half an hour later O'Gar phoned me from the jeweler's, telling me that Halstead had positively identified two pieces—a string of pearls and a topaz brooch—as articles Leggett had purchased there, gifts for his daughter.

"Fine!" I said. "Now will you do this? Go out to Rhino's house and put the screws on his woman, Minnie Hershey. Frisk the joint, rough her up, the more you scare her the better, but don't stay too long, and then beat it, leaving her alone. I've got her covered. I'll give you all the explanations later."

"I'll turn her white," O'Gar promised.

Dick Foley was in the operatives' room, writing a report on a warehouse robbery that had kept him up all night. I chased him out to help Mickey Linehan with Minnie.

"Both of you tail her if she leaves her joint after the police are through," I instructed him, "and as soon as you put her anywhere, one of you get to a phone and let me know."

I went back to my cubbyhole and burned cigarettes. I was destroying the third one when Eric Collinson called up to ask if I had learned anything yet.

"Nothing definite, but I've got prospects. If you aren't busy you might come over here and wait with me."

He said, very eagerly, that he would do that.

Five minutes later Mickey Linehan phoned:

"The high yellow's in the Primrose Hotel on Mason Street."

The phone rang again by the time I had put it down.

"This is Watt Halstead," a voice said. "Can you come down?"

"Not right now. Perhaps not for several hours. Is it—?"

"It's about Edgar Leggett, and it's quite puzzling. The police brought in some jewelry this morning, asking if we could tell whether it belonged to Gabrielle Leggett. I recognized a string of pearls and a brooch which her father bought from us last year—the brooch in the spring, the pearls at Christmas. After the police had gone I, quite naturally, phoned Leggett, and he took the most peculiar attitude. He waited until I had told him all about it, then said, 'I thank you very much for your interference in my affairs,' and hung up. What do you suppose is the matter with him?"

"God knows. Thanks. I've got to run now, but I'll be in as soon as I can."

Eric Collinson had arrived while I was listening to the jeweler's story.

"Just a minute," I told the blond youngster, "and we'll dash out on what might not be a false alarm."

I called Information, got Fitzstephan's number, had it rung, and heard his drawled "Hello."

"You'd better get going with your book-borrowing, if any good's to come of it," I advised him.

"Why? Are things taking place?"

"Things are."

"Such as?"

"This and that, but it's no time for anybody who wants to poke into the Great Leggett Mystery to be dillydallying with pieces about unconscious minds."

"Come on," I told Collinson, putting the phone down and leading the way to the elevators.

He had a Chrysler roadster around the corner. We got in it and bucked traffic and traffic signals for the ten blocks that lay between our starting point and the Primrose Hotel, a gaudy establishment of the fly-by-night variety, run by an ex-tent-showman named Felix Weber.

I made Collinson drive past the hotel to the next corner, where Mickey Linehan was leaning his lopsided bulk against a garage door. He came to us when we stopped at the curb.

"The shine* left ten minutes ago," he reported, "with Dick behind her. Nobody else has been out that looks like any of the birds you told us about."

"You camp in the car and watch the door," I told him. "We're going in. Let me do the talking," I instructed Collinson as we walked back to the Primrose, "and try not breathing so hard. Everything will come out O.K."

At the desk I asked for Weber and was directed to a frosted glass door marked *Manager's Office*. Weber, a little fat blond man with round blue childish eyes and no conscience,

looked up from his desk when we came in, and then jumped up to shake my hand enthusiastically. We were old friends. Ten years back I had just barely missed putting him in the West Virginia bighouse for a swindle, and wouldn't have missed if he hadn't had too much money to spend on witnesses. In the same affair he had just barely missed putting a .45 slug in my body, and wouldn't have missed if he hadn't had too much white mule[†] in him.

I introduced Collinson and said:

"We're looking for a girl who probably came here night before last. Her name is Leggett, no matter what one she's using. A girl of twenty, medium height and build, with a small face, pointed chin, white skin. Maybe she was wearing a brown coat and a brown and yellow hat. She here?"

"I'll see," he said, starting for the door.

"Never mind seeing. If she owes you anything we'll pay it, so you won't have to find out if she does, and collect it, before you let us have her."

He came back from the door, smiling good-naturedly, saying:

"She's in 416, registered as Geraldine Long. What do you want her for?"

"We're going up to see her. The chances are she'll leave with us, so have the bill, if any, ready when we come down."

Outside the manager's door, Collinson put a hand on my arm and mumbled:

"I don't know whether I—whether we ought to do this. She won't—"

"Suit yourself," I growled, "but I'm going up. Maybe she won't like it, but neither do I like people running away and hiding when I want to ask them about diamonds."

He frowned, chewed his lip, and made uncomfortable faces, but he went along with me. We found room 416, and I tapped the door with the backs of my fingers. There was no answer. I knocked again, louder.

Behind the door a voice spoke. It might have been anybody's voice, though probably a wom-

---

an's, but it was too faint for identification, too smothered for us to know what it was saying.

I poked Collinson with my elbow and ordered:

"Call her."

He pulled at his collar with a forefinger and called hoarsely:

"Gaby, it's Eric."

That didn't bring any answer.

I thumped the door again and called: "Open the door." The voice said something that was nothing to me. I repeated my thumping and calling. Down the corridor a door opened and a pasty-faced boy with patent-leather hair stuck his head out to ask: "What's the matter?"

I said, "None of your damned business," and pounded 416 again.

The voice inside rose strong enough now for us to know that it was complaining, though no words could be made out.

Then a bed creaked. Feet rustled on carpet. Presently the key rattled on the other side of the lock.

When the lock clicked, I turned the knob and pushed the door open.

"Good God!" Eric Collinson exclaimed chokingly.

Gabrielle Leggett stood there, swaying a little. Her face was white as paper. Her eyes were all brown, dull, focused on nothing, and her tiny forehead was wrinkled, as if she knew there was something in front of her and was trying to decide what it was.

She had on one yellow stocking, a brown velvet skirt that was wrinkled as if it had been slept in, and a yellow chemise. Scattered around the room were a pair of brown slippers, the other stocking, a brown and gold blouse, a brown coat and a brown and yellow hat.

I pushed Collinson into the room, followed him, and closed the door, turning the key. He stood gaping at the girl, his jaw sagging, his eyes as vacant as hers, though more horrified. She leaned unsteadily against the wall beside the door and stared at nothing with her dark, blank eyes and ghastly, puzzled face.

I put an arm around her and led her to the bed, telling Collinson:

"Gather up the clothes." I had to tell him twice before he came out of his trance.

The girl went docilely across the room with me—if I had let go of her she would have stopped still where I left her—and let me set her down on the edge of the rumpled bed.

Collinson had finished gathering up her clothes when fingers drummed on the door.

"Well?" I called.

Weber's voice, full of curiosity:

"Everything all right?"

"Swell! Will you send a boy down to the corner and tell the man in the Chrysler roadster to drive up to the door and wait. The boy can't miss him—a big man with ears like a pair of red wings and a wide, red face."

With disappointment in his voice, Weber promised to send, and went away from the door. I began dressing the girl.

Collinson dug his fingers in my shoulder and protested in a tone that would have been appropriate if I had been robbing an altar:

"No! You can't—"

I pushed his hand away, growling:

"What the hell? You can have the job if you want it."

He was sweating. He gulped and stuttered:

"No. No. It—I couldn't—" He broke off and walked to the window.

"She told me you were an ass," I said to his back, and discovered that I was putting the brown and gold blouse on backward.

She gave me no more assistance than if she had been a wax figure, but at least she didn't struggle when I pushed her around and she stayed in whatever position I shoved her. Putting on her stockings, I found another physical peculiarity to add to the list Fitzstephan and I had made. There were only four toes on her foot, three small ones—instead of the normal four—beside the big toe. I felt her other foot through its stocking and found it the same.

By the time I had got her into hat and coat, Collinson had come away from the window and was spluttering questions at me. What was the matter with her? Oughtn't we get a doctor? Was it safe to take her out? And when I stood up he took her away from me, supporting her with his long, muscular arms, babbling "It's Eric, Gaby. Don't you know me? Speak to me. What's the matter, dear?"

"There's nothing wrong with her except a skinful of dope," I said. "Don't try to bring her out of it now. Wait till we get her home. You take that arm and I'll take this. She can walk, and there's no use putting on a show for the public. Let's go."

We got her downstairs and into the roadster without attracting any crowds. I sent Mickey up to her room to see what he could find; Collinson and I wedged the girl between us on the seat, and he put the car in motion.

We rode three blocks and he asked:

"Are you sure home is the best place for her?"

I said I was. He didn't say anything more for another five blocks and then repeated his question, adding something about a hospital.

"Why not a newspaper office?" I sneered.

Three blocks of silence, and he started again:

"I know a doctor who—"

"I've got work to do," I informed him, "and Miss Leggett, home now, in the shape she's in now, will help me do it. So she goes home."

He scowled at me, accusing me angrily:

"You'd humiliate her, disgrace her, endanger her life for the sake of—"

"Her life's in no more danger than yours or mine. She's simply got a little more hop in her than she can stand up under. And she took it. I didn't give it to her."

The subject of our argument was alive and breathing between us—even sitting up with her eyes open—but knowing no more of what was going on than if she had been in Finland.

We should have turned to the right at the next corner. Collinson held the car straight, and stepped it up to forty-five miles an hour, staring ahead, his face hard and lumpy.

"Take the next turn," I commanded.

"No," he said, and the speedometer showed a *50*. People on the sidewalks began looking at us as we whizzed past.

"Well?" I asked, wriggling an arm loose from the girl's side.

"We're going down the peninsular," he announced firmly. "She's not going home in that condition."

I grunted, "So?" and flashed my free arm at the controls. He knocked my hand aside, holding the wheel with one hand, stretching the other out to block me if I should try to kill the engine again.

"Don't do that," he cautioned me, increasing our speed another half-dozen miles. "You know what will happen to us all if you—"

I cursed him, bitterly, fairly thoroughly, and from the heart.

His face jerked around to me, full of righteous indignation, because, I suppose, my language wasn't the kind one should use in a lady's presence.

And that brought it about.

A blue sedan came out of a cross street a split second before we got there.

Collinson got his eyes and attention back to his driving in time to twist the roadster away from the sedan, but not in time to make a neat job of it.

We missed the sedan by a couple of inches, but as we passed behind it our rear wheels started sliding out of line. Collinson did what he could, giving the roadster its head, going with the skid, but the corner curb wouldn't cooperate. It stood stiff and hard where it was.

We hit the curb sidewise and rolled over on the lamp-post behind it. The lamp-post snapped, crashed down to the sidewalk. The roadster, over on its side, slipped us out on the lamp-post. Gas from the broken pipe roared up at our feet.

Collinson, most of the skin off one side of his face, crawled on all fours to the roadster and turned off the motor. I sat up, raising the girl, who was on my chest, with me. My right shoulder and arm were out of whack—dead. The girl was making whimpering noises in her chest, but I couldn't see any marks on her except a shallow scratch on one cheek. I had been her cushion, had taken the bump for her. The soreness of my chest and belly told me how much I had saved her.

People helped us up. Collinson stood with his arms around the girl, begging her to say she wasn't dead, and so on. The smash-up had shaken her into semi-consciousness, but she was still too full of narcotics to know whether there had been an accident or a wedding.

I went over and helped Collinson hold her up—though neither needed help—saying earnestly to the gathering crowd: "We've got to get her home. Who can—?"

A pudgy man in plus fours offered his and his car's services. Collinson and I sat in the back with the girl, and I gave the pudgy man her address. He said something about a hospital, but I insisted that home was the place for her. Collinson was too rattled over the girl's various troubles to say anything.

Twenty minutes later we were taking the girl out of the car in front of her house. I thanked the pudgy man profusely, giving him no opportunity to follow us indoors, and Collinson and I led the girl up the blue brick walk and up the front steps.

VI

The girl was now nearly enough awake to answer "No" when I asked her if she had a key. I rang the bell. The door was opened, after a little delay, by Owen Fitzstephan. There was no sleepiness left in his gray eyes; they were hot and bright, as they always got when he found life interesting. Knowing the sort of things that interested him, I wondered what had happened.

"What have you been doing?" he asked, looking at our clothes, at Collinson's scraped face, and at the girl's scratched cheek.

"Automobile accident," I explained. "Nothing serious. Where's everybody?"

"Everybody," he said, stressing the word, "is up in the laboratory. Come here."

He took me across the reception hall to the foot of the stairs, leaving Collinson and the girl standing together by the door, put his mouth to my ear, and whispered:

"Leggett's committed suicide."

"Where is he?" I was more annoyed than surprised.

"In the laboratory. Mrs. Leggett and the police are up there, too. It happened not more than half an hour ago."

"We'll all go up," I decided.

"Isn't that," he protested, "rather unnecessarily brutal—taking the girl there?"

"Maybe," I said irritably, "but it can't be helped. Anyway, she's coked up and better able to stand the shock than she will be later, when the stuff's dying out in her." I turned to Collinson. "Come on, we'll all go up to the laboratory."

I went ahead, letting Fitzstephan help Collinson with the girl.

There were six people in the laboratory: a uniformed policeman, a big man with a red mustache, standing beside the open door; Mrs. Leggett, sitting on a wooden chair in the farther end of the room, her body bent forward, her hands holding a handkerchief to her face, sobbing quietly; O'Gar and Reddy, standing by one of the windows, close together, reading a sheaf of papers that the bullet-headed sergeant held in his thick fists; a gray-faced, dandified man in dark clothes, standing beside the zinc table, twiddling eyeglasses on a black ribbon in his hand; and Edgar Leggett, seated on a chair at the table, his head and upper body resting on the table, his arms sprawled out.

O'Gar and Reddy looked up from their reading as I came in. Passing the table, to join them at the window, I saw blood, a small black automatic pistol lying close to one of Leggett's hands, and seven unset diamonds grouped close to his head.

O'Gar said, "Take a look," and handed me

part of his sheaf—four sheets of stiff white paper covered with very small, precise and plain handwriting in black ink. I was getting interested in what was written when Fitzstephan and Collinson came to the door with the girl.

Collinson saw what had happened in a glance. His face went white, and he put his big body between the girl and her dead father.

"Come in," I said.

"This is no place for Miss Leggett, in her condition," he replied hotly, turning to take her away.

"We ought to have everybody in here," I told O'Gar. He nodded his bullet head at the policeman, who put a hand on Collinson's shoulder and said: "You'll have to come in, the both of you."

Fitzstephan placed a chair by one of the end windows for the girl. She sat in it and looked around the room—at the dead man, at Mrs. Leggett, who had not looked up, at all of us—with eyes that were dull, but no longer completely blank. Collinson stood beside her chair, looking belligerently at me.

I addressed O'Gar loudly enough for the rest to hear:

"Let's read Leggett's letter out loud."

He screwed up his eyes, hesitated, then thrust the rest of the sheets at me, saying:

"Fair enough. You read it."

Not wanting the job, I passed it on to Owen Fitzstephan. Standing beside me, he read:

My name is Maurice Pierre de Mayenne. I was born in Fécamp, department of Seine-Inférieure, in France, on March 6, 1883, and was educated chiefly in England. In 1903 I went to Paris to study art, and there, four years later, I met Alice and Lily Dain, orphan daughters of a British naval officer. The following year I married Lily Dain, and in 1909 our daughter Gabrielle was born.

Shortly after my marriage I had discovered that I had made a terrible mistake, that it was really Alice, and not Lily, whom I loved. I kept this discovery to myself until the child was past the more difficult baby years, that is, until she was nearly five. Then I told my wife, and asked her to divorce me so I could marry Alice. She refused.

On June 6, 1913, I shot and killed Lily, and fled with Alice and Gabrielle to London, where I was soon arrested and returned to Paris. There I was tried, found guilty, and sentenced to life imprisonment on Devil's Island. Alice, who had no part in the murder, and who had been horrified by it, and had gone to London with me only through her love for the child, was also tried, but, justly, acquitted.

If there is any humanity or human likeness left in me, it is not the fault of those who have made Devil's Island the almost perfect hell it is. In 1918 I escaped with a fellow convict named Jacques Labaud on a flimsy raft. Neither of us knew how long we were adrift in the ocean, nor, toward the last, how long we had been without food and water. A week, perhaps, but every hour was a new eternity. Then Labaud died. He died of exposure and starvation. I did not kill him. No living creature could have been feeble enough for me to kill. But when Labaud was dead there was enough food for one, and I lived until I was washed ashore in the Golfo Trieste.

Changing my name to Armand Bacot, I secured employment with a British copper mining company at Aroa, and within a few months became private secretary to Philip Howart, the resident manager. Shortly after that I was approached by a cockney named John Edge, who described to me a plan by which we could defraud the company. When I refused to take part in it, Edge told me he knew who I was, and threatened to expose me. That Venezuela had no extradition treaty with France would not save me, Edge said, since Labaud's body had been cast ashore, undecomposed enough to show what had happened to him, and I could not prove that I had not killed him in Venezuelan waters to keep from starving.

I still refused to take part in Edge's plan and made up my mind to go away. But before I could start, Edge killed Howart and robbed the company safe. He urged me to flee with him, arguing that I could not face the sort of investigation the police would make. That was true, and so I agreed. Two months later, in Mexico City, it became apparent to me why Edge had asked me to accompany him. He had a firm hold on me and expected to use me in crimes that were beyond his abilities. I was determined, no matter what happened, no matter what became necessary, I would never go back to Devil's Island, or to any prison, but neither did I intend becoming a professional criminal. I attempted to desert Edge, he found me, and we fought. I killed him, but it was in self-defense. He struck me first.

In 1920 I came to the United States, to San Francisco, changed my name once more, to Edgar Leggett, and began making a new career for myself, developing some experiments I had made with colors when I was a young artist. In 1923, believing that Edgar Leggett could never now be connected with Maurice de Mayenne, I sent for Alice and Gabrielle, who were then living in New York, and Alice and I were married.

But the past was not dead. Alice, not hearing from me after my escape, not knowing what had happened to me, employed a private detective to find me—a Louis Upton. He sent a man named Harry Ruppert to South America. Ruppert succeeded in tracing me step by step from my landing in the Golfo Trieste up to, but no farther than, my departure from Mexico City. In doing this he of course learned of the deaths of Labaud, Howart and Edge—three deaths of which I was innocent, but of which I most certainly should be convicted if tried.

I do not know how Upton found me here. Possibly he traced Alice and Gabrielle to me. Late last Saturday night he called on me and demanded money. Having no money available at the time, I put him off until Tuesday, when I gave him the diamonds as part payment of his demands. But I was desperate, and I knew what being at Upton's mercy would mean, so I determined to kill him. I decided to pretend a burglar had taken the diamonds, notifying the police. Upton, I was sure, would immediately communicate with me then, and I would make an appointment with him and shoot him down in cold blood. The diamonds would be found in his possession. It would not be difficult for me to fix up a story that would make me seem justified in killing this man whom the police would suppose was the burglar.

But Harry Ruppert—hunting for Upton, with a grudge against him—saved me that killing, himself shooting Upton. Ruppert, the man who had traced me through Venezuela and Mexico for Upton, had also—either by following Upton here or making Upton talk before killing him— learned my identity. With the police after him for Upton's murder, he came here, demanding that I shelter him from them, returning the incriminating diamonds to me, and demanding money in their stead.

I killed him. His body is in the cellar. Out front, a detective is watching my house. Other detectives are busy elsewhere inquiring into my life. I have not been able to satisfactorily explain certain of my acts, nor to avoid contradictions, and, now that I am suspected, there is no chance of keeping the past a secret. I have always known that this would sooner or later happen. I am not going back to prison again.

MAURICE DE MAYENNE.

Nobody said anything for a long moment after Fitzstephan had finished his reading. Mrs. Leggett had taken the handkerchief from her face, listening, sobbing now and then. Gabrielle Leggett was looking jerkily around the room light fighting cloudiness in her eyes, her lips writhing together as if she were trying to get words out but couldn't.

I went to the table, bent over the dead man, felt his clothes. The inside coat pocket was stuffed. I reached under his arm, unbuttoned and opened the coat, took a brown wallet out of the pocket. The wallet was thick with paper money—fifteen thousand dollars, when we counted it afterward.

Showing the wallet's contents to the others, I asked:

"He leave any message besides the one that's been read?"

"None that's been found," O'Gar replied. "Why?"

"He didn't commit suicide," I said. "He was murdered."

Gabrielle Leggett screamed piercingly and sprang out of her chair, pointing a sharp white finger at Mrs. Leggett.

"She killed him," the girl shrieked. "She said, 'Come back here,' and held the kitchen door open with one hand, and picked up the butcher-knife from the drainboard with the other, and when he went past her she pushed it in his back, I saw her do it. I wasn't dressed, and when I heard them coming, I hid in the pantry."

Mrs. Leggett got to her feet, her face washed empty by amazement and grief. She staggered and would have fallen if Fitzstephan hadn't gone over to steady her.

The gray-faced, dandified man by the table—a Doctor Riese, learned later—said in a cold, crisp voice:

"There is no stab wound. He was shot through the temple by a bullet from this pistol, held close, slanting up. Clearly suicide, I should say."

Collinson forced the girl down in her chair again, trying to calm her.

I disagreed with the doctor's last statement, and said so, while my brains were busy with another matter:

"Murder. His letter is the letter of a man who is still fighting. There's plenty of determination in it, but no despair. When he wrote it he meant to go away. If he had intended to kill himself he would have left some word for his wife and daughter. How was he found?"

"I heard," Mrs. Leggett sobbed, "I heard the shot, and ran up here, and he—he was like that. And I went down to the telephone, and the bell—the doorbell—rang—and it was Mr. Fitz-stephan, and I told him. It couldn't—there was nobody else in the house to—to kill him."

"You killed him," I said to her. "He was going away. He wrote this statement, taking the blame for your crimes. You killed Ruppert down in the kitchen. That's what the girl was talking about. Your husband's statement sounded enough like a suicide letter to pass for one, you thought, so you murdered him—murdered him believing that his death and confession would close up the whole business, stop us from poking into it any more."

Her face didn't tell me anything. It was distorted, but in a way that might mean almost anything. I filled my lungs and went on, not exactly bellowing, but making plenty of noise:

"There are a half-dozen lies in your husband's statement—a half-dozen that I know of now. He didn't send for you and his daughter. Mrs. Begg said he was the most surprised man she had ever seen when you arrived from New York. He wouldn't have given Upton the diamonds and then called in the police. He'd have given him money or he would have killed him without giving him anything. Upton didn't come to Leggett with his demands; he came to you. You were the one he knew. His agency had traced Leggett here for you—not only to Mexico City—all the way here, but he and Ruppert had been jailed before they could bleed you. When he got out, he came here and made his play. You got the diamonds for him, and you didn't tell your husband anything about the burglary being a fake. Why? You didn't want him to know that you knew about his South American and Mexican murders. Why? A good additional hold on him, if you needed it? Anyway, *you* dealt with Upton.

"Maybe Ruppert had got in touch with you, and you had him kill Upton for you—a job he'd be glad to do on his own hook. Probably, because Ruppert *did* kill Upton, and he *did* come to see *you* afterward, and you thought it necessary to put the knife in him down in the kitchen. You didn't know that the girl, concealed in the pantry, saw it. Horrified, having known all along that her father had killed her mother, seeing you now kill a man, she got dressed and ran away from this slaughter-house, taking her jewelry to Minnie to sell, drugging herself into forgetfulness.

"You didn't know she had seen you kill Ruppert, but you *did* know you had got out of your depth. You *did* know that your chances of disposing of the body were slim—your house was too much in the spotlight. So you played your only part; you told your husband the whole thing, got him to shoulder it for you, and then handed him his—here at the table.

"He shielded you. He had always shielded you. *You*," I thundered, my voice in fine form by now, "killed your sister Lily, his first wife, and let him take the fall for you. *You* went to London with him afterward. Would you have gone with your sister's murderer if you were innocent? *You* had him traced here, and *you* came here after him, and *you* married him. *You* were the one who decided that he had married the wrong sister—and *you* killed her."

"She did, she did!" cried Gabrielle Leggett, trying to get up from the chair in which Collinson held her. "She—"

Mrs. Leggett drew herself up straight, and smiled, showing white teeth set edge to edge, and came two steps toward the center of the room. One hand was on her hip, the other hanging at her side. The housewife—Fitzstephan's "serene, sane soul"—was gone; this was a wild animal in the form of a blonde woman—except the eyes, which were the animal's own. Even her body seemed now not rounded with the plump-ness of well-cared-for early middle age; it was rounded as a tiger's or panther's is, with cushioned, soft-sheathed muscles.

I picked the gun up from the table and put it in my pocket.

"You wish to know who killed my sister?" she asked softly, speaking to me, her teeth clicking together between words, her lips smiling, her eyes burning. "She—the dope fiend—Gabrielle—she killed her mother. She is the one he shielded."

The girl cried out something unintelligible.

"Nonsense," I said. "She was a baby."

"Oh, but it is not nonsense," the woman insisted. "She was nearly five, a child of five playing with a pistol she had taken from a drawer while her mother slept. The pistol went off, and Lily died. An accident, of course, but Maurice, a sensitive soul, could not bear that the child should grow up knowing that her hand had sent her mother out of this world. Besides, it was likely that Maurice would have been convicted in any event. He and I had been intimate, you know. But that was a slight matter to him. His one thought was to erase from the child's mind all memory of the accident, so she might never remember what she had done, so that her life might not be darkened by the knowledge that she had, even though accidentally, killed her mother."

It wouldn't have been so bad if she hadn't been smiling so coolly as she talked, selecting her words so carefully, almost fastidiously, and mouthing them so daintily. She went on:

"Gabrielle was always, even before she began using drugs, a child of, one might say, limited mentality, so by the time the London police found us we had succeeded in quite emptying her mind of the last trace of memory, that is, of that particular memory. This is, I assure you, the truth of the whole affair. She killed her mother, and her father—to use your quaint expression—'took the fall for her.'"

"Fairly plausible," I said, "but weak in spots. You're trying to hurt her because she witnessed *your* latest murder."

She pulled her lips back from her teeth and started toward me, her eyes flaring, then checked herself, laughed sharply, and began talking again, rapidly, with a hysterical swing or cadence to her words, almost as if she were singing:

"Am I? Then I must tell you this, which I should not tell unless it were true. I taught her to kill her mother. Do you understand? I taught her, trained her, drilled her. Do you understand that? Lily and I were true sisters, inseparable, hating one another poisonously. Maurice—he wished to marry *neither* of us, though he was intimate enough with *both*. You are to understand that literally. But we were poor and he was not, and because he was not, Lily wanted to marry him. And because Lily wanted to, I wanted to. We were like that in all things. But she got him—first—*trapped* him into matrimony.

"Gabrielle was born six or seven months later. I lived with them. What a happy little family we were! From the first Gabrielle loved me more than her mother. I saw to that; there was nothing Aunt Alice wouldn't do for her niece, because her preferring me infuriated Lily. It infuriated Lily, not because she herself loved the child, but because we had always hated one another, had always each tried to take everything from the other. When Gabrielle was no more than a year old I planned what I would some day do.

"When she was nearly five I did it. I taught her a little amusing game. Maurice's pistol, a small one, was kept in a locked drawer high in a chiffonier. I unlocked the drawer, unloaded the pistol, and lay on Lily's bed, pretending I was asleep. The child pushed a chair over to the chiffonier, climbed on it, took the pistol from the drawer, crept across to the bed, put the muzzle of the pistol to my head, and pressed the trigger. When she did well, making little or no noise, holding the pistol correctly in both of her tiny hands, I rewarded her with candy, cautioning her to say nothing about the game to anyone else, as we were going to surprise her mother with it.

"We did; we surprised her completely, one afternoon when Lily, having taken aspirin for a headache, was sleeping in her bed. I unlocked the drawer, but did not unload the pistol. Then I told the child she might play the game with her mother, and I went down to visit friends on the floor below, so no one would think I had anything to do with my dear sister's death. I thought Maurice would be out all afternoon, and intended, as soon as we heard the shot, to rush upstairs with my friends and find that the child playing with the pistol had killed her mother.

"I had little fear of the child's talking afterward. Of, as I have said, no brilliant mentality, loving and trusting me as she did, and in my hands both before and during the official inquiry into her mother's death, it would have been very easy for me to control her, to be sure she said nothing that would reveal my part in the—ah—enterprise. But Maurice, coming home unexpectedly, came to the bedroom door just as Gabrielle pressed the trigger, the tiniest fraction of a second too late to save his wife's life. His subsequent desire to wipe all memory of the deed from the child's mind made any further effort, or anxiety, on my part unnecessary. I did follow him here, and I used Gabrielle's love for me and her hatred of him—which I had carefully cultivated by deliberately clumsy attempts to make her forgive him for killing her mother—to persuade him to marry me, so that Gabrielle, whom he loved, could be kept close to him. *The day he married Lily I swore I would take him away from her—and I did—and I hope my dear sister in hell knows it!*"

Her face had changed as she talked—or chanted—her eyes growing wilder, the wildness spreading down from them, making her face less and less human. By now the last trace of sanity was gone from voice and features. She spun to face the girl across the room, flung an arm out toward her, screamed shrilly:

"You're her daughter, and you're cursed with the same rotten soul and black blood that she and I and all the Dains have had; you're cursed with your mother's death on your hands before you were five; you're cursed with the warped mind and the need for drugs that I've given you in pay for your silly love since you were a baby. Your life will be black as Lily's and mine were black; the lives of those you touch will be black as Maurice's was black; and the—"

"Stop!" Collinson gasped brokenly. "Make her stop!"

Gabrielle Leggett, both hands to her ears, her face twisted with terror, shrieked once—horribly—and fell forward out of her chair.

Reddy was young at the game, but O'Gar and I should have known better than to lose sight of Mrs. Leggett, even for a half-second, no matter how strongly Collinson's gasp and the girl's shriek drew our attention. But we did look at them—if for less than a half-second—and that was long enough.

When we looked at Mrs. Leggett again, she had a gun in her hand, and she had taken a step toward the door.

Nobody was between her and the door. Nobody was behind her, because her back was to the door and by turning she had brought Fitzstephan into her field of vision.

She glared savagely over the black gun, crazy eyes darting from one to another of us, taking another step backward, snarling:

"Don't you move!"

Pat Reddy shifted his weight to the balls of his feet. I frowned at him, shaking my head. The hall or stairs were better places in which to take her alive. In here somebody would die.

She went over the sill, blew her breath between her teeth with a hissing, spitting sound, and was gone down the hall.

Owen Fitzstephan was first through the door after her. The policeman got in my way, but I was second out. The woman had reached the head of the stairs, at the other end of the dim hall, with Fitzstephan, not far behind, rapidly overtaking her.

He caught her on the mid-floor landing just as I reached the top of the stairs. He had one of her arms pinned to her body, but the hand holding the gun was free. He grabbed at it and missed.

She twisted the muzzle in to his body as I—with my head bent to miss the edge of the floor—leaped down at them.

I landed on them just in time, crashing into them, smashing them into the corner of the wall, sending her bullet, meant for the sorrel-haired man, ripping into a step.

None of us was standing up. I caught with both hands at the flash of her gun, missed, and had her by the waist. Close to my chin, the novelist's lean fingers closed around her gun-hand wrist.

She twisted her body against my right arm, which, benumbed in the automobile accident, wouldn't hold. Her thick body heaved up, turning over on me.

Gunfire roared in my ear, burnt my cheek. The woman's body went limp. When O'Gar and Reddy pulled us apart she lay still. The last bullet had torn through her throat.

I went up to the laboratory. Gabrielle Leggett, with Collinson and the doctor kneeling beside her, was lying on the floor. I told the doctor:

"Mrs. Leggett's dead, I think, but you'd better see if there's any chance. She's on the stairs."

The doctor went out. Collinson, chafing the unconscious girl's hands, looked at me as if I were something he didn't like, and said:

"I hope now you're satisfied with the manner in which your work got done."

"I'm not particularly satisfied with the manner," I told him, "but"—stubbornly—"it got done."

Collinson returned his attention to the girl, who had moved an arm.

I walked down the hall toward the stairs, repeating my last three words—*It got done*. I didn't think I was soft-headed enough to have been impressed by Mrs. Leggett's curse, yet I didn't feel that everything was done here. I hadn't the sort of satisfaction you feel when you've completely and finally wound up a job.

The diamonds had been recovered; their going had been explained; and everybody who might have been jailed over their going was dead. There were no loose ends that I knew of. Nevertheless . . . I gave it up, telling myself as I went downstairs:

"Well, if more comes, it'll come."

I was, it turned out, right about that.

THE HOLLOW TEMPLE, BY DASHIELL HAMMETT

A further incident in the "black life" of Gabrielle Leggett

IN DECEMBER BLACK MASK

BLACK MASK, DECEMBER 1928

The Hollow Temple

THE DAIN CURSE

BY DASHIELL HAMMETT

ERIC COLLINSON CAME into my office. There was too much pink in his eyes and not any in his skin. He sat down and said:

"She can't go. They can't let her go. You've got to go with her."

His voice, like his face, was dull and tired and hopeless and bewildered.

"Miss Leggett?" I asked, though I didn't need to; and then: "How is she now?"

"You've killed her."

He spoke bitterly, but without heat, not looking at me; staring at my inkwell, with a beaten look in his eyes.

I ignored the accusation, saying:

"Where is it that she can't go, and that I've got to go with her?"

He replied, still staring at the inkwell, that Madison Andrews was crazy, and so was Dr.

Riese, and so would he—Collinson—be if this thing kept on.

"I thought they were just about as cool and level-headed a pair as you could find."

"But good God!" he exclaimed, "they want to let her go to this Joseph."

"Who is he?"

Instead of answering my question he began complaining that it was all my fault; that if it hadn't been for me, her father and step-mother would still be alive, Gabrielle would know nothing of their "horrible past," nothing of the crime that she herself had committed as the five-year-old tool of her step-mother, and, most important of all, she would not have been made believe that she was accursed—bound to live in blackness herself and to bring blackness into the lives of all who came in contact with her.

"She's better off now than she's ever been," I argued. "I know that, in the shape she was in when it all broke, she was upset a lot by the melodramatic curse her step-mother put on her, or said was on her. But I can't see that she's as bad off as when she was under her step-mother's influence."

He lifted his haggard young face to look at me, and he spoke as if his throat hurt him:

"I'm going to tell you: I didn't think anybody could be as brutal as you were to her."

"Is that," I asked irritably, "why you're here now telling me I've got to go somewhere with her?"

"But what else can I do?" he demanded, puckering his brows, his lower lip drooping down from his teeth. "They're going to let her go. They're crazy, I tell you. And she can't go alone like that—with only Minnie."

"Go with her yourself. You think you—"

"But I can't." Face, voice, and the slant of his wide shoulders were advertisements of hopelessness. "Good God! Don't you think I would? But she won't even let me see her. She's afraid of the curse settling on me. I—I haven't seen her for a week. She wouldn't let me. You've got to go. There's nobody else that's—"

"That's brutal enough?" I suggested.

"You know her, and you know the whole story, and you're already in it. You can take care of her." He took hold of my wrist with a big sunburned hand and pushed his face over the desk toward me. "You've got to go. And you've got to see that nothing happens to her."

I took my wrist out of his hand and growled:

"I haven't got to do anything. I'm not likely to do anything that I know as little about as I do about this. What is it? Where is she going?"

"I told you," he said wearily. "She's going to Joseph's. They're going to let her go. It's Dr. Riese's doing, though Andrews ought to know better. They're crazy. You've got to—"

"Who is Joseph?" I asked.

"That's it. Who is he? What do they know about him? Or about what will happen to Gaby in his Temple? For a man like Andrews to agree to such a thing!"

He put his elbows on my desk, his face between his hands, and stared at the desk-top with dull bloodshot eyes.

"How long since you've slept?" I asked.

"Tuesday," he muttered without looking up, "or maybe Sunday. What difference does it make? You'll go with her?"

"I don't know. Maybe you think you've given me the whole story, but you haven't. You haven't told me anything. Try again? Start with Joseph."

"Another cult," he said impatiently. "He calls his place the Temple of the Holy Grail. I don't know where Gabrielle ran into them, but she's known them for a month or so. I suppose it's the fashionable cult just now. You know how they come and go in California. This Joseph came to see her after her trouble, and now she wants to go to the Temple and stay for a while. They do that—retreats—like the Catholics.

"Dr. Riese—God knows why—said he thought it would be good for her. Andrews said, 'No,' at first, but they persuaded him. He said he had had the cult investigated and it seemed all right. I suppose he meant by that that there was no proof that anybody had ever been murdered there. It's idiotic! What if Mrs. Payson Laurence and Mrs. Ralph Coleman are members? Their social positions won't keep them from being made fools of like anybody else. And Mrs. Livingston Rodman's being a resident of the Temple now doesn't have to mean anything except that she too can be deceived. But Andrews seems to think that because the cult's dupes are beyond suspicion, so must it be. So the old ass has agreed to let Gabrielle go there.

"I don't want her to go, but what can I do? She won't even see me. But I'm damned if she's going there with nobody but her maid, even if Dr. Riese will see her every day. There's got to be somebody there to see that nothing happens to her. You've got to go. I meant what I said about your being brutal, but I know—I know you—she will be safe with you there. You will go, won't you?"

I thought it over without enthusiasm. It wasn't my idea of an inviting job, but the Continental Detective Agency was in business to make money, and I couldn't very well turn down any honest and profitable employment in our line.

Collinson took his face from between his hands and said:

"I don't know what else you may have on hand, but—the money end of it—any amount you charge for your services will be quite all right."

"Andrews is in charge of the girl's affairs," I stalled. "I'll have to see him first."

Collinson said eagerly that that was all right. He had spoken to both Andrews and Riese about engaging me, and they had not only consented, but thought it an excellent idea. Collinson used my telephone to call Andrews and tell him I would be over at his office in a few minutes.

Collinson didn't go to the lawyer's office with me. He said gloomily that if he did he would get into another argument with Andrews, and after a solid week of trying to change the old man's mind he had given it up as a futile business. Leaving me, Collinson gripped my hand violently, asking me to promise all sorts of things concerning the carefulness with which I would guard Gabrielle Leggett. I advised him to get some sleep.

Madison Andrews was a tall, gaunt man of sixty, with ragged white hair, eyebrows and mustache that exaggerated the ruddiness of his face—a bony, hard-muscled face. He wore his clothes loose, chewed tobacco, and had twice in the past ten years been named correspondent in divorce suits.

"I dare say," he told me, "young Collinson has babbled all sorts of nonsense to you. He seems to think I'm in my second childhood—as good as told me so."

"He doesn't think you ought to let her go."

"He has spared no pains in making that known to me," the lawyer said. "But even though he is her fiancé, I am responsible for her care; and I prefer to follow Dr. Riese's advice in this. He is her physician. He insists that letting her go to the Temple for a week or two of seclusion from the world will do more to restore her sanity than anything else that can be done. Can I disregard that?

"Joseph may be—probably is—a charlatan, but he certainly is the only person to whom Gabrielle has willingly talked, and in whose company she has been at peace, since her parents' deaths. Dr. Riese tells me that to cross her in her desire to go to the Temple will be to send her mind deeper into its illness. Am I to snap my fingers at Riese's opinion because young Collinson doesn't like it?"

I said: "No."

"I have learned something of the members of this sect. I know decent, responsible, even prominent people, who are members. Mrs. Livingston Rodman is living there now. I have no illusions concerning the sect: it is probably as full of quackery as any other. But I am not interested in it as religion—rather as therapeutics—as a cure for Gabrielle's mental illness vouched for by her physician. The character of the cult's membership is such that I will consider Gabrielle safe there. Even if I were not quite sure of that, I still should think that no other consideration should be allowed to interfere with her recovery. That, as I see it, comes first."

I nodded my agreement and asked:

"When is she proposing to go?"

"Tomorrow morning. You can go then?"

"Yeah. What is the layout?"

"I'll notify Joseph that you are coming. You are supposed to be a male nurse, and will be given a room close to Gabrielle's. They know of her mental trouble, so your presence there will be quite all right, whether they believe you to be a nurse or not. You needn't go with her. Perhaps it would be best if you were there when she arrives, at, say, eleven o'clock. There is no need of my giving you instructions. It is simply a matter of taking every precaution, seeing that nothing happens to her. Dr. Riese and I have every confidence in your ability to handle it.

Gabrielle's maid, Minnie, will be with her, and Dr. Riese will call every day. Ask for Aaronia Haldorn when you arrive. She is Joseph's wife, I think, and manages the material end of the cult."

"Does Gabrielle Leggett know I'm going?"

"No," Andrews said, "and I don't think we need say anything to her about it. You'll make your watch over her as unobtrusive as possible, of course, and, while she knows you, I don't think that, in her present condition, she will pay enough attention to your presence to resent it. If she does—well, we'll see."

II

From the street, the following morning, the Temple of the Holy Grail looked like what it had originally been—a six-story yellow brick apartment building. There was nothing about its exterior to show that it wasn't one still. I rang the door bell.

The door was opened immediately by a broad-shouldered meaty woman of some year close to fifty. She was a good three inches taller than my five feet six. Flesh hung in little bags on her face, but there was neither softness nor looseness in eyes and mouth. Her long upper lip had been shaved. She was dressed in black.

I told her I wanted to see Mrs. Haldorn. She took me into a small, dimly lighted reception room to one side of the lobby, told me to wait there—her voice was a heavy bass—and went away.

I put my Gladstone bag on a chair, my hat on top of it, and sat down. Drawn blinds let in too little light for me to make out much of the room, but the carpet was soft and thick and what I could see of the furniture leaned more toward luxury than severity.

No sound came from anywhere in the building. I looked at the open doorway and discovered that I was being looked over. A small boy of twelve or thirteen stood there staring at me with big dark eyes that seemed to have lights of their own in the semi-darkness. I said:

"Hello, son."

The boy said nothing, looked at me a minute longer with the cold, unblinking, embarrassing stare that only children can manage, turned his back on me, and walked away, making no more noise than he had made coming.

Looks like I'm going to have a swell time here, I thought, if the two I've seen are fair samples of the joint's occupants—besides Gabrielle Leggett, who's still worse.

A woman, walking silently on the thick carpet, appeared in the doorway, came through it. She was tall, graceful, and her dark eyes had lights of their own, like the boy's. That's all I could see then.

I stood up and asked:

"Mrs. Haldorn?"

"Yes." Her voice, saying that one word, was the most beautiful I had ever heard. It wasn't a voice, it was pure music.

"Madison Andrews told you I was coming?" I said, hoping she would speak more than one syllable this time.

"Oh, you are Miss Leggett's attendant?" The slightest of pauses before the last word told me that she didn't believe in the male nurse pretext. Her voice was all that the first *Yes* had made me think it. "*Yes*, he told me."

She walked past me to raise a blind, letting in a fat rectangle of morning sun. While I blinked at her in the sudden brightness, she sat down and motioned me back to my chair.

I saw her eyes first. They were enormous, black, soft, glowing, heavily fringed with black lashes. They were the only live, human, things in her face. There was warmth and there was beauty in her oval, olive-skinned face; but, except for the eyes, it was unnatural—almost weird—warmth and beauty. It was as if her face were not a face, but a mask that she had worn until it had almost become a face. Even the curving red mouth looked not so much like flesh as like an almost perfect imitation of flesh—softer, redder, maybe warmer, than genuine flesh, but not genuine. Above this face—or mask—uncut black hair was bound close to her head, parted in the middle, drawn down across temples and upper ears to meet in a knot on the nape of her neck. Her neck was long, strong, slender; her body tall, fully fleshed, supple; her clothes dark, silky, part of her body.

She offered me Russian cigarettes in a white jade case. I apologized for sticking to my Fatimas, and struck a match on the smoking stand she pushed out between us.

When our cigarettes were burning she said:

"We shall try to make you as comfortable as possible. We are neither barbarians nor fanatics. I explain this because so many people are surprised to find us neither. This is a Temple, but none of us supposes that happiness, comfort, or any of the ordinary matters of civilized living, will desecrate it. You are not one of us. Perhaps—I hope—you will become one of us. However—do not squirm—you won't, I assure you, be annoyed. You may attend our services or not, as you choose, and you may come and go as you wish. You will show us, I am sure, the same consideration we show you, and I am equally sure that you will not interfere in any way with anything you see—no matter how peculiar you may think it—unless it definitely and disagreeably affects your—ah—patient, Miss Leggett."

"Of course not," I promised.

She smiled, as if to thank me, rubbed her cigarette's end into the ash tray, and stood up, saying:

"I'll show you your room."

Picking up my hat and bag, I followed her out into the lobby, where we entered an automatic elevator. She took me to a room on the fifth floor. Everything in the room, as in the connecting bathroom, was white: white papered walls and painted ceiling; white enameled chairs, bed, table, dresser, fixtures and woodwork; white felt on the floor. None of the furniture was hospital furniture, but the solid whiteness of everything gave it that appearance. There were two windows in the bedroom, looking out over roofs, and one in the bathroom. The only doors were those connecting bathroom and bedroom, bedroom and corridor. Neither had a lock.

I left my hat and bag there and went with the woman to see the room Gabrielle Leggett would occupy. Its door faced mine across a six-foot corridor's purple carpet. The interior was a duplicate of my room's, except that, on the opposite side from the bathroom, there was a small square dressing-room without windows.

"Her maid?" I asked.

"She will sleep in one of the servant's rooms on the top floor. Shall we go downstairs now?"

She took me down to the second floor and pushed back half of a pair of sliding doors, showing me a room dark with walnut paneling and furniture.

"Our dining-room," she said, as she slid the door shut again and moved on along the corridor. "Breakfast and luncheon are usually served in our rooms, but for dinner—at seven—you may either come here or have it in your room, as you prefer. This is the library."

We were at the doorway of a large square room where tan burlaped walls ran up high behind glass-fronted bookcases.

A man turned from one of the cases toward us. He was a tall man, built like a statue, in a black silk robe. His thick hair, rather long, and his thick beard, trimmed round, were white and glossy.

Aaronia Haldorn introduced me to him, calling him Joseph. He came forward to give me a white and even-toothed smile and a warm strong hand. His face was healthily pink and without line or wrinkle. It was a tranquil face, especially the clear brown eyes, somehow making you feel at peace with the world. The same soothing quality was in his baritone voice as he said:

"We are happy to have you here."

The words were merely polite, meaningless; yet, as he said them, I believed that for some reason he was happy. I understood now Gabrielle Leggett's desire to come to this place. I said that I, too, was happy to be there, and at the time I actually thought I was.

We went on, the woman showing me various other rooms, and finally leading me to a small iron door on the ground floor. She opened it and said:

"Our services are held here."

The floor was of white marble, pentagonal tiles. The walls were white, smooth, unbroken except for this door and another exactly like it on the other side. These four straight, white-washed, undecorated walls rose straight up for six stories—to the sky. There was no ceiling, no roof. In the other end of the room—of what had been a room until it had been cut through to the sky—a gray tarpaulin covered something that was shaped like an upright piano, but several times larger than any piano.

"The altar," Aaronia Haldorn explained.

Behind us a soft buzzing sounded.

"That is probably Miss Leggett," the woman said, and we went back through the iron door.

At the elevator I left her, going up to my room. Presently I heard the rustle of people moving in the corridor, going into Gabrielle Leggett's room. I didn't hear her voice, but I did hear Minnie Hershey, her mulatto maid, answering some question Aaronia Haldorn had asked, and I heard the bass rumble of the woman who had let me into the house.

A few minutes later a small frosted globe fixed to the white telephone on my bedside table glowed, and I was asked what I wanted for luncheon. "Anything and coffee will do," I said, and agreed that cold sliced meat and artichoke salad sounded appetizing, declined dessert, and then went into the bathroom to wash.

A maid in black and white brought the meal in to me on a white tray. She was somewhere in her middle twenties, a hearty, pink and plump blonde, with blue eyes that looked curiously at me and had jokes in them.

I said something about the food on the tray looking good. She said, "Oh, yes, sir," without seriousness, put the tray on the table, looked at me out of the corners of twinkling eyes, and went out.

After I had eaten I dug a bottle of King George scotch out of my bag, put it on the table beside the tray, and went into conference with it and a deck of cigarettes. Sounds drifted up through the open windows, but none came from

inside the building until, an hour or so later, the blonde maid returned for the tray.

She pretended she didn't see the bottle. I asked:

"Can I be shot at sunrise for having that here?"

She put up her tawny eyebrows and said:

"I really can't say," gathering up the tray.

"Ever use it yourself?"

"What?" The skin around her eyes twitched. "A shot at sunrise?"

"Yeah. Or now."

She carried the tray toward the door, smiling, saying:

"I couldn't—now. The Village Blacksmith would break my neck if she smelled it on me."

The Village Blacksmith, I guessed, was the big woman with the bass voice.

"Later? When you're through for the day?"

She said, "Maybe," over her plump shoulder as she went through the door.

I spent the afternoon in my room. Dr. Riese came in to see me a little before five o'clock, after visiting Gabrielle Leggett's room. He was a gray-faced, slender, dandified man with a crisp, precise way of turning out his words, usually emphasizing them by making gestures with the black-ribboned nose-glasses that I had never seen on his nose. I had learned that I stood high in his estimation because I had discovered that Edgar Leggett had been murdered, immediately after he—Riese—had pronounced him a suicide.

He told me the girl was in a better frame of mind than she had been since her parents' deaths, and cautioned me against making my surveillance of her too thorough.

"The less she is reminded that she is being guarded, the better for her," he said. "I am glad you are here, but, after all, it is not likely that you will find anything to do."

I promised to manage things so that the girl would see as little of me as possible, and the doctor went away, saying he would be in again in the morning.

I went down to the dining-room for dinner.

There were eight of us at the table: Mrs. Livingston Rodman, a tall, frail woman with transparent skin, faded, tired eyes, and a voice that never rose above a semi-whisper; a man named Fleming, who was young, dark, very thin, with a dark mustache and the detached air of one who had a lot of things on his mind; a Miss Hillen, sharp of chin and voice, scrawny, forty, with an eager, intense manner; a Mrs. Pavlow, who was quite young, with a high-cheek-boned dark face and dark eyes that avoided everybody's gaze; Aaronia Haldorn; and her son, Manuel, the boy who had looked at me from the reception room doorway. Neither Joseph nor Gabrielle Leggett appeared.

The food, served by two Filipino boys, was good. There was little conversation—except that which Miss Hillen made—and none of it religious. She tried to prod Fleming into conversation with questions about Aztec customs. He replied evasively, busy with his own thoughts. Getting nothing from him, Miss Hillen turned to Manuel Haldorn, asking him what he intended being when he grew up, a question any boy hears often enough to be bored by. He smiled at her with a shyness that didn't seem sincere to me—remembering the stare he had given me—and replied that he didn't know—whatever Mama decided was best—and turned his eyes to his plate again.

Miss Hillen's gaze switched to Mrs. Pavlow, whose face suddenly went panicky with embarrassment. Aaronia Haldorn saved her from the sharp-chinned woman's curiosity by asking:

"How are your roses, Miss Hillen?"

Miss Hillen talked roses through dessert and coffee.

III

At nine o'clock I got hold of Gabrielle Leggett's maid—Minnie Hershey—as she was leaving her mistress' room. The mulatto girl's eyes jerked wide when she saw me standing in the doorway of my room.

"Come in," I said. "Didn't Dr. Riese tell you I was here?"

"No, sir. Are—are you—You're not wanting anything with Miss Gabrielle, sir?"

"Just looking out for her, to see that nothing happens. So you and I are really working together. And if you'll keep me wised up, let me know everything she does and says, and what others do and say, and so on, you'll be helping me, and helping her, because then I won't have to bother her."

The girl said, "Yes, sir," readily enough; but, so far as I could make out from examining her dark face, my cooperative idea wasn't getting over any too well.

"How is she this evening?" I asked.

"She's right cheerful this evening, sir. She likes this place."

"How did she spend the afternoon and evening?"

"She—I don't know, sir. She just kind of spent it—quiet like."

No news there. I said:

"Dr. Riese thinks she'll be better off not knowing I'm here, so don't say anything about me to her."

"No, sir, I sure won't," she promised but it sounded more polite than sincere.

At ten-thirty the plump blonde maid who had brought up my luncheon came in to have some scotch and some cigarettes with me. She insisted that we would have to be very quiet, so the Village Blacksmith wouldn't learn that she was there; but I wasn't a lot impressed by her insistence; I knew that as likely as not the girl had been sent up to me.

Her name was Mildred. She was careless, pleasant, a bit tough, and shrewd without being intelligent. She told me she had been working in the establishment for six months, since the present Temple had been opened. It had been donated to the cult by Mrs. Rodman. Mildred's attitude toward her employers' religion was one of tolerant indifference. They were decent enough people, she said. There were no wild parties of the sort that got other cults into the newspapers; and she supposed they had as good a religion as any, but she herself was a Methodist, and that was good enough for her.

She told me that there were half a dozen converts staying there in addition to the ones I had seen at dinner; and that at times there had been as many as twenty or twenty-five of them, all, she added, "real society people." When she asked me what I was doing there, I told her the truth, except that I didn't mention my detective agency connection.

"Is she really cracked?" she asked.

"No, but she's too close to it to be left alone. You've seen her before?"

"She's been here for services, but this is the first time she has even stayed."

"Here often?"

"I've seen her twice."

"See her today?"

"I took her dinner in, but I didn't get a good look at her. It was nearly dark, the lights weren't on, and she was lying on the bed."

Mildred went off at eleven-thirty. A few minutes later I crossed the corridor to put my ear against Gabrielle Leggett's door, keeping it there until my neck got tired—and that's all the good it did me.

I returned to my room, smoked a cigarette, put a flashlight in my pocket, and went for a stroll through the building. The thick carpets that were everywhere made silent walking easy. Lights burned dimly in the corridors. I wandered around for nearly an hour, seeing nobody, hearing breathing through a few bedroom doors, but nothing else. I didn't do any prying, but confined myself to the corridors and more public rooms, like dining-room, library, reception rooms and so on. The iron doors leading to the hollow core of the building where services were held were locked. I tried both of them.

Ten minutes more of listening at the girl's door brought me nothing. I went to bed. At four-something I got up again, put on slippers and bathrobe, and went for another stroll. It was no more profitable than the first.

Dr. Riese visited my room at ten the next morning, apparently quite pleased with the progress his patient was making.

I caught Minnie Hershey in the corridor a little later, tried to get some information out of her, and got nothing but a lot of polite *Yes, sir*s.

When Mildred brought my luncheon in at noon she told me that services would be held at nine o'clock that evening.

In the library, after luncheon, I found Fleming busy making notes from a stack of books. He didn't seem to feel like talking, so I wandered out. The Village Blacksmith passed me in the corridor, paying no attention to me until I spoke, then barely nodding. Aaronia Haldorn came to my room later that afternoon to smoke a cigarette and ask if anything could be done to make me more comfortable. Joseph was in Gabrielle Leggett's room for an hour. I could hear his voice, but, no matter how tight I clamped my ear to her door, I couldn't catch his words.

Before dinner I went out for half an hour's walk in the streets, stocking up with cigarettes, magazines and newspapers.

The shy Mrs. Pavlow didn't appear for dinner. Neither did Gabrielle Leggett, but Joseph was there, and a man and woman I had not seen before. He was a well-tailored, carefully mannered man, stout, bald, and sallow, a Major Jeffries. The woman was his wife, a pleasant sort of person in spite of a kittenish way that was thirty years too young for her.

Joseph, at the head of the table, eating no more than half a dozen good bites, speaking not many more than that number of words, seemed to have the same sort of soothing effect on everyone as he had on me. Even the sharp-chinned Hillen woman prodded nobody with questions. Presently, however, I discovered that there was one at the table who seemed to have escaped this influence—the boy Manuel. I caught him—once, and only for a split second—glancing at his father almost furtively through long lashes; and what I saw in the boy's eyes was either contempt or hatred. I had only his eyes to go by; his face remained angelic. It was only a quick flash that I got of the eyes, but one of those things was in them. I watched the boy surreptitiously through the rest of the meal, but he never looked at Joseph again. He looked often at his mother—somewhat furtively too—but when his eyes were on her there was adoration in them.

I attended the services in the Temple's hollow core that night. The altar, uncovered by tarpaulin now, was a glistening, dazzling, affair of white and crystal in a beam of blue-white light that slanted down from an edge of the roof. The beam was so strong that the altar seemed to quiver in it, to expand and contract. The glare hurt my eyes, tired them, but held them. When I wanted to look around at the congregation I had to fight with my eyes to get them away from the altar.

There were between thirty and forty people there, sitting on white enameled benches. Only ten of them, including me, were men. Men and women sat stiffly on their benches, staring at the dazzling altar with peculiarly fixed, unblinking gazes. Faces seemed white and unreal in the reflected glare, pupils of wide eyes were shrunken.

I saw Gabrielle Leggett on the other side of the room, but she was sitting in the front row, and I couldn't see her face. Minnie Hershey was beside her.

Joseph, in a white robe, moved to and fro in front of the altar, going through some ritual. I didn't know enough about religious ceremony to tell how this one differed from others. It was rather impressive, in a very dignified way. The strained, rigid, attention of the people on the benches gave a tense, expectant, air to it all, as if something tremendous, or violent, or exciting, was about to happen. Nothing of the sort did happen. There was some chanting in which everybody took part. The whole thing lasted an hour and ten minutes.

The congregation went out slowly, not talking much, most of them looking tired and worn, as if they had been through some sort of emotional struggle. I, who knew nothing about whatever spiritual significance the service may have had, felt somewhat the same way myself, probably from staring so long at the dazzling white altar.

I went slowly toward one of the little iron doors, waiting for a closer look at Gabrielle Leggett. Close to the door she passed me, not looking at me. She was thinner than when I had last seen her—ten days before—and what had been barely a suggestion of hollowness around her eyes and in her cheeks then was now a pronounced hollowness. Her small mouth was drawn tight, the lips colorless. She was no paler than usual, because she had always been white-cheeked, but now her whiteness seemed less healthy. Her green-brown eyes were more brown than green, enlarged, blank. She walked as in her sleep, with Minnie beside her.

I tried to catch the mulatto's eyes, but she too was walking blank-faced and dazed.

Those of the congregation who were not staying in the building went away. The others vanished into their rooms. Mildred came into my room for more drinks and smokes. I got no information out of her, nor she out of me.

The house quieted for the night. I left my bed three times at odd hours to prowl through the building. I saw nothing, heard nothing, that was meat to my grinder.

The next day Dr. Riese reported still further improvement in his patient. I wondered what sort of shape she had been in before—if she was better now, as I had seen her last night. I laid in wait for Minnie in the corridor. Her face was not yet clear of last night's daze. I could get nothing out of her.

I had a brief conversation with the boy Manuel that day. I strolled into the library and found him snuggled into a big chair, reading a book entitled *Candide.**

"Morning," I said. "What's exciting in your young life today?"

"Morning," he replied calmly. "What's your opinion of Mildred now? Rather nice legs—hasn't she?—if you like them a bit fat."

---

* Voltaire's 1759 satire on religiosity and blind optimism

I laughed at that one and asked:

"What do you know about it—a young sprout of your age?"

He stared at me coldly for a moment and then returned his big-eyed gaze to the book. Fleming came into the room. I exchanged *Good mornings* with him and went away.

Three more days went by.

On each of them Dr. Riese expressed increasing satisfaction with Gabrielle Leggett's condition. I saw her four or five times in those three days and she didn't look any better to me, but I wasn't a doctor. I gave up trying to get anything out of Minnie. She had gone into a trance; the last time I tried to question her I had to call her three times before she even heard me. I spoke to Dr. Riese about her, but he didn't think it was important.

"Probably just the worry and strain of nursing her mistress," he said. "You know how devoted she is to Miss Leggett."

I said that didn't sound like an explanation to me.

I continued to roam the corridors at night, profitlessly, chiefly because that was about the only thing I could do to earn my pay. New faces came and went. I attended services again—a carbon copy of the first ceremony.

Occasionally I saw and exchanged a few words with Aaronia Haldorn and Joseph. He spent a lot of time with Gabrielle Leggett. Once I asked for his opinion of her condition. He said something about her passing through a spiritual crisis. I felt reassured by his words at the time, but, later, away from him, I thought them over and found that they really hadn't meant anything at all—not anything I could understand.

The plump blonde Mildred came in every evening for an hour or so. We had both given up trying to pump the other, it was now simply a sociable hour or two over whiskey and cigarettes. I went down to the agency one afternoon. There were nine telephone messages and a letter from Eric Collinson on my desk—all demanding assurance that all was well with Gabrielle Leggett. I phoned him that it was.

On the fourth morning, Dr. Riese seemed less sure that the girl was improving; and by the next day he was noticeably worried, though I couldn't get any details out of him. He told me he would be in again to see her at seven that evening.

IV

I spent most of the day fidgeting in and out of my room. The general vagueness of my job in this Temple hadn't bothered me much before—I had had plenty of even more aimless operations in my twenty years of sleuthing—but now that Dr. Riese had found something to worry about—even though it was probably a medical worry and out of my field—I began to get restless, uneasy, irritable.

Dr. Riese did not show up that evening as he had promised. I supposed that one of the emergencies that are a regular part of a doctor's life had held him elsewhere, but his not coming annoyed me.

I sat in my room from half past six on, with my door open, looking at Gabrielle Leggett's door. Mildred took a tray into the girl's room at a few minutes past seven. When she brought me mine I asked her how Gabrielle Leggett seemed to be.

"She's all right, I suppose," she said. "I don't think there's much the matter with her but showing off."

"What was she doing?"

"Sitting at the window, looking out, posing, if you ask me. How is it you're not going down to the dining-room tonight?"

"Tired of eating in the graveyard atmosphere," I said.

At half-past seven Minnie Hershey left her mistress' room, looking with startled eyes through my open door at me, but going on without saying anything. She returned a little after eight, a few minutes before Mildred came up for my tray.

At nine o'clock Joseph appeared, spoke a few words about nothing in particular, smilingly refused the chair I offered him, and went into the girl's room, opening the door without knocking. I cursed him and myself, because he had, for the time he was in my room, chased away my restlessness and uneasiness.

Half an hour later he left the girl's room, nodded at me, said, "Good night," and went down the corridor toward the rear. A couple of the house's inmates passed my door between then and ten o'clock, apparently on their way to their rooms.

At a quarter to eleven Mildred appeared. I asked her not to close the door when she started to. She looked sharply at me, saying:

"I can't stay, then."

"If you knew what a bad humor I'm in you wouldn't want to stay."

She hesitated, lingering for a moment with her hand on the knob, bit her lip, and said:

"Oh, well, I'll come back some time when you're over your grouch," and went away.

At eleven o'clock Minnie Hershey left the girl's room again. I was tempted to stop her and try some questions on her, but didn't. My last several attempts in that line had got me nothing, and I was in too disagreeable a mood for diplomacy. By this time I had given up all hope of seeing Dr. Riese before morning.

Turning off my lights, I sat in the dark, looking at the girl's door and grumbling to myself, cursing the world. At a quarter to twelve Minnie Hershey, in hat and coat, as if she had come in from the street, went into the girl's room once more. She remained inside until nearly one o'clock; and when she came out she closed the door very softly, walking tiptoe, an altogether unnecessary precaution on the thick carpet.

Because it was unnecessary it made me nervous. I went to my door and called softly:

"Minnie."

She tiptoed on down the corridor as if she hadn't heard me. That increased my jumpiness. I went after her, quickly, and stopped her by taking hold of one of her thin wrists.

Her Indian features were expressionless.

"How is she?" I asked.

"Miss Gabrielle's all right, sir. You just leave her alone," she mumbled.

"She's not all right," I growled, "and you know it. What's she doing now?"

"Sleeping."

"Doped?"

She raised angry dark eyes and let them drop again, saying nothing.

"She sent you out to get dope?" I demanded, tightening my grip on her wrist.

"She sent me out to get her some—some medicine, yes, sir."

"And she took some and went to sleep?"

"Y-yes, sir."

"We're going back and have a look at her," I said.

The girl took a quick step away and tried to yank her wrist free. I held it. She said:

"You leave me alone, Mister, or else I'll yell."

"I'll leave you alone after we've had our look, maybe," I said, turning her around with my other hand on her shoulder. "So if you're going to yell, you might as well get started now."

She wasn't at all willing to go back, but she didn't make me drag her.

Gabrielle Leggett's door, like mine and all the guest-room doors, had no lock.

She was lying on her side in bed, sleeping quietly, the bed-clothes stirring gently with her breathing. Her small white face, at rest, with her curly brown hair tumbled over the little forehead, looked like a sick child's.

I turned Minnie loose and went back to my room. Sitting there in the dark I understood why people bit their fingernails.

I sat there for an hour or more and then went for a cruise through the building, drawing the usual blank. In my dark room again, I took off my shoes, sat in the most comfortable chair, put my feet in another, hung a blanket over me, and went to sleep facing Gabrielle Leggett's door, through my open doorway.

Later I opened my eyes for a moment, drowsily, decided that I had only dozed off for a moment, that it was too soon for another trip;

closed my eyes, drifted back toward slumber, and then roused sluggishly again.

Something wasn't right.

I wrestled my eyes open, then closed them. Whatever was wrong had to do with that. Blackness was before them when they were open, and when they were closed. That was reasonable enough, it was a dark, starless night, and my windows were out of the street lights' range. That was reasonable enough—damned if it was!

My door was open, and the corridor lights burned all night. I opened my eyes again. No pale rectangle of light was in front of them, no dim shape of Gabrielle Leggett's door.

I was too much awake now to jump up suddenly. I held my breath and listened, hearing nothing but the ticking of the watch on my wrist. Cautiously moving my hand, I looked at the luminous dial: 3:17. I had been asleep longer than I had thought—and the corridor light had been put out.

My head was numb, my whole body heavy, stiff, and there was a bad taste in my mouth. I got out from under my blanket, and out of my chairs, moving clumsily, my muscles stubborn, and crept on stocking feet to the door—bumped into the door. It had been closed. When I opened it, the corridor light was on as usual. The air coming through the door seemed surprisingly fresh, pure.

I turned, facing into my room, and sniffed. There was an odor of flowers, faint, a bit stuffy, more the odor of a closed place in which flowers had died than of flowers themselves. Lilies-of-the-valley, moonflowers, perhaps another one or two. I had a vague memory of having dreamed of a funeral. Trying to remember what I had dreamed, I leaned against the door-frame and nodded sleepily.

The jerking up of my neck muscles when my head had sunk too low awakened me. I wrestled my eyes open again, standing there on legs that didn't seem part of me, stupidly wondering what it was all about and whether it wouldn't be just as well to go to bed and sleep. While I drowsed

over the thought I put out an arm against the wall, to take some of the strain off my tired legs. The hand—no more a part of me than the legs—touched the light button. I had enough sense to push it.

The light scorched my eyes. Squinting, I could once more see a world that was real to me, and I could remember that I had work to do. I made for the bathroom and doused my face and head in cold water. The water left me still stupid, muddled, but at least partly conscious.

Turning off my lights, I crossed to Gabrielle Leggett's door, listened, and heard nothing. I opened the door quickly, stepped inside, and closed it.

My flashlight showed me an empty bed with covers thrown down across the foot. I put a hand on the hollow her body had made in the bed—cold. There was nobody in bathroom or dressing alcove. There were no signs of a fight. Under the edge of the bed lay a pair of slippers, and a green kimono, or something of the sort, was hung on the back of a chair. There was nothing to indicate that she had dressed before she left the room.

I went back to my own room for my shoes, and then walked down the front stairs to the ground floor, intending to go through the house from top to bottom, silently first. If I ran across nothing—as was probable—then I would start kicking in doors, turning people out of beds, and raising hell until I turned up the girl. I wanted to find her as soon as possible, but she had too long a start on me for a few minutes to make much difference. So if I didn't waste any time getting down the stairs, neither did I run.

I was half-way between the second and first floor when I saw something move—or rather I saw the movement of something without seeing it. It moved from the direction of the street door toward the interior of the house. I was looking at the elevator door at the time, as I descended. The banister shut out my view of the street door. What I saw was a flash of movement through half a dozen of the spaces between the banister's uprights. By the time I had brought my eyes into focus on it, there was nothing to see. I thought I had seen a face, but I knew that's what anybody would have thought they had seen under the circumstances, and I knew that all I had actually seen was the movement of something pale.

The lobby, and what I could see of corridors, were vacant when I reached the ground floor. I moved in the direction that I imagined the moving thing I had seen must have taken—and stopped.

I heard—for the first time since I had awakened—a noise that I had not made. A shoe-sole had scuffed on the stone steps on the other side of the front door.

I walked to the front door, got one hand on the bolt, the other on the key, snapped them back together; and yanked the door open with my left hand, letting my right hand hang within a twist of my gun.

Eric Collinson stood on the top step.

"What the hell are you doing here?" I asked sourly.

It was a long story, and he was too excited to make it a clear one. As nearly as I could untangle his words, he had been in the habit of phoning Dr. Riese for daily reports on Gabrielle Leggett. Today—or rather yesterday—and last night he had been unable to get the doctor on the phone. He had called up as late as two o'clock this morning. Dr. Riese was not at home, he had been told, and none of his household knew where he was or why he was not at home. Collinson had immediately come to the neighborhood of the Temple, on the chance that he might see me, get some word of the girl. He hadn't intended coming to the door—until he had seen me looking out.

"Until you did what?" I asked.

"Saw you."

"When?"

"A minute ago, when you looked out."

"You didn't see me," I said. "What did you see?"

"Someone looking out—peeping out. I thought it was you."

"You mean you hoped and persuaded yourself it was. It wasn't. Who was it? What did he look like?"

"I don't know. I thought it was you, and came up from the corner where I was sitting in the car. Is Gabrielle all right?"

"Sure," I said. There was no use telling him I was hunting for her, and have him blow up on me. "Don't talk so loud. Riese's people don't know where he is?"

"No, and they seem worried. But that's all right if Gabrielle is all right." His haggard young face became pleading. "Could—could I see her? Just for a second? I won't say anything. She needn't know I'm here. Can't you arrange it somehow, please?"

This bird was young, tall, broad, strong, and perfectly willing to have himself broken all up for Gabrielle Leggett's sake. I knew something was wrong, but I didn't know what; neither did I know what I was going to have to do to make it right, how much help I was going to need. I couldn't afford to turn him away; on the other hand I couldn't give him the low down on the racket; that would have turned him into a wild man.

"Come in," I said. "I'm on one of my inspection tours. You can go along if you keep quiet and behave, and afterwards we'll see what we can do."

He came in acting and looking as if I had been St. Peter letting him into Heaven.

I closed the door and led him through the lobby, down the main corridor. So far as I could tell, we had the joint to ourselves.

And then we didn't.

V

Around a corner just ahead of us came Gabrielle Leggett, barefooted and in a yellow silk nightgown that was splashed with dark stains.

In both hands, held out in front of her as she walked, she carried a large dagger, almost a small sword. It was red and wet. Her hands and bare forearms were red and wet. There was a dab of blood on one of her cheeks. Her eyes were clear, bright, calm. Her small forehead was smooth, her mouth and chin firmly set.

She walked up to me, her untroubled gaze holding my troubled one, thrust the dagger toward me, and said evenly, just as if she had expected to find me there, had come there to see me:

"Take it. It is evidence. I killed him."

I said: "Huh?"

Still looking straight into my eyes, she said:

"You are a detective. Take me to where they will hang me."

It was easier to move my hand than my tongue. I took the bloody dagger from her. It was a broad, thick-bladed weapon, double-edged, with a bronze hilt like a cross.

Eric Collinson thrust himself past me, babbling words that nobody could have made out, going for the girl with shaking outstretched hands.

She shrank over against the wall, away from him, fear in her face.

"Don't let him touch me," she begged.

"Gabrielle!" he cried, reaching for her.

"No! No!" she gasped.

I walked into his arms, my body between him and her, facing him, pressing him back with a hand on his chest, growling at him:

"Be still, you."

He put his big lean hands on my shoulders and began pushing me out of the way. I got ready to rap him on the chin with the dagger hilt. Looking past me at the girl, he seemed to forget his intention of forcing me out of his road. I leaned on the hand that was against his chest, moving him back until the wall stopped him.

"Be still till we see what's happened," I ordered.

His hands had gone loose on my shoulders. I stepped back from him, and a little to one side, so that I could see both him and her, facing each other from opposite walls.

"What's happened?" I asked, pointing the dagger at the girl.

She had recovered her calmness.

"Come," she said, "I'll show you. Don't let Eric come, please."

"He won't bother you," I promised.

She nodded at that, gravely, and led the way back down the corridor, around the corner, and to the little iron door that opened into the place where the altar was. The door was standing open. She went first through the door. I followed her, Collinson me. It was dark there under a dark sky. Walking unhurriedly on bare feet that must have found the marble floor chilly, she led us straight toward the altar, a vague dark shape without its tarpaulin.

I got my flashlight out as we walked. When she halted in front of the altar and said, "There," I clicked on the light.

On the first of the three altar steps, Dr. Riese lay dead on his back.

His face was composed, as if he were sleeping. His arms straight down at his sides. His clothes were not rumpled, though his coat and vest were unbuttoned in front. His shirt front was all blood. There were four holes in his shirt front, all alike, all the shape and size that the weapon the girl had given me would have made.

No blood was coming from his wounds now, but when I put a hand on his head I found it not quite cold. There was blood on the altar steps, and on the floor below, where his nose glasses, unbroken, on the end of their black ribbon, lay.

I straightened up and swung the beam of my flashlight directly into the girl's face. She blinked and squinted in the light, but her face showed nothing except that physical discomfort.

"You killed him?" I asked.

Young Collinson came out of his trance to bawl:

"No!"

"Shut up," I snarled at him, stepping closer to the girl, so he couldn't wedge himself in between us. "Did you?" I asked her again.

"Are you surprised?" she asked quietly. "You

were present when my step-mother told of the curse of the Dain blood in me, of how I had murdered my mother before I was five, of my warped mind, of the blackness that would be in my life and in the lives of all that I touched. Is this," she pointed almost carelessly at the dead man, "anything that should not be expected by those who come in contact with me?"

"Don't talk nonsense," I said while I tried to figure out her calmness. I knew she was a hop-head, had seen her coked to the ears before, but this wasn't that. I didn't know what it was. "Why did you kill him?"

Collinson grabbed my near arm and yanked me around to face him. He was all on fire.

"We can't stand here talking," he exclaimed. "We've got to get her out of here, away from here. We've got to hide the body, or put it some place where they'll think somebody else did it. You know how those things are done. I'll take her home. You fix it."

He had nice ideas.

"Yeah?" I asked. "What'll I do? Frame it on one of the Filipino boys, so they'll hang him instead of her?"

"Yes, that's it. You know how to—"

"Like hell that's it," I said. "Not with me."

His face got redder. He stammered:

"I—I didn't mean so they'll hang anybody, really. I wouldn't want you to do that. But couldn't it be fixed for him to get away? I—I'd make it worth his while—any amount. He could—"

"Turn it off," I growled. "You're talking out of my territory."

"But you've got to," he insisted. "You came here to see that nothing happened to Gabrielle, and you've got to go through with this."

"Yeah? You're full of funny ideas, son."

"I know it's a lot to ask, but I'll pay you—"

"Stop it. You've wasted enough time for us." I took my arm out of his hands and turned to the girl, again, asking: "Who else was here when it happened?"

"No one."

I played my light around the place again, even up the walls, on corpse and altar, and discovered nothing I hadn't already seen. I put the dagger beside the body, snapped off the light, and told Collinson:

"We'll take Miss Leggett up to her room."

"For God's sake, let's get her out of this house now, while there's time," he urged.

I said she would look swell running through the streets in bare feet, with nothing on but a blood-spattered nightie.

He jerked his arms out of his overcoat, saying, "I've got the car just down the street; I can carry her to it," and started toward her with the coat held out.

She ran around to the other side of me, moaning:

"Oh, don't let him touch me!"

I put out an arm to stop this. It wasn't strong enough. The girl got behind me. Collinson pursued her and she came around in front. I felt like the center of a merry-go-round, and didn't like the feel of it.

When Collinson appeared in front again, I drove my shoulder into his side, sending him staggering over against the side of the altar. Following him, I planted myself in front of the big sap and blew off steam:

"Let her alone. Let me alone. The next break you make, I'm going to sock your jaw with the flat of a gun. If you want it now, say so."

He got his legs straight under him and began:

"But, good God, you can't—"

I had heard enough of that. I cut in with:

"Stop it. If you want to play with us you've got to stop bellyaching, do what you're told, and let her alone. Yes or no?"

He muttered: "All right."

I turned around and saw the girl—a gray shadow running toward the open iron door, her bare feet making little noise on the marble floor. My shoes seemed to make an ungodly racket as I went after her.

Just inside the door I caught her with an arm around her waist. The next moment my arm was jerked away, and I was flung aside, crashing into the wall, slipping down to one knee.

Collinson, looking eight feet tall in the darkness, stood close to me, storming down at me, but all I could pick out of his many words was a "damn you."

I was in a swell frame of mind when I got up from my knee. It took all my twenty years of the-job-comes-first training to keep my hand off my gun. Bending his face with it would have been sweet.

"There's one coming to you, boy," I promised him, "but it'll wait. We can't spend the whole morning clowning here."

I don't know what his reply was; he mumbled it to my back while I was going over to where the girl was watching us from the doorway.

"We'll go up to your room," I told her.

"Not Eric," she objected.

"He won't bother you," I promised again. "Go ahead."

She hesitated, and then went through the doorway. Collinson looking partly sheepish, partly savage, and altogether dissatisfied, followed me through. I closed the door, asking the girl if she had the key.

"No," she said, as if she hadn't known there was one.

We rode up to the fifth floor in the elevator, the girl keeping me always between her and her fiancé. He stared fixedly at nothing. I studied the girl's face, still trying to dope her out, to decide whether she had been shocked into sanity or deeper into insanity. Looking at her, the first guess seemed most likely, but I had a hunch that it wasn't. At that, I thought sourly, she's no goofier than her boy friend, the big simpleton.

We saw nobody in the corridor between the elevator and her room. I switched on her lights and we went in; I closed the door and put my back to it.

Collinson put his overcoat and hat on a chair and stood beside them, folding his arms. The girl sat on the side of her bed, looking at my feet.

"Tell us the whole thing, quick," I commanded her.

She raised her eyes and said:

"I should like to go to sleep now."

That settled the question of her sanity so far as I was concerned: she hadn't any at all. But now I had another thing to worry about. This room was not exactly as it had been before. Something had been changed since I had been in it not many minutes ago. I shut my eyes, trying to shake up my memory for a picture of it as it had been then; I opened them, looking at it as it was now.

"Can't I?" she asked.

I let her wait for a reply while I put my gaze around the room, checking it up item by item, as far as I could. The only change I could put my finger on was Collinson's coat and hat on the chair. There was no mystery to their being there, and the chair, I decided, was what had bothered me. It still did. I went to it and picked up the coat. There was nothing under it. Then I knew what was wrong; a green kimono, or something of the sort, had been there, and was not there now. I didn't see it elsewhere in the room, and I didn't have enough confidence in its being there to make a complete search.

I wondered what its absence meant while I told the girl:

"Not now. Go in the bathroom, wash the blood off your hands and arms, and get dressed for the street. Take the clothes in there with you. When you come out, give your nightgown to Collinson." I turned to him: "Put it in your pocket and keep it there. Don't go out of this room and don't let anybody come in. I won't be gone long. Got a gun?"

"No," he said, "but I—"

The girl got up from the bed, came over to stand close to me, and interrupted him:

"You cannot leave him here with me. I won't have it. Isn't it enough for you that I have killed one man tonight? Don't make me murder another." She spoke earnestly, but without great excitement, almost as if she were declining an invitation that someone was pressing on her.

"I've got to go out for a while," I said, "and you can't stay alone. Do what I tell you."

"You don't realize what you're doing," she protested in a thin, tired voice. "You know there's a curse on me, and on all who touch me. You know what happened to Dr. Riese, whose only crime was that he was my physician." Her back was to Eric Collinson. She lifted her face so that I could see rather than hear the nearly soundless words on her lips shaped: "I love Eric. Let him go."

I felt sweat in my armpits. A little more of this and she would have had me ready for the cell next to hers: I was actually tempted to let her have her way. I jerked my thumb at the bathroom and said:

"You can stay in there, if you like, but he'll have to stay here."

She nodded her small, suddenly hopeless, face once, gently, and went into the dressing alcove. When she crossed from there to the bathroom, carrying some clothes in her hands, a tear was shiny below each eye.

I gave my gun to Collinson. The brown hand in which he took it was tense and shaky. He was making a lot of noise with his breathing. I told him:

"She's trying to save you from the family curse. She says she loves you. Now don't be a sap. Give me some help this once instead of trouble."

He tried to say something, couldn't, grabbed my nearest hand, did his best to disable it. I took it away from him, and went down to the scene of Dr. Riese's murder.

I had some difficulty in getting there. The iron door through which we had passed a few minutes ago was locked now. I went around to the other one. It too was locked. The lock seemed simple enough. I went at it with the fancy attachments on my pocket knife, and presently had it open.

I didn't find the green kimono inside. Dr. Riese's body was gone from the altar steps, was nowhere in sight. The dagger was gone, and every trace of blood—except where the pool on the marble floor had left a yellow stain—had been mopped up.

Somebody had been tidying up.

I put my flashlight back in my pocket and headed for an alcove off the lobby, where I had seen a telephone. The phone was there, but it was dead. I put it down and set out for Minnie Hershey's room on the sixth floor. I hadn't been able to do much with her, but I knew she was devoted to Gabrielle Leggett, and perhaps I could send her out to do my phoning.

I opened her door—lockless as the others—and went in, closing the door behind me. Holding one hand over the front of my flashlight, I snapped it on. Enough light leaked out to show me the mulatto girl in her bed, sleeping. The windows were closed, the atmosphere heavy, with a faint odor that was familiar—the odor of a closed place where flowers had died, the odor I had smelled in my own room earlier in the night.

I looked at the girl again. She was lying on her back, breathing through open mouth, her face more an Indian's than ever with the peace of heavy sleep on it. Looking at her, I felt drowsy myself. It seemed a shame to rouse her. Perhaps she was dreaming of—

I shook my head, trying to clear it of the muddle settling there. Lilies-of-the-valley, moonflowers . . . that had died . . . death was restful . . . so was sleep . . . little death, somebody called it . . . it was restful . . . sleep . . . sleep . . . the flashlight was heavy in my hand . . . too heavy . . . hell with it . . . I let it drop . . . it fell on my foot . . . puzzling me . . . who touched my foot? somebody . . . Gabrielle Leggett . . . asking to be saved . . . Gabrielle Leggett . . . a job . . . Gabrielle Leggett . . . the job comes first . . . work to do . . .

I tried to shake my head again, tried desperately. It weighed a ton, and would barely creep from side to side. I felt myself swaying, put out a foot to steady myself. The foot and leg were weak, limp, dough. I had to take another step or fall; took it; forced my head up, my eyes open, to find a place to fall, and saw the window six inches ahead of me.

I swayed forward until the window sill caught my thighs, steadying me. My hands rested on the sill. I tried to find the handles on the bottom of the window, wasn't sure whether I had them or not, put everything I had into an attempt to raise the window.

It didn't budge.

I think I sobbed then, and holding the sill with my right hand, I beat the glass out of the center of the pane with my open left.

Air that stung like ammonia came through the opening. I put my face to it, hanging to the sill with both hands, sucking it in through mouth, nose, eyes, ears, and pores; laughing, with water from my eyes trickling down into my mouth.

I hung there drinking air only until I was reasonably sure of my legs under me again, and of my eyesight; until I was able to think and move again, though neither speedily nor surely. I couldn't afford to wait longer. I put a handkerchief over my face and nose and turned away from the window.

Not more than three feet away, there in the black room, a pale bright thing like a body, but not like flesh, stood writhing before me.

VI

It was tall, yet not so tall as it seemed, because it did not stand on the floor, but hovered with its feet a foot or more above the floor. Its feet—it had feet, but I don't know what their shape was. They had no shape—just as its legs and torso, arms and hands, head and face were without shape—without fixed form. They writhed, swelling and contracting, stretching and shrinking, not greatly, but without pause. An arm would drift into the body, be swallowed by it, come out again as if poured out. The nose would stretch down over the gaping shapeless mouth, shrink back up, into the face until it was flush with the cheeks, grow out again. The eyes would spread across the face until they were one enormous eye that had blotted out all the upper face, then contract until there was no eye, then three, then two again. The legs became one thick leg, like a pedestal, then three, then two again. And

no feature or member ever stopped its quivering and writhing until its contours could be determined, its shape recognized.

It, or he, was a thing like a man, who floated above the floor; with a horrible grimacing greenish face and pale flesh that was not flesh, that was visible in the darkness, and that was as fluid, and as unresting, and as transparent, as tidal water.

I knew that I was ninety percent unbalanced, mentally and physically, from breathing the dead-flower stuff. But I couldn't—though I tried to—tell myself that I didn't see this thing.

It was there, within reach of my hand if I had leaned forward, shivering, writhing, between me and the door. I didn't believe in the supernatural—but what of that? Here was a thing that was not a natural thing, and it was not, I knew, a man with a sheet over him, or a trick of luminous paint.

I gave it up. I stood there with my handkerchief jammed to my nose and mouth; not breathing, not stirring—for all I know, my blood may have stopped running. I could say I was waiting to see what happened next; but I wasn't conscious of any intentions at all at the time.

I was there, and the thing was there, and I stayed where I was.

The thing spoke, though I could not have said whether I heard the words or simply became somehow conscious of them:

"Down, enemy of the Lord God; down on your knees!"

I stirred then, to lick my lips with a tongue drier than they were.

"Down, accursed of the Lord God, before the blow falls!"

I moved my handkerchief enough to say:

"Go to hell."

It sounded silly, especially in the croaking voice I had.

The thing's horrible body twisted convulsively, swayed, bent toward me.

I dropped my handkerchief and reached for it with both hands.

I got hold of the thing—and I didn't. My hands were in it to the wrists—into the center of it—were shut on it. And there was nothing in my hands but dampness that was without temperature, was neither warm nor cold.

That same dampness came into my face as the thing's face floated into mine.

I bit at its face—yes—and my teeth closed on nothing, though I could see and feel that my face was *in* its face.

And in my hands, on my arms, against my body, in my face, the thing writhed and squirmed, shuddered and quivered, swirling wildly now, breaking apart, reuniting madly in the black air.

Through the thing's flesh I could see my hands, clenched in the center of its damp body. I opened them, struck up and down inside it with stiff crooked fingers, trying to gouge it open—could see it being torn apart by my fingers, could see it going together again after my clawing fingers had passed—but I could feel nothing but dampness.

Now another feeling came to me, growing quickly once it had started—of suffocation and of an immense weight bearing me down.

This thing that had no solidity had weight, weight that was pressing me down, smothering me. My knees were going soft.

I tore my right hand free of its body and struck up at its face—felt nothing but its dampness brushing my fist.

I clawed at its insides again with my left hand, tearing at this substance that was so plainly seen, so faintly felt. Then on my left hand I saw something else—blood, dark, thick and real, covering the hand, running out between the fingers, dripping from it.

I laughed, got enough strength to straighten my back against the monstrous weight on me, and wrenched at the thing's insides again, croaking:

"I'll gut you plenty."

More blood washed my left hand.

I tried to laugh again, couldn't, choked instead. The thing's weight on me was twice what it had been. I staggered back, sagged against the wall, turning to lie against it.

Pure air from the broken pane, bitter, cold, stung my nostrils, told me—by its difference from the air I had been breathing—that it was not the thing's weight, but the poisonous flower-smelling stuff that was the weight on me.

The thing's pale dampness squirmed over my face and body.

Coughing, I stumbled through it, to the door, got the door open, and tumbled down into the corridor that was now as black as the room I had just left.

As I tumbled, somebody fell over me.

This was no indescribable thing. It was human. The knees that hit my back were human, sharp. The grunt that blew hot breath in my ear was human, surprised. The arm my fingers caught was human, thin.

I thanked God for its thinness. The corridor air was doing me a lot of good, but I was in no shape to battle with an athlete.

I put what strength I had into my hold on the thin arm, dragging it under me as I rolled over on the body it belonged to. My other hand, flung out across the man's thin body as I rolled over, struck something hard and metallic on the floor. Twisting my wrist, I got my fingers on it and knew what it was. It had been in my hand too recently for me to have forgotten the feel of it—the over-sized dagger with which Dr. Riese had been killed.

The man on whom I was rolling had, I guessed, stood beside the door of Minnie's room, with the dagger in his hand, waiting to stick it into me when I came out. My tumble through the door had saved me, making him miss my body with that blade; and in missing he had gone off-balance, tripping over me.

Now he was kicking, jabbing, butting up at me from his face-down position on the floor, with my hundred and ninety pounds draped over his back, anchoring him down.

Holding on to the dagger with my left hand, I took my right hand away from his arm, found the back of his head in the dark, spread my hand on it, and began grinding his face into the floor, taking it easy, waiting for more of the strength that was coming back to me with each breath. A minute more and I would be ready to pick this baby up and get words out of him.

But I had to move before that.

Something hard pounded my right shoulder, then my back, then struck the carpet close to my noodle. Somebody was swinging a club on me.

I rolled off the thin man, thumping his skull with the heavy bronze dagger hilt as I left him. The club-swinger's feet stopped my rolling. I looped my right arm above the feet, took another rap on the back, missed the legs with my circling arm, and felt skirts against my hand.

Surprised, I pulled my hand back. Another blow from the club, on my side, reminded me that this was no place for gallantry. I made a fist of my hand and struck back at the skirt. It folded around my fist: a solid, meaty shin stopped my fist.

The shin's owner snarled in pain above me, and backed off before I could hit out again.

Scrambling up on hands and knees, I bumped my head into wood—a door. A hand on the knob helped me stand up. Not far away the club swished in the darkness again. The knob turned in my hand. I stepped back with the door, into a room, softly closing the door.

Behind me in the room a voice said:

"Go right out of here or I'll shoot you."

It was plump Mildred's voice, frightened. I turned, bending low, in case she did shoot. Enough of the dull grayness of approaching daylight came into this room to outline a thick body sitting up in bed holding something small and dark in one outstretched hand.

"It's me, your little playmate," I told her.

"Oh, you!" she exclaimed, as if in relief, but she did not lower the thing in her hand.

"You in on the racket?" I asked, risking a slow step toward her.

"I do what I'm told, and I keep my mouth shut, but I'm not going in for any strong-arm work, not for the money they're paying me."

"Swell," I said, taking more and quicker steps toward her. "Could I get down through this window to the one on the floor below if I tied a couple of sheets or blankets together, do you think?"

"I don't know—Ouch! Stop!"

I had her gun—a .32 automatic—in my right hand, her wrist in my left, twisting.

"Let go of it," I ordered, and she did.

Dropping her wrist, I stepped away from the bed again, picking up the dagger I had dropped on the foot of the bed. I tiptoed to the door and listened. I heard nothing. I opened the door, and heard nothing; saw nothing in the faint grayness that went through into the corridor.

Minnie Hershey's door was open. The thing I had fought with was not there. I crossed the corridor and went into her room, switching on the lights.

The mulatto was lying as she had lain before, sleeping heavily. I pocketed my gun, pulled down the covers, picked Minnie up, and carried her over into Mildred's room.

"See if you can bring her to life," I told Mildred, dumping the sleeping girl on the bed beside her.

"She'll come around in a few minutes. They always do."

I said, "Yeah?" and went out, down to the floor below, to Gabrielle Leggett's room.

The room was empty.

Collinson's hat and overcoat were gone; so were the clothes she had taken into the bathroom; and so was her nightgown.

I cursed the pair of them bitterly, snapped off the lights, and ran down the stairs to the first floor, feeling as bloodthirsty and violent as I must have looked—battered and torn and bruised, with a bloody dagger in my bloody left hand, a gun in my right.

Going down the stairs, I heard nothing, but when I reached the foot of them, a noise like small thunder suddenly broke out. I stopped until I had identified it as somebody's knocking on the front door. Then I went to the door, unlocked and opened it.

There was Eric Collinson, wild-eyed, white-faced and frantic.

"Where's Gaby?" he panted.

"Damn you," I said, and hit him in the face with the gun.

He drooped, folding forward, stopped himself with his hands on the vestibule walls, hung there a moment, and slowly pulled himself upright again. Blood leaked from a corner of his mouth.

"Where's Gaby?" he repeated, doggedly.

"Where'd you leave her?"

"Here. I was taking her away. She asked me to. She sent me out first to see if anybody was in the street. Then the door shut."

"When?"

"Not a minute ago. Where is she?"

"She tricked you," I grumbled, "still trying to save you from the curse. If you had done what I told—But come on; we'll have to find her."

The reception rooms off the lobby were empty. We left the lights burning in them and hurried down the main corridor.

A small figure in white pajamas sprang out of a doorway and fastened itself on me, tangling itself up with my legs, nearly upsetting me.

Unintelligible words came from it. I pulled it loose and saw that it was the boy Manuel. Tears wet his panic-stricken face; sobs mangled the words he was trying to say.

"Take it easy, son," I said. "I can't understand a thing you're saying."

"Don't let him kill her," I understood.

"Who kill who? And take your time."

He didn't take his time, but out of his sobbing my ears fastened on "father" and "mother."

"Your father's going to kill your mother?" I asked, not greatly surprised.

His head went up and down.

"Where?"

He fluttered a hand at the iron door ahead.

I started toward it, and stopped.

"Listen, son," I bargained. "I'd like to save your mother, but I've got to find Miss Leggett first. Do you know where she is?"

"She's in there with them," he cried. "Oh, hurry! hurry!"

"Right. Come on, Collinson," and we raced for the iron door.

Beyond it, another door opened in the corridor, and the big woman I knew as the Village Blacksmith ran out, toward us, limping as she ran—from the crack I'd given her shin upstairs—and firing a heavy automatic pistol. The reports were deafening in the corridor. Her aim was terrible, playing hell with the ceiling.

I fired twice.

She dropped as I yanked the iron door open.

The white altar was dazzling, almost blinding, again in the beam of white light from the roof-edge. At one end of the altar Gabrielle Leggett crouched, her face turned up into the light-beam. The light on her face was too glaring for her expression to be made out.

Aaronia Haldorn lay on the altar step where Riese had lain. There was a dark bruise on her forehead. Her hands and feet were tied. Most of her clothes had been torn off. Her eyes, glaring at Joseph, held enough hatred to stock hell; her mask-like face was twisted into a fitting setting for the eyes.

Joseph, white-robed, stood in front of the altar, and of his wife. He stood with both arms held high and widespread, his back and neck bent so that his bearded face was lifted to the sky.

In his right hand he held an ordinary horn-handled carving knife, with a long curved blade; in his left a horn-handled, two-pronged fork.

He was talking to the sky, but his back was to Collinson and me, and we couldn't hear his words.

As we ran forward, he lowered his arms and bent over his wife. I was still a good thirty feet from him, Collinson at my side. I bellowed:

"Joseph!"

He straightened again, turning, and when the knife and fork came into view I saw that they were still clean, shiny.

I halted ten feet from the man in white, Collinson stopping beside me.

"Who calls Joseph, a name that is no more?" the priest asked, and I'd be a liar if I didn't admit that, standing there, looking at him, listening to him, I didn't begin to feel that there was nothing so very wrong with anything here or elsewhere in the world. "There is no Joseph," he went on, not waiting for an answer to his question. "You may know now, as all the world shall know, that he who went among you as Joseph was not Joseph, but God Himself. Now that you know, go!"

To any other man I would have said, "Bunk!" and jumped him. To this one I couldn't. I said:

"I'll have to take Miss Leggett and Mrs. Haldorn with me," and said it weakly, indecisively.

He drew himself up taller, and his white-bearded face became stern.

"Go!" he commanded, his voice deep and vibrant. "Go from me before your defiance leads to destruction."

Aaronia Haldorn spoke to me from where she lay tied on the altar steps:

"Shoot. Shoot now—quick. Shoot."

I said to the man:

"You can be Joseph, or God, or Barney Google,* but you're going along to police headquarters. Now put down the knives and things."

"You have blasphemed," he thundered, and took a step toward me. "You must die."

"Stop!" I barked.

He wouldn't stop. I was afraid. I fired.

The bullet hit his cheek. I saw the hole it made.

No muscle twitched in his face; he did not even blink an eye.

He walked deliberately, unhurriedly, toward me.

I worked the trigger, pumping seven more bullets into his face and body. I saw the holes they made.

He came on, deliberately, unhurriedly, no muscle twitching, no sign that he had felt the bullets.

His eyes and face were calm, stern. When he was close to me, the knife in his hand went up high above his head.

He was not fighting; he was bringing retribution to me; and he paid as little attention to my attempts to stop him as a father would to the struggles of a small boy he was punishing.

I was fighting.

The knife glistened up high, and started down.

I went in under it, bending my right forearm against his knife arm, driving the dagger in my left hand at his throat.

I drove the heavy blade into his throat, all the way in till the hilt's cross stopped it. Then I knew I could do nothing more. . . .

I didn't know I had closed my eyes until I opened them. The first thing I saw was Eric Collinson kneeling beside Gabrielle Leggett, turning her face from the glaring light, trying to rouse her. Next I saw Aaronia Haldorn, still lying bound on the altar steps, but unconscious now. Then I discovered that I was standing with my legs apart, and that Joseph was on the floor between my feet, dead, with the dagger through his neck.

"Thank God he wasn't really God," I mumbled to myself.

A brown body in white brushed past me, and Minnie Hershey was throwing herself down in front of Gabrielle Leggett, crying:

"Oh, Miss Gabrielle, I thought that Satan had come alive and was after you again!"

I went over and took the mulatto by the shoulders, lifting her up, turning her to face me.

"How could he?" I asked. "Didn't you kill him dead?"

"Yes, sir, but—"

"But he might have come back in some other shape than Dr. Riese?"

"Yes, sir, I thought he was—" She stopped and worked her lips together.

"Me?" I asked.

She nodded, not looking at me.

VII

I was waiting in Madison Andrews' reception room when he arrived at ten-thirty that morning. He looked anxiously into my face and at my

---

* Sports-loving girl chaser from the syndicated comic strip *Take Barney Google F'rinstance*. First appeared in 1919.

bandaged left hand, and as soon as we were in his private office he asked:

"What is it? Anything gone wrong?"

"Plenty did, but most of it's all right now—except that Dr. Riese is dead."

Andrews looked sharply at my face and bandaged hand again, sat down at his desk, motioned me to a chair, cut off a piece of tobacco, put it in his mouth, pushed a box of cigars at me, and said:

"I'm listening."

"These Temple of the Holy Grail people—Aaronia and Joseph Haldorn—were actors originally. I'm giving it to you as I got it from her and some of the other survivors. As actors they were pretty good—not getting on as well as they wanted to. This religious cult racket had been getting a lot of publicity, and they decided to give it a whirl. They rigged up a cult that was supposed to be a revival of an old Gaelic church back in the days of King Arthur. They brought it to California because our state's known to be a green meadow for anything in that line, and picked San Francisco instead of Los Angeles because the competition was less.

"With them they brought a little fellow named Tom Fink, who had taken care of the mechanical end of things for most of the well-known stage magicians and illusionists at one time or another; and Fink's wife, a big village blacksmith of a woman. They didn't want a lot of converts; they wanted few but wealthy ones. The racket went slow at first, until they landed Mrs. Rodman. She fell plenty, and they worked her for one of her apartment buildings. She also footed the remodeling bill. The stage mechanic Fink had a lot to do with the remodeling, and did a good job.

"They didn't need the kitchens that each apartment in the building had, but Fink found that part of the kitchen space could be used for concealed rooms and cabinets, and that the gas and water pipes and the electric wires that were in them could be adapted to his hocus-pocus with little trouble. I can't give you all the mechanical details now—not until we've had time to take the joint apart. It's going to be interesting.

"I saw some of their work in action—a ghost that was made by an arrangement of lights thrown up on a body of steam rising from a padded pipe which had been pushed into a dark room from a concealed opening in the wainscoting under the bed. The part of the steam that wasn't lighted was invisible in the darkness, showing only a man-shape that quivered and writhed, and that was damp and real without any solidity to the touch. You'd be surprised how weird a trick like that can be, especially when you've been filled with that stuff they pump into the room before they start the vision going. I don't know whether it was ether or chloroform or something else; its odor was nicely disguised with some sort of flower perfume. This ghost—I fought with it—on the level—and even thought I had it bleeding, not knowing that I had cut my hand breaking a window to let in fresh air. It made a few minutes seem like a lot of hours to me.

"There wasn't until the very last—when he went off his base—anything crude about the Haldorns' work. Their services were as dignified and orderly as any could be. The hocus-pocus was all worked in the privacy of the victim's room. First the perfumed gas was pumped in, to get him groggy. Then the lighted steam vision was shown him, with a voice coming out of the same pipe to give him his orders, or whatever he was to be given. The gas kept him from being too sharp-eyed and suspicious, and also weakened his will so that he would be more likely to do what he was told. It was slick enough. The victim could talk about it afterward or not, just as he wished, but its happening in his own room, and the way it was handled, gave it a lot of authority. I imagine they squeezed a lot of pennies out of the customers that way.

"Some friends of Gabrielle Leggett's ran her into the Temple a little while back, and she went there a couple of times. She had enough money—or her parents did then—to make her eligible. When her trouble came and she broke up, the Haldorns decided it was time to play her, and Joseph went to see her. Have you ever seen Joseph?"

"No," the lawyer said.

"Well, he had what he needed. He looked at you and spoke to you, and things happened inside you. I'm not the easiest guy in the world to flimflam, but he had me going. I came damned near thinking he was God at the last. He was young, but he had grown a beard and had had the coloring killed in its hairs as well as in the hairs of his head. His wife tells me that she used to hypnotize him before he went into action, and that most of his effect on people was a result of that. Later he got so that he could get himself in the same condition of his own accord, and toward the last it became permanent.

"Aaronia Haldorn didn't know her husband had fallen for Gabrielle until after she came to the Temple. Until then she thought that he looked on the girl simply as another customer. But he had fallen in love with her, or wanted her, anyway. I don't know how far he had gone in working on her, using his hocus-pocus and her fear of her curse to sew her up, but Dr. Riese finally discovered that everything wasn't going well with her. That was yesterday morning. He told me he was coming back later to see her, and he did come back, but he didn't see her, and I didn't see him—not then.

"He went in to see Joseph before he came upstairs, and overheard Joseph giving instructions to the Finks. He was foolish enough to let Joseph know he had overheard him. Joseph locked him up—a prisoner. They had sent one of the maids up to try to pump me when I first arrived, but after that they let me alone. It was wiser to let me see nothing funny than to try to stir me up with their supernatural stuff. But they had cut loose on Minnie Hershey from the first.

"She was a mulatto, and her negro blood made her susceptible to that sort of thing, and she was devoted to Gabrielle Leggett. They chucked visions and voices at the poor girl until she was dizzy. I had told Dr. Riese that she was going queer, but he refused to take it seriously.

Now they decided to make her kill Riese. They drugged him and put him on the altar. They ghosted her into believing that he was Satan, come up from hell to carry her mistress down there so she couldn't become a saint. Minnie was ripe for it—poor girl—and when the spirit told her that she had been selected to save her mistress, that she'd find the anointed weapon on her table, she followed the instructions the spirit gave her. She got out of bed, picked up the dagger that had been put on her table, went down to the altar, and killed Riese.

"That was the first time they did anything to me. I used to wander around the joint at night. To play safe, they pumped some gas into my room to keep me out of the way—slumbering—while Minnie was doing her stuff. But I was nervous, jumpy, and was sleeping in a chair in the center of the room instead of on the bed, close to the gas-pipe, so I came out of the dope before the night was over.

"By this time Aaronia Haldorn had discovered two things. First, that her husband's interest in the girl wasn't altogether financial. Second, that he had gone off center, was a dangerous maniac. Going around hypnotized all the time, what mind he had—not a whole lot, his wife says—had gone under completely. His success in flimflamming his followers had gone to his head. He thought he could do anything, get away with anything. He had dreams, she says, of the entire world deluded into belief in his divinity, he didn't see that that was any—or much—more difficult than fooling the handful that he had fooled.

"Aaronia Haldorn didn't like either of these things, but the first of them seemed the easiest remedied. She decided that if Gabrielle were sent down to find the murdered doctor, she would probably be shocked into complete insanity, and would be put out of Joseph's reach, in an asylum. She turned a vision and a voice loose on the girl and sent her down to the altar. The shock did upset Gabrielle still further, and worked out, for the time, even better than Aaronia had expected. The curse was never out of Gabrielle's thoughts. Now she took it for granted that this curse was responsible for Riese's death, because of his contact with her. Collinson and I met her in the hall saying she had killed him and should be hanged for it.

"I suspected then that she hadn't really killed him, from the way she talked of the curse; and when I saw him I was sure of it. He was lying in an orderly position. It was plain that he had been drugged before he was stabbed. The door leading to the altar—always kept locked—was unlocked, and she knew nothing about its key. There was a chance that she had been some-body's tool in the murder, but I doubted that.

"Haldorn and his wife both heard Gabrielle's confession that she had killed Riese. The place was scientifically equipped for eavesdropping. Haldorn didn't like that confession. His wife did. He decided that if the body were removed, and I were killed, Collinson would be the only sane witness to the whole thing—except the Haldorns and their allies—and he had heard Collinson trying to persuade me to hush it up. He could count on Collinson's silence.

"Aaronia, planning to spoil her hubby's scheme, went up to Gabrielle's room, got her kimono, wrapped the bloody dagger in it, and stuck it in a corner where the police could easily find it. Meanwhile her husband and the Finks, having removed Riese's remains and cleaned up the place, started to work on Minnie again, to make her kill me. Aaronia crossed them up again, turning on the flower-smelling stuff so strong that it knocked the maid out—put her so soundly asleep that a dozen voices and visions couldn't have stirred her into action.

"Haldorn discovered then what his wife was doing, and he found the dagger wrapped in the kimono. I crashed into Minnie's room just about then, intending to wake her, and Haldorn—or the Finks—turned their ghost loose on me. It gave me hell, and when I finally tottered out of the room, I was jumped by the Finks. I beat them off, got a gun, and went downstairs.

"Meanwhile, Haldorn, up to his neck in a kill-ing spree, condemned his wife to death for her treachery. He had got himself into a fine muddle by this time, and I suppose the only way out that he could see was through continued killing. He still had enough belief in his divinity-shield to take his wife down to the altar before he carved her. She was tied up there when Collinson and I, steered by their son, arrived. I killed Haldorn, but I almost didn't. I put eight bullets in him. Steel-jacketed .32's go in clean, without much of a thump, true enough. But I put eight of them in him—in his face and body—standing close to him and firing point-blank—and he didn't even know it. That's how completely hypnotized he had himself. I finally got him down by driving the dagger through his neck, cutting the spinal cord. God! it was—That's the story."

"And Gabrielle?" Andrews asked.

"The last I heard of her, Collinson was bear-ing her off to Reno, for marriage, not wanting to wait the three days the California law calls for."

The old lawyer's eyes burned at me from under his ragged brows.

"You'd no right to let them go," he roared. "You know she's in no condition to know what she's doing."

"She's not," I agreed. "But I didn't let them go. I was busy, and the first I knew of it was when I got Collinson's note, saying they had gone, two hours later."

Andrews pulled at a mustache corner and glowered at me.

"What about the police? The inquest?" he said. "You know they've got to be here for that."

"Sure you and I know it, but what do they care?"

"I care," he said, "and I engaged you, and I had a right to expect you to protect my inter-ests."

"Yeah. Well, you're her guardian, or whatever you are, and you're a lawyer, so you ought to be able to do something about it—besides yelling."

He glowered at me for another moment and then his face slowly cleared.

"I'm sorry," he said. "I don't like it though, not a damned bit. But it may work out all right, may take her mind off that curse foolishness."

"I hope so," I replied, "but I doubt it. I don't think we're through with the curse yet."

His gaunt body jerked upright in his chair.

"What?" he demanded. "You haven't started believing in—?"

"I haven't started believing anything," I growled, standing up, "except that whatever it is that's hanging over Miss Leggett hasn't been smoked out yet, and that it'll probably be good for a lot more trouble before it is. And I don't believe in curses either—unless they have arms and legs and the rest of the things that make up a human being."

He leaned forward to ask, "Who?"

I shook my head. I didn't know.

He sat back in his chair, smiling.

"Preposterous," he said, and waved me out of his office.

THE BLACK HONEYMOON, BY DASHIELL HAMMETT

The third adventure of the Continental Detective in

"THE DAIN CURSE"

In JANUARY BLACK MASK

Black Lives, the first of the Dain Curse adventures, appeared in the November issue. Until exhausted, copies will be furnished on request at the regular newsstand price.

BLACK MASK, JANUARY 1929

Black Honeymoon

THE DAIN CURSE

BY DASHIELL HAMMETT

ERIC COLLINSON WIRED me from Quesada:

Come Immediately Meet Me Sunset Hotel Do Not Communicate Gabrielle Must Not Know Hurry Need You

The telegram came to me early Friday morning. I couldn't leave San Francisco immediately. Tommy the Rags was being tried for the California Steel and Iron payroll stick-up, and I had to go on the witness stand that day. I was still on it when court adjourned till Monday.

Then I had a date with an ex-wife of Phil Leach. We wanted him for a bank swindle in Des Moines. She had offered to sell us a photograph of him. I made the deal with her, but it was then after six, too late for a train that would put me in Quesada that night.

I ate dinner, packed a bag, got my car from the garage, and drove down.

Quesada was a one-hotel town pasted on the rocky side of a young mountain that sloped down into the Pacific Ocean some eighty miles from San Francisco. Quesada's beach was too abrupt, hard, jagged, for bathing, so Quesada had never got into the summer resort money, but for a while it had been a hustling rum-running port. That racket was dead now—bootleggers had learned there was more profit and safety, less worry and confusion, in handling domestic hooch than imported—and Quesada had gone back to sleep.

I got there at eleven-something that night, garaged my car, and crossed the street to the Sunset Hotel. It was a low sprawled-out yellow building. There was nobody in the lobby except the night clerk. He was a small effeminate man well past sixty who went to a lot of trouble to let me see that his fingernails were rosy and shiny.

When I had registered he gave me a sealed envelope—hotel stationery. My name was on it in Eric Collinson's handwriting. I tore it open and read:

Do not leave the hotel until I have seen you.
Eric Collinson.

"How long has this been here?" I asked.

"Since about eight o'clock. He was here waiting for you for about an hour, until after the last stage got in from the railroad."

"Isn't he staying here?"

"Oh, dear, no. He and his bride got the Tooker place, down in the cove."

"How do you get there?" Collinson was too muddle-brained for me to pay much attention to his instructions.

"You'd never be able to find it at night," the clerk assured me, "unless you went all the way around by the East road, and not then unless you knew the country."

"Yeah? How do you get there in the day-time?"

"You go down this street to the end, take the fork of the road on the ocean side, and follow that up along the cliff. It isn't really a road, more of a path. It's about three miles, a brown house, shingled all over, on a little hill. It's easy enough to find in the daytime if you remember to keep to the right, to the ocean side, all the way down."

I thanked the clerk, let him guide me to a room, told him to call me at five, and was asleep by midnight.

The morning was dull, ugly, foggy and cold when I climbed out of bed to say, "All right, thanks," into the telephone. It hadn't improved much by the time I had put on my clothes and gone downstairs. The clerk told me there was no chance of getting anything to eat in Quesada before seven o'clock.

I went out of the hotel, down the street until it became a dirt road, kept along the road until it forked, and turned into the branch that bent toward the ocean. This branch was never a road from its very beginning, and soon it was nothing but a rocky path climbing sidewise along a rocky ledge that kept pushing closer to the water's edge.

The side of the ledge became steeper and steeper, until the path was simply an irregular shelf on the face of a cliff, six or eight feet wide in places, no more than three in others. Above and behind the path, the cliff rose sixty or seventy feet; below and in front, it slanted down a hundred feet or more to ravel out into the ocean. A breeze from the general direction of China was pushing fog over the top of the cliff, making noisy lather of sea-water at its rocky base.

Rounding a corner where the cliff was steepest—was, in fact, for a hundred yards or so, straight up and down—I stopped to look at a small ragged hole in the path's outer rim. The hole was perhaps six inches across, with fresh loose earth piled in a little semicircle mound on one side of it, scattered on the other side. It wasn't an exciting sight, but it said plainly to even such a city man as I was: *Here, not long ago, a bush was torn up by its roots.*

There was no torn-up bush in sight. I chucked my cigarette away and got down on hands and knees, putting my head over the path's rim, looking down. Twenty feet below I saw it. It was perched on the top of a stunted tree that grew almost parallel to the cliff, fresh brown dirt sticking to its roots.

The next thing that caught my eye was also brown—a soft hat lying upside down between two jagged gray rocks, fifty feet below me, halfway to the water.

I looked down at the bottom of the cliff and saw the feet and legs.

They were a man's feet and legs, in tan shoes and dark trousers. The feet lay on the top of a smooth, water-rounded boulder, lay on their sides, perhaps six inches apart, both pointing to the left. From the feet, the dark-trousered legs slanted down into the water, disappearing beneath the surface a few inches above the knees. That was all I could see from the path.

I went down the cliff, but not at that point. It was a lot too steep there to be tackled by a middle-aged fat man. A couple of hundred yards back, the path had crossed a crooked ravine that creased the cliff diagonally from top to bottom. I returned to the ravine and went down it, stumbling, sliding, sweating and swearing, but reaching the bottom all in one piece, with nothing more serious the matter with me than torn fingers, dirty clothes, and ruined shoes.

The fringe of rock that lay between cliff and ocean wasn't meant to be walked on, but I managed to travel over it most of the way, having to wade only once or twice, and then not up to my knees.

When I came to where the feet and legs lay I had to go waist-deep in the Pacific to lift the body, which rested on its back on the worn slanting side of the boulder, covered from thighs up by frothing water. I got my hands under its armpits, found solid spots for my feet, and lifted.

It was Eric Collinson's body—horribly crushed. There was no back to his head. The water had washed away all blood.

I lugged him out of the water, put him on his back on dry rocks. I couldn't find any marks on him that hadn't apparently been made by the fall. His dripping pockets told me nothing; they held a hundred and fifty-some dollars, a watch, a knife, a gold pen and pencil, papers, letters, and a memoranda book that held nothing informative. There was nothing anywhere in sight to tell me more about his death than the uprooted bush, the hat caught between rocks, and his body had told me.

I left him on the dry rocks, going back to the ravine, panting and heaving myself up it to the path, returning to where the bush had grown. The path was chiefly rough stone. I couldn't find anything on it in the way of significant marks, footprints or the like. I went on.

Presently the cliff began to bend away from the ocean, lowering the path along its side. After another mile there was no cliff at all, merely a brush grown ridge at whose foot the path ran. There was no sun yet. My pants stuck disagreeably to my chilly legs. Water squunched in my torn shoes. I hadn't had any breakfast. I discovered that my cigarettes had got wet. My left knee ached from a twist I had given it sliding down the ravine. I cursed the detective business and slopped on along the path.

It took me away from the sea for a while, across the neck of a wooded point that pushed the ocean back, down into a little valley, up the side of a low hill, and then I saw the house the night clerk had described.

It was a fairly large two-story building, roof and walls brown-shingled, set on a hump in the ground close to where the ocean came in to take a quarter-mile U-shaped bite out of the coast. The house faced the water. I was behind it. There was nobody in sight. The ground-floor windows were closed, with drawn blinds. The second-story windows were open. Off to one side were some smaller buildings and a shed.

I went around to the front of the house. Wicker chairs and a table were on the screened front porch. The screened porch-door was hooked on the inside. I rattled it noisily. I rattled it off and on for at least five minutes, and got no response. Then I went around to the rear and knocked on the back door.

My knocking knuckles pushed the door open half a foot. Inside was a dark kitchen and silence. I opened the door wider, knocking on it again, loudly. I called:

"Mrs. Collinson."

I knew the girl. When no answer came, I went through the kitchen and a darker dining-room, found a flight of stairs, climbed them, and began poking my head into rooms.

There was nobody in the house. Two bedrooms, bathroom, and a cross between a library and a sitting room made up this floor.

In the bathroom—in the tub—was a large bath-towel stained with blood and mud, both still damp.

In one bedroom a .38 automatic pistol lay in the center of the floor. There was an empty shell close to it, another under a chair across the room, and a faint odor of burnt gunpowder in the air. In one corner of the ceiling was a hole that a .38 bullet could have made; under it, on the floor, a few crumbs of plaster. The bed-clothes were smooth and undisturbed. Clothes in the closet, things on the dressing table and in the bureau drawers, told me this was Eric Collinson's bedroom.

Next to it was his wife's, according to the same sort of evidence. Lying on the floor of her clothes closet were a black satin dress, a once-white handkerchief, and a pair of black suede slippers, all wet with mud, the handkerchief also wet with blood. Her bed had not been slept in.

On her dressing table was a small piece of thick white paper that had been folded. White powder clung to one crease. I put the end of my tongue to it—morphine.

II

Quesada was awake when I got back there, a little after nine that morning. My pants were very nearly dry. I changed shoes and socks, got a quick breakfast and a dry supply of cigarettes, and asked the clerk—a dapper boy, this one—who was responsible for law and order in Quesada.

"The marshal's Dick Cotton," he told me, "but he went up to the city last night. Ben Rolly's deputy sheriff. You can likely find him over at his old man's office."

"Where is that?"

"Just two doors down."

I found it, a one-story red brick building with wide glass windows labeled *J. King Rolly, Real Estate, Employment Agency, Mortgages, Loans, Stocks and Bonds, Insurance, Notes, Notary Public, Moving and Storage*, and a lot more that I've forgotten.

Two men were inside, sitting with their feet on a battered desk behind a battered counter. One was a man of fifty plus, with hair, eyes and skin of an indefinite washed-out tan color—an amiable, aimless looking man in shabby clothes. The other was twenty years younger, and in twenty years would look just like the first.

"I'm hunting," I said, "for the deputy sheriff."

"Me," the younger man said, easing his feet from desk to floor. He didn't get up. Instead he put a foot out, hooked a chair by its rounds, pulled it out from the wall, and returned his feet to the desk-top. "Set down. This is Pa," wiggling a thumb at the older man. "You don't have to mind him."

"Know Eric Collinson?" I asked.

"The young fellow honeymooning down at the Tooker place—I didn't know his front name was Eric."

"Eric H. G. Collinson," the older man said. "That's the way I made out the rent receipt for him."

"He's dead," I told them. "He fell off the cliff path last night or this morning—fell or was pushed."

The father looked at the son with round tan eyes. The son looked at me with questioning tan eyes and said:

"Tch. Tch. Tch."

I gave him my card. He read it carefully, turned it over to see that there was nothing on the back, and passed it to his father.

"Go down and take a look at him?" I suggested.

"I guess I ought to," the deputy sheriff agreed, getting up from his chair. He was a larger man than I had supposed, as big as the dead Collinson boy, and, in spite of its slouchiness, his body was full-muscled and trim.

I followed him out to a dusty car in front of the office. Rolly senior didn't go with us.

"Somebody told you about it?" the deputy asked when we were riding.

"I stumbled over it. Know who the Collinsons are?"

"Uh-uh. Are they anybody special?"

"Hear about a Dr. Riese's murder in San Francisco three weeks ago?"

"I read the paper."

"Mrs. Collinson was the Gabrielle Leggett mixed up in that."

"Tch. Tch. Tch," he said.

"And whose father was killed by her step-mother a couple of weeks before that."

"Tch. Tch. Tch," he repeated. "What's the matter with them?"

"A family curse."

"Sure enough?" I didn't know how seriously he meant that. I hadn't got a line on him yet. But, clown or not, he was the deputy sheriff stationed at Quesada, and this was his party.

I gave him the spread-out while we bumped over the lumpy road.

"Mrs. Collinson's father was a French artist named Mayenne. In Paris in 1908 he married a British girl named Lily Dain. She had a sister Alice who wanted him. When Lily's and Mayenne's daughter—the present Mrs. Collinson—was five her Aunt Alice taught her to play a little game with a pistol, which ended in the child shooting and killing her mother. That's what Aunt Alice had wanted, but the outcome wasn't what she wanted: Mayenne was convicted of the murder and shipped to Devil's Island.

"In 1918 he escaped, roamed South America, Central America and Mexico, having to kill a couple of men, according to his story, to keep from being returned to prison, and finally landed in San Francisco, where he took the name Edgar Leggett and made himself a comfortable fortune with some inventions. Alice Dain and his daughter joined him there, and he and Alice married. He didn't know anything about her part in his first wife's—her sister's—death, and the child had forgotten it all long ago.

"In San Francisco things went along smoothly until a couple of blackmailers showed up, a pair of ex-convict-ex-private-detectives who knew about Leggett's past. Alice Dain—Mrs. Leggett then—bought one of them off with some diamonds that didn't belong to her, and the works began to come to light. That's where I first got into it, for the company that had insured the diamonds. Blackmailer number two bumped off number one. When the game got too hot for her,

Mrs. Leggett killed blackmailer number two, and then her husband, trying to shove all the blame on him. I spoiled that, and she tried to gun her way out of the house, shooting and killing herself in the ensuing tussle.

"Before she passed out of the picture, she did her best to fix things all wrong for the girl; telling her about her part in her mother's death; telling her she was cursed with the bad blood, black soul, and so on, that all the Dains had had; predicting that her life would be black and so would the lives of all who came in contact with her. This youngster Gabrielle is way off in the head. Her step-mother had made her that way— maybe there was something in the Dain inheritance to build on—and had kept her that way; and she fell for the curse stuff. She was engaged to Collinson then, but she wouldn't see him after that—afraid of ruining his life.

"Joseph Haldorn and his wife—running that Temple of the Holy Grail where Riese was murdered later—had the girl on their come-on list; and after her parents were wiped out Haldorn persuaded her to come to the Temple for a week or two. Riese, her physician, seemed to think that letting her go was about the only chance of keeping her from going completely nuts—she was damned close to it, and still is. He—Riese— persuaded Madison Andrews, who's her guardian, or who's handling her affairs anyhow, to O.K. it. She went there and ran into more trouble.

"Haldorn fell in love with her. He already had a wife, but his success in hocus-pocussing his converts had made him think he could get away with anything. Dr. Riese came to the Temple every day to see the girl, and presently he discovered that things were being done to her, that she was in danger there. He was foolish enough to let Haldorn know what he had discovered. Haldorn drugged him, put him on the altar, and worked on Gabrielle's mulatto maid—Minnie Hershey—with visions and voices until the dinge* went down and slaughtered Riese, under the impression that he was Satan.

---

* derogatory slang for a black man

"The Holy Grail racket blew up then. I killed Haldorn in the blow-up. His wife, the maid, and one of the Haldorns' assistants—Tom Fink— are in prison now, waiting trial for Riese's murder. Collinson took advantage of the excitement to grab the girl, smother her objections, and carry her off to Reno, where they were married. They had to come back to San Francisco for the inquest, and the girl was in no shape—mentally or physically—for much traveling, so they came down here to honeymoon."

I took Collinson's telegram and note out of my pocket, held them where the deputy could read them without taking his hands from the wheel, and told him what I had done and seen since my arrival in Quesada.

He nodded woodenly, saying:

"Tch. Tch. Tch. He might of been pushed off, all right, but what made you say you thought he had?"

I hadn't said so, but I let it go at that.

"He sent for me. Something was wrong. Outside of that, too many things have happened around the girl for me to believe in accidents."

"There's the curse, though," he reminded me.

"Yeah," I agreed, studying his vague face, still unable to decide whether he was serious. "But the trouble with it is it's worked out too well so far. It's the first one I've ever run across that did."

He frowned over that for a couple of minutes, and then stopped the car, saying, "We'll have to leave the car here. The road ain't so good the rest of the way." None of it had been. "Still and all, you do hear of them working out. There's things that happen that make a fellow think there's things in life—in the world—that he don't know much about." He frowned again as we set off afoot, and found a word he liked. "It's inscrutable," he said.

I let that go at that.

He led the way up the cliff path, stopping of his own accord where the bush had been uprooted. I hadn't said anything about that detail. I didn't say anything while he stared down at Collinson's body at the foot of the cliff, looked searchingly up and down the cliff face, and then went up and down the path, bent far down, his tan eyes examining the ground.

He wandered around that way for ten minutes or more, then straightened up and said:

"There don't seem to be nothing here. Let's go down."

I started to go back to the ravine, but he said there was a better way ahead. There was. We went down it to the dead man.

Rolly looked from the corpse up at the path-edge and complained:

"I don't hardly see how he could have landed just thataway."

"He didn't. I pulled him out of the water," I explained, showing the deputy exactly how the body had been placed.

"That's more like it." He went around almost on hands and knees, looking at, touching, moving, rocks, pebbles and sand. I sat on a boulder, smoked, and watched him. He didn't seem to have any luck.

When he had finished, we climbed to the path again and went on to the Collinsons' house. I showed him the stained towel, handkerchief, dress and slippers; the paper that had held morphine, on the girl's dressing table; the gun on Collinson's floor, the bullet-hole in the ceiling, and the two empty shells on the floor.

"The shell under the chair is where it was," I said, "but that one over in the corner was here, close to the gun when I left."

"What good would moving it over there do anybody?" he objected.

"None that I know of, but it's been moved."

That didn't interest him. He was looking at the ceiling. He said:

"Two shots and one hole. I wonder. Maybe out the window."

He went back to Gabrielle Collinson's bedroom and examined the mud-stained dress. There were some torn places down near the bottom, but no bullet holes. He put the dress back on the closet floor and picked up the morphine paper from her dressing table.

"What do you suppose this is doing here?"

"She uses it," I said. "It's one of the things her step-mother did for her."

"Tch. Tch. Tch. Kind of looks like she might of done it."

"Yeah?"

"You know it does. She's a dope fiend, ain't she? They had had trouble, and he sent for you, and—" He broke off, pursed his lips, then asked: "What time you reckon he was killed?"

"I don't know. Probably last night, on his way back from waiting for me."

"You was in the hotel all night?"

"From eleven-something till a little after five this morning. Of course I could have sneaked out long enough to pull a murder between those times."

"I didn't mean nothing like that," he said. "I was just wondering. What kind of looking woman is this Mrs. Collinson. I never saw her."

"She's about twenty; five feet tall; looks thinner than she really is; light brown hair, short and curly, big eyes that are sometimes green and sometimes brown; very white skin; hardly any forehead; small mouth and teeth; pointed chin; no lobes on her ears, and they're pointed at the top; only four toes on each foot; been sick for a couple of months and looks it."

"Oughtn't to be hard to pick her out," he said, and began poking into drawers, closets, trunks, and so on. I had poked into them during my first visit to the house, and hadn't found anything either.

"Don't look like she did any packing, or took much with her," he decided when he came back to where I was standing by the dressing table. He pointed a thick finger at the monogrammed silver toilet set on the table. "What's the G. D. L. for?"

"Her name was Gabrielle Something Leggett before she was married."

"Oh, yes," he said. "Went away in the car, I reckon. Huh?"

"Did he have one down here?"

"He used to come to town in a Chrysler roadster when he didn't walk. She could only of took it out by the East road. We'll go out thataway and see."

Outside, I waited while he made some circles around the house, finding nothing. In front of the shed where a car had been kept, Rolly examined the ground and gave his verdict: "Drove out this morning." I took his word for it.

We walked along a dirt road to a gravel one, and along the gravel road perhaps a mile to a gray house that stood among a group of red farm buildings. A small-boned, high-shouldered man with a slight limp was oiling a pump behind the house. Rolly called him Debro.

"Sure, Ben," he replied to Rolly's questions, "she went by here about seven this morning, going like a bat out of hell. There wasn't anybody else in the car."

"How was she dressed?" I asked.

"She didn't have on any hat and a tan coat."

I asked him what he knew about the Collinsons; he was their nearest neighbor. He didn't know anything about them. He had talked to Collinson two or three times, and thought him a nice enough young fellow. Once he had taken the missus over to call on Mrs. Collinson, but Collinson had told them she was lying down, not feeling well. None of the Debros had ever seen her except at a distance, walking or driving with her husband.

"I don't suppose there's anybody around here that's talked to her," he wound up, "except of course Mary Nunez."

"Mary working for them?" the deputy asked.

"Yes. What's the matter, Ben? Something the matter over there?"

"He fell off the cliff last night, and she's gone away without saying anything to anybody."

Debro whistled. Rolly went into the house to use Debro's phone, reporting to the sheriff at the county seat. I remained outside with Debro, trying to get more—if only his opinions—out of him. All I got were expressions of amazement.

"We'll go over and see Mary Nunez," the deputy said when he had finished reporting, and then, when we had left Debro, crossed the road, and were walking through a field toward a cluster of trees: "Funny she wasn't there."

"Who is she?"

"A Mex. Lives down in the hollow with the flock of them. Her man, Pedro, is doing a life-stretch in San Quentin for killing a bootlegger named Dunne in a hijacking two-three years back."

"Local?"

"Uh-huh. Down in that cove in front of the Collinsons' place."

We went through the trees and down a slope to where half a dozen shacks—shaped, sized and red-leaded to resemble box cars—lined the side of a stream, with vegetable gardens spread out behind them.

In front of one of the shacks a shapeless Mexican woman in a pink-checkered dress sat on an empty canned-soup box, smoking a corn-cob pipe and nursing a brown baby. Ragged and dirty children played between the buildings, with ragged and dirty mongrels helping them make noise. In one of the gardens a brown man in overalls that had once been blue was barely moving a hoe.

The children stopped playing to watch Rolly and me cross the stream on conveniently placed stones. The dogs came yapping down to meet us, snarling and snapping around us until chased by one of the boys. We stopped in front of the woman. The deputy grinned down at the baby at her breast and said:

"Well, ain't he getting to be the husky son-of-a-gun?"

The woman removed the pipe from her mouth long enough to complain stolidly:

"Colic all the time."

"Tch. Tch. Tch. Where's Mary Nunez?"

The pipe-stem was pointed at the next shack.

"I thought she was working for them people at the Tooker place," he said.

"Sometimes," she replied indifferently.

We went to the shack. An old woman in a gray wrapper had come to the door, watching us while stirring something in a yellow bowl.

"Where's Mary?" the deputy asked her.

She spoke over her shoulder into the shack's dark interior, and moved aside to let another woman take her place in the doorway. This other woman was short and solidly built, somewhere in her early thirties, with intelligent dark eyes in a wide flat face. She held a dark blanket together around her throat. The blanket hung to the floor all around her.

"Howdy, Mary," the deputy greeted her. "Why ain't you over to Collinson's today?"

"I'm sick, Mr. Rolly." She spoke without accent. "Chills—so I stayed home."

"Tch. Tch. Tch. That's too bad. Have you had the doc?"

She said she hadn't. Rolly said she ought to. She said she didn't need him; she often had chills. Rolly said that might be so, but it was best to play safe and have them kind of things looked into. She said yes, but doctors took so much money, and it was bad enough being sick without having to pay for it. He said in the long run it was likely to cost folks more not having a doctor than having him. I began to think they were going to keep it up all day, but presently he brought the talk around to the Collinsons, asking the woman about her work there.

She told us Collinson had hired her two weeks ago, when he took the house. She went there each morning at nine o'clock—they never got up before ten—cooked their meals, did the house-work, and left after washing the dinner dishes, usually somewhere around half-past seven.

She seemed surprised enough at the news that Collinson had been killed and his wife had gone away, but there was no way of telling whether she was as surprised as she looked. Collinson had gone out by himself, for a walk he said, after dinner last night. That was at about half-past six; dinner, for no especial reason, had been a little early.

She couldn't—or wouldn't—tell us anything that would help us guess why Collinson had sent for me. She knew very little about them, except that Mrs. Collinson didn't seem happy. She—Mary Nunez—had it all figured out: Mrs. Collinson loved someone else, but her parents had made her marry Collinson, and so, of course, Collinson had been killed by the other man, with whom his widow had then run off.

I got her away from this romance and asked her about the Collinsons' visitors. She said she had never seen any. Rolly asked her if the Collinsons ever quarreled. She said they did, often, and were never on very good terms: Mrs. Collinson didn't like to have him near her and several times had told him that if he didn't go away from her and stay away she would kill him. I tried to pin the woman down to details, asking what had led up to these threats, how they had been worded; but she wouldn't be pinned down. All she remembered positively, she said, was that Mrs. Collinson had threatened to kill her husband if he didn't go away from her.

"That pretty well settles that," Rolly said contentedly when we had forded the stream again and were climbing the slope toward Debro's.

"What settles what?"

"That his wife killed him."

"Think she did?"

"So do you."

I said: "No."

Rolly stopped walking and looked at me with vaguely worried eyes.

"How can you say that?" he remonstrated. "Ain't she a dope fiend, and crazy in the bargain, according to your own way of telling it? Didn't she run away? Wasn't them things she left behind torn and dirty and bloody? Didn't she threaten to kill him so much that he sent for you?"

"Mary didn't hear threats. They were warnings—about the curse. Gabrielle really believes in it, and she thought enough of him to try to save him from it. I've been through that before with her. That's why she wouldn't have married him if he hadn't have carried her off while she was more rattled than usual—and she was afraid on that account afterwards."

"But who's going to believe—?"

"I'm not asking anybody to believe anything," I growled, walking on again. "I'm just telling you what I believe. And one of the things I believe is that Mary's a liar when she says she didn't go there this morning. Maybe she didn't have anything to do with Collinson's death. Maybe she simply went there, found her employers gone, saw the bloody things and the gun, kicked that empty shell across the room in her excitement, without noticing it, or not bothering about it if she did notice it; then beat it and fixed up that chills story just to keep out of the whole affair, having had enough of that sort of thing when her husband was sent over. Maybe not. Anyway, I want some proof before I start believing that her chills just happened to hit her this special morning."

"Well," the deputy sheriff said, "if she didn't have nothing to do with his death, what difference does all that make anyway?"

All the answers I could think up to that were both profane and insulting. So I kept them to myself.

At Debro's again, we borrowed a loose-jointed touring car of at least three different makes, and ran on down the East road, trying to trace the girl in the Chrysler. Our first stop was at the farmhouse of a man named Claude Baker. He was a lanky, sallow man with an angular face three or fours days behind the razor. His wife was probably younger than he, but looked older—a tired and faded thin woman who might have been pretty at one time. The oldest of their six children was a bow-legged, freckled girl of ten. The youngest was a fat and noisy infant in its first year. Some of the in-betweens were boys, some girls, but they all had colds in their heads. The whole Baker family came out on the unpainted front porch to receive us. They hadn't seen anything, they said; they were never out of bed as early as seven o'clock. They knew the Collinsons by sight, but knew nothing about them. The Bakers asked lots of questions.

Shortly beyond the Baker house, the road changed from gravel to asphalt. Up to that point the Chrysler's tire-marks had told us that it was the last car to travel this road.

Two miles from Baker's we stopped in front of a small bright green house surrounded by rose bushes. Rolly bawled:

"Harve! Hey, Harve!"

A big-boned man of thirty-five or so came to

the door and said, "Hullo, Ben," and came down the walk to us. His features, like his voice, were heavy; he moved and spoke deliberately. His name was Whidden. Rolly asked him if he had seen the Chrysler.

"They went past, hitting it up, around a quarter after seven this morning," he said. "Yes, I saw them."

"They?" I asked, while Rolly asked: "Them?"

"There was a man and a woman—maybe a girl. I didn't get a good look at them—just saw them whizz past. She was driving—a kind of small girl or woman, with brown hair. The man was maybe forty, and didn't look like he was so damned tall. Pinkish face, he had, and gray coat and hat."

"Ever see Mrs. Collinson?" I asked.

"The bride living down the cove? No. I seen him, but not her. Was that her?"

I said we thought it was.

"The man wasn't him. He was somebody I never seen before."

"Know him if you saw him again?"

"I reckon I would if I saw him going past like that."

Four miles beyond Whidden's house we found the Chrysler.

It was a foot or two off the road, on the left-hand side, standing on all fours with its radiator jammed into a eucalyptus tree. All its glass was shattered, and the front third of its metal was pretty well crumpled. It was empty. There was no blood in it. The deputy and I seemed to be the only people in the vicinity.

We walked up and down and around in circles, straining our eyes at the ground, and when we got through we knew what we had known when we started—the Chrysler had run into a eucalyptus tree.

There were tire-marks on the road, and marks that could have been footprints on the ground by the car; but it was possible to find the same sort of marks almost anywhere along the road; and these didn't tell us anything. We got back in our borrowed car and drove on, asking questions wherever we found someone to ask; and all the answers were no.

"What about this fellow Baker?" I asked Rolly as we turned around to go back. "Debro saw her alone in the car. There was a man with her by the time she got to Whidden's. The Bakers saw nothing and it was in their territory that the man would have had to join her."

The deputy scratched his chin and said:

"Well, that could of happened, couldn't it?"

"Yeah, but it might be just as well to go back and talk to them some more."

"If you want to," he said without enthusiasm. "But don't be dragging me into any arguments. He's my wife's brother."

That made it different.

"What sort of man is he?" I asked.

"Mort's kind of shiftless all right. Like the old man says, he don't raise nothing much but kids on that place of his, but I never heard tell that he did anybody any harm."

"If you say he's all right," I lied, "that's enough for me. We won't bother him."

III

Sheriff Feeney—fat and florid, with a lot of brown mustache—and Prosecuting Attorney Vernon—sharp-featured, aggressive, and hungry for fame—came over from the county seat. They listened to our stories, looked the ground over, and agreed with Rolly that Gabrielle Collinson killed her husband. When Marshal Dick Cotton—a pompous, unintelligent man in his forties—returned from San Francisco, he added his vote to theirs. The coroner and his jury were of the same opinion, though officially they limited themselves to the well known "person or persons unknown" with recommendations involving the girl.

Little that was new came out at the inquest. The pistol found in Collinson's room was identified as his. No fingerprints had been found on it. There was a suspicion in a few official minds that I had perhaps seen to that, but nobody said anything definite about it.

The time of Collinson's death was placed between eight and nine o'clock Friday night; the cause, his fall. No marks not apparently caused by it had been found on or in him.

Mary Nunez stuck to her story of being kept home by chills. She produced a flock of Mexican witnesses to back it up. I couldn't find any to knock holes in it.

The marshal's wife—a frail young woman with a weak pretty face and nice shy manner, who worked in the telegraph office—said Collinson had come in early Friday morning to wire me. He was pale and shaky, with dark-rimmed, bloodshot eyes. She had supposed he was drunk, though she had smelled no alcohol.

Collinson's father and brother came down from San Francisco. Hubert Collinson was a big calm man who had taken three or four millions out of Pacific Coast timber and looked capable of taking as many more as he wanted. Laurence Collinson was a year or two older than his dead brother, and much like him in looks. Both Collinsons were careful to say nothing which would suggest that they thought Gabrielle had been responsible for Eric's death, but there was little doubt that they did think so.

The senior Collinson's instructions to me were simply:

"Go ahead. Get to the bottom of it."

Madison Andrews—Gabrielle's guardian—also had come down from San Francisco. He and I had a talk in my room in the hotel. He sat on a chair by the window, cut a cube of tobacco off a yellowish plug, put it in his mouth, ruffled his ragged white mustache, and decided that Collinson had committed suicide.

I sat on the side of the bed, set fire to a Fatima, and contradicted him:

"He wouldn't have torn up a bush as he went over if he was going willingly."

"Then it was an accident. He missed his footing in the dark."

"I've stopped believing in accidents where Gabrielle's concerned," I said. "And he had sent me an S.O.S."

His gaunt body leaned forward in his chair. His eyes were hard and watchful. He was a lawyer cross-examining a witness.

"You think she was responsible?"

I wasn't ready to go that far. I said:

"He was murdered. He was murdered by—I told you three weeks ago that we weren't through with that damned curse."

"Yes. I remember." He didn't quite sneer. "You advanced a theory that the curse was a person, but, as I recall it, your theory didn't include his or her name or motive. Don't you think that deficiency has a tendency to make your theory a little—uh—vaporous?"

"No. Her father, step-mother, physician, and husband are killed, one after the other, inside of two months. I haven't got enough faith in chance to think that just happened to happen, with no connection between the murders."

"Preposterous," he said, irritable now. "We know about her parents' deaths, and about Riese's, and we know there was no connection between them. We know that those responsible for Riese's death are now either dead or in prison, waiting trial. There's no use saying there has to be a connection between them when we know there isn't."

"We don't know anything of the sort," I insisted. "All we know is that we haven't found any connection. Who profits by keeping the girl in trouble?"

"Not a single person, so far as I know."

"Suppose she died? Who would get her money?"

"I don't know. I dare say there are distant relatives in France or England."

"That doesn't get us very far," I growled. "Anyway, nobody's tried to kill her so far. It's her friends who get the knock-off."

The lawyer reminded me that there was no way of knowing whether anybody had tried to kill her—or had succeeded—until we found her. I couldn't argue with him about that.

Her trail still ended where the eucalyptus tree had stopped the Chrysler. Andrews had offered a thousand dollars reward for information that would enable us to find her. Hubert Collinson had added another thousand, with an additional twenty-five hundred for the arrest and conviction of his son's murderer. Half the population of the county had turned blood-hound. Anywhere you went within ten miles of Quesada you could find men walking, or even crawling, around searching fields, paths, hills and valleys for clues; and in the woods you were likely to find more amateur sleuths than trees.

Her latest photographs had been copied and distributed widely. The San Francisco newspapers gave the whole thing a big play; this was the third affair of the sort that she had figured in very recently, and the "curse" was eggs-in-the-coffee[*] for feature writers. I had all the San Francisco Continental operatives who could be pulled off other jobs—six—searching the exits from Quesada, hunting, questioning, and finding nothing. Radio broadcasting stations helped. The Continental's branches in other cities, the police everywhere, had been called on for assistance.

And all this effort had brought us nothing.

I had to return to San Francisco Monday morning for Tommy the Rags' trial. That kept me until noon, by which time I had finished my share in sending him back to Folsom. From the court I went down to the agency. There was a memorandum on my desk:

Phone Owen Fitzstephan, Prospect 2888.

Fitzstephan was a lanky, sorrel-haired novelist who had given me a lot of help on a fake medium job in New York some years before. I had run into him again in San Francisco when I was working on the job in which Gabrielle's father and step-mother had been killed. He had known them, and had given me more help

_____
[*] an item that made the job easy

in swinging that job. So now I didn't waste any time getting him on the wire.

"I've a puzzle for you, or perhaps the solution to a puzzle," he said; "and if you can come up now I'll supplement it with luncheon. Is that enough to bring you?"

I said it was, rode up Nob Hill on a cable car, and within fifteen minutes was going into his apartment.

"All right, spring the puzzle," I said as we sat down in his paper- magazine- and book-littered living-room.

"Any trace of Gabrielle yet?" he asked.

"No. Spring the puzzle," I repeated. "Please don't be literary with me. Don't start with an introduction, and lead up to your climax step by step, creating a lot of suspense and the like. I'm too crude to be impressed that way—it'll only give me a bellyache."

"Oh, very well, then," he said, trying to make his sleepy gray eyes and wide humorous mouth register disappointment combined with disgust. "You'll always be what you are. Have it your own way. At twenty minutes past one Saturday morning—mark my accuracy—my phone rang. A man's voice asked: 'Is this Fitzstephan?' I said, 'Yes,' and then the voice said, 'Well, I've killed him.'

"I'm sure of those words, though they weren't very clear. There was a lot of noise on the line and his voice seemed very distant. I asked, 'Killed who? Who is this?' but I couldn't understand any of his answer except something about money. He repeated 'money' several times. There were some people here—the Marquards, Laura Joines, Curt, and some girl he had brought—and we had been in the middle of a wild argument over the value of immediacy in art. I was anxious to get back to it, and I couldn't make out what the voice on the phone was talking about; so I decided it was a drunken joker, or something of the sort, and hung up.

"Yesterday morning, when I read about Collinson's death in the *Chronicle*, I began to wonder if the phone conversation had anything to do with it. I was at Pebble Beach, having gone down Saturday afternoon for a week-end with the Colemans. I came back last night, intending to tell you about it. This was in my mail this morning."

He picked up an envelope from the table and tossed it over to me. It was a cheap and shiny white envelope of the kind you can buy anywhere. Its corners were dark and curled, as if it had been carried in a pocket for a week or so before being used. Fitzstephan's name and address had been printed on it, with a hard pencil, by someone who was a rotten printer, or who wanted to give that impression. It was postmarked San Francisco, nine o'clock Saturday morning.

Inside was a soiled and crookedly torn piece of brown wrapping paper with one sentence—as poorly printed with pencil as the envelope—on it.

Anybody that wants Mrs. Cullison can have same by paying $10,000.

There was no salutation, no signature.

"She was seen driving away from the house as late as seven-something that morning," I said. "This was mailed here, eighty miles away, in time to be taken from the box in the first morning collection. Funny it should have been sent to you instead of Andrews, who is in charge of her affairs, or old man Collinson, whose daughter-in-law she was, and who's got the most money."

"It is funny and it isn't." The sleepiness had gone out of the novelist's eyes. His lean face was eager. "There may be a point of light there. I've probably told you that I spent two months in Quesada last spring, finishing *The Wall of Ashdod*. I lived in a little two-room house a mile or two from the town, up in this direction though, on the shore. I knew about the Tooker place being vacant, and when Collinson, after their return from Reno, told me he wanted a quiet place to take Gabrielle, I suggested that he go there—if it was still unoccupied—and gave him

a letter to a real estate dealer named Rolly who had the renting of it.

"Now look at this letter. My name is correctly spelled on the envelope, but Collinson is spelled C-u-l-l-i-s-o-n, the way it is pronounced. The letter was sent to me, but starts off, *Any body that*, as if I were to pass the information on to whoever was interested. Does all that mean anything?"

I nodded, saying:

"It might mean that the sender was a native of Quesada who knew you better than he knew the Collinsons, who knew you had sent them down there, who knew your address but didn't know how to reach any of the girl's connections direct."

"Or it might mean," the novelist warned me, "that the sender wanted us to think those things."

"Not likely," I decided. "Except for the wooziness of the printing, which booze, excitement, or both, could have been responsible for, the whole thing looks genuine. It's simple. When your crook gets subtle he usually overdoes it. I'm willing to string along with our first guess. We'll check up your acquaintances down there. J. King Rolly would be the first suspect, but he doesn't look like a murderer and abductor to me, and he knew how Collinson was spelled. However, he's the one man we're sure knew you had sent Collinson down there, so he'll have to be pried into. Who next?"

Fitzstephan made a hopeless gesture with his thin hands. "I knew everybody."

"Which of them knew your address here?"

"None that I know of, but my name's in the phone book."

"Who did you know there," I tried again, "that might be capable of this sort of trick?"

That brought me a long discourse in which it was proven that every man who ever lived was a potential criminal, needing only the right set of circumstances to make him an actual one; that character was a thing which didn't exist, since all men had every trait that any man had, the difference in people being only a matter of which attitude they happened to strike; and that therefore any man in Quesada, or out of it, was, given the necessary circumstances, capable of this sort of trick.

I listened while working on my share of the cocktails, chicken-liver omelette, salad, rolls and coffee that Fitzstephan's Chinese boy had put between us.

"That's nice," I grumbled when the novelist had finished his speech, "and for all I know there may even be some sense in it, but it doesn't help find the girl, and it doesn't help put anybody in jail, so what good is it to me?"

He accused me of having the brains of a detective, and said:

"I haven't said anything to anybody about the phone call and letter—except that I mentioned the call to the people who were here when it came, but that was before I took it seriously. I saved it for you. Should I go to the police now? Or will you take care of that? Would it do any good if I went to Quesada?"

"It might. I'd like to have you down there to go over the ground with me. You know the place, and you're not a bad hand at snooping except when you're being literary. Can you go down for a day?"

"Surely. I was angling for an invitation. We'll drive down the first thing in the morning?"

I thought I had to get back on the job that night. Fitzstephan had a date he couldn't break. He promised to meet me in the Sunset Hotel in the morning.

IV

I went back to the office and put in a Quesada call. I couldn't get hold of Vernon Rolly, or the sheriff. I talked to Cotton, giving him the information I had got from Fitzstephan, promising to produce the novelist for questioning the next morning. The marshal said the search for the girl was still going on, and still without results.

Reports had come in that the girl had been seen—practically simultaneously—in Los Angeles, Eureka, Carson City, Portland, Tijuana, Sacramento, Ogden, San José, Denver, and Vancouver. All except the absolutely ridiculous ones were being run out.

The telephone company could tell me that Owen Fitzstephan's phone call had not been a long distance call, and that nobody in Quesada had called San Francisco either Friday night or early Saturday morning.

I went over to Madison Andrews' office, telling him about the Fitzstephan angle, giving him our explanation of how the novelist had been brought into the affair. He nodded his bony, white-thatched head and said:

"And whether that's the true explanation or not, the county authorities will now have to give up their absurd theory that Gabrielle killed Eric."

I shook my head sideways.

"What?" he asked explosively.

"They're going to think that this was cooked up to clear her," I predicted.

"Is that what you think?" His jaws got lumpy in front of his ears, and his white eyebrows came down over his narrowed eyes.

"I hope you didn't, because if it's a trick it's a damned childish one."

"How could it be?" he blustered. "Don't talk nonsense. None of us knew anything then. The body hadn't been found when—"

"Yeah," I agreed, "and that's why, if it turns out to have been a trick, it'll hang Gabrielle."

"I don't understand you," he said disagreeably. "One minute you're talking about somebody persecuting the girl, and the next minute you're acting as if you thought she was the murderer. Just what do you think?"

"Both can be true," I replied no less disagreeably. "And what difference does it make what I think? It'll be up to the jury when she's found. The question now is, what are you going to do about that ten-thousand-dollar demand, if it's on the level?"

"There's nothing I can do. The letter doesn't say anything."

"Except that you're to get ten thousand dollars ready. Will you?"

"What I'm going to do," he said stubbornly, "is increase the reward for finding her, with an additional reward for the arrest of her abductor."

"That's the wrong play," I assured him. "Enough reward money has been posted. The only way to handle a kidnapping is to come across. I don't like that any more than you do, but it's the only way. Uncertainty, disappointment, fear, nervousness, can turn even a mild kidnapper into a maniac. Buy the girl free, and then do your fighting; but pay what's asked when it's asked."

He tugged at his ragged mustache, his jaw set obstinately, his eyes worried. But the jaw won out.

"I'm damned if I'll submit," he said.

"That's your business." I got up and reached for my hat. "Mine's finding Collinson's murderer, and having Gabrielle killed is more likely to help me than not."

He didn't say anything.

I went down to Hubert Collinson's offices. He wasn't in. I told Laurence Collinson my story and asked him to urge his father to put up the ten thousand dollars.

"That's hardly necessary," he said immediately. "Of course we shall pay whatever is required to secure her safe return."

I caught the 5:25 train south. It put me in Poston, a dusty town twice Quesada's size, at 7:30, and a rattletrap stage, in which I was the only passenger, got me to my destination half an hour later, as a light rain began trickling down.

Jack Santos, a reporter on the San Francisco *Bulletin*, came out of the telegraph office while I was leaving the stage.

"Hello," he said. "Anything new?"

"Maybe, but I'll have to give it to Vernon first. He still here?"

"Up in his room, or he was ten minutes ago. You don't mean the kidnap letter that somebody got?"

"Yeah. He's already given it out?"

"Cotton started to, but Vernon headed him off, told us to let it alone."

"Why?"

"No reason at all except that Cotton was giving it to us." Santos pulled the corners of his thin mouth down. "It's gotten down to a contest between Vernon, Feeney and Cotton, to see who can get his picture and name printed most."

"They been doing anything besides that?"

"How can they?" he asked disgustedly. "They spend ten hours a day trying to make the front page, ten more trying to keep the others from making it, and they've got to sleep some time."

In the hotel I gave "nothing new" to a couple of more reporters, registered, left my bag in my room, and went down the hall to 204.

Vernon opened the door when I knocked. He was alone, and apparently had been reading the newspapers that made a pink, green and white pile on the bed. The room was blue-gray with cigar smoke.

This prosecuting attorney was a thirty-year-old dark-eyed man who carried his chin up and out so that it was more prominent than nature had intended, bared all his teeth when he spoke, and was very conscious of being a go-getter.

He shook my hand briskly and said:

"I'm glad you're back. Come in. Sit down. Are there any new developments?"

"Cotton pass you the dope I gave him?"

"Yes." He posed in front of me, hands in pockets, feet far apart. "What importance do you attach to it?"

"I advised Andrews to get the money ready. He wouldn't. The Collinsons will."

"They will," he said, as if confirming a guess I had made. "And?" He held his lips back so that his teeth remained exposed.

"Here's the letter." I took it out of my pocket and handed it to him. "Fitzstephan will be down in the morning."

He nodded emphatically, carried the letter closer to the light, and examined it and its envelope minutely. When he had finished he tossed it contemptuously to the table.

"Obviously a fraud," he said. "Now what, precisely, is this Fitzstephans's—is that the name?—story?"

I told him, word for word. When I had finished, he clicked his teeth together, turned to the telephone, and told someone to tell Feeney that he—Mr. Vernon, the prosecuting attorney—wished to see him immediately.

Ten minutes later the sheriff came in wiping rain off his big brown mustache.

Vernon jerked a thumb at me, and ordered: "Tell him."

I repeated what Fitzstephan had told me. The sheriff listened with an attentiveness that turned his florid face almost purple and had him panting. When I had finished, the prosecuting attorney snapped his fingers and said:

"Very well. He claims there were people in his apartment when the phone call came. Make a note of their names. He claims to have been at Pebble Beach over the week-end, with the—who were they? Colemans? Very well. Sheriff, see that those things are checked up at once. We'll see how much of his story is true."

I didn't argue with them, but gave the sheriff the names Fitzstephan had given me. Feeney wrote them down on the back of a laundry list and puffed out to get the county's crime detecting machinery going on them.

Vernon hadn't anything to tell me. I left him to his newspapers and went downstairs. The effeminate night clerk beckoned me over to the desk and said:

"Mr. Santos asked me to tell you that services are being held in his room tonight."

I thanked the clerk and went up to Santos' room. He, three other newshounds and a photographer were there. The game was stud. I was sixteen dollars ahead at half-past twelve, when I was called to the phone to listen to the prosecuting attorney's aggressive voice:

"Can you come to my room immediately?"

"Yeah." I gathered up my hat and coat, telling Santos, "Cash me in. Important call. I always manage to have them when I get a little ahead of the game."

"Vernon?" he asked as he counted my chips.

"Yeah."

"It can't be much," he sneered, "or he'd have sent for Red, too," nodding at the photographer, "so tomorrow's readers could see him holding it in his hand."

V

Cotton, Feeney and Rolly were with the prosecuting attorney. Cotton—a medium-sized man with a round dull face dimpled in the chin—was dressed in wet and muddy black rubber hat, slicker and boots. He stood in the middle of the floor, and his round eyes looked very proud of their owner.

Feeney, straddling a chair, was playing with his mustache. His florid face was sulky. Rolly stood beside him rolling a cigarette, looking vaguely amiable as usual.

Vernon closed the door behind me and said irritably:

"Cotton thinks he's discovered something. He thinks—"

Cotton came forward, chest first, interrupting:

"I don't think nothing. I know durned well—"

Vernon snapped his fingers sharply between the marshal and me, saying just as snappishly:

"Never mind that. We'll go out there and see."

I stopped at my room for raincoat, gun and flashlight. We went downstairs and climbed into a muddy car. Cotton drove. Vernon sat beside him. The rest of us sat in back. Rain beat on the top and curtains, and leaked through cracks.

"A hell of a night to be chasing pipe dreams," the sheriff grumbled, trying to dodge a leak.

"Dick'd do a lot better to mind his own business," Rolly agreed. "What's he got to do with anything outside of Quesada?"

"If he'd mind his business there better he wouldn't have to worry so much about what happens down the shore," Feeney said, and he and his deputy sniggered together.

Whatever point there was to this conversation was over my head. I asked:

"What does he think he is up to?"

"Nothing," the sheriff told me. "You'll see that it's nothing, and, by God, I'm going to give him a piece of my mind. I don't know what's the matter with Vernon, paying any attention to him at all."

That didn't mean anything to me. I peeped out between the curtains. Rain and darkness kept me from seeing any scenery, but I had an idea that we were headed for some point on the East road. It was a rotten ride—wet, noisy, and bumpy.

It ended in as dark, wet, and muddy a spot as any we had gone through. Cotton switched off the lights and got out, the rest of us following, slipping and slopping in wet clay up to our ankles.

"This is too damned much," the sheriff complained.

Vernon started to say something, but the marshal was walking away, down the road. We plodded after him, keeping together more by the sound of our feet squashing in the mud than by sight. It was black.

Presently we left the road, struggled over a high wire fence, and went on with less mud under our feet, but slippery grass. We climbed a hill. Wind blew rain down it into our faces. The sheriff was panting. I was sweating. We reached the top of the hill, and went down the other side, with the rustle of sea-water on rocks ahead of us. Rocks began crowding grass out of our path as the descent got steeper.

Once Cotton slipped to his knees, tripping Vernon, who saved himself from a fall by grabbing me. The sheriff's panting was almost a sobbing. We turned to the left, going along in single file, with the surf close beside us. We turned to the left again, climbed a slope, and halted under a low shed without walls—a wooden roof propped on a dozen posts. Ahead of us a larger building made a black blot against an almost black sky.

Cotton whispered: "Wait till I see if his car's here."

He went away leaving us to wait.

The sheriff blew out his breath and grunted: "Damn such an expedition."

Rolly sighed.

The marshal returned, jubilant.

"It ain't there, so he ain't here. Come on, it'll get us out of the rain, anyways."

We followed him up a muddy path to the black house, up on what seemed to be its back porch. We stood there while he got a window open, clambered through it, and unlocked the door.

Our flashlights, which we used for the first time now, showed us a small, neat kitchen. We went in, muddying its floor.

Cotton was the only member of the party who showed any enthusiasm. His face, from dimpled chin to forehead, was the face of a master-of-ceremonies who is about to spring what he is sure is going to be a delightful surprise. Vernon regarded him skeptically, Feeney disgustedly, Rolly indifferently. I didn't know what we were there for, so I suppose I regarded him curiously.

It turned out that we were there to search the house.

We did it, or at least Cotton did it while the rest of us pretended to help him. It was a small house. There was only one room besides the kitchen on the ground floor, and only one—a half-story bedroom—above. A grocer's bill and a tax receipt in a table drawer told me whose house we were in—Harvey Whidden's. He was the big-boned deliberate man who had told Rolly and me of seeing a man in the car with Gabrielle.

We finished the ground floor with a blank score and went up to the bedroom.

There after ten minutes of poking around we found something. Rolly pulled it out from between bed-slats and mattress. It was a small flat bundle wrapped in a white towel.

Cotton dropped the mattress which he had been holding up for the deputy to peep under and helped the rest of us crowd around Rolly's package. Vernon took it from the deputy and unrolled it on the bed.

Inside the towel there were a package of hair pins, a lace-edged white handkerchief, a silver hair brush and comb engraved G. D. L. and a pair of black kid gloves small and feminine.

I was more surprised than anybody else seemed to be.

"G. D. L.," I said to be saying something, "could be Gabrielle Something Leggett—Mrs. Collinson's name before she was married."

Cotton said triumphantly: "You bet it could."

A harsh voice said from the door:

"Have you got a search warrant? You know what it is if you ain't. Burglary, and you know it. Where's your warrant?"

It was Harvey Whidden. His big body in a yellow slicker filled the doorway. His heavy face was dark with anger.

Vernon began:

"Whidden, I—"

The marshal screamed: "It's him!" and pulled a gun from under his coat.

I pushed his arm as he fired at the man in the doorway.

The bullet went into a wall.

Whidden yelled something that the noise of the shot drowned. There was more astonishment than anger in his face now. He jumped out of the doorway and ran downstairs.

Cotton, partly upset by my push, straightened himself up, cursed me, and ran out after Whidden.

Vernon, Feeney and Rolly stood staring after him.

I said:

"This is a lot of fun, but it makes no sense to me. What's it all about?"

Nobody told me. I said:

"This comb and brush were on Mrs. Collinson's dressing table when we searched her house, Rolly."

The deputy nodded uncertainly, still staring at the door. No sound came through it now.

I looked at Feeney and asked:

"Would there be any reason for Cotton planting them on Whidden?"

The sheriff said:

"They ain't good friends." (I had noticed that.) "What do you think, Vern?"

The prosecuting attorney took his gaze from the door, rolled the things in their towel again, and stuffed it in his pocket.

"Come on," he snapped, and strode downstairs.

The front door was open. We saw, heard nothing of Cotton or Whidden. A Ford—Whidden's—stood at the front gate soaking up rain. We got in it. Vernon took the wheel, and drove to the house the Collinsons had occupied. We hammered on the door until it was opened by an old man in gray underwear, put there as caretaker by the sheriff.

The old man told us that Cotton had been there at eight o'clock that night, just, he said, to look the place over again. He, the caretaker, didn't know no reason why the marshal had to be watched, so he hadn't bothered him, letting him do what he wanted; and, so far as he knew, the marshal hadn't disturbed anything, though he might of.

Vernon and Feeney gave the old man hell, and we went back to Quesada. Rolly and I were together on the rear seat.

"Who is this Whidden?" I asked. "Why should Cotton pick on him?"

"Well, for one thing, because Harve's got kind of a bad name, from being in trouble a couple of times back when a little booze used to be run through here."

"Yeah? And for another thing?"

Rolly hesitated, frowning, hunting for words, and before he could find them we had stopped in front of a vine-hung cottage on a dark street corner. The prosecuting attorney led the way to its front porch, and rang the bell.

After a little while a woman's voice called from overhead:

"Who's there? What do you want?"

We had to retreat to the porch steps to see her—Mrs. Cotton at a second-story window.

"Dick got home yet?" Vernon asked.

"No, Mr. Vernon, he hasn't," she said. "I was getting worried. Wait a minute, I'll come down."

"Don't bother. We won't wait for him. I'll see him in the morning."

"No. Wait," she said urgently, and vanished from the window.

A moment later she opened the door. Her blue eyes were dark and excited. She had on a rose dressing gown, in which her frail body looked like a child's.

"You needn't have bothered," Vernon said. "There was nothing special. We got separated from Dick an hour or so ago, and just wanted to know if he had got back. He's all right."

"Was—" Her hands worked folds of her dressing gown over her thin breasts. "Was he after—after Harvey—Harvey Whidden?"

Vernon didn't look at her when he said, "Yes"; and he said it without showing all his teeth. Feeney and Rolly looked even more uncomfortable than Vernon.

Mrs. Cotton's face got very pink. Her lower lip trembled blurring her words:

"Don't believe him Mr. Vernon. D-don't believe a word he tells you. Harve didn't have anything to do with the Collinsons, with either one of them. Don't let Dick tell you he did. He didn't."

Vernon looked at his feet and didn't say anything. Rolly and Feeney were looking intently out through the open door—we were standing just inside it—at the rain. The sheriff's face was red and miserable. Nobody seemed to have any intention of speaking.

I said, "No?" putting more doubt in my voice than I really felt.

"No, he didn't," she cried, jerking her face around to me. "He couldn't—He couldn't have done it." The pink went out of her face, leaving it pale and desperate. "He—he was here that night—all night—from before seven until daylight."

"And your husband?"

"Was up in the city, at his mother's."

"Where does his mother live?"

She gave me the address, in Noe Street.

"Did anybody—"

"Aw, come on," the sheriff protested, still staring at the rain. "Ain't that enough?"

Mrs. Cotton turned from me to the prosecuting attorney again, grabbing one of his arms.

"Don't tell it on me, please, Mr. Vernon," she begged. "I don't know what I'd do if it came out. But I had to tell you. I couldn't let him put it on Harve. Please, you won't tell anybody else?"

The prosecuting attorney swore that under no circumstances would he, or any of us, say a word about it to anybody; and the sheriff and his deputy agreed with vigorous red-faced nods.

But when we were in the Ford, away from her, they forgot their embarrassment and became manhunters again. Within ten minutes they had decided that Cotton, instead of going to San Francisco to his mother's, had remained in Quesada or vicinity till after dark; had killed Collinson; had gone to the city to phone Fitzstephan and mail the letter; and then had returned to Quesada in time to kidnap the girl; planning to use his official position to frame Whidden, with whom he had long been on bad terms, suspecting what everybody else knew—that Whidden and Mrs. Cotton were intimate.

The sheriff—he whose chivalry had prevented my thoroughly questioning the woman a few minutes ago—laughed his belly up and down.

"That's rich," he gurgled. "Him out framing Harve, and Harve getting himself a alibi in his bed. Dick's face is going to be a picture for Puck* when we spring it on him. Let's find him tonight."

"Better wait," I advised. "It won't hurt to check up his San Francisco trip. I can have that done early in the morning. All we've got on him

---

* *Puck* was a humor and political-satire magazine, 1876–1918

so far is that he's tried to frame Whidden. If he killed Collinson and kidnapped Mrs. Collinson, he seems to have done a lot of unnecessary and goofy things."

Feeney scowled at me and defended their theory:

"Maybe he was more interested in framing Harve than anything else."

"Maybe," I agreed, "but why not give him a little more rope and see what he does with it?"

Feeney was against that. He wanted to grab the marshal pronto. But Vernon reluctantly backed me up. We dropped Rolly at his house and the rest of us returned to the hotel.

In my room, I put in a phone call for the agency in San Francisco. While I was waiting for the connection, knuckles tapped my door. I opened it and let in Jack Santos, pajamaed, bathrobed and slippered.

"Have a nice ride?" he asked, yawning.

"Swell."

"Anything break?"

"Not for publication yet," I said, "but—under the hat—the new angle is that our marshal is trying to hang the job on his wife's boy friend, with homemade evidence. The other big officials think Cotton turned the trick himself."

"That ought to get all of them on the front page." Santos sat on the foot of my bed and lit a cigarette. "Ever happen to hear that Feeney was Cotton's rival for the telegraphing hand of the present Mrs. Cotton, until she picked the marshal—the triumph of dimples over mustachios?"

"No. What of it?"

"How do I know. I just happened to pick it up. A fellow in the garage told me."

"How long ago?"

"That they were rivals? Less than a couple of years."

The phone rang, my call. I told Field, the agency night man, to have somebody check up the marshal's Noe Street visit the first thing in the morning. Santos yawned and went out while I was talking. I yawned and went to bed when I had finished.

VI

At a little before ten o'clock the telephone roused me—Mickey Linehan talking from San Francisco. Cotton had arrived at his mother's house between seven and seven-thirty Saturday morning, had slept for five or six hours—telling his mother he had been up all night laying for a burglar—and had left for home at six that evening.

Cotton was in the lobby when I went down there. He was red-eyed and tired, but still determined.

"Catch Whidden?" I asked.

"No, durn him, but I will. Say, I'm glad you jiggled my arm, even if it did let him get away. I—well, sometimes a fellow's enthusiasm gets the best of his judgment."

"Yeah. We stopped at your house on our way back early this morning, to see how you'd made out."

"I ain't been home yet," he said. "I put in the whole durned night hunting that fellow."

"Better get some sleep," I suggested. "Vernon and Feeney are probably still pounding their ears. I'll ring you if anything turns up."

He set off for home. I went into the café for breakfast. While I was eating, Vernon came in and joined me. He had telegrams from Pebble Beach and San Francisco, confirming Fitzstephan's story of having had company in his apartment Friday night, of having spent the week-end with Mr. and Mrs. Ralph Coleman at Pebble Beach.

"I got my report on Cotton," I said. "He arrived at his mother's between seven and half-past Saturday morning, and left at six that evening."

"Seven and half-past." Vernon didn't like that. If the marshal had been in San Francisco at that time, he couldn't have been abducting the girl. "Are you sure?"

"No, but that's the report I got. Excuse me a moment."

Looking through the café door, I had seen Owen Fitzstephan's lanky back at the hotel desk. I went over, hailed Fitzstephan, brought him back to the table with me, and introduced him to Vernon. The prosecuting attorney stood up to shake his hand, but was too busy with thoughts of Cotton to be very interested in anything the novelist could have told him.

Fitzstephan ordered a cup of coffee, saying he had had breakfast before leaving the city. I was called to the phone.

Cotton's voice, but excited almost beyond recognition:

"For God's sake get Vernon and Feeney and come up here. Something terrible's happened."

"What?" I asked.

"Hurry, hurry!" he cried, and hung up.

I went back to the table and told Vernon about it. He jumped up, upsetting Fitzstephan's coffee. Fitzstephan got up too, but hesitated, looking at me.

"Come on," I invited him, "maybe this'll be something you'll like."

Fitzstephan's car was in front of the hotel. The marshal's house was only seven blocks away. Its front door was open. Vernon knocked on the open door as we went in, but we did not wait for an answer.

Cotton met us in the hall. His eyes were wide and blood-shot in a face as hard-white as marble.

He tried to say something, couldn't get the words past his tight-set teeth, and gestured toward the door behind him with a fist that was clenched on a piece of brown paper.

Through the doorway we saw Mrs. Cotton. She was lying on the blue-carpeted floor. She had on a pale blue house dress. Her throat was covered with dark bruises. Her lips and tongue—the tongue, swollen, hung out—were darker, more purplish, than the bruises. Her eyes were wide open, bulging, upturned, and dead. Her hand, when I touched it, was still warm.

Cotton, following us into the room, held out the brown paper in his hand when we turned to him. It was an irregularly torn piece of wrapping paper, covered on both sides with writing—nervously, unevenly, hastily scribbled in pencil.

I was closer to Cotton than Vernon. I took the paper and read it aloud:

Harvey Whidden came here last night—said my husband was trying frame him for Collinson murder—they were after him. I hid him in garret. He said only way to save him was for me to say he was here that night. He was not here that night—but was some other nights when my husband was away. I did not want to say that—he said if I did not my husband would have him hung—I could tell Mr. Vernon and ask him to tell nobody else. I said no—but when Mr. Vernon and men came Harve said he would kill me and self if I did not. So I did. I did not know Harve was guilty then. He told me afterwards. He tried kidnap Mrs. C. Thursday night, but C. nearly caught him. He was afraid C. recognized him. He came in telegraph office Friday right after C. gave me telegram and he read it. I did not know that then. He followed C. that night—pushed him off cliff. Then he drove to San Francisco. He had whiskey and drank it. Then decided to kidnap Mrs. C. anyway. He knew of some man who knew her, and called him up to try to find out who he could get money from—but he was too drunk to talk good. So he wrote him letter and came back here. Met Mrs. C. on road, took her in his car, rubbed out marks where he turned around, and took her some hiding place he has. Below Dull Point. He goes there in boat. That is all I know. When he told me this I told him I would not have anything more to do with him. I am locked in garret now while he is downstairs getting food. I am afraid he will kill me. He is a murderer and I will not help him even if he does.

Daisy Cotton.

The sheriff and Rolly had arrived while I was reading it. Feeney's face was as white and as set as Cotton's.

Vernon bared his teeth at the marshal, snapping:

"You wrote that."

Feeney grabbed it from my hands, looked at it, shook his head and said hoarsely:

"No, that's her writing, all right."

Cotton was babbling:

"No, before God, I didn't, Vern. I planted that stuff on him, I admit that, but that was all. I came home and found her like that, and found this. I swear to God!"

"Where were you Friday night?" the prosecuting attorney demanded.

"Here, watching the house. I thought—I thought they might—But he wasn't here that night, like she said. I watched till daybreak and then went to the city. I didn't—"

The sheriff interrupted, waving the letter, bellowing:

"Below Dull Point! What are we waiting for?"

He plunged out of the house, the rest of us after him. Cotton and Rolly rode down to the waterfront in the deputy's car. Vernon, the sheriff and I rode with Fitzstephan. The sheriff cried throughout the short trip, tears splashing on the automatic he held in his lap.

At the waterfront we changed from the cars to a green and white motor boat run by a pink-cheeked, tow-headed young man called Tim. Tim said he didn't know anything about any hiding places below Dull Point, but if there was one there he could find it.

In his hands the boat produced a lot of speed, but not enough for Feeney and Cotton. They stood together in the bow, guns in their fists, dividing their time between straining forward and yelling back at Tim for more speed.

Half an hour from the dock we rounded a blunt promontory that the others called Dull Point; and Tim cut down our speed, putting the boat's nose in closer to the rocks that jumped up high and sharp at the water's edge.

We were all eyes—eyes that soon ached from staring under the noon sun, but kept on staring. Twice we saw clefts in the rock-walled coast, pushed hopefully in to them, saw that they were blind, leading nowhere, opening into no hiding places.

The third was even more hopeless looking at first sight, but, now that Dull Point was some distance behind us, we couldn't pass up anything. We slid in toward the cleft, got close enough to decide that it was, as we had suspected, another blind one, gave it up, and told Tim to go on.

We were washed another couple of feet nearer before the tow-headed boy could bring the boat around.

Cotton, in the bow, bent forward from the waist and yelled:

"Here it is."

He pointed his gun at one side of the cleft.

Tim let the boat drift in another foot or so. Craning our necks, we could see that what we had taken for the shore line on that side was really a high, thin, saw-toothed ledge of rock separated from the cliff on this end by twenty feet of water.

"Put her in," Feeney ordered.

Tim frowned at the water, hesitated, said:

"She can't make it."

The boat backed him up by shuddering suddenly under our feet with an unpleasant rasping noise.

"That be damned!" the sheriff bawled. "Put her in."

The gun in his hand was leveled at Tim's belly, and the sheriff's eyes weren't sane.

Tim put her in.

The boat shuddered under our feet again, more violently, and now there was a tearing noise in the rasping; but we went through the opening and turned down behind the saw-tooth ledge.

We were in a V-shaped pocket, twenty feet wide where we had come in, eighty feet long, high-walled, inaccessible by land, accessible by sea only as we had come. The water that floated us—and was now leaking in to sink us—ran a third of the way down the pocket. White sand paved the other two-thirds.

A small green motor boat was resting its nose on the edge of the sand. It was empty.

"Harve's," Tim said.

Nobody was in sight. There didn't seem to be

any place for anybody to hide. There were footprints, large and small, in the sand, empty tin cans, and the remains of a fire.

Our boat grounded. We jumped, splashed ashore—Cotton ahead, the rest of us spread out behind him.

Suddenly, as if he had sprung out of the air, Whidden appeared in the far end of the V, standing on the sand, a rifle in his hands.

Anger and utter astonishment were in his heavy face, and in his voice when he yelled:

"You damned, double-crossing—"

The noise his gun made blotted out the rest of his words.

Cotton threw himself down sideways.

The rifle bullet missed him by inches, clipped the brim of Fitzstephan's hat and splattered on the rocks behind us.

Four of our guns went off together, some of them more than once.

Whidden went over backward, his feet flying in the air.

He was dead when we got to him—three bullets in his chest, one in his head.

We found Gabrielle Collinson lying on blankets that had been spread over a pile of dry seaweed in a narrow cave that carried the V ten or twelve feet farther back into the cliff. There was some canned food and a lantern there.

I helped the girl sit up. Her small face was flushed with fever, and she had to whisper because of a cold in her chest; but her mind was clear enough to recognize me and to answer my questions.

She was in no shape for a grilling, but there were things I had to know quick.

She told me she had known nothing about Whidden's first attempt to kidnap her, nor that Eric had sent for me. She sat up all Friday night waiting for him to come back from his walk, and at daylight, frantic, had gone to hunt for him. She had found him—as I had. She had gone back to the house and tried to commit suicide—to put an end to the curse.

"I tried twice," she whispered, "but it was no use. I'm a coward. I couldn't keep the pistol

pointing at myself while I did it. It would jerk away just before I fired. The second time, I tried to shoot myself in the breast, but only hurt my arm a little." She raised her bandaged left arm for me to see. "And then I hadn't even courage to try any more."

She had changed her clothes—muddy and torn from her search along the rocks—had put a rough bandage on her arm and had driven away from the house. She didn't say where she had intended going. I don't suppose she had any destination; she was just going away from the place where the curse had settled on the man she was married to.

She hadn't gone far when she saw a car coming toward her driven by the man who had brought her here. He had turned his car across the road in front of her, blocking the road. Trying to avoid him, she had run into a tree—and knew nothing else until she regained consciousness here. The man had left her here alone most of the time. She had neither the strength nor the courage to try to escape by swimming, and there was no other way.

"Was he the only man ever here?" I asked, remembering Whidden's last words. "Wasn't there more than one?"

"No, just he—the one who went out with the rifle when he heard you come."

"How long had he been here this time?"

"Since before daylight," she whispered. "The sound of his boat woke me."

"Sure of that?"

"Yes."

I had been sitting on my heels in front of her. I stood up and turned to face the marshal, close to him.

"You killed your wife," I said.

He goggled at me. His gun was in his hand, hanging down at his side. I stood too close for him to raise it between us. He stammered:

"Wh—what's that?"

"You killed your wife. She was afraid Whidden meant to, but he's been here since daylight, and she was warm when we found her—after eleven. You found the letter, found that what you had suspected—her intimacy with him—was true, and you strangled her, counting on the letter to hang it on him."

"That's a lie," he cried. "There ain't a word of truth in it."

He pushed back against the others, trying to get far enough from me to bring his gun up. I moved after him, keeping close, getting one hand on his gun, the other on the wrist above it.

He snarled and hit at me with his other fist. The sheriff caught that arm, wrenched it back, growling:

"That'll do."

I twisted the marshal's gun out of his hand.

Feeney and Rolly took him out of the cave.

Vernon stuck his chin up and spoke over it in a satisfied voice, carefully baring his teeth around each word:

"Just as I suspected. We can congratulate ourselves on having brought an extremely difficult affair to a decidedly neat ending."

I was glad somebody liked it. I didn't. Here, for the third time in a very few weeks, the girl had been the center around which crime and death revolved; and for the third time we had discovered everything except what connection there was between the first, second and third times. And, not having discovered that connection, I didn't believe we had brought anything to any kind of an ending.

Whatever or whoever the Curse was—it or he was still loose.

I put all the hypocrisy I had into my voice as I turned back to the girl.

"Well," I said amiably, "let's get back to Quesada."

BLACK RIDDLE, BY DASHIELL HAMMETT

The Continental detective solves the mystery of the "Dain Curse"

IN FEBRUARY BLACK MASK

BLACK MASK, FEBRUARY 1929

Black Riddle

THE DAIN CURSE

BY DASHIELL HAMMETT

"IT DOESN'T MAKE SENSE," I said. "It's dizzy. When we grab our man—or woman—we're going to find he's a goof, and Napa* will get him instead of the gallows."

"That," Owen Fitzstephan said, "is characteristic of you. You're stumped, bewildered, flabbergasted. Do you admit you've met your master, have run into a criminal too wily for you? Not you. He's outwitted you; therefore he's an idiot. Now really. Of course there's a certain modesty to that attitude."

"But he's got to be goofy," I insisted. "Look: Mayenne marries—"

"Are you," he asked wearily, "going to recite that catalogue again?"

"I am. Mayenne marries Lily Dain in Paris in 1908, and their daughter Gabrielle is born. Lily's sister Alice wants Mayenne. When Gabrielle is five, Alice teaches her a game with a pistol, and it winds up as Alice planned, by the youngster killing her mother. But Mayenne is convicted of the murder and sent to Devil's Island. He escapes after some years and comes to San Francisco, where he settles as Edgar Leggett. In 1923 Alice and Gabrielle join him, and he and Alice marry. Call that the prelude if you want."

"I might have called it that yesterday," Fitzstephan complained, "but after hearing it gone over a dozen times today I can't call it anything but damned tiresome."

"You've a flighty mind. That's no good in this business. You can't catch murderers by amusing yourself with interesting thoughts. You've got

---

* Napa State Hospital, a psychiatric facility

to sit down to all the facts you can get and turn them over and over till they click. There's—"

"Stop," he said. "If it must be one or the other, I'd rather hear you discuss your mystery—even for the thirteenth time—than your technic."

"If that's the case, the Leggetts then have five years of peace, until a pair of ex-sleuths who know the family history show up. One of them—Upton—shakes Alice down for a handful of diamonds. The other kills Upton, either on his own account or Alice's, and goes to her for money and concealment. By this time Alice is in a hole, and she tries to pull it in after her by killing the second ex-sleuth—Ruppert. Gabrielle sees the murder. Half-cracked or more, she beats it. Her going gums things for Alice, even though she doesn't know the girl saw the murder; because I, trying to trace the diamonds, have begun to find things wrong with the Leggetts and am hunting for Gabrielle.

"Whatever Leggett knows up to this point, Alice has to go to him now with the works and ask him to take the fall for her. He's got to powder out anyhow, if he doesn't want to be shipped back to the Island, and there's enough chalked up against him that a little more won't hurt. So he comes through with a written confession that he killed Ruppert, that he's to blame for everything. Alice reads his statement, figures it sounds as much like a pre-suicide document as anything else, thinks that's the safest way to play it, and knocks him off—like that. When the trick goes sour on her, she tries to shoot her way out of the house, and, when you and I grab her, succeeds in shooting herself. All that may be part of the prelude too, though it doesn't have to be."

"In any event," the novelist murmured, "it gets you halfway through. Continue, my son, have it over with."

"The shock of all this raises hell with Gabrielle's mind, which wasn't any too strong in the first place, and makes her easy pickings for the Haldorns and their Temple of the Holy Grail cult. They've been working on her for some time, and now they persuade her to come to the Temple for a stay. She wants to go, and Dr. Riese

thinks that letting her go is about the only thing that will keep her from going completely cuckoo. They persuade Madison Andrews, who is in charge of her affairs since her parents' death, to agree—over the objections of Eric Collinson, to whom she's engaged.

"Joseph Haldorn's got a wife, Aaronia, who helps him run the cult racket, but that doesn't keep Joseph from getting a yen for Gabrielle. His success in flimflamming his converts makes him think he can get away with anything. Dr. Riese, coming to see Gabrielle every day, soon discovers that something's wrong, but he hasn't got sense enough to keep it to himself. He lets Haldorn know what he's discovered, and Haldorn has him killed. Then, when Aaronia interferes, Haldorn tries to carve her. I kill Haldorn and one of his associates, Mrs. Fink, and the Holy Grail trick falls apart, landing the survivors—Aaronia Haldorn, Tom Fink, and Gabrielle's maid Minnie—in jail, where they staid till yesterday."

"Till yesterday?" Fitzstephan's sleepy gray eyes woke up. "They've been released?"

"Aaronia and Fink have. Minnie will probably have to stand trial but I don't think any jury will tie Riese's murder on her. She was too plainly spooked into it by Haldorn. There's no chance of hanging it on Fink or Aaronia. They were accomplices in the Temple racket, but there's no proof that they had anything to do with his going crazy and murdering people. They may have—but there's no proof."

"You're watching them, of course?"

"That's what we sprung them for. Well, when the Temple blew up, Eric Collinson grabbed Gabrielle, carried her off to Reno, and married her. They came back to San Francisco for the inquest, and then down here to Quesada, to the house in the cove, a quiet place where she can recover health and sanity. Last Friday Eric wires me, *Come immediately*. I can't get down till late that night. Eric waits here at the hotel for me till after the last train bus is in, and then starts back to his house, but is killed en route—pushed off the cliff by Harvey Whidden, a native with a rum-running record.

"After killing Collinson, Whidden sends messages through you—whose address he knows—demanding ten thousand dollars ransom for Gabrielle's return, and then, after sending the messages, kidnaps her. That same Friday night, Cotton, the marshal here, suspecting what everybody else knows—that his wife and Whidden are chummy—has pretended he was going to San Francisco, but has hidden where he can watch his house, to see if Whidden visits it. Whidden doesn't. When the Collinson murder and kidnapping break, Cotton tries to frame Whidden for it. Whidden, running away, hides in the marshal's house, and makes the marshal's wife tell us that he—Whidden—had been with her the night of the murder.

"When Mrs. Cotton learns what Whidden has done she—so she says—refuses to have anything more to do with him, and is afraid he will kill her to keep her quiet. So she writes a statement giving the whole thing away. Cotton, coming home after Whidden has left, finds the statement. It verifies his suspicion of his wife's unfaithfulness. He strangles her, calls us in, and her written statement seems to be proof enough that Whidden had killed her. Following the statement's directions, we go to Whidden's hiding place and find him there with Gabrielle. He throws up his rifle, yells, 'You double-crossing something-or-other,' and fires. Cotton ducks in time to let the bullet go elsewhere, and we have to kill Whidden. Gabrielle gives Whidden an alibi for Mrs. Cotton's murder by saying he had been with her since daybreak—and the woman had been killed at close to eleven that morning, was warm when we saw her. That means, apparently, that Cotton killed her. He's in the county jail now, insisting on his innocence. Whidden's last words are still unexplained. Gabrielle saw or heard of nobody except Whidden throughout the abduction. They're the facts, brother, as we've got them. Do they make sense?"

Fitzstephan ran long fingers through his sorrel hair and asked:

"Why not? Cotton persuaded Whidden to kidnap Gabrielle. Collinson stumbled on to the plan and had to be killed. According to the plan, Cotton was supposed to see that the other officials didn't get anywhere while Whidden did the actual work. What Cotton did was to make his wife write that statement—I don't know how it hit you, but it didn't read to me like the sort of thing she would have written of her own accord—kill her, and then lead us to Whidden. He was the first man ashore when we reached Whidden's hiding place—to make sure that Whidden was killed resisting arrest before he got a chance to say much. Jealousy would give Cotton sufficient motive for that, surely?"

I shook my head, saying:

"It doesn't click for me, though Vernon and Feeney are figuring it that way. Whidden wouldn't have put himself in Cotton's hands like that. Besides, where would that fit in with the Temple merry-go-round, and the passing out of the Leggetts?"

"I don't know," the novelist admitted, "but are you sure you're right in thinking there must be a connection?"

"Yeah. Gabrielle's father, stepmother, physician and husband have been killed, and her maid jailed, in less than a handful of weeks—all the people closest to her. That's enough to tie it all together for me, but if you want more links you can have them. Upton and Ruppert were the apparent instigators of the first trouble, and got killed. Haldorn of the second, and got killed. Whidden of the third, and got killed. Mrs. Leggett killed her husband, Cotton killed his wife, and Haldorn would have killed his if I hadn't blocked him. Gabrielle as a child was made to kill her mother, and Gabrielle's maid was made to kill Riese, and nearly me. Gabrielle's father left behind him a long statement explaining—not altogether satisfactorily—everything, and was killed. So did and was Mrs. Cotton. Doesn't that look like some one person who's got a system he likes, and sticks to it?"

Fitzstephan nodded slowly, agreeing:

"As you tell it, it sounds like the work of one mind."

"And a goofy one."

"Be obstinate about it," he said. "But even your goof must have a motive of some sort."

"Why?"

"Damn your sort of mind," he said with good-natured impatience. "If he had no motive connected with Gabrielle, why should his crimes be connected with her?"

"We don't know that all of them are. We only know of the ones that are."

Fitzstephan grinned and said:

"You'll go any distance to disagree, won't you?"

I said:

"Then again, maybe his crimes are connected with her because he is."

The novelist let his eyes get sleepy over that, pursing his mouth, looking at the closed door between my room and Gabrielle's.

"All right," he said, looking at me again. "Who's your maniac close to Gabrielle?"

"The closest and goofiest person to Gabrielle is Gabrielle herself."

Fitzstephan got up and crossed the hotel room—I was sitting on the edge of the bed—to shake my hand with solemn enthusiasm.

"You're wonderful," he said. "You amaze me. Ever have night sweats? Put out your tongue and say, 'Ah.'"

"Suppose," I began, but was interrupted by a feeble tapping on the corridor door.

I went to the door and opened it. A thin man of my own age and height in wrinkled black clothes stood in the corridor. He breathed heavily through a red-veined nose, and his small brown eyes were timid.

"You know me," he said apologetically.

"Yeah. Come in." I introduced him to the novelist: "Fitzstephan, this is the Tom Fink who was one of Haldorn's helpers in the Temple."

Fink looked reproachfully at me, then dragged his crumpled hat off his head and crossed the room to shake Fitzstephan's hand. That done, he returned to me and said, almost whispering:

"I come down to tell you something."

"Yeah?"

He fidgeted, turning his hat around in his hands. I winked at Fitzstephan, said, "Will you excuse us for a moment?" and went out with Fink. In the corridor I closed the door and stopped, saying:

"Let's have it."

Fink rubbed his lips with his tongue and then with the back of one scrawny hand. He said in his half-whisper:

"I come down to tell you something I thought you ought to know."

"Yeah?"

"It's about that fellow Harvey Whidden."

"Yeah?"

"He was my step-son."

"You—?"

Floor, walls and ceiling danced under, around and over us. The door to my room roared open, wriggling, a yellow crack curving down it from top to bottom. Tom Fink was carried away from me, backward. I had sense enough to throw myself down as I was flung in the other direction, and got nothing worse out of it than a bruised shoulder when I hit the wall. A door-frame stopped Fink, wickedly, its edge catching the back of his head. He came forward again, folding over to lie face-down on the floor, still except for blood running from his head.

I got up and made for my room. Fitzstephan was a mangled pile of flesh and clothing in the center of the floor. My bed was burning. There was no glass in the window. I checked up these things mechanically while staggering toward Gabrielle's room. The connecting door was open—had been blown open, perhaps.

She was crouching on all fours in bed, facing the foot of the bed, her bare feet on the pillows. Her night dress was torn at one shoulder. Her green-brown eyes—glittering under the brown curls that had tumbled down to hide what little forehead she had—were the eyes of an animal gone trap-crazy. Saliva glistened on her pointed chin. There was nobody else in the room.

"Where's the nurse?" My voice was husky.

The girl said nothing. Her eyes kept their crazy terror focused on me.

"Get under the covers," I ordered. "You're sick enough without getting pneumonia."

She didn't move. I walked around to the side of the bed, lifting an end of the covers with one hand, reaching the other out to help her, saying:

"Come on, get under the covers."

She made a queer noise in her throat, dropped her head, and put her sharp teeth into the back of my hand. It hurt. I put her under the covers, went back to my room, and was pushing my burning mattress through the window when people began to arrive.

"Get a doctor," I called to the first of them, "and stay out of here."

I had got rid of the mattress by the time Mickey Linehan pushed through the crowd that was now packing the corridor. Mickey blinked at what was left of Fitzstephan, at mc, and asked:

"What the hell?"

His big loose mouth sagged at the ends, looking like a grin turned upside-down.

I licked burnt finger-tips and asked, not pleasantly:

"What the hell does it look like?"

The grin turned right-side-up on his red face. He scratched one of his ears—they stood out like loving cup handles—and said:

"More trouble, of course. Of course—you're here."

Deputy sheriff Ben Rolly came in—a tall, big-built, slouchy youngish man with hair, eyes and skin of indefinite tan shades.

"Tch, tch, tch," he said, looking around. "What do you suppose happened?"

"Bomb."

"Tch, tch, tch."

Dr. George came in and knelt beside the wreck of Fitzstephan. George had been looking after Gabrielle since we had rescued her from Whidden the previous day. He was a short, chunky, middle-aged man with a lot of black hair everywhere except on his lips, cheeks and chin. His hairy hands moved over Fitzstephan.

"Damn my soul," the doctor exclaimed. "The man's not dead."

I didn't believe him. Fitzstephan's right arm was gone, and most of his right leg. His body was too twisted to see how much of it was left, but there was only one side to his face. I said: "There's another one out in the hall, with his head knocked in."

"Oh, he'll pull through all right," the doctor muttered without looking up. "But this one— well, damn my soul."

He scrambled up to his feet and began ordering this and that. He was highly excited. A couple of men came in from the corridor. The woman who had been nursing Gabrielle—Mrs. Herman—joined them, and another man, with a blanket. They took Fitzstephan away.

"What's Fink been doing?" I asked Mickey.

"Hardly anything. I got on his tail when they sprung him yesterday at noon. He went from the can to a hotel on Kearny Street and got himself a room. Then he went up to the Public Library and hunted up everything the newspapers have printed about the girl's troubles from beginning to date. Then he went to a lunch-room for some grub, ambled back to his hotel, and camped in his room. He might have back-doored me. His room was dark at midnight, when I knocked off. I got on the job again at six A.M. He showed at seven-something, grabbed breakfast, and a train to Poston, got the stage for here, and came straight into the hotel, asking for you. That's the crop."

"That the fellow out in the hall?" Rolly asked.

"Yeah." I told him what Fink had told me, adding: "The chances are he hadn't given me all he had when the blow-up came. We'll find out when he comes to."

"So Harve was his step-son," the deputy said. "Tch, tch, tch. What about Harve's mother?"

"I killed her in the Temple," I said. "It was her or me."

"Tch, tch, tch. You think this Fink meant the bomb for you, because you'd killed his wife?"

"No. He was standing outside, talking to me,

when it popped. I wonder if it was meant for him, to keep him from telling me what he had come down to tell?"

Mickey said: "Nobody followed him down from the city, excepting me. I reckon I'd better go see what they're doing with him." He went out.

"The window was closed," I told Rolly. "There was no noise, as if something had been thrown through the window, just before the explosion, and there's no broken window-glass inside the room now. It wasn't chucked in that way."

Rolly nodded vaguely, looking at the connecting doorway.

"Fink and I were in the corridor. I ran straight through here into her room. Nobody could have got out of her room without my seeing or hearing them, even if they could have sneaked in there without raising an alarm. The heavy screen I had nailed over her window is O.K."

"Wasn't Mrs. Herman in there?" Rolly asked.

"She was supposed to be, but was out at the time. We'll find out about that. There's no use of thinking the girl—Mrs. Collinson—chucked it. She's been in there, in bed, since we brought her back yesterday. I picked that room out. She couldn't have had a bomb planted there even if she had any reasons for wanting one. Nobody's been in there except the doctor, the nurse, you, Feeney, Vernon and me."

"I didn't say she had anything to do with it," the deputy mumbled, looking vaguer than ever. "What does she say?"

"We can talk to her now, if you want, but I doubt if it'll get us much."

It didn't. Gabrielle lay in the middle of the bed, the covers gathered close to her chin as if she was preparing to duck down under them at the first alarm, and shook her head, "No," to everything we asked her, whether the answer fitted or didn't.

The nurse came in, a big-hearted, red-haired woman of forty-something with a face that looked honest because it was homely, blue-eyed and freckled. She swore by the Gideon Bible that she had been out of the room for only five minutes, just to go downstairs for some stationery, intending to write a letter to her nephew in Vallejo while her patient was sleeping; and that was the only time she had been out of the room all day. She had met nobody in the corridor, she said.

"You left the door unlocked?" I asked.

"Yes, so I wouldn't be so likely to wake her up when I came back."

"Where's the writing paper you got?"

"I didn't get it. I heard the explosion, and ran back upstairs." Fear came into her face, turning the freckles into ghastly spots. "You don't think—!"

"Better look after Mrs. Collinson," I said irritably.

II

Rolly and I went back to my room, closing the connecting door.

He said:

"Tch, tch, tch. I'd of thought Mrs. Herman was the last person in the world to—"

"You ought to've," I grumbled. "You recommended her. Who is she?"

"She's Tod Herman's wife. He's got the garage here. She used to be a trained nurse. I thought she was all right."

"She got a nephew in Vallejo?"

"Uh-huh, that would be the Schultz kid that works at Mare Island. How do you suppose she got mixed up in—"

"Probably didn't, or she would have had the writing paper she went after. Let's lock this place up till we can borrow a San Francisco bomb expert to go over it."

Mickey Linehan was in the lobby when we got down there.

"Fink's got a cracked skull. He's on his way over to the county hospital with the other wreck."

"Fitzstephan died yet?" I asked.

"Nope, and the doc seems to think that if they get him over to where they got the right kind of tools they can keep him alive. God knows what for, the shape he's in. But you know croakers*— that's just the kind of stuff they think is a lot of fun."

"Who's shadowing Aaronia Haldorn?"

"Al Mason."

"Phone the agency and see if you can get a report on her. Tell the Old Man what's happened while you're at it, and see if they've found Andrews."

"Andrews?" Rolly asked as Mickey headed for the telephone. "What's the matter with him?"

"Nothing that I know of—only we haven't been able to find him to tell him Mrs. Collinson is safe. His office—he's a lawyer—hasn't seen him since the day before yesterday, and nobody there will say they know where he is. I saw him that same day, and he didn't say anything about going anywhere."

"Is there any special reason for wanting him?"

"Well," I said sourly, "I don't want to have her on my hands the rest of my life. He's in charge of her affairs; he's responsible for her; I want to turn her over to him."

Rolly nodded vaguely. We went outside and asked all the people we could find all the questions we could think of. None of the answers led anywhere, except to assure us that the bomb hadn't been chucked through the window. We found six people who had been in sight of that side of the hotel at the time of the explosion, and none of them had seen anything that could be twisted into having any bearing on the bomb-throwing.

Mickey came away from the telephone with the information that Aaronia Haldorn, when released from the city prison, had gone to the home of a family named Jeffries—former

_____

* doctors

members of her cult—in San Mateo, and had remained there ever since; and that Dick Foley, hunting for Madison Andrews, had hopes of locating him in Sausalito.

Prosecuting attorney Vernon and sheriff Feeney, with a horde of reporters and photographers close behind them, arrived from the county seat. They went through a lot of detecting motions that got them nowhere except on the front pages of all the San Francisco papers—which was the place they liked best.

I had Gabrielle Collinson moved into another room, and left Mickey Linehan next door, with the connecting door ajar. She talked now—to Vernon, Feeney, Rolly and me—but what she told us didn't help much. She had been asleep, she said; had been awakened by the noise, and then I had come in. That was all she knew.

Late in the afternoon, McCracken, a San Francisco police department explosive expert, arrived; and, after examining all the fragments of this and that which he could find in the blasted room, gave us a preliminary report that the bomb had been a small one, of aluminum, filled with a low-grade nitroglycerine, and exploded by a crude friction device.

"Amateur or professional job?" I asked.

McCracken spit loose shreds of tobacco out—he's one of these birds who chew the ends of their cigarettes—and said:

"I'd say it was made by a guy that knew his stuff, all right, but had to work with what material he could get. I'll tell you more after I've worked this junk over in the lab."

Dr. George returned from the county hospital with the news that what was left of Fitzstephan still breathed. The doctor was tickled pink. I had to yell at him to make him hear my questions about Fink and Gabrielle. Then he told me Fink's life was in no danger, and the girl's cold was enough better that she could get out of bed if she wished. I asked him about her nervous condition, but he was in too much of a hurry to get back to Fitzstephan to pay much attention to that.

"Hm-m-m, yes, certainly," he muttered, edging past me toward his car.

"Quiet, rest, freedom from anxiety," and he was gone.

I ate dinner with Vernon and Feeney in the hotel dining-room. They didn't think I had told them all I knew about the explosion, and kept me on the witness stand all through the meal, though neither of them accused me point-blank of holding out.

After dinner I went up to my new room. The door between it and Gabrielle's was closed. Mickey Linehan was sprawled on the bed reading a newspaper.

"Go feed yourself," I said. "How's our baby?"

"She's up. How do you figure her—only fifty cards to her deck?"

"Why?" I asked. "What's she been doing?"

"Nothing. I was just thinking."

"That's from having an empty stomach. Better go eat."

"Aye, aye, master mind," he said and went out.

The next room was quiet. I listened at the door and then tapped it. Mrs. Herman's voice said: "Come in."

She was sitting beside the bed making gaudy butterflies on a piece of yellowish cloth stretched on hoops. Gabrielle Collinson sat in a rocking chair on the other side of the room, frowning at hands clasped in her lap—clasped hard enough to whiten the knuckles and spread the finger-ends. She had on the tweed clothes in which she had been abducted. They were still rumpled but had been brushed clean. She didn't look up when I came in. The nurse did, pushing her freckles together in an uneasy smile.

"Good evening," I said, trying to make a cheerful entrance. "Looks like we're running out of invalids."

That got no response from the girl, too much from the nurse.

"Yes, indeed," she exclaimed, with too much enthusiasm. "We can't call Mrs. Collinson an invalid now—now that she's up and about—and

I'm almost sorry that she is—he, he—because I certainly never did have such a nice patient; but that's what we girls used to say in training—the nicer the patient was, the shorter the time we'd have him, while you take a disagreeable one, and she'd live—I mean, be there—forever, it seems like. I remember once when—"

I made a face at her and jerked my head at the door. She let the rest of her words drop inside her open mouth. Her face turned red, then white. She dropped her embroidery and got up, saying idiotically: "Yes, yes, that's the way it is. Well, I've got to go see about that—you know—what do you call 'em. Excuse me for a few minutes, please." She went out quickly, sideways, as if afraid I would sneak up behind her and kick her.

When the door had closed, Gabrielle looked up from her hands and said:

"Owen is dead."

She didn't ask, she said it, but there was no way of handling it except as a question.

"No." I sat down in the nurse's chair and fished out cigarettes. "It doesn't seem possible, but he's still alive."

"If he lives"—her voice was husky from the tail-end of her cold—"will he—?" She left the question unfinished, but her husky voice was impersonal enough.

"He'll be pretty badly maimed."

She spoke more to herself than to me:

"That should be even more satisfactory."

I grinned. If I was as good an actor as I thought, there was nothing in my grin but good-natured amusement.

"Laugh," she said gravely. "I wish you could laugh it away. But you can't. It's there. It will always be there." She looked down at her clasped hands and whispered: "Cursed."

Spoken in any other tone, that word would have been—or would have sounded—ridiculous, melodramatic, stagey. But she said it without any feeling, mechanically, as if saying it were a habit. I saw her lying in bed in the dark, whispering it to herself; whispering it to her body when she put on her clothes; to her face when she saw it reflected in mirrors—day after day.

I squirmed in my chair and growled:

"Stop it. Just because a bad-tempered woman works off her hatred and anger in a ten-twenty-thirty* speech about—"

"No, no, my step-mother only put in words what I have always known. I didn't know that she and my mother were cursed too—that it was in the Dain blood—but I knew it was in mine. I knew it from the time I was old enough to compare myself with other children. How could I help knowing? Hadn't I all the physical signs of degeneracy?" She came across the room to stand in front of me, turning her head sidewise, pushing back brown curls with both hands. "Look at my ears—without lobes, pointed at the top. People don't have ears like that. Animals do." She twisted her face to me again, still holding back the curls. "Look at my forehead—its smallness, its shape—animal. My teeth." She bared them—white, small, pointed. "The shape of my face." Her hands left her hair to slide down her cheeks and come together under her oddly pointed small chin. "Look at my hands." She held them out to me. "The thumbs, with those useless joints—hardly different from fingers. I've only four toes on each foot. I've—"

"I'm disappointed in that," I said. "I thought you'd have cloven hoofs. Suppose these things were all as peculiar as you seem to think them? What of it? Your step-mother was a Dain, and God knows she was poison—but where were her 'physical marks of degeneracy'? Wasn't she as normal, as wholesome a looking woman as you're likely to find?"

"But that's no answer." She shook her head impatiently. "She didn't have the physical marks. I have—and the mental ones too. I—" She sat down on the side of the bed close to me, elbows on knees, tortured white face between hands. "I've not ever been able to think clearly, as other people do, even the simplest thoughts. Everything is always a muddle in my mind. No matter what I try to think about, there's a fog between me and my thought, and other thoughts get in the way, and I barely catch a glimpse of the thought I want before I lose it, and have to hunt through the fog and at last find it, only to have the same thing happen again and again and again. Can you understand how horrible that can be? Going through life—year after year—knowing you are and always will be like that—or worse?"

"I can't," I said. "It sounds normal as hell to me. Nobody thinks clearly, no matter what they pretend. People either don't think at all or they go about it exactly as you do. Thinking's a dizzy business—a matter of catching as many of those foggy glimpses as you can and fitting them together the best you can. That's why people hang on so tight to their beliefs and opinions; because, compared to the haphazard way in which they're arrived at, even the goofiest opinion seems wonderfully clear, sane, and self-evident. And if you let it get away from you, then you have to dive back into that foggy muddle to wangle yourself out another to take its place."

She took her face out of her hands and smiled shyly at me, saying:

"It's funny I didn't like you before." Her face became serious again. "But—"

"But nothing. You're old enough to know that everybody except very crazy people and very stupid people suspect themselves now and then—or whenever they happen to think of it—of being not exactly sane. Evidence of goofiness is easily found—the more you dig into yourself the more you turn up. Nobody's mind could pass the sort of examination you've been giving yours—going around trying to prove yourself cuckoo!—it's a wonder you haven't driven yourself nuts."

"Perhaps I have."

"No. Take my word for it, you're sane. Or don't take my word for it. Look. You got a hell of a start in life. You got into bad hands at the very beginning. You were brought up by a step-mother who was plain poison, and who did her best to make a complete ruin of you, and who in the end succeeded in convincing you that you were cursed with some very special family curse. In the past couple of months—the time I've

---

* cheap and melodramatic

known you—all the calamities known to man have been piled on you—and your belief in your curse has made you hold yourself responsible for every item in the pile.

"All right. How's it affected you? You've been dazed part of the time, hysterical now and then, and when your husband was killed you tried to commit suicide but weren't unbalanced enough to face the shock of the bullet in your flesh. Well, good God, woman, I'm only a hired man with only a hired man's interest in your troubles, and some of them have had me groggy. Didn't I try to bite a ghost back in that Temple? And I'm supposed to be old and toughened to crime. This morning—after all you've gone through—somebody touches off a package of nitroglycerine almost beside your bed. Here you are this evening—up and dressed—arguing about your sanity with me.

"If you aren't normal, it's because you're tougher, cooler, saner, than normal. Stop thinking about your Dain blood and think a little of the Mayenne blood in you. You're more like your father than your mother—judging by her sister. You've got more of his blood in you, if appearance is a guide, and owe it more. It's his toughness that has carried you through this far—and will carry you the rest of the way."

She seemed to like that. Her eyes were almost happy. But I had talked myself out of words for the moment, and while I was hunting for more behind a cigarette the shine went out of her eyes.

"I'm glad—I'm grateful to you for what you've said, if you meant it." Hopelessness was in her tone again, and her face was back between her hands. "But, whatever I am, she—my stepmother—was right. You cannot say she was not. Surely my life has been cursed, blackened—and the lives of everyone who has come in contact with me."

"I'm one answer to that," I said. "I've been around a lot recently, and nothing's happened to me that a night's sleep wouldn't fix up." I shut my mouth in time to avoid dragging Madison Andrews in as another answer. Until we found

him we couldn't be sure that nothing had happened to him.

"But in a different way," she protested slowly, wrinkling her forehead. "There's no personal relationship with you. It's simply your work. That makes the difference."

I laughed and said:

"That won't do. There's Fitzstephan. He was a friend of your family, of course, but his presence here was through me—on my account. He was helping me. Why then—a step further away from you than I—should he have got the bomb? I was closer to you than he. Why shouldn't I have gone down first? Maybe the bomb was meant for me? It's reasonable. But that brings us to a human mind behind the whole thing—one capable of making mistakes—and not your infallible and airtight curse."

"You are mistaken," she said, staring at her knees. "Owen loved me."

I decided not to appear surprised. I said:

"Had you—?"

"No, please, please don't ask me to talk about it. Not now—after this morning." She jerked her shoulders up high and straight, said briskly: "A moment ago you said something about an infallible curse. I don't know whether you've misunderstood me, or are pretending to, to make it look more foolish. But I don't believe in your infallible curse—one coming from God or the devil, like Job's, say." She was earnest now, no longer talking to change the conversation. "But can't there be—aren't there people who are so thoroughly—fundamentally—evil that they poison, or bring out the worst in everybody they touch? And can't that—?"

"Maybe there are people who can," I half-agreed, "if they want to."

"No, no! Whether they want to or not. When they desperately don't want to. It is so. It is. I loved Eric because he was clean and fine. You knew him well enough to know he was. I loved him that way, wanted him that way. And then, when we were married—" She shuddered and gave me both of her hands. The palms were dry and hot, the ends of the fingers cold. I had to hold them tight to keep the nails out of my flesh.

I said:

"You're being silly. He was too young, too much in love with you, maybe too inexperienced, to keep from being clumsy. You can't make anything horrible out of that."

"But it wasn't only Eric. Every man I've known—Don't think I'm conceited. I know I'm not beautiful. But I don't want to be evil. I don't. Why do men—why have all the men I've known—?"

"Are you," I asked, "talking about me?"

"No—you know I'm not. Don't make fun of me, please."

"Then there are exceptions? Any others? Madison Andrews, for instance?"

"If you knew him very well, or had heard much about him, you wouldn't ask that?"

"No," I agreed. "But with him it's a habit. You can't blame the curse. Was he very bad?"

"He was very funny," she said bitterly.

"How long ago was that?"

"Oh, possibly a year and a half. I didn't say anything to my father or step-mother. I was—I was ashamed that men were like that to me—and afraid—"

"How do you know," I grumbled, "that most men aren't like that to most women? What makes you think your case is so damned unique? If your ears were sharp enough you could probably hear thousands of women in San Francisco making the same complaint at this moment, and—God knows—maybe half of them would be thinking they were sincere."

She took her hands away from me and sat up straight on the bed-edge. Some pink came into her face.

"Now you *have* made me feel silly," she said.

"No sillier than I do. I'm supposed to be a detective. I've been riding a blooming merry-go-round since this job began—going around and around the same distance behind your curse, suspecting what it'd look like if I came face to

face with it, but never catching up with it. Well, I've got it now. Can you stand another week or two?"

"You mean—?"

"I'm going to earn my wages," I promised her, "and show you that your curse is a lot of hooey. It may take a week or two, though."

She was white-faced and trembling, wanting to believe me, afraid to.

"That's settled," I said. "What are you going to do now?"

"I—I don't know. Do you mean what you've said?"

"Yeah. Could you go back to the house in the cove for a while? It might help things along, and I think you'll be safe enough now. We could take Mrs. Herman and maybe an op or two from the agency with us."

"I'll go," she said.

I looked at my watch and stood up, saying:

"Better get back to bed. We'll move tomorrow. Good night."

She chewed her lower lip, wanting to say something, not wanting to say it, finally blurting it out:

"I'll have to have morphine down there."

"Sure. What's your day's ration?"

"Five—ten grains."

"That's mild enough," I said, and then, casually: "Do you like using the stuff?"

"I'm afraid it's too late for my liking it or not liking it to make any difference now."

"You've been reading Sunday papers," I said. "If you want to break off, and we've a few days to spare down there, we'll use them weaning you. It's not so tough."

She laughed shakily, with a queer twitching of her lips.

"Go away," she cried. "Don't give me any more assurances, promises, please. I can't stand any more tonight. I'm drunk on them now. Please."

"All right. Night."

"Good night—and thanks."

I went into my room. Mickey was unscrewing the top of a flask. His knees were dusty. He turned his half-wit's grin on me and said:

"What a swell dish you are. What are you trying to do? Win yourself a home?"

"Sh-h-h. Anything new?"

"The big officials have gone back to the county seat. The redhead nurse was getting a load at the keyhole when I came back from eating. I chased her."

"And took her place?" I asked, nodding at his dusty knees.

You couldn't embarrass Mickey. He said:

"Hell, no. She was at the other door, in the hall."

III

I got Fitzstephan's car from the garage and drove Gabrielle and Mrs. Herman down to the house in the cove late the next morning. The girl was in low spirits. She made a poor job of smiling when spoken to, and had nothing to say on her own account. I thought it might be because she was returning to the house where her honeymoon had been ended by Collinson's murder; but when we got there she went in with no appearance of reluctance, and there was nothing to show that the place depressed her any further.

After luncheon—Mrs. Herman turned out to be a good cook—Gabrielle decided she wanted to go outdoors, so she and I walked over to the little Mexican settlement on the creek to see Mary Nunez, the Mexican woman who had done her housework before. Mary promised to show up for work the next day. She seemed quite fond of Gabrielle, but not of me.

We returned to the house by way of the shore, picking our way between, over, and around pebbles, sand, boulders, and young mountains. We walked slowly. The girl's forehead was puckered between the eyebrows. Neither of us said anything from the time we left the Mexican settlement until we were within a quarter of a mile of home. Then Gabrielle sat down on the rounded top of a rock that was warm in the sun.

"Can you remember what you told me last night?" she asked, running her words together in her hurry to get them out. She looked frightened.

"Yeah."

"Tell me again," she begged, moving over to one side of the rock. "Sit down and tell me again—all of it."

I did—spending nearly three-quarters of an hour at it. I didn't make such a lousy job of it, either. The fear went out of her eyes as I talked. Toward the last she was smiling to herself. When I had finished she jumped up, laughing, working her fingers together.

"Thank you. Thank you," she babbled. "Please don't let me ever stop believing you. Make me believe you—even if—No. It is true. Make me believe it always. Come on. Let's walk some more."

She almost ran me the rest of the way. Mickey Linehan was on the front porch. I stopped with him while the girl went indoors.

"Tch, tch, tch, as Mr. Rolly says." He shook his grinning face at me. "I ought to tell her what happened to that poor girl up in Poisonville* who got to thinking she could trust you."

"Bring any news down from the village with you?" I asked.

"Madison Andrews's found. He was at the Jeffries place in San Mateo, where Aaronia Haldorn's staying. She's still there. Andrews went there Tuesday afternoon and stayed till last night. Al Mason was watching the place; saw him go in, but didn't tumble to who it was till he left. The Jeffries are away—San Diego. Dick Foley's tailing Andrews now. Al says the Haldorn woman hasn't been off the place. Rolly tells me that Fink's awake, but don't know anything about the bomb; and Fitzstephan's still hanging on to life."

"I think I'll run over and talk to Fink this afternoon," I said. "Stick around here. And—oh, yeah—you'll have to act more respectful to me

---

* reference to Dinah Brand from "The Cleansing of Poisonville"

when Mrs. Collinson's around. It's important that she keep on thinking I'm hot stuff."

"For God's sake bring back some booze—I can't do it sober."

Fink was propped up in bed when I got to him, looking out under bandages. He insisted that he knew nothing about the bomb, that all he had come down for was to tell me about Harvey Whidden being his step-son.

"Well, what of that?" I asked.

"I don't know what of it," he said. "After they let me out, I read in the papers what had happened down here, and I thought I ought to come down and tell you that."

"How much can you tell me about Whidden?"

"Not anything much. Me and him wasn't too friendly. He was at the Temple for a couple of weeks, working for the Haldorns, but they couldn't get along with him, so they let him go."

"You know Madison Andrews?" I asked.

"No. I read about him in the papers. Ain't he that Leggett girl's guardian or something?"

"You don't know him? Aaronia Haldorn does."

"Maybe she does, mister, but I don't. I just worked for the Haldorns. It wasn't anything to me but a job."

The nurse who was fluttering around had become a nuisance by this time, so I left the hospital for the court house and the prosecuting attorney's office.

Vernon pushed aside a stack of papers with a the-world-can-wait gesture, and said, "Glad to see you; sit down," nodding vigorously, showing me all his teeth.

I sat down and said:

"Been talking to Fink. I couldn't get anything out of him, but he's our meat. The bomb couldn't have got in there except by him."

Vernon looked thoughtful for a moment, then shook his chin at me and snapped:

"What's his motive? And you were there. You say you were looking at him all the time he was in the room. You say you saw nothing."

"What of it?" I asked. "He could outsmart

me there. It's his game. The Haldorns hired him because he was an expert at that sort of stuff— had been in charge of the mechanical end of all the best known stage magicians' acts at one time or another. He'd know how to make a bomb, and how to put it down in front of me. We don't know what Fitzstephan saw. Let's hang on to this Fink till Fitzstephan can talk. They tell me he'll pull through."

Vernon clicked his teeth together and said: "Very well, we'll hold him."

I found the local telephone office and put in a call for Vic Dallas' drug store in San Francisco's Mission.

"I want," I told Vic, "about fifty grains of M. and eight of those calomel-atropine-cascara-ipecacstrychnine shots.[*] I'll have somebody pick up the package tonight or in the morning. Right?"

"If you say so, but if you kill anybody, don't tell them where you got the stuff."

I promised not to and put in a call for the agency, talking to the Old Man. He said there were no new reports on Aaronia Haldorn and Madison Andrews, and he agreed to send me another op, MacMan, and to tell him to get a package from Dallas.

I drove back to the house in the cove. We had company. Three strange cars were parked in the driveway, and half a dozen newshounds were sitting and standing around Mickey on the porch. They turned their questions on me.

"Mrs. Collinson's here for a rest," I told them. "Let her alone. If any news breaks here I'll see that you get it, those who let her alone. The only thing I can tell you now is that Fink will be held for the bombing."

"What did Andrews come down for?" Jack Santos of the *Bulletin* asked.

That wasn't a surprise to me, of course: I had expected him to show up now that he was out of hiding.

---

[*] treatments to mitigate the major symptoms of morphine withdrawal

"Ask him," I suggested. "He's administering Mrs. Collinson's estate. You can't make a mystery out of his seeing her."

"Is it true that they're on bad terms?"

"No."

"Then why didn't he show up before this—yesterday or the day before?"

"Ask him."

"Is it true that he's up to his tonsils in debt—or was before the estate came into his hands?"

"Ask him."

Santos smiled with thinned lips and said:

"We don't have to. We asked his creditors. Is there anything to the story that Mrs. Collinson and her husband quarrelled over her being too friendly with Whidden, a couple of days before her husband was killed?"

"Anything but the truth. Tough. You could do a lot with a story like that."

"Is it true that Mrs. Haldorn and Thomas Fink were released to keep them quiet, because they had threatened to tell all they know if they were held for trial?"

"Now you're kidding me, Jack," I said. "Is Andrews still here?"

"Yes."

I went indoors and called Mickey in.

"Seen Dick?" I asked.

"He drove past a couple of minutes after Andrews got here."

"Sneak away and find him. Tell him not to let the newspaper gang make him, even if he has to risk losing Andrews for a while. They'd go crazy all over the front of their sheets if they learned we were shadowing Andrews."

Mrs. Herman was coming down the stairs. I asked her where Andrews was.

"In the front room."

I went up there. Gabrielle, in a low-cut black velvet gown, was sitting stiff and straight on the edge of a leather rocker. Her face was white and sullen. She was looking at a handkerchief stretched between her hands. When I came in she turned to me as if glad to see me.

Madison Andrews stood with his back to the fireplace. His white hair, eyebrows and mustache stood out every which way from his bony pink face. He shifted his scowl from the girl to me, and didn't seem at all glad to see me.

I said, "Hello," and found a table corner to lean against.

He said: "I've come to take Mrs. Collinson back to San Francisco."

Gabrielle didn't say anything. I said:

"Yeah? Not to San Mateo?"

"What do you mean by that?" The white tangle of his brows came down to hide the upper halves of his blue eyes.

"God knows. Maybe my mind's been corrupted by the questions the newspapers have been asking me."

He didn't quite wince. He said, slowly, deliberately:

"Mrs. Haldorn requested my assistance, as an attorney. I went to see her to explain how, in the circumstances, I could not advise or represent her."

"That's all right with me," I said. "And if it took you thirty hours to explain that to her, it's nobody's business."

"Exactly."

"But—I'd be careful how I told that to the half a dozen reporters waiting out front for you. You know how suspicious they are—for no reason at all."

He turned to the girl, speaking quietly but with some impatience:

"Well, Gabrielle, are you going with me?"

"Should I?" she asked me.

"Not unless you especially want to."

"I don't."

"Then that's settled," I said.

Andrews nodded and went forward to take her hand, saying:

"I must get back to the city, my dear. You should have a phone put in, so you can reach me in case of need."

He declined her invitation to stay to dinner, said, "Good evening," not unpleasantly to me, and went out. Through the window I could see him presently getting into his car, paying as little attention as he could to the newspaper men clustering around him.

Gabrielle was frowning at me when I turned from the window.

"What did you mean by what you said about San Mateo?" she asked.

"How friendly are he and Aaronia Haldorn?" I asked.

"I don't know. I know they're acquainted, of course, but nothing beyond that. Why? Why did you talk to him as you did?"

"Detective business. For one thing, there's a rumor that getting control of your father's estate may have helped him to keep his own head above water. Maybe there's nothing in it. Anyway, it won't hurt to give him a little scare, so he'll get busy straightening things out—if he has done any juggling—between now and clean-up day. No use of you losing money along with your other troubles."

"Then he—?" she began, spreading her eyes at me.

"He's got a week—several days at least—to unjuggle in. That ought to be enough."

"But—"

Mrs. Herman, calling us to dinner, ended the conversation.

Gabrielle ate very little. She and I had to do most of the talking until I got Mickey started telling about a job he had been on up in Eureka, where he had posed as a foreigner who knew no English. Since English was the only language he did know, and Eureka normally contains at least one specimen of all the nationalities there are, he'd had a hell of a time keeping people from finding out just what he was supposed to be. He made a long and funny story of it. Maybe some of it was the truth.

After dinner he and I strolled around the grounds while the summer night darkened them.

I told him MacMan was coming down and asked him if Foley had had any news.

"No, he said Andrews came straight here from his home."

The front door opened, throwing yellow light across the porch. Gabrielle, a dark cape over her gown, came into the yellow light, closed the door, and came down to the gravel walk.

"You'll be doing the watch-dog from bedtime till morning," I told Mickey. "Take a nap now if you want. I'll call you."

"You're a darb."* He laughed in the dark. "By God, you're a darb." The grass swished against his shoes as he walked away.

I moved toward the gravel walk, meeting the girl.

"Isn't it a lovely night?" she said.

"Yeah. But you can't go roaming around alone in the dark, even if your troubles are practically over."

"I didn't intend to." She took my arm, suddenly let it go. "Or have you something else—?"

"No."

"Practically over," she repeated when we had reached the road. "What does that mean?"

"That there are a few details still to be taken care of. The morphine, for instance."

She shivered and said: "I've only enough left to last me tonight. You promised to—"

"Fifty grains will be down in the morning."

She kept quiet, as if waiting for me to say something more. I didn't say anything. Her fingers wriggled on my sleeve.

"You said it wouldn't be hard to cure me." She spoke half questioningly, as if expecting me to deny that I had said anything of the sort.

"It wouldn't."

"You said perhaps . . ." the rest of it faded off.

"We'd do it while we were here?"

"Yes."

"Want to?" I asked. "It's no go if you don't."

"Do I want to?" She stood still in the road, facing me. "I'd give—" A sob ended that sentence. Her voice came again, high-pitched, thin: "Are you being honest with me? Are you? Is what you've told me—all that you said last night and this afternoon—as true as you've made it sound? Do I believe in you because you are sincere? Or

---

* excellent

because you've learned how—as a trick of your business—to make people believe in you?"

This girl might be crazy, but she wasn't any too stupid. I gave her the answer that seemed best at the time:

"Your belief in me is built on mine in you. If mine's unjustified, so is yours. So let me ask you a question first; were you lying when you said, 'I don't want to be evil'?"

"Oh, I don't. I don't."

"Well then," I said with an air of finality, as if that settled it. "Now if you want to get off the junk, off you get."

"How—how long will it take?"

"Say a week. Maybe less, but we'll say a week to be safe."

"Do you mean that? No longer than that?"

"That's all for the part that counts. You'll have to take care of yourself for some time afterward, till your system's in shape again, but you'll be off the junk."

"Will I suffer—much?"

"A couple of bad days, but they won't be as bad as you'll think they are, and you've got enough of your father's toughness to stand them."

"If," she said slowly, "I should find out in the middle of it that I can't go through with it, will you—?"

"There'll be nothing you can do about it," I promised cheerfully. "You'll stay in till you come out the other end."

She shivered again and asked:

"When shall we start?"

"Day after tomorrow. Take your usual allowance tomorrow, but don't try to stock up. And don't worry about it. It'll be tougher on me than on you—I'll have to put up with you."

"And you'll make allowances—you'll understand—if I'm not always nice while going through it? Even if I'm nasty sometimes?"

"I don't know." I didn't want to encourage her to cut up on me. "I don't think much of niceness that can be turned into nastiness by a little grief."

"Oh, but—" She stopped, wrinkled her forehead, said: "Can't we send Mrs. Herman away? I don't want to—I don't want her looking at me."

"I'll get rid of her tomorrow."

"And if I'm—you won't let anybody else see me—if I'm not—if I'm too terrible?"

"No," I promised. "But look here: apparently you're preparing to put on a circus for me. Stop thinking about that end. You're going to behave. I don't want too much monkey business out of you."

She laughed suddenly, asking:

"Will you beat me if I'm bad?"

I said she might still be young enough for a spanking to do her good.

IV

Mary Nunez came to work at half-past seven the following morning. A little later Mickey Linehan, in our borrowed car, drove Mrs. Herman in to Quesada, returning with MacMan, a bottle of gin, and a load of groceries.

MacMan was a square-built, stiff-backed man. Ten years of soldiering on the islands had baked his tight-mouthed, solid-jawed, rather grim, face a dark oak. He was the perfect soldier; he went where you sent him, stayed where you put him, and had no ideas of his own to keep him from doing exactly what you told him.

He gave me the druggist's package. I opened it and took ten grains of morphine up to Gabrielle. She was sitting in bed, eating breakfast. Her eyes were watery, her face damp and grayish. When she saw the bindles* in my hand she pushed her tray aside and held her hands out eagerly, wriggling her shoulders.

"Come back in five minutes?" she asked.

"You can take your shot in front of me. I'll try not to blush."

"But I would," she said, and did.

I went out, closed the door, and leaned against it, hearing the rustle of paper and the clink of

_____

* packets of powdered drugs

the water glass touching a spoon. Presently she called:

"All right."

I went in again. A crumpled ball of white paper in the tray was all that was left of one bindle. The others weren't in sight. She was leaning back against her pillows, eyes half-closed, comfortable as a cat full of goldfish. She smiled lazily at me and said:

"You're a dear. Know what I'd like to do today? Take some lunch and go out on the water—spend the whole day simply floating in the sun."

"That ought to be good for you," I agreed. "Take either Linehan or MacMan with you, though. You're not to go anywhere alone."

"What are you going to do?" she asked.

"Ride up to Quesada, over to the county seat, maybe as far as the city."

"Mayn't I go with you?"

I shook my head, saying:

"No. I've got work to do, and, besides, you're supposed to rest."

She said, "Oh," and reached for her coffee. I turned to the door. "The rest of the morphine?" She spoke over the edge of the cup. "You've put it in a safe place? Where nobody will find it?"

"Yeah," I said, grinning at her, patting my coat pocket.

In Quesada I spent half an hour talking to Rolly and reading the San Francisco papers. They were beginning to poke at Andrews with hints and questions that stopped just short of libel. That was so much to the good. The deputy sheriff hadn't anything to tell me. I went over to the county seat. Vernon was in court. Twenty minutes of the sheriff's conversation didn't add to my knowledge. I phoned the agency and talked to the Old Man without learning anything. At the hospital they told me Fitzstephan was certainly going to live.

I drove up to San Francisco, had dinner at the St. Germain,* stopped at my room to col-

lect another suit and a bagful of clean shirts and the like, and got back to the house in the cove a little before midnight. MacMan came out of the darkness while I was tucking the car under the shed. He said nothing had happened during my absence. We went into the house together. Mickey was in the kitchen, yawning and mixing himself a drink preparatory to relieving MacMan on sentry duty.

"Mrs. Collinson gone to bed?" I asked.

"I don't know. She's been in her room all day, and the light's still on."

MacMan and I had a drink with Mickey and then went upstairs. I knocked at the girl's door.

"Who is it?" she asked. I told her. She said: "Yes?"

"No breakfast in the morning," I said.

"Really?" Then, as if it were something she had almost forgotten. "Oh, I've decided not to put you to all the trouble of curing me." She opened the door and stood in the opening, smiling too pleasantly at me, a finger holding her place in a book. "Did you have a nice ride?"

"All right," I said, taking the rest of the morphine from my pocket and holding it out to her. "There's no use of my carrying this around."

She didn't take it. She laughed in my face and said:

"You are a brute, aren't you?"

I said:

"Well, it's your cure, not mine," stuffing the stuff back in my pocket. "If you—" I broke off to listen. A board had creaked down the hall. Now there was a soft sound, as of a bare foot dragging across the floor.

"That's Mary Nunez watching over me," Gabrielle whispered gaily. "She made herself a bed in the attic and refused to go home. She doesn't think I'm safe with you Continentals. She warned me against you—said you were—what was it?—oh, yes—wolves. Are you?"

I said: "Absolutely."

The next afternoon I gave Gabrielle the first dose of Vic Dallas' mixture, and three more at two-hour intervals afterward. She spent the day in her room. That was Saturday.

---

* the St. Germain Cafe on Ellis Street, opposite John's Grill

On Sunday she had ten grains of morphine and was in high spirits all day, considering herself already practically cured.

On Monday she had the rest of Vic's concoction, and the day was pretty much like Saturday. Mickey Linehan returned from a visit to the county seat with the news that Fitzstephan was conscious, but too weak and bandaged to have talked even if the doctors would have let him; that Andrews had been to San Mateo to see Aaronia Haldorn again; and that she had been to the hospital to see Fink, but had been refused permission by the sheriff's office.

Tuesday was a more exciting day.

Gabrielle was up and dressed when I carried her orange-juice breakfast in. She was bright-eyed, restless, talkative, and laughed easily until I mentioned—off-hand—that she was to have no more morphine.

"Ever, you mean?" Her face and voice were panicky. "No, you don't mean that?"

"Yeah."

"But I'll die." Tears filled her eyes, ran down her little white face, and she wrung her hands. It was childishly pathetic. I had to remind myself that tears were one of the regular symptoms of morphine withdrawal. "You know that's not the way. I don't expect as much as usual. I know I'll get less and less each day. But you can't stop it like that. You're joking. That would kill me." She cried some more at the thought of being killed.

I made myself laugh as if I were sympathetic but amused.

"Nonsense," I said cheerfully. "The chief trouble you're going to have is being too full of life. A couple of days of that—then you'll be all set."

She bit her lower lip, finally managed a smile, holding out both hands to me.

"I'm going to believe you," she said. "I do believe you. I'm going to believe you no matter what you tell me."

Her hands were clammy. I squeezed them and said:

"Fine. Now back to bed. I'll look in every now and then, and if you want anything in between, sing out."

"You're not going away today?"

"No," I promised.

She stood the gaff pretty well all afternoon. Of course there wasn't much heartiness in the way she laughed at herself between attacks when the sneezing and yawning set in; but the thing was that she tried to laugh.

Madison Andrews came at half-past five. Having seen him drive in, I met him on the porch. The ruddiness of his face had washed out to a weak orange.

"Good afternoon," he said agreeably enough. "I wish to see Mrs. Collinson."

"I'll deliver any message to her," I offered.

He pulled his eyebrows down and some of his normal ruddiness came back.

"I wish to see her." It was a command.

"But she doesn't wish to see you. Is there any message?"

All of his ruddiness was back now. His eyes were hot. I was standing between him and the door. He couldn't go in while I stood there. For a moment he seemed about to push me out of the way. That didn't worry me. He was carrying a handicap of twenty-some years and twenty-some pounds.

He pulled his jaw into his neck and spoke in the voice of authority:

"Mrs. Collinson must return to San Francisco with me. She cannot stay here. This is a preposterous arrangement."

"She's not going to San Francisco," I said. "If necessary, the prosecuting attorney will hold her here as a material witness. Try upsetting that with any of your court orders, and we'll give you something else to worry about. We'll prove that she might be in danger from you. How do we know that you haven't monkeyed with her money? That you don't mean to take undue advantage of her unfortunate condition to shield yourself now? Why, man, you might even be planning to send her to an insane asylum so the estate will stay in your hands forever."

He was sick behind his eyes, but the rest of him stood up gamely under this broadside. When he had got his breath he swallowed and demanded:

"Does Gabrielle believe this?" His face was purple.

"Who said anybody believed it?" I asked. "I'm just telling you what we'll go into court with. You're a lawyer. You know what we can do with the local court—and the newspapers."

The sickness spread from behind his eyes, pushing the color out of his face, the stiffness out of his bones, but he held himself tall and found a level voice.

"You may tell Mrs. Collinson that I shall return my letters testamentary to the court this week, with an accounting of the estate and a request that I be relieved."

"That'll be swell," I said; but I felt sorry for the old scoundrel shuffling down to his car, climbing slowly into it.

I didn't tell Gabrielle he had been there.

She was whining a little now between her yawning and sneezing, and her eyes were running water. Face, body and hands were damp with sweat. She could not eat. I kept her full of orange juice. Noises and odors—no matter how faint or how pleasant—were beginning to bother her too sensitive nerves, and she was twitching and jerking around continually in her bed.

"Will it get much worse than this?" she asked.

"Not very much. There'll be nothing you can't stand."

Mickey Linehan was waiting for me when I got downstairs.

"The spick's got herself a chive,"* he said pleasantly.

"Yeah?"

"It's the one I've been halving lemons with to take the stink out of that gin. It's a paring knife—four or five inches of stainless steel blade—so you won't get rust marks on your undershirt when she sticks it in your back. I couldn't find it,

_____

* knife

and asked her about it, and she didn't look like I was a well-poisoner when she said she didn't know anything about it, and that's the first time she ever looked like that at me, so I knew she had taken it."

"You're a smart boy," I said. "Keep an eye on her—she's gone on record as saying we're a flock of wolves."

"I'm to do that?" Mickey grinned. "My idea would be that everybody looked out for himself, seeing that you're the lad she dog-eyes most, and it's most likely you that'll get whittled on. What'd you ever do to her? You haven't been dumb enough to trifle with a Mex lady's affections, have you?"

I didn't think he was funny, though he may have been.

Aaronia Haldorn arrived just before dark, in a Lincoln limousine driven by a negro who turned the siren loose when he brought the car into the drive. I was in Gabrielle's room when the thing howled. She all but jumped out of bed, utterly terrorized by this racket that must have been pretty bad in her too sensitive ears.

"What was that? What was it?" she cried between rattling teeth, her body shaking the bed.

"S-h-h," I soothed her. I was acquiring a fair bedside manner. "Just an automobile horn. Visitors. I'll go down and head them off."

"You won't let anybody see me?" she begged.

"No. Now be a good girl till I get back."

Aaronia Haldorn was standing beside the limousine talking to MacMan when I came out. In the dim light her oval face—between black hat and black fur coat—looked more than ever like an olive-tinted, red-mouthed mask. But her enormous black eyes were real enough.

"How do you do?" she said, holding out a hand. Her voice was a thing to make warm waves run up your back. "I'm glad for Mrs. Collinson's sake that you are watching over her. She and I have already had excellent proof of your ability in that direction—both of us owing our lives to it."

That was all right, but it had been said before.

I made a gesture that was supposed to indicate modest distaste for the subject, and beat her to the first tap with:

"I'm sorry she can't see you. She isn't well."

"Oh, but I should so much like to see her, if only for a moment. Don't you think it might be good for her?"

I said I was sorry. She seemed to accept that as final, though she said: "I came all the way from the city to see her."

I tried that opening with:

"Didn't Mr. Andrews tell you . . . ?" letting the sentence ravel out at the end.

She didn't say whether he had or not. She turned beside me and began walking slowly across the grass. There was nothing for me to do but go along with her. Full darkness was only a few minutes away. Presently, when we had gone thirty or forty feet from the car, she said:

"Mr. Andrews thinks you suspect him."

"He's right."

"Of what do you suspect him?"

"Juggling the estate."

"Really?"

"Really," I said, "and of nothing else."

"Oh, I should suppose that would be enough."

"It's enough for me," I said, "but I didn't think it was enough for you." I piled up what facts I had, put some guesses on them, and then took a jump into space from the top of the heap: "When you got out of prison, you sent for Andrews, pumped him for all he knew, and then, when you learned he had been playing with the girl's pennies, you saw a chance to confuse things by throwing suspicion on him. The old boy's woman-crazy; he was duck-soup for a woman like you. I don't know what you're planning to do with him, but you seem to have got him started—and to have got the newspapers started after him. I take it you gave them the tip-off on his high-financing? It's no good, Mrs. Haldorn. Chuck it. It won't work. You could stir him up, all right, make him do something criminal, get him into a swell jam. He's desperate enough now

that people are poking at him. But it'll do you no good. Whatever he does now won't confuse what somebody else did in the past. He's promised to get the estate in order and hand it over. Let him alone."

She didn't say anything while we took another dozen steps. A path came under our feet. I said:

"This is the path that runs up the cliff—the one Eric Collinson was pushed off of. Did you know him?"

She drew in her breath sharply—with almost a sob in her throat—but her voice was steady, quiet, musical when she replied:

"You know I did. Why should you ask?"

"Detectives like questions they already know the answers to. Why did you come down here, Mrs. Haldorn?"

"Is that another whose answer you know?"

"I know that you came for one or both of two reasons. First, to learn how close we had got to the answer of our riddle. Right?"

"I've my share of curiosity, naturally," she said.

"I don't mind making that part of your trip a success. We know the answer."

She stood still in the path, facing me, her eyes phosphorescent in the dim light. She put one hand on my shoulder. The other was in her coat pocket. She put her face closer to mine. She spoke very slowly, as if taking great pains to be understood:

"Tell me truthfully. Don't pretend. This is important. I don't want to do an unnecessary wrong. Wait, wait—think before you speak—and believe me when I say that to lie—to bluff—now will be to commit the most dangerous sort of folly. Now tell me—do you know the answer?"

"Yeah."

She smiled faintly, took her hand from my shoulder, saying:

"Then there's no use of our fencing."

I plunged into her. If she had fired from the pocket she might have plugged me. But she tried to get the gun out. By then I had a hand on her wrist. The bullet went into the ground between us. The nails of her free hand put three red ribbons down the side of my face. I tucked my head under her chin, turned my hip to her before her knee came up, brought her body hard against mine with one arm around her, and bent her gunhand behind her.

She dropped the gun as we fell. I was on top. I remained there until I had found the gun. I was getting up when MacMan arrived.

"Everything's oke," I told him, having trouble with my voice. "See that the chauffeur's behaving."

MacMan nodded and went away. The woman sat on the ground with her legs tucked under her and rubbed her wrist. I said:

"That was the second reason for your coming—though I thought you meant it for the girl. Since we've gone this far, it won't do you any harm and it might do some good to talk."

"I don't think anything will help me now." She got up. I didn't help her because I didn't want her to know how shaky I was. "You say you know." She shrugged. "Then lies are worthless, and only lies would help." She set her hat straight. "Well, what now?"

"Nothing—if you'll promise to remember that the time for being desperate is past. This kind of thing splits up in three parts—being caught, being convicted, and being punished. Admit it's too late to do anything about the first, and—well, you know what California juries, judges and prison boards are."

She looked curiously at me and asked: "Why do you tell me this?"

The answer was, of course, because I was a damned fool; but I said:

"Because being shot at's no treat to me, and because when a job's done I like to get it over with. I'm not interested in trying to convict you of any part in this game, and it's a nuisance having you horning in at the last, trying to muddy things up. Go home and keep yourself quiet."

Neither of us said anything more until we had walked back to her car. Then she turned, held her hand out to me, and said:

"I think—I don't know yet—but I think I've even more to thank you for now."

I didn't say anything, and I didn't take her hand. She asked:

"May I have my pistol?"

"No."

"Will you give my best wishes to Mrs. Collinson, and tell her I'm so sorry I couldn't see her?"

"Yeah."

She said, "Good-bye," and got into the car; I took off my hat and she rode away.

V

Mickey Linehan opened the front door for me. He looked at my scratched face and laughed:

"You do have one hell of a time with your women. Why don't you try getting along with them?" He jerked a thumb at the ceiling. "Better go up and negotiate with that one. She's been raising hell."

I went up to Gabrielle's room. She was sitting in the middle of the wallowed-up bed. Her fingers were in her hair, tugging at it. Her face—wet with tears and sweat—was thirty-five years old. She was making hurt-animal noises in her throat.

I grinned at her from the door and said:

"It's a fight, huh?"

She took her fingers out of her hair.

"I won't die?" The question was a whimper between teeth set edge to edge.

"Not a chance."

She sobbed and lay down. I straightened the covers over her. She complained that there was a lump in her throat, that her jaws and the hollows behind her knees ached.

"Regular symptoms," I assured her. "They won't bother you much, and you won't have cramps."

She remembered the visitor then, and asked me who it had been, asked me about the shot she had heard, and about my scratched face.

"It was Aaronia Haldorn, and she lost her head for a moment. No harm done. She's gone."

"She came here to kill me," the girl said, not excitedly, but as if she knew it positively.

"Maybe. She wouldn't admit anything."

It was a long bad night. I spent most of it in the girl's room, in a leather rocker dragged in from the front room. She got perhaps an hour and a half of sleep, in three instalments. Nightmares brought her screaming out of all three. I dozed when she let me. Off and on through the night I heard stealthy sounds in the hall—Mary Nunez watching over her mistress, I supposed.

Wednesday was a longer and worse day. By noon my jaws were as sore as Gabrielle's, from going around holding my back teeth together.

She was getting the works now. Light was positive, active, pain to her eyes, sound to her ears, odor to her nostrils. The weight of her silk nightgown, the touch of sheets under and over her, tortured her skin. Every nerve she had yanked at every muscle she had, continually. Promises that she wasn't going to die did no good now: Life wasn't nice enough.

"Stop fighting it, if you want," I said. "Let yourself go. I'll take care of you."

She took me at my word, and I had a maniac on my hands. Once her shrieks brought Mary Nunez to the door, snarling and spitting at me in Mex-Spanish. I was holding Gabrielle in bed by the shoulders at the time, sweating as much as she was.

"Get out of here," I snarled back at the Mexican woman.

She put a brown hand into the bosom of her dress and came a step into the room. Mickey Linehan came up behind her, pulled her back into the hall, and shut the door.

Rolly came down from Quesada that afternoon with word that Fitzstephan had come sufficiently alive to be questioned by the prosecuting attorney. Fitzstephan had told Vernon that he had not seen the bomb, had seen nothing to show where it had come from; but that he had an indistinct memory of hearing a noise just after Fink and I had left the room—a tinkling and a thud on the floor close to him.

I told Rolly I'd try to get to the county seat next day, and to tell Vernon to hang on to Fink, that he was our meat.

Gabrielle spent the rest of the afternoon shrieking, begging, and crying for morphine. That evening she made a complete confession:

"I told you I didn't want to be evil. That was a lie. I've always wanted to, always have been. I wanted to do to you what I did to the others, but now I don't want you. I want morphine. They won't hang me—I know that. And I don't care what else they do to me—if I can only get some morphine."

She laughed viciously, wadding the bedclothes in feverish hands, and went on:

"You were right when you said I could bring out the worst in men because I wanted to. I did want to, and I did—except, I failed with Dr. Riese and with Eric. I don't know what was the matter with them. And with both of them I went too far, let them know too much about me. And that's why they were killed. Joseph drugged Dr. Riese and I killed him myself, and then we made Minnie think she had done it. And I persuaded Joseph to kill Aaronia, and he would have done it—he would have done anything I asked—if you hadn't interfered. I got Harvey Whidden to kill Eric for me. I was tied to Eric, legally—tied to a good man who wanted to make me a good woman."

She laughed again, licking her lips.

"Harvey and I needed money, so we pretended he had kidnapped me, hoping to get it that way. He was a glorious beast; it's a shame they killed him. I had that bomb—had had it for months. I had stolen it from father's laboratory when he was making some experiments for a motion picture company. I always carried it with me—it wasn't large. I meant it for you in the hotel room. I was feverish, and I was sure when I heard two men going out of the room, that you were the one who had remained. I didn't see that it was Owen till after I had opened the door a little way and thrown the bomb. Now you've got what you wanted from me. Give me morphine. Have what I've told you written out, and I'll sign it. You can't pretend now that I'm worth curing, worth saving. Give me morphine."

I laughed at her and her confession, reminding her that she'd forgotten to include the kidnapping of Charlie Ross[*] and the blowing up of the *Maine*.[†]

We had some more hell—a solid hour of it, before she succeeded in exhausting herself again. The night dragged through. She got a little more than two hours' sleep, a half-hour improvement over the previous night. I dozed in a chair when I could.

Sometime before daylight I woke to the feel of a hand in my pocket. Keeping my breathing regular, I pushed my eyelids apart till I could squint through the lashes. We had a very dim light in the room, but I thought Gabrielle was in bed. My head was tilted back on the chairback. I couldn't see the hand that was exploring my inside coat pocket, nor the arm that came down over my shoulder, but they smelled of the kitchen, so I knew they belonged to Mary Nunez. She was standing behind me. Mickey had told me she had a knife. Good judgment told me to let her alone. I did that, closing my eyes again. Paper rustled between her fingers, and then her hand left my pocket.

I moved my head sleepily and changed a foot's position. I heard the door close quietly behind me. I sat up and looked around. Gabrielle was asleep. I counted the bindles in my pocket and found that eight had been taken.

Presently Gabrielle opened her eyes. This was the first time since the cure started that she hadn't been awakened by a nightmare. Her face was haggard, but not wild-eyed. She looked at the window and asked:

"Isn't day coming yet?"

"It's getting light." I gave her some orange juice. "We'll get solid food into you today."

---

[*] four-year-old from a wealthy Philadelphia family kidnapped in 1874 and never found
[†] U.S. battleship sunk in Havana harbor in 1898, beginning the Spanish-American War

"I don't want food. I want morphine."

"You'll get food. You won't get morphine. Today won't be like yesterday. You may have a couple of bad spots, but you're over the hump, and the rest of it's downhill going. It's silly to ask for morphine now. What do you want to do? Have nothing to show for all the hell you've been through. You've got it licked—stay with it."

"Have I—have I really got it licked?"

"Yeah. All you've got to buck now is nervousness—and the memory of how nice it felt to have a skinful of hop."

"I can do it," she said. "I can do it because you say I can."

She got along fine until late in the morning, when she blew up for an hour or two. I discovered that cursing her helped, so I finally got her straightened out. When Mary brought her luncheon up I left them together and went downstairs for my own.

When I came back Gabrielle, in a rose dressing gown, was sitting in the leather rocker that had been my bed for two nights. She had brushed her hair and powdered her face. Her eyes were mostly green, with a lift to the lower lids, as if she was hiding a joke. She said with mock solemnity:

"Sit down; I want to talk seriously to you."

I sat down.

"Why did you go through all this with—for me?" She was really serious now. "You didn't have to, and it couldn't have been pleasant. I was—I don't know how bad I was." She turned red from forehead to chest. "I know it must have been disgusting, revolting. I know how I must seem to you now. Why—why did you do it?"

I said:

"I'm twice your age, Gabrielle, an old man. I'm damned if I'll make a chump of myself by telling you why I did it, why it was neither revolting nor disgusting, why I'd do it again and be glad of the chance."

She jumped out of the chair, her eyes wide and dark, her mouth trembling.

"You mean—?"

"I don't mean anything that I'll admit," I said, "and if you parade around with that gown hanging open you're going to catch yourself some bronchitis. As an ex-hophead, you've got to be careful about catching cold."

She sat down on the bed, put her hands over her face, and began crying. I let her cry. Presently she giggled through tears and fingers and asked:

"Will you go out and let me be alone all afternoon?"

"Yeah, if you'll keep warm."

I drove over to the county seat, went to the hospital, and argued with people until they let me into Fitzstephan's room.

He was mostly bandages, with one eye and one side of his mouth peeping out. The eye and mouth-half smiled out of linen at me, and a voice came out:

"Don't ever invite me to any more of your hotel rooms." It wasn't a clear voice, because it had to come out sideways and the novelist couldn't move his jaw; but there was plenty of vitality in it. There was no doubt about its being the voice of a man who was going to live a while.

I grinned at him and said:

"No hotel rooms this time. I'm inviting you to San Quentin. Strong enough to stand up under a third-degree now, or shall I wait a day or two?"

"I ought to be at my best now—facial expressions will hardly give me away."

"Good. Now here's the point: Fink handed that bomb to you when he shook hands with you. That's the only way it could have got in without my seeing it. His back was to me then. You didn't know what he was handing you, of course, but you had to take it—just as you have to deny it now—because otherwise you'd tip us off that you were tied up with Fink and the Holy Grail people, and that he had reasons for killing you."

Fitzstephan said: "You say the most remarkable things. No doubt you know what his reasons were?"

"You engineered Riese's murder in the Temple. Fink, Aaronia Haldorn and Joseph were

accomplices. Joseph was killed. The rest of them put the blame on him—saying he went crazy. That lets them out, or ought to. But here you are killing Collinson and planning God knows what else. Fink's got sense enough to know that if you keep on you're going to let the truth out and drag him and the others to the gallows with you. So he tries to stop you—with me as his alibi."

Fitzstephan said: "Better and better. So I had Collinson killed?"

"Yeah. Hired Whidden, and then wouldn't pay him. He kidnapped the girl, holding her for his money, knowing she was what you wanted. But you made your double-cross stick, by luck."

Fitzstephan said: "I'm running out of exclamations. So I was after her? I wondered about my motive."

"You must have been pretty rotten with her. She'd had a bad time with Andrews, even with Eric, but she didn't mind talking about them. When it came to you, she shuddered and shut up. I suppose she slammed you down hard—and you're the sort of egoist who'd be driven to anything by something like that."

Fitzstephan said: "I suppose. You've suspected me how long?"

"Well, you were standing beside Mrs. Leggett back in their house when she suddenly got a gun to hold us off with, and you were struggling with her when she shot herself. So was I, but your hand was on her gun-hand. There was no proof of anything then. The morning that Fink hoisted you, you and I had gone over the whole story and decided that it was all the work of one mind. You are the one person whose connection with each episode can be traced, who has the sort of mind needed, and who has the motive. I couldn't be sure of the motive until I got my first chance at an undisturbed talk with Gabrielle—the evening after the explosion. I didn't definitely connect you with the Temple crowd until Fink and Aaronia Haldorn did it for me."

Fitzstephan said: "Ah, Aaronia helped you connect me? What has she been up to?"

"She's done her best to set us off sideways

after Andrews, trying to cover you up by gumming the works, even by trying to shoot me."

"She's so impetuous," he said lightly, and turned his head on the pillow so that his uncovered eye looked at the ceiling—narrow and thoughtful. "You really think," he drawled presently, "that you've punctured the great Dain curse?"

"That's what."

"No," he said. "I am a Dain—on my mother's side. She and Gabrielle's maternal grandfather were brother and sister. I insist on the curse. It's going to help save my very dear neck." He squirmed in bed, and his one eye and the one visible side of his mouth smiled together at me—a twisted fraction of humorous triumph.

"You're going to see a most remarkable defense, my son," he went on; "one that will make the papers go into happy convulsions. I promise you that. I'm a Dain, with that cursed blood in me; and the crimes of Cousin Alice and Cousin Lily and Second-cousin Gabrielle, and of the Lord knows how many other criminal Dains, will be evidence in my behalf. The very number of my own crimes will be all to my advantage—nobody but a lunatic could have committed so many and they shall be many. I'll produce crimes and crimes, starting as soon after the date of my birth as will seem reasonable.

"Then there are my books. Didn't most reviewers agree that *The Pale Egyptian* was clearly the work of a sub-Mongolian; and didn't at least one critic insist that the author of *Eighteen Inches* showed every sign of degeneracy? Evidence, my son, to save my sweet neck. And then I shall wave my mangled body at them—an arm gone, a leg gone, part of my torso and of my face—a ruin whose crimes—or perhaps high Heaven—has surely brought sufficient punishment upon him. And the shock, perhaps, has cured me of my criminal tendencies. Perhaps I'll become religious. It'll be splendid. I may wind up with a statue erected to me in Golden Gate Park. Perhaps not—but my neck shall be saved."

"You'll probably make a go of it," I said. "I'm satisfied. You've paid something—and legally

you're entitled to beat the jump if anybody ever was."

"Legally entitled?" he repeated, mirth going out of his gray eye. He looked away, and then back to me. "Tell me the truth—am I?"

I nodded.

"But damn it," he complained, fighting to recover his usual lazy, amused manner, and not making such a bad job of it, "that spoils it. It's no fun if I'm really cracked."

When I got back to the house in the cove, Mickey and MacMan were sprawled on the front steps, smoking. They looked more comfortable than they had been for several days, so I imagined Gabrielle had had a good afternoon.

"Bring any fresh woman-scars back with you?" Mickey asked. "Your little playmate's been asking for you."

Gabrielle was propped up on pillows in her bed, her face still—or again—powdered, her eyes shining happily.

"I didn't mean you were to go away forever," she scolded. "It was a nasty thing to do. I've got a surprise for you and I've nearly burst waiting. Shut your eyes."

I shut them.

"Open your eyes."

I opened them. She was holding out to me the eight bindles Mary had stolen from my pocket.

"I've had them since noon," she said proudly, "and they've got fingermarks and tearmarks on them, but not one has been opened. It—honestly—it wasn't so hard not to."

"I knew it wouldn't be—for you," I said. "That's why I didn't take them away from Mary."

"You knew? You trusted me that much—to go away and leave me with them?"

It would have been idiotic to have confessed that for two days the folded papers had held powdered sugar instead of the original morphine, so I only nodded.

"You're the nicest man in the world." She caught one of my hands and rubbed her cheek into it; then dropped it quickly, frowned her face all out of shape, and said: "Except! You sat there this noon and deliberately tried to make me think you were in love with me."

"Well?" I asked, trying to keep my face straight.

She laughed at me and said:

"You hypocrite. You deceiver of young girls. It would serve you right if I made you marry me, or sued you for breach of promise. I honestly believed you all afternoon—and it did help me. I believed you till you came in just now, and then I saw—" She stopped.

"Saw what?"

"A monster—a nice one, the sort to have around when you're in trouble—but an inhuman monster, just the same, without any foolishness like love in him."

I said:

"Don't be silly. I'd change places with Fitzstephan now—if Aaronia Haldorn was part of the bargain."

VI

Two days later the newspapers blossomed out with Owen Fitzstephan's confession. He had made a high, wide and handsome job of it. Throwing out the decorations, the fictitious parts, and those that didn't have anything to do with us, something like this remained:

He had organized the Haldorns' cult and had come to San Francisco with them. Joseph Haldorn was only a puppet—in the Haldorn family as well as in the Temple. Fitzstephan's connection with them was kept secret, everybody who knew him knew he was a skeptic, and for him to have openly shown his connection would have been to advertise the cult as a fake. Aaronia was Fitzstephan's mistress. He knew his cousin Alice—Gabrielle's step-mother—was in San Francisco, and he had heard through family channels some of the Leggett history. He located her and became intimate with the family, though neither he nor Alice said anything about their relationship. He claimed that Alice became his mistress, too, but that might have been untrue.

He tried his luck with Gabrielle, and the sort of turn-down she gave him made him doubly determined to land her. He was that sort. He managed to get the Haldorns introduced to the Leggetts and had them work on her. When Upton and Ruppert tried to shake Alice down for blackmail, she took her troubles to Fitzstephan and asked his advice. Whether through spite against Gabrielle—a desire to hurt her—or through a desire to turn the Leggett affairs inside out and learn all that he did not yet know, or through pure malice—being a Dain—Fitzstephan deliberately misled Alice, giving her advice that was sure to ruin her and all the family—as it did. He had to kill her in the end; she would have turned against him when she saw what he had done.

Fitzstephan's success there encouraged him to go on with his plans to get the girl, and made them seem more likely to be successful. The Haldorns now had no difficulty in getting her to come to the Temple. They thought his interest in her was purely financial. They didn't know what he had done to the Leggetts. But Dr. Riese stumbled on the truth of his connection with the Temple. That was dangerous for Fitzstephan—it might lead to the truth about the Leggett trouble. Fitzstephan had had a taste of successful murder. He had two easily handled tools—Joseph and Minnie. He had Riese killed. Then Aaronia woke up—discovered that Fitzstephan's interest in Gabrielle wasn't purely financial. Aaronia could and would either make him give up the girl or ruin him. He persuaded her husband that *his* life also depended on Aaronia's death. I had spoiled that, killing Haldorn, and that had seemed to save Fitzstephan for the time—Aaronia and Fink had to keep quiet to save themselves.

By this time, Fitzstephan looked on Gabrielle as his property, bought and paid for by the killing he had done. Each death had increased her value to him, in his eyes. When Eric Collinson had married her, Fitzstephan hadn't hesitated. Collinson must be removed, and he knew who he could hire to do it. He had offered Whidden a thousand dollars. Whidden refused at first, but he wasn't nimble-witted and Fitzstephan was eloquent enough. Whidden had fortified himself with whiskey for the job; and when he had finally done it, he called Fitzstephan on the phone and boasted: "Well, I killed him easy enough and dead enough. Where's my money?"

Fitzstephan's phone came through the apartment house switchboard. He didn't know who might have heard Whidden. He pretended he didn't know who was talking, what was being said, or what it was all about. Thinking he has been double-crossed, and knowing what Fitzstephan wanted, Whidden wrote him a note saying he was taking the girl and holding her for ten thousand dollars. Then he went back to Quesada and got the girl. He had enough drunken cunning to disguise his handwriting, not to sign his name, and to word the note so that Fitzstephan could not tell the police who had sent it without explaining how he knew who had sent it.

Fitzstephan wasn't sitting any too pretty. As soon as he had angled an excuse for coming to Quesada out of me, he came down—some hours ahead of time—and went to the marshal's house to ask Mrs. Cotton—Whidden's mistress—if she knew where Whidden was. Whidden was there at the time. Fitzstephan talked him into something again, explaining everything to Whidden's satisfaction, and assuring him that now everything could be handled so Whidden would get his ten thousand dollars in safety. Whidden went back to his hiding place at daylight. Fitzstephan remained with Mrs. Cotton. She knew too much, and she didn't like what she knew. She was doomed. He had murdered people before, to keep them quiet, and he knew it always worked. If he could get her to leave a signed statement behind, that would help a lot. He got her to do it, but it took him till late in the morning—she suspected what he was up to. His description of how he finally got it wasn't pleasant, but he got it, and then strangled her, barely finishing the job when her husband came home.

Fitzstephan escaped by the back door and joined me and the others at the hotel. He went with us to Whidden's hiding place. He knew Whidden, knew how Whidden would react to this second double-crossing, knew that the sheriff would welcome an excuse to shoot Whidden, and so would Cotton. If neither of them did, he had decided to jump out of the boat with a pistol in his hand, stumble, and shoot Whidden accidentally. He might have been blamed for that—but hardly convicted. Luck was with him. Whidden, seeing him with us, had gone crazy, tried to shoot him, and we had had to kill Whidden.

Fink's bomb had been a small cubical one wrapped in white paper. Fitzstephan had thought it something Aaronia had sent to him, something important enough to risk that sort of sending. He couldn't have refused to take it without opening my eyes, anyway, so he had concealed it until Fink and I left the room. Then he had unwrapped it—and knew nothing else till he came to in the hospital.

Owen Fitzstephan put on the promised show in the court room, and the newspapers went into the happy convulsions he had predicted, and he saved his dear neck. Afterward, Aaronia Haldorn took him away—up in the mountains, I've heard.

Gabrielle topped off her cure with a couple of months in a sanatorium. I've seen her now and then since, usually with a big-shouldered youngster fresh from somebody's college not more than a foot or two from her. Whatever kind of an effect she has on him they both seem to like it.

ABOUT THE EDITORS

Richard Layman is the president of Bruccoli Clark Layman, producers of the *Dictionary of Literary Biography*, and the managing director of Layman Poupard Publishing, producers of the Literature Criticism Series. He has written or edited twenty books on topics in literary and social history.

Julie M. Rivett is a granddaughter of Dashiell Hammett, a Hammett scholar, and a spokesperson for the Hammett estate. She lectures throughout the United States on her grandfather and his works and the impact of American politics on his life and legacy.

Layman and Rivett have collaborated on six books related to Hammett, including *Selected Letters of Dashiell Hammett: 1921–1960*, *Return of the Thin Man*, and *The Hunter and Other Stories*.

PERMISSIONS